THE SUNDERING

— TIME OF LEGENDS —

THE SUNDERING

Gav Thorpe

BLACK LIBRARY

This book is dedicated to Bill, Jes, Andy and Rick.
True Phoenix Kings.

A BLACK LIBRARY PUBLICATION

Malekith copyright © 2009, Games Workshop Ltd.
Shadowking copyright © 2009, Games Workshop Ltd.
Caledor copyright © 2011, Games Workshop Ltd.
The Bloody-Handed copyright © 2010, Games Workshop Ltd.
The Dark Path copyright © 2009, Games Workshop Ltd.
All rights reserved.

First published in Great Britain in 2012 by
Black Library,
Games Workshop Ltd.,
Willow Road,
Nottingham,
NG7 2WS, UK

10 9 8 7 6 5 4 3 2 1

Cover by Stefan Kopinski.
Map by Nuala Kinrade.

A CIP record for this book
is available from the British Library.

UK ISBN 13: 978 1 84970 241 6
US ISBN 13: 978 1 84970 242 3

See Black Library on the internet at
www.blacklibrary.com

Find out more about Games Workshop
and the world of Warhammer at
www.games-workshop.com

Printed and bound by CPI Group (UK) Ltd, Croydon, CR0 4YY

The most tragic tale from the Time of Legends tells of
the fall of the greatest houses of the elves and the rise of
three kings: Phoenix, Witch and Shadow.

There was once a time when all was order, now so distant
that no mortal creature can remember it. Since time
immemorial the elves have dwelt upon the isle of Ulthuan.
Here they learnt the secrets of magic from their creators, the
mysterious Old Ones. Under the rule of the Everqueen they
dwelt upon their idyllic island unblemished by woe.

When the coming of Chaos destroyed the civilisation of the
Old Ones, the elves were left without defence. Daemons of
the Chaos Gods ravaged Ulthuan and terrorised the elves.
From the darkness of this torment rose Aenarion, the first
of the Phoenix Kings, the Defender.

Aenarion's life was one of war and strife, yet through the
sacrifice of Aenarion and his allies, the daemons were
defeated and the elves were saved. In his wake the elves
prospered for an age, but all their grand endeavours were to
be for naught. The warrior-people of Nagarythe found little
solace in peace and in time would turn upon each other and
their fellow elves.

Where once there was harmony, there came discord.
Where once peace had prevailed, now came bitter war.

Heed now the tale of the Sundering.

CONTENTS

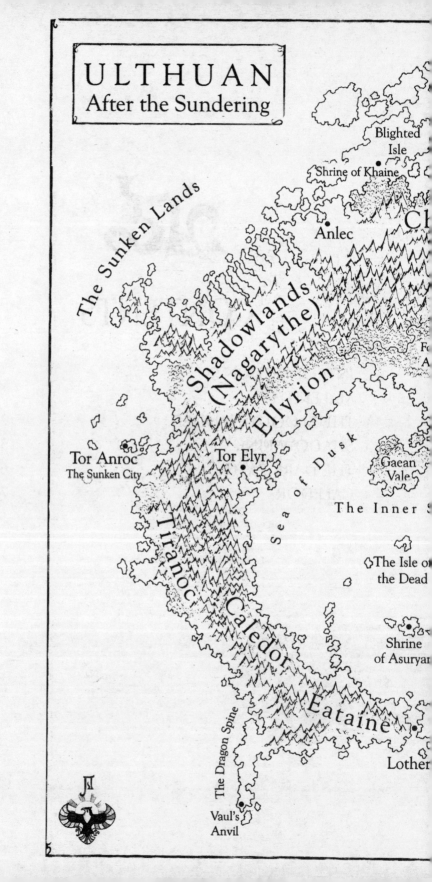

ULTHUAN
After the Sundering

Blighted
Isle

Shrine of Khaine

Ch

Anlec

The Sunken Lands

Shadowlands
(Nagarythe)

Ellyrion

Fo
A

Tor Anroc
The Sunken City

Tor Elyr

Gaean
Vale

Sea of Dusk

The Inner S

Tiranoc

Caledor

◊The Isle of
the Dead

Shrine
of Asuryan

The Dragon Spine

Eataine

Lother

Vaul's
Anvil

The Isles

The Shifting Isles

Chrace

Tor Achare

Forests of
Cothique

Averlorn

Cothique

Forests of
Averlorn

Finuval
Plain

Tor
Yvresse

...an
...le

... Sea

Tower of
Hoeth

Isle of
Dead

Saphery

Yvresse

Sea of Dreams

...rine
...suryan

Eataine

The Shifting Isles

...othern

Introduction

THE GENESIS OF *The Sundering* began a couple of years before it was published, before there was a Time of Legends series to give it a home. It started when I was still working in the Games Workshop Design Studio. I was heading up the new edition of *Warhammer Armies: Dark Elves*, and part of my self-appointed brief was to present a more dark elf-orientated perspective on the events that are portrayed in this book, because frankly most of this stuff had only previously been related in terms of the high elves.

To do this meant going back to the original source material, written by the great William (aka Bill) King. Immersing myself in the ancient history of the elves again, I was struck by how epic and cool this tale was, and was determined to make it as epic and cool from the perspective of Malekith and his followers.

At this point, my thoughts started stretching beyond the background for the dark elves army book, coming up with the notion of a series of Black Library novels that detailed the events of the Sundering and the time that led up to this catastrophic event. I sketched out a rough plan for how the trilogy might work, and prepared a more detailed synopsis for the first novel and sent them down to Black Library (after getting an okay from the Powers That Be that dabbling in this sort of 'historical' fiction was acceptable).

Interesting fact #1: The first titles of the three novels were somewhat different, being *Flames of Treachery*, *Vengeance of the Witch King* and *Rise of the Phoenix King*.

Not a lot happened straightaway, though the Black Library editors liked the idea in principle.

I got on with my life and other work, wrote some other novels and continued with the dark elves army book and other projects.

Maybe a year later (it might not have been quite that long), I had a meeting
with the editors in which they explained this idea they had for a Warhammer series that would, in a way, mirror what was happening with the Horus
Heresy in the Warhammer 40,000 universe. *The Sundering* would fit right in
with their plans for the Time of Legends, and so we returned to the original
proposals and the series was commissioned.

Everything was peachy and I was making good progress on the first book.
As anyone with any experience of life (and in particular publishing) will
know, that is just when a wheel is likely to fall off. In the case of *The Sundering* it began with a discussion about the title of the first book.

The folks at Black Library were very keen to call the book *Malekith*. This
would fit with the titling principles of the other novels being planned, and
would be a strong marketing hook amongst the Warhammer fans. I had a
problem with this, because the character of Malekith did not really emerge
until the final third of the novel, and I thought it would be disingenuous to
name the novel after him when he wasn't a major character.

Interesting fact #2: The main viewpoint character of the trilogy was originally Captain Carathril of the Lothern Guard. He still features in the series,
but nowhere near as prominently.

The cordial but tense discussion that followed resulted in a bit of a stand-
off. Ultimately it is up to the publishers what title they want to put on a
book, but I was feeling uncomfortable about the situation. The wheel was
wobbling but it was still on the axle...

It was then that I had a revelation. I was writing the wrong book!

In fact, I was writing entirely the wrong series, and committing a grievous
tie-in writing sin that I had, in private, moaned about encountering in the
work of a few other writers. You see, Warhammer fans would want to read
all about the characters they know and love/hate from the existing history.
In the other series for Time of Legends they were learning about Sigmar,
Nagash and other luminaries, and I was telling the story of my own character
– Carathril – rather than the figures of legend that the series was supposed
to feature.

Black Library, editors and salesmen alike, were right. It was time to go
back to basics and re-plan the trilogy from scratch. Unlike the other Time of
Legends series that each focus on the exploits of one character over several
novels, I thought it would be good to see the events of the Sundering from
differing perspectives. I have always been keen to show that there is rarely
a definitive line between good and evil, right and wrong. Events are shaped
by people and their goals, ambitions and personality, and the Sundering
presented an opportunity to look at, in particular, the three major players of
the elven discord: Malekith, Alith Anar the Shadow King and Prince Imrik
of Caledor.

Suddenly everything made more sense. This was not so much a series of novels about an historic event, but instead I would be writing something a bit more personal, examining the motives and exploits of three very different characters.

There was a lot of the text I had written that was still useful across the three books, about 30,000 of the 45,000 words I had in place, and as it turns out I have probably enjoyed writing this series far more than I would have done under the initial plan.

And there is still so much more that could be written – other characters to explore and other events to detail. *The Sundering* is a beginning as much as an end, and I hope to return to the great history of the elves at some point in the future.

I hope you enjoy this journey through the dark days of Ulthuan as much as I had fun writing it.

Gav Thorpe
Nottingham, November 2011

MALEKITH

PART ONE

The Passing of Aenarion; the Conquering of Elthin Arvan;
the Grand Alliance; Prince Malekith Becomes
Aware of his Destiny

—◆ ONE ◆—

Broken Legacy

NONE KNEW AT the time that the greatest saviour of the elves would also be their doom. Yet there was one who foresaw the darkness and death to come: Caledor Dragontamer. When Aenarion the Defender, bulwark against the daemons and first of the Phoenix Kings, drew the Sword of Khaine from its black altar, Caledor, greatest mage of Ulthuan, was gifted with a dark prophecy.

Caledor saw that in taking the dire blade forged for the God of Murder, Aenarion awakened the bloodthirsty spirit that had been buried deep within the elves. In Aenarion's line more than any other, the call for war and the thrill of battle was stirred, and across the isle of Ulthuan love of bloodletting was kindled and the innocence of the Everqueen's rule passed forever.

That Aenarion drew the sword at all was born out of grief and anger, and its call haunted him until the day he drove it back into the fell altar of Khaine just before he died. It was that same anguish and loss that drove him to marry the seeress Morathi, whom the Phoenix King had rescued from the grip of Chaos.

Morathi wielded the power of magic without reserve, eager to harness the great energies unleashed upon the world by the coming of Chaos. There were those who saw such practices as obscene and dangerous, and there were whispers that Morathi had bewitched Aenarion. That she craved power was plain for many to see, yet Aenarion was oblivious to their protests and banished them from his presence.

At Anlec, Aenarion and Morathi held court, and in that bleak time their palace was a fortress of war and sorcery. The deadliest warriors came and learnt at Aenarion's hand, while the most gifted spellweavers were taught the deepest secrets known to Morathi. With spell and spear, the warriors of Anlec carved the kingdom of Nagarythe from the grip of the daemons, wielding grave weapons forged in the furnaces of Vaul the Smith God by the servants of Caledor.

IT WAS INTO the midst of destruction and vengeance that Malekith was born, son of Aenarion and Morathi. As was the tradition of those times, a blade was forged for him at the hour of his birth, and he was taught to wield it as soon as his limbs were strong enough to hold it aloft.

From his father, he learnt the skills of rulership and warcraft, and from his mother, Malekith was gifted the power to bind the tempests of magic to his will.

Into Malekith, the Phoenix King poured all of his wisdom and knowledge, but also his thirst for revenge upon the daemons that had taken his first wife and the children borne by her. Into Malekith, Morathi invested her will to achieve anything no matter the cost, and the hunger for glory and greatness.

'Remember that you are the son of Aenarion,' she told Malekith when he was but a child. 'Remember that you are the son of Morathi. In your blood flows the greatest strength of this isle.'

'You are a warrior born,' Aenarion said. 'You shall be fell with blade and bow, and you shall wield armies as lesser elves wield their swords.'

Day after day they told their son this, from before he was old enough to understand their words, to the day Aenarion died.

IT WAS TO the lament of Aenarion that the tide of daemons did not cease, and his constant battles were thus ever in vain. Caledor it was that created the great vortex, which to this day siphons away the power of Chaos and drains it from the world. With the magical energy needed to sustain their material forms now much diminished, the daemons perished, though Caledor and his mages were trapped in stasis within the vortex, cursed to fight against the encroachment of Chaos for eternity. Aenarion gave his life defending Caledor and his mages, and with his last strength returned to the Blighted Isle and restored the Godslayer to the black altar of Khaine.

In the time after the daemons had passed, the great princes of the elves – those warriors and mages who had fought alongside Caledor and Aenarion – came together to decide the path of the future rule of Ulthuan. In the forests of Avelorn, from where the slain Everqueen had ruled, they held the First Council a year after Aenarion's departure.

The princes met in the Glade of Eternity, a great amphitheatre of trees at the centre of which stood a shrine to Isha, the Goddess of Nature, matron of the Everqueen. Grown of twining silver roots and branches, with emerald-green leaves festooned with blooms in every season, the Aein Yshain glowed with mystical power. By the light of the moons and the stars, the First Council convened, bathed in the twilight of the open skies and the aura of the blessed tree.

Morathi and Malekith were there. Dark-haired and coldly beautiful, the seeress wore a dress of black cloth so fine that it appeared as a diaphanous cloud that barely concealed her alabaster skin. Her raven hair was swept back by bands of finely woven silver threads hung with rubies, and her lips were painted to match the glittering gems. Slender and noble of bearing she stood, and bore a staff of black iron in her hands.

Malekith was no less imposing. As tall as his father and of similarly dark eyes, he wore a suit of golden mail, and a breastplate upon which was embossed the coiling form of a dragon. A long sword hung in a gold-threaded scabbard at his waist, its pommel wrought from the same precious metal: a dragon's claw grasping a sapphire the size of a fist.

With them came other princes of Nagarythe who had survived the fighting on the Isle of the Dead. They were dressed in their fine armour, and wore dark cloaks that hung to their ankles, and proudly bore the scars and trophies of their wars with the daemons.

The sinister princes of the north were arrayed with knives, spears, swords, bows, shields and armour wrought with the runes of Vaul, testaments to the power of Nagarythe and Anlec. Banner bearers with black and silver standards stood in attendance, and heralds sounded the trumpets and pipes at their arrival. A cabal of sorcerers accompanied the Naggarothi contingent, clad in robes of black and purple, their faces tattooed and scarred with ritual sigils, their heads shaved.

Another group there was, of princes from the lands founded by Caledor in the south, and from the new realms to the east – Cothique, Eataine, Yvresse and others. At the fore stood the young mage Thyriol, and golden-haired Menieth, son of Caledor Dragontamer.

In contrast to the Naggarothi these elves of the south and east were as day is to night. Though all had played their part in the war against the daemons, these princes had cast off their wargear and instead carried staves and sceptres, and in the place of war helms they wore golden crowns as symbols of their power. They were clad predominantly in white, the colour of mourning, in remembrance of the losses their people had suffered; the Naggarothi eschewed such affectation even though they had lost more than most.

'Aenarion has passed on,' Morathi declared to the council. 'The Godslayer, the Widowmaker, he returned to the altar of Khaine so that we can be free of war. In peace, my son wishes to rule, and in peace we would explore this new world that surrounds us. Yet, I fear peace now is a thing of memory, and perhaps one day to be nothing more than myth. Do not think that the Great Powers that now gaze upon our world with hungry, immortal eyes can be so easily defeated. Though the daemons are banished from our lands, the power of Chaos is not wholly exiled from the world. I have gazed far and wide this past year, and I have seen what changes the fall of the gods has wrought upon us.'

'In war, I would follow no other king,' said Menieth, striding to the centre of the circle formed by the princes. 'In Nagarythe is found the greatest strength of arms upon this isle. The war is over, though, and I am not sure that the strength of Nagarythe lies in tranquillity. There are other realms now, and cities where there were castles. Civilisation has triumphed over Chaos on Ulthuan, and we shall take that civilisation across the seas and the elves shall reign where the gods have fallen.'

'And such arrogance and blindness shall see us humbled,' said Morathi. 'Far to the north, the lands are blasted wastelands, where creatures corrupted by dark magic crawl and flit. Ignorant savages build altars of skulls in praise of the new gods, and spill the blood of their kin in worship. Monstrous things melded of flesh and magic prowl the darkness beyond our shores. If we are to bring our light to these benighted lands, it shall be upon the glittering tip of spear and arrow.'

'Hardship and bloodshed are the price we pay for our survival,' argued Menieth. 'Nagarythe shall march at the forefront of our hosts and with the valour of the Naggarothi we shall pierce that darkness. However, we cannot be ruled by war as we were when Aenarion strode amongst us. We must reclaim our spirits from the love of bloodshed that consumed us, and seek a more enlightened path towards building a new world. We must allow the boughs of love and friendship to flourish from the roots of hatred and violence sown by the coming of Aenarion. We shall never forget his legacy, but our hearts cannot be ruled by his anger.'

'My son is the heir of Aenarion,' Morathi said quietly, menace in her soft voice. 'That we stand here at all is the prize wrested from defeat by my late husband.'

'But won no less by my father's sacrifice,' Menieth countered. 'For a year we have pondered what course of action to take, since the deaths of Aenarion and Caledor. Nagarythe shall take its place amongst the other realms; great in its glory, yet not greater than any other kingdom.'

'Greatness is earned by deeds, not bestowed by others,' said Morathi, striding forwards to stand in front of Menieth. She planted her staff in the ground between them and glared at the prince, her grip tight upon the metal rod.

'It is not to fall upon each other that we fought against the daemons and sacrificed so much,' said Thyriol hurriedly. Clad in robes of white and yellow that glimmered with golden thread, the mage laid a hand upon the shoulder of Morathi and upon the arm of Menieth. 'In us has been awakened a new spirit, and we must temper our haste with cool judgement, just as a newly forged blade must be quenched in the calming waters.'

'Who here feels worthy enough to take up the crown of the Phoenix King?' Morathi asked, glaring at the princes with scorn. 'Who here save my son is worthy of being Aenarion's successor?'

There was silence for a while, and none of the dissenters could meet Morathi's gaze, save for Menieth, who returned her cold stare without flinching. Then a voice rang out across the glade from the shadows of the trees encircling the council.

'I have been chosen!' the voice called.

From the trees walked Bel Shanaar, ruling prince of the plains of Tiranoc. Behind him strode a gigantic figure, in shape as of a tree given the power to walk. Oakheart was his name; one of the treemen of Avelorn who had acted as guard to the Everqueen and tended the sacred shrines of the elves' homeland.

'Chosen by whom?' asked Morathi contemptuously.

'By the princes and the Everqueen,' Bel Shanaar replied, standing to one side of the holy tree of Isha.

'Astarielle was slain,' Morathi said. 'The reign of the Everqueen is no more.'

'She lives on,' said a ghostly, feminine voice that drifted around the glade.

'Astarielle was slain by the daemons,' Morathi insisted, casting her gaze about to spy whence the voice had come, her eyes narrowed with suspicion.

The leaves on all of the trees began to quiver, filling the glade with a gentle susurrus as if a wind whispered through the treetops, though the air was still. The long grass of the glade began to sway in the same invisible breeze, bending towards the Aein Yshain at the clearing's centre. The glow of the sacred tree grew stronger, bathing the council in a golden light dappled with sky blues and verdant greens.

In the shimmering brightness, a silhouette of greater light appeared upon the knotted trunk, resolving itself into the form of a young elf maiden. Morathi gasped, for at first it seemed as if Astarielle indeed still lived.

The maiden's golden hair hung to her waist in long plaited tresses woven with flowers of every colour, and she wore the green robes of the Everqueen. Her face was delicate, even by elven standards, and her eyes the startling blue of the clearest summer skies. As the light dimmed, the elf's features became clearer and Morathi saw that this newcomer was not Astarielle. There was a likeness, of that Morathi was aware, but she relaxed as she scrutinised the girl.

'You are not Astarielle,' Morathi declared confidently. 'You are an impostor!'

'Not Astarielle, you are right,' replied the maiden, her voice soft yet carrying easily to the furthest reaches of the glade. 'I am not an impostor, either. I am Yvraine, daughter of Aenarion and Astarielle.'

'More trickery!' shrieked Morathi, rounding on the princes with such an expression of anger that many flinched from her ire. 'Yvraine is also dead! You conspire to keep my son from his rightful inheritance.'

'She is Yvraine,' said Oakheart, his voice a melodic noise like the sighing of a light wind through branches. 'Though Astarielle remained to protect Avelorn against the daemons, she bid us to take her children to safety. To the Gaen Vale I carried them, where no other elf has trod. There my kin and I fought the daemons and kept Yvraine and Morelion safe those many years.'

At this there were gasps from the Naggarothi, none louder than the exclamation of Malekith.

'Then my half-brother also still lives?' the prince demanded. 'Aenarion's first son is alive?'

'Calm yourself, Malekith,' said Thyriol. 'Morelion has taken ship and sailed from Ulthuan. He is a child of Avelorn, as is Yvraine, and he seeks no claim to the rule of Nagarythe. He is blessed of Isha, not a scion of Khaine, and seeks neither dominion nor fealty.'

'You kept this from Aenarion?' Morathi's tone was full of incredulity. 'You allowed him to believe his children were dead, and raised them separated from their father? You have hidden them from–'

'I am the beloved of Isha,' said Yvraine, her voice stern, silencing Morathi. 'In me is reborn the spirit of the Everqueen. Anlec is a place of blood and rage. It could not be my home, I could not live amongst the taint of Khaine, and so Oakheart and his kind raised me in the manner and place fitting for my station.'

'I see now your conspiracy,' said Morathi, stalking across the glade to confront the princes. 'In secrecy you have muttered and whispered, and kept the Naggarothi from your counsels. You seek to supplant the line of Aenarion with one of your own, and wrest the power of Ulthuan from Nagarythe.'

'There is no power to wrest, no line to break,' replied Thyriol. 'Only in pain and death does Nagarythe prevail. We sent messengers to Anlec and you turned them away. We sought to include you in our deliberations, but you would send no embassy. We gave you every right and opportunity to make the claim for your son and you chose to tread your own path. There is no conspiracy.'

'I am the widow of Aenarion, the queen of Ulthuan,' Morathi snarled. 'When the daemons preyed upon your people, did Aenarion and his lieutenants stand by and discuss matters in council? When Caledor began his spell, did he debate its merits with the peons? To rule is to wield the right to decide for all.'

'You are queen no longer, Morathi,' said Yvraine, ghosting softly across the glade, her steps as light as settling snowflakes. 'The Everqueen has returned and I shall rule with Bel Shanaar, just as Aenarion reigned with my mother.'

'You will wed Bel Shanaar?' asked Morathi, turning on Yvraine.

'As Aenarion wed my mother, so the Everqueen will marry the Phoenix King, and ever shall it be down all of the ages,' Yvraine declared. 'I cannot marry Malekith, my half-brother, no matter what his entitlement or qualities to succeed his father.'

'Usurpers!' shrieked Morathi, raising up her staff. Malekith leapt forwards and snatched the rod from her grip.

'No more!' the prince of Nagarythe cried out. 'I would not have the realm forged by my father torn asunder by this dispute.'

Malekith laid a comforting hand upon the cheek of his mother, and when she was calmed he returned her staff to her. With a last venomous glare at Yvraine and Bel Shanaar, the seeress turned her back upon them and returned to the Naggarothi contingent to glower and sneer.

'I do not seek the throne of Ulthuan to become a tyrant,' said Malekith. 'It is to honour my father and see his legacy fulfilled that I would become Phoenix King. I do not claim this as a right of birth, but surrender myself to the judgement of those here. If it is the decision of this council that Bel Shanaar should wed my half-sister and become king, I will not oppose it. I ask only that you consider my petition this one last time, for it is plain that we have allowed division and misconception to cloud our minds.'

The princes nodded in agreement at these well-spoken words, and gathered together under the eaves of the Avelorn trees. They talked for a long time, until dawn touched her red fingers upon the treetops and the morning mists drifted up from the fertile earth. Back and forth swayed the debate, for some were heartened by Malekith's gentle entreaty and believed that though he was his father's son, he had not wielded the Godslayer and so was not touched by its darkness. Others reminded the council of Caledor's prophecy that Aenarion's line was touched by Khaine, and argued that a child of Anlec could never be freed from its curse.

'We have made our decision,' Thyriol informed the Naggarothi. 'While Malekith is a fine prince, he is yet young and has much to learn about the world, as do we all. Now is a time for wisdom and guidance, not iron rule, and for these reasons we remain committed to the investiture of Bel Shanaar.'

Morathi gave a scream of derision, but Malekith held up a hand to silence her.

'The fate of Ulthuan is not for a single elf to decide, and I accede to the wisdom of this council,' Malekith declared. He crossed the glade and, to the amazement of all, bent to one knee before Bel Shanaar. 'Bel Shanaar shall succeed my father, though he cannot replace him, and with his wisdom we shall herald a new age for our people. May the gods grant our new king the strength to prosper and rule justly, and know that should ever his will falter or his resolve waver, Nagarythe stands ready.'

THOUGH MALEKITH BORE himself with dignity and respect, he was sorely disappointed by the council's decision. He returned to Nagarythe with his mother, and did not attend the ritual wedding of Bel Shanaar and Yvraine. However, he did travel to the Isle of Flame to bear witness to Bel Shanaar's passing through the sacred flames of Asuryan, though the sight stirred within him a kernel of jealousy that he could not wholly quench.

The shrine itself was a high pyramid in form, built above the burning flame of the king of the gods. The flame danced and flickered at the heart of the temple, thrice the height of an elf, burning without noise or heat. Runes of gold were inlaid into the marble tiles of the floor around the central fire, and these blazed with a light that was not wholly reflected from the flame. Upon the white walls were hung braziers wrought in the shape of phoenixes with their wings furled, and more magical fire burned within them, filling the temple with a golden glow.

All the princes of Ulthuan were there, resplendent in their cloaks and gowns, with high helms and tall crowns of silver and gold studded with gemstones from every colour of the rainbow. Only the Naggarothi stood out amongst this feast of colour, taciturn and sombre in their black and purple robes. Morathi stood with Malekith and his followers, the seeress eyeing the proceedings with suspicion.

Astromancers were present too, seven of them, who had determined that this day was the most auspicious to crown the new Phoenix King. They wore robes of deep blues patterned with glistening diamonds in the constellations of the stars, linked by the finest lines of silver and platinum.

The astrologers stood next to the chanting priests of Asuryan, who weaved their prayers around Bel Shanaar so that he might pass through the flames unscathed. Behind the priests sat the oracles of Asuryan; three elven maidens of pale skin and blonde hair, garbed in raiment of silver that shimmered in the dazzling light.

Yvraine and her maiden guard had journeyed from Avelorn to join the ascension of her ceremonial husband. These warrior-women wore skirts of silvered scale edged with green cloth, and carried garlands of flowers in place of their spears and bows, for no weapon was allowed to pass the threshold of Asuryan's temple.

Bel Shanaar stood with the high priest before the flame, and about his shoulders was hung a cloak of white and black feathers, a newly woven symbol of his power and authority.

'As did Aenarion the Defender, so too shall I submit myself to the judgement of the greatest power,' Bel Shanaar solemnly intoned. 'My purity proven by this ordeal, I shall ascend to the throne of the Phoenix King, to rule wisely and justly in the name of the king of gods.'

'Your father needed no spells of protection,' muttered Morathi. 'This is a fraud, of no more legitimacy than the sham wedding to Yvraine.'

Malekith did not hear her words, for his attention and thoughts were bent entirely upon the unfolding ceremony.

As the priests burned incense and made offerings to Asuryan, the oracles began to sing quietly, their verses almost identical but for a few words here and there, which rose into a joyful harmony as Bel Shanaar was ushered towards the flame of Asuryan. The Phoenix King-to-be turned and looked back towards the princes, with no sign of trepidation or exultation.

With a respectful nod Bel Shanaar faced towards the centre of the shrine and walked forwards, slowly ascending the shallow steps that led up to the dais over which the god's cleansing fires gleamed. All present then fell hushed in anticipation as Bel Shanaar stepped within the flame, which turned to a glaring white and forced the onlookers to cast their gazes away lest they be blinded by its intensity.

As their eyes grew accustomed to the bright burning of the flame, they could see the vague shape of Bel Shanaar within, arms upraised as he offered fealty to Asuryan. Then the Phoenix King turned slowly and stepped back out of the flames unharmed. There was a sighing of exhalation as the princes expressed their relief that all went well. The Naggarothi remained silent.

The entourage left, laughing and chattering, save for Malekith, who stayed for a long while gazing at the flame and pondering his fate. The sacred fire had returned to its shifting colours, now seeming dim after its dazzling eruption. To Malekith it seemed as if they had been diminished, tainted by the presence of Bel Shanaar.

Unaware of anything but that burning shrine, Malekith walked slowly forwards, his mind a swirl of conflicting emotions. If he but dared the flame and survived, without the spells of the priests to protect him, then surely it was the will of Asuryan that he succeed his father. Yet what if he was not strong enough? Would the burning of the flames devour him? What then would be left of his hopes and dreams for Nagarythe?

Without realisation Malekith stood directly before the fires, mesmerised by their shifting patterns. The urge to reach out gripped him and he was about to place his hand into the flame when he heard the footsteps of the priests re-entering the temple. Snatching his hand away, Malekith turned from the sacred fire and strode quickly from the shrine, ignoring the priests' inquiring glances.

There were to be many days of feasting and celebration, but Malekith left as soon as the ceremony was complete, his duty having been fulfilled. He felt no urge to linger here, where his father had first thrown himself upon the mercy of the greatest god and been reborn as the saviour of his people. If Bel Shanaar wished to be Phoenix King, then Malekith was satisfied to acquiesce. There were more than enough challenges ahead for him to overcome, Malekith knew, without inciting rivalry and discord. Content for the moment, he journeyed back to Anlec to take up his rule.

⊰ TWO ⊱

Voyage to Elthin Arvan

WITH DETERMINATION AND resourcefulness, Malekith bent his mind to the rebuilding of Nagarythe, as the other princes looked to their realms. In this time, Ulthuan raised itself from the ashes of war, and the cities grew and prospered. Farmlands pushed back the wilderness of Ulthuan as the elves shaped their isle to their liking.

In the mountains, hunters found strange beasts twisted by dark magic: many-headed hydras, bizarre chimera, screeching griffons and other creatures of Chaos. Many of these they slew, others they captured and broke to their will to use as mounts. Here also change had been wrought upon the birds, and the elves became friends with the great eagles who soared upon the mountain thermals and were gifted with the power of speech.

Ships were built and fleets despatched to explore the lands beyond the seas, and the power of the elves grew. Tiranoc, the kingdom of Bel Shanaar, profited greatly from this expansion of the elven realms, as did other kingdoms whose people took ship to found new colonies on distant shores.

Seeing that the future of his lands lay not just upon Ulthuan but across the globe, Malekith decided to lead the Naggarothi forth on an expedition of conquest and exploration. Though he had laboured long in the reconstruction of Nagarythe, ever he had chafed at domesticity and would seek the adventure of the mountain hunts or train with the legions of Anlec.

Not for him the life of security and comfort enjoyed by the princes of Ulthuan, for his spirit burned brighter than theirs, and ever the words of his mother and father sprang to mind. He felt destined for greater things than the building of walls and the collection of taxes, and he appointed many chancellors and treasurers to oversee these duties for him.

In the two hundred and fifty-fifth year of Bel Shanaar's reign, Malekith quit Nagarythe as part of a mighty fleet bound for the east, to the unconquered wilderness of Elthin Arvan. To Morathi he gave the stewardship of Nagarythe. Though the relationship between mother and son had been strained at times, for Morathi could not accept her son's fate as placidly as did he, the two remained close.

Beneath a spring sky the two parted on the wharfs of Galthyr, Morathi wrapped against the chill with a shawl of black bear fur, Malekith in his golden armour. Behind the prince his flagship rose and fell at anchor, her white sails cracking in the breeze, the high tiers of her gilded hull shining in the morning sun. Further out to sea waited a dozen warships of Nagarythe, their black and gold hulls rising and falling upon the white surf, five hundred warriors and knights aboard each vessel; a bodyguard befitting the son of Aenarion.

'You will earn glory on your travels,' Morathi said with genuine affection. 'I have seen it in my dreams, and I know it in my heart. You will be a hero and a conqueror, and you will return to Ulthuan to be showered with praise.'

'I have nothing to prove,' Malekith answered.

'You do not,' Morathi agreed. 'Not to yourself, nor I, not to your loyal subjects. You will make a fine Phoenix King when you return and the other princes see your true worth.'

'Even if they do not, Bel Shanaar is not immortal,' Malekith said. 'I shall outlive him, and there will come a time when the princes must again choose a successor. Then the crown of Ulthuan will return to its rightful line and I shall do honour to the memory of my father.'

'It is good that you leave, for I could not bear to see you wither away in our halls like a rose hidden from the sun,' Morathi said. 'One day your name will be upon the lips of every elf, and you will usher in a new age for our people. This is written in the stars and thus in your destiny. Morai-heg has granted me the wisdom to see it thus, and so shall it be.'

The seeress looked away for a moment, her gaze turning towards the north. Malekith opened his mouth to speak but Morathi raised a finger to silence him. When she looked at her son, he felt her gaze fall upon him like a lamb stood before a lion, such was the intensity of her stare.

'Great deeds await you, my son, and renown equal to that of your father,' Morathi said, quietly at first, her voice rising in volume as she spoke. 'Let Bel Shanaar sit upon his throne and grow rich and spoilt upon the labours of his people! As you say, his time will pass and his line will be found weak. Care not for the judgement of others, but go forth and do as you see fit, as prince of Nagarythe and leader of the greatest people in the world!'

They embraced for a long while, sharing in silence what could not be said.

There were no tears shed at this parting, for the elves of Nagarythe were ever hardened to adversity and loss. For both, this was simply a new chapter in the story of Nagarythe, to be boldly written upon the pages of history with feats of valour and tales of conquest.

SWIFT AND SURE are the ships of the elves, and the fleet of Malekith sailed north and east for forty days, crossing the Great Ocean without trouble. The elves were masters of the seas, the inheritors of the civilisation of the Old Ones that had now fallen, and the world was theirs to claim. Anticipation and excitement filled the sailors and warriors of Nagarythe as they gazed to the east and wondered what spectacles awaited them.

Malekith was filled with energy, and would pace upon the deck of his ship constantly, when not cloistered in his cabin poring over the charts and maps sent back by elven shipmasters who had begun to explore the wide seas and foreign coasts.

He travelled also from ship to ship when he could, to spend time with the other princes and knights who accompanied his expedition. They feasted on fish caught from the seas, and drank toasts to their prince from caskets of wine brought out of Ulthuan. The mood was of a great celebration, as if setting out was in itself a victory. Malekith could not fault them for their optimism, for as they woke each day heading towards the dawn he felt the lure of adventure too. Other ships they saw passing westwards, laden with timber and ores from the new lands. Ever they exchanged news with the captains of these vessels, and each meeting brought fresh excitement at the wealth and opportunities to be had.

The lands of the east were untamed wilderness for the most part. Savage creatures were there, amidst the majestic mountains and dark forests, but also vast untapped resources that could be taken for those with the wit and daring to do so.

Malekith vowed to his followers that they would build a new realm here, and carve for themselves an empire that would dwarf Ulthuan in size and majesty, worthy of the memory of Aenarion. This cheered them even more, for each prince could see himself as a king, and each knight could picture life as a prince. Under Malekith's reign, it seemed as if anything would be possible, and each would have a castle filled with delights set in breathtaking glades and valleys.

Malekith allowed them to forge their fantasies, for who was he to quell their dreams? He had spoken in truth and looked to the wilds of Elthin Arvan as a new beginning; a place where the ghost of his father would not haunt him and the expectations of his mother would not choke him.

As dawn broke on the forty-first day, a commotion ran through Malekith's fleet. Land had been sighted: jutting headlands of white and dark mud flats that stretched for miles. It was not for this that there was much agitation, for the masters of the ships had known they would make landfall that day, but for a great pall of smoke that hung over the northern horizon. A large fire or fires burned somewhere, and Malekith was filled with foreboding. He ordered his captains to turn northwards at once, and up the coast sped the fleet with all sail set, dancing effortlessly across the waves.

Not long after noon they came upon the port of Athel Toralien, one of the first colonies to be founded in these new lands. Her white towers rose up majestically from the sea of trees that grew right up to the coastline, and a great harbour wall curved out into the ocean, surf crashing upon it. As Malekith feared, the city was alight with many fires, and her walls were blackened with soot.

As the Naggarothi fleet tacked into the bay upon which Athel Toralien stood, they found the quays empty of ships. Malekith guessed that their captains had fled whatever disaster had befallen the city, and that Athel Toralien now lay deserted. He was to be proven wrong in part though, for as the ships approached the harbour, a loud cry went up from the lookouts. There was fighting upon the walls of the city!

As the ship of Malekith came alongside a slender pier, he leapt over the side onto the whitewashed planks. In his wake came his soldiers, jumping from the ship in their haste, not waiting for the boarding bridges to be lowered. Calling his warriors to arms, Malekith raced down the pier towards the high warehouses around the edge of the harbour. As he neared the buildings, clusters of elves came out and hurried towards the Naggarothi. Most were women, unkempt and afraid. With them they brought clusters of children with eyes wide in fear, who hung upon their mother's dresses as if they were gripping upon life itself.

'Bless Asuryan!' the womenfolk cried, and hugged Malekith and his warriors with tears streaming down their cheeks.

'Be quiet!' snapped Malekith to quell their effusive thanks and sobbing. 'What evil passes here?'

'Orcs!' they shrieked in reply. 'The city is besieged!'

'Who commands the city?' he demanded.

'No one, my lord,' he was told. 'Prince Aneron left eight days ago, with the fleet and many of the soldiers. There was not enough room aboard the ships for all to flee. Captain Lorhir defends the walls as best he can, but the orcs have war engines that hurl flaming rocks, and have pounded the city for many days.'

The army was assembling on the dockside, and Malekith ordered that the horses be brought from the ships. As the knights readied themselves, he ordered two companies of spears and his best archers to follow him to the walls. As they marched through the city they saw that the destruction was not as widespread as they first thought. The war machines of the orcs were wildly inaccurate and the damaged buildings were scattered across the city. Even as Malekith reached a stairway leading up to the rampart, a ball of flaming rock and tar flew overhead and crashed into a tower, showering dribbles of flame and debris into the street below.

Leaping up the stone steps three at a time, Malekith swiftly reached the top of the wall, which rose some thirty feet above the ground. The curtain wall of Athel Toralien curved around in a semi-circle for more than a mile, enclosing the city against the bay that lay to the south. Beyond lay an immense forest that stretched as far as the eye could see, cut by the straight lines of roads radiating out from the city's three gates.

There were piles of bodies everywhere; of slain elves, and gruesome green-skinned creatures with fanged mouths and slab-like muscles, clad in crude armour. The current attack appeared to be at a gate tower some two hundred yards further along the wall. A motley assortment of elves, some wearing armour, others in robes, beat back with spears and knives against a swarm of the wildly shouting orcs.

More orcs were pouring up from four ramshackle ladders leaning against the wall.

'Form up for advance!' bellowed Malekith, unsheathing his sword, Avanuir.

The spear companies fell into disciplined ranks six abreast, their shields overlapping, a wall of iron points jutting forwards. Malekith waved them to advance and they set off at a steady pace, their booted feet tramping in unison upon the hard stone.

'Clear those ladders,' the prince told his archers before running to the front of the advancing column.

The archers moved to the wall's edge, some standing upon the battlements, and loosed their bows at the savages climbing up the ladders. Their aim was deadly accurate and dozens of the greenskins tumbled to the ground below, black-fletched arrows piercing eyes, necks and chests.

The orcs had gained a foothold upon the wall and more of their number clambered over the rampart, howling and waving brutal cleavers and axes. The Naggarothi advanced relentlessly, as groups of orcs broke from the main body and ran towards them.

When the first orc reached the black-armoured company Malekith despatched it with a simple overhead cut that left its body cleft from shoulder to groin. The next he slew with a straight thrust through the chest, and another with a backhanded flourish that spilled its entrails onto the stones of the wall.

Malekith continued marching forwards, hewing down an orc with every step, his spearmen tight behind him slaying any orc that evaded the prince's deadly attentions. The Naggarothi stepped over the bodies of the fallen savages as they advanced, never once wavering or changing direction as they headed for the knot of greenskins crowding about the ladders. The elves of Athel Toralien took heart with the arrival of their saviours and fought with greater vigour, stopping the orcs from gaining further ground as the Naggarothi closed in.

Wielded by Malekith, Avanuir sheared through shield, armour, flesh and bone with every strike of the prince, and a line of orc bodies trailed him along the wall until he reached the ladders. No clumsy blow from his foes found its mark as he feinted and swayed through the melee.

Signalling his spears to deal with the other ladders, Malekith leapt up to the battlement by the closest, kicking an orc face as it appeared over the wall. The orc reeled from the blow but did not fall. Avanuir swept down and lopped the orc's head from its body, the lifeless corpse tumbling down the ladder, dislodging more orcs so that they fell flailing to the ground.

As he hewed through another attacker, Malekith held up his left hand and a nimbus of power coalesced around his closed fist. With a snarled word of power, Malekith thrust his hand towards the orcs and unleashed his spell. Forks of blue and purple lightning leapt from his outstretched fingertips, earthing through the skulls of the orcs, causing flesh to catch fire and armour to melt. Down the ladder writhed the bolt, jumping from orc to orc, hurling each to the ground trailing smoke. With a thunderous blast, the ladder itself exploded into a hail of splinters that scythed into the orcs waiting at the foot of the wall, cutting them down by the score.

The spearmen had toppled two more ladders, and as Malekith turned from the wall, the fourth and final ladder collapsed, sending the orcs upon it plunging to a bone-cracking death on the hard earth below. The archers turned their shots now onto the orcs who had gathered around the fallen ladders, shooting any that tried to raise up the siege ladders, until the orcs lost heart and began to retreat.

An elf in bloodstained mail emerged from the knot of weary defenders, his helm scored with many blows, and walked slowly towards the Naggarothi company. He pulled off his tall helmet with a grimace, to reveal blood-matted blond hair, and dropped the helm wearily to the stones.

As he approached, Malekith stooped and tore a rag from one of the orcish dead to clean the gore from the blade of Avanuir. The prince raised an inquiring eye to the approaching elf.

'Captain Lorhir?' asked Malekith, sheathing his blade.

The other nodded and extended a hand in greeting. Malekith ignored the gesture and the elf withdrew his hand. Uncertainty played across Lorhir's face for a moment before he recovered his composure.

'Thank you, highness,' Lorhir panted. 'Praise to Asuryan for guiding you to our walls this day, for I feared this morning we had seen our last sunrise.'

'You may have yet,' replied Malekith. 'I have space upon my ships only for my own troops; there is no room for evacuation. I do not think there is escape by land.'

Malekith pointed out over the wall, to where a sea of orcs seethed along the road and beneath the boughs of the trees. Half a dozen huge catapults stood in clearings slashed raggedly from the forest, mighty pyres burning next to them. Scores of trees swayed and crashed down in every direction as the orcs cut timber to build new ladders and more war engines.

'With your aid we can hold the city until the prince returns,' said Lorhir.

'I do not think the prince will be returning soon,' Malekith said. As he spoke, others of the Toralien defenders gathered about to hear his words. 'Why should I and my soldiers shed our blood for this city?'

'With all the favour of the gods, we few could not hold against this horde for another day,' Lorhir said. 'You must protect us!'

'Must?' said Malekith, his voice an angry hiss. 'In Nagarythe, a captain does not tell a prince what he must do.'

'Forgive me, highness,' pleaded Lorhir. 'We are desperate, and there is no one else. We sent messengers to Tor Alessi and Athel Maraya and other cities, but they have not returned. They have been waylaid, or else our calls for aid have fallen upon uncaring ears. I cannot hold the city alone!'

'I cannot throw away the lives of my warriors defending the lands of a prince who would not defend them himself,' Malekith said sharply.

'Are we not all elves here?' asked one of the other citizens, an ageing elf who held a sword with an edge chipped and dinted by much use and little care. 'You would leave us to the tortures and brutalities of these orcs?'

'If this city were mine, I would defend it to my last breath,' Malekith said, appearing to relent. Then his face hardened. 'But Athel Toralien is not my city. We came to the new world to build a new kingdom, not to spill our blood to protect one of a prince who flees for safety at the first hint of menace. Swear loyalty to me, place yourself under the protection of Nagarythe, and I will defend this city.'

'What of our oaths to Prince Aneron?' replied Lorhir. 'I would not be known as a traitor.'

'It is Aneron of Eataine who has broken his word,' Malekith told them. 'Yes, I know him. He stands upon the labours of his father and abandons his people. He is worthy of no oath of fealty. Stand by me, join the Naggarothi, and I will save your city and from here we will conquer this wild and plentiful land.'

The elves huddled together in forlorn conference, occasionally looking out over the walls at the green-skinned army beyond, and at Malekith's stern demeanour.

'Take us with you on your ships, and we will swear our loyalty to Anlec,' Lorhir said finally. 'What can we few hundred do against that tide of hated beasts?'

'Your eyes must be weary,' said Malekith, waving a hand towards the docks. 'Look again.'

The elves gaped in awe as they watched the Naggarothi host disembarking from the warships. In long columns of black and silver they snaked down the piers, banners fluttering above them. At their head came the knights, already mounted upon their black-flanked destriers. Rank upon rank of spears formed up on the dockyard, moving with poise and precision born of a lifetime of training and fighting.

'A thousand knights, four thousand spears and a thousand bows stand at my command,' Malekith declared.

'The enemy is too great for us to hold the city, even with such numbers,' argued Lorhir. 'Prince Aneron had ten thousand spears and he could not hold the walls.'

'His warriors are not Naggarothi,' Malekith said. 'Each soldier in my host is worth five of Eataine. They are led by me. I am the son of Aenarion, and where my blade falls, death follows. Simply swear oaths of fealty to me and I will save your city. I am the prince of Nagarythe, and where I march, the undying will of my kingdom follows. If I so command it, this city will not fall!'

Such was the bearing and greatness of Malekith at that moment that Lorhir and the others fell to their knees, uttering words of loyalty and dedication.

'So be it,' said Malekith. 'The orcs will be dead by nightfall.'

━━◄ THREE ►━━

Slaughter at Athel Toralien

IT WAS NOT long before companies of archers lined the outer wall, and after a few shambolic attacks the orcs soon learned that to approach within a hundred paces was to face certain death. The greenskins tried as best they could to redirect the fall of their catapult shots, but scored only one lucky hit against the rampart while the rest of their fire landed well short or flew over the city into the harbour beyond.

Malekith arrayed his spearmen by companies, near the westernmost of the three gates, and commanded his captains to drive forwards into the enemy. With a fanfare of clarions, the gates were opened and the host of Nagarythe marched forth. At the orders of their commanders, the Nag-garothi stepped out in unison, filing through the gate five abreast, their spear tips shining in the light of the orcs' fires. A wall of black shields went before them, and against this barrier the wild arrow shots of the orcs never found a mark.

The vanguard halted some fifty paces from the gateway as the orcs began to gather into rude mobs, clamouring about their haggard standards, the largest of their kind bullying, bellowing and punching their underlings into a rough semblance of order. The main part of the elven column parted to the left and right, and took up positions in sloping echelon beside the vanguard, to form an unbroken wall of spear points that ran from the north-east to the south-west, one flank guarded by the wall, the other by the sea.

Behind them, half of the archers ran swiftly down from the walls and took up positions from which they could shoot over the heads of their kinsmen.

37

Malekith watched this from the gatehouse, Lorhir and a few other worthy citizens of the prince's new realm beside him.

'We still have a company or more of warriors, and we would not have it said that we did not fight for the future of our city,' said Lorhir.

'I do not doubt your gallantry,' said Malekith. 'But watch, and you will see why no elf may stand in the line of Nagarythe without first passing a hundred years training upon the fields of Anlec.'

The prince signalled to a hornblower stood with the group, and the herald raised his instrument and played out three rising notes. Almost instantly, the battleline of the elves shifted position.

With seamless precision, the companies on the right, nearest the wall, turned and marched northwards, each angled to protect the flank of the company in front. Through the gap thus created came the archers, who spread out into a long line three deep. The shouted commands of their captains still ringing from the wall, the archers let loose a single storm of arrows that sailed high into the air as a dark cloud. The shots fell steeply into the gathering orcs, slaying and wounding hundreds in a single devastating volley.

No sooner had the first salvo hit its mark than another was in the air, and eight more times this was repeated, an unending stream of arrowheads that pierced armour and green flesh and left piles of orcish dead littering the forest and road.

Many of the orcs fled from this ceaseless death, but the largest and fiercest were goaded into action and ran towards the elven line, chanting and screaming. As they approached, their charge gathered more momentum and those orcs that were fleeing turned back and rejoined the attack, bolstered by the headlong assault of their betters. When the green horde was no more than a hundred paces from the elves, the archers let loose a flurry of shots into their ranks, but the onslaught did not cease or even pause.

Malekith gave another signal to his musician and the hornblower let out a long, pealing blast that dipped in pitch. The orcs were no more than fifty paces away, but the lightly armed archers seemed unperturbed. They split their line, every second archer stepping to his right. Through these channels, the spearmen swiftly advanced and then reformed, scant moments before the orcish attack hit.

With a crash that could be heard upon the walls, the orcs hurled themselves at the Naggarothi. Spear pierced green hide and heavy blade cut through shaft and shield as the orcs tried to batter their way through the line with brute strength and impetus. Here and there, elves fell to the sheer ferocity of the assault, but other elves quickly stepped forwards and closed these gaps, leaving no path through the shield barrier. All along the line, spears were drawn back and thrust forwards in a rhythmic pulse, undulating from south to north in a wave that left hundreds of orcish dead.

Against the weight of the orcs' numbers, the elves slowly began to give ground, steadily and calmly taking steps backwards towards the wall as the fighting slowed and then renewed. It was then that Lorhir realised what was happening.

'You are drawing them closer to the walls,' he said in amazement.

'Now see the true strength of the Naggarothi host,' Malekith told his companions.

Two short horn blasts followed by a long piercing note then rang out and the archers still upon the walls moved to the battlements. From here they could fire directly into the orc mass, their shots passing no more than a hand's breadth from their comrades, yet loosed with such accuracy that the Naggarothi were never in danger of hitting their own warriors.

Between the spearpoints and arrows of the Nagarythe host, the orcs' enthusiasm for fighting began to waver. Their leaders bellowed and beat those that turned away from the melee, and took up great swords and axes and hewed at the elves as a treecutter might hack at a log. Encouraged by the spirit of the orcish chieftains, the green horde kept fighting.

The crews of the catapults now tried to direct their fire upon the spearmen, and scored a few hits that opened up holes in the elvish line. However, the archers poured arrows into these breaches to hold back the orcs, while the spearmen reformed again and again to keep the companies steady. Boulders and flaming balls of tar-covered wood fell more upon the orcs than the elves, to the perverse delight of the war engines' crews. It seemed that they cared not who died beneath the crushing shots of their engines.

Now the greater part of the besieging army had been drawn forwards onto the spears of the elves, and Malekith enacted the final part of his strategy.

Another signal from the horn, and the northern gate opened allowing the knights of Nagarythe to ride forth. Pennants streamed from their lance tips, and silver and black gonfalons fluttered from a dozen standard poles as the thousand knights charged the greenskins. With the war cries of Nagarythe upon their lips and the horn blasts of their musicians ringing around them, the knights of Anlec carved a swathe into the flank of the army pressed up against the elven line.

The orcs were defenceless against this manoeuvre, unable to turn to face this new threat without exposing themselves to the spears of the infantry. Spitted upon lances and trampled beneath the hooves of the knights' steeds, hundreds of orcs died in the first impact of the charge. The momentum of the knights carried them forwards into the midst of the orcish host, and the infantry pressed forwards again to ensure that the noble cavalry were not surrounded.

Lorhir gave a cry of dismay and pointed eastwards. Not all of the orcs had yet joined the fray and a group of several hundred now marched swiftly from the far end of the wall. They sprinted eagerly towards the battle and would come up behind the knights, or could otherwise turn through the open gate of the city.

'We must intercept them!' said Lorhir, turning to run towards the steps, but Malekith grabbed him by the arm and halted him.

'I said that you are not yet part of the Naggarothi army,' the prince said sternly.

'But you have no other reserve!' cried Lorhir. 'Archers alone will not deter them, who else will hold them back?'

'I will,' said Malekith. 'If each of my warriors is worth five of yours, then I am worth at least one hundred!'

With that, Malekith turned and sprinted eastwards along the wall. As he ran, he began to chant quickly under his breath, drawing the winds of magic towards himself. He could feel them churning in the air around him, heaving through the stone beneath his booted feet. Though not as dense as the magic condensed by the vortex in Ulthuan, the strands of mystical energy that swirled across the whole world blew strongly here, in the northern parts. Malekith was filled with exhilaration as his sorcery grew in power, suffusing his body with its boundless energy.

With a shout, Malekith drew his sword and bounded up to the rampart before leaping from the wall. Silver wings of magic sprang shimmering from his shoulders and carried the prince aloft.

As he sped swiftly towards the orc reinforcements, Malekith's sword glowed with magical power, a piercing blue light burning from its blade. The light spread until it enveloped the whole of the prince so that he became a gleaming thunderbolt of energy.

The orcs stumbled and gazed upwards in amazement and awe as Malekith sped down towards them, one fist held in front of him, his sword swept back ready to strike.

Like a meteor, the prince of Nagarythe crashed into the orcs in an explosion of blue flame that sent burning greenskins and steaming earth flying for many yards in every direction. Dozens more were hurled from their feet as magical flames licked at their flesh. Smoke drifted up from the crater, revealing the prince crouched on one knee. With another shout he sprang forwards, sword in front of him like a lance point, and the blade slid through the chest of the nearest greenskin.

More out of instinct and natural savagery than bravery, the closest orcs charged towards the prince, their weapons upraised, guttural shouts tearing the air. The prince moved in a blur of speed and motion, slicing and thrusting with his gleaming blade, felling an orc with every heartbeat. Within a few moments, all but one of the orcs were running from the wrath of Malekith.

The creature that remained was a gigantic beast, almost twice as tall as the elven prince. It was clad from head to toe in thick plates of armour painted with dried blood. It regarded Malekith with small, brutish red eyes and flexed its clawed fingers on the haft of the great double-headed axe it carried.

With a grunt it hefted the axe above its head and swung down the blade with terrifying force. Malekith stepped nimbly aside at the last moment, and the axe bit deep into the ground where a moment before the prince had been stood. His sword held idly by his side, Malekith took a few steps to his right as the orc warlord ripped its axe free from the earth in a shower of bloody clods.

With a bellow of anger, the orc swung its axe two-handed, but Malekith easily ducked the wild blow and cut his sword across the shoulder of the warlord, sending shards of armour spinning away. As the orc recovered its balance, the lord of Nagarythe spun around behind it and slashed at its legs, drawing his blade across both thighs, hamstringing the monstrous greenskin.

Falling to its knees, it gave a roar of rage and lunged wildly towards the prince, who stepped backwards as the orc fell flat upon its face. With a deft thrust, Malekith sheared his blade through the exposed shoulder of the orc, and then brought the edge of the blade down upon the wrist of the other arm. The orc howled as its axe fell to the ground, one fist still gripped around its rough wooden haft.

Malekith paced back and forth, eyeing the orc with a contemptuous smile. Helpless now, the orc could do nothing but shout and froth at the mouth. With a flourish, Malekith whipped his sword around for a final time and the orc's head spun into the air with a fountain of blood. It fell to the hard earth at Malekith's feet in a spatter of gore. The prince dug the point of his gleaming blade into the still-helmeted skull and lifted it from the ground for all to see.

The remnants of the orcs were fleeing through the woods, abandoning their war machines, and a great roar of triumph rose up from the ranks of the Naggarothi. Thrice they shouted the name of their prince, each time lifting up their spears and bows and lances in salute. As the knights made sport of chasing the fleeing greenskins through the forest, Malekith returned to his city.

WHEN NEWS REACHED Ulthuan of Malekith's actions, there was much debate and confusion. Prince Aneron travelled to Tor Anroc with many allies and demanded audience with the Phoenix King. The benches around the throne chamber were thronged with nobles and courtiers, and the air throbbed with heated discussion.

A respectful hush fell upon the entry of the Phoenix King, who paced from the great double doors, his long cloak of feathers sweeping across the marble floor. As soon as Bel Shanaar was seated upon his throne Aneron stepped forwards and gave a perfunctory bow.

'Malekith must be punished!' Aneron rasped.

'Punished for what crime?' Bel Shanaar asked calmly.

'He has seized my lands, sovereign territory of Eataine,' Aneron said. 'The city of Athel Toralien was founded by my father and passed to me. This Naggarothi villain has no rightful claim.'

'If you allow Malekith to keep his stolen prize, you set a terrifying precedent,' added Galdhiran, one of the lesser Eataine princes. 'If we can seize each other's lands and claim right of conquest, then what is to prevent us all from doing as we please? Only Nagarythe and Caledor, with their large armies, are served in this manner. You must end this before it begins!'

There were boos and scoffing cries from some amongst the court, and cries of encouragement from others. The tumult continued for some time until Bel Shanaar raised his hand and silence once again descended.

'Are there any that speak on behalf of Malekith?' asked the Phoenix King.

There was a gentle cough, and all eyes turned to the uppermost tier of benches to the Phoenix King's left. Morathi sat amidst a small entourage of grim Naggarothi. She stood languidly and paced slowly down the steps to the floor of the audience hall, her gown billowing behind her like golden dawn clouds.

'I speak not for Malekith, nor Nagarythe,' the seeress said, her voice gentle yet strong. 'I speak for the people of Athel Toralien, left to die in their homes at the hands of the savage orcs by Prince Aneron.'

'There was not room–' began Aneron.

'Be silent,' snarled Morathi, and the Eataine prince stuttered into acquiescence. 'It is not your place to interrupt your betters when they are speaking, Prince Aneron, and the realm of Eataine, forfeited all right to Athel Toralien when they abandoned their duties to protect their citizens.'

Morathi had been speaking to Bel Shanaar but now turned to address the chamber as a whole.

'Prince Malekith usurped no throne,' she declared. 'No blade was lifted against the warriors of Eataine, no blood of fellow elf spilt. The lord of Nagarythe conquered an abandoned city in the grip of the orcs. He saved hundreds of elven lives by his action. That those lands had once belonged to Prince Aneron is of no bearing. If we are to argue ownership in that manner, then perhaps we should ask a representative of the orcs to attend, for they lived there long before we arrived!'

Laughter rippled around the hall at Morathi's suggestion, for Ulthuan had been awash for years with tales of the orcs' brutality and stupidity. The former queen of Ulthuan turned her attention back to the Phoenix King.

'No wrong has been done here,' she said. 'Malekith asks not for reward nor praise, but the simple right to keep what he has fought to claim. Would you deny him that right?'

A greater part of the assembled nobles applauded Morathi's argument. Bel Shanaar considered his position. A large number of Ulthuan's citizenry even now lauded the prince and his heroic defence of the colony city. Prince Aneron had never enjoyed much popularity, even amongst the elves of Eataine, and many enjoyed the snub implicit in Malekith's annexation. The Phoenix King had heard jeers from a large crowd of elves outside the palace during the arrival of Aneron in Tor Anroc.

'I have here one other piece of evidence,' Morathi added.

She gestured to her retainers and one strode down from the benches and passed her a rolled-up parchment. Morathi handed this to Bel Shanaar, who did not open it but merely looked inquiringly at the Naggarothi seeress.

'This is a letter from the people of Athel Toralien,' she said. 'It is signed by all four hundred and seventy-six survivors of the orc attack. They swear loyalty unconditionally to Prince Malekith. Further, they invite their kith and kin to join them in the new lands and are confident that under Naggarothi protection the city will prosper greatly. So, do not simply listen to my opinion, but hearken to the views of the city's people.'

At this there were some cheers from the watching courtiers and princes. Aneron scowled as even some of his fellow Eataine joined in the mockery.

'It appears that a precedent is indeed set,' said Bel Shanaar when the clamour had quietened. 'A prince who quits his property and leaves it unprotected abandons all rights to ownership. We were raised to our station for protecting Ulthuan alongside Aenarion, and we must maintain our rule as guardians of her people. Thus, I make this proclamation. Prince Aneron deserted his lands and his subjects. As Phoenix King, I consider Athel Toralien to have been an abandoned land, and thus suitable for reconquest by any prince. Prince Malekith has established his rightful claim and that shall be recognised by this court. Let this be a warning to all who seek the riches and power available for those in the new world. Go forth in the name of Ulthuan, but never forget your duties.'

Thus was Prince Aneron shamed. With little support for his position, the Eataine prince sheepishly quit the shores of Ulthuan and sailed west to the jungle-crowded coasts of Lustria. Malekith was invested as ruler of Athel Toralien and his conquest of the colonies began in earnest.

—◄ FOUR ►—

Unheralded Allies

ATHEL TORALIEN WAS but the first in a long line of great victories for Malekith and the Naggarothi. They subdued the greenskins of the forests around the city and forged eastwards across the new continent. After almost half a century, Athel Toralien having grown into a teeming port along with other settlements such as Tor Alessi and Tor Kathyr, Malekith looked to found another city further to the east.

Over the years more Naggarothi had made the journey to the colonies, and Malekith's host now numbered over twenty thousand warriors. With this army, he marched along the great river Anurein, which flowed all the way from the mountains to the sea for hundreds of leagues. He put goblin camps to the torch and forced back the beastmen and other vile creatures of the deepest woods.

In the wake of his advance, the Naggarothi cleared the forests and built fortified farms. To the south, other cities were also prospering greatly, and their rulers were eager to seek alliance with the prince of Nagarythe. The forces of other elven lords joined the move eastwards. There were others, too, who were soon to learn about this brilliant general and charismatic leader: the dwarfs.

IT WAS IN the third year of Malekith's great eastward push that he first came across the folk of the mountains.

The forests of Elthin Arvan began to thin as the foothills of the mountains rose up amongst their boughs, and scouts from the Naggarothi host returned to Malekith to report that they had found something unusual in the woods. Large areas of trees had been cut down, not by the crude hacking of beastmen or orcs, but smoothly sawn and felled. They noted that the tracks of booted feet were plentiful, and evidence of large, well-built campfires had been found in the clearings.

Malekith assembled a company of his finest warriors and for several days they marched further eastwards, following the trail as it led towards the mountains.

The elves found the remains of encampments and marvelled at the precision with which tents had been aligned, fire pits dug and the trees hewn to form clearings of almost uniform squares. The ground was trampled by many feet, and there was also evidence that temporary palisades and ditches had also been dug and then removed or filled in. That the strangers were organised was in no doubt, and Malekith ordered his scouts to remain vigilant, day and night.

It was another three days before the elves came upon a path, or rather a road. It began at the largest campsite that they had encountered, and from the tracks that led to the north, west and south, this had been used as some sort of staging area for forays in all directions. The earth was not merely trodden down, but deliberately packed and seeded with stones to make the footing more secure. The road itself was of similar build, stretching away to the south-east, cutting through trees and hills without deviation for as far as the eye could see.

Malekith ordered his warriors to stay off the road, but they followed its course from a little way into the forest, their stealthy advance concealed by the trees. As night fell, the elves saw the glow of bonfires in the distance, several miles away, and plumes of smoke rising across the stars.

Malekith was torn as to what course of action to take. If these unknown woodcutters were hostile, then it would be far better to surround their camp at night. On the other hand, coming upon the strangers in the hours of darkness could possibly lead to surprise and cause the force they were trailing to respond with justified hostility.

In the end, Malekith decided to compromise. He left a few of his swiftest runners near to the road, and ordered them to return with all speed to warn the colonies if he did not return or otherwise send word by daybreak. His most cunning archers Malekith despatched to circumnavigate the camp and wait in ambush should their unknown quarry attempt to fight. They climbed into the branches of the trees and moved above ground from bough to bough, so silent and unnoticed that not even the birds were disturbed at their passing. The others he brought alongside the road and told them to wait a short distance from the camp, ready to provide reinforcements if things went ill.

With two of his lieutenants, Yeasir and Alandrian, Malekith approached along the road, weapons sheathed, their cloaks thrown back across their shoulders so that they concealed nothing that might cause suspicion. As they neared the camp, the elves saw two large braziers burning on either side of the road, casting a wide illumination.

In the light stood a handful of diminutive beings, the head of the tallest no higher than an elf's chest; in build they were stocky, their shoulders and chests broad with muscle, their guts solid and of considerable girth. They were extremely hairy; each sported a beard that reached his waist, and two of them had facial hair hanging almost to the tips of their weighty boots.

Each of them wore a heavy coat of chainmail tied with a thick leather belt with a broad iron buckle. Their arms were bare but for golden torques twisted into intriguing designs, and the noseguards of their helms covered much of their wide faces.

Atop the helms were small crests of leaping boars, or stylised dragons, and three had horns protruding. It was only after careful consideration that Malekith assured himself that these horns were indeed attached to the strangers' headgear and not sprouting from their skulls and passing through holes in their helms. Each held a single-bladed axe, of design unlike anything Malekith had seen before. They each also had a large round shield, rimmed with riveted iron and emblazoned with extraordinary designs of coiling wyrms, anvils and winged hammers.

They were gathered in a group about one of the braziers, talking amongst themselves. The prince's keen hearing caught snatches of a guttural tongue, much like gravel rolling down a slope or the crunch of shingle underfoot. It grated on Malekith's nerves and he just managed to stop his hand straying to the hilt of his sword.

The sentries saw the three elves approaching and turned as one to stare at them. Malekith and his two companions stopped where they were, just inside the circle of firelight, some fifty or sixty paces from the guards. The strange warriors exchanged hurried glances, and then nods from four of them sent the fifth running back into the camp, moving surprisingly swiftly on his short legs.

The two bands stood and simply eyed each other. They remained in this stalemate for some considerable time.

Eventually a party of the dwarfs came marching up the road from the camp, over a dozen of them. One was obviously their leader, his beard braided into four long plaits bound with many golden clasps. Underneath this expanse of bristle Malekith could see a blue jerkin embroidered with gold thread in angular knotwork designs. The others walked deferentially a few paces behind him, their eyes wary, their grips tight on axes and hammers.

Malekith held his hands far out to his sides, to show no hostile intent, though he knew full well that he would still be capable of drawing his blade in the blink of an eye. Yeasir and Alandrian did likewise. A surreptitious glance to the left and right revealed several of the elven scouts hidden amongst the leaves, arrows bent to bows trained on the camp leader as he stomped forwards.

He stopped between the braziers and gestured for the three elves to approach, and then stood with his arms folded solidly across his chest as they walked slowly up the road. Malekith waved his lieutenants to stop about ten paces short of the dwarfs, and took a few more steps. The leader looked at the prince with a frown, though Malekith could not tell if this was an expression of displeasure or the dwarf's natural demeanour – all of them appeared to be scowling.

This close, Malekith could smell the dwarfs as well as see them. He quelled a sneer as an offensive mixture of cave dirt and sweat assaulted his nostrils. The dwarf leader continued to look Malekith up and down, and then turned his head and barked something to his underlings. They relaxed slightly, lowering their weapons a fraction.

The leader proffered a grimy hand and spat something like 'Kurgrik'. Malekith looked down at the grubby paw extended towards him and fought to keep the disdain from his expression.

'Malekith,' the prince said, giving the dirty hand a quick shake before swiftly withdrawing his grip.

'Malkit?' the dwarf said, finally breaking into a thin smile.

'Close enough,' Malekith replied, fixing his face with a pleasant smile learned from many years spent hiding his frustration in the courts of Ulthuan.

'Elf,' Kurgrik said, pointing at Malekith, and the prince could not keep the surprise from his face. The dwarf broke into a wide grin and let out a gruff laugh and then nodded. 'Elf,' he said again.

With a wave, the dwarf leader invited the three into his camp, and as Malekith stepped forwards, the Naggarothi prince gave the most imperceptible nod to the warriors in the trees. Without disturbing a single leaf, they withdrew from sight.

The layout of the camp was as Malekith had surmised from the evidence they had found in the forest. Five rows each of five tents were spread out across a square glade cut into the woods on one side of the road. At the end of each row burned a small and neat fire in deep pits lined with stones.

The dwarfs had all gathered to look at the newcomers, and shamelessly gaped at the tall, slender elves as they walked into the camp, keeping their pace steady so as not to move quicker than their hosts. Dark, inquisitive eyes glared at them from every angle, but Malekith could feel that the looks were of curiosity, not enmity.

For their part, the elves regarded the dwarfs with neutral expressions, nodding politely as they caught the eye of one camp member or another.

The dwarfs led them to the far side of the camp where a large fire was burning, surrounded by low wooden benches. Here the elders sat themselves down, flanking their leader, who gesticulated for Malekith and his comrades to do likewise. Malekith tried to sit down with as much dignity as possible, but on the low dwarfen seat his knees were well above his waist and so he reclined to one side to assume a more comfortable position. For some reason this raised a chortle amongst some of the dwarfs, but it seemed good-natured enough.

Tin tankards were thrust into the elves' hands, and three dwarfs came forwards, two of them carrying a large barrel between them. The third directed them to place it carefully in front of the dwarf leader, and then with great ceremony drove a tap into the keg with a wooden hammer. He poured a small amount of the frothing contents into his hand, sniffed it and then dipped his tongue into the liquid. He thrust a hand towards Malekith with his thumb pointed up and smiled. Malekith smiled in return, but felt it best not to return the gesture lest it was some sign of disrespect.

The chief dwarf than stood up and strutted over to the barrel and filled his golden tankard with the brew. Hesitantly, Yeasir followed suit, sniffing cautiously at his mug's contents. Malekith looked enquiringly at his lieutenant, who replied with a bemused shrug. The other two elves then filled up their tankards and returned to their seats.

Raising his tankard in a way that even the elves recognised as a toast, the dwarf brought his cup up to his lips and downed the contents with three gargantuan gulps. With a satisfied smacking of his lips, he slammed the tankard down onto the bench beside him. Bubbles of foam were stuck upon his beard, and he wiped them away with the back of his hand and winked at Malekith.

Hesitantly, Malekith allowed a dribble of the liquid to pass his lips. It was quite thick, and almost stung his tongue with its bitterness. He could not suppress a quick, choking cough, which elicited more gentle laughter from the dwarfs.

His pride wounded by their good-natured yet mocking humour, Malekith snarled and took a more serious draught of the potion. He fought against the urge to retch as he swallowed, and then gulped down more and more. He felt his eyes watering at its acrid taste, which was as different from the delicate wines of Ulthuan as winter is from summer.

Gulping down the last mouthful, Malekith fought back the bile rising in his throat and playfully tossed the tankard over his shoulder and raised an inquisitive eyebrow. At this the dwarfs erupted into more laughter, but this time it was clearly directed at their leader, who gave a snort, and then a nod of appreciation.

Malekith glanced across to Yeasir and Alandrian, who appeared to be both finishing their drinks. However, out of the corner of his eye, Malekith spied patches of dampness upon the earth close to his companions and suspected that they had used the distraction offered by his performance to pour away most of their drink.

They spent the rest of the night communicating in crude fashion, naming objects in each of their tongues and suchlike. Malekith despatched Yeasir to take word to the others that all was well, keeping Alandrian close by. His lieutenant displayed an unseen gift for language and had already picked up a smattering of dwarfish.

OVER THE NEXT four days, Malekith and Alandrian spent much time with the dwarfs, and invited Kurgrik to the Naggarothi camp. Through Alandrian, it transpired that Kurgrik was a thane, one of the nobles of a mighty city in the mountains called Karaz-a-Karak. As alien as the elves had been in the dwarf encampment, so too were the dwarfs in the elves'.

As host, Malekith offered the dwarfs golden goblets of the finest Cothique wine he had, which the dwarfs quaffed with enthusiasm as the elves sampled their cups with more refinement. The dwarfs were inquisitive, but not offensively so, always polite to inquire, through Alandrian, whether they could inspect the elves' tents, weapons, water casks and all other manner of items. They ran their rough hands over elegantly etched armour with surprising delicacy, and gave approving grunts when they looked at the keen spearheads and arrows of the elves.

As night fell on the fourth day, Alandrian returned from the dwarf camp as Malekith sat in his tent, watching one of his many servants polish his armour. Alandrian brought Yeasir with him and the two lieutenants bowed as they entered the pavilion. Catching the look in their eyes Malekith dismissed the retainer and waved a hand for them to sit upon the plush rugs that served as a floor.

'You have news?' Malekith said, idly swirling wine around a silver goblet.

'Indeed, highness,' said Alandrian. 'Kurgrik intends to leave on the morrow.'

Malekith digested this without comment and Alandrian continued.

'Kurgrik has extended to you an invitation to accompany him back to the dwarf realms.'

'Has he?' said Malekith. 'How interesting. What do you make of his motives?'

'I am no expert, highness, but he seems sincere enough to me,' said Alandrian. 'He says that you may take an escort of fifty warriors.'

'Careful, highness,' said Yeasir. 'Though fifty Naggarothi would be guard enough against Kurgrik's small force, only the gods know what lies ahead. Even if we take the dwarfs at their word, which I don't, you would be relying upon them to provide you with adequate protection against any number of unknown perils. There are orcs and beasts aplenty still, I would say. If they should attack, who is to say that the dwarfs will stand their ground and not abandon you?'

'I do not think that the dwarfs would have ventured this far from their mountain homes if they were cowardly,' said Alandrian. 'There was no fear in them that I could see when they came to our camp, though they were at our mercy.'

'Bravery and duty are not the same thing,' said Yeasir, standing up and starting to pace. 'It is one thing for them to fight for themselves, but would they do so for our prince?'

He strode to the tent door and threw open the flap.

'Every elf of Nagarythe out there would lay down his life for our lord,' Yeasir said. 'Yet not one of them would risk his blood for Kurgrik unless the prince commanded it. I would expect no more from the dwarfs, and quite a lot less if I am to be honest. What if Kurgrik falls? Would his warriors fight on for Malekith?'

'We can demand oaths that they will,' answered Alandrian. 'They value honour highly and I would say that their word is almost as good as any elf's promise.'

'No matter!' snapped Malekith. 'If I am to go, I shall look to myself as ever and not rely upon the dwarfs for my safety. A more fundamental question is whether it is worth my time to go at all?'

'It would be most informative, I am sure, highness,' said Alandrian. 'We can learn much not only of the dwarfs but of the world further to the east.'

'We can judge the size of their armies and the quality of their fighters,' added Yeasir. 'It would be best that we know our foes.'

'If foes they are,' said Alandrian. 'As a gesture of faith and friendship, such embassy could bring us valuable allies.'

'Allies?' said Malekith. 'Nagarythe prospers upon her own strength and needs not the charity of others.'

'I have not made my point clearly, your highness,' said Alandrian with an apologetic bow. 'Ever will the other princes of Ulthuan be jealous of our power, and in Elthin Arvan there is none that can equal the power of Prince Malekith. Though all are of one heart and spirit for the moment, the loyalties of the other realms may well change. Bel Shanaar cares not for the colonies at the present, for they are distant from Tor Anroc. Yet, should his gaze turn upon these shores, how many of your fellow princes would stand by your side if the Phoenix Throne desired control over these lands?'

'And how would the dwarfs guard against that?' said Malekith, setting down his goblet and turning an intent stare upon his captain.

'They are entirely free of influence from Ulthuan,' Alandrian explained. 'With the dwarfs as your friends, you will be the powerbroker in Elthin Arvan and it is Bel Shanaar who will have to tread carefully in his dealings with you.'

'My mind is not made for politics,' said Yeasir, striding back from the door to stand before his master. 'I leave that to you. However, what I have seen of the dwarfs' wargear, it is durable and well made. At the moment we still rely much upon imports from Nagarythe to keep your warriors armed and armoured. If you could secure a more local source for such things, it improves our security.'

'Ever the practical one, Yeasir,' said Alandrian. 'Prince, envisage a treaty between Ulthuan and the dwarfs, for the betterment of both. Who is more fitting to herald such an age than Malekith of Nagarythe?'

'Your flattery is crude and obvious, Alandrian, but Yeasir's practicalities convince me,' announced Malekith, standing up. 'Alandrian, you shall convey my wishes to the dwarf thane that I shall accompany him back to his lands. Press upon him the honour he is being granted and extract whatever assurances your worries require and prudence expects.'

'Of course, highness,' replied Alandrian with a bow.

'Yeasir, I have another task for you,' said Malekith.

'I am ready to serve, highness,' said Yeasir.

'I shall write two letters this night, and entrust them to you before I depart,' said the prince. 'One is destined for Tor Anroc and the hand of Bel Shanaar. I would not have the Phoenix King accuse me of keeping this news from him.'

'And the other, highness?' said Yeasir.

'The other shall be for my mother,' said Malekith with a wry smile. 'Make sure that you deliver it first. If Morathi were to learn second-hand of what happens here, none of our lives would be worth living.'

THE FOLLOWING DAY, Malekith, Alandrian and fifty Naggarothi warriors accompanied Kurgrik as the dwarf thane headed back to the mountains. For the most part, the elves marched in silence alongside their new-found allies, who were equally taciturn. Malekith strolled alongside Kurgrik with Alandrian to translate, and though ever he appeared at ease the prince's eyes and ears were always alert.

Though the dwarfs had been confident enough in their camp, as they set out eastwards, their party became more wary. There were roughly two hundred dwarfs in the group, along with many wagons pulled by sturdy ponies, laden with felled trees. A vanguard of some fifty dwarfs preceded the march half a mile ahead of the main group, who walked slowly but surely alongside the wagons.

All of the dwarfs were armed and their hands were never far from the hafts of their axes and swords as they marched along the road. Ever the dwarfs were watchful, sending out scouts into the woods to warn of ambush.

The pace was not quick; Malekith and the other elves could have moved far more swiftly had they chosen to do so. However, the dwarfs marched relentlessly, and such was the efficiency with which they set and broke camp that they covered many miles each day, never wavering or tiring.

At night, the dwarfs would quickly dig defensive ditches lined with sharpened logs from the carts, and watchful guards patrolled ceaselessly. Kurgrik continued to entertain his guest with beer and such stories as Alandrian could translate.

Four days into the trek, the forests finally relinquished their weakening grip on the lands and were replaced by rising meadows and windswept hills.

The mountains towered ahead, their snowy peaks lost amongst permanent clouds. Even the highest peaks of the Annulii on Ulthuan were diminutive by the standards of these ancient mounts, which stretched across the horizon north and south, seemingly going on forever.

The hills were covered with long grass and bracken, and littered with tumbled boulders swept down from the mountains in ages past. Paths and animal trails led off from the road, but it continued straight on through briar and across moor heading eastwards. As the group came nearer to the mountains, the first of several dwarf-built keeps came into sight.

It was a low, broad structure, only two storeys high, utterly unlike the majestic towers and spires of Ulthuan and quite ugly to Malekith's eye. The fort was crowned with battlements and protected by square towers at each corner. It stood on a hill overlooking the road, with large catapults and bolt-hurling engines upon its walls.

Dwarfs armed with axes and hammers marched out to meet Kurgrik and his curious guests, and as a storm swept down from the mountains, lashing the hills with driving rains and wind, the travellers were quickly ushered inside by the fort's commander.

Within the thick walls, the keep was sparsely furnished, and Malekith found the bare stone depressing. He wondered why the dwarfs did not hide the grey rock with tapestries and paintings. His mood was somewhat mollified as they were brought into a long low hall with a roaring fire pit at the centre. No matter how dreary the dwarfs' aesthetic crudeness, it was preferable to the tempest that was now raging outside.

Kurgrik introduced their host as Grobrimdor, a venerable dwarf of more than four hundred winters whose white beard was half as long again as he was tall. He wore his thick mail coat at all times, and an axe was hung at his belt even as he introduced the more prominent members of the garrison. It was clear to Malekith that despite the storm the dwarfs were still wary of attack.

Grobrimdor and Kurgrik furnished the elves with rough blankets and bowls of thick soup, and then asked politely if Malekith would talk more with them concerning the elves and Ulthuan. With Alandrian to roughly translate, Malekith seated himself upon a low stool by the fire.

'Far to the west, beyond the vast forests, lies the Great Ocean,' the prince began. 'Travel across the high waves for many days and one comes upon the shores of Ulthuan. Our isle is fertile and green, an emerald set upon a sea of sapphire. White towers rise above the tall trees and verdant pastures, against the backdrop of the glittering peaks of the Annulii Mountains.'

'And you live in these mountains, yes?' said Kurgrik.

'Only to hunt,' replied Malekith. 'Except in Chrace and Caledor, where all is mountains and hills and there are no meadows or grass-filled plains on which to live.'

Kurgrik took this answer with a disappointed grunt, but then his eyes lit up with a new vigour.

'These mountains contain gems and gold?' asked the thane.

'Gold and silver, diamonds and crystals of all kinds,' said Malekith.

'And perhaps your king would trade these with our people?' said Kurgrik, getting quite animated.

'It is not for the Phoenix King alone to decide such matters,' Malekith said. 'We have many princes, and each of the realms of Ulthuan is ruled over by such an elf. It is for each to decide the fate and future of his lands and people. I rule Nagarythe, greatest of the kingdoms of Ulthuan, and reign over the colonies to the west of here.'

'That is good,' said Grobrimdor, gesturing for his retainers to bring mugs of ale. 'It is so with us. Our kings rule our cities, and the High King commands from Karaz-a-Karak. Your king must be a great leader to rule over so many princes.'

Malekith stifled his reply before it was spoken and suppressed the urge to glance towards Alandrian. Instead he took a sip of ale, buying time to compose his response.

'Bel Shanaar, the Phoenix King, is a clever statesman and diplomatic with his words,' said Malekith. 'My father, the first Phoenix King, was a great leader. He was our greatest warrior and our salvation from darkness.'

'If your father was king, then why does his son not succeed him?' asked Kurgrik, his knotty brows furrowed with suspicion.

Malekith was again forced to think his response through carefully, lest he betray some weakness or flaw that would offend the dwarfs.

'I will rule Ulthuan when she is ready for me,' said the prince. 'She needed time to heal from a great war fought against the daemons of the north, and so the princes chose not to follow the line of my father but to elevate one of their own to the Phoenix Throne. In the interests of harmony and peace, I do not challenge their decision.'

Both Grobrimdor and Kurgrik nodded and grunted approvingly, and Malekith relaxed a little. His thoughts were still turbulent though. The dwarfs' questions stirred old ambitions, feelings that Malekith had travelled to Elthin Arvan to leave behind. Alandrian, sensing his prince's unease, filled the silence.

'You spoke of trade,' said the captain. 'Our cities grow ever more swiftly with each year. What can your people offer us in exchange for our riches?'

The conversation turned once again to a subject dear to the dwarfs' hearts, and all talk of rulership and succession was forgotten. Malekith spoke little for the rest of the evening and allowed his mind to drift, knowing that Alandrian could later convey any news of import.

Long before midnight the dwarfs showed the elves to their rough quarters. Malekith slept in a large dormitory with his warriors, all of them upon the floor for the dwarfs' cots were far too short for the tall elves.

* * *

HAVING SLEPT POORLY, Malekith woke early in the morning. Many of the dwarfs were already up and about, or had perhaps passed the night without sleeping. The prince swiftly donned a simple robe and cloak and left the dormitory. The dwarfs said gruff welcomes as he passed into the main hall, but did not attempt to stop him. Guided only by whim, Malekith climbed a short staircase and exited out of a squat tower onto the battlements.

The sun was but a dull glow behind the mountains, which reared up into the dark blue skies in an unending line of jagged peaks. A thick mist coiled about the keep, and the breath of the dwarf sentries formed clouds in the air. Droplets of water shone on their beards and iron armour. All was peaceful save for the sound of metallic boots on stone and the jingle of the dwarfs' mail armour.

Malekith stood looking east towards the mountains for some time, until elven voices from below warned him that his companions were stirring. He was about to descend back to the hall when Alandrian hurried from the tower. The lieutenant visibly relaxed upon seeing his prince and his expression turned to sheepish guilt when Malekith raised an inquiring brow.

'I awoke to find you missing,' said Alandrian, striding quickly along the stone wall. 'I thought that perhaps some ill had befallen you.'

'You thought that perhaps I had been taken hostage?' said Malekith. 'That through some sorcery they had spirited me away without a fight?'

'I don't know what I thought, really, highness,' said Alandrian. 'I was suddenly fearful and reminded of Yeasir's warnings.'

Malekith turned back to the majestic view. The fog had all but gone and the mountains were revealed in all of their majesty. The prince took a deep breath and then let it out with feeling.

'I would not swap such sights for the quiet pedantry of the Phoenix Throne,' he declared. 'Who needs to be Phoenix King when glory and conquest await? Let Bel Shanaar wither away in courts and audiences, while the wider world awaits me.'

Alandrian looked unconvinced.

'What is it?' said Malekith.

'It is Bel Shanaar who chooses to stay in Ulthuan and turn his reign into one of domesticity and politics,' said Alandrian, turning his gaze towards the mountains. 'Were you to be Phoenix King, I have no doubt that you would do so at the head of our armies, not from the comfort of Anlec. In time, the princes will see that their king leads from behind them, not from the front. Then they will see the true worth of Nagarythe, and her prince.'

'Perhaps,' said Malekith. 'Perhaps one day they will.'

The two stood in silence for a short while, gazing at the mountains, each content in his own thoughts concerning what they and their dwarfen rulers might herald for the Naggarothi. The sun now rose above the lowest peaks and golden light spilled down upon the hills.

A gruff cough attracted Malekith's attention and he turned to see a dwarf standing in the tower doorway.

'We should rejoin our hosts, highness,' said Alandrian. 'Kurgrik will wish to leave soon.'

'Go ahead and prepare for our departure,' said Malekith, looking back at the mountains but his thoughts far to the west upon Ulthuan. 'I'll be with you shortly.'

OVER THE FOLLOWING days, the dwarfs and elves stopped at several more of the way-forts. Each was as drab as the first and Malekith's expectations of the dwarfs' cities sank with every new sighting of the small, functional buildings.

The dwarfs took the time to spend a night in each of these way-fortresses, to gather news from the garrisons and show off their intriguing guests. The beer they had been presented with at the first meeting was much in evidence, and out of courtesy Malekith deigned to sample the different brews offered to him by each of the keep commanders. Though far from enamoured of the vulgar ale, Malekith soon learned the art of swallowing his allotted draught swiftly, so as to leave as little taste as possible in his mouth. He thought that perhaps this was why the dwarfs also drank so quickly; that they did not really like the taste of their own brews. However, the regularity with which the dwarfs returned to their barrels in an evening suggested otherwise.

When they came into the mountains proper, the dwarfs warned the elves to remain on their guard. Though the forests were the realm of Chaotic denizens and bloodthirsty beasts, the mountains were also home to many orcs and goblins, and other creatures such as trolls, giants and monstrous birds that frequently came south in search of food.

'Many daemons and monsters once besieged our holds,' said Kurgrik, via Alandrian's improving skills as a translator. The foothills were now rising steeply towards the mountains. The column was winding its way along a rough track, Kurgrik riding on his wagon, Malekith and Alandrian walking beside it.

'The sun hid and endless night darkened the mountains,' the thane continued. 'The valleys echoed to the howls and roars of the creatures of the north. They beat upon our gates and hurled themselves at our walls. Many dwarfs died defending their homes against the horrors.'

'We too suffered under the assault of Chaos,' Malekith said. 'Then Aenarion, my father, led the war against the daemons and brought us through the dark times.'

'Grimnir was the greatest of our warriors,' said Kurgrik with a wistful smile. 'Grungni, master of the runes and wise beyond mortals, forged two great axes for Grimnir. With these he slaughtered an army of the beasts. Valaya wove a cloak for her kin, and with her protective gift Grimnir fought against the largest and most deadly foes. Yet for all his fierce skill, Grimnir could not defeat every daemon, for they came forth in an unending tide.'

'As it was on Ulthuan,' said Malekith. 'Without end came the legions of

Chaos. We fought without hope until Aenarion made the final sacrifice. He spilt his blood upon the altar of Khaine in return for victory.'

'Grimnir travelled far into the north with one of his axes and fought to the great gate of the Chaos gods,' Kurgrik said, frowning slightly at the prince's interruption. 'He was never seen again and his axe was lost. He battled into the gates themselves and even now wages war upon the daemons in their own realm, holding back their unending companies.'

'Caledor's vortex closed the gates,' said Malekith. 'It was the magic of the elves that stemmed the daemonic tide.'

Alandrian looked hesitant and did not translate his master's words.

'Why the silence?' demanded Malekith.

'Perhaps it is better that the dwarfs do not know that we trapped their greatest hero within the Realm of Chaos,' Alandrian said with a warning look. 'They may not take kindly to such knowledge.'

'We cannot let them peddle this fallacy,' Malekith insisted. 'It is the strength of the elves, not the dwarfs, that holds back the forces of the Dark Gods.'

'Who is to say that the dwarfen ancestors did not unwittingly aid Caledor's conjuration?' said Alandrian. 'That they suffered under the darkness of Chaos surely gives us more in common with them. Allow them to celebrate their own victories, for they do not tarnish your father's.'

Malekith considered this, not entirely convinced that he could allow the dwarfs to undermine the achievements of Aenarion. A glance at Kurgrik showed the dwarf watching the elves' exchange with friendly bemusement. The prince relented upon seeing the dwarf's ugly, honest face.

'Say that both elves and dwarfs have earned their right to live free upon this world,' said Malekith. 'Tell him that it is my hope that we no longer fight alone, but as allies.'

Alandrian's expression was one of shock.

'What?' demanded Malekith. 'What's wrong with that?'

'Nothing, highness,' said Alandrian. 'Quite the opposite, in fact. That is the most diplomatic thing I have heard pass from your lips in a hundred years!'

The glint of laughter in Alandrian's eyes quelled the angry retort welling up in Malekith's throat, and the prince merely coughed as if clearing his throat.

'Just keep the dwarf happy,' he finally managed to say, suppressing a smug smile.

THEIR JOURNEY TOOK them on for thirteen days before they reached the dwarf city, or hold as it was known to the dwarfs. Karak Kadrin they named it, one of the most northern cities in the mountains.

The location of the city was unmistakable, and as different from the road stations as could be imagined. High ramparts and towers dotted the sides of the pass, overlooking the approaches with sentries and war engines. Immense faces shaped into stylised likenesses of dwarfs were carved into the mountainsides – the Ancestor Gods, the elves were told.

From dark rock were the gatehouses carved, seen for the first time as the road turned to the north edge of the pass and began to wind back and forth up the hillside. They were as two mighty keeps, their foundations made from the mountain itself, thousands of heavy stones painstakingly cut and fitted to form fortifications that rivalled the great sea gates of Lothern. Golden standards glittered in the mountain sun, and banners stitched with angular runes and more of the curious dwarf designs hung from the ramparts.

Between the two immense flanking towers, the gates were closed. Almost as high as the gatehouse, arching far above the pass below, the gate was covered with plates of gold embossed with ancestor faces and symbols of smithying such as anvils, hammers and forges. Warriors clad in chainmail and heavy plates of armour guarded the portal, their expressions hidden behind full-faced helms wrought in the likenesses of fierce dwarf visages.

As the party came within sight of the gate towers, horns began to sound out, filling the valley with long, sonorous peals that rose and fell in harmony with the rebounding echoes. At this signal a much smaller door in the gate opened, though still thrice the height of an elf and broad enough for them to enter ten abreast.

Malekith had been impressed by the outer workings of the hold, but when he passed through the gate he stopped dead in his tracks and looked around in awe. The entrance hall was dug from the bare rock of the mountain, and far from the dreary stone of the way-keeps, it had been fashioned and polished so that it glittered in the light of hundreds of lanterns, every fault and strata a glorious decoration in its own right.

Long and no wider than the main gate, the hallway delved into the mountain, its high ceiling held by great arches carved from the living rock and sheathed in silver. The columns along the walls were cut in the same stylised fashion as the bastions upon the mountainsides; pillars of angular dwarf faces rising into the vaults above.

The lanterns that illuminated this impressive scene hung from thick chains suspended from the high vaults, each lamp larger than a dwarf and glowing with magical light. In the glow of these, the carvings between the arches could clearly be seen, depicting dwarf warriors at war, workers labouring in mines, smiths pounding at the forges and other vignettes of dwarfish endeavour. The floor was covered with regular flags, but each had been painstakingly etched with runes and lines of knotted patterns, the carved channels filled with coloured glass so that the ground was a riot of blues, reds and greens.

More dwarf guards lined the walls, arrayed in a line down each side, garbed in armour chased with gold, their double-headed axes inlaid with precious gems. Messengers had been sent ahead, and the party was greeted with much ceremony.

As they passed through the gigantic gateway the first pair of guards raised their weapons in salute, and so on down the line as the procession made its way along the long hallway. At the far end stood a delegation of dwarfs in brightly patterned jerkins, wearing elaborate helms adorned with horns or wings of gold, and each wore many rings and bracers, necklaces and brooches, so that they sparkled in the lantern light as they moved.

Behind each stood a banner bearer carrying a standard displaying the arms of the dwarf lords, bedecked with golden and silver badges and woven from fine metallic threads of every conceivable hue and shine. As with the other decorations, these were of axes and hammers, anvils and lightning bolts, displayed with such glimmering perfection that Malekith could imagine the royal standard of Nagarythe created in such a way.

Behind the welcoming party stood a door almost as large as the one by which the elves had entered. Cut from a solid piece of wood from some gigantic mountain oak, it was studded with bronze bolts, the head of each identically crafted as a pair of crossed hammers.

The dignitaries bowed low, sweeping their beards to one side with an arm so that they did not brush upon the ground. Malekith nodded his head in return, and the other elves also bowed in welcome. One of the nobles bore a large ornamental mace, and he turned and struck the door three mighty blows, the booms resounding around the hall. A slot opened in the door at about the height of a dwarf's face, and words were exchanged. There seemed to be some kind of argument, but Malekith suspected that this was some form of purposeful exchange whose significance eluded him.

Then the door opened, swinging effortlessly on hinges buried deep within the walls, to reveal the chambers beyond.

The hold was a veritable maze of corridors, halls and galleries, and though he tried to keep track of his path, Malekith soon found he was lost amongst the unending passages and stairwells. They seemed to be progressing up into the mountain, although by a circuitous route that rose and dipped.

The interior of the hold was not quite so grand as the entrance chamber, but still well built and decorated with gems and precious metals. Here and there the route took them past glowing foundries where the heat of furnaces blasted from open archways and the ringing of hammers echoed all around the visitors. There seemed to be little relent from the labour, though occasionally an artisan or forge worker would look up from his endeavours. The impression Malekith was left with was one of constant industry, as dwarfs wearing dirtied smocks and leather aprons busied themselves about the tunnels and rooms.

Eventually they were brought into the audience chamber of King Gazarund. It was a wide, low hall, with shields and banners hung upon the walls. Two long fire pits blazed to each side, the smoke from which disappeared up a cunning series of chimneys and channels to the mountainside far above. A walkway raised slightly above the rest of the chamber ran from the doorway to the throne dais, ascending up nearly twenty feet in a series of stepped rises. Bathed in the flickering red flames, the gold-inlaid tiles of the floor glimmered with ruddy light.

Kurgrik motioned for the elves to halt, and with the other thanes and notable members of the king's council made his way forwards.

King Gazarund sat upon a throne of black granite decorated with more gold tracery. His expression was austere rather than welcoming, and in the firelight his dark eyes shone from under beetling brows. He was bare-armed, save for two intricately wound torques upon each bicep, and he was robed in a simple tabard of blue and white. His beard was thick and black, straggled with stray wisps of grey, and was so long that despite being coiled through loops upon his belt and woven into winding plaits, it still hung almost to the ground. His face was craggy and creased, his skin pocked with the scars of years.

Most distinctively, he wore a golden patch over his right eye, and to Malekith's inner horror it appeared that this covering was riveted into the king's flesh.

The king's crown was set on a table beside the throne, so large and baroque that even this sturdy dwarf would not have been able to bear its weight upon his head. Wings as large as an eagle's splayed from the war-helm, and its cheek guards were studded with dozens of diamonds. In its place, the king wore a simple steel cap, banded with brazen knotwork, a few wisps of unkempt hair escaping from under its fur-lined brim.

The dwarf nobles made petition to the king, or so it seemed to Malekith from his experience of similar ceremonies at the court of Bel Shanaar. The king nodded once and the elves were waved forwards.

With great deliberation, the true ritual of welcoming began, carried out with solemn decorum by the king of Karak Kadrin and his thanes. Malekith and the king exchanged gifts; for the prince a dwarf-wrought brooch of gold, for the king a fine elven bracelet made of silver and decorated with sapphires.

Malekith was presented to the nobles of the hold via a list of unintelligible names that he soon forgot, and then was ushered into the chambers that had been set aside for them to stay.

The bedrooms were accommodating, but far from plush. The furniture was for dwarfs, and so the chairs and beds were distressingly low. Malekith found it easier to kneel before the clay basin upon the wall to wash his face, rather than clean himself at a constant stoop.

There was no fire in the room, but a steady breeze of warm air came from a grated vent upon the wall; Malekith surmised this was somehow redirected from the forges below by some ingenious means. The fabrics upon the bed and chairs were stiff and unyielding, as was the padding in the mattress.

Though Malekith would have preferred something a little more kind to lie upon, it was by no means a necessity for him having spent many of his long years on campaign in the wilderness.

After resting for a short while, Malekith then made it known to the dwarf who stood guard outside his door that he was ready to eat, by the simple expedient of miming food to his mouth and rubbing his stomach. The dwarf nodded in understanding and garbled something in return, and then stood back in his place.

Having called for Alandrian, Malekith again asked for something to eat, only to be told that there was a banquet to be held in their honour that night.

IT WAS A fulsome affair, with much quaffing of ale and long speeches that Malekith did not understand. The feasting hall was bedecked with more banners, and great brass seals displaying the emblems of the various clans and guilds of the hold.

Three tables were arranged down its length, each seating a hundred feasters, and Malekith and his company sat at another table that ran across the head of the hall, along with the king and his most trusted companions.

The food was for the most part palatable, consisting mostly of roast meats and boiled vegetables. Thick gravy and heavy dumplings were also served in abundance, along with pitchers of ale of all varieties and strengths. Malekith had become accustomed to delicately flavoured and fragranced meals, using such herbs and spices as grew on Ulthuan and in the islands on the other side of the world. The menu sat heavily on the prince's stomach, and he could see how the dwarfs were so sturdy of build and wide of girth.

Still, the cooking was done with competence if not finesse, though Malekith despaired of his hosts' table manners at times. Each course was served upon gigantic platters, and once the king had helped himself to whatever he desired, it seemed to become a free-for-all where everybody else was concerned. Ales were slopped over the bare wooden boards of the tables, and Malekith kept a suspicious eye on a puddle of gravy that spread dangerously close to him as the evening progressed.

Kurgrik, sitting on Malekith's left, had taken it upon himself to assist the prince with his dining; assuring himself that his guest was plentifully fed by heaping ladle upon ladle of stew into his bowl, and small mountains of potatoes, roast ducks, barley cakes and other simple fare upon his plate.

Something else that took Malekith aback occurred shortly after the fourth course. There was a pause while the tables were cleared of plates and debris, and all of the dwarfs produced small pouches filled with dried ground leaves. The contents of these small bags they stuffed into pipes of all shapes and sizes, which they then lit and puffed on contentedly for quite some time.

The haze of pipe smoke quickly filled the hall and hung in a thick fug above the table, causing many of the elves to cough violently, including Malekith. Misreading their discomfort as subtle prompts, Kurgrik proffered his tobacco to Malekith. The elven prince declined with a smile and a firm shake of the head, and Kurgrik shrugged and placed his leaf pouch back into the recesses of his robe whence it had come, seeming not to take any offence.

Several more platters of steamed potatoes, venison steaks and immense sausages went by, and then a hush descended upon the hall. There followed several more speeches, which Alandrian attempted to translate as best he could. Most of them spoke about family honour, great tragedies and valour in battle, and after a while Malekith stopped listening to his lieutenant and allowed his mind to drift.

It was then he felt a sharp dig in his ribs and looked around to see Alandrian looking at him pointedly. Casting his gaze around the smoky hall, the prince saw that all eyes were turned upon him.

'It is your turn to make a toast, I believe,' whispered Alandrian with a mischievous smile. 'Shall I translate?'

'I would think it better not to,' said Malekith. 'I know that you have learnt well their strange tongue, but I would not have you accidentally call the king a bloated warthog on my behalf. I shall sound so suitably imperious and charismatic, the exact meaning of my words will not be necessary to convey their spirit.'

The prince of Nagarythe stood up, while Kurgrik leaned over and refilled his tankard with a beer that was so thick and black it could have been mistaken for pitch.

'Your good health!' said Malekith, raising the cup to the hall. The dwarfs sat in respectful expectation, hands hovering close to their tankards. They had no idea what the prince had just said.

'What is the matter with them?' Malekith hissed out of the side of his mouth whilst trying to maintain a genteel smile.

'I think they want something a little, well, longer,' said Alandrian. 'You will have to go on a bit, I believe, to make them think they have been given a proper oratory.'

'Very well,' said Malekith, turning his attention towards the king of the hold. 'Your halls here are mighty, and full of great wonders. I have marvelled at the skills of your people, and I know in my heart that an alliance with you shall bring much benefit to my people.'

A glance towards Alandrian received an encouraging nod, and Malekith continued. Seeing the polite but clueless expressions on the sea of faces before him, the prince decided to indulge himself a little.

'You are very fine people, if a little unwashed and short.'

The elves laughed quietly at this, and taking their cue the dwarfs joined in, chortling uncertainly.

'It has been mostly my pleasure to meet you all, though I have not a clue what your names are, and all of you look pretty much the same to me.'

Another sideways glance at Alandrian was received with a pout of disapproval, but Malekith ignored his aide and carried on with his joke.

'That your mouths produce as much smoke as your chimneys is surprising, and if I do not choke to death before the evening is out, I shall thank the gods for protecting me. I understand that we have only just met, but I hope that in time you will understand the great privilege I have granted you all by allowing you into my presence. There are people of my own homeland who have never been granted an audience with me, and yet here I am, sinking cupfuls of your foul broth and treating you like equals. I am assured that you are an honourable people, and you best well be.'

At this point Malekith stood up and raised his foot upon the table to lean forwards, a feat not difficult for the slender elf, for the table barely came above his knees.

'Know this!' the prince proclaimed, his voice ringing clearly across the hall, focussing the attention of even the most drunkard audience member. 'It will go well for you that we should become friends. The Naggarothi do not treat idly with others, even elves of other realms. Should you wrong us, our vengeance will be sure, swift and deadly. We will burn these halls and we will pile your corpses upon pyres so high that they will rival these mountains. We shall be content to let you dwell in these rocky peaks, and we shall take the lowlands and the forests. Should you oppose us, we will have no option but to drive you before us, as we have the orcs and the beasts and the goblins. I look forward to meeting your High King, for he shall hopefully be of an almost equal standing to myself, and of intelligence enough to treat with me. But I warn you, if I am not impressed with him, I may decide simply to slay all of you. In fact, the next one of you that mispronounces my name might just get my blade through his gizzard. While we may deign to learn your crude language, please do not mangle the heritage of my forefathers and the legacy to my descendants with your ugly lips and thick tongues.'

Raising his goblet once again, Malekith grinned broadly.

'Long may Nagarythe prevail over you all!' he declared.

Before the prince could say any more, Alandrian shot to his feet and gave a shout of celebration, his mug upraised. The other elves, some of them clearly shocked, the rest wearing looks of approval, did likewise; the dwarfs then slowly followed their lead until there was a great rousing cheer that filled the hall with a cacophony of shouting and the slamming of cups upon tables.

'Thank you,' said Malekith, holding up a hand for silence. The dwarfs appeared not to understand the gesture for they continued their banging and clapping.

With Alandrian's hand on his arm pulling him down before he could speak further, Malekith sat, a contented smile upon his face.

This seemed to conclude the round of speeches, and servants came forth bearing great bowls of steaming pudding made from boiled grain and honey, with chunks of stodgy cake to dip into the sweet broth. This was followed by platters of hard cheeses that smelt of diseased goats, as far as Malekith could tell, which were served with small biscuits with the texture and taste of thin slices of dried wood.

Under the stone roof of the hall, Malekith lost all sense of passing time and knew not whether it was midnight or if dawn was fast approaching when the elves were finally allowed to retire to their dormitories. Many of the dwarfs still caroused, though a significant proportion of their number had simply slipped into inebriated stupors at the tables.

For the highest-ranking attendees, the servants brought small pillows, which were carefully placed under the snoring faces of the inebriated lords. The lesser peons were allowed to doze away, their faces in spillages and crumbs.

All Malekith knew was that the banquet had been more tiring than the march, but he went to bed invigorated nonetheless for his overly full stomach, both appalled and yet mesmerised by the strange culture of these people.

On the one hand they were loud, careless and ignorant of any form of etiquette, yet he had seen much evidence that they were also studious, observant, dedicated and loyal. Their attention to detail in matters of craftsmanship equalled that of the elves, and in weapon-making and the construction of mechanical devices their knowledge outstripped that of Ulthuan. That they knew of magic was clear from many of the things Malekith had seen in the hold, yet he had not seen any dwarf openly wielding sorcery, and when Alandrian had enquired on the prince's behalf, he had been met with polite but stern denials that the dwarfs had wizards of any kind.

—◀ FIVE ▶—

The High King

MALEKITH WAS EAGER to continue their journey to the hold of the High King, and was grateful that Kurgrik apparently had a schedule of his own to keep. The thane's shipment of wood was sorely needed for the mines beneath Karaz-a-Karak, and the party, dwarfs and elves, left the city of Karak Kadrin early the next day.

The king came to wave them off, and seemed much more approachable and friendly away from the formality of his court. He shook the hands of each of the elves in turn, and patted Malekith fondly on the arm. He said something in dwarfish, and Malekith smiled and nodded, not bothering to listen to Alandrian's translation.

Malekith and the party did not travel back to the main gates, but were taken by an underground route to another entrance. Though slightly less grand, this portal was no less impressive to the prince, for it led not to the surface but to a vast passageway dug through the bedrock of the mountain. Due south it struck, paved with flags and large enough for many carts and dwarfs to pass each other by with ease.

Lanterns lit the underground highway, and the walls were hewn so smoothly that no shadow darkened them. Great pillars of wood and metal shored up the roof, which was easily four or five times the height of an elf.

For this stage of the journey, they travelled upon the backs of rocking carts. It was not entirely unpleasant, though the lack of night and day began to wear upon Malekith's nerves. After three days, he wondered just how far this tunnel was. After six, he was longing for a sight of sun or stars, or even a storm-filled sky.

Periodically they came across guard stations, not unlike underground versions of the way-forts they had stayed in on the surface. Warriors with strange-looking, mechanical bows patrolled outwards from these subterranean castles.

Branchways and side tunnels broke off from the main road in clustered junctions, and there was always a steady traffic of dwarfs on wagons and on foot. They carried all manner of goods with them: metal ingots, sacks of coal, bushels of crops, mining tools and all manner of other wares.

By the eighth day, Malekith's interest had been restored, for he was now fully realising the extent of the dwarfen realm. They had covered no less than fifteen leagues each day, and so had travelled three hundred and sixty miles or more. The highway went pretty much straight and so he guessed that they were still heading south. If the side passages and other exits each led to other holds and settlements, then the mountains were swarming with dwarfs.

Some of the prince's earlier arrogance dissipated as he pondered the huge implication of an alliance with these people. If the Naggarothi could forge this friendship with speed, then his people would increase the power they already held in the colonies.

Knowing this, he now paid more attention to the dealings the dwarfs had with each other, and tried harder to get a rough grasp of their language from Alandrian. He endeavoured to learn the names of his dwarfish companions: outlandish monikers such as Gundgrin, Borodin, Hagrun and Barrnok. He learned the words for sword, and axe, and that this highway was called the Ungdrin Ankor.

He learned their word for gold, and another, and another, until he was thoroughly confused. During a break, Malekith steered Alandrian into a quiet alcove and confronted his lieutenant on the matter.

'Azgal, churk, bryn, galaz, gnolgen, gorl, konk, thig, ril, skrottiz…' Malekith complained. 'All of these hideous words, and I cannot work out which one means gold! How am I supposed to learn this stupid language?'

'They all mean gold, highness,' Alandrian said patiently.

'Gold's gold!' said Malekith. 'Why do they need so many damned words for it?'

'Gold is, indeed, gold, highness,' said Alandrian, pulling a neck chain from under his robe, upon which hung a small dwarfish amulet he had been gifted by Kurgrik. 'To a dwarf, however, there are lots of types of gold. The gold on the outer edge, with the reddish tinge, is konk. The inner design is made from a slightly softer metal that they call gorl.'

'I understand,' said Malekith, not understanding at all. Alandrian read the doubt on the prince's face.

'We see one metal, which we call gold,' the captain explained slowly, placing the amulet back under his robe. 'The dwarfs see all sorts of different metals and they have a name for each one.'

'So, each word means a different type of gold?' Malekith said. 'Soft gold, hard gold, shinier gold, that sort of thing?'

'That sort of thing, yes, highness,' said Alandrian with a reassuring nod.

'But there can't be that many types of gold, surely?' said Malekith.

'Not physically, no,' Alandrian said. His face screwed up in consternation as he worked out how to explain further. 'To the dwarfs, gold has other qualities, not just physical ones.'

'Such as?' Malekith said.

'Well, there is lucky gold, for a start,' said Alandrian.

'Lucky gold?' Malekith's brows arrowed into a frown.

'Gold that was found by accident, for example,' replied Alandrian.

'Seems strange, but then they are a strange folk,' said Malekith.

'The type of gold also changes depending on where it came from, where it currently is and its own history,' Alandrian continued under the prince's demanding stare. 'There's a word for gold that is an ingot and hasn't yet been made into something. There's a different word for gold that was once made into something else but has been melted down to make something new. There's gold that is for spending, what they call impatient, and gold that is for keeping. That's almost the same word as they use for waiting or patience. Then there's gold that you don't own yet, such as ore or a loan. Of course, that also means there are words for gold that you would like to own, or once owned–'

'Enough!' snapped Malekith. 'So, they have lots of words for gold. I cannot be expected to learn them all.'

'Oh no, highness,' said Alandrian. 'Not even the dwarfs know all the names for gold, apparently. They can make up any name for gold they like and another dwarf will probably understand what they mean.'

Alandrian cast a look over his shoulder at the dwarfs climbing back on the wagons, making ready to leave.

'It's probably best not to mention gold too much, in any case,' Alandrian said. 'Whenever I mention it, they get a queer look in their eyes. Some of them get quite excited. I once mentioned the golden gates of Lothern and Kurgrik almost fainted!'

'So, it is best not to tell them that we have huge treasuries in Athel Toralien?' said Malekith. 'Just in case they come over funny and decide to try to take it?'

'Yes, highness, something like that,' said Alandrian.

Malekith nodded knowingly and glanced over his companion's shoulder to see Kurgrik scowling ever so slightly in the prince's direction. Malekith smiled cheerily and waved, trying to ignore the picture he had of the thane frothing at the mouth and pawing at a coin.

* * *

ON THE TENTH day they turned from the main road, heading west as far as Malekith could judge. Here the traffic increased considerably and Malekith surmised that the capital was not far away. Kurgrik was more animated, and from the comparatively few words that the prince had learned and through the translation of Alandrian, it seemed that they would be at their destination the next day.

Malekith became agitated the closer they came to their destination, and constantly harangued Alandrian to find out more about the dwarfs, and in particular, their High King. On this, Kurgrik proved strangely reticent, saying only that his name was Snorri Whitebeard, and that he was the first to rule over all the holds. The following day, Malekith was to meet this dignitary.

As the caravan readied for the march, Malekith took out his finest cloak from his stores; purple embroidered with golden thread in a design of two dragons coiling about each other. The prince scented his hair with perfumes from his pack, and swept it back over his shoulders with a silver band embellished with five rubies and three diamonds, each cut and polished into an oval as large as a fingertip. Feeling suitably regal, he sat on the wagon at the front of the column alongside Kurgrik. His pride was somewhat punctured by the fact that he had to almost tuck his knees under his chin to fit on the seat.

THE GATEWAY FROM the Ungdrin Ankor to the capital of the dwarf realm was a wide set of golden doors mounted upon a series of gears and cogs that allowed them to be opened effortlessly with a single push despite their immense weight. They were inscribed with many vertical lines of runes, each separated by a sparkling diamond.

The gates were flanked by two pillars of black marble, intricately carved with ancestor faces that glowered at all who approached. The tiles of the floor had an endless array of designs upon them. Kurgrik said something to Alandrian.

'Every clan symbol of the hold is carved into these stones,' Alandrian explained.

Malekith accepted this without word and turned his warrior eye to the gates' defences. Side chambers with stout iron doors looked out upon the corridor, with shuttered windows and murder holes so that defenders could pour arrows into any attacker from almost complete safety. A glance up revealed other openings through which oil could be poured.

Malekith noted all this and, combining it with what he had seen of the great gate of Karak Kadrin, decided that the holds were all but impregnable. With the Ungdrin Ankor to link the cities underground, even protracted siege was impossible, for unless one could control the subterranean highway, there was no way to cut off supplies. Despite these formidable defences, Malekith knew that no stronghold was ever totally secure, but such would be the cost of taking such a city, it was far better to broker a friendship with these people than to anger them.

Dismounting from their carts, Kurgrik and his companions were met with slaps on the back and hearty greetings from their fellow dwarfs as the party passed into the hold. There were curious looks from these dwarfs at the elves, but nothing like the amazement and interest they had raised in Karak Kadrin.

As they progressed into Karaz-a-Karak, the feeling grew more pronounced; these dwarfs already seemed familiar with elf-kind. Recalling Kurgrik's first reaction to Malekith, it seemed that in retrospect the thane had not been surprised to see the elves in and of themselves, but rather to find them in that place.

Malekith's fears were confirmed when they were conveyed by an escort of heavily armed warriors to the throne room of the High King. The chamber was even larger and more opulent than that of Karak Kadrin, and was hung with so many shields, banners and gold emblems that barely a patch of rock could be seen between them. The entire floor was tiled with gold and inset with rubies, and the ceiling was awash with lanterns. More than a hundred steps led up to the dais upon which a large throne was set, similarly bedecked with gold and jewels. Dozens of dwarfs of noble dress and bearing were gathered about the hall.

Most notable of all, and to which Malekith's eyes were immediately drawn, were the two elves stood beside the throne in deep conversation with the king.

One, the prince recognised immediately. He was Prince Aernuis of Eataine, a renowned admiral who had led some of the first ships across the ocean. Nothing had been heard from him for over forty years and it had been widely thought that his expedition had been lost. The reason for his long absence suddenly became clearer to Malekith, and he felt his anger rising at the secretive nature of the prince's dealings with the dwarfs.

The other elf was unknown to the ruler of Nagarythe, but by his bearing Malekith assumed him to be one of Aernuis's councillors. Detecting a change in the atmosphere of the chamber, the elves looked up and saw Malekith striding into the throne room. Though it was hard to tell in the fierce light, it seemed to the prince that their pale faces blanched just a little more.

Kurgrik hurried ahead of Malekith to present the prince to the High King, who was sat on his throne with an elbow upon his knee, his chin rested on his clenched fist. He sat up attentively as Kurgrik approached, and listened intently as the thane spoke for a long while. With a nod, the king directed his stern gaze towards Malekith.

'Happy welcome you are to Karaz-a-Karak,' said Snorri Whitebeard, and Malekith flinched at the mangling of his native tongue, even as he was surprised by the High King's use of it.

'Hello, king,' Malekith replied in his finest Dwarfish, regaining his composure as quickly as he was able. He ignored the smirks upon the faces of Aernuis and his retainer, and saw neither amusement nor anger in the expression of Snorri. 'I Malekith.'

At this the king gave a satisfied nod, and gestured for Malekith to approach up the long stair. Malekith glanced over his shoulder towards Alandrian, and gestured for the lieutenant to follow him. His cloak billowing behind him, the prince of Nagarythe strode up the steps two at a time.

'Malekith?' said the elf whose name the prince did not know. 'You are the last person we expected to see here.'

'So it would seem,' replied Malekith. 'You know me, yet I do not know who you are. Please inform my companion, Alandrian, so that I might know the name of the impudent elf I shall soon slay for not using my full title.'

'Sutherai,' the elf stammered quickly, casting a fearful glance at his prince. Malekith raised an eyebrow in displeasure.

'Your highness,' Sutherai added with a visible shudder.

The High King watched this exchange with what appeared to be an expression of interest, having obviously noted the tone in Malekith's voice and that of Sutherai, if not perhaps understanding fully what had passed between them. Snorri then looked intently at Aernuis, who put on his most obsequious smile and said something in Dwarfish.

'Outrageous!' spat Alandrian from behind Malekith, and the prince turned on his lieutenant with an inquisitive glare. There was also a look of shock upon the face of Sutherai, and one of sudden contrition upon Aernuis.

'The prince just described you to the king as a minor noble, as far as I am able to understand,' Alandrian explained quietly, before quickly adding, 'But do not react too harshly before the High King, I feel that Aernuis has closeted himself closely in his court.'

Malekith absorbed these words and fought back his anger.

'Please announce to the High King my full title, rank and line, so that he might better understand with whom he is meeting,' Malekith said evenly, his eyes piercing holes into Aernuis.

Alandrian spoke at some length, and Malekith realised that his companion was indeed relating every title and rank that Malekith held. The king did not seem overly impressed, but cast a sideways glance at Aernuis, before replying to Alandrian.

'King Snorri asks why it is that elves feel the need to have so many titles,' Alandrian said. 'He is known simply as the High King.'

'Because we value prestige and rank more than you cave-dwelling savages,' was Malekith's mental retort, but he curbed his tongue and paused before replying.

'Tell him that such titles are used only rarely,' Malekith said after a moment's thought, 'such as when lesser nobles forget their place and display a lack of respect.'

This Alandrian truly translated as best he could, and the king looked at Aernuis with a deeper frown, his jaw churning as he considered the events unfolding about him. After a pregnant pause that lasted quite some time, Snorri met Malekith's gaze and there was a peculiar twinkle in his eye. The king then broke into a grin, before laughing out loud. Malekith found himself smiling also, for the High King's amusement was genuine, and there was no hint of mockery in his expression.

Snorri pushed himself from his throne and strode up to Malekith, before grasping his hand and vigorously shaking it and slapping him on the arm. As Snorri returned to his chair of office, Malekith could not stop himself directing a sly smile towards Aernuis while the High King's back was turned, which infuriated the rival prince even further.

The king then muttered something in Dwarfish and ushered them all away with a shooing gesture. Malekith paused to bow before he turned, thinking it prudent to cement this small victory while he could. Aernuis walked beside him as they made their way down the steps.

'Three years I have been here,' Aernuis declared. 'In that time I have worked long and hard to build up the High King's trust for me. You cannot simply stroll into Karaz-a-Karak and expect to be given equal rights as me.'

'Remember whom you are addressing, Aernuis,' replied Malekith. 'I know that these folk despise kinslaying even more than our own people, but if I do not get satisfactory answers from you, I will have your throat slit.'

'In these halls, your threats are idle,' said Aernuis with a snort. 'I have the protection of King Snorri; if you try to cause me harm, it would be like an assault upon the High King himself.'

'We shall see how long that favour lasts,' said Malekith. 'You cannot hide beneath his beard forever, prince. You have wronged me here, and that I will not easily forget, nor soon forgive.'

They had reached the bottom of the steps and parted slightly. Malekith turned and laid a hand upon Aernuis's shoulder, seemingly in friendship from where the High King was sat. In reality, the Eataine prince squirmed under Malekith's iron grip as the Naggarothi lord's fingers dug through his robes, deep into the flesh.

'I look forward to feeding your carcass to the crows,' Malekith said pleasantly. 'The only way you will regain my favour is to make yourself utterly indispensable to my cause. Tell me everything you know about these folk, and how you came to be here, and I may reconsider killing you.'

Aernuis looked into Malekith's eyes, hoping to see some hint of mocking or weakness, but there was none; the Naggarothi's eyes were as hard as flint and as utterly devoid of emotion as a shark's hungry gaze. Looking away, Aernuis freed himself from Malekith's painful grip and straightened the creases in his robe. With a disconcerted look, he turned on his heel and skulked away, enduring the sneers of the Naggarothi still stood at the entrance.

* * *

LATER THAT NIGHT, Malekith supposed, though he could not tell for sure, Aernuis came to the prince's chambers. Aernuis's manner was one of conciliation and he gave a formal bow as he entered, though its impact was somewhat lessened by the fact that the tall elf had already been forced to stoop by passing through the low doorway.

Malekith sat along the length of his short cot with his back against the wall. He was dressed in a flowing purple robe, his armour piled carefully upon the floor, for there was no stand tall enough to hold it. Other items such as his sword and helm were placed neatly on the low shelves of the small room. In his hands he held the dwarf-made brooch gifted to him in Karak Kadrin, and after glancing up at his visitor he returned his gaze to wonder at its workmanship.

'I fear there has been some misunderstanding between us,' Aernuis said. 'I am more than willing to share the spoils that founding a solid relationship with the dwarfs will bring. I am almost alone here, and life amongst these folk has led me into bad habits. I would be honoured to serve in whatever capacity I can, for the benefit of Ulthuan.'

'Go on,' Malekith said without looking up.

'It has taken me many years to build what I have with the dwarfs,' explained Aernuis. 'Only these last three years have I spent with the High King. Before that, I dwelt within Karak Izril, a city as far south again as you have travelled from Karak Kadrin. When we sailed across the ocean, we looked to find passage eastwards, but storms blew us onto the coast southwest of where we now are. Though most of my crew survived the wreck, the ship could not be saved and we were cast upon this strange shore with little in the way of supplies, and with no knowledge of where we had landed.'

'Sounds dreadful,' muttered Malekith, still entranced by his brooch.

'It was,' said Aernuis, ignoring the prince's irony. 'The lands between the sea and the mountains are infested with orcs, vicious green-skinned beasts intent on slaughter and destruction.'

'Yes, I know them,' said Malekith, still feigning disinterest. 'My sword has met more than a few.'

'Goblins riding upon wolves assailed us, and we were driven ever eastwards, into the heart of the desolate wilderness that lies south of here,' Aernuis continued. 'We fought as best we could, but their attacks were constant and gradually our numbers dwindled. For several months we wandered, ever trying to head towards the mountains, but often finding our route cut off by orc camps or marauding warbands. There was little to hunt, and hunger and thirst stalked us as much as the goblins. When but a handful of my ship's company were left, the others decided to head back towards the coast in the hope that some other ship may have followed our course. I knew this to be folly, for we had been driven here only by chance, but they would not be dissuaded from their course of action, so I let them go. Only loyal Sutherai stayed with me.'

'How heart-warming, I'm sure,' said Malekith, tossing the brooch onto a table beside the bed and swinging his feet to the floor so that he faced the Eataine prince. 'So tell me, good admiral, what have you been doing for the last forty years?'

'Sutherai and I made it to the foothills, travelling at night, hiding in stream beds and marshes to avoid detection during the day,' said Aernuis, and his haunted expression as he recalled those times was a testament to the fear that he had felt. 'We came upon a strange building, and thinking it abandoned, we took shelter. The orcs did not approach it, and so we made camp there for some time. It was, of course, a dwarf fort, and six days after we came there, the dwarfs returned. At first they were going to slay us out of hand, but I expect that so bedraggled and pitiful we looked, they stayed their axes. Curiosity saved us, and they took us back to Karak Izril, where we lived for many years.'

Aernuis looked at Malekith's unconvinced expression and sighed.

'I do not expect you to understand our plight,' Aernuis said. 'We were two strangers very far from our own lands. We did not know if there were other elves within a thousand miles, and even if there were, there was no way that we could contact them. Even when we had learned a little of the dwarfen tongue, and they came to trust us more, we could not leave. Where would we go? Out into the wilderness, boldly striking out for friends that in all likelihood did not exist? I felt as if I had stumbled upon all the riches of the world, but had nobody with whom to share them, nothing on which to spend them.'

'Riches?' asked Malekith, dropping his pretence of indifference.

'You have seen how they decorate their halls, the gold and silver they wear, the artisanship of their weapons,' said Aernuis. 'It is but a fraction of the wealth of these mountains. Every hold has vast vaults filled with gems and precious metals, I have seen them. They covet gold like no other thing, and hoard it as a squirrel keeps nuts for the winter. Seeing you, I realised that much has changed since I left Ulthuan, and I think that now we must hold all the varied riches of the wide world in our hands. If we can but broker trade with the dwarfs, you and I will become pre-eminent amongst all of the princes.'

'I am already pre-eminent,' said Malekith.

'Your soldiers are perhaps not so sure,' said Aernuis.

'What do you mean?' demanded Malekith, angrily rising to his feet.

'Sutherai has spoken with many of them, and learned that Bel Shanaar has grown rich and powerful on the proceeds of his empire,' Aernuis said. 'Though your claims here grow by the year, who can say how the fortunes of Nagarythe fare back on Ulthuan? Yet if you can reach agreement with the dwarfs, and act as arbiter between their kings and the Phoenix Throne, it is you who shall hold Bel Shanaar's fate.'

'Alandrian should learn to control his tongue,' Malekith muttered.

'With me by your side, you have a partner ready and willing to speak to King Snorri on your behalf,' Aernius continued. 'Without me, it will take you twenty years or more to earn his trust, and in that time many things can happen. It was by chance that we both met with these folk, but as our cities grow and more of our people cross the seas, how long before others encounter them also? If you fear me as a rival, you must fear time more, for we have an opportunity here to create something that will seal our places in history, but it will not last forever.'

'Perhaps I misjudged you,' said Malekith, and hope filled Aernuis's face, but it quickly dissipated when he saw the Naggarothi's cruel expression. 'I thought you a coward, but instead you are merely a merchant. I am the prince of Nagarythe, a warrior and general, not a trader to barter deals and haggle with lesser entities.'

'And how glorious might be the armies of Nagarythe with the wealth of the mountains in your coffers?' said Aernuis with a smile. 'Dwarf-forged spears in their hands, and dwarf-made arrows in their quivers? You have seen their buildings, sturdy and strong. Crude in look, but we can learn their techniques and turn them to our advantage, to create beautiful palaces in which to pass away our long days, and soaring castles that will defend our realm for eternity. Much of what they make is rough and functional, but if guided by an elven hand, think what their mastery of stone and metal and wood would bring to our people. It is not just trade that this relationship will herald, but a new era of elven dominion.'

'I do not think that they will give up their secrets lightly,' said Malekith.

'They will not,' replied Aernuis. 'But if they will give them up at all, they will give them up to us!'

Malekith sat down again, deep in thought. He imagined the legions of Nagarythe marching upon roads that cut through hills and over bridges that spanned wide rivers and mountain passes. He had seen the odd mechanical bows that many of the dwarfs carried, and wondered what his finest marksmen could do with such weapons.

Only after a while did he remember that Aernuis was still in the room. He looked up at the prince, who was wracked between expectation and dread as he looked at Malekith pondering the future.

'Very well,' Malekith declared. 'You have proved yourself useful to me, and I shall not slay you yet. You may leave me now.'

Aernuis bowed again with as much dignity as he could muster, and then departed. Malekith picked up the brooch from the table and looked at it again, tracing a finger over its entwined patterns. With a smile, he attached it to his robe and stood, calling for Alandrian.

SIX

Beasts in the Mountains

WHAT AERNUIS HAD said proved to be true; the dwarfs were reluctant to treat with any outsiders. However, the Eataine prince's long standing in Karak Izril and his exemplary behaviour in the capital had garnered him a measure of respect, and by association this passed also to Malekith.

The Naggarothi ruler despatched some of his company to return to Athel Toralien, so that proper scribes and diplomats could come to Karaz-a-Karak. The dwarfs laboured likewise, assembling embassies from the many holds across the mountains, for these debates concerned not just Karaz-a-Karak but all of the dwarf empire.

It took the whole of the summer for the preparations to be made, and Malekith was always careful to send regular missives back to Ulthuan so that no suspicion was aroused, whilst conveying as little information as possible so that he would personally remain pivotal to the discussions. This position of influence was helped considerably by the fact that the three elves in the world that had some true understanding of dwarfish were allies of Malekith – Aernuis, Alandrian and Sutherai.

In that time, Malekith also went to great lengths to befriend King Snorri, at first seeking political power but later out of an unexpected but growing affection for the High King. As Malekith's grasp of the dwarfs' language improved, he spent more time with Snorri.

'What is best about Nagarythe?' the High King asked one day.

The two were alone in a reception room of the king's chambers. Malekith sat upon a chair the king had personally commissioned for his tall companion, while the king slouched in a deep armchair upholstered in thick elk hide. The servants had left a keg of ale and a large plate of pies on the low table that lay between them.

'The blue skies,' Malekith answered without hesitation. 'The air is cold and crisp and the north wind stirs the senses. Sometimes she sighs through the pine forests, other times she howls over the mountain peaks.'

'And what do you think of my mountains?' said Snorri. 'Do they compare to your homeland?'

'They are mighty,' laughed Malekith. 'Taller than the peaks of Nagarythe and greater of girth. But I travelled beneath them for the most part and have not yet walked upon them.'

'That will not do!' declared Snorri, jumping to his feet. 'What host am I to show you my rooms and keep from you the beauty of my lands? Do you enjoy hunting?'

'Very much,' said Malekith. 'I have tracked and slain many a monstrous beast in the Annulii.'

'Have you ever killed a troll?' asked Snorri enthusiastically. 'A cragwyrm, or a daggerfang?'

Malekith shook his head. Such beasts were unknown to Ulthuan, at least by the names used by Snorri.

'Then we shall have a troll hunt!' declared Snorri with a wide grin splitting his beard.

TWO DAYS LATER Malekith found himself stood upon a windswept shoulder of rock looking over a deep mountain valley. He was several miles to the north of Karaz-a-Karak, accompanied by Alandrian, the High King and several dozen dwarf escorts. Though the year was well into spring, the mountain air was still chill and the hunting party were swathed in capes and furs. Only a few clouds scudded across the skies, and when the sun broke free the prince could feel his skin prickling with warmth.

Snorri pointed across the valley to a thick forest. The trees were immense in girth, though not tall, not unlike the dwarfs. Square clearings had been chopped into the edges of the woods by dwarfen woodcutters.

'Wutruth,' said the king. 'The strongest trees of the mountains. This forest is older than Karaz-a-Karak, and we cut only five trees every year so that its descendants have time to grow. It is also a haunt of strange and dangerous beasts.'

'That is why we are here,' said Malekith with a smile.

'It is indeed,' said Snorri.

The High King was full of energy as he led the party down a winding track that meandered between rocky crags towards the valley floor. He bounded from stone to stone with an agility surprising for his stature, though Malekith had no difficulty keeping pace with his long, graceful strides. As they walked, Snorri gave a running commentary of everything in sight.

'The peak to the west, with the purple cliffs facing us, is Karag Kazor,' the king said. 'It was upon the fires of her belly that Grungni forged the first of Grimnir's axes.'

A huge flock of dark-feathered birds with bright red beaks swooped overhead and disappeared up the valley.

'Bloodcrows!' exclaimed Snorri. 'That is a good omen! They are scavengers. To see them in such numbers means that there is plenty to eat. Something close by has been killing!'

And so it went on, with Snorri expounding on every type of rock and plant, bird and beast that they encountered. As the sun reached her zenith, bathing the valley in warmth, they reached the well-tended treeline. The forest was dark and clear of undergrowth, the wutruth seeming to claw nourishment from the bare rock.

'If you would like to take a small repast, I'll be back shortly,' said Snorri.

With a handful of dwarf warriors, the High King headed into the woods and was quickly lost in the shadows. The dwarfs that remained sat down on rocks and stumps, and brought forth hard bread and pungent cheeses from their carry-sacks.

Malekith was not hungry and instead watched the dwarfs carefully. They seemed at ease, but every now and then they would glance at their charges. Though the prince considered that they might simply be mindful of their protective duties, he decided that they were present more to protect the High King from any perfidy by the elves.

Snorri returned shortly, a satisfied smile written upon his craggy features.

'Clawed tracks, big ones!' said the High King. 'Not too old either, by my reckoning.'

The king gave the order for the party to get ready to move, which was greeted with quiet, good-natured grumbling. Most dwarfs preferred to stay underground whenever possible, and Snorri's companions were no different. However, they were now used to their High King's strange appetites for sky and fresh air, and indulged him with good humour.

They came across the trail a few hundred paces from the edge of the woods. Malekith bent to one knee to examine them. They were indistinct, the soil here being very thin, but the prince could make out a large footprint as long as his arm and exceptionally broad. It was not unlike orc or goblin tracks, though considerably bigger; four-toed with the marks of ragged claws.

'Troll,' said Snorri with smug confidence. 'You are fortunate. Most trolls will have moved further north by this time of year. This one is either exceptionally stupid or brighter than your average troll.'

'How so?' asked Malekith.

'It could be too stupid to realise it will get too hot for it in the summer,' explained the king. 'Or it could be clever enough to realise that the other trolls have left and there will be plenty for it to eat without competition.'

'Does it make any difference?' said Alandrian.

'Yes and no,' said Snorri with a shrug. 'A stupid troll will be easier to catch, but more likely to attack when caught. A smarter troll might realise it is in danger and try to run away.'

They followed the trail north and eastwards, deeper into the woods. Here and there they found the gnawed remains of an animal carcass or a pile of the foulest-smelling dung Malekith had ever encountered. By this spoor Snorri judged that the troll was close at hand, within a few miles.

'It is afternoon now, so it is likely hiding somewhere in a shady spot out of the sun's gaze,' said the High King. 'There are some caves not far from here that we should explore. It would be good to catch it before nightfall, otherwise it might move away and we'll never find it.'

They continued to follow the tracks, which led towards the caves as Snorri had hoped. Quite some time had passed and the sun was now beginning to slide down behind the peaks to the west. Where Malekith spied the sky through a break in the canopy he saw that clouds were gathering again and the light was fading fast.

The short mountain day was nearing its end when Snorri brought them out of the trees onto a high bluff. A white cliff face opposite was dotted with dark caves, and the High King pointed towards numerous troll tracks on the ground.

'He's here all right,' growled the High King.

Snorri gestured to one of his retainers, who brought forth the king's crossbow. It was a remarkable piece of dwarfish craft, inlaid with gems and silver, its crosspiece and firing lever gilded. As the king loaded his weapon with measured precision, Malekith brought forth his bow from the quiver on his back and quickly strung it. He nocked a black-fletched arrow, casting his gaze towards the caverns only a few hundred paces distant.

'How does one hunt troll?' he asked.

'Some of my lads will go in and flush it out,' said Snorri. 'Or it'll chase them out… One way or another, best to lure it into the open first.'

'And where does one aim for the killing shot?' said the prince.

Snorri laughed.

'This is no bear or stag that can be brought down with a single shaft,' the dwarf said. 'Their brains are exceptionally small, and I've seen a troll carry on fighting with three bolts through its thick head. Their heart is in the chest behind strong bone. Fire is a good bet, for burnt flesh does not regrow.'

In illustration, the king handed one of his bolts to Malekith and pointed to the tip. A small rune was inscribed into the sharpened iron, flickering with a distant flame.

'It might take some bladework to finish it off,' the king added, taking back the bolt.

Malekith pondered this as more than a dozen dwarfs headed across the open ground, flaming brands in their rough fists. He felt no fear, for there was no creature in the world that he could not best. His heart did beat a little faster in anticipation, and the prince could see that Snorri was equally eager to get a sight of their prey.

The High King felt Malekith's gaze and turned to wink at the elf.

'Good fun, eh?' Snorri chuckled.

The torch-bearing dwarfs had now entered the caves and the light from their brands disappeared. Soon enough there came the echo of shouts and three dwarfs came running from a cave entrance to Malekith's left. They glanced over their shoulders, not in panic but to ensure their quarry was following.

A dozen paces behind them emerged the troll.

It was tall and gangling, easily twice Malekith's height, with wiry, muscled limbs and a bulbous stomach. Its head was large and ungainly, with a flattened nose and small, unintelligent eyes. Its hide was like a thick grey scale, hairless save for clumps upon its head and shoulders. Large and frayed pointed ears framed its hideous face, and its mouth was wide and filled with cracked teeth. Its long arms ended in club-like hands, its bony fingers tipped with broken, filthy claws.

The troll gave a keening howl as it lolloped after the dwarfs, stooping to knuckle forwards every few paces, sniffing the air.

Snorri took the first shot, at a distance of some three hundred paces. His crossbow twanged loudly and as the bolt flew forwards its tip erupted with flame. The shot took the troll in the left shoulder and elicited a pained grunt.

The dwarfs scattered further as the troll broke into a run down the gentle slope towards Malekith and the High King. Calming himself, Malekith took aim, his breathing shallow, his senses tuned to the swirl of the wind. He muttered a simple incantation and his arrowhead flickered with blue flame. With a sigh, Malekith released the bowstring and the arrow sped across the open ground and struck the troll directly in the left eye.

The troll fell to the ground with flailing limbs, screeching and gurgling. The prince turned to Snorri, who was still winding back the string on his crossbow.

'No killing shot?' said Malekith with a smile.

'Don't count your gold until the ore's been smelted,' grunted Snorri, not looking up from his task.

Malekith turned back to the troll and stared open-mouthed as it pushed itself back to its feet. The prince's shaft was intact, piercing the eye socket, its flaming tip protruding from the top of the troll's head. It turned its good eye on the hunters and gave an angry roar before breaking into a bounding run that covered the ground with surprising speed.

'Oh...' said Malekith.

Regaining his composure, Malekith loosed three more shots at the fast-approaching monster, each arrow bursting into blue fire as it slammed into the creature's chest. Now even more angry, the troll lowered its head into a reckless charge, its clawed feet churning clods of thin earth from the ground.

Snorri fired another bolt, which punched into the creature's right leg, just above the knee. It stumbled and fell. It stayed on all fours for a moment, shaking its head groggily, before rising once more and resuming its attack.

The other dwarfs began to shout to each other and a flurry of bolts converged on the troll, some missing, others biting into flesh but with little effect. The troll turned on the closest of its attackers, a dwarf by the name of Godri who was one of the king's closest companions. Claws raked across the thane's armour, sending iron rings scattering across the floor with droplets of blood, the dwarf hurled onto his back.

The troll then veered back towards Malekith and Snorri, crimson splashed across its face and arms.

Snorri was still winding back the string of his crossbow and the troll was only a score of paces away. Malekith drew Avanuir and leapt to the attack, the shining blue blade carving a furrow in the creature's ribs as the elven prince darted past. The troll ignored him and bore down on Snorri.

The High King threw his unloaded crossbow into the creature's face and swept out a hand axe from his belt. His first chopping blow lodged into the creature's gut and the troll's momentum barrelled them both over. The two rolled down the slope, the troll biting and slashing, Snorri hacking with his axe.

Malekith dashed after the High King even as the other dwarfs closed in with axes ready. The troll was now on top of Snorri and reared its head back, jaws open wide to bite off the face of the High King.

Seizing his opportunity, Malekith threw Avanuir, guiding the blade with the power of magic. Spinning horizontally, the magical sword scythed through the air. It struck the troll at the base of its skull and sheared off the top of its head, leaving nothing but neck and lower jaw. Avanuir continued swirling past, over Snorri, before looping back again and lancing into the troll's chest.

With a shudder, the troll pitched forwards, pinning Snorri beneath its lifeless bulk.

Malekith was at the High King's side in a moment, and was relieved to see Snorri was still breathing. The dwarf's eyes flickered open, and between the two of them they hauled the troll to one side, allowing the High King to regain his feet.

Foul blood and mucus had spilled onto the dwarf king, matting his beard and staining his mail armour. Drips of gore hung from the brow of his helm, seeping into his braided hair. Snorri used a gauntleted hand to distastefully scrape what he could from his person, and then turned to Malekith and adopted a regal pose, shoulders set, chin held high.

'Congratulations,' said the High King. 'You've killed your first troll!'

THE GROWING FRIENDSHIP between prince and High King was cemented during the latter part of the summer, some twenty days before the negotiations

were due to begin in earnest. Word had come to the capital that an army
of beastmen was gathering south of the massive mountain lake known as
Black Water, and was of such a size that the kings of Karak Varn and Zhufbar
feared an attack against one hold or the other.

Upon hearing this news, and having spent much of the season idle in
the halls of Karaz-a-Karak, Malekith's spirit was roused. Learning that King
Snorri planned an expedition against these Chaos creatures, Malekith went
before the High King in his throne room and offered to lead his company
alongside the dwarfs. Snorri looked doubtful at first.

'The throng of Karaz-a-Karak stands ready at my command,' said Snorri.
'What need do I have for fifty more warriors?'

'In prosperity allies may learn much about each other, but in hardship
they learn what is most important,' said Malekith.

'This is true,' Snorri said with a nod. 'However, we stand upon the brink
of important times, and I would not have my descendants remember me as
the dwarf who risked the lives of his new-found friends.'

'Do not fear for our safety, for we are each warrior-born, none more so
than I,' replied Malekith. 'The army of Nagarythe is the most splendid in all
of Ulthuan and, saving perhaps the throng of your hold, the most powerful
force in the world. Though I have but a relative handful of my warriors present, I would like to demonstrate this to you. We may well become partners
in trade, but in these dangerous times it is as important that we become
comrades upon the battlefield.'

'There is much truth in what you say,' said Snorri with a smile. 'Let it not
be said that I was unwilling to show the elves the true worth of a dwarf with
an axe! In battle we see the proper qualities of courage and discipline, and
perhaps it is time that we had this measure of the elves.'

'And we of the dwarfs,' countered Malekith with a smile.

'Yes, that too,' said Snorri with a meaningful look. Both understood that
to see the other in battle would give each a better appraisal of their prospec-
tive allies, their strengths and, if things went ill, their weaknesses.

So it was that two days after the audience, the Naggarothi readied themselves for battle once more and marched out with the army of Karaz-a-Karak.
Snorri led the dwarfs, and an impressive host it was. Positioned at a rampart
just above the gate, the elven prince had a magnificent view of the wide road
leading down the mountainside, and the rank after rank of warriors issuing
forth.

Every warrior was different, for each provided his own wargear. Some
carried axes, others hammers, while many carried bows or the mechanical
crossbows that the dwarfs now favoured. Upon their shields were a wild
variety of blazons and runes, though common themes of the different clans
became evident as Malekith stood at the gate of the hold and watched the
throng pass out.

Malekith stood with Aernuis, watching the host as it marched forth. The rival prince and his companion would not be accompanying the army; Malekith considered it better that the military spectacle and prowess of his Naggarothi not be undermined by the presence of the two Eataine-born elves. Though Malekith had been careful never to claim that all elves were as brave and strong as the folk of Nagarythe, it was his intent that King Snorri be left with the impression that this was the case.

The dwarfs were gathered into regiments of warriors from the same clan, and marched forth beneath the banners of their families and ancestors. Drummers boomed out martial beats and hornblowers sounded low, mournful dirges. Some carried newly forged weapons, others wielded heirlooms passed down from their forefathers, whose names and histories were as renowned as those that had once wielded them.

Snorri was the most striking individual in the army. He marched at its head flanked on each side by standard bearers, carrying banners woven from metallic threads and icons inscribed with magical runes.

'The one that goes before him bears the icon of the High King,' explained Aernuis. 'The dwarf to his right holds the clan standard of Snorri. On his left is carried the banner of the hold, and the fourth belongs to Snorri himself.'

The king was protected by an all-encompassing suit of armour, under which could be seen a layer of heavy mail. Magical sigils were carved into the polished iron, and these glimmered with energy. His axe was no less spectacular, for three runes of angular design were cut into its blade to bring death to the High King's foes. The two-bladed axe glowed with mystical power and the king held it above his head as if it were no more than a feather, and with it waved the throng forwards on the march. Snorri's war helm was also golden and likewise inscribed with magical symbols bestowing courage and kingship.

'The king's helm was made by Valaya, or so the dwarfs believe,' said Aernuis. 'The runes upon it cast a spell so that any who look upon the High King are inspired and awed; to enemies, the High King appears as a terrifying nightmare that fills their hearts with dread.'

'I feel nothing, nor do I see any nightmarish vision,' said Malekith.

'Then perhaps you are neither friend nor foe,' said Aernuis.

The prince of Nagarythe looked sternly at Aernuis but could see no hint of mockery or insult.

'Perhaps I am simply too far away,' said Malekith.

About Snorri and his standards were gathered many of the hold's thanes, and with them the bodyguard of the king made up of the finest warriors the clans contained. They were armed with great axes and hammers burning with fell runes, and wore mail and plates thick enough to ward away all but the most telling of blows.

These venerable dwarfs had long beards that reached to their ankles; to protect this precious hair they wore segmented armour tied to the braids of their beards so that no enemy cut would deprive them of their fine facial hair. Malekith had learnt much about dwarfs and their beards in his time at Karaz-a-Karak and it was something of remark, indeed suspicion, that the elves grew no facial hair at all. 'Beardling' was a phrase oft-used to describe young dwarfs, and 'beardless' was tantamount to dishonourable, a grave insult amongst dwarfkind.

'They are somewhat of a rabble,' remarked Malekith, watching the dwarfs walk out without particular time or rhythm, each sauntering along at his own rate. They ambled out smoking pipes, eating, chatting and behaving in other un-warlike fashions that gave Malekith the impression that while visually impressive, the dwarfen host lacked the gravitas of his own legions. There was little of the precision and finesse he associated with the steady ranks of his spear companies.

It also told him a good deal about the dwarf attitude to war, for they appeared to be no more concerned that they were marching to battle than if they were out for a pleasant afternoon stroll. Having seen the savage beastmen and wild orcs, Malekith suspected that the dwarfs had faced little opposition to their might, and safe in their holds had not truly been tested in the many years since they first wrested control of the mountains.

It was while considering this that another thought occurred to Malekith. The lack of concern showed by the dwarfs might betray an underlying motive for this expedition. If the confidence of the dwarfs were due to some prior knowledge concerning the nature of their foe, then might not it be the case that all of this display was for the benefit of the elves?

'What have you heard concerning this horde of beasts?' Malekith asked.

'Only that it is sizeable,' replied Aernuis.

'It is awfully convenient that the High King feels it necessary to march out at this time,' said Malekith. 'Perhaps they hope to intimidate me with this display of strength?'

'That could be,' said Aernuis, though there was doubt in his voice.

Malekith laughed inwardly at the thought that the dwarfs believed they could overawe him with such manoeuvres. He had to admire their spirit though, and regretted not having seen the opportunity himself. Perhaps if he had allowed a few dwarfs to travel west with his messengers, to return with tales of how quickly the elven realm was expanding and the size of her armies, then some of the dwarfen truculence might have been dislodged.

'When they see the Naggarothi in battle, they will understand that such tacit threats are fruitless,' said Malekith.

'I am sure that they will, Malekith,' said Aernuis, his tone and expression betraying nothing of his own opinion on the matter.

Perhaps the most intriguing aspect of all the army, and the one that caused Malekith the greatest pause for thought, was its engines of war. While the elves had machines that could hurl spear-sized bolts from the decks of their ships or the walls of a castle, the dwarfs had all manner of ingenious contraptions for the field of battle. Some were small and carried upon the backs of the dwarfs themselves: spring-weighted slings that hurled pots of fire and windlass-loaded bows that fired half a dozen darts with a single shot. Others were grander and were pulled along by teams of ponies upon specially built wagons with broad wheels and sprung-loaded axles.

'These machines, what is their purpose?' asked the prince of Nagarythe.

'Each is built individually by the carpenters and smiths of the hold,' said Aernuis. 'They view the craft of engineering with the same passion as we would a jewelsmith or poet. Each pours his own labour and inspiration into his construction.'

'So each engine is unique?' said Malekith, watching the long line of wagons and limbers winding their way out of the huge gate.

'Yes,' Aernuis replied. 'Like everything else the dwarfs design or make, each engine is named and recorded in their histories, its exploits as vaunted as those of a flesh-and-blood hero.'

'That seems indulgent,' said Malekith. 'I would say the dwarfs dwell too much on the past and do not look to the future keenly enough. That will be their loss, for forward-thinking elves such as I will be able to seize better the opportunities that lie ahead.'

'They plan meticulously, if not with vision,' said Aernuis. 'Though perhaps they lack your flair, they see their rise in strength as inevitable.'

'What is that?' Malekith said, choosing to ignore Aernuis's warning. He pointed at a gigantic bolt thrower that fired projectiles so long that three dwarfs were required to load it.

'*Wolfspear*,' answered Aernuis after a moment's thought. 'If I recall correctly, *Wolfspear* was the first machine to guard the gates at Karaz-a-Karak. The legend has it that it slew four giants when first the hordes of Chaos poured south to besiege the hold.'

'And what about that catapult thing?' said Malekith, indicating an enormous trebuchet followed by a wagon loaded with cunningly carved rocks as large as horses.

'Ah, that is *Gatebreaker*,' said Aernuis. 'A mysterious engine. I once heard an engineer say that it had smashed the dark citadel of Thagg-a-Durz. When I inquired as to who else but the dwarfs had the means to create such castles that required attack, the dwarfs fell silent. Their surly expressions discouraged me from any further inquiry.'

'So, there are enemies of the dwarfs that we do not yet know about?'

'I have heard no other mention of such a race or nation in my time with the dwarfs,' said Aernuis. 'But even when appearing open, there is much that they do not say to us.'

'Well, we shall soon see the mettle of our potential allies,' said Malekith. Without further acknowledgement of the Eataine prince, he turned away and swept down the steps from the rampart, his cloak swirling behind him.

* * *

THE DWARFISH AND elven host marched north along a winding road of brick, which soared over wide valleys on extraordinary bridges that arced over the gorges in breathtaking spans hundreds of feet above the jagged rocks and swirling rivers below. In places, the road seemed to barely cling to the steep sides of the mountain peaks, supported on piles and columns dozens of feet high driven into the mountainside with immense bolts and supported by silver-plated scaffolding.

The air was crisp and sharp, even with the full heat of the sun upon their faces, but the dwarfs walked on relentlessly, seeming never to tire nor complain. They ate on the march, which Malekith thought efficient but uncouth, and as he had seen before, when they made camp every dwarf knew his role and duties and carried out his tasks with little supervision or communication from his leaders.

It was this quiet independence that gave the dwarfs their real strength, Malekith admitted to himself as he watched them break camp the following morning. Each could rely utterly upon his fellows, and the sense of community and brotherhood bound the dwarfs together as a kindred.

The people of Nagarythe he praised for their discipline, their attention to duty and their unending dedication, but he knew his folk would never be lauded for their friendship and hospitality, or for a love of others.

ONWARDS AND NORTHWARDS marched the army, crossing vale and peak with monotonous but speedy advance for two more days. Scouts were despatched by the king to locate the bestial foe, and they returned shortly before nightfall to report that they had seen fires some miles to the north-east.

The king was content to allow the army to rest for the night, though he took pains to point out to Malekith that this was not because the dwarfs could not march straight to battle, but was rather so that he could spend the darkest hours in deliberation with his lieutenants, so that all might know the plan of battle for the coming day.

Before dawn the scouts were again sent out to locate the foe, and they returned just as the army was ready to march, the breakfast fires having been extinguished and the wagons packed with their gear. The beastmen, a savage horde numbering several thousand creatures of greater or lesser size, had spent the night carousing and celebrating, for it seemed that they had recently overrun an isolated brewery further north.

News of this attack was greeted by many curses and much wagging of beards by the dwarfs, who until then had seemed more like the head of a family dealing with an unruly cousin than an army marching to death and bloodshed. Now in the belief that these creatures had attacked their lands, the dwarfs became very serious and Malekith found the change not only swift but extraordinary. The thought that beastmen had assailed their realm filled the dwarfs with a simmering anger.

In a few moments the beastmen had been transformed from potential annoyance to hated enemy, and the dwarf throng made their remaining preparations in what seemed to be considerable haste, eager to attack lest their enemies somehow elude them. Speculation about the attack spread through the army, and as the dwarfs marched out there was a grim mood utterly unlike the atmosphere that had pervaded the host when it had left Karaz-a-Karak.

There was little conversation and a solid purpose had now taken hold. Instead of pipe-smoking the dwarfs ran whetstones over their axe blades and tested the strings on their crossbows. Gear was checked and re-checked, and the thanes moved about the throng issuing gruff commands and reminding the warriors of their oaths.

Steadily the host strode northwards, following the lead of the scouts. Their route took them into a deep valley, with thick stands of pines to either side amongst the rocky outcrops. For several miles the gorge cut through the mountains, its walls becoming ever more heavily wooded.

The column was called to battle order as it neared its quarry, the king and his veterans taking their position in the middle of the host while crossbow-armed dwarfs and more lightly armoured troops made their way forwards. The fire-throwers were sent out to guard the flanks, while the engineers began preparing their machines to be unlimbered.

BEFORE MIDDAY THE gorge opened up into a vast craggy bowl circled by rocks and tall firs. Here the beastmen remained, lazing amongst the smoking remnants of their fires, the smashed and clawed ruins of their spoils littering the ground. Broken barrels and splintered staves lay all about the rocky ground, and upon the pyres could be seen the charring corpses of dwarfs, their flesh ripped and hacked from the bodies.

At the sight of this a deep growling emanated from the throng, and there was much cursing.

A few of the more conscious beastmen saw the army issuing from the gorge and ran about the debris-strewn camp howling and shouting. One picked up a horn from the ground and brought it to up its lips.

Before a note could be sounded, the horned thing collapsed to the ground with a black-shafted arrow in its neck. The dwarfs turned in amazement to see Malekith plucking another arrow from his quiver.

Though the hornblower had been silenced, the beastmen were quickly rousing and rising to their feet, snatching up crude clubs, jagged blades and roughly hewn wooden shields. Their appearance and variety defied description, for each was subtly different from the next.

Many had goat-like heads and legs, with long spiralling horns of an antelope, or curling tusks jutting from their mouths. Others were reminiscent of rams, or scorpions, or serpents. Shapeless things with many limbs and eyes lumbered towards the dwarfs, their mewling cries and senseless roars echoing around the rocky basin.

As the alarm was taken up there came a great cacophony of grunts and shrieks, baying and barking. As well as this clamour, the wind also brought the stench of the camp to Malekith. He almost retched as his senses were overwhelmed with the stink of carrion, rotted blood and dung. His fellow elves coughed and spluttered, and even the dwarfs wrinkled their noses and covered their faces with gauntleted hands.

In size as well as in shape, no two beastmen were alike, for some were in height like the dwarfs, though less broad, with thin, twisted faces and stubby horns. Most seemed of a similar size to the elves, though wider of shoulder and larger of limb. Several were much taller, perhaps twice Malekith's height, with bull heads, bloodstained fangs and huge chests thick with muscle.

Some were almost hairless, others albino or with brightly patterned skins; more still were covered in patches of thick fur of reds, browns and black, or were striped like tigers or spotted as leopards. Long beards trailed from bulging chins, and eyes of black, red and green regarded the approaching dwarfs with a mixture of hatred and fear.

Hooting and wailing drowned out the tramp of dwarfish iron-shod boots as the beastmen gathered into groups about their leaders and came forwards to meet the assault.

As they marched on, the dwarf column spread into a line as space permitted, the missile regiments to the flanks, the more solid clansdwarfs holding the centre. The war machines were dismounted from their carts upon hillocks and rises so that they could oversee the whole battlefield, and as Malekith suspected would happen, all of this was done with few shouted commands, only the occasional beating of a drum or short horn blast. Now that battle was almost upon them, the dwarfs were much more cohesive in their movements, though they still lacked the precise drill and organisation of the Naggarothi.

Malekith positioned himself and his warriors close to the High King's bodyguard, in the hope that Snorri would have a full view of their excellence in battle even once the fighting had commenced. Lacking the numbers for a properly organised line, Malekith arranged his warriors in a single block of bows and spears, the better-armoured warriors to the fore, the archers ready to fire past them at approaching enemies. He stood at the centre of the front rank, Alandrian beside him.

'I see little challenge here,' said the prince. 'A disorderly mob against so many engines and bows will perish without a fight.'

'A shame indeed, highness,' said Alandrian. Like the rest of the company, the captain bore a spear and tall shield. His helm covered most of his face, so that only his mouth was visible and Malekith could not see his lieutenant's expression. Alandrian's tone had been less than enthusiastic.

'I think perhaps you have spent too much time talking and not enough with a blade in your hand,' the prince said sharply.

Alandrian turned, his mouth pursed with anger.

'I am Naggarothi, highness,' the captain declared. 'Warrior-born and fear-less. Do not mistake my desire for peace for cowardice.'

Malekith smiled to himself at the venom in Alandrian's retort and was content that his captain would be as fierce a fighter as he had been in the many long years of their acquaintance.

THERE WAS STILL some considerable distance between the beasts and the dwarfs when the first of the war machines loosed its deadly load. A cluster of rocks each as large as a dwarf's head sailed through the air, and then fell amongst the mustering beastmen, crushing skulls and snapping bones.

A great jeer rose up from the dwarfs at the striking of this first blow, which was to be followed by many more as boulders and bolts began to rain down upon the filthy encampment.

Spurred into decisive action, the Chaotic horde ran forwards, the fastest outpacing the slowest so that there was no line or formation but simply separate groups hurtling towards the dwarfs. Malekith sighed, knowing that even against the dwarfs such a lack of tactics would see the beastmen slain or hurled back before a sword was swung or spear was thrust.

As rocks and bolts continued to take their toll, joined now by crossbow quarrels, and arrows from the elves, Malekith saw that his prediction would be correct. In face of such devastating volleys the beastmen could not main-tain any momentum and their charge petered out as they turned away, and in small groups fled from the death unleashed upon them.

A few of the least intelligent creatures continued their attack and the dwarfs concentrated their missiles upon them. Shambling, slithering monstrosities impervious to fear or pain lumbered forwards driven by the instinct to slay, but were eventually cut down as dozens of rocks and arrows pounded and pierced their scaled and leathery bodies.

Malekith returned his bow to its quiver with another sigh and glanced over at Snorri, wondering if the king would sally forth to hunt down the survivors of the barrage. Malekith was sorely tempted to lead his warriors on into the enemy to display their brilliance at arms, but sudden concern stayed his command.

The High King's attention was focused upon the unfolding scene ahead, but now and then he glanced to his left or right, and at one point turned fully around to stare back towards the valley walls behind the host. Some of the other dwarfs were doing likewise, and Malekith felt a tingle of apprehension.

In the Annulii Mountains of his homeland, the prince knew every sound and scent, but here his senses were unaccustomed to the particular hissing of the wind in the trees, the rattle of rocks and the smell of the air. For the dwarfs, though, this was their home and Malekith knew that their instincts here would be as keen as his were in Nagarythe. Their sudden interest in the surroundings gave Malekith a sensation he had not felt since the daemons had been defeated: worry.

It came to him all at once just how little he knew about this place, and how ignorant he was of its dangers and denizens. He was just mastering his concern when there came a sound that turned his worry to an emotion he had not felt in over three hundred years: apprehension.

It was a horn blast, flat and short. It was not the sound itself that caused Malekith such anxiety, but the direction from which it came. It resonated down the valley, but the prince's sharp hearing told him that it had originated in the trees that covered the eastern wall of the valley, behind the host.

A moment later it sounded again and this time there were answers; other atonal blasts and harsh cries were carried on the wind. Hearing this, the beastmen in the rocky hollow slowed in their flight, then turned and started to come back towards the dwarfs.

Now Malekith saw fully the discipline and cohesiveness of the dwarf army. Snorri barked out orders and received acknowledging shouts from his thanes. The engines and crossbow regiments began to pour their shot into the beastmen again, while the king's bodyguard and nearly two-thirds of the throng turned about and began to array themselves for battle at the valley mouth.

Uncertain what plan was being enacted, Malekith split his company, sending the archers forwards to support the attack against the encampment and turning his spears to face this new threat.

Malekith's mind was racing. How was it that they had become so easily trapped? Had the dwarf scouts not wit or skill enough to detect the ambushers?

Then a darker thought entered the prince's mind; perhaps some greater intelligence, some malign intellect, guided their foes.

There was little time to ponder such questions, for amongst the shouts and the thunder of war machines, there came a new sound. Malekith felt it through the soles of his boots before he could hear it. A trembling of the ground, like the distant rumbling of a waterfall.

He could see nothing amongst the closely growing pines, but the growing thunder in the ground intensified and with a rising sense of unease Malekith realised that it was the pounding of thousands of feet.

A blur of darkness in the air caught his attention and he looked up to see a boulder hurtling through the skies towards the dwarfen line. Armour screeched and bones snapped beneath its weight as the stone crashed into the dwarfs, bouncing and rolling through their ranks.

At first Malekith thought that some strange dwarf machine or other had malfunctioned, or that the beastmen had mastered the use of catapults as he had seen orcs employ such crude engines. More movement drew Malekith's eye up the valley's eastern side and he spied a large figure. It was easily ten times the height of an elf. It was naked but for misshapen rags of tattered hide and bloody sheepskins.

As Malekith watched, the giant stooped and picked up another rock, then hurled the projectile far out over the trees into the army beneath.

From the western woods poured the beastmen, hundreds of them swarming and shouting as they burst from the trees hurling stones and other improvised missiles. They erupted from the cover of the forest close to where a battery of engines had been positioned, and the crews abandoned their machines and formed up to defend themselves. Against such numbers their resistance was brief, and Malekith watched as the bestial horde continued down the hillside towards the dwarf line.

The dwarfs moved to counter this attack, the clan warriors locking their shields together as they advanced to meet the threat. As the distance was closed, the dwarfs hurled throwing axes into their enemies, and in return unwieldy javelins were launched into their armoured ranks. Beastmen fell by the score during this exchange, but only here and there did the sturdy armour of the dwarfs fail.

On and on came the tide of twisted evil, a seemingly unending stream of bloated, frothing beasts and animalistic, howling warriors.

With a shattering clash the charging beastmen met the defiant dwarf line and vicious fighting broke out across the breadth of the army. Though the dwarfs held firm and hacked down their foes with relentless ferocity, still more came, savage and shrieking with the joy of slaying. The beastmen spread out as more and more clambered over the dead to reach the dwarfs, and Snorri sent forwards more of his followers to extend the flanks of his force lest the bestial deluge of vileness surround his army.

While his attention was drawn to the ongoing battle to his left, Malekith recalled that the first horn had sounded from the east, to his right.

He looked over towards Snorri and saw that the High King was deep in consultation with his thanes. Seeing that all the efforts of the dwarfs were directed to the west, Malekith decided the best way to draw attention to the danger from the east was through action.

'Naggarothi, with me!' he shouted, drawing his sword. As one the spearmen raised their shields with an affirmative shout. 'Advance!'

Malekith led his soldiers forwards, towards the spine of the mountainside where the valley met the deep crater of the basin. At another command, they broke into a trot, jogging along swiftly to swing wide of the dwarfs' flank. Dwarfish shouts of anger followed them, but Malekith ignored the noise, judging rightly that the dwarfs mistakenly thought the elves were fleeing.

Snarling and howls now sounded from the woods, and Malekith called his troops to a halt, remembering Aernuis's first encounter with goblins.

Sure enough, dozens of wolves sped from the treeline, carrying goblins upon their backs. The wolves were larger than any normal beast, with foaming maws, dark fur and red eyes. The goblins carried spears and small round shields. From under fur-trimmed helmets, their pinched green faces were split by vicious snarls and hungry leers. Many carried short bows and they loosed off erratic shots as they closed in.

The Naggarothi raised their shields to head height as one, and the small arrows clattered harmlessly aside, lacking the punch of a true elven bow. Still, the goblins made up for in numbers what they lacked in quality and more arrows rained down in wavering and corkscrewing fashion, many falling short. Even as their comrades closed, the goblins paid no heed to the risk of hitting their own kind and continued to shower the elves to little effect.

'Spears to guard!' shouted Malekith.

The Naggarothi lowered their shields just as the first of the wolves raced forwards and leapt to the attack, to be skewered on a spear point, its diminutive rider shrieking as it leapt clear. Another elf thrust forwards his spear, lancing its tip through the goblin's throat. With a twist, the warrior pulled his weapon free and returned to the guard position.

More of the wolves tried a direct attack, seeking to jump amongst the elves to wreak havoc, yet the wall of spears held firm and they and their riders suffered the same fate as the first.

A second wave attacked more cautiously, turning at the last moment to ride in front of the regiment hacking at spear tips, but the Naggarothi pressed forwards a few paces and caught them unexpectedly, slaying many on the points of their spears.

The wolf riders ran back and forth, darting in to attack when they thought the elves' guard was down, but not a single greenskin nor their lupine mounts landed a wound upon the Naggarothi. For all that their attack did no direct harm, Malekith could see more goblins leaving the woods on foot, and saw that his small company would quickly become encircled.

With a snarl, he reached out to the winds of magic and drew power into himself. He felt it writhing within him, crawling under his skin, pouring through his veins. With a chant to focus the unwieldy energies, the prince moulded the coiling magic with his mind.

A golden spear dripping with sparks formed in his left hand, and with a curse upon his lips Malekith hurled the spell at the wolves. The magical spear tore straight through three of the creatures and exploded with a shower of yellow flame. Panicked, the wolves yapped and yelped and turned heel, urged to flee even faster by their cowardly riders.

None too soon, Malekith reorganised his troops to face the goblins now marching out of the woods. The greenskins attempted to circle around the elves, jabbing their weapons towards them and screaming jibes and curses in their foul tongue.

The Naggarothi turned and expanded their formation with ease, spreading out into a semi-circle that presented no flank to the enemy, their backs secured by the outcrop of rock at the valley's entrance. Hissing and spitting, the goblins did not attack at once, and they eyed their slaughtered kin and the dead wolves, the corpses of which lay in heaps about the elven regiment.

'I think they have reconsidered their position,' laughed Alandrian from beside Malekith.

The prince's eyes did not leave the goblins, as more of their number flowed from the woods. Soon there were several hundred of the spiteful little creatures, shouting and taunting, but approaching no closer than a stone's throw.

Something immense crashed through the trees behind the goblins, smashing through branches and splintering trunks.

With a bellow the giant strode out into the valley, having evidently grown bored of hurling rocks from above. In its right hand it held a tree limb studded with shards of broken armour, blades of axes and swords, and bent pieces of shield. Buoyed by their gigantic companion, the goblins began to run further forwards, beating their weapons upon their wooden shields and shouting in their shrill voices.

Above the cries and the clamour of battle, Malekith heard a sudden whistling of air. Turning, he saw a great metal shaft arcing over the dwarfen army, from the direction of *Wolfspear*. The engine's crews had turned the gigantic bolt thrower about upon its hillock in the midst of the dwarf army, much to Malekith's relief.

He followed the trajectory of the massive bolt until it struck the giant full in the chest, smashing through its monstrous breastbone, heart and spine. With an astonished gurgle, the giant lurched forwards two steps and then crashed to the ground, flattening a dozen goblins beneath its bulk. Wails of dismay flooded up from the horrified greenskins, who looked at each other in their panic.

'Kill them,' snarled Malekith, breaking into a run.

Needing no further encouragement, the Naggarothi surged forwards, running hard and fast towards the foe.

Like some small animal frozen with terror as the hawk swoops down, the goblins remained unmoving for several heartbeats. With pitiful shrieks they turned to run as the elves came within a few dozen strides, heading for the safety of the woods.

For all their fright-driven speed, the goblins' small legs carried them across the ground much more slowly than the loping run of the elves, and Malekith overtook the slowest of the greenskins with ease. Striking out to right and left, his sword cleaved through heads and spines. Then the Naggarothi caught up with the bulk of the fleeing rabble, and the butchery began.

Malekith felt the Khaine-fever taking over as he slashed and cut, caring not for the acrid blood that spattered on his lips nor the gore splashed across his golden armour.

His warriors were likewise filled with battle-lust, having spent many long days in the hold of the dwarfs without vent for their energy. Heads and limbs were scattered in the orgy of death, and with rage fuelling their steps the elves chased down the goblins and killed every last one of them.

Only when nothing but entrails and bloodied remains were left did they stop, panting hard not from exhaustion but excitement.

Finally tasting the bitter filth upon his face, Malekith wiped the blood clear of his mouth and looked around. The dwarfs were still fighting hard with the beastmen, and were falling back towards the valley basin, drawing them further from the elves.

Malekith did not know if there were more goblins in the woods, or any other loathsome creature for that matter, and turned the company around to head back to the main battle. From this direction they would drive into the rear of the bestial horde.

Malekith could see the four standards of Snorri Whitebeard above the melee, and chose a line of attack that would see the elves cut through the Chaotic filth to meet up with the High King in the melee.

Now calmed by the bloodletting of the goblins, the Naggarothi advanced steadily, cutting down the beastmen in their path. The largest of the beasts were now fighting hard at the front, leaving the smallest and most cowardly to face the attack of the elves. Most ran before they could be hewed down, though some did not see their peril until it was too late. Their lives ended spitted upon spear shaft or cleaved in twain by Avanuir.

As he cut his way through the beastmen, something disturbed Malekith's concentration. There was shifting in the magic around him. It was dark and heavy and hugged the ground, but something was causing it to sluggishly swirl into the air.

Stopping for a moment and waving his warriors to advance further, the prince focussed his attention on the mystical energy. It was definitely being drawn somewhere else. Following its flow, he looked out over the sprawling battle. Like an eagle seeking its prey, Malekith allowed the magic to guide his eyes, until his gaze alighted upon a peculiar beastman.

Its skin was a pale green, blotched with strange moss-like growths amongst mangy patches of fur, and it wore a tattered cloak of what looked like skin. It was hunched over and a grasping hand protruded from its back. Its horned head was covered with a thick hood of rough, mucus-encrusted cloth. In its gnarled, clawed grip the thing held a long piece of wood to which were bound shards of evilly glowing stone. They scorched into Malekith's magical sense, burning with dark magic.

The shaman lifted its staff and pointed the end towards the elves. Too late, Malekith realised what was happening.

Exerting his will, Malekith tried to seize back the magical power being leeched by the shaman, but he could not stop the vile spell. A thick black cloud of flies erupted from that staff, its buzzing deafening, blotting out all other sound. The swarm lifted above the beastmen and flew straight for the Naggarothi, but it was not the sight of the droning cloud that so disturbed Malekith. He could sense the dark energies writhing within the living fog; like the stench of rot or soured milk the magic flooded Malekith's unearthly senses.

The fly cloud descended on the elves with an ear-splitting hum. Where each fly landed, it brought decay. Armour began to spot with rust, and wooden spear shafts grew weak with mildew. Malekith saw an elf flailing at the swarm with his shield, but within moments it had split and disintegrated into orange dust. Plates of armour cracked, leather split and frayed, and scale links turned to a rusted mass.

Suddenly, like a great inhalation, the magic disappeared. Like a cleansing wind blowing through thick smoke, something new disturbed the mystical flow of energy, dissipating it. The swarm dissolved in the air, leaving the Naggarothi swinging rusted gauntlets and broken spear staves into thin air. The breeze became stronger and then grew into a consuming immaterial whirlwind, like a great gulf that had opened up under the sea to swallow all the waters.

A blazing light caught the attention of the prince, and over the bobbing heads of the embattled beastmen he could just about see a dwarf wielding a metallic globe, stood beside the king. White light poured from runes engraved into the strange sphere, and it was to this that the magical winds were being drawn.

A counter-current formed in the ethereal energy of the magical winds as the shaman tried to fight the power of the dwarfen globe. Something went wrong, though. Malekith could feel the magic becoming barbed and dangerous, like a mellow beast suddenly enraged and revealed to have razor-sharp fangs.

For a moment, Malekith fancied that he saw something on the edge of his vision, a shadow of a shadow not unlike some great daemon in form. It appeared above the shaman and seemed to reach into the beastman with an indistinct hand. Then it was gone, and Malekith fancied that perhaps he had simply imagined it.

With a detonation of magical energy that shredded beastmen and dwarfs for many yards in every direction, the shaman exploded. The ground cracked beneath its falling corpse and the air churned with invisible force. Malekith felt the expanding magical field buffet him as surely as any storm or wave, but the prince gritted his teeth and allowed its gnawing energies to pass him by.

Though Malekith's magical blade and Vaul-forged armour were untouched by the horrifying spell, his warriors were now in poor shape. Some were stuck in their rust-seized armour and rolled upon the ground trying to free themselves; many were pocked with boils and lesions left by the horrific biting of the daemon-flies. Most were now weaponless, amongst them Alandrian, and Malekith could see no option but to order a retreat, much as it bit deeply at his pride to do so. Before he had a chance to issue the command, a new horror emerged for them to face.

* * *

THERE WAS A rumbling of thunder overhead and storm clouds gathered with unnatural speed above the valley. Lightning crackled across the dark canopy and shot to the earth in blinding bolts. A wind from nowhere began to howl down the gorge, bending the trees and whipping grit and droplets of blood into the air.

Pines were sent hurtling in every direction as a terrifying monster erupted from the woods to the east. In form it was not unlike a dragon, though perhaps a little lesser in size, with the scaled legs, body and tail of such a creature. Its hide was a deep crimson, but its talons were of a black as dark as coal. The gigantic centaur-like monster had a red-skinned torso and a pair of arms where the dragon's neck and head would have been. Its head sat upon broad shoulders that were encased in plates of studded armour. Two serrated horns coiled out of its skull and its mouth was little more than a fang-filled slit.

It wielded a pair of identical swords, larger than anything Malekith had ever seen, but true-forged blades rather than the improvised weapons of the beastmen. Energy flickered and crawled upon those cruel swords, whose hilts and crossguards were fashioned from fused spines and whose pommels were made from real skulls. The gigantic beast's eyes were wide and filled with the energy of the storm.

'Shaggoth!' cried one of Malekith's soldiers, and the prince knew it to be true.

The oldest legends of the dragons spoke of such creatures, but Malekith had considered them to be myths from before the rise of the elves; before even the coming of the Old Ones and the banishment of the elven gods. Cousins to the dragons who had ruled the world before the coming of the gods, the shaggoths had bartered their souls to Chaos long before the Dark Gods had arisen to claim this world. If the dragons were to be believed, they had warred with the shaggoths for an eternity until finally the dragons had triumphed and driven their foes into hiding.

With the coming of Chaos, Malekith guessed, the shaggoths had been roused from their lairs, and now one of the titanic creatures stared down at Malekith with death-filled eyes. Lightning arced down from the storm clouds above, striking the shaggoth full on the chest. The creature was invigorated rather than harmed, as coruscating energy rippled across its gnarled skin.

'Our allies watch!' cried Malekith to his elves as those that could move backed away in terror from the apparition. 'Do not shame yourselves! Show no fear! Strike without hesitation! Slay in the name of Nagarythe!'

With lightning still flickering across its flesh, the shaggoth lunged forwards and snatched up one of the Naggarothi in a foreclaw, splintering rusted armour and crushing bones and organs. A sweep of a sword carved through three more warriors, sending their remains spinning through the air. With Malekith's command still ringing in their ears, the Naggarothi closed ranks and attacked, but even those whose weapons had not been undone by the shaman's curse could find no weakness in the scales and hide of the beast.

With a deafening roar, the shaggoth cast the remains of the unfortunate Naggarothi in its claws, so that he smashed back into the company, toppling several more elves. Its swords blazing with energy, the prehistoric monster hacked and chopped with savage glee, slicing great bloody wounds into the regiment.

Summoning what little magical power remained after the dwarfs' counter-spell, Malekith charged in to the attack, Avanuir trailing blue flames as he swept the magical sword towards the beast's underbelly.

The creature reared with an angry bellow and Malekith was forced to leap backwards to avoid a raking claw aimed for his throat. Ducking beneath the swipe of a monstrous sword, Malekith took hold of Avanuir in both hands and hacked at the beast's legs, though even the enchanted blade of Naga-rythe bit only lightly into the armoured skin of the terror.

Alerted by his preternatural senses, Malekith tried to dodge another swing-ing blade, but was caught on the shoulder by the shaggoth's fist and sent wheeling through the air. Landing heavily, the wind knocked from him, Malekith struggled to regain his feet. Pouncing with unlikely speed, the shaggoth grasped Malekith in one of its foreclaws and wrenched the prince aloft. Its right arm swung back ready for the death blow, energy arcing from the blade it held.

With a wordless shout, Malekith drove Avanuir deep into the flesh of the creature's foreleg, causing it to spasm and drop him to the ground. Crawl-ing forwards, Malekith ducked beneath the creature's bulky body and then stood, raking the tip of Avanuir along the softer skin of its underside. Thick, dark blood dripped from the wound and the shaggoth tried to back away so that Malekith would not be hidden by its own body. The prince rolled between its thrashing legs, avoiding an immense sword that dug a great trench in the earth where he had been stood, and drove Avanuir into the base of the shaggoth's tail.

Such wounds would have been grievous against any other foe, but the shaggoth was not even slowed by them. Malekith rolled beneath another attack and barely brought up Avanuir in time to deflect another blow, though the parry sent the magical sword spinning from Malekith's fingers.

Unarmed, Malekith stood up to face the beast, staring defiantly into its black eyes. Intelligence flickered in those inky depths, a recognition of what Malekith was. Other Naggarothi jabbed and hacked at the shaggoth with swords and knives, trying to draw its attention away from their prince. It turned quickly and swept them away with a swing of its tail, hurling them from their feet. Malekith remained where he was stood, hands balled into fists that glowed with magical flame.

The shaggoth loomed over the lord of Nagarythe, its twin swords held high above its head. More lightning arced down from the storm clouds it had summoned, earthing into the tips of those primordial blades. It crossed its blades in front of it in a mocking salute, its mouth twisted with an evil smile.

The first strike caught Malekith full in the chest, lifting him from his feet with an explosion of electricity. Sparks of energy flew from the prince's magical armour as he sailed a dozen feet into the air and then crashed down onto the rocky ground. Pain lanced along his spine and his ribs felt shattered, but Malekith's pride would not let him die on his back.

With a grunt, he pushed himself to his feet, his injuries sending spasms of agony through his body. The prince turned to face the shaggoth once more.

'I am Aenarion's son.' Malekith spat blood onto the ground at the shaggoth's feet. 'My father slew the four greatest daemons that the Dark Gods could send. Armies were laid low by his blade. The world trembled at his tread. All will remember me as they remember him.'

The shaggoth brought down its leftmost blade and Malekith raised his arm to protect himself, the ensorcelled gold of his armour screeching and blazing with light at the impact. The shaggoth's smile died, and its brow furrowed in frustration and anger. Another blow that would have felled trees and shattered stone sent Malekith skidding backwards, his arm broken, a slash across his face.

Spitting more blood, Malekith stood again.

'Your time is long past,' Malekith taunted the beast. 'Our time is now. Go back to your dark hole and pray to your filthy gods that we do not hunt you down.'

With a roar of anger, the shaggoth lashed out wildly, allowing Malekith to easily avoid the blow. Malekith ducked beneath the sword, and then leapt high, fuelled by anger and magic, his blazing fists smashing the shaggoth across the face. Reeling from the blow, the shaggoth took several steps back, shaking its head.

Landing lightly, Malekith readied himself to strike again when the shaggoth let out a great howl of pain. It whipped around, and the prince saw that its tail had been half-severed. There was a flash of light from some source obscured by its gigantic body, and a clawed foreleg whirled into the air in a fountain of thick gore.

Ducking so that he could see beneath the creature's heaving gut, Malekith saw the dwarf High King, blazing rune axe in hand. Each blow cut through flesh and bone without pause, sending the shaggoth staggering from side to side.

Determined that he would not be upstaged by Snorri, Malekith leapt to where Avanuir had fallen and snatched up his blade. Though his left arm was shattered and his insides burned from injuries that could not be seen, Malekith sprinted forwards and leapt upon the shaggoth's back. As it bucked and turned, Malekith ran up the bony crests along its spine. Spitting through gritted teeth from the pain, the prince grabbed one of the shaggoth's curling horns with his crippled left hand and planted a foot upon its shoulder.

With a triumphant cry, he brought down Avanuir across its neck, chopping deep into the thickly muscled flesh. Thrice more Avanuir bit, until the beast shuddered and spasmed and then collapsed to the ground. With a final effort, Malekith sawed the head free and tossed it to the ground beside Snorri, who was awash head to foot with the entrails and sinews of the monster. The beast's remains toppled to the ground, tossing Malekith unceremoniously into the blood-slicked mud next to Snorri.

The High King looked down at Malekith, his eyes glittering behind the visor of his helm. He then gave the curious thumb-up signal the prince had seen the dwarfs use as a sign of approval.

'We'll share this one, I think,' Malekith said magnanimously.

Only then, with his point proven, did Malekith allow himself to pass out.

—◄ SEVEN ►—

An Alliance Forged

WITH THE SHAGGOTH slain and their goblin allies routed or slaughtered, the beastmen had little stomach for the continuing battle and quickly slunk back into the woods. Neither elf nor dwarf was prepared to venture after them, the dwarfs knowing they would never catch their swifter foes, the elves utterly undone by the shaman's spell and the shaggoth's attack.

It was a much slower and wearier march back to Karaz-a-Karak for Malekith. His whole body ached and his back and arm flared with pain every time he took a step. The dwarfs offered to carry him upon one of the war machine limbers, but Malekith refused such indignity. Agonising though it was, he walked alongside the dwarfs, hiding his pain as best he could.

It was a source of pride that those of his warriors still capable of standing did likewise, though seven of them were so badly wounded that he allowed them to be carried on the wagons. The bodies of nineteen others were carried with dignity amongst the dwarfen dead.

The dwarfs were similarly determined to prove their resilience, though a good many had suffered broken bones and deep cuts. Bandaged and hobbling, they marched back to the capital with their heads held high, as high as any dwarf's head could ever reach.

Malekith spent most of those following days with the High King, and was pleased that the heroic display of his warriors and himself had earned much respect in Snorri's eyes. Snorri was much more talkative, and seemed eager that the coming negotiations went well.

* * *

To CHEERS AND great clamour, the throng returned to Karaz-a-Karak and strode through the gates. The dwarfs chanted Snorri's name and came forwards to congratulate their returning warriors. The elves were greeted with similar enthusiasm and were presented with all manner of small gifts and tokens of the dwarfs' appreciation by wide-eyed beardlings and smiling dwarf maidens.

That same night, the High King hosted a banquet for the victorious army, and lavished his warriors and the elves with food and beer. He bid Malekith the honour of sitting at his right-hand side, and gave the prince his own royal drinking tankard. There were many toasts raised, and more speeches, though on this occasion Malekith was far more complimentary to his hosts than he had been in Karak Kadrin. He thanked the dwarfs for their hospitality and spoke of their courage and honour. He pledged his lifelong friendship to their people, and swore an oath of brotherhood with the High King.

This last was a great occasion and marked the dwarfs' absolute acceptance of the elves as their comrades and friends. Whatever the negotiations and trade talks would bring, Malekith now knew that he would forever be an ally of Snorri, and found himself glad that this was so, not only for the power and prestige this would surely bring, but also because Malekith genuinely liked and admired the dwarfs' ruler.

THE DAY AFTER the celebratory feast, Alandrian was summoned to Malekith's chamber. The prince gave him a very personal mission. The lieutenant accepted his orders without question and sought out Aernuis. He found the Eataine prince in one of the upper galleries.

'There is something important we must discuss,' Alandrian said with a conspiratorial tone. 'Come with me.'

Aernuis followed without question as the Naggarothi captain led him out of the hold via one of the many secondary gates, and they walked out onto a windy rampart high up the mountainside.

'Where are we going?' asked Aernuis finally, as Alandrian took them up a winding stair that led up to a cliff face.

'We cannot risk being overheard or seen,' Alandrian confided.

Saying no more, Aernuis ascended the steps and they stood side-by-side upon a wide ledge. Beneath them a swift river had cut a deep ravine, and gushed over a steep fall into a pool surrounded by jagged rocks some two hundred feet below. Spray filled the air and the roar of the water masked all other sound.

'What is it that you have to say?' asked Aernuis.

'I have a message from Prince Malekith,' said Alandrian.

'What is it?' replied Aernuis.

Swifter than a striking snake, Alandrian stepped behind Aernuis and pulled a curved blade from his belt. Grabbing the prince by the chin, he drove the point of his blade into Aernuis's back, cutting through his spine. Aernuis struggled as he collapsed to his knees, his cries muffled by Alandrian's hand.

'You are no longer useful to him,' Alandrian hissed in his victim's ear. 'Malekith has the ear of the High King now, and he remembers the slights against him. He is not known for his forgiving nature.'

Aernuis writhed and wept, but Alandrian's grip was as tight as a vice.

'My prince cannot allow you to live,' the Naggarothi explained. 'He would willingly let his light shine upon your life, but he cannot share power with you. You are beneath him, and your petty ambition would undermine all that he hopes to build.'

The Eataine prince flailed at his assassin but Alandrian easily batted away his grasping fingers. Without any hint of pleasure or regret, the Naggarothi drew his knife across Aernuis's throat and pushed him from the ledge. He stepped forwards to watch the body tumble into the spume. The trail of arterial blood spewing from the wound was soon swallowed up by the fury of the waterfall. Tossing the blade casually after the Eataine prince's corpse, Alandrian turned back towards the stair. He wondered where he might find Sutherai.

FIFTEEN DAYS LATER, the audience chamber of Snorri was filled with a crowd of dwarfs and elves. Though ostensibly mingling and getting to know each other, the two peoples were keeping to their own and only a few brave souls of either race ventured over to talk to the opposite delegation. The High King sat upon his throne and watched all of this with amusement, Malekith stood upon his right.

'It is a shame that your two companions are not here to witness the culmination of their efforts,' Snorri remarked.

'A shame indeed,' Malekith replied without pause. 'I cannot comprehend what possessed them to venture from the city without an escort.'

'Nor I,' said Snorri.

Malekith detected no hint of accusation in the High King's voice, though perhaps the prince's ignorance of the dwarfish language masked some implication in the words.

'I am glad that their disappearance has not caused problems for the negotiations,' Malekith said smoothly. 'It is good that their sudden departure has not formed unfounded suspicions between us. Such an occurrence could have unravelled many months of careful planning.'

'Do you think there is cause for suspicion?' said Snorri, turning a questioning eye upon the prince.

'I think not, but I can see how one might view such matters with suspicion. I do not think that there is any conspiracy at work. Prince Aernuis has long been in self-exile and perhaps the impending talks got the better of his nerve.'

'Whatever his reasons, he is probably troll-fodder by now,' said Snorri, returning his attention to the throng below. 'Or worse.'

'A regrettable end for a prince of Ulthuan,' said Malekith.

They both allowed the hubbub of the hall to wash over them for a while until Malekith felt the need to break the silence.

'Shall we join our parties and bring them together?' the prince said.

'Yes, let's get this pony moving,' said Snorri, stepping from his throne.

FOR MORE THAN a year the talks between the elves and dwarfs progressed, and there were many treaties signed and oaths sworn on both sides. While the rulers and diplomats haggled, the common people of both races got on with the business of the actual trade, reaching local agreements and personal bargains with their opposites.

Malekith recovered from his wounds in time to see the negotiations concluded. Once fit again, he divided his time between Athel Toralien and Karaz-a-Karak, and led the elves to numerous celebrated victories over the creatures of darkness. Bel Shanaar sent the prince a mighty gift in recognition of his achievements: a white dragon from the mountains of Caledor. As his father had done in the time of the daemons, Malekith led the armies of the elves from atop this mighty beast and his foes fell before him. Many times more over the following centuries did the prince of Nagarythe march forth beside the High King, and their friendship was a symbol of the unity between the races of elf and dwarf.

THE ALLIANCE WITH the dwarfs heralded the golden age of the elves; their colonies spread across the globe and the wealth of distant lands flowed into their coffers. Their fleets travelled wherever the elves' desires took them, and cities of gleaming marble and alabaster rose up in the wildernesses of the world.

From Ulthuan the elves spread to every corner of the world, settling in the steaming jungles of Lustria, the savage forests across the great ocean, and upon volcanic isles in the east. The cities of Ulthuan grew with the empire, so that even the meekest of their kind lived in grand mansions amidst great luxury. Everything from the sea to the mountains became the domain of the elves, and in the peaks the dwarfs reigned supreme, their own empire growing vast upon the spoils of the alliance.

Only one land remained free of elvish influence. Eastwards, beyond the mountains of the dwarfs, lay the blasted wastes of the Dark Lands. No elf wished to venture further east, for there was plenty enough for both peoples to enjoy and the dwarfs warned that there was nothing but death and misery in the barren desert.

Thus the elves named the high peaks Saraeluii: the Mountains at the Edge of the World. Truly they were masters of all that they surveyed. Their armies marched at will under the command of the princes, and the evil orc and goblin tribes, vile beastmen warbands and unnameable Chaos creatures were driven into the far north.

Only here, at the very roof of the world, would the elves not venture. It was here that the Realm of Chaos touched upon the world, disgorging its tide of magical energy, warping and corrupting the lands. Having suffered greatly at the hands of daemons before, the elves had no desire to war against the Dark Powers upon the doorstep of their otherworldly realm, and were content to corral the nightmare mutants and monsters upon the bleak ice and keep them from the cities in the south.

Malekith found that his spirit was not quelled by these battles, for his foes were now of little threat, scattered remnants of the huge tribes and armies that had once made the woods their homes. His dragon was slain by a monstrous giant whilst the Naggarothi fought against the last great horde of orcs to beset the elves' lands, and with reluctance the prince realised an age had ended. Elthin Arvan had been tamed, and with that his chance for greater renown would ebb away. So it was that Malekith finally turned his attention to the north, and first went into the cold lands of the Chaos Wastes.

— EIGHT —

The Passing of an Age

HOPING TO REGAIN some of his former passion, Malekith renewed his friendship with the dwarfs of Karak Kadrin, and alongside them took the fight
to the monsters and mutants that came south from the Realm of Chaos.
On occasion the High King would join Malekith in these conquests, and
together they forged along the mountains and across the tundra to bring
civilisation to the icy wilderness.

For a while Malekith was content, his turmoil soothed by the comfort of
battle and his isolation from the politics of the elven princes. With sword in
hand he became master of his own fate once more, and the legends of his
exploits grew in proportion so that again his name was spoken of in awe by
the high and the mighty of the colonies and Ulthuan.

It was here in the bitter cold of the northlands that Malekith first encountered the tribes of men. Some were savage in the extreme, and either took
flight at first sign of the elven and dwarfen host, or sallied forth from their
caves and crude huts to wage pointless battle against their far superior foes.
At first Malekith took them to be nothing more than another barbarian
people, no different or better than the orcs or beastmen.

However, as Snorri and Malekith led an army of dwarfs and elves into
the very north of the Saraeluii, a group of humans came forth timidly from
their rough dwellings to greet them. The humans brought with them gifts
of simple bread and roasted meat. Though they had little more than stone
weapons and heavy sticks, they confronted Malekith and Snorri without
fear, grunting in their basic language.

The High King took the proffered food and in return gave the human chieftain a golden band from his wrist. The man took it and held it up, admiring the gleam of the metal, and a smile cracked his grimy, bearded face. With a shuffling gait, the tribal leader beckoned for the two to follow him back to their caves.

Malekith at first ignored the man, but Snorri was as inquisitive as ever and followed the elder. Relenting, Malekith walked after them, gesturing for his warriors to stand ready should anything untoward occur. Barriers of crudely split wood and curtains of woven grasses and raw animal hides barred the entrance to the largest of the caves, and smoke billowed out of the entrance from the cooking fires within. Ducking through the skins, Malekith found himself in a high, deep cavern.

Half a dozen human females were clustered within, suckling their young. Older women tended a fire over which roasted half the carcass of an enormous deer. The humans looked at their visitors with curious, intelligent eyes, and immediately Malekith recognised that these creatures were not like the orcs or the beastmen. There was something in their gaze that spoke of wisdom and emotion, utterly unlike the unthinking enmity of an orc's stare.

Snorri tugged at Malekith's arm and pointed excitedly to the cave walls. They were painted with many different scenes, interspersed with abstract symbols and crude pictograms. In particular the High King drew the prince's attention to a painting of a small figure, rotund in form and wielding what looked to be an axe. He had a shock of red hair and a long red beard, and fought against a band of daemon-like stick figures with horns and long claws.

'Grimnir,' Snorri said with a grin, and Malekith nodded.

The daubings did look somewhat like the Ancestor God of the dwarfs, who had dyed his hair a fiery orange and wielded a rune axe as he had ventured into the Realm of Chaos to fight the daemons. That had been more than a thousand years ago, but the cave paintings seemed no more than a few years old. Had these humans passed down what they had seen all those centuries ago, Malekith wondered, leaving paintings and tales for the next generation? If it was true, it spoke loudly about their character and intelligence, and Malekith was quietly impressed.

The pair spent a mostly wordless afternoon with the humans, sharing their food and showing them various trinkets and weapons that they carried. The humans were awkward and filthy, but Malekith could see in them a certain nobility of spirit. After they left the camp, promising through signs and gestures that they would return, Snorri and Malekith fell into a long debate concerning what to do with these people.

'They are children of the Old Ones, just as we are,' the High King said. 'They are not creatures of Chaos or darkness, though they are simple and have little civilisation yet.'

'Yet?' said Malekith.

'For sure,' said Snorri. 'Without guidance or protection, they have survived the fall of the Old Ones and the coming of the Dark Gods. With but a small amount of education from us, they will no doubt become useful. They are quick to learn, I reckon, and will be attentive to our lessons.'

'And to what purpose would you educate them?' laughed Malekith. 'Would you have them as clever labourers, or is there a greater intent to your proposal?'

'I would teach them language and writing,' Snorri replied earnestly. 'Not the language of the dwarfs perhaps, but a tongue that we can all understand. They are here for a reason; I can feel it in my bones. It is our duty to shield them from the worst perils of the world and ensure that they prosper.'

'Who are we to judge what should and should not happen?' countered Malekith. 'They have survived thus far by their own wit and strength, and perhaps it is right that we leave them to find their own path. We cannot know the will of the gods and the Old Ones, and I agree that they have a purpose here, but we cannot guess at what it might be. Is it our place to interfere, or to let things take their course?'

'Hmm, there is much in what you say,' said Snorri. 'However, whatever their destiny, I cannot see that it was to be consumed by hideous creatures nor swallowed up by the dark legions of Chaos. Does it not strike you as odd that they thrive here, under the very shadow of the Chaos Wastes? I know from kin who have travelled further north that there are many of these tribes, in the mountains and upon the icy plains. Is it not preferable that we guard against their corruption, so that perhaps they might become a bulwark against the armies of the Chaos Gods?'

'I would sooner see them as backward friends than clever enemies,' said Malekith. 'What if they take what we can teach them and turn our own knowledge against us? With stone axes and flint-tipped spears, they are no threat to us, but who can say what would happen if they learned the means to work metals, to grow into a nation that might one day look upon our domains with envy?'

'There is much we do not know,' agreed Snorri. 'This is no matter to be decided in the course of a single day.'

So the two were in accord, and decided that their peoples would wait and watch. There was much promise in the race of men, but also much that could be perverted and turned to darkness. The elves and the dwarfs would treat their barbaric neighbours with a light touch, allowing them the shelter of their two empires but otherwise only guiding and shaping their future with their presence alone.

FOR AN AGE the world turned and Malekith was content. War and adventure were plentiful and he returned only seldom to Athel Toralien, preferring the wild lands to the increasingly managed and austere realms of his colony. The Naggarothi prince was lauded across all of the colonies, and here he was king in all but name, for even the other princes admired what he had achieved.

Let Bel Shanaar rule over dull Ulthuan, Malekith would tell himself. Let the Phoenix King fill his days settling the arguments of spoilt princes. Glory and renown forever beckoned to the prince of Nagarythe and he grasped his opportunities with both hands.

All was to change.

FOR MORE THAN twelve hundred years the colonies grew and endured, and in that time Malekith's power abroad knew no rival, except perhaps in Karaz-a-Karak. Then came word that Bel Shanaar, now rich beyond measure upon his trade and taxes, planned to travel to the dwarfen capital to meet his peer, the High King. For most in the cities of the forests this was heralded as an event worthy of much celebration. However, Malekith was not pleased.

'What is his purpose in coming?' Malekith demanded of Alandrian. He had just received a letter from Morathi warning of Bel Shanaar's intent.

The two of them sat in a wide chamber at the heart of the prince's winter palace, Malekith's retreat during the season of ice when his armies could no longer march. A fire burned in the dwarf-built grate, and the two elves reclined upon long couches, wrapped in warm woollen robes.

'I cannot know his intent, highness,' replied Alandrian.

'Do not be coy with me,' snapped Malekith. 'What do you think he is up to? My mother claims his rule is weakening on Ulthuan and he seeks to bolster his popularity.'

'Your mother is better placed than I to judge events on Ulthuan, highness,' said Alandrian, and then quickly continued after receiving a cold stare from his master. 'What she says confirms my own belief. Though Tiranoc grows rich, there are some princes who feel that Bel Shanaar does not lead his people. The true glory of our people is in the colonies. On Ulthuan, life has become so luxurious that none need fight nor labour. Fields are not tilled, no game is hunted. All she now desires is sent from the cities across the world: sacks of grain, spiced meats, cut gems and dwarfen trinkets. Ulthuan grows indolent and her people lose themselves in poetry and song, wine and debauchery.'

Malekith frowned and stroked his chin.

'I cannot refuse him directly,' the prince said. 'The other cities are keen for his patronage still.'

'Many are jealous of you, beneath their smiles and plaudits,' said Alandrian. 'They seek strength from the Phoenix Throne so that they might become more independent of Athel Toralien.'

'They simply swap one master for another,' snarled Malekith. 'I helped build them. I keep their lands safe. How do they repay my dedication? They cry to Bel Shanaar and hope that he will shield them from the cruel reality of the world.'

'Perhaps there is opportunity here,' said Alandrian. 'If the dwarfs see Bel Shanaar as weak compared to your greatness, your position grows stronger.'

'No, that will not do,' said Malekith. 'King Snorri believes our people to be united, as are his. If Bel Shanaar is seen as weak the High King will see all elves as weak, including me. He believes that all of Ulthuan and her princes are as strong as Nagarythe and I. We cannot undermine that useful illusion by showing him otherwise.'

'I cannot see how we can turn this to your advantage, highness,' admitted Alandrian.

'Why now?' Malekith mused to himself. 'Why, after one thousand two hundred years does Bel Shanaar visit us now?'

IT WAS A question that was to vex Malekith over the long winter months as he brooded in Athel Toralien. The prince was painfully aware that all the talk in the colonies was of the Phoenix King's visit, his own exploits and glory now forgotten by the fickle, gossiping elves of the other cities.

The prince was further insulted by the news that Bel Shanaar planned to visit the city of Tor Alessi first. Taken at face value, this was reasonable, for the city had been founded by princes from Tiranoc, the Phoenix King's own realm. Yet Malekith knew that this was in fact a subtle slight, for Athel Toralien was paramount in size and power in Elthin Arvan. Athel Toralien was a capital in all but name, more than equal in power to Tor Anroc. Bel Shanaar's intent was to show that despite this, there were lands still beyond Malekith's control.

It was mid-summer when the Phoenix King and his entourage arrived at the Naggarothi city. Malekith ensured that his welcome of the Phoenix King left Bel Shanaar in no doubt as to where the rule of Elthin Arvan truly lay. He recalled the greater part of his army, some two hundred thousand Naggarothi, and lined the road to the city with regiments of black-clad archers, magnificently armoured knights and grim-faced spearmen.

Such military spectacle had never before been seen, on Ulthuan or anywhere else. The Naggarothi host dwarfed the guard of the Phoenix King, even bolstered as the Tiranoc force was by troops from Tor Alessi. Malekith hoped the comparison between the two armies was not lost on the other princes.

Not to be outdone by the Phoenix King's wealth, Malekith lavished his guests with the finest gifts and hosted banquets in their honour for thirty days. Herein was another subtle snipe, for Malekith dedicated each night of festivities to a different guest: one for the Phoenix King and one each for the twenty-nine princes who accompanied him. Malekith's message was clear: Bel Shanaar was the first amongst equals, no greater than any other.

The day before Bel Shanaar was due to leave, Malekith invited the Phoenix King to inspect the warriors of Athel Toralien. They drilled before the city walls, where Malekith stood with his rival upon the massive northern gate tower. A dozen other princes watched with them, forcing Malekith to choose his words carefully.

'I see that you are impressed, majesty,' said Malekith.

'Against what threat do you maintain such a force?' asked Bel Shanaar, turning his gaze from the marching columns of spearmen filing past far below the gatehouse.

'The lands of Elthin Arvan are still home to beasts and orcs,' Malekith said. 'I maintain garrisons in dozens of citadels between the ocean and the realm of the dwarfs. There is also the ever-present threat from the north.'

'Bands of marauders, scattered tribes of thuggish humans?' Bel Shanaar laughed.

'The Dark Gods and their daemonic legions,' said Malekith, and was pleased to see the princes momentarily fearful.

'Caledor's vortex remains strong,' Bel Shanaar said dismissively. 'Such caution is unnecessary.'

'I inherited a duty from my father,' Malekith said, his voice pitched so that it easily carried to the gathered nobles. 'I shall protect my people against any threat, and stand ready to do the same for Ulthuan.'

Bel Shanaar cast a sideways glance at the princes and said nothing. The Naggarothi continued their manoeuvres until the sun was setting over the ocean.

'Well, that was enlightening,' said Bel Shanaar with a clap of his hands. He turned towards one of the gate towers and then spun back on Malekith. 'I regret that I must depart so soon, but there are others who have begged me to attend their cities and palaces. The Naggarothi cannot have me all to themselves, you know.'

Before Malekith could retort, the Phoenix King had moved away and was surrounded by a gaggle of princes. The Naggarothi prince stormed off in the opposite direction. He felt the need to vent his frustration and wondered where Alandrian would be hiding.

THE CULMINATION OF this tour was the Phoenix King's arrival at Karaz-a-Karak. Wishing to display his splendour and power, Bel Shanaar arrived with an entourage of three thousand elves, and a bodyguard of ten times that number. The most high-ranking were housed by the dwarfs, and the others lived in a huge camp that spread for miles along the road that led to the hold.

The greeting ceremony was like nothing either dwarf or elf had ever seen before, as both sides attempted to outdo each other in grandiosity and spectacle. The High King summoned all the kings of the holds to gather to greet Bel Shanaar; hundreds of lesser princes and nobles and every ruling prince of Ulthuan attended the Phoenix King – including Malekith. It was Snorri's wish that Malekith introduce him to the Phoenix King, and out of friendship Malekith therefore attended the reception of the Phoenix King, backed by five thousand of his Naggarothi knights.

The procession was almost a mile long, and more than a hundred banners fluttered above the column as it made its way up the road to Karaz-a-Karak on the appointed day. The dwarfs lined the highway cheering and clapping, and many had been drinking for days on end beforehand to get in the right spirit. Five hundred kings and thanes stood as guard for the High King, each accompanied by his banner and shield bearers, while great runelords and master engineers stood proudly with their guild standards, surrounded by the clan elders of every hold.

As was to be expected there was a huge feast and many speeches, so that the whole thing took more than eight days to complete, for every king and thane had to meet and be formally introduced though many had fought and even lived beside each other for hundreds of years.

Throughout the celebrations Malekith was on hand to offer whatever advice and information the Phoenix King required; he deigned to act as translator for Bel Shanaar. The climax of all this activity came on the eighth night, as the High King and Phoenix King finally stood together upon the throne dais of Snorri's audience hall. Bel Shanaar spoke at length upon the benefits of the alliance and the splendid welcome of the dwarfs. He praised the princes for the creation of this corner of the vast empire, and concluded with an announcement that tested Malekith's tolerance to the limit.

'Elf and dwarf shall be bound forever in immortal friendship,' Bel Shanaar declared. 'As long as our empires endure, may we know peace between us. As a sign of our dedication to this common cause, we shall appoint an ambassador to this court, one of our greatest sons. He is the architect of my empire and the forger of this alliance, and his authority in these lands shall be as mine. His words will be my commands. His will shall be my wish. I name Prince Malekith as embassy to Karaz-a-Karak, and bestow the blessings of all the gods upon his endeavours.'

Malekith fumed inside at these words, and had to fight to keep his expression one of gratitude. 'My empire,' Bel Shanaar had said. 'His will shall be my wish,' a voice raged inside Malekith's head. All that he had laboured and fought to create these many centuries, Bel Shanaar had taken from him with those few words. What right did the Phoenix King have to claim anything that Malekith had made possible?

Ambassador? Malekith already had absolute authority over these lands; he needed no permission from Bel Shanaar. The colonies had been his, wrested from the wilderness and the hordes of darkness by his own hands. Blood he had spilt and agonies he had known in the birth of this great empire, while Bel Shanaar had sat upon his throne in Tor Anroc and gorged himself upon the spoils of Naggarothi endeavour. Holding his ire in check, the prince turned and bowed stiffly to the Phoenix King, avoiding Snorri's gaze lest he recognise some hint of the anger that burned within.

For the remainder of the visit, Malekith excused himself from Bel Shanaar's company, claiming that he was needed back in Athel Toralien. In reality, he sought the sanctuary of the forests, for such was Malekith's anger he could not look upon the face of another elf for several months.

EVENTUALLY THE PRINCE calmed and tried as best he could to return to a normal life. In the five decades that followed Bel Shaanar's visit Malekith sent messages to Morathi frequently, and she replied with equal regularity. Always she was keen to praise her son for his achievements, but there was also gentle admonishment that he ignored his father's legacy on Ulthuan. Ever she had insisted that he return to the isle to take up his birthright, and her writing became even more strident following Bel Shanaar's visit to Karaz-a-Karak. She too had felt the slight caused by the Phoenix King's words and deeds, and Morathi had ranted at length in her next letter, decrying the hypocrisy of Bel Shanaar, who spoke out against supposed decadence in Nagarythe.

In this last matter, Malekith's intuition was roused and he secretively took more interest in affairs back on Ulthuan. He subtly inquired over the coming years as to the nature of life in Nagarythe, both through his missives to Morathi and from loyal Naggarothi who still sailed between the isle of the elves and the colonies.

The news from the merchants worried him on occasion, for there was talk of cabalistic cults dedicated to the more sinister elven gods, and of pleasure sects that lost themselves in luxury and excess. Malekith's suspicions were tempered by the letters of Morathi.

'Jealous of Nagarythe's prominence despite the Phoenix King's court being in Tor Anroc,' she explained in one of her letters, 'many of the ruling princes are waging a subtle and insidious campaign against me and my council. They will not accuse me outright of any misdeed, but through innuendo and rumour imply that we are in league with some unknown dark power.'

Malekith could imagine how the envy of the princes would lead them to such actions, and believed his mother when she assured him that the so-called pleasure cults and dark sects were nothing more than ancient rituals the Naggarothi had always undertaken for the appeasement of the less fondly regarded elven gods.

'The Phoenix King has even hinted that he looks unkindly on the Naggarothi's connections to Khaine,' she continued. 'Our oldest gods he would see forgotten, while he decorates his halls with gold brought to his coffers by the spears of our warriors.'

In his reply Malekith told his mother to do nothing to antagonise the princes or move openly against the Phoenix King, and she promised him it was so, though her tone was ever defiant to their authority.

Something of what Malekith had heard began to seep into life in the colonies. Always the elves had enjoyed wine and song, and the reading of poetry both beautiful and satirical. However, Malekith stayed for months, sometimes years at a time away from the cities, and so the slow but subtle changes wrought upon them seemed more stark to him upon his returns.

A softness of spirit and a laxity that Malekith had detested in Ulthuan began to creep into the culture of Athel Toralien. Many of his subjects were now second- and even third-generation colonists, who had not had to raise a sword in anger to defend their lands, and Malekith feared that the very stability he had fought to bring to this realm was undermining the heart of his people. Not wishing to appear tyrannical, Malekith did not openly oppose the many wine houses and pleasure dens that now seemed to be found in every other building of the city.

Instead, he commanded his council to institute a formal practice of inducting Naggarothi who came of age into the ranks of his army. What once had been tradition Malekith now enforced with law, in the hope that discipline and military life would breed into a new generation the will and power of the elves who had first followed him here.

Malekith's growing contact with mankind awoke his inquisitive spirit, and he was filled with a passion to deepen his knowledge of this race, and also of the shadowy powers that held sway over the Chaos Wastes. Deeper and deeper into the north he ventured, sometimes alone, other times with a host of his warriors. Though the wild forests had all but been tamed by the elves, Malekith drove his armies northwards possessed by a bloodthirsty spirit that worried those who knew the prince well.

It was upon returning from one such campaign that the prince visited his dwarfen allies in Karak Kadrin. The mood in the hold was sombre as Malekith entered the throne room of King Brundin, who had inherited the hold's rule from his father a few years previously. The king was surrounded by solemn-faced nobles, amongst them the venerable Kurgrik whose fortunes had risen considerably since his days of humble logging.

Malekith's oldest dwarf companion turned and hurried down the steps towards the prince, stroking his exceptionally long beard in an agitated fashion.

'What is amiss?' asked Malekith.

'The High King lies upon his deathbed,' said Kurgrik, wringing his fingers through his beard. 'Messengers scour the northlands searching for you. He asks for you, elven prince. You must go to Karaz-a-Karak!'

Malekith glanced up at the throne dais and saw the crowd of earnest, grief-stricken faces, and knew that this was no exaggeration.

'Convey my regrets to King Brundin, but I leave now,' said Malekith.

The prince turned on his heel and ran from the hall. He dashed through the doors, ignoring the shouted concerns and questions of his companions. Down tunnel and across gallery sped Malekith, until he came upon the great gate. Outside, the elves' steeds were corralled on the hillside. Malekith leapt the fence and headed straight for the tallest of the horses, his own mount. He did not wait for saddle or bridle and instead leapt onto the steed's bare back. Malekith turned southwards and the horse broke into a thundering gallop at a whispered word from her rider. Vaulting the corral, the pair sped down into Peak Pass.

Though Malekith journeyed swiftly south, fear that he might arrive too late gnawed at him. When his steed was all but dead from exhaustion, he turned westwards until he came upon one of the elven towers that guarded the borders of the great forest of Elthin Arvan. Here he commandeered a new mount and continued southwards. Driven by worry, Malekith did not eat or sleep, and rode by the light of the moon as much as the sun. After three days he neared the hold of Zhufbar. Dwarfs laboured digging a fresh mineshaft not far from the road, and the prince wheeled his steed towards them. The dwarfs looked up in astonishment, unexpectedly confronted by the ambassador of the elves.

'What news from Karaz-a-Karak?' Malekith demanded.

'No news,' replied their gangmaster, a rugged, tanned dwarf with a greying golden beard and a hook for a left hand.

'The High King still lives?' said Malekith.

'The last we heard, he does,' said the dwarf.

Without further word Malekith heeled his mount into a fresh gallop and sped towards Black Water, where so many years before he had fought alongside the High King. His mind was devoid of fond memories, so possessed was Malekith to see his ally before he passed away. Along the shore he raced, his horse throwing up a wave of spray in its wake as the prince urged his mount on at dangerous speed.

The following day Malekith took the southern road from Karak Varn direct to Karaz-a-Karak. Wide enough for many carts, the road was built of brick and stone, and his passage was swift. He weaved amongst the dwarfen carts until he spied an elven caravan. Bringing his tired steed to a halt before the lead caravan, Malekith dismounted and signalled for the driver to stop.

'Prince Malekith?' said the driver. 'What brings you here?'

'I need one of your horses,' said Malekith, already untying the traces on the foremost of the three beasts drawing the wagon.

'You can ride with me, highness,' offered the driver, but the prince paid him no heed and away he galloped without explanation or payment.

Two more days Malekith rode hard until finally he came before the great gates of Karaz-a-Karak. For the first time he did not marvel at their golden majesty, nor regard with awe the huge towers and buttresses that flanked the huge doors. His steed sweating hard, he galloped up the road. The guards at the gate made to step forwards to bar his route but he did not slow. Recognising the prince and seeing his intent, the guards hurled themselves out of his path, pushing away other dwarfs to clear a passage.

Through the gate raced the prince, the clatter of his horse's hooves on the tiles echoing from the high vaults. Dwarfs were sent ducking into doorways and scurrying in every direction as he pounded through the winding tunnels towards the king's chambers. Only when he saw a crowd of the king's advisors pressed around the door to one of the king's rooms did he slow down. Leaping from the back of the horse, he ran forwards and grabbed the closest of the nobles, a loremaster called Damrak Goldenfist.

'Am I too late?' he demanded.

The stunned dwarf said nothing for a moment and then shook his head. Malekith let go of Damrak and slumped against the wall.

'You misunderstand me, ambassador,' said Damrak, laying a gnarled hand on Malekith's arm. 'The king still awaits you.'

THE SOLEMN BEATING of drums could be heard echoing along the halls and corridors of Karaz-a-Karak. The small chamber was empty save for two figures. His face as pale as his beard, King Snorri lay on the low, wide bed, his eyes closed. Kneeling next to the bed, a hand on the dwarf's chest, was Malekith. He had stood vigil with the ancient dwarf for three days since arriving, barely sleeping or eating in that time.

The room was hung with heavy tapestries depicting the battles the two had fought together, suitably aggrandising Snorri's role. Malekith did not begrudge the king his glories, for was not his own name sung loudly in Ulthuan while the name of Snorri Whitebeard was barely a whisper? Each people to their own kind, the elf prince thought.

Snorri's eyelids fluttered open to reveal cloudy, pale blue eyes. His lips twisted into a smile and a fumbling hand found Malekith's arm.

'Would that dwarf lives were measured as those of the elves,' said Snorri. 'Then my reign would last another thousand years.'

'But even so, we still die,' said Malekith. 'Our measure is made by what we do when we live and the legacy that we leave to our kin, as any other. A lifetime of millennia is worthless if its works come to naught after it has ended.'

'True, true,' said Snorri with a nod, his smile fading. 'What we have built is worthy of legend, isn't it? Our two great realms have driven back the beasts and the daemons, and the lands are safe for our people. Trade has never been better, and the holds grow with every year.'

'Your reign has indeed been glorious, Snorri,' said Malekith. 'Your line is strong; your son will uphold the great things that you have done.'

'And perhaps even build on them,' said Snorri.

'Perhaps, if the gods will it,' said Malekith.

'And why should they not?' asked Snorri. He coughed as he pushed himself to a sitting position, his shoulders sinking into thick, gold-embroidered white pillows. 'Though my breath comes short and my body is infirm, my will is as hard as the stone that these walls are carved from. I am a dwarf, and like all my people, I have within me the strength of the mountains. Though this body is now weak, my spirit shall go to the Halls of the Ancestors.'

'It will be welcomed there, by Grungni and Valaya,' said Malekith. 'You shall take your place with pride.'

'I'm not done,' said Snorri with a frown. His expression grim, the king continued. 'Hear this oath, Malekith of the elves, comrade on the battlefield, friend at the hearth. I, Snorri Whitebeard, High King of the dwarfs, bequeath my title and rights to my eldest son. Though I pass through the gateway to the Halls of the Ancestors, my eyes shall remain upon my empire. Let it be known to our allies and our enemies that death is not the end of my guardianship.'

The dwarf broke into a wracking cough, blood flecking his lips. His lined faced was stern as he looked at Malekith. The elf steadily returned his gaze.

'Vengeance shall be mine,' swore Snorri. 'When our foes are great, I shall return to my people. When the foul creatures of this world bay at the doors to Karaz-a-Karak, I shall take up my axe once more and my ire shall rock the mountains. Heed my words, Malekith of Ulthuan, and heed them well. Great have been our deeds, and great is the legacy that I leave to you, my closest confidant, my finest comrade-in-arms. Swear to me now, as my dying breaths fill my lungs, that my oath has been heard. Swear to it on my own grave, on my spirit, that you shall remain true to the ideals we have both striven for these many years. And know this, that there is nothing so foul in the world as an oath-breaker.'

Malekith took the king's hand from his arm and squeezed it tight. 'I swear it,' the elf prince said. 'Upon the grave of High King Snorri Whitebeard, leader of the dwarfs and friend of the elves, I give my oath.'

Snorri's eyes were glazed and his chest no longer rose and fell. Malekith's keen hearing could detect no sign of life, and he did not know whether his words had been heard. Releasing Snorri's hand, he folded the king's arms across his chest, and with a delicate touch from his long fingers, Malekith closed Snorri's eyes.

Standing, Malekith spared one last glance at the dead king and then walked from the chamber. Outside, Snorri's son Throndik stood along with several dozen other dwarfs.

'The High King has passed on,' Malekith said, his gaze passing over the heads of the assembled dwarfs and across to the throne room. He looked down at Throndik. 'You are now High King.'

Without further word, the elf prince picked his way gracefully through the crowd and out across the nearly empty throne chamber. He stopped halfway towards the throne and gazed up at the high dais. He remembered perfectly the first time he had been here. At the time Malekith's attention had been focused on Aernuis; the High King had barely registered in his thoughts. Now all he could think about was the dwarf now lying still in that small bedchamber.

The throne was empty. Everything was empty. The wars against the orcs and the beasts had been won. The forests had been tamed by the elves and the mountains conquered by the dwarfs. Bel Shanaar had robbed him of rulership of the colonies. It was as if Snorri had unknowingly taken the last days of glory to his grave. His friend was dead and there was nothing else to fight for.

Nothing except the Phoenix Throne.

OVER THE FOLLOWING decade, Malekith became ever more distant from his court in Athel Toralien. As he had done so in Nagarythe, he appointed a wise and well-regarded council of fellow princes and other dignitaries to rule in his stead, and passed on the mantle of ambassador to Carnellios, a prince of Cothique who had been part of the original talks and whom the dwarfs had come to trust. Once content that all was in order, the prince declared that he would go into the north again, for many years, perhaps never to return, and he asked for volunteers to accompany him.

After issuing his proclamation, Malekith set out on a tour of the castles and citadels that protected the lands of Athel Toralien, to extend his offer to all of their garrisons. He picked the finest captains, knights and archers from amongst their number and returned to the city with seventy warriors.

Riding upon the west–east road to Athel Toralien, the prince and his company came upon a great encampment outside the city's walls, stretching for almost half a mile. Great marquees and pavilions housed rich nobles, while more moderate tents were numbered in the many hundreds.

Yeasir was at the east gate to greet his master.

'Thank the gods you have returned,' said the captain, grabbing the bridle of Malekith's steed to allow the prince to dismount.

'Some emergency?' said Malekith, handing the reins to one of his companions. 'An orcish horde perhaps? Beasts from the north?'

'No, no,' said Yeasir. 'There is no threat.'

'Then why do I have an army of vagabonds and princes at my gate?' demanded Malekith, turning to stare at the tent-city stretching along the road.

'They all wish to accompany you on your voyage,' Yeasir said breathlessly.

'All of them?' said Malekith, eyebrows raised.

'Six thousand seven hundred and twenty-eight,' said Yeasir. 'Well, according to the roll of volunteers that Alandrian was forced to begin. They filled the city at first and there was no room in the docks or markets. We had to send them outside, and provided many with shelters.'

'I cannot take more than five hundred,' said Malekith. 'Send away any that have wives or children, and any that have never drawn blood in battle. That should thin out the numbers a little.'

'Yes, highness,' said Yeasir. 'Many are not Naggarothi, do you wish them to accompany you?'

'Only if they swear loyalty to Nagarythe,' said the prince with a frown. 'And I don't want anyone under three hundred years old. I need experience; seasoned veterans.'

'There are eighteen princes of various realms,' Yeasir said. 'What shall I do with them?'

'They seek to glorify themselves in the glow of my deeds,' snapped Malekith. 'Any that are not of Nagarythe, and I mean Nagarythe, not this city, send them home. I will talk to any you feel are worthy of my attention.'

'As you wish, highness,' said Yeasir, bowing as he left.

Malekith stared out along the road as news of his return began to spread through the camp. Horns sounded, and more and more elves came out of their tents and began to converge on the city. Hundreds of them soon packed the road, crying out to the prince for his attention. Malekith turned his back on them and walked into the city. He turned his head to one of the guards.

'Shut the gate until they go away,' the prince snapped.

FIVE HUNDRED ELVES Malekith chose to be his companions; enough to man a ship and fight, but few enough to feed and supply out in the wilds. Almost half were nearly as old as Malekith and some had journeyed with him from Ulthuan. All were without family, for Malekith knew that he ventured into the truly unknown, and whatever perils lay ahead he was determined that his wanderlust would not leave a legacy of widows and orphans.

Alandrian organised the provisioning of the expedition and the repatriation of those who had been turned away. Amongst his many duties he managed to catch up with Malekith one evening.

'Is all ready?' asked the prince, sitting on a low chair upon the balcony of his city house. He gestured for Alandrian to help himself to the contents of a crystal decanter perched on a small table. Alandrian poured himself a goblet of golden wine and sat down.

'If I could make a suggestion, your highness,' Alandrian said delicately. 'Perhaps five hundred and one companions would be better for you.'

'Five hundred and one?' said Malekith, and then he gave a laugh and a nod of understanding. 'You wish to offer your service?'

'I do, highness,' said the lieutenant. 'Yeasir accompanies you, and so would I.'

'It cannot be done,' said Malekith. 'Yeasir has no family. You have a beautiful wife who has borne you two equally beautiful daughters. I could no more rob them of their father than I could cut off a limb.'

'You are destined for great glory,' said Alandrian. 'I have served well and attended my duties with vigour and loyalty. I ask only that I be allowed to continue my service.'

'Your time of service is no more,' said Malekith. He held up a hand to stop Alandrian's protest. 'I have had papers drawn up, declaring you a prince of Nagarythe and the ruler of Athel Toralien.'

'A prince?' stammered Alandrian.

'That is right,' said Malekith, laughing at his friend's stunned expression.

'I was going to wait a while before making an announcement but you have forced my hand. You will be my regent in Elthin Arvan. Yeasir is a soldier first and last, and I will name him commander of Nagarythe, the title I once held when my father was alive. You are a leader, with a patience to match your wisdom and your gift with words. You can best serve me not with spear point but with quill point. Rule Athel Toralien in the finest traditions of Nagarythe. Be ever ready to come to the aid of your homeland. Most of all you must enjoy yourself and take what reward you can from the life the gods have given you!'

Malekith raised his goblet in toast to his companion, who half-heartedly lifted his own, still shocked by the prince's declaration.

─◄ NINE ►─

A Delayed Departure

IN THE MONTHS of preparation before his departure, Malekith received an unexpected visitor. He was sitting in the uppermost chamber of his tower overlooking the harbour of Athel Toralien, reviewing an agreement on the succession of power to his followers. Though he had a palatial mansion, several in fact, within the city and out in the forest, he chose to conduct his business here, in a tower built over the part of the old wall where he had first defended the city against the orcs.

Malekith was just re-reading a particularly complex passage for the third time when he was disturbed from his study by noise from the street far below the open window. There was also much commotion from within the tower, as doors slammed and he heard a great many feet pounding upon the stairs. He tried to ignore the excited shouts and concentrate on the legalistic wording of the document he held, but the ruckus persisted and in frustration he threw the parchment onto his desk and stood up. At that moment there was a hurried knocking at the door.

'What?' he demanded.

The door was flung open by Yeasir, who stepped into the room with a hasty bow.

'I am trying to concentrate,' the prince growled.

'Forgive the disturbance, your highness,' said Yeasir breathlessly, bowing again with more decorum. 'Please look out of your window.'

'My window?' said Malekith.

The prince turned and strode to the open casement and stepped out onto

the small balcony beyond. He stared down at the street below and saw
crowds of elves hastening through the streets towards the docks, some of
them running in their excitement. Raising his head, Malekith looked out
over the roofs of the warehouses to the harbour beyond.

It was a sunny spring day and the calm waters of the bay glittered in the
afternoon light. Dozens of ships bobbed at anchor in the middle of the port,
but all seemed calm and Malekith could see nothing amiss. Then he turned
his gaze further to the south and saw a line of black sails approaching past
the harbour wall.

Shielding his eyes against the glare, Malekith looked at the approaching
ships. There were ten of them, nine unremarkable but for the fact that they
flew silver and black pennants of Nagarythe at their mastheads. The tenth
was what caught Malekith's attention, and the cause of so much interest
from the city folk below.

It glided across the waves without effort, four huge lateen sails filled with
the breeze, surf crashing around the gold-plated ram at its prow. It was larger
than any ship Malekith had ever before seen, in size as large as a castle keep,
spread over three hulls – one central structure flanked by two outrigger hulls
that were each the size of a warship. Upon its deck stood high towers of
dark-stained wood banded and trimmed with shining gold. It was the finest
vessel ever to have crossed the seas, and Malekith was dumbstruck by its
majesty and elegant lines.

Like a lion amongst scavenging dogs, the ship surged through the surf at
the heart of its fleet, before trimly tacking across the wind and gracefully
gliding towards the longest pier. The sound of clarions rang out from across
the waves from the other nine ships, heralding the arrival of their leader.

Malekith fought the urge to leap straight from the balcony and run to
the docks, and instead turned and instructed Yeasir to fetch his cloak and
sword. He stood there tapping his fingers impatiently on the curved parapet
of the balcony, watching as the immense ship slid closer and closer. He
could now see the crew upon the deck, dressed in smart smocks of red and
white, straining at stays to keep the sails full. At some unheard command,
they jumped into action to furl the mainsail, slowing the ship's passage as
it neared the wharf.

Yeasir entered again and fixed Malekith's scabbard to his belt and hung his
purple cloak from his shoulders. Perhaps more hurriedly than he realised,
Malekith strode from the room and descended the long winding stair at the
centre of the tower. Guards at the doors flung them open at his approach,
and Malekith swept past them without a glance, intent on the street outside.

It was thronged with people, and though many parted as they saw him
approach, some were so intent upon reaching the docks that they did not
note his appearance. Yeasir trotted ahead of his lord to clear them out of the
way, and as they realised their error they fell to their knees in apology, and
begged Malekith's forgiveness as he strode past. In this way, Yeasir swiftly

cleared a path to the docks, but upon arriving at the wharfs found the route utterly blocked by the press of elves who had gathered here from all over the surrounding buildings.

A few realised the unmannerly obstruction they were causing, but could only shrug and bow in apology, as they attempted to get out of the way but could not due to the crowds behind them. Such was the hubbub that Yea-sir's shouted commands were barely heard, and in the end Malekith resorted to drastic measures.

Drawing Avanuir from its sheath, he held the fabled sword aloft, its tip pointed towards the cloudless sky. With a word, the prince sent a pulse of magic along the blade. The sorcery erupted into a bolt of flame that shot high up into the air with a piercing screech, attracting the attention of all.

Thus warned of their ruler's approach, the elves began to make way as best they could for the prince, some of them awkwardly leaping onto boats that stood at the water's edge, others pushing into buildings or climbing onto awnings and balconies. As the waves parted before the prow of the approaching ship, so the elves parted in the path of their prince. With a satisfied nod, Malekith sheathed his sword and strode forwards along the widening line between him and the docking vessel.

Malekith walked to the end of the curving pier of white planks and stood with his hands on hips as the immense ship slowly slid around and came alongside. Elves with thick hawsers in hand leapt lithely over the side to the quay to secure the vessel. Amidships, a length of the gunwale soundlessly swung upwards and a wide set of steps slid out of the gap to touch down upon the pier. Malekith walked along the quay to stand at the foot of the docking stairs.

Looking up onto the ship, the sun was behind the vessel, throwing the sails and rigging into stark silhouette. A figure appeared at the top of the ramp, tall and elegant, draped with silky ribbons that danced in the sea breeze. As she strolled cat-like down the ramp, Malekith could see his visitor more clearly, as young and beautiful as he had ever remembered her: Morathi.

The widow of Aenarion walked languidly down from the ship and stopped before Malekith, holding out a hand for him to help her down the last step. He kissed the back of her hand and led her onto the quay, sweeping his cloak out of the way as he did so. Morathi turned her face towards him as they walked along the pier back to the dockside, and she smiled.

'My wonderful son,' she purred.

'Precious mother,' replied Malekith with a formal nod of the head.

As the crowd upon the harbour side could see more clearly, there was shocked whispering, which spread from the end of the pier and out through the assembled elves. A respectful silence then descended and the only sound that could be heard was the cry of gulls in the air and the lapping of the waves against the piles of the quays. Now the elves surreptitiously crowded forwards again, those further back leaning forwards and straining to get a look at the queen-regent of Nagarythe. Many had been born in Athel Toralien and had never seen the seeress.

Mother and son walked serenely towards the tower where the prince had been working, Morathi's hand upon Malekith's. Neither looked at the other, but both gazed out to the crowd with beatific smiles. Malekith's expression was a mask hiding his true feelings, for inside he was in turmoil but he could not show weakness.

Morathi's arrival was most unexpected, and he feared what news she brought. He could think of no reason that was pleasant why she would have abandoned the comforts of Anlec for the colonies. Had she finally driven Bel Shanaar too far and been forced into exile with her son? Was Nagarythe threatened? The ship too was an enigma. It was clearly of Naggarothi design, but no shipyard outside of Lothern was capable of building such a behemoth. How had she come by such a prize, and what was her intent?

Craving the answers to these questions, Malekith forced himself to pace slowly through the streets, accepting the bows and waves of the adoring crowds that were even now still growing in number.

The prince detected a certain smugness in his mother's manner: a pride that he felt was not wholly down to a mother meeting her son. Certainly she had caused quite a stir with her arrival, and Malekith suspected that this was in great part the source of her pleasure. Ever since Malekith had been old enough to notice his mother, he had seen how attention focused upon her, and how only Aenarion's light had shone brighter than hers. As a rock absorbs the heat of a summer midday sun, so Morathi bathed in the quiet adulation of the elven masses of Athel Toralien.

It was some time before they reached the tower overlooking the bay. Glancing over his shoulder as they passed though the doors, Malekith saw that Alandrian had joined Yeasir. He waved Morathi to proceed him up the stairs and turned to his lieutenants.

'Leave us for the moment,' Malekith instructed them. 'Do not go too far, I will be calling for you shortly. Yeasir, please send someone to the docks to ensure that my mother's luggage and servants are taken to the Palace of Stars. We will join her entourage there this evening.'

As the pair bowed and turned to leave, Malekith thought of something else.

'Best send word to my servants at the palace too, and the farmers,' Malekith said, drawing confused looks from Alandrian and Yeasir. 'My mother will have brought many hangers-on, advisors and other menials. There will be a lot of mouths to feed.'

Nodding in realisation, the pair left Malekith, who closed the doors to the tower behind them, shutting out the gaping crowds.

Turning, he leapt up the stairs three at a time, chasing after his mother. Despite his haste, Morathi was already standing beside the balcony window by the time Malekith reached the top of the tower. She turned and smiled as he strode into the room, and held out an arm for him to hold. Sighing, the prince allowed his mother to lay her hand upon his, and led her out onto the balcony. This time, the seeress-queen and prince of Nagarythe were greeted with rapturous cheers and applause. The streets were packed with elves in every direction, and windows and balconies were full as the people of Athel Toralien sought the best vantage point to see their mysterious, glamorous visitor.

'What are you doing here?' Malekith whispered as he waved to the adoring crowds.

'I have come to visit you, my wonderful son,' replied Morathi, not turning her smile from the masses below. 'A mother worries, you know that. Word came to me that you were heading off into the wilds for some ridiculous adventures, so I thought it best that I finally visit your new home before you left.'

'You will not dissuade me,' Malekith warned her. 'I am ready to leave within days.'

'Dissuade you?' said Morathi with a faint laugh. 'Why would I not want you to go? Was it not me that stood upon the quayside when you left Nagarythe, and told you to earn glory and renown for yourself and your people? Have you not done so, and have I not looked upon all that you have achieved with great love and pride?'

'Forgive my misunderstanding,' said Malekith. 'If you are here to lend your support, then I am very grateful.'

Morathi did not reply straightaway, but instead indicated discreetly that they should retire inside. With a final wave and a grin, Malekith stepped off the balcony and his mother followed. Closing the window, Malekith rounded on his mother.

'So why is it that you are here?' he asked, not with accusation but with genuine curiosity.

'It is not my support that you need, at least not in any physical way,' Morathi replied.

Seeing his mother wave a hand towards the bottle upon the desk, Malekith took a clean glass from one of the many cabinets in the room and poured wine for Morathi. She took it with a nod, had a sip and then continued.

'You have been away from Ulthuan for too long. I was of a mind to persuade you to return rather than gallivanting across the wastes, but then I realised that such a course of action would be a fool's errand and only earn me your enmity, perhaps even your disdain.'

'You are right, I will not return to Ulthuan,' said Malekith. 'Why do you think it is so important that I do so now?'

'Not now, but soon,' Morathi said. 'I sense that Bel Shanaar's rule is fading. His usurpation of your relationship with the dwarfs was an attempt to bolster his flagging fortunes. Now that the colonies are well established, all of the kingdoms enjoy the comfort and wealth that the realms overseas bring to us, Tiranoc no less so, nor more so than any others. Nagarythe's most adventurous spirits have departed the shores of the isle, for new generations look to the likes of you to emulate, not to the staid, overly sincere Bel Shanaar. In comfort there is frailty, for a sword must be forged in the burning fires before it can rest in its scabbard. There is no more fire in Ulthuan. Even as her empire continues to grow, Ulthuan herself is diminishing.'

'If Ulthuan has become lessened, then it is the fault of the princes who rule there,' said Malekith, pouring himself some wine.

'That is my point,' snapped Morathi. 'There is none capable of succeeding Bel Shanaar; his court is as weak as he is. Your achievements here have been rightly lauded, but your success has been copied and appropriated and demeaned by others. If only you had returned to us before Bel Shanaar accorded himself and his rule with the dwarfs and stole your victory. It is time to create a new legend for yourself, and return in triumph to reclaim what is rightfully yours.'

'What would you say if I told you that I wish never to return to Ulthuan?' said Malekith. 'What if I have decided that my life is out here, away from the coddling embrace of Ulthuan?'

'Then I would curse you for a fool and cast you out of my life,' said Morathi. 'But that is not really how you think. You do not like Ulthuan, and I cannot blame you. She is like a maiden that you love, gripped tightly within the arms of a less-deserving amour. But, just as you turn away from that sight, within your heart still lingers that love for the maiden, no matter what she does.'

'You are right, of course,' admitted Malekith. 'She is like to me as a lover who has spurned my attentions many times, and yet her gaze lingers upon me always, tempting me with the notion that one day she will accept my advances. However, if what you say is true, then perhaps it is too late for me; the beauty of youth has faded and Ulthuan perhaps is on the decline into infirmity and then a swift passing away. Perhaps it is better this way, that we break our ties to that small isle, and reach out to the wider world.'

Morathi strode across the room, her face a mask of fury, and slapped Malekith across the cheek. In instinct he raised his hand to reply in kind, but Morathi was as quick as a serpent and snatched his wrist in her fingers, her long and sharpened nails digging so deep into the flesh that blood trickled across her hand.

'How dare you!' the seeress hissed. 'Your father gave his life for Ulthuan, and it took his death to save her! I thought I had raised you better than this. I thought that you had not become one of those prancing, preening fools that pass as princes in Bel Shanaar's court. How dare you condemn Ulthuan to death by indifference! Your father laid down his life to protect our isle, who are you to do different?'

Malekith snatched away his wrist with a snarl and made to turn, but Morathi was relentless and grabbed his arm and spun him around to face her.

'You dare to turn your back on me, just as you turn your back on your homeland!' she snarled. 'Perhaps the First Council was right not to choose you; not because of a darkness upon you, but because you are weak and undeserving.'

'What more could I do?' demanded Malekith. 'I have conquered new lands in the name of Nagarythe, and brokered the greatest alliance our people will ever see. What more can I give to Ulthuan?'

'Yourself,' said Morathi. 'When Aenarion died, he left Ulthuan a legacy, and you are part of it. To rule is also to serve, Aenarion understood that. He served Khaine, for there was no other master worthy of his fealty. You must be prepared to serve a high purpose, a great power.'

Morathi paused and took a deep breath, calming herself. When she continued her voice was low but insistent.

'Serve Ulthuan and you will be Phoenix King. Protect her from enemies outside and within and she will embrace you in return. Go into the north and learn of the race of men. Head into the chilling wastes and confront the Dark Gods that hunger over our world. Then return to Ulthuan and take up your place as ruler, to shield us against their unnatural thirst. I fear that only you can protect us against the dangers I have foreseen. I see fire and bloodshed sweeping Ulthuan again. The colonies will burn and all that we hold dear will be cast upon the rocks and be for naught.'

'What have you seen, when will this happen?' asked Malekith.

'You know that there is no future that is certain,' replied Morathi. 'I have simply cast my gaze ahead along the path of my life, and I see death. War will come again and the Naggarothi will be called upon as they were by your father. I warned the First Council that it would be so, but they did not listen. You must learn what you can of Chaos, and of humans, for our future is entwined with both. When you are master of your fate, then return to us and take what has been kept from you for so long. Let Anlec be a beacon of hope again.'

Malekith saw desire and fear in equal measure in the face of his mother, and his love for her stirred him. He laid an arm about her shoulders and pulled her close to him. She quivered, though whether from anxiety or excitement he could not tell.

'It shall be as you say,' said Malekith. 'I shall go into the north and seek whatever destiny awaits me there. I will return to Ulthuan, and I will guard her against whatever comes to pass.'

'And I have a steed worthy of such a journey,' said Morathi, pulling away from her son and leading him by the hand back to the window. She pointed out towards the bay, to the huge ship that now lay in a berth along the quayside.

'She is *Indraugnir*, named after the dragon whom your father befriended and from whose back he fought against the daemons. The two of them died together upon the Blighted Isle, after Aenarion returned the Godslayer to its black altar. It is not yet time for you to ride upon the dragon, but this dragonship shall suffice in the meantime. That fabled name will not go unnoticed by the folk of Ulthuan.'

'She is a magnificent vessel,' said Malekith. 'Yet for all of her glory, she is beyond the means of the Naggarothi to build. I do not understand how she came to be made.'

'We spoke of Ulthuan as a coquettish maiden, and she is,' said Morathi. 'There are many princes who admire her, and who are willing to aid her when she asks in return for the promise of favour. Prince Aeltherin of Lothern is one such admirer, and it is he who built the first of the dragonships and gifted her to you. Others will be built in the shipyards of Lothern over the coming years, but *Indraugnir* is the first and ever will be the greatest in the eyes and dreams of our people.'

'So, you have allies outside of Nagarythe,' said Malekith.

'Many,' replied Morathi. 'Some of the princes of the First Council are dead, by war or age, and their sons now wonder whether their fathers chose rightly. Not all were happy at the time, and a thousand years is a long while to be reigned over by a lesser ruler than Aenarion. There is support for us in every kingdom and across the colonies. The frustration of the common folk builds, for while they live in comfort, their inner spirits are unsatisfied. I do what I can to lift them, to provide their lives with purpose and meaning, but they now live in a world far removed from the times of hunger, fear and deprivation that we knew many centuries ago. They live in idyllic palaces surrounded by a garden paradise, yet many see it for the gilded cage that Ulthuan has become. We pray to the gods for direction, and they answer me through their visions and dreams.'

'I hear much that concerns the gods and your prayers,' said Malekith. 'You tempt fate by courting the twilight pantheon. The likes of Morai-heg and Nethu are not to be toyed with. My father paid a heavy price for the favours of Khaine; do not underestimate the forces you play with.'

'There is no need to be afraid,' said Morathi. 'Only true priests and priestesses perform the actual dark rituals. For the most part these ceremonies are little more than gatherings for feasting and gossiping. Only Bel Shanaar and his deceptively pious coterie feign outrage at some of the rituals, but they know as well as you and I do that Atharti, Hekarti and others cannot be ignored. It is only because we still value the old traditions and the ancient customs in Nagarythe that we are able to perform these rituals at all. Someone must be guardian of the forgotten paths, and if that means that the other kingdoms must turn to us on occasion, then that is all the better.'

'If you move against Bel Shanaar, it will be treason,' said Malekith. 'I know that you seek to undermine his power and influence. Be careful that you do not destroy Nagarythe in the process. No prince of Ulthuan will betray the Phoenix King, and if you move too fast, you will leave Nagarythe friendless and weak.'

'I will make no moves at all,' said Morathi, sitting down in the chair behind Malekith's desk. She swept her long black hair over her shoulder and looked at her son. 'The position of Phoenix King should always command great respect and authority. I would not erode the power of the Phoenix King and leave you a tarnished crown worth less than a copper cap. It is Bel Shanaar that will be found weak, not his rank, and in time the princes will entreat us to help them. Upon the wave of their desire and need will you be swept to the Phoenix Throne and the power of Anlec rightfully restored. I am merely the means for you to achieve this. I cannot become Phoenix King. Only you, the son of Aenarion, can claim what is yours; it cannot now be given, it must be taken.'

Malekith pondered these words in silence, refilling his glass. He walked to the window and gazed at *Indraugnir*. It was well named, for just as the dragon of his father was a foundation of the stories told about him, so too would this ship become a pillar upon which to build the story of Malekith. His mother was deft at manipulating popular opinion, and recapturing the imagination of Ulthuan with this new ship, stirring up the oldest tales of courage and heroism from the time of the first Phoenix King, would set the stage for whatever adventures next befell Malekith.

Yet there are only so many times and so often one can return to the well before it eventually runs dry, and Malekith knew that Morathi's sway over the other princes waned the more she used it. If Bel Shanaar was replaced by another elected Phoenix King, not of Aenarion's line, the precedent set by Bel Shanaar would be sealed in tradition; it would end all hope for Malekith to see Anlec as capital once more.

'And what of the Everqueen?' asked Malekith after much thought. 'Should I succeed Bel Shanaar, I cannot marry my half-sister.'

'It is of no consequence,' said Morathi. 'I have persuaded many of your fellow princes that Bel Shanaar's marriage to Yvraine is merely a technicality required because the Phoenix King must be of the line of Aenarion. You are his son and have no need to marry into the bloodline. If we oppose it, there will be little support for such a sham marriage to be repeated. Though there was once a dream that we might return to the peace of the Everqueen's reign shortly after the war with the daemons, there are few of us surviving now that can even remember the time before Aenarion. The Everqueen is a figurehead and nothing more, the real political power of Ulthuan lies not in Avelorn but in Tor Anroc. She is irrelevant, a priestess raised above her station.'

'What of Morelion?' said Malekith.

'Aenarion's first son lives in solitude in the islands to the east,' Morathi said. 'He has no will to succeed Aenarion, and even if he did he has not the resource nor influence to make a serious bid for the Phoenix Throne. Trust me, and trust in Nagarythe. When you wish to resume your father's duties, there will be those of us ready to raise you up to where you belong.'

'Then I shall await the will of the gods,' said Malekith. 'When the sign comes, I will know it. I shall bring Ulthuan back to greatness and the memory of my reign will echo down through the centuries as loudly as my father's.'

'Good,' said Morathi with an amused smile. 'Now, which of your palaces do you recommend to your weary mother?'

As MALEKITH HAD expected, Morathi was accompanied by a great many retainers: guards, cooks, entertainers, gardeners, food tasters, painters, poets, chroniclers, actors, costumiers, handmaidens, dressmakers, acolytes, soothsayers, priests and priestesses. There were nearly seven hundred in all. All came directly from Nagarythe, and were unlike anything the colonists of Athel Toralien had seen before.

For several decades there had been fewer and fewer émigrés from Ulthuan, and so the most recent styles and fashions remained unseen. Morathi deplored the sheep-like mentality of those elves that followed court styles so slavishly, but was never one to miss an opportunity and so she exploited the somewhat fickle nature of elven taste whenever it suited her.

The seer-queen had carefully cultivated a reputation as a trend-setter and paragon of exquisite aesthetic. She was always at the forefront when it came to patronising an up-and-coming singer or poet, or endorsing some risqué but popular movement. In this way, Morathi managed to appear to move with the times, while Bel Shanaar and his supporters seemed outdated and staid. It helped that through her sorcery, Morathi never appeared to age a single day, even less so than any long-lived elf, while almost imperceptibly the years crept up on the Phoenix King. To young and old alike, Morathi was ever the perfect blend: a guardian of tradition whilst also being a forward-thinking visionary.

Her huge entourage reflected the wide variety of concerns and movements with which Morathi involved herself. From satirical poets who moped about the wine houses hidden behind white veils, to outlandishly tattooed jugglers and fire-eaters who entertained in the plazas, the hundreds of Morathi's followers made their presence felt all across Athel Toralien. Most prominently it was the arrival of the priests and priestesses that changed the city.

Malekith had resisted such developments in Athel Toralien, having been raised by his father to be distrustful of the priesthoods who had denied Aenarion the guidance he had sought. Although Malekith never openly opposed any temple or shrine, he ensured that a priest establishing any such building within the boundaries of his lands soon fell out of favour.

Followers were hard to come by under such circumstances and most priests left within a season of their arrival. With the coming of Morathi's entourage it was as if a flood gate had been opened as priests and priestesses of all descriptions began plying their trade in the city.

In the earliest days of the Everqueen, the elves had worshipped and placated their gods at certain places on Ulthuan sacred to each of them. Elves would travel to these holy grottos, auspicious streams and sinister caves and peaks to entreat with the gods or to offer their praise.

With the elves now spread across the world, Morathi had slowly revolutionised the role of the priesthood. Once they had tended to the shrines that had grown over the sacred sites down through the years. Through Morathi's manipulation, now they were vessels of the gods' power. All were ordained in the time-honoured fashions of the past, but now rather than elves making pilgrimages to the holy places, the priests took the blessings of their gods out across the globe, so that all might still worship Asuryan and Kurnous, Isha and Lileath. Priests could now find spots sacred to their gods in the wider world, and even in the cities of Ulthuan shrines and temples were founded.

Long denied a spiritual release, the citizens of Athel Toralien embraced these newcomers and flooded to their rituals. When the prince complained to Morathi one morning, she laughed away his concerns.

'Your distaste for religion is quite unnatural, Malekith,' the seeress-queen said. The pair walked upon the outermost wall of the city, gazing out across the wind-tossed ocean. 'If you are to rid yourself of your loathing, you will have to overcome your unspoken fears.'

'I am not afraid of priests,' Malekith snorted.

'Yet you never enter a shrine, nor give a moment's praise to the gods,' said Morathi, stopping and leaning her back against the parapet so that the low sun blazed down onto her fair skin. 'Perhaps it is the gods that scare you?'

'The gods have never favoured Nagarythe, I see no reason to debase myself in their name,' the prince countered.

'Yet the gods have their part to play in your life,' Morathi warned. 'It was Asuryan's blessing that made your father the Phoenix King. It was the blade of Khaine that he wielded to free our isle. His first wife was the chosen of Isha. Your blood calls to the gods, and in turn they call to your blood.'

'There are other, stranger and stronger gods now,' said Malekith, his gaze unconsciously straying to the north, to the unseen Realm of Chaos. 'I fear that even Asuryan is now humbled.'

'Then if not for your spirit, embrace the gods for your power,' Morathi said. 'By participating and sponsoring religion, as I have done, you will come to control that from which you are currently distanced. It matters not whether you believe the gods are listening. The important point to remember is that your people do. If they believe you have the favour of the gods, their dedication and loyalty is that much stronger.'

'I will not rule with falsehood,' Malekith said. 'One day we will be free of the gods and the better for it.'

Morathi said nothing in reply, but her face expressed her doubt without words.

AS THE TIME to leave Athel Toralien approached ever closer, Malekith fretted more and more, wishing to be gone. Morathi's arrival had disrupted all routine and semblance of order in the city, as Malekith knew it had been intended to. Knowing how fickle elves could be at times, Morathi had ensured that the spectacle of her arrival, her gift of *Indraugnir* and Malekith's departure would all blend together into a story that would stick in the memory and be debated in the city for many years to come.

Of her vast entourage, only a few handmaidens and gifted seers were returning to Ulthuan with the queen. The rest were, as she put it, her gift to Athel Toralien and the other cities of the east. She had ensured that though Malekith was leaving the colonies that he had almost single-handedly created, his name would live on there in his absence.

When it came to the time for the expedition of Malekith to leave, the Naggarothi prince stood upon the deck of *Indraugnir* as she swayed at anchor in the harbour of Athel Toralien. Alandrian stood with him, as did Yeasir. Morathi was in one of the spacious cabins preparing for the voyage. The three of them looked out over the city, which was more than ten times the size it had been when they had first sailed into the anchorage more than thirteen hundred years before. All knew how much things had changed in that time, and they shared the memory of it without having to say a word.

'Where will you go?' asked Alandrian.

'Out to the snow and the ice,' Malekith said, pointing to the north and west. 'I go to meet my fate, whether glorious or ignoble.'

'It will be glorious, of that I am sure,' said Alandrian with good humour. 'You have been marked by the gods for great things, my prince. It is in your blood to bestride history like a colossus while we mere mortals must labour in your immense shadow!'

'Well, my shadow and I will be moving along shortly,' said Malekith with a smile. 'Feel free to enjoy what warmth and light you can in my absence. If what you say is true, then when I will return I shall eclipse the sun and the moons from several miles away!'

The tide was fair and the prince bid Alandrian farewell. The two parted with Alandrian promising he would keep the city safe, and renewing his loyalty to Nagarythe. Morathi came up on deck just as they were about to depart, to wave to the adulalatory crowds who again lined the dockside to see her. With the wind filling her sails, *Indraugnir* got under way, and by noon the city was out of sight below the horizon.

━◄ TEN ►━

The Call of Khaine

WEST THEY SAILED, as Malekith had said they would. Across the Great Ocean *Indraugnir* carried them, towards an uncharted world. Yet for all their grand destiny, there was a more mundane duty to perform first. Morathi was returning to Nagarythe, and would need to be taken to Galthyr before Malekith's host could continue westwards. Thirty days after setting out from Athel Toralien, aided by a strong wind and *Indraugnir's* swift lines, they sighted the northern isles of Ulthuan.

Standing out from the tossing sea as pinnacles of rock, the northern isles protected the coast of Nagarythe and Chrace from the heavy swells and high waves that were stirred up by the north wind. In their midst rose one island larger by far than all the others, and most westerly of the archipelago: the Blighted Isle. It was here that the Shrine of Khaine was located, a black table of rock from which protruded the Widowmaker, the weapon of Khaine. Morathi knew it well, and she stood at the port rail looking south as the Blighted Isle came into view through the fog and crashing surf. Malekith joined her.

'You think of my father,' said the prince.

'I do,' replied Morathi. 'It was more than a thousand years ago that he flew here upon the real Indraugnir and breathed his last. He is but a memory now, a myth to be told to children who will gasp in awe at his feats, yet not wholly believe them. Even I only truly knew the legendary Phoenix King, for we did not meet until after he had drawn the sword. Even I knew of him only by reputation before that, and of the time before his blessing by

Asuryan there is nothing left but mystery. He is gone from us now, he who was the greatest. There is nothing left of him but you.'

Malekith stood there a while, the spray from the sea wetting his face as he looked at the bleak, dark rocks.

'There is something else that remains,' he said finally.

'What is that?' asked his mother. 'Something that remains of what?'

'Of my father,' said Malekith. 'No one has been to the Blighted Isle since Aenarion returned the sword. He and Indraugnir lie there to this day. We should return their bodies to Anlec where they can lie in state, and all the princes from all over the world will come to pay their respects to the first of the Phoenix Kings. Even Bel Shanaar will have to kneel before his remains and pay homage. All the princes will see that, and when my father is interred in a mausoleum that will rival the pyramid of Asuryan, with the bones of the largest dragon of Caledor standing guard at its entrance, I shall take his armour. The princes will remember Bel Shanaar bowing before that armour and the people will see anew that I am Aenarion's son; Aenarion reborn.'

'Is this the sign for which you have been waiting?' said Morathi. 'Will you now return with me to Nagarythe?'

'Not without my father!' said Malekith.

Calling for a boat and crew to be made ready, the prince then ordered the ship's master to bring *Indraugnir* to a stop. Malekith then changed out of his fine robes and garbed himself in his golden armour, ready to be taken over to the Blighted Isle. Morathi stood at the ship's side as the boat was lowered into the water. She smiled at her son as he leapt up to the rail and seized hold of a rope. With a boyish grin of excitement that Morathi had not seen for hundreds of years, the prince of Nagarythe slid down the rope into the waiting boat.

The boat pushed away and was instantly carried from the ship's side by the surging waves. The fifteen elves of the boat crew erected the mast quickly and turned the boat south, heading towards the south-east end of the isle, the part most sheltered from the prevailing wind and waves. Finding a small inlet, they made the boat secure but only Malekith leapt ashore while the crew tried their best not to touch the cursed rock.

THE BLIGHTED ISLE was devoid of all life; a bleak upthrust of crags that was home to neither plant nor animal. No grasses clung to life in crevasses. No beetles scuttled in the shade beneath toppled boulders. No crabs dwelt in the dark pools of water by the sea's edge. The wind seemed to quieten as Malekith walked inland, picking his way through scattered rocks and stones.

Having no particular course or goal, Malekith wandered for a long while, absently making for what he deemed to be higher ground towards the west of the island, so that he might spy the location of his father's remains. Pulling himself up a rocky ridge, the prince looked to the west and saw that the afternoon had all but passed and the sun was not far from the horizon. Though dismissive of the superstitions of the sailors, Malekith had no desire to be out on the Blighted Isle in the dark, and resolved to find his father's remains and return to the boat before nightfall.

With more purpose, Malekith continued his search, his eyes scanning the valleys and hollows for a glimmer of metal or glint of bone. He found nothing, and was despairing of success as the long twilight shadows surrounded him. He was just beginning to think about returning to the boat and resuming his search the next day when he suddenly paused, caught by a strange instinct.

Though he heard no voice, nor saw no sign, Malekith felt a pull to the south, as if he were being called. The lure was strong, like a singing in his blood. With a last glance towards the setting sun, Malekith followed the strange sensation and turned south, bounding over the rocks at speed.

It was not long before Malekith came to a wide, flat expanse near to the centre of the Blighted Isle. Here jagged black rocks veined with lines of red thrust up into the ruddy skies like a circle of columns. The ground within was as flat as glass and black as midnight. At the centre there stood a block of red-veined rock and something only partly visible shimmered above it. This was clearly the Shrine of Khaine, but as Malekith looked around he could see no sign of his father's resting place nor any remains of Indraugnir. They must have come here, for Aenarion had returned the Sword of Khaine to the very altar close to which Malekith now stood.

Even as his thoughts touched upon the Godslayer, there came to Malekith's ears a distant noise: a faint screaming. Now that it had attracted his attention, the prince looked at the altar of Khaine more closely. As he did so, the sounds around him intensified. The screams of agony were joined by howls of horror. The ring of metal on metal, of fighting, echoed around the shrine. Malekith heard a thunderous heart beating, and thought he saw knives carving wounds upon flesh and limbs torn from bodies on the edge of his vision.

The red veins of the altar were not rock at all, but pulsed like arteries, blood flowing from the altar stone in spurting rivers of gore. He realised that the beating heart was his own, and it hammered in his chest like a swordsmith working at an anvil.

A keening sound, like a note sung by a sword's edge as it cuts the air, rang in Malekith's ears. It was not unpleasant, and he listened to it for a while, drawn by its siren call to take step after step closer to the altar. Finally, the prince of Nagarythe stood transfixed before that bloody shrine just as his father Aenarion had been.

The thing embedded in the rock shimmered before Malekith's eyes, a blur of axe and sword and spear. Finally a single image emerged, of a bulbous mace studded with gems. Malekith was confused, for this was no weapon, but rather reminded him of the ornamental sceptres often carried by other princes. It seemed very similar to the one borne by Bel Shanaar when he had visited the colonies.

It was then that the meaning came to Malekith. All of Ulthuan would be his weapon. Unlike his father, he needed neither sword nor spear to destroy his foes. He would have the armies of an entire nation in his grasp, and would wield them however he pleased. If he but took up Khaine's sceptre, there would be none that could oppose him. Like a vision, the future unfolded before Malekith.

He would return to Ulthuan and go to Tor Anroc, and there cast down the gates of the Phoenix King. He would offer up the body of Bel Shanaar to Khaine and become undisputed ruler of the elves. He would reign for eternity as the bloody right hand of the God of Murder. Death would stalk in his shadow as he brought ruination to the empire of the dwarfs, for such was the power of the elves that they need not share the world with any other creature. Beastmen were put to the sword by their thousands, and the carcasses of orcs and goblins spitted upon poles lined the roads of his empire for hundreds of miles.

Malekith laughed as he saw the rude villages of humans being put to the torch, their menfolk tossed onto pyres, their women with their hearts ripped out, while babies had their heads dashed in upon the bloodied rocks. Like an unstoppable tide, the elves would conquer all that lay before them, until Malekith presided over an empire that covered the entire globe and the fumes of the sacrificial fires blotted out the sun. Malekith was carried forwards on a giant palanquin made from the bones of his vanquished enemies, a river of blood pouring out before him.

'No!' cried Malekith, breaking his gaze from the sceptre and hurling himself face first to the rocky ground.

He lay there for a long while, eyes screwed shut, his heart pounding, his breathing ragged and heavy. Slowly he calmed himself, and opened an eye. There seemed to be nothing amiss. There was no blood or fire. There was nothing but silent rock and the hiss of the wind.

The last rays of the day bathed the shrine in orange, and Malekith pushed himself to his feet and staggered from the circle, not daring to look back at the altar. Knowing that his father would not be found, Malekith gathered his senses as best he could and made for the boat, never once looking back.

Even when he was back aboard *Indraugnir* he ordered the captain to sail north with all speed until the Blighted Isle could no longer be seen. None questioned this command, although Morathi regarded her son with renewed curiosity as he strode to his cabin with unseemly haste.

Sailing further, they came upon the trade lanes of Ulthuan's western ports. Having found none of his father's remains, Malekith refused to return to Ulthuan and instead transferred his mother to one of the many merchant ships returning to Ulthuan from the east. Despite her protestations, Morathi was seen off *Indraugnir* with very little ceremony, and the shocked master of the eastern trader found himself gifted with a small fortune of gold and gems in return for taking the seeress-queen to Galthyr.

By the time they had completed the short journey, during which Morathi had complained constantly and her sorcerers had terrified more than a few of the crew, the ship's captain wished he had asked for more.

⫷ ELEVEN ⫸

The Finding of the Circlet

FOR MALEKITH, HIS new freedom was as intoxicating as wine. He turned *Indraugnir* north and headed for the lands of ice that girded the Realm of Chaos. For several years Malekith and his crew explored the coastline of the frozen northlands, foraying eastwards and westwards in attempts to make charts for future visitors. It proved impossible, as the proximity of the Chaos Wastes and the ever-shifting nature of the ice itself changed the landscape with the passing of every season.

Likewise, any attempt to map the scattered human settlements proved fruitless, for they were nomadic and followed the erratic migrations of elk and other animals. Unlike the men who lived just north of the colonies, these humans were both fierce and terrified. Their weapons and armour were more advanced, forged of bronze, yet there was something about the elves that filled them with horror and they would flee whenever Malekith landed with a shore party.

There was good hunting on the outermost edges of the snowy plains: deer, bears and birds aplenty. The elves fished also, but were forced to head south in the coldest parts of the year, where they traded with other ships for grain and wine. Though some of his followers grumbled about the conditions, most were content, as was Malekith. For many this was the opportunity for them to wrest control from the elements, to forge something entirely new out of the unforgiving wilderness, just as they had done in the forests east of Athel Toralien.

For all the enthusiasm of the Naggarothi, these lands were harsh and resources were scarce. These were not the bountiful forests of the east, but a bleak expanse of unrelenting snow and rock. That the crude humans could survive here was testament that there was some worth in these lands, but Malekith knew that there would be no glittering cities of marble and alabaster. However, he was determined that the north would yield to his will.

Many years after setting out from Athel Toralien, Malekith landed upon an icy coast with the greater part of his followers. They carried their food and tents upon sleds pulled by teams of sturdy horses and were wrapped in coats of fur, and wore thick gloves and boots to protect them from the freezing wind. A few souls were left aboard *Indraugnir* and told to return to this place every fifty days to watch for the expedition's return. With that, Malekith and his warriors forged inland to see what secrets the northern blizzards concealed.

IN THE CHAOS Wastes, the Naggarothi found foes more fell than any they had met before. The lands teemed with monstrous creatures warped by the power of Chaos, and every time that the elves made camp the sentries would be tested by some terrifying winged beast or mindless, shambling thing.

The men of this realm were also far in advance of their cousins further south. Whether from unknown allies or gifted dark knowledge by the Chaos Gods, these humans had thick armour of leather and bronze, and hardened weapons. They wielded swords and axes with surprising skill, and some had shamanic powers and assailed the Naggarothi with spells drawn from the dark magic that swirled in great strength throughout the north.

Many of the humans showed signs of Chaos corruption, and had bloated muscles or bestial faces. No few carried ensorcelled weapons gifted to them by the Chaos gods. Malekith slew a chieftain with bat-like wings and scales instead of skin, who wielded a jagged sword that constantly screamed in some arcane and dreadful language. Avanuir also took the life of a tribal champion who had a snake's body and was clad in armour made of iron-hard bone.

Though Malekith never ventured into the Realm of Chaos itself, often his expedition came close to its uncertain borders. The air shimmered with magical aurorae and crackled with mystical energy. Vast and insane landscapes hovered upon the edge of vision: nightmarish forests of flesh, mountains of bones, rivers of blood and burning skies all lurked beyond the invisible boundary. Even in the Chaos Wastes, the blasted shadowlands surrounding the Realm of Chaos, the daemonic and the unnatural held sway. For the first time in over a thousand years, Malekith pitted his sword against the blades of the daemonic legions of Chaos.

Malekith took ever greater risks, searching for some doom or myth that never materialised. The prince drove his army further and further westwards and northwards, seeking some sign that only he would recognise.

In truth, Malekith was growing ever more despondent. Nearly fifteen years had passed since he had left Athel Toralien and it seemed to the prince that he was no closer to achieving the great glory he desired. There was no army to overthrow, just scattered warbands of humans and transient daemonic apparitions to banish. There were not boundless riches to send back to Ulthuan, just the unending bleakness of snow, rock and ice: an eternal grinding battle of attrition.

With his company much reduced by hardship and fighting, Malekith felt his search growing ever more in vain. Northwards they pressed once more, unto the very edge of the Realm of Chaos. Though he shared his despair with no one else, the Naggarothi could sense Malekith's growing frustration and worried what desperate act he might be considering.

For days they were engulfed by a mighty tempest of wind and snow, and though the Naggarothi struggled onwards eventually Malekith called them to a halt to wait out the unnaturally savage storm.

DURING THE NIGHT, the tents of the Naggarothi camp buffeted by blizzard, Yeasir confronted his lord. The two were alone in Malekith's pavilion, wrapped in their heavy furs as they sat upon the cold ground around a burning magical stone; the only fire that could be lit. Canvas cracked and slapped around them, and the wind howled all about.

'If you but let us know what it is you wish, then we would help you,' said the Naggarothi captain.

'What if I was to tell you that I would dare the Gate of Chaos itself?' said Malekith. 'Would you still follow me?'

Yeasir did not answer immediately but his look of horror was all the reply Malekith needed.

'So there is a boundary across which the Naggarothi dare not cross?' said the prince.

'I would counsel against it, your highness,' said Yeasir, picking his words carefully. 'Yet, if after my protestations were heard you were still intent upon such a course, I would follow you as would the others.'

'And what arguments would you make to dissuade me?' asked Malekith.

'That no living soul has ever entered the Realm of Chaos and returned,' replied Yeasir.

'Is that not the point of such an endeavour?' said Malekith. 'Were we to venture into the heart of Chaos itself and return, would that not be a legend worth telling for a thousand years?'

'If we return,' cautioned Yeasir.

'I did not know that the cold had cut so deeply into your veins, Yeasir,' said Malekith with scorn.

'It is not fear that holds me back,' said Yeasir sharply. 'I would gladly march against any foe, mortal or daemonic, but there is no valour in matching a hundred spears against the might of the Dark Gods! If we were to dare such a thing, we would be remembered as fools led by stupidity and vanity, not glory. Worse still, we would not be remembered at all, for if we should cross over to the worlds beyond and not return, then our tale will end with nothing. "They were lost in the snows of the north," the chronicles would read, and our names would go unremembered.'

Malekith scowled, not out of anger but frustration. He knew that Yeasir's points were valid, but in his heart he yearned for something more. The longer he remained in the north, the more chance that Bel Shanaar would be succeeded by another prince before Malekith's return. The prince of Nagarythe could not bear the thought of slinking back to Ulthuan after all this time, to spend his days living out the fading glories of an age past.

'I will make no decision now,' Malekith declared. 'The morning sun may bring fresh counsel.'

And it did.

BEFORE DAWN, THE storm abated and a calm settled upon the tundra. Yeasir came to Malekith's tent as the sun was breaking, much excited. Following his captain, Malekith emerged from his pavilion to see what had stirred the camp.

To the north, in the growing light of the day, could be seen distant structures. Upon a snow-swept hill, outlandish buildings rose up from the ice, carpeted with white but unmistakable nonetheless. Their exact shape could not be discerned from this distance, but grey and black rock hewn by hand rather than nature jutted at strange angles from drifts and hills of snow. The early morning sunlight sparkled from icicles hanging from strange balconies and glinted from odd-shaped domes. Malekith gave the order for the company to break camp and make ready to march with all speed.

What Malekith had taken to be a few miles turned out to be several leagues, the distance deceptive in the otherwise featureless snow plain. It took hours of marching before the Naggarothi came upon the outskirts of the strange buildings. No outer wall guarded their border and they seemed deserted. In design they were unlike anything the elves had seen before; not of elven, dwarfish or human hand.

The buildings were made of solid stone, but appeared not have been carved from the naked rock but fused seamlessly from some other stone. The walls met at strange angles, and the empty doorways and windows formed odd shapes of darkness, with no corner square. There were no curves either, no rounded arches or elegantly pointed arcs. Some buildings were low, so that their roofs were no higher than Malekith's head, while others had several storeys, each of which was a dozen feet high or more.

To begin, the Naggarothi wandered the wide, uneven streets, up sweeping terraces and lines of stairs that changed in height at every step. The roads joined at irregular intervals, and met in uneven, star-shaped plazas. Other than the cold stone there was nothing else, no wood nor metal, and Malekith judged the settlement to be ancient indeed. After an hour's searching it was clear that the city was vast, larger than anything Malekith had ever encountered.

Here on the edge of the Realm of Chaos, distances could be perversely extended or contracted, and so it was within the city. Short pathways seemed to widen as the elves approached, streets appeared to take longer to walk along than the buildings around them would imply, while eerie avenues that seemed to stretch for miles could be walked along in a matter of moments.

Eventually Malekith and the others ventured inside one of the buildings. It was a grand structure of five storeys, which widened unnaturally as it soared towards the grey skies, its flat walls pricked with hundreds of tiny, dark windows. The lower floor was open, with no internal walls, and the only feature was a wide stairwell that led downwards; there appeared to be no means to reach the upper levels.

Bringing out dwarf-made lanterns that glittered with silver fire, the elves descended the steps. These brought them into a contorted network of passages and rooms, and very quickly Malekith feared they would get lost. He ordered a warrior to stand at each junction with a lamp held aloft, so that no elf was ever out of sight from the route back. In this way, they slowly explored the windowless catacomb. They found no sign of the city's builders, just blank stone devoid of carvings or colour.

After an hour of searching – far longer than Malekith would have suspected by the size of the building above – they came upon another stair. It rose steeply upwards and double-backed and criss-crossed itself in a disturbing way. That it reached far higher than the ceiling was indisputable, though its position, as far as Malekith could tell, put it in the centre of the storey above where no stair had been seen.

Their breath carving clouds upon the cold air, Malekith and his warriors mounted the steps, continuing to leave sentries at each twisted landing so that no elf was out of sight of another. The elves scaled the stairway in a surprisingly short time, and it opened out onto another empty floor, with wide windows through which they could only see the cloudy skies.

Walking to the nearest window, Malekith looked out and then stepped back with a gasp. The stairwell had brought them up to a floor above where they had entered the building, for down below he could see a few of his warriors standing guard at the doorway where they had come in. The city stretched out in every direction as far as he could see, going on and on until it was lost in a grey haze.

Disorientated, Malekith closed his eyes and took a deep breath. Having recovered himself a little, he leaned out of the glassless window, avoiding looking towards the horizon, and hailed the Naggarothi some sixty feet below. They looked up with startled shouts, and their voices came back impossibly distant.

Disturbed, Malekith ordered the Naggarothi to leave, though it took another hour for them to climb down the winding stairway and trace their way back out of the labyrinthine catacomb. There was much distressed murmuring by the Naggarothi, and Malekith's usual confidence had been eroded by the unnatural surroundings. Looking up into the sky, he could see no sign of the sun and so only his internal awareness gave him any sense of the passage of time.

He reckoned it to be mid-afternoon, and knew that in these northern climes the sun would set early at this time of the year, barely passing above the horizon for a few hours. Malekith declared that they would leave the city before night fell and seek out its secrets with renewed vigour the following day.

However, with no sun to guide them, none of the Naggarothi knew from which direction they had entered the city. They retraced their steps as best they could from the footprints in the snow, but these soon petered out and could be found no more, though no snow had fallen since their arrival as far as they were aware. Now even more unnerved, Malekith called for the company to gather, and found that five of their number were missing. None could recall where they had last been seen, and the prince feared that they were lost in the city somewhere, perhaps forever.

Sensing the unease in his warriors becoming panic, Malekith bid them to stay where they were, somewhere amidst the criss-crossing arteries of the city's maze-like roads. Clearly the proximity of the Realm of Chaos was addling their senses, and Malekith could not trust his own eyes. Instead he turned to a deeper sense, of the magic that flowed across the world from the Gate of Chaos.

Closing his eyes and blanking out all other sensation, the prince entered a meditative trance he had learnt from Morathi in his youth. Normally he needed no such concentration to harness the winds of magic, but now he desired finesse and focus and so looked to the lessons of his childhood to give him a centre upon which to concentrate.

Imagining himself as a small speck, a grain of dust upon the ground, Malekith allowed his othersense to reach outwards just a small distance. Magic swirled in all directions, without form or rhythm. Edging out his sphere of awareness, he allowed his mind's eye to encompass a greater part of the city. Here he could detect a more regular stream of power; an underlying flow that poured from one direction. Fixing that point in his mind, Malekith opened his eyes.

Composed once more, Malekith could feel the gentle but persistent surge of Chaos unconsciously, and knew in which direction north now lay. Turning to the south, he ordered the Naggarothi to follow him.

They had walked for perhaps an hour when Malekith felt a different current in the flow of magic. Something close at hand was causing an eddy to form, much like the dispelling stone of the dwarfs. More confident that he could lead his warriors from the city if necessary, Malekith decided to make a detour and investigate this phenomenon. Now that he was aligned with the winds of magic again, Malekith marched unerringly between the grotesque buildings, guiding the company directly to the source of the anomaly.

There was something about the building that disturbed Malekith even more than the others. It was not as tall as some, but was very broad and rose up like a five-levelled ziggurat, though each successive step was slightly misaligned in comparison to the one beneath, so that the whole structure seemed to have been twisted by a god's hand in some prehistoric time. There were archways all around its bottom floor, though nothing could be seen of the upper floors. Though he could not reason exactly why, the building brought Malekith to mind of a temple; to what deity or power, he could not fathom.

Malekith commanded half of his warriors to form a perimeter around the building, which stood alone just off-centre in a huge irregular eight-sided plaza. The other half of the company, Malekith led through one of the slanted archways. They followed the corridors, stairs and tunnels within for some time, but ever their path led them outwards so that they stood in rooms and galleries on the outer edge of each level. Malekith felt magic bubbling around him, and could sense a ward upon the inner walls keeping the magic at bay from somewhere within.

Eventually he found a spot where the magic churned violently, though looking about Malekith could see no physical source for such a disturbance. Holding up a hand to command his warriors to wait, he walked to the point where several streams of energy collided with each other. He stood on that exact spot, nauseated by the clashing magical waves.

Looking around he could see a triangular door that could be seen from nowhere else. He pointed and told Yeasir to follow his directions. Confused but obedient, the captain stalked across the floor of the room, following Malekith's gestures. To Yeasir it seemed as if Malekith guided him towards a solid wall and he hesitated, just a pace from the stone, before the prince's snarling voice bid him to walk forwards once more. With a grimace, his eyes half-closed in expectation of thudding into the wall, Yeasir took a step; he nearly fell over as he found himself atop a strange angular stair, much like the one they had found in the first building.

Through cunning artifice and magic, the stair was impossible to see, as if the door to it stood slightly apart from the world. Once Yeasir had stepped through, he had disappeared from sight, but he returned in moments and waved for the others to follow him.

The stairs led down for a comparatively short stretch, though such concepts as time and distance were becoming increasingly irrelevant in this impossible city. They led into a chamber, utterly black but for the glimmer of the elves' lanterns. The air seemed to suck all the light into itself, and even with the radiance from the lamps Malekith could see barely ten paces ahead.

Stepping cautiously forwards, he found himself treading upon a tiled floor, arranged in a seemingly haphazard mess of geometry yet every tile still fitting perfectly in the insane mosaic. The tiles were as grey as the stone of the rest of the city, but were slightly soft to tread upon, like a thin carpet. Casting the light of his lantern to the right and the left, Malekith could make out dim shapes rising in the gloom: figures stood upon pedestals lining a wide concourse that led away from the door. Malekith raised a hand to halt those following behind, and turned left to inspect the statues more closely.

By the silvery light of the lamp, they looked to be made out of some dull alloy, but as he came within a few paces Malekith could see more clearly that they were skeletons of greying bone. They were not unlike the bones of an elf, or for that matter a man, or dwarf; in proportion they were short of torso and long of limb like an elf, but had the thicker bones of a man, and were of a height little more than a dwarf. Their faces were slender, with a mouth, two eyes and two nostrils that were so disturbingly familiar yet not quite like any skull he had seen, causing Malekith to pause a moment before continuing his inspection.

They were clad in black shrouds that were wrapped about the bodies and shoulders in identical fashion, with hoods raised up on their skulls. Every cadaver wore chains of dark beads, perhaps black pearls, which hung limply from bony wrists and about throatless necks. Each held a serrated, angular sword in its right hand and a triangular shield upon its left arm, both free of any design that Malekith could discern.

The tiles stopped at the line of plinths, and beyond them the floor seemed to be made of the same stone as the rest of the building. Malekith could see nothing in the darkness, the lantern light reflected off no edge or surface, and he had no idea whether there were any other features or if the rest of the chamber was utterly empty.

Walking along the line of inanimate sentries, Malekith could not guess at how far the two lines stretched, but sensed that their course narrowed almost imperceptibly, bringing them together at some distant point as yet out of sight.

Glancing back towards the others, Malekith had another surprise. Though he was sure that he had walked no more than fifty paces, in as straight a line as made no difference, the glimmer of his companions' lanterns was like distant starlight in the gloom, and quite some way off to his left and higher up than his current position.

The prince called out for them to send a party to join him, and his voice echoed off distant walls, bouncing and resounding within a space he judged to be much vaster than the building in which it was supposedly enclosed. With a shiver, Malekith waited for the others to reach him, the light from their lanterns swiftly growing brighter with every heartbeat as if they covered a dozen paces with every stride.

Yeasir was with them and he gazed wide-eyed at the skeletal parade. He said nothing, but his look of concern was not lost on Malekith. With a reassuring nod, the prince turned along the line once more and followed the skeleton-flanked concourse. The pathway did indeed narrow gradually, and led the Naggarothi to a great stepped plinth the summit of which lay in the gloom beyond their lights. Ascending the first few steps and walking around them, Malekith saw that five other lines of skeletons joined the central feature at irregular angles. He rejoined his comrades and ordered a handful of them to stand guard at the bottom of the steps, while the others followed him up the steep dais.

It led onto a plateau, which was impossibly, maddeningly as wide as the base of the steps below. Seven figures sat upon low square stools, more opulent versions of the skeletons below with more dark pearls and brooches of the same black material. Six sat facing outwards, each one facing one of the lines upon the ground below as far as Malekith could tell. They had no hoods but instead wore simple crowns consisting of a narrow band about the skull with a black gem that reflected no light upon their foreheads.

The seventh figure sat facing Malekith, though the prince suspected that he would have faced the intruders regardless of which direction they had approached from. His crown was much larger, of a silver-grey metal, with curling, horn-like protrusions; the only organic shape they had seen since entering the city.

'Highness!' snapped Yeasir, and Malekith turned, his hand on his sword hilt. It was only then that he realised that his other hand had been reaching out towards the skeletal king, to pluck the crown from his skull. Malekith had no recollection of having crossed the dais, and shook his head as if dazed by a blow.

'We should touch nothing,' said Yeasir. 'This place is cursed, by the gods, or worse.'

Malekith laughed and the noise seemed stifled and flat, with none of the ringing echoes of his earlier shout.

'I think this great king rules here no more,' said Malekith. 'This is my sign, Yeasir. What greater statement about my destiny could I make? Imagine returning to Ulthuan with such a crown upon my head, an artefact of the time before.'

'Before what?' asked Yeasir.

'Before everything!' said Malekith. 'Before Chaos, before the Everqueen, before even the gods themselves. Can you not feel it, the great antiquity that fills this place?'

'I feel it,' growled Yeasir. 'There is ancient malice here, can you not sense it? I say again, there is a curse upon this place.'

'You were willing to follow me to the Gate of Chaos,' Malekith reminded his captain. 'Would you rather we left this treasure here and continued north?'

Yeasir's muttered reply was inaudible, but Malekith took it to be his captain's acquiescence. Not that the prince needed the permission of anyone to take whatever he wanted, from wherever he wanted. Magic had guided him to this place and Malekith knew that there was purpose behind it. Whether it was the gods or some other will that had led him here, it was to stand before this prehistoric king and take his crown.

With a smile, Malekith lifted the circlet from the dead king's skull; it was as light as air and came away with no difficulty.

'You have it, now let us leave,' said Yeasir, fear making his voice shrill.

'Calm yourself,' said Malekith. 'Does it not make me kingly?'

With that, the prince of Nagarythe placed the circlet upon his head and the world vanished.

GOLDEN LIGHT BLAZED throughout the immense hall. It did not appear to have a single source, but simply radiated out from all of the walls. Yeasir blinked in the sudden brightness, trying to clear spots from his eyes. As his vision returned, he saw more clearly where they were.

The chamber was vast, larger than any hall he had ever seen on Ulthuan or in the realm of the dwarfs. The walls were impossibly distant, and as Yeasir turned about to look around, he swore that their number increased and reduced, so that at one moment he was standing in a great irregular octagon, at others a triangular chamber.

Disorientated, he looked up and saw a vast ceiling stretching out to the horizon, so immense that he could not see where it met the walls. Huge angular stalactites jagged downwards at strange slants. The ceiling itself was made up of immense plates and surfaces that formed bizarre vertices, and perspective seemed to bend and contract depending on where he looked. Tearing away his gaze from the maddening vista, Yeasir turned his attention to his lord.

To Yeasir, it seemed as if Malekith had been frozen. He stood next to the regal skeleton at the centre of the dais locked in his pose, the crown upon his head, his fingers still touching the strange iron-like headgear. Yeasir leapt forwards with a shout, fearing some bewitchment had befallen his master. Another cry from one of the warriors distracted him and he turned his head to see several of the Naggarothi pointing out across the hall.

Following their fingers, Yeasir saw what he had feared ever since they had entered the ancient hall: the skeletal figures stepping down from their plinths and turning towards the central dais. They also glowed with light, and stalked purposefully forwards, their shields and weapons held ready. Yeasir cast a quick glance at the figures seated around them and was relieved to see that not one of them stirred. Ignoring his transfixed prince, Yeasir dashed to the opposite side of the platform and saw that skeletal warriors were advancing from every direction.

'Form up for defence!' Yeasir commanded, and the Naggarothi came together in a ring of spears and shields that encircled the top of the high podium.

'Prince!' the captain cried out, crossing the dais and laying a hand on his shoulder as if to wake him.

As soon as he touched Malekith, sparks of energy exploded across Yeasir's body and he was flung backwards across the dais, clattering and rolling across the hard stone. His body was numb and his muscles jerked and spasmed as magical energy coursed through him. Gritting his teeth, he fought to control his juddering limbs but felt drained of all strength. He lay there groaning, his arms and legs as heavy as lead, his ears ringing, his vision hazy.

There were more alarmed shouts but Yeasir could not discern the words. In momentary flashes of clarity he could see the Naggarothi archers raising arrows to their bowstrings and loosing them out from the edge of the dais, but he could not see if their shots had any effect. Moaning, he managed to roll to his stomach, and the numbness began to dissipate, replaced instead by gnawing pain in every joint and bone.

He tried to speak, but all he could do was clench his teeth and hiss, as pain shot along the captain's spine and exploded inside his brain. Amongst the buzzing and squealing that filled his hearing, Yeasir caught snatches of shouts and the dreadful clatter of thousands of bony feet marching upon the stone. A panicked thought shot through his pain-clouded mind: we are doomed.

— TWELVE —

Primordial Foes

A KALEIDOSCOPE OF clashing colours swarmed around Malekith. He was filled with the peculiar sensation of rising high up into the air whilst at the same time plummeting down towards some bottomless depth. His head swam and his skin tingled with power. He was lost in sensation, his whole being pulsing and vibrating with unknown energy.

In time – moments or an eternity, Malekith could not tell – the swirling colours began to coalesce around him. They formed into a nightmarish landscape above the centre of which floated the elf prince. The skies boiled with fire and black clouds, and beneath him stretched an arcane plateau that stretched on for infinity: the Realm of Chaos.

In one direction Malekith spied an unending garden, forlorn and decaying, filled with drooping willows and sallow grasses. A miasma of fog and flies drifted up from the overgrown copses of bent and withered trees, and rivers of oozing pus gurgled between fronds of clinging fungi and piles of rotted corpses. Marshes bubbled and boiled and pits of tar gurgled, spewing gaseous vapours into the thick air.

At the centre of the unkempt morass rose up a mansion of titanic proportions: a grandiose but tottering edifice of crumbling stone and worm-eaten wood. Peeling paint and flaking brick stood upon cracked stone and bowed beams, crawling with sickly yellow ivy and immense black roses. Fumes belched from a hundred chimneys and gargoyle-headed pipes spat and drooled gobbets of ichor across cracked tiles and mouldering thatch.

In the smog and gloom shambled daemons of death and plague;

immensely bloated creatures with pustulant flesh and pox-marked skin, and slobbering beasts with slug-like bodies and fronds of tentacles dribbling noxious emissions. Swarms of boil-like mites scrabbled over the sagging walls and roofs of the manse, while a legion of cyclopean daemons, each with a single cracked horn, meandered about the wild gardens chanting sonorously.

Turning his gaze from the filth and squalor, Malekith then looked upon a mighty citadel made up of glimmering mirrors and crystal. Its surface shimmered with a rainbow of colours, translucent yet transparent, shifting with eddies and swirls of magic. Doors yawned like devouring mouths and windows stared back at the prince like lidless eyes. Fires of all colours billowed from the spires of thin towers, sending fountains of sparks trailing down to the ground below.

All about the bizarre palace was an immense maze, of shifting walls of crystal. The twisting, contorted pathways overlapped above and below, and passed across each other through unseen dimensions. Arcing gateways of flame linked parts of the immense labyrinth together, flickering from blue to green to purple and to colours not meant to be seen by mortals.

The skies about the horrifying tower were filled with shoals of creatures that climbed and swooped upon the magical thermals, shark-like and fearsome. Formless, cackling things cavorted and whirled about the maze, flashing with magical power. Daemons with arms that dripped with fire bounded manically along the winding crystal passages, leaping and bouncing with insane abandon. Malekith felt his eyes drawn back to the impossible fortress and saw that a great gallery had opened up.

Here stalked arcane things with multi-coloured wings and bird-like faces, with contorting staves in their hands and robes of glistening pink and blue. One of the creatures paused and looked up at him. Its eyes were like pits of never-ending madness, deep oceans of swirling power that threatened to draw him into their depths for eternity.

Breaking that transfixing stare, Malekith then looked upon a blasted wasteland, surrounded by a great chain of volcanoes that spewed rivers of lava down their black sides and choked the air with their foul soot. Immense ramparts were carved from the mountainsides, huge bastions of dread hung with skulls and from whose jagged battlements fluttered a thousand times a thousand banners of red.

Within the encircling peaks the land was rent by great tears and chasms that welled up with blood like wounds, as if it had been constantly rent by the blows of some godly blade. The skeletons of unimaginable creatures were piled high amongst lakes of burning crimson, and all about were dunes made of the dust of countless bones. Hounds the size of horses with red-scaled flesh and enormous fangs prowled amongst the ruination, their howls tearing the air above the snap and crack of bone and gristle.

At the heart of this desolation grew a tower of unimaginable proportion, so vast that it seemed to fill Malekith's vision. Of black stone and brass was it made, tower upon tower, wall upon wall, a castle so great that it would hold back the armies of the whole universe. Gargoyles spouted boiling blood down its brazen fortifications, and red-skinned warriors with wiry frames and bulbous, horned heads patrolled its ramparts. Upon its highest parapet there stood a thing of pure fury; rage given bestial, winged form. It beat its broad chest and roared into the dark skies.

Shuddering, Malekith turned fully about and stood bewitched by a panorama of entrancing beauty. Enchanting glades of gently swaying emerald-leafed trees bordered golden beaches upon which crashed white-foamed waves, while glittering lakes of tranquil water beckoned to him. Majestic mountains soared above all, their flanks clad in the whitest snow, glistening in the unseen sun.

Lithe creatures clad in the guise of half-maidens cavorted through the paradise, laughing and chattering, caressing each other with shimmering claws. Across emerald meadows roamed herds of sinuous beasts whose bodies shimmered and changed colour, their iridescent patterns hypnotising to the elf prince. Malekith felt himself drawn onwards, ensnared by their beauty.

Suddenly realising his peril, Malekith tore his gaze away from the mesmerising vision. He became distinctly aware that he was being watched and could feel the attention of otherworldly beings being turned in his direction. Feeling as if his soul were about to be laid bare and flayed before the gaze of the Chaos Gods, Malekith felt terror gripping him. He sought somewhere to flee, but in every direction spread the domains of the Dark Gods. With a last dread-driven effort, he wished himself away and was surrounded again by the twirling energies of magic.

When his vision had cleared again, Malekith found himself hovering far above the world, as if stood upon the edge of creation itself and looking down upon the realms of men and elves and dwarfs and every other creature under the sun. He could see the jungle-swathed forests of Lustria where lizardmen scuttled through the ruins of the Old Ones' cities. He saw orc tribes massing in the blighted wilderness, carpeting the ground in tides of green.

Over everything drifted the winds of magic, now more clear to him than they had ever been. The prince saw them streaming from the shattered Gate of Chaos in the north and spreading out across the northlands. He saw the vortex of Ulthuan as a great swirl of power, drawing the energy out of the world. He saw sinkholes of darkness and blazing mountains of light.

In that instant it all became clear to Malekith. The whole world was laid out before him, and he saw as perhaps only his mother had before seen. There were torrents of power that swept across the lands untapped by mortal kind. The very breath of the gods sighed over oceans and plains, down valleys and across forests. From Chaos came all magic, whether good or ill. It was stunning in its beauty, just as a storm-tossed sea can enthral those not caught in its deadly grip.

Malekith lingered awhile, now aware of the crown burning upon his head. It acted as some kind of key, some artefact created by the races that had come before the rise of elves, before even the coming of the Old Ones. It would be easy for him to stay here forever, marvelling at the rich, random choreography of the dancing winds of magic. He could spend an eternity studying their heights and depths with the circlet and still not unlock all of their secrets.

Something nagged at his mind however, a sensation deep within his soul that threatened to break his reverie.

YEASIR STRUGGLED TO his knees, still weak from the magical blast that had cast him down. The alarmed shouts of his comrades grew more urgent as the skeletons began to advance up the steps towards the Naggarothi. Crawling to the edge of the uppermost level, he looked down to see the unliving legion marching implacably onwards, each stepping in synchronicity with all the others, guided by common purpose or will. The arrows of the elves had little effect, most bouncing harmless from the glowing bones of their enemies, others simply passing through them as if they were nothing more than ghosts.

As the first line of skeletons reached the uppermost step, the Naggarothi struck out with their spears, driving silvered points into skulls and ribcages. This had more effect than the arrows and no few skeletons crumbled into bones, their golden light ebbing and then disappearing. Their advance was as inevitable as the coming of the tide though, and even as the first rank fell the second stepped forwards, and the third, and the fourth.

The skeletons' blades were as keen as the day that they had been forged, despite the passage of ages, and they bit into shield and flesh as the skeletons attacked back. Cries of pain and fear began to reverberate around Yeasir as he struggled to pull free his own sword, but the scabbard was pinned beneath him and he had not the strength to lift himself from it.

The elf to Yeasir's left gave a cry and toppled down the steps as an unearthly blade slashed through his throat. The skeleton took another pace forwards into the space the elf had occupied and turned its grinning face towards Yeasir. It raised its arm above its head, the wicked black blade in its hand sparkling with golden light. Yeasir gave a cry and tried to push himself away, but the skeleton stepped forwards again, ready to strike. The captain pulled his shield in front of him just as the sword swung down, and the undead thing's blade rang against it with a dull crash.

Again and again the sword smashed upon the shield, with relentless, metronomic ferocity. After the tenth blow, all the strength was gone from Yeasir's arms and the eleventh strike smashed the top of the shield into his face, stunning him. Dazed, he could do nothing as the skeleton's sword arm rose high again. He stared into the guardian's eyes, seeing nothing but pits of darkness.

The golden light that filled the room flared into white intensity, blinding Yeasir. He shrieked and knotted his eyes shut, expecting to feel the bite of the unnatural blade any moment. No blow came and Yeasir opened a single eye, fearful of what he might see. The skeleton still loomed above him, arm upraised, but its aura had dimmed to a faint glow and it stood utterly motionless.

Yeasir opened his other eye and dared to let out his breath. The captain then heard harsh laughter from behind him and turned his head slowly, wondering what other fearful apparition awaited him.

Malekith stood in the centre of the dais, the circlet upon his head blazing with power. His face was drawn but he was filled with a glow of energy. His expression was one of disdain, divine yet strangely cruel. His gaze was distant. The prince looked at Yeasir for a long while but did not appear to actually see him. The prince flung out an arm and with the gesture the skeletons came to life once more, turning upon their heels and marching back down the steps. Panting with relief, Yeasir watched as they returned to their plinths and once again took up their immobile vigil.

WITH THE POWER of the crown, Malekith could see the magical forces binding the skeletons together and the ancient commands that blazed within their empty skulls. It was simplicity itself to order them to stop, and then with another thought the prince bid them to return to their eternal slumber. All about him the hall was filled with great golden arches and glittering pillars, unseen to all except him.

Given extraordinary awareness by the circlet he could look upon the magic of the ancient architects of the city, the curving galleries and arching balconies constructed from mystical forces that even he had been unaware of. This was why the chamber was devoid of other magic, for it contained its own power, far stronger than that of the fitful winds of magic. Just as air cannot pass into a solid object, so too the winds of magic found no room to creep into the enchantment-filled chamber.

Now gifted the insights granted by the crown, there was no telling how acutely the Naggarothi prince might master the power of Chaos. With the circlet to act as his key, Malekith could work such spells as would make the witchery of Saphery seem insignificant. Had he not looked upon the realm of the Chaos Gods itself? Did he not now know their lands, and had he not dared them and survived?

Elation filled Malekith, more majestic than any triumph he ever felt before. His mother had warned that Chaos was the greater enemy; the perils of orcs and the armies of the beastmen paled into insignificance against those legions of daemons that Malekith had seen. The Chaos Gods plotted and waited, for they had an eternity to ponder their plans and to make their schemes. The elves could not shelter behind the power of the vortex forever,

Malekith realised, for he had felt the slowly growing power of the Chaos Gods even as he had stood in their midst.

It all came together in the prince's mind. The men of the north were vassals of the Dark Gods, and as they prospered and multiplied, so too would the influence of their ineffable masters. There might come a day when the bulwark of the vortex would fail, and again the hordes of Chaos would be unleashed upon the world. Ulthuan was utterly unprepared for such an eventuality. Bel Shanaar could not hope to meet such a threat. It was an apparent truth to Malekith that he alone, with the power of the circlet, now bore the means by which the elves might be protected from this greater doom.

Slowly, with much effort, Malekith took the crown from his head. The great magical architecture faded from his vision and he found himself back in the strangely angled hall beneath the prehistoric city. His Naggarothi surrounded him, staring at their lord with eyes full of wonder and fear.

Malekith smiled. He now knew what he must do.

PART TWO

The Cults of the Cytharai; the Return of the Prince;
Anlec Restored; the Will of Asuryan

—≺ THIRTEEN ≻—

The Malaise of Luxury

EVEN AS MALEKITH embraced the destiny revealed to him by the Circlet of Iron, far to the south on Ulthuan another elf started upon a path that would see him brought into the fates of the most powerful princes of the isle. An unassuming captain of the Lothern Guard, Carathril led a handful of his company along the harbour road. His mission was secret, known only to a few amongst the court of Eataine, but its import was beyond reckoning. That night would set in motion a series of events that heralded the end of the elves' golden age.

White light blazed across the night sky, shining from the thousand windows that pierced the walls of the Glittering Tower. Surf sparkled as it crashed against the rocks upon which the lighthouse was built. By the light of the Glittering Tower ships moved to and fro across the bay, passing into and out of the great portal of the Emerald Gate, beyond which lay the still waters of the Straits of Lothern. Their white sails cast a ghostly shimmer over the calm waters, bathing the sea with radiance.

Past rearing cliffs lined with towers and walls, where the spear tips of sentries could be seen moving endlessly on their patrols, rose up the bulk of the Sapphire Gate, its wrought silver dazzling under the magical light of the giant gems set upon it. In the starlight beyond the Sapphire Gate, a lagoon opened out, tranquil in its stillness, where white beaches climbed out of the quiet waters.

Piers and wharfs crowded with ships of all sizes curved elegantly across the waters. Small jolly boats and pleasure craft hung with golden lanterns drifted along the shore, the laughter and conversation of their revelling passengers echoing across the softly lapping waves. Amidst the forest of tall masts and slender spars of white-decked merchantmen and sleek-sided yachts, the mass of warships loomed large. Immense dragonships rode confidently at anchor, their golden rams and silver-chased bolt throwers shining reminders of their bloody purpose. Darting hawkships tacked back and forth through the sea traffic, their Sea Guard crews ever alert to any danger.

Around the lagoon, the city of Lothern stretched up into the hills. Verdant terraces, abundant vineyards and low-built villas dotted the hillsides, linked together by winding paths of silvery grey that meandered from the shoreline up to the great mansions and slim towers built upon the peaks of Lothern's twenty hills. Quiet reigned over the city; not the peace of contentment but a hush of apprehension.

A languid malaise blighted Lothern, just as it gripped all of the island of the elves. Many elf-folk of Ulthuan had lost themselves in debauchery and excess. What had begun as aesthetic gatherings, readings of darkly poetic works and ceremonies of mutual solace, had become something far more sinister. With blood sacrifices and twisted rituals of debasement, the cultists now pleaded with forbidden powers for release from their woes.

The pleasure cults had drawn in others by offering the simple thrill of experience, for the elves had always been a people who felt sensation and emotion strongly. Let loose from the civilities of polite decorum, some elves had lost themselves in the raw hedonism enjoyed by the cults of excess, indulging every perverse whim and partaking of any forbidden deed.

Few suspected the true extent of the cults' inveiglement into their society, nor the secret machinations that fuelled the midnight conferences of their shadowy leaders. Even fewer knew the true extent of their network, for in outlook each appeared individual and disparate, unique emerging counter-cultures within each realm and city with no connection to the travails of the other kingdoms. So it was that Bel Shanaar and his princes sought to quell the rising power of the cults through political and spiritual means, hoping to forestall the recruitment of new followers and rebalance the distressed psyche of the elven people.

Carathril was intent upon the destruction of a cult recently uncovered in Lothern, and to this purpose he led his warriors along the winding streets of the city.

IN THE MANSE of Prince Aeltherin on the outskirts of the city of Lothern, hidden amongst carefully tended orchards and perfectly appointed gardens, a vile ceremony was reaching its climax.

The air in the marble hall of the elven lord swirled with purple and blue vapours, which billowed from braziers wrought from the twisted bones of animals. Intoxicated by the narcotic fumes, a sea of elves writhed upon the red-carpeted floor. Fishermen and nobles, servants and lawmakers lay together, rendered equally low in their depravity. Some wept at nightmares only they could see, others laughed hysterically, while a few simply moaned in ecstatic pleasure.

Around and about the seething mass stood a dozen priestesses, stripped to their waists, their exposed bodies daubed with symbols drawn in the blood of a fox, their long hair teased into dramatic spines with the fat of the same animal.

The high priestess, Damolien, whispered a low chant, her voice all but lost in the cacophony of joy and misery that filled the high hall. She wore the skin of the slain fox about her shoulders, and on occasion, she would pause and stroke her hands through its fur. Her keen senses further heightened by the narcotic fog, Damolien quivered at the feel of the hairs on her palms and fingers.

A quiet descended as the attendees one-by-one lapsed into a stupor, some still sobbing quietly, others sighing with satisfaction. With a nod, Damolien sent one of her priestesses to fetch Prince Aeltherin, the master of the house, so that he could partake of the ceremony's final stage. Just as the priestess turned towards the double doors that led from the hall, there was a tumult outside. Raised voices and a shriek caused the priestesses to turn as one towards the doorway. Damolien slipped the serrated sacrificial dagger from her waistband a moment before the doors crashed open.

Prince Aeltherin careened into the room, lurching over the somnolent bodies of his guests. Blood spilled from a cut across his chest and crimson droplets flew from his fingertips onto Damolien's face as the prince tripped over a supine figure and sprawled to the ground. Warriors in silver scale armour and wearing white sashes burst through the doorway, their bared swords in hand. Their captain, his tall helm decorated with threads of gold in the likeness of leaping lions, held a sword dripping with blood. He pulled a sliver of parchment from his belt and allowed it to fall open to show the seal of Phoenix King Bel Shanaar.

'PRINCE AELTHERIN OF Lothern!' the captain called out. 'I am Carathril, captain of the Lothern Guard, and I have a decree for your arrest. Surrender to the judgement of the Phoenix King!'

Like a fish flopping upon a riverbank, Aeltherin dragged himself across the now-comatose elves littering the floor. His eyes looked pleadingly towards Damolien.

'Protect me,' Aeltherin hissed.

'Lay down your weapons and surrender in peace,' said Carathril, his voice calm. 'Give yourselves over to the Phoenix King's mercy.'

Damolien smiled. Her tongue flicked out like a serpent's as she licked the blood of Aeltherin from her lips.

'Mercy is for the weak,' she purred, and leapt lithely across the room.

Shrieking like harridans, the other priestesses followed their mistress, their hands flexed like talons, their fingernails sharpened to long points. Carath-ril leapt back from the assault, the point of Damolien's dagger narrowly avoiding his eye. One of his soldiers leapt forwards, sword arm straight, and lanced his blade into the high priestess. She fell without a sound as her disciples hurled themselves at the guards.

The priestesses were vicious and two of Carathril's elves had fallen to their raking claws, their throats opened up, before the killers were despatched by the swords of their fellows. As Carathril stepped distastefully between the unconscious pleasure-seekers, he sheathed his sword and reached a hand out towards Prince Aeltherin.

'Prince, you are wounded,' Carathril said gently. 'Come with us and we will see that your injuries are tended to properly. Bel Shanaar wishes you no ill, only to help you.'

'Bel Shanaar?' snarled the prince. 'An upstart! Usurper! His judgement is that of the crows feasting on a rotted carcass. I curse him! May Nethu take him and cast him to the blackest chasm!'

With a final effort, Aeltherin, hero of Mardal Vale and protector of Linthuin, pulled himself to his feet. With a contemptuous sneer upon his lips, the prince snatched up one of the bone braziers, spilling its fuming coals onto his robes. The diaphanous cloth ignited like tinder, quickly engulfing the prince in blue flames. The flames caught on the carpet as Aeltherin fell and soon the fire had leapt to the tapestries hanging upon the white walls.

Running nimbly amidst the billowing smoke and deadly flames, Carathril and his company dragged to safety as many of the insensible cultists as they could, but the flames grew too intense and still a dozen elves lay helpless amidst the inferno. As one of his soldiers sought to go back into the hall, Carathril grabbed him by the arm.

'It is too late, Aerenis,' Carathril said. 'The fires will claim them. Perhaps they will now know the peace they were seeking.'

—◄ FOURTEEN ►—

The Phoenix King's Court

MAJESTIC EAGLES CIRCLED overhead, their vast shadows flickering across the rough stone of the mountain pass. These were no ordinary birds of prey; they were great eagles, capable of seizing a mountain lion to devour, each wing twice an elf's height in breadth. Carathril reined his steed to a halt and sat there for a moment, gazing up into the blue skies, watching the birds swoop and climb around the snowy peaks of the Annulii. The jingle of harnesses broke his reverie as his accompanying bodyguard, Aerenis, brought his mount to a stop beside him.

The two elves were clad in blue woollen cloaks to guard against the cold of the high mountains, Carathril's edged with golden thread as a symbol of his rank as captain. Each wore a skirt of light scale mail, split at the waist and hemmed with bleached leather, and wide belts decorated with gems and silver. Long white shields hung on their saddlebags, Carathril's painted with the face of a roaring lion, Aerenis's decorated with a single golden rune – sarathai, the symbol of defiance and unyielding defence. Both of the riders wore the tall helms favoured by elven warriors across all of the kingdoms, Carathril's decorated with the lion crest of his family, Aerenis's plain but for the azure plume of a single feather.

They carried leaf-bladed spears and long recurved bows in their saddle packs, and each carried a quiver of white-fletched arrows. Fortunately, they had not had reason to wield such wargear, for their passage had been uneventful.

Despite the seeming tranquillity of the pass neither elf was relaxed. They

163

were crossing through the highest range of the Annulii, where the magical vortex of Ulthuan drew a ring of mystical energy through the mountains. Here magic infused the air and ground; it pulsed and ebbed around the two elves with a barely felt quiver of power. Carathril and Aerenis, attuned to the mystical breezes and flows of the world, unconsciously sensed its presence and strength.

Other creatures were drawn here also, grown large on the unnatural energy like the eagles, but of an entirely less friendly nature. Griffons, with the bodies of massive lions and the heads and wings of giant birds, made their lairs in the mountaintops, while gigantic serpents and bizarre cockatrices lurked in the caves and gulleys swept by the magical winds.

The lieutenant's eyes glimmered from the darkness of his visor as he looked at Carathril.

'Captain?' Aerenis spoke quietly, shielding his eyes against the sun as he followed his captain's gaze. 'What troubles you?'

'It is nothing,' Carathril assured his second-in-command. 'Just a passing fancy, a whim.'

'How so?' asked Aerenis.

'Nothing disturbs them, the great eagles, that is,' Carathril said quietly. 'They eat, and they breed, and they raise their chicks, far removed from our woes. Such freedom, to soar and to hunt, unfettered by anguish or strife. You know, they say that the mages in Saphery can transform themselves into doves or hawks.'

'You would glide upon the breeze as a bird?' Aerenis sounded dubious. Carathril was not known for poetic flights of fantasy. '"They" say a lot of things about those Sapherians, and they are a strange folk that is for sure. But I doubt that they could transform themselves into a bird. Magic does not work so simply, or so I believe. Anyway, why would you want to be a bird? You are not carefree and capricious. What of your duty to Lothern, and your pledge to the Phoenix King? Do these things not give you solace in these dark times?'

'They do, for sure,' said Carathril, turning to Aerenis with a grim smile. 'And with that in mind, we should be on our way to bear tidings to King Bel Shanaar.'

Carathril and Aerenis rode down the winding path of the pass, their horses delicately picking their way along a narrow path of grey cobbles as the valley narrowed into a defile no more than a stone's throw wide. The light of the morning sun had not yet breached the canyon tops, and they plunged into cool shadow.

Above them, the air danced and shimmered and a faint magical aurora played about the barely visible mountain peaks. Occasionally the distant silhouette of an eagle would pass overhead. The rock here was pale and broken, and tumbles of scree and pebbles littered the crevasse floor, so that the two elves were forced to ride slowly, their steeds picking their way carefully between the patches of debris. Scattered whitethistle bushes clung to life under rocky overhangs, the last few brilliant blooms still opening their petals, the first deep red berries bursting into colour on slender, thorned stems. Here and there thin trickles of meltwater from the higher slopes meandered across the path.

Silence descended, broken only by the occasional sighing of the wind across the rocks. They rode on without word for some time, each elf alone with his thoughts. To Carathril's familiar eye, Aerenis seemed distant, perturbed. He rode with a tenseness the guard captain had not seen before.

'Dark thoughts?' Carathril asked, reining his steed across the path to ride alongside his lieutenant. 'The events at the prince's manse disturb you.'

'They do,' admitted Aerenis.

'I am sorry we could not save them all,' Carathril said, guessing his companion's guilt.

'It is more than that,' Aerenis replied. 'Before you pulled me back, I recognised a face I knew. A friend of my sister, Glarionelle, she was there.'

'The flames were too strong; you could not have rescued her.' Carathril said, leaning across to place a comforting hand on his friend's shoulder.

'That I know,' Aerenis said with a nod. He turned his face skywards and spoke as if to himself. 'Though it grieves me it is not the cause of my pain. Why was she there at all? She always seemed so full of life when I saw her. Her laughter came fast and lasted long. What drove her to seek the solace of the forbidden gods?'

Aerenis closed his eyes for a moment and then turned his gaze on Carathril, his dark blue eyes moist with tears.

'How could someone so fair have fallen to such depths?'

Carathril did not reply immediately, but thought for a moment, choosing his words. There was little comfort he could offer Aerenis, for he could not begin to understand his suffering. Carathril was the last of his family, his forefathers had died fighting the daemons and he was without wife or heir. Since the fall of Aenarion only duty and discipline had filled his heart.

'I do not know,' he said, removing his hand and brushing a lock of silver hair from his face. 'Perhaps it was curiosity that lured her, and then passion that kept her snared. I have heard tales, no more than rumours, that not all go to such gatherings willingly. Some are fooled by the coven leaders, others forcibly taken from their homes, drugged and abducted. Those who might have the answers you seek are now dead, for good or ill. Find solace in the fact that we saved some, even if we could not save them all.'

'You are a strong leader and a wise counsellor,' said Aerenis with a rueful smile, meeting Carathril's gaze. A sombre expression replaced the smile and Aerenis glanced away. 'Perhaps it should have been you and not Aeltherin who was prince.'

Carathril laughed with genuine amusement and Aerenis shot him a shocked glance.

'What do you find so amusing?' demanded Aerenis with a frown.

'The blood of princes does not run in my veins,' Carathril explained. 'My father and grandfather did not draw weapons alongside Aenarion, they were not warrior-princes fit to rule these lands. For all my station, for all my swordcraft and authority, I am content to be a servant, for I am the son of farmers, not fighters. While Aenarion and the princes fought, my family sheltered behind their blades, thankful for the protection of their betters. They were slain in fields of corn, not upon fields of blood. I do not feel ashamed, for no matter how mighty a prince becomes, he still needs water to drink and bread to eat. I believe that life and destiny finds a place for us all, and that is a comfort to me.'

'Well, let us hope life has beds for us in Tor Anroc this night!' joked Aerenis, eager to lighten the mood.

Carathril gave his lieutenant a playful shove.

'And one of those golden-haired Tiranoc maidens to warm it for you, no doubt!'

Their laughter echoed along the defile, sending a flock of birds darting into the darkening skies.

THE AUTUMNAL SUN was low on the horizon as Carathril and Aerenis rode through the long grass of Tiranoc. Their descent from Eagle Pass had been swift and they had made good time over the last two days. Once out of the mountains they had allowed their horses full rein and galloped swiftly over the many miles, glad to be lost in a blur of meadows and woodlands.

In Tiranoc, as in all of the Outer Kingdoms, the weather was colder than that of the inner realms, being more exposed to the sea winds than those lands within the circle of the Annulii. Still, the sun had been warm enough to make the ride pleasant for Aerenis and Carathril, and in each other's company they had passed many miles in constant yet trivial conversation.

Ahead, no more than two leagues distant, the city of Tor Anroc rose from upon a white-stoned hill, bathed in the setting sun. About the foothills of the mount clustered white buildings roofed with red tiles, nestled amongst freshly tilled fields, and thin smoke drifted from the farm chimneys. Orange and pink in the dusk light, the foundations of Tor Anroc towered above the plain, and two great roads curved away to the left and right, spiralling around the hilltop to the summit.

From high walls, the blue and yellow flags of Tiranoc hung limply on their banner poles, barely stirred by the still evening air. Towers and citadels carved from the white rock broke above the curving crenellations of the curtain wall, but these in turn were dwarfed by a central spire that pierced the twilight like a shining needle.

Heartened by the closeness of their destination, Carathril and Aerenis guided their steeds into a gentle trot and forged through the wild meadows;

before long they came upon a roadway, flagged with hexagonal red tiles, which cut straight as an arrow towards the city.

Ahead lay walled orchards, where rows of apple and cherry trees clung stubbornly to their golden and red leaves. The harvest had passed and the fields were quiet, peacefully descending into their winter sleep behind hedges of callow flower and kingwood. They had left behind the livestock pastures in the foothills, where shepherds and goatherds had been moving their flocks down from the higher slopes. Soon the droving would begin and the herds would be brought to the markets of the towns surrounding Tor Anroc, and eventually to the capital itself.

The proximity of the city changed the landscape, just as a great tree might dominate a patch of woods or an island break the flow of a river. Here the farms were protected by high walls of white stone, and stood along the road behind gates of silver and gold.

Further back, away from the turnpike and reached only by meandering trails across the fields, stood tall mansions with many-roofed halls and slender towers. Here the nobles of Tiranoc lived in the summer, away from the city. Now only a handful trailed grey smoke from their chimneys; most of Tiranoc's princes had retired back to their city homes to the warmth of open fires, the excitement of winter balls and the intrigue of court life in Tor Anroc. Their horses' hooves clattering on the road, the riders made good speed and the sun was still loitering in the western sky as they rode into the shadow of the high rock of the city.

A great gatehouse barred the road, a bastion upon a wall twice the height of an elf that arched backwards into the mount itself, all carved from the naked rock. Two pale towers flanked the roadway, devoid of openings except for high arrow slits that looked upon every approach. On each of the flat tower tops stood a bolt thrower, mounted upon an assembly of bars and thin ropes so that that they could be swung with ease in any direction.

The golden gate of Tor Anroc lay open, but passage was barred by two chariots, stood side-by-side. Their fronts were carved in the likenesses of eagles and golden wings swept back to form their sides. Two pale grey horses stood motionless in front of each, bound by black leather harnesses; upon the back of each chariot stood two stern warriors, one with a long silvered spear, the other with bow bent and arrow nocked. The sentries watched cautiously as Carathril and Aerenis slowed their mounts to a walk and approached, hands held out from their sides.

'Who approaches Tor Anroc, city of Tiranoc, seat of the Phoenix King?' the spearman on the left called out.

'Captain Carathril of Lothern, bearing missives for his majesty Bel Shanaar,' Aerenis replied as the two halted a dozen paces from the gateway. 'And I, his aide, Aerenis, lieutenant of Lothern.'

'Come, Firuthal, why such caution?' Carathril called out as he dismounted.

The spearman stepped down from the back of his chariot and approached; his face was grim.

'It is not for me to say, friend,' Firuthal said, extending a hand in greeting, which Carathril gripped firmly. 'The guard is doubled on the orders of Bel Shanaar. We are told to patrol the roads and borders, to keep watch for strangers. It is not my place to question our commands.'

'But I am no stranger,' Carathril said, turning and waving Aerenis to join him. 'I bring important news for the Phoenix King, and then perhaps when your watch is complete we can share a jug of wine and speak more freely.'

Firuthal nodded but still did not smile.

'Perhaps,' the charioteer said. 'My watch finishes at midnight; I shall come to find you at the palace.'

'Be sure that you do,' Carathril said, pulling himself back into his saddle with a jingle of harness.

Firuthal quickly trotted back to his chariot and nimbly leapt aboard. With a word, he urged the horses forwards and guided them past Carathril and Aerenis.

'Go quickly, I will send word to the Phoenix King that you are here,' Firuthal told them as he passed, with a glance over his shoulder towards the rising pinnacle of the palace tower. 'He will be eager to hear your messages.'

With a wave, Carathril rode on under the gateway, Aerenis following closely. Beyond, the road split into two and they took the left fork, climbing the hill along its southern slope. The screech of a bird attracted their attention and they looked up to see a hawk racing towards the tower of Tor Anroc: Firuthal's message. As they rode higher, the plains and meadows were laid out around them, stretching from mountain to coast and ruddy in the swiftly falling twilight. Soon low buildings enclosed the road and they were swallowed up by the outskirts of Tor Anroc.

The clatter of pots and the scent of cooking reminded Carathril that it had been some hours since they had eaten, and he hoped that he could swiftly conclude his business with Bel Shanaar and seek a hostelry.

He noted immediately the quiet and calm of Tiranoc. As they passed under a second gateway, through the curtain wall and into the city proper, he noted the lack of people on the streets. Within the city, the road continued its same swirling ascent, curling tighter and tighter about the hilltop, the buildings growing taller with each loop until they passed over the road itself and the pair found themselves riding through a long, lantern-lit tunnel. For a short while, they rode in twinkling lamplight, the jangling of the horses' harnesses and the clipping of their hooves echoing from walls occasionally pierced with high, thin windows and narrow doors.

Frescoes broke the monotony of the white walls, painted in vivid colours, showing harvest scenes and chariot races, deer hunts and marketplaces. Alleys and side streets broke the all-enclosing shaft, but these too offered no view of the sky. The city was now carved out of the stone of the mount, every room, window and door fashioned by masons from the heartrock of the hill. Having been raised in the open avenues of Lothern, Carathril felt a little unnerved and he only realised how uncomfortable he had started to feel when they finally exited the tunnelway out onto a broad plaza surrounding the palace.

Tiled with the same red stone as the road, the courtyard stretched for three hundred paces and it was filled with market stalls and crowds. The cries of stall keepers hawking their wares mixed with the hubbub of bargaining and general conversation. Dressed in flowing robes of white and wrapped with cowls, scarves and cloaks dyed in the same vibrant hues as the tunnel paintings, the folk of Tor Anroc weaved between the stalls at leisure, crossing each other's paths in a slow, complex dance of commerce. In the centre, the tower of the Phoenix King's palace soared into the darkening skies, golden light glimmering from its narrow windows.

'This way,' Carathril said, pointing to the left. A road was kept clear to the doors of the tower, and here a company of charioteers stood guard, fifty of them arrayed in two lines that flanked the approach to the palace.

NONE ATTEMPTED TO bar their arrival, and a retainer came forwards to take the reins of their horses as they dismounted outside the palace gate. The high wooden doors opened before them, showing a vaulted entrance hall lit by gold lanterns. At the far end, a marble stairway spiralled out of sight. A deep red carpet stretched along the hallway and up the stair, and Carathril self-consciously lifted up the hem of his cloak, covered as it was with the grime of many days' travel.

An elf swathed in a flowing robe of blue embroidered in gold with flowing birds came into view, walking swiftly down the stairs.

'Captain Carathril, I am Palthrain, chamberlain to his majesty,' the elf introduced himself with a deferential nod as they met at the bottom of the stairs. His cheeks were sharply angled and his wide eyes dark under a shock of black hair. His movements were measured and precise as he gestured for them to accompany him.

He spoke as he led them swiftly up the steps, his eyes fixed on Carathril's as he did so.

'His majesty is most keen to hear of events in Lothern,' said Palthrain. 'It has been many weeks since we have heard word from Prince Aeltherin, or any of his court, for that matter.'

Carathril hesitated a moment, casting a glance at Aerenis.

'Rest assured, captain, that whatever you tell the Phoenix King I shall know immediately,' said Palthrain.

'Our news will not bring any joy, I am afraid,' said the captain.

Palthrain took this with no more reaction than an understanding nod, though his eyes never left Carathril's.

They passed several landings during their ascent: wide archways leading from the stairs to the hallways and galleries that made up the greater part of the palace. On the fourth level, Palthrain turned them aside and ushered them through the arch into a wide indoor amphitheatre. Wooden benches, empty for the moment, surrounded a central circular floor. At the far end of the hall, in the gap made by the horseshoe of seats, the Phoenix King sat upon a high-backed golden throne; about him stood several other elves of regal disposition.

As THEY APPROACHED, they saw that Bel Shanaar was deep in conversation, his gaze not once straying to the new arrivals. He was dressed in his formal robes of office: layers of white and gold, delicately embroidered with silver swirls and runes. From his shoulders hung a long cloak of white feathers, which draped over the arms of his throne, hemmed with a band of golden thread and sapphires. His face was faintly lined, the only sign of old age any elf endured, and a golden band studded with a single emerald swept back his pale blond hair, showing a forehead creased with a frown. His eyes were bright blue, and he pursed thin lips as he listened intently to the words of his counsellors.

'His majesty, Bel Shanaar, Phoenix King of Ulthuan,' Palthrain whispered reverentially as they crossed the lacquered wooden floor.

He waved his hand gently towards a short, young elf to the Phoenix King's left, who stood with his arms crossed, his expression one of displeasure.

'Elodhir, son of the Phoenix King, heir to the throne of Tiranoc,' said the chamberlain. The family resemblance was clear.

On the other side stood a tall, broad elf dressed in a long sweep of gilded scale armour, bound with a thick black belt, a sword hanging from his hip.

'Imrik of Caledor, son of Menieth,' Palthrain said. 'He is the grandson of that great mage, Caledor Dragontamer.'

'All know of Imrik,' said Carathril, thrilled to see such a legendary warrior in the flesh.

'The third and last of the Phoenix King's advisors is Thyriol,' said Palthrain. 'He is one of the most powerful mage-princes, ruler of Saphery.'

Thyriol's silver hair hung to his waist in three long tresses bound with strips of black leather. He wore multi-layered robes of white and yellows, which constantly shimmered as he fidgeted from foot to foot.

'Thyriol who presided over the First Council?' asked Aerenis, awe in his voice.

'The same,' said Palthrain. His voice rose in volume. 'Captain Carathril of Lothern, your majesty.'

'Thank you, Palthrain,' Bel Shanaar said, still not looking at them.

The chamberlain bowed and left without further word. Carathril and Aerenis were left standing on their own, listening to the discussion.

'We cannot show mercy,' said Imrik with a shake of his head. 'The people need our strength.'

'But many of them are victims as much as they are perpetrators,' cautioned Bel Shanaar. 'They are brought low by their own terrors, and the priests and priestesses play on their fears and manipulate their woes. I have spoken with some who claim that they did not realise how debased they had become. There is dark magic in this, some more evil purpose that we have not yet seen.'

'Then we must find their ringleaders and question them,' suggested Elodhir. The prince took a pace towards his father. 'We cannot simply allow the cults to spread unchecked. If we should allow that to happen, our armies will be eaten away by this menace, our people consumed by their own desires. No! Though it is perhaps a harsh judgement on some, we must prosecute your rule with firm determination and relentless purpose.'

'That is all well and good, Elodhir, but against whom must we prosecute it?' asked Thyriol. As always, Thyriol's words were quiet and meaningful.

As he carefully considered his next words, the elf lord ran thin fingers through his silver hair. His deep green eyes fixed on each of his fellows in turn. 'We all know its root, yet there is not one of us speaks its name. Nagarythe. There, I have said it and yet the world still turns.'

'Tales and rumour are no basis for policy,' replied Bel Shanaar. 'Perhaps our guests bring tidings that will aid our discussions.'

Carathril stood dumbly for a moment, taken aback by his sudden inclusion in the conversation. The Phoenix King and three princes looked at him with inquiring eyes, and the guard captain cleared his throat and gathered his thoughts.

'I bear ill tidings, your majesty,' Carathril said quietly. 'I and my companion have ridden hither with all haste to bring you the news that Prince Aeltherin of Lothern is dead.'

A scowl crossed the face of Imrik, while the others present bowed their heads for a moment.

'It is our misfortune that the great prince fell from grace, your majesty,' continued Carathril. 'I know not how, but Prince Aeltherin became a member of the pleasure cults. For how long, we do not know. It appears that for some time the prince was in league with the dark priestesses of Atharti, and from his position misdirected our efforts to uncover the plots of the cult. Only a chance happening, a name whispered by a prisoner in her sleep, started us on a sinister path that led to the doors of the prince's manse itself.'

'And how is it that Prince Aeltherin does not stand here to defend himself against these accusations?' asked Elodhir. 'Why is he not in your custody?'

'He took his own life, highness,' explained Carathril. 'I endeavoured to reason with him, implored the prince to put his case before this court, but he was gripped with a madness and would not consent. I know not what caused him to act in this way, and I would not dare to speculate.'

'A ruling prince party to these covens of evil?' muttered Thyriol, turning to the Phoenix King. 'Matters are even graver than we would have dared admit. When news of Aeltherin's fall spreads, fear and suspicion will follow.'

'As is the intent of the architects of this darkness, I have no doubt,' said Bel-Shanaar. 'With the rulers of the realms no longer to be trusted, to whom will our citizens turn? When they cannot trust those with authority, the greater the dread upon the minds of our people, and the more they will flock to the cults.'

'And who shall we trust, if not our own?' asked Imrik, his demeanour dark.

'The defection of Prince Aeltherin casts a cloud over every prince,' said Bel Shanaar with a sorrowful shake of his head. 'If we are to lead the people from the temptations of the cults, we must be united. Yet how can we act together when the doubt remains that those in whom we confide may well be working against our interests?'

'To allow ourselves to be divided would bring about a terrible age of anarchy,' warned Thyriol, who had begun to pace back and forth beside the king's throne. 'The rule of the realms is fragile, and the greatest of our leaders are beyond these shores in the colonies across the ocean.'

'The greatest of our leaders sits upon this throne,' said Elodhir, his eyes narrowing.

'I spoke not of one individual,' said Thyriol, raising a placating hand. 'Yet I would wish it that Prince Malekith were here, if only to settle the matter of his people in Nagarythe. In his absence we are reluctant to prosecute investigations within his realm.'

'Well, Malekith is not here, while we are,' said Bel Shanaar sharply. He paused for a moment, passing a hand across his forehead. 'It matters not. Thyriol, what is the counsel of the mages of Saphery?'

The mage-prince ceased his pacing and turned on his heel to face the Phoenix King. He folded his arms, which disappeared within the sleeves of his voluminous robe, and pursed his lips as if in thought.

'You were correct to speak of dark magic, your majesty,' Thyriol said. 'Our divinations sense a growing weight of evil energy gathering in the vortex. It pools within the Annulii Mountains, drawn here by the practices of the cults. Sacrifice of an unnatural kind is feeding the ill winds. Whether it is the purpose of the cults or simply an unintended result of their ceremonies, we cannot say. This magic is powerful but dangerous, and no mage will wield it.'

'There is no means by which this dark magic can be spent safely?' asked Imrik.

'The vortex dissipates some of its power, and would cleanse the winds in due course were the dark magic not fuelled further,' explained Thyriol. 'Unfortunately, there is nothing we can do to hasten this, other than to stop the cults practising their sorcery.'

'And so we return again to our main question,' sighed Bel Shanaar. 'How might we rid ourselves of these cults?'

'Firm action,' growled Imrik. 'Muster the princes; send out the call to arms. Sweep away this infestation with blade and bow.'

'What you suggest threatens civil war,' Thyriol cautioned.

'To stand idle threatens equal destruction,' said Elodhir.

'And would you lead this army, Imrik?' Bel Shanaar asked, turning in his throne to stare intently at the Caledorian prince.

'I would not,' Imrik replied sharply. 'Caledor yet remains free of this taint, and I seek to maintain the peace that we have.'

'Saphery has no generals of renown,' said Thyriol with a shrug. 'I think that you will find the other realms reluctant to risk open war.'

'Then who shall lead the hunt?' pleaded Elodhir, his exasperation clear in his voice.

'Captain Carathril,' said Bel Shanaar. Carathril started, surprised that his presence was still remembered. He had assumed the princes had heard all that they needed, and had been waiting for leave to be excused.

'How might I be of service, your majesty?' Carathril asked.

'I dispense with your duties to the Guard of Lothern,' said Bel Shanaar, standing up. 'You are loyal and trustworthy, devoted to our people and the continuance of peace and just rule. From this moment, I appoint you as my herald, the mouth of the Phoenix King. You will take word to the princes of the realms. I will ask if there is one amongst them who is willing to prosecute the destruction of these intolerable cults. This peril that besets us is no less than the division of our people and the destruction of our civilisation. We must stand strong, and proud, and drive out these faithless practitioners of deceit. The gratitude of our lands and this office will be heaped upon the prince that delivers us from this darkness.'

— FIFTEEN —

A Bold Oath

CARATHRIL FELT WEARIER than he had ever felt before in his long years. For eighty days since becoming the herald of the Phoenix King, he had ridden across the length and breadth of Ulthuan. He had crossed back and forth over the Annulii Mountains; south to the mountains and hills of Caledor where the Dragonriders lived in tall castles amidst the mountain peaks; north to Chrace, where the warriors wore the pelts of fierce white lions hunted by their own hands.

Carathril had crossed the Sea of Dusk and the Sea of Dreams to Saphery, where mages ruled and the fields were tilled by enchanted ploughs and lanterns of ghostfire glittered in the towns. He had taken ship to Avelorn, the beautiful forests of the Everqueen, though he had not met the ceremonial wife of the Phoenix King on his visits, only her stern guard of handmaidens and the priestesses of Isha. In Yvresse, he had sailed amongst the eastern islands and camped under the wooded boughs of the Athel Yvrain. He had become accustomed to the long rides and nights spent under the stars or in strange beds, driven on by his duty to the Phoenix King.

He had borne the tidings of Bel Shanaar to the princes, and as winter closed her chill grip upon the Outer Kingdoms, Carathril had reluctantly returned with their replies: none was willing to lead the soldiery of Ulthuan against the pleasure cults.

Now he rested, as he had done for the past seven days, sitting upon one of the benches in the audience chamber of the palace, lulled half-asleep by the droning of the princes' voices below. For weeks they had arrived and left, seeking counsel from Bel Shanaar and each other, bringing tidings, mostly grim, of events across the realms of Ulthuan.

As far as Carathril could tell, the conflict with the cults of pleasure and excess was growing in intensity. From his own experience in Lothern he knew that it seemed that another sect would emerge even as one was destroyed. It was becoming evident that for some time now, many years likely, the cults had been prospering outside of the cities and large towns. Distant farms and isolated hunting lodges had become meeting places for those drawn to the forbidden rituals of these cults, and here thriving communities had established themselves. Cult members had spread far and wide, and there was no telling how many figures of authority, how many nobles and commanders were now in their grip. Carathril had wanted to believe that the insurgence of dark practices and loathsome ceremonies had been halted, but each revelation dashed his hopes a little further.

The fundamental problem was that each kingdom was confident in its own abilities to combat the emerging fanaticism of the cults, but was suspicious of its neighbours. Even though united under the rule of the Phoenix King, each realm was a sovereign territory of its princes, ruled over in the Phoenix King's name.

The princes had a great amount for which to be worried, and each had a vested interest in protecting the fortunes of his kingdom, for all the ruling families were powerful, militarily, politically and economically. They were descended from the bravest and strongest of Aenarion's captains, who had wielded the magical weapons of Caledor Dragontamer against the daemon hosts. They had a bloodright to rule their lands, and each jealously guarded his domains with the ferocity of a she-lion protecting her young.

No prince could agree to allow another to control the armies of their house, nor could they comfortably consent to having the troops of another realm stationed in their lands. To Carathril's simple mind it seemed as if they ever postured and manoeuvred for aid whilst never offering their own. Once enamoured of these lofty rulers, Carathril was quickly tiring of their political ways. In short, Carathril realised, the majority of the princes – both those that ruled over a realm and those that served them – considered the wider purging of the cults to be somebody else's problem.

It seemed as if a few of the princes felt the same as the herald. Of all the princes, Carathril considered Imrik to be closest to the herald in outlook and opinion. He was plain-speaking, thought of as gruff, even rude, by some of his peers, and feared inaction more than anything.

As the grandson of the great Caledor Dragontamer, he was considered the noblest of all the princes, and this stirred jealousy in the hearts of others. They all feared the power of the kingdom of Caledor, for it was from here the dragon knights hailed, a force greater than any mustered by other realms. As was the way of powerful individuals, many of the princes were loath to surrender control of their forces to another, and for his part

Imrik was unwilling to shoulder the responsibilities he thought were being shirked by the other princes.

Carathril missed Lothern dearly. He had passed through his home city some fifty days earlier to bear news to Prince Haradrin, now ruler of the realm of Eataine. What he had seen, the suspicion and fear in the eyes of his people, made Carathril long to be dispensed from the Phoenix King's service so that he might return and aid his folk. Yet it was not to be, for Bel Shanaar ever sought more diplomacy with the princes, and Carathril was required to be on hand at short notice.

Carathril felt alone amongst these high-ranking personages, for Aerenis had left for Lothern only a few days after they had first arrived. Those few elves that Carathril knew in Tor Anroc were cordial enough, but it quickly became evident that his position as herald not only denied him much time for personal matters and socialising, but also made those around him wary of speaking their mind. They persistently enquired of delicate matters from Carathril, seeking confirmation of rumours and nuggets of information from the Phoenix King's court, and Carathril was reluctant to confide what little he really knew for fear of being seen as a gossip, unworthy of the trust bestowed upon him.

The more Carathril learned of the secretive nature of the cults – of how many of the members led plain and normal lives on the surface but performed hedonistic and despicable acts in private – the more he became distrustful. Eventually, he had decided to forego his rare excursions to the rest of the city and now stayed solely within the confines of the palace when he was in Tor Anroc.

A STIR AMONGST the court roused Carathril as two more joined their number. He recognised them immediately as Prince Finudel, ruler of Ellyrion and his sister, Princess Athielle. They had arrived only two days ago and caused much commotion with promises of cavalry and spearmen for the cause. Carathril leaned forwards, his chin cupped in his hand, and listened to what was being said.

'It matters not if the horsemasters of Ellyrion stand ready to ride forth,' Prince Bathinair of Yvresse was saying. 'Who are they to ride forth against, my dear Finudel? You can hardly lead a cavalry charge through every village and town in Ulthuan.'

'Perhaps you seek to upset the harmony between the realms for your own ends,' added Caladryan, another of Yvresse's nobility. 'It is no secret that of late the fortunes of Ellyrion have waned. War suits those with little to lose, and it costs those who have the means. Our endeavours across the oceans bring us wealth and goods from the colonies; perhaps Ellyrion is jealous of that.'

Finudel opened his mouth to speak, his anger etched in creases across his brow, but Athielle quickly laid a hand on her brother's arm to still him.

'It is true that we have perhaps not prospered as much as some,' the Ellyrian princess said quietly. 'In part that is because we of the Inner Kingdoms must pay the taxes of Lothern to pass our fleets into the Great Ocean. If not for those taxes, I suspect that the Outer Kingdoms would perhaps have less of a monopoly of trade.'

'We cannot be held to account for the quirks of geography,' sneered Prince Langarel, one of Haradrin's kin from Lothern. 'The sea gates must be maintained, and our war fleet stands ever ready for the benefit of all. It is fitting, then, that all should contribute to the cost of maintaining these defences.'

'And against whom do you defend us?' growled Finudel. 'Men? Hut-dwelling savages who can barely cross a river, and an ocean divides us from them. The dwarfs? They are content to dig in the mountains and sit in their caves. The slaves of the Old Ones? Their cities lie in ruins, their civilisation swallowed by the hot jungles. Your fleet is not required, a token of the hubris of Lothern kept gilded by the labours of the other realms.'

'Must every old slight and rankle be dredged up before me every day?' demanded Bel Shanaar, his voice cutting sharply through the raised voices of the princes. 'There is nothing to be gained from this bickering, and everything to be lost. While we argue over the spoils of our growing colonies, our cities here at hand are being devoured by decadence and forbidden pursuits. Would you have us abandon our roots and settle in the newly grown branches of our realm? The world has riches enough for us all, if we could set aside these incessant arguments.'

'The power of the cults grows, that much is clear,' said Thyriol, from where he sat upon one of the ring of innermost benches surrounding the hall. All turned to the mage in expectation.

'The vortex holds the winds of magic in check for the moment, but dark magic is gathering in the mountains. Strange creatures have been seen in the highest peaks, unnatural things spawned from the power of Chaos. Not all things of darkness were purged by the blade of Aenarion and the vortex of Caledor. Hybrid monsters of flesh, mutant and depraved, dwell still in the wilderness. The dark magic feeds them, emboldens them, makes them stronger and cannier. Even now, the passes become ever more dangerous to travel. In the winter when the hunters and soldiers cannot keep these growing numbers of beasts at bay, what then? Will we have manticores and hydras descend into the lowlands to attack farms and destroy villages? If we allow the cults to grow unchecked, perhaps even the vortex itself will fail and once more plunge the world into an age of darkness and daemons. Is there one here with the will to prevent that?'

The assembled princes stood in silence, eyeing each other, avoiding the gaze of the Phoenix King.

'There is one perhaps that has the will,' a voice called out, echoing along the audience chamber from the doorway. Its timbre was firm and deep, filled with authority.

A ripple of gasps and whispers spread through the court as the newcomer strode purposefully across the lacquered floor, the fall of his riding boots sounding like the thunder of war drums. He was dressed in a long skirt of golden mail and his chest was covered with a gold breastplate etched with the design of a dragon, coiled and ready to attack. He wore a cloak of shadow-black across his shoulders, held with a clasp adorned with a black gem set into a golden rose. Under one arm he carried a tall war helm, fixed with a strange circlet of dark grey metal that had jutting, thorn-like spines. A complex headband of golden threads swept back raven hair that fell about his shoulders in twisted plaits tied with rings of rune-etched bone. His eyes were piercing, dark, as he stared at the nervous princes and courtiers. He radiated power, his energy and vigour surrounding him as surely as light glows from a lantern.

The princes parted before the newcomer like waves before a ship's prow, treading and stumbling upon robes and cloaks in their eagerness to back away. A few bowed stiffly or nodded heads in unthinking deference as he swept past to stand in front of the Phoenix King, his left hand, gloved in supple black leather, resting on the golden pommel of a sword hanging in an ebon scabbard at his waist.

'Prince Malekith,' said Bel Shanaar evenly, stroking his bottom lip with a slender finger. 'Had I known of your coming I would have arranged suitable welcome.'

'Such ceremony is unnecessary, your majesty,' replied Malekith, his tone of voice warm, his manner as smooth as velvet. 'I thought it prudent to arrive unannounced, lest our enemies be warned of my return.'

'Our enemies?' said Bel Shanaar, turning a hawkish look upon the prince.

'Even across the oceans, as I fought against vile beasts and brutal orcs, I heard of the woes that beset our home,' Malekith explained. He paused and turned to face the princes and their counsellors. 'Alongside the dwarfs, beside their kings, I and my companions fought to keep our new lands safe. Friends I had that gave their lives protecting the colonies, and I would not have their deaths be in vain, that our cities and our island here would fall to ruin even as we raise sparkling towers and mighty fortresses across the length and breadth of the world.'

'And so you have returned to us in our hour of need, Malekith?' said Imrik haughtily, stepping in front of Malekith with his arms crossed defensively.

'You must also have heard that which vexes us most,' said Thyriol softly, standing up and pacing towards the prince of Nagarythe, stepping between Malekith and Imrik. 'We would wish to prosecute our war against these insidious evils across all of Ulthuan. *All* of Ulthuan.'

'That is why I have returned,' replied Malekith, meeting the mage's keen gaze with his own piercing stare. 'Nagarythe is gripped by this torment no less than other lands; more I have heard on occasion. We are one island, one realm under the rule of the Phoenix King, and Nagarythe will not be party to insurrection, nor shall we tolerate black magics and forbidden rituals.'

'You are our greatest general, our most sound strategist, Prince Malekith,' said Finudel, his voice hesitant with hope. 'If it pleases all present, would you take up the banner of the Phoenix King and lead the fight against these miserable wretches?'

'In you runs the noblest blood of all princes,' gushed Bathinair, one of the Yvressian princes present. 'As you fought the darkness alongside your father, you could again bring the light back to Ulthuan!'

'Eataine would stand by you,' promised Haradrin with a clenched fist held to his chest.

A chorus of pleading and thanks bubbled up from the assembled nobles, but fell silent the moment Malekith raised a hand to still them. The Naggarothi prince turned his head and looked at Bel Shanaar, saying nothing. The Phoenix King sat in thought, his lips pursed, steepling his slender fingers beneath his chin. Bel Shanaar then looked at Imrik's stern expression, an eyebrow raised in question upon the Phoenix King's face.

'If it is the will of the Phoenix King and this court, then Caledor will not oppose Malekith,' Imrik said slowly, before turning away and stalking from the room.

An almost imperceptible expression of relief softened the furrows in Bel Shanaar's frown, and he sat back and gave a perfunctory nod towards the prince of Nagarythe.

'As it pleases this court, so shall I act,' declared Malekith. 'A company of my finest warriors, fighters hardened by war across the seas one-and-all, rides even now to Anlec to announce my return. The army of Nagarythe shall be roused, and no hall nor cave nor cellar shall avoid our gaze. The raven heralds shall ride forth again, and all rumour shall come to our ears so that our foe might not hide. With mercy we shall temper our vengeance, for it is not our desire to slay needlessly those who are simply misguided. By trunk and root we shall tear free this tree of rotten fruit that feeds upon our fair nation, and we shall set free those trapped beneath its dark bower. No matter how high that tree reaches, no matter how powerful or prominent its leaders are, they shall not escape justice.'

─✦ SIXTEEN ✦─

A Journey to Darkness

NORTHWARDS MARCHED THE caravan of Malekith. At their head, the prince led the column from atop an immense black steed bridled with silver and black leather. Behind him rode six hundred knights of Nagarythe, their silver and black pennants snapping in the chill autumn air. With them, they had brought news that already many cultists had surrendered to Malekith's soldiers, throwing themselves upon the mercy of the prince. The people of Nagarythe, long cowed by the cultists who had held sway in Malekith's absence, had come forth from their homes in celebration. Many of Nagarythe's citizens had been forced into serving the cults against their will, enslaved with threats of sacrifice and violence. As if unshackled from a great yoke, they had thrown off the tyranny of the dark priests and priestesses and taken to the streets to proclaim the victorious return of their rightful ruler.

Not only fair wishes from Bel Shanaar accompanied Malekith on his march north; three hundred chariots of Tiranoc went with him as a symbol of the Phoenix King's support. More horsemen had recently arrived from Ellyrion, despatched on the orders of Finudel. Seven hundred reaver knights had crossed the Annulii Mountains along the Unicorn Pass, the Eyin Uirithas, and met the caravan some one hundred leagues from Anlec. In their wake came ten thousand spearmen, assembled from across Eataine and Yvresse; even now they crossed the Inner Sea to join the host that marched against the dark cultists.

With them came a long baggage train, as any army on the march needed an unending tide of supplies to keep it on the move. The wagons of Tor

Anroc were as larger versions of their sleek chariots, each pulled by four high-stepping steeds, the backs of the wains covered with gaily covered awnings and hung with pennants and flags of the kingdom. A hundred in all followed in the army's wake, filled with cooks and fletchers, smiths and ostlers, bakers and armourers and all the gear of their trades. Priests and priestesses came also, of Asuryan and Isha, and astromancers of Lileath, diviners of Kourdanrin and other such soothsayers, chroniclers and clerics as Bel Shanaar had seen fit to grant the expedition.

Though the elves of Tiranoc and Ellyrion were glad of such mystical companions, the Naggarothi, and in particular Malekith, paid them little heed and avoided their gatherings.

Amongst the host rode Carathril, still under oath as Bel Shanaar's herald, to act for the Phoenix King in this endeavour. He felt as much relief and anticipation as the princes, and riding alongside the prince of Nagarythe filled him with a confidence he had never before felt.

ONE BRIGHT MORNING they came upon a stone bridge that soared elegantly across a frothing river. This was the Naganath, which spilled straight from the mountains and across to the sea in a sweeping torrent. Beyond its foaming waters lay Nagarythe.

Malekith's gaze was distant, directed even further north, towards Anlec. His face betrayed no emotion, yet inside his thoughts were mixed. For almost his entire life he had sworn never to set foot here again until he was ready to take his rightful place. Excitement bubbled up inside him at the prospect of the events he saw unfolding in his head. Yet they were tinged with sadness, and not a little regret. Just before they crossed the bridge, Malekith signalled the column to halt and swung down from his saddle. Sensing Carathril's gaze upon him, Malekith turned to the herald and smiled.

'It has been more than thirteen hundred years since I last trod upon those lands,' Malekith said, his voice quiet. 'It has been more than one-and-a-half thousand since I took up the crown of Nagarythe, under the shadow of my father's sacrifice. Of that time, I have spent more of my life upon foreign soil than I have my homeland.'

'It must feel good to return,' said Carathril.

'Yes, it does feel good,' said Malekith with a nod. He nodded even more firmly and then grinned. Then he broke into a laugh and his eyes glittered. 'Very good!'

Carathril laughed with him, realising how much of an understatement he had uttered. Malekith's mood swiftly turned sombre though, and once again he cast his gaze northwards.

'I have been remiss in my duties as ruler,' Malekith said. 'It is in my absence that these depraved and reckless cults have flourished. From my lands, from the realm forged from the blood of my father, has grown a dark canker that poisons the heart of Ulthuan. That is a shame I cannot bear, and I will expunge it.'

'You cannot be blamed for the weaknesses and corruptions of others,' Carathril said with a shake of his head. 'The guilt for this malaise is not yours.'

'Not mine alone, I accept that,' replied Malekith. 'Yet we all bear some responsibility for this degeneration of authority and tradition, and I bear more than most.'

The prince swung himself back upon his steed and turned to face the halted column. His voice rang loud and crisp in the morning air.

'Remember that these are the sovereign lands of Nagarythe,' he cried. 'It is here that Aenarion the Defender built Anlec, and from here that he rode forth to battle the daemons. I do not return to lead an invasion. We do not come here as conquerors. We are liberators. We are here to free this realm from the dark and terrible grip of its depression and immorality. We are here to bring light where darkness has settled. None shall be slain who offers repentance for his misdeeds. None shall be punished who turns from his wayward path to rejoin the side of the righteous. Fight first with your hearts before your swords. Pity those that stand against us, but do not fear them, and do not hate them. It is fear and hatred that has laid them so low, so we shall bring them hope and we shall bring them salvation.'

Malekith drew his sword and held it aloft; its rune-etched blade glimmered with blue fire. His voice rose to a triumphant shout.

'The blood of our forefathers stains this earth! This is Nagarythe and she bows to no darkness! I am prince here, these are my lands! I am Malekith!'

A great roar erupted from the assembled army, from the throats of both Naggarothi and elves of other realms. Malekith sheathed his sword and snatched the standard from the hand of his aide. Wheeling his steed with a flourish, Malekith urged on his mount and galloped across the bridge, the silver and black banner of Nagarythe fluttering above him. Still chanting, the column surged after him.

As THE COMPANY made their way through Nagarythe, the truth of the situation became ever clearer. In the first village they entered, cheering crowds cast petals and blossoms, and a choir of children sang praises to the soldiers accompanied by flutes and harps. The village elder, a venerable elf with silver hair whose tresses reached her waist, presented Malekith with a garland of mountain laurel, and showered thanks upon Carathril and the others as they passed.

Dark-haired maidens presented the marching warriors with bundles of flowers, and a few leapt upon the chariots to hug and kiss the crews. Not even on the carnival days of Isha had Carathril known such celebration, and his heart soared to see the joy in the eyes of the villagers.

As they reached the central square, the mood changed. Here the white-washed buildings were stained with soot, their doors and windows charred. In the centre of the plaza huddled a group of some thirty elves, surrounded by villagers with knives and spears at the ready.

The black dresses and robes of the captives were tattered and bloody, and many bore grazes and bruises. A few bore more severe injuries, cradling broken arms and bandaged cuts. Some had crudely shaven heads, while others had runes of Asuryan daubed with white dye on their exposed flesh.

A handful of cultists regarded the soldiers with defiant and sullen eyes, their faces twisted with sneers; most had vacant gazes of shock, and a few looked down in shame and buried the heads in their hands, weeping. Pity, Malekith had said, and it was pity that filled the prince as he looked upon these poor wretches. Malekith signalled for Carathril to stop, and waved on the rest of the troop. The ruler of these desperate people sat upon his majestic steed and looked down at the prisoners, his face unmoving.

'Traitor!' shouted one of the cultists, a young elf clad only in a loincloth, his bare flesh cut with dozens of small incisions; self-made rather than inflicted by his captors. 'Khaine shall not forgive such treachery!'

Malekith did not react but simply continued to stare at the cultists, though from the corner of his eye he saw Carathril flinch at the mention of the Lord of Murder.

'Ereth Khial will devour you, son of Aenarion!' spat another degenerate, an old man whose black and dark blue robes were torn to shreds.

'Silence!' said Carathril, drawing his sword and urging his steed forwards. The cultists shrank back, cowed by his anger. 'We do not openly speak these names for a reason. That you consort with such gods is proof of your guilt. Save your hexes and curses!'

A lissom elf, her hair waxed into long spines and dyed orange, stood and bared herself to the company with a lewd smile. Scenes of licentious acts were painted in blue dye across her breasts, stomach and thighs.

'Perhaps Atharti's blessings would please you more, my lord,' she said, running a hand over her pale skin. 'There are those here who can attend to your pleasure, whatever your desires may be.'

Malekith waved Carathril back and dismounted. He stood in front of the consort of Atharti. Though she was attractive, it was disgust rather than ardour that Malekith felt. Dark magic polluted her comely body. Hiding his feelings, the prince calmly took off his cloak and wrapped it around her, covering her naked form.

'There is no pleasure in the degradation of others,' Malekith said, stroking the girl's hair. 'It is love not lust that we bring with us. I see fear in your eyes, and that I understand. It is the retribution of mortals not gods that fills you with dread. And I say to this, do not be afraid. We are not here as executioners. We have not come to seek vengeance in blood. Whatever your crimes, you shall be treated fairly and with dignity. We do not judge you for your doubts and your desperation. Your weakness is regrettable but no cause for punishment. Some, I have no doubt, have trodden upon this path willingly and with malice, and in time justice will find them. But even for them, there is mercy and forgiveness. Healers shall attend to your ills, both physical and spiritual. We shall bring forth the darkness that lingers within you, and free you from its grip. In time, you will know peace and harmony once more.'

Malekith ordered that the villagers bring fresh clothes for the captives, and food and water. While the prince marshalled this activity himself, he sent the greater part of the column onwards towards Anlec. Once fed and clothed, the cultists were taken under escort and Malekith resumed the march.

FROM THE VILLAGE, the road turned north-east, towards the mountains, and rose steadily for several miles before cutting into thick woodland. Tall pines formed a wall on either side of the column, and as the day wore on the caravan was swathed with long shadows. No sound could be heard; an eerie quiet stilled all noise from bird and mammal.

'This is a queer land,' Carathril remarked to himself. One of the knights of Anlec heard him and heeled his horse over beside the herald.

'This is Athel Sarui,' the knight told him. 'Forest of Silence' the name meant, but Carathril had not heard of this place before.

'I see why it is so named,' said Carathril. 'Are you from this land?'

'No,' the knight replied quickly, taken aback by Carathril's question. 'No living souls save for the trees live here. It is said that beyond the forest, at the feet of the mountains, there is a great cave. It is one of the Adir Cynath, a gate to Mirai, the underworld. To wander close to the mountains is to risk the gaze of Ereth Khial, and to be taken into her darkness by the rephallim.'

Carathril shuddered at the mention of these forbidding names, of the dark goddess of the dead and her bodiless servants. To hear them spoken openly was unheard of in Lothern, for the cytharai, as the deeper gods were known, were not openly worshipped by right-thinking folk. The cults had embraced the dark promises of these thirsting entities, and by that act even now plunged Ulthuan into turmoil. The knight recognised Carathril's expression of concern.

'Fear not, captain,' he said calmly, and produced a silver amulet from beneath his mail shirt. It was shaped in the symbol of yenlui, the rune of balance, and studded with three shining diamonds. 'This was a gift from a friend in Saphery, it will protect us. Those of us who dwell in the north must oft speak these distasteful names, for many of the darkest shrines to the dwellers beneath lie in our lands.'

'And how is it that the heartland of Aenarion allows such practices?' asked Carathril.

'The cytharai must be appeased, from time to time,' said the knight. 'One does not ignore the gods without peril, especially those of vile and short temper. And does not that blackest of places, the shrine to the God of Murder, lie beyond our northern coast? Once it was that a single priest or priestess would tend the shrines of the nightly lords and ladies. He or she would entreat them to still their vengeance, and placate them with sacrifices.'

The knight cast his gaze downwards.

'On occasion, in desperate times, one must visit these dire abodes, for there are some things beyond even the knowledge of Asuryan and Isha. Even Aenarion sought their wisdom, and that is not to be undertaken lightly. Many are the wards and blessings the priests can bestow upon those who would supplicate themselves before the cytharai.'

'Yet how did worship of gods so abhorrent spread so widely?' said Carathril.

'In indolence or sorrow, more of our people turned to the cytharai to ease their minds, to seek answers to questions perhaps best not asked,' the knight told him. 'Of loved ones long dead; of secrets lost in time; of joys forgotten with the coming of Chaos. Fortified and gratified by their indulgences, these misguided souls opened up the dark mysteries and learned their ways. They perverted the rituals of appeasement and turned them into ceremonies of praise. These dark acts they took with them, ever in secret, and founded new shrines in other lands. In the shadows, beyond the sight of right-minded folk, they practised their evils, perfecting them, luring others into their depravity. For more than five hundred years they have spread across Ulthuan, insinuating themselves into homes and hostels, from the lowliest to the highest. Be aware, the task we now undertake will be neither swift nor easy.'

'And you, how did you not become ensnared or enslaved by these pernicious shrine-folk?' asked Carathril.

The knight tucked his talisman back beneath his shirt and then pulled back his long black hair from the nape of his neck. A scar was there, etched into his skin, in the shape of a curved dagger.

'Who said that I did not?' the knight said. 'For many years I laboured with the blades of Khaine, a holy executioner in Anlec. My father had raised me within the cult, and I knew no different. It was only when he asked me to cut out the heart of my sister that I slew him and fled with her. We travelled across the sea to escape those that hunted us, and in time I met with the prince and told him of the travails of our people. I am Maranith, captain of Nagarythe under oath to Malekith, and it was I he sent to rouse this army ready for his return. I cannot hope to expunge the stain upon my spirit, but if my labours free others from its trap, I shall die content.'

'And I am proud to labour beside you,' said Carathril, extending a hand. The knight gripped it firmly in his own gauntleted fist and shook it firmly.

'What we have started here will change Ulthuan forever, Carathril,' Maranith said. 'Fight with the prince, and history will remember you for eternity.'

CARATHRIL GAVE A nod and rode away. Filled with curiosity, he dropped down the column and pulled his horse to a walk beside the prisoners, observing them. The girl who had so brazenly offered herself to him now seemed demure, wrapped in white linen, her blonde hair washed and plaited, her skin cleansed of its obscene marks. She cast coy glances occasionally at Carathril, the wildness that had filled her eyes before now utterly gone. Carathril smiled at her and waved for her to approach. He dismounted and led his horse as she stepped up beside him.

'Tell me your name,' said Carathril.

'I am Drutheira,' she replied hesitantly.

'I am Carathril, from Lothern,' the herald told her. 'It is uncommon for the maidens of Nagarythe to have straw hair such as yours.'

'I am not from Nagarythe, my lord,' Drutheira said.

'There is no need to call me lord; I am no prince, merely a captain of the guard. You may call me Carathril, or captain, as you please. How come you to be here, then?'

'I am from Ellyrion, captain,' she told him. 'A while ago, twenty years or more, my brother and I were running the herd in the foothills of the mountains. Riders came, clad in black cloaks, and we thought that they had come for the horses. Galdarin, my brother, tried to fight them, but he was slain. They left the horses, but took me. They bore me here, where they had built a temple to Atharti.'

'Twenty years?' gasped Carathril. 'It must have been hideous, enslaved to such diabolic rites.'

'At first I was terrified,' admitted Drutheira. 'They beat me and whipped me, until I could no longer feel pain, I no longer cried. I cared not what happened to me. Then they brought me calmleaf and black lotus, and we feasted and dined in honour of Atharti. I learned the skills of the consort, and daily gave myself to the pleasures of Atharti. When Helreon died, I succeeded her as priestess and learned the inner mysteries of our goddess.'

Her voice had become strident and defiant, but suddenly she paused. Without warning, she began to sob.

'Oh, captain, today is the first day in twenty years I have seen clearly what I have become,' she moaned. 'Other girls I ordered brought to the shrine, and enslaved them as I was enslaved. What terrible things I have seen; have witnessed with joy in my heart. I was lost in the bliss of Atharti, never looking upon those vile acts in the way I see them now. What have I done?'

Carathril hushed her and laid a comforting hand upon her shoulder. She did not look up at him, but instead hung her head and continued to cry. He searched for the words to ease her, but could find none. He was not gifted with a lyric nature, and part of him still reviled what she had become. To give herself, body and spirit, so wholly to the forbidden gods was an idea he found utterly abhorrent. Unable to marry the loathing he felt with the pitiful sight of her so distraught, he chose to remain silent.

They walked thus for some time, until her crying ceased. He turned to see her gazing at him, her face streaked with tears, her eyes shot with red.

'What is to become of me?' she asked.

'As Prince Malekith promised, you will not be harmed,' Carathril assured her. 'In all likelihood, when you are fully cured of this affliction you can return to Ellyrion. I am sure your family think you dead, and would be overjoyed to find you alive and well.'

She said nothing but simply nodded.

'Tell me of Ellyrion,' Carathril said, uneasy with the prospect of more silence between them. He has visited many realms as herald, but wished to hear how Drutheira remembered her land of birth.

'It is fairest in the evening, as the sun sinks upon the mountains and bathes the meadows in gold,' Drutheira told him. 'Pastures of grass as high as your waist, as green as emeralds, stretch out as far as one can see. White horses run wild through the foothills, calling to our herds and leading them astray. We listen to their voices on the breeze; hear them taunting their cousins who are caught beneath bridle and saddle.'

'Does that not make you sad?' asked Carathril. 'Would you not have all horses run free like their wild cousins?'

She laughed, a startlingly beautiful sound to Carathril's ears.

'You are silly, captain,' Drutheira said. 'The steeds of Ellyrion are proud of our friendship, and call their wild cousins stupid and backwards. They love the jangle of harness and the glitter of silver tack. You should see them prance and hear them laugh when they ride forth. They have lush grass to eat and warm stables at night, and call upon their cousins to join them when the winter rains come.'

Carathril was about to say more when he heard his name called from ahead.

'Forgive me, it appears that I am needed,' he said with a rueful smile. 'I would like to talk to you again soon.'

'And I, you,' Drutheira replied. 'Perhaps you could tell me of Lothern.'

'I shall,' he promised, and swung himself upon his horse. He was about to flick the reins and ride ahead when a thought struck him. 'Tell me, Drutheira of Ellyrion, what does my horse think of me?'

She frowned slightly and then smiled. Laying a hand upon the horse's cheek, she leaned close and whispered into his ear. She giggled as the horse neighed and whinnied.

'What?' said Carathril petulantly. 'What did he say?'

'He is very happy to bear you,' Drutheira informed him. 'You have ridden far together, and you look after him well.'

'What is so funny?'

'He said that for all the riding you have done, you have grown to be a heavier not lighter burden to bear with each trip. He thinks you have become a little plump on grain.'

Carathril gave an indignant snort, before laughing himself.

'The palaces of princes would never live to see a herald of the Phoenix King go hungry,' he said. 'Perhaps I need to learn how to say no.'

With a word, he encouraged his steed forwards, breaking into a swift trot. Behind him, Drutheira's smile went unseen; it was a sly expression, filled with a cunning amusement. She returned to the other prisoners and they began to whisper amongst themselves.

As CARATHRIL NEARED the head of the column, Prince Malekith was deep in conversation with one of the raven heralds. The newcomer was mounted upon a jet-black steed and upon his shoulders he wore a long cloak made of dark feathers. He was hooded, revealing only glimpses of his pale, drawn face. The rider held a long-hafted spear, and he had a compact bow tied amongst his saddlebags next to a quiver of black-fletched arrows. The prince of Nagarythe turned to Carathril.

'May I present Captain Carathril of Lothern, herald of Bel Shanaar,' said Malekith. 'This is Elthyrior, one of the raven heralds of Nagarythe.'

'I am honoured,' said Carathril, receiving a silent nod from Elthyrior as his only reply.

'Very well,' said the prince to the raven herald. 'Call your brethren to Anir Atruth, and watch for spies and agents of the cults. We shall meet you there in three days, and then march upon Ealith.'

Malekith commanded his horse into a trot and Carathril did likewise.

'You have never met one of Elthyrior's order before?' asked the prince. 'Not on all your long travels?'

'I know little of the heralds of the northlands,' said Carathril. 'I cannot say what is fact and what is myth, but all I hear is sinister.'

Malekith laughed.

'There is something of a darkness about them, I would agree,' said Malekith. 'Few elves ever meet one of their kind: ever solitary figures only seen on lonely moors and wild mountain passes, and the stories of such encounters are whispered around campfires, and in hushed tones in the wine halls.'

'Where do they come from?' asked Carathril.

'From Nagarythe,' said the prince. 'While we laud the exploits of the greatest heroes of the past, the raven heralds are content to be forgotten. It was my father who founded their company, when the lands were beset by hosts of daemons. Formed of pure magic, the daemons of Chaos could arrive and attack at will, and it was the raven heralds who watched for their appearance and took swift word to the army of Aenarion.'

'And they are loyal to you?' said Carathril.

'They are loyal to Nagarythe,' said Malekith. 'For the moment I am content that their cause and ours are the same. Elthyrior brings grave news from ahead. It seems that we have sparked our foes into action. Upon word of our crossing into Nagarythe, a great many cultists quit Anlec and have marched south. They have made their lair in Ealith, south of Anlec. It is an old fortress, one of the ancient gatekeeps built by my father to protect the road we now travel. We cannot reach Anlec without confronting them.'

'There will be a battle?' said Carathril.

'The raven heralds will act as our outriders, and warn of any ambush ahead,' Malekith said, ignoring the obvious question. 'There are none with eyes as keen as the northern riders, and our enemies will not mark their passing. Our foe will not surrender Ealith meekly back to my rule. Send word to the other captains to gather at my tent tonight, for we must make plans for battle.'

Malekith noticed Carathril frown.

'It is right that we be troubled,' the prince said. 'We should not seek this confrontation gladly, but we must prosecute our cause willingly.'

'I am willing,' Carathril assured him. 'I would cast out this blackness with my own life, were that possible.'

'Be not too hasty to surrender life,' Malekith warned. 'It is not through death but through life that we prevail. I have defended this isle for more than a thousand years, and I have seen many of my comrades sell their lives for no gain while those that survive go on to victory and prosperity. I was raised in Anlec, even as daemons slaughtered and corrupted all about me. My first memories are of spear, sword and shield. My first words were war and death. I was anointed with bloodshed and grew up beneath the Sword of Khaine, and I have no doubt that its shadow lies upon me still. Perhaps it is true that my father's line is cursed, and that war will haunt us for eternity.'

'I cannot imagine what it was like to live in those times,' said Carathril. 'The fear, the sacrifice, the pain of so many lost. I must admit, I offer thanks to the gods that it has been so, and ask that I must never endure what you and others endured.'

'You are wise to do so,' said Malekith. 'One does not seek war for its own end, for it leaves nothing but ashes and graves. However, always remember that though civilisation is built upon foundations of peace, it is only protected through the efforts of war. There are forces and creatures that would see us crushed, driven from the face of the world and dragged into an eternity of darkness. These forces cannot be reasoned with, they cannot conceive of liberty, they exist only to dominate and destroy.'

'But the foes we face are not daemons, they are our own people,' said Carathril. 'They breathe, and laugh, and cry as we do.'

'And that is why we shall show them mercy where possible,' Malekith assured him. 'I have faced grave enemies for my entire life. These last years I have wandered far and wide and seen many amazing and terrifying things. In the forests of Elthin Arvan, our companies fought goblin-fiends that rode upon gigantic spiders and I have battled with stinking trolls that can heal the most grievous wounds. Monstrous winged creatures tossed soldiers aside like dolls in the cold wastes of the north, and savage men caked in the blood of their fellows hurled themselves upon our spear tips. We wept at some of the horrors that confronted us, and I have seen seasoned warriors flee in abject terror from foes not of flesh and blood. But I have also seen such heroism that the greatest of sagas cannot do them justice. I have seen a bow-man leap upon the back of a bull-headed beast and strike out its eyes with an arrow in his hand. I have seen a mother gut a dozen orcs with a knife to protect her children. I have seen spearmen hold a narrow pass for twenty days against an endless horde of misshapen nightmares. War is bloody and foul, yet it is also full of courage and sacrifice.'

'I hope that I have such bravery,' said Carathril. 'I do not know if I would have the strength to master my fear in the face of such sights.'

'I have no doubt that you do,' Malekith said. 'I see the fire that burns within your heart, the dedication to your duty, and I would have no hesitation in having you fight by my side, Carathril of Lothern.'

As THEY RODE, the path veered westwards and brought them from the forest, and by mid-afternoon the head of the column travelled along a high ridge overlooking the northern domains of Nagarythe. Beneath them was spread Urithelth Orir, the great wilderness of Nagarythe.

For sixty leagues westwards and twenty leagues to the north stretched a desolate moorland, broken by stands of withered trees and majestic outcroppings of black rock. Patches of hardy grasses dotted the dark, thin soil, and banks of reeds found purchase along thin rivulets that cut through the hard earth.

To the east the mountains of the Annulii rose abruptly from the bleak flatness, towering in steep cliffs above the lowlands and rising ever higher and higher to the north, the most distant peaks tipped with a permanent white cap. Clouds were gathered about the mountain peaks, but above Urithelth Orir the skies were blue and clear, and the air bit with autumn chill.

The road broke northwards again, as straight as any arrow across the plains, rising and falling gently, crossing the many streams by wide bridges. As sunfall approached, the column halted and made camp. The light of dozens of campfires soon blazed as night swiftly approached, and streamers of smoke obscured the starry skies. Malekith's pavilion was erected at the centre of the camp, within a ring of tents housing his knights. Silver lanterns were brought out and hung on poles, throwing pools of deep yellow upon the bleak ground.

Here and there, the sound of a lute or harp broke the gloom, but their sound was mournful not cheering. Low voices sang old laments, bringing to mind the woes of the past, preparing the warriors for the sorrows that lay ahead.

—◄ SEVENTEEN ►—

The March to Ealith

As DUSK SETTLED, Carathril wandered the camp, seeking out the imprisoned cultists, wishing to speak again to Drutheira. Yet he could not find them and all of his inquiries were met with ignorance. The elves of Ellyrion and Tiranoc assumed they were in the camp of Nagarythe, while the Naggarothi curtly denied any knowledge of their whereabouts. Reluctantly, Carathril returned to his tent, alone and disheartened.

His camp was not far from the central circle. As he ate a supper that was of basic fare brought from Tor Anroc, for there was no hunting to be had in these parts, he heard sounds of laughter and celebration from the Naggarothi encampment. He heard old battle hymns written during the times of the daemon war, lauding the greatness of Nagarythe and its princes. As he washed down a meal of crisp bread and soft cheese with water from his canteen, a messenger arrived from Malekith to take him to the prince's war council. ·

As the guards waved him inside, he ducked beneath the canopy of the pavilion and found himself standing upon thick red carpets laid upon the bare earth. The tent was high and golden lanterns hung from chains around the cloth ceiling, bathing all in a yellow glow. Warmth filled the pavilion from a dozen glowing braziers that gave off no smoke, and the air was filled with excited chatter.

Retainers clad in simple blue coats passed through the assembled captains with ewers of wine. Carathril waved aside a proffered goblet and searched the crowd for a familiar face. There were at least a dozen elves, some dressed

193

in the finery of the Anlec knights; a couple from Tiranoc wore blue and white sashes across their armour, as did Carathril; a trio of elves on the far side of the pavilion wore cloaks of deep red and Carathril recognised them as the leaders of the Ellyrian reavers.

He spied Malekith's second-in-command, Yeasir, talking to the Ellyrians, and Carathril cut his way towards them through the scattered clusters of elven warriors, repeatedly turning down more offers of wine.

'Friend Carathril!' Yeasir called out as he approached. He waved a hand at each of the Ellyrians in turn, as he continued. 'Do you know Gariedyn, Aneltain and Bellaenoth?'

'Not by name,' said Carathril with a nod of greeting.

'I have hoped to speak with you, herald,' said the elf identified as Aneltain. 'But you spend so much time closeted with Prince Malekith, I have not had the opportunity. It must be good to have the ear of a prince.'

'I would not say that I have the prince's ear,' replied Carathril, somewhat taken aback. 'Though I do enjoy Prince Malekith's company.'

'And he yours, I would say,' said Yeasir. 'I have barely exchanged five words with him this past week.'

'It was not my intent to monopolise the prince...' began Carathril, but Gariedyn waved away his protestations.

'Do not apologise,' said the Ellyrian captain. 'We are just jealous, that is all. I am sure that if any of us had been chosen as Bel Shanaar's herald we would enjoy similar attention.'

'So, what does the prince have in mind, then?' asked Bellaenoth. 'Who will he choose to lead the attack on Ealith?'

'The knights of Anlec will have that honour, I am sure,' said Yeasir. He thrust his empty goblet towards one of the waiting servants and had it quickly refilled. Swallowing a mouthful, he continued. 'Ealith belongs to Nagarythe, after all, and it would not do for us to be seen skulking at the back like some timid Yvressians.'

'For my part, I would gladly give you the honour,' said Bellaenoth with a sorrowful shake of the head. 'By all accounts, it is a fearsome stronghold. I would not like to be first in line when we come up against its high walls.'

'That is because you do not know Malekith,' Yeasir assured them. 'He is as brave as a Chracian lion, and as strong as a Caledorian dragon. But, most importantly, he is also as cunning as a Sapherian fox. He would not throw us against such daunting fortifications with no plan. No, I am sure that our noble prince has a scheme for rooting out these troublesome cultists without us having to dash ourselves needlessly against the walls of Ealith.'

'Perhaps the good herald has some insight into this clever ploy?' suggested Gariedyn, and all eyes turned to Carathril.

'Me?' he stammered. 'I am not privy to the counsels of Prince Malekith, much as you may seem to think otherwise.'

Their expressions remained unconvinced.

'Besides,' Carathril added, 'it would not be my place to announce such matters when the prince has chosen not to do so. As a herald, my discretion is paramount.'

'So, you do know something,' said Bellaenoth. Something caught his gaze past Carathril's shoulder and Bellaenoth nodded towards the pavilion's entrance. 'Well, we may find out soon enough anyway.'

MALEKITH STRODE INTO the pavilion, swept up a goblet from the tray of a nearby attendant and downed its contents in a long draught. As he placed the goblet back upon the golden tray, his eyes swept the room, lingering on no one person for any length of time.

'My noble captains,' he said, glad that he had their attention immediately. 'My trusted companions. I must beg your forgiveness for an unavoidable act of perfidy. In these troubled times it is hard to judge who one can trust, and so I judge to trust no one. At least, I must say, I did not trust anyone until now. I could not be sure that the spies of our enemies were not within my camp, and so I have been forced to mislead you all.'

A startled murmur crept around the room, and then died away as the prince continued.

'I have known since I left Tor Anroc that Ealith was held by our foes,' Malekith revealed, pacing further into the pavilion. 'I did not want our enemies to be aware of this knowledge, and so I have kept secret counsel with only the raven heralds, whom I would trust with not only my life, but my realm. As I had hoped, it appears that our foes are confident in their position, knowing that we have not marched forth prepared for siege. To their minds, we must labour to make towers and rams to attack their fortress, and await reinforcements and bolt throwers in order to assault their walls. They believe that they have time aplenty to shore up their defences, and for more of their numbers to gather. Secret covens lurk within the forests and hills around Ealith, ready to sally forth to attack our siege works, ambush our supplies and harass our forces. They are wrong.'

The whispering recommenced, this time excited and intrigued. Two servants brought forth a chair of deep red wood, its high back carved with the likeness of a mighty dragon encircling a slender tower, the throne's arms and legs fashioned as the be-scaled and clawed limbs of the drake. Malekith unclasped his black cloak and cast it upon the throne, but did not sit. He turned to face the assembled captains, his eyes narrowed.

'Knowing the deceit upon which our enemies thrive, I have spread false rumour through their minions,' the prince told them. 'Two of our prisoners have escaped upon stolen horses, bearing news to Ealith overheard from the incautious lips of our warriors. News that we march to Enith Atruth, two days to the west, and another two days' ride from Ealith. The citadel itself lies no more than a day's ride to the north, and our escaped captives will have reached its walls before midday tomorrow. Confident that we tarry in our attack, they will not be ready for our strike. By dusk, Ealith will be ours.'

'Excuse me, highness, but an army does not move as swiftly as a solitary rider,' said one of the Ellyrians. 'Even if we could reach Ealith within the day, it would be impossible to conceal our approach.'

'That is true, Arthenreir,' replied the prince, enjoying his theatrical performance. 'It matters not whether we come to Ealith in a day or a hundred days, we have not the strength of arms to force victory through open battle. And it would not be desirable even if it were so, for I wish there to be as little bloodshed as possible on both sides. Guile shall see our fortunes ripen where might alone proves fruitless.'

'I told you,' whispered Yeasir with a smile. Carathril ignored him and listened intently as Malekith continued.

'Our enemies think Ealith secure against attack, but they are wrong. For many centuries the citadel has been abandoned, and its secrets have been forgotten by most. Not by me, nor the raven heralds. Ealith sits upon a spur of rock, reached only by a single causeway that is overlooked by towers and walls. Or so it would seem to our foes.'

Malekith now dropped his voice to a whisper, and met the gazes of those elves closest at hand, as if confiding in each of them alone.

'In fact, there is another entrance to Ealith,' said the prince. 'There is a passage, carved from the rock itself, which leads from the citadel to the outside. It was built as a means for defenders to sally forth to attack a besieging army from the rear, and leads to a hidden cave more than half a mile from the walls. We shall ride before daybreak, a company of no more than a hundred, and under cover of darkness enter this ancient passageway. It will take us into the heart of the enemy, where we will strike with absolute surprise. The army will march in our wake and there will be no escape. We shall slay or capture their leaders and force the rest to surrender. Without the puppeteers to pull their strings, our enemies are cowardly, decadent hedonists with no stomach for battle.'

'Who is to ride, highness?' asked Yeasir.

'The company shall be split thus: forty of Nagarythe, thirty of Ellyrion, and thirty of Tiranoc's finest riders. No more can we guarantee to approach Ealith unseen, and our strength lies in speed and stealth, not numbers.'

Malekith noticed disappointment well up on the face of Carathril. The Lothern captain was an average rider at best, trained to fight with spear and sword, not with lance and horse. However, he was the herald of the Phoenix King and potentially a useful ally. Malekith raised a hand to attract Carathril's attention and smiled.

'My noble comrade Carathril, you will ride with us, as an honorary knight of Nagarythe. I would not have such a fine heart and sure arm left behind on this adventure!'

'You have my eternal gratitude, highness,' said Carathril with a deep bow. 'It will be my honour to ride amongst such noble companions.'

Once the assembled warriors had departed, Malekith sat on his throne. A few moments later, Yeasir led in a small group of elves covered with dark robes. As they pulled back their hoods, Malekith saw that they were the cultists who had surrendered to him.

The prince of Nagarythe smiled. He had more work for them to do.

DARKNESS STILL SWATHED the camp as Malekith set forth with his riders; the sun was hidden behind the mountains and would be for some time to come. Before they had left, the company had assembled on the outskirts of the encampment and three shadow-swathed raven heralds had passed along their line, blackening harnesses and securing loose tack so that no glint or jingle would give them away. They had handed out long, black cloaks for the riders to wear over their armour, and thus concealed, Malekith's expedition had departed in silence and secrecy.

Now the hundred horsemen followed one of the raven heralds along a winding path northwards, heading down the ridge upon which the army had spent the night. They rode swiftly but not recklessly, and Malekith was glad of the sure-footedness of his mount. Late stars glimmered overhead in the pre-dusk grey, visible now that they had left behind the smoke of the camp. The thudding of hooves in the dirt was the only sound to break the still, and Malekith began to relax, calmed by the steady drumming.

As dawn slowly broke above the mountains, Malekith found that they were riding along an overgrown herder's trail through an expanse of low hills that rose up under the long shadow of the mountains. Their path was criss-crossed with rivulets and streams and the soil was more fertile, giving rise to stands of low bushes and thick clumps of sturdy grasses.

They slowed to negotiate this trickier ground, and at points rode in single file to follow in the tracks of the raven herald who led the way. The second rode sentry at the rear, and of the third there was no sign: he had departed in darkness to scout the way ahead.

They halted briefly mid-morning to ease tired limbs and make a hasty breakfast of bread and cold meats, before riding on. By this time, they had cleared the foothills once more and had made good progress across the rocky moors. Between the heat of the sun high in a clear sky, the thin yet warm cloak wrapped tightly about him and the effort of riding, Malekith did not feel the chill touch of autumn, though the breath of the riders and their steeds steamed in the air.

THEY SAW NOT a soul as they rode, although here and there they passed tumbled-down remains of ancient cottages and towers, scattered across the landscape as if discarded by the hand of some god. There was no road to follow, not the slightest track nor path, and it was clear that these lands had long ago been abandoned. They paused once again in the middle of the afternoon, allowing their mounts to water from a swift-moving brook. A few scattered stones marked the remains of an ancient mill beside the waterway; of its wheel and gears, nothing remained.

Carathril's gaze was drawn to a lone hill, not far from the stream, which rose steeply from the yellowing grass: a mound of bare, blackened rock. At its summit, Carathril could just about see a tumbled monolith, its white stone stark against the darkness of the hillock.

'Elthuir Tarai,' whispered a deep voice, causing him to start. One of the raven heralds stood directly behind him. His black horse stood close by, neither grazing nor resting, but alert and ready. The rider's face was all but hidden in the shadow of his deep hood, but Carathril could see a pair of emerald green eyes. It was Elthyrior.

'What did you say?' said Carathril.

'Yonder hill,' said the raven herald, pointing towards the barren knoll. 'It is the Elthuir Tarai, where Aenarion first wielded the Godslayer in battle. A thousand years ago, there was a town here, called Tir Anfirec, and all the lands about were farms and meadows. The daemons came and unleashed foul sorcery upon the ground, and their curse lingers here still. Upon that mount, Aenarion first drew the Sword of Khaine in anger, and struck down a host of the daemons. I am grandson to Menrethor, who fought here beside the king.'

'Then you are a prince?' said Carathril.

'In name only,' said Elthyrior, looking away. 'These were once the lands of my family, now they belong to nobody.'

'What happened to the town?' asked Carathril.

'It is said that the unnatural blood of the daemons seeped into the earth and poisoned it. The filth of their existence stained the fields and rivers, and Tir Anfirec withered and died like a plant without water. Dark magic saturated every granule, root and leaf, so that cattle died of fever, babes were stillborn and no living thing could flourish. Caledor came to this place and erected a lodestone, even as he planned his creation of the vortex. The waystone, like all the others, siphoned away the dark energy of the daemons, and over the centuries life slowly returned. Not enough for people to return, but sufficient for a few blades of grass and the odd insect nest. Then, perhaps fifty years ago, worshippers of the darkness came here and toppled the stone and undid its enchantments. Now the dark magic is returning, gathering again.'

'Why not raise up the stone again?' said Carathril.

'None in Nagarythe have the knowledge or means,' said Elthyrior. 'At least, none with the will or desire to do so. Perhaps there are loremasters in Saphery that have understanding of such things, and when peace prevails once more, they can restore the waystone. I fear that no living thing shall ever grow again upon Elthuir Tarai, for it was upon that slope that Aenarion sealed his pact with Khaine, and the God of Blood will share it with no other.'

Malekith was calling for the riders to mount up once more. With no further word, Elthyrior leapt into his saddle and his horse quickly wheeled away, leaving Carathril alone with his thoughts. He looked again upon that desolate hill and shuddered, pushing from his mind the frightening images the raven herald's tale had conjured.

AS THEY WENT further north, the lands became more welcoming, now covered here and there with high yellow grass that reached to the riders' knees as they rode. In the full light of day, this dreary heath was more cheering than the dark wilds they had passed through, and the mood of the company lightened considerably. There were scattered conversations along the column, and here and there the riders even joked and laughed, as if to ward away the apprehension that had grown.

Carathril found himself riding alongside the squadron of Ellyrian reaver knights, beside Aneltain who had been chosen by Malekith to lead them. They were more lightly armoured than the knights of Anlec, wearing only breastplates and shoulder guards and trusting in their speed and agility to avoid the foe. Their high helms were crested with long feathers taken from the tails of colourful birds. The Ellyrion steeds were uniformly white, not as broad nor tall as the Naggarothi mounts, and were harnessed with blue-lacquered tack. Each reaver knight carried a short thrusting spear with a broad, leaf-shaped head, and a small but powerful bow, with arrows fletched with blue feathers.

Of all the assembled elves, they were the most garrulous, and chatted freely amongst themselves as they rode. Aneltain was no different and quickly struck up conversation with Carathril.

They talked at first about their homelands, as warriors from different realms naturally do: compared the beauty of their women, the quality of wine and the relative merits of their people. Soon their talk moved on to their current surrounds, as both were strangers in these lands, and then onto the Naggarothi themselves.

'They are taciturn, that is for certain,' said Aneltain. 'Of course, by Ellyrian measure, all other elves are tight-lipped, but these Naggarothi will utter only a single word when ten would be natural, and nothing when one would suffice.'

'Prince Malekith seems eloquent enough,' countered Carathril.

'The prince? Sure, he can weave a speech with the best of them,' admitted the Ellyrian. 'But then, he has been Bel Shanaar's ambassador to the High King of the dwarfs, and from what I hear they are a race not known for their wagging tongues. I suspect he's spent the last two hundred years having to talk just to fill their silence. No, there's something different about these Naggarothi, some shadow upon their spirit that makes me feel uneasy.'

'You distrust them?' said Carathril, his voice dropping to a whisper as he glanced at the knights of Anlec only a short distance ahead.

'That is too strong a word for it,' replied Aneltain. 'I would gladly fight beside them, and I would trust them to watch my back. No, they just make me feel uneasy. There is a grimness about their mood that disturbs me. They don't laugh enough for my liking, and when they do it is with dark humour.'

'It is impossible to understand them, I admit,' said Carathril. 'We cannot hope to think what drives such folk. They are people of Aenarion. Many of them, like the prince, fought at his side. Even those too young to have been raised in those benighted times were raised by parents that were. Perhaps they are right not to laugh, for they have much still to grieve for. They suffered more than most, and their scars run deep.'

'Laughter cures all ills,' said Aneltain. 'It lifts the spirits and banishes dread.'

'I fear there are some ills too heavy to be lifted,' said Carathril. 'I for one am glad that I ride beside them and not against them. A great many of them quit these shores for the new colonies, driven by the need for battle, keen to escape the peace. I cannot understand the mind of one who seeks such peril, but it is the way of the Naggarothi to hail the warrior above other callings. I have no doubt that each one of those riders ahead has drawn more blood across the seas than either of us will do in our lifetimes.'

'That is for sure, and it makes them no less disconcerting,' said Aneltain. 'I have heard that in Anlec they still practise the rites set down by Aenarion: that a spear and sword are forged upon the birth of every child and they are presented to them upon their twentieth year. They learn the names of their weapons before those of their parents, and for their first years sleep upon the inside of a shield as a crib. But, as you say, it is better that we ride to battle with them than against them.'

Having come to this agreement, they then descended into a debate concerning the unique customs of their own homes, and the afternoon passed swiftly.

THE LEAGUES SWEPT past as they rode ever northwards, and the sun was fast dipping towards the west when Malekith called them to halt once more. The company gathered in a circle about their leader. None of the raven heralds were to be seen.

'Night comes quickly, and we must be ready,' the prince announced. 'We are yet out of sight of Ealith, and the raven heralds clear a path through the pickets of the foe so that we might pass. Once they return and bring word that all is well, we ride with all speed. Sariour rises above the mountains before midnight and we must be within the passageway before she spills her celestial light upon us. We cannot know what awaits us inside, and once we move on, I cannot give you clearer orders, for we must move as silently as ghosts.'

Malekith turned about on the spot, meeting the gazes of his company with a fierce stare.

'I have but these words for you,' he said. 'Spare those that surrender, spare not those that resist. I cannot say what horrors we might face, what depravities these cultists have already performed within the walls of their fortress. Let nothing distract you. Guard your fellows and they will guard you. Look to your swords for guidance, for though we are merciful I would have none of us fall this night. Pray to Asuryan, offer thanks to Isha, but remember to save a word for Khaine, for it is into his crimson realm that we must ride tonight!'

With these grim words still ringing in their ears, the company waited in silence, as the sun dropped beyond the sea and plunged them into starlight. A wind grew steadily, blowing chill from the north, and Malekith hugged his cloak tighter about himself. The riders checked each other's gear, to ensure no metal would catch the light and no rogue piece of harness would make noise at an untimely moment.

Malekith dismounted and stretched his legs, pacing to and fro as he waited for the order to move on. He did not linger long, for soon one of the raven heralds returned, almost invisible in the darkness. The prince mounted again, his legs sore from many days spent riding, and soon they were off at a trot on the last stage of their journey.

—◀ EIGHTEEN ▶—

A Foe Revealed

THE RIDERS OF Malekith skirted eastwards before heading south, having circled around Ealith to come at the fortress from the north. Through the gloom, the prince could see the castle in the distance, lit by fires from within so that the walls seemed to glow yellow and red. The keep was upon a great spur of rock that jutted several hundred feet from the surrounding grasslands. Laughter and shrill cries could be heard in the distance and strange shadows danced about the towers.

Upon its highest pinnacle a slender tower reached into the stars, and a strange green light emanated from its narrow windows. Malekith flinched as that light flickered for a moment, filled with the unshakeable belief that he had somehow been seen. Such a thing was impossible though, for the company were as shadows, swathed as they were by the dark cloaks of the raven heralds.

A stand of trees obscured Ealith from view, and Malekith was forced to duck as they rode beneath the boughs into the heart of the copse. Here was almost utter blackness, save for a few glimmers of starlight that broke through the almost solid canopy of leaves. The company dismounted, following the lead of their prince, and walked their steeds further into the trees.

At their centre there rose a great oak, as mighty as a guard tower, and Malekith led his horse between two massive roots and to the others he seemed to disappear. In fact where they thought there was earth and tree was a large opening, as wide and as high as a city gate, the roots of the ancient oak forming a twisting archway. Beyond lay the passageway, walled with grey stone, high enough to mount once more and for three riders to move abreast. At their head, Malekith drew his sword and its blue flame glimmered in the darkness like a beacon. Lanterns were passed down the line and one rider in ten set a glimmering light upon his saddlebags so that those behind could follow. As will o' wisps the company wound along the corridor, plunging deeper and deeper beneath the earth.

Soon the cut stone of the entrance gave way to bare rock, carefully but plainly carved by unknown hands. Malekith felt the corridor rising again and it began to turn to the right in a tightening spiral, and narrowed to the point that they had to ride single file for a short while. As the passage levelled out, at the same height as Ealith's inner walls, it widened again so that five horses could walk side-by-side. Malekith raised a hand to halt the column.

Ahead was a wall of bare rock, with no sign of door or gate. Malekith sat upon his horse in front of the wall and began to chant softly; ancient spell-words whose meanings were lost on the others. As the prince spoke, he traced lines through the air with the tip of his gleaming sword and where it passed a flickering trail of blue fire lingered, sparkling in the darkness. A rune of fire hung in the air, growing in intensity. With a final word, Malekith slashed through the sigil with his blade and a blinding flash filled the corridor. A wide archway now stood where the wall had been, and beyond lay the courtyard of Ealith.

'Ride forth!' shouted Malekith, heeling his mount into a gallop and leaping through the archway.

THE COMPANY BROKE into a charge, lowering spears and lances as they thundered from the secret passageway into the castle. Malekith held his blade at the ready, unconsciously ducking slightly as he passed through the portal though it was easily high enough for a rider to pass.

The courtyard was thrown into pandemonium. A dozen fires burned in bronze braziers, giving off an acrid smoke. Vile runes had been daubed in blood upon the white walls, and clusters of wailing prisoners were chained to each other in small groups. The cultists were taken completely unawares; some had been tending the braziers, others tormenting their captives.

Everywhere cultists leapt up with cries of alarm and shouts of terror as the knights crashed across the pale flagstones with a wall of lances and spear tips, striking down all within reach. Malekith bellowed wordlessly as he cut left and right, despatching a cultist with each blow. The ringing of steel echoed from the high walls, mixed with war cries and the screams of the wounded. Malekith singled out a fresh target: an elf with a pair of serrated daggers in his hands, naked but for a brightly patterned cloak and kilt, standing menacingly over a cowering elf maiden. The cultist turned his head as Malekith charged, his face a mask of dread. The prince did not hesitate, and as he raced past, he slashed downwards with his blade, catching the cultist a deadly cut across the neck.

Panting with excitement, Malekith slowed his steed and cast about for another foe. Dozens of bodies littered the ground, pools of blood spreading across the white paving. Everywhere enemies were flinging down their blades and hurling themselves to their knees with shouts of surrender. A few tried to resist further and were swiftly and mercilessly overwhelmed by the knights. Malekith jumped from his saddle and dashed towards the doors of the central citadel, which towered two hundred feet above the courtyard.

'Ellyrians, stand guard!' the prince shouted. 'All else, follow me!'

The gate had been barred from the inside, but this proved little barrier to the prince of Nagarythe. His sword blazed with magical energy as he raised it high. He brought the enchanted blade down and struck a mighty blow against the door in an explosion of blue fire that shattered the keep gate into charred planks. Without hesitation, Malekith leapt into the hallway beyond.

Though mere moments had passed since the attack had begun, the cultists were recovering quickly. Inside the citadel was a great staircase that spiralled to the upper levels of the tower. Archways led from the entrance hall to chambers all around, and scores of cultists poured from these rooms in a shrieking wave that engulfed Malekith and his company.

Screeching like a wild cat, a female cultist with red body paint and a shaven head hurled herself at Malekith, spitting and biting. He smashed the back of his hand across her face and sent her hurtling to the ground, where she lay unmoving. He barely parried a dagger aimed for his throat, and cut down the ranting zealot who wielded it. All around the elves of Malekith fought back to back, as more of their companions tried to press through the splintered doors to aid them.

As the prince swept out with Avanuir there was another detonation of magical fire, and a dozen cultists were launched high through the air, trailing smoke and burnt flesh, to crash against the walls. Malekith raised up his left hand and blue flame danced from his fingertips. With howls of pain and fear the cultists hurled themselves away, some prostrating themselves and gibbering abjectly, others running back through the doorways to escape the wrath of the prince.

'Upwards!' cried Malekith, pointing towards the stairway.

Carathril joined the prince as he leapt up the steps three at a time, followed by a handful of knights. Others led pursuits into the chambers below. The next level of the citadel was devoid of life and they continued upwards until they reached a wide chamber at the top of the tower. The stairs led them into the middle of a circular room that filled the space of the tower. Here lanterns blazed with the green radiance Malekith had seen from outside, and the eerie light showed scores of elves in horrifying acts of torture and debauchery; a plateau of vileness that would be forever etched into Malekith's memory. All that he heard and all that he had yet seen was not enough to prepare him for the horrors he witnessed in his own lands.

A high priestess, lithe and athletic, presided over the despicable ceremony from a dais littered with corpses and blood. Her white robes were spattered with gore, and a daemonic bronze mask covered her face. Her eyes glowed with a pale yellow light from within, and her pupils were tiny points of blackness in pools of luminescence.

In one hand, she held a crooked staff, wrought from bones and iron, and tipped with a horned skull with three eye sockets. In the other, she wielded a curved dagger still slick with the blood of many sacrifices.

Malekith charged across the chamber, cutting down any cultist who barred his path. He was but a few steps from the dais when the priestess thrust forwards the tip of her staff, and a bolt of pure blackness leapt out and struck the prince full in the chest. The prince's heart felt like it would explode. With a cry of pain torn from his lips, Malekith faltered and fell to his knees. He was as much shocked as hurt, for he knew of no wizard who could best the sorcerous abilities granted him by the Circlet of Iron.

He gazed in amazement at the priestess. She stepped down from the dais with languid strides and walked slowly towards the injured prince, the tip of her staff fixed upon him.

'My foolish child,' she sneered.

THE PRIESTESS LET the sacrificial dagger slip from her fingers to clatter in a shower of crimson droplets upon the floor. With her hand thus freed, she pulled off her mask and tossed it aside. Carathril gave a yelp of astonishment. Though caked with blood, the priestess's lustrous black hair spilled across her bare shoulders. Her face was pristine, the very image of beauty. In her were aristocratic bearing and divine magnificence combined.

Carathril felt himself spellbound. Around him, the other knights gazed dumbly at this apparition of perfection, similarly ensorcelled.

'Mother?' whispered Malekith, his sword slipping from his numb fingers.

'My son,' she replied with a wicked smile that sent a shiver down Carathril's spine; of lust and fear in equal measure. 'It is very rude of you to butcher my servants so callously. Your time amongst the barbarians has robbed you of all manners.'

Malekith said nothing but simply stared up at Morathi, wife of Aenarion, his mother.

'You have been weak, Malekith, and I have been forced to rule in your stead,' she said. 'You trot across the world at the bidding of Bel Shanaar, ever eager to risk your life for him, while your lands fall into ruin. You grovel on bended knee to ask this upstart Phoenix King to rule your own realm. You are a cur, happy to eat the scraps from the tables of Tiranoc, Yvresse and Eataine while your people starve. You build cities across the ocean, and navigate the wide world, while your home festers in filth and decay. You are not fit to be a prince, much less a king! Truly your father's blood does not run in your veins, for no true son of Anlec would allow himself to be so cowed.'

Malekith looked up at his mother, his face twisted with pain.

'Kill her,' he managed to spit through gritted teeth.

As if those words had broken a spell, Carathril found himself able to move again. Sheathing his sword, he snatched his bow from the quiver across his back and set an arrow to the string. As he pulled back his arm, Morathi swung her staff towards him and he leapt aside just as a dark bolt cracked the stone of the floor where he had been standing a heartbeat earlier. As if also broken from trances, the cultists lounging around the room leapt to their feet with snarls and shouts. Malekith pushed himself to his feet, but another blast of Morathi's sorcery hurled him across the floor with a clatter of armour.

This inner coven fought with a feral tenacity, deranged from narcotic vapours and their dedication to Morathi. Carathril tossed aside his bow and drew his sword again as an elf with gem-headed pins piercing her lips and cheeks ran at him with a flaming brand in her hands. Shouts and shrieked curses filled the room and pungent smoke billowed as braziers were knocked over in the struggle. Carathril felt the heat of the brand in the cultist's hands wash over him as he ducked a sweeping attack.

He struck out at the elf's naked legs and cut her down at the knee, sending her toppling to the floor. Even lying upon her back, Carathril looming over her, she hurled abuse and thrust the brand at him. He pushed the tip of his blade into her chest and she slumped to the marble flagstones.

'There will be no welcome for you in Anlec,' Morathi snarled above the din, having retreated to the dais. 'Go back to that usurper and do not return.'

Malekith gave a roar that nearly deafened Carathril and hacked with wild abandon at the cultists who had surrounded him, dismembering and decapitating with wide, sweeping blows. A gap opened up in the melee between the prince and his mother and he stalked towards her, his sword shining with magical energy. A look of panic swept the sorceress's face and she began to back away. Even as Malekith's front foot fell upon the dais, Morathi raised her staff above her head in both hands and a shadow enveloped her, spreading like diaphanous wings to either side. Her body melted and dissipated as those spectral wings beat thrice and swept upwards, and then she was gone.

More knights of Anlec raced up from the stairwell and soon the remaining cultists were slain or pacified. Carathril looked at Malekith, where he still stood upon the dais. Where he had expected to see the prince still in shock or perhaps wrought with grief, instead Malekith was a picture of cold fury. The flame of his blade burned white-hot as he gripped it in both hands before him, and his eyes glittered with barely controlled magic.

The prince's stare moved across the room until it fell upon Carathril, who flinched at Malekith's fell gaze. Carathril was locked in that stare, fixed by two raging orbs of hate, and for a long heartbeat the captain thought that the prince would attack him. The moment passed and Malekith slumped, his sword falling from his fingertips to ring upon the stone floor.

'Nagarythe has fallen into darkness,' he whispered, and now his eyes were filled with tears.

AT DAWN, MALEKITH stood upon the rampart of Ealith and watched the sun rising over the Annulii. In the light of day, the events of the past night seemed dim, distorted. He could barely bring himself to believe that Morathi had been the architect behind the rise of the cults. Now that he considered it, he realised he should not have been at all surprised. It was just like his mother: a network of spies and agents across all of Ulthuan, power over the weak princes and their armies. He cursed himself for allowing Morathi to spread her dark touch into Athel Toralien and feared what he had left behind in Elthin Arvan.

Yet there was logic to her plan that Malekith could not dispel. Had he not already started to use the cultists to his own end? The army of Nagarythe was but one weapon, an unsubtle one at that; the cults of luxury were a far more insidious force and all the more dangerous for it. Morathi had told him as much on her visit to the colonies. Religion and belief could be exploited for power, he had but to steel himself against his distaste to wield them.

A shadow moved up the road towards the citadel and Malekith saw that it was a swift-moving rider: one of the raven heralds. He watched as the dark figure raced up the causeway and through the gates. It was not long before Elthyrior strode up the steps to the wall and gave the prince a nod of acknowledgement.

'Grave news, Malekith,' said the raven herald. 'Ealith is ours, but Nagarythe rises up in support of Morathi.'

'How so?' demanded the prince.

'Some of my company have been corrupted by your mother,' Elthyrior admitted. 'It was they who brought us here, to lure you into the clutches of Morathi. We cannot know her intent, but I believe she sought to turn you to her cause.'

'In that she has failed,' said the prince. 'I have escaped her trap.'

'Not yet,' warned Elthyrior. 'The cults are strong and much of the army is loyal to your mother. Even now they march on Ealith, seeking to surround you and destroy you. There is no sanctuary here.'

'Thank you, Elthyrior,' said Malekith. 'If I could ask but another favour of you. Ride forth with those you know to be loyal to me. Gather what warriors and princes you can and send them south to Tiranoc.'

'And you?' asked Elthyrior.

Malekith did not reply for a moment, for what he was about to say pained him more than any physical wound.

'I must retreat,' he said after a long while. 'I am not yet ready to challenge Morathi and we cannot be caught here.'

* * *

As MALEKITH ORDERED, so it was. The army marched westwards with all speed, ever aware that ahead and behind the worshippers of the forbidden gods were gathering in greater numbers. At Thirech Malekith faced a motley army of several thousand, but the cultists were poorly led and easily shattered by the charges of Malekith's knights, quickly fleeing into the fields and forests around the town.

For four days and five nights Malekith's host marched onwards without relent, seeking the harbour at Galthyr.

Just after dawn on the fifth day after the battle at Ealith, the army rode into sight of Galthyr. Malekith ordered the army to wait out of bowshot from the walls. On the prince's orders, Yeasir rode slowly towards the gate, shielding his eyes against the glare of the morning sun reflected from the white walls. Figures moved upon the parapet, with bows drawn. Yeasir reined his horse to a halt less than a stone's throw from the gate tower.

'I am Yeasir, captain of Malekith!' he called out. 'Stand ready to receive the prince of Nagarythe!'

There was no reply for quite some time, until several new figures appeared upon the gatehouse battlement and stared down at the newcomer. There was a brief consultation between the group, and then one raised a curled golden horn to his lips and let free a clear, resounding note. At the same time, a pennant broke free and fluttered from the flagpole, silver and black.

'The clarion of Anlec!' laughed Malekith. 'And the banner of my house!'

A great cheer welled up from the army as Malekith waved them forwards and the gates opened before them. At a gallop they raced along the road, passing swiftly into the town beyond, the rest of the amy marching with haste behind them. No sooner had the last of them passed than the gates swung closed again with a mighty crash.

Galthyr was half-ruined, with many buildings burnt or collapsed. Wounded soldiers were gathered in the city's squares, tended to by healers of Isha. Malekith spied Prince Durinne walking amongst the casualties and hailed Galthyr's commander as he dismounted.

'I see that we have not been fighting alone,' said Malekith.

'Indeed not,' said Durinne, shaking Malekith's hand. 'Your fleet is safe in the harbour, though only by the valiant efforts of my warriors.'

'Morathi's cultists?' asked Malekith.

'Some amongst the city's populace were her creatures and we drove them out,' explained Durinne. 'They returned two days ago with the armies of Prince Kheranion and Turael Lirain. The prince demanded that I open the gates and surrender Galthyr to his authority. He did not take kindly to having arrows shot at him...'

'You have my thanks,' said Malekith. 'It seems that the list of my allies grows shorter each day. I have not room on my ships for many more, but you are welcome to leave with me.'

'Galthyr can stand for a while yet,' said Durinne. 'When you have left there is little of value here for Morathi to covet. There are other ports already under her sway.'

'Yet she might wish to see you destroyed out of spite for resisting her,' said Malekith. 'Come with me.'

'I will not abandon my city or my people!' Durinne said. 'When the time comes to leave, I have the means to make it happen. Do not spare any more thought on my wellbeing, Malekith.'

Malekith laid a hand on Durinne's shoulder, the gesture expressing the gratitude he felt better than any words he could say.

MALEKITH WAS IN no mood to tarry in Galthyr, for he was sure that even now other ships would be making their way down the coast to blockade the port. Only a few hundred townsfolk remained, but Malekith trusted them not and would not allow them to evacuate upon the ships. The tide and wind were fair, so that no sooner had the host arrived at Galthyr than they left upon *Indraugnir* and another two great dragonships, and seven hawkships. Three more hawkships Malekith sent north, to forestall any pursuing fleet.

Heading south for several days, Malekith's weary force was met by ships from the Tiranoc fleet and escorted to the port of Athel Reinin. Here Malekith left the greater part of his knights, and sent the Ellyrians back to their homeland, warning them not to attack Nagarythe on their own, but to protect the passes across the mountains. Carathril and the charioteers of Tiranoc, who had been forced to burn their chariots at Galthyr, formed a guard for the prince and they rode with all haste. Messages were sent ahead by hawks from the watch towers of Athel Reinin, carrying brief word of what had happened and counselling Bel Shanaar to send troops to his northern border.

ELEVEN DAYS AFTER fighting for his life in Ealith, Malekith found himself back once again in the council chamber of the Phoenix King. He was still shocked at all that had happened; it hardly seemed possible that his world could have changed so much in so little time. He felt sick at the thought of the treachery of Morathi. The prince had requested private audience with the Phoenix King, and had asked Carathril to accompany him in his role as herald to Bel Shanaar, to provide unbiased account. The king was sat upon his throne, dejected and weary, while the prince and Carathril sat upon chairs in front of him.

'You understand that while Morathi holds power, you will never regain Nagarythe?' Bel Shanaar said upon the conclusion of Malekith's tale. 'And to end her grip, she must be imprisoned or slain.'

Malekith did not answer immediately but stood up and paced away from the throne. He despised Bel Shanaar, and despised himself more for needing his help. Whatever his feelings for the Phoenix King, it was clear to Malekith that he would never take his rightful place unless he reigned over Nagarythe once more. He could not fight Morathi alone, and so he was forced to humble himself before this usurper who now sat before him. The simple truth was that Malekith needed Bel Shanaar and would have to put aside his own ambitions for a time. Morathi had abandoned her son and he no longer owed her any loyalty.

'I disown her!' Malekith declared, spinning on his heel. 'Ever she has clawed for power, and whispered in my ear that it is I who should wear that cloak and crown. From the moment of Aenarion's death, she has ceaselessly pushed me to rule this isle. You remember how she screamed and railed when I was the first to bend my knee to you, and ever since she has sought to control me, to force me to power so that she might be queen again. I know not why my father wed her, for she is conniving and vain, and for all my life I remember nothing but her sharp tongue and unbridled ambition. She has cast me aside, and even now, I suspect, she raises up some other puppet in my place. She will not relent until she holds sway over all of Ulthuan, and that is something that I shall not abide.'

'And yet, she is for all that, still your mother,' said Bel Shanaar with concern upon his face. 'If it comes to such, would you be able to drive your blade through her heart? Would your sword arm remain strong as you struck off her head?'

'It must be done, and I would have no other do it,' replied Malekith. 'There is a wicked irony that I should send from this world she who brought me into it. Such considerations are yet far from our immediate concern, for Nagarythe must be reclaimed first. I do not know what hold she has over the other princes and nobles of Nagarythe. I hope that some still resist her, but they will be scattered and few. She will twist and distort my actions to those who waver, so that it appears that it is I who is the aggressor. Our folk are loyal but they are not imaginative. We are raised to obey orders, not to ask questions, yet there are many still who would raise their banners beside their true prince. I shall march to Anlec and overthrow the Witch Queen!'

─◄ NINETEEN ►─

Malekith's War

IT WAS TOO late in the year for Malekith to mount another expedition into his homeland, and so he spent the winter gathering what troops he could from the other princes, while all the while the raven heralds slipped across the border to bring news of what passed in the north. Such reports were disquieting, for it seemed that now she had revealed herself as the witch-sorceress she had long been, Morathi had thrown aside all regard for pretences and now wholly embraced her dark nature.

Nagarythe seethed with activity and to Malekith's further dismay, when spring finally came, unsettling word arrived from the colonies that the same racial ennui that had so beset Ulthuan was now taking hold in the cities to the east. In response to Malekith's requests for troops, Alandrian could only send a fraction of the Naggarothi army from Athel Toralien; the rest he needed to guard against growing numbers of orcs moving into Elthin Arvan from the south.

Other fighters joined the prince's army from Nagarythe; individually and by company they had cautiously made their way south into Tiranoc, risking not only the wrath of Morathi but also the ire of the Tiranoc army guarding the border against any who crossed. Malekith had hoped for many more, but it seemed as if a good many of his former captains and lieutenants were content to serve his mother, either in loyalty or out of fear, while a cadre of princes still faithful to Malekith were isolated in the mountains of Naga-rythe, gathered under the banner of the lords of House Anar.

Malekith had learned well the lesson of Ealith. He knew that the army

213

under his command could not march directly from Tiranoc to Anlec, for the host of Nagarythe would be prepared for such an attack. Yet Malekith did not let despair grip his counsel, and as he sought for support from the other princes, he paid especial attention to befriend Haradrin of Eataine, who had at his command the greatest fleet of the elves and the staunch Lothern Sea Guard. Malekith still had *Indraugnir* under his charge, and with several more dragonships from Lothern he was sure that he would be able to overpower the Nagarythe fleet. Malekith brooded a long while on what few advantages he had, and by the time spring began to thaw the snow in the mountains he had envisioned a bold plan of action.

It began with the army of Tiranoc forming into hosts not far from the Naganath. Knowing well that Morathi's spies and magic would discern such movement, Malekith hoped to lure the Naggarothi into believing that an attack was imminent, and thus draw their forces southwards.

IN THE LAST days of winter, Malekith rode alone into the Annulii east of Tor Anroc. He took with him the Circlet of Iron, and headed into the high peaks. He found himself a sheltered spot and sat upon the ground out of the biting wind. Placing the circlet upon his head, Malekith closed his eyes and allowed the ancient artefact to direct his mind.

Malekith's view raced over the plains of Tiranoc, where frost still clung to the grass. To the Naganath his mind's eye flew, over the icy waters into Nagarythe. He saw the armies of Morathi assembling in the Biannan Moor, and pickets stationed along the length of the river to watch the movements of the Tiranoc hosts. Westwards he spied an army encamped about the walls of Galthyr, though the besiegers seemed content merely to contain Durinne and his army. Further northwards towns and villages were ransacked for supplies and the cultists presided over bloody ceremonies in praise of the cytharai.

Then to Anlec came the prince's vision. In cages of iron throughout the city great beasts from the mountains prowled and roared: savage manticores and screeching griffons, many-headed hydras and hissing chimerae. Around the cages clustered beastmasters with vicious goads and barbed whips, tormenting their captives and feeding them on raw elf flesh. Smiths laboured at magically white-hot fires upon armour plates for the gigantic war beasts, and forged spiked collars with heavy chains. Leatherworkers fashioned sturdy saddles and harnesses studded with rivets and adorned with bones.

Around and about the city were grisly altars to the likes of Ereth Khial, Meneloth, Nethu and other grim deities. Bloodstained chalices stood upon tables draped with cloths of skin, and braziers sputtered with bloodied hearts and charring bones. Wretched and crying, lines of elves in chains and tattered rags were dragged before those savage sacrificial shrines to be cast upon blazing pyres or shredded with wicked daggers in praise of hungry gods.

All was watched over by the cruel nobility of Nagarythe. Princes in dark robes sat upon black destriers draped with silver caparisons, while masked priests with daubed runes upon their naked skin chanted supplications and pleas. The stones of the pavements were stained red, and piles of bones gathered rotting in the gutters to be gnawed upon by impish familiars and scrawny hounds.

As he turned his gaze upon the central tower, the palace of Aenarion, Malekith found his view obscured by a great shadow. He heard a whispering voice: his mother's. He strained to hear what she was saying, but could discern nothing but a murmur. The power of the circlet granted Malekith unprecedented power, and he shuddered to think what unspeakable pacts his mother had made for her own sorcery to blind him.

THE PRINCE SENT word to Bel Shanaar that the Phoenix King should move a greater part of his army to the border. Over the following days Malekith spied upon the movements of the Naggarothi with the circlet. Once he was sure that the legions of Nagarythe marched for the border to protect against attack, Malekith returned to Tor Anroc. He sent swift-flying message hawks to Lothern, ordering *Indraugnir* and a sizeable fleet to set sail and head northwards around the western coast of Ulthuan. Their course was set for Galthyr. Once more using the crown from the north, Malekith saw the Naggarothi fleet gathering about the port, expecting an attack from the sea. More warriors were drawn to the siege, to contest any landing that might be made.

Guided by secret commands from Malekith the raven heralds sowed fear and confusion in the midst of the enemy. They attacked supplies and waylaid companies marching to join the scattered armies. They burned freshly growing crops in the fields and intercepted messengers riding between the Naggarothi commanders and Anlec. Their attacks were concentrated to the west and south, to further the illusion being spun by Malekith's manoeuvres.

Malekith's true attack came not from the west or the south, but from the east. In small companies, under cover of darkness over the course of many nights, the prince moved the greater part of his host into the mountains of Ellyrion. They hid in farms and villages close to the mountains, supported by food stockpiled by Prince Finudel.

When the first moon of the new spring rose, Malekith rode to Dragon Pass, the Caladh Enru, two hundred miles south of Anlec. There he unfurled the banner of Anlec and rallied his army for the attack.

Many thousands strong numbered the host, and amongst them rode princes of Nagarythe and Tiranoc, Ellyrion and Eataine. Sapherian wizards had joined the venture, Thyriol amongst them. As Malekith had foreseen, the possibility of him creating an alliance with Ellyrion had not been envisaged by Morathi and the attack came as a total surprise. In a single day, the garrison of Arir Tonraeir at the western end of Dragon Pass was overrun, and the army of Malekith marched for Anlec.

The army turned northwards, past the twin peaks of Anul Nagrain and across the river Haruth into the plains of Khiraval. Here there had once been farms and pastures for the herds of Nagarythe, but now all had fallen into ruin under the rule of Morathi and the cults. The tumbled remains of abandoned farmsteads jutted from the overgrown fields like broken teeth, and packs of ferocious wolves and monstrous bears had come down out of the mountains to claim Khiraval as their own. The army marched along a highway broken by weeds and marred by cracks and holes. It took them through deserted villages, the empty doors and windows gaping at them like accusing black eyes. The more he saw of what had befallen his proud kingdom, the greater was Malekith's ire.

The Naggarothi commanders in the south were now caught in a horrifying situation. If they were to move north to counter Malekith's attack, they would turn their backs on the Tiranoc hosts at the border. In the end they opted to keep their positions, trusting to the army and defences of Anlec to fend off Malekith's force.

With news coming from the raven heralds that the way ahead to Anlec was clear, Malekith and his army pressed on. Across Khiraval and then north-east towards Anlec through the muddy fens of Menruir they marched. Within fifteen days of crossing into Nagarythe, Malekith's host reached mighty Anlec, the immense capital.

Malekith trusted to the valour of his followers and the poor training of the defenders, who for the most part he reckoned to be wild cultists and not the professional warriors he had artfully drawn far to the south. There was no time to waste, for it would not be long before companies were brought back from Galthyr, and the captains in the south realised that Bel Shanaar had no desire for a costly assault across the Naganath. There was no time for siege to be set, nor any reason to expend energy on pointless parley.

As he had so often done before, Malekith struck hard and fast in his attempt to secure victory.

As the army of Malekith arranged itself for the attack, a clear spring sky bathed the black marble buildings of Anlec, glimmering on a coat of late frost. Silver and black banners snapped in the cold wind from atop the many towers around the high walls, while sentries patrolled back and forth clad in blackened scale and golden helms. The fortress-city reverberated to the tramp of booted feet and the scrape of metal as regiments practised drills in the open squares. The cries of their lieutenants echoed from the stone walls and mingled with the crackle of sacrificial pyres and screams of howling prisoners.

Fearsome was the citadel, for it had been built by Aenarion with the aid of Caledor Dragontamer and was so wrought that no approach was left undefended. Eighty high towers and many miles of thick walls surrounded the city, yet only three gates controlled access in and out, each surrounded by bastions filled with war machines and troops.

The approach to each gate was fraught with peril, for walls extended outwards from the curtain of Anlec and provided points from which the defenders could shoot upon the road for half a mile. Isolated towers, each surrounded by stake-filled ditches, were built in a ring of outer defences, each positioned so that its war engines could cover the next.

Within the circle of towers there was dug a great moat, fifty paces wide. No mere water filled this obstacle, but magical green flames that hissed and crackled fiercely. Only one drawbridge crossed the fire ditch on each road, and this was protected by a keep every bit as fearsome as the gatehouses of the city.

For all the forbidding defences of Anlec, Malekith showed no fear. He sat astride his steed at the front of his army, clad in his golden armour, the circlet of sorcery upon his head, Avanuir blazing in his hand. Behind him were two thousand of his knights, veterans all, hardened in the colonies to the east and led by captains who had fought with Malekith in the chill northlands. They were garbed in golden scale armour and cloaked with purple and black. Their lances glowed with enchantments and runes of protection burned upon their shields. Grim-faced, they eyed the dark citadel of Anlec without dread.

To the north and south of the knights were Malekith's companies of spears, seven thousand in all. Led by Yeasir, they formed up into ranks ten deep, pennants fluttering above them, the sounds of silver horns ringing out the orders. Yeasir strode back and forth along the line, reminding them that they fought for the true ruler of Anlec, exhorting them to show no mercy and to stay firm in the face of their despicable foes. Behind the spears were the lines of archers, three thousand of them, their black bows strung, their quivers heavy with arrows.

Further to the north rode the reaver knights of Ellyrion. Prince Finudel and Princess Athielle had eagerly offered to join Malekith's host, and they trotted forwards at the head of two thousand of their followers. In his hand Finudel held Cadrathi, the starblade lance his father had wielded in battle alongside Aenarion. Athielle waved forwards her troop with the shining white blade Amreir, the winterblade that her mother had used to slay the daemon prince Akturon. White and blue banners flew above the cavalry, emblazoned with images of golden horses. The Ellyrians' steeds were eager, stamping and neighing, and the reaver knights chatted amiably amongst themselves, showing no sign of concern at the imposing fortress confronting them.

The southern wing of Malekith's army was led by Bathinair, prince of Yvresse. He sat astride a monstrous griffon, taken from the mountains of the Annulii as a hatchling and raised to be his war mount in Tor Yvresse.

Redclaw was its name and it was a majestic beast. Its body was that of an immense hunting cat, thrice the size of a horse, patterned with black and white stripes. Its head was that of an eagle, with a high crest of red and blue feathers, and its forelegs were as the talons of some mighty bird of prey, with crimson claws like curved swords. Two wide wings of grey and black feathers swept out from its broad shoulders, between which Bathinair sat mounted upon a throne of white wood, the banners of Yvresse and his house fluttering from its back. He held the spear of ice, Nagrain, its silvered shaft gleaming in the morning light, its tip a blazing crystal stronger than any metal. Redclaw threw back its head and gave a deafening screech, and clawed at the earth in anticipation of the hunt.

Bathinair had not come alone from Yvresse and with him stood another two thousand warriors armed with long spears and carrying blue shields, clad in white robes of mourning.

Charill, one of the princes of Chrace, had come also. He stood upon the back of a chariot pulled by four majestic lions from the mountains of his lands. Each was the size of a horse, and as white as snow. They roared and snarled, pacing eagerly in their harnesses. He wielded the fabled axe Achillar, whose double-headed blade crackled with lightning in his hands. Beside him stood his son, Lorichar, bearing the banner of Tor Achare: the head of a lion in silver thread upon a scarlet background. Both wore long cloaks of lion fur, edged with black leather and hung with many jewelled pendants. Other nobles upon lion chariots flanked the prince, each dour warrior armed with axe and spear and clad in golden mail.

With them came huntsmen from the mountains: blue-eyed warriors with long locks of golden hair bound into plaits, with lion pelts upon their shoulders. They wore silvered breastplates with lion designs, and short kilts threaded with gold. The lion warriors carried heavy axes of differing designs, etched with runes and hung with braided tassels. Their demeanour was as fierce as their namesakes, and they gripped their weapons with eager determination.

Lastly came the princes of Saphery: Merneir and Eltreneth, led by Thyriol. They were mounted upon pegasi: winged horses taken from the highest peaks of the Annulii. Glittering capes of many colours streamed from their shoulders and each bore sword and staff that gleamed with magical power. They circled above the host of Malekith, the sun gleaming from the golden harnesses of their flying steeds.

Malekith saw that all were arrayed ready for battle, and his heart soared at the sight. Not for centuries had he commanded such a host, and the call of his blood sang within his veins. For good or ill, the fortunes of the day would resound down through history, and his name would be recounted for generations to come. The prince was not content merely with posterity, though, and was determined to win victory. He ordered the army to a halt just outside of bowshot from the closest towers and wheeled his steed to face the army. Raising Avanuir above his head, Malekith called out to his army, his voice ringing clearly the length and breadth of the host.

'Look upon this citadel of dread!' he cried, pointing to Anlec with his magical blade, sapphire fire licking along its length. 'Here once hope sprang for our people, and here now glowers our doom! In these halls the ghosts of our fathers reside, and how they must howl at the sight of seeing what was once so great now brought so low! Here was lit the bright beacon of war by Aenarion, now a blackened flame of malice and domination! We are here to extinguish that baleful flare and restore anew the light of the phoenix! You may look and see the unending walls and the cruel towers, but I do not. The might of Anlec is not in her stones and mortar, but in the blood of her defenders and the courage of their hearts. No such strength remains in this benighted city, for all vigour and honour has been crushed from her by the choking chains of misery and slavery.'

The prince then turned his sword upon his army and its point swept along the long rows of warriors.

'Here I see the true spirit of our people!' Malekith declared. 'None come here by bond or bribe, but have marched forth for great and noble cause. We would not see such dark cities across our realms, and all here know in their spirit that today we shall halt the spread of the malignant shadow. Fell Charill! Noble Finudel! Majestic Thyriol! Know these names, and be proud to fight beside them, as I am. In time all here shall be remembered and their names shall be lauded. Unending shall be the appreciation of our people, and cherished shall be the memories of those that fight here this day! Look to your left and look to your right, and fix in your mind the face of your brothers-in-battle. You shall see no weakness there, only determination and bravery. Each here today claims his right to be a prince, for reward comes to those willing to risk all, and never have such dignified companions been assembled since the time of my father. Heroes one-and-all, you are, and as heroes shall the gods heap their praises upon you.'

Malekith then raised his sword in front of his face in salute.

'And forget not that it is I, Prince Malekith, who leads you!' he shouted. 'I am the true lord of Anlec! Scion of Nagarythe! Son of Aenarion! I know not despair, nor fear, nor defeat! With this blade I carved a new kingdom to the east. By my hand our people made grand alliance with the dwarfs. These eyes have looked upon the Dark Gods and did not flinch. Monsters and horrors I have faced and bested, and today will be no different. We shall win, because where I lead, victory follows. We shall win, because it is my destiny to triumph. We shall win, because I will it!'

Malekith then stood in his stirrups and raised Avanuir high above his head. A great cry erupted from the throats of his warriors, shaking the ground. Malekith waved the army forwards.

'Glory awaits!' he cried.

—◄ TWENTY ►—

The Battle of Anlec

AT MALEKITH'S SIGNAL, the army advanced in line, heading towards the bridge across the river of fire. Arrows arced from the roofs of the outlying towers, and the battle began.

With a wild screech, Redclaw beat his wings and bore Bathinair high into the air. The Yvressian prince soared higher and higher, climbing far above the range of the enemies' bows. Likewise did the Sapherian mages circle upwards into the cloudless sky. Behind their shields, the spearmen marched forwards, not once breaking their stride even as more and more arrows rained down upon them.

With a fearsome shriek, Redclaw dived down from the heavens towards the closest of the towers. The archers atop its summit turned their bows towards the descending beast, but their arrows caused no lasting wound upon the griffon's thick hide. Bathinair's lance flashed with power as its point drove through the chests of the defenders, even as Redclaw's talons and beak savaged others upon the tower, rending and tearing.

Another tower suffered at the wrath of Thyriol, who streaked down from above, the tip of his staff blazing with green fire. As his pegasus swooped low over the tower, the mage unleashed his spell, the flames roaring from his staff in the shape of a hawk diving for the kill, exploding amongst the archers and tossing their bodies over the parapet.

More elves rushed up to the tower roof from within, only in time to be blasted by a bolt of red lightning from the staff of Merneir, which shattered the granite bricks of the tower and sent burning bodies and cracked stones

221

tumbling to the charred earth. The army of Malekith surged through the gap between the two towers, while Bathinair and the mages wheeled above their heads, the cheers of the army ringing out to greet them.

The fortified bridge seemed altogether a more daunting obstacle. It consisted of four immense towers, with a drawbridge between each pair, so that the fiery moat could only be crossed by the bridges on each side both being lowered. Atop each tower was a powerful engine, which hurled immense bolts far out across the barren plain. Before his army came within range of these fearsome machines, Malekith signalled for his host to halt.

He rode forwards alone a short way, as if daring the defenders of the towers to direct their machines against him. It was a strange scene; the solitary prince upon his steed staring at the grim castlebridge like a golden lion standing its ground before a gigantic black bear.

Calmly, Malekith raised an open hand into the air. He felt the swirl of magic coursing around him and fixed his eyes upon the moat of flames. Upon his head throbbed the circlet, and the prince could sense the bubbling mystical energies within the flame-filled ditch across his path. He had been master of Anlec and knew the commanding words of the flames, but he could feel other enchantments had been bound into the moat; his mother had known he would try to use the spell words to break this defence. She had not reckoned with the power of the circlet, though, with which Malekith's power was increased five-fold.

In him built energies that would have torn asunder a lesser mage, and as the tide of magic grew, he began to quiver from the surging excitement that filled him. Speaking the command spell, he opened the dam of his mind and unleashed a tide of magic that flowed out of him and into the fire moat. The flames turned black and rose higher as the Naggarothi prince poured all of his will and determination into them, until they climbed a hundred feet into the air.

Now sweating with the effort, Malekith raised up his other hand, his limbs shaking with strain. The magic of the fires wriggled and writhed, trying to escape the grasp of his spell. With gritted teeth, Malekith began to bring his hands closer together and in response the flames of the trench began to coil into tall waves, one on each side of the bridge house.

Malekith brought his hands together with a thunderous clap and the two tides of flame rushed towards each other, utterly engulfing the castle across the entrenchment. Black fire scorched through arrow slits and poured over the roofs of the towers. Ebon flames incinerated elf and machine in an instant, reducing them to clouds of ash that billowed up into the air above the bridge. Even as the ancient planks of the drawbridge began to smoulder, Malekith pulled apart his hands and let loose his grip on the enchantment, the fires washing away and returning to their normal colour.

With a shout of relief and joy, Malekith turned to his army and waved them forwards, his face split by a wide grin. As the spearmen of Nagarythe reached him, he reined in his horse beside Yeasir. The captain looked up at him with suspicious eyes.

'Did you know that was going to work?' Yeasir asked.

'Well,' said Malekith with a smile. 'It's a long walk back to Ellyrion. I would not have wanted to have come all this way for nothing.'

Yeasir's laughter rang in the prince's ears as he wheeled his steed away, riding south to consult with Charill and his Chracian hunters. While Malekith outlined the next stage of his plan to his fellow prince, the Sapherian wizards alighted upon the smoking towers of the bridge and set free the bindings upon the huge drawbridges. They crashed down over the moat of fire, and the path to Anlec was open. Malekith was the first to ride across, his horse cantering forwards with jaunty high steps as the prince made a confident show for his followers.

In truth, the next phase of the attack was the most worrisome for the prince. It was five hundred paces to the closest outcrop of the walls and a further hundred paces through a corridor of arrows and bolts to reach the gate towers. Bathinair and the mages would do what they could to occupy the defenders upon the ramparts, but Malekith knew that speed was their greatest ally here, and even if they moved swiftly, casualties would be high.

As Yeasir led the advance towards the eastern gate, spear-sized bolts from engines upon the walls shrieked into his spearmen, slaying half a dozen warriors with each shot, their fury so powerful that no shield or armour was defence against them. Yeasir shouted himself hoarse urging on his followers in the face of clouds of black arrows, knowing that although there was no true weakness in Anlec's defences, the war machines could not target foes within a short distance of the walls. If the army could reach the safety of the wall's shadow the greatest danger would be passed.

A thousand elves fell as they raced across the bloody field on foot, the knights held in reserve to attack once the gate had been breached. Yeasir was still unclear as to how this was to be accomplished, but after the feat with the fire moat, Yeasir was willing to trust that his lord had an equally accomplished ploy. In fact, Yeasir realised, he was about to wager his life on it.

Some respite was earned for the spearmen by the warriors from the colonies, who moved forwards behind thick wooden pavises. They were armed with new weapons – repeating crossbows made by the dwarfs, which could fire a hail of short bolts in a short space of time. From behind their movable palisades, they unleashed volley after volley of darts at the walls, pinning down the bolt thrower crews and forcing the defending Naggarothi archers to seek cover. The shots did not go wholly unanswered though, as heavy bolts split the timbers of their wheeled shields and punched through to maim and slay those sheltering behind.

Those enemy warriors out of the crossbows' range were beset by the spells of Thyriol, Merneir and Eltreneth. Storms of purple and blue lightning tore along the battlements, leaping from one warrior to the next. Fire spells in the shape of hawks, dragons and phoenixes left a charred ruin of the defenders in their wake. Bolt throwers shattered into splinters under their enchantments and armour glowed with fiery heat, scorching those within. Daggers of white magic sliced through flesh while swords conjured from nothing hacked and slashed at the cultists upon the wall.

Bathinair played his part too. He and Redclaw left a swathe of dismembered and headless bodies along a stretch of the wall north of the gate, until the weight of bow fire from the defenders against him grew so much that he was forced to soar away, both he and his mount bleeding from many wounds. Crimson dripped from the griffon's beak and claws, falling onto Yeasir and his spearmen as the winged beast glided overhead.

The captain had no time to marvel at such spectacles. A third of his warriors lay dead or wounded upon the killing ground, and they were only halfway to their target. Close enough, it appeared, for the defenders to worry that they might yet reach the wall, for the massive gate yawned open in front of them.

From under its great arch there spilled a tide of wild depravity that Yeasir recognised all too well. Nearly naked but for loincloths and gauzy rags, their long hair spiked with gore, cultists of Khaine screamed and shrieked as they charged forwards. A mix of male and female worshippers, their skin daubed with blood, wearing grotesque jewellery made from sinew and innards, the cultists wielded long, serrated daggers and wicked-looking swords. They poured forth from the open gate in a stream of flesh and blood, hundreds of fanatical blood-worshippers.

Yeasir remembered well the feral snarls and wide eyes of the Murder God's chosen disciples, and knew that they were oblivious to everything but the spilling of blood, their battle-frenzy fuelled by the vapours from narcotic incense and potions brewed by the priestesses who ruled their cult.

The Commander of Nagarythe called for the spearmen to slow and rank up, ready to receive the Khainites' charge. In such formation they were more vulnerable to the arrows stinging down from the walls above, and Yeasir had no doubt that the defenders would not hesitate to fire into the forthcoming melee, heedless of the risk to their own comrades; such was the point of unleashing the cultists. With a crash, the gates closed once more.

A thundering of hooves attracted Yeasir's attention, and he turned to see the reaver knights of Ellyrion galloping forwards. They swept around the spearmen, ducking and swaying in their saddles to avoid the arrows raining down from the ramparts. Expertly loosing their bows as they dashed in, the reavers began to pour arrows into the cultists. In-and-out, left-and-right they galloped, sometimes turning nearly all the way around to fire backwards as they raced past their foes. Some turned their weapons upon the walls, their aim impeccable even at speed, their shots picking out any head or limb that could be seen.

The riders formed two circles running counter to each other around the spearmen, and under the cover of their bows Yeasir ordered the advance to begin again, the circles moving forwards to keep position with the spearmen.

When only a few dozen Khainites remained, the Ellyrians broke off their shooting and stored their bows, taking up their spears instead. With Finudel and Athielle at their head, their famous weapons in hand, the Ellyrians charged in. The Khainites would not break before their attack: so intoxicated with blood-frenzy had they become that they fought until the last of them lay dead upon a heap of bodies, his dying breath a curse upon his enemies.

The path was open to the gates and the Ellyrians directed their steeds away, leaving passage for Yeasir and his warriors to enter between the high walls that led to the immense portal. Behind them came Charill and his hunters of Chrace, and behind them the spearmen of Yvresse stood ready to push forwards through any breach.

As the shadows of the walls loomed above them, the spearmen began to glance upwards at their forbidding heights, expecting death to be unleashed upon them at any moment. Yeasir risked a glance backwards, seeking some sign of Malekith's intent. The prince was sat upon his horse a little way back, arms casually folded across his chest. Malekith somehow felt the eyes of his lieutenant upon him and gave a playful wave, before pointing towards the gatehouse.

Yeasir looked up at the menacing towers and saw black-hooded figures appearing at the battlements. They carried bows in their hands and looked down upon the spearmen with arrows nocked.

'Stand ready!' Yeasir shouted, hefting up his shield.

At that moment, the black banner that flew above the gatehouse fluttered and then fell, as if its pole had been cut. In its place there was raised a new standard: white threaded with silver, with a blazon of a clawed griffon's wing upon it. Yeasir stumbled, almost losing his footing in disbelief, for he recognised it as the banner of House Anar.

The warriors of the Anars tossed bloodied corpses over the battlements, and Yeasir saw it was the bodies of cultists and warriors loyal to Morathi, their throats and bellies slit open. The gate ground open again before Yeasir, and he let out a great roar of triumph.

Fearing that the way in might close any moment, he broke into a run, his spearmen close behind. With the lion warriors of Chrace and the spearmen of Yvresse close on his heels, Yeasir was the first to cross the threshold into Anlec. He shouted again as he passed under the shadow of the gate of his home city, exalted at his return.

INSIDE, THE CITY was utterly unlike the home Yeasir had left behind many centuries earlier. The great square beyond the gate had once been dominated by a large statue of Aenarion seated upon a rearing Indraugnir; now instead it was lined with statues of the cytharai. Atharti cavorted naked atop a marble

stone, snakes twining themselves about her limbs. Anath Raema, the huntress, held her bow in one hand and the severed head of an elf in the other,
her waist girded by a belt of severed hands and heads. The god Khirkith was
depicted crouched upon a pile of bones, a jewelled necklace in his hands as
he admired his looted treasure.

There were many others, of gods of destruction and death, and goddesses of strife and pain. A brazier burned before each, sputtering with dire
contents, the bloodstains upon the statues' plinths testament to the foul
practices of the cultists.

When Yeasir had left Anlec, the buildings around the square had been
busy trading forums, bustling with wares from all across the globe. Now
the open-fronted facades had been turned into animal pens, with bars
across their high arches, and all manner of unnatural beasts in the darkness
beyond.

Mutated bears growled and gnawed at their cages, while two-headed
orthruses howled and a stinking fume drifted into the square from the pens
of half-bull bonnakons. Gaseous clouds issued forth from the cages of wild
chimerae and hideously large serpents spat venom through the bars. Other
things wailed, cavorted and roared menacingly from the shadowy confines
of their prisons.

From one cage there billowed a great cloud of smoke, and licking tongues
of flame could be seen lighting the smog. A gate was thrown open and
there came a great screeching, as of many creatures shrieking in concert.
From out of the gloom there emerged a titanic beast, a seven-headed hydra
with flames flickering from its nostrils. Its scales were of deep blue, and
many welts and scars upon its flesh told of its ill treatment by its keepers.
Its heads were protected by plates of golden armour, as was its spined back
and muscled flanks.

Behind the hydra came a pair of handlers wielding vicious goads and
whips, with which they urged the monster forwards, shouting and hurling abuse. Enraged, the hydra stalked forwards, its claws gouging rents in
the stone flags of the plaza, its heads swaying and writhing like a nest of
serpents. From the cage came another of the huge beasts, of red flesh and
silver armour, with blades and barbs hammered into its scales, and spiked
collars about its five necks. Its tail was likewise armoured and beweaponed,
and thrashed left and right as its handlers scourged its sides with the tines
of their long spears and the cruel thorns of their lashes.

Not since the shaggoth had Yeasir known such dread as he looked at the
two behemoths crashing across the square towards his spearmen. Mastering his fear, he called out for his warriors to form a shield wall, though he
doubted such a manoeuvre would be any defence against the monstrous
creatures bearing down upon the Naggarothi.

Growls and roars sounded to the right and the lion chariots of Charill
raced forwards, the prince at their front. The handlers of the foremost hydra

turned their beast towards the Chracians and with another lash from their whips sent it charging forwards.

Seven blasts of yellow fire gouted from the creature's throats, directed towards Charill's chariot. A shimmering blue aura leapt up around the Chracian prince and his lions, a jewelled amulet hanging upon his bared chest glowing bright with power, and the flames lapped around the prince's magical ward without harm.

The lions leapt to the attack, biting and clawing at the hydra's scaled flesh. The hydra's heads snapped forwards, their dagger-like fangs tearing chunks of bloody ruin out of the lions, whose yelps of pain resounded around the square. The hydra reared up with two lions clamped in its fearsome jaws, wrenching them into the air amidst the tangle of their frayed traces, overturning the chariot. Charill and Lorichar leapt free from the splintering wood and twisted metal, and regained their feet as the other chariots attacked.

The Chracians raced past the monster, axes and lion's fangs scoring wounds upon the creature's hide before they swerved away from its whipping tail and snapping heads. In their wake came the hunters, swinging their axes in wide arcs, lodging their blades deep into the creature's tough hide. Though blood streamed from dozens of wounds, the hydra was relentless, powerful jaws and savage claws wreaking red furrows through the Chracians.

Charill bellowed his war cry and joined the attack, Achillar burning with white light in his hands. With the fabled axe he smote a great blow upon one of the creature's necks, severing it utterly, so that neck and head fell to the floor and continued to writhe for a while like a snake. Blood spumed briefly from the injury, but to the Chracian's horror, the great wound swiftly closed over. Flesh bubbled, veins and arteries, muscle and sinew knitted and grew afresh, so that within moments a new head had grown in the place of the old.

Several dozen hunters and the shattered remains of three chariots now surrounded the beast as the Chracians were hurled back by its savagery. With a wordless shout, Lorichar ran forwards, the speared tip of the household banner aimed towards the monster's chest. Lorichar drove the point of the standard deep between the creature's scales, all of his weight behind the blow. His thick muscles straining, his face a mask of effort, Lorichar drove the banner point deeper and deeper.

Yeasir had not the time to see what happened next, for the second hydra was almost upon the Naggarothi.

'Where's Prince Malekith?' Fenrein asked from beside the captain.

Yeasir did not answer, although the thought had also occurred to him. He had not seen the prince since they had entered the city, and the Naggarothi captain dearly wished his lord was beside him; sorcery and Avanuir would make short work of the horrendous creature that now loomed above the Naggarothi.

Unearthly chattering and screeches briefly distracted the lieutenant as he saw more cultists unbarring the other cells. All manner of beasts and monsters ran forth, howling and yammering. Scaled and feathered, majestic and misshapen, the captured denizens of the Annulii poured forth from their dens like a nightmare made real. The Yvressians moved forwards, spears at the ready to meet the bizarre horde.

Yeasir could spare them no more thought as he turned his attention back to the hydra now just two dozen paces away.

He saw it drawing its heads back, and yelled a warning to his warriors. As one they dropped to a single knee and raised up their shields just as the hydra's fire roared out. Yeasir felt his shield heating in his hands, burning at his fingers as the flames engulfed the spearmen. There were cries of pain and the smell of charred flesh filled the captain's nostrils. Surrounded by a pall of smoke, the Naggaroth captain looked up and saw that a great swathe of his company now lay burning upon the ground; many thankfully dead, others screaming and sobbing as they clutched scorched limbs or rolled about on the stone, their hair and clothes alight.

Black-fletched arrows whickered overhead as the archers of House Anar shot from the gatehouse. Their aim was not for the monstrous hydra, but for the cultists cowering behind its bulk. Several arrows unerringly found their marks and the two handlers dropped, bodies and necks pierced and bloody.

Suddenly free of the goading whips and spears of its handlers, the hydra slowed. Three of its heads bent back to examine their unmoving corpses, the other four rose into the air, nostrils flaring as they caught the scent of basilisks and khaltaurs. Fiery venom dripping from its maws, the hydra heaved around its bulk and spied its enemies from the mountains. With deafening hisses issuing from its many throats, the hydra lumbered into a run, heading for the other monsters.

Its closest prey was a gigantic wolf with glowing eyes and iron fangs, which turned at the hydra's approach and leapt at one of its throats. No longer under any control, the hydra tore apart the wolf-thing and barrelled forwards, tail and claws smashing and crushing the lesser creatures before it. All control disappeared as the beasts of the mountains fell upon each other; blasts of fire and lightning danced amongst the mutated creatures and blood of all colours stained the square as the ferocity of the monsters was unleashed. The Yvressians retreated with shrieks of alarm as the ragged corpse of a basilisk was hurled into the ranks, its poisonous blood burning their skin.

Yeasir could not help but laugh, out of relief more than humour. A glance told him that the Chracians had finished off their monstrous foe, though they stood about its body chopping and hacking with their blades to ensure that it regenerated no further.

Malekith's whereabouts still a mystery, Yeasir turned and looked for the prince. He spied him then upon the wall, talking with Eoloran, the prince of House Anar. Telling his spearmen to stand guard for fresh attack, Yeasir left the company and headed towards the steps.

* * *

MALEKITH SAW YEASIR striding up the stairway to the gate wall, and waved him forwards. With the prince stood Eoloran, his son Eothlir and his grandson Alith. All were dressed in silver armour and black cloaks, and carried bows etched with magical sigils. The three were grim-faced, but Malekith was in good humour as he looked at the bloody savagery being unleashed in the plaza below. He introduced Yeasir to his companions, clapping a hand to his second-in-command's shoulder in an encouraging fashion.

'Well done!' the prince exclaimed. 'I knew you would not let me down.'

'Highness?' said Yeasir.

'The city, you fool,' laughed Malekith. 'Now that we are in, it is only a matter of time. I have you to thank for that.'

'Thank you, highness, but I think you deserve more credit than I,' said Yeasir. He looked at the Anars. 'And without these noble warriors, I would still be stood outside, or perhaps lying outside with an arrow in my belly.'

'Yes, well, I have thanked them enough already,' said Malekith. 'It would be best not to give them too much credit, otherwise who knows what ideas they might get.'

'How did they come to be here?' asked Yeasir.

'Malekith sent word to us many days ago,' said Eoloran. He was an ageing elf, of hawkish features and a deep voice. 'When he told us of his intent to attack Anlec, at first we thought him mad. By secret means, he outlined his plans for the attack, and it became clear that this was to be no idle gesture. We were only too happy to play our part in ridding Nagarythe of this wretched regime of darkness. Ten days ago we came into the city, dressed in the manner of Salthites and Khainites, and all manner of other vile worshippers of the cytharai. We met in secret and gathered together to await Malekith's attack. We could not open the gates sooner for the square below was filled with Khainites... Well you know that, since you faced them. Once the square was undefended, we struck as swiftly as we could to take the gate.'

'Well, you have my gratitude, prince,' said Yeasir with a deep bow. He turned to Malekith with a frown. 'I must admit to being somewhat hurt that you did not feel that you could trust me with this counsel, highness.'

'Would that I could have,' said Malekith airily. 'I trust you more than I trust my own sword arm, Yeasir. I could not divulge my plan to you lest it affect your actions in battle. I wanted the defenders to know nothing was amiss until the gates were opened, and foreknowledge of the Anars' presence may well have meant that you held back until the gates were already flung wide. We needed to keep the pressure on so that all eyes were turned outwards rather than inwards.'

Malekith then turned to Eoloran.

'If you would excuse me, I believe my mother is waiting for me,' the Naggarothi prince said, now empty of all humour.

* * *

THERE WAS STILL fierce fighting in the plaza, and the knights of Anlec arrived to take their share of the glory, driving hard into cultists and beasts with their lances. Designed as a fortress, Anlec was laid out in a fashion so that there was no direct route to the central palace. Along twisting streets, harassed by archers from roofs and windows, the army of Malekith advanced cautiously, aware that by alley and underground passage there were many ways by which a foe could come at them from every direction and then melt away into the city.

Fortunately for Malekith, the defenders had committed a greater part of their strength to the defence of the walls, confident that no enemy had ever passed into the city by force of arms. This left the remaining defenders scattered, and as most were simple cultists they attacked in haphazard, uncoordinated fashion and were easily dealt with.

At one stage the advance was halted, as a fearsome figure atop a manticore descended on the column from the skies. Malekith recognised him as Prince Kheranion, and knew him of old.

He wore armour of ithilmar inscribed with protective runes and bound with enchantments of warding, forged in the Shrine of Vaul, against which it was said no mortal weapon would draw blood. The beast upon which the prince rode had the body of a gigantic lion, with bat-like wings that swathed the street in shadow as the traitor plunged down from the air, his mount roaring ferociously.

The knights at the head of the advance were taken by surprise as the prince dropped from above, their armour gouged by his monster's teeth, their horses cast down upon the cobbles.

In his hand the prince wielded the fell lance Arhaluin, the shadowdeath that Caledor had forged for Aenarion before he had wielded the Sword of Khaine. Seeing the weapon in the hands of his foe sent Malekith into a rage. He raced forwards, his steed's hooves striking sparks from the pavement as the prince gathered magical power for a sorcerous blast.

Before Malekith could confront Kheranion, Morathi's captain steered his mount into the air once more and swooped over the rooftops. Moments later he dived into the attack once more, crashing into the Yvressian spearmen further down the road.

For several minutes the prince hit-and-ran in this fashion, halting the advance and allowing other defenders to gather in numbers around the column. Doorways and windows spat arrows into the attackers. Red-robed cultists leapt from hidden trapdoors to snatch warriors and drag them from sight before their comrades could react. Chilling screams began to echo through the streets, unnerving the attackers further.

Beset from above and below, Malekith shouted in frustration and urged the army to move onwards.

The Naggarothi prince knew that ahead lay a wide killing ground, where his army would be vulnerable to attack, but there was no option but to press on towards the palace. Soon the winding streets led them to a rectangular space lined on all sides by high walls punctured with murder holes. As arrows rained down from these narrow slits, Malekith summoned the energy for a spell.

Here, in the heart of Anlec, there was much dark magic, drawn here by the murder and suffering of the cultists' victims. Aided by the circlet, Malekith was able to tap into this flowing energy and harness it. He tried to form a magical shield around his troops, but the dark magic contorted and thrashed in his mental grasp, refusing his will.

With a snarl, Malekith allowed his frustration full vent and let loose a stream of magic as a cloud of black darts that exploded outwards, each small missile twisting and turning to seek out an embrasure or opening. Screams and shouts resounded from the corridors within the walls around the cloister as the darts found their targets, and blood from the slain dribbled from windows and under door.

Kheranion attacked again, plunging downwards with lance ready. Malekith hurled a bolt of lightning at the stooping monster, but Kheranion raised his silvered shield and the spell earthed itself harmlessly within the enchanted guard.

Kheranion was not without some sorcery himself and a dark nimbus surrounded him before erupting into a flock of evil crows that descended upon Malekith's army, pecking at eyes and exposed skin, causing disarray and panic. With a contemptuous sweep of his arm, Malekith dispelled the curse and the crows evaporated into burning feathers.

So intent was Kheranion on his magical duel with Malekith that he did not spy a shape coming upon him from the clouds. It appeared first as a speck, but rapidly grew larger until the shape of Bathinair's griffon could be seen. Hearing its screech, Kheranion turned, but too late. In Bathinair's hand, Nagrain trailed icy shards and its crystalline point bit deep into the muscle and bone where the manticore's right wing met its body. With a strange yelp, the manticore twisted and raked its claws across the chest of Redclaw, and the two snarled and snapped at each other as they dug in their long claws.

Bathinair avoided a thrust from Kheranion as the two monsters locked together and spiralled towards the ground. Nagrain leapt again but Kheranion deflected the attack with his shield, his own magical lance piercing the throat of Redclaw. In its death throes, the griffon clamped its beak about the left foreleg of the manticore and both beasts and riders crashed into a tiled roof before spinning onto the cobbles of the open ground.

The manticore lashed its tail sting forwards, catching Bathinair a raking blow across the chest and sending him flying from the throne upon which he had been seated. Discarding Arhaluin, Kheranion drew a sword whose blade was made wholly of flame. The prince advanced purposefully towards the stricken Bathinair. The manticore righted itself and lunged forwards lopsidedly, its wounded wing trailing uselessly behind it.

Malekith drew Avanuir and urged his horse forwards, eyes intent on Kheranion.

Another shadow eclipsed Malekith for a moment as Merneir swept across the square atop his pegasus, his staff blazing with golden light. With a shout, the mage unleashed a ball of blue fire that hurtled across the open space and detonated with a flash beside Kheranion. The prince was hurled into the air and the manticore flung sideways by the blast. The gold-shod hooves of his steed flailing, the mage descended upon the manticore with his sword, hacking away at its venom-tipped tail while Kheranion shook his head and groggily stood.

Behind the renegade prince, Bathinair rose to his feet also, Nagrain grasped in both hands. His face was a mask of anger as blood trickled across the left side of his face from a cut on his forehead. He swept the point of the spear towards Kheranion and a hail of icy shards erupted from the weapon's tip, slamming into the prince's armour and smashing him from his feet once more. The firesword spun from his grip.

Out of desperation, Kheranion flung forwards an outstretched hand and a blast of power caught Bathinair full in the chest, sending him crashing into the wall a dozen paces distant. The prince collapsed to one knee, panting hard, while Kheranion scrabbled on all fours to reclaim his blade.

Just as Kheranion's fingers curled around the hilt of the accursed sword, Malekith arrived. He leaned low in the saddle and Avanuir carved a furrow into the renegade's armour and bit into his spine. Malekith leapt from the back of his horse as it galloped on and landed cat-like next to the stricken prince. Kheranion stared into Malekith's eyes and saw the prince of Nagarythe's murderous gaze.

'Spare me!' begged Kheranion, falling to his back and tossing away his magical sword. 'I am crippled and no more a threat!'

Malekith saw that this was true, for the prince's legs hung limply from his body as he dragged himself away across the cobbles.

'Perhaps you would have me end your suffering?' said Malekith, taking a step forwards, the point of Avanuir aimed towards his foe's throat.

'No!' cried Kheranion. 'Though I am undone, perhaps my wound is not beyond that of the finest healers.'

'Why would I allow you to live, so that like a pet serpent you could rise up and bite me again?'

Kheranion sobbed with pain and fear, and held up an arm as if to ward away the killing blow.

'I denounce Morathi!' Kheranion shouted, his voice reverberating around the courtyard. 'I will swear anew my oaths to Malekith!'

'You are a traitor, and yet have not the conviction to stand by your treacherous path,' snarled Malekith. 'Betrayal can be forgiven, cowardice cannot.'

With that, Malekith drove the point of Avanuir downwards and Kheranion shrieked, but the tip of the sword stopped a fraction from the fallen prince's throat.

'Yet I also swore to be merciful,' said Malekith, lifting away his blade. 'Though you have done many wrongs against me, I must stand by that oath and offer clemency to those who repent of their misdeeds. Perhaps I will find a way even for a creature as craven as you to make amends.'

With an agonised grunt, Kheranion threw himself forwards and grasped Malekith around the leg and whimpered meaningless gratitudes. Malekith kicked him away with a sneer.

'Pathetic,' the prince rasped, turning away.

— TWENTY-ONE —

A Destiny Manifested

THE CLOSER MALEKITH and his host drew to the central palace, the more disturbing Anlec became. Many of the buildings here had been turned into immense charnel temples, their steps stained dark with blood, the entrails and bones of the cultists' victims hung upon their walls as decoration. Hundreds of braziers burned fitfully, spewing noxious, acrid fumes through the streets. The air itself clung with the stench of death and all was silent save for the crackling of flames and the tread of the warriors on the bloodstained tiles of the streets. They came at last upon the palace of Aenarion, a large building that doubled as the central citadel of Anlec. It appeared deserted, and the broad doors were opened wide. Dismembered skeletons, rotting organs and other detritus littered the steps leading up to the entrance.

Malekith stopped at the foot of the steps and looked up into the beckoning door, seeking an ambush. Lanterns glowed with ruddy light from within, but there was no sign of any other living thing.

Slowly, Malekith ascended the steps, Avanuir in hand. His knights dismounted and followed a short way behind, similarly ready for attack. Malekith paused before he stepped across the threshold and checked one more time for hidden attackers. Satisfied that there was no immediate threat, he strode through the doors into the chamber beyond.

It was as he remembered from a millennium ago. A long colonnaded hall led away from the doors, much like a larger version of the entrance of Ealith's keep. There was no evidence of the murder and slaughter of the rest of the city here. The floor was a vast mosaic of a golden blade upon a storm-filled sky, and Malekith remembered it from when he was a child.

He had crawled upon this floor and happily stroked the golden tiles even as his father had told him of its story, for it was a depiction of a dream, the vision that had beset Malekith's father and spurred him to take up the war against the daemons. Though his father had not known it at the time, it had been the Sword of Khaine calling to him, from hundreds of leagues distant, suddenly awoken from its eons-long slumber by the anger of Aenarion.

The slamming of the doors behind him shattered Malekith's thoughts and he spun around, expecting attack. He heard thuds and thumps as his followers outside attempted to open them, but Malekith knew it would be fruitless; the tinge of ancient magic hung about the portal, spells laid upon it in the time of Caledor.

'Come to me,' a voice echoed along the empty halls, and Malekith recognised his mother's tone.

Still wary of attack, Malekith stalked along the hallway, all childhood thoughts forgotten. His eyes roved across the archways and high galleries, seeking any sign of a hidden assassin, but there was none. Passing through the great doorway at the end of the entrance hall, Malekith came to an antechamber from which two sets of stairs spiralled upwards to the left and right.

The one on the left led to the bedchambers, guardhouses and other domestic rooms on the first floor, while the stair to the right wound higher to the throne room of Aenarion. Without hesitation, Malekith turned to his right and slowly ascended the marble stair, a carpet of deep blue running down its centre. His footfalls made no sound as he walked, and in the silence there came a noise on the very edge of his hearing.

It was weeping, a constant low sob. Stopping, Malekith listened more intently but the noise could be heard no more. Walking again, Malekith heard a distant, dim shriek and a yammering for mercy. Halting once more to listen, the sound faded away again, leaving only silence.

'Spare us!' said a voice behind Malekith, and he spun, sword in hand, but there was nothing there.

'Mercy!' pleaded a whisper in Malekith's right ear, but turning his head he saw only empty air.

'Not the blade!'

'Free us!'

'Give us peace!'

'Justice!'

'Show us pity!'

Malekith twisted left and right, seeking the source of the voices, but he was alone on the stairway.

'Begone,' the prince growled, holding up Avanuir.

In the flickering glow of the blade, Malekith finally saw movement: ghostly figures dimly reflecting the blue glare of Avanuir's fire. He could see the spirits only in glimpses, and saw flashes of headless bodies, children with their hearts ripped out, mutilated women and victims of all kinds of vile torture. They reached out with broken hands, skin hanging in flaps from mutilated arms. Some were eyeless, others had their mouths stitched shut or their cheeks pierced with spikes.

'Get away from me!' snarled Malekith, turning and leaping up the stairs, casting glances over his shoulder as he hurried upwards. The swirling ghosts chased the prince up the steps and he slashed at them with Avanuir, parting their insubstantial forms with its glowing blade.

Panting, he reached the upper landing and stood before the high double doors that led to the throne room. Soundlessly, they opened inwards, bathing Malekith in the golden light from many lanterns within.

At the far end of the hall sat Morathi, clad in a draping wind of golden cloth that obscured very little of her nakedness. She held her staff of bone and iron across her lap, her fingers toying with the skull at its tip. Morathi sat in a simple wooden chair next to the mighty throne of Aenarion; which was cut from a single piece of black granite, its back shaped like a rearing dragon, of which Bel Shanaar's throne was but a pale imitation. Magical flame licked from the dragon's fanged maw and glowed in its eyes.

Malekith's eyes were drawn to the throne above all other things, ignoring even his mother, for this was the strongest memory he had of this place; of his father girded for war sat upon that immense chair, in counsel with his famed generals.

The memory was so vivid that Malekith could hear his father's soft yet strong voice echoing around the throne room. The prince was but a child, sat in the lap of his mother beside the Phoenix King, and Aenarion would occasionally pause in his conversation and look down upon his son. Always stern was that look; not unkind, yet not compassionate either, but full of pride. For years Malekith had gazed back at those strong, dark eyes and seen the fires that raged behind their quiet dignity. Malekith imagined that he alone knew the sinister spirit that hid within, clothed in the body of a noble monarch, masked against the eyes of the world lest it be recognised for what it truly was.

The soul of a destroyer, the wielder of the Godslayer.

And the sword! There across the Phoenix King's lap lay Widowmaker, Soulbiter, the Sword of Khaine. Even at a young age, Malekith had noticed that only he and his father ever looked upon its blood-red blade, for all other elves averted their gaze and would look anywhere else but directly at it. It was like a secret shared between them.

'Yet you did not pick up the Blade of Murder when it was offered to you,' said Morathi, dispelling the illusion that had so gripped her son.

Malekith shook his head, confused by the enchantment cunningly wrought upon him by his mother. Truly they were real memories she had stirred, but her spell had made them as tangible as life, if only for a moment.

'I did not,' replied Malekith, slowly, realising that Morathi had seen into his thoughts and learned of his episode on the Blighted Isle, of which he had spoken to nobody.

'That is good,' said Morathi. She was sat in stately pose, despite her near-nudity, and exuded regal poise. Not here the barbarous priestess who tore living hearts from the breasts of her victims; not the seductive, wily seeress who wove lies with every word and manipulated all around her into a tapestry to her liking. Here she was as queen of Nagarythe, full of quiet majesty and grandeur.

'The sword controlled your father,' the queen said, her tone hushed, reassuring. 'Since his death, it has yearned for you to seek it out. I was worried that you would be ensnared by its power as well, but I am proud that you resisted its bloodthirsty call. None can truly be its master, and if you are to rule, then you must be master of everything.'

'I would rather the world was devoured by daemons than unleash that fell creation upon it again,' Malekith said, sheathing Avanuir. 'As you say, once drawn it will consume its wielder until nothing but blood remains. No person can become a king with its power, only a slave.'

'Sit down,' Morathi said, waving a hand of invitation towards the grand throne.

'It is not yet my place to sit there,' replied Malekith.

'Oh?' said Morathi, surprised. 'And why is that?'

'If I am to rule Nagarythe, I shall rule it alone,' said Malekith. 'Without you. When you are slain, the army of Nagarythe will be mine again. I shall hold power over the pleasure cults and with them secure the Phoenix Throne.'

Morathi remained silent for a moment, looking at her son with ancient eyes, gauging his mood and motive. A sly smile then twisted her lips.

'You mean to slay me?' she whispered, feigning shock.

'While you live, always will your ambition be a shadow upon mine,' said Malekith, angry at his mother's charade. 'You cannot help but be my rival, for it is not in your nature to serve any but yourself. I cannot share Ulthuan with you, for you could never truly share it with me. Even my father was not your master. I would exile you, but you would rise up again in some forgotten corner, a contender for everything that I aspire to.'

'Cannot share power,' Morathi said, 'or will not?'

Malekith pondered for a moment, examining his feelings.

'Will not,' he replied, his eyes full of intent.

'And to what is it that you aspire, my son?' Morathi said, leaning forwards eagerly.

'To inherit my father's legacy and rule as Phoenix King,' Malekith replied, knowing the truth of the words even as he spoke them. Never before had he so openly admitted his desire, not even to himself. Glory, honour, renown; all but stepping stones towards his ascension to the Phoenix Throne. The circlet had revealed to him the true nature of the forces that now ruled the world, and he would not stand by while Ulthuan slowly succumbed to them.

'Yes, Chaos is strong,' Morathi told him.

'Stay out of my thoughts,' Malekith snarled, taking an angry step forwards, his hand straying to the hilt of Avanuir.

'I need no magic to know your mind, Malekith,' said Morathi, still gazing fixedly at her son. 'There is a bond between mother and son that does not need sorcery.'

'Do you submit yourself to your fate?' Malekith said, ignoring her obvious reminder of their relationship; an attempt to stay his hand.

'You should know better than ask such a pointless question,' Morathi replied, and now her voice was stern, harsh even. 'Have I not always told you that you were destined to be king? You cannot be king unless you are prince of your own realm, and I will not surrender it willingly. Prove to me that you are worthy of ruling Nagarythe. Prove to the other princes that the strength within you is greater than any other.'

At some silent command, four figures emerged from the shadows, two to Malekith's left and two to his right. They were sorcerers by their garb, two male and two female, swathed in black robes, tattooed with dark sigils.

Malekith struck out with a blast of magic, materialising as a thunderbolt from his fingertips. Instantly Morathi was surrounded by a shadowy sphere of energy, which pulsed as the bolt struck it. Her adepts unleashed spells of their own, fiery blasts that rushed in upon Malekith in the guise of howling wolf heads, and the prince cast his own shield of darkness to ward them away.

The sorcerers and sorceresses closed in, hurling fireballs and flares of dark power. Malekith protected himself, drawing in more and more magic from the energy seething around the throne room as the spells cascaded towards him.

Morathi sat contentedly upon her chair while her followers unleashed their hexes and curses, watching with interest as Malekith countered each. Churning and bubbling, magic flowed around the hall, growing in intensity as both Malekith and his foes reached their minds out further and further, drawing energy from the city outside.

'Enough,' barked Malekith, letting free the energy that he had pulled into himself, releasing a blast of raw magic not shaped by any spell.

The power blazed, surrounding each of the dark wizards, filling them with mystical energy; more than they could control. The first, a red-haired witch, began to quiver, and then spasmed so hard that Malekith heard her spine snapping as she flopped to the ground. The other sorceress screeched in agony as her blood turned to fire and exploded out of her veins, engulfing her in a tempest of lightning and flames. The third of them flew into the air as if struck, his nose, eyes and ears streaming with blood, his ragged body smashing against the distant wall. The last was consumed by the ravening magic and collapsed in upon himself, crumpled like a ball of paper until he disintegrated into a pile of dust.

'Your followers are weak,' said Malekith, rounding on Morathi.

The seeress remained unconcerned.

'There are always more minions,' she said with a dismissive wave of a beringed hand. 'That trinket upon your head gives you impressive power, but you lack subtlety and control.'

Quicker than Malekith's eye could follow, Morathi's hand snapped out, her staff pointed at his chest. He fell to one knee as his heart began to thunder inside his ribs, drowning him with pain. Through the haze of agony, Malekith could feel the slender tendrils of magic that extended from Morathi's staff, almost imperceptible in their delicacy.

Whispering a counterspell, Malekith chopped his hand through the intangible strands and forced himself back to his feet.

'You never taught me that,' said Malekith with mock admonition. 'How unmotherly to keep such secrets from your son.'

'You have not been here to learn from me,' Morathi said with a sad shake of her head. 'I have learned much these past thousand years. If you put aside this foolish jealousy that consumes you, then perhaps I can tutor you again.'

In reply, Malekith gathered up the coiling magic and hurled it at the queen, the spell materialising as a monstrous serpent. Morathi's staff intercepted it, a shimmering blade springing from its haft to slice the head from the immaterial snake.

'Crude,' she said with a wag of her finger. 'Perhaps you impressed the savages of Elthin Arvan and the wizardless dwarfs with these antics, but I am not so easily awed.'

Standing, the seeress-queen held her staff in both hands above her head and began to chant quickly. Blades crystallised out of the air around her, orbiting her body in ever-increasing numbers until she was all but obscured from view by a whirlwind of icy razors. With a contemptuous laugh, Malekith extended his will, looking to knock them aside.

His dispel met with failure, however, as Morathi's magic swayed and changed shape, slipping through the insubstantial grasp of his counterspell. A moment later and the shardstorm tore through the air towards him, forcing the prince to leap aside lest they rip the flesh from his bones.

'Slow and predictable, my child,' Morathi said, stepping forwards.

Malekith said nothing, but lashed out with his sorcery, a whip of fire appearing in his hands. Its twin tips flew across the room and coiled about Morathi's staff. With a flick of his wrist, Malekith wrested the rod from his mother, sending it skittering across the tiled floor. With another short hand motion Malekith dashed the staff against the wall, shattering it into pieces.

'I think you are too old for such toys,' said Malekith, drawing Avanuir.

'I am,' snarled Morathi, her face contorting with genuine anger.

Something invisible scythed through the air and connected with Malekith's legs. He felt his shins crack and his knees shatter and a howl of pain was wrenched from his lips as he crashed to the floor. Letting Avanuir fall from his grasp, he clutched at his broken legs, writhing and screaming.

'Stop making such a noise,' said Morathi irritably.

Making a fist, she wove a spell that clenched Malekith's throat in its grip, choking him. The pain befuddled his mind, and as he flailed and gasped he could not muster the concentration to counter the spell.

'Focus, boy, focus,' spat Morathi as she stalked forwards, her fist held out in front of her, twisting it left and right as Malekith squirmed in her mystical grasp. 'You think you are fit to rule without me? I expect such ingratitude from the likes of Bel Shanaar, but not from my own kin.'

The mention of the Phoenix King's name acted as a lightning rod for Malekith's pain and anger, and he lashed out, a sheet of flame erupting from him to engulf the queen. She was unharmed, but had released her spell to protect herself. Malekith rolled to his side, coughing and spluttering.

The prince was then flipped to his back and he felt a great weight upon his chest. Numbness enveloped him as the weight pressed down harder and harder, and Malekith fought against losing consciousness. As black spots and bright lights flickered in his vision, he thought he glimpsed a shadowy, insubstantial creature crouched upon his chest: a slavering horned daemon with a wide, fang-filled maw and three eyes. Pushing aside the aching of his body, he tried to focus his mind, but his body would not move.

Morathi stood beside her son, looking down dispassionately. She reached down and grasped Malekith's helm in one hand and pulled it from his head. The queen regarded it closely for a moment, her eyes analysing every scratch and dint in its grey surface, her fingers lingering close to the circlet but never touching it. Gently, she crouched beside Malekith and placed the helm behind her, out of reach. Malekith fought back a surge of panic. He felt strangely naked and powerless without the circlet.

'If you do not know how to use it properly, you should not have it,' she said gently. She laid a hand upon his cheek, caressing him, and then placed her fingers upon his forehead as a mother soothing the brow of a fevered child. 'If you had but asked me, I would have helped you unlock its real power. Without it, your magic is weak and unrefined. You should have paid more attention to what your mother taught you.'

'Perhaps,' Malekith said. With a shout of pain, he swung his gauntleted fist at Morathi, punching her clean in her face and sending her slamming to her back. 'I learned that from my father!'

Stunned, Morathi lost her concentration and her spell evaporated. Malekith felt the invisible weight lifting from his body. With an effort, he drew magic down into his ruined legs, fusing bone back into place, knotting muscle and sinew together.

Whole again, the prince stood, looming over Morathi. With a flick of his hand, Avanuir jumped from the floor and landed in his grasp, its point a finger's breadth from Morathi's face, unwavering.

His face grimly set, he swung Avanuir over his left shoulder and brought it down in a backhand sweep towards Morathi's neck.

'Wait!' she shouted and Malekith's arm froze, the blade no more than a hand's span from the killing blow.

It was no spell that had stayed his hand, but the tone in her voice. It was not desperation or fear, but anger and frustration, as she had used so many times before when he was a child about to do something wrong.

'What?' he asked, confused by his own reaction.

'Use your mind, think about what is for the best,' said Morathi slowly. 'How will this truly aid you?'

'What do you mean?' Malekith said with narrowed eyes full of suspicion. He lowered Avanuir but kept the blade ready to strike the moment he detected the merest hint of a conjuration.

'Do you think that killing me will give you the throne of Nagarythe?' Morathi said, lying as still as a statue, her gaze never moving from her son's eyes. 'Do you think that my death will usher you to the rule of Ulthuan?'

'It cannot harm my cause,' Malekith said with a shrug.

'But it will not help it,' Morathi said. 'Slay me here, unseen by any other, and the truth of your victory will never really be known. "Malekith slew his mother," the chronicles will say, and then the deed will be forgotten, hidden away like a shameful secret.'

'And if I let you live?' Malekith asked warily.

'I will turn the cults to your bidding,' said Morathi. 'You cannot hope to control them, and without me they will splinter and either turn against you or simply vanish altogether.'

'If I let you live, you will use the cults of luxury against me,' said Malekith. 'You will undermine my power even as it grows until I am forced to treat with you. Do not think I will be so easily fooled. Better that you die here even if it means I must start afresh.'

'There is another way, Malekith,' Morathi told him. 'For the cults, you can imprison me as hostage against their loyalty. What better symbol of your new power than to see the sorceress-queen of Nagarythe bound in chains? Better yet, present me as your captive to Bel Shanaar. Your mercy will earn you great credit in the court of the Phoenix King and amongst the other realms. Would you be known to them as a merciless killer, or as a magnanimous victor? Which do you think they would choose as Bel Shanaar's successor? They have scorned your inheritance once already, naming you as a bloody slayer unfit to rule. Will the blood of your mother change their minds?'

'I care not concerning the opinions of lesser princes,' said Malekith, raising Avanuir again to strike.

'Then you are a fool!' spat Morathi. 'If you would wrest the crown of

Ulthuan by force, then go now to the Blighted Isle and take up the sword your father wielded, for you will need it. If you would perhaps take up your rightful inheritance and reign in glory, then you must make the other princes your followers. Already they look up to you; many would have you replace Bel Shanaar right at this moment. Woo them! Show them your kingly virtues, and the blood of Aenarion will prove its worth.'

For a second time, Malekith lowered his blade. He looked deep into his mother's eyes, seeking some deceit or falsehood, but saw only sincerity.

'You would be humbled before all of Ulthuan,' Malekith said. 'Your station, your rank would be worthless.'

'I care as little about such matters as you,' Morathi said. 'I am confident in you, and have much patience. When you become Phoenix King, I will be rightfully restored to my proper position. I have humbled myself before priests and gods to gain what I have. It is no hardship to masquerade for a while as prisoner to Bel Shanaar.'

Malekith sheathed Avanuir and lifted his mother to her feet. He laid a hand upon her shoulder and pulled her close.

'I will spare you,' he whispered to her. 'But if you wrong me, or play me false, I shall kill you without a second thought.'

Morathi clasped her son in a tight embrace, a hand on the back of his head, her lips close to his ear.

'You have proven that to me,' she sighed. 'That is why I am so proud of you.'

─◄ TWENTY-TWO ►─

The Wheels of Power Turn

As MORATHI HAD predicted, there was much rejoicing when news of Malekith's victory spread across Ulthuan. Once Anlec was firmly under his control the prince rode to Galthyr to lift the siege there. The Naggarothi commanders threw themselves on Malekith's mercy and swore new oaths of loyalty to the prince. By secret command from Morathi, many of the cultists vanished into the wilds and their leaders hid themselves amongst the folk of Nagarythe. Prince Malekith sent word to the other rulers of Ulthuan that some measure of order had been restored, and feasts of celebration were held across the isle.

Malekith escorted Morathi south to Tor Anroc, accompanied by the three Sapherian mages Thyriol, Merneir and Eltreneth to guard against any sorcery from the seeress. With a great show of humility, Malekith went incognito through the towns and villages, sparing his mother the spite of the elves she had all but enslaved.

Many days after leaving Anlec they came to the citadel of the Phoenix King, now an immense palace with a hundred halls and fifty spiralling towers. Swathed in black cloaks, they rode through the gate and were met by Palthrain. No words were said for all had been pre-arranged. The chamberlain ushered the small group through the long corridors and vaulted galleries to the heart of the palace, to the throne room of Bel Shanaar.

The floor was paved with white gold and the walls hung with six hundred tapestries picturing landscapes from the wide realm of the elves. Magical dwarf-forged lanterns bathed all in a pearlescent glow as Malekith pulled

245

back his hood. The prince and his companions strode along the hall to stand before Bel Shanaar, who was sat upon his throne deep in thought. Imrik was there, as were Bathinair, Elodhir, Finudel and Charill.

'My king and princes,' said Malekith. 'Today is a portentous occasion, for as I vowed, I bring before you the Witch Queen of Nagarythe, my mother, Morathi.'

Morathi cast off her cloak and stood before her judges. She was dressed in a flowing blue gown, her hair bound up with shining sapphires, her eyelids painted with azure powder. She appeared every inch the defeated queen, dejected but unrepentant.

'You stand before us accused of raising war against the office of the Phoenix King and the realms of the princes of Ulthuan,' Bel Shanaar said.

'It was not I that launched attacks against the border of Nagarythe,' Morathi replied calmly. Her gaze met the eyes of the princes in turn. 'It was not the Naggarothi who sought battle with the other kingdoms.'

'You would portray yourself as the victim?' laughed Finudel. 'To us?'

'No ruler of Nagarythe is a victim,' replied Morathi.

'Do you deny that the cults of excess and luxury that blight our realm owe their loyalty to you?' said Bel Shanaar.

'They owe their loyalty to the cytharai,' said Morathi. 'You can no more prosecute me for the existence of the cults than you can impeach yourself for assuming the mantle of Asuryan's chosen.'

'Will you at least admit to thoughts of treason?' said Elodhir. 'Did you not plot against my father and seek to undermine him?'

'I hold no position in higher regard than that of the Phoenix King,' Morathi said, her eyes fixed upon Bel Shanaar. 'I spoke my mind at the First Council and others chose to ignore my wisdom. My loyalty is to Ulthuan and the prosperity and strength of her people. I do not change my opinions at a whim and my reservations have not been allayed.'

'She is a viper,' snarled Imrik. 'She cannot be allowed to live.'

Morathi laughed, a scornful sound that reverberated menacingly around the hall.

'Who wishes to be known as the elf who slew Aenarion's queen?' the seeress said. 'Which of the mighty princes gathered here would claim that accolade?'

'I will,' said Imrik, his hand straying to the silver hilt of the sword at his waist.

'I cannot condone this,' said Malekith, stepping protectively in front of his mother.

'You swore to me in this very chamber that you would be ready for such an end,' said Bel Shanaar. 'Do you now renege on your oath?'

'No more than I renege on the oath that I would show mercy to all those who asked for it,' said Malekith. 'My mother need not die. Her blood would serve no purpose but to sate the Caledorian's vengeful thirst.'

'It is justice, not revenge,' said Imrik. 'Blood for blood.'

'If she lives, she is a threat,' said Finudel. 'She cannot be trusted.'

'I cannot decide this,' said Malekith, addressing the princes. He then turned his eyes upon the Phoenix King. 'I will not decide this. Let Bel Shanaar decide. The will of the Phoenix King is stronger than the oath of a prince. Is the word of the son of Aenarion to be as nothing, or is there yet nobility enough in the princes of Ulthuan to show compassion and forgiveness?'

Bel Shanaar gave Malekith a sour look, knowing that all that had passed here would be reported by means both open and secret to the people of Ulthuan. Malekith tested his judgement, and there was no course of action that would not damage his reputation with those who wanted to see weakness.

'Morathi cannot go unpunished for her crimes,' Bel Shanaar said slowly. 'There is no place to which I can exile her, for she would return more bitter and ambitious than before. As she enslaved others, so shall she forfeit her freedom. She shall stay in rooms within this palace, under guard night and day. None shall see her save with my permission.'

The Phoenix King stood and glared at the sorceress.

'Know this, Morathi,' said Bel Shanaar. 'The sentence of death is not wholly commuted. You live by my will. If ever you cross me or seek to harm my rule, you will be slain, without trial or representation. Your word is of no value and so I hold your life hostage to your good behaviour. Accept these terms or accept your death.'

Morathi looked at the gathered princes and saw nothing but hatred in their faces, save for Malekith's which was expressionless. They were like wolves that had cornered a wounded lion; knowing that they should slay their prey while they could, yet still fearful that there was fight left yet in their enemy.

'Your demands are not unreasonable, Bel Shanaar of Tiranoc,' she said eventually. 'I consent to be your prisoner.'

WITH MORATHI IN custody, Malekith returned to Anlec, to secure his lands against the cultists that still held sway over some parts of the kingdom. On the surface, a measure of order was restored, though in truth the agents of Anlec were now spread wider and further than ever before. Over the passing years a sense of security grew on Ulthuan once again; but it was a false sense, fostered by the machinations of Malekith.

In ones and twos the cultists began to gather again, now more careful than ever. Their leaders sent messages to each other by their secret ways, and the heads of the dark priesthoods emerged in new guises in Anlec. As councillors and advisors, Malekith masked these magisters within his court, holding over them the threat of exposure to ensure their loyalty to him.

For two decades relative peace prevailed. Often Malekith travelled to Tor

Anroc to consult with Bel Shanaar, and ever the prince of Nagarythe would decry his own failure to capture all of those who had been henchmen to his mother. He offered what help he could to the other kingdoms, and spent as much time in the palaces of his fellow princes as he did in Anlec, fostering harmony and friendship.

On these travels he would also visit his mother, supposedly to check on her wellbeing and to accept a repentance that was never offered. On the twentieth anniversary of his mother's imprisonment, Malekith rode alone to Tor Anroc and was granted a private meeting with his mother by the Phoenix King. They were brought together in the majestic gardens at the centre of the palace of Tor Anroc. High hedges hid them from view as they walked across the plush green lawns, their soft words masked by the splashing of fifty fountains.

'How is the hospitality of Bel Shanaar?' asked Malekith as the pair walked arm-in-arm down an avenue of cherry trees laden with blossom.

'I endure what I must,' replied Morathi.

She led Malekith to a bench of ornately carved pale wood and they sat beside each other; the mother's hand on the son's knee, the son's hand on the mother's shoulder. They sat in silence for a while, both with their faces turned to the bright sky, the sun bathing their skin with her warmth. It was Malekith who first broke the peace.

'All is well in Anlec also,' he said. 'My mercy is now legendary. The cytharai worshippers captured by the princes demand that they receive the same opportunity for repentance as you were granted. They come to Anlec and I hear their confessions and apologies.'

'How many hide beneath your shadow?' asked Morathi.

'Many thousands, all utterly loyal to me,' said the prince with a smile.

'So you stand ready to move soon?' asked the seeress.

'Not yet,' said Malekith, his smile fading. 'Imrik yet resists me in the court of the Phoenix King.'

'Imrik will never be won over,' said Morathi. 'Not only is he jealous, he is shrewd. He guesses our intent, but cannot prove any wrongdoing.'

'Nagarythe also is not yet united,' said Malekith with a solemn shake of his head.

'How so?' asked Morathi.

'There are some princes and nobles who are still fearful of my power,' said Malekith. 'Eoloran of the Anars is chief amongst them. They wish to impose self-rule upon their lands in the mountains.'

'Then Eoloran must be killed,' said Morathi briskly.

'I cannot,' said Malekith. 'Since your fall, his influence has grown considerably. Not only do some Naggarothi nobles hold him in high esteem, some commanders of my armies are under his sway. His lands overseas are highly profitable. Before I can eliminate him, I need him to fall from grace.'

Morathi said nothing for a moment, her eyes narrowed in thought.

'Leave that to me,' she said. 'Word will come to you when you can act.'

'I will not ask what it is that you plan,' said Malekith. 'Yet, I do not understand how it is that you can do anything from here, right under the eyes and ears of Bel Shanaar.'

'Trust your mother,' said Morathi. 'I have my ways.'

The skies were greying and a cloud obscured the sun. Now in shade, the pair stood and walked back to the palace, each lost in thought.

As Morathi had predicted, Imrik of Caledor remained steadfastly suspicious of Malekith's motives, and shunned the prince's overtures of alliance and comradeship. It mattered not though, for through subtle rumour and devious innuendo, Malekith spread the idea that Imrik was jealous of Malekith's popularity. The prince of Nagarythe never spoke out openly against his opponent, and was always ready to praise Imrik's deeds and the calibre of his lineage. He even went so far as to say that, but for the grace of fate, Imrik's father would have been Phoenix King instead of Bel Shanaar. While appearing to be a great compliment, this had the desired effect on the other princes, who had always harboured envy of Caledor's status. Such comments flamed the embers of rumour that Imrik felt wronged that his father had not been chosen by the First Council.

One thousand, six hundred and sixty-eight years after first bowing his knee to Bel Shanaar, Malekith stood ready to make his claim to be Phoenix King. He needed a catalyst that would act as a spur to action on the princes. With a carefully orchestrated series of events, Malekith planned to plunge Ulthuan into brief turmoil once more, so that he could arise from the flames of conflict and claim his birthright.

It began innocently enough, with news that Malekith's warriors had arrested Eoloran Anar, when evidence had come to light that the lord of House Anar had been corrupted by worshippers of Atharti. Cultists rose up out of hiding all across Nagarythe and elsewhere in Ulthuan, supposedly in response to the persecution of a prominent leader. Those who disbelieved the charge against Eoloran were incensed and they too spoke out against Malekith.

Confusion reigned in Nagarythe, as claim and counter-claim spread from town to town, and violence soon followed. None could say for sure who started the killings, but soon there was bitter fighting between those loyal to the Anars and the cultists. The other princes looked on in disbelief as Nagarythe quickly descended into anarchy, where loyalties were so fractured that families were divided and brother fought against brother. Amidst the chaos, Malekith appeared to be doing what he could to restore order, but even his armies seemed fractured by the factions now contending for power.

The battles that had begun in Nagarythe rapidly spread to other parts of Ulthuan as the cults came out of the shadows and struck at the princes.

Palaces burned and citizens were killed on the streets as Ulthuan erupted into bloody infighting. Malekith fought hard to restore his rule in his own kingdom, but the populace had turned against him, for one reason or another. He was forced to quit Anlec with a few thousand loyal troops, and he called upon Bel Shanaar to give him sanctuary.

SO IT CAME to pass that in the autumn of that year, Malekith dwelt in Tor Anroc, and came before Bel Shanaar with a plea. The two were alone in the Phoenix King's throne room, for the princes of the court had returned to their realms to restore what order they could.

'I would make right my mistake,' said Malekith, standing before the Phoenix King, head bowed.

'What mistake have you made?' asked Bel Shanaar.

'In my desire to seek accord with the worshippers of the forbidden gods, I have allowed them to spread unseen and unchecked,' Malekith replied. 'I have allowed myself to be lured into a web of deceit, and was fooled into believing that House Anar were my enemies. Nagarythe now burns with hatred, and I am cast out.'

'What would you have me do?' said the Phoenix King. 'I cannot command your subjects for you.'

'I would have peace restored, so that bitter enmities might be settled and wrongs put to right,' said Malekith, raising his gaze to meet the inquiring stare of Bel Shanaar.

'We all wish that, I am sure,' said Bel Shanaar. 'However, I cannot grant it by simply wishing it so. I ask again, what would you have me do?'

'We must be united in this,' said Malekith earnestly. 'The cults flourished before because we each acted alone. All of the princes must speak with one voice. All of the kingdoms must come together to defeat this dark menace.'

'How so?' said Bel Shanaar with a frown.

'The oaths sworn here many years ago to stand against the cults still hold true,' said Malekith. 'The princes of Ulthuan are still of one purpose on this matter.'

'I do not yet see what you ask of me,' said the Phoenix King.

'As one army we must fight, under one general,' said Malekith. He strode forwards and grasped Bel Shanaar's hand in both of his, falling to one knee. 'As did my father, the army of Ulthuan must be wielded as a single weapon. Each realm in turn shall be cleansed, and no traitor will go unpunished this time.'

'The armies of Ulthuan are not mine alone to command,' Bel Shanaar said slowly. 'I have already pledged the support of Tiranoc, and that has not changed.'

'All have pledged support and even now muster their forces for their own wars,' Malekith said. 'Though perhaps our need has grown greater, more princes than not swore in this chamber to lend their aid.'

'Yet, it is the very magnitude of the situation that will force them to have second thoughts,' Bel Shanaar said. 'It is one thing to ask them to send a few thousand troops to quell cultists and malcontents. To mobilise the militia, to gather their full armies now, on the cusp of winter, is a much greater undertaking. What they have promised and what you now ask is not the same thing.'

'We do not have time to stand idle,' Malekith growled. 'Within a season, civil war could engulf this island. I cannot go to each of the princes in turn and ask for their renewed pledges. You must call the rulers of the kingdoms to a council, so that the matter can be settled.'

'That is within my power, for sure,' said Bel Shanaar. 'For some, the journey to Tor Anroc will take some time, though.'

'Then call them to the Shrine of Asuryan upon the Isle of Flame,' suggested Malekith, standing. 'Thirty days hence, all princes will be able to attend, in the place where you were accepted by the king of gods to succeed my father. We shall consult the oracles there, and with their guidance choose the best course of action for all.'

Bel Shanaar considered this in silence, stroking his chin, as he was wont to do when deep in thought.

'So shall it be,' the Phoenix King said with a solemn nod. 'In thirty days we shall convene the council of princes in the Shrine of Asuryan to determine the destiny of our people.'

── TWENTY-THREE ──

A Council Convened

CARATHRIL STAYED IN Tor Anroc for several more days after Bel Shanaar's proclamation, while heralds were despatched to the princes of Ulthuan. In that time he spoke to Palthrain the chamberlain and others, gauging the mood of the folk of Tiranoc. They were resolute but afraid, was his conclusion. Beyond the Naganath now stood a terrible foe, who could sweep down over Tiranoc at any time. Acting on Malekith's advice, Bel Shanaar despatched an army of twenty thousand elves to the north, to patrol the border and guard the bridges across the Naganath. If the prince of Nagarythe was correct, the cults would not make their next move until spring, for only the desperate or the foolish started a campaign in winter. This was the hope of Bel Shanaar and his council: that the princes would agree to Malekith's mobilisation and send their forces to the west.

Just before Carathril was due to leave for Lothern to take word to Prince Haradrin, he was called to the audience chamber by Bel Shanaar. When he entered, he found himself alone with the Phoenix King, and the doors were closed behind him.

'Come here, Carathril,' the Phoenix King said, waving the captain forwards. 'You ride today for Eataine, yes?'

'This morning, your majesty,' said Carathril, stopping just before Bel Shanaar's throne. 'A ship awaits me at Atreal Anor once I have crossed the mountains, and it is less than a day by sail from Lothern to the Isle of Flame. I felt it better to ensure the other heralds were well prepared before leaving.'

'Yes, you have performed your duties with great dedication and precision,

Carathril,' said Bel Shanaar. He opened his mouth to continue but then stopped. With a finger, he beckoned for Carathril to come closer, and when the Phoenix King spoke, his voice was but a whisper. 'I have one other duty for you to perform. We must gather our forces as Prince Malekith has said, but I am not convinced that it is he that should lead them. Though he seems determined enough to prosecute this war, it is by no means certain that he is entirely free from the influence of Morathi.'

'He resisted well enough at Ealith, I saw it with my own eyes,' said Carathril. 'Also, do we not cast away our greatest weapon if Malekith does not lead the army? If not under the command of the rightful prince of Nagarythe, do our forces not appear to be invaders rather than liberators?'

'I fear that is a poison already spread far by Morathi,' replied Bel Shanaar. 'The Naggarothi have been set against the other realms long before this day; ever have they been independent of thought and deed. Many in Nagarythe, not least Morathi, believe Malekith to be the true successor to Aenarion, and see me as usurper. By giving over command of our armies to the prince, it may be taken as a sign of weakness on my part. I will be seen as ineffective, unable to lead my own subjects. Another must command the army of Ulthuan, in my name alone. I will force Malekith to agree to this condition before I leave for the Isle of Flame.'

'I understand, your majesty,' said Carathril. 'Yet, I still do not know what duty it is that you ask of me.'

The Phoenix King pulled forth a parchment scroll from the folds of his robes and handed it to Carathril.

'Keep this safe, on your person at all times,' the Phoenix King said.

'What is it?' asked Carathril.

'It is better that you do not know,' said Bel Shanaar. 'You must pass it to Prince Imrik at the council.'

'That is all, your majesty?' said Carathril, wondering what message could deserve such secrecy.

'Let no other see it!' insisted Bel Shanaar, leaning forwards and grasping Carathril by the wrist. 'Let no other know that you bear it!'

Bel Shanaar sat back with a sigh, and then smiled.

'I trust you, Carathril,' he said.

BEFORE NOON, CARATHRIL had set out, the missive of the Phoenix King hidden in a leather canister under his robes, next to his heart. With him rode Prince Elodhir and a contingent of Tiranoc knights, to ensure the council was ready for the arrival of the Phoenix King. For Carathril, the journey was unremarkable; he had ridden back and forth across Eagle Pass dozens of times since becoming herald for Bel Shanaar. For six days they rode eastwards, crossing the mountains without incident, and met with Prince Finudel on the eastward side of the pass, just south of his capital at Tor Elyr. The two companies joined for the two days of journeying to Atreal Anor, where they took separate ships. Carathril was bound for Lothern to meet with Prince Haradrin, while Finudel and Elodhir were to set course straight for the Isle of Flame, to prepare the Shrine of Asuryan for the council.

Both ships travelled south and east across the Sea of Dusk, westernmost of the two bodies of water that made up the Inner Sea, skirting the coast of Caledor. Their southerly route took them away from the Isle of the Dead at the centre of the Inner Sea, where the mage Caledor Dragontamer and his followers still stood, locked in eternal stasis within the centre of Ulthuan's magical vortex. Rather than pass by the ill-fated isle, the ships navigated the Strait of Cal Edras, between Anel Edras and Anel Khabyr, which formed the outermost pair of islands of a long archipelago that curved out from Caledor towards the Isle of the Dead. Once through the Cal Edras, the ships parted company.

There were many ships in the Bay of Whispers, plying trade between the coastal villages of Caledor and Saphery, passing in and out of the Straits of Lothern. Carathril spoke to a few of the other crews, and found them to be mostly unaware of the true extent of the tragedy that had happened in the north.

Word had spread of Malekith's expulsion and despite this setback many seemed confident of the prince's ability to reclaim Nagarythe. Carathril chose not to disavow the sailors of their current optimism, knowing that it would be upon ships that news of any disaster would spread fastest, setting panic like a fire in the heart of Ulthuan.

As they sailed onwards towards Lothern, Carathril wondered if his view of life had once been as blinkered as that of his fellow elves. They seemed to be preoccupied with their own dreams and ambitions, and did not give much thought to other forces outside of their immediate lives. He concluded that he had been the same; believing that the cults had been a problem but never once considering the extent to which they had infected the society of Ulthuan, never seeing the threat they truly posed.

The docks at Lothern were as busy as ever, packed with merchantmen returning from the burgeoning colonies or readying to depart with cargoes of goods from the realms of Ulthuan. In a way, it heartened Carathril to see the life of his home city bustling and progressing as if nothing had happened; yet deep inside he knew that this was all soon to change and that his people were utterly unprepared.

For over a thousand years since Bel Shanaar's election as Phoenix King, relative peace had reigned over Ulthuan. War and bloodshed was something brought back in stories from across the seas, and the elves had become complacent, perhaps even indulgent. Now Carathril could see that it was that very security and comfort, the social ennui of an entire people, which had allowed the pleasure cults to flourish so well.

There was no guard to greet Carathril at the Prince's Quay, for his arrival was to be kept secret lest cultists in Lothern learned of what Malekith and

Bel Shanaar planned. He rode quickly through the city, allowing the chatter and crowds to flow around him unnoticed. So disturbed had Carathril become, so anxious of what the future held, that there was no joy in his homecoming. His thoughts were dark as he rode up the winding streets to the hilltops where the manses and palaces of the nobility were built.

The palace of Prince Haradrin was not a fortress like Tor Anroc or Anlec, but rather a wide spread of houses and villas set out in ornate gardens upon the mount of Annui Lotheil, which overlooked all of the city and the straits.

Carathril made directly for the Winter Palace, where he knew Prince Haradrin would be staying. The sentries at the gate recognised him as he approached and stepped aside without word to let him pass.

Prince Haradrin granted him audience immediately, in a great domed hall, its ceiling cunningly painted so that as light from the windows struck it at different times of the day it pictured the movement of the sun in a summer sky and then descended into a glowing twilight.

Before the assembled court Carathril relayed the recent news as concisely as he could, and the princes listened intently and without interruption.

'Bel Shanaar calls upon the princes of Eataine to remember their oaths to the Phoenix Throne,' the herald concluded.

'And what does Bel Shanaar expect from Eataine?' asked Prince Haradrin.

'The Sea Guard and Lothern Guard must stand ready to fight, highness,' said Carathril. 'He calls for Prince Haradrin to attend a council upon the Isle of Flame.'

'Who else shall be at this council?' asked Haradrin.

'All of the princes of Ulthuan are expected to attend, to pledge their support to the Phoenix King's cause,' said Carathril with a small bow of deference.

'Though now herald to Bel Shanaar, you were born of Lothern, Carathril,' Haradrin said, standing up from his throne and walking closer. 'Tell me truthfully, what is Bel Shanaar's intent?'

Carathril felt the letter to Imrik against his skin but kept his gaze steadily upon the prince.

'He would rid our people of the curse of the cults,' Carathril said evenly. 'War is coming, highness.'

Haradrin nodded without comment before turning to his courtiers gathered about the throne.

'Eataine will stand beside Tiranoc,' he declared. 'Send word to the Sea Guard that they should return to Lothern. They shall patrol the Bay of Whispers and bring word to me of all that passes on the ships of the Inner Sea. We shall not yet raise the call to arms, but upon my return be ready to do so. If war is to be our fate, Eataine shall not flinch from her duty.'

CARATHRIL WAS CONTENT to spend the following days wandering the city, safe in the knowledge that his part in these matters had been played. He would accompany Haradrin to the Isle of Flame, deliver the Phoenix King's letter to Imrik and then await the arrival of Malekith and Bel Shanaar. Carathril had resolved that he would ask the Phoenix King to absolve him of his duty as herald so that he could return to his rightful station as a captain of Lothern. While he had been content to march alongside Malekith on his expedition, if full-scale war was to come, Carathril wanted to fight with his own folk, in the army of Eataine.

As he walked the city, Carathril inquired after Aerenis, but of his friend he heard nothing. Wherever he asked, Carathril heard conflicting tales of his lieutenant's whereabouts. Shared acquaintances told Carathril that his friend had been seen little since returning from Tor Anroc those many years ago. Many thought he was on constant duty at the palace, attending the prince, others thought he had been despatched to one of the outlying towns to train young spearmen. Some claimed that he had resigned his commission and sailed over the sea to a new life.

Though disturbed by the lack of information concerning his friend, there was little Carathril could do further, for he was due to sail with Prince Haradrin to the Isle of Flame. The time came when the royal entourage was ready to depart, three days before the deadline set by Bel Shanaar. Carathril was given a berth upon Haradrin's elegant eagleship, although by rights he was not yet part of Lothern's guard again.

As the ship set sail and moved away from the wharf, Carathril looked back at Lothern, seeing it as if for the first time. He looked at the great statues of the gods surrounding the bay: Kurnous the Hunter, Isha the Mother, Vaul the Smith and Asuryan the Allfather. He had barely noticed them before, having grown up with them in sight. Now he looked again at their stern faces and wondered what part they would play in coming events. He also wondered if there were, out in the city somewhere, hidden cellars with images of the darker gods: shrines to the like of Nethu, Anath Raema, Khirkith, Elinill and the other cytharai.

The immense gold and ruby gate to the Inner Sea was open, and hawkships darted ahead of the prince's vessel to clear a path between the crowd of fishing boats, pleasure barges and cargo ships. Once out of the Straits of Lothern, the ship's captain set full sail and the eagleship danced across the waves, gliding across the water at full speed. The sun shone overhead and the blue waters glittered, and for a while at least Carathril was content to stand at the rail and marvel at the beauty of Ulthuan; happy to forget his woes as he lost himself in the sparkle of water and the blue sky.

They sailed overnight with reduced sail, and it was mid-morning when they came into view of the Isle of Flame. Though Carathril had passed it many times before on his way to Saphery, Cothique and Yvresse, the Shrine of Asuryan still amazed him. The white pyramid rose up from a marbled courtyard set within an open meadow. The walls of the shrine blazed with reflected sunlight, bathing the grass and surrounding water with its majesty.

The isle itself was surrounded by gently shoaling white beaches and long piers stretched out into the water. There were four vessels already moored as they hove into the dock: the ships of other princes already arrived on the isle.

─◄ TWENTY-FOUR ►─

An Act of Infamy

It was the day before Bel Shanaar and Malekith were due to leave Tor Anroc for the council upon the Isle of Flame when the Phoenix King commanded the prince of Nagarythe to attend him in his throne room. Malekith walked quickly to the audience chamber, his instinct for intrigue curious as to what the Phoenix King had to say.

'I have been thinking deep upon your words,' Bel Shanaar proclaimed.

'I am pleased to hear that,' said Malekith. 'May I ask what the nature of your thoughts has been?'

'I will put your idea to the princes,' said Bel Shanaar. 'A single army drawn from all kingdoms will prosecute this war against the vile cults.'

'I am glad that you agree with my reasoning,' said Malekith, wondering why Bel Shanaar had brought him here to tell him what he already knew.

'I have also been giving much thought to who is best qualified to lead this army,' said Bel Shanaar, and Malekith's heart skipped a beat in anticipation.

'I would be honoured,' said the prince of Malekith.

Bel Shanaar opened his mouth to say something but then closed it again, a confused frown upon his brow.

'You misunderstand me,' the Phoenix King then said. 'I will nominate Imrik to be my chosen general.'

Malekith stood in stunned silence, left speechless by the Phoenix King's announcement.

'Imrik?' he said eventually.

'Why not?' said Bel Shanaar. 'He is a fine general, and Caledor is the most stable of all the realms at the current time. He is well respected amongst the other princes. Yes, he will make a good choice.'

'And why do you tell me this?' snapped Malekith. 'Perhaps you seek to mock me!'

'Mock you?' said Bel Shanaar, taken aback. 'I am telling you this so that you will speak in favour of my decision. I know that you have much influence and your word will lend great weight to Imrik's authority.'

'You would raise up the grandson of Caledor over the son of Aenarion?' said Malekith. 'Have I not forged new kingdoms across the world at the head of armies? If not my bloodline, than my achievements must qualify me above all others.'

'I am sorry that you feel this way, Malekith,' said Bel Shanaar, unabashed. 'The council will endorse my choice, you would do well to align yourself with me.'

At this, Malekith's frayed temper snapped utterly.

'Align myself to you?' he snarled. 'The hunter does not align himself to his hound! The master does not align himself to his servant!'

'Choose your next words carefully, Malekith!' warned the Phoenix King. 'Remember who it is that you address!'

The Naggarothi prince mastered his anger, biting back further retorts.

'I trust that my protest has been recognised,' he said with effort. 'I urge you to reconsider your decision.'

'You are free to speak your mind at the council,' said Bel Shanaar. 'It is your right to argue against Imrik, and to put forward yourself as candidate. We shall let the princes decide.'

Malekith said nothing more, but bowed stiffly and left, silently seething. He did not return to his chambers, but instead made for the wing of the palace where his mother was kept in captivity. Ignoring the guards at the door to her chambers, he knocked and then let himself in.

The chambers were well furnished, with exquisitely crafted furniture and splendid tapestries upon the walls. Though a prisoner, his mother had lost none of her aesthetic, and over the years had built up quite a collection of art and other ornaments. All of the finery however was somewhat overshadowed by the silvered runes carved upon the walls: mystical wards that kept the winds of magic at bay and thus denied Morathi her sorcerous power. They were a precaution Bel Shanaar had insisted upon.

There was no sign of her in the reception room, and Malekith strode through to the dining chamber beyond. There Morathi sat at a small table, a plate of fruit before her. She plucked a grape from the platter and looked up at him as he stormed in. She said nothing but simply raised an eyebrow inquisitively.

'Bel Shanaar will name Imrik as the general of the army,' growled Malekith.

Morathi dropped the grape back onto the plate and stood up.

'You think he will win the vote?' she asked.

'Of course he will,' snapped the prince. 'He is the Phoenix King, after all, and Imrik would be the best choice after me. If Imrik is made commander of the army, then Bel Shanaar has as good as named his successor. My chance will have passed and Ulthuan will be doomed to a slow dwindling under ever-lesser kings. My father's legacy will be cast upon the ashes of our history and his line will dwindle and die. I cannot allow that to happen.'

'Then Bel Shanaar must not be allowed to put forward his arguments,' said Morathi quietly. 'The time for plotting and patience has come to an end. It is time to act, and swiftly.'

'What do you mean?' asked Malekith. 'How will I prevent Bel Shanaar making his declaration?'

'You must kill him,' she said.

Malekith paused, surprised at himself for not immediately dismissing the idea. In fact, the thought appealed to him. He had waited sixteen centuries to become Phoenix King, a long time even for an elf. Why settle for becoming general of Ulthuan and waiting the gods only knew how long for Bel Shanaar to die of natural causes? Better to take the initiative and see the gambit out for good or ill.

'What must I do?' Malekith asked without hesitation.

'Palthrain is one of my creatures,' Morathi said. 'Long has he been my spy in Tor Anroc. He will hide certain objects in Bel Shanaar's chambers, as evidence of the Phoenix King's worship of Ereth Khial. These will be discovered by you, and you will go to Bel Shanaar's rooms to confront him with this proof. When you arrive, he will be dead, having poisoned himself rather than face the truth.'

'He leaves on the morrow for the Isle of Flame,' Malekith snarled in frustration. 'There is no time to fabricate such a plot!'

'Fabricate?' laughed Morathi. 'You are so short-sighted sometimes, my dear son. The evidence is already in place, and has been for years. Long have I mulled over how to rid us of this wretched swine, and now the time has come. See Palthrain and get the poison from him. Find some pretence to visit the usurper and give him the poisoned wine. Everything else will already be taken care of.'

Malekith paused, considering the implications of what he was about to do.

'If what you say is true, how is it that you have not acted before?' said Malekith. 'Why have you suffered embarrassment and captivity when you could have struck down he who vexes us both?'

Morathi stood and embraced her son.

'Because I am a loving mother,' she said quietly. Standing back, she smoothed the creases in her dress. 'If Bel Shanaar had been slain, Imrik would have stood ready to take his place, as he does now. There would be war between Nagarythe and Caledor. I could not hand you such a poisoned chalice. Now you are stronger and your claim will be agreed by the princes. Imrik's lone voice will not be an obstacle.'

'Surely Palthrain is more trusted than I am,' said Malekith, sitting down on an elegantly carved chair. 'It will be easier for him to administer the poison.'

Morathi shook her head in disappointment and crossed her arms.

'Palthrain will not become Phoenix King with this act,' she said sternly. 'Show me that you have the will to succeed your father. More than that, prove it to yourself. The throne is there for the taking. Only by your own hand can you take it and deserve to sit upon it. Bel Shanaar was given his rule by others. True kings seize it for themselves.'

Malekith nodded wordlessly, struck by the truth of his mother's words. If he could do this one simple thing there was nothing that would stand between him and his dream of ruling Ulthuan.

'Come on!' said Morathi, clapping her hands as if to chivvy along a wayward child. 'You will have plenty of time to practise your speech to the princes on the voyage to the Isle of Flame.'

'I will be Phoenix King,' murmured Malekith, savouring the thought.

Upon leaving his mother, the prince sought out the chamberlain. He took Palthrain to the gardens where they could speak in privacy, and informed him of his desire to enact his mother's plan for assassinating Bel Shanaar. Palthrain took this news without comment, merely telling Malekith that Bel Shanaar was wont to take his evening repast at sunset. He agreed to meet the prince by the Phoenix King's rooms just before then, and would provide him with the deadly wine.

For the remainder of the day, Malekith fretted in his chambers, pacing back and forth. Though he did not doubt that what he was doing would ultimately be for the benefit of all, he worried that the plan would somehow be forestalled. He wanted to speak to his mother again, but knew that to visit her so soon after their last meeting might arouse suspicion.

As the day wore on, doubts clawed at Malekith's nerves. Could Palthrain be trusted? Even now, was the chamberlain fulfilling his true loyalty and reporting the plot to the Phoenix King? Every footstep in the corridor beyond the door to his chambers set Malekith on edge, as he suspected the approach of Bel Shanaar's guards.

Pacing like a trapped animal, barely ready to believe that success was so close, Malekith prowled and brooded in his rooms, unable to settle. He constantly strode to the window to check the progress of the day, as if by his will alone he could bring the sunset more quickly.

After an eternity, the sun was finally upon the horizon and Malekith set out from his rooms to meet Palthrain. He kept his expression genial as he passed servants and guards in the corridors. He then realised that he was not normally so cordial and set his face in a determined frown instead; an expression with which all in Tor Anroc were now very familiar.

In the corridor around the corner from Bel Shaanar's main chambers Palthrain stood with a tray upon which stood a silver ewer and goblet, and a plate of cured meats and bread. Palthrain passed him the tray but Malekith's hands were shaking and the chamberlain quickly retrieved it.

Malekith took deep breaths, trying to calm himself as if summoning the power for a difficult spell. Ignoring the purposefully blank expression of Palthrain, the prince took the tray once more, now in control of his body.

'Are you sure this will work?' demanded Malekith. 'It must be final!'

'It is used in certain practices of the Khainites, to numb the senses,' Palthrain replied. 'In small doses it will render its victim incapable for several hours. With the amount I have put in the wine, it will be fatal. At first he will be paralysed. Then his breathing will become difficult as his lungs freeze, and then he will fall pass away.'

'No pain?' said Malekith.

'Not that I am aware of, highness,' said Palthrain.

'What a pity,' said Malekith.

THE NAGGAROTHI PRINCE walked down the passageway to Bel Shanaar's chambers, forcing himself to stride slowly so as not to garner attention. He knocked at the door and waited for Bel Shanaar's call for him to enter.

The Phoenix King was sat at a writing desk, no doubt penning corrections to his speech for the council.

'Malekith?' he said, startled.

'Forgive the intrusion, your majesty,' said Malekith with a low bow. He stepped across the room and placed the tray on the desk.

'Why are you here?' asked Bel Shanaar. 'Where's Palthrain?'

'I apologise for waylaying him, majesty,' said Malekith. 'I wished to bring you your wine as a peace offering.'

'Peace offering?'

'I wholeheartedly wish to offer my apologies,' replied Malekith, pouring the poisoned wine into the goblet. 'I spoke out of misplaced anger earlier, and I caused great offence. My anger is not with you, though it might have seemed that way. I have endeavoured to earn your trust and to be a loyal subject, and it is my failings not yours that have led you to choose Imrik. I will be happy to support your choice.'

The prince passed the cup to Bel Shanaar, his face a mask of politeness. The Phoenix King frowned and for a moment Malekith feared that he suspected something. The Phoenix King took the goblet however, and placed it on the desk.

'Your apology is accepted,' said Bel Shanaar. 'I do trust you, my friend, but you have personal concerns that far outweigh any duty to me. I choose Imrik not just on ability, but on the fact that I would have you address the problems of your kingdom without distraction. I would have you direct your energies solely to restoring your rule, not pandering to the whims of other kingdoms.'

The goblet remained on the desk.

'Your consideration heartens me greatly,' said Malekith, keeping his eyes fixed firmly upon the Phoenix King lest he dart a betraying glance towards the wine.

'You will offer your support in the council?' Bel Shanaar asked, finally lifting the cup to his lips and taking a mouthful of the wine.

It was not enough for the poison to work and the prince silently willed Bel Shanaar to drink more.

'When the debate rages, none will argue harder than I,' said Malekith with a smile.

Bel Shanaar nodded and took another sip of wine.

'If that is all, then I wish you a fair evening and look forward to sailing with you in the morning,' said Bel Shanaar with a polite nod.

Malekith stood there watching for some sign of the poison's effect.

'What are you staring at?' asked the Phoenix King.

'Is the wine not to your satisfaction?' said the prince, taking a step closer.

'I am not thirsty,' said Bel Shanaar, placing the goblet back on the desk.

Malekith twisted and picked up the goblet and sniffed it.

'It is very fine wine, majesty,' he said.

'I am sure it is, Malekith,' said Bel Shanaar, pursing his lips. His voice became more insistent. 'However, I feel a little sleepy all of a sudden. I shall retire for the night and see you in the morning.'

Stifling a frustrated shout, Malekith lunged forwards and seized Bel Shanaar by the throat. The Phoenix King's eyes widened with terror as Malekith forced open Bel Shanaar's mouth and emptied in the contents of the goblet. The goblet tumbled from the prince's fingertips and spilt a cascade of red droplets over the white boards of the floor.

Clamping one hand over the Phoenix King's nose and mouth and dragging his head back by his hair, Malekith choked the king until he swallowed the deadly draught. He then released his grip and stepped back to watch his future unfold.

'What have you–' panted Bel Shanaar, clawing at his throat and chest.

Malekith lifted the parchment from the desk. As he had suspected, it was a draft of the Phoenix King's speech for the council. Thinking it better that no evidence of Bel Shanaar's support for Imrik was found, he crossed the room and tossed it into the fire burning in the grate. Turning, he saw that there was still life in Bel Shanaar's bulging eyes.

Malekith padded forwards until he was very close, and bent towards the dying elf's ear.

'You brought this upon yourself,' the prince hissed.

With a last gurgle, Bel Shanaar died, his face purple, his tongue lolling from his mouth. Malekith stood for a moment, absent-mindedly looking at the contorted face, not quite believing that it was almost over.

'Well, I have to leave you now,' he said at last, affectionately patting the Phoenix King's head. 'I have a throne to claim.'

—◄ TWENTY-FIVE ►—

The Wrath of Asuryan

PARTIES FROM YVRESSE, Cothique, Saphery and Ellyrion camped upon the meadows surrounding the shrine, in a pavilion town of bright reds, blues and whites. The banners of the princes flew from standard poles above the tents, and mailed sentries stood guard on the perimeter. A place had been set aside already for the prince of Eataine and his contingent, and while Haradrin's servants laboured at the dock to unload the wares and stores of the camp, Carathril went to the shrine itself.

The outer parts of the temple were open rows of columns decorated in relief with images of Asuryan in many guises: as a loving father, a swooping eagle, a rising phoenix and others. Between the colonnade and the shrine proper stood the Phoenix Guard, the sacred warriors of Asuryan, with glittering halberds and high-crested helms. Their white cloaks were embroidered with patterns of red and blue flames leaping up from their hems, and their scale armour shone with gilding.

All were silent, for they were avowed to never speak; each had passed into the Chamber of Days, where the history of Aenarion was recorded, and so too all the histories of the Phoenix Kings yet to come. Past, present and future were laid bare within that secret hall, and the Phoenix Guard were forbidden to speak of the knowledge they now guarded.

Two of the Phoenix Guards stepped forwards and lowered their halberds to stop Carathril as he walked under an arched entrance into the shrine. Carathril presented the seal of the Phoenix King and they let him pass. Inside, Carathril found himself in an antechamber, a small room unadorned

267

but for a carving of a great phoenix over the closed door opposite. Stoops of clear water flanked the doorway, and Carathril paused to wash his hands and face.

He opened the door and moved further in, to find himself in a wide gallery that ran around the outside of the central chamber. Phoenix Guards barred any route to the left or right and Carathril walked ahead, passing through another archway into the holiest of shrines on Ulthuan.

His gaze was immediately drawn to the sacred flame. From nothing it sprang, hovering without fuel over the middle of the chamber, burning blue then green then red then golden, shifting colour every few moments. It gave off no heat that Carathril could feel, but he felt a wave of calmness wash over him as he approached. There was not a crackle or hiss of burning; the flames were as silent as their guardians.

'Do not approach too closely,' warned a voice beside Carathril, and he turned to see an ageing elf wrapped in a blue and yellow robe, leaning upon a staff tipped with a golden likeness of a phoenix. Carathril recognised him immediately as Mianderin, the high priest of the shrine, who had presided here for as long as Carathril could remember. His attention thus drawn from the flame, Carathril noticed that there was much activity in the central chamber, as priests and acolytes brought forth tables and chairs and arranged flame-patterned rugs upon the floor in readiness for the council.

'All will be ready for tomorrow,' said Mianderin. 'Is there something with which I might help you?'

'No,' said Carathril, shaking his head. 'No, there is nothing... except, perhaps, you might furnish me with some information.'

'What is it that you wish to know?' the high priest asked.

'Has there been any word from Prince Imrik?' said Carathril.

'A messenger arrived yesterday,' said Mianderin. 'Both he and Prince Koradrel are hunting in the mountains and could not be located. By choice, I would presume.'

Carathril's heart sank; how was he to present Bel Shanaar's message to Imrik now? He hoped that whatever the missive contained, it was not important to the business of the council.

'Thank you for your help,' he said distractedly.

'Peace be upon your life,' the old priest said as Carathril turned away. The captain paused and looked back.

'I most fervently hope so,' said Carathril before heading out of the shrine.

IT WAS GONE noon on the day appointed for the council to begin, and still there had been no sign of Bel Shanaar, nor Malekith, Imrik or Koradrel. In all there were nearly two dozen princes gathered, some leaders of realms, others powerful nobles in their own right, as holders of land or commanders of troops. As Carathril had seen before, they conspired and bickered in an almost casual fashion, directing vague slights against one another whilst making promises of cooperation and partnership. Though they had been sent word of the unfortunate events of Nagarythe, none knew fully why they had been asked to come, and as the day wore on without sign of the Phoenix King, tempers began to fray and arguments broke out.

Some of the princes, Bathinair chief amongst them, complained bitterly of the disrespect done to them by Bel Shanaar's tardiness. There were whispered threats of returning back to their lands, but they were persuaded to stay by courteous argument from the likes of Thyriol and Finudel. The presence of Elodhir did much to calm the situation, who spent every moment apologising for his father's delay and assuring that it would be worth the princes' while to remain and hear what he had to say.

It was late afternoon, and the autumn sky was just beginning to darken when the huge ship *Indraugnir* glided effortlessly to the quay, the flag of Nagarythe flying from her masthead. There were claps and cheers, some of them ironic, as Malekith strode down the ramp onto the wharf, followed by several dozen of his armoured knights.

Retainers of the prince swarmed over the gunwales, quickly unloading sacks and chests onto the pier. Malekith waved for the princes to predede him inside and they did so, leaving Carathril, the Phoenix Guards and a few other retainers outside with the knights of Anlec.

'Prince, what of the Phoenix King?' said Carathril, falling into step beside the swiftly striding Malekith. The prince did not reply but simply shooed Carathril away with a fluttered hand. Slighted, Carathril gave a snort and stormed away towards the quay.

INSIDE THE SHRINE, the princes and their aides had seated themselves around a horseshoe of tables that had been set up before the sacred flames, and in a chair directly in front of the flames sat Mianderin, his staff of office held across his lap. Other priests moved around the tables filling goblets with wine or water, and offering fruits and confectionaries.

The table nearest the entrance was empty, reserved for Bel Shanaar. Malekith stood behind it, earning himself frowns from Mianderin and a few of the princes. He was flanked by two knights who carried wrapped bundles in their hands. The prince of Nagarythe stood there, leaning onto the table with gauntleted fists, and stared balefully at the assembled council.

'Weakness prevails,' spat Malekith. 'Weakness grips this island like a child squeezing the juices from an over-ripened fruit. Selfishness has driven us to inaction, and now the time to act may have passed. Complacency rules where princes should lead. You have allowed the cults of depravity to flourish, and done nothing. You have looked to foreign shores and counted your gold, and allowed thieves to sneak into your towns and cities to steal away your children. And you have been content to allow a traitor to wear the Phoenix Crown!'

With this last declaration there were gasps and shouts of horror from the princes. Malekith's knights opened their bundles and tossed the contents upon the table: the crown and feathered cloak of Bel Shanaar.

Elodhir leapt to his feet, fist raised.

'Where is my father?' he demanded.

'What has happened to the Phoenix King?' cried Finudel.

'He is dead!' snarled Malekith. 'Killed by his weakness of spirit.'

'That cannot be so!' exclaimed Elodhir, his voice strangled and fraught with anger.

'It is,' said Malekith with a sigh, his demeanour suddenly one of sorrow. 'I promised to root out this vileness, and was shocked to find that my mother was one of its chief architects. From that moment on, I decided none would be above suspicion. If Nagarythe had become so polluted, so too perhaps had Tiranoc. My arrival here was delayed by investigations, when it was brought to my attention that those close to the Phoenix King might be under the sway of the hedonists. My inquiries were circumspect but thorough, and imagine my disappointment, nay disbelief, when I uncovered evidence that implicated the Phoenix King himself.'

'What evidence?' demanded Elodhir.

'Certain talismans and fetishes found in the Phoenix King's chambers,' said Malekith calmly. 'Believe me when I say that I felt as you did. I could not bring myself to think that Bel Shanaar, our wisest prince chosen to rule by members of this council, would be brought so low. Not one to act rashly, I decided to confront Bel Shanaar with this evidence, in the hope that there was some misunderstanding or trickery involved.'

'And he denied it of course?' asked Bathinair.

'He admitted guilt by his deeds,' explained Malekith. 'It seems that a few of my company were tainted by this affliction and in league with the usurpers of Nagarythe. Even as I confided in them, they warned Bel Shanaar of my discoveries. That night, no more than seven nights ago, I went to his chambers to make my accusations face-to-face. I found him dead, his lips stained with poison. He had taken the coward's way and ended his own life rather than suffer the shame of inquiry. By his own hand he denied us insight into the plans of the cults. Fearing that he would not keep their secrets to himself, he took them to his grave.'

'My father would do no such thing, he is loyal to Ulthuan and its people!' shouted Elodhir.

'I confess to having deep sympathy with you, Elodhir,' Malekith replied. 'Have I not been deceived by my own mother? Do I not feel the same betrayal and heartache that now wrenches at your spirit?'

'I must admit I also find this somewhat perturbing,' said Thyriol. 'It seems... convenient.'

'And so, in death, Bel Shanaar continues to divide us, as was his intent,' countered Malekith. 'Discord and anarchy will reign as we argue back and forth the rights and wrongs of what has occurred. While we debate endlessly, the cults will grow in power and seize your lands from under your noses, and we will have lost everything. They are united, while we are divided. There is no time for contemplation, or reflection, there is only time for action.'

'What would you have us do?' asked Chyllion, one of the princes of Cothique.

'We must choose a new Phoenix King!' declared Bathinair before Malekith could answer.

As HE APPROACHED the quay, Carathril watched the Naggarothi labouring on Malekith's ship. Amongst the throng, he spied a familiar face: Drutheira. Her hair was bleached white with a few blackened locks, but still the herald recognised her. Carathril pushed his way through the servants to where she stood on the dock, picking up a bale of cloth. She saw him approach and smiled.

'Carathril!' she gasped, grabbing his hand in both of hers. 'I thought perhaps never to see you again! Oh, this is joyous indeed!'

'Perhaps you can tell me what has happened to the Phoenix King?' said Carathril, and her smile faded.

'Why would you care about him?' she asked. 'Are you not happy to see me?'

'Of course,' said Carathril, uncertain. Seeing Drutheira had suddenly muddled his thoughts. Her eyes were glistening like mountain pools. Carathril struggled to concentrate.

'How is it that you come to be here?' he stammered. 'Why are you in the employ of Malekith?'

'He is a most noble prince,' she said, laying her hands upon Carathril's shoulders. A shiver of energy ran through him, setting his nerves alight at her touch. 'Glorious and magnanimous! When he is Phoenix King we shall all be well rewarded. You too, Carathril. He thinks very highly of you.'

'Malekith, the Phoenix King?' stammered Carathril. Something was wrong but he could think of nothing but Drutheira's pale flesh and the fragrance of her hair. 'Bel Shanaar is Phoenix–'

'Hush now,' said Drutheira, her voice a sighing breath. She stood on tiptoe so that her face was in front of his, her breath a breeze upon his cheek. 'Do not trouble yourself with the affairs of princes. Is it not marvellous that we can be together?'

'Together? What?' said Carathril, stepping away from her.

This attraction was not natural. Something thrashed inside Carathril's head, screaming for freedom. As soon as he broke her touch on him, his mind began to clear.

'You shall be his captain and herald, and I one of his handmaidens,' Drutheira said patiently, as if explaining herself to a child. 'We can live together in Anlec.'

'I am not going to Anlec,' said Carathril. Whatever Athartist enchantment she had woven was beginning to fade. Carathril's thoughts raced to catch up with what she had said. 'What has happened to the Phoenix King?'

She laughed, a sinister sound, and the gleam in her eye stirred fear in Carathril's heart.

'That fool Bel Shanaar is dead,' she said. 'Malekith will be Phoenix King, and he will reward well those that support him.'

Carathril stumbled back a few more paces, his mind reeling. In his confusion, he tripped over a coil of rope and sprawled to his back. Drutheira was over him in a moment, crouching close, her hand cupped to his face.

'Poor Carathril,' she purred. 'You cannot stop destiny, you must embrace it.'

Once again her touch dazzled Carathril before a moment of clarity engulfed him, as if a distant voice spoke to him: Bel Shanaar was dead and Malekith sought to become Phoenix King in his place. 'This cannot be allowed,' the voice said, 'Malekith is not fit to rule.' With a snarl, Carathril pushed Drutheira backwards and regained his feet. He stumbled into a run, heading back down the pier.

'Treachery!' he called. 'Beware!'

A few of Malekith's retainers tried to grab him, but he barged them aside and slapped away their grasping hands as he sprinted down onto the dock.

'To arms!' he shouted. 'Infamy is afoot!'

The Anlec knights drew their swords. Some turned towards Carathril, the rest advanced upon the shrine. Ahead of them the Phoenix Guards brought their halberds up to the ready.

'Is that your intent?' asked Thyriol with a glance at the other princes.

'If the council wishes it,' Malekith said with a shrug.

'We cannot choose a new Phoenix King now,' said Elodhir. 'Such a matter cannot be resolved quickly, and even if such a thing were possible, we are not our full number.'

'Nagarythe will not wait,' said Malekith, slamming his fist onto the table. 'The cults are too strong and come spring they will control the army of Anlec. My lands will be lost and they will march upon yours!'

'You would have us choose you to lead us?' said Thyriol quietly.

'Yes,' Malekith replied without hesitation or embarrassment. 'There are none here who were willing to act until my return. I am the son of Aenarion, his chosen heir, and if the revelation of Bel Shanaar's treachery is not enough to convince you of the foolishness of choosing from another line, then look to my other achievements. Bel Shanaar chose me to act as his ambassador to the dwarfs for I was a close friend with their High King. Our future lies not solely upon these shores, but in the wider world. I have been to the colonies across the oceans, and fought to build and protect them. Though they come from the bloodstock of Lothern or Tor Elyr or Tor Anroc, they are a new people, and it is to me they first look now, not to you. None here are as experienced in war as am I. Bel Shanaar was a ruler steeped in wisdom and peace, for all that he has failed us at the last, but peace and wisdom will not prevail against darkness and zealotry.'

'What of Imrik?' suggested Finudel. 'He is every bit the general and fought out in the new world also.'

'Imrik?' said Malekith, his voice dripping with scorn. 'Where is Imrik now, in this time of our greatest need? He skulks in Chrace with his cousin, hunting monsters! Would you have Ulthuan ruled by an elf who hides in the mountains like a petulant, spoilt child? When Imrik called for an army to be gathered against Nagarythe, did you pay him heed? No! Only when I raised the banner did you fall over each other in your enthusiasm.'

'Be careful of what you say, your arrogance does you a disservice,' warned Haradrin.

'I say these things not as barbs to your pride,' explained Malekith, unclenching his fists and sitting down. 'I say them to show you what you already know; in your hearts you would gratefully follow where I lead.'

'I still say that this council cannot make such an important decision on a whim,' said Elodhir. 'My father lies dead, in circumstances yet to be fully explained, and you would have us hand over the Phoenix Crown to you?'

'He has a point, Malekith,' said Haradrin.

'A point?' screamed Malekith as he surged to his feet, knocking over the table and sending the cloak and crown upon it flying through the air. 'A point? Your dithering will see you all cast out, your families enslaved and your people burning upon ten thousand pyres! It has been more than a thousand years since I bent my knee to this council's first, wayward decision and saw Bel Shanaar take what Aenarion had promised to me. For a thousand years, I have been content to watch your families grow and prosper, and squabble amongst yourselves like children, while I and my kin bled on battlefields on the other side of the world. I trusted you all to remember the legacy of my father, and ignored the cries of anguish that rang in my blood; for it was in the interest of all that we were united. Now it is time to unite behind me! I do not lie to you, I shall be a harsh ruler at times, but I will reward those who serve me well, and when peace reigns again we shall all enjoy the spoils of our battles. Who here has more right to the throne than I do? Who here–'

'Malekith!' barked Mianderin, pointing towards the prince's waist. In his tirade, Malekith's waving arms had thrown his cloak back over his shoulder. 'Why do you wear your sword in this holy place? It is forbidden in the most ancient laws of this temple. Remove it at once.'

Malekith stood frozen in place, almost comic with his arms outstretched. He looked down at his belt and the sheathed sword that hung there. He gripped Avanuir's hilt in one hand and pulled it free, then looked up at the princes, his eyes narrowed, his face illuminated by magical blue fire.

'Enough words!' he spat.

* * *

CARATHRIL DUCKED BENEATH the sword of a Naggarothi knight and then rolled forwards, back onto his feet, before leaping aside to dodge another blade swung at his chest. He had no weapon of his own; why would he have come armed to such a council? It was a decision he was swiftly regretting.

Another knight thrust his sword at Carathril's throat and the captain swayed aside just in time and grabbed the knight's arm. With a twist, he broke the Naggarothi's elbow, the sword cascading from his enemy's grip to embed itself point first in the marble tiles of the shrine's surrounds.

He swung the knight around into the path of another blade, which lanced between his captive's shoulders and jutted from his chest just a hand's span from Carathril's face. Hurling the dead knight backwards, Carathril snatched up the fallen sword and parried another blow. Risking a look over his shoulder, Carathril saw that he was still more than a hundred paces from the shrine, and everywhere the Phoenix Guards fought against the knights. The only noise they made was the clash of their halberds upon sword and armour. With a grunt, Carathril shouldered aside another foe and made a break for the entrance.

'IT IS MY right to be Phoenix King,' growled Malekith. 'It is not yours to give, so I will gladly take it.'

'Traitor!' screamed Elodhir, leaping across the table in front of him, scattering goblets and plates. There was uproar as princes and priests shouted and shrieked.

Elodhir dashed across the shrine, and was halfway upon Malekith when Bathinair intercepted him, sending both of them tumbling down in a welter of robes and rugs. Elodhir punched the Yvressian prince, who reeled back. With a snarl, Bathinair reached into his robes and pulled out a curved blade, no longer than a finger, and slashed at Elodhir. Its blade caught the prince's throat and his lifeblood fountained across the exposed flagstones.

As Bathinair crouched panting over the body of Elodhir, figures appeared at the archway behind Malekith: black-armoured knights of Anlec. The priests and princes who had been running for the arch slipped and collided with each other in their haste to stop their flight. The knights had blood-slicked blades in the hands and advanced with sinister purpose.

Malekith was serene; all trace of his earlier anger had disappeared. He walked slowly forwards as his knights cut and hacked at the princes around him, his eyes never leaving the sacred flame in the centre of the chamber. Screams and howls echoed from the walls but the prince was oblivious to all but the fire.

Out of the melee, Haradrin ran towards Malekith, a captured sword raised above his head. With a contemptuous sneer, the prince of Nagarythe stepped aside from Haradrin's wild swing and thrust his own sword into Haradrin's gut. He stood there a moment, the princes staring deep into each other's eyes, until a trickle of blood spilled from Haradrin's lips and he collapsed to the floor.

Malekith let the sword fall from his fingers with the body rather than wrench it free, and continued his pacing towards the sacred fire.

'Asuryan will not accept you!' cried Mianderin, falling to his knees in front of Malekith, his hands clasped in pleading. 'You have spilt blood in his sacred temple! We have not cast the proper enchantments to protect you from the flames. You cannot do this!'

'So?' spat the prince. 'I am Aenarion's heir. I do not need your witchery to protect me.'

Mianderin snatched at Malekith's hand but the prince tore his fingers from the haruspex's grasp.

'I no longer listen to the protestations of priests,' said Malekith and kicked Mianderin aside.

His hands held out, palms upwards in supplication, Malekith walked forwards and stepped into the flames.

CARATHRIL LEANED AGAINST a column, catching his breath. He had seen several knights enter the shrine, but the fighting outside was almost done. White-robed corpses littered the plaza alongside black-armoured bodies. Pushing himself upright, his heart hammering, Carathril took a step towards the shrine.

At that moment the ground lurched and flung Carathril from his feet.

The earth beneath him shook violently and columns toppled around him as the Isle of Flame was gripped by an earthquake. The isle heaved violently, tossing Carathril to the left and right before sending him hurtling into a falling pillar. He narrowly rolled aside as more masonry showered down from the cloister, crashing upon the cracking marble tiles.

Overhead dark clouds instantly gathered, swathing the island in gloom; lightning flickered upon their surface and a chill descended. Thunderous growling shook the earth underfoot as the herald forced himself back to his feet. Amongst the roaring and crashing, Carathril heard a terrifying shriek: a drawn-out wail of utter pain that pierced his soul.

WITHIN THE SHRINE, prince, priest and knight alike were tossed around by the great heaving. Chairs were flung across the floor and tables toppled. Plaster cracked upon the walls and fell in large slabs from the ceiling. Wide cracks tore through the tiles underfoot and a rift three paces wide opened up along the eastern wall, sending up a choking spume of dust and rock.

The flame of Asuryan burned paler and paler, moving from a deep blue to a brilliant white. At its heart could be seen the silhouette of Malekith, his arms still outstretched.

With a thunderous clap, the holy flame blazed, filling the room with white light. Within, Malekith collapsed to his knees and grabbed at his face.

He was burning.

He flung back his head and screamed as the flames consumed him; his howl of anguish reverberated around the shrine, echoing and growing in volume with every passing moment. The withering figure silhouetted within the flames pushed himself slowly to his feet and hurled himself from their depths.

Malekith's smoking and charred body crashed to the ground, igniting a rug and sending ashen dust billowing. Blackened flesh fell away in lumps amidst cooling droplets of molten armour. He reached outwards with a hand, and then collapsed. His clothes had been burned away and his flesh eaten down to the bone in places. His face was a mask of black and red, his dark eyes lidless and staring. Steam rose from burst veins as the prince of Nagarythe shuddered and then fell still, laid to ruin by the judgement of Asuryan.

Soon, all of Ulthuan would burn.

THE BLOODY-
HANDED

──◀ ONE ▶──

A Cruel Slight

In the two hundred and fifty-fifth year of the reign of Phoenix King Bel Shanaar, the citizens of Athel Toralien became elves of Nagarythe. Abandoned by their princes and left to the depredations of an orc siege, the city and its people were delivered from death by Prince Malekith and the grateful populace swore fresh oaths of loyalty to their Naggarothi saviour.

Under the command of Prince Malekith, Athel Toralien grew; in size, in population, in riches, in esteem and in power. From the western coast of Elthin Arvan, the armies of the Naggarothi marched eastwards and behind their shields and spears the elves of the city built towns and farms, laid roads and bridges, raised up castles and citadels; taming the wilderness of the colonies and fashioning the land into a likeness of their ancestral homes back on the isle of Ulthuan.

For more than thirteen hundred years, Athel Toralien prospered under the guidance of Malekith. When the prince declared that he was to leave the colonies and seek his destiny in the harsh wastes of the North there were many that feared for the future fortunes of the city.

In the docks and wine houses, forest mansions and farms, there was much speculation; elves are naturally disposed to rumour and politics and such a momentous event was a topic even the most introverted spirit felt required comment. In a high tower upon the wall above the harbour, the gossip was no less animated, though there was one amongst the small group of elven maidens who was full of confidence.

'My father is every part the city ruler,' declared Hellebron.

Her maid, Liannin, murmured assent as she brushed her mistress's long hair. Hellebron's father, Alandrian, had been newly named a Prince of Nagarythe and she was enjoying the sudden but deserved elevation in status. 'Princess Hellebron' had a fine sound to it.

'He has run Athel Toralien in all but name for fifty years, while Malekith has busied himself with his battles and adventures,' the young princess continued. She straightened the gold chain around her pale throat, centring its large ruby pendant. The sunlight cast a glow from the gem, dappling Hellebron's slight face with scarlet. 'You will see that this can only be a change for the better.'

'For you, perhaps,' said Ariendil, a dark-haired elf maiden ten years Hellebron's senior. Hellebron's two other friends, Mithalindin and Druithana, kept their expressions neutral, though their eyes flicked between Ariendil and Hellebron, watching carefully. 'No doubt the sun of your house continues to rise. I hope that you do not leave the rest of us in darkness.'

Hellebron giggled. 'How poetic!'

The princess stood up and shooed away her maid, smoothing the creases in her silk dress. 'I am sure my father's patronage for your families will continue. You are still my friends, after all. Perhaps we can all be princesses in the future.'

As Liannin was leaving, the door to the chamber flew open, crashing against the white wall. The maid stumbled back as Lirieth strode into the room. Though twenty years younger, Hellebron's sister was so like her that the pair might have been mistaken for twins. Her dark gaze roved around the room, taking in each of the elves in turn before settling on Hellebron.

'Ah, sister, there you are!' Lirieth's voice was mellow, even in her excitement. 'Do you never spare a glance out of the window?'

'What is it?' asked Druithana.

'Have a look,' said Lirieth.

Hellebron said nothing. She pushed Ariendil gently aside and stepped up to the high window overlooking the harbour.

It was a sunny spring day and the calm waters of the bay glittered in the afternoon light. Dozens of ships bobbed at anchor in the middle of the port. A line of black sails approached the harbour wall. There were ten ships, nine unremarkable but for the fact that they flew silver-and-black pennants of Nagarythe at their mastheads. The tenth was the cause of so much interest.

It glided across the waves without effort, four huge lateen sails filled with the breeze, surf crashing around the gold-plated ram at its prow. Hellebron had seen many great ships pass in and out of Athel Toralien, but none matched the majesty of this vessel. In size it was as large as a castle keep, spread over three hulls – one central structure flanked by two outrigger hulls that were each the size of a warship. Upon its deck stood high towers of dark-stained wood banded and trimmed with shining gold. Hellebron caught her breath and knew at once that such a ship must bear the most noble of passengers. She wondered if the Phoenix King had returned, but it seemed unlikely that such an event would go without announcements and preparation.

Like the most graceful maiden at a dance, the ship glided through the rest of the fleet before trimly tacking across the wind towards the longest pier. The sound of clarions rang out across the waves from the other nine ships, heralding the arrival of their leader.

'Who are they?' Ariendil asked, peering over Hellebron's shoulder.

'They bear flags of Nagarythe,' said Druithana, standing on tiptoe to see past the much taller princess.

'We will not find out by staying here,' said Hellebron. She spun away from the window, forcing her companions to step back, and turned to her maid. 'Go and fetch our cloaks and outdoor shoes.'

'Yes, mistress.' Liannin hesitated, an unspoken hope lingering on half-parted lips.

'Yes, you can come with us,' said Hellebron. 'You would only pester me with questions if you did not.'

'Thank you, mistress.' Liannin smiled, bobbed a curtsey and hurried out of the room.

'We'll have to be quick,' said Ariendil, back at the window. 'It looks like every person in the city is coming out for a look.'

Refraining from unseemly haste, Hellebron readied herself for when Liannin returned, sweeping a crimson cloak about her shoulders and fastening it with a silver clasp in the shape of a dragon's head. She pulled on black calfskin boots, picking off a few stray threads clinging to the brushed hide. Liannin proffered a mirror and helped Hellebron pin up her hair so that it fell in a cascade down her right side.

'Let us see what this fuss is about,' Hellebron announced when she was presentable. She looked at the others, who were watching her expectantly. 'Come on, no time for dithering.'

Liannin did her best to forge a path through the thickening crowds, but further progress became impossible a few streets from the docks. Hellebron and Lirieth gave a commentary on what was happening, the sisters a head taller than their friends and able to see further over the sea of elves.

'The large ship is just coming alongside the quay now,' said Hellebron.

'Look!' The pitch of Lirieth's voice rose sharply as she levered herself onto tiptoe, one hand on Hellebron's shoulder. 'It's Prince Malekith!'

Hellebron saw him too; dressed in a fine robe of black, his purple cloak trailing, scabbard slapping his leg as he strode purposefully towards the wharf. Soon he was also having difficulty with the press of elves.

'Is your father there?' asked Liannin.

Hellebron scanned the crowd but caught no sight of Alandrian.

'Yeasir is with the prince; no sign of father,' said Lirieth.

At that moment, a ball of blue fire screamed into the air, rising above the crowds.

'What was that?' asked Druithana.

'Prince Malekith sent up a bolt from Avanuir to clear a path,' laughed Hellebron. 'You should see them all scurrying out of the way, it's delicious!'

There was nothing more to report, though Hellebron and Lirieth kept their friends occupied with observations on the appearance and fashions of several other noble ladies, most of it uncomplimentary.

Hellebron was distracted from her dissection of the jewellery of an elf called Larissia by the arrival of the ship at the quayside. 'They are lowering a ramp now,' she told the rest. A guard captain with a particularly tall crest on his helm moved across her view. Hellebron hissed in irritation and glared at Lirieth. 'What is happening? I cannot see!'

'There is someone coming off the ship, but I cannot see her clearly. She is embracing the prince. Oh, by the gods!'

Lirieth followed this exclamation by covering her mouth in surprise, eyes wide. The group shrieked over each other, demanding to know what was going on. The guard captain moved slightly. Hellebron could see Prince Malekith and his companion moving back from the quay. The elf with him was tall, with white skin and raven-black hair. Even at this distance, she radiated beauty and power, and the way she walked with Malekith could only mean one thing.

'It's Morathi!' Hellebron nearly squealed the queen's name in her excitement. 'By all the gods, Morathi has come to Athel Toralien!'

Hellebron was engulfed by a barrage of questions from her friends; they wanted to know what she looked like, what she was wearing, was she carrying her famous staff? Hellebron ignored them and gazed longingly at Malekith's mother, feeling the grace and poise that flowed from every movement. More than that, Hellebron could feel her excitement merging with the rest of the crowd. The adoration for the wife of Aenarion, the first Phoenix King, was palpable.

Hellebron's heart stirred with conflicted feelings. She experienced the elation of the others, and at the same time she became keenly aware of a sudden jealousy. It was not directed at Morathi in person, but was envy for the reaction the queen elicited. Her mere arrival, as grand and elegant as it had been, had brought the city to a halt. Hellebron wondered what it would be like to hold such attention, to have such power and authority.

'I have to meet her,' Hellebron said to Lirieth. 'Can you imagine it? We have to speak with father! He will be able to arrange it.'

'Imagine what, dearest sister?' said Lirieth.

'Imagine anything, of course,' said Hellebron, shaking her head at her sister's ignorance. 'We could travel to Anlec; be proper princesses in the court of Morathi. Athel Toralien is nice enough, but it is not Anlec. The latest fashions, brave princes to court us, poets writing verses about our beauty. Oh, sister, it will be wonderful!'

THE WHITE-AND-BLACK TILES of the hallway echoed with the tap of Hellebron's boot as she waited for the call to enter Morathi's chambers. The princess clasped her hands tightly, to prevent nervous fidgeting. She wished there was a mirror in the hallway, so that she could see her hair and the hang of her dress one last time. Liannin had gone, and there was nobody else around to check. Convinced that the complex braids and small spearwall of pins holding her hair in place had come apart without her noticing, she stared at her faint reflection in the window at the end of the hall.

A gentle cough attracted her attention. Hellebron spun back towards the door to see a shaven-headed attendant looking at her in amusement. The handmaiden had a tattoo of a blood drop on each pale cheek, and her dark dress was embroidered with silver runes, many of which Hellebron did not recognise.

'Queen Morathi is happy to see you now.'

Still sure that her hair resembled an unseemly bird's nest, Hellebron lifted her chin and smiled. With purposeful steps, she entered Morathi's chamber. The attendant closed the door behind her, and suddenly Hellebron realised that she was alone with the queen.

Morathi reclined on a low couch beneath an open window, the breeze causing the locks of her hair to dance like black flames. Beyond stretched the city, and past the wall the fields and forests of Elthin Arvan. Hellebron had eyes only for Morathi, who wore a shimmering gown of gold and purple, her lips blood-red, her skin white as snow.

For all the queen's relaxed pose, Hellebron was instantly intimidated by her presence. Morathi's eyes were fixed upon Hellebron, sizing her up as a mountain lion might regard its next potential meal. Hellebron's feel for magic, an unconscious sense that all elves possessed, detected amazing power. The elf maiden's skin prickled at the sensation even as she felt a slight sickness in her gut.

Hellebron dismissed the brief nausea as nerves. She swallowed hard and realised that she had been blankly staring at Morathi for several heartbeats. The queen's expression was expectant and Hellebron realised she was meant to say something.

She stooped into a curtsey, sweeping her long dress backwards, dipping her eyes from Morathi's.

'I am more honoured than I could possibly say, your majesty,' Hellebron said as she straightened, eyes still downcast. Even as the words passed her lips, Hellebron recoiled from them, realising she was gushing. She took a steadying breath and forced herself to meet the queen's unmoving gaze. 'Thank you for seeing me.'

Morathi's reply was to wave a hand heavy with silver rings towards a straight-backed chair at the foot of the couch. Hellebron sat stiffly, hands in her lap, while Morathi regarded her with half-closed eyes, looking like a contented cat.

The queen said nothing and Hellebron wondered if she was meant to say more. She realised Morathi was toying with her, enjoying her discomfort. Hellebron stopped a frown just before it creased her forehead and forced a smile instead.

'I hope that you have found our little city to your liking, your majesty,' she said.

Morathi nodded and swung her legs off the couch to sit straighter, one arm trailing languidly along the seat's back.

'Athel Toralien is a fine city, and its people have been a delight.' Morathi leaned towards Hellebron. She stroked her chin with a slender finger while her dark eyes fixed upon the princess from under thick lashes. 'What is it that you wish from me, child?'

Hellebron was about to ask what the queen meant by the question, but Morathi's hand snapped up, silencing her.

'Do not feign innocence or ignorance, girl. While there are those that simply luxuriate in my presence, I see that you want something. Tell me what it is, and spare me any flattery.'

Hellebron met the queen's bluntness with her own.

'I wish to enjoy your favour; to travel back to Anlec with you and be a part of your circle.'

Morathi's laughter was barbed, cutting at Hellebron's hopes.

'You? You wish me to associate myself with you?' said the queen. 'Many desire such a thing, but few are chosen. What would you offer me by way of return for this favour?'

'My father is th–'

'Your father serves my son. I do not need you to ensure his obedience.' Morathi sat back and her expression softened. 'Tell me, child, what skills do you possess? What do you know of magic?'

'Very little, your majesty,' Hellebron replied. 'Perhaps under your tutelage I coul–'

'No, you could not. Any talent above the ordinary that you might possess would be clear for all to see by now.'

'There are few spellweavers in the colonies, your majesty,' said Hellebron, trying to keep calm, her protest muted. 'There is little opportunity for mystical study here.'

'Yet if magic were your calling, you would have found a way. I have no time for those who allow their ambitions to be so easily thwarted. Perhaps you sing well?'

'Only tolerably so, your majesty.'

'A gift for poetry?'

'No more than children's rhymes, I must admit.'

'At least tell me that you can dance.'

Hellebron sighed.

'I fear such dances as we have here are old-fashioned by the standards of Ulthuan. I have friends who are more graceful.'

Morathi pouted with disappointment, a delicate frown knitting her brow.

'Your honesty is rare, child.'

'I would rather be honest now, than caught as a liar later, your majesty. Any false claim I might make would easily be proven so, given time. I have nothing more or less to offer than my dedication.'

Morathi gently shook her head.

'Then you have nothing to offer at all. All of Nagarythe is dedicated to me, and sycophantic captains and nobles are in easy supply. What need do I have for another fawning hanger-on?'

'None, your majesty.'

Hellebron held back tears, determined that the queen would not see any weakness in her.

'A noble attempt, child,' said the queen. 'But your lips quiver and I see in your eyes that you are already broken with shame. Do not think that pity will sway me either. You are weak and spoiled, like so many of your generation. I am disappointed your father has not raised you better; I expected more from Alandrian's daughter. Perhaps your mother is to blame.'

The dam broke and Hellebron broke into sobs, burying her face in her hands. She felt Morathi stand. The queen laid an arm across Hellebron's heaving shoulders and whispered in her ear.

'Remember this shame, my pretty child,' said the queen. 'Remember this moment of frailty, and realise that the future of Nagarythe is in the hands of those far stronger than you. Come to me again when you have something to give to our people.'

Hellebron felt a tight grip on her arm and wiped a hand across her face as Morathi pulled her up.

'I am sorry,' Hellebron said.

'Sorry for me, or sorry for yourself, child?'

Turning imploringly to the queen, Hellebron saw there was no sympathy in those dark eyes, as black and hard as granite. The queen guided her to the door and almost shoved Hellebron back into the hallway, where the bald attendant looked at the dishevelled princess with a sly smile.

'Morai-heg is cruel, and she has laid upon you an unremarkable destiny, Hellebron,' Morathi said. 'Tomorrow I will not even remember your name.'

The handmaiden entered and the door shut, the sound of its closing like an axeblade to Hellebron's dreams.

As soon as she was alone, the princess straightened, wiped the tears from her cheeks and darted a dagger-stare back towards the door. She cursed herself for resorting to tears – tears that had worked for so many years on her father and mother – and cursed again for not trying harder to impress the queen.

It did not matter. Hellebron knew the queen would see through whatever guile she could muster. Morathi had been wrong though; Hellebron was not weak. There were those who thought she was fey and feckless, but it was just an act. It was far easier to get others to do things for you if they thought you could not do them yourself. Morathi was immune, it seemed.

Her pride smarting from the encounter, Hellebron strode along the hall, determined that she would prove Morathi wrong. She was a princess and she deserved better. Though she did not know how, Hellebron would make Morathi see how foolish she had been to discard her with such contempt. She could not learn magic, and no amount of tutoring would make her a fine dancer or singer, but somehow Hellebron would find a way to gain that which she believed should be hers. She would go to Anlec as a rightful princess of Nagarythe.

Yes, Hellebron thought, one day Morathi will remember my name, and she will see me for what I am.

──◀ TWO ▶──

Lord of Murder

THOUGH HELLEBRON GAVE only a vague account of her encounter with Morathi – and assumed an outlook of indifference, if not antipathy, to the court of Anlec despite her earlier enthusiasm – it was clear amongst the society of Athel Toralien that she had been snubbed by the queen. Nothing was mentioned directly to Hellebron, but she noticed the hidden smirk in the eyes of others, and in casual asides that subtly demeaned her credentials as a true princess.

Never one to back down from confrontation, Hellebron did not hide away from the whispered accusations. She attended every gala and masque, hosted parties in her father's chambers and held her head high whenever she was in public.

In private was another matter. When alone, disappointment flooded her spirit. For all her determined thoughts after seeing Morathi, Hellebron could see no means by which she could advance her status. She suffered twofold already: by her location in the colonies and by her birth to an administrator who was a prince in name but not blood.

It did not matter in Nagarythe that Athel Toralien was one of the greatest cities of the colonies, and that it held the key to the future of the Naggarothi people. There was ever a doubt about the city in the hearts of Nagarythe-born elves, for it had been saved by the prince, and was a conquered territory in the eyes of Naggarothi law. The princes and commanders of Nagarythe were happy to wear the gems and gold that came through the port, but in their eyes Athel Toralien was only marginally Naggarothi, putting it slightly

287

above the other kingdoms of Ulthuan, but not by much of a margin.

So Hellebron suffered in secret, bearing the veiled insults and the back-handed compliments with a smile whilst every night tears wet her pillows and anguish kept sleep at bay.

Following Morathi's grand visit, Athel Toralien changed. The queen had brought with her many priests and priestesses from Nagarythe. Although they were made less than welcome by Prince Malekith, who had little time for the foibles of gods and goddesses, they flourished after his departure into the wastes of the North.

The various sects became part of the social fabric of the city and Helle-bron participated like all the other high-born elves. The popularity of one deity over another waxed and waned like fashions of jewellery and styles of poems; for a season the elite of the city would attend the sombre remem-brances of the dead watched over by the priests of Ereth Khial; for half a year the licentious dancing and erotic displays in the temple of Atharti; and during the summers bands of nobles rode forth on long hunts and sacrificed their kills to Anath Raema.

The ceremonies of the sects became a regular part of the social calendar, and Hellebron did her best to attend the most favoured events and lavish her attention on the highly regarded holy leaders. Despite her dedication, she was always at the periphery; never chosen to speak at a sacrifice, never mentioned as a benefactor, never offered the chance to be drawn into the greater secrets of the cults despite her enthusiasm to learn more.

For five years Hellebron politicked and patronised, but her standing never benefitted. Despair threatened again with the realisation that reli-gion did not promise the answers to her ambitions. The cult leaders were narrow-minded, the priests and priestesses vying with each other for great-est acceptance and acclaim. Divided, no single sect would attract the sort of power needed to impress Morathi, not here in the hinterlands.

One hot summer evening Hellebron sat staring out of the window. She looked at the huge expanse of the Great Ocean and bitterly imagined the great towers of Anlec on Ulthuan far to the west. As the sun set on the golden waves, she felt that Nagarythe might as well be on another world for all her chances of reaching it. For sure, her father would pay for a ship and send her to Anlec, but Hellebron would not go there with nothing to offer; even if her father's riches were greater than those of many ancient royal families, to turn up at the wharfs of Galthyr with no reputation would put Hellebron in the same category as the daughter of a farmer or merchant.

A knock on the door broke her contemplation. She swept back a few rebel-lious locks of hair, affected a wistful pose and called for the visitor to enter.

'Evening greetings to you, sister,' said Lirieth as she stepped inside, shad-owed by a tall captain wearing bright armour chased with sapphires on the breastplate.

'Greetings, sister,' said Hellebron, standing. She inclined her head politely towards the officer. 'This must be Maenredil.'

'It is my pleasure and honour to meet you, princess,' said Maenredil. His hair was jet-black, swept back over his shoulders with a band of gold. His eyes were animated, gauging Hellebron swiftly before roaming about the chamber, taking in every detail. 'You are as beautiful as your sister.'

Hellebron still felt a shiver of pleasure at being called a princess, and she could see amusement in the eyes of the army captain. Her sister had chosen her paramour wisely; Hellebron had sworn *she* would never marry less than a prince.

'I have something I want you to see,' said Lirieth. 'Maenredil has somewhere to take us, something you have not seen before.'

'That is a vague invitation, sister.' Hellebron's gaze slid over to Maenredil. 'If this is some form of Athartist orgy, I must decline. Though there are many pleasures of the flesh to be enjoyed, I cannot bring myself to do so in the company of my own sister.'

To his credit, Maenredil looked away, embarrassed. Lirieth did not seem to notice.

'No, it is nothing like that, sister. It is a warrior's ceremony.'

'I have no desire to watch soldiers marching back and forth,' said Hellebron.

'It is so very different from that,' said Lirieth with a giggle. 'I do not want to spoil the surprise, but please, come with us. What else would you do tonight? Sit here, grudging the stars their prettiness and the waves their melodious voices?'

Hellebron looked at the two of them, standing arm-in-arm just inside the door. Maenredil's playful look had returned.

'I think you will find this evening enlightening and entertaining,' said the captain. 'There have been very few ladies allowed to attend this gathering, but those who have speak nothing but praise of it.'

'Very well,' Hellebron said, pretending an air of vague interest. In truth, she was intrigued. She had not seen her sister so enamoured of another elf since she had been a child, and if nothing else it would be wise to spend some time with Maenredil in order to gain a better understanding of a potential brother-in-law.

When Hellebron enquired what attire would be required for this event, she was told they would be leaving the city. With the aid of Liannin, she quickly picked out some riding clothes, braided her hair tight and pulled on a pair of long boots. They were already riding along the east road when the sun finally disappeared behind Athel Toralien. Maenredil brought out a riding lamp and they followed its glow as he led them from the main road, turning south towards the forests.

They rode on until the only light was Maenredil's lamp and the swathe of stars above. As the track wound beneath the eaves of the forest, Hellebron could see glimmers of orange ahead: torchlight. Soon they caught up with other elves, riding and walking to the south. Most wore armour; a few were dressed in more courtly robes.

They came upon a wide clearing, lit by a single fire as high as the branches. In the ruddy glare Hellebron could see hundreds of elves. Smoke drifted between the trees and lingered under the branches like a red mist. Hellebron could smell more than burning wood; a scent both acrid and sweet that she could not place.

'A dedication to Anath Raema?' Hellebron sighed. 'I have attended more hunting sacrifices than I care to remember. Really, this is quite disappointing, sister.'

Lirieth's reply was a smile and a nod towards the pyre. Maenredil helped Lirieth from her mount and did likewise for Hellebron. He hooked arms with both of the sisters and led them to the edge of the clearing. Closer to the fire, Hellebron thought she could recognise the strange odour in the smoke: roasting boar. She looked for a carcass on the flames but could see nothing. Squinting, she saw some bones amongst the burning logs and now that she was in the clearing, she could see the ground was dark, made of packed ash from many previous ceremonies.

They waited in silence for some time, until Hellebron was thoroughly bored. A study of the other attendees provided little distraction; almost all were soldiers of various ranks. Clad in their armour with swords on their hips, they waited patiently, saying nothing.

'When is something going to happen?' whispered Hellebron. 'I am going to stink of smoke for the whole night.'

'Hush,' said Maenredil. His tone was mollifying rather than curt, but Hellebron smarted nonetheless. She was a princess and should not be addressed in such a way, especially by a simple captain.

Her protest died on her lips as the crowd parted to her right. An elf of senior years – seven hundred, at least – paced slowly from the treeline. He was naked except for a cloth of red wrapped about his waist. The fabric looked strangely stiff until Hellebron realised that it was matted with dried blood. The elf's exposed chest was criss-crossed with a tracery of fine scars, as were his arms. His white hair was wound into wild braids, which splayed from his head like a hydra. In one hand he held a long knife with a serrated edge, in the other a large, golden-rimmed clay goblet.

Behind him came two lines of attendants, ten of them, wearing nothing but red cloaks. Two were maidens, the rest were male. All of them were painted with crimson runes; more blood, Hellebron guessed. Each of them held a different implement: variously shaped blades, hooks, platters and cups.

The high priest stopped just before the flames and turned to face the gathered elves. Silhouetted against the fire, he raised his arms and tilted his head back. Hellebron stepped back in shock as an otherworldly screech emanated from the priest's throat, unlike anything she had heard before; part the wail of an injured animal, part the roar of a savage predator.

The attendants added their voices to the long cry, each shrieking at a different pitch, their screeching spreading out through the forest. Several dozen elves in the crowd shouted also, wordless howls that made Hellebron think of pain and hunger.

The priest's hands dropped. He crossed his arms over his chest, silencing the gathering.

'Praise Khaine!' His voice was as dry as tinder, but carried across the clearing. 'Let us give our thanks for victories past, and seek His divine hand in our future conquests. Praise the Lord of Blood, the Prince of Death, for delivering our enemies to our blades.

'Many of you march forth to the south and east, where a horde of the troublesome beast-creatures has gathered in the dark woods. Give your praise tonight and bring Khaine's curse on your foes tomorrow. Let them know the red wrath of His attention and with His name upon your lips strike down those who would despoil our lands. Let Khaine drink deep of the offerings that we give Him this night, as we promise to sate His hunger for flesh and slake His thirst for blood upon the field of battle.'

The priest's head turned left and right as he studied the crowd. Hellebron felt his eyes upon her and stepped to one side, unconsciously shielding herself behind Maenredil. The priest's gaze moved on and she breathed a sigh of relief. She shuddered, though could find no reason for the momentary fear that had gripped her.

'It is good to see new faces amongst the familiar,' continued the priest. 'Our Lord Aenarion, founder of Nagarythe, King of Ulthuan, would be proud to see those that follow in his footsteps. Did not the Lord of Murder place his blessing upon the troubled brow of Aenarion and deliver us from the daemons? Did not Aenarion take up the holy blade of Khaine to smite our enemies? Now, as then, Khaine looks upon the bloody deeds wrought in his name and is pleased.'

Hellebron felt light-headed. Through the fog of her thoughts, she realised that there was something besides wood and flesh burning on the pyre; a narcotic of some kind. She was no stranger to some of the more exotic leaf and root available from the colonies even further to the east, but she had only occasionally indulged, and always in the company of those she knew well. Deep down she objected to being drugged without her consent, but any protest she might have made stayed deep inside, held in check by the soporific effect of the vapours she was breathing.

She looked at Lirieth and saw that her sister was wide-eyed, hanging on the priest's every word. Maenredil's face was flushed, his breathing coming in short pants. Struggling to focus, Hellebron saw others in the crowd were similarly affected, baring their teeth, hands clenched into tight fists. She swayed as she turned back to the priest, who had continued to speak.

His words lost meaning, and the heat of the flames was like the burning of ice on Hellebron's skin. It was a pleasant sensation, relaxing and invigorating at the same time, like a languid dance with a handsome suitor that promised more vigorous activity later. Hellebron felt the weight of her cloak on her shoulder pressing into her flesh and flung it to the ground, glad to be free of its cloying grip.

At the touch of her hand on her skin, she trembled with excitement. She ran her long fingernails down her throat, delighting at the experience. Every sense was heightened: the chanting of the priest and his disciples; the smoke; the crackle of flames; the touch of the breeze; the softness of the ground underfoot.

Hellebron longed to heighten and sustain the feeling. She ripped off her boots and cast them aside, revelling in the touch of the bare earth on the soles of her feet. Her clothes were too tight, constricting, a barrier between her and the world. She gripped the collar of her loose shirt and was about to pull herself free from its woven prison when she felt Maenredil's hand upon her shoulder.

The sudden intervention startled Hellebron out of her trance. Still intoxicated, she felt no embarrassment or regret at her actions, but became suddenly aware that she was not alone.

Something snarled and growled in the darkness beyond the firelight. For a moment Hellebron was afraid; some creature stalked the woods, perhaps the bloodthirsty spirit of Khaine Himself. She shrank closer to Maenredil for protection; saw that Lirieth held his other arm tightly, eyes wide with excitement, a thin trail of blood leaking down her chin where she had bitten her lip.

Something stumbled through the undergrowth.

The firelight reflected from two eyes in the darkness, coming closer. The elves were hushed, all attention on the approaching creature. In the silence, a harsh panting reverberated around the clearing.

The beast of the forests emerged. It was roughly the height of an elf, far broader in shoulder and chest. Its head was like that of a goat, with six curling horns; hair covered its arms and legs, and though upright, it walked on hooves rather than feet.

Hellebron shuddered, but nobody else seemed the least bit concerned. It was only after her initial shock that Hellebron noticed the beastman's arms were bound behind its back. A short way behind, several Naggarothi soldiers followed, their spears at the ready.

The beastman glared with red eyes, scowling and grunting at the assembled elves, angry and confused. With a snarl that exposed rows of pointed teeth, it lunged towards the audience. The closest guard reacted instantly, swinging the butt of her spear against the back of the creature's legs, sending it sprawling into the packed ash underfoot. The soldier followed up, rapping her spear against the creature's jaw, stunning it.

Hauled to its feet, the beastman staggered as it was thrust towards the high priest. The attendants swarmed around the sacrifice, forcing it to its knees, grabbing hair and horns to pull back its head, exposing its huge chest and vein-corded throat. The high priest gently drew the tip of his dagger across his own chest, cutting a thin line through the skin. A single drop of blood seeped from the wound. The high priest allowed the blood to drip into the goblet he held.

He turned towards the fire, raising the cup in toast.

'I offer up myself, for all blood runs swift in your name, mighty Khaine.' The high priest swung back towards his congregation. 'In time, we all pray to give up ourselves in Your name, upon the field of bloodshed.'

'Praise Khaine,' whispered the crowd.

Hellebron's eyes were fixed on the beastman as the high priest loomed over it, swathing the creature in shadow. The knife flashed in the firelight and a line of red appeared across the dark skin of the beast's chest. Again and again the knife swept down, lightly touching, razor-sharp. Soon blood was streaming from two dozen wounds across the beastman's body and arms. The cuts were so fine Hellebron thought they looked like bright red spiders' webs. Blood oozed across the beast's rough skin, matting its body hair, collecting in folds of flesh.

The attendants hauled the beast upright and blood surged from its injuries, spattering onto the dark ground.

'Let this be the first of many lives You will taste in the days to come!' yelled the high priest. 'Praise Khaine!'

He plunged his dagger into the creature's gut.

'Praise Khaine!' chanted the crowd.

Braying wildly, the beastman thrashed, but was thrown to the ground. Four of the attendants leapt upon the creature, driving long nails through its wrists and ankles, pinning it down. The others set to work with their blades and hooks, cutting through skin, fat and muscle, exposing bone and organs. Piece by piece, the beastman was opened up and laid out for all to see.

Hellebron was fascinated. She was rapt by the intricacy of the work. Every stroke of dagger was lovingly applied, a deadly caress of a gesture. The blood was hypnotising, the essence of life gradually leaking from the creature it sustained. Slippery tubes and strangely coloured organs were pulled free, while an attendant applied sharp cutters to the creature's ribs, splaying them open one at a time until the heart and lungs were exposed. All the while, the priest filled his cup with gushing crimson.

'Praise Khaine!' shrieked the high priest.

'Praise Khaine!' roared the crowd.

The high priest finished the work, handing the goblet of blood to an assistant so that he could cut free the wildly beating heart. It spasmed in his hand for a moment, pumping blood across his exposed flesh.

'Praise Khaine!' The cry echoed through the woods. Hellebron realised her voice was amongst those raised in adoration.

The high priest cast the bloodied heart into the flames of the fire, face turned to the sky. Hellebron looked up and it seemed that the stars burned red for a moment. She could feel the energy swirling around the clearing; in the air, in the ground, in the elves around her.

This was power. This was power she could touch, control, shape to her design.

The goblet of blood was being passed around the worshippers, who each took a sip. Hellebron fidgeted as it made its way around the clearing, anxious to partake of the beastman's strength, desperate to feel the blessing of Khaine.

Lirieth drank first, wetting her lips, a brief wrinkle of distaste on her brow. Maenredil took a mouthful, swallowing with relish. He grinned at Hellebron, exposing his blood-flecked teeth and crimson gums.

Hellebron almost snatched the goblet from his hands. She was the last. She downed the contents in one draught, tasting iron and forest and hunger. The thick fluid rolled down her throat and filled her with warmth – not the warmth of the blood, but something else. She wiped fingers around the rim of the goblet and licked the last sticky patches from her fingertips.

Hellebron was suddenly aware that all eyes were turned to her. Murmurs of disquiet rippled through the crowd. She turned an enquiring look at Maenredil.

'The last of the blood is for Khaine, to be poured on the flames,' the captain said quietly.

Horrified, Hellebron swung around to the high priest.

'I meant no disrespect!' she declared. 'I did not know.'

The high priest said nothing as one of his attendants snatched the goblet from Hellebron's grasp.

'Wait!' snarled Hellebron. She grabbed the goblet back and shoved the protesting attendant to one side. She stalked across the clearing and stopped just in front of the high priest, thrusting the goblet back towards him.

'Take it,' she said.

The Khainite priest took hold of the cup, but Hellebron did not let go, pulling it to her stomach. With her other hand, she seized the high priest's wrist, pulling forwards the hand that held the sacrificial dagger.

'I offer my blood as apology to mighty Khaine.'

Hellebron forced the high priest's hand down, cutting her chest with his blade. Blood welled from the wound and dribbled into the goblet. The sensation was almost overwhelming, a white heat that burned through to her heart.

'Praise Khaine!' she shrieked, pushing the high priest away.

The Khainite looked at Hellebron in confusion. Frustrated, she snatched the goblet from him and strode to the fire. Upending the vessel, she threw her own blood into the flames.

'Accept this offering, Lord of Death, Prince of Murder!' Hellebron raised the cup above her head and turned to the others. 'Bless me with Your divine anger. Gift to me the rage eternal.'

She fell to her knees, tears of joy streaming down her face. The elves stood in shock for a moment.

'Praise Khaine!' the cry came, started by Maenredil. The rest of the congregation took up the call, and Hellebron fell to her belly, writhing in pleasure, screaming prayers to the Lord of Slaughter.

She did not know how long it lasted. Eventually the red haze that had clouded her vision subsided. The others were leaving; Lirieth and Maenredil stood to one side, waiting for Hellebron. She became aware of the stinging pain above her breast. Dried blood caked her shirt. After-images fluttered in her mind; of the dying beastman, the rising flames, her blood upon the dagger. She could not believe it was over so soon.

Hellebron stood, dusted the ash from her clothes and turned to the high priest.

'I beseech you, prophet of Khaine, to teach me more,' she said. She grabbed his dagger-hand again and held the knife's point to her chest, just above her heart. 'Let me serve Khaine with my life, or else I must offer Him my death.'

The Khainite smiled and cupped a blood-caked hand to Hellebron's cheek. Hellebron looked deep into his eyes and for a moment thought he would plunge in the dagger.

The Khainite's murderous look passed. He pulled back the knife.

'You have been touched by Him in a way that is rare, my child,' said the priest. 'I will come to you tomorrow, and we shall see if you wish to stay true to this path.'

'I am of a single mind,' said Hellebron. 'I shall be Khaine's mistress, devoted to him in every way.'

'Tomorrow,' said the Khainite. 'When the sun is up and your flesh has cooled, we will see if you still feel the same way. That is my last word for the moment.'

Hellebron stepped back and nodded. Turning away, her step was light as she crossed back to Maenredil and Lirieth. Her eyes had been opened. She could feel Khaine's touch upon her spirit, always there but now awakened. She knew what she must do.

Hellebron had found the purpose she had been seeking. As a priestess of Khaine, she would travel to Anlec, accorded all the respect and awe due to her position. None save Aenarion would be a greater servant to Khaine.

━◄ THREE ►━

The Path of Blood

HELLEBRON WAS NOT even sure which gristly organ was the heart. She rummaged around inside the goblin's chest, looking for something that might be a main artery. Her knife slashed here and there until a fountain of acrid blood splashed across her face.

'Found it!' she declared gleefully, ripping free the organ.

Lethruis, the high priest, smiled patiently. Hellebron squeezed the last of the dark blood into the chalice and then dropped the heart onto a brazier, where it hissed and spat. Shadows danced on the walls and ceiling of the small stone chamber. She looked doubtfully at the ooze in the cup.

'Do I have to drink this?' she asked.

'If the sacrifice is not good enough for you, what will Khaine think of it?' said Lethruis.

Hellebron conceded the point with a sigh and raised the cup to her trembling lips. She stopped and stooped to take a breath of the narcotic smoke coming from the brazier. The burning dreamroot filled her lungs and her body relaxed.

'This may help,' said Lethruis. He sprinkled a ground substance into the goblin blood. 'Bladesbane makes the blood taste sweeter and the effect of the dreamroot will be enhanced.'

Believing it was better to get the whole thing over with, Hellebron took a mouthful and swallowed quickly, gulping down the goblin's essence before she could taste it. It was unpleasant, having none of the vitality of the beast-man blood she had tasted at the first ceremony.

'Praise Khaine,' she said, emptying the remaining contents of the goblet into the brazier. The flames almost died, but not quite. They burned low and blue for a moment before growing in strength and returning to their normal colour.

Lethruis nodded with satisfaction. 'You are an able student,' said the priest. 'You are attentive, dedicated and willing to learn.'

'Thank you,' said Hellebron, taking a cloth proffered by Lethruis to wipe her lips.

'For more than a hundred days you have come to me to learn the ways of Khaine,' said Lethruis. 'If you wish to truly master the arts of the Lord of Murder, we must spend more time together. Coming here every few days is not enough. If you truly wish to be a disciple of Khaine, you must renounce your life and spend all of your time in His service. Unless you are willing to do this, there is no point in continuing.'

'But you will be leaving Athel Toralien,' said Hellebron. 'You want me to travel with the army? Leave the city?'

Lethruis shrugged. 'If you are not willing to put yourself wholly within Khaine's bloody embrace, I will teach you no more.'

'My father would disapprove.'

'Not all sacrifice is made with knife and blood, Hellebron,' said Lethruis. 'You face a choice. Do not rush your decision. Come to me in two days' time, the night before we leave for the new campaign.'

Hellebron nodded, gave a quick bow of respect and left the shrine room. She walked slowly up the steps from the underground chamber, still light-headed from the dreamroot and bladesbane. The short stairwell took her to an open dome, the roof and columns carved from black granite, engraved with runes of Khaine.

The army mustering field stretched around her, an expanse of black and purple pavilions, corrals, storehouses, armouries and kitchens. The Nagga-rothi were preparing to march far to the east and south, claiming fresh lands for Prince Malekith and Ulthuan.

Walking across the packed dirt, Hellebron's head throbbed as the effects of the narcotics wore off. She felt another pain too: the pain of indecision. Lethruis was forcing her to make a simple choice, but the choice was not so simple. Did she really want to give up her inheritance as the daughter of Athel Toralien's ruler? Could she go without the comforts she had been raised to enjoy, to live in some dark shrine and traipse back and forth across the world following the armies?

This gave her pause. She remembered what it was that had drawn her to Khaine, aside from the monumental sensation of potency and energy derived from the sacrifice: power. High priests were influential, and the role of Khaine within Nagarythe's army and the ties to Aenarion were powerful tools. All of that power was for nothing, if Hellebron could not take it with her when she finally travelled to Ulthuan.

She came to a well, drew up some water and washed the blood from her hands and face. A nearby red-walled tent was set aside for the priest and acolytes. Hellebron ducked inside, stripped off her bloodstained robes and pulled on a dark red dress, fixing it with a thick black belt.

All about the tent were the accoutrements of Khaine; the chalices and knives, pendants and engraved saws. A circlet of black-enamelled iron sat upon a small altar stone. Hellebron had never seen Lethruis wear the Crown of Sacrifice, and wondered what it signified. She knew only its name, and resolved to ask the high priest when she returned.

The brief distraction settled her thoughts. Throwing in her lot with Lethruis would not aid Hellebron's cause one bit. It would mean nothing to Morathi; Hellebron would just be one of many priests and priestesses of Khaine that served with the armies of Nagarythe. Hellebron had to do more. Just as Morathi had brought the worship of Ereth Khial, Morai-heg, Anath Raema and other gods and goddesses, Hellebron would bring the power of Khaine to the people of Athel Toralien.

Lethruis was too much of a traditionalist, but he was a true priest. For the moment he was a useful fount of knowledge. For the moment only. When she had learned all she could learn from the high priest, Hellebron would chart her own course. She had spent days in her father's library, researching the history of Nagarythe, reading over and over of the founding of the kingdom by Aenarion. The tales of Aenarion's wars bearing the Sword of Khaine, the Widowmaker, thrilled her. She learnt how the God of Murder had laid his blessing upon the Naggarothi so that they might banish the daemons that had beset Ulthuan.

Many had forgotten that legacy. While the pleasure-seekers lost themselves in drug-addled orgies, and the morbid poets sang the praises of Ereth Khial, the heart of Nagarythe had been left by the wayside. Hellebron was a princess now, her father a proud soldier and one of the most powerful elves in the colonies. It was her duty to remind the people of their great history, and ensure that the realms of Nagarythe remained strong, pure to the traditions of Aenarion.

She would bring Khaine to the people of Athel Toralien and create a second Anlec in Elthin Arvan. As a prophetess of Khaine, she would eclipse the mundane achievements of the other priests.

Hellebron rode back to the city, mind full of this vision, of an army of followers sworn to Khaine, ready to do her every bidding. She remembered Morathi's spectacular reception in Athel Toralien, and dreamed of the day she too would be welcomed by a cheering throng and her name would be sung by poets for generations.

PRINCE ALANDRIAN TOOK the news better than Hellebron had expected.

'It will be good for you to learn something of our people beyond these walls, and of a world not confined by tapestries and cushions,' said her father. He leaned forwards in his chair and rested his arms on his scroll-littered desk. 'Lirieth should go with you too.'

Hellebron hesitated. The conversation was going too well and she expected some kind of caveat was forthcoming.

'Once you are out of sight of the city, you are beyond my power,' said Alandrian. 'You will be afforded no special treatment, by the priests or the commanders of the army. It is good that you desire to grow stronger, but you will have to do so by your own means.'

'I understand, father,' said Hellebron. She looked at his sincere face and realised that this was not simply a talk to rouse her spirits; he meant every word he was saying. He was not going to disown her, but he was not going to use his influence on her behalf either. 'When Lirieth and I return, we will be a credit to the family.'

'You and your sister must look after each other,' he said. 'I know that the two of you are close, but you will need each other more than you think.'

'What if Lirieth does not want to come?' asked Hellebron.

'She will,' said her father, smiling fondly. 'She adores you, and if you ask her to follow, she will.'

Hellebron considered this. It was a responsibility she had not foreseen. It was one matter to tie her fate to the cult of Khaine, another to make the same choice for her sister. But had it not been Lirieth who had first introduced Hellebron to the Khainites? And Lirieth would be happy to accompany Maenredil on his campaigns.

'I will not pressure her, father, but if she chooses to come with me, we will grow stronger together.'

Alandrian nodded. 'One other thing, daughter,' he said. 'If you are to learn the way of Khaine, as I and many others did, you must seek not only the ceremony and sacrifice; you must embrace all of Khaine's gifts and learn to wage war. It is this that is Aenarion's legacy to the Naggarothi; do not forget it.'

It was Hellebron's turn to nod. 'I will study the many bloody ways, in the shrine and upon the battlefield. We will show those in Nagarythe that the true spirit of the Naggarothi still flows in Athel Toralien.'

Prince Alandrian walked around the table and embraced Hellebron, stroking her long hair.

'You will make me very proud, I am sure,' he said. The two parted, the prince leaving his hand on his daughter's arm for a moment. 'All of Athel Toralien will be proud.'

And Morathi, thought Hellebron. Would the queen be impressed? Hellebron's star would shine so bright in the colonies, Morathi would be forced to recognise her achievements.

HELLEBRON AND LIRIETH bade a sincere farewell to their father and quit the city of Athel Toralien. The lives of elves are not measured in days or seasons, or even years. The sisters saw their first battle in the foothills of the mountains to the south of Athel Toralien. While she chanted the praises of Khaine and invoked the blessings of the Lord of Murder, Hellebron watched the Naggarothi cut down an army of Chaos-twisted beasts. She admired the cruel efficiency of Nagarythe's host, striking with sure and deadly precision like the knife of Lethruis.

A score of wounded foes were brought back to the camp that night and the pyre of Khaine burned high. Hellebron and Lirieth took their places with the other acolytes, bearing the sacred implements of Khaine while Lethruis despatched the sacrifices. Those Naggarothi warriors who had performed exceptionally during the battle were anointed with the blood of their fallen enemies, receiving the praise of Lethruis and the blessing of Khaine for their violent endeavours.

By day the sisters drilled with the soldiers, learning to fight as one part of the whole, two spears amongst several thousands. By night they listened to Lethruis's tales of Aenarion and his war against the daemons. With each story, Hellebron's ambition grew and she knew she had picked the right path. In Khaine's service was the glory of myth, and amongst the Naggarothi there was no greater glory.

Hellebron showed greater patience than in any other endeavour she had embarked upon. She suffered the long marches, the weary dawns and the harrowing confrontations with orcs and beastmen without complaint. She revelled in the sacrifices to Khaine, and gathered a small following of her own amongst the warriors, who cheered her flourishes with the dagger and her eloquent praises to the Lord of Murder.

For two decades the sisters followed the armies of the Naggarothi; fighting in the spear line, and performing the rituals of Khaine upon the eve of battle and the many nights of victory. Under the tutelage of the captains and the stern eye of Lethruis, Hellebron learnt the secrets of spear and sword, dagger and chant.

Lirieth was no less accomplished. The pair fought and offered praise beside each other, and so grew inseparable. Swept up in her dedication to Khaine, Lirieth spurned Maenredil's advances until the captain grew bored and the two ended their tryst. The sisters fought for each other, for their brothers-in-arms, and for Khaine. Lethruis often referred to them as the Daughters of Murder, an epithet Hellebron quickly adopted.

Across the wild mountains, dark forests and windswept grasslands of Elthin Arvan, the Naggarothi swept all before them. At times they fought alone, and at others they were joined by the small armies from the other colony-cities. Such alliances were fraught with tension; the Naggarothi felt that other elves were hanging on the tails of Nagarythe, and for their part the soldiers of other kingdoms were suspicious of the Naggarothi ceremonies and their apparent love of killing.

Lethruis forbade his acolytes from speaking to the elves of other kingdoms, but when she had the opportunity, Hellebron ignored the proscription and would pass on the secrets of Khaine to those few who were willing to listen. With each passing year, she became more convinced that Lethruis was small-minded and jealous of her popularity. The high priest was content to preach his bloody sermons to his own, but Hellebron sought to spread the word of Khaine beyond the Naggarothi.

Three times over the following twenty years, the army returned to Athel Toralien. Hellebron weighted down her expectations on that first triumphant parade, and took the praises and cheers of the city's people as one amongst many. On the second visit, she entered the city as a priestess of Khaine, but it was Lethruis who addressed the crowds and extolled the virtues of Khaine. Hellebron smarted at this glory-stealing but said nothing. Instead she listened to the advice of Lirieth, who spoke of patience and dedication.

On the third visit, Hellebron was dismayed. The folk of Athel Toralien were easily bored and while the Daughters of Murder had been the subject of tales and gossip for a few years, interest in their exploits soon waned. The success of the Naggarothi armies was taken as fact, and each victory was celebrated with less enthusiasm than the last. The beastmen of the North were all but exterminated, and the orcs of the East had been driven out by the dwarfs. The lands of Elthin Arvan were almost as safe as a pasture in Cothique, but the Naggarothi were a forceful people and would not quit their wars.

Hellebron chafed at being one amongst many; both in battle and in the cult of Khaine. She and Lirieth sought out the greatest swordmasters and the most accomplished captains in order to learn new skills, of blade and command. Some were willing teachers, happy to pass on their skills. Others were vain elves, many hundreds of years old. These the sisters ensnared with favours of the flesh, seducing them with their beauty, manipulating them to pass on all that they knew before discarding them.

Word of these exploits reached Lethruis, and the high priest punished the sisters harshly, forbidding them from attending the Khainite ceremonies. Hellebron longed to challenge Lethruis for control, but the old priest was too canny to be tricked, and too unimaginative to share her grander vision for the cult of Khaine.

Robbed of a stage, Hellebron and Lirieth's popularity within the army dwindled. In defiance of Lethruis, they held their own dedications to Khaine in secret, performing their bloody acts before a select audience of the most influential captains and warriors. Compared to the dogmatic, time-worn displays of Lethruis, these sacrifices were energetic and fresh. Hellebron allowed others to plunge the dagger into the orcs and goblins and beastmen that had been captured, sharing in Khaine's glory, while Lethruis stubbornly maintained himself as the conduit between the elves and their bloodthirsty god.

Crossing the lands belonging to the colonies of other kingdoms, the Naggarothi marched almost to the deserts of the south. Here the orcs had gathered, far from the cities of the dwarfs and elves, and it was here the army of Athel Toralien would test itself again.

AN ORCISH SETTLEMENT had been located by the outriders and the next day would bring fresh bloodshed. Lethruis had demanded that Lirieth and Hellebron attend him for the pre-battle rites, yet gave them no part to play in the ceremony. Hellebron silently fumed as she watched Lethruis despatch the sacrifices without fuss, cutting out their hearts while he droned out the same tired platitudes to Khaine he had spoken for hundreds of years.

She watched the small crowd – barely a third of the army had bothered to attend – and knew that even here, amidst Nagarythe's most fervent warriors, the worship of Khaine was slipping away. The soldiers chanted 'Praise Khaine' with hollow eyes and lifeless voices, and the sight of it tore at Hellebron's heart.

Twenty years of hardship she had spent trying to create a myth for herself, and even the small glories she had achieved were ebbing away with every monotonous chant. The battle of the next day would likely be the last for many years to come, and Hellebron's future would drift away into a life of grey obscurity.

When the last heart was tossed into the flames, Hellebron wanted to seize Lethruis and throw him in after it. It was not only her ambition that the tired priest was destroying; more fervently than ever she wanted the praise of Khaine to be shouted from the lips of every elf, and though he spoke the sacred words and told the tales, Lethruis was destroying Aenarion's legacy with every lacklustre ceremony and insipid dedication. Khaine, who through Aenarion had saved the elves, would fade into obscurity, leaving Hellebron's people weak and vulnerable.

When the crowd had wandered away, Hellebron and Lirieth returned to their tent. Hellebron was silent for some time as the two sisters sat sharpening their weapons.

'Nobody will care!' said Hellebron, no longer able to hold in her frustration. 'Tomorrow will be seen as just another battle against the barbaric greenskin tribes. Hunting hawks are held in higher regard than we are.'

'We are still doing Khaine's work, sister,' said Lirieth, sweeping her stone along the edge of her curved sword. 'Blood will still be spilt.'

'It is not enough!' snapped Hellebron, tossing her blade to the rug-covered ground in exasperation. 'How many have fallen to us, my sister? A thousand spirits sent to Khaine on the battlefield and in the fires, but it stirs not a word from those who should be praising our names.'

'Then we must give the storytellers something to tell,' said Lirieth. She held up her blade and inspected the edge. Satisfied, she sheathed the sword, placed it to one side and drew out a serrated dagger. 'A tale can only be told so many times, sister. If it is glory that you seek, you must give the people something new. They are fickle, so we must capture their imagination.'

'Or perhaps we have simply been away too long and our faces and names go unremembered,' said Hellebron. She picked up her sword, whispered an apology to Khaine for disrespecting her weapon, and drew her stone along it with a keening shriek.

'I think you would be disappointed, sister,' said Lirieth. 'If you hope to return now and receive the adulation that was poured upon Morathi, you will not receive it.'

Hellebron snarled. 'Ingrates and sycophants, all of them,' she said. 'What is it that Morathi possesses that we do not?'

'A legacy,' said Lirieth. 'She was Aenarion's queen, and for that she will be forever revered. Unless you plan to marry a Phoenix King, you will need something else to excite the people.'

'Prince Malekith has never taken a wife...'

'I was jesting, sister. If Malekith has not married yet, it is unlikely he ever will; and if he chose a bride, there are other Naggarothi princesses far higher up the list than you or I. Whatever renown we seek, we must earn it. Was not that the point, when we set out? If you merely want to marry into reputation, you could do so at any time.'

Hellebron tested the edge of her sword, effortlessly slicing a piece of cloth. Satisfied, she used the rag to wipe a smear from the silver-inlaid blade. She saw the reflection of her face and paused, admiring herself for a moment. She knew she was beautiful, but beauty was not unique. She stared hard at herself, her ruby-red lips, the darker paint around her eyes, the whiteness of her dyed hair and pale skin.

'Fear,' she said.

'What do you mean, sister?'

'The people fear Morathi as much as they respect her. She is a sorceress without equal. Her entourage intimidates people with their strange customs and mysterious powers. Alone she is forbidding, but as a leader she embodies something far greater. We must get some followers of our own, sister.'

'Father once said that the nature of power is twofold,' said Lirieth. 'On the one hand, those with power promise reward to those that serve them well; on the other, they offer punishment to those that fail to serve. What have we to offer on either count?'

'On the second, we have all the power we need,' said Hellebron. She held up her blade, touching its tip to Lirieth's dagger. 'Death. Perhaps it is time that Khaine feasted on better fare than degenerate beasts and the gristle of orcs?'

'Why sweeten every meal with our own blood, when the whole banquet could be as succulent?' Lirieth said with a smile, picking up her sister's intent.

'Tomorrow, during the battle,' said Hellebron. 'We will show the true desires of Khaine. We will give the army a sacrifice it shall never forget!'

—◄ FOUR ►—

Anointed in Battle

THE FOLLOWING MORNING heralded an inauspicious start. The sky was filled with grey, and light rain dampened the mood of the Naggarothi camp. The ground underfoot was boggy, broken by glistening rocks and deeper patches of marshland. In the haze, nothing could be seen of the mountains to the east and the wilderness was swathed in a melancholy gloom.

Scouts had returned during the night, confirming a large orc encampment to the south-east, made of rough hide tents and little else. It was hard to estimate enemy numbers, but the scouts agreed it was between ten and fifteen thousand – perhaps half a dozen tribes or more forced together by the advances of the elves and dwarfs. There was little hope that the battle would be anything of remark; a small, dispirited enemy army and the mediocre weather would provide little sport or spectacle for the battle-hungry Naggarothi.

Their calls dulled by the rain, the clarions of the Naggarothi summoned the host to arms. In lines of silver, black and purple, the elves mustered. Spear companies formed up, flanked by regiments of bowmen, and warriors armed with repeating crossbows fashioned by the dwarfs. Bolt-thrower crews dismantled their machines where they had been set to guard the camp, and trudged into place behind the main lines. Prince Malriad, commander of the army, mounted his silver-mailed charger and took his position at the head of the knights of Athel Toralien, their pennants hanging limply from their lances.

The sun broke briefly through the grey, glistening from moisture-dappled mail and the tips of spears and arrows. The dazzling effect was fleeting as the clouds thickened and the rain grew in strength. The braziers around the camp hissed, the canvas of the tents flapped and cracked; the warriors of Nagarythe stood in miserable quiet, all eagerness quelled by the filthy weather.

Riders were sent south, to spy upon the orcs and goblins. In the wake of the scouts, Malriad signalled the advance and the trumpets sounded the order to form a column. Hellebron and Lirieth took their place, flanking the standard of their company, long shields upon their left arms, leaf-headed spears in their right hands, swords and knives at their hips. They gave each other a knowing glance from beneath the brows of their silver helms.

'It will be as we decided?' said Lirieth.

'It will,' replied Hellebron.

'What are you two whispering?' asked Nhalek, the standard-bearer.

'Khaine's business,' hissed Hellebron. 'Mind your own.'

The company set off at a steady march, third in the column; the knights formed the vanguard, with a regiment of crossbows behind. Another four thousand Naggarothi followed, a winding snake with a spine of banners and silver spearpoints. There were no roads and the Naggarothi tramped through the long grass; the hems of their robes were soon soaking wet, boots slicked with mud.

Hellebron ignored the slapping of wet material against her legs and gripped her spearshaft tightly, hiding her excitement. If any day needed the spark of bloody spectacle, it was today.

IT WAS MID-MORNING, as grey and lifeless as dawn, when the scouts returned with news that the orcs were leaving their encampment and moving westwards towards the coast. Bands of wolf-riding goblins prowled the wilderness, but they were incompetent pickets and the scouts had returned unseen. The greenskins were unaware of the army bearing down upon them.

The army was heartened by the news as it rippled through the ranks. Prince Malriad gave the order to increase the pace of the advance. The Naggarothi broke into a swift jog, the elves covering the ground with loping, easy strides, effortlessly negotiating the knots of bushes and undulations scattered across their path. The harnesses of the knights' steeds jingled along with the knee-length mail coats of the infantry.

The rain stopped just before midday, though the sky was still overcast. The wind picked up the closer the host came to the coast, a westerly wind finally catching the flags and pennons, snapping them from their shafts while it tousled crests of blue and red and purple and black from the helmets of the elves.

The air was tinged with salt. Hellebron licked her lips, remembering the taste of blood. The ground was firmer underfoot, the mire of the wastelands giving way to rockier terrain. She saw the scouts galloping back from the south-west and it was not long before the clarions were ringing with the signal to break column and form the line for attack.

As the Naggarothi host spread to the north and south, Hellebron caught her first glimpse of the greenskin horde. The ground rose ahead and a sea of orcs and goblins thronged the slope. They clustered beneath crude standards made of skulls and bones. The largest orcs bustled through the horde, shouting and punching to establish their dominance.

Small goblins mounted on the backs of grey-furred wolves waited at the edge of the army, peering at the approaching elves from beneath fur-brimmed helms, their small fists nervously gripping the bent shafts of stone-tipped spears. More of the smallest greenskins were bullied into position at the front of the greenskin army, a ragtag mob wielding daggers, short swords, wooden clubs and round shields.

A change in the breeze brought the stench of the greenskins wafting over the elves. It was a wet mixture of dung, rotting offal and mulch, like the smell of an animal's body left to the worms beneath a thick forest canopy. Hellebron barely reacted; she had drunk the blood of a dozen orcs and goblins and was all but immune to the disgusting taste. Around her, others were not so lucky; there were murmurs of distaste and snarled insults were spat at the filthy enemy.

At the heart of the opposing army several dozen burly orcs sat on the backs of immense boars. Their mounts were clad in scraps of spiked armour, jutting tusks sheathed with metal. The orcs wore crude jerkins of untanned hide, their green skin pocked with scars and marked with tattoos and war-paint. Angry red eyes glared at the elves; crude swords and brutal cleavers waved in defiance.

'Look, trolls!' Nhalek pointed to the south.

More than a dozen of the huge creatures ambled down the slope behind a mob of goblins. Each troll was thrice the height of an elf – five times that of a goblin – with a pot belly, short legs and gangling arms. Their skin was a deep greenish-blue, heads flat, ears long and tattered like a ragged parody of the elves'. The trolls wore scraps of cloth and random pieces of toughened leather, but their skin was harder than any armour the orcs could make. Clawed hands held up splintered tree-limbs and clubs made of bone studded with rivets.

At the rear of the orc army, a train of goblins was hauling a war machine into position. It was a laughably crude attempt at duplicating the catapults of the dwarfs. A ramshackle construction of red-daubed wood and splitting ropes, the stone-thrower looked as likely to fall to pieces as hurl a boulder. Under the lash of an orc overseer, the goblins hammered spikes into the ground to secure the engine, while others slowly winched down the throwing arm and yet more gathered together what rocks they could find for ammunition.

Hellebron caught a whisper travelling along the elf line from the south.

A ripple of discontent swept through the ranks until it reached Hellebron's company. The rumour was that the scouts had spotted a wyvern the night before, but today the huge creature was nowhere to be seen. Hellebron looked up and scoured the clouds for a sign of the half-dragon but saw nothing. Others were looking skywards too, uncomfortable at the thought of a wyvern dropping upon them unseen.

Not for the first time, Hellebron noticed how calm the army was before battle. While the orcs bustled and massed in anarchic fashion, the quiet ranks of elves waited patiently for the orders of their commander. Speartips made straight lines of silver, and shields created an unbreakable wall of black and red. The musicians sounded the commands, short blasts that readjusted the line as the orc army took shape, the regiments marching without haste into their new positions.

It was the calm before the storm, the cold hearth before the fire is lit.

For a moment Hellebron wondered what the greenskins were thinking, looking down the hill at the silent lines of warriors. She dismissed the thought; orcs and goblins were stupid creatures, incapable of acknowledging the majesty of the vision before them. They were equally incapable of knowing when they stared defeat in the face. Time and again the Naggarothi hosts had slain their armies and burned their barbaric villages, but still the greenskins tried to fight.

Violence was the only language they understood. They had to be made to understand: these lands belonged to the elves.

Drums rumbled through the orc and goblin horde. At first the beat was scattered, a noise without rhythm or purpose. Slowly the drums came together, banging out a slow beat which was picked up by the orcs with weapons on shields and stamping feet. Crude horns took up the call, brash and tuneless. The orcs added their voices, defying the elves with deep bellows while the screeches of the goblins cut across the bass chanting.

The beat gradually sped up, the chanting grew louder, the clamour washing down the hill in a vain attempt to intimidate the Naggarothi.

Prince Malriad broke from his knights, followed by the bearer of his personal standard. The two riders galloped along the line and took up a position facing the elf army. Malriad drew his sword, his black steed stamping and swaying.

'We can do better than that!' cried the prince.

'For Aenarion!' the elves called out in a single voice, bringing up spears and lances with a crash that momentarily eclipsed the banging and ranting of the greenskins.

'For Prince Malekith!'

The thousands of warriors took a step, presenting their shields and spearpoints towards the orcs, the thud of feet shaking the ground.

'For Nagarythe!'

This last was a deafening roar, a challenge cried from the throat of every Naggarothi.

Not to be outdone, the orcs increased their clamour, howling and shouting in their guttural language, no doubt hurling insults and making empty boasts. Their leaders, huge creatures taller and broader than the elves, stomped up and down in front of their subordinates, baring their long fangs and snarling.

Perhaps overcome by fear or excitement, the crew of the stone-thrower unleashed their war engine. Its arm snapped forwards. A cloud of fist-sized rocks arced into the air. Thousands of eyes from both armies followed their path.

With an explosion of mud, the stones fell to the ground at least a hundred paces short of the elven line. The wind carried Naggarothi laughter up to the orcs, infuriating them even more. The most unruly mobs headed down the slope, lumbering towards the elven line. Fearing to be left behind, other warbands hurried after until the whole greenskin army was on the move, pouring haphazardly down the slope.

With a flourish of his blade, Malriad rode back to his knights. The slap of ropes announced the firing of the bolt-throwers. Spears sped across the narrowing gap as dark blurs. Where they hit, orcs were flung back into the ranks following, spitted by the barbed shafts.

Hellebron caught Lirieth's eye and the two sisters nodded to each other. The battle was about to begin in earnest and their opportunity would soon be lost.

The two sisters broke from the front rank of the company and walked purposefully towards the onrushing greenskins. Lirieth brought out a phial of deep red liquid and took a mouthful before passing it to Hellebron. She swallowed the rest of the drug-laced blood and tossed aside the crystal bottle. The ireleaf and venomblossom worked immediately, sending a thrill of energy through her. Her pulse raced and her breath came in gasps as the narcotic potion coursed through her system.

The Daughters of Murder cast aside their shields and spears as an astounded whispering gripped the Naggarothi army. They shed their mail coats and tossed away their helmets. Buckling their weapon belts around their semi-naked bodies, the sisters drew their swords and daggers and turned to face their comrades.

'We need no altar to make sacrifice to Khaine,' Lirieth called out. 'This battlefield shall be our temple. Our war cries shall be our litany. To slay is to pray!'

'You call us the Daughters of Murder,' shouted Hellebron. 'Today we offer our blood and spirit to Khaine and dedicate ourselves to the Lord of Death alone. We shall be the Brides of Khaine.'

There were laughs and a few disparaging remarks from the incredulous Naggarothi. Hellebron glared at the army, bared her teeth and snarled.

'Let there be no doubt that we are Khaine's chosen,' said Lirieth. 'We will not shelter behind shields or clad ourselves in armour, for if Khaine desires our blood, He is free to take it! Our blades shall be our defence, as Khaine teaches us. Kill and not be killed, that is the truth of Khaine.'

A lone figure broke from the lines and hurried towards the pair. It was Lethruis, swathed in a bloodstained robe. His face was twisted with rage as he bore down on the two sisters.

'This is a disgrace!' he snarled. 'Cease this disrespect immediately.'

'It is you who are the disgrace!' shouted Hellebron.

Lirieth sheathed her weapons and seized Lethruis. The priest struggled but Lirieth's grip was like iron as she forced him to his knees in the mud. Hellebron sprang forwards, her knife stopping a hair's breadth from Lethruis's throat. The priest fell still, terrified eyes fixed on Hellebron. The other acolytes ran from the army, crying out in dismay.

'Come no closer!' warned Hellebron.

'Who here would risk the displeasure of Khaine?' Lirieth cried out. 'Who amongst the Naggarothi would turn their back on He who blessed Aenarion and has laid the gift of death into our hands?'

'What are you doing?' The demand came from Prince Malriad. The commander rode up to the group and swung down from his horse, one hand moving to the hilt of his sword. 'It is you who dare Khaine's wrath by laying hands on His priest.'

'He is no true adept of Khaine.' Hellebron poured all her scorn into every word. She raised her voice so that the closest warriors could hear. 'In every battle, we lay our lives upon the edge of Khaine's blade while Lethruis and his cronies look on.'

'It is time that changed,' said Lirieth. 'Khaine demands sacrifice and all we offer Him is the sour blood of goblins and the filth of beastmen.'

'This is madness,' said Lethruis. 'The enemy are almost upon us.'

'There is no victory without Khaine's blessing,' said Hellebron. 'Did not Aenarion lay himself before the judgement of Khaine when he took up the Widowmaker?'

'We offer you a choice, priest,' said Lirieth. 'Your promises to Khaine must be fulfilled. Did you not say that we all pray to give up ourselves in Khaine's name, upon the field of bloodshed? Take up a blade now and fight for the glory of Khaine and Nagarythe, or we shall offer up your blood to him this moment!'

'You are insane, both of you,' wailed Lethruis. 'I cannot fight!'

'No, you cannot,' said Malriad. 'You demand our obedience and offer up prayers to Khaine on our behalf. The Brides of Khaine are right; we have no need for you. The blood on our blades is offering enough.'

Hellebron looked up in surprise. Though the drugs fogged her brain, she sensed opportunity, greater than any she had hoped to create. She had thought that Lethruis would either fight – and die, for he had no skill at arms – or she would kill him herself. Here was an even better solution.

'You are our commander, the wielder of this army, the weapon of Khaine,' said Hellebron, thrusting her knife into her belt to place a hand on the prince's breastplate. She could hear the orcs pounding closer. Arrows cut the air from both armies and the shouts of the wounded joined the bellows of the greenskins.

'Quickly, now, our brave prince!' Lirieth snapped, guessing her sister's intent. 'Renew your pledges to Khaine with the blood of this coward and lead your army to victory.'

'Or believe his lies and bow your knee before a priest that can only slay the weak and defenceless,' added Hellebron.

Malriad drew his sword and stepped over the cowering Lethruis. Hellebron's breath caught in her throat as Lirieth let go of the priest and stepped away.

'For Khaine,' Hellebron hissed.

The prince plunged his sword into Lethruis's throat. The priest fell back, blood spraying from the wound. Hellebron and Lirieth sprang to the body, allowing the arterial fountain to soak their clothes, daubing the fresh blood on their faces and naked arms.

The heady thrill of the moment almost caused Hellebron to faint. The blood dripping down her skin, the scent of it in her nostrils and the taste on her lips was exquisite. She glanced at Malriad and saw concern, even regret, in his eyes. The deal with Khaine was not yet fully sealed.

Dipping her fingers into the wound upon the priest's neck, she turned to face the prince. With slow purpose, she drew the rune of Khaine upon his cheek, the blood glistening on Malriad's pale skin.

'Khaine blesses you, Prince, and hungers for the praise of your blade,' she said.

The other acolytes approached uncertainly. They eyed the two blood-drenched sisters and the army commander, and looked with a mixture of horror and contempt at Lethruis's lifeless body.

'Do not fear, brothers and sisters,' said Lirieth. 'You were victims of Lethruis's lies. Khaine has spoken through us and we will lead you on the true path of worship. Take him away.'

'Wait,' said Hellebron as the cortège lifted up the limp body. She worked quickly with her dagger, cutting open the dead elf's chest. With swift incisions, she freed the heart and pulled it out, lifting the organ over her head for all to see. 'There is no life without death; no heart beats without Khaine's blessing!'

As the dead priest was carried away, Malriad mounted his horse and rode back to his knights, bellowing a stream of orders to his subordinates. Hellebron looked at the orcs for the first time. They were perhaps a hundred paces away. Crook-shafted arrows fell into the grass nearby and another boulder sailed overhead. She looked back to her company and saw them as strangers. They looked so different from here, a faceless wall of metal and cloth.

She turned her eye upon Lirieth, knowing she shared her sister's appearance. She was a fearsome sight, her face a mask of blood around bright eyes, her hair slicked with dark red.

The two of them stood side-by-side, weapons bared, as the orcs closed in. Hellebron felt no fear, though a sea of foes descended upon her. The ireleaf pulsed through her body, fuelling her righteous rage; the venomblossom filled her limbs with strength and set her heart thundering. The taste of Lethruis's blood was fresh on her lips, sweeter than any wine of Cothique. She could hear Lirieth's sharp breaths and feel the warmth of her sister's body next to her.

'For Khaine, my sister,' said Lirieth. 'Let the red flood begin.'

'For Khaine,' Hellebron replied.

THE ORCS WERE a mass of metal and green flesh bearing down upon Hellebron. Bestial grunts filled her ears; glaring red eyes and snarling, fang-filled mouths filled her vision. Her sword and knife felt as light as air in her hands. She would not stand idle, to be swept away by the onrushing tide.

Hellebron sprang to meet the orcs head-on, Lirieth just a pace behind her. The blood caked on Hellebron's skin felt more solid than any armour and the power of Khaine buzzed along every nerve.

Her first blow slit open the throat of an orc, almost taking off its head. Hellebron laughed, exulting in the freedom. With spear and shield she had been one of many, disciplined and orderly. Now her spirit was let loose, unencumbered by drill or command.

The onrushing orcs swept around her. She dived and dodged between their brutish bodies, blades licking out to cut deep wounds upon faces and limbs. Even in the tight press of bodies, she was ever-moving, fending off crude blows while her weapons wove a bloody, mesmerising pattern.

It was utterly reckless, but Hellebron did not care. She laughed again as she slipped aside from a shield swiping towards her; shrieked with delight as she ducked beneath a swinging cleaver.

A crash of metal engulfed her. She turned, pulling the edge of her sword across the back of an orc's neck, and saw that the Naggarothi had countercharged. A line of spears drove into the orcs, punching through leather jerkins, piercing eye sockets, slashing and stabbing.

Cutting down another greenskin, Hellebron came face-to-face with Lirieth. Her sister's eyes were wide with excitement, just as they had been during Hellebron's first Khainite sacrifice. They shared a glance and wheeled away. Spinning on her heel, Hellebron drove her dagger into the open mouth of an orc, forcing the point up into its tiny brain. She whipped her hand back as its jaws instinctively snapped shut. She heard the ring of metal on metal and glanced over her shoulder to see Lirieth's sword, less than a hand's span from her back, an orcish blade spinning to the ground.

'It is not only Khaine who watches over me, sister,' said Hellebron, ducking beneath Lirieth's extended arm to drive her sword into the gut of an orc raising a club to strike down her sister.

Lirieth swept low, her blade cutting through the leg of the orc. Hellebron ripped her sword free from its stomach as it fell, swaying to her right to avoid the edge of a shield thrust towards her. She kicked the shield to one side and pounced, driving her knife into the side of the orc's neck.

The orcs fell back from the sisters and the spears, turning to run. Hellebron heard the call of a clarion signalling to hold the line, but it was drowned out by the rushing of blood, the beat of her heart.

'Let none escape!' she shrieked, turning on the Naggarothi. The warriors halted, torn between their desire to run down the orcs and the command ringing from the musician. 'Khaine demands their deaths!'

Lirieth and Hellebron leapt after the fleeing greenskins. Caught up by their display, the Naggarothi surged after them, ignoring the shouts of their captains. Like a blood-tipped spearhead, the company fell upon the routed greenskins, plunging deep, cutting the orcs down as they tried to flee.

Hellebron dashed after the enemy, hacking at their exposed backs, slicing through hamstrings and spines.

'Sister!'

Lirieth's cry halted Hellebron instantly. She slid to a stop amidst the mud and gore, suddenly aware that the ground was shaking. Turning to the right, Hellebron saw the orc boar-riders thundering down the hill towards her. The spearmen hurriedly re-formed their ranks, drawn out of formation by their hasty pursuit of the greenskins.

The orcish cavalry was almost upon Hellebron. She could smell the stench of the boars, feel the ground trembling, see the clods of dirt kicked up by the creatures' metal-shod trotters. The orcs hunched over their mounts, gripping thick ruffs of hair as reins, iron-tipped spears lowered for the charge. She could feel the angry excitement of the greenskins as they swept down upon their seemingly doomed prey.

A glance back showed Hellebron that she was too far from the safety of the swiftly assembling phalanx; to run now was to invite a spear in the back.

Hellebron picked out the largest rider, a dark-skinned beast almost twice as big as an elf. The orc wore plates of stiffened hide, dyed black and strengthened with spiked rivets; links of mail hung from its armour, no doubt looted from dead dwarfs. Its helm was a simple metal bowl, with leather flaps hanging to either side of the creature's howling face.

With a flick of her wrists, Hellebron brought up her sword and dagger. She met the orc's stare with her own fury, her lips curling back from blood-flecked teeth even as the orc opened its huge mouth to bellow at her.

Hellebron waited, snarling and hissing, as the orc rushed closer and closer. She could feel the steaming breath of the boar and its rider, smelled the stench of dung. The orc's battered speartip was coming straight towards her, aimed at her chest. Hellebron's eyes narrowed as she watched the spearhead cutting through the wet air, droplets of water splashing from the iron.

At the last moment, Hellebron brought up her knife, knocking the spear away by just enough. As it passed her right shoulder, she jumped forwards, planting her foot between the eyes of the boar. As the creature's momentum carried it forwards, Hellebron sprang into the air, her sword chopping down into the shoulder of the rider as she somersaulted.

Landing in the mud, she dived to her right to avoid the next boar, rolling to her feet in front of another. Hellebron caught the spearshaft of the rider under her arm and cut through the orc's wrist. Unbalanced, the orc toppled from the boar with a crash. A moment later, she drove the captured spear through its cheek, pinning the greenskin to the ground.

More orcs rode past, too slow-witted to react to Hellebron. She slammed her sword into the chest of one as it desperately tried to haul its boar into her. The shock of the impact almost threw her off her feet; only by an acrobatic twist did she not end up face-first in the mire.

And then the orcs were gone, thundering on into the spear company.

Hellebron spun round to see what had become of Lirieth. The boar-riders smashed into the front rank of the Naggarothi, hurling back the elves, stabbing and trampling everything in their path. Rocked but not broken, the surviving Naggarothi parted before the charge and then fell upon the flanks of the orcish mob, quickly surrounding them.

In the chaos of shields, spears and swords, Hellebron caught a glimpse of a pale figure dragging an orc from its mount, dagger punching repeatedly into the creature's chest; Lirieth was alive and still fighting with the fury of Khaine.

Hellebron's arms and legs moved heavily now, and her head began to thump. She gasped for air and felt a pain in her ribs. Looking down, she saw a spreading bruise through her slashed clothes. There was also a cut on her shoulder she had not felt, and her muscles trembled with fatigue.

She felt the same as she did after a sacrifice; the venomblossom was beginning to wear off. The ground underfoot was uneven, ripped up by the charging boars. Hellebron stumbled on a tussock of grass, her legs like lead. Scrunching her eyes against the pain, she slowly turned to see what was happening along the rest of the line.

To the north Prince Malriad and his knights were scattering hundreds of goblins, riding down the small greenskins, hacking with swords and axes. Beyond them Hellebron saw the green-scaled body of the wyvern, dark bolts protruding from its flesh, ragged holes torn in its limply flapping wings. Another salvo from the bolt-throwers thudded into the monster, hammering into its exposed belly. Of its rider there was no sign.

All around, the Naggarothi were advancing victoriously. Riders darted to and fro, carrying the orders of the commander as the remnants of the greenskin horde fled back to the west. Closer at hand, the boar-riders were falling to the spears of the elves.

The Naggarothi had not avoided death either. Wounded elves dragged themselves through the muck or were borne away on stretchers by their comrades. Weapons and shields lay scattered along the line next to the mail-clad bodies of the dead. A few banners flapped from broken poles, dropped into the mud. Orcish icons had also been discarded, their rusted iron faces and skull totems looking forlornly at the destruction.

Grunts and snorts from wounded orcs attracted Hellebron's attention. Some hobbled away clutching gaping wounds and nursing broken limbs. Others lay beneath the carcasses of their boars, bones crushed. A few continued to snarl viciously, staggering and crawling around with their blades and mauls, wounds ripped across their faces, missing arms or legs.

Thrusting her dagger into her belt, Hellebron pulled open a pouch and took a pinch of crushed purple petals. She chewed quickly, ignoring the bitter taste; venomblossom was much more palatable mixed with blood.

It took a moment for the narcotic to have its effect. As quickly as it had failed, her energy returned. The pain disappeared, leaving her feeling as fresh as if she had woken from a full night's sleep.

She saw the spearmen moving across the field, slaying the wounded enemy.

'Do not kill them!' Hellebron cried out, striding back to the Naggarothi. 'Take them alive. For the blessings He has given us this day, Khaine's hunger will be great tonight!'

LED BY HELLEBRON and Lirieth, the celebrations of the Naggarothi were raucous and lasted for several days. Espousing her philosophy that all could worship Khaine equally, Hellebron organised rituals that allowed the warriors and camp-followers to participate in the gory festivities. Nearly two hundred greenskins of varying size and condition had been taken prisoner and each night for three nights they were brought out to be offered up to the Lord of Murder.

Prince Malriad officiated over the greatest rite on the first night, carving apart the remains of Lethruis, denouncing the dead priest as a traitor to Khaine, Nagarythe and Prince Malekith. As Lethruis charred in the flames, Hellebron announced that a new age of the Naggarothi was dawning. With the prince by her side, she exhorted the army to be proud of their deeds, to remember the debt they owed to Khaine when they returned to their homes.

Lirieth opened up the stores of the cult, giving out venomblossom, dreamleaf and shadowdust to those that were most demonstrative in their praise of Khaine. Every company had their own pyre and their own sacrifice; some despatched the greenskins quickly, with solemn ceremony; others followed Hellebron's lead, inflicting horrendous wounds upon the resilient orcs before finally slashing out their organs and hurling them onto the fires; some even offered up their own blood, cutting themselves with their weapons to sprinkle their crimson offerings on the fires or drink each other's life fluid.

The smoke of the fires blotted out the sky. A great charnel pile grew downwind of the camp, where the cracked and burned bones of the greenskins were heaped upon the ashes of the pyres. Given release from their tiresome duties by Hellebron, the former acolytes of Lethruis were savage, screeching and screaming as more and more blood was spilt, urging on the meekest observers to come forwards and take up the sacrificial daggers in Khaine's name.

On the third and final night, as the last of the captives was thrown alive into the flames, the orc's howls of agony dying away to silence, Hellebron and Lirieth strode out before the crowd, clothed only in dried blood, their hair twisted and matted with the gore of their victims.

'We are free!' Lirieth declared. 'Khaine has set us free!'

'The spirit of Khaine fills each of us tonight,' said Hellebron. 'Tomorrow, the fires will die, and we shall wash the blood from our blades. Yet Khaine will hunger still. He has gorged on the bounty of our might as we have known victory by the strength of His blessings. By the blood of elves was Ulthuan saved; by the blood of great Aenarion himself were we delivered from disaster. By our bloody work have we wrested these lands from savagery, and for the moment we might be fooled into thinking that peace will prevail.

'This world of ours will never know peace, for Khaine will never be sated. It may be a year, ten years or a hundred, until we are called upon to shed our blood again. Yet in those quiet hours, in those days of false repose, never forget that there still live the things of darkness that seek to destroy our lives, steal our spirits and enslave us to their accursed whims.

'We can never afford to let Khaine slumber. Without His gift, without His bloody will to guide us, we will grow lax, we will grow weak. Our enemies will return and we shall be destroyed. Keep Khaine in your hearts, hold Him there for the strength He gives us.'

'For Khaine!' Lirieth led the cry, holding up her bloodied knife.

'For Khaine!' the army cried in return, brandishing their weapons.

Hellebron looked out at the sea of faces, the flicker of the flames causing their eyes to dance with cruel glee. She saw the bloodstained swords and daggers and spears, and finally felt the adoration she so long had feared might never come. As the Naggarothi called out Khaine's name again, Hellebron basked in the moment, sweeter still than anything she might have imagined.

This was glory. This was power.

Tomorrow they would march to Athel Toralien. Not this time the ignominy, the quiet reception. This time her name would spread, her deeds on the lips of every elf of the city.

Khaine had shown her the way, and she would repay him.

—◄ FIVE ►—

The Cult Grows

LETTERS AND MESSENGERS were sent ahead of the army to announce the home-coming of Malekith's faithful warriors. Hellebron and Lirieth wrote a letter to their father, insisting that he organise suitable celebrations for their triumphant return. Though they did not tell him of what had happened, they proudly informed Alandrian that their names were being lauded throughout the army, and that he should demonstrate his pride by granting the army the grandest honours and celebrations he could devise.

Hellebron added her own private message, showering her father with praise and thanks for his support. She told him that things would change in Athel Toralien when she returned, and that soon there would be no elf who doubted his rule of the city. He would emerge from Malekith's shadow, a great prince in his own right, and his name would be forever marked upon the chronicles of the Naggarothi.

When the heralds returned, they brought word from Alandrian. Hellebron read with glee that there was much excitement in the city, stirred up by Prince Malriad and the other nobles. Alandrian promised that there would be a gala reception for his daughters and that no expense would be spared in celebrating the success of the army.

So it was with considerable anticipation that Hellebron woke on the morning the army was due to enter the city. While Lirieth still slumbered, Hellebron stepped from their tent. The air was chill, the sun not yet above the horizon. Torches and braziers illuminated the long rows of pavilions, the stillness only broken by the clinking of armour as the guard patrols walked their rounds.

To the north, less than half a day's march away, Athel Toralien waited for her. Hellebron walked to the edge of the camp, her cloak wrapped about her, bare feet stepping lightly on the dwarf-built road along which the army was camped.

A stream glittered ahead, lit by silver lanterns lining a wide bridge. Hellebron walked to the edge of the water and looked down into the slow-running rill. She could see little of her face, her reflection distorted. Her hair fell in long braids, her face narrow, pale, nicked here and there by slender scars from tiny wounds she had inflicted upon herself in the deepest throes of the Khainite rituals.

She threw off her cloak and stripped away her short dress. Sliding into the water, she gave a girlish giggle as the cold enveloped her, prickling her skin. Closing her eyes, she ducked beneath the water, immersing herself completely, the mud of the bottom pushing up between her toes as the gentle current caressed her flesh.

She turned onto her back, still submerged, and looked up through the water. The light of the lamps swayed and flowed above her, so that it felt like she was swimming in starlight. She held up her hands, reaching towards the shimmering light; hands that had shed so much blood. Her slender fingers had delved into the innards of sacrifices beyond counting, each now a blur in her mind, her memory fogged by repetition and intoxication.

Hellebron drifted, rising to the surface. With gentle motions, she steered herself back towards the bank, enjoying the utter calm. She knew that the moment she set foot back in Athel Toralien, her true grasp for power would begin. There would be many who would see her as a threat, and just as she had sacrificed Lethruis for her goals, there would, in time, be those amongst her followers who would see Hellebron as the opposition.

Many times over the years of subservience and frustration, Hellebron had questioned her ambition and the hardships it would entail. Such doubts had always been short-lived, dismissed with the start of the next day.

Floating serenely in the river, she asked herself a subtly different question: was this what she really wanted? There would be more pain to come, more sacrifice, of that she was sure. If her commitment to this life was not total, she would falter.

There was Lirieth to consider as well. She was part of the growing legend, and Hellebron knew that her sister would do anything for her. Where Hellebron led, she would follow, out of love and duty. Lirieth had embraced Hellebron's hunger, taken it as her own, given up her own life so that Hellebron would thrive. Hellebron could not abandon her sister now; could not ask her to step aside to give Hellebron centre stage. Was it her right to make this decision for her sister, to embroil Lirieth in this destiny without offering her a chance to forge a different path?

The sun was creeping into the sky, lighting the broken cloud with red and purple. Sounds came from the stirring camp as more of the army awoke.

Soon Hellebron would be the centre of the storm, caught in the work of the preparations for the march, the turmoil of the army's homecoming, and whatever lay beyond. This was her last chance, her very last chance, to think clearly about what she wanted.

Immediately Hellebron's thoughts went back to Morathi, the sneer on the queen's face, the scorn in her voice. The calm seeped away through the water, leaving Hellebron boiling with indignation; as enraged and offended as when she had stepped out of Morathi's chambers.

She did not want to please Morathi, nor did she want to impress Morathi. Hellebron realised that it was not recognition or approval that she sought; this life she had chosen went far beyond that. Hellebron wanted Morathi to know the hurt she had heaped – probably knowingly – upon her. Morathi would rue her arrogance and be forced to concede Hellebron's greatness.

All other thoughts vanished with this conclusion. Nothing else mattered. Khaine would be her key to power, her means to rise up and stare Morathi in the eye without shame. Anything less would be an abject failure; an admittance that Morathi had been right to dismiss her so contemptuously. Never again would Hellebron feel so small, so insignificant.

Hellebron exploded out of the water, full of vigour. Throwing on her clothes, she stalked back to the camp, mind brimming over with plans. Doubt was for the weak. She would rise to the heights of power or she would die trying; anything less would be a betrayal of herself, her sister and Khaine.

DESPITE THE ASSERTIONS in Prince Alandrian's letter, the people of Athel Toralien were less than enthusiastic about the return of Malriad and his army. The garrison of the city was turned out to give full honours, lining the walls and gate towers with banners and clarions to mark the return of the Naggarothi, but there were no elves lining the road to the city, no festivals of dancing and song to welcome the army home.

Flanking Malriad, Hellebron and Lirieth passed through the shadow of the main gatehouse into the square beyond. There were several hundred elves dressed in their fineries waiting, holding flowers and gifts; most of them the families of the returning warriors. Children dashed from the crowd to greet their fathers, while wives, mothers and fathers looked on with stern pride.

When all had marched into the city, formed up in their companies, Alandrian appeared. A wooden stage had been built at the eastern edge of the square, hung with bright garlands and silver chains. The early afternoon sun blazing down, the ruler of Athel Toralien strode to the middle of the podium, wearing his finest armour, a cloak of pure black trailing from his shoulders.

It was with a strange shock that Hellebron remembered her father had not always been a civic ruler; he had fought to save this city from the orcs and had marched with Malekith to scour the lands of evil. Alandrian had been present the first time the Naggarothi had met the dwarfs. She had heard the stories growing up, but it had never seemed important to her. Now he was there, wearing the silver-and-gold mail he had worn during those days of adventure and glory. For a moment she forgot her annoyance at the lacklustre reception and revelled in a moment's pride for her father.

'By the grace of the gods, our noble warriors are returned to us,' declared Alandrian. 'You are the embodiment of what is great about the Naggarothi and are the embodiment of Nagarythe's finest traditions. The day we forget the travails that our brave soldiers face, the day we discard our duty to the brave and the fierce, is the day we give up the right to call ourselves Naggarothi.'

A few other local dignitaries trooped onto the stage and declaimed a few vague welcomes and platitudes. Though the rigid ranks of warriors listened attentively, Hellebron could sense their disappointment, and knew that it reflected badly upon her. To keep her followers intrigued on the long march home, Hellebron had regaled them with promises of the fanfares and celebrations that awaited them. Now her promises had proved to be empty and Hellebron fumed; partly at herself for her naiveté, mostly at her father for his empty assurances.

Eventually the dreary welcoming ceremony concluded. As soon as the trumpets sounded the dismissal, the companies broke ranks and flooded into the rest of the city, gathering up such family and friends as awaited them.

Hellebron took a step towards the stage but stopped, feeling a hand on her arm. Lirieth pulled Hellebron close, darting glances towards the nobles assembled on the stage.

'Do nothing rash, my sister,' warned Lirieth.

'It is an insult,' said Hellebron. 'Of all people, father should have known how much this meant to us. It is simply unacceptable.'

Hellebron moved to walk away but Lirieth's grip tightened, holding her back.

'We are back in civilised lands, sister,' she said. 'Tread carefully. All is not lost. Do not let your anger compound this sorry situation.'

Lirieth delved a hand into a small pouch at her belt and pulled out a few grey leaves.

'Dreamwood,' she said. 'Chew a few, it will help you to calm down.'

Hellebron eyed the sedating herb for a moment, uncertain. She liked her anger, it gave her purpose, gave her strength. Seeing the imploring look in her sister's eyes, knowing despite her frustration that Lirieth was right, Hellebron snatched up the leaves and put them into her mouth. She crushed them relentlessly between her teeth, until their soothing effect spread through her body. Her limbs lightened and her breathing slowed. The afternoon light grew dimmer, the white of Athel Toralien's buildings softer.

The mellowing effect took the edge off Hellebron's anger, but she could not dismiss her annoyance entirely. Linking arms with Lirieth, she forced herself to pace serenely to where her father was standing at the bottom of the steps leading up to the stage. Already retainers were taking down the garlands and banners and carpenters were dismantling the podium.

Alandrian's first look was full of apology; aided by the dreamwood, Hellebron felt her ire ebb away a little further. She took her father's offered hand, kissed the palm and then stepped up to give him a fulsome embrace. Lirieth did the same.

'Circumstance has thwarted us,' said Alandrian, reaching his arms across the shoulders of his daughters, pulling them close. 'The harvest is coming in and a trade convoy to Galthyr is setting off tomorrow. I am afraid that the purses of the people have more influence than I do at such times.'

Alandrian steered them towards the road leading to the north of the city, where the family palace sat on the highest hill above the harbour. Hellebron could see the red-tiled roof of the central tower above the manses and villas of the noble quarter.

'All is not in vain, though,' the prince continued, his tone lighter. 'Tonight you will be hostesses of the most glittering gala Athel Toralien has seen in many years. All the great and the rich will be coming, many of them old friends of yours.'

Hellebron bit back a retort; this was not some birthday to be celebrated with wine and song, but a decisive moment in the history of the city. The heralds should be crying the news from every street corner, the poets singing verses of the glories to come.

She felt Lirieth's hand clasp hers behind Alandrian's back and was reassured by the touch. Twenty years they had worked towards that moment; they could afford to wait a little longer.

'That sounds wonderful, father,' said Hellebron. 'I am sure we will make a lasting impression.'

THE FESTIVITIES TOOK place in the warm autumnal evening, spread throughout the gardens and courtyards surrounding the villa and towers of Prince Alandrian. Several dozen of the most influential citizens of Athel Toralien were there, in all their finery and jewels. Red-robed servants moved through the mingling elves with platters of exquisitely prepared food from across Elthin Arvan, and wine from the vineyards around the city. Late-flowering plants wreathed the arches and gateways linking the patios, terraces and lawns, filling the air with a heady melange of scents.

The prince wore a short-sleeved, black robe woven from local wool, and a golden necklace of dwarf design, on which hung a ruby mined from the mountains to the south. The food was served upon lacquered platters of wood from the surrounding forests, the wine drunk from porcelain goblets fashioned in the crafts quarter of the city. Not a grain, grape or blossom had come from Ulthuan.

It was a finely balanced display by Alandrian; not only a display of his personal wealth and influence, but a reminder of the strength of the colonies, and Athel Toralien in particular. Its message was one of shared fate and it was not lost on the attending dignitaries. The gossip was of the colonies, Ulthuan barely mentioned except in passing remark. Many of the elves had never been to their home isle; first- and second-generation colonists who thought themselves equally Naggarothi and Toralii.

Hellebron entered the social fray with Lirieth by her side. The sisters were identically clad, wearing long dresses of crimson silk, cut to expose arms, legs and chests, bordering on the improper. Their hair was outlandishly styled, dyed to match their clothes, outrageously braided and spiked, held in place with skull-headed pins. Their lips were coloured deep red, their eyes shadowed with black, their pale flesh whitened further to create a mask-like appearance. Each wore a rune of Khaine fashioned in a silver pendant, and heavy armbands inscribed with dedications to the Lord of Murder.

As if this were not cause enough for comment, Hellebron and Lirieth were armed. While a few of the princes present wore sheathed swords, the twin curved daggers in the belts of the sisters were highly unorthodox.

The chatter died away as the two of them strolled arm-in-arm down the steps into the courtyard outside their chambers. Stillness reigned for a moment, the quiet broken only by the wind rustling the leaves of the ivy on the walls and scattered, astonished gasps. Hellebron kept her expression placid even as her heart leapt with the thrill of so much attention. Not even Morathi would have drawn away the eyes of the onlookers.

In a carefully orchestrated display, Liannin emerged from the knot of servants and approached the sisters with a tray carrying two crystal goblets filled with what looked to be a dark red wine. Hellebron took one and handed it to Lirieth before raising the other to her lips.

The sisters drank in unison, staining their lips darker still. They emptied the goblets and placed them back on the tray, the remains of their contents sticking thickly to the crystal. Hellebron delicately wiped a droplet from the corner of her mouth and smiled at the staring guests.

All were staring with horror and distaste as they realised that the goblets contained not wine, but blood. Hellebron noted with particular pleasure the consternation on the faces of many of the city's high priests and priestesses. No doubt rumour of the sisters' exploits had spread through the city as the soldiers of the army had returned to their homes. The leaders of Athel Toralien's many sects were gathered together, whispering fiercely to one another.

It was Alairiath, high priestess of Anath Raema that stepped forward as spokesperson. Her hair was a carefully managed mane of wild blonde, woven through with the small bones of animals. She wore many necklaces of fangs and claws from a variety of beasts, hung upon threads of sinew. Her robe was stitched together from dozens of pelts, her cloak a single shaggy mass of bear fur. She carried a small ornamental spear, and the golden buckle of her broad belt was moulded in the likeness of a snarling wolf in profile.

The priestess's eyes flitted around the crowd, numbers growing as more guests were drawn in from the other gardens. She glanced back once at her peers, seeking encouragement, and stopped a few steps from the sisters.

'Where is Lethruis, the anointed of Khaine?' Alairiath tried to speak boldly, but Hellebron detected a tremor of apprehension and noticed that the priestess dedicated to the Merciless Huntress refused to meet her gaze.

'We killed the traitor,' said Lirieth. A shocked ripple spread through the crowd.

'He failed Khaine, and for that he was punished,' said Hellebron.

'His heart was cut out and his body consigned to the ashes of infamy,' Lirieth continued with the lilt of a laugh in her voice.

Alairiath opened her mouth twice without saying anything.

'We are the Brides of Khaine,' said Hellebron. 'The Prince of Slaughter speaks through us, and has made His displeasure known. Khaine will no longer be the outcast, shunned by those who owe their lives to His continued indulgences.'

'You murdered Lethruis? This is unacceptable.' This came from Melthis, leader of the sect dedicated to Nethu, the warden of the city's mausoleums and tombs. He wrung his layers of white robes and looked at Hellebron and Lirieth with pleading eyes. 'You should not have destroyed his body!'

Hellebron grinned, showing the flecks of blood staining her bright teeth.

'Lethruis lived by the power of Khaine, why should he not die by the same?' she said. 'He was Khaine's own, spirit and body, and to Khaine we sent both.'

'We do not come here with threats,' said Lirieth, addressing all of the gathered elves. 'We seek only parity, and the freedom to practise our worship with the same understanding that the rest of you enjoy. Long have we treated Khaine poorly, the patron of Aenarion, founder of Nagarythe, greatest of all elves.'

'No longer,' continued Hellebron. 'Tomorrow we shall divine a suitable aspect for a new shrine to the Bloody-Handed One and in time all will be able to pay their respects to the god who delivered us from disaster.'

'This will not be tolerated,' snapped Khelthion, high priest of Ereth Khial.

As leader of the Cult of the Dead, paying homage to the bleak goddess that held the power of life and death, Khelthion was the unspoken leader of all the cults. Many believed he could call upon his patron to unleash the Rephallim, bodiless spirits that could bring nightmares and even tear an elf's life from a sleeping victim. The rich paid the sect handsomely to pass and receive messages from the deceased, and to maintain the expensive sarcophagi in the Halls of the Eternal Sleep where their ancestors lay.

'Who are you to speak of intolerance?' All eyes turned to Prince

Alandrian, who stepped up beside Lirieth, a scowl creasing his face. 'Do not forget the lean times that existed under the rule of Prince Malekith. Was it not I that welcomed you to our city, so that our people might be at peace with their gods, that Athel Toralien would know prosperity, and so that you could spread your messages of worship and placation? I have been a patron to you all, and I will treat the dedication of my daughters with no less respect. Or would you have it that I withdraw my support, cast you all from the city to peddle your prayers and ceremonies in the farms and wild lands?'

'It is not wise to offend the cytharai,' said Khelthion, striding up to Alandrian. 'Their ways are subtle and their displeasure brings doom to mortals.'

As quick as a flash, Hellebron was next to the high priest, her curved dagger under his chin, the point pricking at his throat.

'Khaine is not subtle in His displeasure,' she purred. 'Yet He is the most easily vexed of the gods and is not slow to anger. If you laud Ereth Khial so highly, perhaps you would not be averse to meeting Her soon?'

'You wouldn't dare.' Khelthion's assurance was absolute as he stared sideways into Hellebron's eyes. His arrogance reminded her of Morathi.

'Do not test me,' said Hellebron.

'It is one thing to murder Lethruis amidst an army of warriors, it is another to kill a priest in cold blood in full view of so many witnesses, in the heart of our city.'

'It is,' said Hellebron, drawing the dagger across the high priest's throat. 'This is sweeter still.'

Blood spilled onto the white paving, splashing Hellebron's bare feet. She pushed Khelthion towards Lirieth, who deftly caught the dying elf. Lirieth glanced at her sister, received a nod of approval and plunged one of her daggers into Khelthion's chest. Alandrian took a step towards his daughters but was halted by a quick glance from Hellebron. He turned his attention to the other elves and saw what she saw: utter horror and deep fear. Yet here and there amongst the crowd of faces were those that looked on with appreciation, perhaps glad to be rid of Khelthion's domination.

'Do something!' Hellebron did not see who made the demand, but there were scattered whispers of assent.

'Do what?' said Alandrian. 'You think that no elf has ever died by the hand of another? Khaine will take what is His. This is a religious matter; it is no concern of mine.'

Ashen-faced servants arrived to take away Khelthion's corpse but Hellebron stopped them.

'He has been taken by Khaine,' she said. 'Not for poor Khelthion the unending twilight of Mirai. It is his privilege to join King Aenarion and the other sons of Ulthuan who have laid down their lives in blood.'

Lirieth took up the line.

'The fires will send his spirit into the next world,' she said. 'This very night, you are all invited to witness this miracle of transformation. At midnight the flames will be lit and you shall see the splendour and majesty of Khaine's work.'

HELLEBRON WAS TAKEN aback by the number of elves that attended the sacrificial cremation of Khelthion's remains. Many were elves involved with the other sects, who glared with disapproval behind their leaders. There were several hundred soldiers and a handful of captains who had fought alongside Hellebron and Lirieth; notably Prince Malriad came along with many of his household.

And there were the ordinary people of Athel Toralien, morbidly intrigued by this sudden turn of events. While the ruling princes, chief merchants, fleet-owners and sect leaders were focussed upon the future of Athel Toralien, the rest of its citizens still listened intently for news from Ulthuan; such news left even the most insular elf aware that Nagarythe was in the throes of a religious renaissance under the rule of Morathi. There had been a small but noticeable influx of new colonists in the past few years, with whispered tales of conflicts with cults and persecution by zealots of all persuasions.

It was with a mixed air of expectancy and apprehension that Athel Toralien witnessed the renewed energy of Khaine's followers. Hellebron kept the ritual brief, speaking of the blood of birth, and of the rebirth of Khaine's power. Though ignorant of developments in Ulthuan, she spoke of a time when the elves would again need to look to their blades; the Chaos Daemons were caged but not defeated and who could say what threat the barbaric humans might present in the future?

Khelthion's body was cut apart with all the gory spectacle Hellebron could muster. She saw in the crowd those elves who were feeling for the first time the same sense of fascination she had experienced. This was not a dirge-laden ceremony of mourning presided over by the adepts of Ereth Khial; it was a vital, invigorating celebration of life and death, of the thin bladestroke that separates the two; a testament to the frailty of the mortal form.

Though many of the audience departed as the ceremony reached its climax, and no few that remained were aghast at what they saw, Hellebron and Lirieth kept the crowd rapt with theatrics and masterful oration. Throughout was the promise that Khaine would give the elves the strength to protect themselves; and the threat that Khaine would also find those who failed to give Him due homage.

The power of the crowd was a phenomenon that had always amazed Hellebron. As the chants to Khaine echoed along the streets from the mouths of soldiers and mariners, captains and traders, princes and scholars, Hellebron marvelled at the sway that popularity and vogue had upon her fellow elves. In the thick of battle, it had been the weight of the many that prevailed, and this was no less true of the ongoing tussles for power that existed in Naggarothi society.

When the flames were dying and the last of the crowd had returned to their homes – sated or terrified, it did not matter – Hellebron remained with Lirieth and her father.

'It is a dangerous thing that you seek to wield,' said Alandrian, as Lirieth and Hellebron washed themselves of the stains of sacrifice. 'You are my daughters and I will do all in my power to further your cause. Be warned, there are some things I cannot protect you against: jealousy, fear and ambition will create many enemies for you.'

'Rest easy, father,' said Hellebron. 'Tonight is but a beginning, a first step. The people will learn that Khaine's way is the straight path, and its rewards come swiftly.'

'I saw it tonight, in the eyes of many that watched,' said Lirieth. 'There were those who did not see the body of Khelthion, but instead the dismembered corpse of another; a rival, a lover who spurned them, a spoiled sibling. We will have enemies, but Khaine will provide the cure for many ills that others seek to expunge from their lives and that will bring even more allies.'

Alandrian said nothing for a moment. He looked at his two daughters and down at the puddle of blood-tinged water spreading across the cobbles.

'You cannot let loose this beast,' he said quietly. 'You must keep it on a tight rein, or it will turn and devour all of us.'

'Our hands, and yours, will be firm upon the leash, father,' said Hellebron. 'The other sects are weak, their leaders apathetic. They have practised their rites and yet the people of Athel Toralien still have their share of woes and disappointments. The time is nigh for a new wind to sweep the city clean, and the people will see the truth for what it is.'

HELLEBRON'S CONFIDENT PREDICTIONS were borne out over the following days. Alone or in small groups, the elves of the city visited the sisters at their new shrine. They left gifts of gems and gold and silver, and promises of support for Khaine and his burgeoning cult. Some came to Hellebron and Lirieth with their complaints, accusing rivals in business, society and love of being enemies of Khaine and traitors to Nagarythe.

Within a few days, Hellebron already had a sound idea of who were her greatest opponents. Chief amongst them were the other sect leaders and their most dedicated acolytes. There was gossip of a backlash, of the other cults combining forces to show the upstarts their real place in society. Hellebron scorned such threats and assured her new followers that Khaine gave his blessings to those who took power for themselves. She reminded her growing number of disciples that it had been Aenarion who had chosen to take up the Sword of Khaine and it was through action, not words, that the Naggarothi would grow to even greater heights of power and wealth. Hers were the words of the future, not the past.

Of greater concern was the news of one particular critic, who had been an outspoken opponent to the rise of all the sects and who had now turned her ire on Hellebron and Lirieth.

Her name was Mirieth, and she was their mother.

She had been estranged from the family for many years, and the sisters' decision to leave Athel Toralien had been the final divide between them and their mother. For more than twenty years they had not spoken, to each other or about each other. Mirieth was now speaking against the cult of Khaine and sending letters to all the nobles of Athel Toralien. There was even rumour that Mirieth would despatch messages to the other cities of Elthin Arvan, to enlist the aid of princes from other kingdoms.

'Let her write her indignant letters,' Hellebron said in reply to Lirieth's concerns. Always the younger of the two had reserved some fondness for their mother, though Mirieth had been dead in Hellebron's heart for many years. 'Her pleas will fall on deaf ears.'

'But her family is powerful in Nagarythe, sister,' said Lirieth. 'Her brother is one of Morathi's favourites and her uncle a powerful prince. Father's split from mother has made him unpopular in many circles and this may be the excuse his enemies need to crush him. This is what he meant when he warned against the course we are taking.'

Hellebron stared at her sister with annoyance.

'Do you have doubts?' she said. 'Do you wish to go back on our oaths to Khaine, on the promises we made to ourselves?'

'Not at all, sister,' said Lirieth. 'The hand of mother's family may be strong, but its reach cannot cross the ocean so easily. I am warning against overreaction. Athel Toralien is unpopular yet desirable, and it would take but a small incitement for many powerful folk of Nagarythe to take a keener interest in our affairs.'

'What is it that you think I would do?' said Hellebron. 'I am not so ungrateful that I would murder the elf that gave me life! Let Mirieth rant and write for all she is worth; for that matter, let them all rave against us; their opposition only strengthens our cause.'

'The will of the people will be known, and in the end they will force us to act,' said Lirieth. 'When the mob is baying for the blood of our rivals, that is the moment we will strike.'

Hellebron considered this. There was a certain appeal to letting her opponents create their own downfall, but for this to be guaranteed they would need a nudge in the right direction.

'We cannot allow the others to be too meek,' she said. 'If we overstep the mark, it will be too easy for them to accuse us of being power-hungry and selfish; yet we must weigh against that the peril of being too meek ourselves. We enjoy the seduction of novelty for the moment, and we must make some steps towards securing our position while the favour is with us.'

'You have something in mind? Something that is not too obvious?'

'I do, sister. The arrogance of Khelthion was opportune, but the other cult leaders will not repeat his mistake. And it is the appeal of the sacrifice that will draw followers to our cause. We must find another candidate for Khaine's cruel intentions, one who is an important supporter of our rivals but not directly part of a sect.'

The two of them spent some time looking over Hellebron's copious notes, examining the names provided to them by those elves hoping to settle a personal score. Many were petty matters, of interest only to a few; many others were too important for Hellebron to act against, knowing that their allies would no doubt reciprocate.

Sifting through the spite of the Naggarothi took some time. Liannin entered with two gleaming lanterns and placed them upon the hooks on the chamber walls. Hellebron barely noticed her, but looked up as the maid hesitated by the door. Liannin bowed her head in deference, but there was clearly something on her mind.

'Speak,' said Hellebron. She stood up and raised Liannin's chin with a finger. 'Do I not consider you almost a second sister? What troubles you?'

'I am afraid,' said Liannin.

'Has someone said something to you?' asked Lirieth, setting aside the scroll she was reading. 'Has someone made a threat?'

'Not against me, and not in any direct way,' said Liannin. She grasped Hellebron's arm and looked at the two sisters with concern. 'It is you that I fear for. There is rumour that Anellion, Khelthion's successor, will denounce you to the city and is bringing a powerful person from Ulthuan to do the same. A friend of my cousin works at the docks and says that Anellion despatched a messenger aboard a fast ship yesterday.'

'To whom was this message sent?' Hellebron guided Liannin to a chair and eased her into it. 'Did you get a name?'

'Khorlandir,' said Liannin.

The name was familiar but Hellebron could not place it. She looked at Lirieth to see if her sister remembered. Her sister's brow was furrowed with consternation.

'I know that name,' said Lirieth. 'I heard it from the lips of Lethruis.'

The mention of Lethruis sparked recollection in Hellebron's mind.

'Was it not from Khorlandir that Lethruis learnt the secrets of Khaine?'

'It is so, sister. He must be powerful indeed, perhaps even a high priest in Anlec. It would not go well for us if he were to come to Athel Toralien.'

'No it would not,' said Hellebron. She noticed Liannin listening closely to the conversation. She stood behind the maid and laid a hand on her shoulder. 'Do not be afraid. You have done well to warn us of this. It would be a great use to us if you could find out anything more that Anellion intends. Can you do this for us?'

Liannin looked up with grateful eyes.

'Of course, I will keep my eyes open and my ears ready,' said the maid. Again there was a moment of hesitation and Hellebron waved Liannin to continue. 'If it is not too much to ask, I would like to attend one of your ceremonies. I was not able to see you the other night.'

Hellebron and Lirieth smiled at each other.

'That would not be a problem at all, dear Liannin,' said Lirieth. 'It was remiss of us not to invite you.'

'Not only will we ensure that you can attend our next dedication, we will make you our guest of honour,' added Hellebron.

With a grateful smile Liannin stood up, squeezed Hellebron's hand affectionately and hurried towards the door.

'Thank you,' said Liannin. 'If it would be all right, I would like to bring some other friends; servants of other great families.'

'Bring whomsoever you would like,' said Hellebron. 'The more, the merrier!'

LIANNIN PROVED A useful spy and the following day returned with news that the priest, Anellion, had an illicit lover, a silversmith who lived in the crafts quarter near the waterfront. Anellion often spent much time with her, ostensibly to procure jewellery and other accoutrements for his followers, but the two were more than trader and customer.

This information coincided nicely with a planned ritual the following night. After the display with Khelthion's body, the sisters' new adherents would be expecting something equally spectacular.

AS THE MOONS slipped out of sight, the pair ghosted through the empty streets of Athel Toralien. They were clad in robes of dark grey, swathed in black cloaks, shadows in the darkness. They found the silversmith's store without incident and entered unseen. Slipper-covered feet padding soundlessly on the polished wooden floor, they made their way through the shop and upstairs to the living quarters.

Through the archway they spied a couple, ageing in years, asleep upon a great bed. They carried on, checking the other rooms, until they found the dark-haired lover of Anellion lying curled up beneath a woollen blanket, her pretty face bathed in the golden light of a lamp hanging from a roof beam outside.

Lirieth pulled something from her waistband; a long pin with a short wooden handle. She pushed its tip through the wax seal of a small phial and pulled it free, a single droplet of liquid hanging from its end. Leaning over the silversmith, Lirieth pricked the side of the maiden's neck, drawing blood.

The girl awoke with a start, hand reaching to the pain in her neck. Hellebron clamped a gloved hand over the silversmith's mouth as she was about to scream. The girl struggled for a moment and then suddenly fell limp as the dreamvine toxin spread to her brain. The silversmith stared at the ceiling with unseeing eyes, her mouth slack.

'Listen to us very carefully,' said Hellebron, stooping to whisper into the maiden's ear. 'When you awake in the morning, you will remember nothing of this save the instructions we are about to give you. You will follow these commands without hesitation. Do you understand?'

The girl nodded vaguely.

'Good,' said Lirieth. She drew a dagger from her belt and curled the silversmith's limp fingers around its handle. 'Listen well.'

THE LANTERNS HAD all been extinguished, leaving the flames of the pyre as the only light in the plaza. The walls of the houses and businesses around the square danced with shadows and the gathered elves were bathed in an orange glow.

Hellebron was pleased to see an even larger crowd, almost a thousand elves. As before there was a mixed mood, and she could clearly see groups from the other cults clustered about their priests, ready to make trouble; as word of the Khainites had spread through the city, the other sects had rallied their followers too. There was a mood of confrontation but Hellebron knew that the event of the night would precipitate something far stronger than some glares and heckling.

Lirieth began with the usual preamble, praising the strength of Khaine, conjuring visions of the great war with the daemons, and the elves' deliverance by Aenarion and the Sword of Khaine.

Hellebron took up the tale, renewing her warnings that the elves would never know peace and reminding the crowd that the Naggarothi were ever at the forefront of battle and needed Khaine's blessing more than any other kingdom.

'Let the spirit of Khaine fill our hearts and make our blood rush!' said Lirieth. 'Who else feels the spirit of Khaine?'

Hellebron and Lirieth stalked back and forth in front of the audience, naked blades in their hands, eyes scanning the crowds.

'Who would open themselves up to the Prince of Blood?' cried Hellebron.

There were some shouts from the elves; those who had worshipped under Lethruis now followers of the Brides of Khaine.

'Praise Khaine!' a voice shouted from the mass. The call was taken up and repeated, growing in ferocity.

A piercing shriek split the chanting and an elf maiden broke from the throng, a curved dagger in her hand. It was the silversmith, her eyes wild, her clothes ragged as she tore at her dress.

'I feel the spirit of Khaine!' she screeched. She fell to her knees in front of Hellebron, head back, an agonised cry coming from deep within. It was a primal noise, of fury and pain. 'It burns! My spirit is on fire!'

Another figure emerged, shouldering through the press of elves. It was Anellion, in all his priestly accoutrements.

'Maineth, what madness is this?' he said, grabbing hold of the silversmith's arm to drag her to her feet.

Maineth ripped herself from his grip and staggered towards the pyre. Her whole body trembled, the dagger wavering in her hand. She looked at Anellion with glazed eyes before turning that mad stare upon the rest of the elves. Maineth seemed to be struggling with something, the knife weaving a random pattern in front of her.

Hellebron and Lirieth watched intently, silently offering up their prayers to Khaine that the dreamvine would work.

'I cannot do it!' screamed Maineth. Hellebron took a step to intervene, but Maineth stumbled away from her outstretched hand. 'I cannot give you the one I love, take me instead!'

Maineth plunged the dagger into her exposed chest. Blood spilled onto the cobbles as she fell backwards, crimson frothing at her lips. The crowd exploded into uproar. The rival priests and their followers hurled accusations while Hellebron's faithful cried out to Khaine. The undecided amongst the crowd screamed in horror, or broke down weeping.

Anellion ran to Maineth and knelt down, lifting her head to his lap. He pulled the dagger free and flung it away, blood coating his hands and arms, staining the gold-and-white thread of his robe. He ran his fingers through her hair, staining her locks with crimson, smearing more blood on her face.

The high priest looked up at Hellebron with a hate-filled gaze. Gently lowering Maineth to the ground, Anellion stood up, shaking with rage.

'Khaine takes His own,' said Lirieth, stepping up beside her sister, knife held ready.

Hellebron was still shocked by the silversmith's actions; she had been instructed to attack Anellion, but this was even better. Gathering her wits, she faced off against Anellion.

'That anger you feel, that rage that courses through you, that is Khaine's gift,' said Hellebron. 'You cannot blame the priests for the actions of their god. Khaine chose you for His sacrifice for this night; be thankful that your lover chose to give herself in your place.'

'This is an attack upon me, on the sect of Ereth Khial,' said Anellion. 'Do not think that such a thing will go unpunished.'

'And who will deliver your vengeance?' said Lirieth. 'Ereth Khial? Anath Raema? Atharti? No, it is the power of Khaine that you desire. It is Khaine that you must turn to when you wish to strike down in hate and fear. Khaine has made His choice and found you unworthy.'

Hellebron noticed a disturbance in the crowd; Anellion's followers and their allies were scuffling with the Khainites. It was too soon for such open confrontation.

'Cease your petty struggling!' she shouted, pointing her dagger at the brawling elves. 'Tonight a sacred act has taken place. Do not despoil the sacrifice of this beautiful moment with your mortal prejudices. Maineth has given her spirit to Khaine and we must consecrate her flesh to Him.'

Lirieth stooped over Maineth's corpse, her blade above the wound in her chest.

'No!' Anellion launched himself at Lirieth. The Bride of Khaine stepped easily aside and swung the back of her fist into his jaw, sending the priest tumbling to the ground.

'Do not anger Khaine further with this interference,' snarled Hellebron, standing between Anellion and his lover's body. 'He has claimed one of us tonight, do not draw His eye upon yourself.'

Tears streamed down Anellion's face as Lirieth crouched over Maineth and cut out her heart. She lifted it reverentially to the crowd, who were now subdued, finally realising what had happened.

'Praise Khaine,' Lirieth said softly. 'Take this sacrifice and stay Your bloody hand from our lives. Be sated with this offering of blood and flesh.'

She threw the heart into the flames and fell to her knees. Hellebron did the same, bowing down to the fire. Behind them, other elves followed their lead, bowing their heads and kneeling down in worship.

'Praise Khaine.' It was not a victorious shout but a frightened whisper from hundreds of elves.

Unseen, Hellebron smiled.

THE EFFECT OF Maineth's self-sacrifice was felt all across Athel Toralien. Hellebron and Lirieth were inundated with callers seeking protection from Khaine's wrath. Many came simply to give praise, but there were a good number who wished to learn all the ways of Khaine; not just the prayers and rituals, but also to fight in Khaine's name.

Lirieth and Hellebron welcomed these new acolytes. With their father's money and influence they took over one of the villas that looked out onto the sacrifice square. Craftsmen were brought in to convert the house into a temple. Over many days, a black granite statue depicting Khaine was raised at the gate, and iron braziers erected along the walls, burning with magical flame. The Brides of Khaine gathered their most promising followers and began to school them in the arts of war, introducing them to the various drugs that allowed them to fight without fear or fatigue.

For their part, the other sects conceded temporary defeat. Fearful of what happened to Maineth, the other priests and priestesses restricted their protests to their own gatherings. Hellebron was content not to push the matter; her focus was on securing her hold on those that came flooding to the new shrine.

Many of these new Khainites were desperate, haunted by the tale of Khaine possessing Maineth and forcing her to commit suicide. They regularly cut themselves and offered up their blood to Khaine, hoping that such smaller sacrifices would keep the Prince of Blood at bay. Hellebron and Lirieth presided over these bloodletting ceremonies, ensuring that their followers did not inflict any wound too grievous, giving assurance that Khaine's thirst could be slaked if the blood was offered with suitable humility.

Autumn turned to winter, winter to spring and a new rhythm of life set-tled in Athel Toralien. Hellebron's sect numbered several thousand, larger even than the following of Ereth Khial. As she consolidated her power, Hellebron's thoughts turned to wider matters. It was not enough to be the strongest cult in Athel Toralien; to dominate entirely the Khainites would need to extend their power beyond the city.

The Brides of Khaine despatched their most trusted and able followers to several other cities around the colonies. Their task was simple: to recruit elves from other kingdoms into Khaine's fold. This was a risky mission, for though the Naggarothi had no qualms about the Prince of Blood, worship of Khaine was not welcomed by other kingdoms. These heralds would work in secret, subtly extending their influence, attracting those who were willing.

Over the next year, Hellebron's confidence grew further. With a strong but as yet incomplete hold on the city, the shrine's coffers swelling with dona-tions, she wrote a letter to Khorlandir, high priest of Khaine in Anlec. In that letter, she extolled the virtues of the Khainites and told Khorlandir of what she had created in Athel Toralien. It was her hope that word of what she had done would begin to circulate in Anlec, paving the way for her eventual arrival. Perhaps, she thought, even Morathi might hear the name Hellebron again.

As another winter turned to spring, Hellebron received word back from Khorlandir. He praised her work in Khaine's name and reassured Hellebron that such dedication would not go unrewarded.

The letter also contained a warning. The rise of Khaine in Athel Toralien was part of a greater movement, and in Nagarythe the other sects were becoming more desperate to halt the popularity of the Khainites. Khorlandir told Hellebron to be wary of any move by the other priests in the city, concerned that rival cults would choose to direct their jealousy against the Khainites isolated in Athel Toralien.

Though Hellebron was disposed to dismiss such concerns, Lirieth was quick to guard against overconfidence. From Liannin, who had proved her-self an enthusiastic and popular, and exceptionally useful, member of the sect, the sisters learned that there were whispers of discontent; almost two years had passed since Maineth's dramatic self-sacrifice and many followers were becoming disenchanted with the Brides of Khaine. Lirieth suspected agitators from the rival sects were stirring up trouble, but even Liannin was unable to point out any of the ringleaders driving the quiet rebellion.

Before Hellebron could devise a plan of action, more worrying news filtered up from the mass of followers. Several elves were missing, and the finger of blame was directed at the priests of Ereth Khial. It was claimed that cultists following the Goddess of the Dead had stolen into the homes of the Khainites and snatched them away, though no witnesses could be found to swear this as fact.

'There are no feathers without a hawk,' Lirieth said to Hellebron one afternoon, as the two of them sat in a small antechamber next to the main temple hall mixing the secret potions and salves used by the Khainites. 'It is as Khorlandir warned: the other sects are building to some larger move against us.'

'They seek to sow division within our company,' said Hellebron. She took a pinch of powder from a flask and used a pestle and mortar to mix it with crushed venomblossom. 'If we fail to respond, our leadership will be questioned and unrest will spread.'

'We need another living sacrifice,' said Lirieth. 'The blooding does not engage as many of our followers as it once did.'

At that moment the curtain of the chamber parted and Liannin entered carrying a steaming pan of water. She set it down next to the sisters and was about to leave when Lirieth caught her by the arm.

'What is the feeling amongst our brothers and sisters?' Lirieth asked.

'They are angry more than afraid,' replied Liannin. She looked very different from the maid she had been, her skin whitened with dye, her hair and lips black. Tiny scars of many cuts covered her arms and shoulders, and she had branded a small rune of Khaine onto her left cheek. 'They see these kidnappings as a challenge to Khaine.'

'We must strike back, and hard enough that there will be no retaliation,' said Hellebron. She looked at Liannin. 'Send out the word to our followers that tonight we shall hold a special ceremony. Lirieth, gather our best fighters and bring them here before dusk. It is time that we sent a message that cannot be ignored.'

HELLEBRON AND LIRIETH stalked through the streets at the head of fifty of their most zealous followers. All of the Khainites were armed with swords and daggers, and they carried burning torches with them. As they passed across the city to the temple district, the slamming of doors and rattle of window shutters greeted them. Even those elves with no interest in religion could not be ignorant of recent developments, and the grim sight of the Khainites sent many elves to flight, fearful for their lives.

Rather than confront the supporters of Anellion directly, Hellebron led her followers to the shrine of Atharti. The pleasure-seekers were an easy target, mostly the young and disaffected who indulged in casual liaison and gross intoxication. The temple of the pleasure goddess was a high, narrow hall with column-lined steps leading up to the main entrance. Above the threshold was a frieze, an indecent image of entwined bodies, with a flowing inscription beneath: 'There is no life without pleasure'.

Hellebron broke into a run, her followers dashing up the steps behind her. There was no door to bar their path and they flowed through the high arch quickly. Inside the temple, the soporific incense of the Athartists lingered on the air, a few dim lanterns shining purple through the haze.

The worshippers lay in scattered groups upon the carpeted floor, in various states of undress. A few looked up with drug-addled eyes as the Khainites spread across the chamber, weapons in hand. Lying naked upon her altar, the high priestess Ilintalia turned languidly towards the newcomers, a half-smile upon her lips.

Hellebron grabbed the priestess by her curled white hair and wrenched her from the altar. Ilintalia squealed with pain but was unable to offer any firmer resistance as Hellebron dragged her back towards the street. Others were roused by her cry, but so intoxicated were they that the Khainites had no problem hauling them to their feet; there was not even need for any bindings.

Surrounded by the bared blades of the Khainites, the Athartists stumbled and slouched towards the street, mumbling in confused fear. A few were regaining their senses, shock washing away the effects of their indulgence. Their protests were swiftly silenced by punches and kicks.

Back across the city marched the Khainites, their hostages huddled in the midst of the mob. There were questions and accusations hurled from doorways and windows as the cultists passed, but Hellebron said nothing and her followers were under strict instructions to harm nobody but their rivals.

Liannin had done her part of the task well and the congregation of Khainites was so large that it spilled out of the temple and into the square where those first ceremonies had been held. Liannin herself stood by the doorway, dagger in hand, as the Khainites laughed and jeered at the feeble Athartists.

Ilintalia was rousing from her fugue and began to wriggle desperately. Hellebron and Lirieth seized the priestess and heaved her into the air, carrying her into the temple upon their shoulders, impervious to her struggles. A great cheer greeted them from within, where the Khainites were packed shoulder-to-shoulder, leaving only a small space in front of the fire pit. They parted to let the Brides of Khaine reach the bloodstained stone altar set before the pyre, hurling insults at Ilintalia.

The sisters dropped the Atharti priestess onto the slab, dazing her. While Lirieth brought forth manacles to chain Ilintalia, Hellebron darted into the antechamber and emerged a moment later with a golden chalice; its contents a potent mix of narcotics.

Without a word being said, Hellebron brought out her knife, slicing its blade across the wrist of their captive. Blood poured from the long wound, to be caught by Hellebron in the wide-brimmed cup. She used her knife to stir the contents and then took a long draught.

Already excited by the taking of the sacrifices, Hellebron's whole body burned as the concoction of blood and drugs took effect. She passed the chalice to Lirieth, who drank swiftly and then gave the goblet over to Liannin to share with those close at hand.

Hellebron stood over Ilintalia, dagger raised. The crackle of the flames and the panting of the congregation added to the noise in her head. The smoke from the fire was no thicker than the fog of her thoughts as she searched for some incantation or prayer to accompany the sacrifice.

She stared out at the expectant faces of her followers, more of them trying to cram in through the door than would ever fit. They didn't care for words, they wanted only one thing: blood!

Hellebron drove the dagger into Ilintalia's breast, again and again, stabbing and slashing in a frenzy of bloodlust. She ripped out her sacrifice's heart and raised it to her lips, tearing a chunk from the organ with her teeth. Crimson spilling down her chin and chest, she presented the trophy to the crowd.

'Praise Khaine!'

The shrine shook with wild shrieks and roars. Hellebron cast the heart into the flames. She felt like she was floating, buoyed up by excitement and adulation. The Khainites bayed for more and another of the Athartists was roughly deposited onto the altar as Ilintalia's corpse was taken away and cut to pieces by Khainites who sought to take their own souvenirs of this glorious night.

This time Lirieth took her turn, more sedate in her actions, carefully cutting open her sacrifice, the young elf's weeping and cries of agony a chorus of praise to the Prince of Murder. Not until she plunged her dagger under his exposed ribs did he die, a plaintive wail ripped from his lips.

Outside, frustrated Khainites fell upon the other prisoners in a storm of shredding blades and ripping hands. Bones and blood littered the cobbled square as the cultists tore apart their sacrifices, chanting praises to Khaine, tossing garlands of entrails to each other like obscene playthings.

Long into night the murder continued, charnel smoke billowing from the temple to swathe the stars, hundreds of voices echoing through the streets of Athel Toralien while the common citizens cowered in their homes.

THE GREAT SACRIFICE of the Athartists did not go without retaliation. The following night, Khainites were set upon by mobs from the other temples and dragged to the altars of other gods. Flames flickered above the city as the homes of Khainites were set on fire. No opponent dared approach the shrine itself, nor strike against Hellebron or Lirieth.

When dawn came and the dead were counted, more than a hundred Khainites had been slain, and half that number of other cultists. Hellebron spoke to her followers and promised them that Khaine would not let these crimes go unpunished. Knowing that many in the city were not aligned to any particular sect, Hellebron was determined that the Khainites would be held in highest dread; she could not allow any other cult to oppose her.

The following night, the Khainites were let loose and running fights broke out through the streets around the temple district. None could match the savagery of the blood cultists and hundreds died, slain on the road or dragged screaming to the altar.

Dawn brought no peace as the battles continued. The sun rose upon a city stained with bloodshed, the streets littered with corpses. Hellebron stood at the door of the temple with Lirieth by her side and exhorted her weary followers to continue.

The clatter of hooves on pavement echoed across the square and a troop of knights rode into view. More than a hundred riders filed into the plaza, lances lowered and swords unsheathed. Behind them came rank upon rank of soldiers with bows and spears, spreading into the streets around the temple of Khaine.

The knights' captain steered his mount towards the shrine and stopped a short distance from the Brides of Khaine. Hellebron did not recognise him.

'By order of Prince Alandrian, all religious cults and sects are to cease this disorder immediately.' The captain glared at Hellebron. 'That includes you. Your father is very unhappy.'

'We are fighting to defend ourselves,' said Lirieth. Hellebron was too furious for words; how dare her father interfere now, at the moment of her triumph?

'There will be no more fighting,' said the captain. 'All temples are to be closed and there will be a curfew from dusk to dawn. Any found continuing this sectarian insolence will be arrested and tried as traitors.'

'I demand to see my father!' shrieked Hellebron.

'We have friends within the army,' said Lirieth.

The captain laughed.

'Any soldier of Nagarythe who disobeys the commands of Prince Alandrian will be executed without trial or appeal. As for your father, he sent me here to bring you to him.' The captain's humour faded.

'You are both under arrest.'

—◄ SIX ►—

Khaine's Legacy

IN THE DISTANCE, the horizon was smudged by the dark green of the forests, broken by the glittering snake of a river. To the north, Hellebron could just about see the ploughed fields of the farmlands, while closer at hand the land rippled with heather-covered hills. Directly beneath the narrow window the tower's gardens exploded with colour, filled with the full bloom of spring. White pebble paths led between the flower beds to an immaculate lawn where servants were clipping the grass, moving on their knees in a row.

It was a very picturesque prison.

The gardens were bordered by a high hedge, and Hellebron could see the glint of the soldiers as they patrolled the road beyond. If she leaned out, she would look down on the helmets of the warriors guarding the tower door.

The first year had been the most difficult. Hellebron had ranted and raved, broken the furniture a dozen times, smashed the gilded mirrors, set fire to the expensive rugs, but her father had not relented in his decision.

The second year Hellebron had spent in deep thought, fantasising a hundred ways by which she might escape. She had skill enough with a sword to break free, but she was half a day from the city. No horses were kept in the stables and she would be caught before she ever sighted Athel Toralien; even if by some chance she reached the city, there was little hope of entering without being seen. The alternative was to head east, but a life of exile would be as bad as imprisonment, with none of the comforts.

The third year Hellebron had spent writing letters to her sister, who languished in similar confinement far to the north. Lirieth's replies told of the great cliffs on which her gaol stood, and the waves that crashed day and night.

Hellebron had no doubt that her letters were opened and read, and that anything of suspicion would be reported to her father. That had not stopped her from communicating her plans and desires; the two sisters thought so alike, they were able to discern the subtlest meaning in the seemingly bland correspondence. Lirieth wrote always of patience; Hellebron urged her sister to remain strong.

Prince Alandrian visited frequently. At first, Hellebron had refused to see him, going as far as to throw missiles at him out of the window. When he stopped coming, she had written to him, apologising for her behaviour, hoping that perhaps she could reason with him, or maybe even tug on his emotions enough to secure her release.

Her father had offered a simple choice: renounce her dedication to Khaine or remain imprisoned. Hellebron had given no answer, and spent much time considering her response. She would not be able to renounce Khaine in name only; there would be many elves only too willing to spy on her to ensure she stayed true to her word. To give up her position as a Bride of Khaine would be to admit defeat and cast aside all the ambition that she harboured.

This Hellebron could not do, and with reluctance told her father that she would not renounce her love of Khaine. He had nodded, perhaps even with a hint of pride, and told her that the offer would always be open to her.

Three and a half years was not a considerable time in the reckoning of the elves, but to Hellebron it was a slow torture. Day by day she knew her dreams were slipping away. Her father had allowed Liannin to remain as maid, and through secret messages she sneaked out of the tower, Hellebron continued to send words of encouragement to her followers and in return received news of what passed in Athel Toralien and the other cities.

After a ban lasting a year, Alandrian had capitulated to the continuing demands of the cults, and the temples had been reopened, even the shrine to Khaine. Without Hellebron and Lirieth, the Khainites were a much lesser force, returned to the status of military indulgence rather than a true sect. Now and then a beastman or greenskin, even the occasional human marauder from the North, would be brought to the city to appease the Bloody-Handed God. It seemed that Lethruis had won from beyond the grave.

A knock on the door broke Hellebron's thoughts.

'Enter.'

Liannin opened the door, consternation showing in her face.

'Prince Alandrian is here to see you,' said the maid.

'He was here only three days ago,' said Hellebron. 'Why has he returned so soon?'

'He has not said anything to me,' said Liannin. 'He is waiting for you in the South Hall.'

Hellebron nodded and stood.

'Tell him I will join him as soon as I am presentable.'

Liannin departed, closing the door softly, leaving Hellebron alone with a sudden rush of thoughts and questions. Only something of immediate and high importance would have brought her father back. Hellebron sat in front of the mirror and brushed her hair, calming herself, pushing aside the flood of speculation that sprang to mind. She changed into a short-sleeved evening dress, tied back her hair with a golden clasp, and took a deep breath.

It was always important to remember she was a princess.

'THERE IS CIVIL war in Nagarythe.'

Hellebron stared open-mouthed at her father at this announcement. She shook her head, thinking she had misheard. Alandrian was sitting at the head of the long dining-table, a fire burning in the grate behind him. He stood and looked into the flames as he continued.

'Prince Malekith has returned to Ulthuan from his travels in the North and Morathi attempted to keep the throne from him.' Alandrian talked stiffly as if reciting from a letter. 'I learned this only yesterday, and the news itself is many days old. The ship's captain who brought it to me says that Malekith has entered Anlec, and Morathi is to be taken to the Phoenix King's court and charged with treason.'

Hellebron laughed, long and hard; so long that tears rolled down her cheeks and she had to hold on to the edge of the table to keep herself upright. All the while, Alandrian looked at his daughter with confusion. Eventually Hellebron regained some modicum of control.

'Morathi is to be tried by Bel Shanaar and the other princes?' Hellebron laughed again, imagining the queen's humiliation. 'This is wondrous news, wondrous news indeed!'

Her father did not see any humour in the situation.

'Nagarythe is tearing itself apart,' said the prince. 'There are factions still loyal to Morathi fighting against the followers of Malekith.'

Hellebron settled again, mind suddenly alive with possibilities.

'These troubles will spread to Athel Toralien,' she said. 'You were Prince Malekith's lieutenant. It was the prince who handed control of the city to you. The cults owe their allegiance to the lapdogs of Morathi, puppets of masters in Anlec these past years. Your enemies will see this as an opportunity to remove you.'

'This has occurred to me,' Alandrian said, sitting down again. He waved Hellebron to sit next to him and laid a gauntleted hand on the table in front of her, an imploring gesture. 'I have a new proposal for you.'

'Ask anything, father.' Hellebron smiled sweetly, hope rising in her heart. 'Anything at all.'

* * *

HELLEBRON HAD TO wait for two more years while her father manoeuvred and politicked in Athel Toralien, slowly replacing or moving officials known to be adherents to the other cults, promoting army officers loyal to him alone, currying favour with the other princes of the city and making secret pacts with the most powerful merchants.

When all was ready, a mounted guard of honour came to collect Hellebron. Lirieth was with them and the sisters shared an emotional reunion, with many tears of joy and embraces. After so much time, now that she was so close to achieving the dominion she craved, the ride to Athel Toralien seemed an eternity to Hellebron. Her father was about to hand her the city like a sweetmeat on a platter, and still Hellebron's thoughts were full of grander designs. Control of Athel Toralien was not the summit of her ambition; that lay across the ocean in Anlec, and with Morathi imprisoned by the Phoenix King in Tor Anroc, there would never be a better time.

In the late summer afternoon, the city was bathed in sunlight, and Hellebron was filled with energy at the sight. Light sparkled from golden towers and silver roofs, bright against the clear sky. She looked at the high walls to the city that had been denied her for so long, and imagined the people of Athel Toralien going about their lives without an inkling of what was about to befall them.

Her thoughts turned to her rivals, the priests and priestesses of the other sects, who had no doubt laughed at her incarceration and joked with each other about the ill fate of the Brides of Khaine. Soon they would learn how dire was the price for denying Khaine, as would any that opposed His return to glory.

As they entered the city, Hellebron was immediately aware of a subdued atmosphere. Everywhere she looked there were soldiers; no doubt the citizens of Athel Toralien had noticed their increasing numbers over the preceding days.

Several princes were waiting inside the gate, their royal guards drawn up around them. Hellebron recognised Malriad and a couple more; the other three were unknown to her, princes from Nagarythe who had fled Ulthuan during the last years of Morathi's reign.

Maenredil was there too, wearing the crest of a commander. Lirieth waved at her former lover, who smiled in return and called his companies to attention. They lowered their spears in salute as Hellebron and Lirieth rode past, much to the sisters' amusement.

Alandrian waited for them at the centre of the square inside the gate. He was dressed in his finest armour, long cloak trailing over the rump of his horse, a golden shield on his arm. He looked every part the prince he was, and it was with a surge of pride that Hellebron bowed her head to her father and reined in her steed beside him.

'This will not go without some effort,' said Alandrian. 'Our preparations have not gone entirely unnoticed. Your mother suspects something is amiss and has called a rally of the people in the market. At the last count there were more than a thousand listening to her endless speeches.'

'What of Anellion and the other cult leaders?' asked Lirieth.

'They have been gathering their followers to the temples, suspicious of the activity. They cannot truly suspect what we have planned.'

Hellebron looked around at the assembled soldiers and then at her father.

'When do we start?' she asked.

FLAMES LIT THE city, pushing back the night. The whole temple quarter was burning, and the screams of those trapped in the temples echoed with the crackling of the blaze. The crash of fighting had died down from its earlier climax, as bands of Khainites and soldiers hunted down the last of the other cultists.

Hellebron and Lirieth had led the attacks, bursting into the temples with spear and blade to cut down all opposition. Many of the meeker cultists had surrendered and were now being led in long lines to the square outside the temple of Khaine. This time Hellebron would not make the mistake of despatching all her sacrifices in a single night; there were enough prisoners to last for a good while if she was able to temper her followers' enthusiasm.

The Brides of Khaine were outside the temple of Anath Raema watching the adepts of the Vengeful Huntress being dragged from their shrine. Lirieth laughed as one of the older priests stumbled and fell flat on his face. The soldiers heaved him up and hauled him along the street, his feet dragging on the paving.

The clatter of hooves announced the arrival of Maenredil. The commander looked aggrieved as he dismounted.

'Is there something amiss?' asked Hellebron.

'That is one way of saying it,' said Maenredil. He cast about uncomfortably for a moment before he fixed on Lirieth. 'It is your mother. She has led a march on your father's villa and is demanding that the purge be ended.'

'So?' said Hellebron. 'Ignore her.'

Maenredil switched his gaze to her, resignation written across his face.

'It is not so simple. She has several thousand people with her. Her defiance is a challenge to your father; open opposition to his rulership. She is demanding that he surrender his reign to her.'

'Then our father should deal with her,' said Lirieth. 'Why is it our concern?'

'You have been away a long time,' said Maenredil. 'The situation in the cult of Khaine has... changed.'

'What do you mean?'

Maenredil flinched at the harshness of Hellebron's question. The commander took a breath.

'With both of you out of the city, Prince Malriad took it upon himself to become our leader. There are many that are still loyal to you, including him, but if you wish to come back as our leaders, there are opponents within the cult who must be swayed. Your mother's open insolence gives weight to their arguments that you are not strong enough to lead. For the moment Malriad has them under control, but if nothing is done, you will be abandoned as being too weak. They say that your father will not be ruler forever, and that without him you will be unable to protect them.'

Lirieth sighed while Hellebron snarled a curse.

'We will deal with this,' said Hellebron. 'Find us horses and we will ride with you to see this mob.'

MIRIETH'S INFLUENCE HAD grown considerably during her daughters' absence. A staunch critic of the cults for many years, she had seized upon her husband's ban to gain wide support for her movement. Many were tired of the cults and their leaders, and thousands had left their homes to join Mirieth in this protest.

As Hellebron and the others rode into the square, Mirieth was standing in front of a line of spearmen stretching across the gate to Alandrian's palace. Alandrian waited on a balcony beyond the wall, surrounded by his supporters. There were several sporting the accoutrements of Khainite priests – faces that Hellebron didn't recognise. They were usurpers, their power built upon the endeavours of Hellebron and Lirieth.

The followers of Mirieth stood in silent protest; people from all walks of life and all parts of the city. A short distance away Hellebron's followers glowered at the protesters, blades in hand, as they stood over the cultists taken prisoner. These Khainites gave a cheer as the sisters appeared. Hellebron looked up at the dignitaries with Alandrian and noted their scowls of displeasure. It was obvious that this minor insurrection within the cult was not to their liking.

Mirieth turned as the Brides of Khaine dismounted. For a moment, Hellebron could not decipher the look on her mother's face. Then realisation slowly dawned: it was pity. Pity born out of love, no doubt, but a stinging insult to Hellebron's pride. Pity was for the weak. It had not been pity that had sent Aenarion to the Blighted Isle to take up the Sword of Khaine. It had not been pity that had driven Malekith to save this city from the orcs. Pity was an affectation of the lesser kingdoms and it had no place in the heart of a Naggarothi.

The two sisters approached Mirieth slowly, wary of some trap. The mood of the crowd changed, their sullenness becoming anger as the architects of the purge came closer. Hellebron and Lirieth stared them down, matching the crowd's anger with their own. The quiet, simmering rage of the Toralii that the sisters had once used for themselves was now turned on the Brides of Khaine.

'I know that you have no love for me, but listen to what I have to say,' said Mirieth. Hellebron stopped a pace from her mother and glared. Mirieth met that hate-filled gaze without fear, her pale blue eyes unwavering as she studied her daughter's face. Mirieth's eyes glistened, hinting at tears held in check. 'It is time for this madness to stop.'

'And you think you have the power to stop it?' said Lirieth.

Mirieth turned to the crowd and raised her arms, silence following swiftly.

'Our homeland is divided,' she said to them, but the words were directed at her daughters, and their father watching from above. 'Nagarythe teeters on the brink of destruction, not by the machinations of others, but brought about by our own selfishness. We have forgotten the lessons left to us by Aenarion. Before he took up the Widowmaker, Aenarion offered himself to the other gods and they rejected him. Only when he sacrificed his life in the Flames of Asuryan did the gods listen.'

Now Mirieth turned back to Hellebron and Lirieth, but her voice was still pitched to carry across the square.

'Aenarion did not sacrifice himself for the glory of Khaine. Aenarion sacrificed himself for the survival of our people. It was to banish death and misery that he laid down his life. It was out of love for all elves, Naggarothi and others, that Aenarion took up the Blade of the Blood Prince, knowing the doom he brought upon himself. It was to banish anarchy, dispel disharmony, that Aenarion turned to Khaine, as the last choice. It was in anger and grief that he became the Bloody-Handed King.'

Mirieth extended two imploring hands towards her daughters. She fell to her knees while tears streamed down her face.

'It is with love, not hate, that I tell you this. Do not let Khaine claim your spirits. He will devour you, and through you devour us all. You still have a choice, to change direction and tread upon a path of light rather than walk the dark roads of death. Your ambitions are fleeting, for all mortals must die eventually, no matter how grand their status or how vast their army.

'And when you are dead, how shall you be remembered? As heralds of strife? As kinslayers and murderers? Even Aenarion, in the fiercest grip of Khaine, never raised his sword against another elf. Nagarythe is in turmoil; let Athel Toralien become a beacon of peace and hope, a new Anlec. Let your legacy be one of harmony, of understanding, of love.'

Hellebron stood over her mother and laid a hand on her shoulder. She looked over to her followers, who waited like beasts about to pounce. Her gaze passed over Mirieth's followers, many of them in tears, fear written on the faces of others.

Last, she looked up to her father's palace. Alandrian stared down with arms crossed, his face an expressionless mask. Around him the chief Khainites sneered and glared, contemptuous of Hellebron and her sister.

Hellebron knelt in front of Mirieth. She raised her mother's face and placed a kiss on each of her cheeks. Leaning close, she whispered in Mirieth's ear.

'It is too late for peace,' said Hellebron. 'If I do not do this, another will. Better to rule with Khaine's blessing, than serve without it.'

Hellebron surged upright, dragging Mirieth with her. Her dagger flashed. Blood spilled from her mother's throat. Letting Mirieth's body fall to the ground, Hellebron held aloft the bloodied knife and stalked towards the wailing crowd, Lirieth at her heel. Some turned to run, others defiantly held their ground but cowered back when Hellebron was a few steps from them.

'Khaine has come to Athel Toralien,' she snarled. 'You have a choice. Accept Khaine as your patron and give your life to Him, or deny Him and give your deaths instead!'

Hellebron whirled around and pointed her dagger at the senior Khainites and her father.

'I have just killed my mother for the glory of Khaine. I did it swiftly and with love. Any other elf that stands in my path will not be so fortunate!'

The followers of the Brides of Khaine fell upon the protesters like a hungry pack. Screams echoed around the square as the elves fled from the Khainites. On the balcony above, Alandrian had withdrawn, leaving the Khainite priests looking down nervously at the carnage below.

Lirieth and Hellebron lifted up their blades and cried out in unison, knowing the city was theirs.

'Praise Khaine!'

SHADOW KING

PART ONE

The Child of Kurnous; Strife in Nagarythe;
A Trailing Shadow; The Treachery of Malekith

ONE

The Young Hunter

IN THE DAYS of the first Phoenix King, Aenarion the Defender founded the realm of Nagarythe in the harsh north of Ulthuan. Under his reign the Nag-garothi – as Aenarion's people were called – studied long the arts of war and forged a formidable army to defeat the daemons of Chaos.

At Anlec, greatest fortress of the elves, Aenarion held court with his queen, Morathi, and they brought into the world their son, Malekith. Aenarion fell at the very moment of his victory and the rule of Nagarythe passed to his son. Prince Malekith formalised the promises of his father and secured the lands and wealth of the many princes who had fought by Aenarion's side. Yet, ever a warrior and a wanderer, Malekith departed for new wars in the colonies.

Second only to the great Caledor Dragontamer in Aenarion's esteem was Eoloran Anar, the Phoenix King's standard bearer. To his stewardship Male-kith gave the lands of eastern Nagarythe in the hills and mountains of the Annulii. In Aenarion and Malekith's name Eoloran would rule, and there was peace and prosperity for an age.

Eoloran was a wise prince and was content to raise the power and privilege of House Anar without conflict, though he sent his son Eothlir to fight in the colonies for a time so that he might know something of war. His wife having died in the war with the daemons, Eoloran became reclusive, though always ready to answer the calls of the lesser nobles of Nagarythe. Other, more ambitious princes grew in renown and the deeds of Eoloran faded from memory except within the halls of Elanardris.

With Malekith gone from Nagarythe to conquer new realms for the elves, the seed was sown for division. Jealous of the power granted to Eoloran, though he did not wield it often, Morathi wove tangled politics to isolate the Anars from the rest of Ulthuan while all the while strengthening her grip upon Anlec and Nagarythe. It was not a topic Eoloran wished to discuss with his family, who were left to wonder what the ancient elf planned to revive his family's fortunes, or if he had any plan at all. He forbade any of the Anars from visiting Anlec and instead was content to petition his fellow lords with letters reminding them of their support from the Anars in centuries past and their ancient vows to one another. Eoloran's son, Eothlir, tried as best he could to maintain the status of House Anar, but he knew that there was a change coming. He could not define what it was that alarmed him; it was a flicker in the corner of the eye, a sound on the edge of hearing, a distant scent on the wind that cautioned him.

It was the Season of Frost, in the one thousand and forty-second year of the reign of Phoenix King Bel Shanaar. At the home of the Anars, the wind had turned north and brought with it the chill of winter down from the mountains. Snow flurries drifted from the highest peaks in long, fluttering streamers of white. The furthest reaches of the pine forests were dusted with snow as the bitter weather crept down the mountainsides day by day. Maieth was wrapped in a long shawl of dark blue wool as she stood in the gardens of the Anars' manse. Eothlir, her husband, placed an arm around her and smiled.

'There is a warm fire within, why do you stand outside in the cold?' he asked.

'Listen,' she said. They both stood in silence, and the only sound to be heard was the sighing of the wind. Then, faintly, there was a call, the croak of a crow.

'A single crow in winter,' said Eothlir. 'A bad omen, do you think?'

'Yes,' she replied. 'Though no more an omen than a houseful of sudden guests come here from Anlec seeking sanctuary.'

'It is but a temporary arrangement,' said Eothlir. 'One day Prince Malekith will return. He will rein in Morathi's excesses. We must be patient.'

'Excesses?' laughed Maieth, with bitterness not humour. 'Butchery and perversion are not "excesses"!'

'There are those who protect her, you know that,' said Eothlir. 'But there are as many who see her rule as tyranny and resist her.'

'When?' demanded Maieth, pulling herself free from her husband's arms to stare at him. 'For many years they have done nothing; we have done nothing.'

'She is the mother of the Prince of Nagarythe, the bride of Aenarion; it would be treason to move against her directly,' said Eothlir. 'For the moment it is sufficient that we rule our lands and keep them free of her taint. If she tries to take our power overtly, she will find greater resistance than she expects.'

'And what of Tharion, Faerghil, Lohsteth and the others who now sleep in our beds, afraid of returning to Anlec?' asked Maieth. 'Are they not also princes of Nagarythe? Do you realise that they once thought that Morathi would never be so bold as to go against them directly?'

'Would you have me a traitor and usurper?' snapped Eothlir. 'Or worse, would you be a widow, and your son fatherless? In Anlec, Morathi holds sway, but here in the mountains her reach is short. She may try to pick us off one-by-one, but as long as we are united, she cannot move against us. Fully a third of Nagarythe's armies are abroad with Malekith. Another third owe allegiance to my father and his allies. Morathi cannot conjure soldiers from thin air, no matter her powers of seeing and scrying.'

'Your father holds half of the warriors in Nagarythe, and yet what does he do?' said Maieth with scorn. 'He hides here and writes letters. Are we not all sons and daughters of Nagarythe? Our armies should be camped outside the gates of Anlec, demanding restitution from Morathi for the wrongs she has done our people.'

'And what of Malekith, Aenarion's heir, our rightful ruler?' said Eothlir, grabbing his wife by the shoulders. 'Do you think he will look kindly upon those that raise arms against Anlec without his consent? Would he welcome those that threaten his mother? I tell you now, my father would die of shame to be thought of as a traitor, and so he rallies support in the only way he can.'

'Hush now,' said Maieth quickly, embracing her husband.

Turning, Eothlir saw a young elf, no more than thirty summers old, walking down the wide steps from the mansion. He was dressed in hunting leathers edged with dappled fur and bound with leather thongs, and in his hands he held a slender black bow and a quiver of arrows.

'More practice, Alith?' called Eothlir, disentangling from his wife's arms. 'You already know that there is not a lord in the mountains that can match your eye and hand.'

'I know nothing of the sort, Father,' said the boy sombrely. 'Khurion says that his cousin from Chrace, Menhion, can strike a pinefowl in flight at a hundred paces.'

'Khurion says many things, my son,' said Maieth. 'If we believe all that he claims, then his cousins, all four of them, would be the match for any army in the world.'

'I know that he exaggerates,' said Alith. 'However, I have made a wager with him, to call his bluff. In the spring I will contest with Menhion, and I shall uphold the honour of House Anar. Until then, I must practise further while the snows still hold back.'

'Very well, but be back before dusk,' said Eothlir.

ALITH NODDED AND walked away, slinging the quiver over his shoulder. He knew that his parents thought him distant, morose even. They whispered and fell silent when he was around, but he was observant and keen-eared and knew that all was not well in Nagarythe. The manse was full of refugee princes who had chosen not to support Morathi and her hideous cults.

He also knew, perhaps even where his father and grandfather did not, that this matter would be settled not with diplomacy but with force. He thought much of his family for avoiding direct confrontation with the rulers of Nagarythe, but he knew that one day he would lead House Anar and he was determined that the manner of the world in which he ruled would be better than that of today. Others would follow him not out of fear, but out of respect; it was never too early to earn respect, though often too late.

Leaving the formal gardens through a silver gate in the high hedge, Alith strode up into the hills that heaped up higher and higher upon the shoulder of Suril Anaris, the Mountain of the Moon. The whole mountain and its surrounds were the lands of the Anar, granted to Alith's grandfather by Aenarion himself. Though inhospitable in winter, they were abundant with game and fowl, and the lower meadows still made good pasturing for goats and sheep. These would be his lands one day, and so he walked them as often as possible, getting to know them as he knew the house where he had been born.

Today he went north and east, along the Inna Varith. The cold river flowed down from caves hidden upon the slope of Suril Anaris and fed the lands of Elanardris with fresh water until it disappeared back underground at the Haimeth Falls many miles to the south.

Picking his way along the winding bank, Alith watched the silver darting of fish in the clear waters, leaping and swimming through the rocky rapids. Needing to get to the northern side of the river the young elf leapt nimbly from rock to rock, heedless of the torrent sweeping past his feet, unmindful of the slicked stones upon which he stepped.

From here he found an old track that led further up into the hills, twisting around dark boulders and leafless bushes. It was some time before he came under the eaves of the pine forest, and set foot upon a frosted carpet of needles. Alith's light tread left barely a mark in the crisp mulch as he broke into a jog, speeding swiftly under the overlapping branches of the trees.

Alith was guided by an inner sense, attuned to the distant warmth of the sun behind the clouds, the wind upon his face and the subtle slope of the ground beneath him. As clearly as if he had a map, he cut eastwards through the woods, along the flank of the mountainside. In the branches above birds swooped to and fro while four-legged, whiskered hunters snuffled through the patchy undergrowth, unaware of his passing. His route brought him to an outcropping of rock that pushed several hundred feet up through the trees, and at its foot there was a low cave. Cloud had flowed down the mountainside and swathed the clearing with a fine greyness that dulled colours and muted sound.

Ducking inside the gap in the rock, Alith came to a wider cavern, dark but for the trickle of sunlight through the entrance. He reached out to his right and his hand came upon a torch of bound branches held within a sconce on the cave wall. He spoke a word; a spark lit within the torch's head and swiftly took flame. With this light, he walked further into the cavern.

The cave opened into a wide natural nave, shaped over thousands of years. Stalagmites and stalactites had met in ages past, forming glittering pillars much like the columns of a grand cathedral. It was not just a temple in appearance, for Alith had come to one of the shrines of Kurnous, the Hunter God. The glow of the flickering brand danced across dozens of skulls placed in niches around the cave wall: of wolves and foxes; bears and deer; hawk and rabbit. Some were gilded, others inscribed with delicate runes of prayer and thanks.

All were gifts to Kurnous.

Though worshipped much more in Chrace, whose hunters were renowned throughout Ulthuan, Kurnous was still acknowledged elsewhere in those communities that had not moved to the ever-growing cities. In Elanardris the Hunter God was held in high esteem, the ways of the wilds not yet swept away with the formality of Asuryan or the other gods.

It was a feral shrine, with a dirt floor scattered with dead leaves. The walls were painted with hunting scenes, of predator chasing prey. Some were ancient and faded; others were brighter and more recent. Alith knew that others came here, though he had never encountered another hunter visiting the shrine.

Alith had no such grand offering this day, though in the past he had fashioned such sacrifices for the Wolf of the Heavens. He knelt before the altar – a rocky plinth strewn with twigs, ash and detritus. There was a hole bored into the rock where he set the torch, and then he gathered up a mound of broken sticks and dried leaves. Snapping a single brand from the torch, he lit the small fire and breathed it into greater life. He spoke a few words of thanks and dropped the burning stem onto the miniature pyre.

Alith then pulled something from a pouch at his belt: a thin sliver of venison from the last deer he had slain, a dozen days ago. He skewered the meat on a forked piece of branch and set it atop the fire where it hissed and spat.

Alith then sat cross-legged before the altar and took his bow across his knees. With his hands upon it, he whispered a few words to Kurnous, thanking him for the kill he had offered and asking for grace in his hunts to come.

Head bowed, Alith sat for a while longer in silent contemplation. He tried to put aside his worries and focus on the hunt to come. He pictured himself stood atop the peak of Suril Anaris, the sun bright upon his face, the wilderness laid out before him. He pictured the trails the animals followed; the pools where they drank; the runs where they hunted. From within, the landscape of Suril Anaris opened up before him. There were still many dark patches: places where Alith had not yet travelled.

After paying due homage, Alith stood and left the cave, the venison still burning behind him. With another word of power he quenched the torch and placed it back in its holder ready for the next visitor; him or another, it did not matter. Stooping low, Alith ducked out of the cave – and then stood frozen.

Just ahead of Alith, in the thickening mist, stood a stag. It was a monumental creature: its shoulder higher than Alith was tall, with a spread of antlers wider than the young prince's outstretched arms. Its coat was white, save for a flash of black down its chest. The stag watched Alith with deep brown eyes, neither aggressive nor alarmed.

The young elf straightened slowly and stared back. The stag bent its head and shook its antlers, scratching at the ground with a hoof. Alith was convinced this was some sign sent by Kurnous, but could not fathom its meaning. The stag was becoming more agitated, and arched back its head and let loose a long bark. Alith took a step forwards, his hand outstretched in a placating gesture, but the stag suddenly looked to the west and then bounded away into the forest.

Alith turned his gaze to where the stag had looked and saw a figure beneath the eaves of the trees. He was mounted upon a black horse and swathed in a cloak of dark feathers. The rider's head was cowled and nothing could be seen of his face.

Unconsciously, Alith reached for his bow, and turned his head to grasp it from the quiver. As soon as he looked back, the rider was gone. Alith strung an arrow and dashed across the open ground to the edge of the trees where the rider's horse had been. There was no mark upon the ground, the frosted pine needles undisturbed by foot or hoof.

Two bizarre events so close together left Alith feeling unnerved, and he glanced around the rest of the clearing but could see nothing. Taking the arrow from his bow, he broke into a run and headed straight back towards the manse, all thoughts of hunting forgotten.

THE HEIR OF House Anar chose not to share his two strange encounters with his family, who had enough to contemplate without the fanciful tales of their son. The experience faded in his memory over the winter and spring until even he was not sure whether it had truly happened or been some kind of waking dream. Thoughts of strange omens and mysterious riders were replaced in the young elf's mind with more pressing concerns: love.

The day before midsummer, Alith savoured the warmth of the sun upon his skin. He wore a short sleeveless gown of white silk, his face, arms and legs exposed to the pleasant heat as he lay on his back staring up into a cloudless sky.

'That is not something I see too often,' said Maieth, sat on the grassy hill next to her son. Behind them the large manse of House Anar, capital of Elanardris, rose up from the slope of the mountain, its white walls bright in the sunshine. Elves were gathered in groups around the gardens, talking and drinking, taking sweetmeats and delicacies off trays from servants liveried in silvery grey.

'What is that?' asked Alith, turning to his side and resting on one elbow.

'A smile,' his mother replied with one of her own.

'I cannot be sad on a glorious day such as this,' declared Alith. 'Blue skies, the glow of summer; these things cannot be touched by darkness.'

'And?' said Maieth with an intent look at her son. 'There have been many such days this year, and yet I have not seen you this happy since you loosed your first arrow.'

'Is it not enough that I am content?' said Alith. 'Why should I not be happy?'

'Do not be so coy, my reticent child,' Maieth continued playfully. 'Is there not some other reason for this unbounded joy? Something to do with the midsummer banquet tomorrow?'

Alith's eyes narrowed and he sat up.

'What have you heard?' he asked, returning Maieth's gaze.

'This and that,' his mother said with a dismissive wave of her hand. 'I met with Caenthras just before I came up here. You must know him; he is the father of Ashniel.'

At the mention of the elf maiden's name, Alith looked away. Maieth laughed at his sudden discomfort.

'So it is true!' she said with a triumphant grin. 'I take it from your carefree happiness today, and the smitten expression you've worn whenever Ashniel has been around, that she has agreed to attend the dance with you?'

Alith's face was one of consternation as he replied.

'She has,' he said. 'Dependent on her father's permission, of course. What did he say to you, exactly?'

'Only that you run around in the woods like a hare, and dress like a goat-herd more than a prince,' said Maieth.

Alith was crestfallen, and moved to stand. Maieth leant over and stayed him with a hand on his arm.

'And that he would be delighted for his daughter to court the son of the Anars,' she added quickly.

Alith stopped and paused before breaking into a wide grin.

'He said yes?' said Alith.

'He said yes,' Maieth replied. 'I hope you have been practising your dancing, and not spending all of your time with that bow.'

'Calabreth has been teaching me,' Alith assured his mother.

'Come,' she said, standing up and reaching down a hand to Alith. 'You should greet Caenthras and thank him.'

She pulled her son up by the hand. Alith stood hesitantly, eyeing the gathered elves as if they were a circling pack of ice wolves.

'He has already said yes,' Maieth reminded him. 'Just remember to be polite.'

— TWO —

Darkness from Anlec

FOR THE ELVES, who each live for an age of the world, time passes quickly. A year to them is as a day to men, and so their schemes and relationships develop slowly. Alith Anar, young and impatient, wooed Ashniel for two years, from midsummer to midsummer, through letters and courtship, dances and hunts. Entranced by the cool beauty of the Naggarothi maiden, the young Anar prince put aside his greater concerns and for a while was happy, or at least relished the promise of future happiness. So it came about that he listened little to the whispered worries of his parents and spent less time in the wilds, instead closeting himself in the study and library of Elanardris learning poetry to impress his amour or listened to tales from his mother, ancient legends of those two divine lovers, Lileath and Kurnous.

To pledge his love for Ashniel, Alith commissioned the finest craftsmen to weave for her a cloak of midnight-blue, studded with diamonds like stars, the constellations drawn in fine traceries of silver thread. Having read into the astronomical texts of the family, Alith had devised the design himself, representing the skies above Ulthuan on the day of Ashniel's birth. This labour he did in secret, even from his family, for he wanted to present Ashniel with this gift on the coming midsummer's night and would risk no warning of it reaching the ears of his loved one.

As evening fell on the night of the festival, servants came out with magical lanterns to hang upon the boughs of the trees in the gardens. The golden dusk was augmented by the yellow glow of the lanterns, which turned to pools of silver as the sun disappeared and the stars scattered across the skies. Chatter filled the air as dozens of elves walked the patios and paths of Elanardris's exquisitely designed surrounds, accompanied by the clinking of crystal goblets and the patter of fountains.

Alith flitted through the scattered crowds of guests like a shadow, his eyes seeking Ashniel. The cloak nestled under Alith's arm, wrapped in silken paper brought from the colonies to the west. The package was as light as a feather, but felt like a leaden weight. Excitement and fear vied inside Alith as he skirted around a plush lawn and headed back towards the paved area where food was being served.

As two guests parted for a moment, Alith spied Ashniel's pale face. Bathed in the lamplight she was beautiful, her expression one of poise and dignity, her grey eyes glittering. Weaving through the milling elves, Alith made straight for Ashniel and was but a few steps from her when a tall figure came up in front of him, forcing Alith to stop sharply. Glancing up as he was about to step around the obstacle, Alith saw the face of Caenthras, one eyebrow raised in suspicion.

'Alith,' said Prince Caenthras. 'I have been looking for you.'

'You have?' replied Alith, taken aback and suddenly worried. 'Whatever for? I mean, how can I be of service?'

Caenthras smiled and laid a hand on Alith's shoulder.

'Do not look so petrified, Alith,' said the lordly elf. 'I do not bear ill news, merely an invitation.'

'Oh,' said Alith, brightening up. 'A hunt perhaps?'

Caenthras sighed and shook his head.

'Not all of our lives revolve around the wilds, Alith. No, I have visitors from Anlec at my house who I wish you to meet: priestesses who will divine the future for yourself and Ashniel. I thought that if the augurs go well, we might discuss the details of the union of our two houses.'

Alith opened his mouth to reply but then realised he did not know what to say. He clenched his jaw to stop himself saying something stupid and simply nodded, trying to appear sagely. Caenthras frowned a little.

'I thought you would be pleased.'

'I am!' said Alith, panicking. 'Very pleased! That sounds wonderful. Although... What if the priestesses say something bad?'

'Do not worry, Alith. I am positive that the omens will be good.'

Caenthras glanced over his shoulder towards Ashniel and then at the package under Alith's arm. He nodded and pulled Alith closer, hugging him to his chest as he steered the youth through the crowd of elves surrounding Ashniel.

'My daughter, light of the winter skies,' said Caenthras. 'Look what I have found lurking nearby like a mouse in its hole! I believe it has something to say to you.'

Caenthras shoved Alith forwards and he stumbled a few paces and stopped in front of Ashniel. He looked up into those grey eyes and melted, the poem he had rehearsed again and again in the library slipping from his memory. Alith gulped, trying to recover his wits.

'Hello, my love,' said Ashniel, leaning forwards and kissing Alith on the forehead. 'I've been waiting for you all evening.'

Her perfumed scent, distilled from autumn wildflowers, filled Alith's nostrils and he was dizzy with the smell for a moment.

'I have this for you,' he blurted, stepping back and thrusting out the package.

Ashniel took the gift, ran her hand over the soft paper and gave an admiring look at the intricately knotted ribbon that bound it. With Alith's aid, she slipped the ribbon free and let the silk paper flutter to the floor. Alith took the neck of the cloak and flung it open, revealing its shining glory. There were appreciative gasps from the other elves and a pleased smile played upon Ashniel's lips.

Alith glanced around and saw that many more elves had gathered upon the patio and several dozen were watching the unfolding spectacle, his mother, father and grandfather amongst them. It occurred to him that perhaps he had not been so devious in his secrecy as he had thought.

'Here, let me,' said Caenthras, stepping forwards and taking the cloak from Alith. He swung the cape around Ashniel's neck and deftly fixed the crescent moon-shaped clasp upon her right shoulder. Seeing the gift upon Ashniel, the words sprang back to Alith unbidden.

'As the stars light the night, so you shine upon my life,' he said, clasping his hands in front of him, his eyes rising to the heavens. 'As the world turns under their gaze, my life unfolds under yours. Where bright Lileath gazes down upon us with her beauty, her radiance is as nothing compared to the light that shines from you.'

There were more gasps from a few of the assembled elves and whispered comments, complaining that Alith should not compare the beauty of a mortal to that of the Moon Goddess. Alith ignored them, knowing that they were simply being prudish.

'My heart burns as the sun and I would have your soul reflect its light,' concluded Alith.

Ashniel's expression was one of refined amusement as she looked at the other maidens in the crowd, pleased with their jealousy. She cupped Alith's cheeks in her hands and smiled.

'Though Lileath spurned Kurnous, I shall not follow suit,' she said. 'The hunter has caught his prey with this most dazzling of traps and I cannot escape.'

There was a cheer, soon joined by more, and Alith and Ashniel found themselves at the centre of a jostling mass of elves eager to congratulate them and examine the fine cloak. Alith let it all wash over him, feeling a calm descend that he had not felt anywhere else except on the mountain tops with an arrow notched upon his bow. Contented, he took a glass of wine from a servant and raised it in toast to Caenthras, who nodded appreciatively and then disappeared into the gathered elves.

THE MOONS WERE barely above the mountains when Gerithon, the chancellor of the Anars, hurried from the house to speak with Eoloran and Eothlir. Alith excused himself from Ashniel and joined his father and grandfather.

'He insists that he speak with you,' Gerithon was saying.

'Then bring him through,' said Eoloran. 'Let us hear what he has to say.'

'Yes, let him speak his mind in front of us all,' said Eothlir.

With a resigned sigh, Gerithon walked back into the manse. For a moment Alith wondered if this visitor was perhaps the dark rider he had first seen in the forest several years earlier. Ever since that encounter Alith had spied the elf – or what he supposed to be an elf though he could not know for sure – several times more, watching the young prince from a mountain ridge or beneath the boughs of a wooded copse. Always the rider had disappeared before Alith could approach, and left no tracks for him to follow.

Alith had spoken of this strange watcher to nobody, fearing that it would cause alarm without bringing answers. But the elf Gerithon escorted from the manse was not the rider, or if he was then he wore a different guise, for he was dressed in the manner of one of the pleasure cultists.

The stranger was clad in swirling layers of purple robes, each diaphanous, but overlaid upon his body in such a way that where they overlapped they concealed his nudity and preserved a little dignity. His right brow was pierced with a silver ring from which hung an oval ruby, and a similar jewel hung from the left side of his nose. The hair that hung to his shoulder was dark but bleached white towards the tips, braided with beads of blue and red glass. Alith noticed that for all his decadent appearance, the newcomer wore a sheathed sword at his belt – a long, thin weapon with a crossguard fashioned into the likeness of two hands cupping the blade.

'My princes,' the stranger said with a low bow. 'Allow me to introduce myself. I am Heliocoran Haeithar. I have ridden from Anlec to speak with you.'

'There is no message from Anlec that we wish to hear,' said Eoloran.

Most of the party attendees and a few servants were gathering around the stranger and hostility filled the air. Heliocoran seemed oblivious to the situation and continued regardless.

'Her majesty, Queen Morathi, wishes to invite the house of Anar to an audience,' said Heliocoran. He looked around at the guests. 'And I extend that invitation to any prince present here, upon my own authority.'

'Queen Morathi?' spat Eothlir. 'When last I heard, Nagarythe was ruled by Prince Malekith. We have no queen.'

'It is unfortunate that the whispers of Bel Shanaar have been allowed to settle here and take root,' said Heliocoran smoothly. Upon close inspection, Alith saw that the envoy's eyes were odd, his pupils disturbingly small, while the green of his irises almost completely obscured the white. This was accentuated by a thin trace of kohl that brought the messenger's eyes into stark contrast in an unsettling fashion.

'We shall determine for ourselves what is truth and what are lies,' said Eoloran. 'Say your part and then leave.'

'As you wish,' said the herald with another exaggerated bow. 'The realms of the other princes are in concert against Nagarythe, and wish to make Malekith their puppet. He fears to return to Ulthuan under the present conditions. Dear comrades of our prince are held hostage against his loyalty. That is the truth of it. The Naggarothi have been betrayed by Bel Shanaar, he who usurped the Phoenix Throne from the heir of Aenarion. For these past many years Bel Shanaar has grown more and more vocal in his opposition to our traditions and customs, and Queen Morathi wearies of his hypocrisy. She calls out to all princes, captains and lieutenants still loyal to the true rule of Nagarythe, and bids them to travel to Anlec so that she might hold counsel with the greatest of these lands.'

His voice had become strident, but again dropped to a soft hush, and his manner became one of pleading confidant rather than bombastic herald.

'Innocent elves have been slain and imprisoned by the minions of Bel Shanaar, the Usurper Phoenix; persecuted for pursuing their leisures and beliefs, hounded for following the ancient rites of our people. If you allow this conspiracy to proceed unchallenged, Nagarythe shall fall and her power squabbled over by weaker bloodlines than stand here. If you would see your lands taken and your children chained and your servants and labourers whipped into misery, then stay here, stand idle and do nothing. If you would see Morathi preserve the inheritance of Malekith so that he might reclaim his rightful position as heir to Aenarion and ruler of Ulthuan, then return with me to Anlec.'

'Though I have no love for Morathi, I have none either for Bel Shanaar,' said Caenthras, stepping to the front of the ring of elves surrounding Heliocoran. 'If the warriors of the Phoenix King come to my lands, will Anlec send help?'

'That is for us to discuss in the council,' replied the messenger.

'What assurances do we have that this is not some trick?' asked Quelor, one of the princes allied to the Anars. 'Who says that bare cells and iron chains do not await us in Anlec?'

'Such division gives sport to the agents of our enemies,' said Heliocoran. 'To set Naggarothi against Naggarothi, that is the aim of our adversaries. Queen Morathi can give no assurances that the doubts sown by the spies of our foes cannot undermine. Instead, she appeals to your sense of duty and to the strength that flows within your veins. All here are true sons and daughters of Nagarythe, and each knows it is their right and their responsibility to uphold the honour of this realm. Lest you wish to be ensorcelled by the cowardly wizards of Saphery and see our dominions overseas taken by the merchants of Lothern and Cothique, heed Queen Morathi's warnings.'

'You do your position justice,' said Eoloran. 'Never have I heard such bile cloaked with such sweetness. You have said your piece, and now be gone from my lands.'

'You cannot stand aside in this battle, Eoloran,' said the messenger, and his tone was frank. 'For years now the house of Anar has refused to choose where its loyalties lie, and has gathered its friends close to protect it against the harms of this conflict. Now it is time to make your position plainly known. You may choose the correct path, and defend your lands against invaders from the other kingdoms, and your reward shall be in the sustaining of your line and the strengthening of your position. Yet you must stand against the misguided will and might of Bel Shanaar and his sycophants.

'If you choose to side with the usurpers, then you may well endure for a time, but dire shall be Queen Morathi's wrath on those who betray Nagarythe. You will be cast from power, scorned by those who once respected you and you shall spend the rest of your days as landless wanderers.'

'And so the threat is made,' said Eothlir. 'You would have it that we stand between a cliff and the ocean, and must dash ourselves against the rocks or else drown.'

'Then tell me, Eothlir, what does your heart say?' said Heliocoran. 'What have I said that you know to be untrue? Do you trust Bel Shanaar so much that you would throw in your lot with him?'

Gerithon hurried from the manse once more, looking agitated.

'There are armed soldiers outside, my prince,' he said. 'Three dozen, at least, that I could see. Their leader is arguing at the gate.'

'Why would a herald come armed for fighting?' said Eothlir, pointing to the sword at Heliocoran's waist. 'What is the meaning of these warriors before our doors?'

'These are not safe times,' said the herald. 'The agents of Bel Shanaar prowl the wilds like packs of feral hounds. You of all should know that we must protect ourselves. It would be most unfortunate if some foe were to waylay your family.'

'Get out!' roared Eoloran. 'Take your bribes and your threats and be away!'

Heliocoran flinched from the outburst as if menaced by a blade, and shrank back towards the house. With a snarl he turned and ran, pushing his way through the elves and hurling aside a serving maid who fell amid the splintered smash of crystal platters. No sooner had he disappeared into the manse than Eothlir was storming after him.

'With me!' he cried. 'He will open the doors and let in his soldiers!'

Alith did not chase directly into the house with the others, but instead ran for the east wing to his chambers. The high window was open and he leapt inside and flung open the chest at the foot of his bed where his bow and arrows were kept. With a straining gasp he swiftly strung his bow, and snatched up his quiver.

Wrenching open the door, Alith raced into the corridor and then along the wood-panelled passageway to the dining hall at the front of the manse. Shouts and the sounds of fighting echoed around the mansion. Striding to the windows, Alith saw that a group of black-armoured warriors had forced their way through the gate of the outer wall and were gathered about the colonnaded portico and were fighting to get inside, pushing at their companions to get through the door.

Opening the wide double doors that led to the entrance hall, Alith was confronted by the sight of his father and grandfather fighting back-to-back, wielding swords wrested from their foes. Meanthir and Lestraen lay bleeding upon the floor, possibly dead, and three of the envoy's warriors were also slain.

Taking up his bow, Alith shot one of the attackers in the thigh, saving his grandfather from a cut aimed towards his shoulder. In the space this created, Eoloran leapt forwards and thrust his blade past the guard of another warrior, cutting him across the arm. Other elves loyal to the Anars came rushing in from the opposite wing of the house, carrying swords and daggers taken from the walls of the great hall. Caenthras arrived, wielding a long spear, and drove its point into the back of one of the elves fighting Eothlir.

There came a deafening crash of glass from the eating hall and Alith turned to see dark-garbed soldiers breaking through the high windows, blades in hand. He shot the first to climb through, but two more jumped in swiftly behind the slain elf. Alith loosed another arrow but with a dull ring it merely caught a glancing blow on the golden helm of his target. Even as Alith whipped another arrow from the quiver across his back, the warrior turned and rushed towards him.

Jumping aside from the outthrust sword of his foe, Alith strung the arrow and loosed it in one fluid motion, the arrowhead punching through the elf's breastplate. Wounded, but not killed, the warrior gave a hoarse shout and swung his sword at Alith's neck. Alith swayed backwards but the point of the blade slashed across his tunic and a line of blood welled up from his wounded chest. Biting back a cry of pain, Alith whipped the tip of his bow into the face of his opponent, who fell back with a hand to his eye.

Tharion appeared at the doorway with a two-handed sword and chopped the elf's legs from beneath him, before giving a cry of alarm. Turning, Alith saw three more warriors advancing towards him, while a fourth made for the fire blazing in the great hearth. He saw the warrior snatch up a branch from the fireplace and take a step towards the tapestries hanging on the wall opposite the windows.

Without a thought, Alith nocked an arrow and took aim between the advancing elves. Breathing out slowly he loosed the arrow, which buried itself in the neck of the elf with the brand. The flaming branch fell from his dead grasp and thudded harmlessly on the stone floor.

The heir of Anar had barely time to loose another shot, which pierced the shoulder of his target, before Caenthras and Tharion were leaping forwards with their weapons, roaring ancient battle cries. Alith was struck by the ferocity of the two ageing princes; veterans of Aenarion's army and skilled warriors both.

Caenthras's spear took one of the dark-clad elves in the throat, who jerked like a puppet without strings before collapsing in a heap. Tharion parried a blow aimed towards his legs and spun his wrists to bring his heavy blade down across his foe's sword arm, severing it at the elbow. A backhanded strike hurled the elf back with his breastplate rent open, his lifeblood gushing over his black robes.

The clatter of hooves on cobbles attracted Alith's attention and he dashed to the windows. He saw Heliocoran wrestling with a tawny steed, trying to swing himself up into the saddle. As Alith climbed through the window, careful to avoid the slivers of shattered glass still protruding from the frame, Heliocoran mastered his mount. With much whipping of the reins, he turned his horse across the courtyard towards the main gates.

As the herald raced away, Alith's aim was obscured by the line of fir trees on either side of the roadway leading from the gate, and he leapt for the porch. Gripping the scrolled top of a column with one hand, he swung himself up onto the portico. From here, he could see the length of the courtyard to the gateway.

A soldier in the colours of House Anar stumbled from the gatehouse ahead of the messenger, blood dripping from a wounded leg. Heliocoran stooped low in the saddle and swept his sword across the warrior's chest as he sped past, felling him with a single blow.

Alith knelt on the roof of the portico and took aim. The clashing of swords and cries of battle below him drifted out of his thoughts as he focussed his mind and body on the dwindling figure of Heliocoran.

He imagined himself in the woods, stalking a boar or deer. He adjusted his line of shot for the wind sighing against the left side of his face, and raised his bow a touch so that his shot would not fall short of his rapidly fleeing prey.

Lit only by flickering lanterns, the herald was all but swathed in darkness and he was a moment from escape, but Alith could see his position clearly in his mind's eye.

With a whispered prayer to Kurnous, Alith loosed the arrow. The black-fletched missile streaked into the darkness, its point glimmering with firelight from the torches upon the walls of the courtyard. He heard a cry as it struck home. Heliocoran slumped upon his steed but did not fall, and then passed out of sight through the gatehouse.

Three of the fleeing messenger's warriors staggered out from the entrance hall onto the roadway beneath Alith, and he loosed three arrows in quick succession, taking them down with a single shot each. Eoloran, Eothlir, Caenthras and others ran out, stopping when they saw there were no more foes. Eoloran looked over his shoulder at his grandson.

'Did any of them escape?' Eoloran demanded.

'I hit Heliocoran, but I do not know if the wound is mortal,' Alith confessed.

Eoloran cursed, and signalled for Alith to climb down from his vantage point.

'That is the last of them,' said Eothlir. 'More will come. How soon, we cannot know. It seems that House Anar has chosen a side.'

Though his father's face was grim, this pronouncement brought pride to Alith's heart. Since he had been born, House Anar had been content to play no greater part in the affairs of Nagarythe. All of that had changed. Morathi had as much as declared war on House Anar, and Alith was pleased that his idleness would soon come to an end. He was Naggarothi, after all, and battle was in his heart and glory called in his blood.

Now was the chance for him to prove his worth and earn the renown that surrounded his family; a renown he had felt had not yet been his to rightfully share.

He hid a smile as he lowered himself down to the tiled ground below.

—◄ THREE ►—

The Prince Returns

NEARLY A YEAR had passed since the attack on the manse; many days filled
with frenetic activity and tension. Eoloran and Eothlir were afraid that
the warriors of Anlec would come upon them at any time, falling upon
Elanardris before its defences were made ready. Riders made haste to all
corners of the Anars' realm, to lesser princes and commanders, to muster
their soldiers at the ancestral home and ready for battle. Other princes, from
House Atriath and House Ceneborn, both long allies of the Anars, chose
Elanardris to make clear their defiance of Anlec.

For all the fears of House Anar, the threats of Heliocoran did not mate-
rialise into action. All of the summer, autumn and spring, troops loyal to
Eoloran came and camped upon the hills that surrounded the mansion,
nearly ten thousand in all. The standard of House Anar fluttered atop the
manse, white with a golden griffon's wing upon it, and from the banners of
the regiments assembling at the call of their lord.

Yet Alith was disappointed. Fully half of their troops had not responded to
the call to arms. Many had turned back the messengers and bid them return
to Eoloran to convey their refusal to act against Anlec. This grieved Eothlir
too, for Alith could see the strain written upon the face of his father when
these messages were passed on.

Alith guessed, as did Eothlir and others, that these dissenters had succumbed to the bribes and threats of Morathi. None could say if their part
was simply to step aside from their duties, or if there was some darker plot
to be uncovered. Would Eoloran's own turn against him? Would they raise

arms against their former master? It was this uncertainty that taxed the counsels of the Anars as they made ready. From where was the greatest threat
– the legions of Anlec or traitors close at hand?

THE GREAT HALL of Elanardris was full of elven princes and lords, all trying
to speak at once. Alith sat in the corner close to the empty fire grate and let
the babbling pass him by. He heard his grandfather's voice raised, calling
for quiet.

'I did not ask you all to come here for us to fight with one another,' Eoloran declared. He was sat at a table set across the hall, flanked by Eothlir and
Caenthras, a few of the other Naggarothi princes stood behind him. 'Already
there is enough division in Nagarythe, we need not add to it.'

'We demand that action is taken,' called out one elf, a lesser noble of
southern Nagarythe called Yrtrian. 'Morathi has taken our lands and forced
us from our homes.'

'And who is this "we" that can make such demands?' Caenthras answered
sternly. 'Those who did not resist the cults that grew up under their noses?
Those who stood idly by while Morathi's agents eroded their claim to lord-
ship? Where were these calls for justice a year ago when Morathi declared
the Anars traitors to Anlec?'

'We have not the means to defend ourselves,' said Khalion, whose domain
bordered Elanardris to the west. 'We place our trust in the greater houses,
which we have supported with taxes and warriors for many centuries. Now
has come the time for that support to be returned.'

'Warriors and armies?' laughed Eoloran, silencing all. 'You would have me
march to Anlec and throw down the rule of Morathi?'

There were a few calls for just such a thing to happen and Eoloran held up
his hand to quieten them.

'There is no means by which our armies can match those of Anlec,' said
the lord of House Anar. 'Not against a land filled with hostile cultists and
those enthralled to Morathi's power. I have offered sanctuary to you all, and
that offer comes with no price. Yet it also comes with no guarantees. For
a year Morathi has been content to stay her hand, burdening our greater
houses with the turmoil of lesser families, knowing that as she grows stronger, our ability to act grows weaker.'

Eothlir stood and scowled at the assembled nobles.

'If Morathi moves more directly against us, we will fight,' he announced.
'Despite that, we cannot, we will not, start a war with Anlec. The lands in
the mountains are still safe haven for any that would escape the tyrannies
of Morathi, and here we shall stand resolute. It is not for the Anars to cast
away the hopes of the future through rash action. We have faith in Malekith
and await his return. Under his rule, your titles and rights will be restored
and you will be glad of the protection you received.'

'And when will that be?' demanded Yrtrian. 'Has any here heard word of Prince Malekith these past years? He cares not for our woes, if he even knows of them.'

This started a fresh round of shouting and recrimination, and Alith stood up with a sigh and eased his way out of the hall. Such had been the bickering for four seasons, since the confrontation with Heliocoran. The Anars had waited for the first blow to land, but it had not come. For a year they had patrolled their borders and taken in those fleeing the plight that had engulfed the rest of Nagarythe, and it seemed that the self-appointed Queen of Anlec was content to allow her enemies to hide in the mountains. Alith chafed at the inactivity but could see that there was little the Anars could do to mount an offensive against Morathi's stranglehold on power.

As he had often done during such bickering conclaves, Alith left the nobles to their arguments and went to his chambers to take up his bow and arrows. Seeking solitude, he quit the manse and headed up into the mountains. Alith did not know for what he searched, and trod the old game trails guided by whim, heading ever eastwards, deeper into the mountains.

His greatest lament was that he had seen little of Ashniel in the past year. Caenthras had been wary of allowing her to leave the confines of his mansion and Alith had been spared little opportunity to visit her as he played his part as heir of the Anars. In his bedchambers he had a chest filled with letters she had sent, but their polite affection gave him little comfort.

Conflicted between depression and anger, Alith sat himself down upon a rock close to a babbling stream and dropped his bow upon the ground. He looked up into the summer sky, where white clouds scudded across the sun. In just one year everything had changed, and yet nothing had, and he could see no way by which the current stalemate would be broken – not in any way that would be good for the Anars.

A flicker of white caught his eye and Alith snatched up his bow and stood. Amidst the tumbled rocks and bushes a little further down the brook he spied an antlered head dipping to the waters. It was the white stag he had seen outside the shrine of Kurnous.

Padding softly along the bank of the brook, Alith sneaked from boulder to bush to boulder, closing in on the magnificent beast. It stood at the water's edge, head held high. It looked towards him and Alith shrank back into the shadow of an overhanging outcrop. The stag seemed unperturbed and lazily walked down the mountain back towards the forest.

Alith followed at a distance, careful not to approach too closely lest he startle the beast, but always keeping it in view. Their path took them under the eaves of the pine trees, ever eastwards into lands that Alith had not yet explored. As he stalked the stag Alith realised there were few landmarks to guide his passage and feared for a moment that he would get lost in the endless trees. The fear soon disappeared when he came upon a clearing, not large but big enough for the sun to break through overhead. Whatever happened, Alith would be able to make his way westwards towards Elanardris.

The stag stood in the sunlight, basking in its warmth. The elf moved closer and saw that the black mark upon the beast's chest was no random pattern but a crude representation of Kurnous's rune. Clearly the stag was some omen or guide sent by the god of hunters.

As before, the white stag suddenly started and bounded away northwards. Alith rose up and gave chase but was barely into the clearing before the deer disappeared from view amongst the lengthening evening shadows.

Stopping, Alith glanced around the clearing and his eye settled upon a shadow just under the eaves to the west. Without thought Alith fitted an arrow to his bow and loosed the shaft at the apparition. The shadow swayed for a moment, seeping into the darkness, and the arrow sped into the woods beyond. The shadow reappeared, more clearly a figure. In a heartbeat Alith nocked and loosed another arrow, but with similar failure to hit his mark. The silhouette had simply merged with its surrounds as the missile had passed.

'Wait!' the figure called out in elvish, its voice deep, tinged with the accent of northern Nagarythe. 'I would not have you waste more of your fine shafts.'

Alith bent another arrow to his bow nonetheless and watched warily as the tenebrous apparition emerged into the sunlight. He was dressed all in black with a cloak and hood of feathers concealing his body and face. The stranger showed his open palms and then reached up to pull back his hood.

The elf had skin as white as snow and emerald eyes that shone in the sun, his face framed by long black hair free of any tie or circlet. His expression was solemn as he glided slowly forwards, his hands held up in a sign of peace. Alith's quick eyes noted the empty scabbard at the elf's belt but he did not relax the tension on his bowstring.

'Alith, son of Eothlir, heir of the Anars,' the stranger said, his voice low and quiet. 'My name is Elthyrior and I bear important tidings.'

'And why would I listen to an elf that skulks in the shadows and stalks me as if I were his prey?' demanded Alith.

'I can only offer my apologies and hope for your forgiveness,' said Elthyrior, lowering his arms to his sides. 'I have not spied upon you out of spite, but only to observe and keep you safe.'

'Keep me safe from what? Who are you?'

'I have told you, I am Elthyrior. I am one of the raven heralds, and I was guided to watch you by my mistress.'

'Mistress? If you are an assassin of Morathi, strike now and let us settle this.'

'It is Morai-heg that claims my loyalty, not the Witch Queen who sits upon an usurped throne in Anlec,' said Elthyrior. 'The crow goddess came to me in a dream one night many years ago, before you were even born. In the mountains she sent me to find you, the child of the moon and the wolf, the heir of Kurnous. The one that would be king in the shadows and hold the future of Nagarythe in balance.'

Alith pondered these words, but they meant little to him. In myth, there was no child of the moon and the wolf, for Lileath and Kurnous had parted without son or daughter. He knew of no other king than Bel Shanaar.

'I do not understand why you think I am the one you seek. What message does the crone goddess have for me? What fate has she seen for my line?'

Elthyrior did not speak for a moment and ghosted softly towards Alith until he was stood but two paces from the tip of the youth's arrow.

'My message comes not from the Queen of Ravens, but from Prince Malekith.'

CLOUDS HAD GATHERED at the peak of the mountain, obscuring the sun and chilling the wind. Alith fixed his eyes upon Elthyrior to discern any malign intent. The raven herald returned his stare without hostility, awaiting Alith's response. The two stood as such for some time, Alith warily eyeing Elthyrior.

'You have spoken with Prince Malekith?'

'Last night, on the northern border of Tiranoc at the Naganath River,' said Elthyrior.

'Surely we would have heard ere now that the prince had returned,' said Alith with a frown.

'In secrecy has he come back, or so he thinks,' said Elthyrior. 'Even now he marches north to reclaim Anlec.'

'Then the Anars and their allies will march with him!'

'No,' said Elthyrior with a sorrowful shake of the head. 'Morai-heg has shown me something of what will come to pass. Malekith will not reach Anlec. He is not yet ready to reclaim his lands from the rule of his mother.'

'Perhaps, with our help…' started Alith.

'No. The time is not yet right. All of those in Nagarythe that would see Malekith restored to the throne rest at Elanardris, but the hope that they hold will be dashed if they march now.'

'I cannot make this decision, why come to me?'

Elthyrior looked to leave but then stopped and turned back to Alith, his stare intent.

'I go where I am bid, though I know not all of the reasons,' the raven herald said softly. 'You have a part to play in these events, but what they are I cannot say. Perhaps fate itself does not yet know your role, or it will be for you to decide. I cannot ask you to simply trust me, for you do not know me at all. All I can give is the warning I bring: do not march with Malekith. But you cannot say these words came from me.'

'You give me this knowledge and then expect me to keep it hidden? My father and grandfather, they should hear this.'

'Your grandfather has little love for my kind, and none for me,' said Elthyrior. 'Words from my lips would be as poison to his ears, for he still blames me for the death of your grandmother.'

'My grandmother?'

'It is not important,' insisted Elthyrior. 'Know only that I am not welcome at Elanardris, and nor will be my words. The Anars must not march yet. Your time will come.'

Elthyrior saw the conflict in Alith and leant forwards with earnest intent.

'Can you swear that all who live under the banner of the Anars can be trusted?' asked the raven herald.

Alith thought about this, and though it pained him to realise, he could not in all honesty say that there were no agents of Anlec at Elanardris. There were simply too many elven nobles – and their households – for him to be sure of anything. Elthyrior recognised the consternation in Alith's face.

'If not for the reasons I have given, than for the secrecy desired by Malekith I ask you not to speak. This news will come to your family soon enough, but let it be from the lips of others. If the prince desires to come unheralded, it is for us to acquiesce to that wish. Every warning that our foes have may turn things against us. I tell you this only so that you might guide your family to the correct decision.'

Alith shook his head, casting his gaze to his feet for a moment while he collected his thoughts.

'When will…' he began, but when he looked up, Elthyrior had gone. There was no sign of the raven herald, only the shadows beneath the trees and a single crow swooping over the tips of the pines.

─◄ FOUR ►─

Herald of Khaine

ONCE AGAIN ALITH found himself returning to Elanardris with a secret to keep, one which burned at him more than ever. Elthyrior's revelation that Malekith had returned had stoked the fires in Alith's heart and he longed to announce to his family that the war for Nagarythe had begun. Yet for all his desire, Alith was haunted by the sincerity in Elthyrior's face and tone. It was as a messenger bringing grave news rather than cause for celebration that Alith remembered the raven herald and so he kept his silence.

It was not long before Alith was relieved to hear a messenger from the lands westwards had come to Elanardris bearing the tidings of the prince's return. The manse was abuzz with activity as word spread Caenthras and the other allied princes at the home of the Anars.

Three days after Alith's meeting with Elthyrior, Eoloran called the princes and nobles into the great hall to discuss their plan of action. This time Alith sat at the high table with his father and grandfather, though he was uncertain what he would say. Elthyrior's warnings to stay in Elanardris were at the front of his mind, but he sensed that the others were keen to march forth and meet with the returning prince.

'This is joyous news indeed,' exclaimed Caenthras. 'The day long hoped for has arrived and the cruel shackles of Morathi's reign can be cast aside. Though we have chafed at those bonds placed upon us by concern for the safety of our kin, now we can let loose our spirits and fight.'

There was much approval to this from the gathered elves, not least from Eothlir. Alith's father stood up and cast his gaze over the hall.

'For too long we have suffered, afraid of Morathi and her cults,' he declared. 'We have been slaves to that fear, but no longer! Word comes to us that Malekith marches for the fortress at Ealith, and from there he will retake Anlec. It is not only our duty but our privilege to aid him in this endeavour. This is a battle to reclaim not only our own lands, but all of Nagarythe.'

Again there was assent from the others and Alith struggled to remain silent. The mood in the hall was martial, the assembled Naggarothi given a vent for years of frustration. Alith could not think of the words that could turn such a rising tide of anger, not least in part because he felt it himself. He was torn between his own desires and the warning of Elthyrior.

Alith suddenly became aware that all eyes had turned to him and realised that he had stood up. He glanced at his grandfather and looked out at the hall filled with expectant faces. If he were to speak against his father, he would invite scorn, perhaps pity. They would not listen and would think him a coward. He was heir to House Anar and all expectation was that he would raise his own voice in defiance of Anlec.

He stood in silence a moment longer, tortured. There was a whisper of disquiet and frowns appeared on the faces in front of Alith. He swallowed hard, his heart beating fast.

'I too feel the desire for retribution,' Alith announced. There were nods of approval from the crowd and Alith held up a hand to forestall any optimism. 'This is a grave time, and calls for measured heads not fiery hearts. I have learnt much wisdom from my grandfather, not least the virtue of patience.'

There were a few heckling complaints but Alith continued.

'If Prince Malekith himself had called for our aid, I would proudly ride out on this campaign. Yet, he has not. It is presumptive of us to raise our blades against our fellow Naggarothi without invite from our true lord. If we take it upon ourselves to exact vengeance for the wrongs done against us, what difference would there be between those of us who hold true to the ideal of freedom and those who would enforce their tyranny with warriors?'

The grumbled complaints turned into derisive shouts. Alith dared not look at his father and instead focussed on one of the elves at the front of the crowd.

'Khalion,' said Alith, reaching out a hand. 'What has changed between yesterday and today? Do you not trust in our prince to restore your lands and bring back the rule of law we desire? Why would we be so ready to unleash the cloud of war now, when under the sun of yesterday we strove for peace? Our grief consumes us, eats at our spirits, but we must not feed it with the blood of our fellow elves. Only by leave of the prince did we claim our lands and we owe it to him to respect that authority. Draw blood and we may yet start the war we have so long wished to avoid. We must temper our feelings with caution, lest our actions have consequences beyond what we see.'

There was disgust clearly written on the faces of the elves and many waved dismissive hands and sneered at Alith.

'Care not for their scorn, Alith,' declared Caenthras, striding to stand beside him. The venerable lord glared at the other elves, cowing their disrespect. 'I value your reasoning and admire your courage and honesty. I do not agree with your arguments, but I think no less of you for voicing them.'

Alith let out his breath in a long sigh and sat down, closing his eyes. He felt a hand on his shoulder and looked up to see his father.

'The youngest of us might yet speak with the greatest wisdom,' said Eothlir. 'I know that none here will march forth unless it is beside the banner of the Anars, and so we face a tough decision. Long we have pondered what might become of us in these dark times. For my part, I would have us go forth to whatever destiny awaits, rather than hide here while it sneaks upon us. I am not the lord of the Anars, though.'

All attention turned to Eoloran, who was sat with one elbow on the table, his chin cupped in his hand. His eyes swept the room, spending more time upon Alith than any other. Straightening, he cleared his throat and laid his hands palm downwards on the table.

'My instinct has ever been to avoid conflict, that much you all know of me,' said the head of House Anar. 'Long we have endured turmoil and darkness, and it seems that stability and light can return to our lives. Though I hear your words, Alith, I am left with a singular fear. Malekith makes his bid now, and I cannot have it be said that the Anars stood by and watched it fail. It is beholden upon us to ensure the prince's success, for the peace and prosperity of all our people in the times to come. Long we have watched and waited, biding our time for the prince's return. That time has come. Unless you have some greater argument to make, I have reached my decision.'

Alith opened his mouth to speak but realised he had nothing else to say, no further argument he could put forwards to keep the Anars safe in Elanardris. He shook his head and sat back. Eoloran nodded and looked at his son and grandson.

'The Anars march at dawn!'

IT WAS WITH a sense of foreboding that Alith marched with the other warriors of the Anars. From across the hills and mountains the army had gathered, responding to swift-riding messengers despatched by Eoloran to muster just south of Elanardris. The host marched west, numbering some twenty thousand warriors, heading for the ancient citadel of Ealith.

The Anars went forth on foot, the rough terrain of their lands not suited to cavalry; since the time of Aenarion they had fought with bow and spear rather than horse and lance. The elves moved swiftly nonetheless, and would reach Ealith in four days.

Alith strode alongside his father at the head of a company of bowmen, the honoured guard of House Anar. For the most part they walked in silence, Eothlir's mood grim as was the atmosphere of the whole endeavour. Never before had the elves marched to war against other elves.

As twilight was spreading its shadow across the hills, Alith spied a crow flying overhead, towards the west. He followed its path and saw, just for a moment, a black-swathed rider silhouetted atop a ridge. The rider vanished into shadow in a moment, but Alith was left in no doubt that it was Elthyrior.

When the army stopped to make camp, Alith excused himself from his father, promising to bring back some game for their supper. Bow in hand, Alith picked his way quickly through the growing lines of tents and headed westwards.

Leaving behind the fires of the camp, Alith found his way lit by starlight alone. After some time, he reached the ridge upon which he had spied the dark rider and nimbly climbed its steep slope, jumping from boulder to boulder until he reached the summit. The white moon, Sariour, was rising and by her light Alith looked all about, seeking some sign of the raven herald. Some distance away on the far side of the ridge he caught sight of a black steed, standing docilely in a hollow. He took a step towards it but then stopped as he heard the sound of a whetstone on metal.

Turning around, Alith saw Elthyrior sitting on a rock just behind him, sharpening a serrated dagger. As before the herald was swathed in his cloak of raven feathers, his face all but hidden. Moonlight shone from his bright eyes, which followed Alith closely as he walked over and sat beside Elthyrior.

'I am sorry,' said Alith.

'Perhaps some things cannot be changed,' replied the raven herald. 'Morai-heg weaves across the skein of our lives and we must do the best we can with the threads she leaves us. None will hold you to account for the decisions of others.'

'I tried,' sighed Alith.

'It is of no matter,' replied Elthyrior. 'The path is taken; we cannot turn back, though your army must do so.'

'It is too late, my grandfather is resolute on marching to Ealith,' said Alith.

'He will not reach the citadel,' said Elthyrior. 'Malekith will take Ealith but it is a trap set by Morathi. Even now, tens of thousands of warriors and cultists close in on him. If you march to his rescue, you will also be caught. I warned that it was not yet time and nevertheless the Anars have stirred Morathi's wrath.'

Alith was incoherent for a moment, trying to comprehend what Elthyrior had said.

'Malekith trapped?' he finally managed to say.

'Not yet, and the prince is canny enough to avoid the snare,' said Elthyrior with a slight smile. 'I ride now to warn him of the danger. By dusk tomorrow, others will come from Ealith, sent by the prince. Be sure that your grandfather listens to what they have to say. Add your voice to theirs if need be. The Anars must turn back now or you will not see Elanardris again.'

Alith bowed his head and clasped his hands to his cheeks as he tried to think. When he sat up he expected Elthyrior to have gone, but the raven herald had not moved.

'Still here?' asked the young Anar.

Elthyrior gave a shrug.

'My steed is swift and I have time enough to enjoy the night air for a while.'

Alith took this without comment and stood up. He started down the slope and turned at a call from Elthyrior.

'I'll save you some time,' said the raven herald and tossed something towards Alith. He caught it out of instinct and found it to be a bundle wrapped in several broad leaves bound with strands of grass. Looking back to the ridge, he saw that Elthyrior had disappeared this time.

As he picked his way down the slope, Alith opened the parcel: two snow hares trussed together by their hind legs.

As Alith made his way back down the ridge, something to the north caught his eye. Looking closely, he saw the telltale flickers of many fires on the horizon. Not knowing the portent of this discovery, he hastened back to the camp, running directly to his father's tent.

Eothlir was deep in conversation with Caenthras, Eoloran, Tharion and Faerghil. They looked up angrily as Alith breathlessly burst through the door flap.

'The enemy are close,' blurted Alith, discarding the brace of hares upon the ground. 'There are campfires to the north.'

'Why have our pickets not seen them?' demanded Eoloran, glaring at his son.

'They lie beyond a ridge to the west,' Alith intervened to save his father's shame. 'It is only by chance that I saw them.'

'How many fires?' asked Caenthras.

'I cannot say for sure,' said Alith. 'Dozens.'

Eoloran nodded and gestured to Tharion to hand him a hide tube. He pulled a broad parchment from within and laid the chart out upon the table.

'Roughly where did you see this encampment?' Eoloran asked, beckoning Alith closer.

Alith looked at the map and found where he was currently stood. He traced his path westwards to his clandestine meeting with Elthyrior and located the area of the ridge he had been on. His finger then followed a line roughly northwards while he recalled the scene to his mind. The trail stopped upon a line of hills that stretched from north-east to south-west.

'They made camp somewhere at the base of these hills,' he said. 'I do not think they will have seen our fires unless they are looking for them.'

'Then we still have the element of surprise,' growled Eothlir. 'We should make ready to strike as soon as dawn rises.'

'What if they are a foe we cannot face?' asked Alith, recalling Elthyrior's dire warning.

'We must ascertain their strength first,' said Eoloran with a nod, more cautious than his son. He looked at Tharion and Eothlir. 'Assemble a small group of scouts and spy upon our foes so that we might know their strength and disposition.'

'Alith, you will guide us to where you saw these fires,' said Eothlir and Alith nodded, glad to have been included in his father's thoughts. 'Tharion, pick out the keenest-eyed warriors in your company and send them to me. Then ensure that all will be made ready to march come the rise of the sun.'

Tharion nodded and picked up his tall helm from a side table. He grinned briefly and then left.

'Beware of sentries,' said Eoloran. 'If the enemy are unaware of us, it should remain so. Count their numbers and observe them, but do nothing else without my command.'

He stared intently at Eothlir to ensure his point was understood, and Alith's father nodded in agreement.

'Do not worry, lord,' said Eothlir. 'I'll not scare them away and deprive you of the chance to lead the Anars in battle again.'

EOTHLIR ASSEMBLED A handful of elves at the edge of the Anar encampment. Swathed with dark cloaks, they set out before midnight, following Alith's lead. He took the small group westwards up the ridge, heading slightly north of where he had met Elthyrior. Though he doubted that the raven herald had remained close by – or that he would be seen against his wishes – Alith thought it best not to risk any discovery.

From the top of the ridge the campfires could clearly be seen. Alith took the time to count them. There were more than thirty fires, two of them exceptionally large. The undulating nature of the foothills meant that the enemy camp would be out of sight until the party was almost on top of it, and so Eothlir marked the direction by the stars in the clear sky and headed north-east.

After a short time the second moon ascended in the west, a sliver of bright green that spilled its sickly light over the Annulii foothills. The elves travelled swiftly over the rugged hillsides, no more distinct than the shadows of the rocks and trees around them. Sariour had set and the shadows had deepened by the time the sounds of the enemy camp came to them on the wind.

The enemy made no pretence of secrecy; piercing shrieks sounded occasionally, accompanied by roars of approval. Harsh laughter drifted towards the scouts and Alith cast an anxious glance towards his father, worried by what they would find. Crouching low, the group crested a low hill and saw the Naggarothi camp laid out before them.

A mass of black conical tents encircled an immense pyre, in the light of which Alith saw cavorting figures, their shadows flickering upon earth slick with blood. Figures flailed and cried out in agony upon the flames. Alith saw a huddled mass of elves bound with spiked chains, kicked and tormented by their captors.

As he watched, one of the prisoners was taken from the group and dragged crying towards the pyre. There she was tossed to the ground at the feet of a male elf stripped but for a daemonic metal mask and ragged loincloth made of skin. Alith recognised him immediately for what he was – a high priest of Khaine, the Lord of Murder. He held a long blade in his hand, shockingly similar to the one Elthyrior had been sharpening, and for a moment Alith feared that the raven herald had led him astray. However, the elf in the mask was taller than Elthyrior, his hair dyed white and beaded with raw bone.

Alith watched reluctantly as the priest's victim was dragged to her feet. The Khainite slashed her across the arms and chest and cultists hurried forwards with bowls made from skulls to fill with the blood that spilt from the wounds. They clawed and bit at each other as they tried to catch as much as possible, before raising the obscene cups to their lips and taking deep draughts.

Weak, the captive fell to her knees. The priest grabbed a handful of her hair and cut the skin from her scalp, tossing the bloody trophy onto a pile behind him. Screaming in pain, the maiden was again hauled to her feet, her feeble struggle no match for her captors as she was spitted upon a spear and driven into the fire. Another great cheer rose up from the camp, chilling in its adoration of the slaughter.

'We cannot see them all from here,' said Anadriel, an elf-maiden who Alith had known for as long as he could remember. For years she had helped those who had displeased Morathi escape the clutches of the cults and brought them to Elanardris. Her sharp features were set impassively, and Alith could only guess how many times before she had witnessed the horrors unfolding below. 'We need to move closer.'

Eothlir nodded, signalling for Anadriel to lead the way. They followed a snaking trail down the hillside, plunging into a grove of trees. Anadriel led them surely between the thin trunks, heading for the light of the fires.

All of a sudden she stopped, her bow in hand and an arrow ready. Alith glanced ahead and saw two figures silhouetted against the firelight. He slowly bent an arrow to his bow and joined Anadriel, glancing to the left and right to see if there were any others close at hand.

'You take the one on the left,' she said, her eyes fixed on the staggering cultists, a male and a female. It was clear what the couple intended, and disgust welled up inside Alith as he watched the pair trot hand in hand into the woods, their bodies smeared with blood.

'Now,' sighed Anadriel and Alith let go the bowstring. The arrow sped surely between the tree trunks and took the male elf in the throat. Anadriel's shaft hit the eye of his companion. Both fell without a sound. Undiscovered, the party moved forwards again until they were hidden in the shadows of the tents.

Alith turned at the sound of metal scraping and a brief, wet noise. His father had a cultist's body cradled in one arm, his knife bloody in the other hand.

'Swiftly, the distraction of the ceremony will not last forever,' said Eothlir, lowering the corpse to the ground and dragging it further into the darkness.

They made their way stealthily through the tents until the words of the high priest could be clearly heard. Eothlir despatched Anadriel and Lotherin to the left and right to count the enemy's number.

Alith felt a hand on his arm and realised that he had made to stand, his bow in hand. Eothlir gave him a shake of the head.

'Tomorrow,' he whispered. 'Tomorrow we make them pay.'

'What of those yet to be sacrificed?' demanded Alith. He felt an almost physical pain at the thought of what was about to happen. Eothlir simply shook his head again, eyes averted.

Alith forced himself to listen to the tirade of hatred spilling from the high priest.

'Hearken to me, the Herald of Khaine. As the libations of the King of Blood pour over us, let us remember that which Khaine calls upon us to do. Cast out the impure and make testament to their weakness with the offerings of their flesh. Raise your voices in praise of their deaths, and take strength from the Lord of Murder so that you might strike down those who would scorn our bloody master!'

A vicious baying and howling welled up from the assembled elves. The high priest raised his left hand above his head and in the grip of his fist a gory heart dripped blood down his arm.

'Mighty Khaine, look upon these offerings and be placated. Grant us your power so that we can slay the traitor who has disowned you, and slaughter his misguided followers upon the pyres of your glory.'

More screeching accompanied this proclamation as the cultists worked themselves into a shrieking horde.

'Let he who has turned his back upon you be cut down and his organs thrown upon the fires in repentance for his misdeeds. Let the ill-begotten heir of your chosen son perish in the ashes of vengeance. Let crimson retribution spill from his corpse to wash away the perfidies of his deeds.'

The priest tossed the heart into the crowds, who fought over their prize like a pack of wild dogs. The Herald of Khaine's voice was calmer though it still carried easily across his followers.

'We are many, they are few,' he told the Khainites. 'Even now the hated foe thinks he is on the brink of victory. Little does he suspect the agony that awaits. His is a false victory, devoid of Khaine's blessings. Even as he rejoices in his empty triumph, he crows at the heart of a trap. None shall leave Ealith alive. Death to Malekith!'

'Death to Malekith!' chorused the crowd, at the crescendo of their frenzy, slashing at their chests and arms with daggers, matting their hair with their own gore. The mob descended upon the remaining captives. Alith turned away, filled with a mixture of loathing and dread. The blood-curdling cries of the Khainites reverberated around the camp, thousands of voices raised in bloodthirsty praise that made Alith's skin crawl. The wind gusted towards him and the stench of charring flesh wafted between the tents, causing him to gag.

There was a flutter of shadows to the left and Lotherin returned, his face grim. Alith noticed a cut upon his cheek and blood upon his hands.

'Ten thousand Khainites, perhaps many more,' Lotherin told Eothlir. 'There is a further camp to the west, where there are trained warriors of Anlec: perhaps another five thousand spears and bows.'

Eothlir nodded at this news, his expression distant. Anadriel rejoined them shortly after and confirmed Lotherin's estimate. There were several thousand cultists attending the rituals and many thousands more scattered across the camp in narcotic stupors.

'I have seen enough,' said Eothlir, signalling for them to move back out of the camp. 'Tomorrow we must be ready for battle.'

ALITH PROWLED HIS grandfather's tent like a trapped wolf, pacing back and forth as he listened to the army commanders making their plans. The words of Elthyrior gnawed at him, their sinister warning vague but nagging. As Eoloran outlined the disposition of the Anars' companies, Alith's exasperation took hold.

'Wait!' he barked, and suddenly felt the stares of the others fall upon him. He calmed himself before continuing, looking directly at his father. 'You heard the words of the Herald of Khaine. Malekith is trapped at Ealith and we cannot hope to reach him. What purpose do we serve by throwing ourselves into the grip of our foes?'

'What other course would you suggest?' asked Caenthras, his voice cold with scorn. 'To slink back to the mountains to await Morathi's ire? We must push forwards and link up with Prince Malekith, unite our strength.'

'And if that strength is spent in this one fruitless endeavour?' countered Alith, trying to present himself as reasoned rather than fearful though the elven lord's anger had shaken him. 'On a hunt, one might get a single shot to fell the prey. The hunter learns when to shoot and when to wait. If we loose our shaft too soon, our target knows us and can react.'

'And if one dithers, the opportunity for the killing strike may be missed,' growled Caenthras. He took a breath and cast his gaze at Eoloran, who was scowling at the noble's outburst, before returning his stare to Alith. 'Forgive my anger, Alith. For long years we have waited, seeking the moment when we can attack. To hesitate invites disaster. I would not be content to sit in my hall and see that moment pass by, nagged by doubts that we stood idle when we should have acted. And on what would we base our strategy? The boastful rhetoric of an intoxicated priest? We cannot be sure that Malekith's position is as forlorn as the Herald of Khaine would have his followers believe.'

Alith smarted at the intimation in Caenthras's words but held his retort, knowing that Elthyrior had presaged the Herald of Khaine's words but unable to reveal this knowledge. Caenthras turned his attention back to Eoloran and rested his fists upon the table on which the map charts were spread.

'Though perhaps we cannot aid Malekith directly, we can still help. An attack now will distract the foe, drawing the eyes of some away from the prince. If we do nothing, the thousands that camp north of us will march on Malekith's position, closing the trap. Should we not intervene? Should we not do what we can to weaken that trap?'

'Your strategy has merit,' said Eoloran. 'The fewer forces Malekith must face, the better his chances for escape.'

'I have another fear,' added Alith. 'Who guards Elanardris while we fight here? Who is to say that Morathi's next blow will not fall upon our homes rather than us? What victory is there to win tomorrow only to return to our lands to find them in the clutches of our enemies?'

This argument bit home and a look of anguish passed across Eoloran's face. His gaze flickered between Alith and Caenthras, and then rested upon Eothlir.

'My son, this is not my decision alone,' Eoloran said heavily. 'Though I am lord of the Anars, I am steward for their future under your rule. You have been silent. I would hear what you have to say.'

'Give me a moment to think,' said Eothlir.

He walked slowly from the pavilion and left the others in silence. Caenthras pored over the charts on the table, avoiding the gazes of others, while Alith took up a stool and sat to one side. The quiet was heavy with anxiety and Alith longed to leave, having said his piece. He forced himself to remain, though he could sense the resentment of some of the elves present, not least Caenthras. Fearful of alienating the father of the one he loved, part of Alith hoped that Eothlir judged in Caenthras's favour and would allow Alith to make amends. Though Caenthras had seemed supportive before, Alith did not know how the proud elf would take the decision going against him.

The tent flap opened with a snap and all looked up. There was purpose written on Eothlir's face.

'We fight,' he declared. 'We cannot stand by while atrocity is committed, though only fate knows at what price. The crimes of the cultists cannot go unpunished. For good or ill, there is a time when we must look to others and a time when we must look to our own. Prince Malekith must be restored to the throne for the future of Nagarythe and we must play whatever part we can.'

'I concur,' said Eoloran. 'Tomorrow we slay the Khainites and then we shall look again at what course of action we must take. Are we agreed?'

Caenthras nodded his assent immediately. Alith stood slowly and looked at his father and grandfather.

'None will fight harder than I,' he declared. 'We will avenge.'

WITH THE DAWN sun glinting on speartips and armour, the army of the Anars broke camp and marched north. It was Eoloran's strategy to come upon the cultists as swiftly as possible, before they moved further west towards Malekith at Ealith.

The Khainites would be ill-disciplined and eager to attack, so the lord of the Anars split his host into three parts. At the fore he sent swift-moving scouts who would circle to the flanks of the enemy and remain out of sight until the battle began. Alith was tasked with leading the right wing of this attack while Anadriel commanded the left. Eoloran was very specific that these flanking forces would target the disciplined Anlec warriors and draw them out of the camp. It was imperative that they were pulled away from the main fighting line but were not allowed to engage the scouts directly. Alith was to withdraw as soon as the enemy came close, dragging their foes away from the Khainites.

Meanwhile, Eothlir and the spear companies would form the main advance to take up a defensive position on the hills overlooking the enemy camp. The remaining archers, under Eoloran, would rain down their arrows upon the cultists and goad them into an unfavourable attack up the slopes.

Alith was tense with anxiety and excitement as he marched northwards at the head of five hundred elves. The rugged terrain and dawn twilight concealed the force and soon they moved out of sight of the main part of the Anar host. Alith realised that this was real and not some story; that he was in charge of a company of elves marching into battle. Unlike his grandfather and father he had never commanded other elves, and the experience was very different to the lone hunts he enjoyed so much. For the first time he truly felt as a lord of the Anars, gripped equally by the glory and the heavy responsibility.

His thoughts turned to Elanardris and his mother, knowing that she would be at the manse wondering what became of her family. He was determined to return with pride. His mind swiftly moved to Ashniel. Would she be impressed? Alith was convinced that she would be. She adored her warrior-father, and Alith's experience in battle would surely increase his standing in her eyes.

As the sun rose and the scouts moved swiftly north, Alith allowed himself to daydream a little, picturing the scene of his triumphant return. Ashniel would be stood on the steps of the porch at the manse, a flowing dress tugged by the breeze, her hair streaming. Alith would run up the long path and they would embrace, her tears of joy wet on his cheeks. So gripping was the fantasy that Alith stubbed his toe on a rock, bringing him back to the present in a flash of pain. Chiding himself for his immaturity, Alith checked on his warriors and saw that none had seen his stumble, or were polite enough to feign disinterest. Realising that soon he would need all of his focus and skill, Alith gritted his teeth, gripped his bow tighter and strode onwards.

THE THOUGHTS OF Alith's father were very different. He was no stranger to battle, having spent several hundred years in the colonies before returning to Elanardris to start a family. This time was different. His army did not face savage orcs and goblins or bestial creatures from the dark forests of Elthin Arvan; his foe this day was one he had never thought he would face. Even in the dark times that had shrouded the latter years of Morathi's rule, Eothlir had never envisaged fighting against his own people. The fight at the manse had been instinctual, reacting to attack. Now he found himself leading several thousand of his subjects to purposefully slay other elves.

The thought was disquieting, not least because Eothlir felt no inevitability about the battle ahead. He could have convinced his father to return to Elanardris with their weapons still sheathed, but he had chosen not to. As the tramp of booted feet sounded around him, Eothlir was perturbed by the notion that he wanted this conflict. He worried that the same desire for bloodshed that drove the Khainites to their depraved acts nestled somewhere in the dark recesses of his spirit.

His concerns brought to mind a tale his father had once told him. Eoloran had only spoken of the event once and refused to be drawn on it again. The event Eoloran had related had taken place shortly after the Phoenix King had drawn the Widowmaker from the altar of Khaine, the infamous weapon that was said to hold the power to slay gods and destroy armies. Eoloran always refused to speak of the Sword of Khaine by name, often calling it simply the Doom or 'that infernal blade'. There would be a haunted look in his eye as he spoke of the Widowmaker, a distant memory of sights that Eothlir would never see, even in nightmare.

The particular story recalled by Eothlir concerned fighting at Ealith, the same fortress that Malekith currently held. A great army of daemons had appeared in the mountains and swept down across the hills, over the lands that would one day be ruled by the Anars. The raven heralds, Aenarion's swift-moving eyes and ears, had brought word to the Phoenix King at Anlec and he had set forth with his host to confront the legion of Chaos.

At Ealith Aenarion made his stand and during an endless night of fighting through which the skies shimmered with ghostly lights and the ground itself burned underfoot, the daemons hurled themselves at the citadel's walls. Though the greater part of the Chaotic host was destroyed, Aenarion was intent on their utter annihilation. Atop his great dragon Indraugnir, the Phoenix King led his army from the fortress, Caledor the Mage at his side, Eoloran and a hundred other great princes behind him. Eoloran had described the battle-fever that had gripped him, the jubilant singing of Khaine that rang in his ears from 'that infernal blade'. He remembered nothing else but the constant slash of sword and thrust of spear, and a joyous love of death in his heart.

Eoloran had spoken of that time with shame, though the cause in which he had slain with such happiness and abandon had been the most righteous: the survival of the elves. Eothlir could never truly understand what the war against the daemons had meant for an entire generation, but if the self-loathing he felt was but a tenth of their woe he could imagine the horrors that disturbed their dreams.

Another memory came to mind, much more recent: the recollection of the Herald of Khaine's vile sermon and the sacrifices heaped upon the pyre. Unless Eothlir would see such slaughter across all of Ulthuan, this blight had to be stopped. It had consumed Nagarythe and it was clear to Eothlir that such barbarity would spread if left unchecked. The thought fortified his resolve and so he pushed aside his worries until a time when he could allow himself the luxury of doubt and compassion. He realised he must fight without joy or anger, for such temptations could awaken the ancient call of Khaine that still rang down through the centuries from the time of Aenarion.

Today he would slay his fellow elves; tomorrow he would mourn them.

ALITH AND HIS small company crept through the hills surrounding the Khainite camp, wary of sentries. Their caution proved unnecessary, for not a single figure was standing watch and as Alith came to the brow of a hill he could see that the encampment was quiet, the depraved cultists within sated by the debauchery of the previous night.

There was more activity further north and west, amongst the pavilions of the Anlec warriors. Their captains strode between the tents, bellowing orders to assemble their archers and spear companies. At first Alith thought that perhaps they had detected Anadriel's scouts and were responding. After short observation, his fears calmed as the soldiers of Anlec formed up in disciplined ranks in the wide spaces at the centre of their camp, parading and drilling for their officers. Their activity was nothing more than the regular movement of troops in camp.

Circling eastwards, Alith allowed the Khainite camp to disappear from sight, though the smoke from its fires ensured that the archers knew where it was at all times. The sun broke strongly over the mountains to the east, casting its dawn glow across the hillsides. Despite the sunlight, the air was still chill and the breath of the archers misted in the air.

Judging that he had come north of the Khainites, Alith headed directly westwards, towards the Anlec camp. His caution returned as they neared. In scattered groups the Anars' warriors flitted from bush to rock to tree, remaining out of sight. It was not long before they were crouched just beneath the summit of a steep hill, ready to move forwards and overlook the Anlec tents.

Signalling to a couple of his warriors – Anraneir and Khillrallion – Alith sneaked to the brow of the hill and looked out over the formations of the Anlec army. They were still practising their spear and bow drills, moving with precision and speed in a well-rehearsed choreography of simulated battle.

Alith waited nervously for a while, not knowing whether Anadriel was yet in position. He watched the skies as much as the enemy and was relieved when he saw the flitting shape of a hawk dashing from the west, climbing and swooping over the foe's camp. The hawk circled for a while and then flew low, its wingtips brushing the grass of the hillside. With a cry, it settled upon the leafless branch of a bush not far from Alith's right hand. He held up his arm and the hawk swept forwards to land on his wrist, its talons gripping his flesh firmly but not piercing the skin.

'We will attack now,' Alith whispered to the bird, which bobbed its head in acknowledgement before beating its wings and launching into the air once more. Alith watched it skirt around the Anlec encampment and then disappear into a small copse of short firs on the westward side of the camp.

Alith nodded to Anraneir and Khillrallion. They turned and slithered down the hill to pass the word to the other archers. Soon the company of elves were all hidden in the long grass at the hilltop, readied arrows at their bowstrings. Raising himself up to a half-crouch, Alith took a final look at his target.

The outskirts of the camp were no more than a hundred paces away, where several sentries stood with spear and bow, their eyes gazing across the hillsides.

'Now!' barked Alith, loosing his shaft at the closest sentry. The arrow took Alith's victim low in the chest, punching through the silvered breastplate he wore. He collapsed with a shout as more arrows whistled through the air, cutting down the other guards.

The warriors of Anlec were professional fighters and responded quickly. They formed into marching columns, archers to the front, and split into companies. A vanguard of roughly a thousand warriors advanced at a quick march, cutting through the lines of tents along wide paths left for just such a reason. As they did so, Alith and his warriors shot their arrows high into the air, allowing them to fall at a steep angle amongst the ranks of the warriors. Though dozens fell to the deadly shafts, the column continued its implacable advance.

Behind the vanguard, more companies were surging out of the camp towards Alith. Bass horns sounded from the Naggarothi warriors, sending a chill across Alith's skin. Those same notes had once signalled the attack of daemons, calling the loyal followers of Aenarion to war. It seemed perverse to Alith that he and his warriors were now deemed the aggressors, fighting against the armies of Anlec. The tramping of boots sounded heavily in the morning quiet, accompanied by the jingling of mail and the scrape of metal.

There were other pained shouts from the far side of the camp and Alith glanced across the expanse to see the arrows of Anadriel's company filling the air to the west. The Anlec vanguard continued on its course while the companies behind hesitated at a shout from their commander, unsure whether he was responding to a feint or a real attack.

'Keep shooting!' ordered Alith, standing fully to loose a stream of arrows into the Anlec warriors.

The vanguard had reached the edge of the camp and the archers split from the spears. Soon, black-shafted arrows were singing their way through the air back towards the Anar scouts. Alith heard shouts of pain and looked to his left to see several elves lying in the thick grass, arrows protruding from their bodies. Two were not moving, two more quickly pulled free the shafts and bound their wounds.

The spearmen were no more than seventy paces away and the storm of arrows from the camp's defenders became relentless. A dozen more were wounded as the cloud of shafts fell amongst the Anar scouts.

'Carry the dead, help the wounded!' yelled Alith, letting loose a final shot at the advancing spearmen. 'Head north-east, draw them from the Khainite camp.'

Under the barrage of arrows, the scouts slinked back down the hillside and cut to their right. At a run, they broke from their cover and followed Alith down the dell and up the mound on the opposite side. Here Alith called for them to halt, once more out of sight of the archers in the camp, and they turned their bows upon the spearmen as they crested the hill in front.

The spearmen fell back from the hilltop, and reappeared shortly after, flanked by their supporting archers. As he called for his scouts to retreat once more, Alith wondered how Anadriel was faring and if the Khainites had yet responded. Focussed on the enemy ahead of him, he realised that it was going to be a long morning.

THE HAWK CIRCLING high above signalled to Eothlir that Alith and Anadriel were about to start their attacks. All was ready above the Khainite encampment as well. He was stood beside Eoloran looking down on the Khainites. In his left hand Eothlir carried the furled banner of House Anar, in his right he held the golden blade Cyarith, the Sword of Dawn's Vengeance. The weapon felt warm to his touch, feeding upon the rays of the morning sun that broke over the mountains, its keen edge glittering with magical energy.

Behind Eoloran stood Caenthras, a curling ram's horn decorated with bands of silver in his hand. At a nod from the lord of the Anars, Caenthras raised the instrument to his lips and let forth a long pealing note, high in pitch. Three times more he sounded the blast, the notes echoing from the hillsides and reverberating across the camp below.

Eothlir waited a few moments while the stupefied elves roused themselves at the sound of the horn. He saw the Herald of Khaine striding from a pavilion with bloodstained walls, his burnished mask gleaming. The priest was gesticulating wildly, summoning his followers from their slumber. When a good number had gathered around their leader, Eothlir let slip the knot upon the standard and the great flag unfurled. He lifted it high so that the symbol could clearly be seen.

Planting the banner into the soft turf of the hilltop, Eothlir took a step forwards. Caenthras blew another long, high note to ensure that all eyes were upon the hillside.

'Behold the mighty Eoloran Anar, lord of these lands,' shouted Eothlir. 'You are trespassers in this realm. Lord Anar demands that this ragged mob departs immediately and slinks back to the dark holes that spawned it. He renounces the accusations of cowards who would slaughter those that cannot protect themselves, and dares his unworthy foes to match their blades against true warriors. He is not without mercy and will hear the pleas of all who beg forgiveness for the crimes they have committed. All who recant their false faith will be granted the peace of Isha.'

Eothlir took a step back as Caenthras sounded the horn once more to signal the declaration was complete.

'That should get their attention,' said Eoloran with a grim smile. 'I think the "peace of Isha" part in particular will get them going.'

Eothlir could not help but smile himself, knowing that the taunts would have precisely the effect he had intended. He glanced over his shoulder and saw the thousands of the Anars' warriors standing ready out of sight. Archers were lined up just below the crests of the surrounding hills, the spear companies arranged behind. Banners slapped in the morning air and the sun shone from the keen edges of speartips and the points of arrows. Dressed in dark blue, the host looked like a deep lake glittering in the sunlight.

'Here they come,' muttered Caenthras.

Eothlir turned his attention back to the camp to see several hundred Khainites racing from the tents towards the Anars. He shook his head slightly, almost embarrassed by the ease with which the ploy was working. Truly their foes had given up any right to be considered sane and civilised folk.

Eoloran turned and marched down the hill, signalling for the archers to move forwards. He crossed to join the right wing of the army as the first of the Khainites reached the foot of the slope in front.

These were the worst fanatics, utterly heedless of their own lives as they charged forwards, knives and swords in their hands, their skin patterned with bloody handprints, their hair slicked into gory spines. Their headlong rush did not falter as the thousands of archers appeared at the summit of the hill.

Eothlir heard his father give the command and watched without emotion as a black cloud of shafts filled the air. The arrow storm dropped down the hillside, falling upon the cultists in a dark mass. Not a single charging Khainite survived that first volley.

The Herald of Khaine was mustering a more coherent force. His hoarse screams could be heard on the wind as the high priest and his underlings moved along the unsteady line of Khainites, sprinkling them with blood from the sacrifices, exhorting them to slay the offenders of the Lord of Murder. As during the ceremony of the night before, the cultists were baying and howling and screaming, offering praises to Khaine or simply giving wordless voice to their seething rages.

Drums joined the cacophony of bellows and shrieks, pounding out a rapid beat that thundered from the hillsides. Just hearing their martial rhythm caused Eothlir's heart to thump faster, his pulse singing in his ears. That there was some magic woven into the incessant drumbeats was inescapable as he felt his anger rising and had to fight the urge to charge forwards. A glance showed that Caenthras and the others were suffering similar temptation.

'Hold fast!' Eothlir called out. 'Await my command!'

He raised his right arm outwards and held out Cyarith at shoulder level, as if it were a barrier to the thousands of spearmen waiting behind him. His hand trembled for a moment, the grip of the ancient sword growing ever hotter in his palm as his excitement fuelled its magic further. Eothlir could feel the sword drawing in energy from the air around him, and he licked his dry lips.

The Herald of Khaine strode forwards at the head of thousands of his followers. The drumbeats continued and were joined by the pattering of bare feet on hard soil. The cultists' screeching had become a singular chant – 'Khaine! Khaine! Khaine!' – which caused Eothlir's skin to crawl as dark energies churned in the skies above. Though the air was clear, the redness of the dawn light deepened, turning to a crimson shroud above and around the elves. Eothlir's magical senses thrummed to an invisible pulsating, in tune with the rapid beating of his heart.

Advancing faster than his warriors, the Herald of Khaine stopped a dozen paces in front of them. He theatrically drew two knives from his belt and Eothlir almost flinched at the sight of the sacrificial daggers. Though impossible for even an elf to see at that distance, Eothlir could feel the runes of Khaine etched into the blades, a burning mark in his mind.

Crossing his arms so that he held out each blade to the opposite shoulder, in one fluid motion the Herald of Khaine drew their edges across his chest. Blood welled up from the wounds as he flung his arms out to the sides. Droplets of crimson fluid flew from the tips of the blades and hung in the air.

A sickness gripped Eothlir as he watched the droplets dissipate into a growing red mist, a cloud of blood that increased in depth until the Herald was obscured from view. The cloud continued to expand, rolling up the hillside towards Eothlir and cascading down the slope to envelop the Khainites.

'Shoot!' Eothlir called out to his father, realising that soon the enemy would all be hidden.

Eoloran did not question the command of his son and signalled for his archers. In long lines they loosed their missiles upon the chanting mob below. Many Khainites fell to the volley, pierced by the Anars' arrows, but soon the survivors were swathed in the red mist. The archers continued to shoot into the roiling mass as it boiled towards them, though with little hope of finding their marks.

Eothlir realised that soon the whole hill would be engulfed by the enchantment and the archers rendered useless. Without waiting for any order from his father, he turned to the spearmen upon the slopes behind.

'Advance to your positions, quickly!' he bellowed, raising his sword above his head and swinging it forwards as if he could drag the spear companies into position. Horn blasts signalled the advance and soon the steady march of thousands of booted feet sounded on the hillside.

The crimson fog was at the summit of the hill and within moments Eothlir could taste blood upon his tongue as the unnatural cloud swallowed him into its ruddy depths. Trickles of blood ran down his face and stained his silver mail, gathering in pools between the fine links. His grip upon Cyarith became slick and, looking down at his hand, Eothlir realised that so tight was his fist, his nails had drawn blood from his palm, his own blood mixing with the roiling cloud around him.

Dark figures appeared in the fog around him, ruddy shapes silhouetted by the rising sun behind them. With a sigh of relief, Eothlir saw familiar faces – Thorinan, Casadir, Lirunein and others loyal to the Anars. Elegant white shields to the front, black-hafted spears levelled forwards, the warriors of House Anar gathered around their commanders.

HUNDREDS OF ARCHERS lined the hilltops surrounding the Anlec camp, more than a match for the bows under Alith's command. The scouts were dispersed along a ridgeline looking west towards the Anlec warriors, taking what cover they could amongst the scattered bushes and high grass.

A tap on the shoulder drew Alith's attention to Anraneir, who pointed to the south. Alith could see a strange hue in the distance, a red miasma that swathed the hills surrounding the Khainite encampment. He did not understand what he saw, but knew it did not bode well.

At that moment, Alith heard the tramping of boots resounding from beyond the hillside opposite. Though the source of the noise was hidden from view, after a while it was clear that the sound was moving southwards. With his apprehension rising, Alith realised that the Anlec spearmen were heading out of the camp towards the main Anar army, content that the archers protected them.

'It seems our prey does not wish to bite on the bait any more,' said Anraneir.

Alith nodded, his brow knotted in thought. The plan had been to draw away the Anlec warriors, but it had failed. There was little that a few hundred bows could do against such a host if the enemy considered them no threat.

'We have to get their attention,' said Alith, backing down the slope of the hill and gesturing for Anraneir to follow him. 'When the prey eludes the hunter, the hunter turns to Kurnous.'

Anraneir looked on in puzzlement as Alith drew an arrow from the quiver at his back. The young noble rang a finger thoughtfully along the shaft from feather to tip, his finger lingering on the sharp arrowhead.

Alith then spoke the word of fire used in the shrines of Kurnous and the arrow's head sprang into flame, burning bright yellow. Angling his bow high into the air, Alith fired the flaming arrow in the direction of the camp. The flickering of the fire sailed high into the air and then disappeared out of sight.

'Spread the word to the others,' said Alith. 'Target the camp with fire.'

Anraneir smiled appreciatively before hurrying along the line of scouts to pass on Alith's orders. Alith took out another arrow and repeated the process of lighting its head, before shooting again. Soon flares of light arced out from along the hillside, descending into the camp beyond the enemy archers. Alith could not tell how many shafts found a mark, but after several volleys, thicker, blacker smoke rose into the air.

'It's working,' Anraneir laughed, returning to Alith's side.

Crawling forwards to the brow of the hill, Alith saw that the Anlec archers were advancing, arrows nocked to their bows. If the scouts simply retreated directly away from their advancing foes, they would soon be out of range of the camp.

'Circle to the north, keep out of sight,' commanded Alith, stowing his bow and crawling back to Anraneir. 'Though I have danced very little, I know enough that one should take the lead.'

'And what a merry dance it shall be,' said Anraneir.

THE RED MIST obscured all sight beyond twenty paces, and Eothlir was tense as he peered into the shifting depths, seeking some sign of the enemy. Their howling and shouting was getting closer, but the sound was muffled by the unnatural fog.

'Silence!' Eothlir bellowed and within moments the lines of spearmen had fallen still, so that not a clink of armour or whispered word broke the quiet.

Eothlir listened carefully to the approaching noise of the Khainites. It seemed loudest to his left.

'Look to the west!' he warned.

No sooner had the words left his lips than a dark mass appeared in the gloom, quickly resolving into running figures. Thousands of Khainites poured up the slope, yelling and panting, wielding wicked daggers and swords with serrated blades. Their faces were twisted into leers of hatred and masks of total fury as they charged.

The cultists hurled themselves at the Anar spearmen, leaping from their feet a few paces distant and descending with flashing blades. Shields were raised to ward off the blows and the clash of metal echoed dully through the mist. Anar battle cries and praises to Khaine filled the air along with the chime of blades meeting.

Eothlir could not see clearly what was happening, but soon his concern was drawn directly ahead as more Khainites came rushing up the slope.

'Take prisoners if you can,' growled Eothlir. 'My father would question those who plot with Morathi. Take the Herald of Khaine alive, if possible.'

The cultists were barely a dozen paces away and sprinting towards the Anars. Eothlir raised Cyarith in one hand and slipped a dagger from his belt with the other. When the cultists were no more than six paces away, the Anar prince leapt to the attack, Cyarith cutting the head from one Khainite while his knife slashed across the bare chest of another.

Dodging a blade aimed for his face, Eothlir parried another attack and drove the point of his sword into the throat of a third cultist. A moment later, the spearline crashed into the Khainites all around him, unleashing the chaos of battle.

The wall of speartips scythed down the foremost cultists and the Anars pressed on, stabbing with their spears and smashing aside their wounded foes with their shields. The controlled ferocity of the phalanx was more than a match for the raw aggression of the Khainites, who were thrust back by the counter-attack.

'Keep to the high ground!' bellowed Eothlir, worried that the momentum of the spearmen would carry them too far down the slope.

Keeping their line, Eothlir's company backed off to the crest of the hill. The Khainites renewed their assault, ducking beneath the spears to hack at the legs of their enemy. Eothlir parried, chopped and slashed with Cyarith, cutting down any cultist that approached. The wounded of both sides were quickly mounting, as injured elves fell into the grass crying out in pain. The Khainites were unheeding of their losses and pushed on, driven by their bloodthirst. The spearmen were resolute in the face of the deranged murderers, stepping forwards to fill the holes in the line left by the fallen.

Caught in the maelstrom of blades and screams, Eothlir could do nothing but fight for his life. He chopped the arm from a raging cultist and drove his dagger into the groin of another. Blades shrieked from his armour as he punched a Khainite in the face, his gauntlet breaking bone. A wide swing with Cyarith severed the leg of yet another foe, who tumbled down the slope still screaming obscenities.

Eothlir felt a wave of dismay, almost like a chill breeze upon his flesh. It came from the right, accompanied by shrill cries of pain and lamenting wails. Cutting through more cultists, Eothlir pushed his way towards the disturbance. As he shouldered aside one of his own warriors, the melee opened up and Eothlir saw the Herald of Khaine.

The blood-drenched high priest was surrounded by a pile of several corpses, his long daggers held out to each side. Scarred runes upon his flesh burned with dark flame and his daemon mask writhed and snarled with magic. Leaving ghost-like red shadows in his wake, the priest leapt forwards and slashed with his right-hand blade, the dagger slicing clean through a shield and sending the arm holding it flying through the air. No blade or armour could hold against those Khaine-cursed daggers, and more elves fell to their wicked attentions in moments.

A spearman dragged himself to his feet behind the Herald of Khaine, leaning heavily on his weapon. With visible effort, the warrior thrust his spear into the priest's back until the point lanced from his stomach.

The Herald of Khaine fell to his knees, but only for a moment. Surging upright, he turned, ripping the spear from the elf's grasp. A hand flicked out and a dagger appeared in the spearman's face, sending him screaming to the floor. Snapping the shaft transfixing him, the Herald of Khaine ripped free the spear and cast the two parts upon the ground. Blood gushed from the wound and spilled onto the ground at the priest's feet.

'Accept this offering, my most beloved of lords!' the Herald cried out, lifting his bloodied hands into the air.

Black flame enveloped the Herald of Khaine's fingertips, spread down his arms and then coruscated across the priest's wounded body. His flesh cracked and burned, but as the flakes fell away they revealed untarnished skin, and the grievous wound was no more.

As the magical fire flickered and faltered, the Herald stepped forwards and stooped to pull his knife from the dead spearman. In moments the Herald was attacking again, cleaving a bloody path through the Anars' warriors.

Eothlir slashed his way through the throng of cultists surging forwards in the gory wake of their leader. He cut at arms and legs, plunged Cyarith through breastbones and hewed through necks in a constant whirl of blades.

'Face a true son of Nagarythe!' roared the Anar prince as he burst from amongst the falling bodies of his foes.

The Herald of Khaine whirled to face Eothlir, white flame burning in the eyeholes of his mask. The glare of that unnatural gaze froze Eothlir with terror for it seemed as if he looked into the eyes of the Bloody-Handed God himself.

'Your agony will be most pleasing to my lord,' crowed the Herald, his voice harsh, edged with the ring of metal. 'None triumph in battle without his blessing, and your fate is sealed.'

The Herald of Khaine dashed forwards, breaking the link between his eyes and Eothlir's. Out of instinct, the prince ducked and threw himself to the right, narrowly avoiding the priest's daggers, which screamed as they cut the air.

Rolling to his feet, Eothlir knocked aside the next blow with the blade of Cyarith and lunged forwards with his knife. The Herald swayed away from the jab and backed off, stepping quickly on the balls of his feet. He wove his knives in a complex pattern, their fluid movement mesmerising. Eothlir kept his eyes fixed upon his opponent's mask, ignoring the horror that crawled up his spine from the entwining sigil drawn in the air by the knife blades.

Eothlir dropped his left shoulder and then spun to the right, Cyarith flicking out to catch the wrist of the Herald. The priest's hand spun through the air still clutching its baleful dagger. Eothlir jumped back as the Herald struck back as quick as a serpent, the tip of his knife flashing less than a finger's width from Eothlir's throat. Edging sideways, Eothlir looked for an opening to attack the Herald's good arm, hoping to disarm him of the weapons that gave him so much power.

Just as he saw his opportunity, Caenthras dashed past, roaring with anger. He held his spear two-handed – Khiratoth, the Ruinclaw – and drove its point clean through the Herald's chest. Blue fire erupted from Khiratoth, tearing the Herald of Khaine apart, the priest's body exploding into a pall of smoke-wreathed destruction. Without a backwards glance, Caenthras charged through the dissipating remains of the priest and into the cultists, who had momentarily stopped their attack, dismayed at their leader's demise.

Caught unawares by Caenthras's sudden attack, Eothlir hesitated a moment, trying to clear his head. Though some cultists broke and ran from Caenthras, many crowded forwards, growling and snarling, hungry for vengeance. Eothlir gathered his nerve as the spearmen around him closed ranks and prepared to face a fresh assault.

DESPITE ALITH'S BEST efforts, the Anlec host had pushed his scouts out of bowshot from the camp. The enemy stood just out of range, serried ranks of spearmen glowering from the opposite hilltop. The sun was nearing midday as the two forces faced off against each other, their commanders waiting to see what happened next.

'So, we have their attention, what do we do now?' asked Anraneir.

'Something is troubling me,' replied Alith, giving voice to a doubt that had been slowly growing within. 'I see bows and I see spears, but I see no horses. The armies of Anlec are based upon archers, spearmen and knights.'

'So, where are the knights?' asked Anraneir, looking over his shoulder as if to see enemy cavalry approaching at that moment.

'Perhaps the Khainites ate their steeds,' laughed Khillrallion.

'I would guess that they have moved ahead towards Ealith, to threaten Malekith,' said Alith.

'What if they return?' Khillrallion said with a grimace. 'We cannot outrun knights.'

'We must remain here so that the Khainites receive no reinforcement,' said

Alith. 'For better or worse, there is little we can do about the situation. If we withdraw, the warriors will simply move south and attack my grandfather's army.'

'It would be wise to have a plan for what happens if their cavalry show up,' said Anraneir.

Alith looked around, seeing only the scattered bushes and trees of the Annulii foothills. Though these were his family's lands, he did not know them with the intimacy of the mountains. He might well have been in Saphery or Chrace for the little local knowledge he had.

'This might help,' said Anraneir, proffering a rolled-up parchment. Alith took it and let it fall open, revealing one of Eoloran's maps.

'Where are we now?' asked Alith, wishing that he had paid more attention at the war council.

With a sigh, Anraneir pointed to the north-west and then to the map.

'Ealith lies that way, we're on the edges of the foothills, here,' the scout explained. 'If we need to hide from cavalry, I suggest the Athrian Vale, north and east of here. If enemy cavalry approach, we can be under the eaves before they're upon us.'

'Provided that we get enough warning,' added Khillrallion.

'Good point,' said Alith. He nodded at Anraneir, handing back the map. 'Take five scouts and head north to keep watch for unpleasant arrivals.'

Anraneir placed the map back in his pack and set off at a trot, calling out names. Alith tapped his fingers on the broad silver buckle of his belt, seemingly deep in thought. The spearmen opposite had remained in place and gave no sign that they intended to attack.

Alith turned suddenly towards Khillrallion.

'Any suggestions for what to do now?' asked Alith.

Khillrallion thought for a moment, a smile creeping across his lips.

'I know some good songs…'

WHOEVER COMMANDED THE Anlec force, Alith admired his patience, if not his loyalties. Noon came and went and the black-armoured warriors stood guard against an attack from the scouts, standing in silent ranks while the air grew hotter and hotter. It would have been foolish to chase the lightly-armoured elves, for there was no hope of catching them. Instead, the Anlec officer was content to wait. The enemy's contentment unnerved Alith. He fretted that he was missing some kind of trick, and worried that his opponent knew something Alith did not – such as when the cavalry would be returning.

Every now and then, Alith led his scouts forwards a little way, shot some arrows at the Anlec ranks and then withdrew to a new position. He did this mainly out of boredom, though he justified it to himself with the notion that such harassment would be sapping the morale of his foes. The truth was that his scouts were left with perhaps half a dozen arrows each, and if the enemy decided to come after them there was little they could do except run.

As midday passed into mid-afternoon, Alith looked constantly to the south for some sign of his father and grandfather; he gazed to the north for warning of approaching cavalry. He was confident that the main force would be victorious over the Khainites, but as time passed he longed to see the banners of the Anars appearing over the hills.

'LOOK,' SAID KHILLRALLION, nodding to the south.

'Finally,' Alith sighed as he saw the telltale silvery shimmer of armoured warriors crossing a distant hilltop.

The enemy commander had also noted this development. Ignoring the scouts, his companies turned quickly southwards and deployed to meet this new enemy. Alith was about to give the order to close in behind the Anlec columns when a shout drew his attention to the north.

'Riders!' yelled Anraneir, running along a ridgeline to the north. 'Hundreds of them!'

'North-east!' bellowed Alith, rising to his feet. 'Run!'

The scouts sprinted down the slope, leaping nimbly over bushes and rocks. Keeping a swift but steady pace they headed towards the woods of Athrian Vale, casting glances to the north. Alith spied a cloud of dust on the horizon, growing nearer with some speed, though the riders themselves were yet hidden from view.

'Faster!' he urged his warriors, picking up speed.

THE TREES OF Athrian Vale came into view as Alith reached the crest of a tall hill. In the vale below, a stream meandered down from the distant mountains. Slender pines crowded to the river's banks and spread out across the deep valley where the waterway widened, an expanse of trees large enough to conceal the fleeing elves.

Alith could feel the ground trembling from thousands of hoofbeats, a rumbling that grew louder and louder as he sprinted towards the first few trees scattered around the border of the woods. The jingle of harnesses was audible too, as were shouts. Ducking beneath the branches of a tree, Alith risked a glance to his left and saw long lines of riders cresting a hill barely two hundred paces away.

Swathed in the dust thrown up by their galloping mounts, the riders appeared through the murk. These were not the sinister black-armoured knights of Anlec. They were dressed in bright blue and white, with armour of silvery mail. Their banners bore blazons of white horses and horses' heads and their helms were decorated with gaily-coloured feathers.

'Ellyrians!' laughed Alith, sliding to a stop on the fine carpet of needles beneath the gloom of the trees. He knew not how they came to be here so far from home, but grinned widely at the sight. He turned and jogged back to the edge of the wood to watch the reaver knights of Ellyrion sweep down the hillside. Other scouts stood close at hand looking at the same spectacle.

The riders carried leaf-bladed spears in their hands and the bright tack of their steeds glinted in the sun. As they came closer, Alith could see their faces, and the sight sent a shiver running through his body. They were grim of expression as they lowered their spears for a charge. Others had bows in their hands and loosed arrows at the fall gallop, the shafts falling towards Alith and his scouts.

'Into the trees!' he yelled, bounding towards the nearest trunk and leaping up into the branches with the surefootedness of a cat. Climbing higher through the pricking needles, he ran to the end of one branch and crouched there.

'Friends!' he shouted out, cupping his hands to his mouth to be heard over the panting of steeds and the thunder of hooves. 'Stay your weapons!'

Dozens of reavers converged upon the tree, bowstrings bent and arrows nocked. A knot of knights came forwards beneath a long pennant displaying a silver horse on a circle of blue, the banner decorated with a white mane.

'House Anar!' shouted Alith though he did not know whether the name would be of any import to the Ellyrians.

A rider with a golden helm topped with a horsehair crest rode from the circling elves, his spear couched beneath one arm, a gold shield embossed with a rearing stallion on the other.

'I am Prince Aneltain of Ellyrion,' the elf called out, shielding his eyes against the sun to peer at Alith.

'Alith Anar,' replied Alith, standing up warily. 'Announce your allegiance and explain your presence in our lands.'

'I have sworn loyalty to the Phoenix King and have just this past night ridden to war alongside Prince Malekith, rightful ruler of Nagarythe. I head for the Pass of the Unicorn to take word back to Prince Finudel, my liege.'

Alith leapt nimbly from the branch and landed in the long grass not far from Aneltain. He raised a hand in welcome as the mounted elves closed in around him, circling menacingly.

'I am son of Eothlir, grandson of Eoloran Anar,' Alith announced. 'We fight the same foe as you.'

Alith turned and pointed to the south.

'Even now, the warriors of House Anar fight the traitors of Anlec. Your presence would be most welcomed by my grandfather. Later you can tell us how Prince Malekith fares at Ealith.'

Aneltain leaned over and said something to one of his knights, who brought out a curling horn of gold and sounded a series of notes. At the ringing command, the Ellyrians broke away from the trees and formed into long columns once more, leaving Aneltain alone with Alith. The Ellyrian prince nudged his horse closer to Alith and bent down in the saddle to speak to him. Closer, Alith could see a fresh cut upon the prince's cheek and the dirt of hard travelling on his cloak.

'Ealith was a trap,' Aneltain said with a woeful shake of the head. 'Malekith retreats westwards to take ship at Galthyr. You would do well to return to your homes. We will speak more of this once the enemy at hand are destroyed.'

Before Alith could utter any answer Aneltain had wheeled his horse away and broken into a gallop, heading for the front of his army. Another clarion burst set the knights moving forwards, cantering away to the south, heading for the army of the Anars.

LAUGHTER FILLED EOLORAN'S pavilion, a sound that Alith had not heard for some time. Aneltain and his Ellyrian captains toasted the victory with silver cups of wine. Eothlir was smiling also, though Eoloran's expression was pensive.

'You have the thanks of House Anar,' said Eoloran, raising his own goblet towards Aneltain.

'As you have already told us a dozen times, Eoloran!' replied the Ellyrian prince. 'You owe us no gratitude, for without your host we would have faced the Khainites alone. It was by fortune, or perhaps the weavings of Morai-heg, that Prince Malekith asked me to lead some of my number directly south. Had he not done so, the knights we destroyed not far from Ealith would no doubt have been a match for your army.'

Alith wondered at these words, having already heard from Aneltain that Malekith had sought the Ellyrian out after the battle for Ealith and directed him to ride back to Ellyrion along the Unicorn Pass. It seemed more than coincidence that Elthyrior had promised Alith others would come to confirm his warning that Malekith was trapped. He had no doubt that the rightful ruler of Nagarythe was aware of what the Anars were doing and had sent aid in their direction. As before, Alith chafed at having to withhold this information, knowing that to announce what he knew would betray the pact he had made with Elthyrior.

'Do you think Malekith will reach Galthyr?' asked Caenthras, looking up from the map table where he had been staring at the charts since Alith had arrived. 'By what route will he march to the port? In whose hands will he find it?'

Aneltain shrugged.

'I cannot answer those questions, any more than you can,' said the prince. 'I entered Nagarythe for the first time only days ago. These are not my lands; I know nothing of their people. I will say that if any of us can escape the clutches of the cultists, it is Malekith. His army is strong and the march not overly long. The prince himself is the greatest warrior and most skilful commander I have ever seen. His personal fleet waits at Galthyr and I hope that the city's rulers remain opposed to Morathi.'

'That is a rare hope in these times,' said Eothlir, becoming serious. 'Yet it is heartening to think that it is not the Anars alone that would resist the power of Anlec.'

'Will Malekith return?' asked Caenthras, staring intently at the Ellyrians.

'Not before spring, I would say,' said Eoloran. 'Though he has not suffered true defeat as yet, this attack seems to have been... hasty, I would say. One does not merely walk up to Anlec and knock on the gates to be allowed entry.'

'We must do what we can to pave the way for that glorious return,' said Eothlir. 'Morathi knows Malekith's intent now, and all surprise is lost. We have raised our weapons against Anlec as well, and we do not know when the return blow will come.'

'We should harass a few more of Morathi's armies, keep her busy while Malekith regroups,' said Caenthras. 'When Malekith returns, he should not face a united, well-composed foe.'

Alith was worried by these words and the look of consideration on Eoloran's face. The Anars had suffered little in the battle that day; Elthyrior's warning had to relate to matters not yet known to Alith.

'That would be unwise,' said Eothlir, much to Alith's relief. 'Now that we have truly stirred up the wasps' nest, we should seek sanctuary in Elanardris.'

'From what little I heard from the raven heralds, that would seem the best course of action,' said Aneltain.

The mention of the raven heralds drew Alith's attention immediately, and also that of his grandfather.

'Raven heralds?' said Eoloran, his eyes narrowed with suspicion. 'What dealings have you had with those dark riders?'

Aneltain was taken aback and gave a defensive shrug.

'They act as Malekith's scouts and brought us to Ealith by secret ways,' replied the Ellyrian. 'Word came to us at the citadel that armies from the north and west and south were converging at Ealith to trap the prince and destroy his army. I fear that House Anar will fare no better if you remain out in the open.'

'Already we have helped Malekith,' Alith said, directing his words towards his father and grandfather. 'The army we have crushed today will not threaten Malekith, and we have bought him time to make his retreat, as was Caenthras's suggestion. Our losses are comparatively few as yet, but if we remain here that might not hold true for long. And who can say what forces will march on our homes once Malekith has slipped away?'

Eoloran sat down behind the map table and rubbed the side of his nose, as he was wont to do when deep in thought. He closed his eyes, seeming to block out the rest of the world as he contemplated his decision.

'We return to Elanardris,' he said, eyes still closed.

Alith stopped himself from crying out with relief. The anxious energy that had filled him since his meeting with Elthyrior drained away and he suddenly felt very tired. He excused himself from the continuing discussions and made his way to his tent, exhausted but happy. Elanardris would remain safe and soon he would see Ashniel again.

━❰ FIVE ❱━

Clothed in Darkness

IT SEEMED TO Alith that the winter wind was more bitter than any that had come before. It brought swirls of snow down from the mountains, but it was not just the cold that clawed at Alith, it was the feeling of being trapped.

From the high mountain path, the young Anar looked south and west across Elanardris. He could see the manse, the gardens swathed in snow. Smoke drifted from the house's three chimneys, billowing southwards on the stern breeze. Beyond the manse, the meadows and hills were laid out in a pattern of dark walls and hedges cutting through the white blanket. The white-walled farmhouses and guard towers could barely be seen, located only through their brightly tiled roofs and the telltale wisps of smoke.

Beyond that, almost at the horizon, the hills of Elanardris gave way to the undulating plains of central Nagarythe. Here the cloud-swathed sky was shrouded by a darker smog, the fires of a huge encampment. The army of Anlec squatted like a brooding black beast on the borders of the Anars' realm, waiting for the snows to cease. At this distance, and through the snow flurries brought down from the north, even the keen eyes of Alith could make out little detail. The enemy camp spread like a stain over the white hills, lines of black shapes that stretched from north to south.

The druchii, his grandfather had called them: dark elves. They had turned from the light of Aenarion and the lord of gods, Asuryan. Eoloran no longer regarded them as Naggarothi. They were traitors to the Phoenix Throne and betrayers of Malekith, their rightful prince.

Their foes thought the same of the Anars. They considered Eoloran's refusal to acknowledge the authority of Anlec as a slight against Aenarion's memory. Alith knew this from the interrogations of prisoners taken after the last battle, when the druchii had attempted to force their way up into the hills. It had been a foolish, desperate assault before Enagruir tightened her wintry grip on Nagarythe. The druchii had been stopped by Eoloran and Eothlir – again, for there had been three such attacks since Malekith had returned – and the dark elves were content to wait for conditions to improve and their numbers to swell further.

Alith's loneliness had been increased by the lack of contact with Ashniel. Far from giving him the triumphant homecoming Alith had imagined, Ashniel had been moved by her father to one of the lord's castles higher in the mountains, far from the enemy. Occasionally Alith would receive a short letter from her, in which she professed her regret at their parting and her wish that they would see each other again soon. Alith had little enough time to reply to these letters, for he spent most days up in the mountains keeping watch on the druchii host. Try as he might, he had little leisure to spend composing poetry and declarations of love and knew that such missives as he managed to send were brusque and clumsy.

As these morose thoughts occupied Alith, a lionhawk, her plumage white to camouflage her against the snows, swept down with a shriek from the mountain clouds. She circled around Alith and the group of scouts around him, and then settled on his wrist. Alith listened to her chirping and cawing for a moment, nodding in understanding as the bird relayed the message from Anadriel.

He stroked the lionhawk's head in thanks before raising his arm and allowing her to fly back to her nest. She would come again when called.

'A rider, on the Eithrin Ridge,' Alith announced to the twenty elves accompanying him. They were all dressed in robes of white trimmed with dark bear fur, enchanted with the greatest blessings of stealth and secrecy known to the dedicants of Kurnous. Even this close, it was hard for Alith to see where elf stopped and snow began. 'Anadriel is moving in from the southwest; we shall intercept this spy from the north-east. Quickly now, we don't want Anadriel to steal our glory!'

Many times the scouts had intercepted druchii warriors attempting to spy upon the Anars' army and defences. As far as Alith knew, not a single one had escaped to take news back to the druchii commanders. This one was different. It was obvious that nobody would be able to cross the Eithrin Ridge unobserved, especially on horseback, and so the druchii had concentrated their forces to the west and north. Alith's instinct told him that this uninvited visitor was not a spy, and wondered if Elthyrior had finally been caught out.

However, there was no solid reason to suspect that this stranger was the raven herald. Alith had heard nothing from Elthyrior since their parting before the battle with the Khainites, and guessed only that he had reached

Ealith safely and persuaded Malekith to send Aneltain south. Elthyrior could be dead, a captive of Morathi, or hidden in whatever lairs the raven heralds used to avoid the attention of their enemies.

As wintry spirits, the scouts made their way across the snow-covered rock, heading towards Eithrin Ridge. They flitted through the sparse trees, deftly running across the snow, moving sure-footedly over patches of sun-glittering ice. As they made their way down the mountainside, the shadow of Anil Narthain fell upon them and the air grew colder. Alith blew on his fingers as he jogged, keeping them warm so that he would not fumble with his bow if the stranger proved to be a threat. The snow crunching underfoot, Alith and the other archers ghosted southwards, eyes fixed ahead for any sight of the interloper.

It was mid-morning before Alith crested a rise, coming out into the winter sun, and saw the intruder. It was not Elthyrior. Although the elf was some distance away, Alith could see that he was shorter than the raven herald, and he was dressed in a grey cloak beneath which could be seen flashes of golden scale and white robes. The intruder was leading his horse, striding across a long snowdrift that had built up on the flanks of the Eithrin Ridge. Alith signalled wordlessly to the others to spread out and circle to the east to come at the stranger from several directions.

For a short while Alith lost sight of his quarry as the rocky slope dipped sharply and then rose up again. Pulling himself up the steep wall of the snow-filled crag, Alith caught sight of the stranger again, standing some three hundred paces away. He had stopped and was looking around quickly, and for a moment Alith wondered if the intruder had spied one of the scouts.

A keening cry overhead announced the presence of Anadriel's lionhawk, and only moments later six figures that before had been invisible stood up. Standing in a semi-circle some hundred paces from the stranger, they were dressed in the same style of clothes as Alith's warriors and had arrows bent to their bows. Alith rose to his feet and dashed across the snow, fitting an arrow to his bowstring.

The stranger had raised his arms and thrown back his cloak, revealing no scabbard at his waist, only the long knife that any traveller in the wilds would be sensible to carry. He was exchanging words with Anadriel and Alith caught the end of a reply.

'...need to speak to Eoloran and Eothlir,' the stranger called out.

Anadriel saw Alith and his scouts approaching from the opposite direction and lifted a hand in brief greeting. The stranger turned slowly to look at Alith. His expression was calm, confident even. He pulled back his hood with deliberate slowness, revealing reddish-yellow hair tied with golden thread. He was certainly not from Nagarythe.

'Name yourself,' Alith called out, stopping some fifty paces from the elf, his arrow aimed at the stranger's chest.

'I am Calabrian of Tor Andris,' the elf replied. 'I bear messages for the lord of the Anars.'

'We know the manner of messages that Morathi would send,' said Alith. He lifted up his bow and arrow. 'You know the manner of our replies.'

'I come not from Anlec, but Tor Anroc,' Calabrian said patiently. 'I carry missives from Prince Malekith.'

'And what proof do you offer?' demanded Alith.

'If you would allow me to approach, I will show you.'

Alith relaxed his arm and brought down his bow. Letting go of the arrow, he waved for Calabrian to come closer. The messenger lowered his arms and stepped up to his horse. He drew something from his saddlebags and held it up. It was a scroll case. Calabrian walked purposefully, glancing at the other scouts, the case still held clearly in view. Alith signalled for him to stop a few paces away and stepped up to him with an outstretched hand. Calabrian placed the casing in Alith's grip and took a few paces further back, his eyes unwavering from Alith's face.

The seal on the case was certainly that of Prince Malekith, and was unbroken. It was light, and so Alith doubted it contained a concealed weapon. Just to be sure, he tucked the case into his belt rather than return it.

'That message is for Eoloran Anar alone,' said Calabrian, stepping forwards. In an instant, Alith was ready, bowstring taut, the arrow pointed towards Calabrian's heart. The messenger stopped. 'I have other assurances, but only Eoloran will understand them.'

'I am Alith Anar, grandson of the lord you seek,' Alith assured the other elf. 'I will take you to the manse and there you will meet Eoloran Anar. Be warned, though, that if your claim proves to be false, you will not be treated well. If you wish, we will take you to the border of Elanardris directly and you can return to your master unharmed.'

'My mission is vital, the prince made that very clear to me,' said Calabrian. 'I offer myself to your judgement and mercy.'

Alith regarded Calabrian for a long time, seeking some hint of deception. There was none that he could see. A glance over the messenger's shoulder showed that Anadriel was inspecting Calabrian's horse and saddlebags.

'She will find nothing out of the ordinary,' said Calabrian, without looking around. 'A few personal items and those things needed when travelling in the grip of winter; that is all.'

Alith did not reply but simply waited for Anadriel to complete her search.

'All is well,' she called out eventually. 'No weapons of any kind.'

'These are dangerous times to be travelling unarmed in Nagarythe,' said Alith, his suspicion returning. 'How is it that you could pass without fear through the Anlec host that sits upon our doorstep?'

'I came not directly from the south, but crossed the mountains from Ellyrion,' explained Calabrian.

'A dangerous crossing,' said Alith, unconvinced.

'Yet it is one that I had to make,' said Calabrian. 'Though I do not know the detail of Prince Malekith's message, he left me in no doubt as to its importance and urgency. When I have Prince Eoloran's reply, I must return by the same route.'

There was earnestness in Calabrian's expression that convinced Alith.

'Very well,' said Alith, lowering his bow and returning the arrow to its quiver. 'Welcome to Elanardris, Calabrian of Tor Andris.'

ALITH WAS NOT surprised when Calabrian had insisted that only Eoloran, Eothlir and Alith were allowed to be present when Prince Malekith's message was opened. The messenger had requested that he be brought to the manse in secret, and made it plain that he only trusted the Anars and feared that agents of Morathi were present in Elanardris. Alith left him with Anadriel on the slopes north of the manse while he consulted his father and grandfather.

So it was that in the darkness of the cloud-swathed night, Alith led Calabrian to the summer house that stood in the eastern stretch of the garden. A single lamp burned within as Alith entered and gestured for Calabrian to follow. A ewer of spiced tea sat steaming on the low table in the middle of the single-roomed building, fluted cups arranged around it. The smell was sharp and Alith crossed quickly and poured himself a hot drink, warming his hands on the delicate cup.

Eoloran was stood at the window, gazing to the south, swathed in a fur-lined robe of deep blue, calfskin gloves upon his hands and his breath misting in the cold. Eothlir was sat on one of the benches that lined the white walls of the summer house, the scroll case in his hands.

'You said that you would offer further assurances as to the veracity of your claims,' said Eoloran, still looking out into the darkness. 'Make them known to me.'

Calabrian cast an appealing glance towards Alith, who poured a drink for the messenger. Sipping gently, Calabrian turned to Eoloran.

'Malekith instructed me to say "The light of the flame burns brightest at night",' said Calabrian, intoning the words with deep solemnity.

Eoloran spun around and glared inquisitively at Calabrian.

'What does it mean?' asked Eothlir, taken aback by his father's reaction. When Eoloran replied, his voice was quiet, distant.

'Those words were first spoken by Aenarion. It was before Anlec was built, just after the daemons had ravaged Avelorn and slain the Everqueen. I remember it well. He had vowed vengeance for the death of his wife and the slaying of his children, and in grief had decided to draw that accursed blade. I argued against him. I warned Aenarion that... that weapon was not for mortals to wield. I could see that his rage would consume him, and said as much. Those words were his reply. He left atop Indraugnir that night and flew to the Blighted Isle. When he returned, the Aenarion I had known was no more and a life of bloodshed followed. How do you know this phrase?'

'You will have to ask Prince Malekith,' said Calabrian, setting his empty cup on the table. 'He bade me to learn the words but offered no explanation. I trust that you believe my story?'

Eoloran nodded and gestured for Eothlir to pass the scroll case.

'Only Aenarion and I were present when those words were spoken, but it seems reasonable that Aenarion might use them again in the presence of his son,' Eoloran said.

Taking the case, Eoloran examined the seal and, satisfied that it remained intact, broke the circlet of black wax with his thumb. He pulled open the end of the tube and slid out a single piece of parchment. Placing the case carefully on the table, he opened the scroll.

'It is a letter,' said Eoloran. He scanned the elegant script for a moment and then began to read aloud, his voice breaking with emotion.

For the eyes of Eoloran Anar, beloved of Aenarion, true protector of Nagarythe. First I must thank you, though words cannot do justice to the debt I owe you for your support. I have heard that you marched to my aid at Ealith, and though that endeavour was ultimately to fail, I escaped and that is due in no small part to the presence of your army. I understand the great risk that you took in showing such support and assure you that you will be honoured and repaid when I reclaim the rule of Nagarythe. Truly you were a friend to my father and, I hope, an ally to me.

Eoloran paused, clearing his throat, a tear forming in his eye. He swallowed hard, brushing away the memories with a wipe of his hand across his brow. He continued in a clearer voice, his calm demeanour returned.

Alas that I must entreat further aid from you at this time. What I ask is dangerous in the extreme and I will not hold it against you should you feel unfit to comply. Please respond through my messenger, Calabrian, who can be trusted with the deepest of secrets. However, I must ask that you tell no more of your people than necessary of what I now request, lest word of it reach the ears of Morathi, by conventional means or via other, more deceitful paths. I march upon Anlec with the first thawing of the spring. Even now, my army assembles in Ellyrion, far from the prying eyes of my mother and her spies, while other forces loyal to the Phoenix King draw their gaze southwards. I am confident that I will reach Anlec, but the defences of the city are little short of impenetrable.

I ask that you take such warriors as you deem utterly trustworthy and infiltrate Anlec, there to stand ready for my attack. I cannot say at what time the stroke shall fall, so you must set out for the city come the first sun of the spring. No army can breach the gates of Anlec, but should they be opened before me I stand ready with a host of warriors the likes of which have not been seen upon Ulthuan's shores for an age. I wait with anticipation for your speedy reply and wish you the blessings of all the gods.

I remain your loyal ally and grateful prince.

'Then there is the rune of Malekith and his seal,' Eoloran finished.

'That is a considerable request,' said Eothlir as Eoloran passed the parchment to him.

'We are going to help, aren't we?' said Alith.

'Yes we are,' replied Eoloran, surprising Alith with the speed of his answer. It was unlike Eoloran to take such a decision with so little consideration. 'Had the prince commanded us to hurl ourselves at the walls of Anlec, I would comply. For the sake of Nagarythe, and all of Ulthuan, Morathi cannot be allowed to continue as ruler. The prince must be restored if we are ever to know peace again.'

Eoloran stood in thought for a moment, rubbing at his chin. He looked at Calabrian, who had stood meekly listening to the contents of the letter he had carried on such a dangerous journey.

'How much of Malekith's intent do you know?' asked Eoloran.

'No more than you,' the messenger replied. 'I left Malekith in Tor Anroc and knew nothing of his plan to move his army to Ellyrion. Nor of his intent to assault Anlec.'

'Then I shall write a reply to your master, and you will be taken across the mountains to Ellyrion,' said Eoloran. 'With Anar guides to lead you, I am sure that your return journey shall be less fraught than the one that brought you here.'

'Who shall we send with him?' asked Eothlir. 'Perhaps more importantly, who shall we take with us to Anlec? And by what means will we get there unheralded?'

'Anadriel and the other scouts who met Calabrian already know of his presence here,' said Alith. 'They are all trustworthy, kin to the Anars each of them. Anadriel knows the mountains as well as I, perhaps even better. I can think of no better guide, nor a more skilful warrior.'

'I would have you take Calabrian, Alith, and then return to the manse to keep our lands safe for our return,' said Eothlir. 'To risk every lord of the Anars on this one quest seems careless, and to abandon Elanardris would be perverse.'

'No,' said Eoloran, cutting across Alith's protest. 'Alith has proven himself in battle, and a finer eye cannot be found in Elanardris. If he is to have a future as a lord of the Anars, he fights with us. There are many who can see to the defence of Elanardris in our absence, and if Malekith marches on Anlec I would say that our foes' priorities will quickly change!'

Alith was profoundly grateful for his grandfather's opinion, but remained quiet lest an outburst change Eoloran's mind.

'For the moment,' said Eoloran with a look at Alith, 'he can run down to the house and bring me back parchment, ink and a quill.'

'Of course,' said Alith, bowing his head in thanks. As he left the summer house, he heard his father's voice quiet but angry, but his words were lost as Alith headed down the path towards the manse.

THE WINTER DAYS dragged on as heavy cloud sat upon the mountains, the snow sometimes coming in blizzards and at other times in more gentle flurries. Anadriel took Calabrian across the mountains to where the borders of Nagarythe, Chrace and Ellyrion met, and sent him south to Malekith.

By secret paths and unknown vantage points, the scouts of the Anars spied upon the enemy camps, noting their numbers and positions. All of this was passed to Eoloran to chart the disposition of his foes. With Alith and Anadriel, the lord of the Anars plotted the route by which a small group of warriors could evade the enemy and leave Elanardris unseen. Twice more Calabrian dared the dangerous route across the mountains to confer with the Anars, bringing assurances from Malekith that his attack was ready and returning with the renewed promises of Eoloran. Then the winter's grip tightened, blizzards ruled the peaks and there came no further word from the prince.

Thirty warriors were chosen by Eothlir, as those most trusted and most capable. All had served the Anars for centuries, several of them distant cousins to Alith. Amongst them were Anadriel, Anraneir, Casadir and Khillrallion. Eothlir began to refer to these warriors as the Shadows, as it would be in secrecy rather than strength that they would succeed.

The Shadows met each other every few days, to discuss the route from Elanardris to Anlec. Khillrallion tested the pathways out of Elanadris and returned several days later to confirm that he had not seen another elf in all of that time. While these practical steps were taken, Eoloran turned his hand to a different form of subterfuge: promulgating a falsehood to his allies that would explain his coming absence.

Through Caenthras, the ruler of the Anars spread the word that he had been in contact with Prince Durinne of Galthyr, a port in the west of Nagarythe. Eoloran let it be known that the two were arranging to meet, and would confirm their alliance and mutual support in the spring. Caenthras took this news with enthusiasm, and would often speak of how he wished for Malekith's return. Eoloran kept his silence on this matter, uncertain of Caenthras's reaction should he know the truth. The old warrior had been invigorated by the fighting against the Khainites and was clearly chafing at the imprisonment imposed by the besieging army. It was Eoloran's fear that Caenthras would march out to join Malekith if he knew the truth, leaving Elanardris unprotected, though it pained him to lie to his friend.

Each day Alith would awaken and look to the skies, hoping to see the first sun of spring. In Nagarythe, the winters were deep and harsh, but once the north wind turned to the west and the clouds broke, spring and then summer would come quickly. The sign that Malekith was ready to attack grew closer with every morning.

ALITH WAS CURLED up on a bed of leaves at the back of a cave, at one of the watch positions overlooking the druchii army. A slight noise caused him to wake instantly, reaching instinctively for the naked sword that lay beside him. Someone was silhouetted against the slightly paler circle of the cavern entrance. A smokeless lamp glowed into life to reveal the face of Anraneir. He was smiling broadly.

'Come, sleepy one, and look at this,' he said, stepping aside.

Alith sprang up and strode to the opening, guessing Anraneir's cause for happiness. There was an almost imperceptible warmth on the breeze, which came from the west. Looking to the east he saw the first red rays of the sun cresting over Anulir Erain, the White Mother who was the tallest of the mountains south of the manse.

'The first spring sun!' laughed Alith. Anraneir hugged Alith in his joy, and the young Anar shared his enthusiasm. The sun signalled a very perilous time for them both, but the prospect of action after such a bleak winter was exciting.

'We should head back to the manse today,' said Anraneir. 'Your grandfather will no doubt wish to leave tonight,'

'Best wait for Mithastir to replace me here,' said Alith. 'Someone still needs to keep an eye on the enemy. You should go now, since it would raise questions why you are here and not at your post.'

'Of course,' said Anraneir, deflated by Alith's practicality. With a waved hand and a whispered word he dimmed his lantern and disappeared into the gloom.

Alith sat cross-legged on the ledge outside the cave, gazing down at the pinpricks of campfires far below. He whispered a chant in praise of Kurnous as he waited for Mithastir to arrive, thanking the Lord of the Hunt for bringing the early spring. Alith took it as a good sign from his patron.

SINGLY AND IN pairs, the Shadows gathered in a small copse of trees known as the Athelin Emain close to the southern border of Elanardris. Alith was one of the first, and waited in the darkness for the others to arrive. As the moons glowed from behind thin clouds, Eoloran and Eothlir finally made their appearance, clad in dark cloaks like the rest. It was the first time Alith had seen his father and grandfather dressed in this fashion, entirely unlike the statesmanlike robes or shining armour he was accustomed to seeing. The ruler of the Anars gathered his warriors beneath the boughs of a great tree, the dim moonlight streaming through the naked branches to cast dappled shadows on the ground.

'We must pass the druchii line before sunrise,' said Eoloran, looking at the thirty Shadows. 'We all know the path which we take, and the danger should we be discovered. I offer you one last chance to return to your homes. As soon as we set foot beyond these trees we are committed to this journey, all the way to Anlec and whatever fate Morai-heg has reserved for us. Some of us, perhaps all of us, may not return from this fight, and it may be a fool's errand that we run.'

There was silence from the others. Alith was eager for them to start out, to put an end to the waiting and planning.

'Good,' said Eoloran with a grim smile. 'We are as one mind. Lauded shall be those that march with me today, and great shall be the gratitude of the Anars and Prince Malekith.'

With that, Eoloran turned south and the Shadows began their perilous quest.

It was not long before the Shadows encountered their first difficulty. Casadir had moved ahead of the main group as lead scout and returned just as Eoloran and the others were leaving the cover of Athelin Emain. They had planned to head directly westwards before turning north, but Casadir brought alarming news.

'The druchii have shifted the southern boundaries of their camp,' he reported as the others gathered at his surprise return. 'Cultists have moved south of the road.'

'Can we go around them?' asked Anadriel.

'Certainly,' replied Casadir. 'Though if we wish to remain out of sight we would have to travel through the fens of the Enniun Moreir. Who can say how many days that would add to our journey?'

'Arrive at Anlec too late or risk discovery, that is no small choice,' said Eothlir. He looked at his father. 'I would put my vote on speed and directness. The risk of being seen is one that we can control, while the delays are beyond our measure to manage.'

'I concur,' said Eoloran. 'It would be of little use to arrive too late and be trapped outside the walls with Malekith.'

'Perhaps there is even an opportunity here,' suggested Alith. He turned to Casadir. 'How large would you say is the cultist camp? How close are they to the others?'

'Two hundred cultists, maybe less,' said Casadir. 'They are camped on the lee side of the hills, on the banks of the Erandath, some distance from the bridge at Anul Tiran.'

'What are you thinking?' asked Eothlir as Alith stayed silent for a moment.

'We can address two problems with one solution,' said Alith. 'I say we kill the cultists in their camp, and take on their guise. Clothed as cultists we can move freely along the roads rather than avoid them, speeding our journey by many days.'

'What if the alarm is raised?' asked Eoloran. 'What you suggest risks a battle that we cannot win and an end to our journey before it has begun.'

'The cultists will be unprepared and we will use stealth as our weapon,' replied Alith, nodding as a plan resolved in his mind. 'From what we saw of the Khainites, they have no military discipline. They expect no attack, and more than likely will be lying in their tents stupefied and unaware.'

'I saw very little movement,' added Casadir. 'It would be very simple to come upon them unseen, if we choose confrontation.'

'Kill them in their sleep?' said Eothlir. 'What you suggest fills me with a deep distaste. We are not assassins, we are warriors.'

'And what of those that have fallen beneath their blades already, and those that would be sacrificed in the years to come should Malekith fail?' growled Alith. 'Too long has justice been absent from Nagarythe. It is all well and good to march out gloriously with banners flapping and clarions blaring, but in this war there are battles to be fought unseen by others. Are we not the Shadows for a reason?'

Eothlir's expression showed his uneasiness, but he turned to his father rather than reply. Eoloran shook his head slowly, unhappy with the decision he faced.

'You did not see what we saw in the Khainite camp,' Alith said. 'Though you may think it cold-blooded murder that I propose, we at least will have the dignity to give our victims a clean and painless death. They will not be tossed screaming onto fires nor have their living bodies desecrated by abuse! Does the hunter regret every life he takes, or does he know that it is the way of the world that some die so that others may live? He cannot pity the stag or the bear, no more than we can pity those that have chosen to prey upon their own kind.'

'You make a powerful argument, Alith,' replied Eoloran. 'To move cloaked in the guise of the enemy would be a great advantage, especially when we come to Anlec. Though we have pondered long on our journey to the city, this gives us a means by which we might enter unknown. We must accept that there is darkness in all shadows, and take strength from the promise that such deeds as we are about to commit are so that others may not know such sacrifice.'

With attack decided, the Shadows broke into groups of three and set out, circling around the cultist encampment. It was past midnight when they had come to their positions, and all about the camp was quiet. The orgy of celebration Alith had seen with the Khainites was absent, but clouds of narcotic vapours drifted from bone-wrought braziers. That the cultists were in a drugged stupor seemed likely.

Coming to the closest tent, a high pavilion of purple cloth, Alith moved to the front at a crouch, dagger in hand. There was no movement from within and only the sound of slow breathing. With a glance around to ensure he was unobserved, Alith opened the flap and slipped inside.

There were seven elves within, all entwined in nakedness upon a huge carpet made of several furred skins sewn together. A lamp with red glass glowed in one corner, bathing everything in vermillion. Two of the elves were male, the others female, the bare flesh of all marked with runes drawn in blue dye. Amongst the swirls and shapes, Alith recognised the rune of Atharti, a goddess of pleasure.

They were utterly still as Alith crouched above the closest. He could smell the fragrance of black lotus, a powerful narcotic that gave vivid dreams when smoke from its burning petals was inhaled. Drawing up his scarf across his mouth and face, Alith leaned forwards and brought his blade up to the sleeping maiden's neck. The dagger shone in the ruddy light and Alith paused.

To kill in the heat of battle was one thing, but to purposefully slay a defenceless victim was unlike anything Alith had ever done. His hand began to tremble at the thought and a sudden fear gripped him. Then the memories of the Khainite ceremony resurfaced in his mind and his hatred for what he had witnessed quelled all revolt.

With a smooth, almost gentle motion, Alith drew the knife across the side of the elf maiden's neck, slicing the artery. Blood spurted from the wound, a crimson shower that soaked the fur underfoot and pooled on Alith's black boots. Fighting down his disgust, Alith moved to the next, and the next, and the next.

It was soon over and without another glance at those he had slain, Alith left the tent and moved on, blood dripping from his dagger.

'By whose leave do you travel on the road?' demanded the Anlec captain, his sword half-drawn from its sheath. Behind him stood several dozen warriors armed with barbed spears and covered from neck to knee in long coats of blackened mail, their faces hidden behind heavy aventails that covered their noses and mouths.

It was not the first patrol the Shadows had encountered on the road to Anlec, and each meeting had been a fraught experience for Alith and the others. Dressed in the garb of Athartists and Khainites and other cultists, the Anars had hidden their weapons in swathed bundles upon their packs and had no means to defend themselves if their enemies attacked.

The whole journey had been nerve-wracking, the masquerade a thin defence against inquiry. The group of elves had travelled along the main road to the capital for seven days, avoiding other parties where possible. Though they looked the part of cultists, they knew nothing of the rituals and workings of the cults and were forced to avoid others on the road. This had led to several instances of the Shadows being forced into the wilds at night so that they were not asked to share camps.

The number of soldiers on the road had been a problem as well. It was clear that Malekith's plan to draw attention to the south was working and the Shadows had passed by thousands of warriors marching towards the border with Tiranoc. For the most part these companies had been too preoccupied with their own fates to notice a small group of cultists, but there had been several times, such as this, when bored officers had decided to investigate.

'I did not know that the roads were barred to those who travelled to pay homage to Queen Morathi,' said Eoloran, bowing apologetically. Alith could imagine the self-loathing his grandfather felt at having to utter such words, but pride was the least casualty of their subterfuge.

'There's war afoot, you should know that,' snarled the captain. 'The roads must be clear for the queen's armies.'

'We would offer no obstruction, my noble friend,' said Eoloran, keeping his gaze downcast. 'In fact, we travel to the temples of Anlec so that we might entreat the gods to bless the endeavours of Morathi's favoured warriors. We are not fighters, and we owe everything to the great soldiers of Nagarythe who would protect us against the persecution of Bel Shanaar.'

It was a well-rehearsed turn of phrase, which Eoloran had devised after much thought, and it seemed to be working on the captain.

'There is little room in the city for vagabonds and wanderers,' he said. 'I warn you that there is a levy upon the people of Anlec to provide more warriors for the army. I see nothing of value in this motley band, but it is the queen's decree that all stand ready in defence of our realm.'

'You are right, we know little of war and battle,' said Eoloran. 'Yet, should our enemies threaten, none will fight harder than I in the defence of Nagarythe and her great traditions.'

Alith was forced to turn away and cough to conceal a short laugh at his grandfather's wordplay. Certainly the Anars would fight hardest to restore Malekith to the throne.

The captain mulled over this answer for a time. Having wearied of the lack of sport provided by Eoloran, he waved the Shadows aside, forcing them onto the muddied grass bank that lined the road. With glowers at the group as they passed, the soldiers formed up and marched on, leaving the Shadows in peace.

Eoloran urged them onwards, keen to put distance between the Shadows and the soldiers, and only after some time did he speak more freely again.

'I judge that we are no more than a day from Anlec, and we must be on our wits,' he warned. 'So far it seems that Malekith's ploy is working, for if the druchii suspected any attack on Anlec, all roads would be closed. We must enter the city before the threat is known, lest the gates be barred against all entry prior to our arrival. I feel that events will quickly come upon us. We must put haste before caution. We must reach Anlec before nightfall tomorrow.'

ANLEC WAS MORE of a fortress than a city, though massive in size and home to tens of thousands of elves. It was the greatest citadel in the world, built by Aenarion and Caledor Dragontamer to hold against the tide of daemons that had assailed Ulthuan. Immense walls encircled the city, bolstered along its circumference by twenty towers, each a small castle in its own right. Black and silver banners flapped in the spring wind from a hundred poles and the glint of weapons could be seen as hundreds of guards made their patrols along the battlements.

There were three gatehouses, each grander than the manse of Elanardris and protected by war machines and dozens of soldiers. The gates themselves were immense portals wrought from blackened iron and enchanted with the most powerful spells of Caledor. Walls extended like buttresses from beside the gates, creating a killing field into which bolts and arrows and spells could be cast upon any attacker. A ring of outer towers, each garrisoned by a hundred warriors, protected the approaches. Perhaps most daunting was the great moat of fire that encircled the entire city, which burnt with a magical green flame and could only be crossed at three mighty drawbridges.

It was across one of these bridges that the Shadows walked, the heat and crackling of the flames to either side. The sun was setting behind Anlec; the city rose out of the gloom like a black monster, spires and towers its horns and claws.

Once this place had been the beacon in the darkness, the fortress of Aenarion the Defender. Now the sight of its black granite buildings sent a shudder of fear through Alith and he cast a glance at Eothlir and Eoloran. Not for many centuries had they come to the city, ever since Morathi had usurped rule from the chancellors and councils left by Malekith. The stories of the dark rites and bloody rituals were enough to make the skin crawl, and the sight of the city left Alith's father and grandfather with pale, pinched faces.

They crossed the killing ground swiftly. Alith glanced up at the high walls to either side and lamented silently, fearful for any warrior doomed to assault Anlec. No doubt many thousands of loyal elves would lose their lives when Malekith attacked. Pushing these sombre thoughts from his mind, Alith heartened himself with the knowledge that the Shadows had arrived. It would be their purpose to ensure the gate opened to save those warriors from such a bloody fate. Seeing Anlec firsthand strengthened Alith's resolve and he took no small measure of pride in the idea that the Anars would play such a pivotal role in the war for Nagarythe.

Fires could be seen through the yawning maw of the open gate, flickering from the dark stone of the flanking towers and the huge arch of the portal. A chill swamped Alith as the Shadows passed into the gatehouse, as if all light had been extinguished. He suppressed the urge to glance backwards as the city swallowed them.

— ⫷ SIX ⫸ —

Anlec Restored

THE NIGHT WAS torn by the screams of sacrificial victims and the screeching entreaties of wild cultists. Alith stood at the window of the abandoned garrison tower and looked over Anlec. Fires of different colours broke the darkness, while bloodthirsty mobs ran amok in the streets below, fighting each other and dragging off the unwary to be sacrificed to the dark gods of the cytharai.

The Shadows had made their lair in a deserted building not far from the northern arc of the city wall. Once it had been home to hundreds of soldiers, but they had been moved south to confront the threat from Tiranoc. Like many parts of Anlec, the area was eerily quiet, the cultists preferring to keep to the centre of the city where the great temples were found. There was strength in numbers as the cults vied with each other for dominance.

There were chambers below the tower that the Anars had not ventured into since their first exploration, appalled by bloodstained floors and barbed manacles, broken blades and wicked brands. Shuddering at the thought of the torments that had been visited upon fellow elves, they had closed the doors and kept to the upper storeys.

'I had no idea that we could fall so low,' said Eoloran, appearing at Alith's shoulder. 'In this place of all, where once there was such dignity and honour, it pains me to look upon what we have become.'

'We are not all the same,' said Alith. 'Morathi has spread weakness and corruption, but Malekith will bring strength and resolve. There is still a future worth fighting for.'

419

Eoloran did not reply and Alith turned to look at his grandfather, to find that he was gazing at Alith with a smile.

'You make me proud to be an Anar,' said Eoloran, touching Alith's shoulder. 'Your father will be a great lord of the house, and you will be a fine prince of Nagarythe. When I see you, memories of the ancient past disappear and pain goes away. It is for the likes of you that we fought and bled, not these wretches that cavort through Aenarion's city.'

Eoloran's words warmed Alith's heart and he grasped his grandfather's hand.

'If I am so, it is because I have your example to follow,' said Alith. 'It is the fine legacy that you will leave us that stirs me, and I call myself Anar with such pride that I cannot put it into words. Where others faltered and fell into the darkness, you have stood unflinching, a shaft of light for all to follow.'

Eoloran's eyes glistened with tears and the two embraced, drawing comfort upon each other's love and putting aside the horrors that lay outside.

Breaking away after some time, Eoloran turned his eyes back to the window and his expression hardened.

'Those that have perpetrated these atrocities must be punished, Alith,' he said quietly. 'But do not confuse punishment with revenge. It is fear and anger, jealousy and hatred that feed these cults, stirring those darkest emotions that lie within us all. If we stay true to our ideals, the victory will be ours.'

FOR NINE DAYS the Shadows concealed themselves within the heart of the enemy. For the most part they stayed out of sight, but singly and in pairs they dared the city on occasion, to gather information and food. The daytime was less perilous than the night, for the orgies and sacrifices of the night before left the cultists sated for a while and the streets were quieter.

While the cultists ruled the night, the garrison of Anlec held sway in the daylight, patrolling the streets vigorously to ensure that total anarchy did not consume the city. It became clear that Morathi held the various forces in balance, indulging the cults to retain their support, yet reining back their excesses enough to ensure that some semblance of order was maintained.

It was late afternoon on the ninth day when Alith and Casadir took their turn to go out into the city and find out what news they could. Garbed in their elegant robes, swords concealed beneath the folds of cloth, the pair headed for the main plaza outside the palace. There was a guard of soldiers upon the steps that led up to the huge doors of the citadel, and a throng of elves was massing in the square.

There was a hum of conversation, an edge of fear to the atmosphere that drew Alith's attention.

'Let us split up and see what we can hear,' he said to Casadir. 'I will meet you back here in a short while.'

Casadir nodded and headed off to the right, passing in front of the steps.

Alith turned left, towards the market stalls that had been set up on the edge of the square. He moved along the stalls, seemingly browsing the sellers' wares yet he was alert to the hubbub around him. Amongst the usual fare of a market there were more sinister goods on sale. Ritual daggers inscribed with evil runes, talismans of the cytharai and parchments filled with incantations to the underworld gods. As he eyed a silver amulet forged in the shape of Ereth Khial's sigil, Alith heard a passer-by mention the name of Malekith. Turning, he followed the group of elves across the square. Amongst the languid strolls of the other elves, these five moved with purpose towards the street of temples that lay to the west.

'Riders came in early this morning,' one was saying. Though the air had not yet thrown off the full chill of winter, she was dressed in a diaphanous veil that was wound loosely about her body, her pale flesh exposed for all to see. Upon her back were scars in the shapes of runes, and her flesh was pierced with rings of gold. 'My brother was at the south gate and overheard what was said to the guards. The riders told the garrison that Prince Malekith advances on Anlec with an army.'

This was greeted with twitters of fear from the other elves.

'Surely he won't attack the city?' said one.

'Are we safe here?' asked another.

'Perhaps we should flee,' suggested another.

'There is no time!' said the first, her voice shrill. 'The riders say that the prince is but a day's march away. His wrath will fall upon us ere sundown tomorrow!'

A thrill of excitement pulsed through Alith on hearing these words. He longed to follow the group further but they had turned up the steps that led to the shrine of Atharti and he had no desire to enter that damned place. Cutting down a side street, Alith circled quickly back towards the square and there he found Casadir waiting for him.

'Malekith is close,' Casadir whispered as Alith came up to him. 'I heard a captain of the guards sending his company to the walls to make ready the defence of the city.'

'He is but a day away,' said Alith as the two of them walked together back towards the abandoned barracks. 'Or so some believe.'

'Morathi is keeping this news secret for the moment,' said Casadir. 'She fears that there will be panic if the people find out that the prince is about to besiege Anlec. Perhaps we should spread the word, and hope that we can cause fear and confusion and hinder her plans.'

'That might be a good idea, but I would speak with my father first,' said Alith.

'I will linger a while longer and see what else I can learn,' said Casadir. 'I will return to the tower before dusk.'

'Be careful,' said Alith. 'As this news spreads, I fear hysteria will grip many of the cultists. The sacrificial fires will burn high this night.'

Casadir nodded reassuringly and disappeared into the gathering crowds. Alith headed for the Shadows' lair at a brisk pace, keen to move quickly but fearful of attracting attention. If Malekith was indeed but a day away, his approach having been kept secret by Morathi's warriors, the Anars had little time to prepare their plan of action. Though the prospect filled Alith with excitement, he felt an underlying dread that the Shadows would fail and the prince would be destroyed upon the city's walls.

As ALITH HAD predicted, the night was punctuated by much rowdy behaviour, the beating of drums and the blare of horns as word spread of Malekith's approach. Amongst the mayhem of the cultists' tribulations and celebrations, the tramp of marching feet reverberated around the city as the garrison turned out and such forces as were near at hand were brought back to Anlec. The Shadows kept to their dark tower whilst this hysteria gripped the druchii, fearful of being set upon in the streets.

Alith spent a sleepless night with the others, alternating between keeping watch for intruders and discussing the coming events with his father and grandfather. When the rosy haze of dawn crept across the horizon, barely glimmering over the stone wall of the city, Alith was in the highest chamber of the tower with Eothlir and Eoloran. In the light of the dawn and by the fires of torches along the ramparts, they could see a great many warriors standing ready to receive an assault.

A singular question had vexed Eoloran since their arrival at Anlec and he gave voice to it again as the sun crept onto the sill of the window.

'From which direction will Malekith attack?' he asked, though posing the question to nobody in particular. 'We must know which gate needs to be opened.'

'I have heard conflicting reports,' said Eothlir. 'Some believe he marches direct from Tiranoc and comes from the south, while others have said that he comes from Ellyrion in the east.'

'From his messages, we know the prince intended to muster his army in Ellyrion,' said Alith. 'The east seems the most probable direction.'

'That does seem likely, but such is the confusion that I have even heard tell that he comes from the west, having landed at Galthyr. While I suspect that you are right, Alith, it is not beyond the bounds of reason to wonder if his plans have changed, either through his own decision or forced by the actions of the druchii. A wrong assumption would not only cost us our lives but could damn Nagarythe to this torment for many more years to come.'

'Then we must see for ourselves what is the truth,' said Alith.

'And from where would you look?' said Eothlir. 'The walls are full of warriors and no tower save for the citadel is high enough to see any distance.'

'When faced with only one path, no matter how dangerous, that is the route we must take,' said Alith. 'I will scale the citadel for a vantage point that will give us sufficient warning of Malekith's approach. We need time to order ourselves and reach whichever gatehouse he assaults, and for that we need to know his intent as soon as possible.'

'If only there were some way we could send or receive word from the prince,' said Eoloran. 'A bird, perhaps?'

'I fear that Morathi's eye will be alert to such things, and we risk revealing ourselves for only an uncertain gain,' said Eothlir. He paced to the window and back, obviously distressed. 'It seems unwise to send out a solitary spy, Alith.'

'Better that only one is caught than all, and I would not ask any other to risk themselves,' said Alith. 'Do not be too disheartened. Anarchy still holds sway over much of the city, though I am sure before long Morathi will instil a greater fear in her followers than Malekith. The shadows are still deep at this early hour and a lone figure moves unseen where many would attract attention.'

'I am still not certain,' said Eoloran.

'Then you'd best bind me and leave me here, for I intend to go!' snapped Alith, who then fell silent, taken aback by his own determination. He continued in a more measured tone. 'I promise I will not take any unnecessary risks, and if I hear word that confirms Malekith's plan I shall return immediately and dare nothing. All eyes are outwards at this moment, none will see a solitary shadow.'

Eoloran said nothing and turned away, giving his assent yet not able to say as much. Eothlir stepped in front of Alith and placed a hand upon the back of his son's head. He pulled him closer and kissed his son upon the brow.

'May all the gods of light watch over you,' said Eothlir, stepping back. 'You must be quick, but in your haste do nothing rash.'

'Believe me, I would like nothing more than to return whole and unharmed!' said Alith with a nervous laugh. He waved away his father's concerns and headed for the door.

Alith stripped off the cumbersome Salthite robes he had been wearing and adorned himself with a simple loincloth and red cloak, such as might be worn by a Khainite. He wrapped a ragged sash around his waist in which he placed a serrated knife. Thus disguised, Alith slipped from the tower without a word to his fellow Shadows.

The street directly outside was empty and the tower itself concealed the view from the walls. Hugging close to the side of the street, where tall-roofed buildings had once housed thousands of warriors, Alith headed for the centre of the city.

Feeling that he would arouse less attention on the main roads than if he were seen skulking through alleys and side streets, Alith took the most direct route to the central plaza, coming at the palace of Aenarion from northwest. Here were many of the homes of Anlec's rulers, most empty while their noble owners commanded troops on the wall or were with their soldiers far to the south. Leaping over garden walls and flitting past bubbling fountains,

Alith looked for a means by which he could gain entry to the citadel.

Where once the spire of Anlec had stood alone in the centre of the city, the passing centuries had brought more buildings, each getting closer and closer to the palace. Though the square south of the citadel was open, generations ago the houses of the nobles had joined to the northern wall of the palace and it was here that Alith headed.

As easily as he had once jumped from rock to rock on the mountainsides of his home, Alith leapt into the bare branches of a tree close to the porch of one of the manses. From here he jumped onto the roof. Sliding past an open dormer window, Alith stooped low to avoid being seen and ran along the angled tiles at the ridge of the steep roof. There was some distance between the manse's gable and the wall of the citadel and Alith took the leap at a run, hurling himself over the drop. His fingers found a hold on the age-worn stones of the wall and, after a moment of scrabbling, his naked toes also found purchase. Spider-like, Alith shimmied to the top of the wall. After peering over to ensure he was unobserved, he slipped through the tall crenellations onto the rampart beyond.

His vantage point was no better than that elsewhere and he could see no further than the curtain wall of Anlec. He needed to climb higher if he was to get a good view of the surrounding plains and witness the arrival of Malekith.

Keeping to the western side of the citadel, still shrouded from the rising sun, Alith climbed up turrets and minarets, sidled along ledges and clawed his way up steepling roofs until he was far above the city. Pausing beneath the sill of an arched window, Alith glanced down and saw figures on the streets below, made incredibly small by distance. There was a great throng in the central plaza and the street of temples was full of people. Elsewhere there were very few elves. Alith could see over the walls, but only to the dark west, the direction least likely to reveal Malekith. He needed to look east, to confirm that Malekith's army indeed approached from that direction.

Crawling along a narrow gutter, Alith came to the edge of a roof overlooking the top of an open turret below. Three warriors stood guard at the door beneath him, but their eyes were looking outwards, seeking the same thing he was. Ignoring the soldiers, Alith pulled himself across the gap above their heads and silently climbed higher.

The sun bathed Alith with its warmth as he rounded the golden pinnacle of a minaret. The sensation gave him a sudden flash of memory. He remembered lying on the lawn of the manse with his mother, talking about Ashniel. It was with guilt that Alith realised he had not thought of Ashniel since leaving Elanardris, so possessed had he been of the coming mission. The memory heartened him, for if they succeeded today, Malekith would regain his throne and Ashniel would no longer be bound to her safe retreat in the mountains.

Spurred on by his desire, Alith looked around for surer footing and saw a balcony not far above him. With a spring, he grabbed hold of the curving stone supports beneath the balcony and pulled himself up to an elegant balustrade. A huge windowed door stood open, leading into a darkened chamber.

Alith heard voices and froze.

After a moment, he relaxed as the voices receded into echoes. Standing to one side of the door so that he could not be seen from within, Alith had the chance to look out properly. Everything to the south and east was laid out before him. The roads running from the gates travelled directly away from the city as far as the horizon, broken only at the raised bridges across the fire moat.

For some time Alith stayed there, seeking some clue that would confirm Malekith's approach. As time dragged on, doubt gnawed at Alith's resolve, his expectation slowly leeched from him as the sun rose higher and higher. On occasion there would be the sound of footfalls within the citadel and Alith held his dagger ready in case someone came upon him.

Even as the last of Alith's hope was waning, he spied a flashing to the south-east. Shading his eyes, he looked more carefully. It was the unmistakeable glint of sunlight on metal. Dust rose on the horizon and Alith watched in awe as the host of Malekith marched towards the city.

Alith had never seen so many warriors. Thousands upon thousands of knights, spearmen and archers advanced, spreading far to either side of the southern road. As the army came nearer and nearer, Alith saw white chariots pulled by fierce lions, and the banners of other realms flapping above the endless ranks of warriors: Ellyrion, Yvresse, Tiranoc and Chrace. Front and centre were the silver and black standards of Nagarythe, the warriors of Prince Malekith. At this distance, Alith could see nothing of the prince, though his black-armoured knights were visible. Winged creatures circled in the clouds above the army: three pegasi and a mighty griffon with riders on their backs.

It was clear that Malekith marched for the southern gate, his army forming up towards the drawbridge in that direction. Relieved, Alith was about to start his long climb down when raised voices from within the citadel attracted his attention. He risked a glance into the chamber and found it was empty. However, through an archway at the far side of the room he could see an inner hall and his heart skipped a beat when a tall figure crossed into view.

She was tall, majestic, her black hair spilling down her back in languid curls. She wore a purple gown of gossamer cloth, which wreathed about her white skin like smoke. There was a strange shadow about her, a barely visible miasma of darkness that seemed to teem with a life of its own. Alith fancied he saw tiny glaring eyes and fangs appearing in that shadowy mist. In her hand the matriarch held an iron staff topped with a strange horned skull and her hair was bound by a golden tiara set with diamonds and emeralds.

Morathi!

Alith was spellbound by her beauty, though he knew in his heart that she was utterly wicked. Her back was to him but the curve of her shoulders and hips stirred a passion inside Alith that he had not known he possessed. He longed to lose himself in that lustrous hair and feel the touch of that smooth skin beneath his fingers.

The sound of voices broke the enchantment and Alith realised the sorceress-queen was not alone. Black-robed figures passed back and forth across the archway, their heads shaved bald and tattooed with strange designs. He could not hear the words being said and against the promise he had made his father, Alith slipped into the chamber to come closer to the hated Witch Queen.

From this new position Alith could see more clearly into the central hall. He recoiled from what he saw. Beyond Morathi burned a multi-coloured flame, which recalled to Alith the tales of the Flame of Asuryan that had blessed Aenarion at the dawn of time. Yet there was nothing holy about these fires, their licking tongues strangely jagged and angular. A half-formed shape dwelt in the middle of the twisting flames. Though indistinct, made up from but also not part of the flames, it looked like the face of a bird, perhaps an eagle or a vulture, shifting between two different appearances. Its eyes glittered with power and to Alith the flames looked like a pair of immense wings furled around some otherworldly creature.

'Their time will come,' intoned a solemn, deep voice that resounded around the hall. The words came from the flames, but did not seem to be elvish, though Alith understood them easily. It was if the words came from a language that bound all other languages together, utterly recognisable and yet totally different.

'The winding road forks many times,' warned another, with a cackle.

'And we see where all paths lead,' said the first voice.

'But not when,' responded the second.

Alith was confused, for both voices seemed to come from the flaming apparition, yet they had about them the tone of an argument.

'And in return for this undertaking, I shall expect to be rewarded.' Morathi cut across the bickering, her voice as luxuriant as her body. 'When I call, I will be answered.'

'It makes demands,' said the screeching voice.

'Demands,' echoed the deeper voice with a guffawing laugh.

'I do not fear you,' said Morathi. 'It is you that came to me. If you wish to return to your infernal place with no bargain made, I shall not stop you. If you wish to return with what you came for, then you will treat me as an equal.'

'Equal?' the creature's shrill voice bit like splinters inside Alith's ears and he winced at the sound.

'Equal in all things, we are,' said the deep voice, reassuring and gentle. 'As partners we make this trade.'

'Remember always that there are things a mortal can do, places a mortal can go, that are beyond your reach, daemon,' said Morathi. A trickle of dread ran down Alith's spine at the mention of daemons and he was gripped by the urge to flee. Shaking, he mastered his fear and forced himself to listen on. 'It was our kind that bound you to the prison that holds you. Should you wish to reach beyond that prison, it is with mortal hands that you must work.'

'Always so arrogant,' mocked the sharp voice. 'Mortals imprisoned us? You would do well to know that no prison can keep us for all time, and no barrier holds us wholly back. There will come a reckoning with mortals, oh yes. A reckoning.'

'Shut up, you stupid old crow,' said the other voice. 'Do not listen to his idle chatter, queen of the elves. Our deal is set, our pact is made. Your followers shall go into the north and teach the humans of the sorcerous ways and in exchange the power of the Everchanging Veil shall be yours.'

'I mark this pact with blood,' said Morathi. Her staff tip lashed out towards one of the sorcerers and he was suddenly swathed with blood from hundreds of small cuts, his screams echoing around the hall. With a contemptuous sweep of her staff, Morathi hurled the still-shrieking acolyte into the fires. The flames burnt brightly for a moment, almost blinding, while harsh laughter resounded from the walls.

'Your fate is woven,' said the daemon. With another flash the flames disappeared, leaving the hall in darkness.

Alith blinked to clear the spots from his vision. It was a moment before he realised Morathi had turned and was heading towards the archway. In a panic, Alith sprinted back out onto the balcony and threw himself over its rail, grasping hold of the supports as he dropped. He clung there, grimacing, as he heard the tap of narrow-heeled boots clicking on the stone above. When Morathi spoke next, her voice was almost on top of Alith and his skin crawled at being so close to the sorceress-queen.

'How remarkable,' Morathi said. 'I thought the fires beyond him. It seems as if my son has grown up finally.'

'Do you not feel its presence, majesty?' hissed one of the sorceresses. 'The circlet upon his helm, it burns with the ancient powers.'

'Yes,' said Morathi with a sigh. 'Has he the will to wield that power though? We shall soon see. It is an artefact from before Ulthuan was raised from the seas. Be wary, my darlings, or we shall all suffer the consequences.'

'Prince Malekith has crossed the fires, your majesty,' said another acolyte. 'What if he takes the city?'

'Send your familiars out to spread the word to the others, our agents in the mountains and the cities,' purred the queen. 'A single battle does not win a war. Should he enter Anlec, he will come to me.'

Footsteps receded into the citadel and Alith let out his breath in an explosive gasp, almost losing his hold on the pitted stonework. There was too much to think about and not enough time to consider everything. Alith focussed on what was important: the Shadows had to open the southern gate, and quickly.

THERE WERE FEW elves on the streets of Anlec, and those that were spared no second glance to thirty Naggarothi garbed in short mail coats and cloaks of black who marched along the road with bows in hand and grim looks on their faces. Shouts and cries echoed down from the walls, but from within the city it was impossible to know how the battle progressed. Now and then Alith saw one or other of the pegasus-riding mages sweep down to the ramparts unleashing magical fire or forks of lightning. The screams of the dying grew in number as an elven prince atop the back of a majestic griffon crashed into the soldiers upon the walls. His icy lance and the claws of the monster gouged great wounds in the druchii regiments. All else save for the clouds of arrows that passed back and forth was hidden from view.

'Wait!' hissed Eoloran as the Shadows came into sight of the wide plaza behind the south gate. The open square was filled with elves howling and screaming: Khainites. Their priests and priestesses moved amongst the shrieking mob, sprinkling them with handfuls of blessed blood, exhorting them to slay the city's attackers for the glory of Khaine. Hateful oaths to slay Malekith echoed from the gate and surrounding buildings. Some of the Khainites fell to their knees, wailing and snarling, dousing themselves with blood from silver chalices, slicking their hair and painting runes upon the flesh with the blood of their companions. Bodies littered the flagstones where the most frenzied worshippers had fallen upon their fellows with knives and bare hands. The skin and flesh had been torn from them, their organs plucked free and devoured by the demented cultists.

Looking up towards the high towers of the gatehouse, Alith could see a great deal of activity. Archers were gathering from the surrounding walls, pouring their arrows into some foe close at hand.

'We must take the gatehouse!' hissed Alith, taking a step.

'We will be butchered,' replied Eothlir, grabbing Alith by the arm and dragging him back as the other warriors took shelter in the shadow of the wall.

'Malekith's soldiers will all be killed,' said Alith, snatching his arm from his father's grasp.

'And so will we,' snarled Eoloran. A bell rang out three times from the direction of the citadel. A moment later a loud grinding echoed across the courtyard. Eoloran pointed towards the gate towers. 'Look!'

The huge gates of Anlec swung open with a rattle of heavy chains. On the gate towers, naked slaves were bent to two great wheels as their druchii masters lashed their backs with barbed scourges. Like a dam being opened, the Khainites flooded out of the city, whooping and screaming with murderous delight.

The gates closed with a shuddering thud as the last of the Khainites passed through. The courtyard was empty and silent, save for the distant battle cries and clash of war from beyond the walls.

'Now is our chance!' said Eoloran, waving Alith and the others forwards.

Bows and arrows readied, the Shadows ran swiftly across the gate square. As had been discussed before setting out from their hiding place, Alith and Eothlir led half of the Shadows towards the eastern tower while Eoloran took the rest towards the western tower. Eoloran's group disappeared through the doorway whilst Alith was still a dozen paces from the other tower.

A figure clad in chainmail appeared at the doorway right in front of Alith. The druchii's eyes widened with shock a moment before an arrow from Anadriel took him in the cheek, hurling him against the stone of the tower. Alith leapt past and was engulfed by the torchlit gloom.

The stair spiralled to the right and Alith dashed up the steps in bounding leaps, the other Shadows closely on his heels. No other druchii came down and as Alith burst from the door at the top he found himself looking out across the plains of Anlec and the army of Malekith.

He had only time to register rank upon rank of spears and knights and archers before movement to his left caught Alith's eye. There were dozens of warriors on the wall next to the tower and the closest were turning towards him.

Without thought, Alith aimed and loosed his first arrow, which punched through the gilded breastplate of the closest warrior. As he nocked and shot his next, Eothlir and the other Shadows fanned out around him to add their own missiles to the volley. Within moments, two dozen druchii lay dead and wounded upon the stones.

'The gate wheel,' said Eothlir, pointing up to the next level of the tower above the parapet.

'Five with me, the rest hold the door,' ordered Alith, running to a flight of steps atop the gatehouse wall. He rammed his bow into its quiver and drew his sword as he bounded up the final few steps to the roof of the tower.

The slavemasters were ready and a cracking whip lashed out to greet Alith as he ran onto the open space. Pain bit through his left arm and he glanced down to see the sleeve of his shirt in tatters, a bloody wound on his forearm. Snarling, he ducked beneath the flailing barbs that snaked out towards him and launched at the whip's wielder. The druchii drew a knife with his free hand but Alith was too quick, driving the point of his sword into the slavemaster's bare chest.

More burning pain screamed across Alith's back as another wicked blow tore at his cloak and flesh, ripping through to the muscle. He stumbled but Casadir was there, dashing past to cut the whipmaster's arm at the elbow. A reverse slash took the elf's head clean off.

The emaciated slaves at the wheel threw themselves at their tormentors, battering and swinging with the chains of their manacles. As Anadriel helped him to his feet, Alith spared a glance across to the other tower and below. He could see black-armoured bodies tossed over the parapet by the Shadows. Much further down, in the killing ground between the outcrops of the walls, a phalanx of spearmen pressed towards the gate, their shields raised against the arrows falling upon them.

'The gate!' shouted Alith, grabbing the nearest slave and pushing him back towards the capstan. 'Open the gate for your freedom!'

Alith lunged onto the nearest bar of the wheel and heaved, the weeping slaves taking their places around him. Fire burned along Alith's spine and he bit back a scream of pain as he bent all of his strength to the task. With a clank-clank-clank the chains tightened and gears turned.

'Keep going!' yelled Casadir from just behind Alith. 'The gate's opening!'

The wheel gathered momentum and within moments ran freely as the gate beneath swung open on its own weight. Alith flopped to the ground with a curse. Casadir dragged him sideways from under the feet of the following slaves as the wheel continued to spin.

With a thunderous crash, the gates slammed against the walls.

Shouts of joy and laughter echoed up from the spearmen below and Alith pulled himself up with Casadir's help and staggered to the parapet. Thousands of warriors streamed into the city. On the wall, Eothlir stood upon the battlement, the unfurled banner of the Anars held high in his hand.

As Casadir bound Alith's wounds with the remains of his cloak, a cry of dismay came from the other Shadows atop the tower. Looking down into the square inside the gate, Alith saw that the druchii beastmasters had unleashed their monstrous creatures upon the army of Malekith. Two enormous hydras advanced on the spearmen, smoke and fire billowing from their jaws.

As the first of the monsters closed on them, the spearmen formed a shield wall, their weapons jutting like silver spines. With a clatter of wheels on stone, the chariots of Chrace charged through the gate and swung around the spearmen. Drawn by white lions, the chariots headed straight for one of the hydras; their prince, a tall elf wielding a gleaming double-headed axe, led the charge.

To the right, more cages were opened and a stream of unnatural beasts loped, skittered and slithered across the stones. Taken from the Anullii and the wastes across the sea north of Ulthuan, the Chaotic monsters lurched forwards, driven by the goads and whips of the beastmasters. More spearmen moved up beside the Naggarothi, their blue banners marked with the symbols of Yvresse.

Alith turned his attention back to the Naggarothi warriors as the flicker of flames and the roars of the lions echoed across the courtyard. The other hydra was almost upon the spearmen. The creature drew back its heads and a shouted command cut across the cacophony filling the square. As one, the spearmen dropped down, raising their shields above their heads. Fire spewed from the hydra's heads, lapping against the shields of the warriors. Some fell, wreathed with smoke and fire, their cries shrill. As the flames dispersed a bank of charnel smoke drifted away from the scorched warriors.

'Kill the handlers!' gasped Alith, drawing his bow.

A shower of arrows fell upon the beastmasters behind the hydra and each fell, pierced by several shafts. As the Shadows turned their missiles upon the other druchii emerging from the cages, Alith watched the hydra.

Suddenly free of the goading whips and spears of its handlers, the hydra slowed. Three of its heads bent back to examine their unmoving corpses, the other four rose into the air, nostrils flaring as they caught the scent of basilisks and khaltaurs. Fiery venom dripping from its maws, the hydra heaved around its bulk and spied its enemies from the mountains. With hisses issuing from its many throats, the hydra lumbered into a run, heading for the other monsters.

'Alith!' Eoloran called up from below. 'Come down here.'

Casadir tightened the knot on the makeshift bandages around Alith's torso and then took off his own cloak and fixed it around Alith's shoulders. With a nod of thanks, Alith trotted down the stairs. The pain had subsided but his back was numb, and twice he almost stumbled as he hurried down the steps.

Coming out onto the rampart, Alith found his father and grandfather in conversation with a majestic elf lord clad in golden armour. He was dark of hair and eye, taller and broader than both Eoloran and Eothlir. He turned as Alith walked out of the tower, a smile on his lips.

'Alith, I would like you to meet a very special person,' said Eothlir, laying an arm across his son's shoulders and pulling him forwards. 'This is Prince Malekith.'

Alith bowed out of instinct, his eyes not leaving the prince's face. Malekith leaned forwards and took Alith by the arm, pulling him upright.

'It is not you that should bow, it is I,' said Malekith, and then he did so, sweeping aside his cloak and lowering himself to one knee for a heartbeat before standing again. 'I owe you a debt that will not easily be repaid.'

'Free Nagarythe and I will consider us even,' said Alith.

'Alith!' snapped Eoloran, but Malekith waved away his rebuke with a laugh.

'He is of the Anars, that is for sure,' said the prince. He turned his gaze back to Alith and his expression was earnest. 'I agree to my part of the bargain. The tyranny of Morathi will end today.'

The prince's attention was drawn to a captain of the spearmen who was striding up the steps to the wall. Malekith waved him forward.

'This is the noble Yeasir, commander of Nagarythe and my most trusted lieutenant,' said Malekith. Yeasir nodded his head in greeting, somewhat uncertainly. Malekith clapped a hand to the shoulder of his second-in-command.

'Well done!' the prince exclaimed. 'I knew you would not let me down.'

'Highness?' said Yeasir.

'The city, you fool,' laughed Malekith. 'Now that we are in, it is only a matter of time. I have you to thank for that.'

'Thank you, highness, but I think you deserve more credit than I,' said Yeasir. He looked at the Anars. 'And without these noble warriors, I would still be stood outside, or perhaps lying outside with an arrow in my belly.'

'Yes, well I have thanked them enough already,' said Malekith. 'It would be best not to give them too much credit, otherwise who knows what ideas they might get.'

'How did they come to be here?' asked Yeasir.

'Malekith sent word to us many days ago,' said Eoloran. He went on to explain the plan devised with Malekith and how the Anars had infiltrated the city.

'Well, you have my gratitude, prince,' said Yeasir with a deep bow. He turned to Malekith with a frown. 'I must admit to being somewhat hurt that you did not feel that you could trust me with this counsel, highness.'

'Would that I could have,' said Malekith airily. 'I trust you more than I trust my own sword arm, Yeasir. I could not divulge my plan to you lest it affect your actions in battle. I wanted the defenders to know nothing was amiss until the gates were opened, and foreknowledge of the Anars' presence may well have meant that you held back until the gates were already flung wide. We needed to keep the pressure on so that all eyes were turned outwards rather than inwards.'

Malekith then turned to Eoloran.

'If you would excuse me, I believe my mother is waiting for me,' the Naggarothi prince said, now empty of all humour.

PART TWO

Exile in Tiranoc; A Usurper's Folly;
Hope Restored; A Banner Falls

—◄ SEVEN ►—

A Bitter Parting

CONVERSATION AND LAUGHTER spilled across the lawns of the Anars' manse in harmony with the pattering of fountains, against a low backdrop of flutes and harps. Three pavilions of red and white, hung with golden chains studded with precious gems, dominated the gardens. Within and without these huge tents, the guests of the Anars strolled and talked, enjoying the midsummer sun.

Nearly twenty years of relative peace had seen the fortunes of the Anars wax again and many of the wealthiest and most powerful nobles of Nagarythe attended Alith's ascension gala. It was his coming-of-age, an occasion of great celebration for the family and their allies. Even Prince Malekith had sent his warmest regards, though his business in the court of Anlec had prevented him from attending, a distraction he professed to regret deeply.

Eoloran had not been surprised by the prince's absence, and Alith also knew well that while Malekith had restored his rule, the problems of the Naggarothi were not yet wholly behind them. Many of the cultists' leaders had escaped capture and hidden, in Nagarythe and other realms of Ulthuan. There was an occasional murmur of uprising, though such demonstrations as happened were local and easily curbed by Malekith's warriors.

The threat of Morathi had receded but not disappeared. Malekith had promised mercy for his mother and the former queen was a prisoner of the Phoenix King in Tiranoc. Though Bel Shanaar forbade her visitors save for her son, and she was kept guarded in chambers lined with magical wards, there were some that believed Morathi still orchestrated the actions of the cults from afar.

Such worries and suspicions were far from Alith's mind on this momentous day. Not only was he a true lord of Elanardris and a prince of Nagarythe, he was also about to make a declaration that he had longed to make for many years.

As the afternoon sun sank towards the horizon, the attendants of the manse marshalled the guests into the main marquee. Censers puffed wisps of fragrant smoke into the air, filling the space with the fresh perfume of mountain flowers. Bunches of white-petalled hill roses and ruby-bloomed caelentha decorated the poles that held up the high roof. Servants swayed effortlessly through the throng with platters of silver, laden with the most exquisite delicacies of Ulthuan and her distant colonies.

A stage of white wood had been erected at one end, gilded with the griffon's wing crest of the Anars. Upon a high-backed chair, Eoloran looked out upon the sea of guests that filled the tent and spilled out onto the grass beyond. His visitors were dressed in their finest clothes, with feathery hats and glittering crowns, bejewelled armlets and necklaces, gowns embroidered with silver thread and hemmed with gilded stars.

Eothlir stood to his father's right hand and Alith to the left. Caenthras stood beside Eothlir while Alith was flanked by Ashniel. She looked resplendent in a gown of soft yellow, which was gathered up in silken billowing clouds about her arms. Golden chains bound her hair in a complex of braids and a single oval diamond hung on a golden necklace around her alabaster neck. She exuded serenity amongst the hubbub of the elves, maintaining an air of cool and noble poise. Alith continually glanced sideways at his love, feeling her beauty lap upon him like the gently cooling waves of a lake's shore.

When all the guests were assembled, Eoloran stood and raised his hands in greeting.

'My most noble friends, welcome to Elanardris,' he declared with a smile. 'It is my honour to have such fine company to witness the ascension of my grandson to adulthood. Many times he has proven his worth, and it is right that we now give praise to his achievements.'

There was a whisper of assent and a forest of hands rose in the air holding crystal goblets and golden cups filled with dark wine. Eoloran took a chalice from a low table set before his throne and raised it in both hands above his head.

'I am Prince Eoloran Anar, lord of Elanardris,' he intoned, his voice quiet and assured. 'My blood hath passed into my son Eothlir, and from he into his son, Alith. My grandson hath come of age this day and upon him now fall the duties of a lord and prince of Ulthuan.'

He took a sip of the wine and lowered the chalice.

'As we gave blood to defend our people alongside great Aenarion, now we take of this wine in remembrance of the sacrifice he made,' Eoloran said solemnly. He drank once more. 'Blood we have shed again to restore peace to these lands, and Alith gave of himself in that conflict. Though we all wish it that such brave deeds are never needed again, my grandson has shown he has the mettle and the spirit to prevail against the darkness that would threaten our homes and our society.'

The mood in the marquee had become sombre as the crowd of elves nodded sincerely, while a few wept silently at the memory of what had befallen Nagarythe. Eoloran allowed his audience to hold their thoughts and memories for a while, his head bowed in meditation as he also contemplated the dark acts he had committed in his life. Straightening, he smiled again.

'Yet it is not for the past that we mark this day, but for the future. Alith is, as are all our children, our legacy to each other and the world. As I pass over this chalice, so I pass my hopes and dreams to the generations to come, and wish them the peace and happiness we have also enjoyed. Into their stewardship we place our great civilisation, from Elanardris to Anlec, Tiranoc to Yvresse, Ulthuan to the far colonies. Into their guardianship we entrust the prosperity of our people, from farmer to prince, servant to king.'

Eoloran turned and proffered the chalice to Alith, who took the goblet with slow ceremony.

'Upon this day of my passing from childhood to adulthood, I accept the duties that fall to me,' Alith said. 'As I have enjoyed the privilege and harmony to learn and grow beneath the boughs of my father and grandfather, I now extend the protection and wisdom of my position to those that will come after.'

Alith then lifted the cup to his lips and took a mouthful of wine. He savoured the deep, rich taste before swallowing, taking in the import of the ceremony just as he imbibed the liquid. No more a child, he was a true lord of House Anar. Pride filled him. Pride that he was Anar, and pride that already he had shown himself worthy of the title of prince.

Alith realised he had closed his eyes. Opening them, he saw expectation in the faces before him: his father and grandfather, Caenthras and Ashniel, and the dozens of elves who had come from across Nagarythe to witness this. Lowering the goblet, Alith smiled and applause filled the tent, with no few shouts of happiness and encouragement.

Caenthras stepped up, hands raised for silence. As quiet descended eventually, the elven lord looked at Alith, his expression thoughtful.

'Let me congratulate Alith on his ascension,' said Caenthras, crossing the stage to embrace the newest prince of the Anars. 'And also let me invite him to say to you all that which we have spoken about between ourselves for many years.'

Suddenly self-conscious, Alith stepped away from Caenthras and turned to Ashniel. He took her left hand in his, still holding the wine in his other.

'On this day of my ascension, it is now time for me to declare to the world that which has been plain for all to see,' said Alith. He looked out towards the audience, joy washing away his nervousness. 'A year hence from this day, House Anar and House Moranin will be joined not just by alliance and friendship, but also by marriage. It is my intent to marry Ashniel and she will become a princess of the Anars as I become a prince of the Moranins. A more profound love I cannot imagine, nor a more fitting dedication to the future than to pave the way for the new heir of the Anars and many more generations to follow.'

'I bless this union between our houses,' said Eoloran.

'I am proud to call Alith a future son,' added Caenthras.

Alith took another sip of wine and held the goblet to Ashniel's pale lips. Her eyes glittered as she looked at him. Her fingers curled around his hand, cool to the touch, and tipped the cup so that the wine wetted her lips and no more. Lifting the chalice away, Ashniel kissed Alith on the forehead, leaving the lightest smudge of red on his brow. She turned with delicate precision, kissed her father upon the cheek and then addressed the crowd.

'There are not the words yet created to express my feelings at this moment, though poets have bent their skills to such labour for a lifetime to fashion them,' she said. 'In the Anars there is great strength, and in my house also. The blood of princes runs deep in Nagarythe, in our bodies and in the land. The generations to come from this lineage will be fair and noble, brave and strong, compassionate and wise. All that is great in the Naggarothi will be made greater yet.'

Alith hooked Ashniel's arm under his and they walked down the short steps from the stage, to be surrounded by the surging elves, who pushed forwards to congratulate the couple and shower them with embraces and kisses. The sides of the marquee were thrown back and the gentle summer breeze stirred the perfumed mists and cast the petals of the flowers into the air above them.

ALITH WAS AWAKE immediately. He did not know what had woken him, but a moment's listening brought sounds of a commotion from the main part of the manse. Evening sun streamed through the unshuttered window; a last defiance against the swiftly approaching Season of Frost. Alith did not remember falling asleep, though upon the table beside his bed lay half-open a lengthy tome by Analdiris of Saphery, analysing the warrior-poetry of Elynuris the Accepter.

Pushing aside the grogginess from his unplanned nap, Alith pulled himself from the bed and straightened his clothes. He heard his father call his name. As he opened the door, Alith found two servants bustling down the corridor, lanterns in their hands.

'What is it?' demanded Alith, grabbing the arm of Cirothir as he jogged past.

'Warriors are marching along the road, prince,' said the servant. 'Your father awaits you at the front of the manse.'

Alith hesitated, deciding whether to fetch his bow. He decided against it, twenty years of peace having eased the paranoia that had once gripped the Anar household. In all likelihood, the soldiers were merely a guard of honour for an important guest. Grabbing a cloak from the chest at the foot of his bed, Alith hurried to the foyer and out onto the courtyard.

Eothlir was there with several other retainers. Eoloran was currently away from the manse, signing a treaty with one of the other noble houses, while Maieth was with Ashniel at the manse of the Moranins making arrangements for the wedding. Father glanced at son with raised eyebrows.

'I have had no word of any important visitor,' said Eothlir. Alith noted that his father had a short sword strapped to his belt. It seemed Eothlir was less willing to forget the troubles of the past.

The clatter of hooves echoed into the courtyard and riders came to a stop just beyond the gateway. Alith could see a column of a few dozen knights, with black pennants on their silver lances. Their leader swung down to the road and crossed quickly to the side of the gate, where Gerithon was standing. There was a short exchange between the two and Gerithon bowed and turned towards the manse with an outstretched arm.

The figure strode purposefully along the pavement, his black-enamelled armour glistening like oil, his dark cloak swirling in his wake. Alith relaxed as the figure came nearer and removed his helm: it was Yeasir, Malekith's captain and commander of Nagarythe. Eothlir seemed set at ease as well, and stepped forwards to meet the Anlec officer.

'You should have sent word, we would have arranged a more suitable welcome,' said Eothlir with a smile, extending his hand. Yeasir's face showed no joy at the encounter and he shook Eothlir's hand only briefly.

'I am sorry,' the lieutenant said, his eyes alternating between Eothlir and Alith. 'I do not bear good news.'

'Come inside and we will hear you,' said Eothlir. 'Your soldiers are welcome to make their camp in our grounds.'

'I fear you will not be so hospitable when you hear what I have to say,' said Yeasir, clearly uneasy. 'I am here to place you under house parole, on the order of Prince Malekith, ruler of Nagarythe.'

'What?' snarled Alith, stepping forwards, stopped only by the outstretched arm of his father.

'Explain yourself,' demanded Eothlir, forcing Alith back. 'Malekith counts House Anar amongst his allies, even his friends. For what reason does he command this arrest?'

Yeasir's expression was pained, and he sent a longing glance back towards his knights.

'I assure you that Malekith has no ill intent towards House Anar,' said the captain. 'If your offer still stands, I would gratefully accept the welcome of your manse.'

Alith was about to tell Yeasir that he had already overstayed such welcome as he deserved, but Eothlir caught his eye and shook his head.

'Of course,' said Eothlir with a nod. 'Your knights may stable their horses and take rooms in the servants' wing. Gerithon!'

The steward came trotting down the path, casting worried looks over his shoulder at the fearsome riders outside the gate.

'Our visitors are to be extended every hospitality as guests,' said Eothlir. 'Please inform the kitchens and make ready such spare bedding as we have available. Commander Yeasir will be accommodated in the main house.'

'Of course, my lord,' said Gerithon, bowing. He hesitated before continuing. 'And how long might your guests be staying?'

Eothlir looked at Yeasir, who sighed.

'Probably for the winter, I'm afraid,' he said, avoiding Eothlir's stare.

'Is it me, or has the weather turned chill quickly this year?' said Alith, wrapping his cloak tight around his body. 'Or perhaps it is something else in the air that makes me shiver.'

Alith stalked back towards the house but a shout from his father caused him to stop and turn.

'Wait for us in my chambers,' Eothlir called out. 'Once everything has been attended to, we will join you there.'

Alith gave no nod or word of assent and merely strode away, his mind full of turbulent thoughts.

WHILE ALITH WAS seething with anger, Eothlir was the picture of patience and understanding. The pair were on the balcony outside Eothlir's chambers with Yeasir, looking at the mountains rising up wild and sharp beyond the ordered nature of the garden. Eothlir and Yeasir were sat on divans, a low table laden with decanter and goblets between them, though nobody had taken a drink. Alith stood staring at the Annulii, his hands fiercely gripping the balcony rail.

'I understand that this must come as something of a shock,' Yeasir was saying. 'No doubt it is some ploy to embarrass or discredit House Anar, and we will be able to put the matter aside in a short time.'

'Who would accuse the Anars of being cultists?' said Eothlir. 'What evidence did they present?'

'I cannot say, for I do not know,' replied Yeasir. 'Prince Malekith vowed before the Phoenix King himself to hunt down the cults, and even his own mother languishes in imprisonment because of that oath. Accusations have been made against the Anars and he is bound by his honour to treat them as equal with any other. You understand that to display any favour or prejudice in this matter would undermine the prince's rule?'

Eothlir acceded grudgingly to this logic with a shallow nod of the head.

'This is a deliberate attack on the Anars,' growled Alith, gazing out towards the mountains. He turned and directed his glare towards Yeasir. 'It is plain that this is some move by the cults to avert the prince's gaze away from them. They seek to divide those that would see them destroyed. Whoever made these accusations is a traitor, performing the deeds of a master other than Malekith.'

'Though I have no name to give you, Prince Malekith assured me that his source is being investigated no less than your family,' said Yeasir.

'What can we do to make this pass away swiftly?' asked Eothlir as Alith turned away again.

'I must conduct a thorough search of the manse and grounds,' said Yeasir. 'As we all know, there is nothing of an incriminating nature to be found, but that must be proved to the prince and his court. Without further evidence, this baseless allegation can be disregarded just as many others have been since the cults scattered on Malekith's return. Many have used such false accusations to settle old scores.'

'I cannot give permission for this,' said Eothlir, and raised a hand to quell Yeasir's argument. 'My father is still lord of the Anars and you must await his return before any search is made.'

'I understand,' said Yeasir. 'Thank you for seeing the difficult position in which I find myself.'

'Gerithon will convey you to your quarters shortly and you are welcome to join us for dinner,' said Eothlir, standing up.

'I think I will go hunting,' muttered Alith, pushing past Yeasir and storming out of his father's chambers.

EOLORAN WAS MOST unhappy by the turn of events he encountered when he returned to Elanardris, though he realised he had no option but to acquiesce to Yeasir's search. The knights were exceptionally thorough, examining every room and corridor and alcove in the manse, searching for amulets and idols that would betray the Anars as worshippers of the cytharai. They scoured the wine cellar and the library, and pulled up the carpets from the halls to seek hidden trapdoors.

Yeasir busied himself with measuring the dimensions of the manse and its rooms, to locate any dead spaces or voids that might conceal a shrine to the lower gods. Despite his personal dislike for events, Alith was impressed and intrigued by Yeasir's diligence. Several days after the search had begun, as he was setting out through the gardens to go hunting, Alith saw the captain on the southern lawn, pacing up and down the rose beds that bordered it. He held parchment in one hand on which he scribbled measurements with a piece of charcoal.

'What do you expect to find out here?' said Alith, crossing over the grass. Yeasir stopped suddenly, surprised.

'I, well, I am looking for concealed entrances,' he said.

'You think we have some grotto beneath the garden, festooned with the bones and entrails of our victims?'

Yeasir shrugged.

'If I cannot conclusively say that you do not, the doubt remains. I am convinced of the innocence of your family, but Malekith needs proof not assurances. The Anars are not the only noble family to have come under suspicion, and some of the things we have found I would spare you description. Complacency now, when so much has been achieved, would only strengthen those that would undermine the true authorities of Ulthuan.'

'The prince has placed a great deal of trust in you,' said Alith, sitting cross-legged on the grass.

'A trust that has been earned over hundreds of years,' said Yeasir, rolling up the parchment. 'He named me commander of Nagarythe in return for the loyalty I have shown him. I was with the prince when he saved Athel Toralien from the orcs. I marched with him across Elthin Arvan and have commanded armies in his name, both in the colonies and here in Nagarythe.'

'I hear that you went with Malekith into the north, as well,' said Alith lightly. Yeasir frowned and looked away.

'That is true, but none of us that came back speak of what happened there,' said the captain. He looked northwards and closed his eyes for a moment. When he opened them, Alith saw fear unlike any he had witnessed before in a Naggarothi. 'There are things on the edge of the Realm of Chaos best left forgotten there.'

Alith considered this with pursed lips.

'I have heard it said that the northlands changed Malekith,' he said after a while. 'He is more serious now, less inclined for adventure and battle.'

'Some adventures and some battles make us realise what it is we want from life,' said Yeasir, fiddling with the charcoal, staining his fingertips. 'Prince Malekith came to the conclusion that his place was here, on Ulthuan, as ruler of Nagarythe. It seems he was right to return when he did.'

'If only he had returned to us sooner,' Alith said with a sigh. 'Perhaps we might have avoided much bloodshed and anguish.'

'The prince was not ready to return earlier, and would not have been able to do what he needed to do,' said Yeasir. 'I am thankful that I was not in Nagarythe to suffer under the rule of Morathi, but that darkness has passed.'

'Has it? What of the cult leaders that escaped justice? What of those depraved worshippers who fled Anlec and Nagarythe?'

'They will be hunted down and brought before Malekith. It is his decree, and I have never seen him fail in something he has set his mind to, even when others thought it impossible.'

Yeasir was about to say something else but stopped.

'What is it?'

'Thank you for talking with me, Alith,' said the captain. 'I know the business that brings me here is unpleasant, but I would have you bear me no ill will for following the orders of our prince.'

Alith considered this for a moment and saw the earnest expression of Yeasir. He remembered the commander's profuse gratitude on the walls of

Anlec and realised that Yeasir believed he owed his life to the Anars. He was an elf of much honour, Alith decided, and if he trusted the judgement of Malekith then he would have to trust Yeasir as well.

Alith stood and extended a hand to the captain, who took it gratefully.

'We are both Naggarothi, and we are not enemies,' said Alith. He glanced towards the clouds gathering overhead. 'I must go hunting before the weather turns against me. When you are done with our gardens, I will take you up to our hunting lodges so that you might see that we have nothing to hide there either.'

'And perhaps catch myself one of the famed Elanardris deer?'

'Perhaps, if your eye is as good for shooting as it is for prying!' laughed Alith.

THE LAST DAYS of the short autumn were drawing to a close, and dark clouds settled around the peaks of the Anullii, pregnant with snow. Yeasir had concluded his exhaustive searches and had not found any evidence of cult activity by the family or their followers. The commander sent word to Anlec along with a complete list of his findings, or lack of them. As Yeasir apologetically explained to his hosts, until he received fresh orders from Malekith he was still bound by the command to keep the Anars under watch. Alith had become almost unaware of the silent knights stationed around the manse and grounds, and they interfered little in his daily life.

The wind was veering to the north with each day, and soon the snow would come again. In the mid-morning just a few days before winter's arrival, Alith was in the side room of his chambers reading Thalduir of Saphery's account of birds in the Saraeluii, the huge mountain realm of the dwarfs that marked the eastern bounds of the colonies in Elthin Arvan. He studied the intricate watercolour paintings, marvelling at the diversity of birds of prey. He hoped that one day he would travel to Elthin Arvan and hunt beneath the wide woods and across the towering mountains of the colonies.

The rattle of carriage wheels in the courtyard broke his thoughts and he placed the delicate silk-bound book upon the table beside him. He stood and went to the high window that overlooked the front gardens of the manse. Several carriages marked with the crest of House Moranin had drawn through the gateway. Excited that Ashniel might be among the passengers, Alith quickly changed from his hunting leathers, which he dressed in when at leisure to do so, and threw on a more formal robe of soft black wool and a wide belt of whitened leather. He tied back his long hair with a thong of woven silver thread and headed downstairs.

On coming out of the main foyer, Alith saw Ashniel gazing from the window of one of the coaches, and he waved. She saw him but her look was blank and a grave doubt began to fill Alith's heart. She drew the curtain closed.

Alith made to walk over to her, but Caenthras stepped down from the lead coach and intercepted him.

'Go fetch your father,' the elven lord said gruffly. 'Bring him here.'

'A lord of House Anar receives guests in the proper manner, he does not hold his councils on the porch,' Alith replied. 'If you would wait a moment, I will have a servant inform my father of your arrival.'

'Your petulance is unbecoming,' said Caenthras. 'Take me to your father.'

Alith still fumed inside at Ashniel's indifference, but acquiesced to Caenthras's demand and led the prince into the house. He knew his father was in the library.

Caenthras followed Alith in silence as they mounted the winding stairs that led up to the second storey of the manse. Alith seethed, wanting to demand what was happening, but he held his tongue, fearing to anger Caenthras even further. Perhaps, a small part of him said, he had misread the situation. His head knew this to be foolish, that something grim was afoot, but Alith said nothing.

Eothlir was sat at a broad desk of white-stained wood, which was littered with maps held down with goblets, plates and other assorted items. The library was not large, barely a dozen paces across, but every wall was lined floor to ceiling with shelves holding scrolls and bound tomes of varying age and subject.

Alith had spent little time here as a youth, no more than required by his tutors, for his passion lay under the open skies and not with written lore. He had preferred his lessons to be practical not theoretical, and had constantly taxed the patience of his teachers with his disdain for poetry, politics and geography. These days he found a little more comfort indoors and the library had a great many maps and diaries from travellers to the colonies. He fondly imagined that at some time he would go to those strange lands with Ashniel by his side.

Eothlir's expression was welcoming as he looked up at the disturbance, but this changed to one of concern when he saw the stern look of Caenthras.

'I fear I am not going to like what you are about to tell me,' said Eothlir, picking up a ewer of water and proffering it towards the lord of the Moranin family. Caenthras declined the drink with a shake of his hand.

'You are not,' Caenthras said. 'You know that I hold no house in higher regard than yours, save for that of Prince Malekith.'

'That is nice to hear, but I think that you are about to demonstrate otherwise,' said Eothlir.

'I am,' said Caenthras. 'My loyalty lies with Nagarythe and my family above all others, and so when I am faced with a decision it is that loyalty which steers my thoughts.'

'Enough, my friend,' said Eothlir. 'Say what it is you have to say.'

Caenthras still hesitated, his eyes fixed on Eothlir, giving not even the slightest glance to Alith who was stood beside his father.

'Ashniel has been invited to attend at the court of Anlec, and I have accepted on her behalf,' said Caenthras.

'What?' snapped Alith. Eothlir did not reply, but shook his head in confusion.

'There have been many wounds between Anlec and the east of Nagarythe, and this is a great opportunity to heal those injuries,' continued Caenthras. 'Think of what good can come to the eastern princes with our voice heard in Malekith's court.'

'And what of the wedding?' said Alith.

Only now did Caenthras look at Alith. His expression was stern.

'Ashniel travels to Anlec before the winter comes,' said the elven lord. 'You are free to join her there in the spring if you wish. Not before then, for she has many duties that need attending to upon her arrival, and I fear she has much to learn about court life in the capital. She does not need the distraction of your presence for the moment.'

'That is unacceptable!' snapped Alith. 'She is to be my wife and yet you have made this decision without consultation with me.'

'She is my daughter,' replied Caenthras, his voice quiet and dangerous. 'Even when you are wed she is my responsibility. I would not have Ashniel waste her life in the woods and mountains when she could achieve so much more in Anlec.'

'One day I will be lord of those woods and mountains,' said Eothlir. 'So will my son. Have you such disdain for us that you prefer the company of the fashionable elite of Anlec? Those who not twenty years ago were all too ready to bend their knee to Morathi and her cults?'

'Times have changed, Eothlir,' said Caenthras, calming his voice. 'Malekith is the new power in Nagarythe, and perhaps one day across Ulthuan.'

'You would see him made Phoenix King also?' asked Eothlir.

'It is the only natural conclusion to events that I can see,' continued Caenthras. 'If you back his claim as heir of Aenarion, then you must feel, as do others, that it is his right not to rule just Nagarythe, but all of Ulthuan.'

'I feel your logic is flawed, Caenthras,' said Eothlir. 'I have no concern who wears the Phoenix Crown and the feather cloak. It is stability and prosperity in Nagarythe that I fought for, not some wider goal.'

'Then it is you who has been deluded,' said Caenthras. 'Or perhaps your father, from whom you have taken all your misguided counsel. Maybe there is more to the accusations of treachery than I first gave credit. What loyal son of Nagarythe would not see Malekith crowned as Phoenix King? Would the Anars see themselves as successors, perhaps?'

'Be careful what you next say,' said Eothlir, standing. 'It seems House Anar has few enough friends at the moment, but House Moranin would do well not to be added to the list of our enemies.'

'And so the ploys of Morathi come full circle, and innuendo and threats have become your weapons, is that right?' spat Caenthras.

'Morathi was correct in one thing,' said Eothlir with a sneer. 'The time to fight was upon us, and those battles have not all been fought. There can be no bystanders. I tell you that House Anar has nothing to do with the cults and if you turn from us, you only fan the fires of falsehood that have smouldered in Nagarythe since Malekith's return.'

'I have come out of courtesy for your family, and for you, whom I once named friend,' said Caenthras, controlling his anger with considerable effort. 'I thought you would offer me the same respect. I will not speak against you, Eothlir, but I cannot aid you. I hope that one day, in not too many years, we can meet again and put this behind us and be companions once more. I wish you no ill, Eothlir, but I cannot countenance moving against the will of Anlec.'

With no further word, Caenthras spun on his heel and stalked from the room. Eothlir's face was a mask of anguish, torn between ire and woe. Alith stared out of the doorway at Caenthras's retreating back, his teeth grinding.

'See that they leave without incident,' Eothlir said, before waving Alith away and sitting down to bury his head in his hands.

Alith hurried after Caenthras, who returned to his caravan and gave the signal for them to depart. The young Anar watched the coach of Ashniel, hoping to see her draw back the curtain and give him some indication of her feelings, but it was not to be. The coach rattled from the courtyard without the slightest glimpse of her.

Alith silently cursed House Moranin, and he cursed the cowardly Caenthras even more. With a snarl he strode towards the house, the servants and soldiers in the courtyard fleeing before his foul mood like sheep from a stalking wolf.

As when he was a child, Alith sought sanctuary in the wilds of Elanardris, despite the misgivings of his father and the bitter weather. He would walk out into the cold peaks sometimes to hunt, on other occasions simply to be away from any other soul.

On this day he was sat on a rock at the bank of a thin stream, skinning and cleaning a mountain hare he had shot. As he stooped forwards to clean his blade in the almost-frozen water, he caught the reflection of a black shape in the sky: a crow.

'It has been a long while,' said Alith, straightening.

'Yes it has,' replied Elthyrior, sitting down beside Alith. As before, the raven herald was draped in his cloak of shadowy feathers, his face hidden in the depths of his hood. Only his green eyes showed. 'And you know that my appearance is not a glad tiding.'

Alith sighed and finished cleaning his knife, slipping it into his belt as he turned towards Elthyrior.

'And what new threat arises?' he said. 'Perhaps the dwarfs have built a fleet of ships made from rock and cross the ocean to sack Ulthuan? Or maybe the Sapherian mages have turned themselves all into rampaging goats?'

'Your attitude is unbecoming for a prince of Ulthuan,' snapped Elthyrior. 'Allow the grace of your bloodline to show through.'

Alith sighed again.

'I am sorry, but I have much in my mind of late. I suppose you warn me not to go to Anlec?'

Elthyrior sat back in surprise.

'How could you know this?'

'Nothing else has changed recently that would warrant your return after twenty years,' explained Alith. 'Always you come when there is a decision to be made, to warn against one course of action or the other. It is the way of Morai-heg to lay these dilemmas before us and laugh as we try to navigate our way through the tangled web she has woven.'

'Do you know why you cannot go to Anlec?'

'Bad things will happen, though of an enigmatic nature I am sure.'

Alith stood and looked down at Elthyrior.

'What can I say to you? I cannot promise that I will not go to Anlec. Ashniel is there now, and if you tell me it is unsafe for me there, I cannot believe that it is safe for my betrothed. Your words make me more inclined to go to her, not less.'

'Ashniel is lost to you, Alith,' Elthyrior said sorrowfully, standing and placing a hand on Alith's shoulder. 'Anlec is not the place you think it is.'

Alith laughed and cast aside Elthyrior's gesture of sympathy.

'You expect me to believe you? You think a few rumours would break the bond that lies between us?'

'Soon there will be more than rumours,' said Elthyrior. 'Since Malekith's return I and others of my order who are loyal to Nagarythe have followed the spoor of those cultists that escaped. They have not been idle, in Nagarythe and elsewhere. Though they are more hidden than ever before, there are ways to find them and learn their secrets. The accusation of the Anars is part of a grander scheme, though what its aim is remains unknown to me. Though word has not yet reached Elanardris, there have been attacks and uprisings in several parts of Nagarythe. The cultists have returned, but this time they declare not for Morathi but for Eoloran of House Anar!'

'That cannot be! You know that we are free of any taint.'

'And yet they protest at the arrest of your family, and so give truth to the lie. Anlec is not safe for the Anars, and I fear that Elanardris will be a haven for little longer.'

'Yeasir...'

'Perhaps,' said Elthyrior. 'He should be watched closely. I do not think he knows truly his part in this, he is but a piece on a game board for a more powerful player.'

'Who is this player? Morathi?' Alith waved away his own concern. 'She is held captive in Tor Anroc, I cannot believe that she still wields the power over the cults that she once had.'

'You know of the saying, "As the parent, so too the child"?'

'You cannot surely suspect Malekith of being the architect of this deception?'

'I cannot *surely* know anything,' laughed Elthyrior, a bitter sound. 'This is a game played with deceit and misdirection. It is played in shadows and with the minds of elves. Yet, I am not a player, I can only follow the moves as they are made and report them to others.'

'So do you know who any of the players are?'

'Morathi, for certain, though at a distance,' said Elthyrior. 'Malekith certainly moves some pieces, though for his own ends or those of some other cause I cannot say. Others in his court are also tied to the strings of their puppets, though it is hard to follow the threads back to the hand that controls them. As I have warned before, you cannot afford to trust anyone save yourself.'

'So what am I to do? It seems as though there is little we can do to defend ourselves against accusation if the cults treat us as their own. It seems we are pieces being played, and have no control over the game or its rules.'

'Then you must find a player on your behalf, and change the board in your favour.'

Alith turned away and gazed at his rippling reflection in the icy water.

'The Phoenix King,' he said. 'There is no greater player in Ulthuan.'

Elthyrior gave no reply and when Alith turned he saw that the raven herald had, as usual, disappeared without warning. A long caw echoed from the mountainsides and then Alith was left alone with the wind and the babbling of the stream.

ALITH BROODED ON Elthyrior's words for several days, weighing up the courses of action he could take. Each day brought the risk that news would come of the cults' uprisings in defence of the Anars, and Alith feared that such tidings would stir Yeasir to firmer security. As midwinter approached, he also knew that travel from the mountains would be all but impossible and, stirred by this vague deadline, called his family together to discuss with them his thoughts.

Unobserved by Yeasir, his soldiers or any of the servants, Alith gathered his family in the chambers of his grandfather. Eoloran was sat beside the crackling fire, while Eothlir and Maieth stood hand-in-hand gazing out of the ice-freckled window.

'I am leaving Elanardris,' Alith announced as he closed the white-panelled door to the chamber.

'For where?' asked Maieth, crossing the room to stand in front of her son. 'Surely you do not think to travel to Anlec in such harsh weather.'

'It is not for Anlec that I am bound,' Alith told them. 'The Anars are being used, and we do not have the means to reveal this deception. I will go to Bel Shanaar and ask for his intervention.'

'That would not be wise,' said Eoloran. 'It is not the business of the Phoenix King to involve himself in matters internal to Nagarythe. Other princes and nobles will not take kindly to interference from Tor Anroc. He knows little of what happens here, and is an uncertain ally.'

'An uncertain ally is better than no ally at all,' said Eothlir. 'House Moranin has all but deserted us, no doubt for the benefit of Caenthras's reputation. Our friends have been few for many years. I think Alith is right that we need to seek strength as times turn against us.'

'Some will say such a move is in defiance of Malekith's rule,' said Eoloran. 'Should we not have the confidence of our prince, then we have nothing.'

'We do not know the counsels Malekith receives,' said Alith, moving to sit in the chair opposite his grandfather. He leant forwards earnestly. 'While we can keep our faith with Malekith, are you so sure that what he is told is the truth? Do not his own oaths of honour make him susceptible to lies told by others? If Bel Shanaar is an uncertain ally, Malekith has not yet proven himself a certain master.'

'What of Ashniel and the wedding?' said Maieth. 'Caenthras has not ruled out the union between the houses. If he were so turned against us, he would not allow Ashniel to be married. There is hope there, Alith. It is my fear that you would risk that alliance by involving the Phoenix King. Caenthras is a strong advocate of Nagarythe's independence from the Phoenix Throne.'

Alith shook his head sadly, and gave voice to a conclusion that had troubled him since Ashniel's departure.

'There will be no wedding,' said Alith. 'Though he says one thing to us, I believe that he has turned Ashniel against me. He treads upon the line between friend and foe, not wishing to associate openly with the Anars but willing to keep alive what connection he has should he find the need for us again. In Anlec, I would be the fly trapped in the web. I cannot go there, and in refusing I snub House Moranin and give Caenthras greater excuse to be displeased with us. I wonder how long it is that his goals and ours have been at odds, and it seems that he has positioned himself to benefit whatever the outcome.'

'I am so sorry, Alith,' said Maieth. She crouched beside her son with a tear on her cheek, and stroked his hair. Alith leaned forwards and kissed her on the head and pulled her up.

'I feel as though I had been blinded but now I see the light,' he said. 'Though I loved Ashniel, I realise that my feelings were never returned. This was ever a match of politics, made by Caenthras and dutifully carried out by Ashniel. I saw her when she left and there was not a sign that she was sad at our parting. What I saw as calm nobility was no more than cool aloofness.'

Alith found his embarrassment rising and became angry, standing up and balling his fists.

'How much she must have thought herself clever, seeing the ignorant Anar come at her slightest call, like the hawk to its master,' he snarled. 'She has played me for a fool, and I filled my part all too well for her. I have read again those letters that she sent me, and think on the conversations we have had, and ever the affection was from me to her, while her own love was but an imagining I had conjured for myself! I am sure she amuses her maids in

Anlec with tales of her tame prince, telling them how I will come running to her in the spring with the gentlest flick of my reins!'

Maieth embraced Alith, running her hand down his back. He allowed himself to enjoy the comfort of her love for a while and then gently pushed her away.

'Though I have been wronged, it is not out of spite that I turn to the Phoenix King,' said Alith. 'I believe that there is genuine danger for the Anars, and it will come soon.'

'What sort of danger?' asked Eothlir. 'How do you know this?'

'First I must tell you that I cannot say from where I gained this information,' said Alith. He held up his hand when Eothlir opened his mouth to object. 'I have given my word, but if you trust me then have faith that what I am to tell you is true.'

'Always we will believe you, Alith,' said Eoloran with a concerned look. 'Tell us what it is that you know.'

'There have been demonstrations against Malekith's house arrest of the Anars,' said Alith.

'So there are those who we can count upon as allies,' said Eothlir. 'I do not see–'

'By cult leaders,' Alith interrupted sharply. 'The cultists make a pretence that we are of their ilk, and thus we will be condemned alongside them. For whatever reasons further their cause, the cults speak openly in praise of the Anars and there is no defence we can make that will stop the accusations that will surely follow.'

'I do not see how Bel Shanaar can help us,' said Maieth. 'Why will he not believe our enemies as well?'

'There is no guarantee that he will not,' said Alith. 'That is why it is I that must go to him. Better that we put some case before the Phoenix Throne than no case at all.'

Alith waved for his mother to be seated and when she had done so, he stood behind her, his hands on her shoulders.

'I have given this my deepest consideration,' he told his family. 'It is not wise that all three lords of the Anars, present and future, are trapped in Elanardris. One of us must leave here so that whatever happens, the cause of the family can be championed beyond these walls. We cannot send a servant to do this, no matter how trusted, for whoever entreats the Phoenix King to help must carry the full authority of the house. I am the most free to leave without question, for Yeasir and his guards are content to allow me to go hunting without escort. They will not expect a swift return and so I can gain a day, perhaps two, ahead of any pursuit that might be sent after me. No one else enjoys that freedom from scrutiny. When my absence is noted, it can be said that I have perhaps fled for Anlec, unwilling to wait until the spring to see Ashniel.'

Alith paused and gave a meaningful look to his father and grandfather. 'I am also the most expendable, should things go ill in one way or another.'

'You are not expendable to me!' said Maieth. 'You are my son and I would see you safe before all other considerations.'

'None of us are safe, Mother,' replied Alith sternly. 'It is not in me to hide here and await the inevitable. The last time we were pressed by the power of Anlec, it was only through the strength of our alliances that we were able to resist our foes. This time the Anars will be forced to stand alone unless we can find help from another source.'

Eoloran and Eothlir exchanged a long look with each other, reading each other's thoughts from their expressions. It was Eoloran who spoke first, standing and gripping Alith's arm.

'It is pointless to express regret on things that we cannot change, and I cannot fault your reasoning. I will write letters of introduction to produce for Bel Shanaar. We know each other of old though many hundreds of years have passed since we last spoke. I believe that the Phoenix King will give you fair hearing, though I cannot guess his response.'

'Do not go openly,' warned Eothlir. 'Morathi dwells in Tor Anroc and though imprisoned I am sure she has her spies at hand. If the Phoenix King is to aid us, then it must be kept secret as long as possible. I understand why Malekith returned to us without announcement, as the element of surprise is one of the greatest weapons we can yet rely upon.'

'When do you plan to leave?' asked Maieth. 'Tell me you will not be going immediately.'

'A day or two at the most,' said Alith. 'Though Yeasir has not yet heard of the cultists' support for us, he will soon and then we cannot say how he will react.'

'Yeasir and his few dozen knights are little threat to us,' said Eothlir. 'Should we need to be rid of his scrutiny it is easily accomplished.'

'No!' said Eoloran. 'We must be beyond reproach, even when no one will believe us. Yeasir is here under lawful authority and we have accepted as such. We must do nothing that adds further fuel to the fires of suspicion.'

'How will we hear from you, or contact you?' asked Maieth. 'Is there a messenger we can trust?'

'There is one who I may be able to use, but I cannot name him now,' said Alith. He directed his gaze to Eoloran. 'If he does come, you will know him and you must trust him, as I do. I cannot say any more.'

Maieth threw her arms around Alith once more, stifling a sob.

'I will write that letter,' said Eoloran, bowing before leaving the room. Eothlir laid his arms about the shoulders of his wife and son, and the three of them stood sharing the silence for a while longer.

IT WAS THREE days before Alith was ready to set off for Tor Anroc. His hunting trips roused no suspicion in the warriors from Anlec, and under the cover of these excursions Alith was able to stockpile a small amount of food and clothes in one of the watch-caves in the mountains. On the seventh morning after meeting Elthyrior he was set to go.

He said no goodbyes to his family as they had already said their farewells several times. Alith was eager to leave now that his mind was set – for practical reason of the deteriorating weather and also driven by the urge to act against the forces aligning in opposition to House Anar. He did not depart early, keeping to his usual routine of heading into the mountains mid-morning. Grey clouds swathed the sky though the snow had lightened in the past few days. As he left the manse, Alith saw Yeasir with his knights drawn up for inspection in the courtyard. Alith waved cheerfully and cut eastwards through the gardens, leaving by the gate in the high hedge that bordered the lawn.

FREE FROM THE eyes of Yeasir and his warriors, Alith turned south-east and made directly for the cave where he had stashed his provisions. It was past midday by the time he had climbed up to the empty watch post and the snow was falling heavily. The air was filled with flurries of white and Alith was unable to see more than a dozen paces ahead. The wind tugged at his grey hood and cloak and swept his long hair across his face as snowflakes settled on his fur-lined hunting coat. His boots were crusted with ice as he strode purposefully across the snow drifts towards the south. Glancing back, Alith saw the falling snow obscuring the faint footprints his light tread had left. Smiling at being free once more, Alith hiked his pack higher onto his shoulders and pressed on.

The snow continued relentlessly for the whole day and into the night. Alith spared himself only short breaks from his walking, taking shelter beneath overhangs and in craggy defiles to drink spice-seasoned water from his flask and eat a little of the carefully wrapped rabbit and bird meat he had cooked over the previous days. As twilight fought through the thick clouds he looked for somewhere to stay for the night.

After much searching, Alith located a small knot of trees further down the mountainside. He climbed into one of the larger pines and quickly wove a rudimentary roof from the branches above. With the worst of the snow kept away, he sat with his back to the trunk, his legs along the branch, and fell into a light sleep.

ALITH WOKE BEFORE dawn and was suddenly aware that he was being watched. Opening his eyes just a fraction, he saw a large crow perched on the end of the branch. With a wry smile, he opened his eyes fully and looked around for Elthyrior.

The raven herald was squatting in the snow a little way off, rousing a small fire into life. A thin wisp of smoke drifted up through the branches. Elthyrior looked up as Alith stood.

'I am happy to see that my warnings do not fall upon deaf ears,' he said.

'I am sorry if I was harsh when we last met,' said Alith, dropping down from the tree. 'Often one knows that something is amiss but refuses to look upon the truth. I knew that all was not well with Ashniel, but would not believe myself. One should not shoot the messenger if the tidings are bad.'

Elthyrior waved Alith closer.

'I wish that I could bring better news on occasion, but it is not the task of the raven heralds to be bearers of happiness,' he said. 'In war and hardship our order was founded, and so our eyes and ears are ready for that which brings misery not joy.'

'It must be lonely,' said Alith, crouching beside the fire. A thought occurred to him. 'Is it safe to have a flame? The smoke might be seen.'

'There is nobody to see it, not here,' said Elthyrior. 'You chose your path well, keeping high up the mountains. Where do you intend to go from here?'

'I thought to head south for another two days until I come to the Naganath. Then follow the river west before turning south towards Tor Anroc.'

'I would counsel against that,' said Elthyrior, shaking his head. 'Bel Shanaar has his army stationed on the Naganath, watching the border. There is little chance your journey to Tor Anroc will be unobserved. Should you be found crossing from Nagarythe you will be taken into custody and brought before Bel Shanaar in full view.'

Alith swore gently.

'I do not know Tiranoc,' he said. 'Now that we speak of it, it seems foolish that I could reach the Phoenix King without suspicion. Even if I make it to the city, how do I contact Bel Shanaar?'

'I have no answers for your second question, but for the first I would say to keep on the southern path until you come to the Pass of the Eagle. Turn westwards and head to Tor Anroc from there. Only a few days to the south the weather is more welcoming and some travellers still pass between Ellyrion and Tiranoc at this time of the year. I am not saying you will go without being noticed, but coming from the east will attract less attention than the north.'

'Thank you,' said Alith. 'I do not know how I would ever survive without you to guide me.'

'Then you must learn, for I cannot be relied upon,' Elthyrior replied. His voice was quiet but stern. 'You are not my only concern, and you are an adult. I am your ally but I cannot be your guardian and guide forever. You know the right paths to take, but you argue with yourself constantly. Trust your instincts, Alith. Morai-heg speaks to all of us in our dreams and feelings. If you do not trust her, and many are wise not to, then find another in whose light you are happy to follow.'

Alith considered this for a moment, warming his hands at the fire.

'You did not answer my first point,' said Alith. 'Are you lonely?'

As if in reply, the crow cawed and flapped down to land upon Elthyrior's shoulder, nestling into the raven feathers that made up his cloak.

'Loneliness is an indulgence for those with the time to spare for it,' said Elthyrior. 'Some fill the emptiness with the meaningless chatter of those around them. Some of us fill it with a greater purpose, more comforting than any mortal company.'

'Then tell me one other thing,' said Alith, seizing the moment of companionship he felt with the raven herald. 'Have you ever loved?'

Elthyrior's face was a mask as he replied.

'Love was taken from my family in the time of Aenarion. Perhaps it may return before I die, but I think it unlikely. There will be little love for any of us in the years ahead.'

'Why? What have you seen?'

'I dream of black flames,' said Elthyrior, gazing deep into the fire. When he turned his attention to Alith, the Anar prince flinched from the icy stare of those emerald eyes. 'It is not a good omen.'

ELTHYRIOR TRAVELLED SOUTH with Alith for the best part of the next day, leaving him just before dusk.

'I cannot be found within the borders of Tiranoc,' the raven herald told Alith. 'They will think me a cultist, and my pledge is to the protection of Nagarythe and it is here that my powers are strongest. From here you can easily find your way to Eagle Pass.'

The snow stopped at about the same time and Alith pressed southwards into the night while the going was fair. His path took him across several streams and a broad river – the headwaters of the Naganath that marked the border between Tiranoc and Nagarythe. Crossing the water, he moved from the realm of Prince Malekith into the kingdom of Bel Shanaar. He truly was on foreign soil.

Looking westwards the sky was clearing and out on the plains many miles away he saw the dim flickers of camp fires. There the armies of the Phoenix King watched their neighbour. It seemed that Bel Shanaar was not yet convinced by the twenty years of peace that had followed Malekith's return. Alith was beginning to share his doubts.

─◄ EIGHT ►─

A Dark Plan Revealed

TIRANOC WAS CERTAINLY warmer than Elanardris. The wind kept steady from the west, bringing air from the hot climes of Lustria across the seas and holding the wintry chill at bay. The sky was overcast though and the square that adjoined the great palace of the Phoenix King was all but empty. A few elves hurried from one place or another, eager to spend little time out of the warmth of the city's thousands of fireplaces.

Alith sat on a marble bench close to the wall surrounding the plaza, looking at the ceremonial gateway that led into the palace. Two white, circular towers soared above, each with a pointed gilded roof and capped with braziers that burnt with magical blue fire – a sign that the Phoenix King was in residence.

The city was utterly different to Anlec. Tor Anroc had been built and rebuilt in times of peace, of winding roads and open spaces, while the Naggarothi capital clung to its warlike past with its forbidding walls and garrison houses. Built around and into a solitary mountain that speared up from the plain of Tiranoc, Tor Anroc was partly opened to the sky and partly a maze of winding tunnels lit with silver lanterns. There was colour and light everywhere Alith looked, utterly unlike the grim greys and black of Anlec's naked stone.

He didn't like it at all. The city was for show and little else, like the enormous gatehouse to the palace. The city was dominated by the manses of princes and other nobles and vast embassies containing lords and ladies from the other kingdoms of Ulthuan. Most of the folk of Tiranoc dwelt in

455

towns that surrounded the capital, riding in by wain and horse each day and returning home at nightfall. Only those close to the Phoenix King could afford to stay in the city.

Alith had been in Tor Anroc for three days. He had followed Elthyrior's instructions and travelled along the roads from Eagle Pass. He had been relieved if not also a little disturbed that his entrance into the city amongst a group of merchants went unremarked. It was fortunate for his personal circumstance, but it was clear that after so many travails across the isle the vigilance against the cults and their agents was weak, even here where the ruler of the elves lived. There were guards at the gates and on the walls, but they watched the masses passing with only vague interest.

For three days Alith had come to the plaza and thought on how he might enter the palace and contact the Phoenix King in secret. He had listened to the market stall traders gossiping and the exchange of rumours between the visiting nobles picking at the merchants' wares. Fashions in clothing and literature, talk of the colonies and the romances of the princes and princesses of Ulthuan dominated, and there was little spoken about Nagarythe, or Prince Malekith. It occurred to Alith that the Naggarothi were treated like distant cousins, occasionally wayward and attracting attention but otherwise left to their own means. If one did not pry too hard, one would not see things that might be unpleasant.

The hosts of Tiranoc camped close to the banks of the Naganath told Alith a different story, and he was astounded that having such a garrison in place caused so little remark amongst the Tiranocii. Even Morathi's imprisonment was old news and Alith had not heard her name spoken once in the time he had been in the city.

Alith admitted that he was at a loss concerning what to do next. His paranoia was such that he was loath to announce himself to any but Bel Shanaar, though as a prince of Nagarythe he could have simply walked up to the gates and demanded an audience with the Phoenix King. He had caught word that Bel Shanaar regularly held open sessions during which any elf could petition him, but also had detected an undercurrent that such audiences were not truly open and all petitioners were questioned and vetted prior to being allowed to come before the Phoenix Throne. A public audience would do Alith little good even if he could gain entry – the hall would surely be full of others to see Bel Shanaar and he would have no privacy to express his concerns to the Phoenix King.

As midday came, the market began to fill with elves as they made their way in from the towns and farms around the city. Alith wandered amongst the growing crowds, his grey and brown wilderness clothes at odds with the swirling robes and gaily coloured dresses of the urbane elite of Tiranoc. Fortunately most took him for a servant of some kind and paid him no attention as individuals in power often do when close to those of lesser station.

It was this invisibility that gave Alith an idea.

That night he stayed in the city, though the boarding house cost him a good proportion of the silver coins his father had furnished him with. After dark, when the gates were closed, the city took on a different life. Lanterns of red and blue sprang into life and those more modest elves who still lived in Tor Anroc finished their labours and came out. The wine houses threw open their doors and cellars and the merchants packed up their stalls to patronise these establishments.

Alith entered one of these drinking halls close to the palace and was pleased to see a variety of customers in the livery of the Phoenix King. Some were ageing retainers, most were young pages, maids, ostlers, cleaners, cooks and other mundane chore-workers looking for a way to establish themselves in court life. Alith picked a likely group – three male elves and four female – and bought a generous pitcher of hot spiced wine. This cost most of his remaining money and he hoped the expense was not in vain. He filled a tray with eight red-enamelled clay goblets, and the jug, and sat down with the palace servants.

'Hello,' he said, handing out the cups. 'I'm Atenithor. I'm new to the city and I'm wondering if you could help.'

'Is that an Ellyrian accent?' asked one of the maidens as Alith began to pour the wine. She was petite, for an elf, and her smile was warm and genuine. Alith took her to be a little younger than him, but only by a decade or so.

'Chracian,' he said, feeling that if someone knew the difference they would already have known he was Naggarothi. He guessed that few folk of Nagarythe would be found in the city.

'I'm Milandith,' said the girl, extending a hand. Alith shook it and there were peals of laughter from those around the table.

'One kisses the hand in greeting,' said one of the male youths. He took Alith's hand and quickly pursed his lips to the middle knuckle. 'Like so. I am Liaserin. Pleased to make your acquaintance, Atenithor.'

Alith returned the gesture, trying not to look self-conscious. In Naggaroth, a simple handshake was considered sufficient greeting, and perhaps an embrace for those who were family or well-regarded.

'It seems I have already displayed my ignorance.' Alith laughed off his embarrassment. 'It is a good job that I have some friends to steer me straight. I was a hunter, you see, and one does not get much time to learn the niceties of city life on a mountainside.'

He then went around the table kissing the hands of the others, nodding his head in deference as they told him their names.

'What brings a hunter to Tor Anroc?' asked Lamendas, a female elf that Alith judged to be a little older than the others, perhaps in her eightieth or ninetieth year.

'Ambition!' Alith declared with a grin and raised eyebrows. 'My father is a famous hunter in the south of Chrace, but it seems that the princes don't value his work as much as when he was young. I realised that if I am to make a name for myself it was either Tor Anroc or the colonies, and I've never been one for ships!'

There was more laughter, friendlier. Alith could feel his new companions warming to his presence and continued.

'Naturally, I am looking for a position at the palace. Might I enquire how one goes about securing such employment?'

'Well, that depends on what you can do,' said Lamendas. 'Not much need for a hunter in a palace.'

'Butchery,' Alith replied quickly. 'A hunter learns to use a knife as well as a bow, and so I thought perhaps I might make myself useful in the kitchens.'

'You might be in luck,' said Achitherir, a boy of perhaps no more than thirty years. 'The cooks are always looking for more help. Every banquet the Phoenix King holds is attended to by more guests than the last. You should speak to Malithrandin, the Steward of the Fires.'

'Malithrandin?'

Milandith, who was sat on Alith's right, leaned close to him and pointed towards a table close to the fireplace. There were six elves of more senior years arguing intently over a piece of paper. Her other hand brushed Alith's thigh gently but deliberately as she sat back.

'My father, he sits with the other stewards,' she said, placing a hand on Alith's knee beneath the table. 'I could introduce you if you like.'

'That would be most helpful,' said Alith, making to stand. Milandith's grip on his knee tightened and forced him to stay seated.

'Not now, the stewards would be most perturbed to have their leisure interrupted by us,' she said. 'I will take you to him in the morning.'

'Where might I find you in the morning?'

'Well, if you pour me another glass of wine,' Milandith purred, 'you'll find me lying next to you...'

MAGICAL LIGHT FLICKERED from the lantern in the corner of Milandith's small room, dappling everything in a muted yellow and green. Alith lay staring at the ceiling, feeling the warmth from Milandith beside him. He wondered if he had made a terrible mistake. It would have been unforgivable for him to sleep with Ashniel before they were wed and Caenthras would have been right to demand serious reparations for such an act, not to mention the dishonour Alith would have brought to the Anar name. Perhaps things were different for the lower orders? There had certainly been no hint of reproach or suspicion from the other servants when Milandith had brought him back to her quarters in one of the palace's long wings.

A thought occurred to Alith that brought a smile to his face. What would be Milandith's reaction if she learnt that she had bedded a prince of Ulthuan, heir to one of the most powerful families in Nagarythe, no less? As he dwelt on this, his mood darkened again. The encounter, passionate and honest, had been nothing like his dealings with Ashniel. There had been none of the coquettish flirtation and implied physicality, simply the mutual desire of two people. Maybe Ashniel had deliberately held back her attentions, to lead him on and tease rather than fulfil?

He felt Milandith stir next to him and looked to his left, letting his gaze linger on the smooth curve of her naked back and her thick curls of brown hair spilling onto the golden pillow. She rolled towards Alith, eyes half-opened.

'I would have thought your exertions would have left you ready for sleep,' she murmured, stroking a hand across his bare chest.

Alith leant across and kissed her on the cheek.

'I have a lot to think about,' he said. 'The city seems to offer many charms that a simple hunter is not used to.'

Milandith smiled and stretched, allowing herself to fall onto him, her head on his chest. She curled her fingers into his hair.

'The city has many delights to be enjoyed, but I would have thought that this one was not new to you,' she said sleepily.

Alith did not reply and she looked up at his face. Her eyes widened in shock and she covered her mouth, suppressing a light laugh.

'I did not know Chracian hunters were so chaste!' she giggled. 'Had I known, I would have been more… gentle.'

Alith laughed with her, feeling no embarrassment at his inexperience.

'If you could not tell that this was my first time, then I must have some natural talent!'

Milandith kissed him on the lips, cupping his face in her hands.

'Beginner's luck, perhaps?' she said. 'Of course, there is a simple way to find out.'

Any other thoughts fled Alith's mind as he held Milandith close; Nagarythe, Caenthras, Ashniel, the cults, all banished in a moment of peace and contentment.

ALITH WORKED HARD in the kitchens and, when time allowed, learnt as much as he could about the Phoenix King's palace. When not preparing boar or venison or rabbit or wildfowl for the cooks, his attention was divided between exploring the layout of the palace and socialising with the other staff, particularly Milandith. In this last case, Alith learnt a great deal of gossip over goblets of wine and in whispered, dreamy conversations lying in bed late at night. Milandith was naturally inquisitive and outgoing, and seemed to know much about the routines and rituals of palace life, as well as a good number of the hundreds of servants and guards that populated the citadel. Alith felt a little guilt about exploiting their relationship in such an underhand way, but Milandith seemed always ready to teach her new lover about Tor Anroc and its ways, and was honest about her own desire for companionship and intimacy without deep commitments required from either of them.

What Alith had learnt did not fill him with confidence. Bel Shanaar was only rarely alone, his days filled with audiences and meetings with persons of importance. His family – his son Elodhir principal amongst them – were also a constant presence during less formal occasions. When matters of state or family did not require his attention, the Phoenix King was shadowed by his chamberlain, Palthrain. Much as Gerithon managed many of the affairs of Elanardris for Eoloran, Palthrain was Bel Shanaar's chief advisor and agent. He oversaw the running of the palace, and every member of the staff from the maids to the captains of the guard ultimately owed responsibility to him. His dealings were not confined purely to the domestic, and he was pivotal in many negotiations between Tiranoc and the other kingdoms.

One other figure attracted Alith's attention, mentioned in passing by Milandith one evening. His name was Carathril, a slightly melancholy elf who served as the Phoenix King's chief herald. He was from Lothern and as Alith inquired more he learnt that Carathril had once been a captain in the Lothern Guard and had acted as Bel Shanaar's emissary when Malekith had first tried to retake Anlec and been thwarted at Ealith. That Carathril knew a little about Nagarythe and the prince intrigued Alith and he decided that he would attempt to make the acquaintance of the herald at the earliest opportunity.

Alith had been in the palace for nearly twenty days before such a circumstance arrived. Most of his labours in the kitchen, which he found surprisingly pleasant to perform for they were not taxing and gave him time to cogitate on other matters, were usually finished by mid-afternoon. This gave him until the evening to conduct his shadowy investigations before the expectations of social interaction required him to spend time with his fellow servants after dark. On this particular day, Alith was presented with the chance to enter the Phoenix King's great hall.

It was an open audience, as Alith had heard about, and such members of society as were able to beg, bribe or sneak their way into the hall were allowed to observe the proceedings. Dressed in his nondescript white robes, Alith was easily able to join a group of elves as they made their way into the central chamber, and then split from them to take a seat on the benches at the top of the tiers of seats surrounding the auditorium.

As he made his way up the steps, Alith spied a lonely-looking figure sat somewhat apart from the others, far from the crowds who jostled for places on the lowest benches nearest Bel Shanaar. From his appearance, livery and disposition Alith guessed this to be Carathril, and he walked around the top tier of the seats and sat down beside the elf.

'Are you Carathril?' he asked, deciding it was better to speak plainly than try to elicit what he needed by subterfuge.

The elf turned in surprise, and then nodded.

'I am the Phoenix King's herald,' he said, extending his hand towards Alith.

'You can call me Atenithor,' said Alith, kissing Carathril's hand. The herald took it away a little too quickly and Alith judged that he was as uncomfortable with this Tiranoc convention as Alith. 'I find it strange also.'

'What's that?' said Carathril, who had turned his attention back to the procession of elves making their way through the open doors.

'The hand-kissing,' said Alith. 'I'm not from Tiranoc either, and I find it most peculiar.'

Carathril did not reply and instead raised a finger to his lips for quiet and nodded towards the doorway. Alith looked down and saw Palthrain enter, dressed in a coat of deep purple with a wide blue belt studded with sapphires. He stood to one side and bowed.

Alith laid eyes upon Bel Shanaar for the first time. The Phoenix King was stood erect and proud, dressed in a flowing robe of white decorated with golden thread in the design of phoenixes rising from flames. Upon his shoulders he wore a cloak made of white and black feathers that trailed behind him. His austere face looked straight ahead, and atop his head he wore a magnificent crown of gold that sparkled in the sunlight that came from the windows surrounding the dome of the hall. Bel Shanaar paced evenly along the chamber and came to his throne. Pulling his lustrous cloak to one side, he sat down and gazed around. Even from this distance Alith could see the Phoenix King's sharp eyes passing over those in the hall, missing nothing. He resisted the urge to flinch when that steely stare fell upon him.

'Bring forth the first of the petitioners,' Bel Shanaar declared, his voice deep and carrying easily to every part of the hall.

'It's really not that exciting after twenty years,' Carathril said quietly. 'It's not as if anyone asks anything of import at these events. Usually the petitions are nothing more than an excuse to highlight some new trade opportunity, or announce a marriage or death. It's just for show, all of the real business happens when the doors are closed.'

'I would dearly like to see that some time,' said Alith, also keeping his voice low. The benches around them were not quite full but there were plenty of other elves close at hand who would have little difficulty hearing the conversation. 'I hear that you have been to Nagarythe.'

'I once had the honour of marching with Prince Malekith, it is true,' said Carathril. 'That is also old news, though once my exploits were remarked upon by the greatest of princes.'

'I too have fought with Malekith,' said Alith, his voice the barest whisper.

Carathril directed a sharp look at Alith and leaned closer.

'You come clothed as a servant, yet you claim to have fought with the prince of Nagarythe,' said the herald. 'One or the other, or perhaps both, are a deceit.'

'Both are true,' Alith replied. 'I serve in the palace kitchens, and I have met Prince Malekith. I would like to speak to you, but this is not the place.'

Carathril darted a suspicious glance at Alith but then nodded.

'There is more to you than a simple kitchen serf,' Carathril said quietly, his eyes fixed upon Alith. 'You are clearly not exactly what you say you are, even if what you have told me already is true. I do not know what your interest is in me, but you should know that I am but a messenger, I bear no power in the palace.'

'It is simply your attention that I desire,' said Alith. He sat back and breathed a sigh. 'I know that you have no reason to trust me, and I can make no argument here that would convince you. If you would agree to meet me soon, name the place and time of your choosing and take whatever precautions you see fit – though we must be able to speak alone.'

'I do not like intrigue,' said Carathril. 'It is one of the things that mark me out from everyone else in the palace. I will speak with you, but if I do not like what I hear I will call for guards and you will be turned over to Palthrain. My agreement to see you is no promise.'

'And I ask for none,' said Alith. 'When and where shall we meet?'

'There will be an interval soon enough, you can come with me to my chamber,' Carathril said. 'I see no point in waiting any longer than that.'

Alith smiled in thanks and turned his attention back to the proceedings below. Carathril had been right, it was a dull affair as petitioner after petitioner came to give praise to the Phoenix King and ask for his blessing for some venture or other. Others came to complain about the taxes levied by Lothern for passing the Sea Gate, while one thought it most important that Bel Shanaar knew of his intention to sail to Lustria to secure timber for his village in Yvresse.

AFTER THE TENTH such meeting, Palthrain announced that this session was ended. Servants came into the hall bearing platters of sliced meats and trays laden with small cups and decanters of fragranced waters and the juices of exotic fruits. These were then passed into the audience so that they might refresh themselves.

'Time to go,' said Carathril, standing.

Alith followed the herald down the steps onto the main floor, where Carathril turned and bowed to Bel Shanaar. The Phoenix King nodded in greeting and darted an inquisitive look at his herald's companion. Alith bowed also, avoiding Bel Shanaar's gaze lest he react in some way that aroused suspicion. When Alith straightened he saw that the Phoenix King had turned his attention to his son.

CARATHRIL LED ALITH towards the northern towers of the palace and up several winding flights of stairs. This area had been out of bounds for Alith, for only those servants that possessed the seal of the Phoenix King could enter, something far above a lowly kitchen worker. Carathril passed between the guards at the doorway of the fourth storey without incident, Alith following meekly behind. A few steps along the corridor, Carathril shot a warning glance at Alith: a reminder that the Phoenix King's soldiers were close at hand should Carathril need them.

They walked down a long carpeted corridor – the passageways of the servants' quarters were bare stone – and Carathril turned to the right into another passage. He opened a broad door on the left of the corridor and waved Alith inside.

The herald's quarters consisted of two rooms. The first was a square reception area with low couches and tables and a small fireplace. Through an open archway beyond, Alith saw the bedchamber, which was sparsely furnished.

'I spend very little time here,' Carathril explained, noticing the direction of Alith's gaze. 'I have found it best not to make my chambers here too home-like, otherwise I would be doubly homesick.'

'Doubly?'

'I already miss Lothern greatly, though my service to the Phoenix King is an honour and a duty I would not relinquish on a whim,' said Carathril, closing the door and motioning for Alith to sit himself down. 'I return there often enough to remind me of what I love about the city, but not frequently enough to satisfy my desire to be there.'

'Yes, it is a hard thing to leave behind our homes,' Alith said with true sympathy. He had been away from Elanardris for only a short time but had frequently found himself wishing to return swiftly. Leaving aside the painful memories of Ashniel, he still found he loved the mountains as much as anything else in the world.

'Yes, and there is a curious thing,' said Carathril, sitting down opposite Alith. 'I have travelled across all of Ulthuan, and I have learnt many things that other, less cosmopolitan observers might miss. You call yourself Ateni-thor, which I believe is Chracian in origin, yet your voice betrays that you are not from there. If I am not mistaken I would say you were Ellyrion, perhaps.'

Alith smiled and shook his head.

'Close, but not correct,' he said, leaning against the back of the couch with one arm. 'I am Naggarothi. You would not recognise my accent as such though, as I come from the east, close to the mountains.'

'I have never been there,' said Carathril.

'That is a shame, for not only have you missed the breathtaking beauty of Elanardris, but also the counsel and friendship of House Anar,' said Alith.

'I am bid to go where the Phoenix King pleases, not to choose my destinations,' replied Carathril with a sigh. 'If my duties have not taken me there, it is because Bel Shanaar has no cause for me to visit.'

'That may well change,' said Alith. 'I think that the Phoenix King's interest in Nagarythe is going to increase greatly in the near future.'

'How so?' asked Carathril, frowning as he leaned forwards.

'I shall speak the open truth now, for I trust you, though I do not know why, and I wish you to trust me,' said Alith.

'Bel Shanaar says that I have an honest face,' Carathril said, and a smile played on his lips, the first sign of humour Alith had seen from the herald. 'I am his most trusted subject after his family and chamberlain. Anything you tell me will be taken in full confidence provided that it does not threaten the Phoenix King. My position here is entirely founded on my reputation for absolute discretion.'

'Yes, I have heard the same from others,' said Alith. He stood up to address Carathril. 'I am Alith, son of Eothlir, grandson of Eoloran Anar. I am a prince of Nagarythe, come to Tor Anroc in secret to seek the aid of the Phoenix King.'

Carathril said nothing. He sat and looked at Alith for a long while, the smile gone from his face. Then it returned, broader than before.

'You have a tendency for the dramatic, Alith,' he said. 'You have my attention.'

Alith crossed the room and sat beside Carathril.

'I must speak with the Phoenix King in private,' said Alith. 'Can you help me?'

Carathril leaned away from Alith's earnest plea and again sat in silence for some time, scrutinising his guest. Eventually he stood and moved to a cabinet against the wall. From this he drew out two crystal goblets and a bottle of silvery wine. He poured two measures, precise in his actions, and placed the bottle back in the cabinet. He offered one of the glasses to Alith as he sat down again. Alith took the drink but did not sample it. Instead he studied Carathril's face for some sign of his intent.

'You put me in a very difficult position,' said the herald. 'I cannot take your claims at face value, not yet. However, if what you say is true and your coming here is a secret, then I am severely limited in what inquiries I can make without revealing your presence.'

'I have a letter of assurance from my grandfather, in my room,' offered Alith, but Carathril waved away the suggestion.

'I am in no position to judge the veracity of such a document,' he said.

Again the herald pondered his decision, staring at Alith with the tenacity and vigilance of a hawk trying to guess the next movement of its prey. Alith remained silent, knowing that there was nothing he could say that would sway Carathril's choice.

Eventually Carathril nodded to himself, having reached a decision.

'Bring me this letter and I will deliver it – unopened! – to Bel Shanaar,' he said. 'If the Phoenix King assents to see you, then I have performed my duty. If not, then I fear that things may go ill for you. Though from outside you might think that we are complacent of the cults and other wrongdoers, in truth our watch has not faltered nor have our suspicions waned.'

Alith put down his goblet on the floor and grasped Carathril's hand.

'I cannot thank you enough for this kindness,' said Alith. 'I will bring you the letter at once, and hope that the Phoenix King judges it to be true.'

'I will wait for you outside the south-east dining hall,' Carathril said, standing up. He opened the door to indicate the conversation had ended.

Alith strode to the door, eager. Remembering his manners he stopped before leaving and turned to bow to Carathril. The herald returned the bow with a nod and waved Alith away.

NEARLY A WHOLE day of fretting followed Alith's encounter with Carathril. The heir of the Anars was distracted during his evening revelry with Milandith and the other servants that formed the clique of the kitchens, and he decided to retire early – and alone – to his room. The next morning he set to his work in the kitchens, glad of the distraction yet unable to clear his thoughts of his concerns. Had he been right in trusting Carathril? Would Eoloran's letter convince the Phoenix King? Even if Bel Shanaar consented to a meeting, how could it be arranged without being observed?

Every time the kitchen doors opened, Alith looked up sharply, not sure whether to expect a messenger or soldiers. His diverted state drew scowls from the chief cook, a domineering elf called Iathdir who ran the kitchen as a captain of the guard commands his company.

At mid-afternoon word came down that Bel Shanaar had requested a light meal in his chambers. Much to the concern of Malithrandin, no kitchen servants were free as all were in attendance for a feast being held by Princess Lirian, Elodhir's wife. Malithrandin commanded Alith to carry the tray of herb-crusted meats and spiced bread the Phoenix King had requested, and led the way towards the heights of the palace where the royal quarters were found.

Here the corridors were wide and stately, lined with mosaics of cut gems and sculptures both classical and modern. Alith had no time to admire the art, not that he had much inclination to do so, as Malithrandin strode purposefully along the passageway casting impatient glances over his shoulder. They also passed guards dressed in light mail and breastplates of gold, with pairs of swords – one short, the other long – hanging at their hips. They ignored Malithrandin but gave Alith disdainful glares as he hurried past. At the end of the long corridor was an unassuming door of white-stained wood. Malithrandin knocked lightly and then opened it, waving in Alith.

The rooms within surprised Alith. Beyond the unadorned door lay the opposite of the flamboyant decoration and dress of court. Here was the simple beauty of the dove compared to the strutting grandeur of a peacock.

The Phoenix King's personal chambers were minimally but exquisitely furnished, and even Alith's awkward eye could recognise the elegance of design and craftsmanship in the fluted legs of the high tables, the delicate juxtaposition of geometry and natural shapes in the carvings around the fireplace. All was white, including the carpeted floor. The only colour was the Phoenix King himself, who sat close to the fire in a robe of shimmering scarlet, a weighty book open on his lap. Out of his robes of office and crown, he had a more approachable air, and reminded Alith of his grandfather, though Eoloran's expression was usually more severe.

'Put it down there,' Bel Shanaar said, pointing to a low table to one side of the Phoenix King.

Alith did so, with a bow. Bel Shanaar leaned forwards, examining the contents of the platter. He carefully picked up a slice of cooked meat between thumb and finger and as he straightened the Phoenix King glanced at Alith, unobserved by Malithrandin who was still stood by the door.

'Is this Yvressian loin?' asked Bel Shanaar, waving the sliced meat in front of Alith.

'That is Sapherian loin, your majesty,' replied Alith.

'Really?' exclaimed the Phoenix King. 'And what is the difference?'

Alith hesitated and glanced towards Malithrandin.

'Oh, you might as well leave us, steward,' said Bel Shanaar with a dismissive wave of the meat cut. 'My guards can escort your companion back to the kitchens when I'm done.'

'Yes, your majesty,' Malithrandin said stiffly, bowing as he left, though Bel Shanaar had already returned his attention to Alith.

'Well?' said the Phoenix King. 'What is so special about Sapherian loin?'

'It is smoked for three years, your majesty, over chips of mage-oak and whitegrass,' replied Alith, who was glad that Iathdir had taken it upon himself not only to improve Alith's butchery skills but also his general knowledge of meat preparation. 'After that, it is soaked in–'

'You can dispense with the pretence, Alith,' said Bel Shanaar. He delicately folded the thin meat into a small packet and popped it into his mouth. Alith waited patiently while the Phoenix King chewed deliberately. Swallowing, the Phoenix King smiled. 'Your acting is as good as your carving. Tell me, why should I not call my guards and have you arrested as an assassin?'

Alith opened his mouth and then shut it, taken aback by the accusation. He quickly rallied his thoughts.

'Have you not read the letter from my grandfather?'

'I am addressed as "your majesty",' Bel Shanaar said calmly. 'Even if you are a prince, I am still your king.'

'Of course, your majesty, my profound apologies,' Alith replied hastily.

'This letter indeed comes from Eoloran Anar, of that I am certain,' said the Phoenix King, pulling out the parchment from inside his robe. 'It makes assurances of the bearer and requests that I offer you every assistance that I am able. Other than that, it tells me nothing. It tells me not of your intent, nor of the loyalties of your grandfather. I know Eoloran Anar of old, and respect him very much, but it appears he does not extend me the same courtesy. It has been more than seven hundred years since I have seen Eoloran in my court. How do you explain this?'

Again Alith was unsure what to say.

'I cannot speak for my grandfather, your majesty, or his actions, or lack of them, your majesty,' he replied. 'I know only that he has also shunned the court at Anlec and has withdrawn from a public life to enjoy introspection and the comforts of Elanardris.'

'Yes, that sounds like the Eoloran I fought with at Briechan Tor,' said the Phoenix King. He thrust the letter back into his robe and waved Alith to sit down on the chair opposite. 'Nagarythe is an enigma to me, Alith, and I cannot say that I wholly trust you. You come in secret to my palace and masquerade as a servant. You waylay my chief herald and arrange a meeting in which only you and I should be present. My only comfort is that enchantments are woven about this chamber and any blade that passes the door would be revealed to me. So, I feel safe enough, I suppose. What is it that you want me to do?'

'I am not sure,' confessed Alith. 'All I know is that the Anars, a loyal family of Nagarythe and Ulthuan, are victims of some political game or vendetta, and we cannot withstand this on our own.'

'Tell me more,' said Bel Shanaar.

Alith then related the recent history of the Anars, from before the return of Malekith and the travails with Morathi, to their recent indictment and arrest as suspected cultists. Alith was not much of a storyteller and frequently he related events in the wrong order, forcing the Phoenix King to ask questions or press Alith to highlight some pertinent point that he had skipped earlier. Throughout, though, Alith kept secret the existence of Elthyrior and was vague when Bel Shanaar quizzed him on how he had come by a certain piece of information or other.

'You know that there is little I can do to act directly in the lands outside Tiranoc,' Bel Shanaar said when Alith was finished. 'The people of the kingdoms answer to their princes and the princes answer to me. Perhaps if it were some other realm than Nagarythe I might be able to intervene, but there has never been anything less than cool relations between the Phoenix Throne and Anlec.'

The Phoenix King stood and paced to the high, narrow window, the afternoon sun bathing his face. He did not turn around as he spoke, perhaps unwilling to look at Alith as he delivered his decision.

'I cannot act unless your grandfather petitions me directly,' he said. 'Or perhaps your prince, Malekith, though that would seem unlikely. Your opponents have woven their tapestry of lies with considerable skill it would seem, and nothing has occurred that would threaten the authority of my position.'

Bel Shanaar turned and there was sympathy written across his face.

'All I can offer you at the moment is the sanctuary of Tor Anroc and my palace,' he said. 'I will keep safe your secret, and in fact I will do what I can to make your life here as pleasant as possible without revealing who you are or drawing attention to your presence. You are, of course, free to return to Nagarythe whenever you wish, and I will provide papers and escort to the border to ensure your safety if you do so. I will also make discreet inquiries with Malekith as to his current plans and thoughts, though I will leave out any direct mention of the Anars. If you wish, I can arrange for a message to be delivered to your grandfather, and perhaps he will come to Tiranoc and speak openly of these problems with me. Whatever pressures I can bring to bear on the matter will be brought, but I can offer no promises.'

THE WINTER PASSED slowly for Alith, though it was not without event. Bel Shanaar was careful not to reveal Alith's true identity, but by subtle means was able to extend his patronage to the young prince. It was made known that the Phoenix King deemed his new servant too old and too sophisticated to work as a kitchen boy, and so Alith was, through the stewards, elevated to a member of the court staff, attending to the ruler of Tiranoc and his family. In particular, Alith's duties were directed towards the comfort of Yrianath, Bel Shanaar's eldest nephew. This new position required that Alith had the seal of the Phoenix King and he found his freedom to explore the palace greatly increased.

Alith's ascent was something remarked upon by the other servants for a short while, but it was not the first time Bel Shanaar had shown favouritism to a particular elf in the household and most of the staff speculated that Alith's star would soon wane. Though graceful and diligent, he was considered somewhat uncouth for a future career at court, and those jealous of his sudden rise in esteem put down Alith's promotion to an eccentric fondness of the Phoenix King for the rural, oafish mannerisms Alith occasionally exhibited.

With his rise in position Alith felt a change in his relationship with Milandith. A bearer of Bel Shanaar's seal, Alith was privy to parts of the palace his lover was not, and so frequently she interrogated him on the latest gossip from the royal family. Alith became acutely aware that the passion that had brought them together was diminishing, and where once Milandith had viewed him as a source of pleasure she now regarded him as a bottomless well of information. The irony that their expectations of the relationship had been exchanged was not lost on Alith. Milandith's constant delving disturbed him, through a combination of his natural reticence and discretion, and growing feelings that any gossip might be a disloyalty to the family of Bel Shanaar.

Alith was keen not to draw attention to himself nor make an enemy of Milandith and her friends, so over the course of the winter Alith saw less and less of her and began to feign disinterest in her advances. Sure enough, as midwinter passed, he heard rumour that Milandith had abandoned her pursuit of Alith and turned her amorous attentions upon one of the guards. Over a pitcher of Yvressian wine, Alith and Milandith agreed that what they had enjoyed had now passed and they were to go their separate ways with no ill-feeling.

Though his secret was now safer, Alith's loneliness increased. He felt trapped in the palace and missed his home. The mountains of Tiranoc were several days away, and even though the winter was far less harsh here than in Nagarythe, he could not spare the time to go hunting there.

His isolation was not helped by the absence of any news from the north. Bel Shanaar assured Alith that he had despatched a messenger to Elanardris, but Alith feared that the herald had been waylaid, or that his family found it impossible to reply. Information from Nagarythe was sparse, and during the winter months the icy waters of the Naganath seemed to separate the kingdom from Tiranoc as much as any ocean.

So it was a frustrated, lonely Alith who wandered the corridors of the royal palace, or could be found upon the walls of Tor Anroc at dawn, gazing to the north. A few of his new friends expressed concern for this behaviour but Alith was quick to assure them that he was simply feeling a little weary and homesick and promised that he would be more entertaining when spring returned.

Yet when spring came, there was no surcease to Alith's worries. Merchants who had tried entering Nagarythe had been turned away at the border without explanation. What little news that came south was startling. There was fighting between the army of Anlec and pleasure cultists, and even in Anlec it seemed as if Prince Malekith struggled to maintain his rule. Some of his princes had turned against him and supported the cults, while others remained neutral, waiting to see where this latest power struggle would leave Nagarythe. Alith became quite agitated and enquired as to the names of those families involved, but not once were the Anars mentioned, for good or ill.

As these disturbing tidings found their way to the capital, Alith resolved to head back to Elanardris. By means of Carathril, he sent word to Bel Shanaar of his intent and in reply was brought again to the Phoenix King's chambers.

Bel Shanaar's expression was drawn as he stood beside the high arched window that looked out over the south of Tor Anroc. He turned as Alith closed the door.

'I cannot allow you to leave Tor Anroc,' said the Phoenix King.

'What?' snapped Alith, forgetting his manners entirely. 'What do you mean?'

'I mean that it would be unwise of me to allow you to leave my protection at this time,' said Bel Shanaar. 'And I do not think it would be to your benefit either.'

'But my family will need m—'

'Will they?' said Bel Shanaar, his expression stern. 'Are you so great a warrior that if they are involved in the fighting you will swing the tide in their favour?'

'That is not what I meant, your majesty,' said Alith, regaining some of his composure.

'Then perhaps they think you are unsafe here, away from this violent dispute, and would be better protected in Nagarythe?'

Alith shook his head, confused. He *knew* he should return to Elanardris to help, but Bel Shanaar was distracting his thoughts with these questions.

'I am sure they think me safe, your majesty,' said Alith. 'It is my duty to aid my house if they are in peril.'

'Is it not also your duty to keep alive the future of that house?' said Bel Shanaar, his expression as unrelenting as his words. 'Though it pains me to say this, you may already be the last of the Anars. Would you see that name die to satiate curiosity? Would you risk every future generation of the Anars because you are afraid of your uncertainty?'

Alith did not answer but his expression made it plain that he would indeed do such things. Bel Shanaar frowned deeply.

'Let me make myself as clear as a mountain lake, Alith,' said the Phoenix King. 'I am not allowing you to leave these palaces until there is more clarity in this matter. I have given you the benefit of my patronage but these new developments in Nagarythe are disturbing – open fighting between Malekith's soldiers and the sects – and I wish to know where you are at all times.'

Alith guessed the intent behind the words.

'You are keeping me hostage, in case the Anars are traitors.'

Bel Shanaar shrugged.

'I must consider all eventualities, Alith,' he said. 'While at this time I believe that you and your family are loyal, that loyalty is to Anlec and Nagarythe. Where the loyalty of the kingdom resides is as yet uncertain. It would be foolish of me to allow a potential spy, one who knows much about Tor Anroc, to return to Nagarythe. It would be foolhardy not to keep what means I have for negotiation with your house. Your house decided to bring me in as a player of this game and so my fate is woven into yours. I will use all of the pieces at my disposal.'

Alith stared dumbfounded at this statement, quite unable to believe what he was hearing.

'I demand your word of parole that you will not attempt to leave my palace. If you refuse, I shall have you imprisoned,' said Bel Shanaar. His expression softened as he crossed the room to stand in front of Alith. 'I bear you no ill-will, Alith, and I give my prayers to the gods that your family is safe and that Nagarythe swiftly overcomes this current turmoil.'

It was plain to Alith that he had little choice in the matter. If he refused to give his oath, he would be thrown into the cells beneath the palace. Not only would he lose his freedom, even amongst such momentous times this scandal would not go unseen and questions would be raised over his identity. That risked his life and his family's fortunes. He took a deep breath, collecting his thoughts.

'By such gods as might bear witness, I swear as a prince of Nagarythe and Ulthuan to remain under the protection of Bel Shanaar, and to make no attempt to leave Tor Anroc until such time as he gives me leave or circumstances change.'

Bel Shanaar nodded.

'I wish it were otherwise, and when you become lord of the Anars you will understand that with power come hard decisions. If I learn of anything, I will pass this on to you, and you must promise to do the same for me.'

'I will, your majesty,' said Alith with a formal bow. 'Is there anything else that I might attend to whilst I am here?'

Bel Shanaar shook his head.

'No, that is all.'

THE LAST FINGERS of summer were struggling to keep their grip on Tor Anroc when Alith began to overhear reports from Bel Shanaar's commanders at the northern border, telling of how the skies above Nagarythe were filled with smoke. They sent scouts over the river and found villages in ruins, burnt to their foundations, corpses littering their streets. Seers proclaimed a great darkness was sweeping down from the north, and these rumours soon rooted themselves in the populace of the city.

Word came via the heralds of other princes that the cults were on the rise once more. For twenty years they had stayed hidden, plotting and growing. At some unheard command they attacked the soldiers of Ulthuan's rulers, desecrated shrines and temples to other gods, and kidnapped the unwary.

Even in Tor Anroc there were small sects found practising rites to Atharti and Ereth Khial, and their members fought to the death rather than be taken prisoner. Paranoia gripped the palace at the resurgence of the cults, and hundreds of soldiers were brought back from the border to police the citadel and the surrounding city.

Fifteen days after the violence began, Alith received a message telling him that his presence was required by the Phoenix King. Alith hurried to the south hall as he had been instructed, and entered to find a great many of the princes of Tiranoc and their households gathered there, along with a small army of attendants and councillors. Alith could not see what was happening and surreptitiously made his way to the front of the crowd.

Bel Shanaar and his son Elodhir were stood beside the throne at the end of the hall, and Alith could see that Carathril was also in attendance. But it was the figure standing with them that drew Alith's eye. He wore a suit of golden armour, decorated with the design of a coiling dragon, and a long purple cloak that hung to the floor. The warrior wore a long sword at his waist – unusual in that most elves were not allowed to bear arms in the presence of Bel Shanaar – and under one arm he held an ornate warhelm decorated with a silvery-grey crown. His features were severe, his hair black and his eyes glittered with a dark light.

It was Prince Malekith.

'I have three thousand soldiers and knights that need billets,' the prince was saying. 'Once again I find myself putting practicality before pride, and must ask for sanctuary and the hospitality of Tor Anroc.'

Bel Shanaar regarded Malekith calmly, no hint of his thoughts betrayed.

'This is a grave situation indeed, Malekith,' said the Phoenix King. 'Doubtless the woes of Tiranoc are not of the magnitude of Nagarythe, but here also the cultists seek to usurp just rule. I am afraid that such aid as I may have been able to provide in times past is now impossible.'

'I need nothing from the Phoenix King, save his patience and understanding,' said Malekith with a slight dip of the head. 'Those that seek to oust me from power have revealed their hand, and this time when I strike back my blow will find every mark. There are many in Nagarythe that fight to protect my rule. Anlec is currently denied me by these wretches. I need a place to rally those forces loyal to me. Soon enough I will commence a new campaign to free Nagarythe of this vileness, for good this time.'

Malekith's expression was severe, his manner exuding anger, a deep rage that set his jaw twitching, his eyes fierce. Alith had seen that expression once before, when Malekith had spoken of seeing his mother after taking the gate of Anlec.

'Though surprise has garnered some victories for my enemies, they haven't the means or the courage for a true war,' the prince continued. 'I offered clemency before. Now I offer only swift retribution.'

'It is in the interest of all of Ulthuan that Nagarythe returns to stability as soon as possible,' said Bel Shanaar. 'I cannot deny you the right to shelter, but I must warn you that no other Naggarothi may cross the border without invitation. Is that understood?'

'I agree,' said Malekith. 'At a time when it is difficult to know friend from foe, I commend your caution. Now, with your pardon, I must see my mother.'

At this Bel Shanaar paused. Alith knew that Malekith had visited Morathi on several occasions since her incarceration two decades earlier, and it seemed an expected request considering Nagarythe was in such disarray. Even so, the mere mention of the former sorceress-queen sent a shiver of fear through Alith, mixed with a deep-rooted hate. The hall was silent as the elves waited in expectation of the Phoenix King's reply.

'Of course,' Bel Shanaar said eventually. 'Though I have no love for Morathi, I would not deny you.'

Malekith again bowed in thanks and, accompanied by Elodhir, strode from the hall. Bel Shanaar and Carathril left by another archway, and as soon as the Phoenix King had gone chattering broke out amongst the crowd.

'What has happened?' Alith demanded, grabbing the arm of the nearest elf. The page looked at him with astonishment.

'Cultists have retaken Anlec and Prince Malekith has been deposed,' said the elf, with a haughtiness held by those who consider themselves important for having heard news moments before any other. 'It seems those Naggarothi fiends are fighting amongst themselves again.'

Alith stayed his tongue at this remark and instead walked quickly from the hall. He made his way back to his room in the servants' quarters and there sat on his bed, staring at the stone floor. He could make no sense of it. How could the cults have gathered such power unseen? How had they survived Malekith's diligent purging? Unable to comprehend what had occurred, Alith's mind was blank, numbed by the dire news.

FOR THREE DAYS the palace was chaotic. Rumours and claims spread through the residents and servants alike. Lodgings were found for the small army Malekith had brought south with him, and Alith was busy attending to the errands of his masters and mistresses. Yrianath was preoccupied with matters pertaining to Tiranoc's trade and how it might be affected by the situation in Nagarythe, which held considerable power in the Elthin Arvan colonies. Distracted, Yrianath often overlooked Alith's presence, allowing the heir of the Anars to overhear things that in normal times would have remained secret.

Malekith called upon the Phoenix King to assemble the princes of Ulthuan in council. They were to meet at the Shrine of Asuryan upon the Isle of Flame: the most sacrosanct of places where Aenarion and Bel Shanaar had been elevated to Phoenix King. Alith watched Carathril leave along with many other messengers, the chief herald's expression grim and distant.

Alith had his own distractions. His ignorance of how affairs in Nagarythe were unfolding was driving him to the point of madness and he spent each night unsleeping, toying with the idea of breaking his oath to the Phoenix King and fleeing Tor Anroc. Yet each morning he realised that the means by which his house might be saved lay here at the capital, not in the north, and so he remained.

Preparations were made for the Phoenix King's expedition to depart for the Isle of Flame. Elodhir had already departed and when Bel Shanaar left, control of the palace would fall to Yrianath, as the next prince of mature age. This made for much work for Yrianath's councillors and servants, who were kept busy at all hours to apprise themselves of every development. Despite his exhaustion, Alith still found no solace in sleep and became so irritable that others avoided him when they had the chance.

Frustration almost spilled into violence when Alith overheard a group of nobles speaking foully of the Naggarothi, blaming them for every ill that had befallen Ulthuan in recent centuries. It was only the accidental intervention of one of the stewards, calling upon Alith to attend to Yrianath, which prevented the young Anar from striking the nobles.

All of this frenetic activity reached a calm equilibrium the day before the Phoenix King was due to leave. In a rare moment of peace, Alith was in the gardens, staring wistfully at a marble sculpture of a waterfall. It was refined and finely detailed, but lacked all of the majesty of the real thing. Rivers cascaded down the mountains of Elanardris with thunderous power, sending spray and fog across the surrounding slopes. The gentle tinkling of this fountain seemed ludicrous and trite in comparison.

'There you are.'

Alith turned and found Milandith sitting beside him on the white bench. She wore a green silken dress, her braids woven into showers of hair that spilled across her shoulders. In the autumn sun she was as pretty as Alith had ever seen her and for a moment he was lost in admiring her beauty.

'Why such worries?' asked Milandith, running a hand across Alith's brow as if to smooth away the creases of his frown.

'Do you not think these are dark times?'

'They are,' she said, grasping Alith's right hand in both of hers. 'Yet what is there that we can do? The princes will meet to decide, and we will be ready to help them.'

She laughed, a peculiar sound to Alith's ear given the grimness of his mood.

'I would not like to have such responsibility,' she said. 'Can you imagine? Trying to decide what to do about all of this? Raising armies and waging wars are not in my nature.'

But they are in mine, Alith thought. He was a son of House Anar and if battle was to be waged, he would be there to wage it. He looked at Milandith, soaking in her innocence and beauty. How simple it would be, he thought, to make the masquerade real. He could live in peace as Atenithor of Chrace, a servant to Prince Yrianath and nothing more. He could renew his relationship with Milandith, and perhaps they would wed and have children. Bloodshed and murder, darkness and despair would be the realm of princes and he would live out his life as a simple soul.

But that could not be. Not only did guilt gnaw at his heart, duty ingrained in him since he had been born stiffened his resolve. He could no more hide from this than a rabbit could hide from one of his arrows. He was Alith Anar, heir to a princedom of Nagarythe, and he could not pretend otherwise.

'You are distracted,' said Milandith, unhappy. 'Perhaps I am boring you?'

'I am sorry,' said Alith, forcing a smile. He ran his fingers lightly over Milandith's hair and cheek, his fingertips coming to rest on her chin. 'I am distracted, but not by the sort of distraction I would like.'

Milandith returned his smile and stood, pulling him up by the hand.

'I think I can find just the sort of distraction you need,' she said.

ALITH DOZED, FEELING the heat from Milandith beside him. In his half-asleep state he could hear doors banging elsewhere in the servants' quarters and feet running outside but he chose to ignore them. The moment had passed though, and the real world was beginning to intrude again upon the blissful ignorance brought about by Milandith's attentions. Hoping to set aside his pain for a while longer, Alith leaned across the bed and nestled his face in her unkempt hair, kissing her lightly on the neck. She murmured wordlessly and, eyes still closed, laid a hand upon his back, gently stroking his skin, tracing the whip-scar with a finger.

Suddenly there was a furious knocking at the door. A moment later it crashed open. Both of them shot upright as Hithrin, Steward of Halls, burst into the room. There was a wild look in the elf's eyes, bordering on terrified hysteria. His wide gaze settled on Alith.

'There you are!' he cried, running across the room and grabbing Alith by the arm. 'Your master calls for all his servants to attend!'

Alith snatched his arm away and shoved Hithrin backwards, though the steward was supposedly his superior.

'What?' snapped Alith. 'Can I not have a moment's peace? What could be so urgent?'

Hithrin stared dumbly at Alith for a moment, his mouth opening and closing without sound. He swallowed hard and then blurted out his news.

'The Phoenix King is dead!'

─◄ NINE ►─

Darkness Descends

THE GREAT HALL was in pandemonium. Elves of all ages and stations had come from across the palace to hear what had happened. Yrianath stood beside the Phoenix Throne, Palthrain and many other nobles and councillors with him. As Alith pushed his way through the throng, there was an air of panic and desperation. Some elves were shouting, others weeping, many stood in shocked silence, waiting to hear the words of Yrianath.

'Be calm,' he cried out, raising his hands, but the cacophony continued until Yrianath raised his voice to a roar. 'Silence!'

In the stillness that followed only the rustle of robes and quiet sobbing could be heard.

'The Phoenix King is dead,' Yrianath said solemnly. 'Prince Malekith found him in his chambers early this morning. It would seem that the Phoenix King took his own life.'

At this there was another outburst of anger and woe, until Yrianath signalled again for the elves' attention.

'Why would Bel Shanaar do such a thing?' demanded one of the nobles. It was Palthrain who stepped forwards to answer the question.

'We cannot know for sure,' said the chamberlain. 'Accusations had come to Prince Malekith that the Phoenix King was embroiled with the cults of pleasure. Though Malekith disbelieved such claims, he has sworn in this very hall to prosecute all members of the cults, regardless of station. His own mother is still imprisoned in this palace. When the prince went to

Bel Shanaar's chambers to confront him with the evidence, he found the Phoenix King's body, with the marks of black lotus on his lips. It seems that the charges were true and Bel Shanaar took his own life rather than face the shame of discovery.'

The hall shook with a rising clamour as the elves surged forwards, making demands of Palthrain and Yrianath.

'What charges?'

'What evidence was presented?'

'How can this have happened?'

'Are the traitors still here?'

'Where is Malekith?'

This last question was asked several times, and the call grew louder and louder.

'The prince of Nagarythe has departed for the Isle of Flame,' said Yrianath when some measure of order had been restored. 'He seeks to inform Elodhir of his father's demise, and to take guidance from the council of princes. Until Elodhir returns from the council, we must remain calm. The full facts of what has occurred here will be brought to light, rest assured.'

Though still much distressed, the elves were somewhat quietened by this statement and instead of angry shouts, a conspiratorial murmuring filled the hall. Alith ignored the buzz of gossip and the tearful lamentations and turned to Milandith. Her cheeks were wet with tears and he clasped an arm around her and pulled her close.

'Do not be afraid,' he said, though he knew his words to be a lie.

A STRANGE ATMOSPHERE enveloped the palace over the following days. There was little activity and Alith could sense that his fellow elves were each trying to come to terms with what had transpired. Few were willing to talk about their shock and grief, which was unusual in itself, and fewer still would mention the circumstances surrounding Bel Shanaar's death. There was an undercurrent of suspicion, formless and unspoken but palpable.

Alith's first thought was to leave the city, now that he was no longer bound by his oath to Bel Shanaar, but he decided against this course of action. Though events could threaten to expose him, he heard no hint or rumour concerning his arrival not long before Bel Shanaar's demise. To leave hastily would perhaps invite more attention than staying.

Instead, Alith stayed close to Yrianath, as required by his position and as his curiosity desired. The prince was as shocked as any by the tragic turn of events and seemed content to await Elodhir's return rather than take any lead himself.

Bel Shanaar's body was made ready for interment in the great mausoleum of his family in the depths of the mount beneath Tor Anroc. The funeral proceedings could not start without Elodhir, and so the elves found themselves in a spiritual limbo, unable to publicly express their grief. For once, Alith missed the idle chatter that used to distract him so much. In the echoing quiet of the palace his dark thoughts resounded all the more.

SIXTEEN DAYS HAD passed when new arrivals caused a great stir in the palace. Alith had been attending to Yrianath, who was in discussions with Palthrain concerning the funeral arrangements of Bel Shanaar. A herald entered hastily, announcing that he had come from the Isle of Flame.

'What news of Elodhir?' asked Yrianath. 'When can we expect his return?'

At this, the herald began to weep.

'Elodhir is dead, among many other princes of Ulthuan,' he wailed.

'Speak now, tell us what has happened!' demanded Palthrain, grabbing the messenger by the arms.

'It is a disaster! We do not know what happened. A mighty earthquake shook the Shrine of Asuryan, and there were signs of violence. When we entered, only a few princes had survived.'

'Who?' insisted Palthrain. 'Who survived?'

'A handful only came out of the temple,' said the herald, almost buckling at the knees. 'So many nobles dead...'

The herald swallowed hard and straightened, wiping a hand across his eyes.

'Come,' he said, turning towards the door.

Alith followed a little way behind Palthrain and Yrianath, and they seemed content to allow him, if they even noticed his presence. The herald took the group across the courtyard and out of the great gate of the palace where a large crowd had gathered. There were many carriages, each draped in white awnings. Tiranoc soldiers held back the throng, casting their own shocked glances back towards the coaches. Palthrain forced his way through the crowd and Alith followed in his wake.

The chamberlain pulled back one of the white curtains and Alith caught a sight of Elodhir, lying upon a bier inside the carriage. His face was as white as snow and he was laid upon his back, arms folded across his chest. Yrianath gasped and looked away. Just before Palthrain allowed the curtain drop back, Alith thought he saw the red mark of a wound across the dead prince's throat, but so brief was the glimpse that he could not be sure.

Another elf came striding through the carriages. She was clad in silver armour and a black cloak. Alith immediately recognised her as Naggarothi and shrank back towards the other elves, though he did not know her. She spoke briefly to Palthrain and pointed at one of the other carriages. An expression of dread passed over Palthrain's face before he composed himself. Without a word, he turned and hurried back into the palace.

Yrianath sent the captains of the guard to bring more soldiers from the city. With a stone-faced expression the prince gave instructions for the staff of the palace to begin moving the dead Tiranocii nobles inside. Alith was pleased not to be counted amongst the number tasked with this unpleasant chore, and stayed out of sight as best he could.

THE GRISLY LABOUR was interrupted by shouts of dismay from the crowd around the gates. Alith turned to see Palthrain ordering elves out of his path. He was followed by a contingent of the Naggarothi warriors who had come with Malekith. They created a line through the thronging elves and behind them strode another.

She was tall and stunningly beautiful. Her long black hair fell in lustrous curls about her shoulders and back, and her alabaster skin was as white as the stone of the gate towers. Her dark eyes were fierce and Alith flinched from their gaze as the elf stared scornfully at the assembled watchers. Alith knew her immediately and felt fear grip his heart.

Morathi.

The crowd fell back in fear as she swept through the gate, the train of her purple dress streaming behind her, boots ringing on the flags of the road. Her full lips were twisted in a sneer as she surveyed the frightened mass. As soon as she came within sight of the carriages, her entire attention was fixed upon them and so swift was her stride that Palthrain had to run to keep pace.

He led her to one of the coaches and Morathi threw back the coverings with a beringed hand. She fell to her knees and uttered a shriek, an awful wail that pierced Alith's mind and echoed from the walls of the palace. Looking beyond Morathi, Alith saw what lay upon the board of the wagon.

It was a blackened mess and at first Alith did not recognise what it was. As he forced himself to look closer, Alith saw streaks of gold that had melted into rivulets and then solidified, and links of chainmail burned into charred flesh. It was the figure of an elf, obscene in its desecration. Two unblinking, unmoving eyes stared out and half of the elf's body was seared down through flesh and muscle, revealing burned bone. Dark flakes fluttered from the corpse, drifting on the wind. Alith stepped a little closer and could make out something of the design on the figure's breastplate, though it was much disfigured. It was the remnants of a coiling dragon.

At that moment Morathi rose to her feet and wheeled towards the watching elves. Her eyes were orbs of blue fire and her hair danced wildly in an unseen gale while sparks erupted from her fingertips. With cries of fear, the crowd turned and ran from the sorceress.

'Cowards!' she shrieked. 'Look at this ruin! Face what your meddling has brought about. This is my son, your rightful king. Look upon this and remember it for the rest of your wretched lives!'

Elves were shouting and screaming as the stampede continued, pushing and pulling at each other as they tried to press back through the gatehouse. Alith ignored them, transfixed by the apparition of Malekith's corpse. He felt sick, not just from the sight, but also from a foreboding that welled up in his stomach and froze his spine.

The tramp of many booted feet echoed around the plaza, joined by the clattering of hooves. Such elves as remained scattered ahead of a column of black-clad spearmen and knights: the rest of Malekith's warriors. Like a black snake they advanced from around the palace and for a moment Alith feared that they would attack. They did not.

Instead they formed a guard of honour three thousand strong around the carriage as Morathi climbed aboard. Alith looked to the Tiranocii warriors to intervene, but those that had remained were afraid to confront the grim-faced soldiers in front of them. He did not blame them, and was rooted to the spot by the stern lines of spears and the immobile knights. Morathi signalled to the driver and the carriage moved away with a rattle of wheels and the crunch of the marching Naggarothi.

One of the captains of the Tiranoc guard stepped forwards, somewhat cautiously, hand on sword hilt at his waist. Palthrain intercepted the warrior and put a hand to his chest.

'Let them go, Tiranoc is well rid of them,' said the chamberlain. Without incident the Naggarothi left the plaza down the tunnel-road to the east, and then were out of sight.

With that, Prince Malekith passed out of Tor Anroc for the final time.

THERE WAS A deathly hush in the grand hall and an air of reverence surrounded the two bodies laid in state upon marble slabs either side of the Phoenix Throne. Though Bel Shanaar's death remained contentious, he had ruled over Ulthuan for one thousand, six hundred and sixty-eight years and was accorded due respect from all present. Thousands of elves had filed past the Phoenix King's remains, preserved by the attentions of priests dedicated to Ereth Khial, the blemishes of his poisoning removed by priestesses of Isha. Alith noted that Elodhir's body wore a collared robe that concealed his neck and so was unable to confirm the wound he had thought he had seen in the carriage.

The doors had been closed after five days and only the household of the princes remained. Alith was in attendance to Yrianath, as were other servants to their masters and mistresses. The hall was almost empty, for many nobles from Tiranoc had travelled with the Phoenix King to the council of princes and not returned alive. The bodies of some had been brought back from the Isle of Flame and were with their families in the manses around the huge palace. Some had not returned at all and their fate remained unknown.

'A grievous wound has been done to Tiranoc,' declared Yrianath. He seemed just as stunned as when he had first looked upon Elodhir's corpse. Beside him were Lirian, Elodhir's widow, and the dead prince's son, Anataris. She was draped head-to-foot in white robes of mourning, her face concealed behind a long veil, the babe in her arms swathed in white cloth. Of her expression, Alith could see nothing.

'Tiranoc will not stand idle in these times,' Yrianath continued. Though his words were meant to be defiant and stirring, his voice was hollow. 'We shall prosecute by whatever means those who have heaped this hurt upon us, and taken from Ulthuan its rightful ruler.'

There was a discontented rustle of voices and Yrianath frowned. He cast his weary eyes over the nobles.

'Now is not the time for whispers and secrets,' the prince said, gaining some vigour. 'If there are any present who wish to speak their mind, they are free to do so.'

Tirnandir stepped forwards with glances to the rest of the court. He was the eldest member of the court after Palthrain, born just twenty years after Bel Shanaar's ascension to the throne and respected as one of the Phoenix King's wisest advisors.

'With what authority do you make such promises?' the noble asked.

'As a prince of Tiranoc,' replied Yrianath.

'Then you claim succession to the rule of Tiranoc?' asked Tirnandir. 'By tradition, the line does not pass to you.'

Yrianath looked confused for a moment and then turned his eyes upon Lirian and Anataris.

'Bel Shanaar's heir was Elodhir, and Elodhir's heir is no more than three years old,' said Yrianath. 'Who else would you propose?'

'A regent, to claim rule until Anataris comes of age,' said Tirnandir. It was clear from the nods of other council members that this had already been discussed in private.

Yrianath shrugged.

'Then as regent I will make these promises,' he said, uncomprehending of any cause for objection.

'If a regent is to be appointed, then he or she need not be of the descent of Bel Shanaar,' said Illiethrin, the wife of Tirnandir. 'You are no more than six hundred years old, there are many in this hall better suited to the role of regent.'

Palthrain intervened before Yrianath could reply.

'These are uncertain times, and our people will look to us for leadership,' said the chamberlain. 'It is not proper that the stewardship of Tiranoc passes far from the royal line. Other realms are facing the same woes as we, and surely our enemies will exploit any dispute to their own purposes. Yrianath has a claim by blood that is strong, and with such advisors as are gathered here, his policies can yet be wise. To do otherwise invites claim and counter-claim by those who seek to undermine the true rule of Ulthuan.'

'And where is that true rule to be found?' snapped Tirnandir. 'There is no Phoenix King, and we have had no word from the council of princes regarding a successor. Morathi has been let free once more, and her ambition will not have been dimmed by twenty years of imprisonment. No doubt she will put forth some claimant of her own. Does the elf we choose here also take on the Phoenix Crown and cloak of feathers?'

'I do not seek the Phoenix Throne,' Yrianath said hastily, holding up his hands as if to ward away the suggestion. 'It is for Tiranoc that I will act. Other kingdoms shall surely look to themselves at this time.'

There was angry muttering and Palthrain raised his hand for silence.

'Such a matter cannot be decided in a moment,' he said. 'All concerns can be raised and deliberations made in due course. It is unseemly to squabble in this fashion, here beside the body of our Phoenix King. No, this will not do at all.'

'We will talk on this matter again when respect has been paid to the deceased and the memory of our lord properly regarded,' said Tirnandir with an apologetic bow. 'It is not division we seek, but unity. Ten days hence we will convene again and make such petitions as are required.'

The nobles bowed to the bodies of the dead, and a few nodded their heads to Yrianath as they left, but several darted suspicious glances at the prince. Alith believed Yrianath beyond reproach, for he had been in the prince's entourage for several seasons and seen or heard nothing to raise his suspicions. However, the sudden removal of both Bel Shanaar and Elodhir had left the subject of succession wide open for debate, as Alith suspected those who had perpetrated the deaths had intended.

Though these lofty concerns occupied a little of Alith's thoughts while the final arrangements were made for the twin funerals, he was mostly concerned for events in Nagarythe. He decided that as soon as the ceremony was concluded, he would head north and rejoin his family. Who could say what chaos reigned with Prince Malekith dead?

THE BURIAL RITES of the Phoenix King and his son would be long, even by elven standards, and were due to last ten days. On the first day, Alith joined a long line of mourners who passed by the dead to celebrate the lives of those who passed. Poetry was recited praising the achievements of Bel Shanaar as both a fighter in the time of Aenarion and a king in times of peace. Under his auspices, the elven realm had grown every year, so that the colonies of Ulthuan stretched across the world to the east and west. The alliance with the dwarfs in Elthin Arvan was lauded by a choir of three hundred singers, and this irritated Alith more than he had thought it would. In those conversations he had shared with Yeasir at Elanardris, the commander had made it clear that it was Prince Malekith who had forged the friendship with the dwarfs and Alith was inclined to agree.

The second day was spent in silence, the whole of Tor Anroc eerily quiet as the populace meditated upon the memories of Bel Shanaar and Elodhir. Some would write down their thoughts in verse, others kept their recollections to themselves. This period of solitude gave Alith time to sit in his room and think deeply on what had happened. His thoughts were never focussed on one thing, and he reached no conclusion as to what had passed or what he needed to do next. He longed more than ever to return to the mountains and the support of his family.

Thinking of Elanardris took Alith onto a dark path, and he horrified himself with all kinds of fearful imaginings of what might await his return. He had received no word from family or friend for almost a year and he did not know whether any were still alive. The frustration he had felt over that period welled up inside him in one wave and he vented his anger and fear with violence, smashing lamps, tearing at the sheets on his bed and driving his fists into the walls until his knuckles were bleeding heavily. Panting, he collapsed onto the floor, weeping uncontrollably. He tried without success to fight back the images of torment that assailed him, until long after midnight he fell into an exhausted sleep.

WHEN HE AWOKE, Alith found himself refreshed, though no more optimistic than he had been the night before. Though shared by no other, his personal outpouring had cleared his mind and he knew what he needed to do. His decision to remain at Tiranoc for the ceremony of burial was simply an excuse to delay his inevitable return. While ignorance tortured Alith for the most part, it also gave him hope, a hope that might be crushed as soon as he returned north. He realised he was being immature, seeking reasons to keep himself in this vacillating state, and set about packing up such possessions as he would need on the journey.

There was a knock on the door and Alith pushed the half-filled pack beneath his bed before opening it. It was Hithrin, who glanced at the destruction Alith had wrought the night before but made no comment.

'We are to attend our master, Alith,' said the steward, not unkindly. 'He is to receive an important guest at midday. Tidy yourself up and come to his chambers as soon as you can.'

Hithrin gave Alith a look of sympathy and then walked away. The look was like a barb to Alith's pride and he busied himself clearing up the ruin he had made of the room and dressed himself carefully. This menial activity allowed him to gather his thoughts after the interruption and he weighed up whether to attend to Yrianath or depart straightaway. Alith decided to remain a little while longer, intrigued to find out what manner of guest would call upon Yrianath at this time of mourning.

THE RECEPTION FOR Yrianath's visitor was a sombre, stately affair. Alith, amongst the other servants, had prepared a simple cold luncheon in the lower east chamber, a small hall overlooked by two galleries. Just before the prince's guest was due to arrive, the servants were asked to leave and Alith filed out with the rest of them.

He was perturbed by this secrecy and slipped away from the other staff as they made their way back to the servants' quarters, doubling back to the hall. Using the serving stairs normally employed to bring trays of food and drink to parties gathered on the galleries, Alith slipped unseen into the main chamber. High windows lined the south and north walls of the hall, but shed little light on the galleries, which were usually lit by lanterns when in use. From the hazy gloom, Alith peered down into the hall.

Yrianath was sat at one end of the long table, the platters of food arrayed before him. He picked nervously at their contents until there was a resounding knock at the door.

'Enter!' Yrianath called out, standing.

The door opened and a functionary bowed low before ushering in the prince's visitor.

Alith suppressed a gasp and shrank back towards the wall as Caenthras strode into the chamber, resplendent in armour and cloak. Yrianath hurried forwards and greeted the Naggarothi prince at the near end of the table.

Alith began to panic. Why was Caenthras here? Did he know of Alith's presence, and if so what was his purpose in coming to Tor Anroc? The urge to flee before discovery gripped Alith and it took all of his nerve to remain where he was. He told himself that he was over-reacting, and that if he were to remain a while longer he would soon have the answers to these questions. He slipped forwards to the balustrade and nervously looked down on the elves below.

'Prince Caenthras, it is a pleasure to welcome you,' said Yrianath. 'Long have we yearned for news from beyond the Naganath. Please, sit down and enjoy what hospitality one can in these dark times.'

Caenthras returned the bow and placed his helm upon the table. He followed Yrianath to the food and sat down at Yrianath's right as the prince seated himself.

'These are indeed dark and dangerous times,' said Caenthras. 'Uncertainty holds sway over Ulthuan and it is imperative that authority and order are restored.'

'I could not agree more, and may I offer my condolences to all in Nagarythe, who have also suffered the loss of a great leader,' said Yrianath, pouring wine for himself and his guest.

'I am here as official embassy for Nagarythe,' said Caenthras, picking up the goblet and swirling its contents. 'In order that any turmoil is dealt with, it is vital that the rulers of Ulthuan work together. It is a woe to us, then, that so many realms are as yet without leaders, and we know not with whom to discuss these matters. I hear that Tiranoc is embroiled in such a debate at the moment.'

'I think embroiled is perhaps too strong a word...'

'Is it not true then that there is disagreement over who will succeed as ruling prince?'

Yrianath hesitated and sipped his wine as a distraction. Caenthras's forceful stare did not waver and Yrianath put down his glass with a sigh.

'Issues have been raised over the succession,' he said. 'As the oldest blood descendant I have offered to act as regent for the time being, but there is opposition from some of the other court members.'

'Then I should tell you that Nagarythe supports your claim to Tiranoc,' said Caenthras with a broad smile. 'We are strong believers in tradition, and it is fitting that the relatives of Bel Shanaar succeed him.'

'If you could but convince my peers of my case, then the matter would be settled,' said Yrianath, leaning towards Caenthras with earnest intent. 'I do not seek division, and a swift end to this matter is the best outcome for all concerned, so that we might turn our attention to graver issues.'

'Most certainly,' said Caenthras, patting Yrianath's hand. 'Stability is the key.'

Caenthras helped himself to a little food, arranging it carefully on his plate. When done, he cocked his head to one side and directed a thoughtful gaze at Yrianath.

'I would say that the word of one prince, an outsider at that, would do little to sway the opinion of the Tor Anroc nobles,' said the Naggarothi. 'As a sign of support I am willing to petition certain other princes and officers of Nagarythe to travel to Tor Anroc and speak on your behalf. I am sure that having such allies will increase your standing and strengthen your claim beyond reproach. It is, after all, unity that we seek at this time.'

Yrianath considered this for a moment, but Alith could already see the trap being laid. If Yrianath wanted to be leader of Tiranoc he needed to do so from his own strength. Had not the Anars suffered greatly of late for relying too much on the support of others? Alith wanted to warn the prince not to agree, to tell him that it was a false bargain, but he dared not reveal his presence to Caenthras. Instead, he remained mute and watched the terrible plot unfold.

'Yes, that would seem a good course of action,' said Yrianath. 'I see no problem with that.'

'Then might I impose a certain request upon you?' said Caenthras.

Here it comes, thought Alith as he watched Yrianath drawn towards the lure like a fish.

'Your northern border is closed to the Naggarothi,' continued Caenthras with a disarming shrug. 'It is only by chance that I met one of your officers who would vouch for me, and thus allowed me to pass into Tiranoc. I fear such embassies as would come south on your behalf will not be so fortunate. I wonder if perhaps you could write me several letters of passage, which I might send to my fellow princes to act as permission to cross the Naganath with their bodyguards?'

'Well, yes, of course,' said Yrianath. 'I will give you the seal of my princedom as a guarantee of safe passage. How many would you need?'

'Let us say a dozen,' said Caenthras, smiling. 'You have many allies in the north.'

'A dozen?' replied Yrianath, flattered. 'Yes, I see no reason why that cannot be arranged.'

The prince's expression of happiness then faded and his shoulders slumped.

'What is the matter?' asked Caenthras, the picture of concern. 'Is there some problem?'

'Time,' muttered Yrianath. 'Deliberations are due to recommence at the ending of the funerals, only seven days hence. I fear my supporters will not arrive in time to swing the debate, and my rivals already arrange their arguments against me.'

'I have riders ready to go north at once,' said Caenthras. 'I cannot guarantee that our friends will be able to reach Tor Anroc in seven days, but perhaps you could delay proceedings in some fashion.'

Yrianath brightened at this suggestion.

'Well, the discourse of court never runs swiftly,' he said, as much to himself as his companion. He gave Caenthras a determined look. 'It can be done. I shall provide you with my seal before night comes. I am sure that a final decision can be averted until I can make my strongest case.'

Caenthras stood and Yrianath rose with him. The Naggarothi extended a hand, which the prince shook enthusiastically.

'Thank you for your understanding,' said Caenthras. 'A new alliance between Nagarythe and Tiranoc will no doubt set our people on the path to greatness again.'

'Yes, it is time that history took its place behind us and we looked to the future once more.'

'A most progressive and commendable attitude,' said Caenthras. He turned for the door but then looked back at Yrianath after a few paces. 'Of course, we will keep this arrangement between us for the moment, yes? It would be counter-productive if your opponents were to hear of what has passed between us.'

'Oh, that is for sure,' said Yrianath. 'You can rely on my secrecy, as I can on yours.'

Caenthras gave another nod and a smile and then left. Yrianath stood for a moment tapping his fingers upon the tabletop, obviously happy. With a self-assured stride, he walked out of the room, leaving Alith alone in the silence.

As he had listened to the exchange between the princes, Alith's fear had disappeared, to be replaced by anger. It was clear that Caenthras had long been manipulating events in Nagarythe to increase his own standing, and had worked against the Anars even as he had pretended to be an ally. Alith did not know how long this treacherous, selfish goal had driven Caenthras, but he looked on everything the prince had done with suspicion. Caenthras had once been a true friend of the Anars, of that there was no doubt, but somewhere, at some time, he had chosen to take a different path. The betrayal burned inside Alith, igniting the jealousy, fear and frustration that had been swirling inside him since Ashniel had been taken away. Now that Caenthras's plots were involving the rule of Tiranoc, there was a clear danger to all of Ulthuan.

Caenthras had to pay for his duplicitous crimes.

THE RITES OF passing for Bel Shanaar and Elodhir continued for the next seven days. There were ceremonies of mourning led by the greatest poets of Tiranoc, who recited anguished requiems to the Phoenix King accompanied by dirgeful wailings and choruses of weeping maidens. Alith found these recitations utterly lacking in originality or special significance, bland oratories of loss and woe that spoke nothing of those who had died. In Nagarythe, such verses would be filled with true lamentation for those who had been taken away, composed by the families who had lost a loved one. In all, Alith found these professional mourners to be overblown and impersonal.

The next day heralded the first of several rituals of sanctity during which the rightful priests and priestesses of Ereth Khial prepared the bodies and spirits of the deceased for the afterlife. These spiritualists were unlike the cults of the dead that had risen in Nagarythe. They sought not to converse with the supreme goddess of the underworld, but to protect the souls of the departed from the attentions of the ghost-like rephallim that served the Queen of the Cytharai. As with the mourners, Alith was left a little confused. In Elanardris it was well understood that the spirits of the dead would go through the gate to Mirai, there to dwell forever under the watchful eye of Ereth Khial. There was no fear, only acceptance that death is the natural conclusion to life.

Unlike the wild chanting and sacrifices Alith had witnessed in Anlec, these true priests bathed the bodies in blessed water and used silver ink to paint runes of warding on the dead flesh. He watched from the back of the attending crowds as they made whispered intonations to placate the rephallim, and wove chains of beaded gold around the limbs of the departed so that they would be too heavy for the vengeful ghosts to carry away.

During the funeral, Caenthras was housed as a guest of Yrianath and Alith had to move warily, to avoid discovery by the Naggarothi prince. He spied on the pair whenever the opportunity presented itself, which was rare, but was nearly always clever enough to pass on some duty that required his presence to another of Yrianath's household. On occasion Alith was forced to take extreme measures to avoid being seen by Caenthras, ducking into doorways or running down halls on hearing his approaching voice. At one time he even resorted to hiding behind a curtain, something Alith had thought only occurred in children's tales.

Simply killing Caenthras would not be as easy as Alith had first thought. Certainly slaying him without being caught was quickly looking impossible, as the prince never seemed to be out of company, either of Yrianath, Palthrain or some functionary of the palace.

While the keen edge of his hatred for Caenthras remained undiminished, as Alith observed the prince from afar, his vow to slay him was mollified by a desire to visit upon him the same ruin as he had perpetrated against the Anars. A simple knife in the back in the darkness would only cause more suspicion and grief, while an open challenge would reveal his presence and raise all number of unpleasant questions regarding his presence in the palace at the death of Bel Shanaar. On top of that, Alith was pretty certain that in a straight fight with Caenthras, the veteran of the wars against the daemons would surely win.

If Alith could understand more the nature of Caenthras's scheming he would be able to bring about a more just downfall than simple death. Alith wanted Caenthras exposed and shamed before his life was ended. To do that he needed to know everything about Caenthras's plans, his allies and his minions. That would mean awaiting the arrival of the other nobles who would vouch for Yrianath's accession. For the time being, Alith was patient enough to stay his hand and see what was unveiled.

THE DAY CAME for the final interment of the dead rulers of Tiranoc, and tens of thousands of elves travelled to the capital to pay their respects and witness this last journey. There were, some commented, few princes and nobles from other realms. Speculation was rife on why this might be so. The more pragmatic observers simply mentioned the travails that had beset Ulthuan's rulers of late and suggested that most would be busy keeping order in their own lands. The more conspiracy-minded locals believed that there was a deliberate snub implicit in the absence of so many worthwhile citizens of Ulthuan. A few elves, after encouragement from friends who should probably have known better, even went as far as to say that the Phoenix King's death was held in such suspicion by the other kingdoms that they feared to come to Tiranoc.

Alith's own conclusion was that those princes who had survived the tragedy at the Shrine of Asuryan, of which there were very few by many accounts, had far more important things to do than doff their crowns to a dead body. Though some in Tor Anroc had forgotten, the uprising from the cults that had preceded the council of princes was still ongoing. It was the nature of folk to concentrate on their own perils and woes, and none in Tiranoc could consider the grief of other people to be anything like as great as theirs. For the sake of peace, Alith kept these opinions to himself when asked to venture his thoughts on such matters.

THE BODIES OF Elodhir and Bel Shanaar were set in state upon the backs of two gilded chariots, each pulled by four white steeds. Three hundred more chariots rode in escort with the departed, followed by five hundred spearmen and five hundred knights of Tiranoc. Yrianath, Lirian, Palthrain and the other court members were also driven in chariots, decorated with chains of silver and flying the pennants of their houses, following behind the body of the Phoenix King.

Alith and the other servants were gathered in the plaza outside the gatehouse, which had been cleared of all other elves, so that they might witness the passing away of their former lords. Alith watched the thousands-strong cortege wind its way out of the palace grounds and take up station in the square. The golden chariots then emerged and all present gave up a great shout, declaring their farewells to the fallen king and prince. Sonorous pipes sounded from the towers of the palace to warn the city below, and the blue flames of the gatehouse flickered and died.

Alith had not known Bel Shanaar well, and had cause to resent some of his actions. Yet he could not stop tears forming in his eyes as he watched the procession clatter out of the plaza. Thus had passed the first Phoenix King since Aenarion, and the world ahead lay uncertain. No matter what came next, Alith knew that an age had ended and felt in his core that his generation would not know peace. Blood had been shed, the kingdoms of Ulthuan were divided and there were those who seemed determined to drag the elves down into darkness.

WITH THE PHOENIX King and his son interred within the sepulchres at the heart of the mountain, the business of the palace was soon abuzz with the succession. The servants were full of opinion as to who would be the more suitable prince to rule. However, all of their heightened speculation was to be for nothing. Yrianath claimed a sickness had befallen him, brought about by the grief of the funerals, and would not be able to participate in any debate whilst he was under the influence of this affliction.

'It must be a tremendous burden,' said Sinathlor, guard captain of the towers where Yrianath's chambers were located. He and several others of the prince's household were in the common room of their quarters, drinking autumn honeywine. Alith sat a little way apart, attentive to the discussion but far enough away that he need not participate directly.

'I am not surprised that he has been set low by this malady, not surprised at all,' added Elendarin, Stewardess of the Halls. She swept back her white hair and gazed at her companions. 'He has always been of a delicately sensitive disposition, ever since he was a child. His empathy for the people's grief is a tribute.'

Alith suppressed a disparaging remark at this saccharine observation, but Londaris, Steward of Tables, was not so polite.

'Ha! I have never seen anything so obviously false in my life,' he declared. 'This very morning, I found the prince on his balcony taking in the dawn sun and he seemed as fit as a hunter's hound.'

'Why feign such weakness?' argued Sinathlor. 'Surely that gives argument to Tirnandir and his cronies?'

Alith was fascinated by the professional loyalty of the household of each noble, who would argue the cause of their master and mistress in the fiercest of debates, yet as soon as their role and duties changed would switch their defences to their new lord or lady. It was not so with Gerithon, whose family had served the Anars since Eoloran had founded Elanardris, or the other subjects of the house who owed their loyalty alone to their prince and their kingdom.

'Yes, it does,' Londaris was saying. 'That is why I think it a risky move. I am sure the prince knows best, but I cannot see at the moment what advantage he gains.'

Another thing that occurred to Alith during the debate was that all of the elves present had a personal stake in the unfolding events. If Yrianath's bid succeeded, they would be members of the ruling household of Tiranoc, with all of the privilege that entailed. It was in their own interests to see the court's decision favour their master.

'He gains time,' said Alith, sensing an opportunity. 'Have you not noticed that of all the visitors who have requested to see him, only the Naggarothi, Caenthras, has been admitted? Not even Lirian, who is the ward of our lord since the death of her husband, can see Prince Yrianath. I fear that this illness may not be the fault of the prince at all, but some ploy by the Naggarothi envoy.'

There were frowns from some of the elves, but nods from others.

'What have you heard?' demanded the Fire Master, Gilthorian.

Alith held up his hands as if in surrender.

'I know nothing more than I am saying, I assure you,' he replied. 'Perhaps it is simply idle speculation on my part, for I am still a novice in the ways of politics. Yet it occurs to me that this envoy has Yrianath's ear by some means, and their meetings are always held in secret. Not even Palthrain attends them, and he supports Yrianath's claim. I do not know what this means, but it makes me wary.'

The others attempted to question Alith further and then took up his line of reasoning when he declined. It was, they agreed, somewhat suspicious for a Naggarothi prince to arrive in Tor Anroc during the funeral, and Caenthras certainly had unprecedented access to Yrianath. Though no conclusions were drawn, Alith went to his bed that night content that he had stirred up an unwitting force of spies on his behalf. He hoped the rumour would spread to other households and perhaps the nobles themselves, so that they might pay closer attention to Caenthras's activities.

ON THE SEVENTH night after the conclusion of the burial ceremonies, at a time when the demands for Yrianath to come to the court were becoming louder and louder, Alith was woken by the thud of booted feet in the corridors above his room.

He dressed quickly and slipped quietly out of his chamber. The palace was in a new tumult and Alith followed the other servants as they made their way towards the main halls. He froze when they came out into the courtyard at the centre of the palace grounds, for stood there were rank upon rank of spearmen and bowmen, several thousand of them. They were not dressed in the white and blue of Tiranoc, but in the black and purple of Nagarythe. Alith immediately ducked back inside, his heart beating.

The Naggarothi princes had arrived, and they had not come alone.

━< TEN >━

A Loyal Traitor

ALITH ARRIVED IN the corridors outside Yrianath's chambers just in time to see Caenthras and an escort of Naggarothi entering the prince's rooms. Alith ducked down a servants' stairwell as the group emerged, Yrianath in the midst of the imposing warriors, looking much distressed. There was nothing Alith could do, even if he had been armed. He slipped away down the stairs to the floor below, where Lirian lived.

As he emerged from the stairway, a group of Naggarothi, four of them, rounded the corner. Alith turned to run but the closest leapt forwards and grabbed his arm, hauling him back into the passageway.

'Please,' Alith begged, falling to his knees. 'I'm just a poor servant!'

The warrior sneered as he hauled Alith to his feet.

'Then you can serve us, wretch,' he snarled.

Alith smashed the heel of his hand into the soldier's chin and as the warrior fell, snatched free the sword at his waist. The blade cut the throat of the next before the Naggarothi could react. The remaining pair split, coming at Alith from both sides.

Alith parried the first blow and leapt backwards as the point of a sword stabbed towards his chest. His return attack crashed against the shield of the warrior to his left and his arm jarred from the impact. Alith's heart was in his throat as he dived beneath another swinging blade, rolling on his shoulder to come up to a guard position a moment before the other warrior launched a furious assault. Blow after blow rang from Alith's sword as he backed down the corridor, heading towards Lirian's chambers.

In a momentary respite from his assailant, Alith used his free hand to tear down a tapestry upon the wall, hurling it at the warrior. He followed up with a jumping kick, the ball of his foot smashing into the swathed figure, sending him toppling to the carpeted floor.

The other leapt over his fallen comrade, but Alith had expected this and lunged, chopping at his foe's leg. Blade bit into armour and rings of mail scattered across the corridor in a spurt of blood. The Naggarothi fell to the ground, a cry of pain torn from his lips. Alith drove the point of his sword into the warrior's exposed neck.

The remaining soldier disentangled himself from the tapestry but lost his sword and shield in the process. As he bent to retrieve his weapon, Alith brought his blade down hard on the back of his head, splitting the warrior's helm and biting into his skull.

Panting, Alith straightened and assured himself that his foes were dead. He leant the sword against the wall and hurriedly unfastened the belt of one of the soldiers, wrapping it around his own waist. Sheathing his stolen blade, he ran down the passageway to the royal chambers.

THE TWIN DOORS were open and there was no sign of anyone within. Alith stepped cautiously inside, ears alert for any sound, but there was none. A quick glance through the doors and archways leading from the antechamber confirmed that the Naggarothi had already taken Lirian and her son.

Alith could spare no further thought for the missing heir to the Tiranoc throne. The Naggarothi would be searching the whole palace and sooner or later he would run across opposition he could not avoid or overcome. It was inevitable that he would be recognised by someone. He needed to get out of Tor Anroc.

Alith assumed that the Naggarothi had entered by the main gateway, and so headed through the palace towards the north towers, hopefully ahead of any search parties. He kept to the side corridors and hidden stairwells used by the servants to move about the palace unseen by their masters. As he came closer to the servants' quarters he could hear yells and cries from ahead.

He changed route, cutting eastwards across the lawn of a night garden, skimming from column to column, through moonlight and shadow, along the edge of the cloister. Beyond were the outer parts of the eastern wing, and from there he would be able to reach the formal gardens at the back of the palaces.

Several of the ground-floor windows were unshuttered and open, and Alith jumped through the closest. He heard tramping feet echoing from bare stone to his right and so turned left at a run. His headlong sprint brought him out into one of the smaller gateyards that led out of the palace into the grounds. He was about to haul open one of the solid wooden gates when he heard footsteps behind him.

Turning, Alith saw more than a dozen spearmen entering the paved square. He saw a flash of white amongst them: Lirian carrying Anataris. The nearest warriors levelled their weapons and advanced slowly. Alith drew his sword and put his back to the closed gate.

'Wait!' the officer at the back of the group called out. Alith recognised the voice.

The small troop parted and the captain strode forwards. Though much of his face was concealed by his helmet, Alith could see that it was Yeasir.

The commander of Nagarythe stopped suddenly on seeing Alith. For his part, Alith was unsure what to do. If he turned his back to open the gate they would be upon him, and if he tried to fight, he would have no chance of victory.

'Put down your weapon, Alith,' Yeasir ordered.

Alith hesitated, flexing his fingers on the grip of his sword. He glanced at Lirian, who seemed oddly calm. She nodded reassuringly. Alith reluctantly let go of the sword, the clatter of its fall like a mournful knell as it echoed around the gateyard. Alith slumped back against the gate, raising his hands in a gesture of surrender.

Yeasir handed his spear to one of his soldiers and approached, his gauntleted hands held up in front of him, palms upwards.

'Do not be afraid, Alith,' said the captain. 'I do not know how you come to be here, but I am not your enemy. I mean you no harm.'

Yeasir's words did not relax Alith in the slightest and the young Anar's eyes darted around the yard seeking some other avenue of escape. There was none. He was trapped.

'Come, quickly,' said Yeasir, waving a hand over his shoulder.

Lirian, her baby in her arms, trotted forwards. As she did so, Yeasir gestured to one of his warriors.

'You, give me your bow and arrows,' snapped the commander. The soldier complied, slinging his quiver from his shoulder and passing it to Yeasir. To Alith's surprise, the Naggarothi captain handed them on to him and then stooped to pick up the discarded sword.

'There is little time to explain,' said Yeasir as he slipped the weapon into the sheath at Alith's waist. 'This is a most fortunate encounter for both of us. Now you can take the heir of Tiranoc to safety.'

A handful of the soldiers stepped forwards and opened the gate, letting in the moonlight from the gardens beyond. Lirian hurried through.

Alith could say nothing and stood shaking his head.

'Morathi has returned to Anlec and not all are pleased,' Yeasir said hurriedly. 'She wishes to punish Tiranoc for what happened to Malekith – it is not safe to be here. There is a haven to the east; I have told Princess Lirian its location. I will do whatever I can to delay pursuit, and will join you there in a few days' time. My wife and daughter are hidden there also, and together we will head east to sanctuary in Ellyrion.'

'What?' was all that Alith could muster.

'Just go,' snarled Yeasir. 'I must report the escape of the princess to the others and a search will soon follow. I will come to you and explain all.'

With that Yeasir shoved Alith unceremoniously through the gate, which closed soundlessly behind him. Lirian was already hurrying along a paved path ahead and Alith ran to catch up. Sounds of fighting echoed from the towers of the palace as the three of them headed into the night.

YEASIR LED HIS troops into the great hall, where other parties of Naggarothi had brought the various members of the court, as directed by Palthrain. The chamberlain stood beside the Phoenix Throne with Prince Yrianath and Caenthras. The last of these frowned when he saw Yeasir.

'You are unaccompanied,' said the Naggarothi prince.

'It seems our prey has eluded us for the moment,' replied Yeasir lightly. 'She will not get far, not with a child to care for.'

'That is unfortunate,' growled Caenthras.

'You believe she is still in the palace?' asked Palthrain.

'It is unlikely that she will quit Tor Anroc,' said Yeasir. 'Where else would she go? We are upon the brink of winter and the princess is no expert of the wilds. Tomorrow we will begin a search of the city.'

'I expected more of you,' Caenthras hissed quietly as Yeasir took his place beside the others.

'Though I may not be a prince, I am still Commander of Nagarythe,' Yeasir replied, keeping his tone level. 'Do not forget that.'

Caenthras remained sullenly silent as Palthrain called for the attention of the fearful Tiranocii nobles.

'There is no cause to be afraid!' the chamberlain announced. 'These warriors are present at the request of Prince Yrianath. In these uncertain times, it is important that we all remain vigilant for the corrupt amongst us, and our Naggarothi allies are here to help.'

'You invited them here?' said Tirnandir, his voice dripping with scorn.

'Well, I...' began Yrianath, but Palthrain cut across him.

'It is imperative that we choose a new prince to succeed Bel Shanaar, who might treat with our allies with authority,' said the chamberlain. 'Prince Yrianath has declared himself fit to be regent. Are there any present that oppose his claim?'

Tirnandir opened his mouth and then shut it again. Like all the other assembled courtiers, his eyes strayed to the Naggarothi warriors lining the hall, their swords bared and spears in hand. Palthrain waited for a moment and then nodded.

'As there is no objection raised, I declare that Prince Yrianath shall be our new regent, until such time as Prince Anataris comes of age to assume his rightful position. Hail Yrianath!'

The Naggarothi shout was far louder than that of the Tiranocii, who mumbled their praise and exchanged fearful looks.

'These are unprecedented times,' continued Palthrain. 'When faced with usurpers and traitors, we must act swiftly to ensure the safety of all loyal elves and prosecute those that would undermine the true rulers of Ulthuan. To that end, Prince Yrianath will enact the following laws.'

Palthrain then produced a rolled-up parchment from the sleeve of his robe and handed it to Yrianath. The prince took the scroll uncertainly and, prompted by a stare from Palthrain, unrolled it. His eyes scanned the runes upon it, widening with shock. A fierce glance from Caenthras quelled any protest and Yrianath began to read aloud, his voice wavering and quiet.

'As ruling prince of Tiranoc I decree that all soldiers, citizens and other subjects give their utmost cooperation to our Naggarothi allies. They are to be extended every courtesy and freedom whilst they aid in the protection of our realm. You are to obey the commands of such officers and princes of the Naggarothi as if they were mine. Failure to comply will be considered an act against my power and punished by death.'

Yrianath's voice broke at this point and he swayed as if about to faint. Eyes closed, he steadied himself and then continued reading.

'Due to the uncertain loyalties exhibited by some within the army of Tiranoc, I also decree that every soldier, captain or commander is to surrender his weapons to our Naggarothi allies. Those who secure our faith will be allowed to return to their positions as soon as practical. Failure to comply will be considered an act against my power and punished by death.'

A profound silence had fallen upon the hall as Yrianath's words settled in the minds of the Tiranocii. The prince's eyes glimmered wet as he continued, casting plaintive glances at those he had unwittingly betrayed.

'My last decree of this accession is to temporarily disband the court of Tiranoc until such investigations surrounding the demise of Bel Shanaar clear those present of involvement in this unspeakably vile act. I hereby take all authority to rule as regent and my word is law. Such commands as issued by former members of the court have no validity and should be disregarded until confirmed by myself or our Naggarothi allies. Failure to comply will be considered an act against my power and punished by death...'

There was open discontent, a ripple of whispers, short-lived as Caenthras stepped forwards and took the scroll from Yrianath. The Naggarothi's expression was stern.

'In order to comply with the wishes of your new prince, you will all be escorted back to your homes and placed under house arrest. You will be called for in the following days to account for your actions.'

With a gesture from Yeasir, the Naggarothi soldiers ushered the assembled nobles towards the open doors. When the Tiranocii had been escorted out, Palthrain turned to Caenthras.

'That went better than I expected,' said the chamberlain. 'Now our work can begin.'

* * *

DAWN HAD YET to creep above the mountains when Lirian led Alith to a stretch of wooded hills north and east of Tor Anroc. The pair had spoken little on the journey, much to Alith's relief. He had no words of comfort and though he had known about the conspiracy between Caenthras and Yrianath, he had suspected nothing of what was to unfold from that partnership. As they silently followed road and path, and finally cut across the meadows of outlying farms, Alith had tried to make sense of what had happened.

They walked steadily uphill through the darkness of the trees, Lirian clutching Anataris to her chest. Alith studied the princess out of the corner of his eye, seeing strain on her face. She was dressed in a light robe, utterly unsuitable to cross-country travel and very much stained and ragged. Her usually perfectly arranged hair fell in blonde disarray and her eyes were red from suppressed tears. There was bleakness about her expression that echoed the emptiness in his heart.

Alith tried to think of words of comfort that he might say but he could find none. Every turn of phrase seemed trite or nonsensical. He could offer no reassurance for he felt none himself. Everything had fallen apart, and as far as Alith could work out, it all pointed back towards Nagarythe. He found that he had far more questions than answers and wished that he had been able to find out more from Yeasir.

Lirian stopped and wordlessly pointed to the left. In the gloom Alith could just about make out the darker shape of a cave opening. Drawing his sword, he signalled for the princess to hide behind a tree. Stalking ahead, Alith heard whispered voices. Both were female.

Coming to the cave he found a small group huddled around a shuttered lantern, the dim light barely reaching the cave walls. There were three elves, two female and a child wrapped in a bundle of blue cloth. Both of the adults were clad in heavy robes of deep blue and embroidered shawls of the same colour. The older of the two, perhaps seven or eight hundred years of age, jumped to her feet, a dagger in her hand. She stepped protectively in front of her younger companion and the baby.

'Friend,' said Alith, swinging his sword to one side. The terrified elves remained unconvinced and he tossed the blade out of the cave. 'I am here to help, Yeasir sent me.'

His protestation was met with fearful looks and Alith returned outside, calling for Lirian. The princess walked warily through the trees and would not enter the cave until Alith stepped inside. The two groups of elves looked suspiciously at each other for a moment.

'Who are you?' asked the younger elf. 'What do you want?'

'I am Alith Anar, friend of Yeasir,' Alith replied. 'I am escorting Princess Lirian and her son.'

'What is happening, where is my husband?' demanded the elder of the pair. 'Where is Yeasir?'

'He is in Tor Anroc, misdirecting the pursuit,' replied Alith. 'What is your name?'

'Saphistia,' she told him, placing the knife back in her belt. 'This is my sister, Heileth, and my son, Durinithill. When will Yeasir come?'

'I do not know,' said Alith, leading Lirian by the arm. He gestured for her to sit beside Heileth. 'He instructed me to wait here but promised he will join us soon. Have you any food or drink?'

'Of course,' said Heileth.

She stood and carefully handed the child to his mother and then turned to a row of packs laid against the rock wall. She brought out a waterskin and several small cups and passed them to Alith. Wrapped packets of cured meats followed.

'Anar is not a trusted name in Nagarythe these days,' said Saphistia as Alith poured water for each of them.

'Lies,' snarled Alith. 'We have been victims of a campaign to discredit our house. Yeasir trusts me, and so should you.'

Alith did not wait for any further comment and left the cave to retrieve his sword from the fallen leaves outside. He stayed there a while, scanning the woods for any sign of pursuit. There was none. Ducking back inside, he grabbed a cup and some food.

'I'll keep watch,' he told the others before swiftly retreating again.

He had no desire for company and sat with his back against a tree. He barely tasted the spiced meat, his thoughts far away in Nagarythe. When Yeasir returned Alith would leave and go north. Yeasir could run to Ellyrion if he wished – he had his family with him. Alith would return to Elanardris to discover what had befallen his kin.

Dawn brought no sign of any other elf, friend or foe. Alith looked into the cave and found all within were asleep. Taking his bow in hand, he set off to find some fresh food.

'SO IT SEEMS that your assumptions were wrong,' said Palthrain. 'The princess has escaped the city.'

Yeasir did not reply, but simply hung his head, feigning shame. He was alone in the great hall with the chamberlain and he longed to strangle the traitorous noble, but knew that he needed to keep his own loyalties concealed if he was to rejoin his family.

'Two days have been wasted,' continued Palthrain. 'Two days ahead of your forces.'

'I believe they are on foot. Our riders will swiftly catch them,' said Yeasir.

'They?'

'Yes, it is also my belief that the princess has help,' Yeasir said quickly, keeping his expression bland whilst inwardly he cursed his slip of the tongue. 'A soldier perhaps, or a servant. I cannot imagine that Lirian has the wit to contrive such an escape on her own. She is a spoilt Tiranocii bitch.'

'And when were you going to appraise me and Caenthras of this conclusion?'

Now Yeasir allowed his anger to show.

'While you may take some credit in creating this situation, remember that I am commander here! You are not even Naggarothi, so be mindful of your accusations. Morathi might be mildly distressed should anything happen to you, but we are a long way from Anlec. Bad things, unseen events, happen in war. If you were a Naggarothi, you would know that.'

Palthrain seemed unconcerned by Yeasir's threats.

'So what is your plan to continue the search?' asked the chamberlain.

'She will not go north, that takes her closer to the Naganath,' said Yeasir.

'But much of Tiranoc's army is camped in that direction. The princess might seek sanctuary with them.'

'Possible but unlikely,' said Yeasir. 'I very much doubt that she trusts anybody in Tiranoc at the moment. I think she will go west, heading for the coast. There she will be able to take ship to any other realm in Ulthuan.'

'Why would she trust other kingdoms when she does not trust her own?'

'She might not, but the sea is the greatest obstacle to recapturing her. If she has headed south or east, we will be able to catch her before she reaches Caledor or Ellyrion. If Lirian reaches a ship, we have no means of pursuing her.'

'I can see there is reason in your argument,' Palthrain said, leaning upon the arm of the Phoenix Throne.

'I was not asking your permission,' said Yeasir.

'Of course not,' Palthrain replied smoothly. 'Still, it might be better that you inform Caenthras of your plan so that you can... coordinate your forces.'

'What of Yrianath?' said Yeasir, keen to steer the topic of conversation away from the question of who had authority amongst the occupying soldiers. Morathi had charged the commander to lead the warriors, but many of those troops were direct subjects of Caenthras and owed their loyalty to the prince. 'He is little use as a regent until we have the heir in our possession.'

'Yrianath gives us a veil of legitimacy for the time being,' said Palthrain. 'He understands his position very well, as do the other members of the court. Once we have Lirian and her brat, Yrianath will be able to conduct affairs with the other kingdoms as we desire.'

Yeasir nodded and turned towards the door. Palthrain's words reached him at the end of the hall.

'That is, of course, assuming you actually *find* Lirian.'

Yeasir stopped but did not turn.

'When this is done, there will be a reckoning,' he whispered to himself before striding away.

* * *

FOUR DAYS HAD passed since the flight from Tor Anroc and there had been no sign of Yeasir. Saphistia was becoming distraught and repeatedly urged Alith to head back to the city to find out any news concerning her husband. Alith flatly refused to do so, saying that he would not leave the group unprotected.

'How long must we stay here?' asked Lirian as the fourth day turned to the fourth night. The princess had regained little life, and spent most of her time listlessly wandering around the cave, whispering to her son.

'We wait until Yeasir arrives,' replied Saphistia.

'What if he doesn't come?' the princess said with a long sigh. 'He could be dead already.'

'Don't say such a thing!' snapped Heileth.

Saphistia merely directed a venomous gaze at Lirian and retired to the back of the cave where the two children were laid upon beds Alith had made from leaves and a cloak. There was another opening beyond, which led into a network of water-carved tunnels that ran through the hills. This was to be their escape route if they were discovered, and Alith had spent some time exploring them at night while Heileth had kept watch. If the worst occurred, there was a small tunnel they could use to head north, and Alith had assembled a small trap made of branches and rocks that could be used to block the route to delay any pursuit.

'It was a grand procession,' Lirian said idly. 'All of those banners and chariots.'

'What was grand?' asked Heileth.

'Elodhir's funeral,' the princess replied, her voice distant, her gaze directed at nothing in particular.

'Stop talking about funerals,' hissed Saphistia. 'Yeasir is alive. I would feel it if he were dead.'

'Elodhir died so very far away,' said Lirian. She turned her empty eyes to Saphistia. 'I didn't feel a thing.'

Alith quit the cave with a shake of his head. He offered praise to any gods listening, asking if they would deliver Yeasir soon so that he could leave the bickering group behind. Even as he formed these thoughts, a movement amongst the trees caught his attention. In a moment Alith had his bow in hand and an arrow to the string.

Listening, Alith could hear the muffled hoof-beats of several steeds and soon he saw a figure leading half a dozen horses across the leaf mould. Alith slipped behind a nearby tree, arrow aimed at the new arrival. A few heartbeats later and Yeasir came into view. Alith stepped out and lowered his bow.

'You do not know how pleased I am to see you,' Alith called as he walked down the hill.

'Your celebration may be short-lived,' replied the commander. 'I cannot stay long.'

'How so?' Alith asked as Yeasir joined him. The pair walked towards the cave, the horses trailing obediently after them.

'Caenthras's forces are close by,' said Yeasir. 'It is not yet safe to leave and I must return before my absence is noted.'

When they came to the cave, Saphistia ran to the cavern entrance and embraced her husband tightly.

'Thank the gods that you are safe,' she gasped. 'I feared the worst with every passing moment.'

Yeasir calmed his wife, kissing her on the cheeks, before turning his attention to his son. He picked up the babe from where he lay swaddled in a blue blanket, and held him close to his chest, his eyes lingering lovingly on Durinithill's small face.

'He has been so brave,' said Saphistia, clasping her arm around Yeasir's. 'Not a whimper or a tear the whole time.'

As if emerging from a sleep, Yeasir then straightened and handed the child to Heileth.

'I have brought steeds and more supplies,' he said. 'I must divert the pursuit further south today, and tonight I will return. Then we can leave before the search begins afresh in the morning.'

Lirian stirred at the back of the cave.

'What of Yrianath?' she asked. 'Perhaps you could rescue him also?'

Yeasir shook his head sadly.

'Yrianath is caught in his own folly,' said the commander. 'Palthrain and Caenthras watch him every moment. It is you and your son that must be kept safe. Without the true heir their claim to any legitimate rule is weak.'

Yeasir then shared another long embrace with his wife, and as they parted his face betrayed his pain. For a brief moment, Alith thought that Yeasir would not go, and he wondered what it was like to share such love.

His expression full of stern resignation, Yeasir tore his eyes away from his loved ones and left the cave. Alith followed him out.

'There is something I wish to speak to you about,' said Alith.

'Be quick,' said Yeasir.

'I am returning to Nagarythe,' Alith told him. 'I cannot go with you to Ellyrion. I must go to my family.'

'Of course,' said Yeasir, his eyes straying for a heartbeat towards the cave. 'Keep them safe until tonight, and then you may follow whichever path you need.'

Alith nodded. He watched Yeasir head off through the woods, heading to the west, until the commander had disappeared from sight. He sat down on a rock and began his melancholy watch.

NOT FAR FROM the cave a figure swathed in magical shadow watched Yeasir leaving. He swung into the saddle of his black horse, his raven-feathered cloak swirling behind him. Silently, he steered his steed south, riding swiftly.

* * *

A SENSE OF foreboding filled Yeasir as he crossed the plaza towards the palace. As he came to the gatehouse, he saw Palthrain standing with a small company of warriors. Yeasir's heart began to pound. Something was wrong.

'How fares the search?' the chamberlain asked, his manner off-hand.

'No success today,' said Yeasir as he stepped past.

'Perhaps you would have more luck if you did not waste your time visiting secret caves,' said Palthrain.

Yeasir whirled around to confront the chamberlain. A sly smile crossed Palthrain's lips.

'Did you think you could betray us?' he said.

Yeasir ripped his sword free and lunged before the guards could react. The blade punched through Palthrain's robes, sliding effortlessly into his gut.

'I'll see you in Mirai,' hissed Yeasir, dragging his sword from the blood-bubbling wound.

He cut the arm from the first warrior that approached and drove its point through the throat of the second. Yeasir dodged aside from the spear of a third and broke into a run, sprinting through the gateway.

Running to the corral that had been made where the market had once stood, Yeasir jumped onto the back of a horse and urged it into a gallop. Three Naggarothi attempted to bar his path but he rode straight through them, snatching the spear from the grasp of one of them as he passed. With the echo of thundering hooves resounding from the walls, he passed into the tunnel-street that wound down through the mount of Tor Anroc.

There were shouts of alarm from behind Yeasir but he paid them no heed, growling at his mount to run as fast as possible. Elves threw themselves from his path as he raced through the city. His heart was pounding with the hooves of his steed and he was gripped by a breathless panic. Everything in the world seemed to disappear around him. All that existed was the thought of his wife and son.

DUSK WAS SETTLING on the fields of Tiranoc as Yeasir's headlong rush across the countryside continued. He spared no thought for his steed falling foul, his every intent upon the wooded hills ahead. In the ruddy light Yeasir could see armed figures marching into the woodland.

Steering left, he sought to overtake the warriors. He ducked as he came to the edge of the trees, branches whipping at his face and shoulders. A glance to his right confirmed that several hundred Naggarothi were converging on the cave.

His horse stumbled on a root and Yeasir almost fell. With a ragged gasp, he righted himself and urged the horse onwards. The glint of armour and weapons could be seen in the gloom ahead.

With a last effort, Yeasir forced his mount up the hillside that led to the cave, cries from the warriors around him sounding through the trees.

'Alith!' he shouted as the cave came into view. The young Anar leapt up from where he was sat, his bow suddenly in hand.

Yeasir reined his mount to a skidding stop, sending a cloud of leaves swirling in the air. He swung himself down to the ground and ran for the cave.

'We are undone!' said the commander.

Saphistia and Heileth dashed from the cave. Yeasir waved away the attentions of his wife.

'Take the children and flee!' he rasped. 'The enemy are at hand.'

Even as he spoke these words, the first of the Naggarothi could be seen advancing through the woods. They pointed up the hill towards the cave and hastened their attack.

'Flee!' cried Yeasir, grabbing Saphistia and shoving her towards the cave. She fought back, slapping away his arm.

'You are coming with us!' she said, tears streaming down her face.

Yeasir relented for a moment, pulling her close, his arms tight around her. He caught the scent of her hair and felt the warmth of her against his cheek. Then hollowness gripped him, welling up from the pit of his stomach, and he pushed Saphistia away.

'Take Durinithill and go,' he said hoarsely. 'Protect our son, and tell him that his father loved him more than anything else in the world.'

Saphistia looked as if she would stay, but Heileth grabbed her arm and dragged her towards the cave. With a wordless cry, Yeasir bounded after them and threw his arms around Saphistia for a last time.

'I love you,' he whispered and then pulled away.

Yeasir looked at the Naggarothi stalking through the woods and his sorrow was burned away by a bright anger. His body was aflame with rage, his hands trembling with the emotion. He had known little peace in his long life. He thought he had found it, but there were those who would rob him even of this small contentment.

'I will fight beside you,' said Alith.

'No!' Yeasir told him. 'You must keep them safe.'

The Naggarothi were barely a hundred paces away. Yeasir could hear the echoes of his wife and companions' shrill voices from the cave.

'Get them away from here,' he hissed. 'There is a darkness claiming Ulthuan. You must fight it.'

Alith hesitated, his eyes flicking between the cave and the closing Naggarothi. With a resigned sigh, he nodded.

'It has been my honour,' said Alith, grasping Yeasir's shoulder. 'I have met no truer son of Nagarythe and I swear that if need be I will give my life to protect your family.'

ALITH WAS NOT sure if his words had been heard, for all of Yeasir's focus was on the approaching warriors. Alith ran to the cave mouth and turned back. The black-clad Naggarothi were advancing more cautiously, in a line a dozen wide, shields raised and spears lowered.

Yeasir faced the dark mass coming through the trees; sword in his right hand, spear in his left. He appeared relaxed, already accepting of his fate. One might have thought the commander was simply taking in the fresh evening air. Yeasir spared not one glance back, his stare fixed upon those that would slay or enslave his family. Alith had never seen such courage, and though he knew what he must do, he felt a great shame that he was being forced to run.

Yeasir raised the spear defiantly above his head and his voice rang out, the cry of a commander who had bellowed orders over the din of a hundred battles.

'Know who you face, cowards!' he shouted. 'I am Yeasir, son of Lanadriath. I am Commander of Nagarythe. I fought at Athel Toralien and the Battle of Silvermere. I marched with Prince Malekith into the north and faced the creatures and daemons of the dark gods. I was the first into Anlec when Morathi was overthrown. Ten times ten thousand foes have felt my wrath! Come and taste the vengeance of my spear and the ire of my sword. Come to me, brave soldiers, and face a true warrior!'

Yeasir lifted up his sword also and his next cry caused the advancing soldiers to halt, sharing fearful glances with each other.

'I am Naggarothi!'

Yeasir broke into a run, heading down the slope at full speed. As he came to the line of shields, he leapt into the air, his spear flashing downwards. With a crash of metal, he plunged into the soldiers. Screams of pain and dread resounded over the hillside as a swathe of warriors fell before the commander's assault. In moments a dozen bodies littered the ground and the dead leaves were spattered with blood. Yeasir's sword and spear tip were a silvered whirlwind, cutting down everything within reach.

Then Yeasir was lost from view as the soldiers swarmed forwards and surrounded him.

Alith was choked with despair but his heart burned with pride as he turned into the cave. He followed the others and plunged into the darkness.

━◄ ELEVEN ►━

A Beacon of Hope

ONCE MORE ALITH found himself in the mountains, though this time he was not alone. The group had ridden north from the caves and then turned eastwards. Alith's craft had allowed them to avoid their pursuers in the foothills before turning north again. It was the morning of the sixth day of their flight when Lirian reined her horse in beside Alith's.

'Why are we heading north?' she asked. 'The Pass of the Eagle is south. There is no way north to Ellyrion.'

'We are not going to Ellyrion,' Alith told her. 'We head for Nagarythe.'

'Nagarythe?' Lirian gasped. She tugged her horse to a stop and Alith paused beside her. 'Nagarythe is the last place we need to go. It is the Naggarothi who want to take my son!'

Heileth came alongside.

'What is the delay?' she said.

'He is taking us to Nagarythe,' Lirian said shrilly, as if accusing Alith of wanting to kill them all in their sleep.

'Not all of Nagarythe is ruled by Morathi,' Alith said. 'We will be safe in the lands of my family. Safer than anywhere else. The cults are everywhere, even in Ellyrion. Do you trust me?'

'No,' said Lirian.

'How can we be sure you will not abandon us?' said Heileth.

'I gave my vow to Yeasir to protect you,' replied Alith. 'It is my duty to see you all safe.'

'And what is the word of a Naggarothi worth these days?' said Lirian.

507

'Perhaps we should return to Tor Anroc and ask them?'

'Not all Naggarothi are the same,' Alith replied hotly. 'Some of us still value honour and freedom. We are the true Naggarothi. We have a name for those who have occupied Tor Anroc – druchii.'

Lirian was still uncertain, though Heileth looked more convinced. She was also Naggarothi and understood better the divisions that had grown there. She turned to Lirian and spoke softly.

'What Alith says is true,' she said. 'Not all Naggarothi pray to dark gods nor seek to enslave others. If you do not trust Alith, do you trust me?'

Lirian did not reply. She urged her horse away and turned back down the trail they had been following. Alith leaned forwards and grabbed the reins to stop her.

'We are going to Nagarythe,' he said quietly.

Lirian looked into his eyes and saw no compromise there. She lowered her head and turned back to the north.

ALITH HAD NEVER loved Elanardris so much as he did the moment they crested the ridge at Cail Anris. He stopped his horse and looked at the hills and mountains. He had wondered at times whether he would see such a sight again. For a moment he was lost in the beauty of the white slopes and the wind-swept grass. The autumn clouds were low, but here and there the sun broke through to dazzle from the peaks. The air was crisp and cool, and Alith took a deep breath.

The others had stopped with him, gazing in wonder, both at their surrounds and the change in Alith.

'Is this your home?' asked Saphistia.

Alith pointed north and west.

'The manse of the Anars lies over those slopes,' he said. 'Past those woods upon the shoulders of Anul Hithrun and two more days of riding.'

A movement in the skies caught Alith's eye and he was not surprised to see a crow dipping down over the hillside. It landed on the branch of a short bush not far away and cawed once before setting off again, heading south.

'I shall fetch us some fresh food,' said Alith. 'Go on ahead. I'll not be far away nor gone long. It is safe here.'

He turned his horse after the crow and set off at a gentle trot, his eyes keen for any sign of Elthyrior.

Coming around a pile of moss-covered boulders, Alith saw the raven herald sat on a rock, his horse nearby nibbling at the grass. The crow was perched on Elthyrior's shoulder and gave Alith a beady look as he dismounted and walked his horse closer.

'I should have expected your welcome,' said Alith. He let the horse walk free and sat down beside Elthyrior.

'I would have said it was coincidence, but I know the ways of Morai-heg better than that,' replied the raven herald. 'I was heading north when I happened to see you. What news from Tiranoc? I have heard little, but that has been enough to worry me.'

'Caenthras and others have usurped power in Tor Anroc,' Alith told him. 'I am escorting the true heir of Bel Shanaar to keep him out of Morathi's clutches. I have had no word from Nagarythe for almost a year. What manner of welcome can I expect in Elanardris?'

'A good one,' said Elthyrior. 'Morathi has other concerns than the Anars at the moment. Her army is split between those who were loyal to Malekith and those who have sworn fealty to her. She thinks the Anars are a trouble of the past, no threat to her.'

Alith took this without comment and Elthyrior continued.

'All of Ulthuan is in upheaval,' he said. 'Only a handful of princes survived the massacre at the Shrine of Asuryan.'

'Massacre?'

'Surely. Though it is hard to piece together what occurred, some treachery unfolded there. The cults have been patient, growing their strength, and now they strike. Attacks and murders plague the other kingdoms, turning their eyes inwards whilst Morathi readies for war.'

'War?' said Alith. 'With whom? It is one thing to occupy leaderless Tiranoc, it is another to march to battle against the other princes.'

'And yet that is her intent, I fear,' said Elthyrior. 'Once she has full control of the army again she will set Nagarythe against all of Ulthuan.'

'Then perhaps we should allow her to indulge this folly,' said Alith.

'Folly?' Elthyrior laughed bitterly. 'No, it is not folly, though there are risks. Ulthuan is an isle divided. No single realm can stand against Nagarythe. Their armies are small and untested, and no doubt there are traitors loyal to the cults in their ranks. Of all the kingdoms, only Caledor perhaps has strength to hold if the others do not unite.'

'And surely they will unite when they see the threat,' said Alith.

'There is nobody to unite them, no banner that they can come together beneath. The Phoenix King is dead. Who else would the princes follow? Whether it was some part of a grander scheme or simple opportunism, the death of Bel Shanaar and so many princes has left Ulthuan vulnerable. If Morathi can strike quickly enough, in the spring I would say, then nobody is ready to hold against her.'

As he absorbed this, Alith absent-mindedly plucked a long stem of grass and began to tie it into intricate knots. Occupying his hands allowed his thoughts to clarify.

'It occurs to me that the longer Nagarythe is unstable, the more time the others have to recover from this disaster.'

'I would agree,' said Elthyrior. 'What do you have in mind?'

'A banner, you said,' replied Alith. 'There must be a rallying call to all of those Naggarothi who would see the druchii menace opposed. The Anars can issue such a call.'

'The Anars did not fare so well last time they attempted to defy the will of Anlec,' said Elthyrior.

'Last time we had a traitor in our midst – Caenthras,' snarled Alith. 'We were unprepared for the foe we faced, isolated and outnumbered. This time there can be no doubting our cause. There can be no divided loyalty, and those families that perhaps once feared Morathi's anger and did nothing will know that they cannot simply stay silent any longer.'

Elthyrior directed a doubtful look towards Alith.

'How I wish that were true,' said the raven herald.

He started walking towards his horse when Alith called out.

'We are likely to need your eyes and ears in the days to come. Is there any way that I can contact you?'

Elthyrior mounted his steed, pulling his cloak over its flanks.

'No,' he said. 'I come and go at the whim of Morai-heg. If the All-seeing One thinks that you need me, I shall be close at hand. You know how to find me.'

The crow leapt from his shoulder and beat its wings thrice before soaring past Alith at head height. It gave a loud screech and climbed into the air. Alith watched it circle higher and higher until it was just a speck.

'I…' he began, turning to where Elthyrior had been. The raven herald was gone, without the slightest beat of hoof or jangle of tack. Alith shook his head in disbelief. 'Just for once, I wish you'd say goodbye properly.'

ALITH HAD QUITE an entourage by the time he was on the road to the manse. Loyal subjects of the family came out of their houses and stores to rejoice at his homecoming. Their cheers and smiles were just a little too desperate though, and the strain of the split within Nagarythe showed on their faces. Alith did his best to remain confident, playing the part of the lord of the Anars, but in his heart he knew that their woes were far from over.

The commotion brought a small crowd from the manse. Soldiers and servants came out of the gates and gazed in astonishment at the return of their master. Alith spied Gerithon amongst them, who sent several of his staff running back to the house. When Alith had reached the gate, his father and mother were striding across the courtyard, trying to hurry yet remain dignified at the same time.

Alith had no such pretension. He jumped from his horse and pushed his way through the knot of elves, receiving claps on the back and heartfelt welcomes. He broke into a run and met his mother halfway to the manse.

The two of them shared a deep embrace, Maieth's tears wetting Alith's cloak as she buried her face in his chest. Eothlir joined them, wrapping his arms around both of them. His expression was austere but there was a gleam in his eye that betrayed his joy at seeing his son alive. Alith was grinning widely. Then he remembered his charges.

Turning to the gate, Alith saw Lirian, Saphistia and Heileth sitting on their horses and gazing around in shock. Servants helped them down, taking the children for a moment before returning them. Alith performed the introductions quickly, mentioning only the names of his companions. Though he knew they were safe here, he did not want idle chatter to spread concerning Lirian and her son.

'We need to talk,' he said to Eothlir and his father nodded, waving them towards the house.

'Gerithon will ensure our guests are looked after,' he said.

'Where is Eoloran?' Alith asked as they walked along the paving.

'He'll be waiting inside,' said Maieth.

Indeed he was. Alith's grandfather was in the main hall, sat at the end of the table with his fingers steepled to his chin. He looked up as Alith entered, his face a blank mask. Alith felt a sudden nervousness at Eoloran's behaviour, and feared that he had done something wrong by returning. Or perhaps he should have returned earlier?

'You have been away a long while, Alith,' Eoloran said solemnly. His facade broke as a smile crept into the corner of his lips. 'I hope you have been busy with important matters to neglect your family for so long.'

'More than I can ever tell you,' laughed Alith, striding to his grandfather and embracing him. 'Yet, I will try to.'

Gerithon appeared at the doorway.

'Your guests will be quartered in the east wing, lord,' he said.

'Thank you, Gerithon,' Eoloran replied. 'And please ensure that we are not disturbed.'

'Of course,' Gerithon intoned with a shallow bow. He backed out of the hall and closed the doors soundlessly.

Alith gave as brief a summary as he could concerning the events in Tor Anroc and the circumstances of his departure. The others listened intently without interruption, but as soon as he was finished they had a barrage of questions.

'Do you think the Tiranocii will resist?' asked Eoloran.

'They will try, and they will fail,' said Alith. 'The court is held hostage and the army has no direction. If Morathi were to cross the Naganath, I doubt there is much that Tiranoc can do to stop her.'

'Tell me more of Caenthras,' demanded Eothlir. 'What was his part in all of this? Is he knowingly complicit?'

'It was Caenthras who entrapped Prince Yrianath, Father,' Alith replied. 'Though I doubt he is the sole architect of this usurpation he is certainly one of its chief agents. I saw banners of his house amongst the warriors that arrived.'

'You are sure that Yeasir fell?' Alith's father continued. 'Perhaps his troops will not be so happy to fight under Caenthras.'

'Some were loyal to Yeasir, but I do not know how many,' said Alith. 'And amongst those there were none that he trusted with the location of his wife and child. I do not think the druchii will turn on each other, if that is your hope. And Yeasir definitely fell. No warrior save perhaps Aenarion himself or Prince Malekith could have fought such numbers alone and survived. His family is now my responsibility.'

'And we will help you bear that,' said Maieth. 'Now, tell me more about Milandith...'

'There will be time enough later to hear about Alith's romances,' Eothlir said. 'First we must decide what we will do next.'

Alith nodded, knowing that it would be well into the night before such a decision was reached. Maieth fluttered a hand at her male relatives and stood up. She stood behind Alith and laid her hands on his shoulders.

'You can't hide from me forever,' she said, kissing him on the top of the head. She walked away and then looked back as she opened the door. 'I'll find out what you've been up to!'

'Give me Morathi's torturers before an inquisitive mother,' said Eothlir when Maieth had left the room.

Alith nodded in fervent agreement.

—◄ TWELVE ►—

Dark Fen

As ELTHYRIOR HAD predicted, the druchii were intent on subjugating all of Ulthuan. Over the course of the following winter Anlec strengthened its grip on Nagarythe, pushing back those factions opposed to Morathi's return. Elanardris again became a safe haven for these dissidents, including princes and captains. Thousands of Naggarothi warriors made camp in the foothills of the mountains. Durinne, lord of the port of Galthyr, resisted for the whole of the winter, but fresh forces besieged the city when the snows began to thaw and the druchii were victorious. They took many ships that had sought winter harbour, and with this fleet nowhere on Ulthuan was beyond their reach.

By mid-spring, the armies of the druchii marched. With Tiranoc divided, they were able to control the passes eastwards and advanced into Ellyrion. Their navy prowled the coast to the north and west, only kept from the shores of Caledor and Eataine by their fear of the powerful fleet at Lothern. All the while, the Anars expected the fury of the druchii to fall upon Elanardris, yet the blow never came. Morathi, perhaps out of arrogance, saw no threat from the mountains and was determined to subjugate the other kingdoms as swiftly as possible. The questioning of commanders captured by Anar raids confirmed as much: when Ulthuan was under Morathi's control, she would have time enough to deal with the Anars.

The Anars led sorties into the rest of Nagarythe, but were unable to mount any kind of meaningful offensive. Wary of being surrounded or leaving Elanardris unguarded, Eoloran and Eothlir could not bring their full strength against the druchii. Thousands of refugees had fled into the mountains around the Anars' lands. Food and other resources were scarce, and so the Anars fought a guerrilla war, hitting the druchii columns as they marched to Tiranoc, then withdrawing before their foes gathered their strength.

In this time, the Shadows were reformed, with Alith as their leader. Their numbers swelled to several hundred of the most deadly warriors in Elanardris, and Eoloran tasked them with disrupting the druchii as much as possible.

Under Alith's leadership, the Shadows terrorised their foes. Driven on by his memories of the Khainite camp and the occupation of Tor Anroc, Alith was merciless. The Shadows did not fight battles. Instead, they crept into camps and killed warriors in their sleep. They raided villages supplying the druchii armies and destroyed food stores and burnt down the homes of those that supported Morathi. Nobles loyal to Anlec soon began to fear for their lives as Alith and his Shadows hunted them down, slaying them upon the dark roads or breaking into their castles to kill them and slaughter their families.

IT WAS WHILE returning from an attack on Galthyr, during which the Shadows burnt half a dozen ships in the harbour with their crews still aboard, that Alith next met Elthyrior. A year had passed since the massacre at the shrine, and for all the psychological damage the Anars had inflicted, Alith knew that they had achieved little real gain. Yet what Elthyrior told him gave him some hope.

'There is a new Phoenix King,' said the raven herald.

The pair had met in a copse of trees not far from the Shadows' camp on the northern edge of Elanardris. It was night-time and neither moon had yet risen. In the darkness the raven herald was invisible, a disembodied voice amongst the trees.

'Prince Imrik has been chosen by the other princes and, thank the gods, he has accepted the Phoenix Throne,' Elthyrior continued.

'Imrik is a good choice,' said Alith. 'He is a warrior, and the realm of Caledor is second only to Nagarythe in strength. The dragon princes will be a firmer test for Morathi's warriors.'

'He has taken the name of King Caledor, in memory of his grandfather,' Elthyrior added.

'That is curious,' replied Alith. 'It is not without merit. It is well that the other princes are reminded that the blood of the Dragontamer runs in the king's veins. Do you know anything of his intent?'

'He intends to fight, but more than that I cannot say,' said Elthyrior.

'Perhaps there is some means by which we can send a message to Caledor,' said Alith. 'If we could join forces in some way...'

* * *

IT WAS WITH this thought that Alith returned to the manse to consult with his father and grandfather. Several messengers were sent south, but the Naganath was well patrolled. The bodies of three heralds were found upon stakes on the road to Elanardris, dismembered and flayed.

The winter passed without reply, and the fate of the last messenger remained unknown. What little news that reached the Anars was not encouraging. Despite King Caledor's appointment, the other realms still appeared much divided, especially those to the east that had yet to suffer the full wrath of the druchii. Far from joining forces behind Caledor, the princes were more concerned with protecting their own lands, so that Tiranoc, Ellyrion, Chrace and Eataine suffered greatly at the hands of the advancing armies.

IT WAS LATE spring when a bloodied herald rode up to the manse and demanded an audience with Eoloran. The lord of the Anars summoned Eothlir and Alith to the great hall.

'I am Ilriadan, and I bear tidings from the Phoenix King,' said the messenger. He had been given fresh clothes and a wound on his arm had been bandaged. He sat at the long table with the others, food and fortified wine laid before him.

'Tell us what you know,' said Eothlir. 'What news of the war?'

Ilriadan drank a little wine before answering.

'There is little to comfort those who resist Morathi's expansion,' he said. 'King Caledor does what he can to stem the attacks but the druchii, as you call them, have gathered their strength and no force the Phoenix King can yet muster matches them. He is forced to retreat from their advance, slowing it for a time and little more.'

Eoloran was disconcerted at these tidings. He sighed and bowed his head.

'There is no hope that the Phoenix King can mount an offensive?' he asked quietly.

'None at all,' said Ilriadan. 'His princes do what they can to rouse the dragons of Caledor to fight with them, but few of them remain willing to aid the elves. Without the dragon princes, the army of Anlec is too strong.'

'Is there any effort that we might make that will aid the Phoenix King in his cause?' asked Eothlir.

Ilriadan shook his head.

'The druchii hold several castles and towns in Ellyrion and Tiranoc,' said the messenger. 'The Phoenix King thought to raze the lands ahead of their advance, but the other princes have refused, and say that they will not starve their own people. Morathi consolidates her hold on what she has already gained and we fear a fresh offensive next year.'

'I cannot believe that in all of Ulthuan there is not the force that can match our foes,' snapped Alith. 'Nagarythe is strong, but surely the other kingdoms can muster an army to match!'

'You are Naggarothi, you do not understand,' said Ilriadan. 'You are raised as warriors. We of the other kingdoms are not. Our armies are small compared to the legions of Nagarythe. What warriors we did have, most left our shores to forge the colonies, and those that remain have never seen battle before. The druchii have beasts from the mountains that they unleash upon us, and deranged cultists that lust for blood and do not fear death! Many Naggarothi have returned from Elthin Arvan to swell the numbers of Anlec's host. Each of them is a veteran of war and a match for every five of ours! How can we fight against such an army, a monster driven on by a hate of its foes and a terrible fear of its commanders?'

The Anars all remained silent, absorbing the realisation that there would be no help from outside Nagarythe.

'We train such soldiers as we can, but King Caledor cannot throw his untried forces into reckless battle against such a superior foe,' said Ilriadan.

'How long before your army can fight?' said Eoloran.

'Two years, at least,' came the reply, and this was answered by a chorus of sighs.

'Not all is despair,' Ilriadan added quickly. 'The druchii do not have the ships to breach the Lothern gate and so cannot dare to cross the Inner Sea. Caledor to the south still holds strong, and the enemy face fierce opposition to fight their way through Chrace. The Phoenix King's cousin rules there and was not at the shrine, so Chrace is united under his rule. The mountains will not be as forgiving as the plains of Tiranoc. Should they pass Chrace, the druchii face Avelorn. Isha will not suffer such dark creatures in her forests and the spirits of the woods will fight beside the warriors of the Everqueen. Not all of those whose lands the druchii have occupied have capitulated, and maintaining their grip will sap their strength. In speed and surprise they have gained the advantage, but time is a weapon on our side. The victories of this past year will not be so easy to achieve in the next, and in the year after... Well, let us not get ahead of ourselves.'

THE ANARS WERE forced to conclude that they could do no more than they were already. They fortified the hills of Elanardris as best they could, expecting attack at any time. From this haven, the Shadows sallied forth on their raids and the warriors of Eoloran menaced troops moving along the eastern roads.

The situation in the mountains worsened as those fleeing Chrace crossed from the east, daring the treacherous peaks to get away from the druchii scourge. There had been little enough food to begin with and thousands more mouths needed feeding. Alith was forced to redirect the attentions of his Shadows. They ambushed the druchii caravans to steal supplies and raided grain houses. They attacked isolated patrols and stole their baggage – tents, clothes and weapons that the Anars needed. Alith feared that the Shadows had been turned from feared warriors into quartermasters, but Eoloran was adamant that the refugees needed to be provided for.

ANOTHER BLEAK YEAR passed, and another. Chrace was almost overrun. Groups of hunters held out in their mountain lodges, but the roads to Avelorn were open to the druchii. In this way, Ellyrion was surrounded, though Prince Finudel still held his capital at Tor Elyr.

Scattered word came from further east. In the lands of Saphery, some of the mage-princes of that realm had been lured to Morathi's cause by the promise of sorcerous power. Though outnumbered by the loyal mages, these sorcerers waged war with their kin. The meadows were blasted by magical fire, the skies rained down comets and the air itself seethed with mystical energy.

The druchii had dared an attack on Lothern, seeking to gain control of the formidable sea gate. The assault had been repulsed with heavy losses on both sides, the loyalists only claiming victory after King Caledor arrived with the army of his kingdom. That realm remained secure against the druchii advance and, like Elanardris, became a sanctuary for those from Ellyrion and Tiranoc pushed out by the warriors of Anlec.

Still the Anars waited for the time to strike.

IT WAS NOT until the fourth year of the war that the druchii advance stalled. Hawks carrying messages from the Phoenix King arrived at the manse with the coming of the spring. Eoloran read these with some satisfaction.

'The dragon princes have ridden forth at last,' he told Alith and Eothlir. 'King Caledor has used the Eataine fleet to gather together his new army on the border of Ellyrion and is advancing north.'

'That is good news indeed,' said Alith. 'When he reaches Tiranoc, we should strike out to join him.'

'I fear that we may extend ourselves too soon,' replied Eoloran. 'We must judge the right time to strike for the greatest effect.'

'We cannot afford to be too cautious,' argued Eothlir. 'Though our army is not so large as Caledor's, it is in the right place to threaten the druchii. We cannot hold much longer, and certainly not another winter. Would you wait until Caledor is upon the borders of Elanardris before acting?'

'You go too far!' snapped Eoloran. 'I am still lord of this house!'

'Then act as a lord!' replied Eothlir. 'Lead out the army now! This is our best chance for victory. As we helped Malekith at Ealith, we can do the same for the Phoenix King. Bite into the heart of our foes and force them to bring back warriors from Ellyrion and Tiranoc. Our raids accomplish little, they have become nothing more than an annoyance to Morathi. Let us gather what warriors we can and act boldly.'

'It is folly,' said Eoloran with a wave of his hand. 'Who will protect Elanardris?'

'The Chracians and Tiranocii have enough warriors to hold the hills until our return.'

'Leave my lands in the hands of outsiders?' Eoloran laughed scornfully. 'What manner of prince would I be?'

'One who can swallow his pride to do the right thing,' said Eothlir.

Alith watched the argument with horror. His father and grandfather had quarrelled on occasion before, but he had never seen them both as angry. Always they had debated on principles but now they attacked each other.

'You think it is pride that steers me?' Eoloran roared. 'You think those helpless thousands camped in the mountains are of no concern?'

'They have no future unless we act,' Eothlir replied, chillingly calm in the face of his father's ire. 'They will starve or freeze to death by the end of the year, for we cannot continue to feed and clothe them. The only way to end their suffering is to end the war. Now!'

Eoloran strode towards the door and snarled over his shoulder.

'It will be your lands that you are throwing away, not mine!'

As the hall reverberated from the slamming door, Eothlir sat down and stared out of the high windows.

'What should we do?' asked Alith.

Eothlir looked up at his son, his eyes bleak.

'I will fight, no matter what the wishes of your grandfather,' he said. 'You are not a child, what you do is your decision.'

'I will fight as well,' said Alith, needing no time to think it over. 'I would rather try for victory and fail than suffer this wasting death that grips us. We can only get weaker the longer we wait.'

Eothlir nodded and reached up a hand to pat Alith on the arm.

'Then we will fight together,' he said.

EOTHLIR MUSTERED SOME fourteen thousand warriors in all. Each was Nagarythe-born and knew that he fought not only for his life but for the lives of future generations. This force marched westwards, to the edge of the foothills of Elanardris. To the east the rear of the host was protected by the mountains, while to the west and south stretched the marshes of Enniun Moreir – Dark Fen. To the north lay the broken ground of Urithelth Orir.

One thousand cavalry were sent north, all the riders that Eothlir could gather. Their target was the druchii camp at Tor Miransiath. With them had ridden a herald, Liasdir, who bore the banner of the Anars. He would announce that Elanardris was defiant of Anlec and would never bow down before the Witch Queen. They were the bait for the trap, for such an affront to Morathi would never be tolerated by the druchii commanders.

The remaining thirteen thousand soldiers, of whom more than half were archers, took up a horseshoe-like position at the crests of the hills, the open segment facing westwards. Each warrior had brought as many shafts as could be found in Elanardris and was ready to unleash a storm upon the enemy. The spearmen arrayed themselves into phalanxes in front of the bowmen, their shields overlapping to form a wall against the missiles of the enemy. The army was not hidden, for this was designed to be a gesture of defiance to goad the druchii into a hasty attack.

The cavalry would lure the druchii into the treacherous marshland, where Alith and his Shadows had spent two days, marking out the surest routes for the riders to follow. The riders would remove these markers as they retreated, leaving their pursuers mired and easy targets for the archers. Eothlir was determined that he would draw the ire of Anlec; if the Anars could inflict a sufficient defeat upon their foes, Morathi would have no choice but to bring troops back from Ellyrion, easing the pressure upon King Caledor.

Eothlir sent out the riders just before midday. Timing was everything. As the skies darkened the journey across the marsh would get ever more dangerous and the druchii casualties would be all the greater for it.

ALITH STOOD BESIDE his father, sword in hand. His Shadows were hidden amongst the mounds and reeds of Enniun Moreir to snipe the enemy as best they could, but Eothlir had insisted his son stayed close to him during the battle.

The enemy arrived at about the time Eothlir had hoped. Shrill whistles from the Shadows announced the coming of the cavalry and it was not long before Alith could see the riders picking their way along the trails, the last in each column tossing aside the rods the Shadows had used as markers. Upon reaching the hills, the knights cut to the north, ready to counter-attack against any foes that attempted to flank on the right. Liasdir split from the other riders and dismounted next to Eothlir, driving the banner pole into the turf of the hillside. Drawing his sword, he looked at his lords.

'There are quite a lot of them,' he said with an uncertain smile. 'I hope we are doing the right thing.'

Eothlir did not reply, his gaze was fixed on a dark mass moving through the marshlands. Like a spreading blot, the druchii army advanced slowly. It was as if a black mist followed them, and Alith could sense sorcery in the air. His skin crawled at the touch of the dark magic and could feel it seeping down from the mountains behind him, drawn by the enchantments of the druchii.

Larger shapes could be seen amongst the lines of infantry. Hydras splashed through the marsh, their bellows and roars sounding out like a challenge.

'Musicians!' called Eothlir.

Trumpeters raised their instruments to their lips and let out a long blast that echoed across the hills. The note filled Alith with pride, a pealing signal of refusal. Somewhere behind Alith voices rose in song and Eothlir turned in surprise. From one company to another the sound spread, the battle anthem of the Anars ringing from fourteen thousand throats. The rousing song rose in pitch and volume, sweeping away the noises of the druchii beasts.

Alith's heart thundered along to the rhythm as the verses recounted the feats of Eoloran during the time of Aenarion and recalled the battles to claim Elanardris from the daemons. When the tenth and final verse was finished, a deafening shout engulfed the hills.

'Anar! Anar! Anar!'

Alith joined in and saw also that his father cried out the family name, his sword held aloft.

'Anar! Anar! Anar!'

The druchii were close enough to judge their numbers. Alith guessed there to be at least thirty thousand foes. He was thankful that there were no knights, but less pleased that the army presented a wall of silver and black. All were Naggarothi soldiers, not a single cultist amongst them. They were battle-hardened and disciplined and would be deadly enemies.

The first arrows from the Shadows began to find their mark when the druchii were no closer than five hundred paces to the Anar line. The casualties inflicted were few, but the effect was considerable. Already hard-pressed to find a footing in the marsh, the druchii tumbled into the mud when their comrades' corpses tripped them. Standard bearers fell and the banners dragged up from the fen sagged wetly against their poles. Captains looked around fearfully as the Shadows picked their targets with deadly accuracy.

Alith knew from the battle at Anlec that the greatest weakness of the hydras was the handlers that goaded them. Unfortunately, it seemed that the druchii had also learnt that lesson, and the whip-armed elves tried as best they could to keep the bulk of their beasts between them and the Anar scouts. As they advanced, they steered their monsters between the regiments of spearmen, so that the Shadows could not draw aim upon them.

Here and there the druchii returned the shots of the Shadows. Archers tried to find their mark, but the scouts were well hidden. Companies carrying mechanical bows that fired several shots in quick succession poured bolts at their elusive enemies and the Shadows fell back, flitting from cover to cover.

Pace-by-pace the druchii continued their advance, harried by the Shadows and slowed by the sucking mud of Dark Fen. All the while the sun lowered towards the west and gloom descended.

Anar archers started their volleys as soon as the druchii were within range, the elevation of the hills allowing them to loose their arrows farther than their foes. Each company let free with a cloud of arrows in turn. The rate was not remarkable, but it was sustained. Storm after storm of black-feathered shafts fell into the druchii and they died in their hundreds. The dead sank into the mire and piled up on the firm ground; the warriors following behind were forced to shove aside these grisly mounds to keep to the meandering paths.

As more and more of the Anlec warriors fell, Alith felt the first glimmer of hope. Though he had readily agreed to his father's decision to sally forth from Elanardris, he had doubted whether it would achieve anything – little more than a diversion to provide small relief for Caledor's army to the south. Watching the druchii suffer in their thousands gave him a grim satisfaction.

Eventually the druchii archers and crossbowmen came within two hundred paces and began to loose their missiles against the Anars. The spearmen raised their shields while the archers above knelt behind them and continued to shoot, though with less venom than before.

When the druchii were almost at the edge of the marsh, the final part of Eothlir's plan was put into action. As well as marking out trails, the Shadows had laid a slick of oil on the water of the fens. At Alith's signal, the Shadows sent flaming arrows into the mire. The flames caught quickly, dancing across the marsh to engulf the leading ranks of the druchii spear companies. Burning warriors flailed at the fire and dashed to and fro in panic, spreading it further.

Alith began to laugh at the predicament of his enemies, but stopped himself when he caught a stern look from his father.

'You should not take joy in death,' said Eothlir. 'To revel in destruction is to desire it, and it is on that path that these unfortunate souls have trodden.'

'You are right, Father,' Alith said, bowing his head in apology. 'It is my happiness at success that gives me good humour, but I should not forget the price being paid for our victory.'

Victory certainly seemed likely. The first of the druchii that had survived the torrent of arrows and the conflagration were struggling from the marsh and pushing up the rise towards the Anar army. Spearmen came first, raising their shields above their heads to protect them from the archers. They remained resolute in the face of the volleys, forming their ranks again, allowing their numbers to grow rather than advance piecemeal towards the waiting phalanxes.

When several hundred warriors had assembled on the slope, two hydras flanking them, the druchii continued their advance. A drum boomed out the marching beat and the spearmen lowered their weapons to the attack and strode forwards. The hydras hissed and screeched, flames licking from their many mouths, a pall of smoke surrounding their scaled bodies.

'We must deal with those monsters swiftly,' said Eothlir. He turned to Nithimnis, one of his captains. 'Go to the companies of Alethriel, Finannith and Helirian and tell them to engage the hydra on our right. Signal for the cavalry to attack on the flank.'

The captain nodded and dashed off, heading for the warriors on the right flank. Eothlir moved his attention to Alith. 'Send word to your Shadows to lure away the hydra on the left.'

Alith gave a low, keening whistle and moments later a hawk skimmed across the hillside, bobbing over the heads of the archers and spearmen. Alith extended his arm and the bird landed on his wrist. He bent close and whispered in the language of the hawks, relaying Eothlir's message. The hawk twisted its head left and right and then leapt into the air with beating wings. It swooped down towards the fen, disappearing amongst the tangle of rushes and bushes.

It was not long before arrows with flaming heads began converging on the hydra. Though each did little damage, the weight of fire was enough to scorch its flesh, while some arrows found their mark in its eyes, mouths and softer underbelly. Its hide was slicked in places with oil from the marsh and the flames took hold, setting alight its flank and back. Enraged, it swung towards the source of its irritation, fire roaring from its mouths. Turning aside from the spearmen the hydra stomped down into the fens, sinking to its shoulders in the thick mud, more flames streaming from its screeching maws.

At fifty paces, the advancing druchii broke into a charge. This was not the wild attack of cultists, but a determined and cohesive thrust towards the Anar spearmen. The two walls of warriors met with a resounding crash and the true battle began.

Though they had suffered heavy casualties, the druchii numbers were still their greatest advantage. More and more of them emerged from the fen, to widen the line of attack or lend their presence to the companies already engaged. Archers and crossbowmen began to shoot into the troops stationed at the crest of the hill and a vicious exchange of missiles raged above Alith's head.

Alith watched the fighting with a careful eye. The Anar line was holding strong, the advantage of higher ground allowing them to plunge their spears over the shields of their foes whilst their attackers tried to gain some momentum as they pushed uphill. Faced with several hundred spearmen, the hydra on the right was causing a good deal of carnage, tossing aside warriors with its jaws and smashing more to the ground with its immense claws. The elves were not wholly outmatched. Thick blood streamed from dozens of wounds in the hydra's scaled skin and three of its seven heads swung limply against its chest.

The ground began to shudder under Alith's feet and he looked past the hydra to see the riders of Elanardris charge. Spears lowered, they crashed into the hydra, running down its handlers and driving their weapons into the creature's flesh. Horses whinnied and riders cried out as the monster's tail lashed viciously through their ranks, crushing elves and breaking the legs of their steeds. The spearmen redoubled their efforts and Alith watched as two of the hydra's legs gave way, its tendons severed by spearpoint and sword. The infantry clambered over its body, jabbing and stabbing relentlessly while the cavalry swept on, galloping into the flank of the druchii regiments.

The attack sent the druchii scattering down the hillside, some of them tripping over hummocks and dips or the bodies of the fallen. The knights did not push too far and at a signal from their captain wheeled their mounts around and retired back to the north to ready for another charge.

Again and again the druchii surged up the hill, only to be met by a wall of spears. Their commanders tried to turn the left flank of the Anars, furthest from the cavalry. Eothlir despatched his thousand-strong reserve to counter the threat, forcing the druchii regiments back towards the centre.

Alith could not count how many were dead and wounded. Certainly the druchii were at less than half the strength they had brought to the battle. His own side's casualties were far less, though there were gaps appearing in the line where the druchii had met some success. He was confident nonetheless, of both his father's ability and the resolution of the warriors. He had not yet needed to draw his sword and the battle was being won.

Shouts of alarm drew Alith's attention and he turned to see many of the archers looking skywards and pointing to the north-east – back towards Elanardris. Alith saw immediately their cause for concern: an immense black shape moving swiftly through the clouds.

'Dragon!' bellowed Alith, ripping free his sword.

THE DRAKE PLUNGED down towards the rear of the army, an oily cloud trailing from its mouth. It was the largest beast Alith had ever seen, at least as long as a ship from smoking snout to barbed tip of tail. Its serpentine body was as straight as an arrow, huge wings held stiff as it glided soundlessly downwards, four legs ending in massively clawed feet extended towards the ground. Upon its back rode a figure clad in shining silver armour. He was sat upon a throne-like chair, twin pennants trailing from its back. On his left arm he carried a shield taller than an elf etched with a rune of death. In the right hand he wielded a lance longer than two horses, its tip a dark crystal that streamed black flames.

Arrows rose up from the archers, but they might just as well have been throwing sticks at a city wall for the injury they caused. With a gargantuan beat of its wings, the dragon stopped in the air above the archers, the buffet of wind hurling dozens of elves from their feet. A huge cloud of thick vapour issued from its mouth, engulfing hundreds. Alith watched as skin flaked and flesh melted in the noxious mist. Choked screams sounded across the hill as the archers fell to the ground, grabbing madly at their faces, screaming in terrifying agony.

The dragon climbed upwards again, and Alith was filled with the urge to run. Its yellow eyes seemed to look directly at him. Its teeth were like long swords and its red claws glistened like fresh blood. The dragon's black scales glimmered in the setting sun, so that it seemed to be made of glowing embers.

Dozens of dreadful thoughts clamoured for Alith's attention, but one was louder than all of the rest: how had the druchii come by such a creature? The dragons of Ulthuan dwelt beneath the mountains of Caledor. Not since the time of Caledor Dragontamer had all but the youngest been coaxed from their centuries-long slumber. Yet the truth was right before him, in all of its horrific glory.

The monster was circling higher, getting ready to swoop again. It let forth a piercing shriek that set Alith's ears ringing. So dire was that noise that hundreds of warriors broke into flight, dropping their spears, shields and bows so that they might run all the faster. Alith had never witnessed such panic before.

'Alith!' he heard his father shouting and realised Eothlir had been calling his name since the dragon had first appeared. Looking over his shoulder, Alith saw that the druchii were surging up the hill towards them. All along the line the spearmen were being pushed backwards.

Alith turned his full attention on these attackers, bringing up his sword. The druchii came at a gentle run, still shoulder-to-shoulder. With a shout, Alith plunged forwards moments before the two lines of warriors met.

His first blow chopped the head from a jabbing spear, while he rammed his shoulder into the warrior's shield. Snatching a dagger from his belt, Alith plunged the blade back-handed into the druchii soldier's neck. His next sword thrust took another druchii in the chest. Something caught his shoulder and he felt a stab of pain. Twisting, he smashed the back of his fist into the jaw of a third warrior before bringing his sword down across the druchii's face.

Everything devolved into a chaotic melee: Alith, Eothlir and the others shouting and fighting, the druchii snarling and stabbing.

'Hold the line!' bellowed Eothlir. 'Push them back into the fens!'

Hundreds of spearmen gathered around their commander, with bitter war cries on their lips and blood upon their armour. Alith heard a gasp of pain and glanced to his right. Liasdir fell to the ground, blood gushing from a wound in his back. He grabbed hold of the banner to pull himself to his feet but another druchii spearman lunged, thrusting his weapon through Liasdir's chest. Falling, Liasdir dragged the banner down into the bloody grass.

Eothlir batted away a spear and stooped to pick up the fallen standard. Cutting the arm from yet another attacker, he raised the flag above his head.

'Fight on, Anars, fight on!' he cried.

A SHADOW SWAMPED Alith, blotting out the twilight. A rushing of air filled his ears and he looked up a moment before the dragon landed, crushing dozens of druchii and Anars alike beneath its bulk. Eothlir swung towards the monster, sword raised. His eyes widened in rage as he recognised the rider.

'Kheranion!' he spat. Alith knew the name only from rumour, and that told of how the renegade prince had been spared at Anlec by Malekith. He had been a scourge of those Naggarothi opposed to Morathi's rule, one of the most brutal slaughterers in Nagarythe. It was claimed that his back had been broken by Prince Malekith but he had been healed by dark sorcery, kept alive by potions made from the blood of his victims.

The prince's face was twisted into a cruel sneer framed by white and silver hair. He said nothing as he thrust his flaming lance. Alith gave a hoarse shout as the black-flamed iron burst through Eothlir's body, sending boiling blood steaming into the air. As quick as he had struck, Kheranion wrenched the lance free.

Eothlir staggered backwards a step and righted himself. He turned slowly towards Alith and then fell to his knees, his sword falling out of view into the trampled grass, the standard of the Anars fluttering from his grasp. Blood bubbled up from Eothlir's throat, foaming from his mouth. Alith's greatest horror came not from this, but from the look in his father's eyes. They were wide and wild, filled with utter terror.

'Flee!' Eothlir croaked before pitching into the mud.

KHERANION'S MOCKING LAUGHTER drifted to Alith's ears. Alith gave a wordless scream of despair and rage, and hurled himself towards Kheranion and his monstrous steed. He had taken barely two steps when someone grabbed his arm and yanked him aside. Stumbling, Alith tried to wrest his arm free, but found himself grabbed roughly by many hands and bodily lifted away.

'Let me go!' screamed Alith, struggling as best he could as more spearmen surged forwards to put themselves between the dragon and their lord. 'Let me go!'

The army was broken by the death of their commander. Thousands of Alith's followers turned and ran, while a brave few hundred formed up to sell their lives dearly and stall the pursuit. Alith felt himself dragged up the hill. Desolation swept through him and he went limp, tears coursing down his face.

Sobbing, he let his warriors carry him to safety.

— THIRTEEN —

The Fall of House Anar

UNDER THE COVER of night, the remnants of the Anar army retreated eastwards towards the mountains only to find that more druchii barred their way. Forced to turn southwards, Alith stumbled numbly alongside his warriors, too scared to think of what had happened and too tired to wonder what might yet come to pass. It was if he sleepwalked, placing one foot in front of the other out of habit.

With the druchii close on their heels, Alith's lieutenants turned the army westwards again, seeking sanctuary in the marshes of Dark Fen. For twenty-three days they hid amongst the waterways, scattering for cover as the beat of dragon wings sounded overhead, travelling by night alone. The army splintered as companies and individuals sought to avoid the pursuit, each going their own way. Some were lost in the marshes, some made it far south only to be picked up by druchii patrols along the Naganath.

Those that stayed with Alith survived, though not through any action or decision of the prince. He was happy to follow instructions from the likes of Khillrallion and Tharion. The warriors began to whisper that Alith's mind had been broken, and they were not far from the truth. Alith was possessed by a waking nightmare, unable to rid himself of the vision of his father's death. Over and over he saw Eothlir fall beneath the lance of Kheranion, smelt the noxious stench of the dragon's breath in the air and heard his father's last, desperate command.

Eventually the druchii relented in their hunt and the survivors drifted eastwards again, heading for Elanardris. For two more days they trudged

527

through the mists of the fen, exhausted, hungry and dispirited. That night they made camp just south of where they had fought the army of Anlec, though no warrior dared investigate the battlefield, fearful of what they might find there.

At dawn, smoke could be seen to the east, rising from the mountains. These were not wisps of campfires: towering columns of thick black smoke hung over the foothills like a shroud. Filled with foreboding, Alith and the army hurried towards the rising sun.

They came to the first burnt-out village just before midday. The white walls of the buildings were stained with soot and contorted, charred corpses could be seen within. They had been shut inside when the buildings had been set on fire. Along the road they found more bodies, mutilated in all manner of hideous ways. Scraps of flayed skin were hung upon the walls that bounded the fields, and garlands of bones and flesh were strung from the bare branches of trees.

More horrors followed as Alith hurried on. Naked bodies were nailed upon the blackened stones of towers and barns. The heads of children had been woven into the thorny stems of rose bushes like obscene replacements for their missing blooms. Symbols of the cytharai were daubed in blood everywhere Alith looked.

The survivors of the battle wept, some throwing down their weapons to cradle the remains of loved ones discovered, others breaking from the army to go to their homes. Alith's warriors deserted in their hundreds and he let them go. He could no more insist that they stay than he could stop them breathing.

By mid-afternoon, Alith had no more revulsion left. If he had been numb before, now he was utterly empty, devoid of any thought or emotion. The slaughter was simply too vast to comprehend, the atrocities too outlandish to remember. The refugee camps had been attacked and the dead were scattered about the fields in huge piles of cadavers. Some had died swiftly, cut down where they had been caught, but many showed signs of barbaric abuse, having perished of raw agony from the wounds inflicted upon them. Carrion-eating birds had come down from the mountains in great flocks and they lurched away heavily as the elves approached, gorged on the macabre banquet laid out for them.

ALITH FELT NOTHING as he saw the clouds of smoke billowing from within the walls of the manse. From his first sight of the smoke at dawn the previous day he had expected to see this and had already experienced such cold dread that he no longer registered the fact that the nightmare was real.

Coming through the gates, Alith thought at first that the walls of the manse had been changed into something else, or that the lengthening evening shadows were deceiving him. As he stumbled closer he saw that the ruined house was festooned with the bodies of elves, pinioned to the walls with metal spikes. All but a few hung limply, but a handful stirred at his approach.

He recognised the bloody remains of Gerithon nailed to the door and dashed to him. Spikes pierced his elbows and knees, driven into the hard wood of the door, and his blood dripped into a ruddy pool at his feet. The Anars' retainer raised his head a little and opened one bloodshot eye; the other was closed shut with a clot of blood dripping from a gash across his forehead.

'Alith?' he croaked.

'Yes,' Alith replied, taking a canteen of water from his pack. He tried to give some to Gerithon but the other elf turned his head away.

'Water will not save me,' he whispered. His eye wandered for a moment and then settled again on Alith. 'They took Lord Eoloran alive...'

This news was like a bolt of lightning. For a moment Alith felt elation that one of his family had survived. The next moment came the crushing realisation that his grandfather would suffer a far worse fate than death. With thoughts of family Alith raised Gerithon's head with a hand under his chin.

'What of my mother?' he demanded.

Gerithon closed his eye slowly in reply.

'Do not let me die in torment,' the chamberlain whispered.

Alith stepped away for a moment, unsure what to do. Others had come into the grounds of the manse and were wandering around, gazing with horror at the despicable cruelty on display.

'Bring them down!' snarled Alith, filled with a sudden energy. He pulled his knife from his belt and drew it quickly across Gerithon's throat. Blood trickled over his fingers and Alith flicked it away. 'Give peace to those that have not yet succumbed, and bring all of the bodies to the manse.'

Under Alith's instructions, the elves gathered the remains of those loyal to the Anars and arranged them inside the house. There were also druchii bodies amongst the dead, for the Chracians and Tiranocii had been true to their oaths and had fought to defend Elanardris. These Alith ordered to be left for the crows and vultures.

Undertaking this sombre task, Alith was blind to those whose bodies he carried. In his eye they were just a blur, not the faces of friends, servants and loved ones. He may have carried Maieth's body, he did not know. That she was amongst the dead was certain, he did not need to know by what manner she had been slain.

As dusk shrouded all in darkness once more, Alith and his followers brought wood and oil from their stores and with this turned the manse into a great pyre. Alith set a torch to the fuel and then turned away. He did not look back as the flames grew quickly, pushing back the night with their glow. His ears were deaf to the roaring and crackling, and his nose caught no stench of flesh and smoke.

All that he had was gone, and all that was left was a shadow, and as a shadow he walked towards the mountains.

* * *

ALITH BARELY REGISTERED the others around him as he made his way up the slope. He was aware of nothing; not the grass beneath his feet, not the cold air nor the stars glittering above. Soon he passed along the secret trails into the forest and was alone. He carried on a little further, each step harder than the last, until finally he fell to his knees with an anguished cry torn from his lips. He raised his head and howled like a wolf, giving vent to the rage and despair that was all he had left. Long and piercing was that cry and it echoed from the trees and slopes, mocking him.

When he could screech no more, he tore at the grass, ripping out great clods of earth and tossing them in all directions. He pulled free his sword and swung at the naked branches, hacking and slashing without thought. His stumbling assault brought him to a winding beck and he tripped, splashing into the freezing water. Even the shock of the icy brook did not shake the madness that gripped him. He pulled himself to his feet and waded upstream, cutting the water with his blade and hurling insults at the sky.

He came upon a still pool, shining in the white moon. Casting his sword aside, he threw himself down onto the rocks, his head in his hands. The coldness seeping up from the water filled him, but it was as nothing to the bitter chill in his heart. An icy void was all that remained, and its touch numbed every part of his body.

For a moment or an age he sat there, staring at his reflection. He did not recognise the elf trapped in the still water. There were scratches on a face marked by streaks of soot and filth cut through by the traces of tears. The eyes that stared back at him were dark and wild. This creature was not the son of the Anars, it was some dishevelled, abandoned thing swathed in pity and disgust.

Gripped by another fit of self-hatred, Alith took out a knife and hacked at his hair, and for a moment the blade hovered close to his throat. The temptation struck him to pull the dagger across, to end his misery as he had ended the misery of all those the druchii had tortured.

Yet for all his grief, he hesitated. It would be weakness to avoid his punishment. Hubris had destroyed his family – they had dared to believe themselves strong enough to resist Anlec – and they now lived on only in memory. When he died, the Anars would be no more, and that was a shame he couldn't bring upon them.

Alith let the knife fall from his fingers into the pool.

As he sat gazing into the water, Alith began to feel and hear and smell again: the tinkling of the stream, the resin of the pine trees. His keen ears could hear burrowing creatures rummaging amongst the fallen needles and the flutter of bats' wings. Owls screeched and hooted, fish splashed, branches creaked.

And then there came the cawing of a crow.

A shadow appeared beside Alith. He looked up into the face of Elthyrior. The raven herald's expression was as unmoving as a mask, showing neither sympathy nor scorn. His eyes were unblinking, staring at Alith.

'Begone,' said Alith, his voice a harsh and broken growl.

Elthyrior did not move, nor did his gaze.

The urge to strike the raven herald swelled within Alith. Unreasoning loathing filled him, and in his mind Alith blamed every ill that had beset him on Elthyrior. That calm gaze taunted him.

A snapping twig broke through Alith's thoughts and he stood, casting a glance over his shoulder. In the dim moonlight that penetrated the trees, he saw a small group of figures: three maidens and two children.

Alith walked towards them unsteadily, blinking. As he came closer he saw that this was no illusion. Before him stood the refugees he had brought out of Tiranoc.

'I took them from Elanardris before the druchii came,' Elthyrior said, answering Alith's unasked question. 'We must take them to safety in Ellyrion, as you should have done before.'

The words seeped slowly into Alith's mind, to be joined by the memory of the oath he had sworn to Yeasir. Alith looked at each of them in turn, feeling nothing. What did he owe to the shade of a dead commander? He turned his bleak look upon Elthyrior.

'You would be wise to leave,' said Alith. 'Without me. There is a cloud upon my life and you would do well not to stand beneath it.'

'No,' Elthyrior replied. 'There is nothing to keep you here, no reason to stay. This is not your destiny.'

Alith laughed bitterly.

'And what new tortures does Morai-heg have planned for me?'

Elthyrior shrugged.

'I cannot say, but it is not your place to dwindle into nothing here,' he said. 'It is not in you to let those who killed your family go unpunished, for all that you blame yourself and me. You deny it, but there will come a reckoning, and you will be the instrument of that vengeance. Remember your oath to slay Caenthras?'

The mention of the elven lord's name sparked in Alith's heart and for a moment he felt something. The smallest ember of a fire began to burn inside him.

'And what of the other druchii?' Elthyrior continued. 'Do they lay waste to Elanardris without retort? If you will not avenge them, then take up that knife and drive it into your chest, for though you still breathe, you are all but dead. I cannot offer you comfort, nor sympathy. I am also the last of my line, and perhaps you will be the last of yours. My deeds are the last testament to the memory of a father murdered and a mother killed and a sister taken by the daemons. Would you have the last act of the Anars be remembered shamefully, of their lands razed and their people slaughtered?'

'No,' snapped Alith, his vigour strengthening.

'Would you have the druchii claim to have wiped out the Anars?'

'No,' Alith replied, clenching his fists.

'Would you forgive those that have brought this doom upon you? Would you forget their misdeeds and seek sanctuary in your self-pity?'

'No!' Alith snarled. 'I will not!'

Alith plunged into the pool and retrieved his dagger and sword. Splashing onto the bank, he saw Heileth, Lirian and the others shrink back from him, their eyes fearful. Far from being ashamed of their reaction, Alith drew strength from their dread. As if in response to his mood the moon hid behind a cloud and the small clearing plunged into darkness. In that darkness Alith felt himself growing. The twilight poured into him, the shadows claiming him for their own.

There was fear in the darkness and he would become that fear. The druchii murderers would scream their guilt from bloodied lips and beg for a forgiveness that did not exist. They had claimed the darkness for themselves, but it was not theirs alone to rule. The night might belong to them, but the shadows would belong to Alith.

'Let's go,' he whispered.

PART THREE

The Wrath of the Ravens; War with Nagarythe;
The Shadow King Awakes; The Witch King

—◄ FOURTEEN ►—

Pursued by Darkness

THEY MADE CAMP just before dawn, in the lee of an overhang upon the western slope of Anul Arillin. Elthyrior warned them that it was unwise to move by day and then slipped away, back along the path they had followed.

The group shared a silent, cold breakfast. Alith sat apart, chewing a chunk of cured meat, staring at the peaks ahead as the first rays of sun broke over them. The sight that had once filled him with such joy did not move him in the slightest.

'Get some sleep,' he told the others, before climbing up the overhang to keep watch. Glancing down, he saw them gather together under their blankets, like birds seeking each other's warmth in a nest. He longed for the sight to stir something in him: a memory of his mother, the hint of the passion he had felt with Milandith. Instead, his thoughts turned to Caenthras and the other druchii. Only then did he feel anything, a deep anger that heated him far more than the rising sun.

ELTHYRIOR RETURNED NOT long after the sun had fully cleared the peaks. He arrived hurriedly, panting, and Alith saw that there was a slight cut upon his brow.

'We are being followed!' he said breathless, stooping to stir the sleeping elves.

'Who?' said Alith as he jumped down from the overhang.

'Renegades of my brethren,' snarled Elthyrior. 'Though perhaps it is I who has been named the renegade. They have thrown in their lot with Morathi,

535

and I suspect they did some time ago. They tried to trap me but I escaped. We must hurry though, for they will not be far behind!'

The party readied themselves as swiftly as possible and followed Elthyrior east and south, climbing up the shoulder of Anul Arillin. Alith and Elthyrior carried the babes so that Lirian, Heileth and Saphistia could better keep pace. They followed no track, and instead hiked across bare stone and along the rocky banks of streams, so that they left little trail.

'It will not delay them for long,' Elthyrior told Alith as they helped the maidens scramble over a tumble of boulders damming a narrow stream. 'The raven heralds have means other than eyes and ears to follow their quarry.'

Onwards and upwards they marched, breaking only occasionally for rest and drink. Part of Alith hoped the raven heralds would catch them, longing to exact the first retribution against the druchii. For all his desire for a confrontation, he put aside his own wants, knowing that it would be a greater blow against the druchii cause to keep alive the sons of Yeasir and Elodhir.

By mid-afternoon they had crested a ridge on the southern side of the mountain. Alith turned to look down the slope, Elthyrior stepping back to stand beside him. Far below, faint black shapes could be seen moving amongst the rocks: the raven heralds.

Alith watched for a moment, and saw that there were five of them, perhaps more. Each led a horse as black as his raven-feathered cloak.

'Their steeds will be more of a hindrance than help in the mountains,' said Elthyrior. 'We should make as much gain as possible before we reach the plains of Ellyrion and their mounts become an advantage.'

'Then let us continue,' said Alith, turning his back on the pursuers.

ALITH HAD NEVER spent a night so high up in the Annulii. The magical vortex created by Caledor Dragontamer swept through the mountains, drawn by the waystones erected across Ulthuan. Magic flittered on the edge of visibility and a deeper sense inside Alith could feel its strength. Mystical winds vied with each other, twining and splitting, eddying and gusting across the slopes. Each successive draught brought a strange sensation, of lingering hope, or deepening despair, warmth or chill, wisdom or rashness. Though he had lived close to the mountains for all of his life, this was the first time he had truly felt their presence.

Not only the magical winds disturbed the travellers' rest. Howls and roars echoed from the peaks as warped animals defended their territories. Here in the wilderness, wyverns and manticores, hydras and basilisks prowled the darkness. The same creatures the druchii had enslaved for their armies wandered the peaks, enormous predators that were more than a match for Elthyrior and Alith's blades.

Though Alith was no stranger to mountaincraft, in these unfamiliar surrounds he was as dependent on Elthyrior's guidance as the rest of the group.

The raven herald had a sense for the terrain and its inhabitants that went beyond familiarity and experience. He had taken them on circuitous tours to avoid the nests of monsters, and sometimes they had doubled back on a whispered warning from Elthyrior. As the others slept, Alith questioned Elthyrior on this.

'I have told you before that I follow a different path, one laid down by Morai-heg,' explained the raven herald. 'That path leads neither to good nor ill, save that I do not believe my mistress wishes me to end my existence in the gullet of some Annulii beast.'

'But how can you tell where to find this path?'

'One cannot think about it,' said Elthyrior. 'It is an instinct, a knowing within that guides me. It is something that cannot be seen or heard or smelt, only felt in your heart. Morai-heg tugs us this way and that as she is wont, and most pull back against her thread, refusing to accept her wisdom. I accept the fate she has woven for me and allow her hand to turn me left or right, to stop me or urge me on as she sees fit.'

Alith shook his head at this, uncomprehending.

'But if Morai-heg has chosen our fate already, then what of the decisions we make?' he asked. 'Surely we are more than puppets for the gods?'

'Are we?' said Elthyrior. 'Aenarion, for certain, dared the gods' wrath to save his people, yet did not Khaine claim him as his own? Did not Bel Shanaar offer himself to the mercy of Asuryan before he became Phoenix King? Even Morathi wields her power only from the pacts she has made with the darker gods.'

'And why should I care for such gods when they clearly do not care for me?'

'You should not,' said Elthyrior, eliciting a frown of confusion from Alith. The raven herald stoked their small fire as he continued. 'The gods are what they are, old and young, lower and higher. Only a fool attracts their attention or makes demands of them. The druchii do not realise this, thinking they are free to exhort the cytharai without consequence as long as the sacrifices are fresh. But what happens if they are victorious? What if all elves become druchii and Morathi reigns in terror across the world? There can be no peace, no harmony, no balance in such a civilisation. Such dark gods thrive on strife and discord, so there can be no pleasing them.'

Elthyrior turned his earnest eyes upon Alith, fierce in their intensity.

'That is why we cannot allow the druchii to win,' he whispered savagely. 'They are the doom of our people, and their victory will condemn us to a bloody death at our own hands. Our people cannot live in anger and hate for all time.'

'Is it not too late?' said Alith. 'The druchii have already divided our people and brought war, and only more bloodshed and war can follow.'

'Only if one lives without hope,' replied the raven herald. 'We can fight to achieve peace, knowing that no peace is preserved without further war. Once we lived in utter bliss, but that can never be regained. All we can hope for is balance, in ourselves and in our people.'

Alith pondered this for a while and Elthyrior left him to his thoughts. Talk of harmony and balance meant nothing to Alith except to reassure him that only the death of the last druchii would bring peace: to his people and to him.

FOR ELEVEN MORE days they stumbled and clawed their way across the mountains, buffeted and chilled by the winds. Elthyrior and Alith pressed the others to keep moving, though Heileth, Saphistia and Lirian were soon wearied by the labour. At times it was if they walked without thought, following the lead of their escorts in silence. Though Elthyrior would occasionally relent and call for the group to stop, Alith spared only the slightest thought for his companions. He regarded their presence as a necessary annoyance, a duty to be fulfilled that kept him from pursuing his true goal. By sunlight and starlight he led them on until they could walk no further and only then would he allow them to sleep.

In all this time they saw nothing of their pursuers. Elthyrior would sometimes remain behind to keep watch, but whenever he reappeared he reported that they were alone. The news brought little cheer to Alith, for as Elthyrior warned the raven heralds would soon close the gap upon them once they were out of the mountains.

Having crossed the back of the peaks, the going became easier as the steepest peaks quickly gave way to the shallower mounts of Ellyrion. Within the encircling wall of the Annulii, the weather was warmer and the winds gentler, and they made swift progress. For three more days they descended, leaving behind the barren peaks, finding themselves once again amongst sparse forest and grassy valleys.

It was with a mixture of relief and trepidation that the party made camp in a dell nestled at the foot of the mountains. Alith stood atop a steep hill nearby and looked across Ellyrion. Dawn was rising and in the growing light he could see the grasslands of the Ellyrians stretching out to the south and east. As the sun rose it bathed the grass in its ruddy light, creating a glowing sea that undulated in the wind. Perhaps once Alith may have marvelled at the natural beauty of the plains, but his only thought was that there would be nowhere to hide in such open country.

'We should head south and find a river to follow,' said Elthyrior, striding up the slope.

Alith replied with a quizzical look.

'I do not know these lands, and neither do you,' Elthyrior explained. 'But the herds of the Ellyrians need water as much as elves, so a river will give us the greatest chance of reaching a settlement.'

Alith shook his head.

'We cannot be sure of the loyalties of any Ellyrians we meet,' he said. 'I have heard only that Prince Finudel has sworn to aid King Caledor. We need to make for Tor Elyr as directly as possible.'

'And you know the way to Finudel's city?' Elthyrior replied with a doubtful look.

'While you learnt to speak with crows and listen to Morai-heg, I was shut up in a study with my tutors who thrust maps of Ulthuan beneath my nose,' said Alith. 'Tor Elyr lies south of here, just east of the Eagle Pass from Tiranoc. It is situated on an inlet of the Inner Sea where the rivers Elyranath and Irlana meet the waves.'

Elthyrior nodded, impressed. Then a new doubt crossed his face:

'Eagle Pass is at least eight days' march to the south,' he said. 'And that is if we suffer no delay from our frail companions. The dark riders will surely catch us before then.'

'Not only that, but the druchii hold the pass,' Alith said with a grim smile. 'I would be surprised if we could reach Tor Elyr unhindered, but it is there we must deliver our charges. There is a forest between the Elyranath and the Annulii, Athelian Toryr, which should provide us with some cover.'

Alith pointed south to illustrate his point. In the dawn gloom a darker shadow could be seen on the eastern flanks on the mountains, starting just at the horizon.

'We can reach Athelian Toryr within two days,' he added.

Elthyrior thought about this for a moment, lips pursed.

'There is an alternative,' said the raven herald. 'The Ellyrian herds wander the meadows; we could find one and secure ourselves some steeds.'

'Steal horses?' Alith replied with disgust, though his disregard for the idea quickly passed as he considered the thought. He nodded appreciatively. 'If we see such a herd before we reach the forest, then perhaps you are right. For the moment, we head south, following the hills.'

Elthyrior signalled his assent and the pair returned to the camp.

THEY SET OFF as the sun climbed higher in the sky, trusting to swiftness rather than darkness for safety, following the hills to the south-west at the feet of the Annulii. Now that he had a plan, Alith's mood lifted slightly at the thought that soon he would be free of this burden, free to pursue his own war against the druchii.

He gave that matter some thought as they walked, daydreaming of the punishments he would exact upon Caenthras and the others once he had the opportunity. Gone was the shattered emptiness that had consumed him after the fall of Elanardris. He imagined returning to Nagarythe with more warriors, to challenge those who ruled from Anlec.

With these darkly entertaining thoughts, the time passed quickly, and soon it was midday. They came across a stream running swiftly down from the mountains and stopped a while to drink, fill their canteens and catch fresh fish to eat. Alith felt none of the pleasure of this simple activity, his mind fixed solely on thoughts of the future. He was only aware of the delay, which nagged silently at him as he stooped into the waters to snatch up fish with his bare hands while Elthyrior kept watch to the north.

Having refreshed themselves and eaten, the group moved on, following the path of the stream. It meandered to the south and Alith hoped that this would lead them to the Elyranath. Ahead the slopes of the mountains darkened with trees, still more than a day's travel away. Alith pushed them on, seeking the sanctuary of the woods.

THE NEXT DAY brought fresh hope, for the stream they followed came to a greater river, which Alith was convinced was the Elyranath. It swept powerfully from the north, heading almost directly south.

'If only there were boats,' said Saphistia. 'We could rest and travel swiftly at the same time.'

With this in mind, they searched the banks of the river but could find no sign of such craft. It seemed the Ellyrians preferred their steeds to water. The search was not entirely in vain, for just upriver the waters widened and slowed at a ford. Elthyrior and Alith both spied fresh hoofmarks on the banks to either side, many horses having stopped to drink before moving off to the east.

'I see no print of boots,' remarked Elthyrior. 'I would say the horses are not tended.'

'Or perhaps the riders simply did not dismount,' countered Alith. 'Either way, neither of us can say how far the herd has travelled since crossing. It could be many hours away by now.'

'There is a means by which we might find out,' said Elthyrior, turning away.

Alith and the others watched as the raven herald strode away from the river, up a small rise to the west. Here he sat upon its crest, almost hidden in the long grass, with his legs crossed and his arms held out to either side of him. He remained unmoving for some time and Alith chafed at staying in one place for so long. Continually his gaze strayed to the north, his eyes searching the hills for any sign of the dark riders.

Just as Alith was about to interrupt, irritated at this unnecessary delay, Elthyrior lifted his head back and let out a long whistling sound, which deepened into a low cawing. The noise swirled around Alith. The cry rose and fell in volume and pitch, creating harmonious echoes within itself, as if it came from many throats. Alith could feel the magic bound within the call lifting up, spreading higher and higher, and he turned his gaze to the clear skies.

He saw nothing at first. After a moment a black speck appeared to the north. Another came from the south, swiftly followed by several more. Other dark dots converged from every direction, revealing themselves as crows as they neared. Alith guessed there to be several dozen as they flocked together high above the hill, wheeling and swooping, the cacophony drowning out Elthyrior's ululation.

An eerie silence then followed. One-by-one the crows dipped to the hillside, settling in the grass on and beside the raven herald until he was obscured by a shuffling, ruffling crowd of feathers and beaks. The crows hopped and fluttered around Elthyrior, each cawing out in turn, as if in council. Alith watched with amazement as Elthyrior stood, the flock leaping into the air, circling around him.

With a sweep of his hand, Elthyrior bid the birds to leave and in a great mass they climbed into the air, shrieking their farewells. As suddenly as they had arrived they were gone, each flying back the way it had come.

The raven herald walked down the hillside, his expression grim.

'I have news, both good and ill,' he said. 'The herd that crossed the river has no guardians, and is but a short walk to the east, beyond that next line of hills.'

'That is the good news?' asked Heileth.

'It is,' replied Elthyrior. He turned to the north and pointed towards a towering white cliff they had passed early that morning. 'The dark riders are close on our heels, passing that bluff. If we cannot take steeds they shall be on us before nightfall.'

'Perhaps we can find a more defensible position further into the hills,' suggested Alith.

'It will be to no avail,' said Elthyrior, shaking his head. 'They will come at us in the darkness, clothed in shadow. I do not know if they mean to kill us or capture us, but we cannot fight them. There are eight of them, and we have no bows with which we might even the odds.'

'We must get horses!' said Lirian, clasping her son protectively to her chest as if the riders were bearing down on them at that moment. 'We can't allow them to catch us. Think what terrible things they will do to us!'

Elthyrior looked to Alith, seemingly happy to abide by his judgement. Alith considered his options and liked none of them, but for all that he wracked his mind he could not conceive of any better plan.

'We'll make for the herd,' he announced. 'If we cannot fight, then the swiftest flight is our best option.'

Though he sounded confident, Alith had no hope that they would outrun their pursuers. Perhaps for a day or two they would stay ahead, but it was still a long way to Tor Elyr and the dark riders would be relentless. If they came across a place that they could defend with any surety, he resolved they would stop and fight rather than be caught unawares.

As they headed east, Elthyrior walked beside Alith.

'There is something else that you should know,' he said quietly.

'What is it?'

'I did not want to alarm the others, but my summoning of the crows will have been felt by my former brethren. Just as they can spy for me, the crows will spy for them. Such birds have little loyalty. The dark riders will soon know that we are mounted and will ride all the harder to catch us.'

NIGHTFALL FOUND THE group riding into the eaves of Athelian Toryr. As Alith had feared, though their stolen mounts proved faster than travelling on foot, their progress had not been as swift as it could have been. He did not have much horse riding experience, having had little opportunity to learn in his youth, while all except Elthyrior were unused to riding without saddle and harness. The Ellyrian steeds had been docile enough, and ran like the wind when urged, but Saphistia and Lirian, carrying their sons, had been afraid to give their steeds their full run. At times they had been forced to slow to a walk as the path wound round loops in the river or crossed other streams, and Alith knew such things would not delay the dark riders.

Picking their way slowly under the tree canopy, the fugitives continued south by the dim starlight that broke through the leaves. Alith constantly looked over his shoulder, expecting to see shadowy riders closing on them at any moment. Elthyrior seemed content, his gaze fixed ahead, or perhaps he simply accepted that there would be no warning of attack.

As the pale light of Sariour breached the roof of leaves, they came across a clearing, the stumps of felled trees stretching for several hundred paces. The smell of sawdust hung in the air.

'These have been freshly hewn,' said Elthyrior.

'There may be a lodge close at hand,' said Alith. 'Spread out and seek a path.'

The group did as he asked while Alith halted and turned back the way they came, keeping watch for pursuit. It was not long before he heard Heileth calling from the north-west. Alith guided his horse into a trot with a word, crossing the clearing swiftly. He found Heileth at the edge of the open area, Lirian and Elthyrior already with her. A wide trail in the fallen leaves and undergrowth struck out to the north, into the hills.

Saphistia soon joined them and, dismounting, they followed the path speedily, Alith at the fore, Elthyrior guarding the rear. Ahead something white shimmered in the moonlight. As he came through the trees Alith saw that it was a lodge, built of narrow planks, painted white. It had a steep tiled roof and a stone chimney, though the narrow, arched windows were dark and no smoke could be seen.

Elthyrior appeared and signalled for the group to halt before vanishing to the left. Alith drew his sword and turned about, seeking any sign of danger. A few roosting birds flapped from tree to tree and nocturnal hunters rummaged amongst the undergrowth. An owl called in the distance, but all else was still, even the wind. The starlight came fitfully through the branches, dappling the pathway and the clearing beyond.

Elthyrior emerged from the right, having circled the lodge.

'It is empty,' he told them. 'Whoever felled the trees has moved further south today.'

'Should we stay, or move on?' asked Lirian. 'Anataris is so tired, as am I. Can we not rest here for a while? Perhaps the riders will pass us by.'

'And then be between us and Tor Elyr,' said Elthyrior. 'No, we should not stop.'

Alith was about to agree when Elthyrior sharply raised his hand, warning for silence. The raven herald slowly drew his sword and waved Lirian towards the lodge.

'Get inside,' he whispered, his eyes fixed upon something out in the woods.

Alith followed his gaze, but could see nothing. He took Heileth by the arm and led her to the door, Lirian and Saphistia following close behind. When they were inside, Alith brought the horses around the back of the lodge, where a small stable was built against the back wall. Having hidden the mounts, he returned to the front of the building, where Elthyrior was crouched beside a tree close to the path.

Keeping low, Alith joined the raven herald. Peering around the tree trunk, he allowed his eyes to lose focus, looking for movement rather than detail. Things scratched in the dirt and shuffled in the leaves but he saw nothing else.

Then, no more than two hundred paces away, he spied a shadow. It moved slowly, seeming to seep from one tree to the next, momentarily blotting out the patches of starlight. Once he was aware of it, Alith watched more closely, following its course as it approached from the north, skirting around the edge of the clearing.

'There are three more to the south,' said Elthyrior, his voice nothing more than the barest sigh.

The raven herald tapped Alith on the arm and motioned slowly towards the lodge. Rising, the pair stepped backwards, inching away from the path. There was another hoot of an owl and Alith realised the call came from no bird. The shadow ahead stopped for a moment and then changed direction, heading directly across the clearing towards them.

Elthyrior sprang up, dragging Alith by the arm. The two bolted for the lodge, swerving left and right. An arrow whistled past, catching Alith's cloak before thudding into the wooden frame of the door. Another hit the door itself as Elthyrior wrenched it open.

'Get away from the windows!' the raven herald snarled. At his instruction Saphistia, Lirian and Heileth cowered behind the stone hearth, the two children huddled tight amongst them.

The inside of the lodge was a single open room, with windows to the north, south and east, the fireplace to the west. A long table with two benches dominated the centre of the lodge. Sheathing his blade, Alith crossed to the other side and looked out.

There was another shadow, a few dozen paces away, watching.

'Help me,' said Elthyrior, motioning towards the table. Between them, they managed to tilt it upon its side and scraped it across the leaf-patterned tiles to block the doorway.

Glass shattered as an arrow sped into the room, glancing off the mantel of the fireplace. Several more followed, snicking from the hearth. Alith crouched beneath the southern window and glanced out. He saw the flickering of a flame and then a flash of orange as a fire-tipped arrow sped towards the window, landing just short, smoke spiralling up from the sill.

'They'll burn us out!' hissed Alith as more flame-arrows came through the windows, thudding into the benches and skittering from the floor.

Heileth darted forwards, tamping down the burning arrows with her cloak, her demeanour calm. Another missile sped inwards and caught her in the leg just below the knee and she fell backwards with a suppressed squeal of pain. Alith grabbed her under the arms and hauled her to the others. A quick glance showed that the wound was not deep.

'Bind it,' he said, looking at Saphistia. He heard the sound of tearing cloth as he turned back to the windows.

The fire-arrows had not done much damage to the seasoned wood of the lodge, but smoked fitfully where they had hit. Alith glanced towards the back of the lodge and saw a raven-cloaked figure moving closer to the stable.

Alith leapt through the broken window with a crash, snatching his sword free. The raven herald straightened in surprise as Alith dashed across the ground between them. The druchii tossed aside a bow and a gloved hand pulled free a slender blade as Alith reached his foe.

Alith swung back-handed towards the raven herald's head. His enemy ducked and Alith almost lost his footing, stepping to his right to regain balance. The herald lunged, raven-feather hood falling back, revealing a cruelly beautiful face. Alith was almost caught by the thrust, momentarily stunned by the maiden's appearance.

He raised his sword to parry another blow, stepping backwards again until he sensed the stable wall at his back. Dodging to the left, he avoided the next attack, the herald's sword carving a furrow in the white planks.

Alith spun away from the next thrust, bringing his sword swinging up. The blade cut into his foe's arm, under the shoulder, and blood sprayed in the starlight. The raven herald gasped, lurching away, and Alith swiftly followed, driving the point of his sword into her back. She twisted as she fell, blood dribbling from her lips and running down her pale chin. Her eyes were filled with hate.

A shout from Elthyrior brought Alith back to the window to see flames flickering along the eastern wall, lapping at the window. The fire was taking hold and smoke was quickly filling the chamber despite the broken windows. Lirian was sobbing in the nook beside the fire, bent protectively over her son.

A flash of panic crossed Elthyrior's face as he realised the peril of their situation. If they stayed inside the smoke would choke them, if they left they would be easy prey for the raven heralds' bows.

'Out the back,' snapped Alith, gesturing to Saphistia. He took Durinithill as she clambered through the window and then handed back Yeasir's son, gesturing for Lirian to follow.

'Wait!' said Elthyrior. He pointed towards the southern windows. 'Listen!'

Alith froze, his breathing still. He could hear nothing for a moment, but then his keen ears detected something at odds with the sounds of the forest. It was a tremor, distant but powerful. Dashing to the side of the lodge he saw white shapes moving quickly through the woods.

Riders!

From the south and east the Ellyrian reavers came, upon pearl-white steeds, dashing amongst the trees with reckless speed. There were dozens of them, galloping between the boles, bows in hand. The raven heralds turned in shock as the Ellyrians thundered across the clearing and streamed up either side of the path. One of the heralds loosed arrows as they approached, felling three knights before the shafts of the other Ellyrians found him, hurling him into the bushes with four arrows in his chest. The surviving raven heralds fled, disappearing into the shadows between the shafts of starlight, skimming from trunk to trunk before vanishing completely.

The riders of Ellyrion quickly encircled the lodge and Alith was struck by the memory of his first encounter with these headstrong folk, so many years ago. He searched their stern faces but recognised none. Climbing back into the lodge, Alith helped Elthyrior pull the table from the door and the two of them stepped out, dropping their swords to the ground.

'Once again it seems I owe my life to the proud knights of Ellyrion,' said Alith, forcing a smile.

The knights' captain, his silver breastplate chased with sapphires in the form of a rearing horse, urged his steed forwards. He stowed his bow and brought forth a long spear whose tip flickered with magical energy.

'Do not be so glad to see me,' he said fiercely. 'In Ellyrion, spies and horse thieves are punished with death.'

—◄ FIFTEEN ►—

The Clarion Sounds

THOUGH THEIR HANDS were not bound, Alith was in no doubt that he and the others were prisoners of the Ellyrians. They had ridden south with an escort of a hundred knights, who constantly darted suspicious glances at the Naggarothi. Anataris and Durinithill had been taken away, despite the wailed protestations of their mothers. Though it was a callous act, Alith knew he would have done the same.

Five days after their capture, the Ellyrians brought them to Tor Elyr. To the east the Inner Sea sparkled in the afternoon sun, waves crashing upon a steep pebble shore. Two glittering rivers wound towards the coast from the north and west, converging on the capital of Ellyrion.

The city was unlike anything Alith had ever seen. Built upon the confluence of the rivers and the sea, Tor Elyr was a series of immense islands. These isles were linked by bridges, graceful arches covered with turf so that it seemed as if the meadows rose up of their own accord and spanned the water.

The towers of the Ellyrians were like ivory stalagmites, open at the base, soaring high upon circles of carved columns above spiralling stairs. Not a paved path or road could be seen, all was grassland, even under the platforms of the towers.

White horses roamed freely within and without, gathering in herds to crop the lush grass, trotting over the bridges alongside their elven companions. White ships with figureheads of horses with golden harnesses bobbed on the water, their huge triangular sails reflecting the sun. It was as different

547

from bleak Nagarythe as the summer is from winter. All was warmth and openness, even the skies were cloudless, their deep blue mirrored in the waters of the Inner Sea.

There were many looks at the group as their captors led them through the wide, winding avenues of Tor Elyr, crossing from island to island. There was a babble of talk as they passed and the Ellyrians were not restrained in voicing their disapproval as insults and curses followed Alith.

They came to the great palace, alone upon an isle at the mouth of the rivers, larger than the manse of Elanardris, though not nearly so grand as the citadel of Tor Anroc. The palace was shaped as an amphitheatre, a huge enclosed field surrounded by an arch-broken wall and six towers built upon hundreds of slender pillars. At the centre of the arena rose a stepped hill, runes of white carved into the turf, a circular stage of dark wood and silver at its summit.

About this circle stood tall banner poles, each hanging a standard from one of the great houses of Ellyrian. Blue and white and gold fluttered in the gentle breeze, topped with streaming tails of horsehair. At their centre were two thrones, their backs carved in the likeness of rearing horses that appeared to be dancing with each other. Ellyrian nobles were gathered upon the stage and hillside, some on foot, some upon the backs of haughtily stepping steeds. All turned to look at the new arrivals, their expressions unwelcoming.

The rightmost throne was empty save for a silver crown upon its seat. On the other sat Princess Athielle, and the sight of her stirred within Alith feelings he had thought gone forever. Her hair reached to her waist, spilling across her shoulders and chest in lustrous golden curls, braided in places with ruby-studded bands. She wore an elegant sleeveless gown of light blue, garlanded with dark red roses and embroidered with golden thread and more red gems. There was also a golden hue upon her skin, glowing in the sunlight.

The princess's eyes were a startlingly deep green flecked with brown, beneath a brow furrowed with anger. Lips pursed, Athielle regarded Alith and the others with a smouldering ire that did nothing to abolish Alith's admiration; if anything her intemperate expression only served to display a fiery disposition that attracted him more.

'Dismount,' commanded Anathirir, the captain who had taken them prisoner.

Alith duly slipped from the back of his horse and immediately stepped towards the thrones. Knights closed in swiftly, placing themselves between Alith and their co-ruler, their speartips directed towards him. There could be no danger, for Alith and Elthyrior had no weapons.

'Bring them,' said Athielle. 'Let me see them.'

The knights parted and, urged on by the presence of the riders, the group walked towards the princess. She stood as they stopped a few paces short, and strode from her throne. Taller than Alith, arms folded across her chest, Athielle walked back and forth in front of them, her eyes taking in every detail.

Alith bowed briefly and opened his mouth to speak but Athielle recognised his intent.

'Say nothing!' she snapped, a finger raised to silence him. 'You will speak only to answer my questions.'

Alith nodded in assent.

'Who here is your leader?'

The captives exchanged glances, and the eyes of the others eventually fell upon Alith.

'I speak for all of us, Lady Athielle,' he said. 'My name is–'

'Have I asked your name?' Athielle interrupted. 'Is it true that you took from our herds by the ford of Thiria Elor?'

Alith darted a glance at the others before answering.

'We took horses, it is true,' he said. 'We were–'

'Did you have permission to take these horses?' Athielle continued.

'Well, no, we needed–'

'So you admit to being horse thieves?'

Alith stuttered for a moment, frustrated by the princess's interrogation.

'I'll take your silence as agreement,' said Athielle. 'In these times, save for the slaying of another elf there is no greater crime in Ellyrion. Even now my brother fights to free our lands from the Naggarothi menace, and we find you in our borders. You came across the mountains to spy for Morathi, did you not?'

'No!' said Heileth. 'We were fleeing Nagarythe.'

'But you are Naggarothi?' Athielle turned her full intent upon Heileth, who shrank back from her wrath.

'I am not,' said Lirian. She cast a plaintive glance back towards the knights. 'Please, princess, they have taken my son.'

'And how many sons and daughters of Ellyrion have been taken by this Naggarothi war?' Athielle retorted. 'What is one child amongst so much destruction?'

'He is the heir of Bel Shanaar,' said Alith, drawing gasps from the Ellyrian nobles. Athielle turned her glare back upon him, her expression doubtful. Then she laughed, without humour.

'The heir of Tiranoc? Out of the wilderness with a ragged party of Naggarothi? You expect me to believe that?'

'Highness, look at me,' said Lirian, her voice growing in insistence. 'I am Lirian, widow of Elodhir. We have met before, at Bel Shanaar's court, when Malekith first returned. I was not so unkempt then as I am now, and my hair was almost as long as yours.'

Athielle cocked her head to one side as she studied the Tiranocii princess. Her eyes widened with recognition.

'Lirian?' she whispered, covering her mouth in horror. Athielle skipped forwards and threw her arms around Lirian, almost crushing her with the intensity of her embrace. 'Oh, my poor child, I am so sorry! What has become of you?'

The princess of Ellyrion stepped back.

'Bring the children here,' she snapped, her sudden anger focussed upon Anathirir. Shame-faced, the captain hurriedly gestured to his knights and within moments two rode forwards and handed the babes back to their mothers.

'And who are you to have delivered this gift to us?' Athielle said, looking at Alith.

'I am Alith,' he said solemnly. 'Last lord of House Anar.'

'Alith Anar? Son of Eothlir?'

Alith merely nodded. To his surprise, Athielle then hugged him tight as well, squeezing the breath from his body.

'You fought beside Aneltain,' Athielle whispered. 'I have so longed to meet a lord of the Anars to thank them for their aid.'

Alith's hands hovered close to Athielle's back, unsure whether he should return the embrace. Before he had decided, she broke away, a tear in her eye.

'I am so sorry,' she said, addressing all of them. 'Such wickedness as Morathi has unleashed has spawned a darkness in all of us! Please forgive my suspicions.'

Alith almost laughed at the transformation in the princess. Faced with such earnest contrition, there was little else he could do.

THE HOSTILITY WITH which the group had been greeted was matched by the Ellyrians' hospitality once Athielle had given her blessing. Spacious chambers were given over to them in the palace, and Alith found himself attended by several servants. He found their constant presence a distraction and despatched them on pointless errands so that he could be by himself. His quest for solitude was waylaid by an invitation from the princess to attend a feast that night.

Alith was conflicted as his servants led him out into the great arena. Deep within, he longed to leave Tor Elyr having discharged his duty to Lirian and the others. The memories of razed Elanardris haunted his thoughts and he nurtured this bleak remembrance, drawing resolution from his bitterness. Yet the thought of spending more time with Athielle, of forgetting the woes that had burdened him, teased him. This desire made him feel weak and selfish, so it was in a sour mood that he stalked from the palace to join his hosts.

The meadow-hall had been filled with long tables and hundreds of lanterns glowed with a rainbow of colours, dappling the ground with green and yellow and blue. Ellyrian knights and nobles strolled along the tables, sampling the many drinks and delicacies on offer. Their chatter was light and drifted out into the evening sky, and there was much laughter. Alith cast his gaze across the crowd, seeking a familiar face, but saw nothing of Elthyrior, Saphistia or the others. Athielle had not yet arrived.

A few of the Ellyrians tried to engage him in conversation, wandering over in small groups to meet their strange guest. His civil yet curt replies soon rebuffed their attempts at friendship, and the sympathetic looks of the departing nobles did nothing to ease the residual anger he felt. To Alith, it seemed impossible that such a banquet could be held while elves fought and died not so very far away, the future of Ulthuan hanging in the balance. It was such a far cry from what he had left in Nagarythe that he was taken by the urge to leave immediately. He wanted no part of this false display of gaiety and wellbeing.

As he resolved to depart, Athielle made her entrance. Flanked by a bodyguard of knights, she rode into the arena upon a high-stepping white stallion, her long tresses flowing behind her like a cloak. Diamonds glittered in the harness of her steed and flashed like stars from the threads of her blue gown.

The crowd parted before the princess and she rode quickly up to her throne while her knights wheeled away, picking their way easily through the mingling elves. Athielle dismounted with a flourish and sent her horse running with a whispered word. Servants were on hand with platters of food and goblets of wine, but she ignored them, casting her gaze across her assembled subjects. Her eyes stopped when they fell upon Alith, who was stood away to her left, far from the rest of the elves.

Athielle beckoned him to approach. Taking a deep breath, Alith strode up the throne hill, ignoring the looks directed at him from the other Ellyrians. His eyes were fixed upon Athielle, as hers were upon him. The princess smiled as Alith reached the stage and extended a hand in greeting. Alith took her hand in his, bowed and kissed her slender fingers.

'It is my pleasure to see you again, princess,' said Alith. To his surprise he realised that he meant these words, all his misgivings having been dispelled by her warm smile.

'And it is an honour for me, prince,' Athielle replied. She turned and whispered something to one of her retainers who slipped away.

'I hope that you are finding your stay in Tor Elyr more comfortable than your journey here,' she said, gracefully withdrawing her hand before sitting upon her throne.

Alith hesitated before replying, not wishing to be dishonest but cautious not to voice his misgivings.

'The hospitality of your city and people are a great credit to Ellyrion,' he said.

Servants returned carrying high-backed chairs, which they arranged around the throne. As Athielle waved for Alith to be seated, she looked away with a broad smile.

'You need not suffer my company alone, Alith,' she said.

Before Alith could dispute that such an encounter was anything but pleasant, Athielle pointed past him. Alith turned to see Lirian, Heileth and Saphistia walking up the hill, clad in flamboyant dresses of silk and jewels. There was no sign of the children, or Elthyrior. Alith's companions seated themselves around him, looking comfortable in their finery, pleased with the attention being heaped upon them.

'Our vagabond maidens have been restored to their glory,' said Athielle. 'Like fine steeds that need to be well-groomed after a long ride through briar and wood.'

Alith murmured his agreement, for his companions looked every part the nobles that they truly were. Still, there was something stiff about the beauty of Lirian, like a finely rendered statue, which reminded Alith too much of Ashniel. Heileth and Saphistia were more familiar, being Naggarothi, but even they had taken on an otherworldly air with the pampering of their attendants. Alith returned his gaze to Athielle, admiring all the more her natural beauty. Though her appearance was as meticulously designed and styled as the others, Alith saw a light within her, a glow of life that couldn't be swathed by all the gems and cloth in Ulthuan.

Alith tried to dismiss these thoughts but Athielle leaned forwards towards him, her scent enveloping him. It was the perfume of Ellyrion itself: of fresh sea air and grass, of open skies and rolling meadows.

'You seem uncomfortable, Alith,' said the princess. 'You are not at ease.'

'I am perplexed,' said Alith. 'If you will pardon the question, I must ask how it is possible that so many Ellyrians can be brought here, while the Naggarothi wage war upon all of Ulthuan?'

A scowl marred Athielle's perfect features and Alith felt a stab of regret at his words.

'You come to us in a brief moment of respite. Even now my brother fights in the north, defending these lands.' Her tone and expression relented as she continued. 'Is it wrong to enjoy these fleeting moments of peace? If we do not treasure our lives as they can be without war, what is it that we fight for? Perhaps it is a failing of the Naggarothi that they could find no contentment within themselves, that only in action and not quiet do they measure the success of their lives.'

Athielle's words stung Alith and he looked down, shamed. He had no right to bring his own darkness here, to taint the light of the festivities of others, but for all his misgivings, a part of his soul protested against acquiescence. This was an illusion, a fake revelry that tried to defy the blights of Ulthuan, hollow and meaningless.

Alith curbed his tongue, wishing to cause no further offence. Athielle was speaking to the others, but her questions and their replies were faint in Alith's ears. Only after some time did he look up, stirred by movement. Lirian, Saphistia and Heileth were leaving the throne-stage. Alith stood and mumbled a few parting words, and then he was alone with Athielle and her court.

'I see that my attempts to lighten your mood have been for naught,' said Athielle. 'Please, sit, and we will talk of matters that are perhaps of more concern to you.'

'Forgive my mood, princess, I am not ungrateful for your kindness,' Alith said, taking his seat again. 'I have suffered more than any from this war and it is not in me to put aside my woe. I would have it that every day could be spent as this one, but wishing it will not make it so.'

'I will not deceive you, Alith,' said the Ellyrian ruler, her mood serious. 'The war has not gone well of late. King Caledor's gains of the summer have been reversed and we expect the Naggarothi to march again for Tor Elyr before the end of the season. I do not know if we can hold them this time, for they seem reckless in their hatred and determination to crush all opposition.'

'There is no alternative but to fight,' Alith replied. 'I have seen the horror of Morathi's rule, the wickedness of her followers. It is better to fight and die than submit to such barbarous slavery.'

'And how will you continue to fight, Alith?' asked Athielle. 'You are a prince without a realm, a leader without an army.'

Alith said nothing, for he had no answer to the question. He knew not how he would fight, only that he must. He refused to entertain the hopelessness that churned within him; refused to consider any thought of surrender. The blood in his veins burned, his heart set to racing at the merest contemplation of the druchii and the wrongs they had heaped upon him.

He looked up at Athielle and she shrank back from his piercing stare.

'I do not know how I will fight,' Alith said. 'I do not know if any will fight with me. While I still draw breath, I will not suffer a single druchii to live. This is all that is left of me.'

THE SEASONS PASSED differently in Ellyrion, the weather far milder than in Nagarythe, and Alith became unsure how long he had spent in Tor Elyr. The passing days melded into an interminable limbo, and Alith felt the same frustrations that had beset him in Tor Anroc. He had no plan, no course of action to follow, only the burning desire to do something.

He spent little time with the others he had arrived with; Elthyrior had disappeared soon after their coming, and the rest were quickly adjusting to court life in their new home. Alith found the Ellyrians intolerable company, even more garrulous and overly friendly than the serving folk of Tor Anroc. The wide meadows surrounding the city had none of the bleak charm of Elanardris, the sun-drenched fields only serving to throw his own cold feelings into stark contrast. The Inner Sea held no appeal for Alith either, nothing more than a means to travel further east, away from Nagarythe.

So it was that he spent much of his time alone, brooding on his fate. The

Ellyrians soon came to shun his company, and he encouraged this. He even turned down requests from Athielle to join her, driven by a self-torturous need to deny himself any form of pleasure. Alith came to hate and love his own suffering, taking comfort from his bitter thoughts, confirming his own dark suspicions about his fellow elves.

WHEN EVEN THE clement weather within the Annulii began to grow colder, Prince Finudel returned from his campaign. Alith joined the Ellyrian court to welcome the prince, and was introduced by Athielle that evening. The three of them met alone in the prince's chambers, high within one of the palace's towers. Alith again related the circumstances surrounding his exile from Nagarythe.

'All that I desire is to strike back at those who have destroyed my family and my lands,' Alith concluded.

'You wish to fight?' said Finudel. The likeness between him and his older sister was remarkable, though Finudel was even more animated and prone to changes of mood. The prince paced to and fro across the circular room, his hands in constant motion, seeking activity.

'I do,' said Alith.

'Then you will soon have the opportunity,' replied Finudel. 'You were not the only Naggarothi to have crossed the mountains. They joined with us as we pursued an army of cultists. Many spoke highly of you, Alith, and they will be heartened to hear that you are alive.'

'I am glad that others have evaded the clutches of Kheranion and his army,' said Alith. 'How many have made the crossing?'

'A few thousand in all,' said Finudel. 'They are camped to the west with my army. It would do me a great service if you would lead them into battle beside me.'

'Nothing would give me more satisfaction,' said Alith. 'Against whom are we to fight?'

'The druchii have retaken the Pass of the Eagle, its eastern reaches no more than three days from here,' Finudel said. 'I ride out again tomorrow.'

'And I ride out as well,' said Athielle. 'We cannot allow our foes to approach Tor Elyr. As you see, our city has no walls to defend, no keeps to hold the druchii at bay. We must meet them in open battle, and must do so with all of our strength.'

'We must deal with this threat,' added Finudel. 'In the north, there are still those who were once our subjects who have been swayed by Morathi. They are a blight within Ellyrion but they cannot be swept away whilst the threat from the west remains.'

'I will fight for Ellyrion as if they were my own lands,' said Alith. 'The druchii will pay a bloody price for their treachery.'

─< SIXTEEN >─

Blood on the Plains

CHEERS GREETED ALITH'S arrival at the Naggarothi camp, but the enthusiasm of his followers was soon quelled by his dour expression. Amongst those that thronged towards him from the tents, Alith recognised many faces. The former Shadows Anraneir and Khillrallion were there, with Tharion, Anadriel and several others who had fought at Dark Fen. All seemed pleased to see him, but there was a drawn, haunted look about their faces.

'We feared for you, lord, when you disappeared from Elanardris,' said Anraneir. 'We thought you dead, or worse.'

'You were not wrong,' replied Alith. 'Though I am not dead in body, I suffer all the more for it.'

Some of the captains exchanged worried glances at this, but remained silent.

'What are your orders, prince?' asked Tharion.

It struck Alith as strange that one of his father's closest friends, who had fought beside Eothlir in the colonies, would look to him for leadership. Alith considered the question for some time.

'Fight until your last breath, and with that last breath spit out your hatred of the druchii.'

THE ARMY MOVED westwards towards the Pass of the Eagle, a force of several hundred knights riding ahead of the host to spy the position of the enemy. The Naggarothi marched alongside the Ellyrian spearmen and archers, and Alith walked with them, choosing to accompany his warriors on foot rather than ride with Finudel and Athielle.

555

Two days from the pass, scouts returned with word of the druchii army. Messengers asked Alith to attend the Ellyrian prince and princess so that they might devise a strategy. They met just after midday, as the army took a break from its march along the southern bank of the Irlana River. Beneath a pavilion roof of blue and gold, the commanders sought the counsel of each other whilst they refreshed themselves with water from the river and fruits brought from orchards further south.

'We are outnumbered, that is for certain,' they were told by Prince Aneltain, who had met Alith whilst returning from the ill-fated expedition to Ealith more than twenty-five years earlier. It was Aneltain's warriors that formed the vanguard and the prince had troubling news. 'Forty thousand infantry at least, and some ten thousand knights. Few are cultists, most are soldiers trained in Anlec.'

'That is nearly ten thousand more warriors than we have mustered,' said Athielle. She paused to take a bite from a red apple, her expression pensive.

'It is, but we have the greater number of cavalry,' said Finudel. 'We have twice as many riders.'

'These are knights of Anlec, not reavers,' said Alith. 'You cannot count their strength by numbers alone.'

'And the reavers of Ellyrion carry bows,' countered Finudel. 'And ride swifter steeds. The druchii knights can chase us for a year and a day and they will never catch us.'

'They do not need to chase us, brother,' said Athielle, finishing the apple, tossing the core towards her horse, Silvermane. 'The enemy know that we must stand at some time, to protect Tor Elyr.'

'Why?' asked Alith. The other elves directed surprised looks towards him. 'Why do you need to protect Tor Elyr?'

'Fifty thousand of our subjects live in the city,' said Finudel, a touch of anger in his voice. 'We could not abandon them to the cruel intent of the druchii.'

'Evacuate them,' said Alith. 'By land and ship, have your people leave the city. It is only stone and wood, after all. Why hang such a weight about your necks when you have such a swift army?'

'It matters not,' said Athielle. 'Though many of us can ride away from the druchii, even in Ellyrion there are not enough horses for every elf. Half our force is on foot.'

'Have them hide in Athelian Toryr, where the enemy will not happily follow.'

'Hide?' spat Finudel. 'You would have us allow the druchii to ravage our lands at will, leaving us destitute and homeless.'

'Better that than make food for the crows,' Alith replied. 'While you live you can fight.'

'We will not run like cowards,' said Athielle. 'Too many have done so and paid the price later. The Naggarothi only grow stronger the longer we delay confrontation.'

Alith shrugged.

'Then we will fight them,' he said. 'It would be wise to attack while they are still in the pass, where their numbers will count against them. Ambush them from the slopes, lure them onto your blades and surround them.'

'A rock-strewn valley is no place for cavalry,' said Aneltain. 'We would surrender the advantages that we possess.'

'We will meet them upon the open field, and fight as Ellyrians,' said Finudel.

'It is clear you have already set your minds on one course,' growled Alith. 'No argument I can make will convince you of the error of your actions. If you do not wish to hear my counsel, why did you ask me here?'

'And who are you to tell us better?' said Finudel. 'A dispossessed prince; a wanderer with nothing but hate.'

'If you would suffer the same fate as I, then do as you say,' snarled Alith. 'Ride out in glory, with your banners streaming and your horns ringing. You think that because you have defeated the druchii before that you will have victory today? They do not fight on your terms, and they will win. Unless you crush them, kill every one of them, they will not relent. Morathi drives them on, and their commanders fear her far more than they fear your knights and spears. Have you mages to match their sorcery? If you win and they flee, have it in you to chase them down, slay them as they run? Is it in your noble hearts to butcher and kill, so that they will not return?'

'Darkness cannot be defeated by further darkness,' said Athielle. 'Did you not hear what I told you in Tor Elyr? It is because the druchii despise peace, loathe life, that they must be defeated. If we become the same, we have lost that which we fight for.'

'Fools!' said Alith. 'I will have no part of this folly. The true Naggarothi have already paid the price for thinking that they can stand face-to-face against the might of Anlec. The corpses of my mother and father are testament to that course of action.'

Alith stormed from the pavilion, scattering the Ellyrians in his path. He strode through the camp, heedless of the shouts that followed him. Despair vied with rage inside him: despair that the Ellyrians would die; rage that the druchii would gain an important victory.

HIS CAPTAINS MET Alith as he entered the Naggarothi camp. They immediately sensed his foul mood and followed in silence as he cut between the assembled regiments towards his tent. A glare from Alith halted them at the door as he ducked inside.

Alith sat listening to the musicians of the Ellyrians calling them to the march. The ground trembled beneath the tread of horses and elves as Finudel and Athielle mustered their army. Let them march to their pointless deaths, he told himself.

It was Khillrallion who dared his foul temper, standing calmly upon the threshold of the pavilion, hands behind his back.

'The Ellyrians have broken camp, prince,' he said quietly.

Alith did not reply.

'Should we make ready to march as well?'

Alith looked up at Khillrallion.

'We will follow behind,' he said. 'If they call for our aid, I will not deny them.'

Khillrallion nodded and withdrew, leaving Alith with his tumultuous thoughts.

FINUDEL AND ATHIELLE chose to make their stand upon the meadows of Nairain Elyr, less than a day's march from the mouth of Eagle Pass, where the Irlana flows from the mountains and loops widely to the north before continuing east towards the Inner Sea. The Ellyrians put their infantry upon the right, with their flank protected by the river, while their cavalry they kept to the left, giving them the freedom of the wide fields to the south. Alith encamped his small army, four thousand in all, even further to the south. Here he stayed within his tent, and dismissed all visits from his lieutenants.

The following dawn Alith was roused from his sleep by Tharion.

'One of the Ellyrians wishes to see you,' said the captain.

Alith nodded and signalled for the messenger to be brought to the pavilion. A few moments later Tharion entered with Aneltain in tow. Alith nodded in greeting but did not rise from his cot.

'The druchii have been spied by our scouts,' said the Ellyrian. 'They will be upon us before noon.'

'And you still intend to meet them in open battle?' asked Alith.

'There is no other choice,' replied Aneltain.

'Send your infantry across the river, and take your riders to the east,' said Alith, his tone off-hand. 'That is one alternative to throwing your lives away in this pointless gesture.'

'You know that we will not retreat,' said Aneltain. He took a step forwards, his expression imploring. 'Fight with us and we can win.'

'Four thousand spears and bows will not win this battle,' said Alith. 'Even Naggarothi spears and bows.'

'Then at least promise that you will hold this position,' said Aneltain. 'At least give Finudel and Athielle your assurance that you will defend the southern flank.'

Alith looked at Aneltain with a frown, sensing the accusation implicit in the request.

'I swore to defend Ellyrion as if these were my own lands,' Alith said sharply. 'I do not make such oaths lightly. Though I do not agree on this course of action, I will not abandon my allies.'

Aneltain's relief was palpable as he bowed in thanks.

'I remember a time when it was I that came to the aid of the Anars,' he said. 'I am glad that I was not wrong to do so.'

Alith pushed himself from his bed and strode up to Aneltain, staring him in the eye.

'Perhaps you think that I owe you this favour?' snarled Alith. 'You think that I feel some debt?'

Aneltain stepped back, aghast at Alith's aggression. His expression of gratitude became one of anger.

'If you do not feel the debt, then I will not claim it,' Aneltain said fiercely. 'If it does not matter to you that brave Ellyrians died restoring Malekith to his throne, and Chracians and Yvressians as well, then perhaps you should consider who it is that you wish to fight for.'

'I do not fight *for* anyone!' roared Alith, forcing Aneltain to retreat quickly to the tent's opening. 'I fight *against* the druchii!'

With a venomous glare, Aneltain left, shouting for his horse to be brought to him. Tharion directed a sharp glance at his prince.

'Would you have us left with no allies?' said the veteran captain.

'No allies would be better than poor allies,' Alith replied, slumping back onto his bed. 'They talk of honour and glory, as if that counted for anything. They do not understand the manner of foe they fight, even though they have looked it in the face a dozen times. Fear is all the druchii understand, and fear is a power we can wield as well if we choose. Morathi and her commanders do not fear the cavalry charge or the volley of arrows. No, it is the darkness they have unleashed, it causes them to pause for thought, wakes them in the cold hours before dawn. They look over their own shoulders, dreading to see who wields the knife for them. Fear binds them more than loyalty, and with fear we will break them apart.'

Tharion considered this for a moment, doubts scribed upon his brow.

'What is it that you fear, Alith?'

'Nothing,' he said. 'There is no pain that can be visited upon me that I have not already felt. There is no torment I can suffer that my memories do not inflict upon me every day. I have nothing left to be taken away, save this existence that hurts me with every breath. I do not seek death, but I have no fear of being sent to Mirai. There I will find my family again, and take vengeance upon those that killed them. Beyond even death my hatred will continue.'

Tharion shuddered and turned away, terrified by the look in Alith's eye.

ALITH STOOD AT the edge of the Naggarothi camp, looking out over the two armies as the druchii advanced. In long lines of silver, white and blue, the Ellyrians stood their ground against the encroaching black host. White steeds stamped and whinnied, sharing the excitement of their riders. A hundred banners streamed from silver poles, and golden horns were lifted to lips to let forth peals of defiance.

The reaver knights were split into two forces, one led by Finudel, the other by Athielle. The princess sat upon Silvermane at the head of the closest division, her long hair flying free in the wind, her slender form encased in silver armour studded with sapphires. In her hand she held aloft a white sword, the winterblade Amreir, and upon her left arm hung a shield in the shape of a horse's head, its mane a flowing mass of golden thread.

Finudel was no less impressive. He carried Cadrathi, the starblade lance forged by Caledor Dragontamer, whose head burned with a golden flame. In gold panoply sat the prince, a cloak of deep red flapping from his shoulders. His steed Snowhoof, sister to Athielle's mount, was enveloped by a long caparison of gilded ithilmar, every scale of armour inscribed with a rune of protection.

Studying the druchii, Alith saw that their standards also bore runes, of bloodthirsty gods and wicked goddesses. Many had painted or embossed symbols of cults upon their shields, twisted script that seethed with dark magic. In columns the Naggarothi advanced, black and silver snakes whose coming was heralded by the tramping of thousands of boots.

The knights of Anlec turned to the south, to face the reavers. Harsh battle cries and shrill horns announced their challenge to Finudel and Athielle while black and purple pennants snapped upon golden lances. Their steeds were black, with chamfrons of silvered armour decked with blades, flanks covered with shining links of mail.

Sorcerers and sorceresses there were too, prowling amongst the regiments, their magic coiling and weaving around them. Dark clouds swathed the sky at their commands, flickering with lightning, thunder matching the crash of the army's advance. The shadow of the storm swept over the plains, shrouding both armies in gloom.

Glancing at the heavy skies, Alith saw a dark shape, enormous and winged. Despite his earlier words, for a moment he was gripped with fear as the dragon circled menacingly. His father's bloodied face flashed in front of Alith, and his muscles twitched with the memory of the terror that had filled him.

'Kheranion,' Alith snarled, allowing his anger to flood away all dread.

Turning on his heel, Alith shouted for his captains. They came running from across the camp and waited breathlessly for their commander's decree.

'We attack,' said Alith. 'Sound the muster, gather your regiments. Today we will slay these druchii dogs and send a message back to Anlec. Bring me the head of Kheranion.'

There was no argument from the lieutenants, who hurried back to their companies, calling for musicians and banner bearers to signal the attack. Alith returned to his tent and took up bow and arrows, given to him by Khillrallion.

'Shadows, to me!' he called upon returning outside. Soon he stood at the centre of a circle of black-swathed archers, bitter survivors of Dark Fen.

'Today I lead the Shadows again. The enemy bring their own darkness, and that suits us well. Show no mercy. Every arrow brings death. Every sword thrust is vengeance. Every drop of blood is owed to us. We will be the nightmares once more, and the druchii will remember well why they fear the Shadows.'

IN ALL, MORE than two hundred of the Shadows had survived the disaster at Dark Fen, and clad in their black cloaks they followed Alith westwards, circling around the right flank of the druchii host. The rest of Alith's army stood ready at the camp, with orders to engage the enemy if they came too close. Not until Alith returned from his foray were they to move forwards.

It was the druchii that started the battle. They had brought with them repeater bolt throwers: war engines that hurled half-a-dozen spear-sized shafts with each salvo. The opening volley from ten of these machines screamed into the air above the advancing druchii and plunged down into the Ellyrian infantry. To Alith it was clear that Kheranion thought the reaver knights unable to match his columns and sought to destroy the spearmen and archers first and then drive away the cavalry with weight of numbers.

Alith found it curious that the druchii prince remained in the skies, observing the unfolding battle from the back of his black dragon. At Dark Fen he had only become involved when it was obvious that the Naggarothi were losing. Perhaps he was a coward? Or perhaps there was some other reason Kheranion feared to commit to the fighting.

As he pondered this, Alith signalled for the Shadows to halt. The long grass of Ellyrion reached above waist height and provided ample conceal-ment for the scouts. The storm overhead continued to growl and rumble, growing in intensity, shrouding the meadows with a yellowing gloom close to twilight. In the darkness, the Shadows readied their bows and waited for Alith's next command.

As he looked at the druchii army, Alith was surprised to see that they had brought no hydras with them. He had no idea why they had left their mon-strous war-beasts behind, but was pleased that such was the case, though it was small comfort when he remembered the dragon climbing and swoop-ing through the storm clouds.

The druchii halted their advance just out of the range of the Ellyrian bows as the repeater bolt throwers continued to unleash their deadly volleys. The closest of the war machines was about four hundred paces from the Shad-ows, its crew working quickly to replace an empty magazine.

'Split into fives, target the bolt throwers,' Alith told the others. 'I want the crews dead.'

In small groups, the Shadows broke away, flitting through the long grass towards their targets. Alith and his four companions headed directly for the closest while the other Shadows fanned out around the rest of the battery. Companies of spearmen stood close to the war machines, guarding against any attempt by the Ellyrians to circumvent the main line, but their attention was focussed to the east not the south and the Shadows approached unseen.

Alith stooped in a crouch about seventy paces from the repeater bolt thrower. He fitted an arrow to his bowstring, rising just enough to see his target. The bolt thrower was crewed by two druchii, protected by breast-plates and helms but no heavier armour. Having removed the empty shaft box from the top of their engine, they were carrying a new magazine of bolts back to the war machine.

'Now,' Alith said calmly, sighting upon the leftmost of the two druchii.

With a gentle exhalation, Alith loosed his string and the black-fletched arrow whistled just above the tips of the grass, taking his target in the right shoulder. Another shaft hit him in the thigh, punching deep through the flesh and out the other side. The druchii dropped his burden, spinning to the ground while three arrows found their mark on his companion, one of them hitting him through the eyehole of his helmet's mask.

The only sound was the clatter of the magazine tumbling from their dead grip, easily lost in the wind. Alith dropped down and made his way to the war engine as quickly as possible, exchanging his bow for a long hunting knife. With occasional glances to check that he was unobserved, he reached the bolt thrower.

Alith sawed at the rope coils that provided the tension for the war engine's mechanism. His sharp blade quickly parted the cords twisted around one launching arm and the rope fell slack. It would take hours to restring the machine, but for good measure Alith used the tip of his knife to pry out the trigger mechanism from the main body of the machine. He levered out several springs from the delicate workings and tossed them into the grass.

Satisfied with his work, Alith began to head back southwards, keeping a close eye on the nearby druchii regiments.

As the other Shadows unleashed their attacks and more war machines were dismantled, the captains of the spear companies realised something was amiss. The rate of fire had fallen dramatically and officers turned back towards the bolt throwers to find out why. There were shouts of alarm as black shadows flitted between the engines. The captains' commands ringing in their ears, the druchii warriors brought up their weapons, their eyes searching the grass for the mysterious archers.

Alith made a long screech of a hawk, the signal for the Shadows to withdraw and rejoin him. He kept his eye on the closest regiment of druchii, who had begun to wheel in his direction, though they were several hundred paces away. Alith could not believe that the Shadows had been seen, but then amongst the front rank of armoured warriors he spied a slender, semi-naked figure.

It was a sorceress, her long white hair flickering like the lightning in the clouds above, her pale flesh painted with runes of mystical power. She lifted a slender arm and pointed in Alith's direction, turning to the captain marching beside her.

Even as Alith saw motes of magic dancing from the sorceress's fingertips he felt a strange pressure, a build-up of dark magic in the air around him. A moment later a crackling bolt of energy leapt from the druchii's hand, exploding just to Alith's left, hurling him sideways with the force of its detonation.

Picking himself up, Alith saw a charred circle of grass, at its centre the distorted, broken body of Nermyrrin, her skin blackened, her eyes nothing more than dark holes from which two wisps of vapour coiled. More magical blasts leapt across the meadow as the sorceress advanced with her bodyguard, setting the grass alight and hurling smoking bodies into the air.

'Fall back!' Alith called out, picking up the remains of Nermyrrin. She was strangely cold to the touch. 'Bring the dead!'

One hundred druchii spearmen locked their shields as the Shadows covered their retreat with arrows. The sorceress stepped back into the press of bodies, shielding herself from harm as black shafts felled the warriors around her.

Alith stowed his bow and hiked Nermyrrin's body over his shoulder. Turning away from the druchii, he hurried back through the grass, sensing the presence of the other Shadows around him moving swiftly but stealthily across the meadow. A glance back showed that the spearmen had been called to a halt, and mocking shouts followed the Shadows as they headed back to the Anar camp.

The druchii's contempt was ill-placed. Half of the druchii war machines could no longer fire and the crews of several more were dead. Without the weight of fire from their machines to pressurise the Ellyrians into an attack, the druchii were forced to continue their advance. Drums rolled once more and horns blared as the massive shape of Kheranion's dragon swooped down over his army. The monstrous creature landed in the midst of the host for a moment, the druchii general atop its scaled back bellowing orders to his lieutenants. Alith had barely taken three breaths before the dragon sought the skies again, lifting itself higher and higher with powerful sweeps of its clawed wings.

Alith noted this with interest, realising that Kheranion was taking great pains to spend as little time as possible on the ground. Clearly the strength of the dragon and its lance-wielding rider were on the attack, smashing into the foe at speed. For the moment, Alith could think of no way of grounding his enemy though, and so turned his attention to other matters.

NEITHER SIDE WANTED to commit themselves to the attack. The Naggarothi and Ellyrians closed within bow range of each other, exchanging clouds of arrows. The reavers led by Athielle darted forwards to loose volleys before wheeling away out of range of the repeater crossbows of their enemies. All the while the menacing knights of Anlec stayed in the reserve, waiting for the crucial moment to unleash their devastating charge.

The druchii wizards conjured up storms of blades that slashed through the Ellyrians, and cast spells that wracked their enemies with bone-deep agony, searing their flesh and stripping away skin. There was little the Ellyrians could do to counter these spells, and they were suffering badly from the disadvantage.

Alith called his Shadows to him again as they gathered on the edge of the camp.

'Hunt the sorcerers,' he said. 'Make every shot count. Attack and then fade north and we'll regroup on the right of the Ellyrian infantry.'

The Shadows nodded their understanding and melted away into the greyness, Alith following. For some it would appear foolhardy, sneaking between two armies about to engage each other. Alith knew better. Across Nagarythe the Shadows had tormented and terrorised the druchii using the same tactics. Approach close and unseen, kill the enemy and then vanish. It made soldiers think they faced more foes than they actually did, and made commanders fear for their safety. The disruption would serve the Ellyrians well and Alith hoped that Finudel and Athielle were wise enough to take advantage when the time came.

Alith approached the closest druchii at a crouch, sliding effortlessly amongst the grass blades, barely another ripple amongst the swaying caused by the storm winds. He was close enough to hear the chatter of the spearmen as they stood in their ranks waiting for the order to advance.

'These horse fondlers are no match for Naggarothi blades,' one lieutenant said, drawing harsh laughter from her comrades.

That the druchii still dared to call themselves Naggarothi bit at Alith's temper. They had spurned all right to that claim when they had turned on Malekith, the heir of Aenarion, and cast him from Anlec. They were traitors – dark elves – and nothing more. Alith forced himself to relax, aware that the enemy were little more than two dozen paces away. With deliberate slowness, he drew up the hood of his cloak, whispering a few words to draw his hunter's magic into its fibres.

Alith felt the vaguest shimmer of energy tingle on his head and shoulders. To him nothing changed. To another, Alith would have disappeared; one moment a black-swathed figure, the next nothing more than bending grass stems. Thus concealed, Alith rose gently until he was standing at his full height. The front rank of the spearmen was directly ahead of him, so close he could have thrown an arrow at them. Their captain was a female druchii with red-dyed hair bound into plaits with bloody sinew, and a scar cut across her face from chin to right ear. Her eyes were a piercing ice-blue and Alith resisted the urge to flinch as that cold gaze was directed straight at him. The captain did not see him at all, her eyes staring just past his shoulder at the Ellyrians some distance beyond.

Alith took his bow from the quiver on his shoulder and calmly set an arrow to the string. Pulling up his weapon, he sighted along the shaft, lining up the arrowhead with the captain's throat. Alith enjoyed the tension as he pulled back his right arm. He revelled in the moment, the captain ignorant of her imminent death, the power he held to bring about that fate. A satisfied smile danced briefly on Alith's lips as he watched the druchii turn at some comment from her standard bearer, grinning with teeth filed to sharp points.

Without ceremony, Alith let go of the bowstring. The arrow hit its mark perfectly, spearing through the captain's neck. Blood frothed from her mouth and sprayed from the wound as she collapsed, spattering the other druchii. Shouts of horror rippled through the dark elves and Alith savoured the uncertainty, the panic. Alith silently lowered himself back into the grass and slipped away.

As he crept northwards he spared glances for the work of the other Shadows. Alith watched as company banners fell, sorceresses were pinned by shafts and lieutenants toppled to the ground with grievous wounds. Alith could feel the disconcertion spreading through the druchii ranks, but not all of the Shadows went unobserved. Alith also saw repeater crossbows scything through the long grass with their missiles, and companies of warriors dashing forwards with their spears to hunt down their ambushers.

THOUGH THE ATTACKS of the Shadows caused scattered confusion, the druchii pressed on, sweeping Alith's warriors northwards before them. Thirty of his warriors did not join their leader, their bodies lost out on the field. The black host of Kheranion resolutely advanced into the teeth of the arrowstorm coming from the Ellyrians, forcing Finudel to order his infantry to withdraw towards the river. The reaver knights formed up to protect the retreat as Alith and his Shadows joined the move, stalking unseen alongside the Ellyrian regiments.

Kheranion's commanders split their force, sending a third of their infantry towards the retreating Ellyrians while the remaining spearmen and archers advanced on the reavers, the knights of Anlec ominously shadowing them. Finudel and Athielle ordered their riders south knowing that they could not contend with the enemy's numbers directly. Alith was horrified to see the Ellyrians thus split, the druchii pushing forwards between the two wings of the infantry and cavalry.

Hidden within the high grass on the bank of the Irlana, Alith realised he had made the same mistake. The rest of his army was still at the camp to the south, on the other side of the druchii host. Alith instinctively looked into the storm clouds, seeking Kheranion's presence. He saw the dragon to the west, beating its wings slowly to keep station in the strong wind, drifting southwards above the reavers as the Ellyrians pulled back from the attacking army.

Kheranion's full plan was then revealed. The druchii infantry lengthened their lines, creating a barrier that kept the Ellyrian infantry penned in at the edge of the river. The black-armoured Anlec cavalry came forwards at last, winding columns of grim riders snaking between the companies of spearmen and repeater crossbowmen, their lances lowered. In their hundreds the knights gathered, sinister squadrons of black and silver, their faces hidden behind ornate visors.

'There's nowhere else to run,' said Lierenduir, crouched close at hand to Alith's left. 'Those knights will sweep the Ellyrians into the water.'

'At least that means the Ellyrians are forced to fight,' replied Alith. 'Better that they battle to the last elf than try to flee.'

'What of us?'

Alith looked around, analysing the immediate vicinity. The river broadened to the west where the meadows were flat, opening out into a ford at least five hundred paces wide. On the far side the trees of Athelian Toryr stretched down almost to the northern bank, the depths of the forest hidden in shadow. Alith nodded towards the crossing.

'When the charge comes, head for the ford,' he said. 'We'll disappear into the woods if necessary.'

'What about the others at the camp?'

'There is nothing we can do for them at the moment,' said Alith. 'We can try to draw some of the druchii across the river and into the trees, to buy the others time to head south and join with Caledor.'

Lierenduir looked pained at Alith's fatalism but said nothing, turning his gaze back to the ranks of the Anlec knights. Ellyrians and Naggarothi waited in disturbing silence, each hoping for the other to show some indication of their intent. With several of the druchii magic wielders slain by the Shadows, the storm above was abating, though thunder broke the quiet occasionally and flickers of lightning crawled across the thinning clouds. To the east, shafts of sunlight pierced the gloom, shining from the armour of the reavers. At this distance Athielle was nothing more than a golden gleam amongst the silver and Alith was suddenly concerned for the princess. Against the dark swathe of Nagarythe the army of Ellyrion seemed pitifully few.

Alith thought back to the sweeping bridges and boulevards of Tor Elyr, the white towers that would be blackened and broken if the druchii were victorious. He cared nothing for the city itself, but the memory of his coming there, of meeting Athielle, lingered with him. Her refusal to allow the city to be sacked told Alith all he needed to know about Athielle, of her love for her people and her home. That thought brought more painful memories, of scorched Elanardris and Gerithon nailed upon the door to the manse.

In his mind's eye the two scenes overlapped, so that he saw the arena-hall of Tor Elyr, Finudel and Athielle dead upon their thrones, elves and steeds lying in bloodied heaps around them. Such was the fate they had dared by resisting the druchii, and Alith felt a stab of shame at his harsh words to them. They had chosen to risk all, not for glory or honour, but for survival. Athielle's warning repeated over and over in his mind:

'It is because the druchii despise peace, loathe life, that they must be defeated. If we become the same, we have lost that which we fight for.'

Looking across the meadows of Ellyrion it was as if she said the words again, so clear was her voice to Alith. He fixed his gaze upon that distant shimmer of gold, dismissing the nightmare visions of destruction that haunted him. Then Alith turned his eyes upon the ranks of the druchii, the unending lines of black and purple, the wicked signs upon standards proclaiming their bearers' unfettered depravity.

'Gods curse us all,' he snarled, standing up fully.

The other Shadows cast glances at their leader, brows creased with concern. With an almost lazy slowness, Alith nocked an arrow to his bow and sighted upon the Anlec knights. With a grim smile, he loosed the shaft. He followed its course as it looped over the meadow and struck a knight's horse in the neck. The steed reared and then fell, crushing its rider beneath its dark bulk.

As Alith fitted and loosed another shaft, the Shadows joined him, a ragged volley of arrows arcing towards the knights. Several more of the riders fell to the missiles, their black-armoured corpses tumbling from their saddles.

Alith turned to Khillrallion.

'Give me your hunting horn,' said Alith.

Khillrallion pulled out a curled ram's horn from his belt and ran through the grass to place it in Alith's outstretched hand. Alith looked at the gold bands that coiled around the horn, seeing flickers of lightning reflected in the metal.

Alith lifted the instrument to his lips and blew a note that rose in pitch and then swung into a long bass tone. Squadrons of knights were turning their horses towards the sound, their angry shouts heard even at this distance. Again and again Alith sounded the notes, the Anar call for attack. Tossing the horn back to Khillrallion, Alith knew not whether Tharion would hear the command, or how the captain would respond. All Alith was sure of was that today would not be the day he ran away to fight another day.

Today Alith would stand and fight, and fall if necessary.

ALITH GAVE SILENT praise to Finudel, or perhaps Athielle, as he heard answering horn blows from the Ellyrian host. Spurred into action, the archers on the river bank lifted their weapons and unleashed a salvo against the druchii knights, a shower of white-feathered shafts glittering through the storm gloom. The Shadows added their own arrows to the attack. The spearmen raised their voices in a bold war cry and formed up for the advance.

Ahead of them, the knights of Anlec were thrown into disarray. Alith could see their officers arguing, and judged that they debated whether to confront the threat of the infantry or turn their attention to the hated lord of the Anars that had taunted them. Indecision reigned for a while and the Ellyrian infantry closed in under the cover of a hail of arrows.

Some semblance of order was finally restored and three squadrons of knights wheeled towards Alith, six hundred riders in all. The rest of the cavalry urged their mounts, breaking into a run towards the advancing Ellyrians.

Alith had no time to spare for the coming clash; the knights were bearing down fast upon the Shadows.

'Into the river!' Alith cried, knowing that they would not outpace the riders in a race to the ford.

Alith leaped from the high bank into the flowing waters as the knights broke into a charge. His breath was knocked from him by the cold river, and for a moment the current buffeted and wrestled him beneath the surface. Breaking back into the air, Alith unfastened his cloak, which hung like an anchor from his shoulders. Freed of its constrictions, Alith struck out towards the far shore with confident strokes, the other Shadows around him in a shoal of black and grey, discarded cloaks swirling downriver.

A glance over his shoulder showed Alith that the knights had reined in their mounts at the water's edge, unwilling to plunge into the swirling waters. Insults and curses followed the Shadows as they swam away, before the knights' officers signalled for them to continue west towards the ford.

Halfway across the river, Alith looked to his left, at the receding knights, and tried to judge whether they would complete their circuitous journey to the far side before the Shadows. He was confident that the riders would still be crossing the ford when he set foot on dry land. To the right, the battle between the Ellyrian infantry and the druchii was in full tumult. The other knights had smashed through several of the spear companies already, their path marked by a litter of bodies. From the river's surface, Alith could see nothing of the reavers or his own army and he hoped that they fared well. Knowing that he could do nothing else for the moment, Alith focussed on swimming, driving himself swiftly through the water.

PANTING, ALITH DRAGGED himself through the reeds and pulled himself up onto the northern bank of the Irlana. The other Shadows followed, slipping into the grass like dark otters, glistening with water. Alith shuddered from the wet, the warmth of the sun still kept at bay by the dark clouds, the wind stealing the heat from his body.

'What now, prince?' asked Khillrallion. Alith was taken aback for a moment by the use of his proper title. Bedraggled and cold, he certainly did not feel like a prince. 'Alith? What now?'

Westwards Alith could see the first of the knights surging from the ford amidst spumes of water. Northwards stood the dark forest of Athelian Toryr, sanctuary from the Anlec riders.

'Into the woods,' Alith said, wringing water from his sodden shirt. 'We'll try to lure them into the trees. Get up into the branches and shoot them from out of harm's way.'

The Shadows did not hurry; there was plenty of time to reach the forest before the knights would catch them. They restrung their bows with dry cord taken from waxed pouches, emptied water from their quivers and flicked droplets from the feathers of their arrows in preparation for the fight to come.

They were just over halfway to the trees, perhaps a hundred paces from safety, when the foremost Shadows stopped and signalled for the others to wait. Alith hurried forwards to where Khillrallion was staring beneath the thick canopy of leaves.

'I think I saw something moving,' said Khillrallion.

'*Think* you saw?' said Alith, peering into the darkness. 'Saw what?'

'I don't know,' Khillrallion replied with a shrug. 'A movement in the shadows. See, there it is again!'

Alith followed the direction of Khillrallion's finger under the eaves of the wood. Sure enough, there was something in the darkness, indistinct and motionless. Alith knew immediately what it was: a raven herald.

As he looked, he saw more riders sitting silently in the gloom upon unmoving steeds, little more than patches of deeper black amongst the shadows. Alith could not focus on them and could not accurately judge their number, but at a guess he thought it to be more than several dozen rather than less.

'Morai-heg has a cruel humour,' hissed Alith with another glance westwards. Most of the knights had crossed the river, and the first squadron had formed up and was advancing swiftly and purposefully towards the Shadows.

Khillrallion gave Alith a look of incomprehension.

'Raven heralds,' Alith explained. Khillrallion looked back at the woods with fresh fear, his hand reaching for an arrow. The other Shadows followed his lead as word of the danger spread in whispers, readying their weapons.

'They will have surely seen us,' said Alith. 'Why do they not attack?'

'Perhaps they would prefer to have us run down by the knights rather than risk themselves?'

Alith was not satisfied by this answer and continued to stare at the vague shapes between the trees as if he could discern their intent in some way. The noise of the approaching knights grew louder but Alith refused to take his eyes from the raven heralds. What were they waiting for?

As if in reply, something moved through the tops of the closest trees. A flitting black shape landed on a branch at the edge of the woods. A single crow lifted its head and let out a loud cawing.

Alith laughed for a moment, not quite sure he believed what he saw and heard. The other Shadows were looking at him quizzically as Alith stood up.

'Target the knights,' Alith said, pulling free his bow.

'The heralds will run us down in a heartbeat!' protested Galathrin.

Alith looked at the Shadows, seeing uncertainty in their expressions.

'Trust me,' he said before redirecting his attention to the approaching cavalry, nocking an arrow to his bowstring.

ALITH FELT NOT a moment of doubt as the knights of Anlec broke into a gallop. Everything dropped away: his worries, his fears, his anger. Alith stood in a moment of calm, his breath coming slow and steady, limbs light, movements precise and focussed. As he looked at the approaching riders, Alith saw every detail as if it were frozen in time. Droplets flew from the manes and tails of their horses, surrounding the squadrons in a fine mist. Water glistened on the black rings of the knights' armour. Golden lancetips and silvered helms sparkled with reflected lightning.

At three hundred paces Alith took aim at the knight bearing the banner of the closest squadron, closing fast. The arrow sped into the storm-wracked sky and then fell, striking the charging knight in the head. As he slumped sideways, the standard fell from his grasp but the following knight swayed to one side and snatched up the falling flag before it touched the ground. Alith let fly another arrow, but the wind gusted and carried the shot short to disappear into the grass in front of the knights. Adjusting his aim, Alith shot again, the shaft spinning away from the raised shield of another knight.

At two hundred and fifty paces, the rest of the Shadows were also shooting. Alith reached back and his fingers fell upon a lone flight, the last of his arrows. He took it out with measured slowness and examined its shaft and feathers for any damage. There was none and he fitted it to his bowstring, his hands working without conscious thought.

At two hundred paces, Alith released the string and his final shot soared towards the knights. It struck one of the lead riders in the shoulder of his lance arm, spinning him from his mount to be trampled by the hooves of the following knights. Alith placed his bow in its quiver and drew his sword.

At one hundred and fifty paces Alith saw blackness moving under the trees. The ground was shuddering under the impact of the charging horses, but it was the stillness of the woods that drew his attention. In a long line the raven heralds burst from the woods, eerily silent. Several hundred feather-cloaked riders streamed from between the trees, ghosted by a strange darkness, moving impossibly fast. Behind them came a great flock of beating black wings and raucous cries, hundreds of birds pouring from the woods in a billowing cloud of feathers and snapping beaks.

The raven heralds loosed a volley from their bows as they closed, the squadron of knights closest to the woods thrown into a confusion of falling knights and tumbling horses. Stowing their bows, the riders brought out narrow-bladed spears, tips lowered full-tilt.

At one hundred paces from Alith the raven heralds hit the knights, driving into their flank like a black dagger. Caught utterly unawares, dozens of the Anlec cavalry were cast down by the spears of their attackers. The shrill whinnies of horses and the panicked shouts of elves rebounded from the trees as the raven heralds continued on, cutting through the knights towards the river.

The lead riders turned to see what had happened, dragging their mounts to a standstill.

'Attack!' bellowed Alith, raising his sword and breaking into a run. He did not look to see if the other Shadows followed.

The closest knights twisted left and right, caught between the raven heralds and the Shadows. Alith covered the gap at a full sprint, his blood surging as he sped through the long grass.

One of the knights dragged his horse around and tried to charge but Alith was too close, nimbly leaping aside from the lance point directed towards his chest. With a shout, Alith grabbed the knight's arm and used it as a lever to jump up behind the rider.

Alith drove his sword into the knight's back, the point cleaving through cloak and mail. Tossing the elf's body aside, Alith slipped from the steed's haunch as it galloped on, the knight's dead grip tight on the reins, his body dragged through the grass.

Alith threw himself down as another lance flashed towards him, its point passing a hair's-breadth above his head. Diving between the legs of the knight's steed, Alith swept upwards with his blade, cutting through the cinch of the saddle. With a shout the knight toppled sideways, crashing heavily beside Alith. The Anar prince drove the point of his sword through the knight's visor and then looked for a new foe.

Ahead the fight between the knights and heralds had become a vicious melee. Swords rang against each other and curses were spat. Horses fought as well, flailing hooves and gnashing teeth at one another while their riders slashed and stabbed. It was no place for an elf on foot and Alith kept his distance with the Shadows, looking for stragglers to ambush.

A knight staggered from the fighting, clutching his arm. Blood flowed freely down his mail skirt as he fell to one knee. The Shadows pounced, driving their swords into him. As Alith wrenched his blade from the dead knight's chest, he cast his eye over the battle.

The Anlec cavalry had been beaten on the first charge, yet though they had lost more than half their number they fought on stubbornly. Those of Alith's followers that still had arrows occasionally loosed a shaft into the swirling press of bodies, picking off such targets as presented themselves. Naggarothi corpses of both sides were trampled beneath iron-shod hooves while the wounded tried crawling to safety. The Shadows tended to the injured raven heralds with bandages torn from their cloaks; and to the wounded knights with their swords.

The crows whirled and swooped around the fight, adding to the confusion. They fluttered into the faces of the knights, pecking at exposed lips, digging their beaks into visors seeking eyes. Some of the flock had settled on the corpses, tearing at cloaks and robes, clawing at any exposed skin, peeling strands of bloody flesh from the fallen.

Alith noted that the carrion birds feasted only on the slain knights, avoiding the dozens of raven herald corpses that were heaped in the long grass.

The knights fought to the last elf, a captain clad in ornately etched armour of silver and gold. He had discarded his lance and struck out at his enemies with a long sword whose blade flashed with magical fire, every blow he landed cutting through body or limb with ease. His identity was concealed by a full helm styled in a daemonic, snarling face, his eyes hidden in shadow. As his horse turned and wheeled, the raven heralds pulled back from the druchii officer, a dozen of their number already lying dead around him.

Without any spoken command, several of the riders stowed their spears and brought out their bows as the circle widened around the captain. The druchii realised what was about to happen and kicked his steed into a run, levelling his sword for a final charge. Eight arrows converged on him before he reached the raven heralds, taking him in the head and chest, flinging him ignominiously to the blood-wetted grass amongst those he had slain.

THE RAVEN HERALDS gave no cheers of victory, waved no weapons in celebration. They weaved their horses around the piles of the dead and injured, their speartips seeking any surviving foes. Alith watched without emotion as they plunged their spears into any knights still drawing breath, and then he turned away to look to the south.

Alith could not see much beyond the river, only a chaotic mass of white and black pitted against each other. He saw the banners of Ellyrion mingled with the standards of Nagarythe, and could make little sense of the confusion. Manoeuvre and strategy had played its part, but the battle would ultimately be decided by strength, skill and courage.

A shadow fell across Alith and he looked up into the face of a raven herald. He held a blood-stained spear in his right hand, his arms and gloves slick with crimson. Emerald eyes shone from the depths of his hood and Alith smiled.

'Morai-heg must have some devious plan for me indeed, to save me once again,' said the lord of the Anars.

'It was not The Allseeing One that brought me here,' replied Elthyrior.

'Then by what guidance do you come to my rescue?'

'By the request of Princess Athielle,' said Elthyrior. 'On the first night after our arrival, she asked me to return north and bring back those heralds that still opposed the darkness of Anlec.'

'Your intervention is timely, nonetheless,' said Alith.

'The battle is not yet won,' Elthyrior said, nodding out across the river. 'Finudel and Athielle are attacking and Kheranion makes his final move.'

Alith spun quickly and searched the skies. To the south-east a black shape descended like a thunderbolt. Wings furled, thick vapour streaming from its mouth and nostrils, the black dragon plunged earthwards towards the reavers. For a moment it seemed as if the beast would slam into the ground, but at the last moment its wings flared open and the dragon levelled just above head height, its claws raking a massive furrow through the ranks of the Ellyrian riders, carving through elf and steed alike. As the monster climbed back into the sky it lifted up two more riders, flinging them to a bone-crushing death amongst their kin as it banked away.

Alith saw this destruction at a distance, unmoved until his eyes fell upon the small shape of a golden rider: Athielle. The dragon soared over her reavers, arrows pattering harmlessly from its thick hide.

Alith cast about for a spare steed, for there were many left riderless after the fighting. He ran to the closest, the unarmoured horse of a dead herald, and leaped onto its back.

'What do you think you can achieve, Alith?'

Alith did not reply, but simply urged the horse into a gallop, heading for the ford. He glanced over his shoulder constantly, keeping watch on the dragon as it circled and dived down, mauling yet more Ellyrians before spiralling back towards the clouds. At this distance Alith could hear nothing of the slaughter. The carnage being wrought was like a tableau picked out in a tapestry, a representation of something horrific yet almost beautiful.

Water splashed up Alith's legs as his steed forged across the ford but he did not notice, nor did he feel the bite of the wind on his skin or hear the splash of the river. His eyes were fixed on Athielle and her reavers; Finudel's companies of riders were already driving into the rear of the druchii fighting close to the river. The dragon continued to menace the Ellyrian cavalry; with fang and noxious breath it gouged holes in the reavers. Many of the riders were fleeing the beast, but around Athielle a knot of several hundred held their courage, sending showers of ineffectual arrows towards their monstrous tormentor.

The horse reached the opposite bank and surged up through the reeds, almost toppling Alith. He swayed wildly and as he righted himself his gaze passed to the south. For a moment all thoughts of Athielle and the black dragon were dispelled.

Alith saw his army marching northwards to the aid of the princess, but it was not this that stunned him so. Behind them came another host, many thousands strong, in lines of silver, green and red. Above the army four lithe shapes swept through the air, two red and two a deep blue in colour.

The dragon princes of Caledor!

ALITH CALLED HIS steed to halt with a word and sat in amazement as the four dragons glided effortlessly over the plains, flying so low that their wingtips almost brushed the grass. Fire snaked from their mouths, leaving a trail of grey haze whipped into vortices by their beating wings. Each dragon bore a rider upon a throne, long pennants of red and green streaming from poles and lance tips.

Alith gave a shout of wordless joy at the sight, and then fell silent, admiring the power and grace of the dragons as they swept onwards towards Kheranion's army. The druchii commander seemed unaware of his peril as he and his monstrous steed ravaged Athielle's bodyguard.

Two of the Caledorians broke to the left, heading towards the battle at the river. They flew past Alith barely fifty paces away, gusts of wind from the dragons' wings washing over Alith as they sped on towards their foes. The other two dragon riders peeled to the right, straight towards Kheranion.

THE DRUCHII PRINCE laughed as he plunged his lance through the gut of another Ellyrian. Beneath him, Bloodfang tore and ripped and shredded with teeth and claws, revelling in the slaughter. Kheranion fixed his eyes upon the gold-armoured princess, imagining the agonising delights he would visit upon her that night. He would take her alive, and her brother, and shame them both before handing their broken remains to the priests and priestesses of Khaine.

With this in mind, Kheranion wrenched back on the gilded chains that served as Bloodfang's reins, arms straining to pull in the beast's bloodthirsty enthusiasm. The dragon swept a rider from his horse with raking claws and looked back at its master, lips rippling with annoyance.

'Do not harm the princess!' Kheranion commanded. 'She is mine!'

Bloodfang gave a growl of disappointment but offered no argument, turning his bloody attentions back on the Ellyrians. His jaws snapped shut around the head of a horse, decapitating it in one bite. A lash of Bloodfang's barbed tail speared three more riders, buckling breastplates, smashing ribs and pulverising vital organs.

The path was almost clear to Athielle; barely a dozen more reavers stood in Kheranion's way. He could see the princess clearly as she fixed him with a contemptuous stare from beneath the flowing waves of her long hair. Kheranion wondered how defiant she would be when that hair had been cut from her scalp and her beautiful features had felt the caress of a dozen blades. The prospect sent a thrill of excitement through the prince and he urged Bloodfang forwards again.

Bloodfang took a step, striking out with a clawed wing to send more knights tumbling, and then stopped. The dragon arched his neck, nostrils flaring, and then turned suddenly to the left.

'What are you doing?' demanded Kheranion, heaving back on the chains with all of his strength.

Bloodfang ignored his question and bunched his muscles, ready to spring into the air. Kheranion quickly cast about for the source of the dragon's distemper. Looking south the prince saw two immense shapes hurtling through the sky towards him.

'Khaine's bloody mercies,' Kheranion whispered as Bloodfang hurled himself into the air, the dragon's wings creating a downdraught that sent riders tumbling, toppling horses to their flanks. Kheranion could feel his mount's heart thundering, hammer-like vibrations pounding through the seat of the prince's saddle-throne and along his spine. Bloodfang's breaths came in stentorian blasts, clouds of oily vapour forming a fog around rider and beast as the dragon strove to gain more height.

The foremost dragon rolled right and then turned sharply left, the prince atop its back angling his long lance over the monster's neck. Bloodfang twisted away and the lance bit through the membrane of his right wing, ripping a large and ragged hole in the scaled skin. In a flash the dragon flew behind them, crashing its tail against Bloodfang's flanks as it passed.

The other Caledorian steered his mount higher and the great creature folded its wings into a stoop, coming at Bloodfang from above. Kheranion twisted in his saddle and set the butt of his magical lance against Bloodfang's flesh to absorb the impact, angling the point towards the approaching dragon prince. Bloodfang's wounded wing spasmed and faltered in its beat, sending the dragon lurching to the right, taking Kheranion's lance tip away from his foe.

Kheranion stared at his rival. The Caledorian's snarling face was framed with a shock of platinum blond hair that streamed back in the wind of the dragon's descent. There was nothing but anger in the prince's deep blue eyes as they met the druchii's gaze. Kheranion met that gaze with a curse upon his lips, a moment before the Caledorian's lance hit home.

Its tip sheared through Kheranion's breastplate in an explosion of magical fire, piercing a lung and shattering his spine. The prince was already dead as the impact lifted him from his throne, breaking his legs as he was torn free from the lacquered straps that had secured him there. His grip broke and the chains fell from his dead grasp. The Caledorian twisted his lance with a flick of his wrist, sending Kheranion's body spiralling to the ground far below.

The first dragon circled around and raked its claws across Bloodfang's snout, shredding skin in a spray of thick scales. Bloodfang gave a roar and spewed forth an immense cloud of poisonous gas. Pumping his wings, blood streaming from the injury, the black dragon turned and raced away, heading for the Inner Sea.

Rising into the clouds, freed of Kheranion's mastery, Bloodfang fled.

—◄ SEVENTEEN ►—

A Bitter Fate

WITH ANELTAIN AS escort, Alith rode into the Caledorian camp. He had already met with Tharion and learned that over four hundred of his warriors had fallen in battle and more than twice that number were badly wounded. The arrival of the Caledorians had turned the balance, but the druchii had fought on fiercely, breaking only as the sun dipped towards dusk. The army of Anlec had fled back towards the pass, pursued by the vengeful reaver knights and the dragon princes.

There was an air of celebration in the encampment. Fires burned and songs and laughter drifted between the red and white tents. The pavilion of the dragon princes rose high above the rest of the camp, its roof held up by three mighty poles, flags of Caledor streaming from their tips.

Warriors came to take their horses as they dismounted outside the open flaps of the huge tent. Entering, Alith found himself in a swirl of elves; Caledorian and Ellyrian. The conversation was animated, eyes were bright and faces flushed with victory and wine. The four dragon princes were holding court at the centre of the pavilion, still bedecked in their blood-spattered armour. With them stood Athielle and Finudel, smiles upon their faces.

All turned at Alith's approach, but it was Athielle's reaction that he noticed. Her expression grew sombre and she stepped away, placing her brother between her and Alith. Before Alith could speak one of the Caledorians interrupted, his voice deep, his tone unwelcoming.

'What do we have here?' said the prince, his deep blue eyes gauging Alith coolly.

'I am Alith Anar, prince of Nagarythe.'

'A Naggarothi?' replied the Caledorian with a dubious eyebrow raised, recoiling slightly from Alith's presence.

'He is our ally, Dorien,' said Finudel. 'Were it not for Alith's actions I fear your arrival would have found us already dead.'

The Caledorian prince regarded Alith with contempt, head cocked to one side. Alith returned the look with equal disgust.

'Alith, this is Prince Dorien,' said Finudel, breaking the awkward silence that had rippled out through the nearby elves. 'He is the younger brother of King Caledor.'

Alith did not react to this, meeting Dorien's stare.

'What of Elthyrior?' Athielle asked, stepping past her brother. Alith broke his gaze from Dorien to look at her. 'Where is he?'

'I do not know,' Alith replied with a shake of the head. 'He is where Morai-heg leads him. The raven heralds took their dead and vanished into Athelian Toryr. You may never see him again.'

'Anar?' said one of the other Caledorians. 'I have heard this name, from prisoners we took at Lothern.'

'And what did they say?' asked Alith.

'That the Anars marched beside Malekith and resisted Morathi,' replied the prince. He extended a hand. 'I am Thyrinor, and I welcome you to our camp, even if my intemperate cousin will not.'

Alith shook the proffered hand quickly. Dorien snorted and turned away, calling for more wine. As he marched off through the crowd, Alith saw that the prince walked with a limp.

'He is in a grumpy mood,' said Thyrinor. 'I think he has broken his leg, but he refuses to allow the healers to look at it. He's still full of fire and blood after the battle. Tomorrow he will be calmer.'

'We are grateful for your aid,' said Athielle. 'Your arrival is more than we could have hoped for.'

'We were brought word of the druchii marching along the pass four days ago and set out immediately,' said Thyrinor. 'I regret that we cannot stay here, for we are needed in Chrace. The enemy have all but overrun the mountains and the king sails with his army to thwart them at the border with Cothique. Tomorrow we continue north and then through Avelorn to strike at the druchii from the south. Today is an important victory, and Caledor recognises the sacrifices made by the people of Ellyrion.'

Alith suppressed a snort of derision, turning away to hide his expression of disgust. What did these folk know of sacrifice?

'Alith?' said Athielle, and he felt the princess at his shoulder. He turned back to her.

'I am sorry,' said Alith. 'I cannot share your enthusiasm for today's victory.'

'I would think you happy that Kheranion is dead,' said Finudel, joining his sister. 'Is that not some measure of payment for your father?'

'No,' Alith said quietly. 'Kheranion died swiftly.'

Athielle and Finudel fell silent, shocked by Alith's words. Thyrinor stepped up beside Finudel, proffering a goblet towards Alith. The Naggarothi prince took it reluctantly.

'Victories have been few for us,' said the Caledorian. He raised his own glass in toast to Alith. 'I give you my thanks for your efforts and those of your warriors. Were the king here, I am sure he would offer you the same.'

'I do not fight for your praise,' said Alith.

'Then what do you fight for?' asked Thyrinor.

Alith did not reply immediately, aware of the coldness that gripped his heart and the warmth of Athielle so close at hand. He looked at the princess, gaining a small amount of comfort from the sight.

'Forgive me,' Alith said, forcing a slight smile. 'I am weary. Wearier than you can possibly imagine. Ellyrion and Caledor battle for their freedom and I should not judge you for matters that are not your responsibility.'

Alith took a mouthful of the wine within. It was dry, almost tasteless, but he feigned a nod of appreciation. He raised the goblet beside Thyrinor's and fixed his gaze upon the Caledorian.

'May you win all of your battles and end this war!' Alith declared. His eyes flickered to Athielle to gauge her reaction, but her expression was unreadable, her brow slightly furrowed, lips pursed.

'We should not impose upon you any longer,' said Finudel, guiding Athielle away with a touch on her arm. She gave a last glance at Alith before being steered into the crowd of Caledorian nobles.

Alith returned his stare to Thyrinor.

'Will you fight to the last, against all hope?' Alith asked. 'Will your king give his life to free Ulthuan?'

'He will,' replied Thyrinor. 'You think that you alone have reason enough to fight the druchii? You are wrong, so very wrong.'

The prince left Alith with his thoughts, calling his cousin's name. Alith stood motionless for a while, staring into his cup. The red wine reminded him of blood, its taste still bitter upon his tongue. He wanted to let the goblet drop from his fingers and leave, to put as much distance as he could between himself and these nobles of Ellyrion and Caledor. They fought the druchii, and they spoke fine words against them, but they did not understand. None of them truly knew what they fought against.

As he looked at the elves within the tent, hiding his disdain, Alith spied a familiar face: Carathril. The herald was stood somewhat apart from the crowd, his expression one of discomfort. Carathril met Alith's gaze and waved him over.

'You are the last person I expected to see here,' said Alith as Carathril gestured to a bench and sat down. Alith stayed on his feet.

'It seems I am destined to serve another king as herald,' Carathril replied heavily.

'And is he a king you serve gladly?'

Carathril considered this, his expression pensive.

'He is a leader of action and not words,' the herald said. 'As the commander of our armies, I would wish for no other.'

'And when the war is over?'

'That is not yet our concern,' said Carathril. 'It would be unwise to worry about a future so uncertain. You would do well, Alith, to align yourself with Caledor. He has strength, and determination in abundance. With his aid, your lands in Nagarythe can be restored.'

'I have learnt well the harsh lessons of the last few years,' said Alith. 'A ruler can no more reign through the power of others than a cloud can move against the wind. We looked to Malekith and he could do nothing to halt the doom of the Anars. We turned to Bel Shanaar and he failed us. I have no more time for kings.'

'Surely you would not fight against Caledor?' Carathril said with genuine horror.

'In truth? I cannot say,' Alith said with a shrug. 'The future of Nagarythe is my only concern; let your king and his princes do what they will. I am the last loyal prince of Nagarythe and I will restore the rule of the righteous to my realm. Caledor has no sway over the Naggarothi, only from their own can they be led.'

WHILE DORIEN LED his Caledorians northwards, Alith chose to stay in Ellyrion. His army had suffered much and even he could see that they were in no position to wage further war for the time being. With Finudel and Athielle's permission, the Naggarothi built a camp on the plains not far from Tor Elyr and spent the winter recovering their strength.

The conversation with Carathril had unsettled Alith and raised many questions he did not yet know how to answer. Where would he fight, and for what cause?

He certainly could not bow his knee to a Caledorian, for all that others spoke highly of the new Phoenix King. The rivalry between Nagarythe and Caledor was ingrained, an unconscious suspicion of the southerners. The debacle with Bel Shanaar had proven to Alith that the title of Phoenix King was worthless; he could no more fight for a foreigner's crown than he could give his life for a blade of grass or the leaf of a tree.

Alith cared little for the fate of the Tiranocii, when he even spared a thought for them. They had sown the seeds of their own doom; the weakness of their leaders had brought about the occupation. While Bel Shanaar had reigned, Tiranoc had revelled in its status, its princes and nobles growing powerful and rich from their positions. Bel Shanaar was dead and now they looked to the east and south, to a Phoenix King from Caledor to save them. Tiranoc's fall of fortune was not lost on Alith, but he had no sympathy for the kingdom.

Ellyrion was a different matter. The Ellyrians had fought the druchii, and suffered the consequences of their opposition with the death of thousands. Alith also had enough self-awareness to recognise that his regard for Ellyrion was also due in part to his feelings for Athielle. But Ellyrion was not his home. He felt uncomfortable on the wide plains, exposed beneath the blue sky.

While the wounded healed and Tharion set about the reorganisation of the Anar regiments, Alith brooded alone, often riding out to the Annulii to walk in the foothills and contemplate his fate. He hoped that he would meet Elthyrior, but the raven herald remained unseen.

Pathless and lost, Alith taunted himself with memories of Elanardris in flames, of his father's death and the torments his grandfather undoubtedly suffered in the dungeons beneath Anlec. No course of action he conceived brought comfort to Alith; no destiny he could lay out for himself brought the answers he sought.

As summer, hot and beautiful, fell upon Ellyrion, Alith's mood changed. The shining sun and the verdant grassland turned his thoughts to Athielle, and he felt a deep longing to see her again, to know how she fared. Just as he had doubted himself that moment in the gardens with Milandith, Alith wondered if it was weakness to indulge the feelings he had for the princess.

IT WAS WITH a mixture of reluctance and excitement that he rode to the capital alone, having sent word to Athielle and Finudel that he wished to discuss the progress of the war. In truth the wider war was irrelevant to Alith. Neither side had won any great victory nor suffered any terrible loss. Only two battles had been fought since the engagement on the Ellyrion plain, both on the borders of druchii-assaulted Chrace. For the moment it seemed that both sides were content to maintain their current positions, building their strength further.

Alith was greeted with little ceremony, as he had requested in his letter. Retainers of Finudel met him at the edge of Tor Elyr and rode with him in silence to the central palaces. A small delegation led by Aneltain waited for the Anar lord in the amphitheatre and took him to a circular hallway in the north of the palace.

Finudel sat alone to one side of the hall, which was lined with curving benches in readiness for audience. High windows allowed the sun to stream down in shafts, casting rainbows upon the white floor. Reaver pennants hung between the windows, tattered and stained, honouring those that had given their lives in the war. Alith could not count their number; there were hundreds of them, perhaps thousands even, each marking the death of a brave knight.

Finudel looked up with a smile as the small group approached. He wore a light robe of white decorated with intricately flowing lines of blue and gold thread that made Alith think of the rising sun shining on waves. Finudel stood and nodded in greeting.

'Welcome, Alith,' said the prince. 'I hope that you are in good health.'

'I am,' replied Alith. He looked around the room, confused. 'Where is Athielle?'

Finudel's smile faded and he gestured for Aneltain and the others to leave. When they had gone, he motioned for Alith to sit on the bench opposite him. Alith did so, a frown creasing his brow.

'The princess? I wished to speak with you both.'

'I do not think that is wise,' said Finudel.

'Oh?'

Finudel looked out of the nearest window for a moment, gaze distant, clearly uncomfortable with what he was about to say. When he looked back at Alith his jaw was sternly set but there was sympathy in his eyes.

'I know that it is my sister that you really come to see,' said the Ellyrian prince, measuring every word, eyes searching Alith's face for reaction. 'I have seen the way that you look at her, and I am surprised you have kept yourself from Tor Elyr for so long.'

'My duties as a–' began Alith but Finudel cut him off.

'You deny yourself on purpose,' said Finudel. 'You think of your feelings for Athielle as a weakness, a distraction. You have doubts, about yourself and about her. That is natural.'

'I'm sure th–'

'Let me finish!' Finudel's tone was abrupt but softly spoken. He lifted a finger to emphasise his point. 'Athielle is quite taken with you as well, Alith.'

Alith felt a flutter in his chest as he heard these words, the stirrings of a long-dead feeling: hope.

'She will not say what occupies her thoughts, even to me, but it is plain that she wishes to see you again,' Finudel continued. 'No doubt she has some foolish notion that the two of you might have some kind of future together.'

'Why are such thoughts foolish?' said Alith.

'Because you are not a good match for her,' said Finudel, his expression apologetic but certain.

'I am a prince of Ulthuan, let me remind you,' said Alith hotly. 'Though my lands have been taken away, one day I will restore Elanardris to its former glory. There is not a prince on the isle who has not suffered some misfortune and waning of circumstance in this war.'

Finudel shook his head, disappointed.

'I do not speak of title or lands or power, Alith,' he said. 'It is *you* that is not a match for my sister. What would you offer her? Would you take her to Nagarythe, a bleak and cold land, and ask her to leave her people and join yours? Would you be content to allow her to stay here in Tor Elyr while you pursue this vengeful course you have taken? Allow her to drift about this palace, pining for your return, uncertain whether you lived or died?'

Alith opened his mouth to rebut the accusations, but Finudel continued.

'I am not finished! There is another course that you could follow. Athielle obviously cares nothing for your loss of power, or your lack of lands and subjects. It is *you* that enamours her. I cannot fathom her thoughts sometimes. Perhaps it is because the two of you are as night and day that you feel drawn together. Who can understand the twisted paths our hearts follow? If you feel as I think you do, you must ask yourself what you are prepared to sacrifice for her.'

'I would give my life for your sister,' said Alith, surprising himself, though Finudel merely shook his head.

'No, you would give your death for her, and that is not the same thing,' said the prince. 'Would you renounce any claims to your title in Nagarythe, and live here in Ellyrion? You cling to your revenge like a child clings to its mother, seeking some meaning from its emptiness. Would you resolve to banish the dark memories that haunt you, which drive you to seek the deaths of your enemies? Could you do such things even if you desired it?'

'I cannot change who I am,' said Alith.

'Cannot or will not?'

Alith stood and paced away, frustrated by Finudel's words.

'What right have you to make such demands?' Alith demanded.

'I do not make these demands for myself, but for my sister,' Finudel replied calmly. 'Do not tell me that you have not asked these questions of yourself. Surely you are not so obsessed with this bloody quest of yours that you thought Athielle would merely fit her future around yours?'

Alith growled, but his anger was not for Finudel, it was for himself. The prince's words, his doubts, gave voice to a lingering dread that had existed within Alith since he had first seen Athielle.

'You present me with a choice I cannot make,' said Alith. 'At least not here, not now.'

'It is a choice you have already made,' said Finudel. 'You simply need to recognise which way your heart has cast its vote. I have a suite of rooms already prepared for you, you can stay here as long as you wish provided that you do not try to contact or see Athielle. It would be a cruelty to stir her hopes if you do not intend to live up to them.'

'Thank you for the hospitality, but I do not think I can remain so close to Athielle without seeing her,' said Alith. 'Should I wish to meet her, I have the means to do so despite your precautions and guards. I do not want to go against your wishes, but I do not trust myself to leave her alone, so I will not stay.'

Alith quit the hall and found Aneltain waiting outside. The Ellyrian, normally talkative and inquisitive, remained quiet as he saw Alith's troubled look. He called for Alith's horse to be brought from the stables and they waited in silence.

Mounting his steed, Alith turned back towards Aneltain and extended a hand in farewell. The Ellyrian gripped it firmly and patted Alith on the arm.

'I feel that I will not see you again for some time, Alith, if at all,' said Aneltain.

'You may be right,' said Alith. 'Take care of the prince and princess, and of yourself. Though I cannot claim to be your friend, I wish you every fortune in the dark times ahead. Stay strong, and as you enjoy the sun and the light, think of us that must dwell in the darkness. I must go. The shadows beckon me.'

Alith rode away without another glance back, at Aneltain or the palace where Athielle remained. Did she perhaps look out of a window high on a tower and see him leave? Did she stand at a doorway, watching him go, perhaps not realising that he had no intention of returning?

Probably not, Alith told himself with a bitter chuckle. It had been a fantasy, a sliver of a dream that had brought him here, but Finudel had been absolutely right. He could not leave the shadows while the druchii remained, and he would not drag Athielle down into the darkness. Love was simply not part of Alith's future.

Only emptiness remained.

━━◄ EIGHTEEN ►━━

The Call of Kurnous

ALITH RODE NORTH for several days, unwilling to return to his Naggarothi and wanting to get far away from Tor Elyr: from Athielle. He made no haste as he rode. There had been a time when he would have enjoyed the sun above, the fresh air and the wild meadows. Now he did not even see them. His thoughts were ever inward as he tried to wrestle a spark of bright truth from the darkness that had enveloped his heart.

As soon as he had left Tor Elyr Alith had known that he would not return for Athielle. Finudel had been correct, there was no life for him here; no life that he could share with Athielle. Across the mountains, Elanardris was a burnt ruin, his family destroyed, his people slaughtered or scattered. There was nothing in the world that Alith could hold on to, draw strength from. Like a leaf bobbing upon a bubbling stream, Alith was adrift on a current of violence and strife, unable to choose his course or destination.

Northwards Alith rode for day after day, guided by nothing more than a whim. He hunted rabbit and deer on the plains and kept away from the mountains, which were so like Elanardris and yet not his ancestral home.

Sometimes he rode by night and did not sleep, other times he meandered for days on end, fishing and hunting, not moving north nor turning back south. He did not count the sunrises and sunsets and lost track of how much time had passed since he had left Tor Elyr. It did not matter.

One sun-drenched afternoon, Alith saw a huge forest to the north-east and he turned his mount towards it. Following the curve of the Annulii, Alith headed towards Avelorn, the realm of the Everqueen.

* * *

TALL AND ANCIENT were the trees of Avelorn, growing upon the far bank of the winding river Arduil that marked the boundary of Ellyrion. It was a remarkable change of scenery. On the south-west banks the land mounded upwards into the plains and meadows of the horse-folk; on the far side a dark mass of foliage obscured the whole horizon, the tips of the mountains only dimly seen far beyond the immense spread of leaves.

Alith called his horse to a halt on the near bank of the river and looked out over the clear waters to the gloomy forest. Brightly coloured birds fluttered from branch to branch, their screeches and shrill chirps unwelcoming. Furred things snuffled in the undergrowth searching for roots and berries. Honeybees the size of Alith's thumb hummed to and fro, moving across the last blossoms clinging to the branches.

Alith was filled with a melancholy air. It was not so sharp as the depression that had often gripped him since Black Fen. There was no bitterness in his mood, only an ennui brought upon him by the doleful scene played out across the river. Avelorn was neither bright nor dark; it simply was what it was. Though a brisk wind blew across the plains at Alith's back, the branches of Avelorn remained motionless, still and quiet, sombre for eternity.

Birthplace of the elves, some philosophers had called it. The spiritual heart of Ulthuan; blessed by Isha and ruled over by the Everqueen. Alith had no desire to meet Avelorn's mysterious lady. His life of late had been full enough of princes and kings and queens. Alith's whim had brought him this far, to the furthest extent of Ellyrion, but he felt no inclination to go any further. Likewise, he had no desire to turn away, for southwards lay only more strife and the distracting presence of Athielle.

He sat for the rest of the afternoon watching the forest, seeing it change as the sun set. The shadows lengthened and the gloom deepened. In the twilight, feral eyes glittered from the dark, watching Alith closely. The day birds roosted and fell quiet, their cries replaced by the haunting calls of owls and night falcons. The underbrush came alive with a multitude of small animals; mice and shrews and other creatures ventured out under the cover of darkness.

There came a sound that sent a shiver down Alith's spine, of excitement rather than fear. It was the howl of a wolf, soon raised in chorus with other lupine voices. It came from the right, to the east, and moved closer. Alith turned his gaze in the direction of the sound but could see nothing between the dark boles of the trees.

A crash of leaves and snap of branches drew his attention, and Alith glimpsed a flash of movement. Something white leapt over a bush and disappeared behind a tree. Alith followed its progress and a moment later saw it in full: a white stag.

It swiftly disappeared from sight and the growl of the wolves grew louder. Unthinking, drawn by some instinct within him, Alith dismounted and waded into the river, following the noise. Soon the water was too deep to wade and he struck out with powerful strokes. His bow and sword were still in his pack on the horse's back, but he gave them no thought. He was filled with the urge to follow the stag.

A warm breeze sighed against Alith as he pulled himself onto the far bank, using the root of a tree for purchase. The wolves were close now; Alith fancied he could hear their panting and the pad of feet on mulch. Without hesitation he plunged into the undergrowth and entered Avelorn.

ALITH HEADED IN the direction in which he had last seen the white stag. At an easy run, he cut along winding trails and leapt over sprawling roots. The howl of a wolf echoed close at hand, to his left, and was answered from his right. Ignoring the hunting pack, he ran on, swift and sure.

The last of the sun disappeared and plunged Alith into darkness. His eyes quickly adjusted and he did not slow his pace, feeling his way between the rearing trunks of the ancient trees as much as he guided himself by sight. Now and then he glimpsed white ahead of him and he quickened his pace, until he was short of breath from the exertion.

Snarls and growls surrounded Alith but he was heedless of their threat. He had been seeking a guide and the stag had come to him. He was determined that this time he would find out where it wanted him to go.

Alith broke into a small clearing and stumbled to a halt. The stag was stood just ten paces away, head tossing as it sensed the wolf pack closing in. Alith glanced to his left and right and saw silvery wisps encircling the clearing; the flash of yellow eyes and the heavy pant of the wolves were all around him.

As one the pack advanced to the edge of the clearing. He counted fifteen wolves, and there were others still moving around the periphery. The stag stood rigid, eyes wide with panic, muscles quivering with exhaustion. It lowered its head and scuffed the leaf-strewn ground with a hoof.

The wolves glared at Alith and the stag from the bushes, pacing back and forth, uncertain. A few sat on their haunches and watched patiently, tongues lolling from their mouths. They were the largest wolves Alith had seen, their fur a mix of dark grey and glittering silver. He felt the piercing gaze of their opal eyes upon him, gauging him, watching for any weakness.

'The two-legs is lost,' growled a voice behind Alith. He spun to see a massive wolf stalking into the clearing. It was almost as tall as the stag, its shoulders as high as Alith's chest. Its fur was thick, a deep ruff of black running down its back, its tail thick and bushy. As it spoke, Alith saw fangs as long as his fingers, each as sharp as a dagger point. All these things Alith noted in an instant, but the creature's eyes kept his attention. They were a bright yellow and seemed to flicker with orange flames.

'Smell fish,' said another wolf. The beasts spoke in the language of Kurnous, the same tongue Alith used with the hawks of the mountains. 'Crossed river.'

The pack leader, for such was the black-maned wolf, took another pace, ears flicking.

'Our hunt,' the wolf said. It took a moment for Alith to realise the wolf was addressing him.

Alith glanced over his shoulder at the stag, which was standing motionless a few paces behind him. It appeared calm, one eye fixed on Alith.

'My hunt,' said Alith. 'Stag is mine. Follow long time.'

The blackmane snarled, lips rippling away from its savage teeth.

'Your hunt? No fangs. No hunt.'

Alith drew his hunting knife from his belt and held it in front of him.

'One fang,' he said. 'Sharp fang.'

The wolves yapped and wagged their tails in amusement and the leader padded even closer, standing only a few paces from Alith, muscles taut, tail rigid.

'Sharp fang, yes,' said the leader. 'We many fangs. Our hunt. You prey.'

The rustle of leaves betrayed other wolves advancing into the clearing, growing in confidence. Alith could not defend himself against all of them. He looked again at the stag, mind racing. He recalled the words of Elthyrior – that he should not second-guess the gods but should follow the instincts they had placed within him. He remembered also the shrine to Kurnous where he had first seen the white stag. It was a place of sacrifice, where the slain were laid upon the altar of the Hunter God. The black flash of Kurnous's rune upon the stag's breast burned in Alith's mind.

Kurnous was the god of the hunter, not the hunted. The stag was his gift to Alith.

'My hunt!' snapped Alith.

He leapt towards the stag and threw his left arm over its neck even as he drove the point of his knife into the rune of Kurnous, plunging its blade deep into the deer's heart. The stag leapt away, breaking from Alith's grasp, blood spuming from the wound. Taking a faltering step the stag fell to its side, back arched, and within moments was dead.

A cacophony of growls and barks surrounded Alith as he turned on the wolf leader, bloodied blade in hand.

'One fang, sharp fang,' Alith said. He strode to the stag and grabbed an antler, pulling up the animal's head. 'Plenty food. Our kill.'

The blackmane stopped, muscles bunching to lunge. It eyed the dead deer and then Alith's knife.

'Our kill?' said the wolf.

Alith let go of the antler and knelt beside the carcass, cutting around the wound he had inflicted. He pulled free a hunk of raw flesh and tossed it towards the blackmane.

'Our kill,' Alith said again, cutting more meat for himself. He waited until the pack leader took the offered meat, gulping it down in one mouthful. Alith took a deep bite, the still-warm blood dribbling over his chin, coating his hands. He could feel the power of the stag passing into him, firing his senses.

Cautiously the wolves approached. Alith stood up and stepped away, blood smeared on his clothes. The spirit of Kurnous raged within him, setting his heart to pounding, relishing the taste of the deer in his mouth.

As the wolves set upon the body of the white stag, Alith raised his head and howled.

WAKING SHARPLY, ALITH felt hot breath on his cheek and warmth all around him. He opened his eyes and glanced around, finding himself in the dimness of a cave, the early sun creeping through the entrance. The wolf pack lay around him, their breaths and snores reverberating quietly around the cavern. He was laid between two of the beasts, close but not touching.

The iron taste of blood filled his mouth and Alith licked his dry lips. He became aware of his own nudity, his exposed flesh slicked with cracking patches of dried crimson. His hands were similarly stained, blood beneath his fingernails and worked into the creases between his fingers. Blood smeared the muzzles of the wolves around him and matted the fur of their chests.

Alith remembered nothing of the night before, save for flashes of red, the tear of skin and the crack of bones. He dimly recalled the exultation he had felt, the victory of the kill that eclipsed his pleasure of any other hunt. Though he found his surroundings strange, he sensed no threat, no discomfort. No guilt. Some part of him that had lain hidden had been awoken, given freedom to show itself for the first time. He felt its aftertouch lingering inside, a savagery and fierce joy that had taken control of him but was for the moment sated.

Sitting up slowly, Alith discovered he still wore his belt, bloodied knife sheathed at his waist. Beyond the cave entrance he saw a wall of trees and ferns, blocking all sight beyond a dozen paces. He heard the gushing of a waterfall close by and the sound stirred in him a deep thirst.

Delicately, Alith stood, careful not to wake the wolves around him. As he picked his way between the slumbering hunters, he spied the enormous form of the blackmane, sprawled languidly next to a large female at the centre of the cave. Seeing the pack leader brought back the memory of his confrontation and he shivered at the recollection, realising that he had been but a heartbeat away from sharing the fate of the white stag.

Stepping out into the dawn Alith was surprised he felt no chill, unclothed as he was. The sun barely peeked through the treetops but he was warmed with a heat from inside.

Alith turned to his right, following the sound of water. The ground outside the cave was scuffed and marked by the paw prints of much use and the reek of the wolves' spoor was heavy in the air. The cave was a split in a rearing grey cliff face hung with ivy and other creeping plants. Far above

Alith's head, more trees grew at the top of the butte, their roots jutting over the edge. Walking along its base, he came to a shallow pool, fed by a beck that tumbled down a gully etched through the cliff face.

Alith squatted by the pool and dipped his hands into the clear water. It was cold and refreshing and he splashed his face and the back of his neck, the sensation sending a thrilling ripple across his skin. Though his thirst was sharp, Alith washed away the stains from his bloody feast before raising a cupped hand to his mouth. A waft of hot breath struck his back and Alith whirled, water flying from his fingers.

Blackmane stood barely two paces away, several other wolves not far behind their leader. Droplets of water glistened on the fur of Blackmane's face. He looked up at Alith with his head cocked to one side.

'Young sun, early to wake,' growled Blackmane. 'Two-legs leave?'

Blackmane's hackles were rising and he ran his thick tongue over blood-stained teeth. It was clear that Blackmane still wanted to kill him.

'Thirst,' replied Alith, glancing back at the pool. 'Not leaving.'

'You hunt, you kill with pack,' said Blackmane. 'One of pack?'

Alith paused and in the moment of hesitation, Blackmane took a step. Alith held his ground, knowing that to show the slightest sign of weakness would be to invite attack. The other wolves regarded Alith with curiosity, but he felt no animosity from them. It did not matter, Blackmane would be more than a match for Alith if he chose to fight.

'One of pack,' Alith said.

'Who pack leader?' demanded Blackmane, advancing another step.

'You pack leader,' said Alith.

Blackmane snapped his jaw a couple of times and settled back, haunches tensing, his tail curling over his back.

'Show me!' snarled the wolf.

Alith was at a loss for a moment, until he saw the other wolves behind Blackmane cringing from their leader, dropping their bellies to the ground, their ears flattened against their heads. Alith did as best he could, falling to all fours and resting his chest on the dirt, his eyes fixed on Blackmane.

The pack leader straightened, towering over Alith. His eyes narrowed with suspicion and Alith met his gaze, not daring to move in the slightest. After some considerable time, Blackmane relaxed, ears flicking, and stepped away.

'Drink,' said Blackmane, before turning his back on Alith and stalking back to the cave.

Alith breathed a sigh of relief and sat back, his heart hammering. One of the other wolves approached him, a female with a silver streak along the top of her muzzle, and Alith tensed again, expecting another confrontation. None came, and the wolf licked his chin and cheek, her heavy tongue rasping against Alith's skin.

Turning back to the pool, Alith dipped in his hand once again and finally took a mouthful of water. Fighting the urge to drink heavily, Alith drank a few more mouthfuls and then stood. He reached down and stroked the head of the nearest wolf, scratching it behind the ear.

'One of the pack,' the wolf said, tail wagging. Some of the other wolves gave reassuring whufs and gathered around Alith, rubbing their furred bodies against him. Guided by his four-legged companions, Alith returned to the cave.

—◄ NINETEEN ►—

Child of the Wolf and the Moon

ALITH SLEPT WITH the wolves for most of the day and woke as the sun was setting. He felt calm; a peace had descended upon him that he had not felt for many years. Stretching, he returned to the pool for another drink while the rest of the pack roused themselves for the next hunt.

Blackmane was amongst the last to wake, the fierce pack leader prowling from the cave, still suspicious of Alith. Alith deferentially dropped to his hands and knees without thought as Blackmane stalked past towards the water.

Rays of dusk streamed through the treetops as the wolves gathered around Blackmane. The pack headed northwards at a steady pace and Alith kept up with them with ease. Not far from the cave, the pack split, some of the wolves heading off in pairs, others alone. In this way they could cover more ground searching for a potential kill.

Alith could only follow their lead, staying close to the older female that had befriended him that morning. Her fur was a speckled dark and light grey that reflected the light, and Alith named her Silver. He had also dubbed a few others from instantly recognisable features: Snowtail; Broken Fang; Old Grey; One Ear; Scar. The others of the pack were still indistinguishable from each other in Alith's eyes.

From what he knew of wolves, most of the pack would be the offspring of Blackmane and Old Grey; a few of the others were stragglers like himself adopted by the pair. More than half were male, and they were of all ages, Blackmane and Old Grey being the eldest, with several young that Alith judged to be little more than a year old. The youngest playfully danced and wrestled with each other, swiping their paws across the muzzles of their rivals in mock fights, nipping at each other's necks and hindquarters in practice for killing prey.

Alith faced another difficulty in communicating with his new companions. They rarely spoke in Kurnous's tongue, preferring to express themselves with stance and position, the subtleties of which were entirely lost on Alith. He had already learnt not to meet Blackmane's eye; doing so always drew bared fangs and the need for Alith to quickly fall to his stomach in appeasement. Alith was most perturbed by this, as none of the other wolves seemed to suffer Blackmane's wrath so vehemently. As he ran alongside Silver, he pondered why Blackmane had allowed Alith to join at all if the pack leader felt such antipathy towards the two-legged arrival. There was no means by which Alith could ask this question, the language of Kurnous being devoid of any means to express such emotional concepts.

A howl to the east signalled that prey had been located. Silver stopped and sat back, raising her head to respond in kind. After receiving a reply, she quickly broke eastwards. Other howls sounded around Alith while the pack located each other. Within a short time, Alith found himself surrounded by converging silvery-grey shadows slinking through the twilight that shimmered through the canopy of the forest.

It was Scar that had found something. The male was sat on the lip of a rise, looking northwards, occasionally letting loose a howl to bring the other wolves to the hunt. The pack picked up the scent of prey, their tails straightening with excitement. Blackmane trotted into view and Alith drew back behind Silver. The other wolves let out an excited mix of barks and wails until Blackmane snarled them into silence.

Blackmane's mate, the one Alith called Old Grey, took the lead, forging down a steep bank covered with fern fronds. The air was filled with rustling as the wolves closed in on their quarry, clouds of spores floating in the dusk light. Alith followed closely behind, keeping bent low to avoid being seen. The pack slowed as they neared their prey, their voices falling silent as they did so. Alith could not tell what it was they hunted; the press of trees prevented him from seeing what the wolves could smell. He kept behind Silver as the wolves gathered together, stalking through the underbrush with purpose.

It was then that the wind brought to him the scent of deer, sharper than he had ever smelt it in the mountains of Elanardris. The musk set his heart beating faster, awakening an urge to chase and kill. He took deep breaths to calm himself and kept his gaze far ahead, seeking some glimpse of the herd.

At the bottom of the dell, Old Grey turned to the left and followed a shallow rivulet upstream, the ground rising higher and higher into the outermost reaches of the Annulii foothills. Alith realised with a shock that he was already a considerable distance from the Ellyrion border, deep within the realm of Avelorn. It occurred to him that he had never been in such danger – armed only with a knife and devoid of all armour – yet he felt no nervousness. It was as natural to him to stalk naked through these woods as it had been for him to stand upon the mountainside with bow in hand.

Despite the excitement of the chase, there was a peace in Alith's heart. Although he had only been with the pack for a day, he already felt a bond with them from sharing their food and sleeping with them the night before. It was not since his early days with Milandith that he had felt such closeness, such welcome familiarity.

Old Grey stopped as another howl split the air, not far to the north. The wolves closed in on Blackmane making uncertain noises, one or two of them whimpering. The howl sounded again and was taken up by other lupine throats, rising in pitch and volume. Blackmane's hackles rose and he stood with quivering legs, alert and enraged. He let loose a howl of his own, long and deep. The rest of the pack took up the call, issuing a challenge to the unseen newcomers.

The answering wails seemed to come from many places and of different tones, but Alith had learnt enough about wolves to know that they changed position and their howls to give the impression of greater numbers. Blackmane's pack was large and it was unlikely the interlopers outnumbered them. For all that, it was only Blackmane that showed no signs of fear. The other wolves punctuated their howls with quiet whimpers, their ears pressed back in distress, their tails rigid with tension.

The howling contest continued for some time. Blackmane stood his ground as the other pack's cries came louder and closer. All then fell quiet, save for the sighing of the wind in the leaves and the trickle of the water-course down the middle of the tree-filled dell. The pack spread out a little, more than half of them moving a little way downwind, the direction from which any attack would be most likely. Blackmane stood on a rock barking, like a general ordering his regiments into position before a battle. Silver edged her way to the north and Alith followed for a few strides until Blackmane's voice cut through the stillness.

'Two-legs, come close,' the grizzled wolf snapped at Alith.

Alith did as he was told without hesitation, crouching beside the boulder upon which the pack leader was standing.

'Fight likely,' said Blackmane, turning his golden eyes on Alith. There was no sign of the pack leader's earlier aggression; Alith fancied that he detected a kinder tone in the old wolf's voice. 'Stay close. Sharp fang kill stag quick. Sharp fang not kill wolf quick. Two-legs tall, neck safe. Protect legs. Bite throat. Bite neck.'

Alith nodded in understanding and then caught himself, realising that the gesture meant nothing to Blackmane.

'Bite throat, bite neck,' said Alith.

Blackmane turned his attention away and Alith settled back on his haunches, his eyes seeking any sign of movement in the rapidly darkening forest. A cool breeze eddied down the steep valley.

A howl that Alith now recognised as Old Grey's echoed from ahead. Alith drew his knife but stayed crouched behind the rock, his glance flicking between the trees and Blackmane. The pack leader was stood erect, tail trembling, lips drawn back as a deep growl reverberated from his throat. Alith quivered from the vibrations of Blackmane's warning and from the rush of blood surging through his body. Leaves rustled close at hand as the other pack members drew closer to Blackmane, taking up guard in a circle around their leader.

Some of the younger wolves began to whimper, sensing the agitation exuded by the adults. They laid down in the ferns, ears flattened, shoulders hunched tight, while the older pack members stood protectively over them.

THE FIRST OF the rival pack appeared a short distance away to the right, bounding lightly over a fallen tree trunk, hairs bristling along her back. She stopped as she saw Blackmane and the others and was quickly joined by five more wolves, all of them nearly as large as Blackmane, all considerably older.

Blackmane turned towards the newcomers and snarled, his teeth glinting in the setting sun.

'Go!' he snapped. 'Our hunt!'

Now that he was becoming more familiar with the wolves' behaviour, Alith thought he detected a hint of uncertainty in the interlopers. They all stood with fangs bared and eyes narrowed, but the occasional nervous flick of their ears betrayed a lack of confidence.

'No hunt,' said the female. Alith saw that her jaws were bloodstained and she held herself awkwardly, favouring her left hind leg.

'She is wounded,' Alith whispered to Blackmane.

'Our hunt,' Blackmane repeated, ignoring Alith. 'Go back!'

A shiver of fright rippled through the rival wolves, and they sank lower to their bellies, giving up their pretence of aggression. Only the female stood her ground, her gaze constantly moving between Blackmane and the other members of his pack. Her eyes finally settled on Alith and she gave a startled yelp and flinched.

'Two-legs!' she yowled. Edging backwards, she started a constant whining that was taken up by the others of her pack.

Their reaction spread to several of Blackmane's wolves, who began to make inquiring barks, seeking reassurance from their leader. A few looked with suspicion at Alith and bared their teeth.

Blackmane glanced at Alith and then returned his attention to the strangers.

'Two-legs hunt with us,' he said. 'One of pack.'

'Many two-legs come,' said the female. 'Hunt with long fangs. Kill many. Not eat.'

'Two-legs not hunt wolf,' said Blackmane. 'Go now!'

'Two-legs kill wolf,' the female insisted, stepping forwards again. 'Long fangs and sharp fangs. Mate dead. Many packs killed.'

'How close?' Alith asked, standing up. This earned him a growl from Blackmane and more whimpering from the strangers, but he ignored both and walked forwards, slipping his knife back into its sheath. 'How close two-legs?'

'We run for two suns,' said the female hesitantly. 'Try to fight. Many killed. Two-legs not chase. Two-legs come from high ground. Come this way.'

'Many two-legs?' asked Blackmane, leaping down from the rock and padding between Alith and the other pack. Old Grey, Scar and a few others moved forwards also, backing up their pack leader with growls and snarls.

'Many, many two-legs,' the female answered. 'Many long fangs. Many sharp fangs. Two-legs fight other two-legs.'

Alith was taken aback by this revelation. He had suspected that the Chracians had come south over the mountains, fleeing the druchii. Now it seemed the druchii had come to Avelorn as well.

'All two-legs kill wolves?' he asked.

'Black two-legs kill wolves,' the female replied. 'Black two-legs bring noise. Black two-legs bring fires. Black two-legs burn other two-legs.'

Revulsion lurched in Alith's stomach at the thought of the druchii coming here. It could only mean that Chrace had been overrun at last, and Avelorn was now under threat.

'Two-legs come here?' Blackmane asked. In reply, the other wolf merely whimpered and flattened her ears. 'Two-legs come, we fight.'

'Not fight,' whined the female. 'Two-legs come with long fangs. They kill, not fight.'

'Our hunt!' snarled Blackmane. 'Not run!'

'Our two-legs has sharp fang,' added Old Grey.

'Two-legs has no long fang,' said the other wolf. 'Sharp fang not fight long fang.'

It was now that Alith realised 'long fang' was the wolves' expression for a bow; most likely the dwarf-made repeater crossbows the druchii brought back from the colonies of Nagarythe in Elthin Arvan. The wolves would have no chance to fight against such hunters, and would be slaughtered by the vicious druchii out of a sheer pleasure for killing.

'We run,' Alith said, turning to Blackmane. The pack leader snarled and snapped his jaws but Alith did not back down. 'Cannot fight long fangs. Long fangs kill many wolves. Wolves kill no long fangs.'

For a moment Alith thought Blackmane would attack. The wolf bunched his muscles, preparing to pounce, his tail as straight as a rod behind him.

'We run,' said Old Grey. 'Long fangs kill cubs. We run. Find new hunt.'

'No!' Blackmane rounded on his mate. 'Two-legs come, two-legs keep coming. Pack runs, pack keeps running. Better fight not run. Make two-legs go away!'

'Not run, hide,' said Alith. 'Black two-legs hunting other two-legs. Not hunting wolves. Wolves hide, two-legs go away.'

Alith knew this to be a lie; given any opportunity the druchii would scour Avelorn with sword and flame. The only chance for survival for the pack would be to lie low until the forces of the Everqueen and her subjects could push back the druchii advance.

The other wolves continued to argue, but Alith did not listen. He was confused by his own reaction. Why did he care whether the wolves lived or died? If they killed even a single druchii, would that not be a victory? He wondered what had happened to the hatred that had burned within him only two days before. Why did he not feel like striking out against the druchii?

A glance back at the worried pack gave him his answer. He saw the cowering cubs, heard the whimpers of their guardians. This was a family, and though they were not elves, they no more deserved to be sacrificed to the druchii's bloodlust than the people of Ellyrion, or any other creature of Ulthuan. The druchii despised all that they could not control, and they would come to Avelorn with their whips and their chains to tame the wilds. Morathi craved domination over all creatures, not just her fellow elves. Alith realised that Morathi must hate the Everqueen even more than she hated Caledor; an incarnation of purity and nobility that Morathi could never defeat save through force.

'We hunt,' Alith said suddenly, cutting through the wolves' argument. 'Not fight, hunt! Kill in darkness. Hunt two-legs.'

'Hunt two-legs?' said Old Grey. 'Not good. We kill two-legs, more two-legs come to kill.'

'I am two-legs, I know two-legs,' Alith told the wolves as they padded back and forth uncertainly. 'Black two-legs bad. Black two-legs kill and kill and kill. Other two-legs fight black two-legs and wolves hunt black two-legs. Two-legs afraid.'

Blackmane was staring intently at Alith, his posture more relaxed.

'Two-legs hunt with long fang, sharper than fang, sharper than sharp fang,' said the pack leader.

'Yes,' said Alith. 'Not fight long fang. Hunt two-legs. Hunt at night. Hunt quiet. Kill two-legs and hide. Come back and hunt two-legs again. Not fight.'

'Two-legs need long fang to hunt,' said Blackmane. 'Long fang sharper than sharp fang.'

'I have no long fang,' Alith replied. Save for his knife, his possessions had been abandoned.

'Water has long fang,' said Blackmane. 'Two-legs take long fang and hunt.'

Alith was confused, unsure what Blackmane was telling him. Frustration welled up within the elf, unable to speak properly with the rest of the pack.

'Water has long fang?' Alith said.

'Old long fang,' said Scar, a grizzled-looking wolf with a greying muzzle and the jagged remains of a wound across his right shoulder. 'Long fang in water old as forest, older. Wolves not need long fang. Two-legs need long fang. Long fang hide from two-legs. Only bright face of night show long fang.'

Scar's words bordered on the meaningless, but his tone was low, almost reverential. Alith sifted through the jumbled phrases trying to discern any sense, but the wolf's references were entirely lost on him.

'Yes,' agreed Blackmane. 'Water hide long fang. Bright face of night come soon. Two-legs take long fang. Hunt black two-legs. Pack hunt.'

'Show me long fang,' said Alith, realising that the wolves were speaking of a real place.

'Bright face of night show long fang,' said Scar. 'Six more suns before bright face of night come.'

Slowly understanding dawned on Alith as he pieced together the strands of the wolves' story. 'Suns' were days, and in six days' time the moon Sariour would be full: the bright face of the night. Whatever it was the wolves were talking about, it could only be seen by the light of the full moon.

'Good,' said Alith and Scar wagged his tail appreciatively. 'Hide six suns. Bright face of night show long fang.'

'Hide six suns,' said Blackmane, his words punctuated with snarls. 'Watch black two-legs. Two-legs take long fang. Hunt black two-legs.'

THE STRAGGLERS THAT had been fleeing the druchii were welcomed into the pack by Blackmane, and the wolves headed east to seek a lair. As they travelled, the howls of other packs could be heard, all of them moving southwards and eastwards away from the mountains.

They encountered other animals retreating from the druchii invasion. Herds of deer threw aside their usual caution, risking the attention of the wolves rather than be caught by the invaders. The pack still needed to eat and the terrified deer proved to be easy prey. That dusk, Alith again gorged himself on fresh flesh, filled with the thrill of the hunt and the energy of the kill.

Over the following days the pack moved into the territories of rival wolves. Each sunrise was heralded by a cacophony of howls as the two packs strove to assert their dominance. Each time neither side was willing to retreat and the two packs came together. Clearly outnumbered, the rival wolves nevertheless stood their ground, daring Blackmane to attack. On the first occasion, Alith feared that there would be bloodshed, but Blackmane surprised him, and the rest of his pack. He told the other wolves of what was happening and warned them to head east. The other pack became fearful and begged Blackmane to help them. The old leader was reluctant, but Alith persuaded him to allow the pack to grow even larger.

Three more encounters ended the same way, and the pack grew to over fifty in number. Alith was reminded of the mustering of regiments at

Elanardris. The growth of the pack came with the same problems the Anars had faced. There were more mouths to feed and the huge pack was forced to range far and wide to seek food, their prey having also been driven away by the presence of the druchii. This slowed down the pack and one night Alith could smell the fires of the druchii camp and hear their raucous celebrations on the wind.

That night Blackmane told the pack they could not hunt but had to run as swiftly as they could, to keep the druchii from catching them. Always the wolves headed east, but the druchii were never more than a day's travel behind as they drove into the heart of Avelorn.

As the pack continued to move, some of their number would break off, alone or in pairs, and head northwards to spy upon the druchii. They returned with news that the druchii were burning many trees and had slain hundreds of creatures from the forest. Alith tried to find out the druchii numbers, but the best the wolves could tell him was 'a flock' and 'many packs'. On the eighth night since coming to Avelorn, Alith convinced Blackmane to allow the elf to see for himself the strength of the enemy.

HAVING ACCLIMATISED QUICKLY to the sounds and rhythms of the forest, Alith was confident as he set out at dusk, following back along the path the wolves had taken. As the sun set and the forest was plunged into starlight, he turned northwards and kept a fast but steady pace. He ran for most of the night, stopping only to drink occasionally, the moons rising and falling before he first smelt the smoke of fires drifting through the trees.

Slowing to a walk, Alith saw distant flickers of orange and red. The stench of the charnel fires drifted to him on the gentle wind, a choking mix of woodsmoke and burning flesh. Swathed in almost total darkness, Alith stalked towards the camp with dagger in hand.

Amongst the long and wavering shadows cast by the pyres, Alith spied several sentries. He watched for a while, noting the routes of their patrols and the timing. For all of their depravity, these druchii were disciplined and organised and at first Alith could see no way past the cordon. It was only after further observation that Alith noticed the sentries kept their gaze groundwards; none of them looked up into the trees as they patrolled. And why would they? As far as the druchii knew, there was no threat from the leaves and branches above their heads.

Smiling grimly, Alith slipped forwards silently and climbed the bole of a tree overlooking one of the patrol paths. He waited patiently in the branches, not a muscle moving, his breathing slow and shallow, eyes scanning the path below for the approach of an enemy.

As Alith had predicted, one of the guards came marching between the trees with spear and shield ready. His eyes never once looked up as he passed below Alith.

Alith soundlessly dropped down behind the druchii and plunged his knife into the side of his neck, killing him instantly. Quickly stripping the body, Alith took the clothes and armour before dragging the corpse into a nearby bush so that it would remain unseen.

Clad in the uniform of the slain soldier, Alith headed towards the druchii camp.

WITH A SWAGGER Alith had often seen affected by the druchii, the lord of the Anars strolled into the enemy camp. He knew that his Naggarothi features would blend in with the druchii, and it was far easier to avoid detection in plain sight than to skulk in the shadows. As he expected, there were no challenges and the elves of the camp never gave him a second glance. To walk so boldly in front of his enemies sent a frisson through Alith's body. It pleased him immensely to masquerade as one of them; an invisible foe ready to strike at their heart.

The druchii force was not as large as Alith had first feared. He guessed by the size of the camp that there were three or four thousand in this army, almost half of them cultists of Khaine. He was surprised by this, noting that the worshippers of Khaine seemed to be gaining power over their rivals. He saw a few Salthite totems and heard chants to Ereth Khial, but it was the sacrificial pyres to the Lord of Murder that dominated the ceremonies.

As he walked between the black and red pavilions and weaved his way between stupefied cultists, Alith detected an atmosphere of desperation. It was intangible, but Alith could feel an edge in the words of the priests as they raised their voices to the cytharai, imploring for their favour. The braziers sputtered not with the organs of elves, but with the hearts and livers of deer and bear and wolf. Alith saw not a single elven prisoner.

As he walked, Alith noted the layout of the camp. The cultists were confined to the centre, surrounded by the tents that housed the soldiery. Morathi's commanders were taking no chances with their unreliable allies, keeping a close watch on the cultists. Combining this observation with the lack of cultists in the army on the Ellyrion plain, Alith wondered if Morathi was finally tiring of her sectarian lackeys. They had been useful to her in claiming power, but now their presence created more chaos and problems for the druchii.

Alith was also able to compare his experience in the camp with the time the Shadows had spent in Anlec. Many of the warriors were younger, less than three hundred years old. In times past, such youngsters would never have been allowed to march in a Naggarothi host. It gave Alith hope to see this, knowing that with every year that the druchii were held back, their numbers would dwindle. Morathi's gambit had been to seize Ulthuan before the princes could organise themselves in the wake of Bel Shanaar's death. It seemed that the actions of the Anars had perhaps helped in some way to prevent this. Alith doubted whether history would remember the brave deeds of his house, or the tragedy at Black Fen, but it gave him some momentary pride to recall them. For the first time since the massacre, he was able to look back on that day with a feeling other than hatred and misery.

He had seen enough to convince him that the druchii were vulnerable. If they stayed together, they would eventually be found and destroyed by the Chracians or the warriors of the Everqueen. If they split... Alith would be waiting for them with his newly met friends.

ALITH CUT SOUTH through the camp, moving at a nonchalant walk, his spear over one shoulder, shield slung on a belt across his back. He left the circle of pyres and strolled into the darkness, the only light the flicker of firelight from a spearpoint or link of mail. He saw a sentry a little apart from the others and approached, gently humming the battle anthem of the Anars. The warrior carried a bow and a long sword hung at his waist.

Alith deliberately snapped a twig beneath his foot and the guard turned at Alith's noisy approach, relaxed and unwary.

'You should see some of those Athartists,' Alith said with a leering look. 'You could stretch them any which way you want and they wouldn't make a whimper.'

'I wouldn't mind the odd scream or two...' the guard said with a lewd chuckle.

'I've had my fill already, why don't you go and enjoy the festivities,' suggested Alith, half-turning back towards the camp. 'I drank some moonleaf tea and I can't sleep a wink. I'll keep watch. You never know when we'll be attacked by a badger or something!'

'I'm not so sure,' replied the sentry, glancing between the beckoning fires and the looming shadow of the commanders' pavilion.

'Oh well, if you want to stay here in the dark...' said Alith, taking a step back towards the glow of the flames.

'Wait!' hissed the guard. Alith smiled to himself before turning around to face the soldier.

'I won't tell anybody, if you won't,' Alith said with a smirk. He enjoyed the dilemma playing out on the druchii's face. His indecision, his uncertainty, gave Alith a sense of power over him. He wasn't sure why he toyed with the elf in this way, when he could have easily surprised and overpowered him. There was something about making the druchii dance to the tune of the Anars that was immensely gratifying.

Alith stood next to the druchii and laid his arm across his shoulders.

'I don't think the commander is going to let them stay that long,' Alith added, imagining himself tying the hook onto the end of a fishing line. It was almost too easy to enjoy. Almost.

'I heard as such,' said the guard. 'He said it was "bad for discipline", or something like that.'

'It is a bit of a distraction,' said Alith.

As quick as a serpent, Alith slipped behind the warrior and tightened his arm around his victim's throat and neck. The sentry barely had time for a few choking gasps before he slumped into Alith's arms.

'A terrible distraction,' Alith whispered as he hefted the unconscious elf across his shoulders and headed into the woods.

TARMELION WOKE WITH a thunderous headache and a biting soreness in his chest. He felt dizzy and did not risk opening his eyes immediately. As he recovered his senses, fear gripped him. He could feel nothing, except for a throbbing in his wrists and ankles and a sharper pain in his chest. He was cold. There was something sticky on his face.

Opening his eyes, Tarmelion found himself looking at the leaf-strewn ground, some distance away. It took a moment for him to realise that he was hung from a tree branch, naked, with blood dripping from a cut in his chest.

'How long before you bleed to death?' a voice asked him from above. Something shifted its weight on the branch and Tarmelion began swaying gently. He craned his neck to catch sight of his tormentor but he could not twist his head far enough to see. He caught a glimpse of a shadowy figure just above him, but it moved out of sight as soon as his eyes fell upon it.

'Who are you?' Tarmelion begged, the pain in his chest growing as his heart began to beat faster, forcing more blood from the wound.

'Why are you here?' the voice asked. 'What do you want with Avelorn? How many more of your kind are coming?'

'I don't know!' sobbed Tarmelion, already terrified out of his wits. He could remember nothing of how he came to be in this place. His last memory was talking to one of the other sentries outside the camp. 'What are you?'

He repeated this question again and again, tears streaming from his eyes, the blood rushing to his head and spilling across his face from the gash above his heart. All became silent save for the distant patter of blood drops hitting the leaves far below.

The branch creaked and a moment later Tarmelion was confronted by a horrifying apparition. A face appeared right in front of him, upside-down and covered in blood. It was smiling. Tarmelion shrieked and tried to get away, straining every muscle, sending himself swinging dizzyingly from side to side. The face followed him, close enough he could smell blood on its breath. The smile faded and the creature bared bloodstained teeth at him.

'You are going to tell me everything you know,' the thing snarled.

HAVING LEARNED WHAT he wanted, Alith knocked the druchii unconscious and cut him from the tree. He carried him back towards the camp and left him close to one of the paths. Avelorn was the subject of many strange tales and dark legends, and it served Alith well that the sentry be found and spoke to his comrades of his terrifying encounter with a bloodthirsty denizen from the forest. It would sow more doubt in the hearts of the druchii and add to their fear of this unnatural place.

Alith stripped off the druchii clothes, glad to be rid of them for they had been ripe with the stench of fire and death. He did this not only for his personal comfort, but because he was afraid the smell of the druchii would mask his own scent and confuse the wolves. If he came upon the pack in such a fashion, they would attack without question and perhaps only later realise their mistake. Better to walk as nature intended. He kept the bow, arrows and sword.

Dawn came as Alith was making his way back through the woods at a swift run. The chorus of howls that greeted the sun allowed him to steer towards the pack's location. They would be on the hunt at this time, padding sleekly through the early morning twilight in search of prey. He felt the same urge and slipped an arrow to the bow. Slowing, he searched for tracks and soon came across a run used by rabbits. A surge of excitement welled up inside Alith at the thought of catching his prey and it took all of his willpower to remain calm. The bow trembled in his hand; he wanted to cast it aside and hunt with knife and teeth.

What was it that he had awoken with the slaying of Kurnous's stag?

IT WAS DUSK once again before Alith caught up with the rest of the pack, which had made its lair in a thin grove of trees beside a wide lake. Silver was the first to greet him with barks and licks and Alith ruffled her fur and stroked her chest in return. They were interrupted by Scar.

'Two-legs come,' said the wolf, turning away without waiting for acknowledgement.

Alith gave Silver a parting pat and followed Scar down to the water's edge. The lake was quite large, easily more than a bowshot wide and twice as long, aligned roughly north to south. The water was crystal-clear, a perfect mirror of the ruddy skies fringed with the silhouettes of the trees. Scar turned northwards and followed the edge of the lake, which was marked by a ribbon of shore upon which only grass grew, sloping gently down to the bare earth at the lake's bank.

In the twilight Alith saw Blackmane at the northern end of the lake, sitting attentively at the water's edge. The pack leader stared out towards the middle of the lake. Alith followed his gaze but could see nothing. There was no wind and not even a ripple disturbed the lake's surface.

'Water holds long fang,' said Scar as they approached Blackmane. 'Two-legs take long fang, hunt other two-legs.'

Scar sat down to the right of his leader and Alith crouched down on the other side. Blackmane had not moved a muscle for the entire time, but now turned his head and looked at Alith.

'Long time, many lives, since two-legs came to forest,' said Blackmane, his voice quiet, respectful. 'Long fang in lake before two-legs came. Long fang old as forest.'

Blackmane returned to his vigil, his immobility a reflection of the utter stillness that surrounded the lake. Alith sat cross-legged and waited also, comfortable in the silence. His mind drifted, memories and feelings swirling together, pictures forming in his mind's eye on the tranquil water.

He had always craved space and peace. Having grown up with no brothers or sisters, there had always been somewhere he could find away from other elves, to listen to his thoughts alone. He remembered gala banquets in the great hall and on the lawns. He recalled long days spent with tutors in the library, trying to absorb the knowledge they were imparting, their voices becoming a drone while his mind wandered to the mountains. He had enjoyed the company of his friends, but their presence was something that could be chosen. When he wanted companionship he had been able to find it, and when he wanted solitude, the wilds had always beckoned.

As he allowed himself to drift into a trance-like state, Alith's senses sharpened. He could hear the playful yaps and yelps of the pack across the lake and the chirruping of birds in the trees. Blackmane's breathing was slow and regular, while Scar panted with excitement. The evening air was cool on Alith's skin, but not unpleasant. He felt the weight of the quiver across his back and realised he still held the bow he had taken from the druchii sentry. These objects felt out of place, and he stood and strode across to the line of trees encircling the lake clearing. He took off the accoutrements of war and placed them beside a tree, noting its position so he could return for them later. Completely naked once again, he returned to Blackmane's side.

Alith quickly fell back into his contemplative state. All turmoil gone, Alith sensed something else. It was magic. Since the time of Aenarion and Caledor, the winds of magic had been drawn into the Vortex of Ulthuan and Alith had grown up knowing but not really noticing the immaterial winds that swept through the mountains of his home. He had felt their coil and eddy as he gave thanks to Kurnous, and had enjoyed their suffusing energy when he had called upon them to shield him from view or guide his aim.

Here, in Avelorn, the magic was different, of an entirely older order. It was rooted in the trees, lingered in the grounds and was contained in the waters of the lake. Having focussed on this realisation, Alith noted that the lake was particularly strong in mystical energy. It reminded him of silver-yellow rain, of calm dew on an autumn morning or the scent of a spring flower. There was potential here, life that was ancient and eternal. This was the magic of the Everqueen, the source of her power. It was this that the druchii – Morathi – wanted to desecrate. The druchii could never enslave such a power and so they sought to deny it to their foes. It was their way, to destroy that which they could not claim, to taint that which could create.

A sharpness, a sudden spike in the magic of the pool, brought Alith out of his waking dream. He opened his eyes slowly, as if from a long and refreshing sleep. The twilight had gone, replaced by a clear sky full of stars and the full moon. Alith turned to Blackmane, but realised with a shock that both the pack leader and Scar had left him. He sat alone on the edge of the lake.

Even as he wondered why the wolves had brought him here, Alith saw something shimmering in the middle of the lake. He took it to be the reflection of the moon above and stood for a better look. The glimmer of light was not the moon, which strangely did not reflect on the water at all. The source of the light was within the water, at the bottom of the lake.

Alith looked around him, suddenly disconcerted. In the night the trees seemed different, the lake more menacing. It was a sheen of black; even the stars did not show on its surface. Only that light in the depths illuminated the scene, dappling the shore and the surrounding trunks and branches with a silvery hue.

Alith fought back his fear with reason, pushing aside the animalistic instincts that had suffused him during his time amongst the pack. It was not dread that filled the clearing, but there was something that tugged at Alith's heart. It was a deep sorrow, a longful mourning. He sensed that a great tragedy had occurred at some time in the distant past. It was neither a memory nor a sensation he could define, but there was something about the bleakness of the scene that told him of an emptiness and loss of hope that only he could understand; something as alone as he was called out to him from the waters.

Alith waded into the lake, warm against his skin. He felt as if he strode into a pool of quicksilver, meeting slick resistance. Pushing forwards, he began to swim, striking out towards the strange light with slow, measured strokes. His passage made not a single ripple and no splash spoiled the silence. He kicked his legs and swam faster, but still the lake was as calm as it had been when he first laid eyes upon it.

Though he swam, Alith could feel no sense of motion or time and he could not tell for how long he forged towards that light. It grew neither stronger nor weaker but remained constant, bathing him in its glow. Had the lake been normal, he could have crossed it a dozen times over without too much effort, but Alith found his breath coming in short gasps, his limbs tired. It felt like he had been swimming for an eternity but he pressed on, ignoring the burning of his muscles and the pressure in his chest. The light surrounded him, dragging him forwards.

When he knew he was above the light source – and he did not know how but he just knew – Alith stopped and treaded water for a moment. He looked down but all he could see was the white and silver that engulfed him. Taking a deep breath, he plunged downwards, towards the sunken moonlight.

Down and down he swam until his lungs were fit to burst. Down even further he went, his world now a bubble of silver that embraced him. Part of him wanted to stop, wanted to turn and break for the surface, fearful of drowning. Another part of Alith welcomed the oblivion the light offered. Yet still another part of him heard a voice.

It was a female voice, which Alith recognised as if in distant remembrance, but he did not know whether the voice came from the water or inside his own head. The voice reminded him of safety and boredom but he could not place it. It told him a story as he swam, the words coming to mind as if recalled, yet Alith did not know from where the memory might come.

In the age before the elves the gods were as one with the world and the heavens. They played and schemed and fought with one another. And loved. Greatest of the godly lovers were Kurnous the Hunter and Lileath of the Moon. For eternity Kurnous wooed Lileath but the two of them could never meet, for Kurnous dwelt in the endless forests of the world and the Moon Goddess haunted the skies. To show Kurnous that his love was not unrequited, Lileath petitioned Vaul the Smith to create a gift for the Hunter. She poured her love and her soul into that gift and bade Vaul to take it to Kurnous as a token of her affection. Khaine the Warrior, ever jealous of Kurnous and Lileath's love, intercepted Vaul as he returned from the moon. He demanded that Vaul give him the gift that Lileath had commissioned. Vaul refused, telling Khaine that it was not for him. At this Khaine grew very angry and threatened to torture the crippled Smith if he did not give him Lileath's gift. Vaul refused again and instead passed the gift to Isha to hide it from Khaine. Isha, Mother of the World, proclaimed that none save for Kurnous would ever find the token of Lileath's love. Shedding a tear, she cast the gift down from the heavens to the world. Vaul suffered greatly at the hands of Khaine for his defiance, but the Smith-God did not know where the gift was hidden. When Khaine released him, Vaul told Kurnous of what had happened. Kurnous was the God of the Hunt and there was nothing he could not find, but the gift of Lileath eluded him. Every month she looked down upon the world and stared at her gift, so that Kurnous might follow her gaze. Yet the Hunter never found it before the elves came and the gods were forced to dwell evermore in the heavens. So it was that Kurnous and Lileath would remain apart for eternity and Kurnous's children would howl their love for Lileath every full moon.

Alith felt something in his grasp, solid yet flexible. He tightened his grip on it and turned, heading for the surface. The glow diminished around him while fatigue and lack of breath played tricks on his mind, confusing him with glimpses from his past and a cacophony of noise. His heart thundered and his body screamed in pain along every vein and fibre of muscle. His prize tight in his hand, Alith pushed upwards, feeling the strength leaking from him, the last bubbles of air streaming from between his gritted teeth.

With an explosive gasp and a spume of water, Alith broke the surface of the lake. The starlit sky spun and the moon swirled. His whole body was numb, save for his right hand, which was pained by the tightness of his grip. Alith took in great lungfuls of air and after a while the pain and dizziness receded, though he still felt as weak as a newborn cub. Only when the rushing in his ears had stopped and he could feel the water against his skin once more did he look at what he held.

It was the most beautiful bow he had ever set eyes upon. Crafted from a silvery metal that glittered in the moonlight, its tips were each decorated with a crescent moon. No droplet of water clung to its length and its string was all but invisible, finer than a hair. It felt as light as air in his grasp and perfectly balanced for his hand. It was warm to the touch, reassuring, almost loving with its presence.

Alith heard noises from the edge of the lake. Looking around he saw that the moon was just above the treetops, almost gone from view. In the dim light he could discern the shadowy shapes of the wolf pack, spread around the shore of the lake. Dozens of pairs of eyes glittered in the shadows, watching him. Keeping himself afloat with gentle kicks and sweeps with his free arm, Alith kissed the bow and held it triumphantly above his head.

All around him the wolves howled as the Children of Kurnous cried their love for Lileath.

⚔ TWENTY ⚔

The Taming of the Wolf

ALITH WAS BREATHLESS as he ran through the woods. Glancing over his shoulder, he could see the knights chasing him, ducking beneath branches as they steered their heavy mounts between the trees. More than a dozen of them had given chase when Alith had shot their captain as they patrolled southwards from their camp. The thud of the horses' hooves reverberated from the steep sides of the wooded dell as Alith led them towards the pack.

Alith put in a fresh spurt of speed and cut to his left, disappearing from the knights' view. He leapt onto a rock and from there jumped into the branches of a tree with the swiftness of a squirrel. He ran lightly along the branch and crouched next to the trunk, peering between the leaves at the approaching riders.

The foremost rider signalled for the pursuers to slow as he passed Alith's hiding spot. Alith felt a tremor of fear as the small column came to a walk and paced by below him, their eyes scanning the trees for any sign of their prey.

'Halt!' called the lead knight, holding up his hand. 'It has stopped running.'

Alith caught his breath and his heart began to race. He glanced at the ground beneath the horses but knew he had left no tracks as he had run. He also knew that he could not be seen easily. His pale skin was obscured by mud and blood he had painted across himself, and immobile he was all but indistinguishable from the bark of the tree.

Slowly shifting position, Alith turned his attention to the knights' leader, wondering what sense it was that had alerted the rider. He was armoured as the others in heavy silver plate, his dark grey steed protected by a caparison of light mail and a black enamelled chamfron gilded with the rune of Anlec. A high war helm protected the rider's head, decorated with a plume of long black feathers that swayed as the knight looked to his left and right. There was something else on the knight's helmet, a band of gold that held in place a mask that Alith could not see until the rider turned fully around and stared directly at him. Alith gasped at what he saw.

The golden mask depicted a thin, snarling face sculpted with angular cheeks and diamond eyeholes. It was not the fierce expression of the war mask that so alarmed Alith, but what was set into it. A pair of blue eyes were bound to the mask above the eyeholes, a net of fine golden thread passing through the glistening orbs and the metal of the helm; real eyes that moved with a life of their own. A fine trickle of blood ran down the sides of the mask from these as they tracked back and forth, seeking something. They swivelled in unison towards Alith and the rider straightened as if startled.

For a moment Alith was locked in the unearthly stare of those magical eyes. He was transfixed with horror, not only of his discovery but by the means with which he had been found.

'There, in the tree!' the rider cried out, pulling free his sword and pointing towards Alith.

The knights' exclamations broke Alith's trance and he pulled himself higher into the branches with one hand, unslinging the moonbow from his back with the other. He felt the gift of Lileath pulse in his hand, mirroring his heartbeat. Angry shouts rose towards him as he lifted an arrow to the impossibly thin string. He pulled back on the shaft, with no more resistance than he would have from passing his hand through the air. Sighting on the knight with the abomination of a mask, Alith could hear the bow whispering to him, offering soothing encouragement. He could not discern the words, and doubted he would understand their language even if he could clearly hear them. Their tone was reassuring, relaxing him, quelling the trembling in his hands.

Alith loosed the arrow and it sprang from the moonbow as a flash of white, cutting straight through the breastplate of the knight and out of his back to bury itself up to the fletching in the leaf-strewn ground. A gaping hole in his body, the knight toppled sideways and crashed lifelessly into the dirt. As he had done since finding the moonbow, Alith marvelled at its power; it was strong enough to send a shaft through a tree bole yet so light that he could balance it on a fingertip.

Alith shot another of the knights, the angle of the arrow passing down through the rider's shoulder and splitting the spine of his steed. Both collapsed in a heap. With no means to shoot back, the knights turned and fled, one more of their number falling with an arrow through his back as they galloped back up the dell.

With moonbow still in hand, Alith dropped back to the ground. He felt a wave of revulsion wash through him as he stepped towards the knight with the grotesque helmet. Turning him over with his foot, Alith stared at the horrid contraption of gold and flesh wound into the helm. He knelt down for a closer inspection and saw that the wires holding the eyes in place passed through the helmet and into the face of the wearer. Though the knight was dead, the eyes continued to follow Alith, staring at him wherever he moved.

Forcing himself to look at those eyes, he regarded them with distaste, but also a feeling of recognition. There was something about their lidless stare that seemed familiar. Then it came to him: these were the eyes of the sentry he had interrogated. A sorcerer in the druchii camp had laid an enchantment upon them to seek out Alith, and gifted them with the ability to see him wherever he hid.

Disgusted, Alith drew his sword and sliced through the golden bindings, spilling the eyes to the ground. They swivelled amongst the leaves, still staring accusingly at Alith. With a lurch in his stomach, Alith brought his sword down onto them and hacked them into viscous pieces. As he straightened, Alith wondered if the unfortunate sentry had survived the donation of his eyes. It would be like the druchii to blind him for his error, rather than grant him the ignominy of death.

Stowing the moonbow and his sword, Alith retrieved his precious arrows and turned down the dell to head back to where the pack was waiting in ambush. He would have to tell them there would be no hunt today.

FOR A DOZEN days after finding the moonbow, Alith and the wolves assailed the druchii, but the opportunities to strike back at his hated foes were few. The enemy advanced relentlessly, driving the pack before them. The wolves tried to head north and circle back to the west but after a day they ran into another druchii host; this one coming directly south and heading for the Ellyrion border. Eastwards the black regiments marched, unwittingly herding Alith and the wolves before them as they pressed on towards the Aein Ishain, shrine to the goddess Isha and home to the court of the Everqueen.

Save for the phases of the moon, Alith had not counted the passing of the days, but he started to worry about time once more. How far was it to the Everqueen, and how fast were the druchii moving? Was the spiritual ruler of Avelorn aware of the danger that pressed so hastily into the forests?

This last question Alith dismissed as soon as it came to him. These were the lands of the Everqueen and she was bound to them in ways far beyond a prince's connection to his lands. The death of the beasts and the burning of the trees would be known to her, as Alith felt the cuts on his bare feet and the grazes on his skin. No, the Everqueen would not need warning of the threat that loomed over Avelorn.

Unable to hinder the druchii advance, Alith was at a loss regarding what course of action to take. Having seen the strength of his enemy, Blackmane wished to flee eastwards even further, down through the isthmus of Avelorn and into the Gaen Vale. Here the old wolf believed his pack would be safe from the druchii, though he would not tell Alith why he felt such surety.

IN THE FOLLOWING days Alith noticed a change in the forests. The nature of the trees altered, becoming even larger and older than those of the outer woods. Bramble and bracken barred their way and often Alith was forced to crawl after the wolves through natural culverts and along tunnels of sharp briar. Walls of thorns turned them northwards or southwards, and Alith was convinced the forest itself was trying to keep them from moving eastwards.

Sixteen days after drawing the moonbow, Blackmane's pack came to the borders of the Gaen Vale. No elves save for Malekith's half-brother and half-sister – and the Everqueen herself – had ever travelled to the Gaen Vale, but the legends surrounding it were many. Some claimed it was the spiritual heart of Avelorn, of all of Ulthuan, where Isha had cried out her last tears before she left the world for the heavens. Other tales told that the Gaen Vale was the birthplace of the first Everqueen, the mortal incarnation of the goddess.

That strange spirits lived in the Gaen Vale was beyond dispute. The forest had a consciousness of its own in those dark depths. The trees could walk and talk, infused with the life of Isha. Legend claimed that these spirits protected Morelion and Yvraine, the first children of Aenarion, from the attacks of the daemons. The Everqueen sought counsel from the forest's immortal guardians and Alith believed that they would be no friends of the druchii.

Alith cared not for the legends of Isha, but he could recognise sanctuary. Separated from the mainland of Ulthuan by the narrowest strip of land, the Gaen Vale could be easily defended against the druchii. So he followed Blackmane as the pack forced their way towards safety, the druchii ever close on their heels.

AS NIGHT FELL on Alith's thirtieth day in Avelorn, they came to the northern end of the isthmus. The skies were swathed with thick cloud, the forest bathed intermittently by the white light of waxing Sariour and the sickly green of the Chaos moon. A mood of unease spread amongst the pack, a feeling of foreboding that Alith shared. The air tasted strange and Alith wondered if the druchii conjured a foul sorcery to stain Avelorn with their dark magic. The wolves gathered close together, the pack rubbing against each other for reassurance, their mewls and whimpers sounding in the darkness. Blackmane strode confidently through his charges, his bark bringing comfort to the scared pack.

Alith was filled with the sensation of being watched, but though he scanned the trees for any sign of an interloper, he saw nothing. Then he became aware of movement and the whimpering of the wolves increased. Alith sensed it now. The breeze brought with it a different scent, that of autumnal rot and mouldering leaves. Shadows shifted at the edge of Alith's vision, but when he turned to look he saw nothing but bushes and trees. Eerie creaks and the swish of leaves filled the air. Things whispered in the undergrowth, a susurrus that came from every direction and none. Though he could see nothing, Alith was in no doubt that the forest was moving.

The trees were getting closer.

THE PACK GATHERED around Blackmane, Alith at his side. A near-impenetrable wall of trees surrounded the elf and wolves, branches reaching high overhead to blot out what little light crept through the clouds. A thicket of brambles had grown up around the trees, creating a thorny fence.

Alith drew the moonbow and nocked an arrow, glancing nervously all around. Even Blackmane's fierce confidence had disappeared and the pack leader hunched at Alith's side, ears flat against his head, eyes wide with fright.

Something shifted to Alith's right and he turned, bow raised.

'Not welcome,' said a voice on the wind, reminding Alith of the rustle of leaves in the wind. One tree stood a little further forwards from the others, a huge bowed oak heavy with leaf. It shuddered and acorns fell to the ground in a loud patter. 'Leave us.'

'Black two-legs come,' said Blackmane, standing up and taking a pace towards the arboreal apparition. 'Kill. Burn. We run.'

The tree might have twisted slightly towards Blackmane, though it could well have been a trick of the moonlight.

'Wolves may come,' the voice said. 'Two-legs must not.'

'Why would you deny your ally sanctuary?' demanded Alith, speaking in elvish. 'I would fight to protect these lands from the druchii.'

'Come here,' the treeman said, bending a branch in Alith's direction like a beckoning arm.

The elf approached cautiously, moonbow still in hand. He stopped a few paces from the treeman and saw a gnarled face in the bark, far above his head. Knots made for eyes and a split in the bark formed a mockery of a mouth, though neither moved as the treeman spoke.

'What manner of elf runs wild with the wolves?' the treeman asked.

'I am Alith, last of the Anars,' the elf replied, stiffening with pride as he spoke. The treeman said nothing and Alith continued. 'I am the son of the wolf and the moon.'

At this the trees around the trees began quivering violently, branches clashing, leaves fluttering. Alith did not know if this signalled anger or amusement, but he kept calm.

'I request passage to the Gaen Vale, to seek sanctuary from those that would hunt me down and slay me,' Alith said, taking the arrow from the string of the moonbow and placing both in his quiver. 'Or worse,' he added.

A branch reached out and laid leafy fingers upon Alith's brow, their touch as light as a feather. A moment after it had settled, the branch whipped away with a crack.

'No,' said the treeman, its voice deepening to a rumble. 'There is no place for you in Gaen Vale. You bring darkness with you. Death is in you. Only life is welcome in this place. You must go.'

'The darkness follows me, but it is not of my making,' said Alith, thinking of the pursuing druchii. 'I will help you fight!'

'The darkness is drawn to you, and you are drawn to it,' the treeman said, slowly straightening. 'You cannot pass into the Gaen Vale.'

Alith was aware of the eyes of the wolves upon him, Blackmane's stare the most intent. The wolves could not follow the words, but Alith's narrowed eyes and tense posture told them what they needed to know about the exchange.

'We go?' asked Blackmane. 'Hide?'

'Yes,' said Alith. 'You go. You hide.'

'Two-legs come,' said Blackmane.

'No,' said Alith, turning away from the treeman to focus on the wolves. 'Two-legs not come. Two-legs will hunt. Wolves will hide.'

'No!' snarled Scar, trotting from the pack. 'Two-legs hunt, wolves hunt.'

'Wolves hunt,' echoed Blackmane.

'Cubs not safe,' said Alith. 'Cubs not hunt. Black two-legs come soon. Wolves hide.'

'Cubs hide, wolves hunt,' said Blackmane. 'Pack hunts with two-legs.'

Alith wanted to argue, but there were no words to express what he knew. The druchii would come this way, in ever-increasing numbers. The wolves had to flee, to head to safety in the Gaen Vale. Yet there was no way he could convince them of their peril. Alith would have to leave them.

'Two-legs not run,' said Silver, joining Scar. It was as if the wily female had read Alith's mind. 'Two-legs stay with pack. Pack protects.'

'Black two-legs kill pack!' snapped Alith, causing Silver to shrink back as if he had taken a swipe at her. Alith felt a pang of guilt, but continued, knowing that he had to make the wolves understand the danger. 'Many, many black two-legs. Kill many, many wolves. Wolves run!'

Alith turned his back on the pack to a chorus of yelps and howls. He ignored them and strode westwards, away from the Gaen Vale. He'd taken only a few paces when he heard the padding of feet. Glancing over his shoulder he saw Scar, Silver, Blackmane and nearly two dozen other wolves following him.

'No!' Alith yelled, stooping to snatch up a handful of dirt. He flung it at the wolves with a wordless shout. Turning away, Alith stormed through a gap that had opened in the thorny barricade.

'Don't let them follow me!' Alith called out in elvish, his voice catching in his throat.

'We will protect them,' the treeman's haunting voice called back. The thorns writhed and within moments the gap was sealed once more.

Howls and snarls echoed through the trees, following Alith as he stalked into the darkness with tears in his eyes.

ALITH WEPT FOR the rest of the night, sitting on the root of an enormous tree. He wondered why the gods could be so cruel. They tempted him with love and peace and then took away that which he desired most: Ashniel; Milandith; his family; Athielle; the wolf pack. In his grief he was reminded of Elthyrior. *Loneliness is an indulgence for those with the time to spare for it. Some fill the emptiness with the meaningless chatter of those around them. Some of us fill it with a greater purpose, more comforting than any mortal company.*

Alith had entered Avelorn thinking he had found a purpose, but it had not been so. Had he been wrong to slay the stag? He thought not. Had Kurnous intended him to run with the pack? It seemed likely. If so, then what had it brought Alith save for more woe?

Alith heard a gentle whisper and without thought reached to the quiver on his back and brought forth the moonbow. He stroked a finger along the silvery metal, relishing the warmth. He held it to his cheek, his tears running along its length, soothed by its touch.

Here was the reason he had been brought to Avelorn.

Cradling the moonbow to his chest, Alith stood and took a deep breath. It was up to him to find his own purpose. Others could blame fate, or the gods, or luck. Alith was empty of blame, save for his hatred of those that had brought this woe upon Ulthuan. His fate had not been made by Kurnous, nor his father and grandfather, not even by Bel Shanaar. All that had happened to Alith had one source and one source alone: the druchii.

He had been a leaf on a river, pulled by currents beyond his control. Forced to fight. Forced to run. Forced to hide. That would change. The stag would run and be hunted down. The wolf chose its prey. Now was the time to act, not react. For too long the druchii had been allowed to choose the tune. That feral love of the hunt that Kurnous had awoken stirred in Alith's breast.

He looked to the north, where the druchii made their camps and despoiled the forest. With the moonbow Alith could slay many of them. They would come for him and he would elude them, just as the Shadows had done. But it was not enough. Even with the moonbow, he could not slay enough druchii to halt them, to turn the war against them. The lone wolf was no threat to them.

Moonbow in hand, Alith turned to the south-west, towards Ellyrion. He could not hunt alone, but he knew where he would find his pack.

—◄ TWENTY-ONE ►—

An Oath Fulfilled

ALITH RAN FOR many days, heading south across Ellyrion, filled with the spirit of the hunt. Clad in naught but his weapons, he avoided the herds of the Ellyrians, travelling by day and night. He did not pause to kill and drank sparingly, possessed by the vision of his new war against the druchii. As packs his warriors would hunt, like the Shadows of old.

By the dark of night he crested a hill and looked south. To the east the lights of Tor Elyr glittered on the waters of the Inner Sea. He hesitated for just a moment, a last pang of regret upon seeing the city where Athielle lived. It was gone in an instant. To the south he saw the shrouded lanterns of the Naggarothi camp.

Approaching the camp, Alith was called upon by a picket to identify himself. It was only when he saw the astounded look upon the sentry's face that Alith became aware of his outlandish appearance. The Naggarothi eyed Alith for a long time, struggling between joy and incredulity as the prince made himself known.

'Send word to Khillrallion and Tharion that I wish to see them immediately,' said Alith as he strode unashamedly into the camp.

'My prince, where have you been?' asked the warrior, following a little way behind his lord. 'We feared that you were dead or taken prisoner.'

'Such a thing will never happen,' Alith replied with a grim smile. 'The druchii will never catch me.'

Alith sent the soldier ahead to fetch his lieutenants and made directly for the rough lodge that served as his quarters. More Naggarothi came from their huts and tents to stare at their returning prince. Alith ignored their inquisitive gazes, though he noted that while many were astounded by his appearance an almost equal number seemed to focus upon the moonbow in his hand.

Tharion came running through the camp as Alith reached the door to the lodge.

'Prince Alith!' the commander cried out with a mixture of relief and surprise. 'At first I did not believe it!'

There followed much inquiry as to the prince's whereabouts and actions, all of which Alith refused to answer. His experiences in Avelorn were his alone, to share with no other. All that his people needed to know was their prince had returned, and with fresh purpose.

When Khillrallion arrived, he brought with him another elf: Carathril. Alith was as surprised by the herald's presence as Carathril was by Alith's appearance. They greeted each other coolly, both unsure of each other's agenda.

'What brings the herald of the Phoenix King to my camp?' Alith asked as they walked into the main room of the lodge. He carefully placed the moonbow on the long table, before removing his belt and quiver and laying them to one side. Alert and dignified, Alith sat at the head of the table and gestured for the others to sit.

'Carathril is here at my request,' said Tharion, exchanging a glance with Khillrallion. 'When you disappeared we were at a loss. We sought the advice of King Caledor as to how we might best aid his cause. We have been discussing joining Caledor in his next campaign.'

'That will not be required,' said Alith. He turned to Carathril. 'However, your journey has not been entirely in vain. Return to your master with the news that the druchii have invaded Avelorn in strength. Even now they are probably at the border of the Gaen Vale.'

Carathril took this news with a frown.

'And how are you aware of this?' asked the herald.

'I have returned from Avelorn, and saw the druchii for myself,' Alith told the group. 'I fear Chrace is now entirely overrun, and the eastern kingdoms would do well to prepare their defences for a fresh onslaught by Morathi.'

Alith fancied he could see the questions burning in the minds of the others but none were voiced.

'That is grim news,' said Carathril. 'I will convey this to King Caledor. However, my reason for being here has not changed. I wish to discuss how best you might aid the Phoenix King in his war against the druchii.'

'Please leave me alone for a moment with the Phoenix King's herald,' said Alith, keeping his tone neutral.

'Perhaps we could, hmm, fetch you some clothes, prince?' suggested Tharion.

'Yes, do that,' Alith replied absently, his gaze fixed on Carathril. He continued when the others had left the room, finally allowing his anger to show.

'I am not some hound to be called to heel! I fight for my lands and my heritage, not for the Phoenix Throne. I will wage my war against the druchii in whatever way I see fit, and will suffer no interference or questions. Protect Ulthuan and its people, but know this: Nagarythe is mine.'

'You would set yourself up in opposition to the Phoenix Throne?' said Carathril, his face a picture of disbelief. 'You claim Nagarythe as yours? What makes you any different from Morathi? By what right can you claim such rule?'

'I am Naggarothi. The cold of winter runs in my veins. The legacy of Aenarion beats in my heart. My father and grandfather have given their lives to Nagarythe, not for glory or renown, but out of duty and love. I do not seek Nagarythe for myself, but to keep the land safe from the ambitions of others. The Phoenix King's grandfather chose to leave Anlec and found his own realm in the south, and by that action relinquished any claim to rulership over Nagarythe.'

'You owe loyalty to nothing,' said Carathril, bowing his head with sadness. 'You would make yourself a king, yet you would rule over barren waste and have no subjects. You will become a king of shadows.'

Alith smiled at Carathril's choice of title and remembered Elthyrior's words from so many years ago. *'In the mountains she sent me to find you, the child of the moon and the wolf, the heir of Kurnous. The one that would be king in the shadows and hold the future of Nagarythe in balance'.*

Since that first conversation, the raven herald had insisted that Alith should plot his own course, should follow his destiny without complaint. Alith found truth in that message. He had become the prime hunter, the leader of the pack. The druchii were his prey and he would never give up his pursuit of them.

Alith looked at Carathril, still smiling. The herald did not share Alith's amusement. The prince nodded.

'Yes, that is *exactly* what I will become.'

WHEN CARATHRIL HAD been abruptly dismissed, Khillrallion and Tharion returned with boots, robe and cloak for Alith. They also brought a pail of water and soap but Alith waved these away.

'We cannot win against the druchii in open war,' Alith told them as he pulled on the robe and fastened the broad belt around his waist. 'Not by our own strength. There are simply too few of us left.'

'Then we should fight alongside the Ellyrians or Caledorians,' said Tharion.

'No!' snarled Alith. 'We will continue to fight where we have always done, where it pains the druchii most: in Nagarythe. It could be years before Caledor is ready to march north in strength, and what will we find as liberators? A spoiled wasteland, destroyed by darkness and battle, and Anlec tumbled into stones, humbled. If Caledor invades Nagarythe he will destroy everything to cast out the druchii; everything that we would give our lives to protect. We can wage a different war, one that will eat at the druchii from within. Weakened, they will lose their war in the other realms and we will stand ready to claim power.'

'You would see us all become Shadows?' said Tharion, guessing Alith's intent.

'I would,' replied the prince. He wished to gaze outside but the hall had no windows. Instead he looked deep into the flickering light of the fire. 'Elanardris is no more; every crack and shadow will be our new home. The dark woods, the fens, the hills will conceal us. Not a single druchii will walk in Nagarythe without looking over his shoulder. Not a single army will march on the roads without fearing every outcrop and vale. This is a test of will, and we cannot flinch. For every one of ours that dies, a dozen druchii must be sent screaming to Mirai. For every drop of blood we give, we take a river in return.'

'Retraining all of your warriors will not be swift,' warned Khillrallion, sat upon one of the benches. 'Many have spent a lifetime in the ranks, learning discipline and the craft of open battle. These are not the skills of the Shadow, and they have no experience.'

'We will divide the army between you and the other remaining Shadows, that's roughly fifty warriors each,' Alith declared. 'In Athelian Toryr they can learn the ways of the woods, be tutored by the wisdom of Kurnous. In the mountains and the passes they will come to know the secrets of rock and snow.'

'And what of weapons?' asked Tharion. 'We have less than a thousand bows for more than three thousand warriors, and that many Shadows will need a forest of arrows.'

'I will see what the Ellyrians can provide for us for the time being,' said Alith. 'In the end, our warriors must learn to make such things for themselves, or take them from their slain foes, for it is only thus that we will be able to continue to fight in Nagarythe. Just as the shrines of Kurnous exist as stores for the hunters in the wilds, we shall set up caches across Nagarythe, hidden from the eyes of our foes and made secret by enchantments. Remember that we will be Shadows, homeless and untraceable. The army must learn to hunt what it needs, to pass without notice, to leave no sign of their presence.'

'You are asking a lot,' said Khillrallion.

'Those that cannot learn will be left behind,' snapped Alith. He glared at his two captains, daring them to speak out. For a moment he bared his teeth and narrowed his eyes, much as Blackmane had done to cow his pack. 'I am your prince and these are my commands!'

Khillrallion nodded in silent acquiescence while Tharion leaned away from Alith, shocked by his ferocity. Alith relented and held out a placating hand towards the pair.

'We must be strong, stronger than ever before,' said the prince.

'As you wish, lord,' said Tharion, standing and giving a formal bow. 'I swore an oath to your grandfather and father, yet I have not had opportunity to give it to you until now. I will serve House Anar and its prince until the end of my days. As my lord bids me, so shall I act. By Asuryan and Isha, by Khaine and Ereth Khial, I am bound by this oath to you.'

Alith watched Tharion as he marched from the hall, looking at Khillrallion only when the ageing elf had left.

'Two years,' Alith said. 'In the spring two years from now, we will return to Nagarythe and begin our shadow war. I look to you to make sure that we are ready. I would have no other captain to aid me.'

'And I would have no other prince to follow,' Khillrallion replied with a wink. His mood then became sombre. 'Twice I thought I had lost you, and yet you have returned. Yet, neither time do I think the prince I knew has come back.'

'I will be a prince for only a little while longer,' Alith said. 'When we return to Nagarythe, I shall be the Shadow King.'

FOR MOST OF the year the Naggarothi trained in their new style of war. Alith sent petitions to Finudel asking for weapons, which the prince granted as best as he was able. No mention was made by either of them regarding Athielle. Finudel informed Alith in one letter that she had heard news of his disappearance but not his return. Alith assured Finudel it was better that she believed him gone, lest she leave the city and come to the camp. Such an encounter would not be to the benefit of either.

The following winter, as far as the Ellyrians could tell, Alith's army simply disappeared. Riders brought news to Finudel and Athielle that at dawn they had passed the Naggarothi settlement and found it deserted where the night before it had been filled with life. No tracks told of where they had gone, and nothing remained of their occupation; not a single arrowhead or cloak, link of mail or water bottle had been left behind. Nearly three and a half thousand elves had vanished.

Alith had led his warriors into Athelian Toryr, dispersing them through the forest and mountains. Each of these groups was led by a former Shadow, respectfully known as shadow-walkers by the other warriors for their ability to move without trace. Alith led no cadre himself, but moved between the groups, monitoring their progress and instilling them with his bitter ethos.

For another year they continued to train, living in the wilderness without supply or support. The shadow warriors honed their archery and their stalking, and learnt the words of Kurnous that would bring fire to dead wood or summon hawks to be their messengers. They slept in tree branches or beneath arching roots, made pillows of rocks and lairs of caves. By Alith's design, no group knew where the others dwelt, and they were ordered to avoid each other as the wolf packs avoid their rivals. If one was seen by a shadow warrior from another cadre, the shadow-walkers would punish them, setting them arduous tasks of survival. To some it may have seemed cruel, but to Alith it was essential that his army be self-sufficient, not only physically but mentally.

Alith hardened the minds of his warriors as much as their skills. Whenever he visited a cadre he would speak to them at length, reminding them of the ills done to them by the druchii, passing on his own thirst for revenge, stirring up the dark passions that seethed beneath the civilised faces of all Naggarothi. He wanted his warriors not only to be skilled but to be as savage as the wolves, merciless and determined.

'When you look at your foe, do not see another elf,' he would tell them. 'See them for what they are: creatures less than animals. Remember that your enemy is responsible for all of your woes. It is he that cast you from your homes, tortured your friends and slaughtered your families. You can have no compassion for those you will slay, for it will be rewarded by failure. Hesitation is death, doubt is weakness. The druchii tore your lives from you and threw them upon sacrificial pyres, and anointed their priests with the blood of your kin. The ghosts of the fallen wander Mirai, wailing in grief for the wrongs done to them, pleading with the living to avenge them.

'Do not long for peace, for there can be none while any druchii still draw breath. Embrace war as the crucible of your valediction, the means to purge this stain upon our people. Swear oaths of vengeance, not to me or your companions or to the uncaring gods, but to fallen mothers and fathers, dead sisters and brothers, slain sons and daughters. Take the darkness that the druchii have created and rob them of its power. You are the blade that will strike down the wicked. You are the shadow warrior, the faceless bringer of justice.'

As the last days of autumn gleamed upon the red and yellow leaves, Alith called the groups together, assembling them in the foothills at the eastern end of Eagle Pass. By night they made camp, gathering silently by the dying light of Sariour and the ruddy glow of the Chaos moon.

'We are ready,' said Alith, his quiet voice the only sound to break the stillness. 'The wait is over, the fighting begins anew. By dawn we will be heading towards Tiranoc and war. I will not ask you to follow me, for you have all proven your loyalty to our cause. I will not exhort you to acts of bravery, for you have all shown great courage to be here. I will only say that this is our moment of truth. Let the princes of the east fight their great battles and hurl the lives of their subjects away in futile resistance. It is here, in the west, that this war will be won. We fight for loved ones lost. We fight for futures blighted. We fight to reclaim a land that was once gloried above all others. We fight for Nagarythe.'

'For Nagarythe,' came the hushed answer from the army.

As the shadow warriors melted away into the darkness, heading westwards along the pass, Tharion approached Alith and fell in beside his prince.

'Is it wise to march on the brink of winter, lord?' asked Tharion.

'Armies do not march by winter, but we are not an army,' Alith replied. 'We are hunters, remember. In rain and wind and snow and baking sun we stalk our prey, across moor and mountain, river and fen. Let the druchii worry about moving armies in the grip of the ice, with their wagons and their baggage. Let them stand helpless as we burn their towns and kill their folk, as we were once helpless against the legions of Anlec.'

Tharion nodded in understanding, and Alith saw a dark fire in the veteran's eyes. It was the same look that Alith saw whenever he chanced upon his reflection in a pool or patch of ice.

THE ATTACKS OF the shadow warriors came as a shock to all of Ulthuan. News quickly spread amongst the druchii and their enemies. At first Alith kept his army together, overrunning the eastern watch towers of Eagle Pass, ambushing druchii patrols on the road and waylaying their messengers. Isolated by the growing snows of winter, druchii garrisons huddled in their camps, casting fearful gazes into the night. They whispered that the shadow army was made up of the spirits of those sacrificed to Ereth Khial, who had escaped her underworld domain to wreak their vengeance.

Alith learnt of this and laughed at the superstition of his prey. He used their fears as weapons, terrorising the druchii at every opportunity. Before their attacks, his warriors hid in the shadows and made wailing cries to unsettle their foes. They called out names they had overheard, accusing the druchii of being murderers. Howling like wolves the shadow warriors prowled just beyond the light of the fires, allowing the sentries vague glimpses of movement before disappearing. With whispered spells the shadow-walkers cast a gloom upon the fires, dimming their light and sending the druchii into a fearful panic.

Then the shadow warriors unleashed the fury of their bows. Storms of black shafts enveloped the camp, each one unerringly finding its mark. Never once seeing their attackers, the druchii died by the hundreds, screaming and panicked. And always the shadow warriors left a few survivors, allowing them to escape so that they would take their dread and horror to others. The shadow warriors retrieved their arrows from the dead and left the bodies for the crows and vultures. Each dawn heralded a new column of smoke as a camp or caravan burned, and the druchii would look to the mountains and wonder if the next night would be their last.

AT KORIL ATIR, at the height of the pass, the druchii had built a keep to watch to the east and west. For two days the greater part of the shadow warriors marched, bypassing the camps and wayforts along the pass. A few bands were sent by Alith to harass the druchii garrisons at the Ellyrion end of the pass, obscuring the shadow warriors' true location.

At midnight, the shadow warriors gathered on the slope below Koril Atir. The citadel's battlements rose in a jagged spire above the valley, silhouetted against the sliver of Sariour as the white moon descended in the west. Thin pennants fluttered from the flagpoles in the strong mountain winds, but that same wind brought no sound save for the screech of owls and the occasional roar of a hunting beast.

The keep was the most ambitious target yet and Alith could sense the trepidation of his followers. It was one matter to attack poorly defended camps, another to storm a fortress. Alith had confidence though. This would be no frontal assault, with screaming battle cries and siege engines. Surprise and stealth would bring the shadow warriors a greater victory than any army of Ellyrion could achieve. It was his intent not only to send a message to the druchii that none of their lands were safe, that no army or fortress offered them protection; Alith wanted the princes of the east, and the Phoenix King in particular, to understand just how dangerous the shadow army could be. The Anars would never be underestimated again.

WHEN THE MOONS had disappeared and all was dark, Alith led his followers towards the citadel. Lanterns burned from the narrow windows of the tower, but there was still much shade to conceal Alith and his army. By the light of these lamps, Alith could see warriors patrolling the battlement, ruddy light gleaming from spearpoints and helms.

Alith led the first wave of shadow warriors, circling around the keep and moving on the citadel from the north along the butte on which it stood, picking their way across the cliff face itself. The stones of the tower were closely set, with no sure purchase for toe or finger between them. However, the shadow warriors used knives and climbing spikes to scale the wall, quietly driving their points into the mortar that held together the giant blocks. Alith and fifty warriors slowly made their way up the tower wall, pausing whenever they heard the tread of boots above, cautiously advancing when the danger receded.

Alith was reminded of the time he had scaled the citadel of Aenarion in Anlec. He wondered if any sorcerous ward protected Koril Atir. He could feel the vortex churning through the Annulii and nothing else, but he was not a mage by any means and much dark magic was subtle and difficult to detect. If there were magical barriers, he would have to overcome them; there was simply no way he could prepare for every eventuality.

Reaching the battlement, Alith waited until a pair of patrolling sentries passed. He slipped through the embrasure behind the guards and padded forwards on soft feet, knife ready for the kill. He heard a soft grunt behind him and glanced behind to see Khillrallion hauling himself over the battlement. The two of them exchanged nods and darted forwards, slicing the throats of their prey and toppling their bodies to the rocks below with fluid movements.

Alith leaned over the wall and signalled for the shadow warriors to finish their ascent to the rampart. When all were upon the top of the wall, Alith cupped his hands to his mouth and mimicked the cry of a snow owl. Within moments he heard shouts from the far side of the tower, on the south approach, as the remaining shadow warriors made their presence known. Flaming arrows arced through the night sky and it was not long before feet were pounding up the wooden steps within the tower.

Dozens of the garrison poured from the doorways onto the rampart and Alith's contingent struck with bow and sword, cutting down the druchii as they emerged. Their dying cries mingled with the shouts of the Anar warriors on the other side of the tower, adding to the confusion. Their bodies were dragged aside and Alith led his warriors into the red-bathed interior of the keep. The distinctive rattle of repeater crossbows sounded from below as the defenders shot from arrow slits on floors within the tower. These needed to be dealt with quickly. Alith signalled for Khillrallion to take half of the shadow warriors and deal with the missile troops. Alith would head for the main gate with the rest.

Just like Anlec, Alith thought with a satisfied smile.

As DAWN'S ROSY gleam reached the citadel, Alith ordered his warriors to bring the bodies of the slain druchii to the main gate, and to raid the armoury for spears and other weapons. Several Ellyrians were found in the tower's dungeons, tortured and bloody. Alith gave them clothes and weapons and sent them east upon the mounts once used by the citadel's messengers.

'When asked who liberated you, say that your saviour was the Shadow King,' Alith told the Ellyrians as they departed.

The Anar prince stood at the gate, seven hundred slain druchii piled around him. With a meaningful look at his warriors, he snatched one of the corpses by the ankle and dragged it to the open gate. He grabbed the front of the corpse's shirt and leant it against the black-painted timbers.

'Spear,' he snapped to Khillrallion, holding out a hand. The shadow-walker brought a weapon to his leader and stepped back. 'It is not enough that we kill our enemies. They fear their mistress in Anlec far more than they fear death. We need to send the druchii a message even their depraved minds can understand: even in death they are not safe from our revenge.'

With that, Alith thrust the spear two-handed, its point passing through the throat of the druchii corpse and into the gate. Alith gave the shaft a twist to ensure it was stuck fast.

Taking his knife from his belt, Alith cut a rune into the forehead of the dead druchii: thalui, the symbol of hatred and vengeance. He tore open the elf's shirt and across his chest carved another: arhain, the rune of night and shadows. Examining his handiwork, Alith wiped the blade clean on the rags of the corpse's shirt and placed it back in his belt.

Alith looked at his warriors, seeking any sign of disgust or horror. A sea of faces watched him blankly, a few with deep intent. Alith nodded to himself and pointed to the mounds of the dead.

'Send a message,' he told his shadow warriors.

* * *

'IT IS GRIM reading, my prince,' said Leothian, bowing obsequiously as he handed the parchment scroll to the lord of Tor Anroc.

Caenthras ignored the subservient herald and turned to the messenger's companion, one of the lieutenants tasked with guarding Eagle Pass. The Naggarothi prince fidgeted on the throne of Bel Shanaar, uncomfortable with its design. The three elves were swallowed up by the massive emptiness of the great hall of the palace, their voices echoing coldly from the bare walls and high ceiling.

The audience benches had been removed, and all petitioners were forced to stand or kneel before their new master. It was one of the few changes in Tor Anroc that had pleased Caenthras; the mewling Tiranoc nobles were still allowed to live by the direct order of Morathi, but they now knew their proper place.

'Tell me, Kherlanrin, why I should let you live,' Caenthras said heavily.

The warrior stifled a glance towards Leothian and kept his eyes downcast.

'I would gladly fight a foe that faces us in battle, but I can no more defeat this enemy than I can nail shadows to the ground,' Kherlanrin said quietly. 'Our soldiers awake in the morning to find their commanders dead, their despoiled remains hanging from trees outside the camp, with not a guard or other soldier harmed. Horses with the corpses of our scouts tied upon the saddles are sent into our camps, the mouths and eyes of their dead riders stitched shut, their wrists bound with the thorny stems of mountain roses.' He shuddered and continued. 'I found a squadron of knights that had been moving between Arthrin Atur and Elanthras. Their throats were slit and the bridles of their steeds had been nailed into their faces.'

'The situation is unacceptable,' said Caenthras. 'Anlec demands results. I will give you another ten thousand warriors, as many as I can spare. As soon as the snows abate, you will lead them into the pass and bring me the heads of these rebels. I want to know who leads them and I want to find out by looking at his dead face. Is that understood?'

The pair nodded and retreated swiftly when Caenthras dismissed them with a wave of his hand. The whole situation was embarrassing. The assault on Avelorn was faltering because Caenthras's commanders were fearful to march along the pass. This left the Ellyrians free to support Avelorn from the south. Caenthras had no idea how much longer Morathi's patience with him would hold, but he was determined that his would not be the first head on the block when that patience finally failed.

ON A FRESH spring day Alith looked down at the sinuous columns of black from atop a steep cliff, Khillrallion beside him.

'They will spend all of the seasons of Rain and Sun looking for us,' said the shadow-walker. 'The druchii will divide their forces to sweep the pass, and then we will strike at each part in turn.'

'No, that is not my intent,' said Alith with a grim smile. 'These warriors come from the west. Morathi's commanders have emptied their camps to search for us, leaving Tiranoc all but unguarded. They think that we cannot slip past so many eyes. They are wrong.'

'We go to Tiranoc?'

'To Tor Anroc, no less,' said Alith.

TEN DAYS AFTER the druchii offensive began, Alith was far to the west, hiding in the caves where he had first sought sanctuary with Lirian and the other refugees. With him he had brought only the shadow-walkers, leaving the rest of the army to the east, to amuse themselves at the expense of the druchii as they saw fit. He had brought only former Shadows because what he had planned was beyond the skill of those so recently trained. When Alith explained his intent to the others he was met by confusion and incredulity.

'It is a great risk that you take,' said Khillrallion, giving voice to the concerns of his comrades. 'And for little gain.'

'You are wrong if you think this is merely a personal vendetta,' said Alith. 'Consider the despair of our foes when they realise that nowhere is safe for them, not even the palace of an occupied city. It will sow division in the druchii ranks, and cast doubt in the minds of their leaders. Think of their dread when they learn that no number of soldiers can keep them safe, no wall or gate can keep out the shadows that hunt them. We must not only be merciless, we must be daring! We will terrorise our foes and infuriate them at the same time. No locks or bars will keep us out! We will steal the swords from their belts and the gold from their treasuries. Not only will they fear us, they will hate us for our audacity. We will drive them mad, send them thrashing at illusions while we laugh at them from the darkness.'

'I am not sure it can be done,' said Gildoran.

'It can and it will,' Alith replied calmly. 'Did we not open the gates of Anlec under the noses of the druchii? Did I not scale the palace of Aenarion, and spy upon Morathi as she performed her dark rituals? Tor Anroc is as nothing compared to the perils of Anlec.'

'And you ask us to risk our lives in this endeavour?' said Gildoran. 'Some would think it vanity.'

'I do not *ask* anything!' Alith growled, losing patience. 'I command and you obey. I am the Shadow King, and I have made my will known. If you cannot live with that, then leave, go east and live amongst the Ellyrians or the Sapherians or the Cothiquii. If you would be a Naggarothi, you will follow me!'

'Forgive me, prince,' said Gildoran. 'It shall be as you say.'

Mollified, Alith clapped an arm to Gildoran's shoulder and looked out at his shadow-walkers. The prince was genuinely excited by the prospect of what he was about to do, the first time in several years.

'Good!' said Alith. 'Death to the druchii!'

* * *

SITTING ON YRIANATH'S throne, Caenthras looked up as the doors of the great hall opened and a messenger entered quietly. She was dressed in a long robe of deep purple, silver medallions in the shape of elongated skulls hanging on slender chains from her belt. Caenthras recognised her immediately: Heikhir, one of the Anlec heralds. The Naggarothi prince glowered at the emissary as she strolled languidly along the hall. No doubt she carried more demands from Morathi.

'I bear tidings from your queen,' said Heikhir with a bow. Her actions were deferential, but Caenthras sensed mockery in their exaggerated precision. He knew that the court in Anlec considered him a failure. The treachery of Yeasir had ensured that. Far from being the power he had envisioned, he was little more than a puppet of Morathi, in turn manipulating her gutless mouthpiece, Yrianath. At least Palthrain had had the good grace to get himself killed to leave Caenthras in sole command of Tiranoc.

'What is it?' Caenthras asked wearily.

'The queen yet awaits your latest report on the hunt for the rebels in Eagle Pass,' said Heikhir.

Caenthras shrugged.

'Every soldier that can be spared scours the pass for these ghosts,' he said. 'If the queen were to command me to lead the army I would drive on into Ellyrion. These attacks are nothing more than a distraction.'

'These attacks are a direct affront to Queen Morathi,' Heikhir said pointedly. 'Can you find no more troops?'

'Not without weakening our defences on the border with Caledor,' said Caenthras. 'Perhaps she could spare me a sorcerer or two from her little coterie, to use their magic to track these... rebels?'

'The pretender king fights in Cothique, what threat is there from the south?' Heikhir asked, ignoring the question.

'Enough,' Caenthras replied. 'Or perhaps Morathi would prefer the dragon princes to simply fly over Tiranoc and attack Anlec directly?'

Heikhir laughed but there was no humour in her tone.

'I shall report that your efforts are... ongoing.'

Caenthras did not have the will to argue. It mattered not at all what he said, Heikhir would take back whatever message she thought most pleasing to her mistress. For a moment Caenthras considered writing a letter, to put his concerns into record. He dismissed the idea. For one thing, he was too tired. For another, he doubted it would ever get delivered.

'Is there anything else?' he sighed.

Heikhir shook her head with an impish smile and then bowed. Caenthras stared daggers into her back as he watched her leave.

Caenthras stood with some effort, weighed down by his worries. He turned to the door on his left, to make his way back to his chambers. He stopped in mid-stride. In front of the door there stood a shadowy figure, swathed in black.

'Who are you?' Caenthras demanded. 'Did Morathi send you?'

The stranger shook his head slowly, the movement barely visible in the depths of his hood.

'Did you come with Heikhir? What do you want?'

In reply, the figure drew back his hood. For a moment Caenthras did not recognise who it was, but then realisation dawned. The face had not changed much, but its expression had. Once it had looked at him with fawning desperation but the face he looked upon was filled with utter contempt.

'Anar!' snarled Caenthras as he realised several things at once: that Alith was the leader of the 'rebels' in Eagle pass; that his capture would bring Caenthras renewed favour from Anlec; and that he would take some personal pleasure from killing the last of the wretched House Anar. The ruler of Tor Anroc reached to his waist for his sword and then remembered that he had none – his blade was still in his bedchamber.

Alith had not moved; his eyes were fixed on Caenthras.

'I will call for the guards!' Caenthras declared, suddenly less certain of himself.

'And I will disappear,' Alith replied quietly. 'Your only chance of capturing me is to defeat me by your own hand.'

Caenthras looked around the hall for something he could use as a weapon, but there was nothing. Grimacing, he turned back to Alith.

'You would kill an unarmed enemy?'

'I have done so already, hundreds of times,' Alith said.

'You have no honour.'

'I have seen what happens in so-called fair fights,' Alith told him. 'The honourable usually lose.'

Alith reached over his shoulder and pulled forth a magnificent bow, made of a shimmering metal, decorated with twin symbols of the moon. Caenthras's stomach lurched as Alith fitted an arrow to the impossibly thin bowstring and raised the weapon.

Caenthras considered his options. It was doubtful he could cross the hall and grapple Alith before he loosed his shaft. There was nowhere to hide. If he called for aid, Alith would still shoot and then slip away, no doubt.

'You have been wronged, I admit that,' Caenthras said, taking a step forwards. 'By me, I know.'

'Wronged?' Alith spat. Caenthras flinched at the scorn in the young warrior's tone. 'Because of you my family is dead, my people slain or enslaved and my lands are a razed wilderness. By your hand, thousands of true Naggarothi have died. Your ambition has welcomed vile war and spread darkness across all of Ulthuan. And you say you have done wrong?'

'Please, Alith, show some mercy,' Caenthras pleaded, taking another step.

'No,' Alith replied, letting go of the bowstring.

* * *

ALITH STOWED HIS bow and pulled free his sword. Crossing swiftly to Caenthras's body, he pulled the arrow from his prey's left eye and chopped off Caenthras's head, placing the bloody trophy in a tightly woven sack. Alith headed back towards the door by which he had entered, but then stopped. He walked back to the corpse and gave it a hard kick in the ribs.

'I'll see you in Mirai, you bastard,' Alith whispered. 'I'm not finished with you.'

HORNS AND SHOUTS and other clamour roused Yrianath from his fitful slumber. He awoke to find an elf dressed in the livery of his servants shaking him. He did not recognise the face, but that was not unusual. The Naggarothi regularly changed his staff to ensure he had no one with whom he might conspire.

'What is it?' he asked groggily.

'Fire, my prince,' the servant gasped. 'The whole palace is on fire!'

Instantly awake, Yrianath leapt from his bed and grabbed the robe proffered by another attendant. He could smell smoke and as the two servants ushered him out of the chambers he could see the flicker of flames at the eastern end of the corridor.

'You will be safe in the gardens, lord,' the first servant told him, steering Yrianath towards a stairwell half-hidden behind a tapestry. 'We'll use the servants' way, it'll be quicker.'

Yrianath allowed himself to be led down the spiralling steps and along a narrow corridor. They passed rooms and passages he had never seen before, but he spared them not even a glance. Other servants were hurrying past in the opposite direction, on their way to fight the fire.

The group passed through one of the smaller kitchens and out into a wide herb garden. From here, Yrianath's escorts turned right and led him through an arch in a hedge. Yrianath found himself in a circular garden, bordered by the hedgerow and night-flowering hisathiun.

'Wait here a moment, prince,' the servant instructed him. Yrianath was not used to taking orders from his subjects, but he was confused and so stood where he had been left as the two attendants vanished into the darkness.

He waited there for a moment, turning his eyes up to the towers of the palace where flames flickered from the windows and a blot of smoke swathed the stars.

'Do you have any regrets?' a voice asked him from the darkness. Whirling around, Yrianath searched the night garden but saw nothing.

'Who's there?'

'Your conscience, perhaps,' the voice replied. 'How does it feel to have the deaths of so many on your hands? What do you think history will say of Prince Yrianath?'

'I was tricked! Trapped by Palthrain and Caenthras!'

'And so you did the honourable thing and took your own life... No, wait, that isn't what happened, is it?'

'Where are you?' Yrianath demanded, continuing to turn on the spot, seeking his interrogator. 'Show yourself.'

'Do you feel guilty?'

'Yes, yes I do!' Yrianath shrieked. 'Every night I am haunted by what I have done. I know I was foolish, short-sighted. I meant no harm!'

'And what act of contrition would you perform to make amends?'

'Anything, oh gods, I would do anything to put this right!'

Something shimmered in the darkness and a sheathed dagger fell at Yrianath's feet.

'What should I do with that?' he asked, staring at the knife as if it were a poisonous serpent.

'You know what to do. I suggest slitting your throat would be quickest.'

'What happens if I refuse?' Yrianath flicked the dagger away with the toes of his bare foot.

'This happens,' said the voice, directly behind Yrianath. There was a flutter of cloth and a black-gloved hand closed over his mouth, stifling his scream. Yrianath felt a hot pain in his back and then everything went numb. Blackness swallowed him and he fell.

ALITH REMOVED THE prince's head and placed it in the sack with Caenthras's. He would have spared Yrianath the indignity if he had been brave enough to take his own life. Instead, he would also be used as an example. A glance confirmed the fire raged in the palace, its ruddy light creeping across the gardens.

Keeping to the shadows, Alith headed for the boundary wall.

CLOUDS SWATHED THE mountains to the east, turning to a blood-red as the sun rose. A pall of smoke hung over Tor Anroc, the scorched towers of the palace rising as blackened spires over the city. Here and there embers glowed, flickering through glassless windows.

There had been panic on the streets, but the druchii commanders had stamped down ruthlessly on the citizens of Tor Anroc, accusing any that were found outside of being arsonists, slaying them on the spot. Fear shrouded the Tiranocii capital as much as the swathe of smoke.

'I'm glad I wasn't at the palace last night,' said Thindrin, slouching against the battlement of Tor Anroc's eastern gatehouse. The druchii's spear and shield were leant against the stonework next to him.

'For sure,' replied his companion, Illureth. 'I think that those that died in the fire were the lucky ones. The Khainite witches will have plenty of bodies for their pyres tonight when Caenthras is finished.'

'Or perhaps he'll send them into Eagle Pass, for the rebels to torture,' said Thindrin. His vicious grin turned to a frown. 'I'm not certain which is worse: witches or rebels.'

'For sure,' Illureth said again, suppressing a yawn. The sentry glanced absently over the rampart. Something caught his attention. 'What is that?'

Thindrin looked down to the roadway leading up to the gate and saw an indistinct shape, tall and thin in the dawn gloom. For a moment he took it to be a person, but then dismissed the notion. There was another shape, of the same size and height, on the other side of the road.

'I don't know,' he said. 'Stay here, I'll take a look.'

Thindrin snatched up his spear and shield and jogged casually down the steps inside the gate tower. He signalled to Coulthir at the gate to open the small access door. Ducking through, Thindrin walked a few paces along the road. Two spears had been driven into the turf either side of the paved slabs, and something round hung from each. As the light brightened and Thindrin walked closer, he saw what it was. His spear dropped from his grasp and clattered on the flagstones.

Thindrin gathered his wits for a moment and turned back to the gatehouse.

'You better send for the captain!' he called out.

Upon the spears were the heads of Princes Yrianath and Caenthras; the rune of shadow carved into the forehead of the first, the rune of vengeance cut into the cheek of the second.

TWENTY-TWO

Blades of Anlec

As THE LEGIONS of Anlec had brought misery and dread to Ulthuan, so Alith's shadow warriors visited terror and woe upon the druchii. They ranged across Tiranoc and Nagarythe, sometimes even daring Anlec itself to kill members of the courts and mutilate their bodies with symbols of dread: shadow and vengeance. Rarely did they gather in any numbers, so that the Naggarothi armies could not know whether to march south or north, to patrol the mountains or sweep the marshes and plains.

Alith would sometimes call a halt to the attacks, for dozens of days at a time. The first time he did this, the druchii believed that perhaps the mysterious Shadow King had been caught or slain. They were wrong, and in one night Alith unleashed coordinated attacks across the druchii-held territories, assassinating commanders, burning camps and stealing supplies. The next time there was a lull, the druchii were more fearful than when they were being attacked. The dreaded anticipation of what the Shadow King would inflict upon them next occupied their waking thoughts and tormented their dreams.

They were not disappointed. On midsummer's day, an army marching east towards the Eagle Pass vanished. It set out from Tor Anroc and never made it to the garrison at Koril Atir. No bodies were found and there was no sign of ambush; five thousand warriors were simply never seen again.

THE WAILING OF the elf maiden diminished quickly to a whimper and then fell silent as her blood spilled from her throat and spread into a pool upon the marble floor. Morathi contemplated her crimson reflection for a while, pleased with what she saw. Six years of constant war might have taken their toll on her underlings but she remained as fresh and beautiful as she had been on that momentous day so many centuries before.

She smiled at the recollection of her own naïveté of youth even as she recalled the thrill of power she had felt during that first sorcerous bargain. She had not known then quite how far that fateful encounter with the daemons would take her, but she regretted not a single step along the path. It was true that the swift victory she had once envisaged was now beyond her grasp, but nevertheless the war progressed well.

She dismissed the distracting thoughts with a shake of her head, her long curls of hair sending a thrill through her body as they tickled her shoulders. She fought back the urge to indulge in the sensation and lifted the blood-stained knife in her hand. Delicately, she pricked the tip of her thumb and allowed a single droplet of her own blood to fall into the pool made by the sacrifice. Where it touched the offering, her blood spread in a slow ripple, forming shadows of deeper red. The shadows became more defined, showing a scene of the mountains. Clouds scudded across the red sky and hung about crimson peaks. With a word she focussed the vision, zooming in to Eagle Pass. Her magical eye swept over a column of warriors and knights as they marched eastwards to confront the army of upstart Imrik. They would not be victorious but they would distract the usurper king long enough for other parts of her plan to be set in motion.

A discreet cough pulled her attention towards one of the archways leading into the chamber. A functionary dressed in silken robes bowed low and the sorceress beckoned him in with a beringed finger.

'Your guest awaits your pleasure, majesty,' said the servant.

'Bring him up immediately,' Morathi replied. She turned back to the scrying pool, instantly forgetting the servant's presence.

'Who is it?' someone asked from one of the adjoining rooms. His voice was hoarse, a whisper wracked with pain. 'Is it... Hotek?'

'No, it is not,' Morathi replied. 'He labours still, but his work will be complete soon enough. No, our guest is someone else, who brings very good news indeed.'

The scrape of a metal-shod foot on stone announced the arrival of Morathi's guest. He stood in the archway clad in armour that had been tested much, scratched and dented in many places. His black hair was swept back with a silver band and the right side of his face was livid with a long scar, his eye on that side a blank white orb.

'Prince Alandrian, how good of you to come,' Morathi said huskily.

'Milady,' replied Alandrian with a bow. 'It is my honour to finally come here and see you in person after all these years.'

'Yes it is,' said Morathi. 'But it is one that you deserve. What news of my reinforcements?'

'I have left a strong garrison at Athel Toralien and the siege is ongoing, majesty,' said Alandrian, unconsciously lifting a hand to his ruined face. 'The other colonies have been emptied of troops who now sail for Ulthuan. Five hundred thousand of your bravest and noblest warriors will be on these shores before winter.'

The prince's smile was mirrored by Morathi.

'That is good,' she said. 'While you await your troops, there is a small matter I want you to deal with.'

'I understand you wish to be rid of the so-called Shadow King,' replied Alandrian. 'With your support, I will have his head on a lance by the time the fleet arrives.'

'You will have all the support you need,' said Morathi. She looked through the archway from which the other voice had come, her expression suddenly pained. 'It vexes us that all is not well in Nagarythe. I expect you to restore stability as you did in Athel Toralien.'

'It will be done,' Alandrian replied with another bow. 'I will bring you the head of the Shadow King myself.'

'I trust that you will,' said Morathi.

'Yeasir was a traitor,' the husky voice said from the adjoining chamber, its wavering tone hinting at delirium. 'You would not betray us, Alandrian?'

'Yeasir was once strong, but when asked for true sacrifice he weakened,' said Morathi. 'Alandrian has already proven his loyalty in that matter, haven't you, Alandrian?'

'Khaine called to my daughters and they answered willingly,' said Alandrian. 'That their mother did not agree was unfortunate for her, majesty. I regret her lack of wisdom but I cannot regret her death.'

'I am told that your daughters' studies go well and that they have progressed far in the arts of Khaine,' said the sorceress-queen. 'I can barely recall their demure attendance to me in Athel Toralien those many years ago. Tell me, are they as devoted to their father now as they were when last we met?'

'Not as devoted as they are to the Lord of Murder,' said Alandrian, his scarred face creasing into a wry smile. 'I am very proud of them and I do not doubt that one day they will make all of Nagarythe similarly proud.'

Morathi took a few steps towards Alandrian and laid a gentle hand upon his ravaged cheek.

'I could fix that for you, my dear,' she said. 'You could be as handsome as you were when we first met.'

'Thank you, majesty, but I must decline,' said Alandrian. 'My scars remind me of the price of overconfidence. A mistake I will not repeat.'

'You always... had the most sense... of us all,' the whisper announced between hissing intakes of breath.

Alandrian said nothing for a moment, but dared a glance towards Morathi. The sorceress was distracted, still with a hand on his cheek, staring into the adjacent room. He turned slightly to follow her gaze but Morathi stepped in front of the prince, obscuring his view. She drew her hand back slowly and shook her head.

'Not yet,' she said quietly. A golden tear formed in her eye. 'Soon enough you can see him.'

THE CRIES OF gulls and crash of waves masked what little noise was made by the shadow army. The tang of salt on the air reminded Alith a little of Tor Elyr, a taste unfamiliar to one who had lived most of his life far from the sea. The Shadow King felt ill-at-ease. The headlands of Cerin Hiuath, less than a day's march south of Galthyr, were relatively exposed in comparison to the shadow warriors' usual hunting grounds. The moorlands to the east provided cover for the two hundred warriors to approach the coastal road, but the tops of the cliffs were all but devoid of features to offer concealment.

Despite his misgivings, Alith had brought a force here to strike at a worthy prize. Word had come to the Shadow King that several of Morathi's court, leaders of the various cults that vied for power within Nagarythe, were to take ship at Galthyr and sail north to join the druchii armies in Chrace. Knowing that the route direct from Anlec would be closely watched, the cult magisters were to take a more indirect route, travelling south-west before heading up the coast to the port. The possibility of killing or capturing these influential cultists was too tempting to pass up, and so Alith had hurriedly put out the command to several of the shadow warrior cadres to join him in the west.

For two days since they had gathered the shadow warriors watched the coast road for signs of the entourage. Alith expected them to be travelling with little protection: any large force moving out of Anlec would have attracted unwanted attention. If his two hundred warriors were not enough for the task, they would simply withdraw without being seen. Although the shadow warriors' daring had become part of the myth surrounding the Shadow King, the truth was that Alith thought himself a cautious commander, risking his warriors only when the odds were in his favour or, as now, the gains of victory warranted additional gambit. In this way the shadow warriors had suffered only a few dozen casualties since they had begun their campaign.

If the cultists were as careful as Alith thought they would be, they would travel fast and light, hoping to avoid detection. The fact that the course of the war in Avelorn and Cothique had lured these primates out of Anlec was in itself a victory of sorts, upon which Alith intended to capitalise as much as possible. The disappearance of the cult leaders would send their followers into disarray for some time, the power struggles and internal conflict ravaging Anlec and leaving the druchii vulnerable to further attacks. It was pleasing to Alith to turn the cults' weapons of disorder and fear against them, inflicting upon them the woes they had engineered for the princes of Ulthuan for several centuries. As they lived, so would they die.

Shortly after midday, one of the shadow warrior scouts came running hard from the south. He breathlessly reported his news to Alith and Khillrallion.

'Riders, lord, coming fast along the road,' the scout told them. 'I would say no more than thirty of them.'

'Are they the counsellors?' asked Khillrallion. 'Are they the ones we hunt?'

'I believe so,' said the shadow warrior. 'There are some twenty knights, the others are armed but dressed in fineries. One of them has long white hair braided with black roses, which matches what we know of Diriuth Hilandrerin, the magister of the cult of Atharti. He is responsible for the massacres at Enen Aisuin and Laureamaris. Another rides under a red banner marked with the dagger of Khaine, which was borne by the warriors of Khorlandir during the first siege of Lothern. I do not recognise the others but they wear many of the profane symbols of the cults.'

'They are our prey,' said Alith. He half-turned his head for a moment as he heard the faintest of whispers from the moonbow in the quiver upon his back. 'I can feel it in my bones. Their darkness comes before them like a wave.'

'Make ready for the ambush,' Khillrallion told the shadow warrior. 'Send a hawk to us when our quarry have passed your position. We will come at them from north, east and south and trap them.'

Alith nodded his assent; this was the plan he had outlined to the shadow-walkers a few days earlier.

'I want prisoners if possible,' the Shadow King reminded his companions. 'These creatures may be able to tell us much of what passes in Anlec, and of forces loyal to them in the other kingdoms. For the violence and suffering they have unleashed upon us, their deaths should be neither swift nor painless.'

The messenger set off at a run as Khillrallion departed to bring news of the imminent attack to the other shadow-walkers. Alith stayed where he was, in the shadow of an outcrop of rock directly overlooking the road. The coastal path was broad and paved with white stone, winding its way along the edge of the land less than a bow's shot from the crashing seas. He had picked a stretch of the road where the coast heaped into rough hills and dropped away sharply to jagged rocks at the water's edge. The ambushers had not only the advantage of surprise but also position. The shadow warriors had the ambush site well scouted, and despite the scarcity of cover most of them could be concealed within a few hundred paces of the road and would strike before being seen. The rest were to remain out of sight further east, to move in as a reserve should resistance be stronger than anticipated.

Alith drew forth the moonbow and gave it a loving stroke.

'More blood for you today,' he whispered as he fitted an arrow to the string.

* * *

ALITH HEARD THE riders before he could see them. Hooves pounded on the cobbles of the road as the druchii made a dash for the comparative safety of Galthyr. He waited, fighting back tension and excitement, and cast a glance behind him to ensure that none of his warriors could be seen. In this regard the Shadow King was very pleased. Even though he knew where each shadow warrior lay in wait, not a single one caught his eye.

A troop of ten knights were the first to come into view, their silver armour gleaming in the summer sun, their black uniforms and banners streaming in the sea breeze. Alith let them pass without hindrance. A short distance behind, perhaps only a few dozen paces, the rest of the party galloped: ten more knights formed up around a knot of lavishly dressed nobles and retainers.

When the magisters and their bodyguards were almost level with Alith, he rose from his hiding place, moonbow ready. He was a heartbeat from letting loose the string when a shout from behind him drew his attention. Furious that one of his warriors had betrayed their presence, Alith turned to see what had happened. His anger quickly became alarm when he saw what had caused the cry.

Along the hills to the east a line of warriors appeared, regiment upon regiment of warriors in black and purple advancing beneath long banners. Crossbowmen formed into lines on the flanks as spearmen and swordsmen advanced in the centre. On and on they came, thousands of druchii.

Alith spared no time trying to answer the question that hammered into his brain at the first sight of the army: how did so many warriors come to be here? Rather than ponder that which he could not answer, Alith leapt immediately to a more pressing issue: how to escape?

The twenty knights had come together in a single squadron on the road and faced eastwards, barring any route to the north; their charges continued along the road and were quickly disappearing from sight.

Running figures from the south – shadow warriors shouting warnings as they approached – told Alith they there was no sanctuary in that direction either.

'To me!' Alith called out. 'Rally to me!'

The Shadow King watched the wave of black-armoured warriors advancing from the east as the shadow warriors gathered around him. A glance at the sun told him that the druchii had timed their attack well; they would be at the road some time before the first evening shadows fell.

'We have been lured into a trap,' Alith said hurriedly as the shadow warriors clustered around him. They crouched in a circle, partially concealed by the grass of the hills. Some stared intently at Alith with desperation in their eyes, others cast nervous glances at the knights on the road or allowed their gaze to be drawn to the army in the east. The riders close at hand seemed content to stay out of bow's reach. Why would they not? Alith thought, there is no need to attack with so many reinforcements on the way.

'The sea is our only escape,' Alith said. 'We must reach the waters and then swim south and come ashore at Koril Thandris. From there, we separate and make our way east, to meet again at Cardain.'

'The knights will charge if we attempt to cross the road,' said Khillrallion. 'We cannot outrun warhorses.'

'Then we must kill the knights first,' said Alith with a shrug.

'Bows against fully armoured knights?' asked one of the shadow warriors, a young elf called Faenion.

'There are only twenty of them,' snapped Alith. 'Shoot at their horses; on foot they will be little match for us. When the road is clear, we head down to the shore a little way to the south, where there is a shingle beach.'

At this the shadow warrior who had come from the south before the ambush spoke again.

'There are more knights moving up the road from that direction,' he said with a shake of his head. 'At least fifty of them. I do not think we can reach the sea that way before they cut off the road.'

Alith growled in frustration. It was not just the fact that he had been caught out that upset him; he had enjoyed so many successes of late his luck had been bound to run out at some point. What worried him more was the precision with which the trap had been set. The bait had been irresistible and the enemy had guessed exactly where and when he would strike. The Shadow King wondered for a moment if he had become too predictable, but dismissed the notion as soon as it came. Whoever had masterminded this particular trap had simply got the better of him this time.

'We'll have to climb down the cliffs,' Alith said at last. 'Slay the knights at hand and get to the clifftops. From there we'll just have to take our chances amongst the rocks.'

The shadow warriors exchanged worried glances and there were a few murmurs of dismay.

'The enemy will not wait for you to regain your courage!' snarled Alith, pointing a finger towards the lines of black steadily closing from the east. 'Follow me, or stay here and die.'

Alith stood up and strode purposefully towards the Anlec knights on the road. He lifted up the moonbow and sighted along the shaft, his aim settling on a rider at the front of the formation. The arrow leapt from the string and took the knight full in the chest, punching through iron and tearing from his back to pass through the throat of the rider behind him.

Startled, the knights took a moment to collect themselves ready for a charge, in which time Alith felled three more with another shot. Lowering their lances, the knights urged their steeds into a full gallop and thundered towards the shadow warriors. Alith watched them coolly. On the Ellyrion plains and in the forests of Avelorn, he had learnt the reputation of these deadly riders was greater than their actual strength. When he might once have trembled at the armoured warriors bearing down on him, he felt only contempt.

Another shot from the moonbow sliced through the neck of the lead horse and buried itself in the chest of the following steed, sending both crashing to the ground. The other shadow warriors sent their own arrows arcing into the knights in a series of deadly volleys and before the knights had crossed half the distance from the road all were dead or lying wounded in the grass.

A look over his shoulder confirmed to Alith that the approaching army was now closing fast.

'To the cliffs, follow me,' he shouted, stowing the moonbow and breaking into a run directly towards the sea.

Alith led the retreat, casting glances over his shoulder towards the approaching druchii host as the shadow warriors reached the road. The enemy were advancing quickly but Alith and his warriors would be at the cliff edge before their repeater crossbows were in range. A look to the south revealed the knights coming along the road; they too would not reach the shadow warriors before they were safely moving down the cliff. Though the situation was not good, Alith was more confident than when he had first seen the banners rising over the hills. Despite this he did not allow himself to relax.

'Keep moving!' Alith ordered as several of his warriors took up positions to shoot at the oncoming druchii. 'No rearguard will hold them back.'

When he was a few dozen strides from the cliff edge Alith caught his first glimpse of the sea. He marvelled at the unending dark blue horizon but as he continued forwards he saw the wider expanse of the ocean. High waves rolled in towards Ulthuan, far stronger than the tides of the Inner Sea he had witnessed at Tor Elyr. Ignoring his own command, he stumbled to a halt, mesmerised by the spectacle. As far as he could see in every direction stretched the Great Ocean, dwarfing him with its size. Far beyond lay the jungles of Lustria, where the descendants of the Old Ones' servants clung to civilisation. Ruined cities and steaming mangroves, treacherous swamps and ancient treasures awaited bold adventurers and explorers.

Alith realised how little of the world he had seen. He had never been to Elthin Arvan to the east, or the colonies of Elithis, or the towers of the elves far to the south. Had it not been for the civil war, would he have ever visited Ellyrion or Avelorn?

Shouts from his shadow warriors broke Alith's reverie and he snapped back to the current situation. His companions were pointing down to the seas and there he saw something that sapped his confidence as quickly as it had returned: three black ships at anchor not far from the shore.

Reaching the cliff edge, Alith looked down to gauge the difficulty of the descent. The cliff was not quite vertical, the strata of rocks pronounced in light and dark bands, the surface pitted with many holes and ledges. It was not the most difficult climb Alith had attempted. The cliff was not the problem, the greatest dangers were at their feet where surf crashed against jagged rocks and swirled in strong currents through jutting piles of tumbled boulders.

Something black and heavy blurred through the air close by Alith, quickly followed by other projectiles. Several shadow warriors were thrown from their feet with long shafts jutting from their bodies as the ships loosed their deadly bolt throwers. The swish of spear-sized missiles filled the air as more shadow warriors were cut down by another volley.

Along the cliff face warriors threw down their weapons to lighten themselves, some of them tearing off their cloaks and boots as well. Many hesitated, staring in horror at the black ships lurking out to sea or transfixed by the bodies of the slain.

'Keep moving!' Alith yelled again, unfastening his cloak and tossing it to the ground. Looking left and right he saw his followers pulling themselves over the cliff to begin the long descent. He grabbed the quiver from his back, ready to cast it aside, but hesitated. The moonbow gleamed in the sunlight. He could not abandon such a hard-won prize. Pulling it free, he passed the moonbow over his shoulder, threw away the quiver and then swung himself over the clifftop.

The shadow warriors were nimble and well-versed in climbing, and soon most of them were halfway down the cliff. Bolts from the lurking vessels hammered into the grey stone, some of the shots finding their mark, sending shadow warriors tumbling down to the frothing surf below. Rock shrapnel splintered from the iron heads of the bolts as they crashed into the cliff face, shredding Alith's clothes and grazing skin. One bolt missed his foot by the smallest of margins, pulverising the rock on which he had been stood. Alith scrabbled to find a new grip as he swung dangerously from one hand.

Panicked shouts and cries of pain mixed with the sound of the waves as Alith dropped from one handhold to the next, swinging from ledge to outcrop, his fingers finding purchase in small cracks, his toes making solid footing out of striations no wider than a finger.

More and more of Alith's warriors were falling to the bolt throwers, their screams drowned in the thunder of the sea as they plummeted into the swirling waves. Perhaps a quarter of their number had already been lost.

'They'll kill us all!' Alith bellowed to his followers. 'Leap into the water!'

The shadow warriors were too fearful of jumping to their possible deaths, but to Alith it was more certain that their doom would come if they remained on the cliff face.

'With me!' he cried, letting go his handholds and pushing out with all of the strength in his legs.

Wind battered Alith's face and tore at his hair as he fell towards the seas. He saw the foaming spume hurled into the air by the sharp pinnacles of the reefs, but it was the rocks below the water that he feared more. He closed his eyes and angled into a dive with a silent prayer to the sea god Mannanin upon his lips.

Hitting the water was like being kicked by a horse, forcing all of the air from Alith's body. He banged his right arm against something and immediately lost all feeling in his hand. He was engulfed by a storm of bubbles, tossing him this way and that, threatening to dash him against the rocks. He was turned upside down, twisted back and forth by the fierce eddies, the water colouring red from his wounds. Light and dark whirled as he rolled between the surface and the forbidding depths. Coldness seeped into his flesh and gnawed at his bones.

Alith struck out, fighting against a surge that threatened to drag him deeper and deeper into the water. One-handed he clawed his way to the bubbling surface, buffeted and buoyed by the heaving waves. Twice more the current snapped at his legs, pulling him under, filling his mouth with salt water. He coughed and spluttered, and gave a howl of pain as he was thrown into the sharp edge of a spire-like reef, a long gash torn across his stomach. The current tugged at the moonbow, its string cutting deep into Alith's arm. It tangled with his legs and batted against his face, but Alith would not relinquish his prized weapon.

Stroke by painful stroke, the Shadow King forged through the waters. He managed to gain his bearings and turned south, away from the druchii ships. A look back to the cliffs confirmed that the druchii army had arrived. Crossbowmen unleashed a storm of quarrels from above, picking off those shadow warriors who did not possess the courage to make the leap into the sea.

Slicks of red stained the water, and Alith had no idea how many warriors had been lost. He saw several, Khillrallion among them, clinging to the rocks, gasping for breath. They were sheltered in the lee of a giant pinnacle that stood apart from the rest of the cliff like a huge grey needle. Alith swam over to them and grabbed a handhold in the cracked surface of the rock.

'We cannot stay here,' Alith panted. He pointed upwards, to the gathering druchii troops, too breathless to say anything further. Khillrallion nodded in understanding and signalled for the others to follow.

Exhausted, Alith pushed away, unable to spare any more thought for his followers. He needed all of his strength and focus just to stay alive.

TWENTY-THREE

The Night of Dark Knives

MORATHI'S DISPLEASURE WAS not usually a survivable experience, but Alandrian held his nerve as he strode up the steps of Anlec's palace. It was true that he had not captured or killed the enigmatic Shadow King, but he had come much closer than anyone else in the last six years. He was not foolish enough to believe that Morathi would simply forgive him his failure, but Alandrian had already devised a new plan to ensnare the elusive renegade; a plan that would not only bring success but also be an act of contrition on his part. He had even taken the bold step of requesting an audience rather than awaiting the queen's summons.

Upon entering the throne chamber, Alandrian was taken aback by the smile that Morathi wore. She sat upon a chair beside the great throne of Aenarion, swathed in a voluminous robe of white fur and black silk, her bared arms and legs pale in the lamplight. Her whole demeanour was welcoming, its openness more disconcerting than a scowl.

Alandrian suppressed a shudder as he felt dark magic crawling across his skin and fancied he saw flittering shapes in the shadows at the edge of vision. Half-heard voices whispered and twittered around him, and he struggled to ignore their taunts and promises, focussing on the sorceress-queen.

'Majesty,' said Alandrian, bowing long and low. 'I offer my deepest apologies for the lack of success in apprehending the deviant who has so vexed your thoughts of late.'

'Stand up,' said Morathi, her voice neither cruel nor kind. She continued in the same matter-of-fact tone. 'We could waste a great deal of time, with me reminding you of your failings, and you offering apologies and excuses. Let us assume that such a conversation took place in the manner we both anticipated.'

Alandrian felt a flutter of fear. Was he to be presented no opportunity to argue his case? Perhaps he had overestimated his position and influence.

'With that in mind, I am sure your arguments would conclude with an offer to make amends,' Morathi continued, her voice softening.

She stood and beckoned to a group of shadowy figures who had been lurking in the darker recesses of the hall. Three sorcerers – two female, one male – came out of the gloom, clad in robes of dark purple, their skin dyed with archaic symbols that set Alandrian's teeth on edge. He had never been comfortable with sorcery; it seemed a dangerous weapon to wield.

'These are three of my most promising protégés, Alandrian,' Morathi said, gliding effortlessly across the hall towards the prince, her sorcerers falling in behind her. Alandrian swallowed hard, eyes flicking from Morathi's alluring eyes to the harsh stares from her disciples.

The sorceress-queen stopped in front of Alandrian and placed a finger to his lips as he was about to speak. Alandrian felt a thrill of energy surge through him from her touch, stirring his heart, awakening urges he had not felt since the sacrifice of his wife.

'Hush, prince, let me finish what I have to say,' she said, her voice as soft as a velvet caress. 'You have another plan to apprehend the Shadow King, if I am but merciful and generous enough to grant you another chance. Something like that, was it?'

Alandrian nodded dumbly, not trusting himself to speak. Between the dark magic clouding his senses and the sensuous presence of Morathi, he was quite unable to gather his thoughts. He quivered uncontrollably, caught between lust and abject terror, both emotions stemming from the same cause.

'Good,' said Morathi, stepping back and crossing her arms across her perfectly formed chest, her weight on one leg, her smooth thigh exposed through a slit in her robe. Alandrian forced himself to keep his gaze on her equally beautiful face, dismissing the temptation to reach out and stroke that delightful skin. 'I am not known for my mercy, nor my generosity, but I would offer nothing less to one who has known such favour from my son and has given so much in the service of Nagarythe. Your past actions and loyalty far surpass those of my other subjects, and you may rest easy for the moment, knowing that you also have my favour, despite the recent setback you have suffered.'

Released from Morathi's spell, Alandrian recovered his wits and was about to offer his profuse thanks, but was stifled by a slight shake of the head from the queen.

'Don't grovel,' she said, 'it's beneath you.'

She turned with a sweep of her arm, hair swirling in a dark cloud about her shoulders. Alandrian had to look away as Morathi prowled back to her chair, hips swaying. He looked at her again only when she was seated, regal and austere once more.

'Tell me how my faithful minions might help you in your efforts,' Morathi said.

'I fear that there is no bait that we can now dangle that will lure the Shadow King into a trap,' Alandrian said, speaking confidently, glad that his speech was well rehearsed, for his thoughts had been scattered by Morathi's actions. Just as she had intended, he realised. 'If we are to slay this scorpion, we must find his nest and drag him out by the tail.'

'I agree,' said Morathi. 'How do you plan to find him when so many thousands of others have failed?'

'I have been studying the attacks of his warriors, in great detail,' Alandrian explained. 'At first they appear capricious, striking east and west, north and south without pattern. But there is a pattern there, I have seen it before.'

'Really?' said Morathi, leaning forwards with interest, one hand stroking her delicate chin. 'What have you seen?'

'In Elthin Arvan I became a keen hunter; the forests there teem with game,' Alandrian said, cautiously taking a step forwards. 'Some chase boar, others prefer deer, but I was not interested in those things. I much preferred to hunt those that also hunt. If you can best the hunter at his own game, you have truly proven yourself.'

'A trait I find most appealing at the moment,' Morathi said with a smile, her eyes alight with a glimmer of silver fire. 'Please, carry on.'

'The Shadow King hunts like a wolf,' Alandrian announced with a grin. 'It is difficult to discern, but it is there. Nagarythe is his territory and he patrols it regularly, putting his mark on one area before moving on to the next. In any given year he could strike anywhere, but it has been six years now and his thoughts are known to me. The attack near Galthyr is an aberration created by us and I must discount that from my thinking. After his next attack we will know where he has been and, more importantly, I know where he will have moved to. We will strike swiftly, take him unawares.'

'All of this sounds very worthy, but what is it that you need from me?' Morathi asked.

'Nagarythe is too large an area for your sorcerers to cover with their scrying powers, especially when looking for something constantly moving,' Alandrian explained. 'I can only estimate the Shadow King's presence in a general area, too large to sweep by conventional means without alerting him to our presence. Between my theory and the abilities of one of your sorcerers we should be able to locate the Shadow King with precision.'

'And how will you deal with him once you know where he is?' Morathi inquired, sitting back and crossing her arms again.

'If you would indulge me for a moment, majesty?' Alandrian asked, receiving a nod of assent in return.

He left the hall briefly and returned with two other elves, females so alike as to be twins. They wore breastplates and vambraces of gold chased with rubies carved with runes of Khaine, which flickered with a bloody light. Their silver hair was drawn back into long tresses bound with sinew and circlets of bone; bright blue eyes stared out of masks of painted blood. Each carried numerous blades: several daggers at their belts and in their boots; pairs of long swords hanging from their waists; matched scimitars upon their backs; boots and fingerless gloves armoured with spikes and blades. Even their fingers were hung with rings armed with curving talons of gilded iron.

'Two of Khaine's most promising slayers,' Alandrian announced with a proud smile. 'I present my precious daughters, Lirieth and Hellebron.'

Morathi stood and walked forwards again, her expression appreciative. She nodded, gauging the two warrior-maidens closely.

'Yes,' Morathi purred. 'Yes, they would be very fine weapons indeed. You need someone to guide them to the target.'

Morathi turned and looked at her disciples, before gesturing to one of the females. She was short and slight in comparison to Alandrian's assassins, her dark hair cut at the shoulder. Her skin was even paler than the queen's and her hair was shot through with streaks of icy silver, giving her the appearance of a winter spirit. She regarded the Khainites coolly, lips pursed, eyes analysing every detail.

'This one is the best at scrying,' Morathi announced. 'Get her close and she will be able to find the Shadow King for you. Step forwards, dear, and introduce yourself to the prince.'

The sorceress did as she was bid, giving a perfunctory nod of the head.

'It will be my pleasure to serve you, Prince Alandrian,' she said, her voice as cold as her demeanour. 'My name is Ashniel.'

ALITH'S LAUGHTER WAS echoed by a few of the other shadow warriors, but many did not share his sanguine view on his close encounter upon the cliffs. Both Khillrallion and Tharion had voiced concerns that Alith was becoming reckless, though they had couched their misgivings in more polite terms.

Some of the survivors of the ambush Alith had sent further east, to recuperate from their wounds and spread the word of what had happened; Alith was aware that the druchii would try to claim some form of victory from the affair and wanted his continued survival to be widely known. The others he had brought to this haven and some of the shadow-walkers had been summoned for an impromptu conference, at one of several sanctuaries the shadow warriors had created across Nagarythe.

Alith held court in a farmhouse a short distance from the town of Toresse in the south of Nagarythe; a place that had once been populated by a mix of Naggarothi and Tiranocii and had suffered greatly as a result while Prince Kheranion had lived. Many of the inhabitants had been killed or enslaved as 'half-breed' and all discontent had been violently put down by the prince's soldiers. Like many other brutalised towns and villages, Toresse had become a centre of quiet dissent against druchii rule that had found new hope with the coming of the Shadow King. The owner of the farm moved around the table with loaves of bread and cuts of lamb, casting awestruck glances at his guest.

'I am the rat that nips the fingers of those who try to catch me,' joked Alith, searching through the wine bottles on the table seeking to refill his goblet. 'There is nothing more frustrating for our foes than success snatched away at the last moment.'

'Our foes might call the deaths of more than a hundred warriors a success,' Tharion said sombrely. He gave a maudlin shake of the head and stared into his half-empty cup. 'We have grown arrogant with our success, believing ourselves untouchable.'

Alith's humour dissipated and he directed a frown towards Tharion.

'Every cause demands sacrifice,' said the Shadow King.

Tharion looked up and met his lord's stare with a bleak gaze.

'No cause is furthered by pointless sacrifice,' he said. 'Just ask the thousands that have burned on the pyres of the cultists.'

'You compare me to the leeches that have sucked the life out of Nagarythe?' snarled Alith, hurling aside his goblet. 'I have asked no elf to risk any more than I risk myself. I do not send my followers out to die while I remain safe behind castle walls. I gave you all a choice, one that you freely accepted. I repeat that now, to you and every shadow warrior. If you no longer believe in our cause, if you feel you can no longer fight the war we must fight, you are free to leave Nagarythe. If you remain, I expect you to fight for me, to follow me as your rightful king. I demand much, I know, but it is nothing less than I demand of myself.'

'You misunderstan–' began Tharion but Alith cut him off.

'Now is the time to strike again!' he declared, turning his attention away from Tharion to address the others in the room. 'While the druchii pat each other on the back and tell each other how close they came to catching the Shadow King, we will visit upon them a fresh humiliation, a punishment for their hubris.'

'*Their* hubris?' muttered Tharion.

'Forgive him, lord,' cut in Khillrallion before Alith could reply. The shadow-walker took Tharion by the arm and pulled him up. 'He has been most distressed by the thought that you might be taken from us, and he is not used to strong wine.'

Tharion snatched free his arm and smoothed out the creases in his shirt sleeve. He looked at the assembled shadow warriors, somewhat unsteadily, and then focussed on Alith.

'We fight for you, Alith,' Tharion murmured. 'You are the Shadow King, and we are your shadow army. Without you, there is no us. Are no us?

Whatever. Don't get yourself killed trying to prove something you've already proven.'

Tharion pushed his way across the room followed by glances from the others, some angry, others sympathetic. The slam of the door brought a disconcerted silence, many looking to Alith, some avoiding each other's gaze out of embarrassment.

'He's just a little drun–' began Khillrallion.

'He is in danger of becoming a mother hen, a smothering hen even,' said Alith. 'I am no helpless chick, and neither are my brave, my very brave shadow warriors. That is the nature of the hunt. Succeed and eat, fail and starve.'

Alith rounded on the others, anger written across his face.

'Do you think I want my followers to die?' he snapped. 'Did I ask for our families to be butchered and our homes destroyed? I did not choose this life, it chose me! The gods and the druchii have made me what I am, and I will be that thing because our people need it. I do the things I do, terrible things, we do the terrible things we do, so that those that come after us might not have to do the same.'

Alith ripped off his woollen shirt and turned his back on the shadow warriors, showing them the scar of the whip blow he had suffered in Anlec. He turned back to face them, pointing to more wounds upon his body and arms, those from the flight at the cliffs still livid.

'These injuries are as nothing to the suffering our people endure!' he raged, scattering the bottles with a sweep of his arm. He looked upwards but in his mind's eye did not see the beamed ceiling but rather the everlasting heavens where the gods were said to dwell. 'A cut, a bruise, what do they mean? True torment is in the spirit. The spirit of a whole generation crushed by the evil of the druchii. What more must I give to spare them what I have experienced?'

Alith stooped and picked up a bottle from the floor. He brought it down on the edge of the table, smashing it. Staring again at the gods only he could see, he raised the broken pottery to his chest.

'Do you want more blood, is that it?' he cried out. 'Perhaps you want me dead? Like my mother and father. No more Anars. Would that satisfy you?'

Khillrallion grabbed his lord's arm and wrenched the broken bottle from his fingers, tossing it aside. He said nothing and simply laid his arm across Alith's shoulders, pulling him close. The Shadow King pushed him away and half-turned before stumbling and falling to his knees.

'Why me?' Alith sobbed, burying his face in his hands, blood streaming as his fresh wounds reopened.

The other shadow warriors gathered close, patting Alith on the shoulder and laying comforting hands on his head.

'Because you are the Shadow King,' said Khillrallion, kneeling next to his leader. 'Because nobody else can do it.'

* * *

THE FOLLOWING MORNING no mention was made of Alith's outburst. The discussion amongst the shadow warriors after Alith had departed had been one of solidarity with their leader. They knew they could never share the burdens he had chosen to bear, and had reaffirmed their faith in each other and the Shadow King. Some had remarked that it was all too easy to think of the Shadow King and forget the Alith Anar that was obscured by the title: an elf barely into adulthood who had lost everything and taken it upon himself to become the spirit of vengeance for all of them.

After breakfasting, Alith called his band to him and took them south, coming upon the waters of the Naganath before midday. From the concealment of a boulder-strewn hillock, Alith pointed westwards, to a stone bridge that arced over the river, a fortified tower at each end. The river was narrow and fast, less than two hundred paces wide.

'The Ethruin crossing,' Alith told his warriors with an impish smile. 'It is the most direct route between Anlec and Tor Anroc. In the summer the closest crossings are two days west or a further day and a half east. In the winter the ford at Eathin Anror is impassable, adding another day to the journey if one wishes to go by the eastern route. Imagine Morathi's irritation when next an army marches south only to find the bridge gone?'

'Irritation, lord?' said Tharion. 'Two garrisoned towers seem a tough nut to crack only to cause some irritation.'

'You're missing the point, Tharion,' said Alith. 'I *want* the druchii to come after me. It was a close thing at Galthyr, but I have learnt the lesson. Our enemies will divert valuable resources to finding *me*. They are used to the attacks of the shadow warriors, but the Shadow King, well he is the source of all their frustrations. I want to mock them. I want them so mad that they'll do whatever they can to find me. When they do that, they will make a mistake and we will exploit it, whatever it turns out to be. Imagine having to double the garrison on every crossing in Nagarythe. Every storehouse and grain barn will need guarding. While they scrabble around for the Shadow King, the other shadow warriors will roam free and cause anarchy.'

'You think that being deliberately petty will rile them even more?' asked Tharion.

'I wanted them scared, but their near-success will allay some of that fear, for a while at least,' said Alith. 'That being the case, I must select a different shaft for my bow, one that will not strike deep but will strike many times. Like the persistent wasp, I shall sting them again and again, each wound not sufficient to kill, but enough to infuriate. If they think they can get the better of the Shadow King, I will prove them otherwise. Just when they think I'm done, I'll be back, again and again, stinging them until they cry. They can swat and flail until they are screaming and breathless, and still I'll come back!'

'I understand,' said Tharion. 'One other question, though.'

'What?' replied Alith.

'How do we make a bridge disappear?'

ALITH WAS HEARTILY sick of the stench of fish. It was in the fisherman's smock he wore, in his hair, under his fingernails. He sat in the shadow of the fishing boat's sail as it slid gently along the Naganath towards the Ethruin bridge. Druchii soldiers stood at either end of the span, checking the occasional carts and wagons that crossed the border. More warriors could be seen drilling close to the northern tower.

All was as it had been for the last fifteen days. The druchii were content to let the flotilla of boats pass up and down the river, as they had done so for hundreds of years. The white-painted vessels warranted barely a glance, so familiar were they. All of the boats were from Toresse. Their owners did not know what Alith had intended, but had been willing to aid the Shadow King if it meant discomfort for their overlords.

As the boat lowered its mast and passed under the bridge, Alith slipped over the bulwark into the water, along with the other three shadow warriors hiding amongst the crew. They swam swiftly to the brick bank beneath the bridge and pulled themselves out of the water. Removing several of the blocks to reveal a hiding place, Alith pulled out wool-wrapped bundles of tools: broad chisels and mallets with cushioned heads.

The four of them pulled themselves up by means of a web of narrow ropes that had been constructed under the bridge, hung from hooks that had been screwed into the mortar of the bridge itself. Taking up their places, backs to the water rushing below, they continued their work, carefully chipping away at the mortar, the soft taps of their muffled hammers hidden by the gurgle and swirl of the Naganath. When a stone had been sufficiently loosened, they brought out wooden wedges, knocking the supports into place to keep the bridge intact for the time being.

In this painstaking fashion Alith and his followers had taken apart the bridge block by block, using the wedges and the natural pressure of its arch to keep the structure in one piece. The ropes that held them out of the water were also passed through holes cut in the thick ends of the wedges, allowing them to be pulled free at a later time.

Nearly two-thirds of the bridge had been thus prepared for demolition, by small teams of shadow warriors working in shifts from dawn until dusk. It was muscle-aching and mind-numbing work, lying virtually immobile in their rope cradles, repetitively working away at a finger's length of mortar at a time.

Until midday Alith and his companions laboured, when the fishing fleet returned and they were picked up, another team of shadow warriors replacing them. The boats were moored at Toresse and Alith stepped onto the quay to find Khillrallion waiting for him. The shadow-walker was pensive.

'Bad tidings, friend?' Alith asked.

'Perhaps,' said Khillrallion. The two of them turned off the road that led into the town and made their way along the reed-strewn bank of the river. 'Tharion is missing.'

'I saw him only this morning, as I left on the boats,' said Alith. 'He cannot have gone far.'

Khillrallion's expression was part-grimace and part-smile.

'I sent some of the others to look for him, but though he was late to the lesson he has learned the arts of the shadows well. There is no sign of where he has gone.'

'Sometimes we all need some time alone,' Alith reasoned.

'Not Tharion,' Khillrallion argued. 'He has never been shy in speaking his mind amongst others, and has no problem confiding his woes to me. He feels his age and a misplaced guilt over the fall of Elanardris.'

'Misplaced?' said Alith. 'None of our guilt is misplaced, we all must accept that we played a part in the downfall of the Anars, even if our intentions were the opposite.'

'I would suggest you do not say such things to Tharion, if we find him,' said Khillrallion. 'Since Cerin Hiuath he has been preoccupied with the dynasty of the Anars. He is of a far older breed than you and I, one of your grandfather's generation. We all despise what has become of Ulthuan, but it is only those that were there when she was saved from the daemons who really feel what has been lost. They gave their blood once to save our people, and they thought they did so in order that we who came later would not have to.'

'But why has this affected him now?' asked Alith. He sat down at the river's edge and Khillrallion sat beside him. 'For six years we have fought the druchii.'

'You have become the Shadow King, but Tharion can only see you as Alith Anar, grandson and son to two of his closest friends, the last of their line. For you Elanardris is now a memory, the shadow war has become your new legacy. For Tharion, that lineage, that tradition, is still embodied in you. You are not the Shadow King, you are the last of the Anars. He does not trust the Caledorians or the Chracians or any of the others to restore that which has been lost in our lands. Only while you live can he still cling to the hope that the glory of Elanardris, all of Nagarythe, might be restored. He fears that if you die, all hope dies with you.'

Alith pondered this without comment. He had endured some of Tharion's stubbornness and old-fashioned thinking out of a sense of duty to the veteran. In truth he tried not to dwell on the ageing elf too much, for Alith could not think of Tharion without also thinking of Eoloran, possibly dead, more likely languishing in some cell in Anlec. In all he had found it better not to think too much about the past, only the promise of revenge held by the future.

Alith thought about Tharion's concerns, as voiced by Khillrallion. Perhaps he was too possessed of being the Shadow King that he had forgotten who he was beneath the title. But that person lived in constant pain, surrounded by dark memories and feelings of impotence. The heir of the Anars had been powerless; the Shadow King was powerful. It brought its own woes and pain, but they were as nothing compared to the agony that awaited him once he had fulfilled his oath. What then? Alith asked himself. Who would he be when the shadow war was over? Perhaps Tharion would know.

'Find him for me,' Alith said quietly, laying a hand on Khillrallion's arm. 'Tell him that I need him with me, and I have something very important for him to do.'

THARION HAD STILL not been found when the time came for Alith to enact the second part of his plan. It was dusk, thirty days since the peril of Cerin Hiuath, and the Shadow King was poised to prove that he was not dead. Alith and his warriors were concealed amongst the trees and rushes that bordered the river east of the bridge. The boats and their crews were at the Toresse quays, ready for the signal to come downriver.

As darkness fell, several lights could be seen to the north, in woods that bordered the Anlec road. Flickering red and thin columns of smoke betrayed the presence of several fires. Their presence did not go unnoticed by the watchers in the guard towers and soon the trumpets were calling the garrison to order. Spear and sword companies were mustered at the north end of the bridge, their commander shouting excited commands. With a tramp of feet, the force marched to investigate.

When they were out of sight, Alith and the shadow warriors slipped out of hiding, bows ready. The towers would not be completely abandoned, but Alith knew he had enough warriors to deal with those druchii that remained.

The Shadow King led his fighters to the north tower, approaching the bridge silently. A cluster of figures stood atop the battlement gazing to the north. As at Koril Atir, the shadow warriors soundlessly scaled the walls of the tower. The druchii had hung chains festooned with barbs and spikes beneath the battlements to prevent such a move. Alith and the others bound their hands with cloth and pulled them gently aside to allow each other to pass.

Once on the rampart, it was a matter of a single volley to fell the guards, though two let out piercing cries of pain as they died. Alith had considered this and ran to the south side of the tower.

'Come quickly!' he cried out across the river. 'We caught some of the Shadow King's scum! The others are getting away! Quick!'

Alith split his warriors, sending some into the tower to ensure every room was clear, keeping the rest atop the tower. It was not long before the gate of the other guard house swung open and a stream of several dozen warriors emerged onto the bridge.

'Wait until they're close,' Alith told the warriors crouched behind the embrasures even as he waved the druchii to hurry up.

When the enemy were halfway across the bridge, Alith gave his shadow warriors the nod. They rose up behind the battlement and unleashed a storm of arrows at the druchii, cutting down half of them. They turned tail, fleeing towards the far end of the bridge, only to be met by another contingent of shadow warriors that had swum across the river to cut off their retreat.

As the last of the sun's rays glimmered and then disappeared, Alith had control of both ends of the bridge. Looking to the east, he saw white shapes ghosting down the river: the sails of the fishing fleet. After mooring their ships, the crews swarmed over the bridge with more lengths of rope, which they tied to the net already hanging under the bridge. The elves crowded the banks of the river, a dozen to each rope. Alith took his place, gripping the rope tight.

'Heave!' he bellowed, pulling with all of his weight.

The wedges resisted at first, but after a moment there was a shift as the elves strained on the ropes. First one wedge fell free, and then another. Alith exhorted his company to a greater effort and with one pull the supports were dragged free. With a drawn-out grinding, the keystones fell into the river and the whole bridge collapsed after, sending up a splash that spattered Alith with water. Waves lapped over the banks, wetting Alith's feet.

Already the ship crews were jumping aboard their vessels, ropes still in hand, dragging the stone blocks out of the river's depths. As each block was hauled over the bulwark, a slipknot was loosened and the stone fell free onto the deck. The fisherman had assured Alith that the twelve boats would be sufficient to move the stones upriver, where they would be dropped back into the river, hidden but never forgotten.

The Shadow King turned to the warrior behind him, a youngster named Thirian.

'Time for some heavy lifting,' Alith said with a wink.

With a mixture of disappointment and relief, Khelthrain led his warriors back down the road. Whoever had lit the campfires had decided to flee rather than face his soldiers. On the one hand it was a shame that the insurgents had eluded him; on the other, Khelthrain was glad he had not faced the terrifying apparitions that so many other captains had fallen prey to. Not wishing to be out in the wilds while there remained the potential of ambush, he had quickly turned the column around and headed back to the safety of the towers. It was in generally light spirits that he marched along the road to his guardhouses, mentally composing the report of the incident he would have to send to Anlec. The orders had been explicit: *any* sighting or possible sighting of the so-called shadow warriors was to be passed on, with specific details of time and place.

The reassuring presence of the two towers rose up in the starlight and Khelthrain's thoughts began to turn to his bed. It was a pity that he would be sleeping alone, unlike some of those lucky wretches who had garrisons in the towns and cities, but at least he was out of the way and rarely bothered by the rulers in the capital. Ambition had never been high on Khelthrain's priorities, and a certain degree of middle-rank obscurity suited his nature.

Something seemed wrong as they approached the northern tower. Khelthrain wasn't sure what was amiss. He could see several figures standing immobile atop the battlements and the gate was closed. Then it struck him. He could see the glitter of the river beyond the gatehouse where he should have seen dark stone.

Khelthrain stopped dead in his stride, the warrior behind him clattering into his back, almost knocking the commander from his feet. The warrior bent to help him and then straightened, eyes wide with surprise.

'Captain?' he said hesitantly. 'Where is our bridge?'

THERE WERE DOZENS of maps of Nagarythe arranged over three tables. Alandrian paced between them with a sheaf of parchments in one hand.

'Here,' he said, pointing to a village where grain intended for horse fodder had been stolen.

A functionary, barefoot and clad only in a black loincloth, stepped forwards with a quill and a pot of red ink. He delicately marked a cross on the map at the indicated place, adding it to the many such marks already made.

'And here,' Alandrian continued, indicating an attack on a patrol out of Ealith.

'Oh, wait…' the prince whispered. He stopped and read the next report again, letting the others shower to the floor. 'Oh, yes. You're a cunning bastard, aren't you?'

'Prince?' said the servant.

Alandrian ignored him, striding to the map of the Naganath area. He stared at the chart for some time, his mind firing fast. He traced a finger eastwards along the Naganath. No, there was nothing there. The Shadow King wouldn't be dull enough to take another bridge. But he would go eastwards. Always after his most daring escapades he went east, back towards the mountains. It was like a homing instinct.

Alandrian brought another map to the top of the pile, of the area north and east of Toresse. He scoured the landmarks and settlements, seeking something of significance. A yellow circle caught his eye.

'This?' he demanded, gesturing to the servant. 'What is this? At Athel Yranuir?'

The functionary peered at the map, brow creased in thought.

'It is a tax house, prince,' he announced. 'Tithes are gathered there before being brought by armed column to Anlec.'

'And when is the next collection due?'

'Give me a moment, prince, and I will find out,' said the servant.

While he was gone, Alandrian stared at the map. The servant's information would confirm it, but Alandrian already had a strong suspicion about the Shadow King's next move. Eastwards he would go, away from the torrid time he had suffered at Galthyr, away from his joke at Toresse. But he wouldn't go too far east before striking again, not while he was still riding high from his prank.

'The harvest taxes will be collected in four days' time, my prince,' the servant announced as he entered. 'A contingent of knights will be moving out of Ealith tomorrow.'

Alandrian closed his eyes, blocking out everything save his knowledge of the Shadow King. Four days was not a long time to prepare. Would the Shadow King be able to put together an ad-hoc plan at such notice? Did he even realise the opportunity that awaited him?

It didn't matter. If Alandrian was the Shadow King, that's where he would be. He knew it.

'Please send word to Lady Ashniel, and to my daughters,' Alandrian said, his eyes snapping open. 'Ask them to prepare for a ride. We have a wolf to catch.'

'Shall I also send warning to the troops at Ealith and the garrison of Athel Yranuir?' the servant inquired.

Alandrian looked at the servant as if he had suggested that the prince dance naked around the room singing children's songs.

'Don't be ridiculous,' he said. 'Why spoil the fun?'

THERE WAS AN aesthetic pleasure in the contrast between gold and red: gold of coin and red of blood. Alith wiped a thumb across the face of the coin, smearing the crimson across the rune of Nagarythe imprinted upon it. Blood money, he thought, smiling at the joke.

He tossed the coin to Khillrallion, who was sweeping piles of money from the tables into a heavy sack. Another five shadow warriors did likewise in other counting rooms while a further twenty-five kept watch, stationed on the tiled roof and at the narrow arrow slits that served as windows.

Alith strode to one such embrasure, checking the time. The sun had set and the Chaos moon was already easing above the mountains, its sickly glow heavy behind the gathering clouds. The tax collectors were on their way; he had learnt as much from the gasped confessions of the druchii who had guarded the money. He glanced towards their bodies, faces and mouths glistening from molten gold that had been poured down their throats as punishment for such greed. It was unlikely the knights would arrive during the night, giving the shadow warriors plenty of time to take everything and disappear.

Rain pattered on the stone road outside, and Alith peered again into the gloom, irked by some sense he could not quite define. He had been on edge since coming to Athel Yranuir. The town was unremarkable save for the counting house, neither a safe haven for the shadow warriors nor dominated by the druchii. Alith had noticed the elders' hall showed signs of perversion to Khaine – bronze braziers in the archways and bloodstains upon the steps – but he had seen no other signs of the cults' sway.

The attack had gone just as he had planned and not a single shadow warrior had been wounded. There was no reason for his disquiet, and Alith dismissed it as understandable paranoia following his experience at Cerin Hiuath. In some ways he welcomed the thrill of uncertainty. It added an edge of excitement that he had not felt in some time, a feeling of being alive.

Between the darkening skies and the growing downpour, Alith could barely see the other buildings around the tax house. He looked out across the market square and could dimly see the elders' chambers on the far side. To the left stood a row of craftsmen's stores, their fronts enclosed by blue-painted boards. To the right were winehouses and stables. The former were empty, having been closed at Alith's first appearance. The people of Athel Yranuir would not hinder the shadows warriors, but they would not help, and had vanished as soon as the fighting had begun. Alith could not blame them; most folks feared reprisals from Anlec for aiding the shadow warriors.

'We're almost finished,' announced Khillrallion. Alith turned to see him hefting a laden sack onto a pile beside the main door.

'Good,' said the Shadow King. 'There should be wagons and horses at the stables. Send Thrinduir and Meneithon to fetch two.'

Khillrallion nodded and left the room. Alith heard him relaying the order and turned back to the square, ill-at-ease. He glared at the concealing rain, wondering what it was that his eyes could not see but his heart could feel. He cast his gaze higher, seeing the tops of the enormous evergreen forest that surrounded the town, which shared its name. Perfect cover for his forces to use if the knights arrived from Ealith. He was worrying about nothing.

'ARE YOU SURE?' Alandrian asked again.

Ashniel nodded once, her face showing a glimpse of irritation. Alandrian looked away, unable to meet the sorceress's gaze. Her eyes had become glistening orbs of black, which reflected an exaggerated version of Alandrian's face when he looked into them: a cyclopean mask of scar tissue.

'He is there,' she said calmly. 'He is touched by Kurnous and he leaves a trail upon the winds. It passes quickly but I can sense it. Your assumption was correct.'

'Do we get to kill him now?' asked Lirieth, baring teeth filed to points and capped with rubies.

'I want to taste his blood,' said Hellebron, panting with excitement. 'I've never tasted the blood of a king, shadow or not.'

'He'll taste like wolf meat,' laughed Lirieth. 'Isn't that right, magic-weaver?'

Ashniel turned away with a sneer while Alandrian smiled at his daughters' enthusiasm. Truly they had embraced the changes of these new times and he was certain they would both enjoy great success and power in the regime that was rising to rule Ulthuan.

He didn't understand much of it himself, being of a far older breed, but he knew opportunity when it came and had exploited this one to its full potential. Morathi had brought her priests and sorcerers to Athel Toralien and it had irked Malekith, but when the prince had left for his campaign in the northlands Alandrian had seen the wisdom of allowing them to flourish. He had been careful to curb too many excesses, wary of allowing the colony to devolve into the kind of barbarism Yeasir had warned was gripping Anlec.

That foresight had paid off. The Cult of Khaine was fast-growing, second in power only to Morathi's court. His daughters were well placed to ride the bloodthirsty stallion trampling upon the heads of the other sects of Ulthuan. In the shorter term, they had developed skills that were profoundly useful in this current matter.

'Yes, you can kill him soon,' the prince said. While there were advantages to bringing in the Shadow King alive, dead was safer for all involved. One did not bring Khainite assassins to take prisoners.

Rain began to fall, splashing through the needle canopy above. In the darkness, the lights of Athel Yranuir shone between the trees. A murmur from Ashniel caused him to turn.

'I sense he is getting ready to leave,' the seeress said, staring through Alandrian at some otherworldly sight. 'We must move now.'

ALITH WORKED WITH the others, carrying the bags of gold from the treasure house to the carts in the square. His hair was plastered across his face, his clothes sodden and chafing. It seemed an inglorious end to what should have been one of the great tales of the shadow warriors. He shrugged and exchanged a smile with Casadir as they passed in the doorway.

'It rains on the druchii as well,' remarked the shadow warrior.

'They have roofs to cover them tonight,' replied Alith. 'We'll be sleeping in the woods.'

'I wouldn't have it...' Casadir's voice trailed off and his eyes narrowed. Alith looked over his shoulder into the town square to see what had alerted him.

Four figures approached through the rain, walking calmly towards the shadow warriors. They were hard to make out, but there was something about their demeanour that fired Alith's instinct for danger.

'Everyone inside!' he hissed, waving the shadow warriors into the trove.

The shadow warriors barred the door and Alith called out the orders, positioning his warriors at the casements and sending them up the spiral stairs to the roof tower.

'Oh...' exclaimed Khillrallion, looking out of one of the windows. 'That's not good.'

'What is it?' Alith demanded, stepping to the window.

'Best not to look,' said Khillrallion with a haunted expression, standing between Alith and the embrasure. They jostled from side-to-side until Alith shoved Khillrallion out of his path and strode up to the narrow opening. He gazed out into the night to see what had caused Khillrallion's consternation.

He saw a druchii in the ornate silver armour of a prince, sword in his left hand, a shorter blade in his right. He was flanked by two outlandish maidens, Khainites by their dress and weapons. Water sparkled from bared metal, the edges of their blades glinting menacingly. For all of their fearsome appearance, Alith did not quite understand Khillrallion's discomfort.

His eye was drawn to a fourth figure, a little way behind the others. She wore a heavy purple robe tied with a belt studded with diamonds. In the light of the Chaos moon her skin took on a pale green tone, the white streaks in her hair standing out in the darkness like lightning strikes. Her face...

Her face was known to Alith. The eyes were whirling orbs of magic and the expression one of cold indifference. But her lips, thin, and her delicate nose and chin were all too familiar.

Alith fell back from the window with a groan of pain, the sight of Ashniel like a physical wound in his gut. Alith stumbled to his knees, moaning wordlessly.

'I told you not to look,' rasped Khillrallion, grabbing Alith by the shoulders and hauling him to his feet. There was panic in the Shadow King's eyes, the look of a child suddenly finding himself lost and alone.

Alith took a step towards the door, mindless, and Khillrallion hauled him back.

'You can't go out there,' said the shadow-walker. 'They'll cut you to pieces.'

'I want the Shadow King!' a deep voice called from outside. 'Nobody else has to die.'

Alith was regaining something of his composure but was still unsteady on his feet.

'It is her, isn't it?' he whispered.

Khillrallion nodded. There was nothing he could say. Alith closed his eyes, steeling himself, and then looked out of the window again. The prince and Ashniel were still there; the two Khainites were nowhere to be seen.

'Be on your guard,' snapped Alith, his instincts taking control. 'Watch the door and the roof!'

A tense silence descended, broken only by the rattle of rain on the rooftiles and the splash on the square outside. Alith went from one arrow slit to the next, trying to find where the Khainites had gone. It was not long before Khillrallion called him back to the front of the building.

Outside, the Khainites flanked the prince once more. At their feet knelt two children: one a boy, the other a girl. They gripped their captives by the hair, pulling back their heads, curved daggers at their throats.

'I want the Shadow King,' the prince called again. 'These will only be the first two if you do not come out.'

Alith snatched the moonbow from its quiver and took a step towards the door before Khillrallion tackled him from behind, both of them tumbling to the floor.

'You cannot go out there!' the shadow-walker repeated as Alith kicked himself away and got to his feet. Several of the shadow warriors had closed in, standing between their lord and the doorway. Their expressions betrayed their agreement with Khillrallion.

'Have it your way!' came the pronouncement from the square.

Alith leapt to the window in time to see arcs of blood streaming from the two children, the Khainites' blades flashing in the rain. Spilled blood merged with the puddles as the small bodies were dropped like rag dolls.

'Shall I have them fetch two more?' the prince taunted. 'Perhaps some even younger this time?'

'No!' wailed Alith. He wheeled on the shadow warriors, lips curled back in a snarl. 'We cannot allow this!'

The shadow warriors by the door looked resolute.

'We'll deal with this,' said Casadir, pulling back the heavy bolt.

'If they want the Shadow King, they shall have him,' Alith said, fitting an arrow to the string of the moonbow. 'Kill the Khainites first. Leave the sorceress to me.'

Alith looked out of the window as the door was thrown open. Arrows sped through the darkness. In a whirl of shining metal, the Khainites swung their blades and cartwheeled away, the arrows ricocheting from their swords. At a nod from their master, they came forwards at a run.

More arrows sliced through the rain to meet them. With supernatural speed, the pair somersaulted and swirled, dodging every missile. They reached a full sprint and would have been at the door in moments. Several of the shadow warriors leapt out into the square to meet their charge while Casadir swung the door shut behind them. The clang of the bolt rang heavily in Alith's ears, like the locking of a condemned elf's cell.

Alith felt the bite of every cut with a gasp as the Khainites sliced through the four shadow warriors without breaking stride. Throats were slit, tendons severed, limbs lopped away. It was over in a heartbeat, the remains of Alith's followers lying at the Khainites' feet, blood running in rivulets across the flagstones. One of the Khainites lifted a dagger to her mouth and licked the blade clean. She turned to her companion with a feral grin.

'More dog than wolf,' she said.

The two took up defensive stances next to each other, one fixed on the doorway, the other looking to the warriors on the roof.

'Can we have some more playthings?' the Khainite with bloodied lips called out.

'This has to end!' said Alith, crossing quickly to the doorway.

'Yes it does,' agreed Khillrallion. Behind Alith, the shadow-walker glanced at the others and received nods of understanding.

'CAN I KEEP one as a pet?' asked Lirieth, darting a quick glance over her shoulder towards her father.

'Bring me the head of the Shadow King and you can have whatever you desire,' Alandrian replied.

He felt a chill and looked to his right. Ashniel was standing beside him. The rain around her was turning into snowflakes, freezing on her skin, tiny icicles hanging from her long eyelashes, her hair rimed with ice.

'It's true what they say in Anlec, isn't it?' said the prince. 'You really are a cold-hearted bitch.'

Ashniel turned a haunting smile towards him but said nothing.

The door to the tax house slammed open again and the shadow warriors poured out, some with bows in hands, others grasping swords. Lirieth and Hellebron spun around each other as they deflected the hail of arrows, cutting through the shafts in flight.

Ashniel stepped forwards and threw out a hand. Alandrian felt the warmth leeched from his body as the air around her churned with ice and blackness. A storm of snow-white shards flew from her fingertips, scything into the shadow warriors. Frozen droplets of blood tinkled to the ground where the chill wind slashed through flesh, skin turning blue from cold at their slightest graze. Bows dropped from numbed fingertips and arrows splintered in the air.

Under the cover of the arrow volley the other shadow warriors had charged forwards, meeting the Khainite sisters blade-to-blade. Iron chimed against iron, but the fight was over in moments, Lirieth crouching low to cut the legs from her foes while Hellebron struck high, decapitating everyone within reach. The scene more closely resembled a butcher's yard than a town square by the time they had finished. Lirieth stooped and with a flick of her wrist, cut free the heart from one of her victims. She sheathed her other weapon and flicked the still-warm organ to her free hand. With a pout, she raised it above her head, squeezing hard, blood streaming down her arm and splashing onto her face.

'Praise Khaine!' she shrieked.

There was a flicker of movement at the doorway. A cloaked elf appeared with a silvery bow in hand. Quicker than the eye could follow, he loosed an arrow. The shaft took Lirieth in the throat, ripping her from her feet, sending her sprawling onto the wet flagstones.

Hellebron screamed, a sound of pure rage, and leapt forwards. Another arrow sang through the air but she cut it aside. She dodged the next with a spinning leap, her long bound bringing her within striking distance of her foe. Her left hand lashed out, its blades barely missing the face of her enemy. The right hand found its mark, plunging a slender sword under the ribs of her prey, its point erupting in a fountain of blood from his right shoulder. Blood bubbled from his lips as Hellebron ripped the blade free and twirled, slashing head from neck.

Flicking droplets of blood from her blades, she sheathed her weapons and prised the magnificent bow from the elf's dead fingers. Hellebron turned and held her trophy towards Alandrian, who clapped appreciatively.

'I think we best make that a gift to Morathi,' said the prince and Hellebron's shoulders sagged with disappointment. Alandrian pointed to the shadow warriors who had been incapacitated by Ashniel's enchantment. 'You can do what you like with those.'

Alandrian's eye was drawn to a pair of shadowy shapes fleeing across the rooftop. Ashniel raised her hand to unleash another spell but the prince stopped her.

'Let them go,' he said. 'Let them take the news to the others. The Shadow King is dead!'

TWENTY-FOUR

Strength of Elanardris

THE MOOD AMONGST the shadow warriors was shock and dismay. Summoned by Tharion, they had come here, to the ruins of Elanardris, to hear what the future held for them. Many were at a loss without Alith's leadership and there were whispers of doubt that the shadow army could continue without him.

Tharion sensed a shift in the war. The news of the Shadow King's demise quickly spread. With one act, the balance of favour had moved, the druchii regaining their former aggression, sensing weakness in their foes. Their sweeps of the wilderness for the shadow bands became bolder, while the shadow warriors, who had long believed in the myths of their own invulnerability, became more timid. They had survived and prospered with their daring, but now they were too often surrendering the initiative to their foes. The momentum of the war was changing.

Tharion knew exactly what was happening: the hunters were fast becoming the hunted again.

With Alith's passing command had fallen to Tharion, who had gathered his followers in the ruins at Elanardris as a reminder of what they fought for. Hundreds of them were hunched around the fires, faces drawn, expressions bleak.

'We cannot allow these reverses to continue to sap morale,' Tharion told them, standing upon what had once been a wall separating the east gardens from the summer lawn. 'If the druchii do not fear us, we have failed.'

'We will continue the fight!' said Casadir, the only shadow warrior to have escaped Athel Yranuir. He looked around at the others, but their support was half-hearted.

'How do we fight without the Shadow King?' a voice called from the darkness. 'Our enemies grow stronger while we diminish.'

'It is true,' said another. 'I have come from Chrace, and the tidings are grim. A new force has arrived in Ulthuan, brought back from the colonies by Morathi. I do not know exact numbers, but tens of thousands of warriors, all of them hardened in many campaigns, have made landfall in Cothique. I fear the kingdom will be under Morathi's sway by the end of the year.'

'We must redouble our efforts here, to ensure that Caledor can concentrate all of his warriors on this new threat,' said Casadir.

Tharion sighed and then frowned.

'It will not be as simple as that,' he said. 'With fresh armies in the east, Morathi's commanders are likely to bring back much of their existing force to Nagarythe, to rest and resupply for a fresh offensive next year.'

'More targets for us,' growled Casadir, and there were words of assent from other shadow-walkers.

'That is true to a certain extent,' said Tharion. 'What will be more important will be the thousands of troops coming back to Nagarythe. No doubt they will not stand idle while we continue our attacks.'

The significance of this began to sink in and there was a disquieted whispering amongst the shadow-walkers.

'What do you propose that we do, lord?' asked Anraneir. 'The returning armies will use Dragon Pass and Phoenix Pass; perhaps we could gather in strength there and attack them on the move?'

'They will be expecting that,' Tharion said with a shake of his head. 'There are less than two thousand of us left, these six years of fighting having taken a steady toll. We could harass the druchii columns without committing our strength, but that will not serve our ends well. A few hundred dead here or there is of no meaning to them.'

'We can still hurt the druchii, of that I am convinced,' said Anraneir. He shrugged. 'I cannot see how, just yet. If we were to bring all of our forces together, we might be able to strike back powerfully once more, but to do so risks discovery and ultimate defeat.'

'We are growing fewer, that cannot be denied,' Tharion said quietly. 'In a war of attrition we have no hope of victory. What else can you tell us from the east, Tethion?'

'The wider campaign is at a stalemate, unless these new druchii forces turn the tide against us,' the shadow-walker announced. 'The enemy possess Nagarythe, Chrace and Tiranoc, and much of Ellyrion and Cothique. Lothern is frequently besieged. Cultist uprisings continue to plague those cities and realms not yet under the sway of Anlec. There is rumour that the mages of Saphery battle with some of their number who have been swayed to the path of dark sorcery.

'Even the realm of Caledor is not free from the taint of corruption. While the Phoenix King pursues the greater war, the cults have infiltrated his mountain realm to sow discord. Many Caledorians support the king but would look to the defence of their own realm before expending the lives of their kin for the protection of the other kingdoms. Earlier this year, several priests of Vaul were discovered to be in league with Anlec, making magical weapons and armour for the druchii and smuggling them north through Tiranoc. Their leader fled, having stolen the sacred hammer of his god. I am sure that he labours in Anlec now, forging new weapons for the princes of Nagarythe.'

'Is there no report that might give us hope?' asked Tharion.

There were shakes of heads and disconsolate sighs all around the fire.

'Then it is time that I revealed to you why I have brought you all here,' Tharion continued. 'I spoke with the Shadow King before he left for Athel Yranuir. I shared with him my doubts and he listened. He gave me instructions, which we will all follow.

'The shadow army will come together again,' he declared. There were happier murmurs from the shadow-walkers but Tharion cut them off with a gesture. 'Not for a battle. We have never been victorious by pure force of arms. Guile and deception are weapons as useful to us as bow and sword, and with guile and deception we must lure the druchii into a position more favourable for us.'

Some of the elves nodded; the faces of other betrayed incomprehension.

'The druchii are full of confidence. They have a right to be. If we stand face-to-face against this resurgence, we risk becoming overwhelmed. No, we will not fight that way. We will lie low, bide our time and wait for the right opportunity. The druchii will think they have crushed us. We will allow them this illusion of victory, it is only our pride that is wounded by it. Their eyes will turn elsewhere, to the fresh campaigns in the east, and they will believe Nagarythe safe under their control. Then, and only then, we will strike again, rising up from the shadows to deal a blow to our foes that will make them hate and fear us more than ever.'

'And where would you have us hide?' asked Casadir. 'If we scatter into the populace we risk discovery by the cults, if we continue to live in the wilds as we do now, then why not continue the fight?'

Tharion stood up and spread his arms, encompassing their surrounds. The tumbled stones of Elanardris glowed ruddily in the firelight, already overgrown by moss and creepers, the once-carefully maintained gardens reverting to wilderness.

'Here we were born, and here we will be reborn,' Tharion declared. 'For some time I have been thinking; thinking about the past and the future. Though Morathi may control the lands of Nagarythe, there are many that suffer under the yoke of her tyranny. There are those who are sympathetic to our cause, amongst the downtrodden folk who labour for Morathi and her minions. Those that can be wholly trusted we will bring here, adults and children alike, and found a new generation of shadow warriors. This war will not end soon and we must look to the future.'

Tharion began to pace around the fire, meeting the gazes of the shadow warriors.

'Have no doubts, no matter what happens we will never surrender. It is possible that none of us will see victory in our lifetimes, and so we must lay down the foundations for our army to continue the fight after we have passed on. While there remains any spirit of defiance to Anlec and resistance to the druchii, our enemies can claim no victory. Elanardris is no more, consigned to bitter history, bare stones and memories of better times the only testament to the dynasty that once thrived here. I will not rebuild the manse, nor replant the gardens. It is not in the bricks and the mortar that Elanardris found strength, but in the blood of its people and the power of the land. These are our lands still, and they need a people to live in them. While we draw breath and struggle, Elanardris will not wholly die.'

BY SECRET MEANS, word was brought to the disaffected and disloyal Naggarothi, those who served out of fear rather than loyalty. They were encouraged to desert, though few ever made it to Elanardris. In ones and twos they came, slipping away from their homes and garrisons under cover of darkness, to meet the shadow warriors in out-of-the-way places. Sometimes whole families came, making the journey on foot through the briars and across the moors, seeking sanctuary in the mountains.

Wary of infiltration by agents from Anlec, Tharion personally vetted every hopeful, killing out of hand any that caused him the slightest suspicion. There were some, he knew, that were innocent, but the lives of so many depended upon absolute security. It was essential that the druchii remained oblivious to the subtle stream of refugees fleeing their oppression. The slightest notion that all was not as they desired would bring down the wrath of Anlec.

The old refugee camps had long been swept away by the years and so the shadow warriors and their charges set to building new shelters. Hidden in caves and in the hearts of the mountain woods, they stored food and clothes, blankets and water.

Under roofs made of woven branches, in shelters made of rockpiles, in hollows behind waterfalls and in reed-covered huts in the marshlands, the new people of Elanardris eked out their existence. Tharion always felt an eerie calm when he visited these places, their inhabitants quiet, thankful for their salvation but extremely cautious. They spoke little of the lives they had left behind, and few cared to speculate on the future. Even the children were quiet; there were few sounds of innocent joy and laughter was a rarity. Survival became the goal; to avoid discovery and see another dawn was measured a success.

Despite Tharion's earlier belief, the druchii did not withdraw their exhausted, bloodied armies from the fighting in the east. The reinforcements from the colonies were simply added to their numbers and Morathi's commanders pushed them even harder. Nagarythe was made a little safer by this aggression, though the rest of Ulthuan suffered for it.

The shadow warriors patrolled the borders but did not attack unless necessary. Tharion wanted no attention to be paid to the shadow army, their lack of activity reinforcing the belief that the Shadow King's death had led to their dispersal. It gnawed at his pride to allow the druchii to gloat over this, but pride was an easy sacrifice when so much was at stake.

In the spring of the eighth year of the shadow war, a child was born in Elanardris, the first since the war had begun. There was little celebration, for everybody's mood was mixed. That new life had come to a land once desolate was a blessing, but there were many that wondered what sort of life, what manner of world the young girl would see when she grew older.

More newborns followed in the coming years. Tharion wondered what type of people they would grow into. He passed on Alith's edict that all youngsters were to be raised in the traditions of the Anars and when old enough would be trained in the craft of the shadow warrior. They would learn to hunt and fish, to wield sword and bow, and speak the secret words of Kurnous. Though there was no present end of the war in sight, Tharion hoped daily that such endeavour would prove unnecessary. He wanted nothing more than the children of Elanardris to grow up strong and full of pride, and in peace.

The new lord of Elanardris also worried what character of person would be made by this upbringing. Raising children with hate for the druchii clawed at his conscience, but he had made a promise that the Shadow King's teachings would be passed on. The symbols of vengeance and shadow became the sign of Elanardris. They were painted on cave walls and carved into the bark of trees. Amulets and brooches were fashioned in their shape. This concerned Tharion, reminding him of the cults they fought against, but he could not deny the people their right to express their fear and their hope, to cling to these symbols in the wake of Alith's passing.

The years passed slowly, each brief summer a time of worry when druchii armies were on the move; every winter a tortuous hardship when food was scarce and the winds blew cold from the north and the snows heaped upon the roofs of the bivouacs. Some of the shadow warriors took families, others vowed to remain alone. They kept vigil over the land of the Anars, hidden watchers ready to slay at a moment's notice. Their deadly skills were little used, the unforgiving mountains as much of a deterrent to any druchii interest as a wall of spears and a forest of bows.

With each year the memory of the Shadow King was celebrated with a hunt. The shadow warriors chased deer through the woods of the mountains, and offered up a share of their prey to Kurnous and the Shadow King.

With each year, Tharion tried to remember the Shadow King less and Alith Anar more, but it was difficult. His exploits were told around the campfires, and as bedtime stories to the youngsters. The elf who had been a legend while he lived quickly became a myth after his death. Some of those that lived in Elanardris did not even know that he had a name, calling him only by his title. Tharion tried to keep alive the memories of the elf behind the myth, but he sometimes felt like he was swimming against the tide. These people were desperate and a character out of fable was more comfort to them than a mortal of flesh and blood who had once dwelt in the lands they now occupied. It gave them succour to believe that some spirit watched over them. The more knowing of their number declared that the Shadow King was a wolf not a shepherd, more likely to be bringing vengeance in Mirai than he was to be watching over a flock.

It was a harsh existence but the folk of Elanardris endured, listening for news of the wider war while they kept themselves hidden. A stability of sorts grew in the area, the shadow society developing new traditions and codes, new beliefs and practices. Nobody knew who first coined the phrase Aesanar – the New People of Anar – but it helped that they had a name for themselves. Tharion was bestowed the title First Lord of the Aesanar by the people he ruled, his position a regency for when a new claimant to the title of Shadow King would emerge. Pragmatic and resourceful, the Aesanar healed and grew, waiting for the day when one would arise to lead them back into the war; waiting for the day the shadow war would begin anew.

In the thirteenth year of the civil war, nine years since the flag of the Anars had fallen at Dark Fen, that day came.

By FIRELIGHT THE shadow-walkers met once more in the shadows of the old manse. Tharion had called them together at the request of Casadir. The shadow-walker had been reluctant to explain why, saying only that he had met a messenger with important news that they should all hear. Casadir explained this briefly to the assembled shadow-walkers, and impressed upon them the need for secrecy.

All turned as one as a dark figure led a horse into the circle of light, a cloak of raven features upon his back.

'This is Elthyrior, the raven herald,' announced Casadir. There were scattered whispers; Elthyrior was part of the Shadow King legend. Many present had met him before, but several had not.

'Tell us of what you have heard,' said Casadir, sitting down and waving a hand to the space on his right. Elthyrior whispered something to his steed, which wandered out onto what had once been the grand lawn of the summer garden, and then the raven herald sat cross-legged next to the shadow-walker.

'A new power reigns in Anlec,' the raven herald announced, a statement greeted with gasps of shock. 'The druchii talk with reverence of him, a ruler they call the Witch King.'

'Who is this Witch King?' asked Tharion.

'I do not know,' said Elthyrior. 'None that I have questioned or overheard can say for sure. Some believe it is Hotek, the renegade priest of Vaul that fled Caledor several years ago. Others believe Morathi has adopted Prince Alandrian and granted him rule in return for his slaying of Alith Anar.

'I am told that he is blessed by all of the cytharai. I have heard that no weapon can harm him, and he learnt sorcery from Morathi herself. Some of the druchii say the Witch King will be the scourge that wipes away their foes and hails the great victory of Nagarythe.'

Elthyrior's emerald gaze swept across the shadow-walkers, each of them intent upon his words.

'We all know that reality and myth can sometimes be blurred, but I have heard grave claims about this Witch King,' Elthyrior warned. 'Perhaps a more telling question would be "what is the Witch King?". "His gaze shreds skin and flesh from bones", one captive told me. "He burns with the fire of our hatred", said another. All say one thing: he is the true ruler of Nagarythe and soon he will reign over all of Ulthuan!'

'Camp tales and fireside stories, no doubt,' said Tharion. 'Perhaps Morathi fears the war has turned against her, and has conjured up this Witch King to instil fear and obedience in her troops.'

'While there may be some truth to that, I fear the best we can hope for is exaggeration,' said Elthyrior. 'So widespread is this rumour, and so vehemently is it believed, I have no doubt that some new druchii lord has emerged to lead the armies of Nagarythe.'

'What can we do about it?' asked Anraneir. 'Tharion, would you lead the shadow army against this new tyrant?'

'If it is agreed that we will act, then I will lead,' said the First Lord. 'But I am no Shadow King. I do not claim to have the strength and the cunning to outwit such a foe.'

'Without the Shadow King, are we truly the shadow army?' asked Yrain, newly granted the title of shadow-walker. She looked at her comrades with an impassioned expression. 'The Shadow King has power, to rally the weak and put terror in the hearts of the druchii. Does it matter who bears the title?'

'It matters if he cannot deliver,' said Casadir. 'I would not take up that mantle. To be a leader is one thing, to be a ruler is another. The Shadow King must be more than these things. He must be wrath and vengeance, unyielding and eternal. To be a living symbol, an incarnation of what we all fight for, what we all believe in…'

'Is there any elf here who could be such a thing?' Tharion asked. For a moment Casadir smiled, a flicker of amusement that soon disappeared. He shook his head, dismissing any claim he might make.

None answered, each looking at his companions to see if any volunteered. A few shook their heads, either disappointed by this reaction or dismissive of the idea that a new Shadow King could be found.

Elthyrior stood up suddenly, hand reaching to his sword. His gaze was fixed upon something outside the light of the fires, close to the manse building. Some of the shadow-walkers readied their weapons; others looked around nervously.

The flames of the campfires flickered, losing strength. One-by-one they died until only a single flame remained, barely lighting Tharion and those close to him.

'What is it?' hissed Anraneir.

Rustles and panting could be heard coming from the darkness. Golden eyes flashed in the starlight. The shadow-walkers turned this way and that, seeking ghostly shapes that appeared and disappeared in a blink of the eye.

The clouds above the mountains broke, bathing all with the silvery light of Sariour in full bloom. Where there had been darkness and shadow, now stood a figure swathed in black, face hidden within a deep hood. It stood immobile, arms crossed, head bowed.

All around the camp, wolf howls split the air.

'Who are you?' Tharion demanded, sword in hand. 'What do you want?'

'I am the Shadow King,' said Alith Anar, pulling back his hood, 'and I want vengeance.'

── TWENTY-FIVE ──

Return to Anlec

UPROAR ERUPTED, CRIES of disbelief mingled with shouts of celebration and exclamations of shock. The shadow-walkers crowded close, mobbing Alith. Gigantic wolves prowled the periphery, their barks and yaps adding to the noise.

Elthyrior stood apart, watching the proceedings with suspicion. He caught Alith's eye and the Shadow King waved away his followers, telling them he would speak shortly. As Alith strode through the long grass, the shadow warriors set to relighting their fires, the air alive with the hubbub of surprise and elation.

'A trick?' said Elthyrior when Alith reached him.

The Shadow King shrugged and smiled.

'A new myth,' he said. 'Only Casadir knows the truth.'

'And what is the truth?' asked Elthyrior, expression stern. 'It is not right that you deceive your followers in this way.'

Alith indicated for Elthyrior to walk with him and the two left the camp. The Shadow King and the raven herald picked their way along an overgrown path of marble and sat in the charred remnants of the summer house.

'It is a necessary deception,' Alith said, plucking the bloom from a moon-wreath that was growing over the remains of the outbuilding. 'One that I did not begin.'

Elthyrior raised a doubtful eyebrow.

'Truly,' Alith continued. 'I was set to confront Alandrian and his Khainite witches, but Khillrallion struck me over the back of my head. Dazed, I

671

could not stop him taking the moonbow and masquerading as me. Casadir had me halfway up to the roof before I regained my senses. Khillrallion and the others bought my freedom with their lives. It would have been dishonour to have thrown away that which they had so willingly given, and so I ran with Casadir. He is the only other soul that knows what happened.'

'That does not explain your disappearance for the last seven years,' said Elthyrior. 'You abandoned your people.'

'I did not!' snapped Alith. He closed his eyes, forcing himself to relax. 'The tide was turning against us, my people needed a calmer head to rule. Tharion had already suggested to me that we create a new haven in Elanardris and I had agreed. I could not have built what he has built. He has given us a future, one that I could not. Though I did not plan it, my death gave us that opportunity, the pretence for peace we needed. The druchii would be all too ready to believe the shadow army was no more. My death gave my people space to recover, to start a new path. Had I lived, Alandrian would have continued his hunt. Twice he nearly caught me, and both times it cost lives, lives very dear to me. I watched Khillrallion cut down and I realised that the greatest danger to my people was me, and the druchii's hatred of me. I am a symbol, but that works both ways. I am defiance personified, and that rallies the brave to our cause. It also riles the druchii, who lust after domination and control.

'I decided to disappear. I returned to Avelorn for a while and ran with my brothers and sisters again. It was a carefree time, I will admit. But duty nagged at me, and year-by-year I knew I could not find peace, and that while the Shadow King had to die, he could not remain dead forever. I returned to Elanardris last winter and contacted Casadir. He told me of everything that had happened, and only this morning he passed on to me the news that you had arrived.'

'So why return now?'

'You know that answer already,' said Alith, standing and walking to the fallen wall at the front of the summer house. He looked westwards.

'The Witch King,' said Elthyrior.

Alith nodded, not turning around.

'I too heard of this creature. As far as Cothique and Chrace his coming is being proclaimed as the great awakening of the Naggarothi. He fills them with dread and awe in equal measure. I have never heard such devotion uttered amongst the druchii, save for those hopelessly corrupted by the cults. No elf I know could command such loyalty, yet the Witch King rules Anlec and Morathi supports him. I must find out who he is.'

'I fear that we shall all know that before too long,' said Elthyrior. He stood and joined Alith. 'I am glad that you are not dead, Alith Anar.'

'Me too,' the Shadow King replied with a grin.

* * *

ALITH REQUESTED THAT his return be kept secret for the time being. He declined to make any comment on what had happened to him and flatly refused to answer questions regarding his death and resurrection. He simply assured his followers that he had returned to lead them to new victories, still as hungry to punish the druchii as he had always been. There were those that wanted to proclaim his triumphant return across Nagarythe, but Alith bade them to keep their tongues.

'All of Ulthuan will soon know that the Shadow King lives again,' he told them, smiling knowingly but keeping silent when they pressed for further detail.

Alith gave instruction also that the shadow-walkers were to begin restructuring the army, making the shadow warriors ready again for war. This was to be done under the pretence that Tharion was considering launching an offensive against the Witch King, but to be kept quiet to the wider populace of the Aesanar. The shadow army was to meet Alith at the ruins of the manse. When asked when the rendezvous would happen, Alith gave another cryptic reply.

'You will have no doubt when the time to march has come.'

ANLEC HAD NEVER looked so forbidding. Alith had thought it a terrifying fortress the first time he had come here. The druchii had taken its foundations and heaped upon it their warped aesthetic and cruel design. The towers soared higher than ever, the walls hung with silver chains bearing rotting corpses and sharp hooks. Heads were displayed upon long spikes above the gatehouses and the ramparts themselves had been fashioned like rows of slender fangs. Flocks of vultures and crows circled constantly, settling to peck at the disfigured remains on display.

Amongst the purple banners of Nagarythe fluttered standards of red and black, displaying symbols of the cytharai, bedecked with the skulls and bones of those that had displeased the city's rulers. A thousand fires burned in braziers upon the walls, casting a pall of smoke across the whole fortress.

The sound too was awful. The clamour of gongs and bells and drums sounded constantly alongside the caws of the crows and the screeches of the vultures, as the temples performed their bloodthirsty rituals. Shrill cheers and drawn-out screams could be heard through the din. A stench of charred flesh hung on the breeze. Dark magic seethed, creating a palpable air of evil that made Alith shudder. He wrapped his plain blue cloak tighter around himself, filled with a supernatural chill.

Alith took a deep breath and ventured forwards, passing through the western gatehouse.

He had come seeking answers: to know the identity of the mysterious Witch King. But he had another purpose, far more personal. For most of his life the druchii had taken from him: his family, his friends, his love and his lands. They had heaped upon him one more insult that he could not allow to pass. They had taken the moonbow.

Her whispers had disturbed his sleep through the long summer nights in Avelorn. While he had hidden out in the shrines to Kurnous in the Annulii, the moonbow's distant cries of torment plagued his thoughts. He had not spoken of this to Elthyrior, but this was the true reason he had returned. His family were gone. His friends were dead. His lands were wilderness. All of those things he could not bring back. But the moonbow... That he could reclaim.

Within the city, Alith's confidence returned. With a calm assurance, he made straight for the palace of Aenarion. He wasn't sure where the moonbow was being kept, but he knew it was in the citadel somewhere. He would take it from under the nose of Morathi, and in that gesture he would announce the Shadow King's return.

The stair up to the main gates were stained red with blood and guards stood every few steps, cruelly hooked halberds at the ready. Despite the sentries, the doors were thrown open and a steady procession of druchii made their way in and out of the palace. Alith joined the line waiting for entry, ignoring the grim-faced warriors stood to either side. Step-by-step the line moved forwards until Alith passed into the shadow of the citadel.

THE MAJORITY OF visitors continued along the central stairs, no doubt seeking audience with one or other member of Anlec's ruling court. Alith stepped aside, watching not for soldiers but for servants. His time in Tor Anroc had taught him that it was more often the servants' passages that allowed free and easy movement in such palaces. It was not long before he saw a flustered page appearing from behind a tapestry depicting Aenarion riding atop his dragon Indraugnir. Alith wondered if Aenarion had ever known the demented creature he had married, or might have ever guessed the cruelty he would unwittingly inflict upon the world.

Crossing to the concealed entrance, Alith looked up at the huge portrait. Clad in golden armour, the first Phoenix King was every part the noble lord and warrior legend held him to be. Yet there it was, in his right hand, the Sword of Khaine. Even represented in silver and red thread, that grim weapon exuded death. Caledor Dragontamer had prophesied that Aenarion had cursed himself when he drew that fated blade. Perhaps, Alith thought, he cursed us all.

Alith slipped behind the tapestry and found a slender archway. Beyond a set of steep steps led upwards. Alith followed their winding path, not sure where he was heading but content to allow instinct to guide his hand. When he thought he was about two-thirds of the way up the towering bastion of the citadel, he left the stairwell and found himself in a broad gallery lined with alcoves. The alcoves housed marble statues of the princes that had fought with Aenarion. Some of them were defaced, their features chipped away, crude messages scrawled on them with blood. Some were intact, those that still continued to serve the new powers of Anlec. Most of them Alith did not recognise, a few were familiar to him.

He came across one that made him stop. Its features were as his, and it was only after a moment's thought that Alith realised it was a depiction of a young Eoloran Anar. Bloodied nails had been driven into its eyes. Eoloran was dead to all intents, and he was only one of many victims of the druchii that Alith would avenge, yet the reminder of his grandfather stirred something within Alith.

He had come here to reclaim the moonbow, to take back that which had been stolen from him. Was it possible that he could snatch away something else while he was here? Was the real Eoloran Anar still alive? Was he somewhere close by, locked in some dungeon of Anlec? Alith decided that he had time enough to investigate. Turning around, he headed back to the stairwell and descended into the bowels of the citadel.

ALITH HAD EXPECTED a hellish scene, full of agony and torture. In contrast, the dungeons of Anlec were well lit with golden lamps, and silent. He saw no guards, and as he wandered the narrow corridors he found the cells clean – and empty. Not a soul was to be found. Confused, Alith headed back to the main stairs and sought out the servants' quarters, a few levels above the dungeon.

It was a twisted scene of everything he had encountered in Tor Anroc. Maids and pages hurried to and fro, many of them bearing scars and other signs of abuse. Some wore amulets of the darker gods, some dressed in the flamboyant robes of the pleasure cultists. They snarled and sniped at each other in passing, and cringed when their masters swept past bellowing orders and lashing out with whips.

Alith grabbed the arm of a young maiden slinking past with an empty silver tray. She looked at him fearfully as he pulled her to one side.

'Lay a finger on me and you'll answer to Prince Khelthran,' she said, with more dread than threat.

Alith released her immediately and held up his hands.

'I am new here,' he said. 'I don't understand what's happening.'

The maid relaxed, tossing back her raven hair and assuming an air of importance. Evidently he was not the first newcomer to have made such a mistake.

'Which lord do you serve?' she asked.

'Prince Alandrian,' Alith replied quickly, the first name that came to him. The girl nodded.

'You should do well,' she said, indicating with her head that Alith should follow her.

She led him into a storeroom, its shelves empty, dust upon the floor.

'Watch out for Erenthion, he has the cruellest temper of them all,' the servant told him. Alith nodded gratefully. 'And never turn your back on Mendieth, he's a sly one and will stick a knife in you without even knowing your name.'

'Atenithor,' Alith said with a smile, but received a frown in reply.

'The less people that know that, the better,' said the maid. 'Names attract attention, and attention can be very bad for your health.'

'I fear I may already have caught the gaze of some,' Alith confessed, his face a mask of worry. 'I have been set an errand but I know not how to fulfil it.'

'What is it that you've been asked to do?'

'I have a message for… For Eoloran Anar, from the prince,' Alith said quietly, his eyes flicking nervously to the closed door. 'I went to the cells but they are empty!'

The girl laughed but Alith could not judge whether from scorn or humour.

'No prisoners are kept in the citadel!' she giggled. 'They all go to the temples for sacrifice.'

'Then it is a prank?' Alith asked, keeping hidden the knot of worry that tied his stomach. 'There is no such prisoner?'

'There is an Eoloran Anar,' said the girl and Alith nodded with relief. 'But he is not a prisoner. His apartment is in the western tower.'

Not a prisoner? Alith put his confusion aside long enough to ask for directions and then excused himself.

ALITH WAS AGAIN surprised by the lack of guards in the western tower of the citadel. He guessed the druchii were arrogant enough to believe that no one would dare infiltrate the heart of the capital. Following the instructions he had been given, Alith quickly made his way to the floor where Eoloran Anar was said to live. He found himself outside a plain black door, half-open. He knocked and received no reply. With a glance around to check that he was not observed, he opened the door a fraction further and slipped inside.

The room was plainly furnished, lit from a wide window that led out to a balcony. Alith could see a figure sitting in a chair of woven reed, facing the sun. After checking the adjoining bedroom, Alith cautiously made his way outside.

Eoloran Anar sat with the sun on his face, eyes closed. He seemed to be asleep. For a moment Alith was taken back many years, to a time before all of their woes. He remembered sitting in the gardens of the manse, his grandfather taking the sun just like this. Alith would play with his friends until their noise roused his grandfather and he would gently chide them for disturbing him, before rising from his chair to join in their games.

Flames and dark smoke consumed the memory, leaving behind a vision of blasted Elanardris and the bodies of his friends nailed to the manse walls. Alith growled unconsciously as the memory faded away.

'Grandfather?' whispered Alith, crouching next to the ageing elf.

Eoloran stirred, a wordless mutter issuing from his lips.

'Eoloran,' Alith said, louder than before.

His grandfather turned his head, brow creased, eyes still closed.

'Who is that?' he asked, his voice a hoarse whisper.

'It is Alith, grandfather.'

'Begone with your tricks,' Eoloran snapped. 'Alith is dead. You killed them all. Take your apparitions away.'

'No, Grandfather, it really is Alith.'

The Shadow King laid a hand on his grandfather's and gently squeezed it.

'I'm going to take you out of here,' Alith promised.

'You will not trick me this way,' said Eoloran. 'You can blind me but you cannot make me a fool.'

'Look at me, Grandfather, it really is Alith!'

Eoloran turned his head and opened his eyes, revealing two white, lifeless orbs.

'Do you still take pleasure in your handiwork, daemon?' he said. 'I did not give you the satisfaction of my cries when you took my sight, and I will not give you the reward of my dashed hopes now.'

'I'll find you healers, Grandfather,' said Alith, tugging at Eoloran's arm in an attempt to pull him from the chair. 'In Saphery, the mages will be able to give you back your eyes. Come with me, I cannot stay long.'

'You would like me to leave wouldn't you, fiend?' said Eoloran, softly pulling his arm away from Alith's grip. 'How many souls was it that she promised you if I left? One thousand and one? Their deaths will not be on my conscience. You can threaten me, goad me, tempt me like this, but I will not allow you to seal that infernal bargain.'

'You have to come with me,' Alith said, tears in his trembling eyes. 'Please, you have to believe me, it's Alith!'

'I do not have to believe anything. It is torture enough that you keep me in this vile place, where I can smell the sacrifices and hear their screams. You leave open my door and tell me I can leave any time that I wish, but you know I could never do that. My spirit remains pure and when I am taken to Mirai I shall not be haunted by the shades of elves murdered for my freedom. I would stay here a thousand years longer and endure whatever torments you can devise rather than allow that to happen.'

Alith stepped back, quivering from sorrow and rage. He could take Eoloran forcibly, but if what the old elf said was true, his grandfather was not willing to pay the price for freedom that Morathi had set. Alith pulled free the knife hidden in the waistbelt of his robe, thinking to end the old elf's misery. His hand shook violently as he reached towards Eoloran's throat, and then he snatched it back. He couldn't do it. Though it tore at his heart to do so, Alith could only do as he had been raised: respect his grandfather's wishes. He bent forwards and kissed him on the forehead.

'Goodbye, Grandfather,' Alith said, voice choked with emotion. 'Die with peace and dignity.'

One more humiliation to be avenged, Alith thought, his grief becoming the cold fury that had sustained him for many years.

USING THE SAME clandestine means by which he had located Eoloran, Alith learned that the moonbow was kept on display alongside many other trophies taken by the druchii during their conquests. Alith's search led him to a semi-circular gallery overlooking one of the main halls. The chamber below was empty, but several dozen druchii thronged the gallery to view the exhibits. There were several soldiers positioned around the display, looking bored.

Alith loitered in the crowd for a while, looking at the standards of Bel Shanaar ripped from the halls of Tor Anroc; a cloak made from the pelt of a white lion torn from the back of a Chracian prince; the Sunspear, once carried by Prince Eurithain of Cothique; the charred bark stripped from a treeman of Avelorn. Alith hid his disgust at the grisly relics on display, pushing his way around the gallery until he came upon the moonbow.

It was laid upon a purple cushion, the metal dull and lifeless. A plaque beneath read: *Bow of the so-called Shadow King, slain by Hellebron, priestess of Khaine.* Alith stared for a moment, shaking his head. A soldier stood not far to his right, examining his fingernails. Alith weaved through the druchii and came before the warrior.

'I'll just borrow this,' said Alith. His hand flashed to whip the soldier's sword from its scabbard. Alith plunged the blade into the druchii's gut, giving a twist before pulling it free.

Chaos erupted around him as the druchii shouted in alarm. Some tried to grab hold of him and Alith cut them down savagely, kicking aside their bodies as he forged towards the moonbow. Others tried to run but Alith lashed out at any within reach, hacking them down without mercy.

Reaching the moonbow, he snatched it up, feeling it spring into life in his hand. Its warmth seeped up his arm and a chorus of gentle voices hovered on the edge of hearing.

The other guards were closing in with bared blades and Alith leapt to the wooden balustrade that lined the gallery. He was about to drop into the hall below when something caught his eye.

At the apex of the gallery was displayed a simple band of silver and gold, a gem-studded star set upon it: the crown of Nagarythe. Alith ran along the balustrade, leaping over the swing of a guard's sword as he closed in on the crown. Turning deftly, he parried the next blow and sent his sword through the warrior's throat. He spun and kicked another druchii in the face before leaping over him and driving the sword through his back. Alith swung with the moonbow to parry the attack of the next soldier, his sword cutting a thin ribbon of blood across the druchii's face. Alith hammered his shoulder into the warrior's midriff and drove his sword point into his side as he fell.

'I'll take this as well,' Alith laughed. Slinging the moonbow over his shoulder, Alith pirouetted past the next attack and snatched up the crown of Nagarythe in his free hand. He flipped the crown onto his head and ducked as a sword swung for his face. A kick to the knee sent his attacker reeling back and Alith followed up swiftly, showering blows upon his opponent's sword until his defence gave way. Alith drove the sword through his prey's chest and then jumped back onto the balustrade.

With a final flick of his sword, he sent the last soldier stumbling back before somersaulting from the rail. Landing lightly, he raced to the doors, hoping that they were not locked. They were not, and Alith burst out of the hall to find the long antechamber a scene of pandemonium. Servants and druchii nobles were pushing at each other to flee the fracas, while armoured warriors tried to battle their way through the crowd, fighting against the tide of elves.

Alith spied another servants' entrance to his right and jumped nimbly onto the shoulder of a servant. As the elf buckled, the Shadow King jumped again, using the head of a screeching noblewoman as a stepping stone, before throwing himself through the air towards a long banner hanging from the ceiling. Alith grabbed the pennant in one hand and swung above the throng, releasing his grip to send him sailing over the heads of the oncoming guards, breaking his fall with a roll.

Alith ripped down the concealing tapestry as he darted through the archway, flinging the canvas at his pursuers. He dashed down the steps beyond the doorway, ducking through archways and running across landings in a haphazard fashion. He had no idea where he was heading, so it made no difference whether he turned left or right.

Bursting through a double door, Alith found himself in a vaulted reception room, a naked couple writhing upon one of the couches. At the far end was an open window through which Alith could see the roofs of Anlec.

As he ran to the window, Alith drove his sword between the shoulder blades of the rutting male, pinning him to the elf beneath. He could hear the clatter of feet behind him but Alith did not turn around. Letting go of his sword, Alith pulled his thick cloak over his arm and head and lunged through the window at full speed, crashing out onto the tiled balcony beyond.

Alith vaulted one-handed over the rail and swung underneath, feet seeking purchase on the wall of the palace. There was none. Alith dropped another storey, breaking his fall with a roll, his ankle twisting painfully as he landed. Biting back the pain, Alith jumped again, disappearing into a forest of spires that crowned one of the citadel's many minarets.

In a few more moments he had vanished, descending swiftly into the crowds of Anlec.

* * *

THE CAPTAIN OF the guard was virtually prostrate as he entered Morathi's chambers. He kept his eyes firmly fixed on the floor as he crawled forwards, shuddering like a beaten dog.

'We found this, your majesty,' he said, proffering a roll of parchment. 'It was pinned by an arrow to the chest of one of my soldiers.'

Morathi strode forwards and snatched the parchment from his quivering hand. She turned away and then stopped.

'Stand up,' she hissed, not looking back. 'The city is sealed?'

'Yes, your majesty,' the guard whispered back. 'The search continues.'

Morathi rounded on the captain, her eyes holes of pure darkness.

'He's already gone, you imbecile!' she shrieked, slapping the captain across the cheek.

Dismissing her soldiers' incompetence, Morathi turned her back on the captain again and opened the parchment. Behind her the captain slunk towards the door, one hand held to the weal on his face, where Morathi's rings had struck him. Where the blood oozed from the wound it turned black and the captain stopped at the doorway, horrified. A dark bruise spread across his face, bloating his features, dark blood filling up his eyes. With a wet gasp, he fell to his knees and clutched his throat before slumping sideways, a trail of black slime dribbling from his lips.

Morathi read the letter:

Dear Morathi,

Not dead yet, bitch. Send your new thug to Elanardris if you dare.

Alith Anar, Shadow King.

It was signed in blood with the runes of shadow and vengeance.

── TWENTY-SIX ──

The Witch King

SNOW CRUNCHED LIGHTLY underfoot as the shadow army gathered amongst the ruins of the ancient manse. It was a grisly scene, the blackened stones still littered with the bones of the dead druchii, while the scorched earth where Alith had built the pyres was still bare. A tree grew in the middle of what had once been the great hall; ivy and thorny bushes climbed their way into Alith's bed chambers.

For six days the shadow warriors had mustered here on Alith's command, dispersing by night for reasons of safety. Alith felt sure that this day would be the last. Scouts had brought word in the night that a druchii army was camped in the foothills, larger than anything seen for a decade. It had to be the Witch King's host.

Seven days ago, word had reached the Shadow King that Anlec was emptying of its army. At first Alith had thought this host would head south to Tiranoc, perhaps to assault Caledor. The following day he learned that it marched eastwards, towards the mountains.

The time had come to confront this foe. Alith could feel it in the air. The snows were light, the clouds grey over the mountains. There was a strange calm in the wilderness. Dark magic tugged at the edge of Alith's senses. Yes, he told himself, today he would know the truth.

MID-MORNING BROUGHT SHOUTS from the east, where a rider had been spotted coming down from the mountains. Alith sent word that he was to be allowed to approach, knowing that it would be Elthyrior. He would not be anywhere else on such a momentous day.

Sure enough, the raven herald rode into the ruins, his steed picking its way nimbly though the tumbled stones and hummocks of earth that concealed so many of the dead. His hood was thrown back, revealing his pale, pinched features. In his right hand he carried a spear, but something was bound along half its length, wrapped in a waxed canvas shining with water droplets.

Elthyrior spied Alith and directed his steed towards the Shadow King.

'I see it is not only my enemy that I have brought out of hiding,' said Alith as Elthyrior dismounted.

'The time has come to return this,' said the raven herald, handing Alith the bound spear shaft.

'What is it?'

'Cut free the bindings when the Witch King comes,' said Elthyrior, 'and you will see.'

'Do you know who the Witch King is?' asked Alith.

Elthyrior shook his head.

'You have far more eyes and ears than I, Alith,' he said. 'Besides, did you not venture into Anlec to find out?'

'I got distracted,' Alith replied, though he had the decency to blush while he said it. 'I am glad that you are here.'

'There are few of us left, and I do not think the raven heralds will survive this war,' replied Elthyrior. 'Our time has passed.'

Alith was disturbed by this. If there had been one constant throughout his turmoil of so long, it had been Elthyrior. The raven herald had been many things – a guardian, an ally and companion – though never quite friend.

'The Shadow King watches over Nagarythe,' said Elthyrior with a lopsided smile. 'Morai-heg gives way to Kurnous, and moves her all-seeing gaze upon others.'

Alith could think of nothing to say, and so the two of them stood side-by-side in silence, looking to the west. It was not long before the druchii army could be seen, marching along the road from the north-west, cutting across the foothills in ribbons of black. Alith scanned the skies, searching for sign of dragon riders or manticores, but there was nothing. It seemed that Alith's plan had succeeded: the Witch King would confront him personally.

FOR ALL THAT he had experienced, Alith felt a slight twinge of nervousness as the druchii army spread out across the hills. Their number was inconceivable, more than a hundred thousand at a rough guess. Where had so many warriors come from Alith had no idea. Had Morathi hoarded so many troops all of these years, perhaps waiting for the right leader to emerge?

Some distance away the army halted, out of bolt thrower range. The intent was clear: Alith was to feel no immediate threat and stay where he stood.

Whispers and shouts of alarm caused Alith to look at his shadow warriors. They pointed to the skies, where a dragon appeared through the clouds, descending slowly. It was the largest beast Alith had seen, half-again as big as the dragon that had carried Kheranion. Alith was about to call for his army to flee to the hills but stopped as the dragon circled back towards the druchii army, landing in front of it.

A tall figure dismounted, dropping to the ground beside the monster. The air shimmered around him, a haze of dark mists and rising heat. Alith watched closely as the Witch King approached.

He was far taller than any elf, and clad in an all-encompassing suit of black armour. He carried a shield adorned with a gold relief of a hateful rune that burned Alith's eyes when he looked upon it. The sword in his right hand was enveloped by blue flame from hilt to tip, casting dancing shadows on snow.

It was the armour that caught Alith's full attention. When the Witch King was less than a hundred paces distant, striding purposefully up the hill, Alith could see that it was not wholly black, but a ruddy light glowed from within. Wisps of steam swirled around the warrior. Alith realised with horror that the plates and mail of the armour smouldered, every joint and rivet still hot as if recently forged. The Witch King left molten snow and scorched earth in his wake while the air itself recoiled from his presence, streaming away from his body in whirling vortices.

The shadow warriors watched the Witch King carefully, bows in hand. Alith had ordered them not to attack until his command; he needed to know who dared call himself ruler of Nagarythe. Having seen the strength of the Witch King's host, there was no doubt that this warrior commanded the loyalty of Anlec.

As the Witch King advanced through the tumbled remnants of the old gate, Alith's gaze was drawn in by his eyes. They were pits of black flame, empty and yet full of energy. Nothing could be seen of his face save those terrible orbs; the Witch King's head was enclosed in a black and gold helm adorned with a circlet of horns and spines made from a silvery-grey metal that reflected no light.

Remembering Elthyrior's gift, Alith drew his knife from his belt and cut away the cords binding the canvas around the spear in Alith's left hand. He shook the shaft to dislodge the bag, which fluttered away in the wind. Stirred by the breeze a flag snapped out from the shaft, tied with gold-threaded rope.

The banner was tattered and stained, ragged with many holes and frayed stitching at its edges. It had once been white, but was now dirty brown and grey. The design upon it was indistinct but Alith recognised it immediately as a golden griffon's wing: the standard of House Anar.

Alith felt a surge of courage flow through him, dispelling the dread surrounding the approaching Witch King. The banner had flown in this place since the time of Aenarion and Alith drew on its strength, on the power of centuries that even the blood of the Anars could not wash away. Emboldened, Alith stared at his foe.

'By what right do you enter these lands without the permission of Alith Anar, lord of house Anar, Shadow King of Nagarythe?' Alith demanded, raising the ragged banner above his head. 'If you come to treat with me, hear my oath to the dead. Nothing is forgotten, nothing is forgiven!'

The Witch King stopped half a dozen paces away, the heat from his body prickling at Alith's skin. His infernal gaze moved up to the flag. The Witch King sheathed his sword and gestured at the banner, a mere flick of a finger.

The standard burst into black flames and disintegrated into a flutter of charred flakes that were quickly taken away by the wind, leaving Alith holding a burnt staff. He let the smoking wood drop from his fingers.

'House Anar is dead,' intoned the Witch King. His voice was echoing and deep, as if coming from a distant hall. 'Only I rule Nagarythe. Swear loyalty to me and your past will be forgotten, your treachery forgiven. I will grant you these lands to rule as your own, your fealty owed only to me.'

Alith laughed.

'You would make me a prince of graves, a custodian of nothing,' he said. He grew serious, eyes narrowing. 'By what right do you demand such loyalty?'

The Witch King stepped forwards and it took all of Alith's nerve to hold his ground. Strange voices hissed at the edge of hearing – spirits of sacrifices bound within the armour. The heat was near unbearable, causing Alith's eyes to water, his skin cracking with dryness. Alith licked his lips but his mouth was also parched. Worst was the crawling, filthy sensation of dark magic that leaked through Alith, drawing the life from his blood, chilling his heart.

'Do you not recognise me, Alith?' the Witch King said, bending close, his tone quiet, swathed in a charnel aura of burning and death. 'Will you not serve me once more?'

The voice of the creature in front of Alith was cracked and hoarse, but the Shadow King recognised it. A lifetime ago it had spoken words upon which Alith had hung all his hopes and dreams. Once, in the distant past, that voice had sworn to Alith to set Nagarythe free from tyranny and he had believed it. Now it called for him to surrender.

It was the voice of Malekith.

THE DARK
PATH

Fields of golden crop bent gently in a magical breeze as the palace of Prince Thyriol floated across Saphery. A shimmering vision of white and silver towers and dove-wing buttresses, the citadel eased across the skies with the stately grace of a cloud. Slender minarets and spiralling steeples rose in circles surrounding a central gilded needle that glimmered with magic.

The farmers glanced up at the familiar beauty of the citadel and returned to their labours. If any of them wondered what events passed within the capital, none made mention of it to their companions. From the ground the floating citadel appeared as serene and ordered as ever, a reassuring vision to those that wondered when the war with the Naggarothi would come to their lands.

In truth, the palace was anything but peaceful.

Deep within the alabaster spires, Prince Thyriol strode to a wooden door at the end of a long corridor and tried to open it. The door was barred and magically locked. There were numerous counter-spells with which he could negotiate the obstacle, but he was in no mood for such things. Thyriol laid his hand upon the white-painted planks of the door and summoned the wind of fire. As his growing anger fanned the magic, the paint blistered and the planks charred under his touch. As Thyriol contemplated the treachery he had suffered, and his own blindness to it, the invisible flames burned faster and deeper than any natural fire. Within ten heartbeats the door collapsed into cinders and ash.

Revealed within was a coterie of elves. They looked up at their prince, startled and fearful. Bloody entrails were scattered on the bare stone floor, arranged in displeasing patterns that drew forth Dark Magic. They sat amidst a number of dire tomes *bound with black leather and skin. Candles made of bubbling fat flickered dully on stands made from blackened iron. Sorcery seethed in the air, making Thyriol's gums itch and slicking his skin with its oily touch.*

The missing mages were all here, forbidden runes painted upon their faces with blood, fetishes of bone and sinew dangling around their necks. Thyriol paid them no heed. All of his attention was fixed upon one elf, the only one who showed no sign of fear.

Words escaped Thyriol. The shame and sense of betrayal that filled Thyriol was beyond any means of expression, though some of it showed in the prince's face, twisted into a feral snarl even as tears of fire formed in his eyes.

FAERIE LIGHTS GLITTERED from extended fingertips and silver coronas shimmered around faces fixed in concentration as the young mages practised their spells. Visions of distant lands wavered in the air and golden clouds of protection wreathed around the robed figures. The air seemed to bubble with magical energy, the winds of magic made almost visible by the spells of the apprentices.

The students formed a semicircle around their tutors at the centre of a circular, domed hall – the Grand Chamber. The white wall was lined with alcoves containing sculptures of marble depicting the greatest mages of Ulthuan; some in studious repose, others in the flow of flamboyant conjurations, according to the tastes of successive generations of sculptors. All were austere, looking down with stern but not unkindly expressions on future generations. Their looks of strict expectation were repeated on the faces of Prince Thyriol and Menreir.

'You are speaking too fast,' Thyriol told Ellinithil, youngest of the would-be mages, barely two hundred years old. 'Let the spell form as words in your mind before you speak.'

Ellinithil nodded, brow furrowed. He started the conjuration again but stuttered the first few words.

'You are not concentrating,' Thyriol said softly, laying a reassuring hand on the young elf's shoulder. He raised his voice to address the whole class. 'Finish your incantations safely and then listen to me.'

The apprentices dissipated the magic they had been weaving; illusions vapourised into air, magical flames flickered and dimmed into darkness. As each finished, he or she turned to the prince. All were intent, but none more so that Anamedion, Thyriol's eldest grandson. Anamedion's eyes bore into his grandfather as if by his gaze alone he could prise free the secrets of magic locked inside Thyriol's mind.

'Celabreir,' said Thyriol, gesturing to one of the students to step forward. 'Conjure Emendeil's Flame for me.'

Celabreir glanced uncertainly at her fellow apprentices. The spell was one of the simplest to cast, often learnt in childhood even before any formal teaching had begun. With a shrug, the elf whispered three words of power and held up her right hand, fingers splayed. A flickering golden glow emanated from her fingertips, barely enough to light her slender face and brazen hair.

'Good,' said Thyriol. 'Now, end it and cast it again.'

Celabreir dispersed the magic energy with a flick of her wrist, her fingertips returning to normal. Just as she opened her mouth to begin the incantation again, Thyriol spoke.

'Do you breathe in or out when you cast a spell?' he asked.

A frown knotted Celabreir's brow for a moment. Distracted, she missed a syllable in the spell. Shaking her head, she tried again, but failed.

'What have you done to me, prince?' she asked plaintively. 'Is this some counter-spell you are using?'

Thyriol laughed gently, as did Menreir. Thyriol nodded for the other mage to explain the lesson and returned to his high-backed throne at the far end of the hall.

'You are thinking about how you breathe, aren't you?' said Menreir.

'I… Yes, I am, master,' said Celabreir, her shoulders slumping. 'I don't know whether I breathe in or out when I cast. I can't remember, but if I think about it I realise that I might be doing it differently because I am aware of it now.'

'And so you are no longer concentrating on your control of the magic,' said Menreir. 'A spell you could cast without effort you now find… problematic. Even the most basic spells are still fickle if you do not have total focus. The simplest distraction – an overheard whisper or a flicker of movement in the corner of the eye – can be the difference between success and failure. Knowing this, who can tell me why Ellinithil is having difficulty?'

'He is thinking about the words and not the spell,' said Anamedion, a hint of contempt in his voice. He made no attempt to hide his boredom. 'The more he worries about his pronunciation, the more distracted his inner voice.'

'That's right,' said Thyriol, quelling a stab of annoyance. Anamedion had not called Menreir 'master', a title to which he had earned over many centuries, a sign of growing disrespect that Thyriol would have to address. 'Most of you already have the means to focus the power you need for some of the grandest enchantments ever devised by our people, but until you can cast them without effort or thought, that power is useless to you. Remember that the smallest magic can go a long way.'

'There is another way to overcome these difficulties,' said Anamedion, stepping forward. 'Why do you not teach us that?'

Thyriol regarded Anamedion for a moment, confused.

'Control is the only means to master true magic,' said the prince.

Anamedion shook his head, and half-turned, addressing the other students as much as his grandfather.

'There is a way to tap into magic, unfettered by incantation and ritual,' said

Anamedion. 'Shaped by instinct and powered by raw magic, it is possible to cast the greatest spells of all.'

'You speak of sorcery,' said Menreir quickly, throwing a cautioning look at the apprentices. 'Sorcery brings only two things: madness and death. If you lack the will and application to be a mage, then you will certainly not live long as a sorcerer. If Ellinithil or Celabreir falter with pure magic, the spell simply fails. If one miscasts a sorcerous incantation, the magic does not return to the winds. It must find a place to live, in your body or your mind. Even when sorcery is used successfully, it leaves a taint, on the world and in the spirit. It corrupts one's thoughts and stains the winds of magic. Do not even consider using it.'

'Tell me from where you have heard such things,' said Thyriol. 'Who has put these thoughts in your mind?'

'Oh, here and there,' said Anamedion with a shrug and a slight smile. 'One hears about the druchii sorcerers quite often if one actually leaves the palace. I have heard that any sorcerer is a match for three Sapherian mages in power.'

'Then you have heard wrong,' said Thyriol patiently. 'The mastery of magic is not about power. Any fool can pick up a sword and hack at a lump of wood until he has kindling, but a true woodsman knows to use axe and hatchet and knife. Sorcery is a blunt instrument, capable only of destruction, not creation. Sorcery could not have built this citadel, nor could sorcery have enchanted our fields to be rich with grain. Sorcery burns and scars and leaves nothing behind.'

'And yet Anlec was built with sorcery,' countered Anamedion.

'Anlec is *sustained* by sorcery, but it was *built* by Caledor Dragontamer, who used only pure magic,' Thyriol replied angrily.

He shot glances at the others in the room, searching for some sign that they paid undue attention to Anamedion's arguments. There was rumour, whispered and incoherent, that some students, and even some mages, had begun to experiment with sorcery. It was so hard for Thyriol to tell. Dark Magic had been rising for decades, fuelled by the rituals and sacrifices of the Naggarothi and their cultist allies. It polluted the magical vortex of Ulthuan, twisting the Winds of Magic with its presence.

They had found druchii sorcerers hidden in the wilder parts of Saphery, in the foothills of the mountains, trying to teach their corrupted ways to the misguided. Some of the sorcerers had been slain, others had fled, forewarned of their discovery by fellow cultists. It was to protect the young from this corruption that Thyriol had brought the most talented Sapherians here, to learn from him and his most powerful mages. That Anamedion brought talk of sorcery into the capital was a grave concern. Saphethion, of all places, had to be free of the taint of Dark Magic, for the corruption of the power in the citadel could herald victory for the Naggarothi.

* * *

'I am glad you have found us,' Anamedion said with no hint of regret or shame. 'I have longed to shed our secrecy, but the others insisted on this subterfuge.'

The mention of the other mages broke Thyriol's focus and he took in the rest of the faces, settling on the blood-daubed features of Illeanith. This brought a fresh surge of anguish and he gave a choked gasp and lurched to one side, saved from falling only by the burnt frame of the doorway. He had been disappointed but not surprised by Anamedion's presence. Seeing Illeanith was one shock too many.

It was as if daggers had been plunged into Thyriol's heart and gut, a physical agony that writhed inside him, pulling away all sense and reason. The mages who had come with Thyriol began to shout and hurl accusations, but Thyriol heard nothing, just the arrhythmic thundering of his heart and a distant wailing in his head. Through a veil of tears and the waves of dismay welling up inside of him, Thyriol watched numbly as the sorcerers drew away from the door, adding their own voices to the cacophony.

'Everyone but Anamedion, leave me,' Thyriol commanded. 'Menreir, I will call for you when I am finished. We must discuss the latest messages from King Caledor.'

The mage and students bowed their acquiescence and left silently. Anamedion stood defiantly before the throne, arms crossed. Thyriol put aside his anger and looked at his grandson with sympathetic eyes.

'You are gifted, Anamedion,' said the prince. 'If you would but show a little more patience, there is no limit to what you might achieve in time.'

'What is it that you are afraid of?' countered Anamedion.

'I am afraid of damnation,' Thyriol replied earnestly, leaning forward. 'You have heard the myths of sorcery, while I have seen it first-hand. You think it is perhaps a quick way to achieve your goals, but you are wrong. The path is just as long for the sorcerer as it is for the mage. You think that Morathi and her ilk have not made terrible sacrifices, of their spirit and their bodies, to gain the power they have? You think that they simply wave a hand and destroy armies on a whim? No, they have not and do not. Terrible bargains they have made, bargains with powers we would all do better to avoid. Trust me, Anamedion, we call it Dark Magic for good reason.'

Anamedion still looked unconvinced, but he changed his approach.

'What good does it do us to spend a century learning spells when the druchii march against us now?' he said. 'King Caledor needs us with his armies, fighting the Naggarothi sorcerers. You speak of the future, but unless we act now, there may be no future. For seven years I have listened to the stories of horror, of war, engulfing Tiranoc and Chrace and Ellyrion. Cothique and Eataine are under attack. Must the fields of Saphery burn before you do something?'

Thyriol shook his head, fighting his frustration.

'I would no more send lambs to fight a lion than I would pit the skills of my students against Morathi's coven,' said the prince. 'There are but a dozen mages in all of Saphery that I would trust to fight the druchii in battle, myself included.'

'Then fight!' Anamedion demanded, pacing towards the throne, fists balled. 'Caledor begs for your aid and you are deaf to his requests. Why did you choose him as Phoenix King if you will not follow him?'

Thyriol glanced away for a moment, looking through the narrow arched windows that surrounded the hall. He did not see the greying autumn skies, his mind wandering to the ancient past. He saw a magic-blistered battlefield, where daemons rampaged and thousands of elves died screaming in agony. He saw the most powerful wizards of an age holding back the tides of Chaos while the Dragontamer conjured his vortex.

His memories shifted, to a time more recent but no less painful. He saw Naggarothi warriors, skin ruptured, hair flaming, falling from the battlements of Anlec while he soared overhead atop the back of a pegasus. Depraved cultists, dedicated to obscene sacrifice, wailed their curses even as lightning from Thyriol's staff crackled through their bodies.

War brought nothing but evil, even when fought for a just cause. Shaking his head to dismiss the waking nightmare, Thyriol returned his attention to Anamedion, his heart heavy.

'Your father thought the same, and now he is dead,' Thyriol said quietly.

'And your cowardice makes his sacrifice in vain,' Anamedion growled. 'Perhaps it is not Dark Magic that you fear, but death. Has your life lasted so long that you would protect it now at any cost?'

At this, Thyriol's frayed temper finally snapped.

'You accuse me of cowardice?' he said, stalking from his throne towards Anamedion, who stood his ground and returned the prince's glare. 'I fought beside Aenarion and the Dragontamer, and never once flinched from battle. Thirty years ago I fought beside Malekith when Anlec was retaken. You have never seen war, and know nothing of its nature, so do not accuse me of cowardice!'

'And you throw back at me accusations that I cannot counter,' Anamedion replied, fists clenching and unclenching with exasperation. 'You say I do not know war, yet condemn me to idle away my years in this place, closeted away from harm because you fear I will suffer the same fate as my father! Do you have so little confidence in me?'

'I do,' said Thyriol. 'You have your father's willfulness and your mother's stubbornness. Why could you not be more like your younger brother, Elathrinil? He is studious and attentive... and obedient.'

'Elathrinil is diligent but dull,' replied Anamedion with a scornful laugh. 'Another century or two and he may make an adequate mage, but there is no greatness in him.'

'Do not crave greatness,' said Thyriol. 'Many have been dashed upon the cliffs of their own ambition. Do not repeat their mistakes.'

'So says the ruling prince of Saphery, friend of Aenarion, last surviving member of the First Council and greatest mage in Ulthuan,' said Anamedion. 'Maybe I have been wrong. It is not battle or death that you fear, it is me! You are jealous of my talent, fearful that your own reputation will be eclipsed by mine. Perhaps my star will rise higher than yours while you still cling to this world with the last strength in your fingers. You guard what you have gained and dare not risk anything. You profess wisdom and insight, but actually you are selfish and envious.'

'Get out!' roared Thyriol. Anamedion flinched as if struck. 'Get out of my sight! I will not have you in my presence again until you apologise for these lies. You have done nothing today but proven to me that you are unfit to rule Saphery. Think long and hard, Anamedion, about what you want. Do not tarnish me with your vain ambitions. Go!'

Anamedion hesitated, his face showing a moment of contrition, but it passed swiftly, replaced by a stare of keen loathing. With a wordless snarl, he turned his back on his grandfather and strode from the room.

Thyriol stumbled back to his throne and almost fell into it, drained by his outburst. He slumped there for a moment, thoughts reeling, ashamed of his own anger. Righteousness contended with guilt, neither winning a decisive victory. What if Anamedion was right? What if he really was jealous of the youth's prowess, knowing that his own existence was waning fast?

Closing his eyes, Thyriol whispered a few mantras of focus and dismissed his self-examination. The fault was not with the prince, but with his grandchild. For decades he had known that there was something amiss with Anamedion, but had turned a blind eye upon his deficiencies. Now that Thyriol had finally given open voice to his doubts, and Anamedion declared his own misgivings, perhaps the two of them could move on and resolve their differences.

With a sigh, Thyriol straightened himself and sat in the throne properly. Anamedion's small rebellion was a distraction, one that Thyriol could not deal with immediately. He had Caledor's messenger waiting, eager to return to the Phoenix King with Thyriol's answer. The world was being torn apart by war and bloodshed, and against that the petulant protests and naïve philosophies of a grandson seemed insignificant.

Thyriol twitched a finger and in the depths of the palace a silver bell rang to announce that the prince of Saphery wished to be attended.

Anamedion felt the other sorcerers opening the portal they had created for just this situation. The shadow at the back of their hiding place deepened, merging with the shadows of a cave some distance from the palace's current location. Something seethed in the shadow's depths, a formless bulk shifting its weight just outside of mortal comprehension.

Hadryana and Meledir lunged through the portal without word, fearful of Thyriol's wrath. They were soon followed by the other students and Alluthian, leaving only Illeanith and Anamedion.

'Come!' commanded his mother, grabbing him by the arm. Anamedion shook free her grasp and looked at his grandfather.

Thyriol was a broken creature. Anamedion saw an elf near the end of his years, frail and tired, his own misery seeping through every fibre of his being. There was no fight left in him.

'I am not ashamed,' said Anamedion. 'I am not afraid.'

'We must leave!' insisted Illeanith. Anamedion turned to her and pushed her towards the shadow-portal.

'Then go! I will send for you soon,' he said. 'This will not take long, mother.'

Illeanith hesitated for a moment, torn between love of her son and fear of her father. Fear won and she plunged through the tenebrous gateway, disappearing into the dark fog.

When Anamedion returned his attention to Thyriol, he saw that the prince had straightened and regained his composure. For a moment, doubt gnawed at Anamedion. Perhaps he had misjudged the situation. Thyriol's look changed from one of horror to one of pity and this threw fuel onto the fire of Anamedion's anger. His momentary fear evaporated like the illusion it was.

'I will prove how weak you have become,' said Anamedion.

'Surrender, or suffer the consequences,' growled Menreir, blue flames dancing from his eyes.

'Do not interfere!' Thyriol told his mages, waving them back. The pity drained from his face and was replaced by his usual calm expression. In a way, it was more chilling than the prince's anger. 'I will deal with this.'

Anamedion knew that he must strike first. He allowed the Dark Magic to coil up through his body, leeching its power from where it lurked within and around the Winds of Magic. He felt it crackling along his veins, quickening his heart, setting his mind afire. Uttering a curse of Ereth Khial, Anamedion threw forward his hand and a bolt of black lightning leapt from his fingertips.

A moment from striking Thyriol, the spell burst into a shower of golden dust that fluttered harmlessly to the bare stone floor.

Only now did Anamedion see the counterspells woven into his grandfather's robe. The sorcerer's cruel smile faded. The prince's body was steeped in magic, subtle and layered. Dark Magic pulsed once more, bolstering Anamedion's confidence. Thyriol's defences mattered not at all; the wardings were many but thin, easily penetrated by the power Anamedion could now wield.

THE VIEW WAS breathtaking from the wide balcony atop the Tower of Alin-Haith, the vast panorama of Ulthuan laid out around the four mages. To the south and north stretched the farms and gentle hills of Saphery, bathed in the afternoon sun. To the west glittered the Inner Sea, barely visible on the horizon. To the east the majestic peaks of the Anullii Mountains rose from beyond the horizon, grey and purple and tipped with white. Thyriol noted storm clouds gathering over the mountains to the north, sensing within them the Dark Magic that had gathered in the vortex over the past decades.

'I am going to tell Caledor that I will not open the Tor Anroc gateway,' the prince announced, not looking at his companions.

The three other wizards were Menreir, Alethin and Illeanith, the last being Thyriol's daughter, his only child. Thinking of her led the prince's thoughts back to Anamedion and he pushed them aside and turned to face the others.

'I cannot risk the druchii taking control of the gateway from the other end,' Thyriol explained.

The palace of Saphethion was more than a floating castle. It was able to drift effortlessly through the skies because the magic woven into its foundations placed it slightly apart from time and space. From the outside the palace appeared beautiful and serene, but within there existed a maze of halls and rooms, corridors and passages far larger than could be contained within normal walls. Some of those rooms were not even upon Saphethion itself, but lay in other cities: Lothern, Tor Yvresse, Montieth and others. Most importantly, one of the isle-spanning gateways led to Tor Anroc, currently occupied by the army of Nagarythe.

As soon as he had found out that the city had fallen into the hands of the druchii, Thyriol had closed the gate, putting its enchantments into stasis. Now the Phoenix King wanted Thyriol to reopen the gate so that he might send agents into Tor Anroc, perhaps even an army.

'Caledor's plan has much merit, father,' said Illeanith. 'Surprise would be total. It is unlikely that the druchii are even aware of the gateway's existence, for none of them have ever used it.'

'I wish to keep it that way,' said Thyriol. 'The wards upon the gate can resist the attentions of any normal druchii sorcerer, but I would rather not test their strength against the magic of Morathi. Even the knowledge that such gateways can exist would be dangerous, for I have no doubt that she would find some means to create her own. On a more mundane point, I cannot make the gate work only one way. Once it is open, the druchii can use it to enter Saphethion, and that puts us all at risk.'

'The Phoenix King will be disappointed, lord,' said Menreir.

'The Phoenix King will be angry,' Thyriol corrected him. 'Yet it is not the first time I have refused him.'

'I am not so sure that the druchii are still unaware of the gateways, prince,' said Alethin. 'There are few that can be trusted these days with any secret, and I am sure that there are Sapherians who once served in the palace now in the employ of the cults, or at least sympathetic to their cause. Even within the palace we have found texts smuggled in by agents of the druchii to sow confusion and recruit support.'

'That gives me even more reason to be cautious,' said Thyriol, leaning his back against the parapet. 'Tor Anroc is shrouded in shadow, protected from our augurs and divinations. Perhaps the druchii have discovered the gateway and guard it, or even now work to unravel its secrets. The moment it is opened, it will be like a white flare in the mind of Morathi – I cannot hide such magic from her scrying.'

'Forgive me, prince, but to what end do you tell us this?' said Menreir. 'If your mind is set, simply send the messenger back to Caledor. We are no council to give our approval.'

Thyriol was taken aback by the question, for the answer seemed plain enough to him.

'I had hoped that you might have some argument to change my mind,' he said. Sighing, he cast his gaze back towards the mountains and when he continued his voice was quiet, wistful. 'I have lived a long, long time. I have known the heights of happiness, and plunged into the depths of despair. Even when the daemons bayed at the walls of Anlec and the night lasted an eternity, I had hope. Now? Now I can see no hope, for there can be no victory when elves fight other elves. I wish an attack on Tor Anroc, an assault on Anlec, could end this war, but there is no such simple ploy. Not armed force or great magic will end this conflict. We are at war with ourselves and the only peace that can last must come from within us.'

'Do not do this,' Thyriol warned.

'You are in no position to give me commands,' snapped Anamedion. A sword of black flame appeared in his fist and he leapt forwards to strike. Menreir stepped in the way, out of instinct to save the prince, and the ethereal blade passed through his chest. In moments the mage's body disintegrated into a falling cloud of grey ash.

Anamedion swung back-handed at Thyriol, but a shimmering shield of silver energy appeared on the mage's arm and the flaming blade evaporated into a wisp of smoke at its touch.

'You cannot control the power needed to defeat me,' Thyriol said. He was already breathing heavily, and Anamedion heard the words as nothing but an empty boast.

Dispelling the warding that surrounded the room, Anamedion reached out further into the winds of magic, drawing in more and more dark power. A black cloud enveloped him, swirling and churning with its own life, flashes and glitters in its depths. He urged the cloud forward and for a moment it engulfed Thyriol, cloying and choking.

A white light appeared at the cloud's centre and the magic boiled away, revealing Thyriol unharmed, glowing from within. Anamedion could see that his grandfather's pull on the winds of magic was becoming fitful and saw a chance to finish him. Taking a deep breath Anamedion reached out as far as he could, a surge of sorcery pouring into his body and mind.

THYRIOL FELT A hand upon his back and turned his head to see Illeanith next to him.

'Anamedion told me that you have banished him from your presence,' she said. 'He is stubborn, but he is also brave and strong and willing to prove himself. Please end this dispute. Do not make me choose between my father and my son.'

'There are no words that will lift the veil of a mother's love for her son,' replied the prince.

'You think me blind to my son's faults?' snapped Illeanith, stepping back. 'Perhaps I see more than you think, prince. Other matters are always more important to you. For over a thousand years you have lived in the mystical realm; you no longer remember what it is to be flesh and blood. I think that a part of you was trapped with the other mages on the Isle of the Dead, a part of your spirit if not your body. Anamedion has not seen the things you have seen, and you make no attempt to show them to him. You think that you guard him against danger, but that is no way to prepare him for princehood. He must learn who he is, to know his own mind. He is not you, father, he is himself, and you must accept that.'

Illeanith glanced at the other two mages with an apologetic look and then disappeared down the steps from the balcony.

'I miss her mother,' sighed Thyriol, leaning over the wall to peer down at the courtyard of the palace where armour-clad guards drilled in disciplined lines of silver and gold. 'She helped me remember how to stay in this world. Maybe it is time I moved on, let slip this fragile grip that I have kept these last hundred years. I wish I had died in peace, like Miranith. One should not be born in war and die in war...'

The other two mages remained silent as Thyriol's words drifted into a whisper, knowing that Thyriol was talking to himself, no longer aware of their presence. They exchanged a knowing, worried glance and followed Illeanith from the tower, each fearful of their prince's deterioration.

'Sorcery is not an end in itself, it is just a means,' said Anamedion. 'It need not be evil.'

'The means can corrupt the end,' replied Thyriol quietly, his hoarse whisper further proof of his infirmity. 'Just because we can do a thing, it is not right that we should do a thing.'

'Nonsense,' spat Anamedion, unleashing his next spell. Flames of purple and blue roared from his hands, lapping at Thyriol. The ancient mage writhed under its power, sparks of gold and green magic bursting from him as he deflected the worst of the spell, though it still brought him to one knee. 'You'll have to kill me to prove it!'

'I will not kill my own kin,' wheezed Thyriol.

'I will,' said Anamedion with a glint in his eye.

Anamedion could feel only Dark Magic in the chamber and knew that the prince's resistance was all but over. All he needed was another overwhelming attack and this would be finished. He would become prince of Saphery as was his right, and they would take the war to the Naggarothi.

Grasping the fetish at his throat, the rune-carved knuckle bones burning his palm, Anamedion incanted words of power, feasting on the sorcery that was now roiling within every part of his body. He visualised a monstrous dragon, drew it in the air with his mind's eye. He saw its ebon fangs and the black fire that flickered from its mouth. Thyriol attempted a dispel, directing what little remained of the winds of magic, trying to unpick the enchantment being woven by Anamedion.

Anamedion drew on more Dark Magic, swamping the counterspell with power. He focused all his thoughts on the spell, as Thyriol had once warned him he must. He had no time to appreciate the irony, all his mind was bent on the conjuration. He could see the shimmering scales and the veins on the membranes of the dragon's wings. The apparition started to form before Anamedion, growing more real with every passing heartbeat.

In a moment the dragon-spell would engulf Thyriol, crushing the last breath from his body.

Thyriol waited patiently in the Hall of Stars, gazing up at the window at the centre of the hall's ceiling. It showed a starry sky, though outside the palace it was not yet noon. The scene was of the night when the hall had been built, the auspicious constellations and alignments captured for all eternity by magic. Thyriol had come here countless times to gaze at the beauty of the heavens and knew every sparkling star as well as he knew himself.

A delicate cough from the doorway attracted Thyriol's attention. Menreir stood just inside the hall, a cluster of fellow mages behind him and a worried-looking servant at his side.

'We cannot find Anamedion,' said Menreir. 'Also, Illeanith, Hadry-ana, Alluthian and Meledir are missing, along with half a dozen of the students.'

Thyriol took this news without comment. The prince closed his eyes and felt Saphethion around him. He knew every stone of the palace, the magic that seeped within the mortar, the flow of energy that bound every stone. The golden needle pulsed rhythmically at its centre and the winds of magic coiled and looped around the corridors and halls. He could feel every living creature too, each a distinctive eddy in the winds of magic. It would not take long to locate his grandson.

But it was not Anamedion that Thyriol found first. In a chamber beneath the Mausoleum of the Dawn, there was a strange whirl of mystical power. It flowed around the room and not through it, masking whatever was within: a warding spell, one that Thyriol had not conjured. It was subtle, just the slightest disturbance in the normal flow. Only Thyriol, who had created every spell and charm that sustained Saphethion, would have noticed the anomaly.

'Come with me,' he commanded the mages as he pushed through the group. He showed no outward sign of vexation, but Thyriol's stomach had lurched. Mages were free to use their magic in the palace, why would one seek to hide their conjurations? He suspected sorcery. Despite his reasons for being in the Hall of Stars, this was more pressing than his division with Anamedion. His grandson would have to wait a while longer for their reconciliation.

Thyriol whispered something, almost bent double, his eyes fixed on his grandson. Anamedion did not hear what the prince had said. Was it some final counterspell? Perhaps an admission of wrong? A plea for mercy?

For the moment Anamedion wondered what Thyriol had said, his mind strayed from the spell. The distraction lasted only a heartbeat but it was too late. The Dark Magic churning inside Anamedion slipped from his grasp. He struggled to control it, but it wriggled from his mind, coiling into his heart, flooding his lungs. Choking and gasping, Anamedion swayed as his veins crackled with power and his eyes melted. He tried to wail but only black flames erupted from his burning throat. The pain was unbearable, every part of his body and mind shrieked silently as the sorcery consumed him.

With a last spasm, Anamedion collapsed, his body shrivelling and blackening. With a dry thump, his corpse hit the ground, wisps of thick smoke issuing from his empty eye sockets.

THYRIOL KNELT DOWN beside the remains of his grandson. For the moment he felt nothing, but he knew he would grieve later. He would feel the guilt of what he had done, though it had been unavoidable. Thoughts of grief recalled the death of Menreir, his oldest friend. Thyriol had barely noticed his destruction, so engrossed had he been in his duel with Anamedion. Another link to the past taken away; another piece of the future destroyed.

'What did you whisper?' asked Urian, his eyes fixed upon the contorted remnants of Anamedion. 'Some dispel of your own creation?'

Thyriol shook his head sadly at the suggestion.

'I cast no spell,' he replied. 'I merely whispered the name of his grandmother. His lack of focus killed him.'

Thyriol stood and faced the mages clustered around the blackened doorway. His expression hardened.

'Anamedion was young, and stupid, and ignored my warnings,' said the prince. 'Illeanith and the other sorcerers will not be so easy to defeat. There will be more of them than we have seen. The war has finally come to Saphery.'

CALEDOR

PART ONE

*The Dragontamer's Legacy; Ancient Rivalries;
Strife in Nagarythe; Imrik's Self-Exile*

ONE

Pride of Caledor

DURING THE DARKEST years of Ulthuan, the two greatest elves to have lived were at the forefront of the war against the daemons of Chaos. The first Phoenix King, Aenarion the Defender, was aided by Caledor Dragon-tamer, and the two lords of Ulthuan held the daemon hordes at bay for more than a century.

Caledor it was that saw the attacks of the daemons would never cease while the wild winds of magic blew across the world. The Dragontamer studied long and hard the mystical secrets of Chaos, gaining an insight into the immaterial realm beyond any other mortal. Seeing that the magic flowing into the world from the Realm of Chaos in the north sustained the daemons, Caledor set about preparing a mighty spell that would create a vortex of energy on Ulthuan to siphon away the winds of magic. Many were the arguments he had with Aenarion over this course of action; Aenarion feared rightly that the weapons and armour of the elven lords were forged by the same magic that sustained the daemons and without it the isle he ruled would be defenceless.

The two never came to agreement on the matter, and when Aenarion's wife, the Everqueen, was slain, he ignored Caledor's counsel and sought out the Sword of Khaine to strike down the daemon hosts. The Phoenix King became a dark, vengeful warrior, and founded the kingdom of Nagarythe in the north of Ulthuan, and ruled from the citadel of Anlec. The Dragontamer quit his alliance with Aenarion and his own kingdom, named after Caledor, turned its efforts to the creation of the magical vortex.

Though once friends, the two great elves never again wholly trusted each other, but at the moment of greatest peril, Caledor and Aenarion both played their part in the defeat of the daemons. Caledor began his ultimate spell upon an isle in the waters of Ulthuan's Inner Sea. Seeing what the Dragontamer intended, the daemons threw their armies at Caledor and his mages. Aenarion came to Caledor's aid and held back the legions of Chaos to give the mages time to complete their incantations.

Both were to sacrifice themselves. Though victorious, Aenarion and his dragon, Indraugnir, were grievously wounded in the battle. True to the oaths he had made, Aenarion flew north to the Blighted Isle to return the Sword of Khaine to its black altar; neither king nor dragon were seen again. Caledor and his followers became trapped within the eye of the vortex, frozen in time by the spell, doomed to an endless existence as conduits for the magical energy.

Thus the lands of Caledor and Aenarion were left without their rulers; Caledor in the mountains of the south, Nagarythe in the bleak north. The distrust that existed between the two kingdoms did not end with the deaths of their founders, but grew greater. The successors of the elven lords would not surrender power to each other and each claimed credit for the victory over the daemons.

When Aenarion's son, Malekith, desired to inherit his father's position as Phoenix King, the princes of Caledor resisted. They reminded the elves of the other realms that Malekith had been raised in a place of darkness and despair, and that the Dragontamer had prophesied that the descendants of Aenarion would be forever tainted by the curse of Bloody-Handed Khaine.

The First Council of princes chose Bel Shanaar of Tiranoc to be Phoenix King, thus ensuring neither Caledor nor Nagarythe would hold the greatest power in Ulthuan. Malekith accepted this decision with dignity and the Caledorians likewise endorsed the choice of Bel Shanaar.

Under the reign of this new Phoenix King the elves rebuilt their cities and explored the world. Colonies were founded across the oceans, and the influence of the elven kingdoms spread far and wide. Always wary of each other's status and power, Nagarythe and Caledor continued their rivalry for centuries and though peace existed between the two kingdoms, their distrust of each other deepened, the princes of each accusing the other of being jealous, arrogant and self-serving.

So it was with some annoyance, and a little trepidation, that Prince Imrik of Caledor heard the news that Naggarothi banners had been seen approaching his camp. The general of Caledor's armies in Elthin Arvan, the lands east of the Great Ocean, Imrik was grandson to the Dragontamer, younger brother of the kingdom's ruling prince, Caledrian.

The arrival of the Naggarothi was untimely. Imrik and his warriors had spent twelve days pursuing a horde of savage orcs and goblins through the wild lands in the south of Elthin Arvan, and that day would bring their foes to battle.

'The Naggarothi seek to steal our glory,' Imrik said to his companions, his youngest brother Dorien and cousin Thyrinor.

The three sat in Imrik's pavilion, already in their armour of golden plates and silver scale. The herald who had brought the news of the Naggarothi arrival waited nervously for his general's command.

'They believe they can take a victory here and claim these lands for themselves,' said Dorien. 'Send them away with a warning that they trespass on Caledorian soil.'

Thyrinor shifted uncomfortably in his seat and raised a hand to Dorien to ask for his peace.

'It would not be wise to provoke them,' said Thyrinor. He turned to the messenger. 'How many do you say they are?'

'Twelve thousand, my prince,' replied the herald. 'Of which four thousand are knights. We counted them as they forded the Laithenn River.'

'They'll be here well before noon,' said Imrik. 'They marched all night.'

'We should ready our army and attack the orcs before the Naggarothi get here,' said Dorien, standing up. 'They cannot claim credit for a battle that was finished before they arrived.'

'Not yet,' said Imrik. 'I will not be forced into hasty battle.'

'So what would you have us do?' said Dorien. 'Share the glory with those cold-blooded killers?'

'We'll prove ourselves greater,' said Imrik. He signalled for the herald to approach. 'Ride out to the Naggarothi and tell their prince to come to me.'

The messenger bowed and departed swiftly, leaving the three lords of Caledor in silence. Imrik waited patiently, arms crossed, while Dorien paced to and fro. Thyrinor moved to a table and poured himself wine mixed with water, which he sipped with an agitated expression. After some time, he turned on Dorien with a frown.

'Sit down, cousin, please,' Thyrinor said sharply. He swallowed a mouthful of wine. 'You prowl like a Chracian lion in a pen.'

'I don't like it,' said Dorien. 'How did the Naggarothi learn of our pursuit, and how did they catch us so swiftly? And if my pacing vexes you so much, feel free to step outside, cousin. Or would that be too far away from the wine ewers for you?'

'Stop bickering.' Imrik's quiet instruction stilled the pair. 'Dorien, sit down. Thyrinor, drink no more. Our army readies for battle while you squabble like children. Wait.'

Dorien acquiesced and sat down, sweeping his long scarlet cloak over one arm of his chair. Thyrinor emptied his goblet and placed it on the table before returning to his seat.

'How can you be so calm, cousin?' said Thyrinor. 'Do you expect the Naggarothi to be our allies?'

'No,' said Imrik, unmoving.

'You give them opportunity to snub us,' Thyrinor said. He threw up his hands. 'Why attempt an embassy you know will not succeed, cousin?'

'Because they would not,' said Imrik. 'We behave with dignity.'

'As if the Naggarothi care about our dignity,' Dorien said with a snort of derision. 'They will see it as weakness.'

'Do you see it as weakness, brother?' asked Imrik. His eyes fixed Dorien with an intent stare.

'No,' Dorien replied, a little hesitant. 'I know we are not weak.'

'That is all that matters,' said Imrik. 'I care not for the opinions of the Naggarothi.'

Again the elves fell quiet. Outside, the clamour and bustle of the mustering army could be heard. Captains called out for their companies to assemble and piercing clarions signalled the call to battle.

Imrik passed the time in contemplation of the battle to come. The Naggarothi were an unwelcome distraction. He had not become Caledor's most lauded general by allowing himself to be distracted. The prince knew his companions thought him brusque, cold-hearted even; he considered them boisterous and hot-headed. The prince was content with his life. The chance to prove himself in battle, to show his worth as an heir of the Dragontamer, was enough. Even the small exchanges with his brother and cousin left him agitated, and glad to be far from the court of Caledrian. Here in the colonies an elf could make a name for himself with honest endeavour, away from the personalities and politics of Ulthuan.

It had been such constant wrangling that had driven him to Elthin Arvan. Though descended from the line of Caledor, Imrik had little aptitude or desire for magical ability and so had dedicated himself to mastery of the sword and the lance, and the command of armies. He shared his people's distrust of the Naggarothi, but also held them in some grudging respect; their accomplishments in war were unmatched by any other kingdom, including his own.

In particular, he admired their ruler, Prince Malekith. Imrik would never say as much to another elf, but the achievements of Malekith were an example to be followed. Such admiration was shadowed by irritation too; had Imrik not shared his lifetime with Malekith he would have been renowned as the greatest general of Ulthuan. As it was, he was famed in Caledor and amongst a few of the colonial cities that knew of his exploits, but his victories and conquests were otherwise drowned out by the accolades heaped upon the prince of Nagarythe.

Imrik curled his lip in a silent snarl, annoyed that despite his efforts, he had allowed the Naggarothi to interrupt his pre-battle preparations. Dorien and Thyrinor looked at their commander, alerted to his annoyance.

'Call the army to order,' Imrik said, standing up.

He lifted his sword from where it leaned against the side of his chair, and buckled its golden sheath to his belt; his ornate helm he tucked under his arm. The hem of his cloak brushing the intricately embroidered rugs on the floor, Imrik led the other two elves from the tent.

The air was damp and the sky overcast, a thin mist obscuring the heath-lands on which the elves had made camp. The pennants atop the pavilions hung limply in the still air, wet from rainfall in the night. The small town of gaily coloured tents was alive with activity as retainers bustled to attend to the needs of the captains and knights. Spear companies marched briskly to the mustering south-east of the encampment, their silver armour and dark green shields dappled with water droplets.

Imrik turned to the west and strode along a temporary causeway laid across the grass and heather. Gilded harnesses studded with rubies and emeralds jingled as a squadron of knights rode across the pathway ahead, dipping their lances in salute as they passed in front of their general, white steeds stepping briskly. Imrik raised his hand in acknowledgement.

Passing between an open-sided armoury and a store tent, the three princes reached the dragon field. Three of the mighty beasts lazed on the stretch of rocky grassland, expelling clouds of vapour from their nostrils. Two were the colour of embers, with deep red scales and orange underbellies; the third had an upper body of dark blue like twilight, its legs and lower parts the colour of slate. All three raised massive heads on their long necks at Imrik's call.

'Time for battle!' shouted the general.

The dragons heaved themselves up with growls and snorts, yellow eyes blinking slowly. The largest, one of the red-scaled pair, stretched out its wings and yawned wide, fumes smoking from its gullet.

'So soon?' the monster said, its voice a deep rumble.

'Are you tired, Maedrethnir?' said Thyrinor. 'Perhaps you wish you were slumbering beneath the mountains of Caledor with your kin?'

'Impudent elf,' said the dragon. 'Some of us must remain awake to keep you out of trouble.'

'Perhaps you would prefer to walk?' suggested Thyrinor's mount, the blue dragon called Anaegnir. She flapped her wings twice, buffeting the elves.

Young elves in the livery of Imrik's household emerged from the camp, bearing the ornate saddle-thrones and weapons of the dragon princes. When the harnesses were fitted – an involved operation that required much cooperation from the dragons – the three princes pulled themselves up by ropes to the backs of their mounts. They buckled belts across their waists, leaving their armoured legs to hang free across the necks of the beasts. Each was handed a lance by his retainer; weapons forged of silvery ithilmar, three times as long as an elf is tall, garlanded with green and red pennants. The princes took up high shields and hung them from their saddles.

When the retainers had retreated a safe distance, Imrik leaned forwards along Maedrethnir's neck and rubbed a hand along his scales.

'South-east, to the army,' said the general.

Maedrethnir launched into the air, the grass flattened beneath the thunderous flapping of his wings. The other two dragons followed swiftly, and all three princes circled higher and higher above the camp.

The altitude granted Imrik an impressive view of his army assembling. Two thousand knights drew up in squadrons a hundred strong, their banners and pennants rippling as they trotted across the wild heath. To their left, the spear companies formed; blocks of five hundred warriors, nine in all, ranked ten deep behind their standards. Twenty wagons formed a column behind the spearmen, each drawn by four horses and bearing two bolt throwers and their crews. Archers, some three thousand more elves, waited in companies beside the spearmen.

In green and red and silver, the elven host stretched across the dark moorlands. Turning his gaze to the south-east, Imrik could make out the distant curve of a river, rushing down from the high mountains jutting above the horizon. From above it was easy to see the route taken by the orcs; a swathe of trampled grass and bushes that meandered towards the river. The smoke of hundreds of fires obscured the wide waters much farther to the south where the greenskins had made their camp.

As Maedrethnir tilted a wing and dipped towards the army, Imrik heard a distant shout. Looking over his shoulder, he saw Dorien waving his lance to attract attention. When he saw that Imrik was watching, he pointed the lance tip to the west. Imrik told Maedrethnir to turn to the right so he could see what had attracted Dorien's attention.

A column of black and purple wound alongside a narrow stream: the Naggarothi. Their armour glittered with gold, their knights in the vanguard setting a swift pace while the infantry followed as quickly as possible. Imrik spied something else, a shape above the army of Nagarythe.

'What is that flying above the Naggarothi?' he asked.

Maedrethnir turned his head to look, gliding effortlessly in a slow arc towards the other elven host.

'A griffon and rider,' said the dragon, with some distaste. 'Shall we teach them not to intrude upon our skies?'

'Take me to them,' said Imrik.

Beating his wings, Maedrethnir soared higher and turned towards the Naggarothi. Looking back, Imrik saw Dorien and Thyrinor following. With his lance, the general signalled for the other two princes to join the army. Thyrinor took the instruction immediately and turned away; Dorien did so only reluctantly.

As they flew towards the Naggarothi, Maedrethnir dipped his long head towards the ground.

'A rider,' he said.

Imrik looked and saw a lone elf on a white steed, galloping back towards the Caledorian camp.

'Take us down to him,' said Imrik. 'Let's hear the Naggarothi reply.'

The rider reined in his steed as the dragon and prince descended steeply. The horse stamped skittishly as Maedrethnir landed a short distance away, the messenger's steed letting out a whinny of unease. The herald patted the beast on the shoulder and urged his mount closer, so that he could be heard without shouting.

'General, the Naggarothi prince declined your invitation,' said the messenger.

'Does this prince have a name?' Imrik asked.

'He is Maldiar, my prince,' replied the herald. 'A lord of Athel Toralien.'

'Never heard of him,' said Imrik. 'Must be one of the upstarts Malekith made prince before he disappeared into the northern wastelands.'

'Indeed, my prince,' said the other elf. 'He bade me to tell you that the Naggarothi do not accept demands from Caledorians. I am sorry, my prince, but Maldiar also instructed me to tell you to abandon your attack on the orcs and claims he alone has right of conquest in these lands.'

'We shall see,' said Imrik. 'Return to the army and tell my captains to be ready to advance.'

'As you command, my prince.' The herald turned his horse away; it leapt gratefully into a gallop to race away from Imrik and his monstrous steed.

'Let us meet Maldiar,' Imrik told Maedrethnir.

A rumble shook the dragon's chest, which might have been a laugh, and he powered into the sky. Dragon and rider headed towards the Naggarothi, skimming over the heath just above the height of the few scattered trees that broke the rough hillscape.

The griffon rider – Maldiar, Imrik assumed – had noted the approach of the Caledorian prince and directed his own winged mount head-on towards Imrik. As the other prince came closer, Imrik could make out more of Maldiar and his beast. The prince wore silver and gold armour inlaid with rubies; the eagle-like head of his griffon was feathered with blue, black and red, and its hindquarters were striped white and black, its claws the colour of blood.

The griffon let out a high-pitched shriek as the two princes closed in each other. Maedrethnir shook with a deep growl in reply, smoke leaking from his nostrils.

'Force them down,' said Imrik.

Maedrethnir surged higher, climbing above the griffon, and then stooped with wings furled, heading straight for the Naggarothi prince. Neck straight, jaw open, the dragon looked like he would crash into the griffon and rider. At the last moment, he opened his wings and stopped in mid-air, sending a rush of wind over Maldiar. The griffon swayed and dipped in the draught, tumbling a short distance before righting itself. Maldiar's shouted curses drifted up to Imrik but the Caledorian ignored them and pointed to the ground.

With Maedrethnir hovering just above and behind, Maldiar descended, guiding his griffon to land upon an outcrop of rock rising up through the sea of gorse and grass. Imrik and his dragon spiralled around them three times before landing within lance-reach. The griffon was a large beast, three times the size of a horse, but it was dwarfed by Maedrethnir, who loomed over creature and rider with wings outspread, blocking the morning sun.

'How dare you!' rasped Maldiar. 'This is an insult! By what right do you interfere with my rightful progress?'

'I am Imrik of Caledor. You have no rights here. These will be my lands.'

'Imrik? I have heard of you. I have heard of your jealousy of Prince Malekith, and this is a brazen attempt to steal lands that are his by rightful conquest.'

'Those orcs say otherwise,' said Imrik. 'Turn your army back. You are not welcome here.'

'I do not waste my time with Caledorian thieves,' said Maldiar. 'By Khaine's bloodied fist, I should strike you down for this.'

'Please try,' said Imrik. Maedrethnir reared up onto his back legs and let out a deafening bellow. The purple-feathered crest on Maldiar's helm flapped madly and the griffon darted closer, hissing and cawing. Maldiar wrestled with the reins of his mount and pulled it back.

'Your threats are empty, Imrik,' said Maldiar. 'I shall clear these lands of the orcs and claim this region for Nagarythe. Your Phoenix King would think badly of Caledor if you were to dispute such a victory in his court.'

Imrik offered no comment and watched impassively as Maldiar struggled with the griffon's reins for a moment and then directed it into the air. The Naggarothi prince sped back to his army.

Imrik sighed. Maldiar was right, he was not about to attack another army of elves. The only solution would be to destroy the orcs before the Naggarothi could get involved. As Maedrethnir headed cloudwards again, the prince saw that the matter would not be easily settled. The knights of Athel Toralien were some way ahead of the rest of the Naggarothi army, and bearing down fast on the orc camp.

As swiftly as he could fly, Maedrethnir headed back to the Caledorian army. Already the columns were marching out, no doubt ordered forth by Dorien in anticipation of Imrik's return. The knights split into two wings either side of the infantry, holding the line unlike the reckless advance of the Naggarothi. In three columns the archers and spearmen marched south, two heading directly for the orc and goblin camp, the third angling eastwards, cutting off the greenskins' retreat from the river. With the Naggarothi coming up fast, there would be nowhere for the orcs to run.

Imrik soared over the army, the shadow of Maedrethnir passing over the lines of warriors. The morning mist had melted away in the strengthening sun and the clouds above had thinned, leaving patches of bright sunlight on the heathland. Dorien and Thyrinor steered their dragons towards Imrik and took up station on either side of their general, all three dragons easily keeping pace with the marching columns with steady beats of their wings.

'I said they would not listen,' called Dorien. 'We have wasted time treating with the Naggarothi.'

Imrik said nothing in reply. For all the speed of their advance, the knights of Athel Toralien were now dangerously separated from the support of the Naggarothi infantry and war machines. Maldiar had caught up with the swift vanguard and swooped to and fro above the cavalry.

The Caledorian general turned his attention to the real enemy. Bands of wolf-riding goblins criss-crossed the moorlands as pickets. The dragons were easy to notice and the distant sound of brash horns sounded the warning of attack. Through the smog of the fires, Imrik could better see the orc encampment; it was larger than he had anticipated, stretching for some distance along the river bank. He could see the waters fouled downstream of the greenskins, a slick of filth washing away to the south.

The orcs needed no tents for shelter, though there were a few crude stockades holding packs of giant wolves and droves of large boars. Imrik could see orcs and goblins clambering into these enclosures with whips and goads.

Something larger caught his eye. Close to the centre of the camp burned the largest fire, surrounded by ragged banners and crude totems. To one side a scaled, winged beast strained at chains run through rings hammered into its flesh, binding it to the ground. It was almost as large as a dragon, though it had no forelegs, its scales deep green in colour, its head surrounded by horns and a yellow crest.

'Wyvern,' growled Maedrethnir, also seeing the monster. The dragon quivered with anger. 'Twisted spawn of the mountains. We shall slay it.'

'And its master,' added Imrik as a huge orc emerged from the throng of greenskins and approached the wyvern.

The orcs were mustering quickly, gathering in tribal groups around barbaric standards of skulls and bones topped with ugly, fanged faces fashioned from wood. The smaller goblins seemed more reluctant to leave the camp, and clustered together in several crowds behind their larger cousins.

A shrieking cry split the air and the wyvern climbed awkwardly into the air, the orc warlord upon its back. The sound of cheering and roars of approval drifted across the moorlands, joined by a vigorous banging of drums and discordant horns.

Imrik directed Maedrethnir downwards, the pair swooping across the Caledorian army less than a bowshot above. The general signalled to his captains to make ready the battle-line and then soared high again, watching the enemy. Beneath him the two columns of infantry spread out, alternating archer and spear companies, while the bolt throwers were unloaded from their wagons and assembled at the flanks of the long rows of elven warriors. One wing of cavalry rode on to reach the river; the other held back in reserve, ready to press home a breakthrough or counter any reverse inflicted by the orcs.

To the west, on Imrik's right, the Naggarothi cavalry had divided into squadrons, each several hundred strong and riding in an arrowhead formation, their fluttering banners at the apex of each wedge. It looked as if they planned to charge into the heart of the greenskin camp; a reckless strategy. Imrik could see the orcs forming up to face the charge of the knights; masses of fanged, muscled warriors carrying wooden shields and all manner of cleavers, swords, axes and mauls.

For a moment, Imrik had lost sight of the wyvern. He found it again, on the ground at the heart of the gathering orc and goblin horde. The warlord was gesturing madly, trying to convey some rough battle-plan to its subordinates. The wolf-riding packs of goblins were coming together, riding between the Naggarothi knights and the infantry following some distance behind. The goblins harried the elven cavalry with short bows, sending ragged volleys from the backs of their wolves. The shooting had little effect against the heavily armoured knights, but here and there an elven rider fell or a mount was killed, leaving a thin trail of dead and wounded in the wake of their rapid advance.

The orcs had also mustered their cavalry; two masses of boar riders had gathered at the far end of the strengthening orc line, further to the west. Bullied by the orcs, a swathe of goblins was driven east and north, towards the Caledorians. The plan was simple and immediately obvious to Imrik's experienced eye. The goblins would keep the Caledorians busy while the tougher, stronger elements of the army would see off the Naggarothi attack.

The orc warlord's plan could well work, Imrik decided. Maldiar's desire to embarrass Imrik had outweighed his judgement. No matter the prowess of the Naggarothi knights, there were too many greenskins to sweep away with an unsupported charge.

The situation put Imrik in a dilemma. He could rapidly change his own plans and support the Naggarothi attack or he could hold to his position and allow the knights of Athel Toralien to be destroyed.

He raised his lance high, the signal for Dorien and Thyrinor to fly within earshot. They did so, just a little behind Imrik, the tips of the dragons' wings almost touching.

'Thyrinor, tell the army to make general advance,' said Imrik. 'Kill the goblins and attack the orc flank.'

'The Naggarothi won't thank you for rescuing them, brother,' shouted Dorien. 'If they want to dash their lives upon the rocks of pride, let them.'

'Every elf slain by an orc hand is a stain upon the honour of all of Ulthuan,' said Imrik. 'I cannot allow it. Follow me!'

Ignoring his brother's further protests, Imrik called to Maedrethnir to bank to the right and head for the Naggarothi. He did not check to see if Dorien came after him, knowing that despite his brother's ill wishes towards the Naggarothi, he would obey the command of his general.

Dragon and prince climbed towards the clouds, the air growing colder the higher they flew. Imrik's breath came as wisps of mist and his skin was chill by the time they had reached the Naggarothi. He looked eastwards and saw Thyrinor leading the Caledorian attack. Archers and bolt throwers reaped a heavy toll of the massed goblins as the spearmen closed from the front and the left wing of the cavalry swung along the river. Looking down, he saw that the third infantry column was not far behind the knights of Athel Toralien, a short way ahead of the Naggarothi army.

The boar riders could hold their enthusiasm no longer and they raced from the orc lines, spears lowered for the charge. The Naggarothi cavalry had been expecting such a move and the lead squadrons parted before the greenskin assault, leaving them to the following companies. Confused by the manoeuvre the orcs tried to rein in their madly running mounts and anarchy engulfed the riders while they tried to redirect their charge. They were too late, as hundred of lances were lowered and the gold-clad elven knights smashed into their flank.

From his vantage point high in the air, Imrik could appreciate the precision of the charge, three spearpoints of riders hitting the boar riders in echelon; the first charge split the front of the orcs from the rest and the next two hammered into the side of those at the back, cleaving into the dark mass like a golden shaft of light piercing shadow.

The riders that had avoided the boars galloped on, veering to the left to attack the point of the orc line where the orc mobs were fewest in number. Imrik saw what Maldiar intended; to break through between the orcs and goblins and then attack the line from the rear. The Caledorian revised his earlier judgement of Maldiar's generalship. It was a bold tactic, but if it worked the greenskin army would be thrown into turmoil, confronted with marauding knights at their rear and several thousand infantry approaching from the front.

The problem was that once they were behind the orcs, the knights would be trapped against the river, as the orcs had been, and hindered by the boggy ground. They were too far ahead of their support and the greenskins would have time to turn and face them before the infantry arrived.

'What is you plan, brother?' called Dorien.

'To kill orcs!' Imrik shouted back, directing Maedrethnir into a steep dive.

Dorien followed, the two dragons racing to the ground at incredible speed, the wind whipping at the princes' cloaks, threatening to tug the lance from Imrik's grip as he levelled it for the attack. Behind him, the banner poles of the throne-saddle bent madly, pennants snapping.

Maldiar had his own idea for supporting the knightly charge. As his cavalry smashed into the greenskins, his griffon swept over the rear ranks, claws slashing, the Naggarothi prince's sword a blaze of blue fire that sliced through the greenskins by the handful.

As the ground rushed closer, Maedrethnir let out a terrifying roar. Orcs scattered across the moorlands in all directions, forgetting the rampaging knights in their dread. Many were hacked down as they ran, others turned in desperation to fight the elven cavalry but were ill-prepared; the knights of Athel Toralien cut through their ranks as easily as a ship's prow parting water, leaving a mangle of bodies as they continued their charge into the camp.

Dorien and Imrik hit the orcs simultaneously, their dragons bellowing dark fire from their maws, claws raking huge gaps into the orc mobs like ragged welts on green flesh. Imrik's lance gleamed white from the runes etched into it, a trail of dancing motes left in the air as its tip slashed throats and punched through bodies without pause.

As Maedrethnir landed, crushing more orcs beneath his scaled body, Imrik reached back and unhooked his shield. The dragon swept a dozen orcs into the air with a sweep of his tail while more blackish-red flames engulfed twice that number.

Less than a spear's throw away, Dorien and his mount inflicted similar damage, the orcs boiling around him flailing futilely at his dragon with axes and cleavers, their blows bouncing harmlessly from massive scales. Imrik could hear his brother's clear voice, ringing out with a battle-poem of his homeland.

As Maedrethnir snapped his jaws around two orcs, biting them in half, Imrik looked around, wondering what had become of the warlord and his wyvern. He found the answer as a dark blur rushing at Dorien from above and behind the prince.

The general shouted a warning, but it was not needed. Dorien had been playing ignorant and as the wyvern dived in for the attack, the Caledorian prince's dragon lunged from the ground, wings unfurling. The wyvern's jaws and claws missed by less than the length of a sword, though the orc warlord slashed a black-headed axe across the dragon's tail, sending blood and scales showering to the ground.

The two monstrous creatures raced upwards, spiralling and snarling, each seeking to gain height on the other. Dorien's dragon was stronger than the wyvern, rising more swiftly with each beat of his wings. As the wyvern strained to keep pace, the dragon twisted with surprising agility, dipping a wing to plunge down, claws ripping at the wyvern's neck.

Dorien's lance plunged through the wyvern's right wing as the orc warlord swung its axe at the dragon's shoulder, the strangely burning blade slamming deep into flesh. Wyvern and dragon locked together, ripping and biting; Dorien stowed his lance and drew a longsword that glittered like moonlight. Prince and warlord rained blows upon each other as the beasts plummeted, the orc lashing its weapon wildly while Dorien's sword was a shimmering gleam of movement.

Imrik was distracted from the duel by the clatter of arrows against scale and armour. He saw that the orcs around him had fled and in their place a knot of goblins loosed crooked-shafted arrows ineffectually from a bush-filled dell to his left.

'Burn them,' Imrik told his mount.

Maedrethnir swung his head and opened his cavernous mouth. The goblins let out shrill screams a moment before the hollow was awash with smoke and fire. Imrik turned his attention back to his brother in time to see Dorien's dragon heave itself away from the wyvern moments before hitting the ground. With a damaged wing and blood streaming from scores of wounds, the wyvern could not right itself in time and plunged sideways into the moor, shedding scales in a flail of legs and tail. The warlord was tossed clear by the impact, landing head-first in a small stream some distance away.

While Dorien swapped his sword for his lance once more, his dragon circled around the fallen wyvern, bathing it with fire. The grounded beast hissed and roared, ungainly on its two legs, tail thrashing awkwardly in the flames.

'Up,' said Imrik. Maedrethnir bounded into the air and took the general above the battle.

All semblance of two coherent battle lines had been lost. The goblins had broken before the advance of the Caledorians, fleeing back towards their camp in their hundreds while Imrik's knights bore down on them from the direction of the river. Several companies of archers had split from the main host and were pouring volleys of arrows into the orc camp, each shaft tipped by magical white flame.

Beyond the dying wyvern, Maldiar and his griffon were mauling the remnants of the boar riders; the hybrid monster tossed squealing hogs into the air with beak and claws while the Naggarothi prince chopped heads and limbs from the riders. The Naggarothi infantry had now reached the battle, driving the goblin wolf riders before them with spear and arrow. Along the river bank, the Naggarothi knights were reforming, ready to charge again into the fray.

Imrik caught sight of the orc warlord surging up from a thicket of reeds, axe still in hand.

'Let Maldiar argue when I have the warlord's head,' Imrik told Maedrethnir. The dragon gave a deep-throated rumble of approval and turned towards the orc leader. Maldiar had spied the enemy as well and his griffon soared over the Naggarothi advance, speeding towards the warlord.

'A fool races a dragon,' said Maedrethnir, cutting across the moorlands with swift wing beats, the ground rushing past so close that the dragon's wingtips brushed the stands of grass and bushes.

Yet the dragon's dismissive remark was premature; the warlord broke into a run towards Maldiar, shouting madly and waving its axe. Imrik saw a gleam of magical fire as Maldiar raised his sword high and called his griffon into a steep dive.

The warlord slowed to a halt and stood with stocky legs apart, axe in both hands, fixed on the approaching Naggarothi prince. Imrik heard his dragon snarl and could feel the beast's whole body shuddering with effort as

Maedrethnir strained every sinew to close the distance before Maldiar struck.

Imrik could tell he would be too late. Maldiar was already leaning to one side in his saddle, sword held horizontal for the killing blow, the shadow of the griffon racing over the undulating ground, about to engulf the orc.

Both princes were utterly intent upon their prey. If Maldiar missed, Imrik's lance would find the orc's back before the Naggarothi could turn for a second attack. The Caledorian tightened his grip on the lance, glittering point spearing towards the warlord, even as Maldiar's griffon plunged for the kill.

As a snarling blur of red, Dorien's dragon slammed into Maldiar's mount, sending both tumbling into the ground.

Startled, Imrik almost missed his mark, but swung the lance point back on target at the last moment. The ithilmar tip slid effortlessly through the orc's armour, punching out of its chest as Maedrethnir swept past. The shock of the blow almost wrenched the weapon from Imrik's grasp and lifted him against his saddle harness, the orc carried bodily through the air for some distance as Imrik's dragon banked and rose towards the blue skies.

The warlord's dangling body slid from the ithilmar shaft, ripping free the pennant so that it fluttered like a cape as the corpse cartwheeled down onto the rocks and grass. Maedrethnir bellowed in triumph, his roar shaking Imrik's whole body.

Imrik was more concerned with what was going on on the ground below him. Maldiar and Dorien faced each other, swords in hand, their respective mounts looming behind each prince. The general trusted neither to stay their hand, and shouted to Maedrethnir to land close by. Imrik watch the two elves staring at each other and exchanging insults as his dragon circled tightly to reduce speed. Maedrethnir landed on all fours, beside Dorien's dragon; Imrik had already stowed his lance and was pulling at the harness buckles before the dragon's claws had touched the ground.

'Put away your weapons!' Imrik shouted as he swung from the saddle-throne and dropped lightly to the dirt.

'He calls us thieves,' protested Dorien, eyes locked on the Naggarothi.

'I do not take commands from Caledorian cowards,' said Maldiar, his gaze not moving from Dorien.

'Cowards?' snarled Dorien, taking a step. Maldiar raised his sword a little higher in response. 'I will cut off your head for such an insult!'

'You will not,' snapped Imrik, stepping in front of his brother. He grabbed Dorien's sword arm. 'Sheathe your blade, brother.'

'Listen to your master, yapping dog,' said Maldiar. 'Do not test your blade against mine.'

Imrik whirled on the Naggarothi, his hand at his sword hilt in an instant.

'I might yet,' said Imrik.

Maldiar hesitated, his sword tip wavering for a moment before he stood firm again, eyes narrowed, jaw clenched.

'I thought not,' said Imrik. 'The battle is not yet won.'

'I am all but victorious,' said Maldiar. 'The rabble have been scattered, it is only a matter of time before my warriors hunt them down.'

'This is not your victory,' said Dorien, pulling his arm from Imrik's grip and pushing past. 'Your knights would be dead, as would you, if we had not come to your aid.'

'My aid?' Maldiar's face was a mask of sneering hatred. 'Your interference almost lost me this battle.'

'Go away,' said Imrik, pulling back Dorien by the shoulder. 'Destroy the rest of the enemy, brother.'

Dorien looked Imrik in the eye, cheeks twitching. Imrik met the look with a cold stare that his brother knew well. With a parting dismissive gesture, Dorien slid his sword into its scabbard and stalked back to his dragon.

Imrik returned his attention to Maldiar, who had lowered his blade but not sheathed it.

'We shall split the spoils,' said Imrik.

'How so?' replied the Naggarothi prince. He laughed sourly. 'You are welcome to keep the bodies. I shall take the land.'

'No,' said Imrik. 'You shall have the land west of the river, and Caledor the region to the east.'

'Why would I agree to such a thing?' Maldiar put away his sword and crossed his arms defiantly. 'Why would I give half my new lands to you?'

'Some is better than none,' said Imrik. 'If Malekith has complaint, let him bring it to me.'

'You know well that our fair prince campaigns in the north,' said Maldiar. 'He has not set foot in the colonies for nearly fifty years.'

'Do you lack the authority to agree such a bargain?' asked Imrik. Maldiar stiffened, stung by the implication of the question.

'I am a prince of Nagarythe; I speak with the full authority of Prince Malekith and Queen Morathi.'

'Queen Morathi?' Imrik frowned at the mention of Malekith's mother, widow of Aenarion. 'Morathi is queen no more.'

'In Nagarythe she is,' said Maldiar with a sly smile. 'I agree to your terms. It matters not. When Malekith returns, we shall stake our full claim and will not be refused. Enjoy your prosperity while it lasts, Caledorian. Nagarythe grows tired of shedding blood for the benefit of others. You will not make such demands in the future.'

Maldiar spun away and strode back to his griffon. The beast lowered to the ground as the prince grabbed the gem-studded reins. Before he pulled himself up to the saddle, the Naggarothi looked back at Imrik.

'You should be wiser in your words and actions, prince,' Maldiar said. 'Khaine has turned his red gaze upon you, Imrik of Caledor. You should hope that he is not displeased.'

Imrik was taken aback by this mention of the Bloody-Handed God. It was widely known that the Naggarothi were blatant in their worship of the Lord of Murder, and many of the other dark gods of the cytharai, but to hear Khaine's name spoken so openly was a shock even for Imrik. He watched as Maldiar flew away, wondering what was meant by the threat.

'Let us finish this,' Imrik said to Maedrethnir, dismissing the Naggarothi from his thoughts. Such vague insults and threats were typical of his folk.

THE MARCH BACK to the colony of Caledor was a long one, but the Caledorian host was in high spirits following their victory over the orc horde. Imrik did not share the jubilation of his troops, unsettled by the words of Maldiar and the events he had witnessed following the battle. Many of the Naggarothi had gathered up the wounded orcs and, instead of slaying them out of hand as Imrik had ordered his warriors, they were taken back to the camp of the Naggarothi. Imrik did not know for sure what fate had awaited these prisoners, but having heard Maldiar speak of Khaine and seen variations of the Bloody-Handed God's rune upon some of the Naggarothi banners and shields, he had his suspicions.

Word of the orcs' defeat had reached ahead of the army and the walls of the Grey City, Tor Arlieth, and the streets within were lined with celebrating elves. The city was built in the mountain foothills, rising above the huge canopy of forest that stretched from the sea north-west of where the orcs had been slain. Seventeen pale grey towers rose up from the wooded slopes, roofed with blue slate and flying the flags of Caledor. A wall ten times the height of an elf girded the city, with another half as tall around that. Between the two walls were the camps and garrisons of the army, and it was here that the knights and militia paraded to the applause of their people. Garlands of flowers looped from roof to roof, and leaves had been strewn on the pavements. Harps and horns and pipes played from roof terraces and balconies, while below the citizens cheered their warriors' return.

Having flown thrice over the city with his brother and cousin, so that the grateful people could raise up their voices in song and praise of their heroic princes, Imrik descended to the hill upon which the keep and palaces were fashioned from the rock of the mountain. The citadel was built as a representation of a huge dragon, its walls spreading like wings until they merged with the mountainside, the main tower rearing high above topped with a roof of gold. A hundred flags flew from the battlements, each belonging to a noble house of Caledor, and above them all, the banner of the city snapped in the mountain air. Trumpets sounded through the clear air to signal the arrival of the princes, and a guard of honour formed by the huge gates; the dark red wood of the portal carved with a relief of the mountains of Caledor, the shapes of dragons flying above.

The three dragon riders landed on an immaculate lawn that split the wide plaza that surrounded the citadel. Divested of their harnesses and saddle-thrones, the dragons bade their riders farewell and flew up to caves in the mountain overlooking the city. Accompanied by Dorien and Thyrinor,

Imrik strode through the opening gates as the guard company lifted their spears in salute.

Imrik wanted to head to his chambers, but was waylaid in the long entrance hall by Hethlian, the chancellor of the city. Dressed in a long robe of jade green and golden yellow, the ageing elf emerged from a crowd of servants and called Imrik's name. The chancellor was dressed in full ceremonial regalia; a belt of gold and rubies hung about Hethlian's waist, the symbol of his position, and he carried an ornamental sceptre in his left hand, topped with a sapphire the size of a fist, intricately shaped like the petals of a rose.

'Your safe return heartens us all, princes,' said Hethlian, performing a short bow to each of them. 'It is with immense pleasure and pride that I offer my personal congratulations on your victory, as well as the gratitude of the city.'

Imrik thought of more than six hundred elves whose bodies had been carried back to the colony on biers, but said nothing. They would receive their honours in time, he was sure.

'A three-day festival has been declared by the council of elders,' continued Hethlian. 'You will, of course, be our guests of honour.'

'Will we?' said Imrik, startling the chancellor.

'My cousins and I would be honoured to accept your gracious invitation,' said Thyrinor, stepping next to Imrik. 'Yet we are weary from the march home and would appreciate a little time to recover before we discuss the arrangements.'

Imrik looked at Thyrinor, one eyebrow raised, and suppressed a sigh. His cousin's face was impassive, save for his eyes, which held a slight look of pleading. Thyrinor glanced towards Hethlian and nodded with an encouraging smile.

'Yes, we will attend,' said Imrik. Hethlian smiled and bowed again. He opened his mouth to speak, about to launch into a fresh monologue, but Imrik cut him off. 'Has there been news from Ulthuan?'

'Um, yes, several caravans have arrived via Tor Alessi bearing missives and goods,' said Hethlian, quickly regaining his composure. 'Nothing of note, I would say. Trade goes well. The colonies west of Ulthuan continue to grow, though not as strongly as here in Elthin Arvan. Prince Laetan of Cothique became a father to a beautiful daughter in the spring. Bel Shanaar attended the marriage of...' Hethlian's voice trailed away in the face of Imrik's unblinking stare. The chancellor rallied with a brief smile. 'As I said, nothing of note.'

'What of Nagarythe?' said Imrik. 'Or Malekith?'

'No news of Malekith has reached us here,' said Hethlian. 'The borders of Nagarythe are still closed to trade and visitors as far as I am aware. We have, however, received several delegations from Athel Toralien. It seems they are more amenable to contact than their kin back in Ulthuan.'

'There are Naggarothi in the city?' said Dorien.

'A few, yes,' said the chancellor. 'Simple traders, I assure you. You know they have far better connections to the dwarfs than we, and the demands of the city for dwarf goods have never been higher. They come and go infrequently. Is that a problem?'

'There will be if I meet one of them,' snapped Dorien. 'Just keep them away from the citadel, we don't want them prying and poking around here.'

Hethlian had no reply to this and the four elves stood in silence for a moment. Imrik glanced at Dorien with an impatient look.

'I trust that our apartments are in order and food and wine available,' said Thyrinor.

'Yes, you will find everything to your satisfaction, princes,' said Hethlian with a look of gratitude. 'Your servants await you in your chambers. Let me keep you from their attendance no longer.'

The chancellor bowed again and swiftly retreated along the hallway, darting a glance over his shoulder at the princes before disappearing through a curtained archway. Imrik turned towards the corridor leading to the royal apartments, but was stopped after just two steps by a liveried servant.

'What is it?' Imrik snarled at the retainer.

'The chancellor did not mention that a letter from your brother arrived this morning, prince,' said the elf. 'It was sealed with Prince Caledrian's mark, so I left it with your household.'

'Thank you,' said Imrik. 'Anything else?'

'No, prince,' said the servant, backing out of Imrik's path.

Imrik marched along the corridor, boots ringing on the marble floors, Dorien and Thyrinor trailing behind.

'You seem even more irritable than usual, cousin,' said Thyrinor, hurrying to keep pace. 'What is it that so perturbs you?'

'The Naggarothi,' replied Imrik.

'Finally,' said Dorien. 'Have I not long warned you about Nagarythe? We should ban them from the city.'

'It is not the city I am worried about,' said Imrik, taking a turn to the right through a pointed archway, his footfalls muffled by a thick red carpet embroidered with white and yellow rose designs.

'Is it this letter from Caledrian?' said Thyrinor. 'Do you have an inkling of what it contains?'

'No,' said Imrik, 'but when I receive a personal letter from the ruler of Caledor, and not one marked by his court, I fear it bears bad tidings.'

They came upon the double doors to Imrik's apartment. Two servants opened the pale wooden doors and bowed as Imrik paced inside without breaking stride

'I am going to my rooms to get out of this armour,' said Dorien, continuing along the portrait-lined passageway.

Imrik simply nodded, sparing his brother not a glance. The members of the prince's household lined the walls of the foyer. As Imrik walked past his chatelaine, Elirithrin, she stepped forwards with a small silver tray, a white envelope on the platter.

'You wish to see this?' she said.

'Thank you,' said Imrik, plucking the letter from its place as he walked past. 'Bring wine and a cold platter to my study.'

'How did you know?' said Thyrinor, stopping next to Elirithrin. 'That he would want to see the letter, I mean.'

'Experience,' the chatelaine replied with an expression of surprise. 'I have served the prince for two hundred and thirty-eight years. I know his priorities.'

'Of course you do,' said Thyrinor. He hurried after Imrik and entered the shelf-lined study just as his cousin was sitting down behind an ornate desk.

While the offices of other elven nobles housed libraries of prose and poetry, philosophical tracts and genealogical tomes, Imrik's was empty by comparison. One set of shelves was brimming with rolled parchment maps of Ulthuan and Elthin Arvan, another with bound treatises on military matters. The remaining two sets of shelves were sparsely populated with a variety of strange ornaments; amongst them a gilded orc skull with diamonds for eyes, a selection of daggers of both elvish and dwarfish make, several ornate ceremonial helmets, and a silver dragon scale the size of a spread hand mounted on a plaque – supposedly from Aenarion's mount Indraugnir.

Imrik stood again, unfastened his cloak and laid it carefully over the back of his chair before sitting down. From a drawer in the desk, he brought out a gilded letter opener in the shape of a miniature dragonspear, with a broad, leaf-shaped head. He inspected the seal, satisfied himself that it was intact and cut open the envelope with a single stroke.

He ignored Thyrinor hovering at the end of the desk as he read, quickly scanning his older brother's flowing script. The letter was brief and to the point. Caledrian had heard increasing rumours of unrest within the borders of Nagarythe. He feared that the turmoil might spread to neighbouring Tiranoc, Ellyrion and Chrace but Bel Shanaar refused to act. He requested that Imrik return to Ulthuan, with Dorien and Thyrinor if they desired, to represent Caledor in the council of the Phoenix King.

Imrik handed the letter to Thyrinor without comment and leaned back in the chair, arms folded. He watched a frown deepen on his cousin's brow as Thyrinor read.

'Will you come?' said Imrik when he saw that Thyrinor had finished.

'What?' said Thyrinor, who was reading parts of the letter again. 'I don't know. Is it wise that we all go back?'

'I am summoned by Caledor's prince and I must answer,' said Imrik. He leaned towards Thyrinor, one hand on the top of the desk. 'I would like your company.'

'My company?' said Thyrinor with a short laugh. 'I thought you always preferred your own company, cousin, though I thank you for the invitation.'

'I cannot go to Tor Anroc alone,' Imrik admitted with a grimace. 'Court life will madden me beyond belief.'

'Why do you think Caledrian chooses you?' Thyrinor said, moving to a low couch in front of the map store. 'You're not the most diplomatic person to send.'

'Maybe that is why,' Imrik said with a shrug. 'I do not know why Caledrian does not attend himself. I will ask him.'

'It will take some time to make preparations for the journey,' said Thyrinor, placing the letter on the arm of the couch. 'I'll have the staff attend to it.'

'What are you talking about?' said Imrik. 'Preparations?'

'The journey from here to Tor Alessi; booking passage on a ship to Ulthuan; arranging transport from Lothern. That doesn't happen by itself.'

'None of that will be needed,' said Imrik, smiling slightly.

'It won't?' said Thyrinor. He looked closely at his cousin, eyes widening with realisation as he saw his happy expression. 'You want to ride the dragons all of the way back to Caledor?'

'It's quickest,' said Imrik. 'No point wasting time.'

'What about our belongings? The servants? Shall they dangle underneath?'

'They can follow after,' said Imrik. He tapped gauntleted fingers on the desktop. 'Bel Shanaar is known for the luxury of his palace, you will have comforts.'

'But riding all the way?' Thyrinor opened his hands imploringly to Imrik. 'Why?'

Imrik stood up and folded his cloak over his arm.

'We're dragon princes,' he said, tapping a finger against his breastplate. 'Why sail when you can fly?'

━◄ TWO ►━

The Prince Returns

LIKE THE DRAGONS that made the kingdom their home, Caledor was wreathed in smoke and fire. Sulphurous ash clouds obscured the dark peaks of the Caledorian mountains, lit from below by the ruddy glow of volcanoes. Mingled with the billowing fumes were glowering storm clouds that flickered with lightning, the rumble of thunder merging with the crack of eruptions. Streams of hot lava flowed down the slopes; where they met the lakes and rivers, great columns of steam rose into the air. Pocked and cracked, the volcanic rock vented its subterranean fury through hundreds of geysers and fumaroles, while in dormant calderas thick forests grew, lush from the fertile minerals spewed forth in ages past.

It was a place of stark contrasts and harsh beauty, and even Imrik's hard heart stirred at the sight. He was tired from the long journey; twenty days of near-constant flight, the last eleven over the ocean made without break. His fatigue slipped away as he caught sight of Tor Caled, his home city. Nestled in the eastern flank of the mountains, the city was a massive edifice of walls and towers, shaped from the raw element of the volcanoes by the magic of Caledor Dragontamer and his followers. Towers like stalagmites, slender and graceful, rose up from steep hills on the coast; the city's wall flowed down to the water's edge in undulating curves, black stone glistening with veins of red. A moat of lava protected the other side of the city, crossed by a hundred arcing bridges of granite, each protected by two towers at each end. Huge monoliths banded with silver and gold speared from the river of fire, glowing with ember runes that kept the flames at bay.

Not in Imrik's lifetime had any foe tested the capital of Caledor, but in the time of the Dragontamer it had been an unyielding bulwark against the daemons. In those terrible days the flames that had girdled the city had risen as high as the towers, and the bridges had been cast down. Many were the paintings and murals that decorated the palaces and houses of the nobility depicting the epic battles that had been waged over the mountains.

Outside the city were the dragon grounds; a wide expanse of scattered bushes and hard earth populated by underground chambers housing attendants from Tor Caled's noble families. Divested of their harnesses here, the dragons bade farewell to the princes and flew away to their roosting caves deep within the mountains.

Within the wall, the city was no less fortified and imposing. Though centuries of peace had laid a gentler touch upon the battlements and turrets of the grand houses, with many murals and mosaics brightening the hard stone, Tor Caled's founding in war was plain to see. The layout of the streets, unchanged for millennia, wound back and forth up the slope, looked down on by each level above so that defenders could pour arrows and magic into an attacking force. The cliffs that separated the level of the city above each row of buildings were protected by redoubts and embrasures, surrounded by nests of spear-like outthrusts to protect against attack from the air. At each turn, huge gatehouses could be closed to bar the road, twenty in all between the wall and the summit. Even now bolt throwers and sentries stood guard at these watchtowers.

The streets were busy as Imrik, Dorien and Thyrinor took horse and rode up the winding street. The lower parts of Tor Caled were given over to commerce, three turns of the road filled with traders' stalls and the shop fronts of craftsmen. The next four levels were the residences of the normal folk of the city, though even these were magnificent villas with their own gardens; Caledor was not a populous realm and barely a tenth of its people dwelt within the city, the others living in fortified towns throughout the mountains and along the coast of the Inner Sea. Before the pinnacle of the city came the artificers' quarter, where many wonderful and ornamental things were created, and dwarfish wares were on display.

Thyrinor made his excuses here, leaving his cousins to look for a homecoming present for his wife. Dorien and Imrik rode on, occasionally remarking on some shop or stall that had opened or closed in the five years they had been absent. Aside from the details, nothing had changed from the city Imrik remembered, and he was reassured by the sense of unchanging stability.

When they arrived at the palaces, a soaring spectacle of towers, turrets and balconies that delved into the slope of the mountain, they were informed that Caledrian was out of the city attending to business matters. Dorien and Imrik parted and went to be reunited with their families.

Word of Imrik's arrival had preceded him, as he had expected, and his wife Anatheria greeted him at the grand entrance to the palaces. At her side, a young boy stood clutching her long dress, an unruly shock of blond hair obscuring his face. Imrik embraced his wife without comment, and crouched down in front of his son.

'Standing up now,' said the prince, clasping a hand to Tythanir's shoulder. The boy shrank back, blue eyes wide and fearful. Imrik laughed.

'What did I teach you, Tythanir?' Anatheria said sternly.

The boy stepped to one side and stood with feet together, hands gripped tightly against his stomach. He looked at Imrik with studied solemnity.

'Welcome home, father,' said Tythanir, bobbing his head.

'That's good,' said Anatheria, ruffling her son's hair with slender fingers. She looked at Imrik. 'And what do you say, husband?'

'It is good to be home,' said Imrik, pulling his son closer, arm around his shoulders. He planted a kiss on the boy's forehead. 'You grow up fast, son.'

Tythanir grinned and wrapped his arms around Imrik's armoured leg, looking up at his father.

'Did you ride a dragon?' said the boy.

'Yes, son, I did,' Imrik replied. 'One day, so will you.'

Though Imrik had not thought it possible, Tythanir's grin grew even wider and his eyes looked up to the mountains.

'I'll be the most famous dragon prince ever!' the boy declared. 'And I'll lead armies like you and everyone will know who I am.'

'I have no doubt,' said Imrik, with a glance to Anatheria. 'You will become the pride of Caledor.'

Taking the boy's hand, he walked into the palaces, his wife beside him. Tythanir broke from his grasp and ran ahead, chattering to himself as he pointed at the tapestries lining the hallway, each depicting the lords of Caledor on their dragons.

'I will not be staying long,' Imrik told his wife.

'I know,' she replied. 'Caledrian spoke with me before he sent his letter. I think this will be good for us. Your brother is too dismissive of Bel Shanaar, and the other kingdoms find greater favour with the Phoenix King. Your brother's ambassadors have been in Tor Anroc too long and are beguiled and rendered mute by its charms. Our status must be reasserted.'

'I am more concerned with Nagarythe,' said Imrik as the two of them followed Tythanir along the carpet running the length of the long hall. 'Their isolation these last decades cannot bode well. Malekith's absence has left Morathi free to aggrandise herself. The Naggarothi are not only arrogant, they are becoming dangerous. Their grip of the colonies is still strengthening.'

'Then you must persuade Bel Shanaar and the other princes to weaken that grip,' said Anatheria. 'Make them see the danger.'

'You and the boy will stay here,' said Imrik.

'Why?' replied his wife, directing a scowl at him. 'Tythanir has already spent more than half his life away from his father.'

'I do not wish our son to be raised in Tor Anroc,' said Imrik. 'These are important years in his life, and he must learn the traditions of Caledor.'

Anatheria was not placated by this reasoning and quickened her pace to catch up with her son. Imrik ran a few steps and gently grabbed her arm. She snatched it from his grasp but stopped.

'I know that you find your family burdensome, but you are a husband and a father and have responsibilities,' she snapped, keeping her voice low, darting a look at Tythanir. He was engrossed with a suit of dragon armour, running his hands over the inlaid gems. 'You have an heir, as you desired; now you must do your duty by him.'

'I have returned,' Imrik said, raising his voice in annoyance.

'Not by your choice,' said his wife, turning away. 'Always you place duty to Caledor above your family.'

'I will do right by you and my son,' said Imrik, softening his tone. 'That is why you must remain here. Tor Anroc is not an ocean away. I will see Tythanir often enough, both here and there.'

He did not know if his wife heard him. She took her son by the hand and walked away, leaving the prince in the hallway. Imrik shook his head, frustrated. Though Anatheria might never comprehend the demands on a prince of the Dragontamer's line, Tythanir would understand as he grew older. To be a leader of elves was in his blood, a legacy of his great lineage.

Feeling suddenly uncomfortable, Imrik wondered if it was his armour or the weight of something else.

EIGHT DAYS AFTER arriving home, Imrik was told that his brother was returning to Tor Caled within the next two days and was to be met by the court of Caledor. Imrik passed word to the other princes and nobles, sending riders to those who lived outside the city. It was an occasion of some remark as the lords of Caledor assembled; not for centuries had they all been gathered at the capital.

The city was abuzz with rumour, and more than once Imrik rebuked members of his household for indulging in speculation. Tor Caled swarmed with the entourages of the arriving nobles, and gala feasts were held each night to celebrate every arrival. By the light of red lanterns the elves danced and sang in the plazas and streets, needing only small excuse for festivity.

On the morning before Caledrian was due to arrive, another important elf appeared in the city: Hotek, the high priest of Vaul. On hearing this news, Imrik travelled to the main gate to meet Hotek in person and conduct him to the palaces with due ceremony. Though often bored by state functions and the interminable mingling that they entailed, Imrik held dear the oldest customs of Caledor and formally welcomed Hotek.

His deference was not so much to the elf, but to his position, for it was the high priest of Vaul, Hotek's predecessor, who had aided Caledor Dragontamer in the forging of many weapons and artefacts during the war against the daemons. Such help had not been without risk, and several times the shrine at the mount of Vaul's Anvil had been assailed by the minions of Chaos. Though incurred in millennia past, Imrik stayed true to the debt his bloodline owed to the priests, and said as much on greeting Hotek.

'I repay the homage, Imrik,' said Hotek as the two stepped aboard a golden carriage with an awning of green and grey dragon scales. The priest cut a severe figure: his face thin even for an elf, his high cheekbones and brow sharp, his white hair swept back by a band of black leather studded with ruddy bronze. Most remarkable were his eyes, of pure white. Like those that he led in his order, Horek had ritually blinded himself, to share in the suffering of Vaul. He showed no sign of discomfort or disability for the loss, his other senses, including his innate mystical awareness, heightened to compensate for his lack of sight. All the same, Imrik was always slightly disconcerted when talking to a priest of Vaul and kept his gaze away from Hotek's face.

'In you and your family, the honour and strength of the Dragontamer remains strong,' Hotek continued. 'So few there are these days whose call the dragons heed. It is a testament to you that they count you as an ally when so many of their kind have taken the long slumber of aeons.'

As the four horses set off up the steep road, Hotek arranged his heavy blue robes more comfortably and leaned back in his seat. He knitted his fingers across his chest, each digit weighed down by a jewelled ring, and about his wrists and neck were many fine chains of silver, gold and other gleaming metals.

'To what do I owe the pleasure of this invitation?' the priest asked, head turned towards the prince as though he could see him. 'Caledrian's missive simply stated that he was bringing together the full court of Caledor, and that as high priest of Vaul I have by tradition a seat in that esteemed gathering.'

'I do not know for sure,' Imrik replied. 'He called me back from Elthin Arvan to represent Caledor at Tor Anroc, but I have heard no more since my return. The continuing strange behaviour of the Naggarothi concerns him.'

'The Naggarothi?' Hotek attempted to appear casual, but Imrik noticed a sudden tension in the priest's body and voice. 'What concern of the Caledorians are the affairs of Nagarythe?'

'Perhaps none,' said Imrik. 'Even at Vaul's Anvil you must have heard that they have closed their borders. Don't you think that strange?'

'The shrines are beyond the politics and boundaries of individual kingdoms,' Hotek replied, waving a hand airily, relaxed again. 'If the Naggarothi want to keep to themselves, I welcome it. The better for the rest of us to be free of their stern expressions and snide remarks.'

'It is said that they openly worship the cytharai,' said Imrik. 'Khaine for certain, and the other undergods likely. In the colonies, they are quite brazen about it.'

'We do not dictate to others how they choose to appease the gods,' said Hotek with a shrug. 'I know that they endeavour to spread the worship of the cytharai to other kingdoms and cities, but their proselytising falls on ears unwilling to listen for the most part. Better to ignore them and let the metal cool than temper it to hardness with accusations and persecution.'

'Your shrine, it fares well?' asked Imrik.

'Our days as armourers to the princes have thankfully long passed,' Hotek said. 'Today we fashion amulets not swords, rings not shields. And much time is spent in the study of such dwarfen artefacts that come into our possession. They are most remarkable pieces, unlike anything fashioned in Ulthuan. Sometimes crude to look at, I admit, but containing simple yet powerful enchantments.'

The conversation continued in similar vein until they reached the palaces. Imrik passed the care of Hotek to the servants of his older brother and with his duties discharged, spent the rest of the morning playing with Tythanir. At noon, the time of his brother's expected arrival, he made his way to the great hall, which had been set with a ring of high-backed chairs for the council, nearly a hundred in all. Caledrian's throne faced the huge doors, his advisors already waiting beside it and most of the nobles already present.

Imrik took his place to the right hand of the throne, Dorien on the other side, with Thyrinor next to him. The hall soon filled, leaving only a handful of places of nobles that had been unable or unwilling to attend. The muffled call of clarions rang from the citadel walls announcing Caledrian's arrival. The assembled elves stood and awaited his entrance, a quiet whispering rebounding from the painted walls of the hall.

A stamp of feet preceded the opening of the doors. All eyes turned on Caledrian as he entered. The ruler of Caledor was dressed in a long robe of white, patterned with golden thread in curling flames, a wide belt about his waist and a narrow circlet on his head. He strode into the hall without much ceremony, waving a hand in greeting to some of his councillors, stopping to have quick conversations with others. He had an easy smile, and clasped hands and shoulders without unease, but Imrik thought he saw a certain stiffness in his brother's movements that betrayed some burden he carried.

Imrik stepped up to meet his brother as he reached the throne. He embraced Caledrian, as did Dorien, and the three stood together for a moment.

'It is good to see both of you here,' said Caledrian. He glanced past Dorien and smiled at Thyrinor. 'And you, cousin. I wish that our reunion took place in happier times, but I have grim tidings. After the council, we will feast together and become properly reacquainted.'

With that, Caledrian signalled for the council to be seated, though he remained standing. Imrik noticed that another elf had joined the short line of Caledorian dignitaries behind the throne. He was a little stockier than the others, with grey hair and almost white skin; certainly not of Caledor.

He wore a purple robe of light material, so that it flowed from his arms and legs in the slightest draught. He was relaxed yet alert, eyes never still as they took in the details of the hall and its occupants.

'My gratitude to you all for coming here at such short notice,' declared Caledrian, drawing Imrik's attention away from the newcomer. 'There has been much speculation as to my activities of late, so let me put rumour to rest. Not long ago, I received representation from Bel Shanaar.' He waved a hand towards the elf that Imrik had been watching. 'This is Tirathanil, a herald of the Phoenix King. He bore to me alarming news, and we have spent days in debating its import and the wishes of Bel Shanaar. The matters are of such import that, according to custom, I will lay them before this council and conduct a vote to know the wishes of Caledor.'

The prince sat on his throne and paused; the councillors leaned forwards in their seats, anxious to hear what he had to say next, their eyes fixed upon Caledrian.

'For years we have heard of an unsettling rise in the open worship of the cytharai,' he continued. 'Each of us knows tales from the other kingdoms of some of the depravities involved in these rituals, and I am thankful to acknowledge that such practices have not encroached upon Caledor. It is Bel Shanaar's suspicion, and I share it, that these cults are under the sway of Nagarythe. More specifically, that they owe allegiance to Morathi. We are not content to allow this state of affairs to remain unchanged.

'If it is the intent of this council, we shall answer the summons of Bel Shanaar to attend to his court at Tor Anroc, there to discuss what action will be taken. As many of you know, I had already made plans for noble Imrik to act on my behalf, and the greater urgency that now faces us only strengthens my belief in that decision.'

Caledrian looked to Imrik for a moment and then returned his gaze to the council members.

'It is not his will nor mine that Imrik will carry with him, but the will of this council,' said Caledrian. 'No proposal for action has been put forward by Bel Shanaar and I have heard nothing of the desires of the other princes. Thus Caledor will, as in times past, take the lead in this matter. With due respect to the wisdom of the council, it is my belief that the kingdoms must unite in purpose and in arms and destroy these cults wherever they are found. There are those that see no need for action and there are some that even support these cults in secret. We must root out those in thrall to Morathi and bring them before the judgement of the Phoenix King.'

'Why stop there?' said Dorien. There were mutters of annoyance and scowls from the rest of the council; it was not proper form to speak before being invited by the ruling prince. Dorien paid no heed to the whispers of irritation. 'You say it yourself that Nagarythe is the source of this menace. Malekith has abandoned his kingdom and allowed it to fall into barbarism and hedonism. We all know that Morathi is not to be trusted. I say that we subject Nagarythe to the rule of the Phoenix King until Malekith returns; if he ever does. Too long have we allowed our cousins in the north their wayward practices. It is time they were brought to account for it, and stability restored.'

There were nods of agreement from many in the council, and a few members clapped softly or slapped a hand to thigh in appreciation. Imrik agreed with the sentiment, but knew that any direct action against Nagarythe would be tantamount to invasion. He was inclined to believe Caledrian did not desire to go so far, and was certain that Bel Shanaar would never endorse such a thing unless given extreme provocation. Imrik saw no reason to comment, knowing that the council would decide regardless of his opinion on the matter.

Several council members indicated their willingness to speak, Hotek amongst them. The priest received a word from Caledrian and stood up, hands behind his back. He took a few paces towards the throne, and as dictated by convention addressed his thoughts to the ruling prince, though his words were for the whole council.

'I am wary of any persecution of these cults,' said Hotek, his voice soft and melodious. 'Not because I support them, but because we risk escalating isolated violence into a greater strife. I deplore these base rites as much as any of you, and know that for each disturbing story there is possibly another fouler act committed unseen. Unless proof can be presented that these cults are acting in concert, that the hand of Morathi controls them, it would be unwise to raise up arms against our own people. My sect once provided Aenarion and your forefathers with weapons to free this isle from death; we will not provide them to be used against those we are sworn to protect. For the most part these are simple people, not corrupt of heart but misguided or simply indolent and bored. Bel Shanaar has allowed this circumstance to arise by his inaction, it is true, but it would be foolish to over react. It is not too late to allow peace to prevail.'

'A sentiment we all share,' said Caledrian. 'Yet we cannot allow this depravity of spirit to fester any longer. Only by stern efforts have we kept Caledor free of the cults' taint; others have not been so successful. The other kingdoms are uncertain in their power, unwilling to do what is necessary to bring Ulthuan back from the brink of disorder. We must take a lead where others have shirked their duties.'

'Perhaps if we could speak with Tirathanil?' suggested Eltaranir, one of the oldest members of the council, whom Imrik considered as an uncle. He had been a close friend of Imrik's father, Menieth; they had attended the First Council together when Bel Shanaar had been chosen to succeed Aenarion, and it had been Eltaranir that had borne Menieth's body back from the colonies when he had been slain in the wars of conquest.

Caledrian waved to the Phoenix King's herald to come forwards. Tirathanil did so with a slight swagger, pleased with the sudden attention. His pomposity deflated under Eltaranir's scrutiny.

'There is little I can add that your prince has not already told you,' said the herald. 'Yet I will endeavour to answer any questions you have.'

'Has Bel Shanaar received any news of Malekith?' asked Hotek. 'It is dubious to discuss the kingdom of another prince when he cannot represent himself.'

'The Phoenix King knows nothing more of Malekith than any of you,' said Tirathanil. 'That he still lives is likely, and continues his exploration of the northern wastes. As for representation, Nagarythe it was that severed ties to Tor Anroc, despite several attempts by myself and others to make embassy to them. If Morathi still rules, she does not answer the Phoenix King's invitations to court.'

'If she still rules?' Thyrinor pounced on the turn of phrase. 'Why should she not?'

'There is rumour of infighting amongst the Naggarothi,' admitted Tirathanil. 'How extensive or violent it is, we do not know. It is the Phoenix King's assessment that in Malekith's long absence, the princes of Nagarythe struggle for power.'

'Perhaps we should aid whoever seeks to overthrow Morathi,' suggested a voice from the council.

'An outrageous suggestion!' said Eltaranir. 'To meddle so in the rulership of one kingdom is to invite dissent in *every* kingdom. It is only through our pacts of non-interference that we are able to govern as befits each realm. We must be wary of every accusation levelled at Nagarythe. Many princes are jealous of the Naggarothi power and would take opportunity to undermine it. We are not free of such envy; would you have every scurrilous rumour and accusation made against Caledor used as an excuse to pry into our lives?'

The council member who had spoken sat down with a chagrined expression. More than a dozen other elves raised their hands to be acknowledged and a background of whispering began. Caledrian called each in turn to speak, though they added little that was meaningful to the discussion, which went on through the afternoon. Imrik listened to each speech intently, seeking to solidify his own feelings on the matter. His instinct was to act quickly and decisively, but as he heard proposal and objection, his certainty wavered.

By the time the sky was darkening beyond the high windows, Imrik felt ready to speak. He shifted in his chair and caught Caledrian's eye. When the next opportunity presented itself, Caledrian nodded to Imrik.

The prince stood, thumbs hooked into his broad belt. He looked first at Dorien, and then at the rest of the council. The hall was quiet, the private discussions fading away as Imrik turned to Caledrian. Not once had any objection been raised to his appointment as ambassador, and every elf was keen to hear his personal view on the issues.

'We must fight,' said Imrik. He raised a hand for silence as protests echoed around the chamber. 'We cannot attack Nagarythe. No prince can send his warriors into the lands of another without permission. Bel Shanaar must broker an agreement between the kingdoms. Each shall provide forces to the Phoenix King, which will operate under his authority alone. Every kingdom will be purged in turn. Those cultists that repent their associations with the cytharai and desire clemency will receive it. Those that oppose the will of the princes will be imprisoned, or slain if they resist with violence.'

Imrik sat down again.

Silence followed as each elf digested this plan. Caledrian was deep in thought on his throne, his advisors whispering to him.

'Do you think Bel Shanaar will agree?' Imrik asked Tirathanil. All eyes turned on the herald, awaiting his reply.

'In principle, yes,' said Tirathanil. He took a deep breath before continuing. 'I think you will find some support amongst the other princes. With Caledor's support, they will be able to sway the opinion of those that are less committed.'

Caledrian stood up, signalling to Tirathanil to withdraw behind the throne. The prince crossed his arms and swept his gaze slowly around the circle of elves.

'We have a proposal to vote upon, as composed by Imrik,' said Caledrian. 'Make your decision known. I suspend my right of view in this matter. If the council endorses this course of action, it will be final.'

A few elves stood immediately, supporting Imrik's plan. There was some conversation and shuffling, and then the others rose to their feet until only Hotek was left seated. The priest of Vaul smiled and nodded at Imrik, and stood up.

'The vote is unanimous,' declared Caledrian. A self-congratulatory murmur rippled around the ring of council members. The ruling prince looked at Imrik. 'Tirathanil returns to Tor Anroc tomorrow, brother. Can you leave that soon?'

Imrik considered his options. He had no desire for the negotiations his plan would require, and in the short time he had been in Tor Caled he had made efforts to reconcile with Anatheria and make himself better known to Tythanir. It would take some time for other princes to answer Bel Shanaar's call and the wait would be arduous. He could imagine himself kicking his heels in the Phoenix King's palace, forced to pass the time with the Tiranocii nobility in endless banquets and galas.

Yet it would be improper to remain idle in Tor Caled when he had important duties to attend.

'No point waiting,' he said. 'I'll leave tomorrow.'

THE NUMBER OF princes, nobles and envoys tested the capacity of the Phoenix King's palace, which was one of the largest buildings in Ulthuan. Imrik and Thyrinor, having taken ship along the coast of the Inner Sea to Ellyrion and then ridden westwards to Tor Anroc through the Annulii Mountains, found the city bustling; claustrophobic compared to the colonies and Tor Caled.

Imrik was silently grateful for the fact that the Caledorian entourage, which included a handful of scribes and servants in addition to the princes, was accommodated in one of the houses in the centre of the city rather than within the palace itself. This gave Imrik some of the solitude he required, and the events of the first few days of the visit sent the prince into isolated retreat several times.

There were so many people to meet, so many introductions, ceremonies and feasts, Imrik was wholly reliant upon Thyrinor to remember who everybody was and where he was supposed to be. More delegations arrived each day, adding to Imrik's sense of bewilderment. It appeared that many of the attendants did not understand the gravity of the occasion, and saw the convening of the Phoenix King's court as an opportunity to extend their usual festivities and politics. On uncertain ground, Imrik had held his tongue on a number of occasions, advised by Thyrinor to hold his patience and not unduly antagonise anybody; a feat Imrik found difficult, since most elves found his taciturn nature bordering on insult in itself.

There were fewer princes present than Imrik had hoped. Many of the eastern kingdoms had sent ambassadors instead; though they professed to speak and act with the authority of the princes, Imrik could not treat with them as equals as any assurances they made would have to be ratified later by their masters. It meant that the whole business of discussing the growing problems of the cultists and the situation in Nagarythe descended into petty wrangles and interminable discussions about the exact phrasing of a proposal or the true meaning of another delegate's words.

A few princes had made the journey, and Imrik found them to be of a generally more tolerable nature than the other attendants. In particular, he found Thyriol of Saphery to be calm and wise amongst the tumult, and had considerable respect for the mage who had learnt his mystical arts under the tutelage of Imrik's grandfather. Finudel and Athielle, joint rulers of Ellyrion, were also pleasant company. Though both displayed disarming humour and quick wit, they were ever conscious of the importance of the council.

Imrik had spent some time with these three elves listening to their opinions on Nagarythe and voicing the proposal of Caledor to form a united army under the banner of the Phoenix King. Other than a perfunctory greeting when he had arrived, Imrik had spent no time discussing his views with Bel Shanaar, but on the sixth day of the council, he was due to speak before the Phoenix King.

He met with Thyrinor and Thyriol beforehand, and brought up his uncertainty at expressing his plans in a way that would meet favour with the Phoenix King.

'I am not eloquent,' Imrik admitted as the three princes drank fruit juices in the gardens of Imrik's adopted house. Autumn cloud and sun mingled overhead, bathing the immaculate lawn in periods of warmth and shade, while birds and bees flitted about the carefully maintained hedges and trees. 'I am too abrupt. Bel Shanaar will think I am telling him what to do.'

'Perhaps you should phrase your proposals as questions, cousin,' said Thyrinor, reclining on a white stone bench beside a shallow pool of clear water. Bubbles broke the pond as jade-scaled fish swam lazily just under the surface, their bodies glinting. 'Lead Bel Shanaar to come to the answers you wish him to.'

'That is not a gift I have,' said Imrik. 'I was never a good student of rhetoric.'

'Do not be overly concerned by your mannerisms,' Thyriol assured him. Dressed in a rich yellow and gold robe, the Sapherian mage sat in the shade beneath a tree, eyes closed. 'You do not know Bel Shanaar well, but he is well versed in statecraft and will listen not to your words but to your message. It was with some personal difficulty that he has gathered the council. He has critics, and there are those willing to say the Phoenix King is too weak to act on his own.'

'No doubt those whispers were first formed on the lips of Morathi and her lackeys,' said Thyrinor. 'Even in the colonies, there has been quiet but constant campaign against Bel Shanaar; ever with the assumption that Malekith should have been chosen instead.'

'Let them grumble,' said Imrik. 'My father had as much claim as the Dragontamer's successor. Caledor has no love for the Phoenix King, but I will give Bel Shanaar the respect he earns.'

'Grumbles may seem unimportant to you, but every rumour and snippet is valuable here,' warned Thyriol, opening his eyes. 'Even you must be aware that as unpopular as the Naggarothi are, the Caledorians are not high in the affections of the other kingdoms. Your dragons scare them.'

'So they should,' said Imrik. 'It is not Caledor's fault if they have strength when other kingdoms allow themselves to be weak.'

'They are not as weak as they once were,' said Thyrinor. 'The port of Lothern in Eataine is becoming one of the largest cities in Ulthuan, and her fleet dwarfs ours. Cothique and Yvresse have outposts all over the world. Even gentle Saphery, our companion's kingdom, is renowned for the skill and power of her mages. We cannot rely upon the dragons for eternity. Only a handful remain that do not sleep beneath the mountains, and it will not be long before they too choose to slumber.'

'Which is why we're here,' said Imrik. 'The Phoenix King alone can harness that strength.'

'But will he be willing?' Thyrinor directed the question to the mage.

'Bel Shanaar is concerned, but not desperate,' replied Thyriol. 'Your proposal has merit that he will see, but if it is not the desire of the other kingdoms, he will not give your plan his backing.'

'Your voice would lend weight to our argument,' said Thyrinor. 'Not only as the prince of Saphery, but as one who elevated Bel Shanaar to Phoenix King.'

'There is some truth to that,' said Thyriol, smiling faintly. 'Bel Shanaar and I fought against the daemons under Aenarion, and there are few left who can claim such an achievement.'

'We should go now,' said Imrik, glancing up at the sun. Noon was approaching, the appointed hour for his audience with the Phoenix King. 'I would not keep Bel Shanaar waiting.'

The corridors of the outer palace were comparatively quiet; it had been made known that the Phoenix King had set aside the whole day for representations of the princes present, with no lesser agents permitted. There were bows and words of deference to Thyriol from the few other elves they met, and platitudes offered to Imrik, as the princes made their way to the main hall of the palace.

Though they were early, Bel Shanaar's chamberlain, Palthrain, was waiting for them at the hall doors. Palthrain bowed in greeting and offered a few pleasantries.

'Is Bel Shanaar receiving audience yet?' asked Imrik.

'Enter when you wish,' said Palthrain. 'The Phoenix King lends his ear to Athielle and Finudel presently, but they have made it known you are welcome to join the discussion.'

Imrik took a breath and nodded to Palthrain, who signalled for the attendants to open the doors. The hall beyond was vast, its roof held up by slender pillars inscribed with golden runes, the ceiling cunningly painted to represent a spring sky, lit from dozens of arched windows.

At the far end, Bel Shanaar sat upon a throne wrought in the shape of a phoenix, wings outspread. A long cloak of white feathers draped over the throne from his shoulders, hemmed with a band of golden thread and hung with sapphires. The Phoenix King wore formal robes layered in white and gold, delicately embroidered with silver swirls of flame and glittering runes. Elves showed little sign of age, no matter how ancient, and Bel Shanaar's face was only faintly lined despite his centuries of existence. He did not wear the elaborate Phoenix Crown; instead his pale blond hair was swept back with a golden band decorated with a single emerald at his forehead. His eyes were bright blue, alert as Athielle spoke, her voice quiet but carrying along to Imrik by the perfect acoustics of the hall.

'They are raiders, pure and simple,' the princess said. 'They come across the mountains and take unattended herds. It is the worst kind of theft, to steal the horses of Ellyrion.'

'Yet you offer no proof of this larceny,' said Bel Shanaar. 'Your herds go missing and you spring to blame the Naggarothi, when a more likely explanation is some monstrous hunter from the Annulii. A feral hippogryph perhaps, or a hydra?'

'And Nagarythe is not a poor kingdom,' added another prince. Imrik knew him to be Elodhir, the son of Bel Shanaar. 'If the Naggarothi desired horses, they would buy them.'

'Not from us,' said Finudel. 'We have concern that they do not treat their herds well. Their arrogance has become overbearing, their attitude to their beasts verging on cruelty.'

Palthrain made known the arrival of the princes as Imrik, Thyrinor and Thyriol entered the hall. The others ceased their conversation and waited for the arrivals to join them. Palthrain made formal introductions, though all the elves were known to each other.

'It is an honour to welcome the representatives of Caledor to this chamber,' said Bel Shanaar, dismissing Palthrain with a casual wave. 'I hope that your kingdom fares well, and Caledrian also.'

'Our fortunes are as usual,' said Imrik. 'My brother is worried by the rise in the cults that taints much of Ulthuan. Caledor remains free of these sects, but it is not an easy task.'

'And there are those who have laboured in vain to halt the progress of the cults,' said Athielle. 'It is not from lack of watchfulness that these cults prosper. Caledor perhaps owes as much to the patrol of our common border as it does the vigilance of its leaders.'

'No accusation was meant,' said Imrik. 'What has happened cannot be changed. What we do next, that is what must be decided.'

'Imrik has a proposal I believe worth hearing,' said Thyriol, his robes glinting in the sunshine streaming through the high windows. The mage turned to Imrik and nodded.

'Each kingdom alone has attempted to halt the spread of the cults, and failed,' said Imrik. He offered a shrug of apology to Finudel and Athielle. 'It seems to me that this is a problem for all of Ulthuan. Only you, the Phoenix King, can claim authority over the whole isle. Use your position to assemble an army drawn from every kingdom. Appoint a general, or lead the army yourself, and purge the cults from each kingdom in turn.'

The Phoenix King and princes said nothing, perhaps waiting for Imrik to elaborate on his plan. He had nothing else to offer at the moment and stayed silent. Eventually Bel Shanaar stirred, leaning forwards in his throne.

'An army?' he said, quiet but firm. 'That is your solution?'

Imrik glanced at Thyrinor, but received no assurance from his cousin's blank expression.

'The cults are a threat,' said Imrik. 'They need to be dealt with. An army may be uncivilised, but it will be effective.'

'Violence has never been the cure for any ill,' said Bel Shanaar.

'The orcs and beasts of Elthin Arvan disagree,' said Imrik. 'To avoid violence is laudable; to shirk your duty as the defender of Ulthuan is not.'

'Be careful with your remarks,' snapped Elodhir. 'You address the Phoenix King! Do not forget the oaths you swore before the sacred flame of Asuryan. Caledor is yet part of Ulthuan and one of the Phoenix King's domains.'

'I remember my oaths,' Imrik said in return, turning his fierce gaze from Elodhir to Bel Shanaar. 'Does the Phoenix King? He remembers the darkest days of our people. Harsh times that needed harsh answers. The cults have festered too long.'

'Such disrespect will not be tolerated,' Elodhir replied, but Imrik ignored him, his attention focussed on the Phoenix King.

'Silence, my son,' said Bel Shanaar. 'Imrik has some cause for complaint, though he chooses not to sweeten his bitter message with softer words. He is right; I swore oaths to defend Ulthuan against all enemies and perils. That this peril is of our own creation does not make it any better than those that assail us from beyond our borders; in many ways, it is far worse.'

'A show of determination will be enough for many in the cults,' said Athielle. 'Their leaders, those that ensnare the desperate and unwary, they need to be dealt with by the full force of justice. Those who follow, those who simply seek some other meaning to their existence or to lose themselves in senselessness, can be shown the error of their ways without punishment.'

'An army invites resistance,' said Elodhir. 'The threat of violence will prompt the cultists to defend themselves.'

'They have already committed violence,' said Thyriol. The mage's slender fingers tugged at the sleeves of his robe as he spoke. 'Sacrifices have been made, lives taken. There are stories from every kingdom of cults choosing to fight and die rather than subject themselves to the mercy of their prince and his warriors.'

'And that violence will escalate,' said Bel Shanaar. 'The cults are scattered, disorganised and of more spiritual than physical threat.'

'I disagree,' said Finudel. 'They are aided by Nagarythe, of that I am sure.'

'Sure, but without evidence,' said Bel Shanaar. 'You would have me outlaw an entire kingdom based on rumour.'

'Not rumour,' said Athielle, her temper flaring. 'Bodies we have found, of herdmasters slain. Others have disappeared without trace, and the elders of remote towns have been intimidated and murdered.'

'And the Naggarothi dead from these raids?' said Elodhir. 'You have found them?'

The silence of Athielle and Finudel was the only answer they could offer. Elodhir shook his head and looked at his father.

'It seems that we have been offered no greater insight into the problem,' said the Phoenix King. 'We are no closer to a solution than at this time yesterday.'

'Action is required,' said Imrik. 'It is inaction that has allowed the cults to flourish.'

'I will make no hasty decision,' said Bel Shanaar. 'The situation grows more volatile and I would not risk provoking it without good cause. I will consider your position, Imrik. Please take refreshments and rejoin me this evening.'

Imrik was about to offer further argument but saw that the others were already bowing and turning away, accepting the Phoenix King's dismissal.

He did the same, choosing not to risk Bel Shanaar's anger, keeping his sharp words to himself for the moment.

When they had left the hall, Thyrinor beckoned for Imrik to leave the others and the pair found an unoccupied chamber not far from the audience hall. Murals depicting the Tiranoc coast decorated the walls, moving from placid summer shores to winter storms as the scene subtly changed as one looked around the circular room.

There were cushioned benches, and side tables laden with fruit, wine and water. Thyrinor picked up a jug and poured golden wine into a crystal goblet, and then remembered to offer the same to Imrik, who declined.

'I need a clear head,' said Imrik, slumping onto one of the benches. He took an apple from a platter near at hand and bit deeply, savouring the freshness of the fruit. 'Bel Shanaar is too cautious. Yet the more I push him, the less I will achieve.'

'It is for your forcefulness that you were chosen, cousin,' said Thyrinor. He took a mouthful of wine, eyes closed. He opened them after a moment. 'This is really rather good wine. Anyway, it is not Bel Shanaar that you need to worry about for the moment. His concern is the reception he will receive from the other delegations. Finudel and Athielle will back you, of that I am sure. Thyriol too, I would think, as he has offered no counter to our plan. You must persuade the others.'

'How do I do that?' asked Imrik, finishing off the apple. 'It seems to me that no kingdom wishes to take responsibility.'

'Then show them the leadership lacking in Bel Shanaar,' said Thyrinor. 'Why not offer to lead the army?'

'No,' Imrik said immediately. 'I have no desire to do that.'

'Why not? You are a natural general, and you have the respect of many other princes, if not their friendship.'

'I cannot lead the warriors of other kingdoms,' replied Imrik. 'I cannot trust them.'

'But you would trust another to lead them?'

Imrik left the question unanswered. His only concern was the safety of Caledor. That meant ridding the rest of Ulthuan of the pernicious cytharai cults, just as it had meant destroying the greenskins and the forest beasts that threatened the colonies of his kingdom. It was not a role he relished, though it was one he filled with pride. The thought of being answerable directly to Bel Shanaar troubled him; the prospect of working closely with the princes of other kingdoms unsettled him.

'Will you at least speak with the representatives of the other kingdoms?' said Thyrinor, pouring himself a second glass of wine. 'If you gain their backing, Bel Shanaar will have no choice but to support our proposal.'

'And how do I do that?' said Imrik. 'They will see it as Caledor trying to gain more power. They see everything through eyes tinted with envy.'

With a heavy sigh, Thyrinor put his goblet to one side and crossed his arms.

'Are you regretting your decision to accept this duty?' he said. 'I find your negativity arduous to endure, cousin, and others will feel likewise. You bring them doom instead of offering hope. Give them something to put their trust in. If you are to succeed you must support Bel Shanaar and make the others believe in his ability to lead our people.'

'A belief I do not have,' said Imrik. 'Would you have me lie?'

'You can be intolerable!' Thyrinor threw up his hands. 'Why are you here at all, if you have no belief that we can succeed?'

'It is my duty,' replied Imrik.

'Is that all? Do you not fear for the Ulthuan in which your son will grow up?'

'While Caledor remains strong, he will be untouched by this malaise,' said Imrik. 'That is my only concern.'

'Caledor cannot resist the rest of Ulthuan forever,' said Thyrinor, taking up his wine and drinking swiftly. 'The dragons cannot fight against the whispers that scratch at the spirit of our people. The mountains are no bulwark against the insidious nature of melancholy and boredom. If Caledor is to remain free, the rest of Ulthuan must be freed first.'

'I understand,' said Imrik, confused by his cousin's misplaced frustration. 'I see your point. With the backing of Caledor, the Phoenix King will command the authority he deserves.'

'So, will you speak with the others?'

'Yes,' said Imrik, standing. 'But not at the same time. I must speak with each delegation in turn. I cannot stand to be dragged into their bickering.'

'Then I will organise things,' said Thyrinor, finishing his drink. He took a few steps towards the door and stopped. 'Please try to be civil to them.'

For the whole afternoon, Imrik tried as hard as possible to be civil, ignoring the veiled slights directed at Caledor and the innuendo cast upon the delegations of the other kingdoms. He spoke with each group of representatives, outlining the Caledorian plan for a campaign against the cults. Thyrinor did much of the speaking, taking care to emphasise the importance of each kingdom in the grand scheme, ensuring that it was the listeners that believed they would have the most control. By the time Palthrain found the pair in the late afternoon, at least five other kingdoms had indicated their support and promised to make representation to Bel Shanaar; none had yet been willing to declare their support openly.

As before, Imrik found Bel Shanaar, Elodhir, Thyriol, Finudel and Athielle in the king's audience chamber. There were a few other elves around, sitting on the great amphitheatre of benches that surrounded the Phoenix Throne. Imrik ignored them and strode up to Bel Shanaar.

'Have you decided?' said Imrik.

'You have been busy,' replied Bel Shanaar. 'Since our last conversation, I have had constant visitors proposing the idea of an army drawn from all of the kingdoms.'

'I intend no trickery,' Imrik said quickly, sensing he was being accused of some subterfuge.

Bel Shanaar smiled, though he did not deign to share the reason for his amusement. He gave Thyriol a nod and the mage held up a rolled parchment.

'This is the first draft of a declaration,' said Thyriol, handing the scroll to Thyrinor. 'It declares the open worship of the cytharai to be illegal and calls upon all elves to renounce the undergods.'

'That is all?' said Imrik. 'What of the army?'

'One thing at a time,' said Elodhir. 'First we must get agreement that action needs to be taken. When that has been secured, we can discuss what form that action will take.'

'Winter will come swiftly,' said Imrik. 'If we do not strike now, it will be next spring before we can move. It will take many days to gather warriors from the whole of Ulthuan. The call must be sent out immediately.'

'Your presumption is incredible,' said Elodhir. 'We will not let you bully the other kingdoms into agreeing with you.'

'We?' Imrik looked hard at Bel Shanaar. 'Only one elf is Phoenix King.'

'And I speak as prince of Tiranoc also,' said Bel Shanaar. 'Mine is a double burden of rulership. Would you have me declare war on my subjects?'

Imrik heard the noise of others entering, but paid no heed to the newcomers. Anger warred with disappointment in his heart. Before returning to this hall, he had thought progress had been made; in reality very little would be agreed any time soon.

'Captain Carathril of Lothern, your majesty.' Palthrain's voice rang down the hall.

'Thank you, Palthrain,' Bel Shanaar said, still not looking at the arrivals.

Imrik glanced over his shoulder and saw Palthrain bowing and departing, leaving two elves in armour, wearing the colours of Lothern. Both appeared to be officers, but he did not recognise them from the Eataine delegation. He dismissed them from his thoughts as irrelevant.

'We cannot show mercy,' said Imrik with a shake of his head. 'The people need our strength.'

'But many of them are victims as much as they are perpetrators,' cautioned Bel Shanaar. 'They are brought low by their own terrors, and the priests and priestesses play on their fears and manipulate their woes. I have spoken with some who claim that they did not realise how debased they had become. There is dark magic in this, some more evil purpose that we have not yet seen.'

'Then we must find their ringleaders and question them,' suggested Elodhir. The prince took a pace towards his father. 'We cannot simply allow the cults to spread unchecked. If we should allow that to happen, our armies will be eaten away by this menace, our people consumed by their own desires. No! Though it is perhaps a harsh judgement on some, we must prosecute your rule with firm determination and relentless purpose.'

Imrik was taken aback by Elodhir's sudden change of heart. He was not sure what game was being played by Elodhir, and was certain he did not like it. For a moment, he preferred the other prince's opposition to his support, but then realised this was immature.

'That is all well and good, Elodhir, but against whom must we prosecute it?' asked Thyriol. As always, Thyriol's words were quiet and meaningful. As he carefully considered his next words, the mage ran thin fingers through his copper-coloured hair. His deep green eyes fixed on each of his fellows in turn. 'We all know its root, yet there is not one of us speaks its name. Nagarythe. There, I have said it and yet the world turns.'

'Tales and rumour are no basis for policy,' replied Bel Shanaar. 'Perhaps our guests bring tidings that will aid our discussions.'

The Phoenix King and princes looked at the new arrivals, who stood for a moment with their mouths open, surprised to be so quickly drawn into such a discussion. The guard captain, who had been named Carathril by the announcement, cleared his throat and paused for a moment before speaking.

'I bear ill tidings, your majesty,' Carathril said quietly. 'I and my companion have ridden hither with all haste to bring you the news that Prince Aeltherin of Lothern is dead.'

The news did not bode well and Imrik scowled. A death amongst the ruling princes was bound to cause even more delays.

'It is our misfortune that the great prince fell from grace, your majesty,' continued Carathril. 'I know not how, but Prince Aeltherin became a member of the pleasure cults. For how long, we do not know. It appears that for some time the prince was in league with the dark priestesses of Atharti, and from his position misdirected our efforts to uncover the plots of the cult. Only a chance happening, a name whispered by a prisoner in her sleep, started us on a sinister path that led to the doors of the prince's manse itself.'

'And how is it that Prince Aeltherin does not stand here to defend himself against these accusations?' asked Elodhir. 'Why is he not in your custody?'

'He took his own life, highness,' explained Carathril. 'I endeavoured to reason with him, implored the prince to put his case before this court, but he was gripped with a madness and would not consent. I know not what caused him to act in this way, and I would not dare to speculate.'

'A ruling prince party to these covens of evil?' muttered Thyriol, turning to the Phoenix King. Imrik growled at the thought. Caledrian had hinted at such treachery, but to hear it confirmed was grievous news to the Caledorian. Immediately his thoughts went to the other members of the court and which, if any, could be trusted.

'Matters are even graver than we would have dared admit,' said Thyriol. 'When news of Aeltherin's fall spreads, fear and suspicion will follow.'

'As is the intent of the architects of this darkness, I have no doubt,' said Bel

Shanaar. 'With the rulers of the realms no longer to be trusted, to whom will our citizens turn? When they cannot trust those with authority, the greater the dread upon the minds of our people, and the more they will flock to the cults.'

'And who shall we trust, if not our own?' asked Imrik, giving voice to the doubt in his mind, his eyes seeking signs of duplicity in the faces of the others.

'The defection of Prince Aeltherin casts a cloud over every prince,' said Bel Shanaar with a sorrowful shake of his head. 'If we are to lead the people from the temptations of the cults, we must be united. Yet how can we act together when the doubt remains that those in whom we confide may well be working against our interests?'

'To allow ourselves to be divided would bring about a terrible age of anarchy,' warned Thyriol, who had begun to pace back and forth beside the king's throne. 'The rule of the realms is fragile still, and the greatest of our leaders are beyond these shores in the colonies across the ocean.'

'The greatest of our leaders sits upon this throne,' said Elodhir, his eyes narrowing.

'I spoke not of one individual,' said Thyriol, raising a placating hand. 'Yet I would wish it that Prince Malekith were here, if only to settle the matter of his people in Nagarythe. In his absence we are reluctant to prosecute investigations within his realm.'

'Well, Malekith is not here, while we are,' said Bel Shanaar sharply. He paused for a moment, passing a trembling hand across his forehead. 'It matters not. Thyriol, what is the counsel of the mages of Saphery?'

The mage-prince ceased his pacing and turned on his heel to face the Phoenix King. He folded his arms, which disappeared within the sleeves of his voluminous robe, and pursed his lips in thought.

'You were correct to speak of dark magic, your majesty,' Thyriol said quietly. 'Our divinations sense a growing weight of evil energy gathering in the vortex. It pools within the Annulii Mountains, drawn here by the practices of the cults. Sacrifice of an unnatural kind is feeding the ill winds. Whether it is the purpose of the cults or simply an unintended result of their ceremonies, we cannot say. This magic is powerful but dangerous, and no mage will wield it.'

'There is no means by which this dark magic cannot be spent safely?' asked Imrik. He thought of the sacrifice of his grandfather, trapped forever in the eye of the vortex so that such dark magic would not pollute the world.

'The vortex dissipates some of its power, and would cleanse the winds in due course were the dark magic not fuelled further,' explained Thyriol. 'Unfortunately, there is nothing we can do to hasten this, other than to stop the cults practising their sorcery.'

'And so we return again to our main question,' sighed Bel Shanaar. 'How might we rid ourselves of these cults?'

'Firm action,' growled Imrik. 'Muster the princes; send out the call to arms. Sweep away this infestation with blade and bow.'

'What you suggest threatens civil war,' Thyriol cautioned.

'To stand idle threatens equal destruction,' said Elodhir.

'And would you lead this army, Imrik?' Bel Shanaar asked, turning in his throne to stare intently at the Caledorian prince.

'I would not,' Imrik replied sharply. 'Caledor yet remains free of this taint, and I seek to maintain the peace that we have.'

'Saphery has no generals of renown,' said Thyriol with a shrug. 'I think that you will find the other realms reluctant to risk open war.'

'Then who shall lead the hunt?' pleaded Elodhir, his exasperation clear in his voice.

'Captain Carathril,' said Bel Shanaar. Carathril jolted in surprise.

'How might I be of service, your majesty?' Carathril asked.

'I dispense with your duties to the Guard of Lothern,' said Bel Shanaar, standing up. 'You are loyal and trustworthy, devoted to our people and the continuance of peace and just rule. From this moment, I appoint you as my herald, the mouth of the Phoenix King. You will take word to the princes of the fourteen realms. I will ask if there is one amongst them who is willing to prosecute the destruction of these intolerable cults. This peril that besets us is no less than the division of our people and the destruction of our civilisation. We must stand strong, and proud, and drive out these faithless practitioners of deceit. The gratitude of our lands and this office will be heaped upon the prince that delivers us from this darkness.'

Imrik saw Thyrinor's brow raised at this unprecedented declaration.

'Your change of heart is welcome,' said Finudel. 'What has caused it to be altered?'

'A prince is dead,' said Bel Shanaar. 'There can be no path that is not shadowed with darkness from this time on. The path will grow longer if we wait, and Imrik is correct. Matters are reaching a head, and who can say what fresh turmoil in Nagarythe might spread into the other kingdoms. We must act swiftly lest more become lost in the darkness. We cannot give our enemies the winter to move against us.'

'Yet you do not have a general,' said Thyriol.

All eyes turned to Imrik.

'No,' said the Caledorian. 'There are others who have waged war in the colonies, and even a few princes who fought beside Aenarion. They will be capable of leading your army.'

Not wishing to discuss the matter further, Imrik strode from the hall, content that he had achieved his goal. Thyrinor hurried after him and caught up just as the doors were closed behind them.

'This is a great opportunity for Caledor,' said his cousin. 'Be sensible, Imrik. You know that the princes will choose a general from amongst their number, and there will be great prestige attached to the position. Other ranks of importance will be filled, and the esteem of that kingdom will grow further. Bel Shanaar is nearing the end of his natural span, and there are princes that already position themselves to claim the Phoenix Throne.'

'What has that to do with me?' said Imrik.

'Imagine what Caledor could achieve if Caledrian was to become the next Phoenix King?'

Imrik stopped in his stride and turned on Thyrinor.

'And that is your only thought?' he snapped. 'Or perhaps it is your own prestige that occupies your plans? Caledor does not need the Phoenix Crown to be the greatest of the kingdoms.'

'Your accusations are harsh, cousin,' declared Thyrinor, though his embarrassed countenance betrayed his guilt. 'The empowerment of Caledor is to the benefit of all our princes, you included.'

'I want nothing more than I have,' said Imrik, resuming his long stride along the corridor. 'Had I desired more glory, I would put myself forward as Bel Shanaar's general.'

'You are being selfish, to rob your brothers of this opportunity,' said Thyrinor.

'Yes, I am,' replied Imrik. 'Since my coming of age I have done all that has been asked of me without complaint. I have spent most of my life earning riches and glory for Caledor. Now I wish to have the time to see my son grow and learn, and perhaps even give him a brother or sister.'

Exasperated, Thyrinor turned away, leaving Imrik to depart the palaces alone. Imrik crossed the plaza outside the palaces to the house that had been set aside for the Caledorians. The chief of the servants, Lathinorian, met him as he stepped over the threshold.

'A messenger from Prince Caledrian arrived,' said Lathinorian. 'He awaits you in the second chamber.'

'I have no need to send a message,' said Imrik. 'Send him back to Caledrian with the news that we have been successful. I shall convey the rest myself when I return.'

'We are leaving soon, prince?' said Lathinorian. 'Shall we begin preparations for our departure?'

'We leave tomorrow,' said Imrik. 'I am tired of Tor Anroc.'

With that, Imrik headed upstairs to his bedchambers, and left instruction that he was not to be disturbed.

NOTHING BROKE IMRIK'S thoughts; he heard no sound save the wind whistling across the mountains. He looked out of the window and watched Anatheria with Tythanir; the boy was holding a wooden sword and shield and under the instruction of Celebrith making strikes at a small straw dummy set up in the middle of the lawn. The boy had insisted he be allowed to train with a sword. Anatheria had worried her son had been caught up in the dark talk of cults and war that had filled the palace corridors of late, but Imrik had been in no mood to deny his son what he wanted.

The prince knew the peace of the scene was an oddity. Tor Caled had hosted heralds from one kingdom or another for a considerable time; many of them coming to entreat Caledrian or one of his princes to take up the office of the Phoenix King's general. All had been declined. Caledrian had no more desire than Imrik to leave his kingdom during these troubled times, and had forbidden any other prince of the realm from answering the call. He was insistent, with Imrik's support, that Caledor was not entangled in the politics of this new army. When a suitable candidate was appointed, the kingdom would send such warriors as they could spare to fight under another elf.

Thyrinor and Dorien had argued differently, and with some cause. They had claimed it was foolish to allow the other kingdoms to choose a general without Caledor having a say in the matter. If Caledorian warriors were to fight, their princes should know who they would follow. Caledrian had asked if Imrik would return to Tor Anroc to take part in the selection debates, but Imrik had flatly refused.

Having returned once and been sent away again, Imrik was determined that nothing would disrupt his time with his family. His relationship with Anatheria had improved significantly, and Tythanir was growing fond of his father. Imrik was not about to risk these developments by abandoning them again, even if only for a little while.

Entertained by his son's antics, Imrik barely heard the door opening behind him, guessing it to be a servant. It was with surprise that he turned at the sound of his older brother's voice.

'Imrik, I must speak with you,' said Caledrian.

Caledor's ruler was grim of mood, and Imrik could tell from his brother's expression that he was not anxious to have this conversation.

'What is it?' said Imrik. 'You could have sent for me.'

'This is not a discussion between ruler and prince, but between brothers,' said Caledrian, sitting on a couch and looking past Imrik, out of the window. 'I have received Carathril, the Phoenix King's herald. The princes are finally gathering at Tor Anroc to choose a general. Not only that, rumour spreads, that there is outright war in Nagarythe, between Morathi and others who would see her reign ended.'

'Grave news, but to be expected,' said Imrik, turning his back to the window to rest against the sill. 'What of it?'

'I want you to go to Tor Anroc.' Caledrian looked away as he said it, casting his eyes downwards.

'No,' said Imrik. 'Go yourself, or send Dorien or Thyrinor.'

'I cannot,' said Caledrian. 'Dorien will undo all progress made with his rashness and Thyrinor is too willing to accommodate Bel Shanaar. It must be you.'

'Why can you not go? The other ruling princes will expect it.'

'And they will seek to settle past disagreements,' said Caledrian. 'I have not protected Caledor's prosperity by endearing myself to my fellow rulers. My presence would be as disruptive as Dorien's.'

'You said you come as brother, not lord,' said Imrik. 'This sounds like a command.'

'It is not,' said Caledrian. 'I will not force you to go.'

'Nor could you,' said Imrik.

'This will not be like last time,' promised Caledrian. 'Bel Shanaar is on the brink of brokering an agreement between the kingdoms to deal with Nagarythe. This is far more than just a campaign against the cults. The Phoenix King wants to persuade the others to unite and force Nagarythe into negotiation. If Caledor is not present, Bel Shanaar believes the others will baulk at the prospect.'

'What happened to your vow not to interfere in the other kingdoms?' said Imrik. 'Now you speak of invasion.'

'Not a prospect I desire, but one that is forced upon us,' said Caledrian. He crossed the room and laid a hand on Imrik's arm. 'With the revelation of Aeltherin's treachery, it has the other princes distrusting each other more than ever. However, none doubt the integrity of Caledor and her princes. They know that we would never fall under the influence of Nagarythe. More than that, it is you that commands their respect, even if few are willing to admit it. Brother, we are on the brink of war and I need your help. Your presence will reassure our allies and cow those who would seek to oppose action.'

Imrik pulled away his arm and stared out of the window, watching as Tythanir made a clumsy hack at the dummy, Celebrith helping to guide his blow.

'What manner of world will your son see?' Caledrian said behind him. 'Our grandfather gave his life to protect us from the daemons. Our father put his trust in Bel Shanaar, and sacrificed himself for the prosperity of this kingdom. What I ask is not so great a price; just a little of your time.'

The mention of Imrik's forefathers rankled him, but he could not deny what Caledrian said. What reason could he give to refuse? All sounded as vain excuses; in truth they were and Imrik despised himself for clinging to them. Yet the simple fact remained that he did not wish to be Caledor's ambassador, and had even less inclination to get involved with a war against the Naggarothi.

Confrontation was inevitable. Even if Bel Shanaar lacked the courage to act directly against Nagarythe, the purge of the cults would be a blow to Naggarothi esteem. Even if only half of the rumours concerning the strife in Nagarythe were true, it was still far from a stable kingdom.

As he watched Tythanir pretending to be a warrior, Imrik felt a moment of disgust. Of course he wanted his son to grow up skilled with sword and lance and bow; but what right did Imrik have to make that choice for him? There was a good chance that Bel Shanaar would pull back from his utter commitment to eradicate the cults and bring the Naggarothi to heel. Fifty years had passed since Malekith had abandoned his own people; anything could happen in the next fifty if nothing changed.

'I'll go,' said Imrik, his knuckles white as he gripped the window sill. 'Tonight. No delay will make the parting any easier.'

'I love you, brother, and would not ask of this of any other,' said Caledrian, placing his hand on Imrik's shoulder. 'Ensure that Bel Shanaar will see through this campaign to the end, and help the other princes choose a good general. When that is done, I will ask no more of you.'

There was no doubting Caledrian's honest intent, but Imrik knew that such a promise would never be kept. A war was about to be waged on Ulthuan and until it was concluded, there would be no peace for Imrik or any other prince.

THE ATMOSPHERE OF Tor Anroc was even more fevered than during Imrik's last visit. He had left behind Dorien and Thyrinor, wanting no distractions. They had complained bitterly, as Imrik had expected, until he had made it clear he would consider their presence an irritation and a hindrance. Dorien was slightly mollified by Imrik's request that he stay as guardian to Anatheria and Tythanir; as yet he had no family to care for. Thyrinor had been even more stubborn, and only when Caledrian had commanded his cousin to stay in Tor Caled had the matter been settled.

Much had already been decided before Imrik's arrival, for which he was grateful. Having determined to prosecute a campaign against the cultists, it appeared that Bel Shanaar was fully committed, despite Imrik and Caledrian's misgivings on this point.

Several princes had already announced which of their noble houses would bring their warriors to the effort, though Imrik had no such promises from his brother. If all went well, the princes of Caledor would not be required; it had been long years since the dragons of Caledor had fought upon Ulthuan's soil and all in the kingdom desired that such a thing remained a memory. The deployment of such force was not only impractical in a campaign against scattered, small cults, it would incense the Naggarothi without question and force their hand.

So Imrik spent his time in the hall of Bel Shanaar and listened as noble after noble and prince after prince staked their warriors to the cause and their claim to the generalship. Most were given short shrift by the Phoenix King and princes; untested leaders who had not seen battle. It was a problem for all of the kingdoms; their most warlike folk and most accomplished commanders had long quit these shores for a more adventurous life building and guarding the colonies.

On the second day after his arrival, Finudel and Athielle came to the court and pledged the support of Ellyrion. Thyriol made oaths on behalf of Saphery, and volunteered his own magical prowess to the cause. From

Yvresse and Chrace and Cothique princes offered themselves in response to Bel Shanaar's call.

Yet for all the martial talk and posturing, two questions remained: who would lead the army, and where would it be sent? There seemed to be an ongoing struggle between the princes, unspoken but no less tenacious than any battle with armies. Even within the camps of the different kingdoms there was division: some who committed troops wanted to be the first to benefit, while others saw gain in the upheaval falling elsewhere first.

Again and again Imrik turned away those that would see him raised up as the Phoenix King's general. The idea was proposed again by Finudel, two days after he had arrived.

'There is none of us so well equipped for this honour as you,' said the Ellyrian prince, when the council had gathered in Bel Shanaar's hall. 'Save perhaps for the efforts of Malekith, none has achieved greater deeds of arms in recent history.'

'That makes it somebody else's turn,' replied Imrik.

There was some laughter at this, but Imrik's scowl showed he had intended no joke and silenced them.

'We could bring back Aerenthis, perhaps?' suggested Thyriol. 'As warden of Athel Maraya he is experienced in war.'

'He has already declined,' said Bel Shanaar with a long sigh. 'As have Litheriun, Menathuis, Orlandril and Cathellion.'

'Then if no other will take this burden, I shall do it,' said Elodhir.

'A noble offer, but one I cannot accept,' said the Phoenix King. 'I have told you before that the general cannot be of Tiranoc. If this army is to fight under my authority, it must be led by a prince of another kingdom, so that no accusation can be levelled that I favour my own kingdom above any other.'

'There must be some way to resolve this,' said Finudel. 'In Ellyrion, twenty thousand cavalry and ten thousand spears await the command of a general. Who is to lead them?'

'It matters not if the horsemasters of Ellyrion stand ready to ride forth,' said Prince Bathinair of Yvresse. 'Who are they to ride forth against, my dear Finudel? You can hardly lead a cavalry charge through every village and town in Ulthuan.'

'Perhaps you seek to upset the harmony between the realms for your own ends,' added Caladryan, another of Yvresse's nobility. 'It is not secret that of late the fortunes of Ellyrion have waned. War suits those with little to lose, and it costs those who have the means. Our endeavours across the oceans bring us wealth and goods from the colonies; perhaps Ellyrion is jealous of that.'

Finudel opened his mouth to speak, his anger etched in creases across his brow, but Athielle quickly laid a hand on her brother's arm to still him.

'It is true that we have perhaps not prospered as much as some,' the

Ellyrian princess said quietly. 'In part that is because we of the Inner King-doms must pay the taxes of Lothern to pass our fleets into the Great Ocean. If not for those taxes, I suspect that the Outer Kingdoms would perhaps have less of a monopoly of trade.'

'We cannot be held to account for the quirks of geography,' sneered Prince Langarel, one of Haradrin's kin from Lothern. 'The sea gates must be main-tained, and our war fleet stands ever ready for the benefit of all. It is fitting, then, that all should contribute to the cost of maintaining these defences.'

'And against whom do you defend us?' growled Finudel. 'Men? Hut-dwelling savages who can barely cross a river, and an ocean divides us from them. The dwarfs? They are content to dig in the mountains and sit in their caves. The slaves of the Old Ones? Their cities lie in ruins, their civilisation swallowed by the hot jungles. Your fleet is not required, a token of the hubris of Lothern kept gilded by the labours of the other realms.'

'Must every old slight and rankle be dredged up before me every day?' demanded Bel Shanaar, his calm voice cutting sharply through the raised voices of the princes. 'There is nothing to be gained from this bickering, and everything to be lost. While we argue over the spoils of our growing colo-nies, our cities here at hand are being devoured by decadence and forbidden pursuits. Would you have us abandon our roots and settle in the newly grown branches of our realm? The world has riches enough for us all, if we could set aside these incessant arguments.'

'The power of the cults grows, that much is clear,' said Thyriol, from where he sat upon one of the ring of innermost benches surrounding the hall. All turned to the mage in expectation.

'The vortex holds the winds of magic in check for the moment, but dark magic is gathering in the mountains. Strange creatures have been seen in the highest peaks, unnatural things spawned from the power of Chaos. Not all things of darkness were purged by the blade of Aenarion and the vortex of Caledor. Hybrid monsters of flesh, mutant and depraved, dwell still in the wilderness. The dark magic feeds them, emboldens them, makes them stronger and cannier. Even now, the passes become ever more dangerous to travel. In the winter when the hunters and soldiers cannot keep these growing numbers of beasts at bay, what then? Will we have manticores and hydras descend into the lowlands to attack farms and destroy villages? If we allow the cults to grow unchecked, perhaps even the vortex itself will fail and once more plunge the world into an age of darkness and daemons. Is there one here with the will to prevent that?'

The assembled princes stood in silence, eyeing each other, avoiding the gaze of the Phoenix King. Imrik felt the weight of expectation upon his shoulders. He had known this moment would come and done everything he could to avoid it.

He closed his eyes, picturing his son at play, hardening himself to another duty thrust upon him. He opened his mouth to answer.

'There is one perhaps that has the will,' a voice called out, echoing along the audience chamber from the doorway. Its timbre was firm and deep, filled with authority.

A ripple of gasps and whispers spread through the court as Imrik opened his eyes to see a newcomer striding purposefully across the lacquered floor, the fall of his boots sounding like the thunder of war drums. He was dressed in a long skirt of golden mail and his chest was covered with a gold breast-plate etched with the design of a dragon, coiled and ready to attack. He wore a cloak of shadow black across his shoulders, held with a clasp adorned with a black gem set into a golden rose. Under one arm he carried a tall war helm, fixed with a strange circlet of dark grey metal that had jutting, thorn-like spines. A complex headband of golden threads swept back raven hair that fell about his shoulders in twisted plaits tied with rings of rune-etched bone. His eyes were piercing, dark, as he stared at the nervous princes and courtiers. He radiated power, his energy and vigour surrounding him as surely as light glows from a lantern.

The princes parted before the newcomer like waves before a ship's prow, treading and stumbling upon robes and cloaks in their eagerness to back away. A few bowed stiffly or nodded heads in unthinking deference as he swept past to stand in front of the Phoenix King, his left hand, gloved in supple black leather, resting on the silver pommel of a sword hanging in an ebon scabbard at his waist.

Imrik felt relief and anger war within him at the sight of the newly arrived prince; relief that another was willing to take up the mantle of leadership, anger that he had not done so before.

'Prince Malekith,' said Bel Shanaar evenly, stroking his bottom lip with a slender finger. 'Had I known of your coming I would have arranged suitable welcome.'

'Such ceremony is unnecessary, your majesty,' replied Malekith, his tone of voice warm, his manner as smooth as velvet. 'I thought it prudent to arrive unannounced, lest our enemies be warned of my return.'

'Our enemies?' said Bel Shanaar, turning a hawkish look upon the prince.

'Even across the oceans, as I fought against vile beasts and brutal orcs, I heard of the woes that beset our home,' Malekith explained. He paused and turned to face the princes and their counsellors. 'Alongside the dwarfs, beside their kings, I and my companions fought to keep our new lands safe. Friends I had that gave their lives protecting the colonies, and I would not have their deaths be in vain; that our cities and our island here would fall to ruin even as we raise sparkling towers and mighty fortresses across the length and breadth of the world.'

'And so you have returned to us in our hour of need, Malekith?' said Imrik, stepping in front of Malekith with his arms crossed. The Naggarothi prince's overly dramatic entrance summed up everything Imrik believed about Aenarion's son.

'You must also have heard that which vexes us most,' said Thyriol softly, standing up and pacing towards the prince of Nagarythe, stepping between Malekith and Imrik. 'We would wish to prosecute our war against these insidious evils across all of Ulthuan. *All* of Ulthuan.'

'That is why I have returned,' replied Malekith, meeting the mage's keen gaze with his own piercing stare. 'Nagarythe is gripped by this torment no less than other lands; more I have heard on occasion. We are one island, one realm under the rule of the Phoenix King, and Nagarythe will not be party to insurrection, nor shall we tolerate black magics and forbidden rituals.'

'You are our greatest general, our most sound strategist, Prince Malekith,' said Finudel, his voice hesitant with hope. Imrik bit back a retort at this sudden change of allegiance. 'If it pleases all present, would you take up the banner of the Phoenix King and lead the fight against these miserable wretches?'

'In you runs the noblest blood of all princes,' gushed Bathinair, his tone sickly in the extreme. Imrik shook his head in disgust, unseen by the others, for all eyes were on Malekith. 'As you fought the darkness alongside your father, you could again bring the light back to Ulthuan!'

'Eataine would stand by you,' promised Haradrin with a clenched fist held to his chest.

Imrik stepped away, distancing himself from the others as a chorus of pleading and thanks bubbled up from the assembled nobles. They fell silent the moment Malekith raised a hand to still them. The Naggarothi prince turned his head and looked at Bel Shanaar, saying nothing. The Phoenix King sat in thought, his lips pursed, steepling his slender fingers beneath his chin. Bel Shanaar then looked at Imrik's stern expression, an eyebrow raised in question upon the Phoenix King's face.

'If it is the will of the Phoenix King and this court, then Caledor will not oppose Malekith,' Imrik said slowly, before turning away and stalking from the room.

IT WAS WITH a bitter heart that Imrik arrived in Tor Caled with news of Malekith's return. So fortunate was the timing, he suspected the Naggarothi prince to be involved in the rise of the cults. For Imrik, events now seemed too neat to be coincidence. The affair had the stench of artifice about it; created and managed for the further aggrandisement of Malekith.

He said as much to Caledrian, though his brother confessed some measure of relief that Malekith would restore order to Nagarythe. The ruler of Caledor called together the most powerful nobles of the kingdom to discuss his response to the development.

'We have no need to get involved,' Imrik told the council. 'Malekith has taken the duty upon himself. Let him stamp his rule again upon his rebellious people.'

'There is a course of reason that suggests we should not let Malekith operate without counter,' said Thyrinor. 'With the mandate of Bel Shanaar and the blessings of the other kingdoms, he might turn such power to mischief. If Caledor had representation in the army, a force to match Malekith's veterans, balance will be maintained.'

'A wise course, but one that will founder,' said Caledrian.

'How so?' replied Thyrinor.

'Who here will fight for Malekith?' Caledrian addressed the assembled princes and nobles.

'I will not,' said Imrik; a sentiment echoed by the others.

'I will raise no blade beneath a Naggarothi banner,' said Dorien. 'It is an insult to the memory of the Dragontamer to fight with the outcasts of the north.'

Caledrian smiled grimly at Thyrinor, his point made.

'Will you, cousin?' said the ruling prince. Thyrinor glanced at the rest of the council and shook his head. 'Then the matter is settled. No house of Caledor will join Bel Shanaar's army, and the dragons will not fly the skies of Ulthuan.'

'A choice that is yours alone to make,' said Hotek, who had remained silent since the discussion had begun. 'Yet Caledor should show some support to the venture, lest our kingdom be accused of forgetting our duties to the Phoenix King.'

'You have a suggestion, Hotek?' said Caledrian.

'Make a gift of weapons to the cause,' said the priest of Vaul. 'As your grandfather did for Aenarion, let the artifice of Vaul's Anvil be your offering to Bel Shanaar.'

Caledrian looked to the others and received nods of assent.

'It shall be as you say,' he said. 'What must I do?'

'You need do nothing,' replied Hotek. 'I shall see to the forging and delivery on your behalf. It would be fitting if you would travel to the shrine with me to make offering to the priests.'

'Of course,' said Caledrian. 'Whatever you desire shall be yours.'

'For Vaul,' Hotek said pointedly.

'Yes, for Vaul,' Caledrian swiftly corrected himself.

THOUGH THE TIMES that followed were anxious, the path chosen by the princes of Caledor seemed to be wisest. At first troubling news reached them from the north. Malekith's first attempt to restore his rule in Nagarythe ended in failure. This Caledrian and Imrik and the other princes heard from Carathril the herald, who had ridden alongside Malekith on the ill-fated venture.

Though this setback caused some consternation in Caledor, the noble and the wise of that kingdom again decided not to intercede in the war. The first weapons from Vaul's Anvil were finished, six rune-enchanted swords, and were delivered with due ceremony to Bel Shanaar. The gift was accepted graciously, though the Phoenix King was saddened that the dragon princes would not lend their might to the battle.

Though Malekith's first foray into Nagarythe had nearly ended in disaster, much had been learnt of the enemy. Morathi was indeed the chief architect of the cults, and had usurped her son to take control of Nagarythe. Strengthened by the confirmation of this belief, the other princes doubled their efforts to rouse the cults from their cities and towns, declaring them outlaw. They sent more troops to Malekith as he prepared for a fresh offensive in the spring..

During the bleak winter days, Imrik was able to forget the troubles of the north and spend much time with Tythanir. Unlike his brothers and the other princes, he cared nothing for news of Malekith's affairs, believing his part in the unfolding war to have been settled.

One day he took his son into the mountains, onto the peaks above Tor Caled. He showed him the view of the city and told tales of the city's founding by Tythanir's great-grandfather.

'Our blood is in these rocks,' said Imrik, stamping a foot on the frosted ground. 'Beneath it is the fire of the mountains and the caves of the dragons. From the mines in these peaks was brought forth the first ithilmar. Caledor Dragontamer took this wondrous metal to the smiths of Vaul and bade them to forge a blade and a shield and armour for Aenarion.'

'And the other weapons too?' said the boy.

'Later, yes,' said Imrik. 'The first were for Aenarion, who had passed through the flame of Asuryan and been reborn. Next, Caledor gave instruction for the making of his staff, wrought of gold and silver and iron. For his son Menieth, my father, a sword was forged upon the smith god's anvil.'

Imrik drew his sword from its sheath. The blade glittered with inlaid ithilmar, wrought into runes of sharpness and death. In Imrik's hand it weighed no more than a feather, and so keen was its edge, the lightly falling snow could not settle upon it.

'This is the wrathbringer, Lathrain,' said Imrik. He crouched and took Tythanir's hand and wrapped it about the worn hilt, so that the two of them held the sword together. 'To your uncle, Caledrian, your grandfather gave the kingdom. To your other uncle, Dorien, he gifted the standard of Caledor. To me he gave this blade. He died with this weapon in his hands. To wield it is the greatest honour in Caledor, but to bear it is to carry the honour of the kingdom also.'

'How many daemons did grandfather slay?' asked Tythanir, eyes wide with excitement.

'Countless,' replied Imrik.

'What about orcs, and beastmen?'

'Beyond number,' said Imrik.

The child looked at the sword with amazement. He reached a finger towards the blade but Imrik stopped him.

'The edge need never be sharpened,' said the prince. 'Watch.'

Imrik took the sword in his fist and stood up. He pointed to an outcrop of rock, dusted with snow. With an effortless swing, Lathrain sheared off the top, sending it tumbling down the slope. Tythanir laughed at the demonstration.

'Cut something else!' the boy cried out.

'No,' replied Imrik, sheathing the blade. 'It is not a toy.'

Tythanir's lip trembled and his eyes filled with tears.

'I want to see you cut something else,' he said, his voice breaking with sadness.

'One day it will be yours, and you will understand why it is no plaything,' Imrik said, pulling the boy close to embrace him.

'But...' the child started, but Imrik's unflinching stare ended the protestation as it began.

'It is not right to argue,' said Imrik. 'Your mother is too indulgent.'

The boy scuffed his feet and pouted as they walked hand in hand back down the path. It pulled at Imrik's heart to see his son so crestfallen, but he could think of nothing that would ease Tythanir's childish disappointment.

It reminded Imrik of the long days of his own youth, when his father had been away. He had studied diligently, eager to show his father how much he had learnt when Menieth infrequently returned. Great was his father's praise on those occasions, but always paired with a reminder to Imrik of his duties as a prince of Caledor. Imrik remembered how his father would tell him that though Caledrian was the heir, Imrik was the strongest of the three brothers. When Caledrian ruled, Imrik would have to be the protector of the family.

Such thoughts brought Imrik to his happiest memory and he smiled at the recollection. He tugged at Tythanir's hand to get the boy's attention. Tythanir looked up with a scowl, so deep it could have been Imrik's own, and the prince could not help but laugh. This only served to annoy Tythanir further, but as he pulled to get away, Imrik gently dragged him back.

'Would you like to see the dragons?' he asked, and received a wordless shout of excitement in reply, all thoughts of magical swords gone from the boy's mind.

─◄ THREE ►─

The Flames are Fanned

To visit the dragon lairs was no simple expedition, and Imrik was forced to wait until the spring on the vehement instructions of his wife. Tythanir was excited for the whole winter, asking his father every day if they were going to see the dragons. Such was his anticipation, the boy handled every disappointing reply with forced dignity, fearful that the offer would be withdrawn altogether if he made too much of a fuss.

Though Imrik tried to avoid all news of wider Ulthuan, he could not help but hear of the travails from the other kingdoms from his family and other nobles. The cults had risen up against the princes, burning and murdering and bringing anarchy to many towns and cities. Even in Tor Anroc, cults were found, but still the kingdom of Caledor was free from the presence of the cytharai-worshippers.

When the first sun of spring finally touched Anul Caled above the city, Imrik announced that the weather was fair enough to set out for the dragon caves. Though he did not know it, another expedition was setting forth at the same time; Prince Malekith's army marched across the Annulii, destined for the Naggarothi capital of Anlec and a confrontation with his mother.

Dorien and Thyrinor joined Imrik's family on the journey, along with several other nobles whose sons had yet to see the dragons of their homeland. To witness the creatures in their lairs was a birthright and a privilege known only to the Caledorian nobility, and so it was unsurprising that there was much ceremony and celebration surrounding the trip.

It took five days for the caravan to wind its way up to the higher passes of the mountains; a journey a dragon could fly in a day, Imrik thought wistfully as his carriage bumped and rolled over the uneven road. Dozens of wagons carried the families and their servants, each flying the green and red flag of Caledor.

Each morning the children woke with the dawn, gazing hopefully into the cloudy skies for their first sight of a dragon, yet nothing larger than a bird of prey was to be seen. The clouds grew heavier, joined by the fumes and vapours of the volcanoes. The rocks were dark grey and the caravan traversed ancient lava flows, heading higher still.

By late afternoon on the fifth day, they came to the Vale of the Drake, a bleak gorge nestling within the Dragon Spine Mountains. Hundreds of cave entrances broke the slopes like gaping mouths; from many, wisps of steam and smoke curled lazily into the valley.

They left the horses and wagons and went on foot, Dorien carrying a long instrument made from a dragon's horn tipped and rimmed with gold. The princes and their young charges stopped upon a lifeless mound of shining rock in the middle of the vale.

Dorien lifted the dragon horn to his lips and blew a single bass note that echoed for a long time.

'Will the dragons come?' asked Tythanir.

'Hush,' said Thyrinor. 'Listen.'

All stood in silent expectation, the children straining to hear so hard that some of them stood on tiptoe.

'Blow it again, uncle,' said Tythanir.

'Quiet,' snapped Imrik. 'Patience.'

It seemed as if the horn blast continued to reverberate from the cave mouths, long after any natural echoes would have died away. Yet rather than diminishing, the sound grew in strength. All turned left and right, trying to pinpoint the source of the noise. It seemed to issue from every cavern at once.

'There!' hissed Dorien, pointing behind them and to the left.

There was the faintest flicker of light in the smog that crept from the cave, as of distant fire. To the keen ears of the elves came the sound of scratching, as of monstrous talons scraping rock and scales sliding against stone. The answering call to the horn continued, dipping and rising. Imrik's skin prickled at the sound, even though he knew its cause; the breath of a dragon rebounding strangely along the maze of tunnels that riddled the mountains.

Closer and closer came the sound, and brighter and brighter glowed the light. It was a trick of the featureless gorge that the caves seemed small, for Imrik had walked them and knew some to be large enough for a ship to pass into.

With a billowing of fumes, something immense launched itself from the cave entrance; broad wings unfurling to catch the thermals of its own fire, a red dragon soared into the sky. A few of the children shrieked at the sight, but most stood dumbfounded; Imrik remembered his own silent awe and terror when he had stood on this same spot with his father.

As the dragon circled above, Imrik knew it immediately to be his own mount.

'You are fortunate,' he told Tythanir and the others. 'This is Maedrethnir, the oldest of the dragons to remain awake. It is a great honour to meet him. Be sure to show proper respect.'

Necks craning to watch the dragon above, children and adults followed Maedrethnir's progress as his shadow flitted across the mountainsides and disappeared as he rose into the clouds. There were some sighs of disappointment, but Imrik smiled, knowing what to expect. The old dragon was showing off, just as he had done the first time Imrik had seen him.

The whispers from the children turned to gasps as the clouds above the valley began to roil across the sky, lit from within by patches of orange. As the fumes and vapours swirled, a dark shape blurred through the air at their heart. The glow deepened, becoming a blood red that grew more intense with each heartbeat.

Maedrethnir burst from the clouds like a meteor, wreathed in flame and smoke, plunging straight at the elves. At first the children laughed with delight. A piercing cry split the air, building in volume as the dragon continued to dive. The giggles died away and Imrik felt Tythanir slip his hand into his father's, grip tightening as the dragon roared closer and closer.

There were some wails of panic from the youngest children, and anxious murmuring from the others. Down plunged Maedrethnir, flames licking along his body and wings, trailing spirals of black smog. Imrik felt his son tug at his hand and heard him urge his father to move. The prince held Tythanir to the spot. The pulling grew more insistent with every moment, Maedrethnir a comet of flame and scale and claw hurtling towards the barren mound.

Just as the children's screams cut the cold air, the dragon snapped open his wings, soaring over the group so low his wings almost brushed the ground.

The blast of wind knocked the smallest to the ground, Tythanir left dangling in his father's grasp as Imrik's hair and cloak swirled and the air raged around him, reverberating with a crack as the dragon flapped his wings once and climbed away.

Imrik could feel his son trembling and turned, helping him back to his feet. For a moment, tears glistened in Tythanir's eyes, his whole body shaking, his lips bloodied from being bitten.

Recovering from the shock the children's laughter came again, tinged with a mania of relief and joined with the deeper chuckles of their fathers. Above, Maedrethnir tipped a wing and turned sharply, descending to land a short distance away, rock shards sent flying as his claws scraped across the mound.

'A fine display!' Dorien called out. He looked at the young elves, who stood with wide-eyed awe, staring at the dragon just a stone's throw away. 'We thought it time you met the future lords of Caledor.'

Introductions were made, each child brought forwards to bow before Mae-drethnir. As he greeted each, the dragon's breath ruffled hair, causing some to laugh while others retreated quickly, still struck dumb by the experience.

Lastly, Tythanir was presented.

'The line of Caledor himself,' said Imrik. 'My son, Tythanir.'

The boy stepped towards the dragon and placed his hands on his hips defiantly. He stared up into the monstrous face of Maedrethnir, his scowling countenance reflected in the dragon's large eyes.

'That was a very bad thing to do,' scolded Tythanir. 'You frightened every-body. You should say sorry!'

Maedrethnir drew back and looked at Imrik, head cocked to one side in surprise.

'That is no way to pay respect,' snapped Imrik.

'This old creature should bow to us,' said Tythanir. 'Caledor was the Drag-ontamer. We are their masters.'

'You are wrong, boy,' said Dorien. 'Though Caledor first tamed the wild dragons, they are now our trusted allies. They are the source of our king-dom's power and you will show them respect.'

'Bow and say you are sorry,' said Imrik.

'What if I don't?' replied Tythanir.

'I will crush you,' said Maedrethnir, lunging at the boy, one clawed foot held above Tythanir's head. The boy flinched only a little, and despite his annoyance at Tythanir's ill manners, Imrik felt some respect for the young elf standing his ground against the dragon.

'That would be silly,' said Tythanir. 'You are not going to crush me.'

Maedrethnir hesitated and looked at Imrik again, unsure what to do.

'If you do not bow, you will be punished,' said Imrik.

'But it's not fair,' said Tythanir, crossing his arms as he turned to his father. 'I am a dragon prince!'

'You have had good warning,' said Imrik. He nodded to Maedrethnir.

The dragon swung its tail, the tip cracking against Tythanir's backside with just enough force to propel him to the ground. A wail erupted from the boy as he clutched his hands to the offended area.

'His mother will hear of this,' Dorien whispered in Imrik's ear. 'She will not take it kindly.'

'She can take it whichever way she wants,' Imrik replied. 'The boy was rude and he was punished. She spoils him sometimes.'

'Have you learnt the lesson, young elf?' said Maedrethnir, raising the tip of his tail threateningly.

'Yes,' sobbed Tythanir as his father helped the boy to his feet and turned him towards the dragon. He bobbed a quick bow. 'I am sorry.'

'Apology accepted,' said the dragon, lowering his tail.

The boy stepped back and sheltered behind his father, eyeing the dragon carefully.

'Are any of your kin willing to join us?' asked Thyrinor. 'We are honoured by your presence but would like to introduce the young ones to some of the others.'

'They do not wish to be disturbed,' replied Maedrethnir. 'They sleep and will not rouse for infants, even the sons of Caledor's greatest.'

'A shame,' said Imrik. 'It has been a long while since you have graced us in number.'

'And perhaps we will never again,' said the dragon. It was impossible to tell Maedrethnir's thoughts from his reptilian expression but Imrik thought he detected a note of resignation in his words. 'For a long time we have concerned ourselves with the lives of elves, but our interest is dwindling. The peace of slumber beckons strongly.'

'We will not disturb you longer,' said Dorien, bowing to Maedrethnir. 'Pass our regards to your kin.'

Maedrethnir lowered his head on his long neck and looked at each of the children in turn, baring fangs as long as each was tall.

'Learn your lessons well, and pay due respect,' said the dragon. 'If you do, one day you may be worthy of riding upon the back of one of my brothers or sisters.'

There were nods and solemn promises from the boys. With a growl of contentment, Maedrethnir backed away across the mound and launched into the air. He flew a few loops, gouting fire, before gliding back into the cave from which he had emerged.

Imrik sent Tythanir to the others and gestured for Dorien to join him.

'You look concerned, brother,' said Dorien.

'I think Maedrethnir lied,' said Imrik. 'I fear he is the last of the dragons awake.'

'Let us hope not,' replied Dorien. 'It is the dread of the dragons that keeps Caledor safe. If it was known that the power of the mountains is spent, it would go ill for our kingdom.'

'Yes it would,' said Imrik, heart heavy. 'Say nothing of this, not even to Caledrian. He does not need any other worries at the moment.'

'As you say, brother,' said Dorien. 'The day when the dragon princes cannot fly forth will be the day the kingdom falls.'

'Not while I live,' growled Imrik. He patted the sword at his waist. 'The dragons are not our only weapons.'

A FEW DAYS after he had returned to Tor Caled, Imrik was called to the great hall of the palace by Caledrian. He arrived to find his brothers and cousin already waiting for him, along with several others of the city's princes.

Imrik's eye was drawn to a falcon perched on the back of his brother's throne, as placid as a songbird. Caledrian held something in his hand and there was a small velvet bag cast upon the seat of the throne.

'Your message seemed urgent,' said Imrik as he strode along the hall. 'What do you have there?'

'I thought it best if we saw this together,' said Caledrian. 'It was sent by Thyriol of Saphery.'

Caledrian opened his palm to reveal a shining yellow crystal, a small rune etched into each of its many faces. The prince held out his hand, the crystal resting upon it, and read a short incantation from the note that had accompanied it. Imrik felt the flutter of magic in the air, emanating from the stone.

The light of the crystal brightened, growing to a golden shimmer that dappled the floor, walls and ceiling of the hall. Like sunlight streaming through a window, the gleam rippled and moved, darker shapes forming within it. Imrik could sense the magic on his flesh even as the light touched upon his eyes. He noticed the light cast no shadow in the chamber.

A figure resolved from the shifting light, a wavering image of Thyriol standing with arms folded, hands tucked into the sleeves of his robe. Details of the scene behind him could be just about discerned; marching troops and a high tower that disappeared into vagueness. The ghostly figure stared straight ahead, looking at a nondescript stretch of wall behind Caledrian.

'Felicitations, princes,' said the image, the voice seeming to originate in the air itself, leaving no echo. 'I have sped these tidings to you for I have important news from the north. Prince Malekith has assaulted Anlec and been victorious. He has taken Morathi prisoner and reclaimed the rule of Nagarythe.'

The apparition paused and looked away for a moment. He seemed to mutter something and then returned his attention ahead.

'We are keeping the capture of Morathi secret, lest her followers attempt some attack to rescue her,' the mage continued. 'With a small guard, Malekith escorts his mother to Tor Anroc to face the justice of the Phoenix King. Given the grievances of many against her, Malekith has extended invitation to each kingdom to send a single representative to Bel Shanaar's court to learn of the Phoenix King's judgement. Ride swiftly.'

The image wavered and vanished, leaving a faintest glow for a moment within the crystal before that also disappeared. Caledrian closed his fist around it.

'Malekith invites us to Tor Anroc?' Thyrinor was the first to speak, incredulity raising the pitch of his voice. 'He acts if he were Phoenix King, not Bel Shanaar.'

'Malekith has equal accusations to answer,' said Dorien. 'His neglect of his kingdom for fifty years has brought misery to many.'

'I will go,' said Imrik.

'You offer?' said Caledrian, unable to hide his surprise. 'You assume I will ask.'

'You would,' said Imrik, sighing at the inevitability. 'Deny it.'

Caledrian looked embarrassed for a moment and then nodded.

'I cannot,' he said. 'Malekith will ask for clemency for his mother. You must ensure Morathi does not receive it.'

'I will,' said Imrik. 'There is blood on her hands.'

THE PALACE OF Tor Anroc had continued to expand even in the short time since Imrik had last visited. No doubt helped by the gifts of grateful princes, Bel Shanaar had lavishly furnished his chambers. White gold was inlaid on the flags of the floor and no fewer than six hundred tapestries covered the walls of the hall above the benches, each picturing a scene from Ulthuan and lands across the world. It irked Imrik to recognise many from his own conquests, hanging in the palace of an elf that had not lifted a sword to claim the places depicted. From silver chains hanging from the ceiling the chamber was illuminated by dozens of lanterns of dwarfish design, each a subtly different hue of pale yellow.

Bel Shanaar sat on his throne, with Bathinair, Elodhir, Finudel and Charill of Chrace in attendance. Unseen but close at hand, Thyriol stood ready to counter any enchantments Morathi might cast. The princes of the other realms had refused to come, fearing that despite Bel Shanaar's precautions the Queen of Nagarythe would still unleash some last spiteful act rather than face her judgement. Imrik stood with the other princes, waiting for Malekith to make his appearance. There was no conversation, and no audience had been allowed onto the benches.

The Caledorian could feel the trepidation of the others, but even his grave misgivings did not extend so far as to believe this was some trap to ensnare them. Over the past decades, Morathi had been given plenty of opportunity to see the Phoenix King if she planned any physical malice towards him.

The doors opened and all turned their gaze down the hall. Malekith entered with long strides, still clad in his golden armour, a hooded figure cloaked in black following a step behind.

'My king and princes,' said the Naggarothi ruler. 'Today is a portentous occasion, for as I vowed, I bring before you the Witch Queen of Nagarythe, my mother, Morathi.'

Morathi cast off her cloak and stood before her judges. She was dressed in a flowing blue gown, her hair bound up with shining sapphires, her eyelids painted with azure powder. She appeared every inch the defeated queen, dejected but unrepentant.

'You stand before us accused of raising war against the office of the Phoenix King and the realms of the princes of Ulthuan,' Bel Shanaar said.

'It was not I that launched attacks against the border of Nagarythe,' Morathi replied calmly. Her gaze met the eyes of the princes in turn. Imrik studied the others: Bathinair met her stare coolly, Elodhir flinched, while Finudel and Charill looked away in discomfort. Imrik stared back, making no attempt to hide his distaste. 'It was not the Naggarothi who sought battle with the other kingdoms.'

'You would portray yourself as the victim?' laughed Finudel. 'To us?'

'No ruler of Nagarythe is a victim,' replied Morathi.

'Do you deny that the cults of excess and luxury that blight our realm owe their loyalty to you?' said Bel Shanaar.

'They owe their loyalty to the cytharai,' said Morathi. 'You can no more prosecute me for the existence of the cults than you can impeach yourself for assuming the mantle of Asuryan's chosen.'

'Will you at least admit to thoughts of treason?' said Elodhir. 'Did you not plot against my father and seek to undermine him?'

'I hold no position in higher regard than that of the Phoenix King,' Morathi said, her eyes fixed upon Bel Shanaar. 'I spoke my mind at the First Council and others chose to ignore my wisdom. My loyalty is to Ulthuan and the prosperity and strength of her people. I do not change my opinions on a whim and my reservations have not been allayed.'

'She is a viper,' snarled Imrik, revolted by her professed innocence. 'She cannot be allowed to live.'

Morathi laughed, a scornful sound that reverberated menacingly around the hall.

'Who wishes to be known as the elf who slew Aenarion's queen?' the seeress said. 'Which of the mighty princes gathered here would claim that accolade?'

'I will,' said Imrik, his hand straying to the silver hilt of Lathrain at his waist.

'I cannot condone this,' said Malekith, stepping protectively in front of his mother.

Imrik tensed, but stayed his hand. He watched Malekith intently, alert for any violence.

'You swore to me in this very chamber that you would be ready for such an end,' said Bel Shanaar. 'Now you renege on your oath?'

'No more than I renege on the oath that I would show mercy to all those who asked for it,' said Malekith. 'My mother need not die. Her blood would serve no purpose but to sate the Caledorian's vengeful thirst.'

'It is justice, not revenge,' said Imrik. He was reminded of Carathril's tale of the mass suicide of Aeltherin's cult. 'Blood for blood.'

'If she lives, she is a threat,' said Finudel. 'She cannot be trusted.'

'I cannot decide this,' said Malekith, addressing the princes. He then turned his eyes upon the Phoenix King. 'I will not decide this. Let Bel Shanaar decide. The will of the Phoenix King is stronger than the oath of a prince. Is the word of the son of Aenarion to be as nothing, or is there yet nobility enough in the princes of Ulthuan to show compassion and forgiveness?'

Bel Shanaar gave Malekith a sour look, knowing that all that had passed here would be reported by means both open and secret to the people of Ulthuan. Imrik thought that to let Morathi live would be weakness, but he remained silent. He had voiced his opinion on the matter, but the decision rested with the Phoenix King.

'Morathi cannot go unpunished for her crimes,' Bel Shanaar said slowly. 'There is no place to which I can exile her, for she would return more bitter and ambitious than before. As she enslaved others, so shall she forfeit her freedom. She shall stay in rooms within this palace, under guard night and day. None shall see her save with my permission.'

The Phoenix King stood and glared at the sorceress.

'Know this, Morathi,' said Bel Shanaar. 'The sentence of death is not wholly commuted. You live by my will. If ever you cross me or seek to harm my rule, you will be slain, without trial or representation. Your word is of no value and so I hold your life hostage to your good behaviour. Accept these terms or accept your death.'

Morathi looked at the gathered princes and saw nothing but hatred in their faces, save for Malekith's which was expressionless. Imrik sneered at her glance, wishing to be away from her presence. Even now the stench of sorcery hung about the former queen,

'Your demands are not unreasonable, Bel Shanaar of Tiranoc,' she said eventually. 'I consent to be your prisoner.'

FOLLOWING THE IMPRISONMENT of Morathi, a measure of peace was restored. With Malekith again in control of Nagarythe and the support of the pleasure cults curtailed the unrest and violence that had marred Ulthuan subsided. As he had wished, Imrik spent the years in Tor Caled with his wife and son, watching Tythanir grow to become a proud and able youth. The time did not heal the growing estrangement between Imrik and Anatheria; it appeared that as much as she had chastised her husband for his long absences, his continued presence was just as demanding for her.

Despite this, Imrik was content, if not altogether happy. After a life of war and duty, he could not relax wholly and would often visit Maedrethnir to speak of old battles and conquests. The ancient dragon confirmed what Imrik had suspected; the others of his kind were unwilling to leave their lairs and soon he too would join them in the long sleep.

Imrik also found time to travel, to see parts of Ulthuan he had not visited since his childhood. Thyriol hosted Imrik and his family for a season in the floating city of Saphethion. Over a summer, Imrik was the guest of Prince Charill in mountainous Chrace, where he hunted the wild monsters of the Annulii with his distant cousin, Koradrel. The two became friends, Koradrel happy with Imrik's quiet nature and of a taciturn disposition himself.

Throughout, Imrik set about to distract himself from the long pass of days, and came to understand, if not sympathise with, the malaise of boredom that had drawn so many to the cults of the undergods. He even considered returning to the colonies, but on sending letters to his allies in Elthin Arvan learned that there was little challenge remaining for one of his skills.

After more than two decades, the harmony of Ulthuan was shattered again.

— FOUR —

The Council of Princes

'MALEKITH HAS BEEN ousted from power.'

Imrik could scarcely believe the messenger sent by Bel Shanaar. The Tiranocii stood patiently in the great hall of Tor Caled, addressing Caledrian and his brothers.

'Bel Shanaar knows this as a fact?' said Dorien.

'Even now, Malekith has fled Nagarythe with a body of loyal warriors and takes sanctuary in Tor Anroc,' said the herald. 'Some believe the architect of this rebellion to be Eoloran Anar, a dissident who lives in the mountains in the east of Nagarythe.'

'Impossible,' said Imrik. 'All should know Eoloran Anar, standard bearer of Aenarion. His loyalty to Ulthuan is beyond question. Bel Shanaar knows him as an ally.'

'Which is why the Phoenix King does not pay heed to these rumours,' the messenger replied smoothly.

'Though this is distressing, I cannot see how this involves my kingdom,' said Caledrian. 'Have we not been here before, and did not Malekith resolve the situation for himself?'

'With this coup there has been resurgence in the activity of the cults,' said the herald. 'There are riots and burning in cities across Ulthuan. Several princes and lesser nobles have been murdered or taken hostage.'

'They have bided their time,' said Imrik. 'They waited for the others to become lax.'

'It seems so,' said the herald. 'The Phoenix King wishes this renewed unrest to be dealt with swiftly. The proposal to form a united army under his banner will be revisited. However, this time there will be no delays. All princes are instructed to gather at the Shrine of Asuryan on the Isle of the Flame, to appoint the commander of this army. You are to set out at once.'

'Not I,' said Imrik, looking at Caledrian. His brother opened his mouth to speak but Imrik talked across him. 'I have been invited to Chrace by Koradrel and I will go. You have avoided the other princes for too long.'

Caledrian looked as if he would argue, but Imrik glared at his brother to forestall any complaint. The ruler of Caledor reluctantly nodded and turned to Thyrinor.

'I will go to the Isle of the Flame to attend this council, and you will attend me,' he said.

'I have no objection,' said Thyrinor. 'I have never seen inside the Shrine of Asuryan. It will be a privilege to gaze upon the sacred flame that blessed Aenarion.'

'I leave tomorrow,' said Imrik. 'We can ride together to the coast. I will take ship to the north and you to the east.'

'We will send word of the proceedings,' said Caledrian.

'Please do not,' replied Imrik. 'I am not interested. History simply repeats itself. I will be in the mountains.'

Caledrian frowned at this news.

'But should I need your aid, what will I do?' he said. 'No messenger will find you.'

'That is my intent,' said Imrik. 'You will have to deal with this, brother. I cannot help you.'

Arrangements were made with Bel Shanaar's herald, who departed that evening with Caledrian's acceptance of his position at the council. Imrik spent the night with his family, promising Tythanir the head of a hydra as a gift on his return. In the morning, he left the city with Caledrian and Thyrinor, pleased to have avoided embroilment in further intrigue that did not concern him.

THE CHATTER AROUND the horseshoe of tables and chairs in the shrine was of the delay in the arrival of Bel Shanaar and Malekith. Elodhir had arrived from Tor Anroc with the news that his father and the prince of Nagarythe would follow shortly, but even the heir to Tiranoc's throne was now perturbed by their failure to arrive.

'What if the cultists know something of what they plan?' Elodhir said to Thyrinor.

The two of them stood by a table near to the entrance to the pyramidal shrine, the multicoloured pillar of fire known as the flame of Asuryan burning at the centre of the temple. Other princes and their aides had seated themselves in preparation for the council, as they had done several times over the last few days. Seated directly in front of the sacred flames was the high priest Mianderin, his staff of office held across his lap. Other priests moved around the tables filling goblets with wine or water, and offering fruits and confectioneries.

'I would not fear,' Thyrinor said as soothingly as possible. 'Your father is the Phoenix King, and Prince Malekith the most accomplished warrior in Ulthuan. It is most likely fresh information from Nagarythe that delays them.'

'You are right,' said Elodhir. He was about to return to his seat when a young priest entered the shrine.

'A ship bearing the flag of Tiranoc draws in to the wharf,' the elf announced before taking position with his fellows along the white stone walls.

There was a hubbub of discussion and Thyrinor joined Caledrian at the seats and table set aside for the Caledorian representatives.

'About time,' said Caledrian. 'It is probably for the best that Imrik did not come. These delays would have frustrated him to the verge of violence, I suspect.'

'And I expect much wrangling to be the business of the next few days,' replied Thyrinor. 'My cousin's absence has been remarked upon several times. There are those who think he should be here to receive the nomination as general.'

'He made his opinion clear on that before,' said Caledrian. 'If he wishes to have no association with this campaign, I cannot blame him and will respect his wishes. Caledor has taken much from him already.'

'Dorien and I spent almost as much time fighting in the colonies,' said Thyrinor.

Caledrian smiled and patted his cousin reassuringly on the arm.

'And it is remembered,' said the prince. 'Yet it was Imrik my father named as the sword bearer of Caledor, and that is a weighty burden to bear.'

The two of them fell silent as new figures appeared at the shrine door.

Malekith entered and walked behind the table reserved for Bel Shanaar, earning himself frowns from Mianderin and a few of the princes. Thyrinor felt Caledrian's grip on his arm tighten. Something was amiss; Thyrinor had felt it from the moment Malekith had appeared. The Naggarothi prince was flanked by two knights who carried wrapped bundles in their hands. Malekith stood leaning on the table with gauntleted fists, and stared balefully at the assembled council.

'Weakness prevails,' spat the prince of Nagarythe. Thyrinor shuddered at the venom in Malekith's voice. 'Weakness grips this island like a child squeezing the juices from an over-ripened fruit. Selfishness has driven us to inaction, and now the time to act may have passed. Complacency rules where princes should lead. You have allowed the cults of depravity to flourish, and done nothing. You have looked to foreign shores and counted your gold, and allowed thieves to sneak into your towns and cities to steal away your children. And you have been content to allow a traitor to wear the Phoenix Crown!'

With this last declaration there were gasps and shouts of horror from the princes. Malekith's knights opened their bundles and tossed the contents upon the table: the crown and feathered cloak of Bel Shanaar.

Elodhir leapt to his feet, fist raised.

'Where is my father?' he demanded.

'What has happened to the Phoenix King?' cried Finudel.

'He is dead!' snarled Malekith. 'Killed by his weakness of spirit.'

Panic choked Thyrinor, his throat tightening against the shout of dismay that rose from him. He looked to Caledrian, whose face had paled, jaw and fists clenched tightly.

'That cannot be so!' exclaimed Elodhir, his voice strangled and fraught with anger.

'It is,' said Malekith with a sigh, his demeanour suddenly one of sorrow. 'I promised to root out this vileness, and was shocked to find that my mother was one of its chief architects. From that moment on, I decided none would be above suspicion. If Nagarythe had become so polluted, so too perhaps had Tiranoc. My arrival here was delayed by investigations, when it was brought to my attention that those close to the Phoenix King might be under the sway of the hedonists. My inquiries were circumspect but thorough, and imagine my disappointment, nay disbelief, when I uncovered evidence that implicated the Phoenix King himself.'

'What evidence?' demanded Elodhir.

'Certain talismans and fetishes found in the Phoenix King's chambers,' said Malekith calmly. 'Believe me when I say that I felt as you did. I could not bring myself to think that Bel Shanaar, our wisest prince chosen to rule by members of this council, would be brought so low. Not one to act rashly, I decided to confront Bel Shanaar with this evidence, in the hope that there was some misunderstanding or trickery involved.'

'And he denied it of course?' asked Bathinair.

Thyrinor could not comprehend what he was hearing. He moved to rise to his feet, but Caledrian pushed him back to his chair.

'Watch the knights,' Caledrian hissed in his ear.

Thyrinor turned his attention to the black-clad knights of Anlec, who had stepped back and now filled the doorway with their armoured forms, dark eyes glaring from the visors of their high helms, arms crossed over their carved breastplates.

'He admitted guilt by his deeds,' explained Malekith. 'It seems that a few of my company were tainted by this affliction and in league with the usurpers of Nagarythe. Even as I confided in them, they warned Bel Shanaar of my discoveries. That night, no more than seven nights ago, I went to his chambers to make my accusations face-to-face. I found him dead, his lips stained with poison. He had taken the coward's way and ended his own life rather than suffer the shame of inquiry. By his own hand he denied us insight into the plans of the cults. Fearing that he would not keep their secrets to himself, he took them to his grave.'

'My father would do no such thing, he is loyal to Ulthuan and its people!' shouted Elodhir.

Thyrinor was in agreement, but a glance at his cousin showed that Caledrian was not paying attention to Malekith, his eyes instead roving across the other princes, gauging their reactions.

'Bathinair is with Malekith,' Caledrian whispered, quietly pushing his chair away from the table.

'What do you mean?' Thyrinor whispered back, but received no reply.

'I confess to having deep sympathy with you, Elodhir,' Malekith was saying. 'Have I not been deceived by my own mother? Do I not feel the same betrayal and heartache that now wrenches at your spirit?'

'I must admit I also find this somewhat perturbing,' said Thyriol. 'It seems... convenient.'

'And so, in death, Bel Shanaar continues to divide us, as was his intent,' countered Malekith. 'Discord and anarchy will reign as we argue back and forth the rights and wrongs of what has occurred. While we debate endlessly, the cults will grow in power and seize your lands from under your noses, and we will have lost everything. They are united, while we are divided. There is no time for contemplation, or reflection, there is only time for action.'

'What would you have us do?' asked Chyllion, one of the princes of Cothique.

'We must choose a new Phoenix King!' declared Bathinair before Malekith could answer.

Voices erupted across the shrine and princes stood up, gesturing madly at one another. Malekith watched the tumult without emotion. Thyrinor followed his gaze, which was fixed upon the sacred flame.

'I really wish Imrik was here,' Thyrinor admitted.

'Cease this noise!' roared Caledrian, getting to his feet. 'Be calm!'

His shout stilled the shrine.

'We will not find the truth with this anarchy,' Caledrian continued in quieter tones.

'Does Caledrian put himself forward for the Phoenix Throne?' said Bathinair.

The prince of Caledor was stunned by the suggestion.

'I have no such ambition,' he said, looking pointedly at Malekith. 'Yet if there are others here who would stake such a claim, it should be made plain and we should consider it.'

'Is that your intent?' asked Thyriol with a glance at the other princes.

'If the council wishes it,' Malekith said with a shrug.

'We cannot choose a new Phoenix King now,' said Elodhir. 'Such a matter cannot be resolved quickly, and even if such a thing were possible, we are not our full number.'

'Nagarythe will not wait,' said Malekith, slamming his fist onto the table. 'The cults are too strong and come spring they will control the army of Anlec. My lands will be lost and they will march upon yours!'

'You would have us choose you to lead us?' said Thyriol quietly.

'Yes,' Malekith replied without hesitation or embarrassment. 'There are none here who were willing to act until my return. I am the son of Aenarion, his chosen heir, and if the revelation of Bel Shanaar's treachery is not enough to convince you of the foolishness of choosing from another line, then look to my other achievements. Bel Shanaar chose me to act as his ambassador to the dwarfs, for I was a close friend with their High King.

'Our future lies not solely upon these shores, but in the wider world. I have been to the colonies across the oceans, and fought to build and protect them. Though they come from the bloodstock of Lothern or Tor Elyr or Tor Anroc, they are a new people, and it is to me they first look now, not to you. None here are as experienced in war as am I. Bel Shanaar was a ruler steeped in wisdom and peace, for all that he has failed us at the last, but peace and wisdom will not prevail against darkness and zealotry.'

'What of Imrik?' suggested Finudel. 'He is every bit the general and fought out in the new world also.'

'Imrik?' said Malekith, his voice dripping with scorn. 'Where is Imrik now, in this time of our greatest need? He skulks in Chrace with his cousin, hunting monsters! Would you have Ulthuan ruled by an elf who hides in the mountains like a petulant, spoilt child? When Imrik called for an army to be gathered against Nagarythe, did you pay him heed? No! Only when I raised the banner did you fall over each other in your enthusiasm.'

Thyrinor was so incensed by the accusation, words failed him. Before he could speak, another prince was making his voice heard.

'Be careful of what you say, your arrogance does you a disservice,' warned Haradrin.

'I say these things not as barbs to your pride,' explained Malekith, unclenching his fists and sitting down. 'I say them to show you what you already know; in your hearts you would gratefully follow where I lead.'

'I still say that this council cannot make such an important decision on a whim,' said Elodhir. 'My father lies dead, in circumstances yet to be fully explained, and you would have us hand over the Phoenix Crown to you?'

'He has a point, Malekith,' said Haradrin.

'A point?' screamed Malekith as he surged to his feet, knocking over the table and sending the cloak and crown upon it flying through the air. 'A point? Your dithering will see you all cast out, your families enslaved and your people burning upon ten thousand pyres! It has been more than a thousand years since I bent my knee to this council's first, wayward decision and saw Bel Shanaar take what Aenarion had promised to me. For a thousand years, I have been content to watch your families grow and prosper, and squabble amongst yourselves like children, while I and my kin bled on battlefields on the other side of the world. I trusted you all to remember the legacy of my father, and ignored the cries of anguish that rang in my blood; for it was in the interest of all that we were united. Now it is time to unite behind me! I do not lie to you, I shall be a harsh ruler at times, but I will reward those who serve me well, and when peace reigns again we shall all enjoy the spoils of our battles. Who here has more right to the throne than I do? Who here–'

'Malekith!' barked Mianderin, pointing towards the prince's waist. In his tirade, Malekith's waving arms had thrown his cloak back over his shoulder. 'Why do you wear your sword in this holy place? It is forbidden in the most ancient laws of this temple. Remove it at once.'

Thyrinor felt Caledrian tense next to him. Remembering his cousin's words, the dragon prince moved his gaze to the Anlec knights. They too had weapons at their hips, their gauntleted hands upon the hilts.

Malekith stood frozen in place, almost comic with his arms outstretched. He looked down at his belt and the sheathed sword that hung there. He gripped his sword's hilt and drew it free. The Naggarothi prince looked up at the others with eyes narrowed, his face illuminated by magical blue fire from the blade.

'Enough words!' he spat.

Thyrinor sat rigid, transfixed by the glow of fabled Avanuir in Malekith's fist. Caledrian moved behind his chair, grabbing hold of the back in both hands. Thyrinor felt the waves of magic flowing from Malekith's blade, mixing with the mystical draught that poured from the sacred flame, tinged with an aura that now spread from Thyriol.

'You were overlooked before,' said the mage, holding out his hands in a placating gesture. 'I bear in part the responsibility for that choice. Let us do nothing hasty, and consider again our positions.'

'It is my right to be Phoenix King,' growled Malekith. 'It is not yours to give, so I will gladly take it.'

'Traitor!' screamed Elodhir, leaping across the table in front of him, scattering goblets and plates. There was uproar as princes and priests shouted and shrieked.

The knights started forwards and Caledrian leapt to meet the closest, crashing his chair into the Naggarothi's helmed head to send the knight slamming against the wall. Out of instinct, Thyrinor rose to his feet and reached to his belt, but there was no sword there, for all the princes save Malekith had obeyed the strictures of Asuryan.

Elodhir dashed across the shrine, and was halfway upon Malekith when Bathinair intercepted him, sending both of them tumbling down in a welter of robes and rugs. Elodhir punched the Yvressian prince, who reeled back. With a snarl, Bathinair reached into his robes and pulled out a curved blade, no longer than a finger, and slashed at Elodhir. Its blade caught the prince's throat and his lifeblood fountained across the exposed flagstones.

The knight Caledrian had attacked recovered quickly, deflecting the prince's next blow with a raised arm before shoving the Caledorian against a table. In a moment, the knight's sword was in his hand.

Confusion reigned. As Bathinair crouched panting over the body of Elodhir, figures appeared at the archway behind Malekith; more black-armoured knights of Anlec. The priests and princes who had been running for the arch slipped and collided with each other in their haste to stop their flight. The knights had blood-slicked blades in the hands and advanced with sinister purpose.

Thyrinor launched himself at the warrior confronting his cousin, tackling him to the ground. The knight swung an armoured fist, stunning Thyrinor with the blow. He staggered back, vision spinning as the knight surged to his feet and loomed over Caledrian. Past his cousin, he saw the mage, Thyriol, smashed to the ground by an armoured fist while the other princes tried to wrest weapons from the Naggarothi knights.

Malekith walked slowly through the melee as his knights cut and hacked at the princes around him, his eyes never leaving the sacred flame in the centre of the chamber. Screams and howls echoed from the walls. Thyrinor threw himself groggily at the closest knight, grasping hold of his sword arm as it descended, trying to twist the weapon free.

The knight's elbow struck Thyrinor on the chin, sending him sprawling. The distraction gave Caledrian time to recover himself, holding the chair in front of him as a shield. The knight's sword hacked through the chair in a shower of splinters, Caledrian reeling back from the blow.

Out of the melee, Haradrin ran towards Malekith, a captured sword raised above his head. With a contemptuous sneer, the prince of Nagarythe stepped aside from Haradrin's wild swing and thrust his own sword into Haradrin's gut. He stood there a moment, the princes staring deep into each other's eyes, until a trickle of blood spilled from Haradrin's lips and he collapsed to the floor.

Malekith let the sword fall from his fingers with the body rather than wrench it free, and continued his pacing towards the sacred fires.

'Asuryan will not accept you!' cried Mianderin, falling to his knees in front of Malekith, his hands clasped in pleading. 'You have spilt blood in his sacred temple! We have not cast the proper enchantments to protect you from the flames. You cannot do this!'

'So?' spat the prince. 'I am Aenarion's heir. I do not need your witchery to protect me.'

Mianderin snatched at Malekith's hand but the prince tore his fingers from the haruspex's grasp.

'I no longer listen to the protestations of priests,' said Malekith, and kicked Mianderin aside.

As Thyrinor lunged again, the knight turned, sword swinging. The blade's tip scored across Thyrinor's chest and arm, spraying blood. With a wounded cry, Thyrinor fell to the ground, clasping his good hand to the injured limb.

Through the haze of pain, he saw Caledrian seize the knight from behind, wrapping an arm around his throat.

The knight flailed but could not dislodge the Caledorian prince. Thyrinor tried to stand, but his legs gave way and he slumped back to the flagstones. With his other hand, Caledrian wrested the sword from the knight's grip, the weapon clattering to the floor.

A shadow loomed up behind Thyrinor's cousin. He tried to shout a warning, but was too late.

Blood fountained as another knight hacked Caledrian's head from his body with one sweep of his sword. The first knight recovered his weapon and turned on Thyrinor.

Unable to defend himself, he rolled away from the blow, trailing blood, a cry of pain wrenched from his lips. He dived under a table, which shuddered a moment later from an impact. Between armoured legs, Thyrinor glimpsed bloodied bodies on the ground. Entranced by the slaughter, he turned his gaze up and saw Malekith.

His hands held out, palms upwards in supplication, the Naggarothi prince walked forwards and stepped into the flames.

A MOMENT OF silence and stillness engulfed the shrine and every pair of eyes turned to the sacred fire. The flame of Asuryan burned paler and paler, moving from a deep blue to a brilliant white. At its heart could be seen the silhouette of Malekith, his arms still outstretched.

Thyrinor heard a dull rumble, as of thunder, which returned with greater ferocity. The floor trembled beneath him and motes of mortar dust sprinkled down from the ceiling. Pieces of tile pattered onto the table above him and shattered on the flagstones.

With a lurch that flung Thyrinor into a table leg, the ground heaved. Stones erupted across the paved floor, hurling broken fragments. Prince, priest and knight alike were tossed around by the great tumult. Chairs were flung across the floor and tables toppled. Plaster cracked upon the walls and fell in large slabs from the ceiling. Wide cracks tore through the tiles underfoot and a rift three paces wide opened up along the eastern wall, sending up a cloud of dust and rock that choked Thyrinor.

With a thunderous clap, the holy flame blazed, filling the room with white light. Within, Malekith collapsed to his knees and grabbed at his face. He flung back his head and screamed as the flames consumed him; his howl of anguish reverberated around the shrine, echoing and growing in volume with every passing moment.

The pain of that cry pierced Thyrinor's heart, a shrill wail of agony so sickening, so filled with rage and frustration, it twisted his gut and gnawed a path into his mind, where it would dwell forever. The withering figure silhouetted within the flames pushed himself slowly to his feet and hurled himself from their depths.

Malekith's smoking and charred body crashed to the ground, igniting a rug and sending ashen dust billowing. Blackened flesh fell away in lumps amidst cooling droplets of molten armour. He reached outwards with a hand, and then collapsed. His clothes had been burnt away and his flesh eaten down to the bone in places. His face was a mask of black and red, his dark eyes lidless and staring. Steam rose from burst veins as the prince of Nagarythe shuddered and then fell still, laid to ruin by the judgement of Asuryan.

The knights rushed to their prince's aid, while the bloodied and battered princes took what shelter they could as debris continued to fall around them. Lifting up the body of their master, the knights pushed towards the entrance. Several princes tried to bar their escape and were swiftly cut down, their blood spilling onto the dusty flagstones.

Thyrinor staggered out from under the table, and witnessed a scene of stomach-wrenching carnage. Bodies and limbs, of princes and priests, littered the floor. Pools of blood and piles of gore were slick underfoot as he numbly paced around the shrine room looking for survivors.

'So many killed,' he muttered, staring into dead face after dead face.

The princes of Ulthuan were slain. The elite of elven nobility lay dismembered and torn all about Thyrinor and he wept; for what had happened, for what he saw and what he feared would next come to pass.

PART TWO

*The Treachery of Malekith; Race to Chrace;
Imrik Becomes King; The Siege of Lothern;
Avelorn Burns; The War Takes its Toll*

— ◄ FIVE ► —

A King is Chosen

THE INTERIOR OF the shrine was awash with the blood of princes; the walls cracked and broken by the earthquake; the floor littered with debris and bodies. Carathril picked his way through the ruin, a hand over his mouth in horror. The ghastly scene was bathed in a deep red glow from the flame of Asuryan, lending it an even more disturbing sheen.

With a groan, Finudel sat up, pushing aside the armoured body of a Naggarothi knight. His robe was slashed across his right shoulder and blood leaked from a long wound as he staggered to his feet. Carathril dashed to his side and helped him to stand. Finudel looked at Carathril, his eyes glazed and distant, incomprehension written across his features.

'He was the best of us,' murmured Finudel. 'How could he betray us?'

'Who?' asked Carathril, righting a chair with his free hand and lowering the prince onto it. 'Who has betrayed us?'

'Malekith...' Finudel whispered.

A groan attracted Carathril's attention and he left Finudel to search through the morbid pile of corpses, blood slicking his hands and sleeves as he pushed aside the bodies. A hand grabbed at the hem of his robe and Carathril turned to see Thyriol, his face even paler than usual. There was a cut across his forehead and dried blood caked the mage's eyes.

'It is Carathril,' the captain said softly. 'You are safe now.'

'No,' said Thyriol, his voice a hoarse rasp. 'None of us are safe. Malekith will unleash the darkness of Nagarythe upon us all.'

'Malekith is dead,' a voice rang from the far end of the shrine. Carathril

779

glanced up to see Thyrinor, prince of Caledor, where he knelt upon the floor cradling the headless body of his cousin, Caledrian.

'How so?' asked Thyriol, his voice regaining some of its former strength and timbre.

'I saw him step into the sacred flame,' Thyrinor told them. 'Asuryan judged him to be tainted and burnt him alive before casting his body back to us. His knights fled with the remains.'

'I saw them,' said Carathril. 'And Bathinair also.'

'Yes, Bathinair killed Elodhir, with a concealed blade,' said Thyrinor. 'Who can say how long he has been a puppet of Nagarythe?'

They digested this news in silence, until Finudel stirred himself and stood shakily to his feet. He walked hesitantly towards the shrine entrance, one hand gripped to his injured shoulder.

'I thank Asuryan and all gods that Athielle was not here for this butchery,' the Ellyrian said quietly.

'There are too few who were absent,' said Thyriol. 'More than half the ruling princes of Ulthuan lie dead in this chamber. Of those that remain, most are lords of Nagarythe. Malekith's treachery has bitten deep, inflicting a wound from which we might never recover.'

'Malekith may be dead, but Nagarythe remains,' said Thyrinor. 'I fear that Morathi knows full well what her son intended, and even now Nagarythe readies for invasion of the other realms.'

'She will take the death of her son gravely, and will vent her grief and anger upon the rest of us,' said Carathril. 'I see now that the divisions between mother and child were feigned, and that these past months we have been led upon a deadly dance of deception.'

'But there is no one left to lead,' growled Finudel. 'Who will muster the militia? Who will call the spears and bows to war against Nagarythe when the best of our commanders lie dead within this chamber?'

'Perhaps,' said Thyriol. 'Many died here, but there are those alive still that might stand against Nagarythe.'

'You speak of Imrik,' said Thyrinor.

At the mention of the Caledorian prince's name, Carathril remembered a letter entrusted to him by Bel Shanaar. He ran from the temple, leaping nimbly and without second thought over bodies and rubble. He noticed that Malekith's ship had departed, along with the knights and cultists, having hurriedly left their unloaded stores upon the quay. Compelled by nameless worries, Carathril sped between the pavilions of the camp, which were in tumultuous uproar as servants and soldiers dashed about, panicked by the earthquake. He ducked beneath streaming banners and leapt over tent ropes in his haste, dodging effortlessly through the milling throng.

Reaching his tent, Carathril tore aside the door and delved into his pack, seeking the scroll. Pulling it free from its hiding place, he turned back towards the shrine. A warrior in the garb of Eataine recognised him and snatched his arm as Carathril ran past.

'Where is the prince?' the soldier demanded.

Carathril hesitated before replying.

'Prince Haradrin is dead,' he said quietly, lifting the elf's grip from his bloodied sleeve. 'Gather as many soldiers as you can and await my return.'

Carathril ignored the elf's desperate questions and ran back to the shrine, vaulting over the fallen columns in his haste. Entering once more, he saw that several priests had escaped the slaughter, and they were even now tending to the bodies and the devastation, shock and grief scored upon their faces. Thyriol and Finudel were having their wounds bathed and dressed, and Thyrinor picked his way through the fallen princes and their counsellors seeking any still alive. His grim face betrayed his lack of hope in this task.

'What do you have there?' asked Thyriol, as Carathril held up the scroll.

'Perhaps the last wishes of the rightful Phoenix King,' panted Carathril. 'Bel Shanaar entrusted me with this message for Prince Imrik before I left Tor Anroc.'

'Open it,' said Finudel, but Carathril was reluctant.

'Bel Shanaar was adamant that Imrik alone read whatever is contained within,' said Carathril. 'I was to keep it secret from you all.'

'Bel Shanaar has been murdered and Imrik is not here,' said Thyrinor sternly. 'I think it is safe to say that those who have sided with Nagarythe are not here, either, and that we who have survived remain loyal to Ulthuan.'

Though he was not wholly convinced, Carathril relented and broke the wax seal upon the scroll. He read aloud the Phoenix King's letter:

> *To the Esteemed Prince Imrik of Caledor,*
>
> *You must forgive me the subterfuge that surrounds the delivery of this letter, for as you are aware, we live in distrustful times. Events in Nagarythe lead me to believe that the cults and sects that have so plagued our people these many years are but one thread of a dark tapestry woven by those who rule in Nagarythe. Morathi's turn to darkness is absolute, and I cannot bring myself to trust Malekith, though he seems most earnest in his endeavours to bring peace to Ulthuan. I cannot say that there are any in the Northern Realm who remain loyal to the Phoenix Throne.*
>
> *While my heart hopes that war can yet be averted, my head tells me otherwise. Malekith is determined to prosecute a military campaign against the Naggarothi, and in this I am in accord with him. Where our opinions differ is in who is best chosen to lead this action. I cannot wholly trust Malekith, for even if he is not complicit in these events in some way, he is the prince of Nagarythe and son of Morathi and I fear that his resolve may not endure the calamity of fighting those whom we must face; friends and trusted peers of his, and folk of his own realm.*
>
> *It is for this reason that I turn to you, Imrik, and you alone. You have counselled me to decisive action in the past, and so I must entrust*

> *to you the leadership of the assembled armies of Ulthuan. There is none braver, nor accomplished upon the field of battle as you, and in Caledor resides the greatest strength of our isle. While Caledor stands firm and holds true to the ideals of our people, Ulthuan will endure.*
>
> *I shall confront Malekith with my decision before we arrive at the Isle of the Flame. I do not think he will be pleased, to say the least. He will argue in the council for control, and there is much loyalty to him amongst the other princes. Only Caledor's ruler has equal measure of power in this debate, and I hope that I can look to you and your brothers for support in this.*
>
> *If we cannot speak on this matter, any message you have for me can be entrusted to my herald, Carathril, who bears this missive; either by written or spoken word. He is of staunch loyalty and most noble character, and I vouch for him in the highest manner.*
>
> *May the gods bless us all and protect the peace of our lands.*
>
> *Bel Shanaar, Prince of Tiranoc, Phoenix King of Ulthuan*

THYRIOL TOOK THE scroll to read it again for himself, and the princes pondered long and hard over the meaning and import of Bel Shanaar's words.

'We are left with a difficult choice,' said Thyriol. 'The Phoenix Throne stands empty, and a dire threat rises to challenge us. Bel Shanaar may have been gifted rare prophecy in his choice of words, and his entrusting of this letter to his herald. I think it is plain that the Phoenix King would have seen Imrik succeed him if he could have known what was to occur.'

'I agree,' said Finudel. 'Yet, we three here cannot make this decision alone. Just as it was wrong for Malekith to try to take the crown, it is not for less than a handful of princes to place it upon the head of another. Heirs there are, in those realms whose rulers now lie dead upon this floor, who have equal right to make this choice.'

'Though conceived in deceit, Malekith's lies were, like all great illusions, grounded in some truth,' said Thyriol. 'It is unlikely that the army of Nagarythe will march before the spring, and that, at least, gives us some time to prepare.'

'I fear that Malekith was also right that we cannot afford to hesitate,' said Thyrinor. 'If Imrik had come, then perhaps we could have moved more swiftly, but he is still in the mountains and utterly unaware of the drastic course events have now taken.'

'We must send word to him at once, and go to those other realms that now must mourn the loss of so much noble blood,' said Finudel. 'Though we must gather a new council, I do not think there will be any opposition to Imrik taking up the mantle of the Phoenix King.'

'Except perhaps from Imrik himself,' said Thyrinor with a resigned expression. 'He was reluctant to lead the war against the cults when we last spoke, who is to say that he will not feel it his duty to keep Caledor safe first and foremost now that Caledrian is dead?'

'Caledor is strong, that is true,' said Finudel. 'Yet even the strength of

Caledor would not be enough to resist all of Ulthuan if the other realms should fall to Nagarythe's power. Imrik will fight, of that I have no doubt.'

'And how might we bring Imrik to the Isle of the Flame?' asked Thyrinor. 'Messengers could search for many days and not find him. He made it clear he does not want to be found.'

'No one escapes the gaze of the raven heralds,' said Finudel, speaking of the ancient order founded by Aenarion. The suggestion troubled Thyrinor, for the raven heralds were elves of Nagarythe. He was thankful when Carathril objected.

'No!' said Carathril. 'I do not trust them, for they played their part in the deception at Ealith. As you say, they see all, and I cannot believe that they were so misled. Even if some are not in thrall to Anlec, we have no way of telling friend from foe, or of contacting those who would side with our cause.'

'Then you must go, Carathril,' said Thyrinor.

'Me?' gasped Carathril. 'I have no talent for this sort of endeavour.'

'Bel Shanaar had every confidence in you,' said Thyriol. 'I share his confidence. You will not be unaided, there are enchantments known to the mages of Saphery that will help you locate Imrik.'

'I would not know where to begin,' protested Carathril. His first thought was of returning to Lothern, to inter the body of Haradrin in the mausoleum and share in the grief of his people.

'In Chrace, of course,' said Finudel, stepping forwards to lay a hand on Carathril's shoulder. 'You shall have the pick of Ellyrion's steeds to carry you.'

'And a ship travels even swifter,' said Thyrinor. 'Many there are by the wharf, and you are welcome to whichever you choose and a crew for it.'

Thyriol rolled up the scroll and held it in his outstretched hand towards the captain. Carathril looked at the other princes and saw that they were in agreement. A protest stirred in his breast but he quelled it for the moment.

'Most assuredly you have the blessing of Asuryan,' said the mage. 'Who else of those here has been through so much turmoil of late and emerged unscathed?'

Carathril sought for an argument, a reason why he should not go. He longed to return to Lothern, which would reel again at the news that another of its rulers was dead by violence. He was scared, though he could not admit that in such noble company; the wilds of Chrace were dangerous enough in normal circumstances and on the very borders of Nagarythe. He would have to sail past the Isle of the Dead and search in the monster-infested mountains.

Then he remembered the words in Bel Shanaar's letter. Pride and duty stirred within Carathril, burning through the fear in his stomach. He recalled the tattooed and scarred cultists and their depraved rites, his loathing for what would become of Ulthuan if they should be victorious outweighing his dread at the task ahead. He took the letter from Thyriol.

'I shall go,' said Carathril. 'There is no time to waste.'

'We are not so sorely pressed that you cannot spare time to prepare,' said Thyriol. 'You shall not go alone, so we must choose a company of soldiers to guard you, and tomorrow will serve us as well as today. There is much we must make ready, for you and for other messengers.'

—◄ SIX ►—

The Hunters Set Forth

As CARATHRIL BEGAN his voyage across the Inner Sea, the Isle of the Flame was alive with activity. Ships were sent to gather more soldiers to protect the surviving princes and other heralds despatched to warn the kingdoms of what had happened and the proposed election of Imrik. Unknown to those at the Shrine of Asuryan, Bathinair and the Anlec knights bore the body of Malekith westwards. By sorcerous means they arranged for a caravan to meet them on an isolated stretch of the Ellyrian coast and in secrecy they passed over the plains and across the mountains.

They travelled to Tor Anroc, and cloaking the events at the shrine in lies, spread the news of the massacre. In the dismay and confusion, Morathi was allowed to leave with the body of her son and they travelled north to Anlec.

As they passed through one of the massive gatetowers of the city, Morathi sat upon a carriage next to Malekith. She had said nothing since leaving Tor Anroc, and simmered with a rage that surpassed even the anger she had felt when Bel Shanaar had been chosen over her son to be Phoenix King.

'This is no slight on your character,' she whispered. 'This is no mere insult. This is an attack upon Nagarythe, and assault upon the memory of your father. I have been too lenient with these fools. Your death will be avenged.'

She laid a hand upon the shrouded body as tears of fire rolled down her cheeks. She pictured Ulthuan ablaze with war, the usurpers and their petty princes screaming their apologies as her warriors put them to the sword. She would raise monuments to her son as grand as those dedicated to her late husband, and every elf would pay homage to his greatness.

So wrapped up in these thoughts was Morathi that she almost did not notice the quiver of movement beneath her fingertips.

Unsure if she had imagined it, she sat immobile for a dozen heartbeats, her hand resting on the covered chest of Malekith. She decided it had been the carriage jostling over the pavement and was about to take away her hand.

It came again, the slightest tremble.

With a gasp of joy and relief, Morathi pulled back the shroud to reveal Malekith's ravaged face. Where once he had been so dashing, so handsome, a ruin remained. Bone and charred flesh were fused, sinew exposed.

'You are as strong as your father,' she whispered, lowering her mouth to the ragged remnants of her son's ear. She cradled his head against her cheek, and kissed Malekith's burnt flesh. 'You are Aenarion's heir, true king of the elves.'

There was a rattling hiss of breath from the lipless mouth.

As charred skin cracked and flaked, an eye opened, a pale orb in the dark ruin. It stared ahead, sparks of mystical energy dancing in the pupil. The sparks became an ember, became a tiny flame of magic. The flame grew and darkened, the whole eye becoming a flickering hole of dark fire. At its depth, a pinprick of redness appeared.

The skinless jaw opened. A rasp escaped, wordless. Fingers twitched beneath the shroud.

'Lie still, my brave son,' said Morathi, her tears now of relief, dropping like liquid pearls onto Malekith's face. 'Save your strength. I will look after you. You will be restored. I swear it by my own life.'

A ravaged arm pushed up past the edge of the shroud, shedding blackened skin, thin rivulets of blood streaming from the hand. Fingers little more than charred bone curled around the back of Morathi's head, pulling her closer, stroking her hair.

THE WORLD WAS a blur of light and dark, noise and silence, pain and numbness. Voiceless screams echoed in Malekith's ears, shrieking to the slow beat of his heart. Everything burned. Every part of his body was a fire of agony. Even his mind, his spirit, was consumed over and over by the flames, searing into the core of his being.

He welcomed the blackness.

Yet oblivion did not last. There was no respite from the torment heaped upon his body; no pause in the frustration and anger that ate at his thoughts. Every breath he took was like taking the fire of the sun into his lungs. Every slight draught was a gale of razors on his flesh. And the whispers would not stop; the voices on the edge of hearing, goading and laughing, cackling at his folly. Wisps of dust swirled about him, each tiny mote a leering face with pointed teeth. The walls sang to him; sonorous dirges that spoke of bottomless blackness. The light through the window, painfully bright, danced upon his withered form, leaving tiny footprints of ash across his chest.

And so much pain. Unbearable pain. In every pore and muscle, every shredded nerve and scorched artery. To live was to experience unending agony.

The blackness came for him again. He greeted it with open arms.

He revived again. He stood upon the edge of an abyss and stared down into the dark of eternal death. It was so inviting, to take a single step, to fall into the peace of ending. One step. One small step and the agony would cease.

'No,' he snarled, the single word sending shivers of fresh pain through his body.

ON A BRONZE mirror, a scene played out in ruddy monochrome. Ships plied the waters of the Inner Sea, coming and going to the Isle of the Flame. The island itself was shrouded in a fog, obscured from Morathi's viewing by the enchantments of the priests. What went on within the walls of the Shrine of Asuryan was unknown to her, but such frenetic activity on the sea nearby told her everything she needed to know; the rest could be assumed.

Morathi waved a hand to dismiss the image; it was replaced in the full length mirror by her reflection. She took a moment to admire what she saw, running a hand over the curve of her waist and hip, tracing a finger along the delicate line of cheek and jaw. She raked slender fingers through her lustrous hair, shuddering at her own touch.

The moment was interrupted. In the reflection a figure appeared in the doorway behind Morathi. She turned to see Bathinair.

'Thyriol rallies the princes,' he said. He held up a bloodstained, torn parchment. 'Our agents took this message from a Sapherian herald. They seek to elevate Imrik to the Phoenix Throne, your majesty.'

Morathi plucked the tattered letter from Bathinair's hand and glanced at it. She could smell the blood, the ink, and fragrant oil from Bathinair's skin.

'An obvious choice,' she said. 'Why was he not slain with the others?'

'He did not attend the council,' Bathinair explained. 'He ignored Bel Sha-naar's invitation to go hunting in Chrace with his cousin.'

'Then we still have opportunity to sow harm upon our enemies,' said Morathi, the letter bursting into black flame between her fingers. 'Go to the high priest of Khaine, and bring me the deadliest killers in Anlec.'

'Assassinate Imrik before he can be made king?' said Bathinair. 'I like it.'

Morathi stalked across the chamber and seized the prince by the throat, her long black-painted nails drawing blood from skin.

'I do not care for your likes and dislikes,' she snarled, letting a little of the dark magic within her seep into the scratches. Bathinair hissed and spat like a serpent that had itself been bitten, writhing in Morathi's unnaturally strong grip. 'Bring me the assassins and offer no opinion.'

She let go of Bathinair and he stumbled back, hands rubbing at the wounds on his neck.

'At once, your majesty,' he said, eyes fearful.

When the prince had gone, Morathi went to the adjoining chamber. Upon a bier covered in many sheets Malekith lay immobile. He whispered and murmured words too faint to hear. His fists clenched and opened, his head jerking slightly from side to side. She laid a hand on his brow, pained by his delirium. There was no sorcery she possessed that could heal these wounds, inflicted by divine flame.

She smiled. For all Malekith's feverish madness, he was recovering. Day by day she watched him, seeing the tiniest extra life creeping back into ruined flesh. It would take years for him to be restored, if there were no setbacks; time enough to bring all of Ulthuan under the rule of Nagarythe and keep the Phoenix Throne secure for Malekith's triumphant return.

There was a stool beside the bed and she sat down, hand still on his brow. She talked constantly and softly to him, telling the same tales she had told him when he was a child: tales of Aenarion and gods and daemons.

The afternoon passed and Morathi comforted her wounded son. She stopped and went back to the main chamber when she detected the presence of eight elves in the passageway outside, drawing a curtain across the doorway to conceal Malekith from prying eyes.

Bathinair entered, seven others following him through the archway. The assassins had the look of lean, hungry wolves, with pinched faces and tight muscles. Morathi could feel the touch of dark magic like a cloying fog, dripping from their swords and blades, pulsing from vials of poison and rune-crafted jewellery. Blood stained their skin red and slicked their hair. Tiny skulls and runes of Khaine pierced their flesh on rings and studs.

She looked each in the eye, seeing no compassion, no mercy, no kindness, only cold death.

'Good,' she said to Bathinair, stroking his cheek. The prince shuddered for a moment, ecstatic at her touch. 'You may return to the Athartists and cavort with them until I summon you again.'

'Thank you, your majesty,' said Bathinair, leering at the prospect of attention from the hedonistic priestesses and cultists.

When he had gone, Morathi commanded the assassins to kneel. They did so, in a semicircle around her.

'Imrik must be slain,' she told them. 'You will find him and kill him.'

'Where will he be found?' asked one of the killers, revealing teeth filed to points.

'In Chrace,' replied Morathi.

'An elf could get lost for a lifetime in those peaks,' said another. 'How are we to find Imrik?'

'Will your scrying guide us to him?' asked a third.

'The vortex is too strong in the Annulii,' Morathi said. 'No spell can pierce the magical winds.'

'Then you have some trail for us to follow?' said a fourth.

'Close your eyes and I will show you,' Morathi said with a smile.

She chanted, calling on the patrons of the dark winds to bless her spells. She named them in turn, and with each title the magic in the chamber thickened and swirled. Morathi felt it coiling about her, sliding across her flesh, warm and chill, dry and slick. She spat the words of the incantation she had prepared, each syllable like a fizzing on her tongue, each sound a clear note in her ears.

Morathi flexed her fingers and arched her back as the dark magic flowed into and through her. It pulsed along her nerves, setting every sense alight. With centuries of practice, she calmed herself, forcing the magic to her bidding, shaping it with her words and thoughts.

The assassins had their faces turned up to her, eyes closed. She thrust out her hands, bolts of black energy leaping from her fingertips into the eyes of the Khainites. Each thrashed and screamed, falling to the floor with flailing limbs as the sorcery poured into them, fusing with their bodies.

When the spell was cast, Morathi slumped back into a chair, panting and spent. With a fingertip, she wiped a bead of sweat from her brow, eyes closed, breath coming in ragged gasps. She touched the fingertip to her tongue, and tasted the sweet residue of magic on her skin.

Groaning, the assassins recovered, each holding his head, cursing and swearing at the pain. Morathi opened her eyes and stood up. She walked along the line of supine elves, towering over them imperiously.

'You shall know such pain as I feel at Imrik's continued life,' she told them. Stepping over the last, she turned back down the line. 'The pain will lessen with every step closer to your prey, and will grow with every step further from him. I have laid my mark upon you and you shall not know sleep or thirst or hunger until Imrik is dead. Look at me!'

The assassins raised their heads and looked at Morathi with eyes like red glass. A black rune smouldered upon the brow of each, burnt into flesh by sorcery. They winced and writhed, unable to escape the throbbing pain within their heads.

'Kill him and you will know pain no longer,' said Morathi. She pointed a finger to the door. 'The more swiftly you complete your task, the sooner you shall know peace again. Go now to Chrace! Find Imrik! Slay him!'

—❖ SEVEN ❖—

The Road to Chrace

THE WIND WAS fresh from the east, bringing scatters of rain onto the pale wooden decking, casting droplets from mast and sail onto Carathril as he stood at the rail. He had crossed the Inner Sea many times during his duties to Bel Shanaar but he had not yet come to terms with the Phoenix King's death, and in all of those previous voyages he had never felt such urgency and such responsibility.

The sky was heavy with autumnal cloud, matching the herald's dismal mood. Around him, the sailors adjusted the triangular sails at the orders of their captain, squeezing every last measure of speed from their ship. To the bow and stern, and at the mastheads, lookouts kept watch for ships, fearful that another vessel might be under the sway of the Naggarothi or the cultists. On the deck were two hundred seasoned marines; the famed Sea Guard of Carathril's home city of Lothern.

Ahead and to starboard appeared an isle with shallow shores. Grey haze hung about its coast, and coloured lights danced in the sky above. Carathril moved to the port side, not wishing to look upon the Isle of the Dead. It was on that slip of land that Caledor Dragontamer had cast the spell of the great vortex, forever trapping himself and his fellow mages at its heart.

Growing up in Lothern, Carathril had heard all of the sailors' tales. Some claimed the mages could be seen as ethereal figures with arms reaching to the heavens, frozen in time at the moment of their triumph. It was said that the last syllables of that mighty enchantment were still carried on the breeze;

791

that Caledor's final words would come to an elf while he slept if his ship strayed too close to the shore.

Carathril had no desire to test the truth of the tales and he heard sailors and Sea Guard whispering prayers to Mannanin, god of the waters, asking for safe passage and a route clear of the Isle of the Dead.

Due north they sailed after, cutting between the chain of islands that curved across the Inner Sea. For three more days they carried on without pause, and saw no more than the occasional sail on the horizon.

They came into view of the Inner Sea's northern reaches. A forest-swathed shore marked that boundary, broken by the mouths of many rivers. Of all the realms of Ulthuan, it was this one that Carathril had never seen. Avelorn, home of the Everqueen. The thought of it sent a tremor through Carathril, of excitement and quiet fear. A land of boundless forest, Avelorn had always been the heart of elven society. Tor Anroc had been the political capital of Ulthuan, but it was Avelorn that was the elves' spiritual centre. There were some philosophers who claimed the forefathers of every elf had been raised beneath that endless bower of leaves and branches.

In his years of service to the Phoenix Throne, Carathril had never been despatched to the court of the Everqueen, and he had never received a visitor from Avelorn. The Everqueen, Yvraine, daughter of Aenarion and Astarielle, did not concern herself with temporal affairs. Hers was a timeless guardianship, of the isle and its people as a whole. Yet Carathril knew that the Everqueen would be aware of the tumult engulfing her island; other messengers were on board to visit her court and inform Yvraine of the decision to elect Imrik.

To one of the broad rivers sailed the ship, entering the waters of Avelorn as dusk fell. The trees crowded close to the bank on each side, willows that dipped long fronds into the water. Clouds of bats set out from their roosts, dark swathes against the setting sun. Things screeched and howled and roared in the twilight, and Carathril was glad he was on the ship and not the shore.

The river was broad and easily navigable, so they sailed on through the night. As the moons rose, the character of the forest changed again. In the silvery light of Sariour, the trees seemed to dance and whisper in the wind, their secret messages echoing across the waters as a susurrant background noise. The river was teeming with life: fish and frogs and lizards could be seen skimming the placid waters in the patches of moonlight that broke through the cloud. The call of nighthawks and the howls of wolves sounded from every direction and Carathril found sleep impossible.

By dawn, they came to a great bend in the river, turning westwards towards the peaks of the Annulii that could be just about seen rearing in the distance over the canopy of trees. In the light of the dawn, animals came to the waterside to drink. Here and there, the trees opened up into broad glades where herds of deer grazed and foxes stalked through the long grass.

Carathril was convinced he saw other movement too, in the gloom beneath the forest canopy. Not birds or beasts, but the trees themselves seemed to shift. He knew that Avelorn was alive, and from the oldest tales had heard of the treemen that protected the forest; it was a different matter to see such creatures in the shadows, spirits of bark and leaf that creaked and groaned like trees in a strong wind.

A little after noon, they came to a jetty. It was not made of timber, but of the massive roots of a tree extending into the river. A company of armoured warrior-women waited on the shore nearby: the Maiden Guard of Avelorn. Seeing them, the captain steered the ship towards the natural wharf and put the ship alongside the twisting roots.

The captain of the Maiden Guard came to the ship, spear in hand and shield on the other arm, her golden hair falling in waves from beneath her green-gold helm, her eyes a bright green that pierced Carathril's soul. When she spoke, her voice was distant, her eyes unfocussed as if she looked upon something else. Carathril imagined the sighing of leaves and the gentle tumble of water over rocks.

'The whole forest speaks of your coming,' she said. 'I am Althinelle, glade protector and captain of the Maiden Guard. Who is your leader?'

The ship captain waved to Carathril, who hesitantly moved along the rail to address Althinelle.

'I am Carathril, of Lothern, lately of Tor Anroc,' he called down to her. 'I have heralds aboard for the Everqueen and am destined upriver for the mountains of Chrace.'

'We have hoped that you would come,' Althinelle replied. 'Our queen is most distressed. She feels a darkness swallowing Ulthuan and would know its cause.'

'The Phoenix King Bel Shanaar is dead,' Carathril told her. 'Prince Malekith dared the wrath of Asuryan to replace him and was found wanting. The flames consumed him and the shrine all but toppled.'

'Grave news,' said Althinelle. She nodded. 'Send down your heralds and I will take them to Queen Yvraine. You may pass on up the river. For what purpose do you travel to Chrace?'

As the sailors threw rope ladders down to the wharf and the heralds climbed over the ship's side, Carathril hesitated to reply; out of practice rather than suspicion. There could be no hint of the cultists or Naggarothi in Avelorn; the Maiden Guard would ensure the forests were kept free of any cytharai taint.

'Prince Imrik of Caledor is to be found there,' said Carathril. 'Many princes were massacred by Naggarothi at Asuryan's shrine, and Imrik is to be named Bel Shanaar's successor. We must find him and escort him safely to the Isle of the Flame.'

'Very well,' said the Maiden Captain. There was a hint of amusement in her tone. 'We shall send word to the companies at the borders of Chrace to keep watch for your return. The Everqueen will grant safe passage to her future husband. Isha's blessings be upon your life.'

'Please convey my gratitude and regard to the Everqueen,' said Carathril.

Althinelle laughed, the sound touching joy into Carathril's heart.

'Be assured that Yvraine knows of your gratitude and regard, Carathril of Lothern, lately of Tor Anroc.'

The Maiden Captain stepped back. Just as he turned away, Carathril saw something strange; Althinelle's eyes looked blue not green. He shook his head and dismissed the idea as an illusion of the strange forest light. The whole experience left him feeling light-headed and he retired to his cabin to lie down.

He did not intend to sleep, but since he had rested little since the massacre at the shrine, his eyelids felt heavy and he passed into a deep slumber. When he woke, he saw through the cabin window that it was late evening.

He felt refreshed and strong, and for some reason the cabin was filled with the smell of wild flowers.

THE WIND CAME in howling gusts down the valley, bringing an early touch of winter from the peaks. Flurries of snow dusted from the ridges and shoulders of the mountains above and the moons were hidden by a thick bank of cloud.

Despite the gloom, Elthanir could see perfectly well. He followed the winding trail with the sure-footedness of a mountain goat, springing from rock to rock, weaving between the branches of the overhanging bushes and steering easily past outcrops, his feet upon the edge of the shelf, a precipice dropping steeply down to his right.

He did not feel the cold, not the ache of limbs from many days travel, or the hunger that would have gnawed the stomach of an ordinary elf, or the parched dryness of his throat. Only the burning occupied him; the fire behind his eyes that pushed him onwards.

The others followed in silence. None of them had spoken since they had left the palace of Anlec, each consumed by his curse, his inner pain.

As another flurry of wind dusted his cloak and hood, Elthanir stopped at a turn in the path, where it dropped down sharply towards the valley floor. He looked north and recognised Anil Arianni and Anul Sethis, twin peaks that soared above the others, joined by a sharp ridge.

He knew the mountains well, for they marked the edge of Nagarythe. He stared up at the pass known as the Chracian Gate and knew that in a few days the burning pain would end.

THE PARTY EMERGED from the edge of the pine forests onto the highest slopes of Anul Sarian. The snow was light, Imrik's boots barely leaving a mark as he forged up the mountainside, his broad-headed hunting spear over his shoulder. Ahead the trackers had stopped in the shelter of a cluster of snow-crusted boulders, bows in hand.

'Looks like we might get lucky today,' Koradrel said, following behind Imrik. 'Perhaps something a bit more challenging than a stag or bear.'

'With luck,' replied Imrik, glancing over his shoulder.

Both princes were clad in hunting leathers and fur-lined cloaks, the hoods pulled up against the cold breeze. Their woollen leggings were bound with thongs, and knee-high boots protected their feet. Each wore heavy gloves riveted with rings of iron, and breastplates over their padded clothing.

'If nothing comes of this, we shall have to make camp,' said Koradrel, pointing to the sun disappearing to the west, his breath steaming the air.

'No lodges nearby?' said Imrik.

'Half a day's walk to the south,' replied Koradrel. 'There are caves on the north-eastern slopes, with room for all of us.'

The group consisted of twenty elves in all; the two princes, four guides and fourteen retainers leading the packhorses carrying the tents and supplies. All were armed with bows and spears and the huntsmen carried long axes and wore armour. On one of the sleds was mounted a small bolt thrower, a smaller cousin to the repeater machines used in battle. The others were heaped with food, nets, blankets, firewood, spare clothes, lamps and torches, axes for felling trees and shovels for digging pits, wire and chains for snares and traps, and bundles of fresh spears and arrows. In any other kingdom, such a party might look as if they were ready for battle, but in Chrace they were simply essential supplies for a hunting trip.

Imrik considered battle safer, and every elf in the group was alert, watching the cloudy skies, peering into the shadows beneath the pine trees, eyeing every rock and bush.

Like Caledor, Chrace was a kingdom of mountains. In the Dragon Spine Mountains, the dragons hunted down any large beast that wandered into their territory. In the Chracian peaks, it was the elves that had to keep watch for marauding monsters. The vortex of Ulthuan raged through these rocky spires, tinging the air with magic, colouring the clouds and the snow with a glistening half-seen rainbow. The powerful winds of magic had drawn all manner of strange creatures to these lands. Some could be reared as mounts if caught young, such as the pegasi, griffons and hippogryphs. Others were beasts of pure Chaos; the manticores and hydras, basilisks and chimeras.

For centuries they had made their nests and for centuries the highlight of the Chracian calendar had been the monster hunts. The Chracians had honed their beast-slaying skills, mountaincraft and woodmanship to a high art. Several times during his campaigns in Elthin Arvan, Imrik had called upon the expertise of his Chracian allies to rid an area of a troublesome beast.

The prince liked the Chracians as a people, and though they lived at opposite sides of Ulthuan, there was much in common. Though Chrace lacked the raw grandeur of Caledor, and had no claim to a great founder like the Dragontamer, it had its own natural majesty. The people were sturdy in body and spirit, used to the isolation of winter.

That they were fierce warriors was beyond doubt. Many of the retainers, like Koradrel, wore the pelts of the famed Chracian white lions. It was considered a testament to adulthood and prowess for a warrior to hunt one of the massive cats, and no elf was allowed to wear the fur of a white lion unless he had slain it with his own hand. Imrik had killed two such beasts on his hunts, but had refused to wear their cloak of honour; he had jokingly confessed to Koradrel on one hunt that he feared such a thing would confuse the dragons and he would get eaten as prey on returning to Caledor. In truth, he did not feel the right to bear such a badge of strength upon his shoulders. He was just a visitor in these lands; a genuine Chracian hunter lived and breathed these mountains every day.

They reached the position of the scouts and took shelter amongst the rocks. Glad to be out of the wind, Imrik pulled down his hood, took off the band holding back his hair and ran his fingers over his head.

'You see something?' he asked the closest guide, an elf called Anachius.

The guide nodded and pointed along the slope. Imrik saw the darkness of a cave mouth, and the ground in front was trampled and free of snow.

'A lair,' said Imrik with a smile. He tied back his hair and turned to Koradrel. 'What is in there?'

'Let us go and find out,' replied the Chracian, taking his spear from where he had leant it against a rock.

The group cautiously moved out from the boulders, making barely a sound and leaving only the faintest marks in the snow. Imrik took his spear in both hands, breathing shallowly, eyes intent on the cave ahead. Anachius moved in front of the group with another guide, racing swiftly over the rough ground, their lion-pelt cloaks tied tight around their bodies.

The hunters stopped about a bow's shot from the cave entrance while the guides continued ahead. The two elves circled away from the cave, moving through a scattering of rocks. They spent some time examining the ground, pointing at tracks. There followed a brief conversation and then the other guide headed back towards the group while Anachius edged cautiously towards the cave.

'There is definitely a creature inside, or nearby,' said the guide when he had returned. 'There are no feathers that we can see, and the claw marks show that it is a large beast. We found tufts of coarse fur on the rocks, not shed scales, and no sign of burning. The smell of carrion comes from the cave.'

'So not a griffon or hydra,' said Koradrel.

'Not a chimera, either,' added Imrik. 'Such would not leave meat uneaten.'

'True enough,' agreed the guide.

'So what have we here?' asked Koradrel.

The question was answered by a shout from Anachius.

'Manticore!' the guide cried out, sprinting from the cave mouth.

The beast exploded from the cave behind him, the mountainside reverberating with a feral roar. The monster was in rough shape the same as a massive lion, its pelt dark brown and marked with deep orange patches. Two wings like those of an immense bat were curled upon its back and claws like white scimitars scraped across rock as it skidded out onto the slope. Its tail was segmented like a scorpion's, arching over its wings, tipped with a barb as long as a spear. Most frightening was its face: feline but with disturbingly elf-like features, dark against a huge mane of bright red hair.

The manticore bellowed again as the elves readied their weapons. Some raced towards Anachius, shouting encouragement. The monster pounced, wings opening, easily catching up with the forlorn guide.

Anachius turned at the last moment, warned by a cry from Koradrel. He raised his spear as the manticore landed, its rune-carved tip scoring a wound across the creature's cheek. A massive paw swiped away the weapon and sent Anachius crashing to the ground, his arm flopping uselessly.

In a heartbeat the manticore was upon the guide, jaws closing about his torso, almost shearing the unfortunate elf in half.

'Fight or run?' said Imrik.

'Fight!' replied Koradrel. 'A manticore will chase us all of the way back to Tor Achare. Take cover in the rocks!'

Imrik tore his gaze from the vision of the manticore tearing Anachius limb from limb, showering the white ground with blood, organs and splinters of bone, a bass growling echoing after the hunters as they retreated back to the boulders.

Glancing over his shoulder as he ran, Imrik saw that the monster did not feed, but simply ripped apart the guide with wild rage, shaking body parts in its mouth before tossing them away. It continued to stamp and slash with its claws, turning flesh to red ribbons.

Reaching the rocks, Imrik came to a halt beside Koradrel. Looking down the slope, he saw all but two of the other hunters racing towards them with weapons ready. The other two had stopped the horse train and were readying the bolt thrower on its sled.

'They are fearsome but mindlessly aggressive,' said Koradrel. 'We must lure it into view of the bolt thrower. Once we have grounded the beast, we attack as a group. Spears and axes, arrows will do little harm.'

Imrik nodded and adjusted his grip on the spear, one shoulder against a boulder. The manticore had finished its frenzy of destruction and lifted its head, sniffing, head turning left and right, pointed ears swivelling to detect any noise. It let loose another roar and bounded into the air. The manticore's flapping had none of the grace of a dragon's flight, but it powered skywards at speed, scanning the ground for more prey.

Torches had been lit by some of the guides and they ventured from the rocks with the flaming brands in hand, waving to attract the beast's attention and lure it away from the caravan.

The manticore dropped from the skies, forelegs outstretched. The torchbearers flung away their brands and sprinted back to the rocks, the manticore bearing down upon them like a bolt of pure fury.

The elves reached the boulders as the manticore crashed into the ground, snarling and swiping. Imrik could feel the heat of its breath, tainted with the stench of rotted flesh and fresh blood.

The manticore saw him and lunged. Imrik hurled himself behind a boulder a heartbeat before the monster's claws slashed across the rock, sending chips of stone into the air. It growled constantly, and padded to the right, snorting and sniffing. Koradrel appeared to the creature's right and hurled his spear, the weapon punching into the creature's ribs just behind its shoulder. It gave a howl of anger and spun, tail lashing but too slow to catch the swiftly retreating Chracian.

Bunching powerful muscles, the beast looked as though it was about to take to the sky again. One of the hunters emerged from the shadow of the rocks with an axe in hand, bellowing a challenge. The manticore twisted and leapt for the kill, but the hunter rolled beneath its outstretched claws and raked the edge of his axe across its gut. Blood streamed onto the snow.

The hunter surged to his feet and dashed for the rocks, but unlike Koradrel he was too close. The manticore's sting flashed down, punching into the elf's back, the tip of the barb erupting from the hunter's shoulder. He flopped to the ground, convulsing madly as the sting was ripped free, blood and froth erupting from his mouth.

Moving more sluggishly from its wounds, the manticore circled around the boulders, moving up the slope, tail lashing, wings flexing. Imrik looked into its eyes and saw yellow orbs of hatred. The prince wondered what could spawn a beast of such rage.

Bounding forwards two steps, the manticore leapt, landing with surprising agility atop the largest boulder. It peered down into the rocks as the elves scattered, one claw catching Koradrel on the arm as he raced past, pitching him face-first to the ground.

Imrik acted out of instinct, bounding over a rock with spear in hand. The movement diverted the manticore away from the fallen prince and Imrik ducked as the sting whipped towards him, clattering against a rock to leave a trail of thick venom. Imrik stood over Koradrel and thrust upwards with his spear. The blow was hasty and only scored a ragged mark across the manticore's shoulder. In reply, a paw smashed into Imrik's chest, throwing him backwards. His breastplate was buckled, two marks raked across it, but it had saved him from instant evisceration.

Other hunters poured into the fight, swinging long axes and jabbing with spears. The manticore leapt over their heads to another perch, smashing an elf from his feet with its tail as it landed. The Chracians were relentless as Imrik recovered his breath, their weapons forcing the monster to rear up with a roar.

Imrik heard a distant snap and a moment later the manticore's throat erupted in a shower of blood, a bolt jutting from the side of its neck. Flopping sideways, it tumbled down the rock, limbs flailing, tail slashing left and right. A well-placed axe blow severed the sting, blood and poison gushing from the wound.

Still the beast would not be slain. It rolled to its feet, wings unfurling, howling madly. Not wanting the manticore to escape, Koradrel rejoined his warriors, leaping atop the monster's back to drive his spear into its spine. The beast fell again, Koradrel jumping lightly to the ground as the manticore slammed into the rocks. An incautious elf lost a leg to a vicious sweep as the creature lashed out in its death throes.

Contented that it would die without further action, Koradrel called his hunters away a safe distance. Imrik joined his cousin and the two leaned on each other, breathing heavily. The rush of battle filled the Caledorian prince as he looked at the dying monster. Glancing down, he realised how close he had been to sharing its fate; relief combined with battle-lust to send a surge of energy through him. Imrik caught Koradrel's eye and saw the glint there. They both laughed and embraced.

Imrik mastered himself after a while and looked at the dead beast with raised eyebrows.

'So that's a manticore,' he said.

SINCE HE HAD been made a herald by Bel Shanaar, Carathril had crossed the Annulii Mountains many times, yet it never ceased to have an effect on him. Crossing from Avelorn into Chrace, over some of the highest passes in the circle of peaks, he felt the vortex more powerfully than ever before. The magic felt like it tugged at his hair, seeped through the pores of his skin, set his teeth on edge. The clouds that covered the mountains were tinged with purple and red and green, and through rare breaks strange rainbows shimmered against the sunlight, the colours of their curved arcs distorted by the magical field.

The reputation of Chrace as a home for many monstrous dangers was well known and Carathril's company of Sea Guard were constantly alert for attack. Winter was fast approaching these northern climes, and on the third day after leaving the river, the group awoke to find the ground and their tents covered with a light dusting of snow. Carathril had been to Chrace before and was well prepared with a fur-lined cloak and hood, and gloves of soft leather. The Sea Guard had also brought winter clothing, and swathed against the cold wind and flurries of icy sleet, the elves forged on into Chrace.

It was not for monsters alone that the Sea Guard were watchful. The route of the company took them along Phoenix Pass, which crossed the Annulii into Nagarythe. Even keeping to the highlands as much as possible, there was every chance they would run into Naggarothi warriors patrolling the border.

Though the increasingly bitter weather made it more uncomfortable, Carathril decided that they should march by night and seek shelter by day, the better to avoid the Naggarothi. Even then he was constantly nagged by the feeling of being watched; these lands were the traditional haunt of the raven heralds. Carathril had met some of their order, and knew that if they wished to remain unseen, not even the keen eyes of the Sea Guard would spot them.

He was eager to press on and cross back into Chrace as quickly as possible, fearful that the raven heralds would have spied the company as soon as they left Phoenix Pass. Even now, riders could be speeding to Anlec, bearing the news. Such was the situation following the massacre at the shrine, Carathril would expect the Naggarothi to react violently to any trespass on their lands.

For three nights they marched, often following no track at all through the bleak hills of eastern Nagarythe, keeping their bearing by snatched glimpses of moon and stars. For three days they made camp in hollows and caves, eating cold food to avoid lighting fires, wrapped in blankets to keep the wintry air at bay.

On the fourth morning, Carathril did not call the company to a halt, but instead insisted that they pushed on through the day as well. They crossed an icy river that cascaded down from the Annulii and so passed into Chrace. Out in the wilderness they had no hope for relief or reinforcement, and turned eastwards away from Nagarythe as soon as the terrain allowed.

Every now and then Carathril glanced over his shoulder as he marched, expecting to see a feather-cloaked rider on a distant hill or an army of Naggarothi in pursuit. Each time the horizon was bare of foe, just the grey cold skies of northern Ulthuan.

They made camp that night in the lee of a great shoulder of rock and dared to light fires again to melt snow and cook a more wholesome meal. Neaderin, the captain of the Sea Guard, joined Carathril inside his tent as the wind plucked at canvas and howled across the rocks.

'We have reached Chrace, but where now do we search for Imrik?' asked the captain.

Carathril was at a loss for an answer for the moment. The Caledorian prince had deliberately left no word of where he could be found, and all of Thyriol's magic had been unable to locate Imrik within the mystical whorl of the vortex.

'His cousin Koradrel lives in the capital, Tor Achare,' Carathril said after some thought. 'Morai-heg might favour us and we find Imrik there, returned from his hunt. If not, Koradrel's household will surely know where their master has gone.'

'So we head directly east, to Tor Achare?' said Neaderin. 'Or do we journey around the mountains and come at the city from the north?'

It was a difficult decision. Carathril felt the need for urgency, but the short-est path would be the wrong one if they went astray in the mountains or some ill fate befell them. Against this, he measured the extra time it would take to march around the mountains and negotiate the deep forests north of Tor Achare. It was a more certain route but, even allowing for a few days' delay crossing the mountains, would take nearly twice as long.

'We shall take the longer route,' said the herald. 'Though the worst of winter is not yet here, the mountains are not for the inexperienced. And if Imrik hunts in the mountains, we will need directions to locate him.'

'We are Sea Guard, not mountaineers,' said Neaderin. 'This could have been avoided. We should have sailed through the Lothern Gate and around Ulthuan to the northern coast of Chrace.'

'With Prince Haradrin dead, Lothern will be awash with anarchy and suspicion,' said Carathril. 'I was not certain that the sea gates would be opened to us, and even if they were, travel through the port risked many other distractions and delays. I am sorry, but it had to be this way.'

Neaderin sighed and departed, leaving Carathril feeling cold and gloomy. The chill drove his pessimistic mood as much as the task ahead. Even in winter, Eataine was as warm as a Chracian summer and he missed the sun upon the white houses of Lothern and the glittering waters of the port. There would be no easy way to find Imrik, but Carathril contented himself with the thought that although the need to find the prince was pressing, the Naggarothi would not be able to make any move before the spring. Even if they had some malicious intent for the next Phoenix King, the task of finding him would be just as difficult for them; in fact it would be harder for they would have no allies in Chrace to help them.

Slightly eased by this, Carathril tried to sleep, ignoring the numb of cold in his fingers and toes.

THE CRACKLE OF burning logs almost drowned out the whimpers of the woodcutter and his family. His tear-streaked face was lit by the flames of the burning lodge, mingling with the blood seeping from the fine cut upon his brow. Blinking to clear his eyes, the Chracian looked up at Elthanir, his lips bloodied, teeth broken.

'I shall tell you nothing,' the woodcutter managed to say, a string of blood-flecked saliva drooling from the corner of his ravaged mouth.

Elthanir shook his head. He knew he was close. The pain was now just soreness at the back of his head, an ember of the fire that had previously raged behind his eyes. The woodcutter gasped as Elthanir ripped his dagger out of the elf's ribs.

'Imrik,' Elthanir snarled, just about able to concentrate on the word through the fog of pain. 'Where?'

He used the blade on the hunter's arms, cutting where the flesh was most sensitive. It reminded Elthanir of the rituals in the temple of Khaine, though in that gore-soaked shrine there was no point in confession.

The woodcutter grimaced and said nothing, trembling violently. Elthanir stopped his torture, fearing that his victim would pass out or perhaps even die. He looked over his shoulder at the others and nodded. One of them stepped forwards, dragging a young male elf, no more than fifteen years old. In his other hand, he held a knife with a blade heated in the flames of the cabin, oblivious to the burning of his own flesh. The air wavered with heat as he forced open the boy's mouth and held the blade close.

Behind him, the hunter's wife wailed and lurched for her child, but was driven back by a knee to the gut. Her daughter, even younger than the son, struggled in the arms of another assassin, awash with tears.

Elthanir grabbed the woodcutter by his long hair and twisted his head to look at his son. The Chracian sobbed.

'Imrik. Where?' the assassin asked again.

SOMETHING WOKE CARATHRIL. He lay with his eyes closed, feeling a presence close at hand. He could hear nothing except for the wind and the slap of canvas and twang of rope. It was the quiet that disturbed him, as if there was an absence of a sound he expected to hear.

He opened his eyes and saw something darker in the tent with him. Before he could open his mouth to shout, a black-gloved hand clamped over his mouth. A hooded face leaned over him and whispered in his ear, the words a barely heard sigh.

'Do not struggle and do not shout.'

The voice sounded familiar but Carathril could not place it. He felt something lightly brushing his face and realised it was the touch of feathers from the elf's hood. A raven herald!

'You are in no danger, I am here to warn you,' said the shadowy elf. A shuttered lantern revealed a glimmer of red light. The intruder pulled back his hood and revealed emerald-like eyes and jet-black hair. Carathril placed the voice immediately on seeing the herald's face. It was Elthyrior, who had ridden with Malekith and Carathril in the assault on the fortress of Ealith twenty years before.

'Will you remain silent?' said the raven herald. Carathril nodded, realising that had Elthyrior wished to kill him, he would have done so already. The raven herald lifted his hand away and straightened. 'Good. I am pleased that you trust me.'

'I would not say that,' said Carathril.

Elthyrior smiled and sat cross-legged beside Carathril's bed roll. His eyes were sparks of green in the dim light.

'That is probably the wisest position to take,' he said. 'The raven heralds are divided; some for Morathi, some against. I have news for you, but first you must tell me what brings the herald of the Phoenix King into the mountains of Chrace.'

'I might ask the same of a Naggarothi herald,' replied Carathril, sitting up, pulling his blanket to his chest to keep warm. He was disturbed to notice that while his own breath came in little wisps of vapour, there was nothing from the raven herald when he spoke.

'Morai-heg has guided me here, as she guides me to all places of importance,' said Elthyrior. 'Know that I have heard rumour of what happened in the Shrine of Asuryan and Tor Anroc. I believe that you know Alith Anar?'

'We have met,' said Carathril. The exiled Naggarothi prince had come to him for help in asking sanctuary of the Phoenix King.

'Alith still lives and has returned to his family, and so starts upon a path that will lead him into the darkest places,' said Elthyrior. 'I know of the death of Bel Shanaar, and of a great many princes slain at the Isle of the Flame, but I do not know the cause. Morathi has left Tor Anroc and returned to Anlec with the body of Malekith. I see and know many things, but still I do not know what brings the herald of the dead Phoenix King to Chrace with a bodyguard of Lothern soldiers.'

'Why should I tell you?' said Carathril. That Elthyrior knew so much was disturbing and Carathril wondered if he was being kept alive just to divulge the purpose of his mission.

Elthyrior must have read something of Carathril's thoughts in his expression. He took a knife from his belt, wrapped Carathril's fingers around the hilt and pulled the blade to his throat.

'Even a raven herald can be killed,' said Elthyrior. 'The moment you suspect me of falsehood or violence, you can end my life with a simple slash. I shall relieve you of further worry by telling you what I guess to be the situation, and you can simply answer me if what I believe is true or false.'

Carathril thought about this and could see nothing but sincerity in the raven herald's eyes.

'Go on,' said Carathril.

'You seek Prince Imrik of Caledor,' said Elthyrior. He smiled. 'I see from your face that this is true. The prince passed this way in the autumn to go hunting with his cousin, Koradrel. Now a herald of the Phoenix King marches north in haste with a body of soldiers. It is not difficult to link the two facts.'

'Why have you sneaked into my tent?' said Carathril. 'I would trust you more had you approached openly and in daylight.'

'I cannot risk discovery,' said Elthyrior. 'Treachery is the greatest weapon the Naggarothi have in their arsenal at the moment. Can you vouch for all of your soldiers? Are you certain that none of them are connected to the cytharai cults?'

Carathril admitted to himself that he did not have such confidence, but would not say as such to the raven herald. The Sea Guard were loyal to Eataine, and he had come to the conclusion that even if one or two had been corrupted, there was little they could do whilst surrounded by enemies.

'I can tell that you understand me,' said Elthyrior. 'It is with betrayal and suspicion that Morathi and her followers strike their deadliest blows, and we would be foolish to trust anyone but ourselves in these times.'

'You are right,' Carathril said with a nod. 'I am seeking Imrik of Caledor. A few princes survived the massacre and seek to choose a new Phoenix King to succeed Bel Shanaar.'

'Imrik is a good choice,' said Elthyrior.

'I have not said that Imrik has been chosen,' said Carathril.

'No, but that would explain why seven assassins seek him not more than a day from here,' replied the raven herald.

'What?' Carathril almost cut Elthyrior in his moment of shock. He pulled the dagger back from the other elf's throat. 'What assassins?'

'Khainite, the deadliest kind,' said Elthyrior. 'I have followed them for the last five days, since I came across their trail. If you turn east, you will be following in their footsteps. Move swiftly, I fear they already know where to find Imrik.'

'We have to leave at once!' Carathril threw aside his blanket and got to his feet.

'Please wait until dawn,' said Elthyrior. 'It is not far off. And keep my appearance here a secret.'

'I will,' said Carathril. 'Before you leave, can you tell me what happens in Nagarythe? What does Morathi plan? Any news you have would be invaluable.'

'Not all of Nagarythe is under Morathi's control,' said the raven herald. 'The House of Anar resists her. You travelled through their lands on leaving Phoenix Pass, though you did not know it. They will hold back Morathi as long as they can, but they cannot hold forever. Already I fear the cults control Tor Anroc, from what Alith learnt before he fled. It would not be safe for you to travel there, nor any herald of the other princes. The first blows come spring are likely to fall upon Ellyrion and Chrace.'

'And would you have kept this information to yourself had our paths not crossed?' said Carathril, wondering just how much Elthyrior knew about the events that were unfolding.

'It is because I bear this news that our paths have crossed,' the raven herald replied, which did not allay Carathril's suspicions but he decided not to press the matter.

'Which way must we head to catch the assassins?' he asked instead.

'Due east at dawn for half a day,' replied Elthyrior, standing up. He dipped his head in a nod of respect. 'I fear from there the assassins' path will be all too clear.'

'You will follow them also?'

'No,' replied the raven herald with a shake of his head. 'I am already out of Nagarythe and the situation changes quickly. Now that Morai-heg has sent you to me, I will return and watch Anlec for the next move of Morathi.'

'Thank you for coming to me,' said Carathril.

The gloom of the lamp disappeared, leaving the tent in darkness. Carathril heard not a rustle of feather nor the flap of the door, but knew within a heartbeat that the raven herald had gone. He waited for a while, collecting his thoughts, which had been sent into a whirl by Elthyrior. When he was certain the raven herald was away from the camp, he lit a lamp, pulled on his breastplate, vambraces and sword belt.

Leaving the tent, he saw that the sentries around the camp had not moved, and the glow of the fires illuminated the mountainside for some distance. Carathril walked over to the closest picket.

'Anything strange?' asked the herald.

'Nothing,' the sentry replied. 'Not even the birds have disturbed us.'

Shaking his head at the mysterious ways of the raven heralds, Carathril moved to one of the fires where he sat until the first glow of dawn appeared in the east. He sent one of the Sea Guard to fetch Neaderin.

'It's too cold for such an early start,' said the captain as he warmed himself by the fire. 'What could be so urgent?'

Carathril had wondered how he would explain his change of mind without mentioning Elthyrior. He did not want to lie to Neaderin, but nor could he reveal the raven herald's visit.

'I think that we shall take too long if we go around the mountains,' said Carathril. 'Imrik must be crowned Phoenix King as soon as possible, before the Naggarothi respond to events at the Isle of the Flame. With winter coming, it would be better if Imrik left Chrace sooner rather than later. We will head directly east.'

Neaderin gave Carathril a hard look, displeased with this news. The herald had expected some resistance and decided that he was in no mood for a debate.

'I am the appointed commander of the expedition, and I have made my decision,' he said, standing up. 'I want the company breakfasted and camp broken now. If there is anything you need me for, I shall be making my preparations to leave.'

With that, Carathril turned and left the astonished Sea Guard captain and walked back to his tent, trying not to hurry.

—◀ EIGHT ▶—

A New Legend

THE WIND HAD died down and the snow abated, but the late afternoon air was chill as Koradrel led the hunting party back towards the road to Tor Achare. Space had been made on one of the sleds for the bodies of the elves that had been killed by the manticore; another was laden with the hide, head and claws of the beast, for artificers to make suitable trophies.

'It seems we are not alone,' said Imrik, pointing to the west.

A thin column of smoke could be seen against the setting sun, drifting up from the forested slopes of Anul Anrian. Koradrel looked to the west, brow knotted in a frown.

'That's a large fire for a camp,' he said, signalling to one of the guides to join him. The elf jogged to join his prince. 'It could be nothing, but go and take a look. It may be that some monster has caused the blaze.'

The scout trotted off from the path, disappearing quickly beneath the pines that lined the mountainside on either side of the trail.

'What manner of beast could set such a fire?' said Imrik as the two continued on, the caravan of sleds not far behind.

'Who can say?' replied Koradrel with a shrug that set his lion cloak swinging. 'There are all kinds of creatures in these mountains that defy definition; things warped by Chaos and sustained by the vortex.'

'How far to the camp?' asked Imrik. He was feeling tired and his chest was bruised from the manticore's attack.

'Not far,' Koradrel said. He pulled a small clay bottle from a pouch at his belt and unstoppered it. The Chracian passed the bottle to Imrik with a smile. 'This will keep you warm for a while longer.'

'Charinai?' Imrik said, sniffing the bottle's contents. He took a swig of the spiced spirit, which warmed his mouth and throat to leave a pleasant taste of autumn fruits. 'I hope you have more.'

'There is a bottle in my pack somewhere,' Koradrel replied with a grin. 'We can celebrate our kill properly once we reach the campsite.'

Imrik passed the liquor back to his cousin, feeling invigorated by the brew. He glanced again to the west and hoped the smoke was something mundane; he did not feel in the mood for another encounter with Chrace's bestial denizens.

THE SEA GUARD spread around the clearing, spears and shields held at the ready, forming a cordon around the smoking ruins of a cabin. Carathril approached with sword unsheathed, eyes scanning the surrounding treeline for any sign of the perpetrators.

'Here!' Neaderin called out from beside a smaller pile of charred wood, most likely an outhouse of some kind. Two crows flapped away from something at Neaderin's feet, startled by his shout. The captain's voice was tense, and he stepped away from whatever he had found, shoulders hunched.

Carathril crossed the clearing quickly. He stopped dead as his eyes fell upon Neaderin's discovery, his stomach twisting in revulsion.

He was not sure how many bodies there were in the ash, but the size of some of the bones meant that children had been slain. What remained of the burned flesh was hacked and gouged, scattered into the flames. There was blood in the snow. A lot of blood. A short distance away, where the crows had been, entrails had been laid out. The interference of the carrion birds had not dislodged the gory pattern so much that it could not be recognised: a rune of Khaine.

Carathril shuddered as he remembered the places he had seen such depravity before; in the cult lairs of Lothern and the fortress of Ealith in Nagarythe.

'Naggarothi,' said Carathril. 'Assassins sent after Imrik.'

'How can you be sure?' replied Neaderin, not looking back towards the grisly scene. 'This could be the work of Chracian cultists.'

'Unlikely,' said Carathril. 'Had we found such a thing in Tor Achare, I would be tempted to believe you. Here, in the wilderness, it seems too much of a coincidence. These unfortunates were tortured before they were slain. This is a tree-feller's lodge. The only other thing this poor family would know is where to find the best pine groves.'

'So what do we do?' asked Neaderin. 'There is no sign of any trail leaving the clearing. Whoever did this covered their tracks.'

'Or left none,' said Carathril, remembering the strange ways of the raven heralds. If such secrets were known to the assassins, Imrik was in grave peril.

At that moment, there was a call from one of the Sea Guard, who had fanned out to search the treeline. Neaderin and Carathril ran over to see what had been discovered.

'Your assassins made a mistake,' said Neaderin, bending to one knee as the Sea Guard pointed at a patch of snow sheltered between the roots of a tree. Carathril saw a few drops of red on the white.

'They headed north-east,' he said. 'There's nothing else, call your company back. We must hurry if we are to warn Imrik.'

The soldiers rallied to the clearing at the call of their captain and headed out after the assassins, armour jingling as they ran into the woods.

THE SUN HAD almost disappeared behind the mountains and the sky to the east was a deep blue, the first stars visible, the crescent of Sariour appearing over the horizon. Elthanir knew his prey was close. The pain in his head had almost abated, leaving just a dull ache to nag at his thoughts. He could smell wood smoke on the light breeze, coming from a fire to the north. That concurred with the woodcutter's confession.

Sensing this too, the other assassins spread out as they moved through the close trunks of the pine trees. Elthanir began a whispered mantra, the incantation of a spell that drew in the magic of the vortex. Sorcery swirled around him, bending and shifting, seeping into his body.

Glancing at the others, he saw them doing the same. One moment seven black-clad figures stalked into the shadow; the next they were gone.

Stepping so lightly his feet left no mark upon the fallen needles and mulch, Elthanir stalked northwards. Owls hooted and small mammals scurried past, paying no heed to his presence as he slipped between the trees, pulling a recurved short bow from the quiver across his back and quickly stringing it as he walked. Ahead, he saw the distant twinkle of orange that was the campfire. He slid an arrow into place, its tip glistening with poison made from the black lotus. The assassin moved so he could see the fire a little better. There were half a dozen large tents, and hunters clad in lion-pelt cloaks moved about the camp. He settled down against a tree to wait for his victim to show himself.

There was laughter, and scattered verses of song. The Chracians were in high spirits. Elthanir could not remember what it was like to know such joy; the only pleasure he felt came from the act of killing and the infliction of pain.

The last rays of the sun streamed through the branches ahead, mingling with the smoke of the fire. A tent flap cracked and a tall elf emerged, clad in armour, a sword at his hip. He wore no lion cloak and Elthanir recognised him immediately: the Caledorian! Hatred welled up inside the assassin, remembering the agony he had felt, the image of his victim burned into his mind.

Imrik wandered away from the fire, heading to Elthanir's right. He moved from his position, flitting from shadow to shadow, disturbing nothing, the roosting birds overhead oblivious to his presence. He caught sight of his quarry again, standing in a small clearing, looking up into the clear skies.

Elthanir sighted on the prince, raising his bow. He gently pulled back the string, enjoying the tautness in his hand, revelling in the moment of death. With a satisfied smile, he loosed the arrow.

IMRIK ENJOYED THE touch of the fresh air on his cheek after the heat of the camp. The clouds had cleared and he looked up at the stars, remembering the constellations as they had been taught to him by his mother. As he turned his gaze downwards, his eyes caught something close to the edge of the clearing. It was a line of paw marks in the shallow snow, each several times as large as his hand. It was unmistakeably the trail of a white lion.

Just as he looked up, he saw a glint in the air. Reacting without thought, Imrik threw himself to one side, hand pulling his sword free in one fluid gesture, the blade flashing up to slice the arrow in half as it passed within a hand's breath of his shoulder.

Movement to his left caught his eye and he turned and shifted again, this time a dagger spinning end-over-end out of the shadows. Imrik deflected it with the flat of his blade.

'Attack!' he yelled, spinning on his heel, searching for some sign of his assailants. He saw nothing but darkness. 'Assassins!'

He heard the thud of feet and spun around, sword ready.

A lion whose shoulder was as high as the prince's rushed from the woods, fangs bared, its pale fur shining in the starlight. The Caledorian prince met its gaze, looking into deep yellow eyes filled with feral hunger. Imrik leapt aside as the lion raced towards him, just as he expected it to pounce.

The lion ignored him and ran straight across the clearing. On reaching the trees it leapt, paws outstretched. Blood splashed onto a nearby tree trunk, though from what Imrik could not see. Roaring and biting, the lion struggled with something that seemed to be made of shadow. Cuts opened up in its white hide, adding the lion's blood to the mess, but a moment later a hand fell into view, ragged bone jutting from it. There was a piercing wail and an elf clad in black staggered into the clearing.

ALERTED BY A shout, Koradrel snatched up his axe and ran from the tent he shared with his cousin. He heard the roar of a lion and set off at a sprint towards it, fearing Imrik was being attacked by one of the fabled white-furred beasts. The other hunters surged from the camp behind him.

He found his cousin in a small clearing a short distance from the camp, sword in hand, circling constantly, his blade sweeping and chopping in what seemed to be a mad slashing at thin air. Something fluttered on the edge of Koradrel's vision, a hazy mist that parted and reformed at the blade's passing.

As he neared the edge of the trees, Koradrel thought he saw something else, a greater darkness in the shadows behind Imrik. There was definitely movement. Not knowing what manner of spirits attacked his cousin, Koradrel slid to a stop and hurled his axe at the apparition closing in behind Imrik. It whirled across the clearing and struck the deeper shadow, stopping in the air. A heartbeat later, the body of an elf collapsed to the snow, almost cleaved in twain from shoulder to waist by the axe blade.

There were shouts from the other hunters as they encountered more shadowy foes in the woods, and the ring of metal on metal. There were cries of pain as well, and the whicker of darts and arrows cut the air.

THE STUPEFYING EFFECT of the charinai continued to flush from Imrik's body as he raised his sword to fend off another blurred attack towards his throat. As he staggered back the light of the moons broke through the cloud, bathing the clearing in silvery-green light. At that moment, he caught sight of his assailant, a flicker of a figure in the glow of the Chaos moon, swirling with the power of the vortex.

Imrik lunged without thought to drive the point of his blade towards the assassin's face. The shadowy attacker leaned away from the attack, a dagger glinting in the moonlight ringing against Imrik's blade. Even as the moonlight faded behind the clouds again Imrik pressed his attack, slashing his sword left and right, feeling its tip connect with flesh. There was a cry of pain and Imrik thrust high. Blood spattered along the etched blade and the magic of Lathrain flared, white licks of fire erupting along the blade.

Still swathed in shadow, the assassin flailed across the clearing, his clothing burning with pale flame so that he appeared a hazy silhouette of dark cloud engulfed by white fire, darkness and light swirling and battling.

Hearing fresh steps behind him, Imrik turned, sword at the ready. Koradrel raced into the clearing and snatched up his axe from the body of another assassin as more lion-cloaked hunters ran from the woods. One of the Chracians fell, a barbed dart in his arm, blood pouring from eyes and nose as the poison quickly took effect. There was a lighter blur in the dark and a savage growl rebounded from the trees; the white lion still prowled the woods.

'How many?' panted Imrik.

'Four are dead,' said Koradrel. 'I do not know how many still live.'

'There!' bellowed one of the huntsmen, pointing to the south as a dark shape sped from the treeline, the faint light catching a glint on a raised blade.

Three of the hunters leapt to meet the assassin; the first toppled to the ground in the next heartbeat, head falling separately. The other two swung their axes high and low and the crunch of breaking bones broke the stillness. A mangled body appeared, slumped on the ground, a curved, serrated blade falling from the assassin's dead grasp.

Silence reclaimed the woods.

Koradrel and the hunters closed around Imrik, axes held at the ready. They stood in the centre of the clearing, as far from the trees as possible, all eyes turned outwards.

'Above!' shouted Imrik, seeing a haze pass across the moonlit clouds.

His warning came too late as the gloom-cloaked attacker landed in the midst of the group, blood spraying as twin knives flashed. The hunters could not use their axes, afraid their wide swings would hit each other. The band scattered, trying to create space, two more of them falling with pained screams as their throats were cut.

Imrik's sword needed no such room and the prince sprang towards the shadow of the assassin, arm outstretched. The point lanced into something hard and deflected away.

'Duck!' shouted Koradrel and Imrik immediately dropped to the ground.

A moment later the axe head of Koradrel swung over the Caledorian, connecting heavily with the assassin. A severed arm flew from the shadow-shape and the air was split by a piercing howl of pain. Imrik surged to his feet, swinging up his sword, the blade burning as it cleaved through the wounded assassin's breast, slicing through ribs and heart.

After the flurry of violence, peace descended again.

Still Imrik was not sure if all of his attackers had been slain. Nobody spoke as the group reformed around the princes. Every flutter of a leaf or creak of a branch drew the attention of the elves, who peered into the darkness with wide eyes, searching for the slightest sign of a foe.

After some time, Imrik relaxed and sheathed his sword.

'That is the last,' he said.

'Are you sure?' said Koradrel.

'Yes,' replied Imrik, though his eyes said otherwise as they flickered towards a particular tree on the edge of the clearing, between the elves and their tents. Koradrel caught his meaning and gave the slightest of nods.

'Let us return to the camp,' said the Chracian. 'Gather the dead and attend to the wounded.'

The two princes set off towards the trees, weapons in hand. When they were only a few paces from the shadows, the last assassin struck, leaping from the gloom with sword outstretched. Koradrel had been expecting the attack and caught the blade with his axe, turning it aside as Imrik chopped with his sword, slashing down where he thought the assassin's neck to be.

His aim was not far off; the black-clad body that tumbled to the ground had its skull nearly sheared through. Imrik pulled free his blade with a grimace.

'Nobody sleeps tonight,' he said.

'I don't think anybody could after this,' Koradrel replied.

In all, eight hunters had been slain in the fight, three more wounded, one of those in a fever from a poisoned cut and not expected to survive until dawn. All of the elves sat in vigil for the rest of the night, the fires banked high with wood, whispering prayers to Ereth Khial to watch over the spirits of the slain.

Dawn was not far off when the sound of a large body of soldiers could be heard coming up the valley. The Chracians were alert, two of the guides heading down the track to investigate while the rest stood guard at the camp and manned the bolt thrower.

It was a testing wait for Imrik. The fight with the manticore and the attempt on his life had left him feeling drained, his body weak from the exertions of the day. He pulled his sword free and stood with the others, waiting anxiously.

There was no sound of fighting and after a while, the scouts returned with the third of their number who had been sent to investigate the fire. With them came another elf, clad in silver armour.

'Who is this?' demanded Koradrel.

'I know him,' said Imrik, sheathing his sword. 'He is Carathril, herald of the Phoenix King. He can be trusted.'

The Chracians relaxed only slightly as the herald approached the camp. Behind him came a company of warriors bearing shields with the emblem of the Sea Guard.

'In a night of surprises, this is the last thing I expected,' said Koradrel. 'What brings a herald of the Phoenix King to the wilds of Chrace?'

'Grave events have engulfed Ulthuan,' said Carathril. 'Bel Shanaar is dead and a great many of our princes have been slain at the Isle of the Flame. Malekith tried to become Phoenix King and was killed by the flames.'

'Caledrian?' said Imrik, his heart heavy with foreboding,

Carathril shook his head.

'Your brother is amongst the dead,' said the herald. 'Yet Thyrinor survived.'

Imrik swallowed hard at the news. His thoughts flashed back to when he had been told of his father's death and been presented with Lathrain. Emptiness swallowed his heart at the realisation that Caledrian was slain, and the gulf widened as he realised that he was now ruling prince of Caledor.

Carathril beckoned to one of the Sea Guard, who entered the camp bearing a bundle wrapped in waxed leather. The herald took this and walked up to Koradrel.

'These are for you,' he said, eyes downcast.

Koradrel took the bundle and opened it. Inside were a folded banner of red with a white lion's face embroidered upon it and an axe, its double-bladed head like the wings of a silver butterfly etched with forks of lightning.

'Achillar, and the banner of Chrace,' said Koradrel, choking on the words. He looked at Carathril. 'Where are my brother and nephew?'

'Also slain,' Carathril said. He gave a solemn bow. 'You are now the ruling prince of Chrace.'

There were moans and mutters from the other Chracians, and some swore oaths to the gods to find the perpetrators of such a crime.

'The Naggarothi have revealed their true colours,' said Carathril in answer. 'It was knights of Anlec that killed so many at the Shrine of Asuryan, and I have good information that Morathi has been freed and returned to Anlec.'

Carathril reached into his robe and drew out a folded piece of parchment. He handed it to Imrik, who looked numbly at the letter, not understanding its importance. He pushed back the grief that welled up inside him and directed an inquiring look at Carathril.

'Bel Shanaar wrote this to you before he died,' explained the herald.

'The seal is broken,' said Imrik, unfolding the letter.

'Thyriol instructed me to open it,' said Carathril. 'Read it first and then hear my message from him.'

Imrik scanned the letter quickly, saying nothing. Its content came as no surprise, although it seemed now more prophetic than perhaps had been intended.

'What else?' said Imrik.

'Those princes that have survived, Thyriol, Finudel and a few others, have chosen you to become Phoenix King,' said Carathril. He looked at Koradrel. 'They do not expect any objection to the nomination.'

'And they will get none from me,' said the Chracian.

'These are desperate times,' said Carathril. 'The situation has changed. Ulthuan does not need you as a general, it needs you as a king.'

'Why?' said Imrik.

Carathril was taken aback by the question and took a moment to reply.

'You are the best of the princes, and you have the support of your fellows,' said the herald. 'Caledor remains strong, and you will need that strength. You have the dragon princes to come to your call.'

Imrik nodded, accepting each point.

'No other prince who survives can match you, Imrik. They are slain, all but a few of the greatest of Ulthuan. The Phoenix Throne is empty, the crown unworn, and the kingdoms are in disarray.'

'Bad,' said Imrik. 'Very bad.'

'What does this mean?' said Koradrel. 'Malekith dead, Morathi reigns again in Nagarythe, princes slain and assassins in the shadows?'

Imrik looked at the other elves, seeing fear and hope in their expressions. Fear of what had happened; hope that he would protect them. There was no higher calling, no greater duty that he could be asked to fulfil.

'What will become of us?' said one of the Chracians. 'What happens now?'

Imrik took a deep breath and nodded his assent to Carathril and Koradrel. His hard stare met the gazes of those around him and he answered the question that loitered in all of their minds.

'War.'

— NINE —

From the Flames

THERE WAS NONE of the ceremony that had accompanied the crowning of Bel Shanaar. The Shrine of Asuryan was almost empty; the high priest Mianderin and his acolytes prepared their incantations while Imrik waited with the ruling princes that had survived the massacre or been chosen to succeed those who had not. There was one notable absence; no representative stood for Tiranoc. Messages had been sent, but no word had returned of who had succeeded Bel Shanaar; Elodhir had been heir before his death at the hands of Bathinair.

Koradrel had come south with Imrik and Carathril, accompanied by several hundred Chracians summoned from the mountain towns around Tor Achare. Not trusting any other with the task, Imrik had appointed the lion-pelted warriors to be his bodyguard in recognition of their fight against the assassins. He called them the White Lions of Chrace and news of their bravery had quickly spread through the several thousand elves stood guard on the Isle of the Flame. Alongside them were the silent warriors of the Phoenix Guard. Their numbers were diminished, many having fallen to knights of Nagarythe and cultists in fighting outside the shrine while the massacre had taken place within.

Imrik spied the crest of the Phoenix Guard's captain amidst a troop standing at the doorway, and left the other princes.

'Your order has read the secrets held within the Chamber of Days,' said Imrik. 'Written in fire upon the stone are the lives of every Phoenix King.'

The captain nodded once, his expression unmoving.

'And you read Bel Shanaar's doom?'

The captain did not respond, but met Imrik's glare with a steady gaze.

'Is my death written there in flame?' the Caledorian asked.

Again the captain made no gesture of denial or agreement. Snarling, Imrik grabbed the Phoenix Guard captain by the golden clasp of his cloak.

'What use is the wisdom of Asuryan if you keep your tongue?' snapped Imrik. 'You stand silent while our people destroy themselves.'

'He will not answer you,' Mianderin called from within the shrine. 'He will die before he utters any word. Unhand him, Imrik, and behave like a king. It is not for us to know the will of Asuryan, nor to second-guess it. Fate will always prevail.'

Imrik released his grip and stalked back into the shrine, wondering if there was any means by which he might elude the destiny scribed upon the walls of the Chamber of Days. He was greeted by a row of expectant faces. Thyriol was smiling slightly, evidently amused at Imrik's outburst.

'Imrik dies this day,' declared Mianderin, waving the group to gather around the eternal flame of Asuryan. 'As Aenarion and Bel Shanaar before him, he shall pass into the flames and be destroyed by Asuryan's judgement, to be reborn again as the Phoenix King.'

'If I am to die, then my name will die with me,' said Imrik, earning himself a frown from the high priest for the interruption. He ignored Mianderin's sigh of annoyance and continued. 'Imrik will not lead our people to salvation. I will be Caledor, in honour of my grand-father and the kingdom that raised me. Imrik will walk into the flames but Caledor will emerge.'

'May we continue?' said Mianderin. Imrik nodded his assent. 'Today we crown a new Phoenix King, chosen by the princes of Ulthuan to be the first amongst equals.'

'Are we done?' said Imrik.

He started walking towards the flame. Mianderin hurried after him, signalling to his acolytes to light incense burners and begin their chanting. The high priest grabbed Imrik's arm two steps from the flame.

'Not yet,' said Mianderin.

The high priest stepped back and began his own whispering incantation. Imrik stood looking at the flame of Asuryan. There was no heat. His skin prickled with magic and he felt the enchantments of the priests weaving around him. His limbs chilled and his heart slowed.

Two acolytes approached and fastened the long cloak of feathers upon his shoulder guards. Taking a deep breath, Imrik looked to Mianderin, who nodded.

Imrik stepped into the fire.

THE FLAMES BURNED through him, touching every part of his body and spirit. There was no pain, no sensation at all. Imrik felt like a ghost, apart from the mortal world. He could still hear the singing of the priests, but the melody had changed, the pitch moved higher. Imrik swore that a thousand voices were now singing.

He could see nothing but multicoloured fire. He was made of it. He lifted a hand in front of his face and saw nothing save the dancing flames.

Imrik wondered if he was dead.

The cloak felt like wings, lifting him up, borne aloft by the flames. He closed his eyes but nothing changed; still the flames filled his vision. A gentle breeze seemed to wash over him, its touch smoothing away skin and flesh and bone, reducing him to delicate ash; all without the slightest hint of discomfort. Imrik thought that he imagined it.

Sensation returned, the fire coalescing again into his form, creating body and limbs and head and fingers and every part of him from its essence. Opening his eyes, he turned and stepped out of the flames.

THE PRINCES GAVE a cheer, raising their fists in salute to their new king.

'Hail Caledor, Phoenix King of Ulthuan!'

Caledor nodded in gratitude and rejoined his companions. He did not even glance back at the flames.

'What now?' he asked.

'It is tradition that you travel to Avelorn, and be married to the Everqueen,' said Mianderin. 'She is Ulthuan's true ruler, and you must seek her blessing as well as Asuryan's.'

The priest leaned in closer and whispered his next words.

'It is also necessary that you father an heiress to take up the mantle of Everqueen,' said Mianderin.

'No time,' said Caledor. He looked at the princes. 'We need an army. Nagarythe will march soon, if it does not already. There is not a host of a single kingdom that can match them.'

'And what would you do with this army?' asked Aerethenis. The elf was young, barely an adult, and had just inherited Eataine from his slain uncle Haradrin. 'Which lands will you protect with this host?'

'Protect?' said Caledor. 'Ulthuan is too large for one army to guard. We will invade Nagarythe first.'

This caused consternation, particularly among the newly elevated princes. There were words of disagreement and Tithrain of Cothique stepped forwards to voice the complaint.

'We have few warriors to speak of,' said the freshly crowned prince. 'What armies we have defend our lands in the colonies. Not just Cothique, but also Eataine and Saphery. Yvresse still reels from the treachery of Bathinair.'

'You can offer your households,' Finudel said sharply. 'And yourselves. Saphery has mages, Eataine the Sea Guard. All of you have city militia, raised to combat the cults.'

'And they still fight that battle,' said Tithrain. 'If we march on Nagarythe we abandon our homes to unknown peril at the hands of Morathi's agents and assassins.'

'Sooner that than allow the legions of Nagarythe to march into your homes,' said Athielle. She looked at Caledor with fierce eyes and then to Koradrel. 'Chrace and Ellyrion border Nagarythe and will feel the first blow. Tiranoc also, though I fear the absence of their new prince tells me we should expect no aid from that quarter, whatever the reason.'

'Chrace will fight, you already know that,' said Koradrel. 'But the others are right, cousin. I must return and see to the defence of my kingdom first before I can accompany you into Nagarythe. When the border is secure, I will bring such warriors as I have remaining to you.'

Caledor sighed with frustration and looked to Thyriol for support.

'I will send word for those mages skilled in counter-magic to come here, so that we might thwart any sorcery of Morathi and her coven,' said the Sapherian prince. 'Like the others, I have few spears and swords for the cause and many of them must be employed guarding against the enemy that already lurks within.'

Biting back his disappointment, Caledor remembered that he was chosen as king to lead, not be a tyrant. The princes were right to be fearful for the security of their kingdoms. It was not cowardice; it was their first and greatest duty to protect their people.

'Very well,' he said. 'Let us each return to our kingdoms and make what preparations we can. We will return here at the first winter moon, in forty-three days.'

'Be vigilant for all danger,' said Thyriol. 'While we cast our gaze towards Nagarythe, do not let the enemy near at hand slip from your sight. The cytharai worshippers will come in force now that all is revealed. Make no mistake, this is a war now, and we must prevail.'

'Show no mercy,' said Caledor. 'A moment's weakness will doom us all.'

A LONG PEAL shook the bleak mountainside from Dorien's dragon horn, rebounding from the bare rocks, echoes muffled by the low mist. Thyrinor glanced at Imrik – Caledor, he reminded himself – and saw the new Phoenix King's eyes intent upon the cave mouths barely visible though the haze. The new ruler of Ulthuan had passed on the momentous news of his elevation with barely a glimmer of emotion; no more feeling than if he had been reporting the weather over the Inner Sea. Caledor had refused all suggestion of celebration and was even more close-lipped than he had been before.

They had ridden with haste to the lair of the dragons, Caledor almost silent for the whole journey. Thyrinor had tried to prise forth some word concerning the Phoenix King's thoughts, but had failed. Caledor was worried, that much Thyrinor could see, and the way he waited for the dragons to answer the call did nothing to allay Thyrinor's fears. Caledor was tense, hands clenched in fists, arms crossed over his breastplate, jaw clamped shut.

There was none of the show of the last visit. Maedrethnir emerged from a cave to the elves' right and swooped down to the bare hill.

'There is something different about you,' said the old dragon. His nostrils flared wide as he sniffed the air, head weaving back and forth around Caledor. 'Magic touches you. Old magic.'

'I am Phoenix King,' replied Caledor. 'You sense the flame of Asuryan.'

'Phoenix King?' The dragon arched back its neck in surprise. 'Bel Shanaar is dead?'

'War is coming,' said Caledor, ignoring the question. 'Will the dragons ride with the princes of Caledor?'

'You have become even more abrupt, Imrik,' said Maedrethnir.

'I have taken the name Caledor,' said the Phoenix King. 'To honour these lands and the elf that first sought the alliance of the dragons.'

Maedrethnir snorted, though Thyrinor could not tell whether from amusement or derision. Regardless, the dragon bowed its head and launched into the air, circling back to the cave from which he had emerged.

They waited a long time. Thyrinor tried to engage with Dorien, but he seemed to have been infected by his brother's mood and would say no more than a few words in reply. Eventually Thyrinor gave up and sat down on a rock, left to his own dark thoughts.

Dusk was approaching when finally Maedrethnir appeared again. Two more dragons followed him out of the cave: Anaegnir and Nemaerinir. The three dragons landed around the elves, wings cutting swirls though the thickening mist.

'No more?' said Caledor.

'We three are all that will come,' said Maedrethnir. 'No others will answer the call.'

'Three dragons is enough to destroy Nagarythe,' said Dorien. He turned to Nemaerinir, his own mount. 'Thank you for heeding the call.'

'I slept only lightly,' the red-scaled dragon replied. 'Another year and perhaps I would not have answered.'

'Maedrethnir spoke of war and you mention Nagarythe,' said Anaegnir, her voice mellower than the males. 'What evil stirs in the north?'

'Treachery,' replied Thyrinor. 'The Naggarothi try to usurp power and the other kingdoms have little might to respond. The dragons of Caledor will go a long way to restoring the balance of power.'

'To fight elves?' said Nemaerinir. The dragon rumbled deep in his throat. 'An unpleasant business.'

'Yes,' said Caledor. 'Yet one we must attend to.'

'The Naggarothi promote the worship of the undergods,' said Thyrinor. 'They would have all of Ulthuan under thrall of Khaine and Ereth Khial and others should they be victorious.'

'There are worse gods to be in thrall to,' said Maedrethnir.

'Our division makes us weak,' said Dorien. 'A weakness the Chaos Gods will sense and act upon. If the elves fall, who will keep the vortex from failing? The dwarfs? The humans? The orcs?'

'Dorien is right,' said Thyrinor. 'We must fight not just for the fate of ourselves, but for the future of the world. If Morathi and her followers rule, they will bring dark magic and sorcery and the daemons will come again.'

'It shall not be so,' growled Anaegnir. 'We will help you.'

'Good,' said Caledor. 'We ride back to Tor Caled. Meet us at the palaces when you are ready.'

'And then where?' said Dorien. 'The Naggarothi can march straight through Tiranoc and be upon our borders before we know it.'

'They would be foolish to march before spring,' replied Thyrinor. 'We have time to muster the army.'

'The army will wait, but the cultists will not,' said Dorien. 'They will rise up and pave the way for the Naggarothi advance. There will be death this winter, mark my words.'

'A dragon cannot hunt cultists,' said Anaegnir. 'Not unless you wish your cities ruined and your fields burned.'

'You are right,' said Caledor. 'We shall wait for the army of Nagarythe. Then we kill them.'

── TEN ──

Lothern Attacked

As CARATHRIL OPENED the door to the winehouse, swirls of fragrance-laden smoke drifted out into the street. He waved for Aerenis to precede him inside and then entered, closing the door behind him. It was quiet, as was to be expected in the middle of the day, with only a few patrons gathered at a table close to the fire. Carathril recognised them as members of the Palace Watch, again without surprise as this particular wine room was used almost exclusively by members of the princes' guard. One of them, Myrthreir, raised a hand in welcome and beckoned the pair over to the padded bench on which he sat.

'The new Fierean deep red has just finished settling,' said another of the soldiers, Khalinir, as they joined the group. He proffered his glass towards Carathril. 'Try some, it is very fruity.'

Carathril accepted the crystal goblet and took a sip of the wine. It was delicately scented with rose, and was of a fuller flavour than he usually liked but not unpleasant.

'Palatable,' said Carathril with an equivocal look,

He offered the glass to Aerenis.

'I think I will stay loyal to my Sapherian Gold until the winter grape season comes around,' he said, waving away the goblet.

An attendant with long fair hair bound in a single plait down her back made her way over to the table and Carathril ordered a bottle of his favourite wine. Aerenis asked for water.

'I heard Hythreir's *Dissertation on Cynics* last night,' said Khalinir. 'He was performing in the Sapphire Plaza. It was a touch sentimental, if you ask me, but it seemed to get the crowd going, what with all that talk about Aenarion and such. Then again, that is Hythreir, always one for popularity over pedigree.'

'I thoroughly enjoyed his *Musings of a Lothern Trader*,' said Fithuren from the far end of the table. 'Of course, that was before Malekith returned. His humour has changed dramatically, and I do not appreciate some of the darker elements he now uses in his compositions. It seems that he has been getting more and more caught up with his own woes for these last years. One would think that he was the only elf in Lothern with worries and cares, the way he stands there and laments in Opal Square sometimes.'

'It is enough that we must deal with these accursed cults when we are on duty, I do not want to hear about them endlessly when I set down my spear,' said Myrthreir. 'The prince issues proclamation after proclamation, and yet still there are those blind enough to flock to these demagogues and rabble-rousers. Only five days ago, we found a nest of Athartists posing as an embroidery guild in Callhan. I tell you, when we found what they had been picturing with their needles, it sent a shiver down my spine. One of them almost took my eye out with his fingernails, if you believe that.'

'You sent them away?' asked Aerenis.

'Of course we did,' replied Fithuren. 'Until the prince orders otherwise, we send them under escort to Amil Annanian. I hear that another ship left this morning, with nearly two hundred of the depraved souls on board. More than fifty are being tended to by the priests of Ereth Khial.'

'If it means that we do not spill as much blood as we might, then I see no harm in it,' said Aerenis.

'They seem tame enough, once captured,' said Mythreir.

'Most are normal folk,' said Aerenis. 'Some simply want answers or escape, or sympathy. For my part, I do not see the harm in much of what they do. In Nagarythe, I hear, there are blood sacrifices and all manner of bestial behaviour, but here in Lothern most of those we arrest are nothing more than lost souls seeking a path.'

'Their acts are forbidden, even if they do not directly harm others,' said Myrthreir.

'But why are they forbidden?' asked Aerenis quietly. The serving maid returned with their drinks and Aerenis took a sip of his water before continuing. 'The prince and his council decide that Hythreir's poems and performances are sound, whilst issuing decrees against writers such as Elrondhir and Hythryst for being seditious and dangerous. Five years ago, Elrondhir was court poet to Prince Haradrin, now he is a fugitive.'

Carathril had become accustomed to Aerenis's morose moods since he had returned to Lothern. It was a city he had found to be irrevocably changed by the betrayal of Prince Aeltherin and the death of Prince Haradrin, yet even now there were some in the guard and nobility who refused to accept the danger posed by the dark cults.

Rumours and whispers persisted that Haradrin had entrapped Aeltherin in some way, and it was to these conspiratorial allegations that Aerenis now referred. Carathril had spoken many times with his friend concerning the manner of Aeltherin's demise and he knew it haunted Aerenis still, as did the death of his sister's friend, Glaronielle. The prince had burned himself alive, along with his unconscious followers, and the hideous scene still haunted all of those that had witnessed it. Though Aerenis had never admitted as such, it was plain to Carathril that his companion had harboured feelings for the girl he had mentioned; feelings that perhaps he had never expressed to her while she lived.

Now Aerenis had become cold-hearted, turning ever more inwards in his grief as the years had passed. He no longer joked with good humour, and laughed only from bitterness. His company was rare, for he spent most of his off-duty time with his own counsel; Carathril had never insulted his friend by inquiring too deeply concerning where he hid himself away for days at a time.

Lost in his musing, Carathril did not realise that he was being addressed by Myrthreir.

'Carathril?' the royal guard said.

'I am sorry, my thoughts were soaring elsewhere, like the eagles of the mountains,' Carathril said with a glance at Aerenis. If his friend recollected that old conversation, he did not show it, but stared silently into his glass.

'I asked if the Sapphire Company was taking part in this expedition to the mountains tomorrow,' said Myrthreir.

'Yes, I am leading the company to Hal Mentheon to meet with Captain Fyrthril of the Ruby Company,' said Carathril.

'Hal Mentheon?' Aerenis asked sharply. 'You did not mention that before.'

'Why the concern?' said Carathril.

'It is the town where my sister lives,' Aerenis explained. 'I hope that she is safe.'

'We are mustering at Hal Mentheon, but our mission takes us inland to the mountains, somewhere close to the Enullii Caith on the border of Caledor,' Carathril assured his friend. 'I am sure that nothing is amiss in the town, we would have heard otherwise from Fyrthril.'

'Yes, you are probably right,' muttered Aerenis, returning his gaze to his water.

Carathril finished his goblet of wine and poured another, letting the conversation of the others sweep over him, occasionally nodding in agreement at some point or smiling at a witty comment. Aerenis excused himself shortly before dusk, and though Carathril worried about his friend, he was glad of the lightening of the mood that came with the departure of his dour companion. As often happened these days, the talk eventually meandered its way around to the subject of Nagarythe.

'I heard from a Chracian merchant that the army of the Anars is besieged in the citadel of Cauthis, just west of Griffon Pass,' said Khalinir.

'That is old news,' scoffed Myrthreir. 'Naggarothi fighting Naggarothi can be no bad thing for us. I don't know why the prince is so worried. Nagarythe is furthest from Eataine. It's not as if they could sneak through Tiranoc and Ellyrion to attack us without warning, is it?'

Carathril remained silent. He had met Alith Anar and felt some sympathy for those Naggarothi still loyal to the Phoenix Throne. Whatever the fortunes of the coming war, Carathril knew in his heart that the Anars would be forevermore caught between their loyalties. He was thankful that they opposed Morathi. Myrthreir was right about one thing: Lothern was about as far from the fighting as Carathril was likely to get without heading for the colonies.

New recruits were being mustered and one day Carathril knew he would have to march out again beneath the banner of Eataine. For the moment he was content to leave the action and worries to others. Like many of his fellows, his first concern was the safety of his prince and his people. He would fight when ordered, but was trying to enjoy the relative peace while it lasted.

Knowing that he was to march out with his company the following day, Carathril made his excuses and left the winehouse while his willpower and sobriety still allowed.

As he walked back to his quarters along the stone streets of Lothern, he pondered that area of greyness between convivial leisure and the slide into the depravities of the cults. To lose oneself utterly to sensation, to cast aside the fears, doubts and anguishes of rational life was forever a temptation to the elves. The joys of friendship and love were unsurpassed, but so too did Carathril and his people suffer greatly from the blackest depths of anger and woe.

Each walked a perilous path between agony and ecstasy, forever fighting the restless spirit awakened within his heart by the coming of Aenarion; the desire to fight and conquer, to ascend to pinnacles of sensation of which only the elven mind and body were capable.

Carathril felt no such desire himself. His life had been eventful enough and he craved the mundane and predictable as much as the cultists sought stimulation and risk. Comfortable that he could still resist the lures of his elven spirit, and lulled by the wine, Carathril fell asleep relaxed and at peace.

AERENIS WOKE CARATHRIL not long after daybreak, bringing him a tumbler of fresh water from the barracks well and a small loaf of bread with a pat of butter and a pot of glistening honey. Carathril's lieutenant seemed more at ease than he had the night before and the captain remarked upon this.

'I shall see my sister when we reach Hal Mentheon,' Aerenis explained. 'I have not seen her since summer last year, nor my cousins and nephews. Remember, I am country-born, not a child of Lothern like you.'

'Of course,' said Carathril. 'I have no family to miss, but I suppose the city and its people are the closest I have to kin.'

The company was assembled for the march to Hal Mentheon and was soon heading westwards from Lothern to meet up with soldiers from other parts of Eataine. Situated between the Inner Sea and the outer coast of Ulthuan, the kingdom was a beautiful spread of rolling hills and farmlands, gradually rising to the west until it reached the foothills of the Dragon Spine Mountains that marked the border with Caledor.

The one hundred elves made their way along a coastal road at a steady pace, meadows and pastures to their right, shallow cliffs on their left broken by winding paths and roadways leading down to many inlets and beaches. The wind came off the sea, bringing with it salty air and flurries of drizzle from the cloudy sky, but the march was not unpleasant during the frequent breaks in which the sun shone down.

Past midday the company halted for a rest, above a small fishing village nestled in the lee of a white chalk cliff that curved like a waning moon around a green-watered bay. Most of the vessels were out, their white sails and hulls seen against the dark of the sea. Food was unloaded from the company's supply wagons.

Carathril left the company and walked a short distance away to lean against a white-painted stone wall marking the boundary of a farm. Arms resting on the wall, spear and shield next to him, he looked out to the sea and watched the birds flying around the cliff tops, their harsh cries cutting the air above the crash of surf at the foot of the cliff below him.

He moved his gaze further out to sea and looked at the horizon to the south, enjoying the tranquillity of the flat blue expanse of the ocean. Aerenis joined him, handing Carathril a wrapped parcel of bread and cured meat before leaning his back against the wall.

'It's hard to believe there is anything amiss in Eataine on days like this,' said Carathril.

'Perhaps there is nothing amiss,' replied Aerenis. 'Enjoy the peace for what it is.'

'If only it was so simple,' said Carathril. He sighed and closed his eyes, taking a deep breath of sea air and soaking in the warmth of the sun. 'There are enemies closer at hand than we realise. I cannot believe Lothern is totally free of the cults, and the rest of Eataine surely provides shelter for more.'

'Do you wonder if perhaps enemies have been made of the cults when it need not be so?' said Aerenis.

'What do you mean?' said Carathril, turning to his friend.

'There have been a few, like the Khainites, who have preyed on the innocent, but most of them are harmless enough, surely?' answered Aerenis. 'What if some of our people wish to lose themselves occasionally in a pleasant fugue, or wish to converse with the spirits of the dead? Is it worth the suffering it has brought to persecute these people?'

'It is a trap of the spirit,' said Carathril. 'It is the harm it does to our culture, our society, which makes the worship of the cytharai a malaise. You saw what had become of Prince Aeltherin. The cults impair the judgement and erode the moral being of our people.'

'And so you would have every cultist slain?' said Aerenis. 'Is that the solution?'

'I do not know,' replied Carathril. 'It seems inevitable that bloodshed will settle this. The Naggarothi have stirred up their sycophants and their agents, and the cults will respond by moving against the rule of the princes and the Phoenix King. If they surrender peacefully, it could be avoided.'

'I detect the hint of arrogance with that approach,' said Aerenis. 'Why are all the demands heaped upon the cultists? What attempts have ever been made to help them, to incorporate their needs and desires into our society? They have been branded outsiders, now criminals, and you wonder why they disregard the authority of their princes?'

Not having any answer to that, Carathril turned back to the sea. Aerenis was kind-hearted and forgiving, and he made a good point. Yet for all the wrongs that the cultists might reasonably claim had been done to them, Carathril could not forget the grisly scenes he had witnessed at Ealith many years before, nor could he forget the beguiling power that had tried to turn him to the service of the cytharai.

His eye roamed the waves without purpose as he considered Aerenis's words. Looking to the west, he spied a sail coming around the headland, larger than that of a fishing boat. Concentrating, he saw a two-hulled hawk-ship sailing into view, both its sails full in the wind, a light-blue pennant streaming from its masthead.

Another followed, and another.

Surprised, Carathril watched the flotilla tacking into the bay. In all there were eleven vessels, two of them mighty three-hulled dragonships, their decks lined with elves.

'What business has a Tiranocii fleet in Eataine?' he said, glancing towards Aerenis. His companion was staring at the fleet, his expression one of shock and disbelief.

'Your eyes are sharper than mine,' said Aerenis, shielding his gaze from the sun almost directly overhead. 'I think I see soldiers aboard.'

Carathril returned his attention to the approaching ships. Looking more closely, he realised that Aerenis was right. The sides of each ship were lined with elves in armour, carrying shields and spears. As the flotilla came into the sunlight, Carathril saw that the warriors were dressed in black and purple, with banners of the same flying above them.

'Naggarothi!' he snapped. 'They must have taken the fleet of Tiranoc.'

'The Naggarothi are here in Eataine?' Aerenis's reaction was one of confusion more than shock.

'We have to return to Lothern,' said Carathril, pushing himself from the wall.

'I must warn my family.' Aerenis looked as if he had not heard what Carathril had said.

The lieutenant broke into a run, shouting to the others by the road. Carathril headed after him, calling for the company to fall in. There was anarchy and dissent. Some of the warriors, like Aerenis, had family outside the city and wished to return to their homes to warn of the Naggarothi attack.

'They will fall upon Eataine like a cloud of wrath,' Aerenis implored, grabbing Carathril by the sleeve of his robe. 'We cannot leave our people ignorant of the threat.'

Carathril could see that order would not be easy to restore. He darted a look to seaward and saw the first of the hawkships was gliding up to the harbour. The boarding gantries were already being swung over the side.

'Those who will return to Lothern, come with me,' he said quickly, his gaze roving over the company. 'Those that wish to see families safe, go to them as swiftly as possible and bring them to the city. If you cannot do that, I suggest that you head for the sanctuary of Caledor. I do not think the Naggarothi will dare the ire of the dragon princes.'

As nearly a third of the company split away, heading north and westwards, Carathril delayed Aerenis with a hand on his shoulder.

'Fetch your family and bring them to Lothern,' said the former herald. 'Bring as many people from Hal Mentheon as you can.'

Aerenis nodded.

'Make sure you keep the gates open for us,' he said. 'It will take two days and more to reach them and return.'

'I will make sure the prince sends out the army to provide escort for you,' promised Carathril. 'I have to go now. Take care of yourself, my friend.'

'And you, my captain,' said Aerenis.

Carathril stood for a moment and watched as Aerenis hurried along the road, chasing after the dwindling group of silver and green moving quickly to the west. The captain turned back to the east and signalled for the remaining members of the company to form up. He looked down at the harbour and felt a twinge of guilt as lines of black-and-silver snaked from the docked ships into the fishing town. There was nothing his small company could do against the several thousand Naggarothi landing on the shore. His duty was to warn the people of Lothern and ensure the sea gates were closed.

He set off at a brisk march, the company falling in behind, and blocked out the first shouts and screams that were carried to him on the sea breeze.

BANKS OF CLOUD had swept over the countryside, swathing Eataine in darkness, the light of the moons a dim glimmer to the east. In the gloom, dozens of fires burned, stretching along the coast as towns and villages were consumed by flames set by the Naggarothi. From the wall of Lothern, Carathril could see other lights too; the brands carried by the soldiers of the prince stretching in long lines towards the city, guiding the refugees to sanctuary.

There had been pitifully few over the last day and a half; no more than a few thousand had been able to flee the Naggarothi attack. Aerenis had not yet reported back to the barracks and Carathril feared the worst for his friend, though he harboured a small hope that he had reached the city unseen by the captain and was busy attending to his family.

A gong rang loudly over the city and Carathril turned. Bathed in the pale glow of the Glittering Tower, Lothern was quiet, subdued by the Naggarothi offensive. More lights clustered between the two great sea gates, shining from lamps upon the ships of the Eataine fleet; dozens of vessels that had sought safe harbour from the captured Tiranoc ships prowling along the coast.

There had been many who had argued for the prince to open the sea gates and let loose the wrath of the fleet against the raiders, but such counsel had been refused. Aerethenis, nephew to slain Haradrin, had little support in his new position and was loath to risk Lothern's ships; the kingdom's greatest weapon. It was a hard-hearted decision to abandon the folk of Eataine to the merciless Naggarothi, but Carathril agreed with his ruler. There was no sense in risking an invasion of the harbour.

The gates below Carathril swung open again as a crowd of elves surged along the road, escorted by companies of knights with pale-green pennants. The refugees looked haggard, having been harried across the pastures and meadows, and many of the knights were wounded, their armour dented and injuries bandaged. Carathril scanned the faces of the elves passing into the gate and gave a cry of relief when he spied Aerenis.

Carathril dashed down the steps to the square behind the gatehouse. He found Aerenis amongst the crowd, three female elves and two young boys with him.

'Praise Asuryan that you are safe,' said Carathril.

Aerenis looked at him with a bleak expression.

'Asuryan deserves no praise for what has befallen us,' said the lieutenant. 'It was the flame of Asuryan that scorched Malekith and unleashed this war upon us.'

Carathril was shocked by his friend's words and could think of no reply. Aerenis said nothing more as he guided his family across the square, to where residents of Lothern were waiting with food, blankets and healing tinctures.

The thunder of hooves on cobbles caused Carathril to draw back as the knights rode back through the gate. Their captain, his green plume sparkling in the light of the Glittering Tower, pulled his mount to a stop beside the gatehouse.

'Close the gate!' he bellowed. 'The enemy have reached the Anir Morien!'

'What of the rest of the army?' Carathril called out. 'We cannot abandon them.'

The captain looked down at Carathril, his expression one of surprise.

'What army?' the captain said with a bitter laugh. 'Those torches you see are carried by the Naggarothi! A few companies hold Tir Athenor, others have fled to the Inner Sea. The Naggarothi will be at the city by dawn.'

Carathril's chest tightened and his legs weakened at the news. The captain's words had carried across to others in the square. Shouts of dismay and cries of panic echoed from surrounding buildings. Anir Morien was the closest of the watch towers beyond the walls, and if it had fallen the Naggarothi would control an important harbour on the Inner Sea.

The crowd surged further into the city, spreading the dreadful news.

'Man the walls, I shall ride to the prince,' said the knight captain.

Without waiting for a reply, he wheeled his horse away and clattered across the square, leaving Carathril aghast. Having heard the dire tidings, many soldiers were leaving the wall, eager to see their families.

'Back to your posts!' Carathril roared, unsheathing his sword. 'You best serve your loved ones behind your spears and shields!'

A few disobeyed the order and headed into the city, but most were cowed by Carathril's words and filed back into the towers, grim-faced. The former herald sprang back up the steps to the gatehouse and fixed his gaze to the west. The flickers of the Naggarothi torches crept closer as he looked, moving through fields and woods like serpents of flame.

'Sound the alarm,' said Carathril, turning to a hornblower beside him.

The musician wetted his lips and lifted the long white horn to his mouth. He let loose a pealing blast that reverberated across the city. Within moments it was taken up by those in the other towers, the warning echoing across Lothern, bells and gongs ringing out in answer.

In the distance, a greater light broke the night; flames from a burning manse upon a distant hilltop. Carathril could see nothing of the Naggarothi save for the sea of brands coming ever closer.

'Archers!' called Carathril.

He dashed into one of the guard towers and took up a bow and quiver for himself. Returning to the wall, he found several hundred elves assembling to either side of the gate, arrows nocked, eyes straining against the night.

'Mark the fires,' said Carathril, stringing a shaft.

The Naggarothi were still some distance away, well out of bowshot. Something whined in the darkness and a hail of barb-tipped bolts crashed against the stone of the gatehouse a short distance away. Hidden by the darkness, the crews of the Naggarothi war engines could easily see the defenders on the wall and towers.

'Douse the lanterns,' Carathril ordered. 'Pass the word to douse the lanterns.'

Like a blanket draped across the fortifications, the lamps were extinguished, darkness spreading to the north and south, leaving only the faint glimmer of moonlight and the reflected glow of the sea to the south.

The city's bolt throwers returned the volleys of the enemy, launching salvoes of spear-sized shafts towards the approaching glow of the Naggarothi army. The night was silent save for the slap of rope on wood and the swish of bolts cutting the air. Not even a cry could yet be heard, though Carathril was sure the bolt thrower crews would have found some target.

In response, the Naggarothi put out their brands, the guttering of the flames sending a chill through Carathril, the countryside around the city become as dark as the sky. Robbed of their marks, the war engines of both sides were stilled and a queer calm descended. There were mutters and whispers from the elves around Carathril until he silenced them with a sharp word.

All eyes and ears were strained for any sign of the Naggarothi. The stone of the road was like a pale ribbon that wound through the hills until it could no longer be seen in the distance. The wind sighed against the stone and fluttered the banners at their poles atop the tower roofs.

Time passed, the moons sinking lower in the sky, increasing the darkness.

Then came the first noise of the Naggarothi; a distant jingling of mail shirts, the clop of hooves on the road and the padding of thousands of booted feet. Here and there, Carathril spied a brief glimmer of light as the dim glow of the moons reflected off a helm or spear tip.

The air was growing colder still. Unnaturally so, thought Carathril. He could feel the churn of magic in the air and so could the other defenders. Whispers of sorcery spread along the wall and there were muttered incantations to ward away the dark magic.

Still the air grew colder, until the breaths of the soldiers were a mist in the pale moonlight. Carathril flexed his fingers on his bow to ease their stiffness, but would not dip his aim for a moment. He stared intently along the shaft, seeking some target upon which he could loose the arrow, but he saw nothing but vague shadows and glimmers.

The chilling air set his joints to aching and a rime of frost was creeping across the stones of the wall, the flags hanging limply as ice crackled on the embroidered banners. The bow began to tremble in Carathril's grasp and his shoulders ached with the strain of holding it up. Around him, archers were uttering hushed curses, blowing on their fingers, stamping their feet.

Harsh words split the air a moment before a dark cloud of shafts lifted out from the darkness, hundreds of serrated tips shining as they arced up towards the wall. The defenders threw themselves to the rampart as the rain of missiles clattered against the stone. Here and there an elf cried out, pierced by a shaft, as another volley and another swiftly followed.

The barbed cloud seemed unending, the repeater crossbows of the Naggarothi sending a hail of missiles effortlessly through the night. Carathril clenched his jaw, not daring to lift his head above the rampart as chips of stone sprayed around him.

Amongst the rattle of impacts and snap of breaking shafts, the captain could hear the tramp of booted feet getting closer and closer. The Naggarothi were advancing under the cover of their repeater crossbows. They would be at the walls soon if the defenders allowed themselves to be cowed by the flurries of bolts cutting the air.

'Ready your bows!' shouted Carathril, rising up to a narrow embrasure. The archers around him followed his lead, using the wall to cover themselves against the shafts still descending upon them. Bringing up his bow, he saw a swathe of darkness no more than two hundred paces from the wall. Advancing in close formation, shields and spears held high, the Naggarothi presented an easy target. 'Loose!'

A storm of white shafts leapt into the gloom, to be met with cries of pain and surprise. The repetitive snap of the engines in the towers added to the noise, hurling their bolts into the advancing enemy. The sound of mail being punctured and flesh being pierced came from all sides, and within moments the Naggarothi machines were returning fire, sending up showers of stone shards from the parapets protecting the bolt throwers.

Exposed, the archers suffered at the next Naggarothi volley, a score and more reeling back across the wall with vicious shafts in arms and bodies. Some slumped where they had been standing, helms and breastplates pierced.

In the dim light, Carathril spied a knot of several dozen Naggarothi advancing quickly on horseback. They dragged between them a ram fashioned of dark metal, its head that of a griffon wrought from shining ithilmar, borne upon a frame made of thick timbers and bound with iron. More Naggarothi ran behind, ready to man the ram once it was at the gate.

No order needed to be given. Every elf on the walls knew that the Naggarothi could not be allowed to attack the gate. Shafts rained down on the riders, the cries of the cavalry mingling with the whinnying of wounded steeds.

A great clamour filled the square behind Carathril and he glanced over his shoulder to see the knights of Eataine gathering, streaming down the roads of the city to form up in squadrons several hundred strong.

Carathril heard a command to open the gate. Looking down, he saw that the Naggarothi were less than fifty paces from the gatehouse. If the sortie failed, they would be inside the city within moments.

'Do as they say!' he snapped at the elves in the gate tower, knowing that the risk had to be taken. The gate was not yet shored up properly, and once destroyed could not be replaced.

Weights and gears rumbled in the towers as the gate mechanism was freed. Even as the huge oak doors were swinging inwards, the knights were breaking into a charge. Rank after rank, ten knights wide, galloped out of the city with shields ready and lances at full tilt.

The crash of their impact rang against the walls. Carathril could make out little of the fight in the dark, just a swirl of silver-armoured figures and pale horses against the gold-and-black knights of Anlec. War cries and hoarse challenges greeted the charge. Metal rang on metal.

Carathril was forced to duck back behind the parapet as another volley of repeater crossbow shafts sailed through the air. Peering through the embrasure, he could see Naggarothi advancing in long lines, carrying tall ladders between their files, protected by the raised shields of more warriors to each side. He emptied his quiver, loosing arrow after arrow into the oncoming assault, but to little effect.

Several squadrons of knights peeled away from the attack along the road, wheeling into the flank of the spearmen with the ladders. They crashed through the Naggarothi soldiers who fell in their dozens to lance and sword and flailing hooves. Yet not a quarter of the spearmen had been routed when a horn sounded the recall. Fearing to be caught too far from the gate, the wedge of knights turned their horses and rode back to the road, where the lead squadrons were already riding through the gate back to the safety of the city.

At another command, the gates were swung shut just behind the last of the knights. Bars were slide into place and locked as bolts from the Naggarothi slammed into the ancient wood of the doors. Carathril judged that the knights had lost almost a quarter of their number, but the dark-clad bodies littering the road and the space just before the walls were testament to the casualties they had inflicted during the brief sortie.

Further south along the wall there were sounds of fighting, as several companies of Naggarothi had reached the defences with their ladders. For the moment it appeared the attention of the Naggarothi had been driven from the gatehouse and Carathril returned to the guard room to fetch more arrows. Inside were dozens of wounded elves, sitting against the walls or lying on mattresses soaked with their blood. Many bore the marks of the repeater quarrels, and wounded knights were being carried up the wide stairs to have their injuries tended by the priests and priestesses within.

Snatching up a fresh quiver from the rapidly diminishing stock, Carathril returned to his place and looked south. The Naggarothi had given up their direct assault quickly and were falling back towards the hills, the shafts of the defenders following them. To the east, across Lothern, the first ruddy gleam of dawn touched the rooftops and towers.

And so passed the first night of the siege of Lothern, one of many that would beset the city in the coming seasons.

'When will Caledor come?' Mythreir gave voice to the question that had been asked many times; so many times Carathril had tired of hearing it asked.

'Perhaps never,' snapped the guard captain. 'You think Lothern is alone in the Phoenix King's thoughts?'

'It should be highest,' replied the other elf as the two walked along the northern ramparts of the city, looking down at the Inner Sea. To the east, a flotilla of ten ships waited behind the Sapphire Gate, sails trimmed, decks packed with Sea Guard. 'With Lothern besieged, the Naggarothi raid across the Inner Sea without hindrance.'

'And until Ellyrion is secure again, Caledor cannot send relief to the city,' said Carathril, sighing heavily. 'How many times must I explain?'

'Until you make sense,' said Myrthreir. 'Caledor's strategy is wrong and the prince should make better representation. With Lothern delivered, we can control the shore of Ellyrion and supply his army.'

Carathril offered no further reply, annoyed by his companion's obstinacy. Caledor would no more relieve Lothern with the enemy free in Ellyrion than a swordsman would turn his back on an armed opponent. The city held, and held strong, and that was all that mattered.

They reached their destination, a stretch of wall overlooking the Inner Sea that curved away from the Sapphire Gate. Further along the shore the ships of the Naggarothi were beached, having been captured in northern Ellyrion and sailed south in support of the siege. To the north and south, the Lothern Straits were bracketed by enemy fleets. The one saving grace was that the Naggarothi had made no inroads upon the eastern reaches of Eataine, and many of the populace had been evacuated towards Saphery.

It was the sea gates the Naggarothi desired though, and for two long years they had battered the walls with war engines, vile monsters and evil sorcery. This last had become less of a threat since the arrival of Eltreneth last autumn, one of the chief mages of Saphery. Soaring above the city upon his white-winged pegasus, the Sapherian had countered the spells of the enemy, staff wreathed in mystical power, sword blazing.

Now the enemy prepared for a fresh assault. They had built towers and rams concealed from the war engines of Lothern by huge ramparts of earth and timber. They planned to launch this latest attack along the Inner Sea road, that much was clear, and Prince Aerethenis had finally bowed to those who would have the fleet of Lothern let free.

Without ceremony, the Sapphire Gate opened, the roar of water building as the huge portal swung open between the Straits of Lothern and the Inner Sea. Where the two bodies of water met, the sea thrashed and foamed as wave crashed against wave, before slowly swirling and dying away to leave the path clear for the flotilla. The early morning light shimmered from the gleaming decks of the ships as they passed through the open gate, their sails bright triangles of white and blue.

'I heard a new name for them,' said Mythreir.

'What's that?' said Carathril, his attention on the hills through which the Inner Sea road cut towards the city, alert for foes that might attack the emerging flotilla from the coastal cliffs. There was no movement, yet the two hundred archers who stood with bows ready at the rampart did not relax their guard, having experienced much Naggarothi trickery in the past.

'The Naggarothi,' said Mythreir. 'They are being called the *druchii* now.'

'Druchii?' Carathril could not stop a grim smile. The word meant the Dark Ones. It was fitting. Since he had first ridden with Prince Malekith, Carathril had seen the Naggarothi prove themselves capable of the direst acts.

'Druchii it is. Let us keep watch for their wiles all the same.'

The Lothern flotilla sped along the coast at full sail, the pilots knowing every reef and rock around the harbour entrance. Horns blared in the distance as the druchii caught sight of the oncoming ships and Carathril could just make out a burst of activity along the shore as they streamed towards their own beached vessels.

There came a rush of air and a flap of feathers above and Carathril looked up to see Eltreneth soaring overhead mounted on his pegasus. The mage's staff trailed sparks of red and blue fire as the winged horse pitched down towards the cliff tops where the druchii had made camp.

A bolt of black lightning leapt up from the sea of dark pavilions, to be turned away by a shimmering sphere of gold that enveloped Eltreneth. Hails of repeater arrows streamed towards him, yet these too were turned away by his magical shield. Even from a distance, Carathril could feel the ebb and surge of magical energy as the mage and the sorcerers below him battled for control of the winds of magic. Multicoloured fire leapt from Eltreneth's staff, scorching through tent and corral, setting a swathe of the camp ablaze as dark clouds sprang into existence in the air around him, crackling with unnatural energy.

The ships had now come into range of the druchii fleet moving off the beaches. Only a handful of enemy vessels had made the sea when blossoms of white-burning bolts and arrows seared across the waters, catching in sails and rigging, setting fire to decking and masts. Not to be outdone, the druchii fired back with clouds of black shafts, repeater crossbows and bolt throwers raking the decks of the Eataine ships as they closed in.

'Rather them than me,' said Myrthreir as the two flotillas moved amongst each other, turning and tacking, their war machines scything the air between with black- and silver-headed missiles. 'Let me face my death toe-to-toe.'

Carathril was inclined to agree but said nothing. The fighting would get all too personal soon enough as the lightly armed hawkships of both sides manoeuvred around each other, looking for an opening to board. From this distance the naval battle looked more like a stately dance than a desperate contest of bloodshed. The squadrons arced about each other like partners hand in hand, linked by the clouds of arrows instead of arms. Here and there they came together, the war cries and crash of timbers lost in distance so that everything seemed as serene as a masque.

Two druchii ships were already sinking, aflame from bow to stern, tiny figures leaping to the water to save themselves. Another listed heavily, sails tattered, masthead burnt, the rigging a smouldering pile upon its deck. The Eataine fleet had not suffered too greatly from the exchange, but a hawkship had already turned and was limping back towards the Sapphire Gate, a yardarm trailing by ropes over the port side, dragging like a sea anchor. Carathril could see the white of the crewmen's robes as they swarmed around the debris, cutting and hacking to free themselves from the broken mast's dead weight.

Having speared through the first line of the enemy, the rest of the flotilla swooped upon the vessels still landed at the sandy beach. Eltreneth circled above, driving back the Naggarothi who sought to board the ships with blasts of flame and glistening silver clouds of magical blades. Undefended, the beached ships were an easy target for the Sea Guard, who poured flaming arrows into them with volley after volley.

In their attack, the Lothern ships had approached within range of the bolt thrower batteries mounted on the cliff top. They added their shafts to the arrows being fired from the camp, iron-headed spears punching through canvas and timber and flesh as they fired down upon the decks of the ships.

Sited even more advantageously, the engines of Lothern now let loose their fury. From the highest towers on the wall, the bolt thrower captains now spied the druchii's positions and unleashed a devastating storm of shafts onto the cliff tops. Here and there an archer near Carathril loosed a shaft as the war machine crews scurried from cover to cover, the high wall of the city providing ample extra range for their Eatainii longbows.

Carathril did not set an arrow to his bow, knowing that his aim was not so good at such extreme range. Always he had been better with sword and spear. Such skills had been put to the test more than a dozen times since that first night attack, repelling assault after assault on the city walls. Sometimes he had faced the sinister Naggarothi legions, other times cultists fuelled by bestial hatred and frenzy-inducing drugs. On more than one occasion the Naggarothi had gained the wall and threatened to overcome the defenders, but on each occasion the defenders had held firm, rallied by their leaders to drive the enemy back from Lothern.

It was spirit-sapping, the endless tension, the constant waiting for the next attack. The garrison of the city and the few citizens who had remained behind to provide for them were not without supply, from the sea and the east, but such was the ever-present danger of the city becoming surrounded that such food as was brought in was carefully rationed. Water too was always stringently measured, ever since some of the wells in the southern quarter had been found to be poisoned.

That was perhaps the worst part of all; the enemy that hid within. Long had the cytharai worshippers made their lairs and temples unseen in Lothern, and even the discovery of Prince Aeltherin's cabal two decades earlier had not ended them. Now they acted as assassins and saboteurs, a shadowy threat that could strike at any time. Some had been discovered, but so many elves had fled into the city two years earlier it was impossible to guard against attack and patrol the streets at the same time. Lone soldiers heading back to barracks from duty had been waylaid, families threatened and kidnapped and slain, captains and nobles blackmailed, the cultists ever seeking to weaken the strength and the resolve of the city's defenders.

That was one concern that Carathril did not have. He had few friends and no family. He fought for his city alone, and was responsible solely for himself. He did not count the number of his fellow elves he had slain, nor the times he had come so close to death. Two years had numbed him to the fighting, deadening the pain in his spirit that threatened with each attack.

The naval raid was almost finished. Half a dozen druchii ships had been destroyed at the cost of three vessels, the rest of the enemy flotilla fleeing northwards along the coast. Companies of Sea Guard had landed, nearly two thousand in all, and were fighting through the druchii camp to bring down the siege engines and set oil and flame upon the rams. Smoke billowed across the waters of the Inner Sea and the crackle of flames spread along the shore.

A great cheer rippled along the wall as another tower was brought crashing down in an explosion of wood and rope and tarred canvas. It was quickly silenced as horns pealed from further west along the wall. All eyes turned in that direction.

The main druchii army was on the move; not for the city but to the relief of its shore camp. At its fore, the Naggarothi knights galloped ahead, thousands of heavily armoured warriors riding in columns across the fields and hills, intent upon the Sea Guard. Warned from the city, the green-and-blue clad warriors of the navy broke off their attack and covered by archers and bolt throwers upon the ships returned to their vessels, quickly streaming up the gangplanks.

The knights had barely reached the outskirts of the ravaged camp by the time the ships were putting off from shore, their sails hauled up, tacking across the wind to head back towards Lothern. It was impossible to tell how much damage had been wrought by the raid, but the pall of smoke was testament to considerable success.

The elves upon the walls raised their spears and bows and sang songs of rejoicing as the flotilla passed back through the Sapphire Gate. Carathril did not feel like celebrating. He looked along the shore of the Inner Sea to where the druchii were amassing. It was only a matter of time before they came again. He stowed his bow and leaned on the rampart, eyes fixed on the host of the Naggarothi slowly moving back westwards.

How long could Lothern hold, alone against such determined hate?

'When will Caledor come?' Carathril whispered.

⊰ ELEVEN ⊱

The Black Dragons

THE ARMY OF the Phoenix King stretched along the valley in a winding line of silver, red and green against the pale rock. Here and there companies bearing the colours of other kingdoms broke the scheme; the pale-green banners of spearmen from Cothique, the purple standards flying above archers from Saphery.

There were not many, barely four thousand including the five hundred knights of Caledor that rode in the vanguard. If the scouts were correct, at least twice that number of druchii was marching east along the pass, directly towards Caledor's host. For all that, the odds were not all in the enemy's favour.

Maedrethnir soared easily upon the upward draughts coming from the mountains that flanked the pass. The chill air was soothing against his scales, cooling his blood and the fire within. Steam trailed from the dragon's mouth and nostrils as he banked over the army, climbing high on a fresh rush of wind, eyes narrowed as he scanned the mountainsides for any sign of a Naggarothi ambush.

He barely felt the weight of the throne and the Phoenix King upon his back and for a time enjoyed the sensation of flying, allowing the currents of the skies to move him left and right, wingtips leaving thin streamers of vapour in their wake as he glided down through the low cloud.

The dragon felt something else beside the wind; the pulse of magic from the elves' vortex. It was like a thin sheen of oil upon his body, an acrid taste in his mouth, a distant echo in his ears. He remembered a time when he had crossed these mountains without that sickly sensation, when the Everqueen had ruled and the dragons had played in the skies.

Even then Maedrethnir had been old, and his memories stretched back further still, way beyond the fall of the Old Ones and the coming of Chaos that polluted the land. He remembered when this isle had been nothing more than a chain of volcanoes jutting from the ocean. Newly hatched, Maedrethnir had played with the others, hopping from fuming peak to fuming peak on growing wings.

The air had been lighter then, and all the world colder so that the fire inside was but a flicker, not the raging inferno he was now forced to hold back. He rumbled unconsciously with annoyance as he remembered that strange day, many millennia before, when the skies had been split by multi-coloured rifts and the silver starboats of the Old Ones had appeared. The dragons had scattered, terrified by these new arrivals. Many fled to the deepest caves and oceans, but some remained to see what the strangers intended.

The sun had grown larger and the skies had warmed, and the Old Ones built their temples and cities in the jungles that had thrived in the new heat. Many of the dragons had voiced concern, calling to their kin to fight and cast out the invaders. The oldest and wisest knew better, and like those before them they slunk away into the dark corners of the world and waited to see what would pass.

Amongst them had been Indraugnir, Maedrethnir's father. With many of his kin and friends, the ancient dragon lord had sought shelter in the caves of the volcanoes, but even there they had not found peace. Maedrethnir smiled and turned his head to cast a glance at the rider upon his back. What could Caledor know of the disruption his people had caused? He knew nothing of those worrying days and nights when the earth had rumbled and the seas had roared. The Old Ones' servants, the bloated slann, had lifted the isle from the sea bed, the mountains belching forth smoke and flame. The dragons trembled as the caverns they had made their home fell around them, but Indraugnir cautioned them to stay hidden lest the Old Ones destroy them altogether.

In time the lands settled again and the first elves came. Maedrethnir had spied upon them from the mountain fastness with his father and mother, protective of the new clutch of eggs hatching in the darkness beneath the volcanoes. With the Old Ones had come that first taint of magic, and the isle was soon steeped in its presence, lingering in every cloud and upon every blade of grass.

For all of the intrusion, the elves had seemed peaceful enough and the dragons had returned to their lairs and dreamed long dreams of the day when they would be free to roam the skies as they had done before. Indraugnir entertained his children and his allies with ancient stories of the war with the shaggoths and the dragon ogres, and had warned about the dark touch of the Powers Beyond the Skies that had corrupted the dragon's twisted cousins.

'Look there!' Caledor's shout and pointing lance broke Maedrethnir's reverie.

The dragon shook himself from the half-dream, alarmed that the long sleep still beckoned him even though he flew upon the winds. A shiver of expectation ran through Maedrethnir's body as he spied a swathe of dark-armoured figures in the valley below; the vanguard of the druchii army.

'Shall we greet them?' said the dragon.

He needed no reply and tucked his wings tight to dive down towards the valley floor. The wind keened in his ears and rushed across his scales, sweeping away the last somnolent after-effects of his daydream. Heart beating fast, Maedrethnir flexed his claws in anticipation. The elves below were scurrying to and fro in their fright as the dragon and rider descended, their panic stirring Maedrethnir's old hunting instincts.

He was filled with the urge to stoop and rend, to bite and rake claws through the miniscule prey that scattered before his approach. Caught up in predatory excitement, the dragon plunged down, wings opening to slow his descent as he felt the fire building up in his gut, nagging at him to unleash its fury. A roar burst forth, powered by primal desire, the valley echoing to the blast of noise.

Black spears sped up from the scattered rocks and bushes. Maedrethnir dipped a wing and veered as the missiles streaked past. Another volley followed from a second repeater bolt thrower stationed guarding the flank of the druchii, catching the dragon with two of the long shafts. Metal screeched and wood splintered against the dragon's hard scales as two of the bolts bounced harmlessly from Maedrethnir's shoulders. A cloud of arrows from dozens of repeater crossbows engulfed the dragon, pattering from his hide as harmlessly as rain as he crashed through the dark storm of shafts.

More of the larger bolts flew upwards from the druchii war engines. Twisting, Maedrethnir batted two aside with a sweep of his foreleg, the rest missing or bouncing away from the thick scales protecting the dragon's shoulder.

With metal shrieking and bones snapping, Maedrethnir landed in the midst of the archers, smashing half a dozen druchii to a pulp with the bulk of his body. Flame erupted from the dragon's throat, scorching everything within reach as Maedrethnir's neck snaked left and right, the pain from the fire burning at his mouth and gut.

The internal fires exhausted for the moment, he heaved in a great breath, smoke and steam coiling around his face. Caledor shouted something from the dragon's back but he heard not a word of it, consumed by the need to kill. Claws swept out, slicing through armour and flesh like swords, eviscerating, decapitating and dismembering. Turning, Maedrethnir lunged and snapped his jaws around the body of a fleeing elf. Metal links buckled between sword-like teeth. Sheared in twain, the elf's corpse dropped to the ground while rivulets of blood ran down the dragon's throat.

The blood incensed him more, stirring a hunger that had not been sated for several years. Arching back his neck, Maedrethnir bellowed again, venting flames from his nostril in the hunt-frenzy. He was dimly aware of flashing silver around him; Caledor's lance thrusting and slashing through the few archers that escaped the dragon's wrath.

He felt sharpness in his flank, the sudden pain cutting through the red mist of desire that had swamped the dragon's thoughts.

'The bolt throwers!' called Caledor. He lifted his lance to the north, its shaft slick with bright blood. 'Destroy the bolt throwers!'

Smelling terror and death, the scent intoxicating and addictive, Maedrethnir fought back another surge of feral anger. He looked at his right side, where the pain came from, and saw a barbed bolt jutting between his ribs, just below the wing. Snarling, he pulled the shaft free with his jaws, the spear-sized missile disintegrating into wooden shards.

With a last slash of his tail that crushed the bodies of more druchii, Maedrethnir launched himself from the ground, panting as he unfurled his wings and pulled himself higher with every long stroke. The archers quickly disappeared from view as the dragon powered towards the mountainside where three war engines had been positioned amongst the craggy rocks. Another hail of large darts slapped against his hide, shedding scales but doing little serious harm. One of the crews laboured quickly to replace the bolt magazine atop their engine, and towards this pair the dragon angled his flight.

The druchii warriors let the heavy box tumble from their grasp as they turned to flee, Maedrethnir smashing into the bolt thrower moments later in a shower of jagged splinters, snapping rope and twisted metal. The bushes and rocks provided no protection against the sheet of flame that erupted from the dragon's maw, razing leaf and branch, cracking stone and charring the elven warriors within their molten armour. Another cry from Caledor drew the dragon's attention to the left, but too late. A second bolt thrower loosed its salvo of half a dozen shafts, the six spears thudding into Maedrethnir's hindquarters and tail. Most broke upon his scales but two punched home, their barbed points digging into flesh. Lips rippling with anger, the dragon turned and pounced, jaws snapping off the head from one crew member, foreclaw gouging a furrow through mail and muscle, from groin to neck of the other.

Pausing for a moment, Maedrethnir's nostrils widened, drawing in the scents of battle: dread and blood, leather and crushed grass. There was something else, something familiar yet unknown, the slightest touch on the wind. Though he could not identify the smell, it stirred something within the dragon, stabbing into the most primitive parts of his brain as the bolts had pierced his hide.

A flicker of movement caught the dragon's attention; a shadow passing quickly across the rocks of the mountainside. Maedrethnir's head snapped up out of instinct and he spied a winged shape against the clouds. Caledor had seen it also.

'What is it?' asked the Phoenix King.

It was too large to be a manticore or griffon, black against the pale sky. Maedrethnir caught the scent again, shocked by realisation.

'Drake,' snarled Maedrethnir. 'Corrupted and vile.'

Ignoring Caledor's call to wait, Maedrethnir hurled himself into the skies to confront this new threat. The other dragon sensed his approach and turned on a dipped wing, revealing scales as black as pitch and eyes that burned like flame. A fume of green vapours bubbled from between the creature's teeth, embroiling itself and its gold-clad rider in a sickly mist.

'A dragon?' Caledor was awash with confusion and fear. 'How can it be?'

'It has been touched by the Powers Beyond the Skies,' growled Maedrethnir. 'Can you not sense it?'

The black dragon was surrounded by an aura of darkness, and as the two monsters closed on each other Maedrethnir saw that its head was encased in an iron harness studded with black gems, reins of golden chain in the fist of the rider. Its dark flesh bore many scars from old wounds, testament to a cruel upbringing.

It was an abomination. Maedrethnir had known that not all the eggs that had been laid over the centuries had been accounted for. The dragons had believed them to have been stolen by the other predators that dared to share their caves; bulbous-eyed, pale things that scavenged on the remains of the dragons' kills. Now it seemed the mystery was solved; the eggs had been taken by the Naggarothi to hatch and raise and twist to their cause.

'It must be destroyed,' snarled Maedrethnir, beating his wings faster and faster, blood racing through his body.

He felt the butt of Caledor's lance set against his flank as the Phoenix King readied for the first exchange. The other dragon raced down, its rider wielding a barbed trident. Not for an age had Maedrethnir fought another dragon, for mate or territory, but his old instincts were still with him. The other had the advantage of height, but was coming in too steeply in his inexperience.

A flick of the tail and a shifting of his left wing caused Maedrethnir to almost stop in mid-flight. The black dragon plummeted past, claws flailing wildly at Maedrethnir's neck and face, the rider's trident passing harmlessly overhead. Caledor's lance caught the black dragon along the back, its enchanted tip raking a bloody furrow through ebon scales.

Maedrethnir turned and dropped after his descending foe, wings tilting and turning as the black dragon heaved left and right to avoid the pursuit. Smaller than Maedrethnir, the black dragon was swifter in the turn and as Maedrethnir's jaws snapped at his tail, the drake reversed its course and with a rapid beat of wings shot upwards again, heading towards the clouds once more.

More laboriously, Maedrethnir swept out of his dive and into a climb. Each sweep of his more powerful wings brought him closer to his prey, who vanished into the thickening cloud. Growling with irritation, Maedrethnir soared into the white haze, eyes wide for any sign of the other dragon.

'Keep watch behind,' he told Caledor.

Glancing back, Maedrethnir saw the Phoenix King peering left and right through the cloud set swirling by each stroke of the dragon's wings. A screech sounded from the right, muffled by the cloud, and a moment later the black dragon was darting from the gloom, claws outstretched.

Maedrethnir turned towards the attack, but not so swiftly that he could avoid the swooping drake. Diamond-hard claws sank into the flesh of his shoulder as Caledor swung his shield across and deflected the jabbing trident of the rider, the weapon's three tines crackling with magical power.

The black dragon latched on, claws digging deep and deeper; a mistake.

Maedrethnir arched his neck and sank his jaws into the other beast's right wing, teeth sawing through skin and tendon, cracking bone. With a scream that let forth a billowing pall of noxious vapour, the black dragon released its grip and pushed away, damaged wing spurting blood.

The gaseous breath of the drake filled Maedrethnir's nostrils, acrid and burning, searing the dragon's throat and scratching at his eyes. Choking on the fume and momentarily blinded, the old dragon circled cautiously. Caledor was having similar difficulty, coughing and retching, doubled over in the throne-saddle.

The drake appeared briefly to the left, diving down through the cloud before being swallowed by the pale mass. Maedrethnir dropped as well, falling steeply through the sky until he burst from the bottom of the cloud layer into open air. Rolling to his left, he arched his neck and glared at the haze, looking for the shadow of the black dragon.

'There!' shouted Caledor, pointing up and to the right. A flicker of darkness passed to and fro as the Naggarothi and his mount searched the clouds for their foe, unaware that they were far below. 'After them.'

Maedrethnir snorted at the implication that he needed to be told and powered upwards with rapid sweeps of his wings. His wounds were starting to ache, but he pushed aside the pain and flew on, arcing upwards to come at the black dragon from directly below.

Like an erupting volcano, Maedrethnir exploded into the cloud, fire roaring from his gullet to engulf the drake and its rider. Rolling quickly, the black dragon avoided the worst of the blast, but the manoeuvre brought it onto Caledor's lance tip. The ithilmar shaft plunged into the creature's underbelly with a flicker of magical flame. The black dragon gave a howl and lurched sideways, favouring its damaged wing.

Maedrethnir flew above the enemy and then quickly plunged down, rear claws seizing upon the creature's scarred tail. The rider tried to swing his trident around for a thrust but the back of the saddle-throne prevented him. Helpless, the black dragon toppled towards the ground, Maedrethnir upon his back, claws rending great wounds, leaving bloodied welts all over the black dragon's hindquarters and back.

Far below, the two armies clashed. A dark spear of Naggarothi knights plunged through the white mass of Caledor's spearmen while the silver-helmed knights of the Phoenix King outflanked the Naggarothi, curving around the enemy host in long columns. The druchii had brought Khainite cultists with them, a splash of red and naked flesh that hurled itself again and again towards the elves loyal to Caledor, driven back each time by clouds of arrows and war machine bolts.

The chaotic melee became distinct lines and companies as the two dragons plunged ever closer. Bodies littered the rocky ground of the pass, clad both in black and white, the heaped dead testament to the bitter fury of the two armies.

The black dragon snarled and beat its wings ferociously, trying to slow its descent, filthy gas pouring from its wide open mouth. Maedrethnir held firm despite the writhing and struggling of the other monster, claws scraping against the black dragon's spine.

Individual figures could be picked out in the battle; a captain with a red-crested helm waving his sword towards the druchii crossbows; a Naggarothi officer slitting the throat of a fallen spearman; wild cultists hacking at the bodies of the fallen from both sides, ripping free organs; a wall of lances crashing into the flank of the Naggarothi knights as the Silver Helms charged.

No more than a bow's shot from the ground, Maedrethnir released his grip and opened his wings, muscles straining to stop, tendons taut almost to parting. The black dragon twisted, blood splashing onto the rocks, wings beating furiously, but to no avail.

With a thunderous impact, the drake and rider smashed into the rocks, splintering stone and bone in equal measure. The harness holding the saddle snapped with a loud crack and the throne was cast from the dragon's back, splintering against the sharp boulders.

Maedrethnir dived again, leaving nothing to chance. As the black dragon struggled to right itself on twisted legs, wings broken and flopping uselessly, Maedrethnir slammed into the drake. His jaws seized the other dragon's neck just behind the head, spines and fangs snapping from the titanic pressure. His claws raked at the black dragon's underbelly, slashing through scale and muscle, exposing ribs and organs.

With a flap of his wings and a heave of his body, Maedrethnir leapt over the black dragon, twisting the foe's neck in his jaw with a loud cracking of bone. Shaking left and right, Maedrethnir slammed the black dragon's head repeatedly into the rocks, dashing open its skull. Releasing his hold, the red dragon turned and plunged his fangs into the drake's exposed innards, crunching through bone, tearing at its gizzards.

Maedrethnir feasted, gorging himself on the meat of his slain rival. It had been millennia since he had last tasted dragon flesh and he wolfed down huge gulps, cracking open the bones to lap at the marrow. The dragon's blood sang through his body, drowning out the pain of his wounds, blotting out the calls of Caledor upon his back.

Something hard cracked across the top of Maedrethnir's skull, stunning him for a moment. Dazed, he stumbled back from the corpse of the black dragon, seeking the source of the attack.

'The rider is getting away,' said Caledor, hitting the dragon again with the haft of his lance.

Maedrethnir growled at the impudence of the elf, to berate him so. The dragon took a step back towards the corpse of his dead foe but was stopped by more sharp words from the Phoenix King. Maedrethnir wanted to shrug off the rider, to rip free of the harness that bound them together.

Caledor snarled words that bit into Maedrethnir's mind; words of power discovered by the Dragontamer. Cowed, the dragon slumped to his belly and shook his head, trying to dismiss the numbing sensation seeping through his brain. Through the fog of insensibility, he heard Caledor's calm voice.

'Your enemy flees,' said the Phoenix King. 'Chase him down.'

Maedrethnir looked around and spied the Naggarothi scrambling over the rocks some distance away, one leg dragging with a limp. With a snarl the dragon bounded quickly over the boulders, wings half-furled. He loomed over the druchii, who turned and pulled a sword from his belt. The blade glittered with a frozen light that hurt Maedrethnir's eyes and he shied back, almost blinded.

Caledor was not to be denied, his lance taking the Naggarothi high in the chest, punching through breastplate and heart. The druchii slashed wildly with his sword, ringing its blade from the ithilmar lance, leaving a stream of frosty particles in the air. Caledor moved his arm, pushing his weakened opponent to his back, pinning him to the ground.

'Finish him,' said the Phoenix King.

Maedrethnir raised a foreleg and stamped down, crushing helm and head beneath his weight. Blinking away the after-image of the ice-tinged blade, Maedrethnir regained some clarity. The hunting rage subsided, the fire inside cooling in his belly. The dragon shuddered, feeling the sudden pain of his injuries.

He remembered the black dragon, realising with disgust the twisted nature of the beast.

'I must return to my kin,' said Maedrethnir.

'When the battle is won,' said Caledor.

'No!' the dragon replied fiercely. 'They must be told about the black dragons. I must pass the word, raise my kind from their slumber.'

'When the battle is won,' repeated Caledor.

Quick as a serpent, Maedrethnir whipped his head around, fangs slicing easily through the bindings of the saddle-throne. Shrugging his shoulders, he let the construction slip gently from his back, depositing the saddle and Phoenix King unkindly upon the rocks.

'Win your battle, little elf,' said Maedrethnir. 'I shall win your war.'

Before Caledor could recover and speak the taming words, Maedrethnir launched into the air, skimming up the mountainside with swift beats, heading south.

THE SMOG AND the night were no barrier to Maedrethnir's keen sight. The dragon steered between the volcanic peaks as easily as if it were noon and not the darkest night. By the glow of lava and patches of starlight, the dragon soared over the peaks of Caledor, mind and body alive with disgust verging on hatred.

He descended swiftly to the valley of the caves, folding his wings as he plunged into the largest opening. Feet scraping on rock furrowed by millennia of dragon claws, he advanced into the darkness, laboured breaths echoing along the wide tunnel. His right flank was sore and his muscles ached from the two days of constant flight, but the news he bore was too urgent to allow him rest.

He headed directly for the deepest chamber, ignoring the many other passages that twisted away from the main tunnel. The air cooled as he moved further and further beneath the earth, his hot breath coming in great clouds of vapour that condensed upon rock walls worn smooth by the scales of dragons passing in and out.

The chamber was vast, a massive hole in the world ringed with stalactites and stalagmites larger than the towers of the elves, jutting like the fangs of the beasts that slumbered within. Patches of luminous moss and clouds of fireflies gave the appearance of a globe of starry night, the dim green and orange and yellow reflected from crystal veins in the walls and the edges of angular geodes.

The immense cavern dropped down sharply from the tunnel mouth and the dragon opened his wings and leapt into the air, gliding effortlessly between the upthrusts of rock. As he neared the centre of the chamber, the dragons could be seen. A few, those that had begun the long sleep in the last few centuries, still moved subtly, chests expanding slowly or contracting with enormous exhalations and inhalations, the ground around them glistening with ice from frozen vapour.

The others were immobile, only distinguished from their surroundings by the subtle hue of their scales. Many were part of the rock, stalagmites covering their unmoving bodies, melding the dragons with the floor. Spines had become roots for immense pillars that stretched towards the ceiling, limbs were like rivulets of hardened lava, covered with dully glowing patches of lichen.

Maedrethnir settled close to the chamber's heart, surrounded by the eerie gloom. Save for the flutter of large insects that nested with the dragons, nothing moved. The dragon's claws scraped on the rock, sending up showers of stone shards as he turned about, tail lifting to avoid the jagged points of the smallest stalagmites.

The dragon raised himself up, gripping a pillar of rock with a foreclaw and arching his neck. He let out a bellow, the noise filling the chamber, echoing back and forth, rebounding from every angle. Long and hard Maedrethnir roared, until pieces of stalactite broke from the ceiling of the cavern, their crashes adding to the reverberating din.

Closing his mouth, wisps of fire dancing from his nostrils, the dragon waited as the after-echoes of the noise slowly died away.

Something stirred in the darkness, a scrape of scale and scratch of claw. Rock splinters and ice crystals tinkled to the ground as a dragon to his left shifted its bulk, shaking off the layer of centuries. A yellow eye half-opened in the gloom.

There was more movement and noise from all around, as slumbering dragons shook free the drag of the long sleep, coughing dust and flame. A mighty column of rock trembled and then shattered, spilling to the hard floor as a green dragon almost as large as Maedrethnir arched its back, slowly pushing itself up on four trunk-like legs.

'Awake, my kin!' bellowed Maedrethnir. 'Dread times are upon us!'

CARATHRIL STOOD UPON the northern tower of the gatehouse, overlooking the road into Lothern. Around him all was a wasteland. Over five years of siege, the druchii had felled every tree and lain waste to every field, razed every village and farm. Blackened ruins jutted from the bare earth. The stench of death lingered in the air. In the ruins of an outbuilding not far away Carathril could see bodies draped over the rubble, splashes of red on their pale robes, limbs twisted unnaturally. He had seen many such sights these past years, yet each innocent slain raised his anger again and reminded him why the druchii had to be stopped.

Into the square behind him marched a column of elves. They walked wearily, toiling over the uneven white slabs, worn down in their spirits by the battles they had fought. With bleak eyes they gazed at the desolation, some of them weeping, others unmoved and utterly despondent, all the more frightening for that, their gazes dead to the suffering that had been inflicted.

'We are too few,' said Eamarilliel, another captain of the guard. 'We cannot hope to defeat the Naggarothi.'

'They muster again,' Carathril replied dully.

Around the city, columns of black-armoured warriors marched into position. For weeks more ships had come, disgorging reinforcements for the besieging army. Time and again the vessels of Lothern had sailed forth to impede their landings, but they had succeeded only in delaying the next assault, not halting it.

Carathril could see monstrous beasts being goaded forwards by teams of handlers; multi-headed hydras wreathed in the fume of their fiery breath. Drums sounded the call to war, reverberating from the city walls.

'We must hold,' said the former herald, but his voice lacked conviction.

'We are too few,' Eamarilliel said again.

'We were too few last time,' said Carathril. 'Yet the city is still ours.'

Sullen and exhausted, the defenders of Lothern mounted the steps to the wall and took their places at the rampart with bow and spear. From his vantage point, Carathril could see companies of druchii embarking upon vessels at the shore, to sail around the city and attack from the east as well as the west.

'I think this will be the last battle for Lothern,' said Eamarilliel. 'They gather every force they have to throw at us.'

The attack was heralded by a flurry of burning bolts from the Naggarothi war machines. They targeted the great gate, the flaming shafts thudding into the thick wood with the sound of monstrous hail. Sparks flared from the tower and walls as more bolts crashed against the city's defences, spraying the defenders with ripping pieces of metal and wood and stone.

Carathril did not flinch as a bolt careened from an embrasure and speared through three elves just to his right, impaling them against each other. There were shouts for the wounded to be taken away as the druchii drums rolled and the advance began.

Carathril looked down at the vast army, spreading from shore to gate, a slowly encroaching swathe of black and purple. He was forced to agree with Eamarilliel's assessment. The enemy came in three great waves under the storm unleashed by their war engines, leaving no reserves; should the defenders somehow repel the attack there was nothing to stop them sallying forth in pursuit of their defeated foes.

The former herald wondered what had brought about this change of strategy. Was it confidence that the druchii would be victorious? Had some other development forced the enemy to such decisive action? Carathril entertained the thought for a moment, heartened by the idea that the druchii had suffered reverses elsewhere and were stung by desperation.

A forest of ladders rose up from the druchii host, while high towers ground forwards amongst the spear companies, bolt throwers raining missiles from the siege engines while iron-headed rams fashioned in the likeness of many terrifying creatures swung on chains between their spiked wheels. Carathril waited with spear in hand; there were not enough arrows in the city for every warrior and so inexpert marksmen like himself no longer had bows to use. All he could do was wait for the foe to reach the wall.

A tower covered in wetted leathers and furs to protect against fire arrows came straight for the gatehouse, flanked by two immense war hydras to protect against counter-assault. It ground the dead of both sides under its metal-rimmed wheels, barely swaying as horses and other creatures strained at traces to bring it ever closer, whipped on by druchii beastmasters. A ramp like the jaw of some immense monster with metal fangs loomed over the wall, ready to be lowered to disgorge howling Khainites within the tower.

Amongst the cacophony of battle, Carathril was distracted by another noise; shouting from the city behind. He looked over his shoulder and saw with horror smoke rising from the buildings around the Strait of Lothern. Warehouses burned and he could see figures running in the streets carrying flaming brands; the cultists had emerged in force in response to the attack of their Naggarothi masters, perhaps brought forth by secret communication of the besiegers' intent.

Others on the wall had noticed the treachery unfolding within the city behind them and they were torn between guarding their positions and returning to the city to confront this new threat. Squadrons of knights raced through the streets, scattering the saboteurs, but as quickly as they were dispersed the cultists gathered again, ambushing their would-be pursuers with stones, blades and fire.

Carathril did not know what to do. The siege tower was less than a bow-shot away, rumbling forwards steadily. Cultists were entering the square behind the gate, no doubt intent on opening the doors to allow the druchii within. Spearmen streamed down from the towers to protect the mighty portal, which had withstood everything the druchii had thrown against it for the last five years but had no defence against traitors within.

'Archers, hold the wall!' Carathril called out. 'Spearmen with me!'

As he turned towards the steps leading down towards the plaza, Carathril came face-to-face with Aerenis; his friend led a company of his own, promoted to captain during the long siege.

'We must see the gate secured and then return to the wall,' Carathril told the other captain. 'Follow me.'

Aerenis shook his head and stayed where he was. A feeling of dread crept up Carathril's spine as he noticed the strange expressions on the faces of the soldiers in Aerenis's company.

'I cannot allow that, friend,' said Aerenis.

'What madness is this?' demanded Carathril, pushing aside a spearman to confront Aerenis.

'I am sorry, Carathril,' said the other elf, with a look of genuine hurt. 'You should have listened to me.'

Already unnerved, Carathril reacted out of pure instinct as Aerenis's sword slashed towards his throat. He caught the blade on the haft of his spear, the weapon almost knocked from his grasp. Stunned, the former herald barely had time to bring up his shield to ward away the following blow.

'Have you gone mad?' Carathril said, batting away another swipe. 'The enemy will be upon us in moments!'

'The enemy is already here,' said Aerenis. 'Do you not see?'

Horrified, Carathril saw that the rest of Aerenis's company had set upon the spearmen on the wall. Fighting broke out between the two towers of the gatehouse, company against company, while the siege tower lumbered ever closer.

'Why?' said Carathril, jabbing the point of his spear at the traitorous captain.

'You would keep me from beautiful Glaronielle,' said Aerenis, sweeping his blade towards Carathril's legs, forcing him back into the press of the warriors fighting behind him. 'Ereth Khial has granted me the love I always desired.'

'The Queen of the Underworld?' Carathril was shocked. He had never suspected such a thing of his friend, even in his most melancholy of moods. 'That is why you betray your city?'

'With the priests of Nagarythe to aid us, we will bring back the departed and I shall be with Glaronielle as I could not in life.'

Carathril laughed harshly and drove his spear at Aerenis's chest, the attack warded away by the edge of the other elf's shield.

'You will be sent to Mirai to meet Glaronielle, that is sure enough,' said Carathril. 'The priests of Nagarythe will offer you up to Ereth Khial for their own bargains with the Dark Queen.'

The suggestion incensed Aerenis; his expression of morose resignation twisted into a feral snarl, eyes wild. Carathril raised his shield and weathered a frenzy of blows, each numbing his arm with their ferocity.

'I will see Glaronielle again!' raged Aerenis as he rained down blow after blow. 'We will be together and we will wed and have children!'

'You will certainly be together,' snarled Carathril, despising what he saw had become of his friend.

He turned aside the next sword blow with a twist of his shield, spinning Aerenis to one side. In one fluid movement, Carathril lunged, his spear piercing his friend's side below the arm. Aerenis gave a cry of pain and spun to the ground, sword falling from his grasp. Carathril did not hesitate. He dragged free his spear and plunged it into the neck of Aerenis, driving with all his strength, fuelled by anger at the treachery of his friend. The spearpoint crashed off the stone of the rampart, almost severing Aerenis's head from his body.

Wrenching free his weapon, Carathril glanced over his shoulder and saw the looming shadow of the siege tower. The traitorous spearmen had been vastly outnumbered and were all but slain, but their turning had spread anarchy across the gatehouse. The siege engine was less than twenty paces away. Carathril could see the chains holding the ramp quivering, ready to be let free.

'On me!' he cried, standing directly opposite where the assault would come, lifting his spear above his head to rally his warriors 'Fight to the last!'

Carathril glared at the cruel face painted onto the timbers of the tower, staring it down as if it were some real beast to be cowed. He set his shield and spear, legs braced, and waited for the ramp to crash down.

He heard a thunderous crack and a blast of wind threw him to the stones. Suspecting sorcery, Carathril glanced around for a sign of Eltreneth, though he had felt no surge of magic.

A moment later the siege tower exploded into thousands of splinters, bloodied bodies cascading from its ruin as it toppled to the ground. A green-scaled dragon burst from the cloud of debris, corpses and tangles of wreckage hanging from its mouth and claws as it swept up over the gate-house shedding debris.

Carathril stared wide-eyed as the monstrous creature turned sharply and dived down upon the remains of the siege tower spewing fire, incinerating all that had survived its devastating charge.

'There must be a dozen of them,' muttered a spearman lying beside Carathril.

Laughing from shock, Carathril staggered to his feet to see more dragons sweeping back and forth across the druchii ranks. War hydras snarled and spat flame as beasts with scales of red and green and blue and silver and gold rampaged through the Naggarothi army, smashing war engines, ripping swathes through the archers and spearmen, grappling with the enslaved monsters of the druchii.

The former herald recognised the standard flying from the throne-saddle of the largest, a massive red beast; the pennant of King Caledor. The Phoe-nix King's lance cut through armoured knights by the dozen as his dragon slashed and snapped a bloody trail through the mounted Naggarothi.

Carathril dropped his spear and shield and grabbed the spearman's breastplate, dragging him to his feet. He swept his arms around the other elf's shoulders and brought him into a tight embrace as tears rolled down his cheeks.

'Caledor is here,' Carathril wept. 'Caledor has come...'

THERE WAS NO greater thrill than leading a flight of dragons into battle. Dorien laughed from the joy of the experience as his mount swept low over the army of the Phoenix King, Thyrinor, Earethien and Findeir following behind. His dragon, Nemaerinir, rumbled in echo of his laughter, sharing the prince's excitement.

The army marched north, having wintered in Caledor. A brief foray into Eataine had revealed the dire situation at Lothern, but the Phoenix King had also been brought word of a fresh druchii offensive against Ellyrion. The dragon riders had flown to the besieged city as swiftly as possible, smashing the Naggarothi forces in a single afternoon while the infantry and cavalry moved towards Tor Elyr.

Prisoners captured at Lothern had revealed a much greater threat than Dorien could have imagined. All of Nagarythe seemed to be on the march, striking simultaneously for Lothern, Ellyrion and Chrace. The other king-doms could barely muster the troops to quell the murderous cultists within their borders and Caledor had been forced to split the dragon princes. The Phoenix King himself had flown to the Isle of the Flame to call a new coun-cil of the princes of the eastern kingdoms, leaving Dorien in charge of the army.

Dorien had felt the urgency of his brother's words as the Phoenix King had despatched him to the north; the victory at Lothern would be for nothing if Ellyrion was allowed to fall. Dorien had argued hard for all of the dragon princes to fly forth to Ellyrion, but Caledor had refused, claiming that they would be sent to fight across Ulthuan to show that they did not fight for one kingdom alone. It seemed a nonsensical gesture to Dorien but he had not pressed his disagreement, fearing that too much resistance would see him replaced as general by Thyrinor or one of the other princes.

Below the dragons the army followed a straight road that led to the Eagle Pass, where the next druchii attack was expected. The warning had come from Finudel and Athielle, along with a promise to march with the army of Ellyrion. The letter had ended with an impassioned plea for aid that had added to Dorien's sense of haste.

Ellyrion was a land of low hills and rolling pastures, curving between the Inner Sea to the east and the Annulii to the west. The fields the army marched past were deserted, the famous herds of Ellyrion having been gathered at the capital for the kingdom's army. The scars of past battles could be seen from the air; burned settlements and scoured fields where the druchii had been held at bay by the Ellyrians and Caledor's army.

The elves marched throughout the days and for most of each night, resting only for a short while before every dawn. Dorien fretted at the delays, knowing that his dragon riders could have arrived at Eagle Pass several days earlier if they had not been forced to keep pace with the infantry and knights. Every morning he dreaded to receive a messenger from the Ellyrians bringing word that the reinforcements had arrived too late; every morning Dorien dreaded to look to the north-east, towards Tor Elyr, half-expecting to see columns of smoke from a razed city.

Yet no smoke had been seen and no messenger had arrived, and the army was less than a day's march from the eastern end of Eagle Pass. Dorien had commanded that the dragons fly ahead to locate the druchii army if possible and ascertain the whereabouts of the Ellyrians. If the two forces combined, they would be more than a match for any army of Naggarothi – in Dorien's opinion at least, though Thyrinor continued to voice Caledor's warnings against overconfidence.

It was nearing midday when Dorien first noticed darkness on the northern horizon; a glowering storm cloud that stretched far from west to east, lightning dancing against the black thunderhead.

'That is no ordinary storm,' said Nemaerinir. 'It stinks of sorcery.'

'That it does,' replied Dorien, feeling dark magic blowing down on the winds from the Annulii. 'A conjuration of the druchii, no doubt.'

The prince signalled for the other dragon princes to fly closer. He darted a look back and saw his army below, marching as swiftly as possible along the road. Thyrinor drew up alongside him atop Anaegnir.

'It seems that we arrive too late,' said Thyrinor.

'Perhaps not,' Dorien called back. 'We must fly with all haste to see what happens.'

Rising higher, the dragons flew abreast of each other, heading directly for the storm. As morning became afternoon, they approached the dark cloud. The gloom had thinned somewhat and two armies could be seen spread out on the meadows below. The dark army of the Naggarothi was like a spear thrust between two parts of the bright Ellyrian host.

Heavily armoured knights closed in for a charge against the Ellyrian infantry, who had their backs to a winding river on the other side of which spread a thick forest. The Ellyrian reaver knights were further east, an ebbing and flowing line of white horses and silver-clad riders that charged the druchii and retreated again and again, like surf crashing against rocks; like a receding tide, with each withdrawal they were forced further east.

'What's that?' cried Thyrinor, pointing almost directly below.

Dorien could not quite believe what he saw. It seemed as if another army was advancing into the southern flank of the druchii; another army also clad in black and silver and bearing banners of Naggarothi design.

'The traitors fight amongst themselves!' he laughed. 'Perhaps we should leave them to it?'

Thyrinor's reply was drowned out by a bass growl from Nemaerinir that shook the whole of the dragon's body, reverberating up Dorien's spine.

'A black dragon,' Nemaerinir snarled, and banked to the east.

Sure enough, an ebon-scaled drake menaced the Ellyrian cavalry, sweeping low through their ranks.

'Thyrinor, with me,' called Dorien. 'The black dragon is ours! Earethien, Findeir, destroy the Naggarothi knights!'

The other riders lifted their lances in acknowledgement and the dragons divided into two pairs, heading north and east.

The enemy seemed oblivious to the arrival of the dragons, undetected against the storm clouds. The black dragon and its rider were slaughtering the Ellyrians, each scything dive ripping a swathe of dead and wounded through the ranks of the cavalry. As Nemaerinir dived down, Dorien could see the target of the enemy general's cruel attentions; a shining figure of white and silver that rallied the elves against the dragon's attack. As he approached, the prince saw long locks of flowing golden hair and knew immediately that he looked upon Athielle, ruling princess of Ellyrion.

The black dragon crashed into her bodyguard, biting and slashing its way towards the defiant princess. The reaver knights threw themselves into the dragon's path to protect their beloved ruler, only to be ripped apart and crushed.

'He's mine!' roared Dorien, lowering his lance as Nemaerinir tipped towards the black dragon.

'Dorien, wait!' Thyrinor cried in return, his own mount following behind.

The black dragon's jaws snapped shut around the head of a horse, decapitating it in one bite. A lash of its barbed tail speared three more riders, buckling breastplates, smashing ribs and pulverising vital organs.

The way was almost clear to Athielle; barely a dozen more reavers stood in the path of the druchii commander. Dorien aimed his lance at the dragon, judging it to be a greater threat than the Naggarothi general.

Suddenly the black dragon stopped mid-attack. The monstrous creature arched his neck, nostrils flaring, and then turned towards Dorien as he raced closer. The black dragon hurled himself into the air, wings creating a down-draught that sent riders tumbling, toppling horses to their flanks. Clouds of oily vapour formed a fog around rider and beast as the dragon strove to gain more height.

At Dorien's command, Nemaerinir rolled right and then turned sharply left, the prince adjusting to aim his long lance over his mount's neck. The black dragon twisted away and the lance bit through the membrane of his right wing, ripping a large and ragged hole in the scaled skin. In a flash Nemaerinir was behind the foe, crashing his tail against the black dragon's flanks as it passed.

Thyrinor steered his mount higher and Anaegnir folded her wings into a stoop, coming at the enemy from above. The druchii rider twisted in his saddle and set the butt of his magical lance against his mount to absorb the impact, directing the point towards the approaching dragon prince. The black dragon lurched unexpectedly to the right, wounded wing faltering spasmodically, pulling the druchii's lance tip away from Thyrinor.

Dorien gave a shout of annoyance as Thyrinor's lance point hit home. Its tip sheared through the Naggarothi's breastplate in an explosion of magical fire, lifting him from his saddle-throne with a tearing of straps and snapping of wood. The dragon's reins of chain fell from the dead druchii's grip as Thyrinor twisted his lance with a flick of his wrist, sending the body spiralling to the ground far below.

Nemaerinir circled around and raked his claws across the other dragon's snout, shredding skin in a spray of thick scales. The black dragon gave a roar and spewed forth an immense cloud of poisonous gas. Pumping his wings, blood streaming from the injury, the black dragon turned and raced away, heading for the Inner Sea while Dorien and his steed gagged on the noxious fumes left in its wake.

As the filthy cloud dispersed, Dorien turned Nemaerinir after the escaping drake, but Thyrinor flew in front of him, raising his shield to attract his cousin's attention.

'The battle is far from won,' Thyrinor called out. 'We have more urgent matters to attend than pursuing a wounded foe.'

Dorien glanced down and saw the truth of this. Aided by the dragon princes, the Ellyrians were pushing forwards from the river, but the cavalry of Athielle and Finudel were sorely pressed by massed companies of spearmen.

'You are right, cousin,' said Dorien, and he felt Nemaerinir growl with disappointment. 'Let us earn even more gratitude from the Ellyrians by saving their rulers!'

The two dragons descended quickly, but the Naggarothi had time to prepare. Bolts and arrows flew up to meet them as they dived down on the enemy infantry. Dorien gave a yell as a black-shafted missile ricocheted from Nemaerinir's scales and crashed against his right thigh. The enchantments cast within his armour by the priests of Vaul protected him from losing his leg, but pain surged from knee to hip.

'Are you wounded?' asked Nemaerinir, slowing in his descent.

'It is nothing,' Dorien snapped in reply. 'Let us slay these wretched Naggarothi and be done!'

It took only a few passes from the dragons to rout the Naggarothi. The black-clad knights and soldiers streamed back towards Eagle Pass in their thousands, harried by the dragons. Dorien noticed that the Ellyrians did not join the pursuit and remembered the second Naggarothi army to the south. With Thyrinor close behind, he flew towards the large standard of Ellyrion, spying Finudel by its side.

He winced as pain shot up his leg when Nemaerinir landed not far from the prince of Ellyrion, the jolt sending spasms up his back. Biting back a snarl, Dorien called out to Finudel.

'The enemy are on the run, why do you not chase them? I shall deal with the remaining enemy.'

'We must tend to our wounded,' the Ellyrian shouted back. 'And the Naggarothi to the south are no enemies, they are our allies.'

'How strange,' muttered Dorien. He raised his voice. 'I am Dorien, brother of Caledor. You are welcome at my camp this evening.'

'An invitation I will gladly accept,' Finudel replied. 'Is not the Phoenix King with you?'

'He has others matters that demand his attention.'

'I understand. You have the gratitude of all Ellyrion, Dorien. Be sure that we shall shower you with wine and gifts for what you have done for us today. We would be destroyed without you.'

'Yes, you would,' replied Dorien. He realised he was being undiplomatic and added, 'but your bravery and skill are without question.'

'I shall come to your camp at dusk,' said Finudel, choosing to ignore any slight he might have taken. 'My thanks again.'

Dorien nodded and with a word from the prince Nemaerinir flew off. Dorien looked eagerly west, but the Naggarothi were already at Eagle Pass. It would be too much of a risk to follow them into the mountains without support, and the rest of the army would never catch them.

'Come back for some more fun, Naggarothi scum!' he shouted at the retreating army. 'My friends and I will be waiting for you!'

* * *

THYRINOR WAS A little drunk, but he did not care. He had slain a druchii commander that day and had been repeatedly toasted by their Ellyrian guests. For what seemed to be the twentieth time, he described the duel with the black dragon's rider to an eager audience, ensuring he gave Dorien equal credit for the Naggarothi's death. From outside the great pavilion of the princes came laughter and Caledorian victory songs.

When the tale was done, he begged leave of his companions and sought another ewer of wine. He found himself at a table laden with food and realised how hungry he was.

'You must be very proud,' said a voice behind him.

He turned to find Carathril of Lothern. Despite his protestations, Caledor had reinstated him as herald of the Phoenix King, in reward for his part in Caledor's ascension and heroic acts recounted to Caledor by the prince of Eataine. The herald's expression was impassive, morose even.

'You make slaying the enemy sound like a bad thing,' replied Thyrinor, locating a crystal jug of pale wine. 'You have killed more than your fair share, I have heard.'

'And one amongst them I had counted a friend,' replied Carathril. 'We should not ever become enamoured of slaying other elves.'

'No, you are right, my friend,' said Thyrinor, shamed by the herald's words. 'It is love of war that sets the Naggarothi apart from us.'

'I hope that the king understands that also,' said Carathril. He looked up as another group of elves entered the tent and his brow furrowed. 'There are some that embrace hatred as much as the druchii.'

Thyrinor followed Carathril's troubled gaze and saw that Finudel and Athielle had been joined by another elf; a strange individual clad in dark hunting clothes. His pale skin and dark hair marked him out as a Naggarothi. A quiet settled across the gathered Caledorians and the newcomer was quickly the centre of attention. Thyrinor saw Dorien limping towards the newcomer and sensed confrontation.

'Excuse me, friend,' said Thyrinor, hurrying to intercept his cousin.

'What do we have here?' said Dorien, his deep blue eyes regarding the stranger with barely concealed hostility.

'I am Alith Anar, prince of Nagarythe.'

'A Naggarothi?' replied Dorien with a dubious eyebrow raised, recoiling slightly.

'He is our ally, Dorien,' said Finudel. 'Were it not for Alith's actions I fear your arrival would have found us already dead.'

The Caledorian prince regarded Alith with contempt, head cocked to one side. Alith returned the look with equal disgust.

'Alith, this is Prince Dorien,' said Finudel, breaking the awkward silence that had rippled out through the nearby elves. 'He is the younger brother of King Caledor.'

The Naggarothi prince did not react to this, meeting Dorien's stare.

'What of Elthyrior?' Athielle asked, as Thyrinor reached the group. He had never heard of the elf of whom she spoke. 'Where is he?'

'I do not know,' Alith replied with a shake of the head. 'He is where Morai-heg leads him. The raven heralds took their dead and vanished into Athelian Toryr. You may never see him again.'

'Anar?' said Thyrinor, remembering the name the Naggarothi had used. He was from the house of Eoloran Anar, one of the noblest bloodlines in Ulthuan, yet looked as if he had spent his whole life in a backwater village. 'I have heard this name, from prisoners we took at Lothern.'

'And what did they say?' asked Alith.

'That the Anars marched beside Malekith and resisted Morathi.' He extended a hand. 'I am Thyrinor, and I welcome you to our camp, even if my intemperate cousin will not.'

Alith shook the proffered hand quickly. Dorien snorted and turned away, calling for more wine. As he marched off through the crowd, Thyrinor saw the Naggarothi's eyes following him, narrowing as he noticed Dorien's limp.

'He is in a grumpy mood,' said Thyrinor. 'I think he has broken his leg, but he refuses to allow the healers to look at it. He's still full of fire and blood after the battle. Tomorrow he will be calmer.'

'We are grateful for your aid,' said Athielle. 'Your arrival is more than we could have hoped for.'

'We were brought word of the druchii marching along the pass four days ago and set out immediately,' said Thyrinor. 'I regret that we cannot stay here, for we are needed in Chrace. The enemy have all but overrun the mountains and the king sails with his army to thwart them at the border with Cothique. Tomorrow we continue north and then through Avelorn to strike at the druchii from the south. Today is an important victory, and Caledor recognises the sacrifices made by the people of Ellyrion.'

Alith turned away and Thyrinor saw the Naggarothi's fists clench and his shoulders hunch.

'Alith?' said Athielle, stepping towards the Naggarothi. Thyrinor noticed the pain in her expression and shared a concerned look with Finudel. The Ellyrian prince subtly shook his head as a warning against any remark. Alith turned back to the princess.

'I am sorry,' said Alith. 'I cannot share your enthusiasm for today's victory.'

'I would think you happy that Kheranion is dead,' said Finudel, joining his sister. 'Is that not some measure of payment for your father?'

Thyrinor had paid little attention to the ongoing saga of the Anars. In that, he shared Dorien's view that Naggarothi killing Naggarothi was no bad thing. He spied a servant passing with a golden tray filled with wine goblets and swiped a fresh glass.

'No,' Alith said quietly. 'Kheranion died swiftly.'

Athielle and Finudel fell silent, shocked by Alith's words. Thyrinor stepped up beside Finudel, proffering a goblet towards Alith. The Naggarothi prince took it reluctantly.

'Victories have been few for us,' said the Caledorian. He raised his own glass in toast to Alith. 'I give you my thanks for your efforts and those of your warriors. Were the king here, I am sure he would offer you the same.'

'I do not fight for your praise,' said Alith.

Thyrinor bit back a retort at the Naggarothi's rudeness and took a sip of wine.

'Then what do you fight for?' asked Thyrinor.

Alith did not reply immediately. He looked towards Athielle and his expression lightened a little.

'Forgive me,' Alith said with a slight smile. 'I am weary. Wearier than you can possibly imagine. Ellyrion and Caledor battle for their freedom and I should not judge you for matters that are not your responsibility.'

Alith took a mouthful of wine and gave a weak nod of appreciation. He raised the goblet beside Thyrinor's and fixed his gaze upon the Caledorian.

'May you win all of your battles and end this war!' Alith declared. His eyes flickered away for a moment before returning to meet Thyrinor's bemused stare. The Caledorian saw emptiness of spirit in that gaze and was forced to look away, suppressing a shudder.

'We should not impose upon you any longer,' said Finudel, guiding Athielle away with a touch on her arm. Alith gazed longingly after her for a moment before he returned his stare to Thyrinor.

'Will you fight to the last, against all hope?' Alith asked. 'Will your king give his life to free Ulthuan?'

'He will,' replied Thyrinor. 'You think that you alone have reason enough to fight the druchii? You are wrong, so very wrong.'

Alith's presence was deeply unsettling. Thyrinor turned away and called for Dorien, feigning concern for his cousin so that he could leave the Naggarothi alone. He joined Dorien with the other Caledorian princes at the centre of the pavilion, downing the contents of his goblet.

'I don't know about you, but I think I prefer it when the Naggarothi are not on our side,' he said in a hushed voice, fearful that the Anar prince would hear him.

'I don't trust him,' said Dorien, staring over Thyrinor's shoulder to where Alith was in deep conversation with Carathril. 'Finudel is a fool for allying with his sort. Believe me, that Anar will turn out to be a traitor and I would have my throat slit before I agree to fight alongside him. Better that than a knife in the back.'

Thyrinor eyed Alith Anar with suspicion, knowing the truth of his cousin's words. It was not just the Naggarothi's words and demeanour that bothered him. There was a darkness of the spirit that permeated the core of Alith, and

Thyrinor wanted no part of it. Turning away, he pushed the Naggarothi from his thoughts and spied a group of Athielle's handmaidens looking appreciatively at him across the pavilion.

Securing himself a fresh goblet of wine, he headed towards them with a smile.

—◀ TWELVE ▶—

Avelorn Withers

THE FLOWER WAS wilting. Its leaves hung lank and yellowing, stem twisted, pale blue petals ragged-edged as they dropped to the ground. Yvraine knelt beside the plant, sensing the source of its malaise. All of Ulthuan was sickening. Dark magic flowed, corrupting everything it touched. Unspeakable rites were performed in the name of the undergods. The Everqueen's people slew each other across the isle. The harmony of Ulthuan was disrupted and all was falling to disorder.

Yvraine touched an extended finger to a drooping leaf and let free a fragment of her power. Life flowed into the flower and it straightened and coloured, infused with the Everqueen's magic. It was a gesture and nothing more. She could not heal every hurt being wrought upon Ulthuan.

The Everqueen knelt beside the flower and pushed her fingers into the earth, feeling every particle of soil on her skin. Long hair flowing about her face, she closed her eyes and took a deep breath, inhaling the scent and moisture of the bare ground, breathing in the life force of Isha.

She let her mind wander from the mortal shell that others knew as Yvraine, and seeped into the soil, slowly spreading through the Gaen Vale, out into Avelorn and onwards, through every blade of grass and bloom in Ulthuan.

Her spirit wept as her mind felt the crushing tread of the Naggarothi armies over pasture and meadow. She recoiled at the taste of blood in the rivers and streams. Armies camped beneath the bowers of ancient trees and cut them down to feed their fires.

The Everqueen retreated back to Avelorn, dismayed by what she had felt.

Hatred, greed, zealotry, and not just from the Naggarothi. Always it was so, evil rising from evil to feed itself. The filth of Chaos lingered in the air and the water and the ground. Her people would never be free of its touch.

For all her dark thoughts, she knew that there was always hope. From the memories she shared with her many mothers she knew that Ulthuan had seen an age far worse than the present. Life could not be so easily extinguished. The pain of Avelorn still lingered in her heart from when it had been razed by the daemons. The forest had grown again from that perilous time, yet the greater damage had been done. Her father, Aenarion, had taken the Godslayer, and in that single act had welcomed violence into the hearts of the elves forever. The Naggarothi could not be blamed for what they had become, the seed of their evil had been sown generations earlier.

Yet that seed of darkness had been nurtured by evil purpose. The Everqueen's thoughts turned to the architect of this new time of woe: Morathi. It was her spite, her jealousy, her greed that had fuelled this war. All of the blood spilt ran as a flood from Morathi's hands.

That flood had come to Avelorn now. Armoured warriors roamed into the western woods from the mountains of Chrace, killing and burning. They were a scourge upon everything, seeking to tame and conquer nature itself. Yvraine's consciousness moved along branch and root, spying upon the Naggarothi camps. She felt the patter of blood on the grass beneath the sacrificial altars, tasted the charnel smoke of the pyres through her leaves, while animal terror coursed through her roots from the fleeing creatures of the forest.

The sun fell and rose and fell again many times as Yvraine watched the Naggarothi, seeking to divine their purpose. They drove everything before them, wolf beside the deer, fox beside the rabbit, hawk beside the dove. All were united in their dread of the dark slaughter that had come to Avelorn.

Drawn by her anger, the Maiden Guard gathered in the clearing around Yvraine's still form. In the silver-and-gold glow of the Aein Yshain, Isha's favoured tree, the warriors of Avelorn sharpened their spears and strung their bows, waiting for their queen to resurface. They too felt the discord rampaging through Avelorn, and had come to this sacred glade to hear what would be done about it.

There was too much death, and violence would always defeat itself. Yet the forest had to be protected and its people and creatures defended against the malice of Morathi and her soldiers.

Yvraine returned to her mortal form, its skin shining with a faint light as her spirit took its place. She stood and looked upon her army in their golden scale and green cloaks.

'My husband-to-be does not come to our aid,' she said with disappointment. 'He proves as fallible as the others, short-sighted and selfish. He has not yet even come to seek my blessing in person, nor join with me so that the reign of the Everqueen will be sustained. Yet I sense that we will not stand alone. From across Ellyrion comes the army of his brother. Go to them and show them the paths through the forest that will take them to our enemies. Drive them from the glades and the deep woods with spear and arrow, and then return to me.'

Her will made known, Yvraine retreated to the caves beneath the arching roots of the Aein Yshain. She sat upon her throne of curled roots while attendants busied themselves with gourds of water taken from the sacred springs, filling the pools that surrounded the Everqueen's seat. Images shimmered in each pond, showing Avelorn from west to east, south to north. While time passed in the world outside, Yvraine shared the life of the great tree of Isha, each day like a single heartbeat of existence.

After a few moments, she was disturbed from her contemplation by a presence within the sacred glade. Rising from her throne, green and yellow gown flowing like a gossamer waterfall behind her, Yvraine left the chamber and found one of the treemen of Avelorn waiting for her in the glade above.

'Oakheart,' she said. 'Long it has been since you first brought my brother and me to the Gaen Vale and long since you spoke to the First Council. What disturbs you to bring you to my court?'

The treeman moved slowly, limb-branches unfolding, trunk curving gently as if in a wind, to bow before the Everqueen.

'One is coming that should not come,' said Oakheart as he straightened with a quivering of browning leaves. He too felt the waning of Avelorn's power, the autumn blighting what should have been an existence of eternal summer. His voice was quiet, like the sighing of wind through branches. 'He has made pact with the wolves and they lead him to Gaen Vale.'

Yvraine nodded and allowed herself to drift for a short while, seeking this person. She found him, an elf clad in nothing but a sword belt, running with a great pack of wolves.

'You are right, he cannot come to the Gaen Vale,' she said, reclaiming her body with a shudder. 'Yet he cannot be turned away unaided. I sense the spirit of the hunter in him. The time has come for Isha's gift to be passed on. Let the wolves take him to the Lake of the Moon, and see if he has the will to claim Kurnous's prize for himself.'

'And if he still seeks sanctuary in Gaen Vale?' sighed Oakheart.

'He is touched by darkness and cannot come here,' replied the Everqueen. 'Guard the sanctity of our home and turn him away, but do not harm him.'

'As the forest wills it,' said Oakheart.

As the treeman left the glade, Yvraine returned to study the elf from her vision. He was young, barely an adult, and she watched him fight ferociously with a Naggarothi knight. He was brave, but savage at heart. As Isha had chosen Yvraine, so the hunter Kurnous had chosen this elf. The Moonbow of Isha would be enough of a reward for the young elf's brave deeds defending Avelorn; but he would have to put it to use elsewhere. The evil he fought was within him as well as outside, and Yvraine could not risk having such a person in the Gaen Vale at this precarious time.

Leaving the feral hunter to his fate, she dismissed him from her thoughts and returned to her throne chamber to witness the battle against the Naggarothi.

THE FORESTS OF Avelorn were no place for a dragon and Dorien had regrettably been given no choice but to lead his army from horseback; Thyrinor and the other dragon riders had flown further north, to seek out the Naggarothi where the mountains of Chrace shouldered down into the ancient woods.

The Caledorian prince was nervous. It was not the prospect of battle with the Naggarothi that disturbed him – he relished the coming fight – but the strange nature of his environs and his quiet allies. The Maiden Guard had met his army on the border of Ellyrion and Avelorn. In a quiet but determined way, their captain had told Dorien he was to follow her warriors through the forests. No elf was to leave the trail that was set, and though no warning had been given as to what might befall such a wanderer, such were the tales of Avelorn that every elf under Dorien's command knew to obey the edict.

By twisting paths that seemed to spring from the woods at the army's approach, the Maiden Guard had led Dorien through the deep forests, heading ever north and west. When asked about the enemy, the Avelorn warrior-maidens would say only that there were several thousand of them and that they were currently being waylaid. The march took several days, and at night Dorien lay awake in his tent, listening to the murmuring of the trees, the screech of owls and the howling of wolves. Each morning when he left his pavilion, he was convinced the forest had changed. Pathways had opened up from the clearings that had not existed the evening before, and even rivers seemed to have diverted their courses so that the army could pass without hindrance.

Dorien was a native of the mountains and whole days would pass without sight of the sky beyond the thick canopy, fuelling his fears. He considered himself at home in the wilds, like many elves, but it was only on coming to Avelorn that he realised just how tame the wildernesses of Ulthuan had become under the moulding of the elves' desires. Beyond Avelorn every wood and dale had a sculpted quality; carefully managed to appear untamed, yet in comparison to the forest of the Everqueen they were as ordered and safe as a manse's gardens.

The sentries on night watch whispered about the constant creaking and groaning of the woods; of flickers of faerie lights and strange eyes in the moonlight. The Maiden Guard assured Dorien that there was nothing to fear, and hinted that for all the unease the elves of the other kingdoms felt at Avelorn's strange ways, it was nothing compared to the terror being heaped upon the Naggarothi invaders. Dorien was pleased to hear this but could get no answers when he pressed for more information.

After seven nerve-wracking days and nights traversing the wild woods, Dorien was told that the Naggarothi were close at hand. The smoke of fires carried on the breeze, and it seemed that the trees were even more active than before.

'While the Maiden Guard are at home in such a place, my army is not meant for warfare in such close confines,' Dorien complained to Althinelle, the captain of the Maiden Guard.

'There is no need to lament,' she replied. 'Your knights shall have even ground on which to charge and your archers shall have clear fields over which to loose their arrows.'

'While I am thankful for the assurance, I cannot see how we shall lure the Naggarothi onto this open ground you have prepared,' said the prince. 'I fear we will be outmanoeuvred.'

'Our enemies do not yet know the field of battle, but they will have no choice but to come there,' said Althinelle. 'Avelorn will bring them to you. Make ready your army and head due west. Battle will be upon you before noon.'

Offering no other explanation, Althinelle left Dorien to his confused thoughts. The Maiden Guard departed the camp, heading westwards, while the army prepared to march. Dorien mounted his horse and joined the knights of Caledor in the middle of the army, while archers and spearmen were sent forwards in the vanguard to seek the open space of which Althinelle had spoken.

Without the Maiden Guard to lead the way, progress was slower. Dorien gazed constantly up through the leaves to track the rising of the sun, fearful he would miss some appointment whose time and place he did not exactly know.

He had no cause for such fears. Shortly before midday, scouts returned with news that fighting could be heard to the west, though they had not been able to locate the Naggarothi army itself. Following the scouts, the army headed towards the shouts and cries that echoed through the trees.

As if pushed aside by some vast hand, the woods abruptly stopped not far to the west. The trees lined a vast sunlit glade, the floor of which was carpeted in thick grass and meadow flowers. Dorien was amazed by the sight of it, but his wonder was short-lived; on the other side of the clearing, black-robed figures marched into view. Some were helping wounded companions and the sounds of fighting came closer.

More and more Naggarothi emerged, staggering into the daylight, arrows falling on them from the darkness of the wooded eaves of the glade. Several thousand in all hastily gathered their ranks as Dorien's army spread out to north and south, the knights on the right end of the line, ready to sweep around the enemy.

Beyond the Naggarothi the prince could see shapes moving through the woods; he assumed it was the Maiden Guard from the continued sounds of conflict and death that rang across the clearing.

Dorien ordered the musicians to signal the advance and his army paced towards the Naggarothi, spears and bows at the ready. The druchii formed a short, solid line of spears and repeater crossbows, at the heart of which sat a few hundred knights in reserve. There was not a patch of high ground to defend, and the Naggarothi were sorely outnumbered.

'They are fools to stand and fight,' said Laudneril, riding to Dorien's right bearing the prince's household standard.

'I think they would rather take their chances with us than the woods,' said Dorien.

'I do not think they have any choice in that!' Laudneril replied with shock, pointing towards the far edge of the glade.

The trees were moving. It was hard to see exactly how, but the wall of trunks and branches marking the border of the clearing was creeping closer to the Naggarothi. The ground rumbled gently, causing the knights' horses to whinny and stamp.

Arrows sliced the air as Dorien's archers came within range. The druchii crossbowmen ventured closer, casting suspicious eyes at the advancing woods, and returned the volleys with missiles of their own. Though they had marched at least five hundred paces into the vast clearing, the Naggarothi now found the trees no more than two hundred paces from their backs. Keening cries and shrill calls came from all around. To the north and south, the woods closed in as well, girding the clearing with an almost solid ring of trees.

Unable to retreat, the Naggarothi held their ground as Dorien's army pressed in for the attack. The druchii knights cut to the north, seeking to head off Dorien's cavalry, while spear blocks manoeuvred for advantage and the bolts and arrows of both sides passed overhead.

As the two armies converged, Dorien remembered the warnings of his brother. Though the druchii were outnumbered, they were veterans of war, raised in bloody Nagarythe, tested in the colonies. For the most part his own army, save for a core of Caledorians who had seen battle in Elthin Arvan, were largely untested. It was the dragons that had broken the siege at Lothern and routed the Naggarothi at Ellyrion Plains; he wished he had known Avelorn would provide an open field of battle and not sent the dragons north.

He pushed such thoughts from his mind as the two columns of cavalry charged each other. The druchii knights were armoured from toe to scalp in mail and plate, faces hidden behind narrow-visored helmets, their horses protected by chamfrons and scale barding. Black and purple pennants fluttered from lowering lance tips and the ground thundered beneath the iron-studded hooves of their black horses.

Dorien drew Alantair, an heirloom of the war against the daemons. The slightly curved blade glimmered with runes, orange fire playing along its edge from hilt to tip. The Caledorian prince lifted his shield and singled out a foe to attack, guiding his steed with gentle nudges with his knees. He chose a druchii clad in golden armour, a black cloak swirling from his shoulders. His helm was masked with a daemonic face and curling silver horns topped it as a crest. He rode beside a banner of red cloth embroidered with the rune of Anlec in black; a captain, Dorien thought, or perhaps even a Naggarothi prince.

'For Caledor!' the prince bellowed, the war cry answered by the Silver Helms around him.

The Naggarothi were chanting as they charged, a dirge-like chorus in time to the beating hooves of their mounts. Barbed and jagged lance tips gleamed in the sunlight.

At the last moment, Dorien's horse swayed to the left, the Naggarothi's lance smashing into the prince's shield with a crackle of energy. The impact almost threw Dorien from the saddle but he gripped tight with his legs and swung his sword over the horse's head as the two riders passed, the flaming blade shearing through the shield of his foe, sending the druchii's arm into the air.

Dorien had no time to finish off the Naggarothi; another enemy knight crashed into him, lance missing the Caledorian's shoulder by a hair's breadth. Dorien chopped into the back of the druchii as he galloped past.

The impetus of both sides dissipated by the mutual charge, the two forces of knights swirled about each other in a spreading melee. The druchii discarded their lances and drew axes and swords, while Dorien slashed left and right, Alantair's burning blade slicing through flesh and armour. The noise was deafening, metal ringing on metal, the shouts of the warriors, the stamp and whinnying of their steeds.

Bodies of horses and elves piled on the blood-slicked grass as both sides fought mercilessly. Dorien's steed stumbled and righted itself in the gore, leaving the prince open to an attack from his right. An axe blade crashed against the side of his helm, protective runes flaring with magical power. Still, he was dazed, and could only clumsily fend away the next blow with the blade of Alantair. Dorien could feel blood trickling down the side of his neck and his head throbbed. As if in response, the ache in his leg returned. The healers had done everything they could, but there had been no time to properly rest and recuperate.

Another knight surged between Dorien and the attacking druchii, his sword thrusting into the other elf's visor with a spray of blood. The Naggarothi toppled sideways, crashing to the ground. Dorien gave the Caledorian knight a salute of thanks and kicked his steed into the press of cavalry, seeking a fresh foe.

By mutual desire, the two sides slowly parted, seeking clearer ground for another charge. As Dorien had feared, the druchii had matched his knights despite their fewer numbers; there were more bodies of friends than foes littering the clearing. As the squadrons reformed a couple of hundred paces apart, Dorien turned his attention to the infantry. There also the momentum of the attack had been halted and a sprawling fight now raged.

Arcs of black energy revealed the presence of a sorcerer. White-robed spearmen were thrown back by the magical blast, their armour crackling, skin burning. The white glow of protective talismans enveloped Theriun, the prince leading the infantry, as another hail of dark energy flickered along the line. The knights needed to outflank the druchii, but there was no way to do so with the enemy cavalry still threatening. If they charged now, Dorien's squadrons would in turn be attacked in the rear. He cast a hasty glance towards the druchii knights and saw that they were already advancing again.

Dorien could feel the dark magic surging through the air, like a pressure in the back of his skull. The sensation was tinged with the power emanating from Alantair. Yet it was something else that had attracted Dorien's attention to the ebb and flow of the winds of magic. He felt power seeping through the ground, gathering quickly.

The druchii charged again, banners fluttering. Still reorganising themselves, Dorien's Silver Helms hastily formed to face the renewed attack. Dorien fervently wished he had a dragon or two as he watched the block of black and gold bearing down on his unprepared warriors.

The magic of the earth surged. To Dorien it felt as if the ground shifted, so violent was the build-up of mystical energy. Beneath the steeds of the druchii, the grass erupted. Vines with thorns like daggers shot into the air, coiling and snaring, ripping the druchii from their steeds, strangling and tripping horses. In moments, a massive briar enveloped the Naggarothi, tightening around necks and limbs, barbs piercing mail and flesh. The scream of dying horses and the panicked shrieks of the druchii accompanied a dread-inducing creaking and slithering as more and more tendrils burst from the earth, lashing with violent life.

Beyond the clashing lines of infantry, Dorien saw that the forest was on the move again. Only this time shapes emerged from the trees. Massive, gangling creatures with flesh of wood and skin of bark strode into the clearing. Behind them came a host of smaller creatures, bounding and running on branch-like limbs. Winged spirits with small bows flitted about the branches of the treemen, shooting glimmering darts into the backs of the druchii.

With them lumbered giant bears and packs of black-furred wolves raced into the clearing, snarling and slavering. Hawks and owls swept down from the treetops, leading flocks of smaller birds that engulfed the druchii repeater crossbows, pecking at faces, talons scratching.

Looking back at the Naggarothi knights, he saw that all but a few dozen had been slain. The survivors, many unhorsed, hacked their way free of the magical briar. Dorien commanded half of his knights to finish off the enemy cavalry, and ordered the rest to follow him as he pointed his sword at the beleaguered Naggarothi infantry.

As the Silver Helms charged, the treemen reached the line of druchii soldiers. Club-like fists smashed bone and buckled armour. Fingers filled with the power of delving roots prised open helms and punched through breastplates. The spears and swords of the druchii chopped harmlessly at the treemen, who were as impervious to the blows as the mightiest oak. Crushed and trampled, trapped against the resurgent spearmen of Dorien, the druchii died in their hundreds.

The prince's cavalry charge was the final blow. As bears crushed bodies and wolves dragged down fleeing druchii, the knights hammered into the flank of the Naggarothi, cutting them down, smashing them to the ground with the impact of their steeds. His horse flailed its hooves into the face of a spearman while Dorien's blade decapitated another.

The druchii fought to the last, knowing that the forest offered no sanctuary for retreat. Surrounded by elves and spirits of Avelorn, they sold their lives with spat curses on their lips, vowing vengeance from the pits of Mirai. Dorien's arm was sore with the effort of slaying, for the battle continued long into the afternoon.

When it was done, Althinelle came to Dorien. The Maiden Captain's armour was awash with blood, her fair hair stained with gore, her speartip slick. There was something feral about her appearance, and Dorien wondered at the power that had been unleashed by the fury of Avelorn.

Dismounting, Dorien gave the captain of the Maiden Guard a brief bow and sheathed his sword.

'I wonder if Avelorn ever needed us here,' he said.

Althinelle said nothing for a moment. Her features seemed to shimmer with a pale green light, and when she looked at Dorien, it was with eyes that seemed as ancient as the forest around them.

'You have our gratitude, Dorien of Caledor,' said Althinelle. 'We could not defeat this enemy alone.'

'It is my honour to protect the ancestral lands of our people,' said Dorien. He felt the same shimmer of earth magic as he had during the battle, though now it was subtler, more diffused. 'Without Avelorn's intervention, I fear we might not have been victorious.'

'The Naggarothi will come again,' said Althinelle.

'I will leave what troops I can, but they are sorely needed elsewhere,' replied Dorien. 'Cothique is under threat, and my brother will need my aid when he sails there after the council of princes.'

'Send my regards to your brother,' said Althinelle, surprising Dorien. He looked at her more closely and realised that he was no longer addressing the captain of the Maiden Guard. 'Tell him that I look forward to our wedding. And warn him that he should not delay too long before he visits Avelorn; there are precious few moments left to us.'

Dorien dropped to one knee and bowed his head.

'Everqueen,' he said. 'Forgive my brother's tardiness. He has many things on his mind, and I fear that your blessing is not one of them.'

Althinelle-Yvraine laid a hand on Dorien's arm and gently pulled him to his feet. He kept his gaze averted, fearing to look into those deep green eyes again.

'Take your dead from this place,' said the Everqueen. 'You will be guided into Chrace, and from there you may head east and meet Caledor in Cothique.'

'Thank you, Everqueen,' said Dorien. 'And what of the druchii bodies? Shall we dispose of them also?'

Althinelle-Yvraine shook her head and turned to look over her shoulder.

'Avelorn will deal with them,' she said, with what seemed like sadness. 'The forest will sate itself with their remains.'

Dorien looked to where her gaze was directed and saw that the trees of the forest were already enveloping the druchii dead. Roots coiled through the corpses, dragging them down into the shifting earth. It seemed as if blood dripped from the leaves of the trees as they drank deep of the slain.

'Go now.' Dorien saw that Althinelle was herself again. The wildness in her eyes had gone and she seemed as weary as he felt. 'We shall leave a clearing for you to camp tonight. We will head north at dawn.'

Dorien nodded and turned away, shouting for his captains. The sooner he was out of fabled Avelorn, the more comfortable he would feel.

—< THIRTEEN >—

An Age Ends

'A HUNDRED?' SNARLED Caledor. The herald from Yvresse flinched as the Phoenix King thrust himself from his chair and stalked towards the messenger. 'A hundred spears are all that Prince Carvalon can spare?'

'We are a peaceful people,' the herald replied with an apologetic bow. 'Few enough volunteer for the militia and of those, most are required to garrison our towns against the attacks of the cultists.'

Caledor turned on the others in the Shrine of Asuryan, his adopted throne room. Thyriol was with him, as were Finudel and Athielle, Dorien, Thyrinor, Koradrel, Tithrain of Cothique, the high priest Mianderin, and his chief herald Carathril. Representatives of Eataine and Yvresse huddled together, apart from the princes, watching the Phoenix King warily.

'How can I fight a war with no army?' Caledor said. 'For six years we have marched and battled, and the druchii have been held. Now is the time to strike back.'

'Our losses have been heavy too,' said Thyriol. 'Each Naggarothi has trained for two hundred years for this war, and many have been fighting for much longer. You cannot expect our fresh recruits to face such foes with equality. Were it not for your dragons, Ulthuan would have been overrun by now. A counter-offensive is out of the question.'

'So we must simply wait for the next druchii attack?' said Dorien. 'We let them gather their strength again while their cultist lackeys have us chase from kingdom to kingdom? We should march to Anlec and finish this.'

Tithrain laughed nervously and all eyes turned towards the young ruler of Cothique.

'Anlec is unassailable,' said the prince. 'We have all heard the tales of its defences. A river of fire girds its high walls, and twenty towers overlook the approaches. Even if we were to cross Nagarythe intact, we could not take such a fortress.'

'We have a dozen dragons,' said Dorien. 'No river of fire would stop them.'

'Eleven,' said Koradrel, his voice hushed. 'Prince Aelvian and Kardraghnir were slain in Chrace during battle against the Naggarothi. My captains brought me the news last night. Bolt throwers, dozens of them, brought them down from the sky.'

This news was greeted with groans from some and a stony stare from Caledor. Koradrel shrugged.

'It matters not,' said the Chracian. 'To what end would the capture of Anlec serve? Malekith retook his capital and it did him no good. The world has changed. The Naggarothi will never agree to peace.'

'What are you saying?' said Thyriol.

'Extermination,' said Caledor.

The mage fixed the Phoenix King with a narrowed glare.

'And what of the cultists?' said Thyriol. 'Do we kill every last one of them also?'

'If we have to,' said Caledor, matching the mage's gaze. He took no pleasure in the pronouncement, but if Ulthuan was to know peace again, every threat had to be eliminated. 'We are a divided people. Prosperity and opportunity have masked those divisions, but now they have been made clear. The druchii must be slain or driven out of Ulthuan, and any that choose to follow them.'

'As you said, you have no army,' said Finudel. 'You think that you could attack Nagarythe?'

'No,' said Caledor. 'We have only been able to survive because the enemy have split their strength. They occupy Tiranoc, and have attacked Eataine, Ellyrion, Chrace and Avelorn at the same time, seeking swift victory. If we force them to gather in one place, and muster our own strength against them, we risk losing the war at a stroke.'

'Until we have an army that can match the druchii, we cannot test ourselves on an equal basis,' said Thyrinor. 'Our greatest hope is to draw them out and defeat each army in turn.'

'Your dragons cannot be everywhere at once,' said Thyriol. 'How do you plan to halt any fresh advances?'

'We cannot,' said Caledor, sitting down again. He looked at each of the princes, gauging their resolve. He was not reassured by what he saw but continued regardless. 'We must deny the druchii any great victory. We retreat before them, burning the fields, razing the storehouses. Nagarythe is not a fertile kingdom, they depend upon what they take to feed their armies.'

'For how long?' said Tithrain with an expression of horror. 'Those lands feed our people too. It would be ourselves that we also starve. A season, perhaps, we could cope with...'

'For as long as it takes,' said Caledor. 'We will bleed the druchii dry with hunger and battle. We must be resolved to this. Hardship will come, but with it also victory.'

'No,' said Athielle, earning herself a scowl from the Phoenix King. 'The pastures of Ellyrion are too valuable to waste in this way. Our fields and herds have been nurtured for generations, we cannot throw that effort away. It would be a triumph for our enemies.'

Caledor's stare bore down on the princess but she did not flinch. Glancing to Finudel, Caledor saw that he was in two minds, but knew he would side with his sister in any argument.

'What about Chrace?' he said, looking to Koradrel.

'The druchii have continually pillaged most of the meagre crop we grow,' replied the Chracian prince. 'With our hunters at war, the monsters of the mountains grow bolder and attack our farms in greater numbers. What we have left, we need for ourselves.'

'The eastern kingdoms must provide for those beset in the west,' said Caledor. 'If you cannot send soldiers, you must send food.'

'I fear we can offer too little in that regard,' said Thyriol. 'For too long we have relied on the supplies from our colonies. Those supplies have dwindled. Elthin Arvan is in no less turmoil than Ulthuan.'

'If your people will not farm, they will have to fight,' said Caledor. 'Every elf that can carry a spear must be trained. If not, they will die unarmed.'

'And while we raise a new army for you?' said Tithrain. 'What will you do?'

'Wait for the druchii to come again,' said Caledor.

EVERY WHEEZING BREATH was like a rusty nail scratching across Morathi's heart. She bent over Malekith's inert form, seeing the handsome elf he had been, not the ravaged near-carcass that lay on the wide bed. His eyes flickered to hers for a moment and there was recognition. A withered hand reached out to her and she clasped it to her chest as she knelt down beside the bed.

'What news?' the prince of Nagarythe whispered from cracked lips.

'Our underlings disappoint us, my dear,' replied Morathi. 'The upstart Caledor has pushed back our latest attacks. He refuses open battle, using his dragons to hit our armies on the march before withdrawing.'

'He is a coward.'

'No, he is clever,' said Morathi, placing Malekith's hand beside him. She stroked a hand across his bare scalp, skin flaking to the white sheet. 'He knows he cannot beat us, but seeks to stall our victory for as long as possible. Our commanders have played his game too long. I will force him into action.'

'And the other?' said Malekith, rising a little from the bed, eyes intent on his mother.

'It progresses well, my son,' said the sorceress-queen. 'You have done well to survive these years of torment, yet you must hold on longer. Such a work takes a long time to perfect, but when it is done you will be restored to your glory.'

Malekith's ruined face creased into a smile.

'I can wait,' he said. 'My return will be triumphant and none will stand before me.'

'It will be glorious,' said Morathi. 'But we must keep your survival secret still. Your sacrifice in the flames is a symbol to our people, and until your resurrection to full power it is best to let them to continue in that belief. It hurts me as much as you to know that you are denied your position as ruler of Nagarythe, but it is for the best.'

Malekith said nothing and closed his eyes. Morathi stood up.

'I must attend to some unpleasant business. Rest well.'

With a parting look at her son, Morathi left the chamber. She swept across her rooms, gathering a trail of handmaidens and servants in her wake. Walking down the sweeping steps at the centre of Aenarion's palace, she heard wails of torment echoing from the dungeons beneath the citadel.

'I thought I said all prisoners were to have their mouths stitched shut,' she said to one of her attendants.

'I will see the torturers learn the error of their oversight,' the handmaiden replied, eyes glinting with cruel anticipation.

The entourage followed her across the great hall and down the steps of the palace into the plaza outside. Five thousand Naggarothi stood in silent ranks behind their captains and banners. They had been assembled at dawn for her inspection and now the sun dipped towards the horizon.

Dismissing her cabal with a wave of a ringed hand, Morathi crossed the square with long strides, heading directly towards Bathinair, who stood at the front of the small army. The queen stopped in front of him, eyes narrowed.

'Give me your sword,' she said.

Bathinair looked confused but did as he was told, pulling the gleaming magical blade from its sheath. Morathi took it from him and held it up, examining the fine workmanship. The prince's eyes followed Morathi as she stalked past him and beckoned to one of the company captains.

'What is your name?' she demanded.

'Ekheriath, my queen,' the captain replied with a deep bow.

'Would you like to be Prince Ekheriath?' she said.

'Anything to serve you, my queen,' the elf replied with a shorter bow. 'It would be an honour to attend your court.'

Morathi struck more swiftly than a serpent, Bathinair's sword lancing through the captain's gut. He fell with a stifled cry, eyes full of hurt and betrayal. Morathi twisted the sword to the left and right, Ekheriath writhing and moaning with each movement.

'Princes do not fail me,' she said, pulling free the blade.

She delivered a kick to the sprawling elf's face and moved on, beckoning to the next captain with the bloodied sword.

'And your name?' she snarled.

'Nemienath, your majesty,' the soldier said hesitantly, eyes straying to the still-groaning Ekheriath who had slithered to his knees in a spreading pool of his blood, one hand clasped to his wounded gut.

'Would you like to be a prince?'

Nemienath did not reply, eyes darting left and right like a trapped animal.

'Well?' Morathi's snapped question made the captain flinch.

'All who serve you wish to be included in your favours,' he said, not meeting her gaze.

'Kill Bathinair,' Morathi said, thrusting the sword into Nemienath's hand. 'You can replace him.'

Bathinair spun around on hearing this, eyes wild with fear. Morathi smiled approvingly as Nemienath showed no reluctance, dashing across the square with the sword raised for the attack. Bathinair tried to catch the blow on his armoured arm, but the mystical blade sliced through without stopping, shearing just below the shoulder. With a cry, Bathinair fell to the ground, blood spraying. Nemienath glanced back at Morathi before delivering the killing blow, plunging the sword into Bathinair's exposed neck.

Morathi waved Nemienath to approach and kneel before her. He did so, bending to one knee, head bowed. The queen stooped to cup his chin in her hand, lifting his head to look at her, a smile on her ruby red lips.

'What does it feel like to be a prince?' she purred.

'It is an honour, my queen,' replied Nemienath. 'I will bring glory to Nagarythe in your name.'

'You will?' Morathi said sweetly. Nemienath nodded, locked to her gaze. Morathi's smile twisted to a snarl. 'I had to give you a blade to bring me honour! Why have you failed me so many times before?'

Magical energy crackled from her fingertips, engulfing Nemienath's head. Black lightning coursed through his shuddering body, burning and splitting flesh, bursting blood vessels. Morathi let the smoking corpse drop to the marble slabs, Bathinair's sword clattering from the dead grasp.

The queen rounded on the assembled Naggarothi warriors.

'None of you are worthy to serve me!' she cried. 'You are incompetent or you are traitors, I cannot tell which. I give you the might of Nagarythe and you throw it away. I ask you for a simple thing, such a simple thing, but you cannot do this for me. All I wanted was Yvraine's head.'

'The Everqueen, her powers are too great,' one of the warriors called back. 'How do we fight Ulthuan itself?'

Morathi was about to spit back an angry reply, but stopped herself. The anonymous warrior did have a point, though it was no excuse for the defeats suffered. Yvraine possessed the power of the Everqueen, and that was a fine prize. To control Avelorn, to seize the strength of Yvraine would be a better victory than her simple death. There was another reason to see Yvraine humbled before she died. Daughter of Aenarion by his first wife, she had colluded with the princes at the First Council to deny Malekith his right to be Phoenix King. She would beg for mercy at the feet of the true ruler of Ulthuan, and admit that she had been wrong to oppose her half-brother.

'I can match the power of the Everqueen,' Morathi announced, smiling again, pleased with her conclusions. 'When I take her magic from her and see her broken before me, all will recognise the ascendancy of the Naggarothi and the true queen of the elves. Draw together what forces you can, bring forth the Khainites and the beasts of the Annulii. Gather an army worthy of my command!'

THE SKY WAS choked with the burning of Avelorn. A pall of smoke covered the land from the mountains of Chrace to the Inner Sea. Driven on by Morathi, the army of Nagarythe scoured everything in its path, leaving a swathe of ruin through the realm of the Everqueen. Pushed hard by their queen, terrified of her reprisals for any delay, the Naggarothi princes and commanders swept aside all resistance.

As before, Yvraine stirred the forest to its own defence, but this time the Everqueen contended against the magic of Morathi and her cabal of the most powerful sorcerers and sorceresses. Against the dark incantations of the Naggarothi, the enchantments of Avelorn failed and like a blight spreading across a leaf the druchii advance continued.

Fearing the worst, Yvraine sent word to Caledor, reminding him of his duties to the Everqueen. The Phoenix King did not come, but sent Thyrinor and two other dragon princes with an army of ten thousand warriors, for the most part freshly trained troops begged from the eastern kingdoms. On the ships of Eataine, Thyrinor brought this host across the Inner Sea and landed on the coast of Avelorn ahead of the druchii advance. Here he was met, like his cousin and Carathril before him, by the Maiden Guard of the Everqueen. As then, Yvraine spoke through her chosen captain, Althinelle.

'It angers and saddens to me to see such desolation wrought upon the heart of Ulthuan,' said Thyrinor, having dismounted Anaegnir to speak with Althinelle. 'I wish that you had warned us sooner.'

'The outer forests are of no consequence,' replied the Everqueen, her vessel's eyes alight with the green glow of magic. 'It is the Gaen Vale that holds the power of Avelorn. The Aein Yshain must be protected at all costs. This close to the sanctuary of Isha, my powers are at their peak. Morathi believes she has the best of me, but she is wrong. We will draw her on, closer to her prize, and in doing so Morathi will bring about her own demise.'

'A risky strategy,' said Thyrinor. 'To let the druchii approach so close to the Gaen Vale gives us no place to retreat.'

'Yet it is also the perfect site for battle,' countered Yvraine-Althinelle. 'The narrow isthmus will allay some of the advantage of the druchii army and force them on to our bows and spears.'

'I see,' said Thyrinor. 'If that is your will, I shall obey. We will move by ship along the coast and make camp at the Isthmus of the Gaen Vale.'

'Heed the guidance of the Maiden Guard,' warned the Everqueen. 'None set foot upon the Gaen Vale save by the invitation of Avelorn itself. Know that should you break this ban, I will be powerless to protect any trespassers.'

Thyrinor shuddered and nodded.

'Believe me, my queen, none will ignore such warnings,' said the prince. 'With your leave, we will head east and make landfall again in two days' time.'

'Until then, Prince Thyrinor,' said Yvraine-Althinelle. 'The enemy will be close on your heels, do not tarry.'

With a deep bow, Thyrinor headed back to Anaegnir and mounted the throne-saddle upon her back.

'This place is steeped in magic,' said the dragon, flicking her tongue with distaste. 'The air itself is cloying with the pollution of Chaos.'

Thyrinor felt it also; waves of dark magic that eddied down from the vortex in the Annulii, drawn by the conjurations of Morathi and her followers. As smoke polluted the sky, dark magic polluted the spirit. It lay like a shroud on the prince's thoughts and he could not help but fear what would happen if their defence failed and Morathi took possession of the Aein Yshain.

With such power in the hands of the druchii ruler, Ulthuan would be plunged into an age as dark as the time of the daemons. The cytharai cults would rule over the worship of the celestial gods and the elves would be destroyed by their own savagery and sacrifice. As clear as a landscape before him, Thyrinor could imagine the pyres burning day and night and hear the screams of the priests' victims.

He had seen such things writ on a smaller scale throughout Ulthuan, as the cults sowed terror and discord amongst their enemies. The prince felt sick at the memory of the bloodied and charred remains that had been found in secret shrines and around bone-girdled altars.

'I will die rather than live to see such misery,' he told himself, belting himself into the saddle harness. With a flap of wings, Anaegnir was airborne, steering back towards the fleet that lay at anchor just off the sandy shore.

'They are desperate.'

Morathi flicked a gaze of annoyance at the underling who had interrupted her thoughts. The sorcerer shrank bank from her gaze as motes of energy danced in Morathi's eyes. Had she been in a less favourable mood, a dread gaze would have been the least punishment inflicted on the overly talkative minion. Fortunately for him, Morathi shared his assessment as she looked at the army stretched across the narrowest strip of land ahead. This would be the last, futile attempt to hold her back.

Beyond the lines of silver and blue, red and green, lay the Gaen Vale. Morathi could taste its power, glittering like a field of golden stars across the canopy of the forest. The ground on which she was standing throbbed with magic, sending shivers of energy through her even as she coiled strands of dark magic about herself, pushing back the pure touch of the Everqueen's protective enchantments.

'Make ready for the attack,' she announced, gesturing for a beastmaster to bring forward her mount.

The elf led a gigantic winged horse to his queen. Its hide was black, its wings like those of an enormous bat, ribbed and veined. The creature's mane was like fire, bright orange and red, and its eyes were like dark rubies. From its forehead jutted three spiralled horns that had been bound in gold, and from its ears and nostrils hung talismans wrought from black iron in the shape of Khainite runes. The dark pegasus stomped and snorted, tugging back on the reins in the beastmaster's hands, nearly dragging him from his feet.

Morathi snatched the reins in one hand, pouring dark magic into the muscles of her arm, making them as unmoving as stone. The dark pegasus flicked its head hard and tried to rear up, but was brought up short, almost falling over as Morathi stood immobile, holding it in place. It whinnied and dropped down, bending its forelegs so that Morathi could pull herself up to its bare back, nestling between the leathery wings.

'Why are we not yet attacking?' Morathi demanded, seeing that her army had not moved.

'They have three dragons, my queen,' replied a captain, pointing to the smoke-filled skies. Huge shapes flitted against the smog, licks of fire trailing from their mouths. 'If we advance beyond the range of our bolt throwers, they will tear us apart.'

'Sound the attack,' said Morathi. 'Do not concern yourself with dragons.'

With that, she snarled a word of command at her mount and was borne into the smoke-thick skies.

TREPIDATION WASHED THROUGH Thyrinor as he saw a black shape rising from the midst of the druchii army. It seemed as if a dark cloud shrouded the rider, pinpricks of light breaking through like a distant night sky. More than the prince's eyes, his magical sense caused his unease. The pegasus rider was like a hole in the winds of magic, a sink into which all of the magic drained, the force of its accumulation dragging at Thyrinor's consciousness. The closest he had felt to such a sensation was the presence of Thyriol, but where the mage was like a warm glow, the sorceress was a chill void, sucking all life and energy into herself.

Only one elf could wield such power: Morathi.

'She is just a single creature,' said Anaegnir, sensing his fear. 'A fragile thing, easily broken.'

'Morathi has not survived as long as she has by being fragile,' warned Thyrinor. 'The daemons could not destroy her, nor Prince Malekith.'

The dragon snorted and dived, angling to intercept the rising pegasus. The other dragon riders fell after Thyrinor, to the left and right. Beneath them, the druchii army started its advance, lines of spearmen and knights converging into columns to march along the narrow stretch of land. From this height, Thyrinor could see the Inner Sea on both sides, the surf a white border to the left and right of the dark mass of infantry.

Plunging groundwards, the wind tugging at his cloak, Thyrinor felt an expansion of pressure within his spirit. Half-shadows danced in his vision, leering faces formed of thick smoke and air swirled around him. He felt himself at the bottom of a great pit, sinking fast, being swallowed up. He looked up, seeing the swathe of smoke above twisting, coiling like a sea serpent, thrashing from side to side.

'Beware!' he shouted to Anaegnir. 'Go left!'

The dragon did not heed him, but pressed on towards Morathi, jaw open, forelegs extended. Glancing back, Thyrinor saw a huge tendril of whirling smoke streaming down towards him.

'Left!' he shrieked. 'Left!'

The dragon slipped sideways. Too late to avoid the descending column of smoke, Thyrinor and Anaegnir were caught in a maelstrom of choking smog. Buffeted and battered, dragon and rider whirled across the sky, the wreathing smoke following them, growing thicker and tighter with every passing moment.

Thyrinor slashed with his lance, meeting no resistance, yet the fog settled on his shoulders like stone, and constricted about his throat and chest like the grip of a giant. Anaegnir was struggling also, belching flame, head thrashing from side to side as scales buckled and bones creaked.

With a noise of tearing metal, Thyrinor's breastplate caved in, crushing his chest. Ribs splintered even as his helm gave way under the pressure, shards of bone piercing lungs and heart. Anaegnir screeched, wings buckling, bones snapping as the dragon and rider were compressed by the titanic force of dark magic. Crimson streamed from Thyrinor's eyes and ears and nose and mouth, soaking the robe he wore beneath his armour. Drowning on his own blood, the prince flopped sideways in the harness, all air expelled from his body, organs and blood vessels collapsing.

A CHEER WELLED up from the Naggarothi army as the mangled remnants of the Caledorian and his dragon crashed into the forest. Morathi laughed with them, filled with the intoxication of the spell and joy at her enemy's destruction. The other two dragons parted and climbed away, wary for the moment. Morathi directed her steed after the one heading north, a dragon with scales of jade and spines and claws of black. Drawing her ensorcelled blade, Morathi raised the sword in challenge as the pegasus swept up towards the monster above.

The prince atop the dragon drew his own blade, a flash of red against the black of the smoke and cloud. The two riders closed quickly, heading directly for each other, swords lifted ready for attack.

As the two were about to meet, Morathi wrenched hard on the reins, steering her pegasus to the right, while she swept her sword in an arc towards the Caledorian. Black lightning spat from the blade, earthing itself through the dragon rider's armour, dancing along his raised sword. Snarling, Morathi whispered fell prayers to her daemonic allies, drawing on more dark magic as she circled around the dragon, the coruscation of energy moving from the prince to his mount. Scales exploded and spines quivered as the dark magic lanced through the dragon's enormous frame. It gave a bellow and twisted, gouting fire at the sorceress.

The cloud of darkness that surrounded Morathi solidified, turning away the flames as it encased her in a swirling sphere of power. Insulted by the attack, she directed her mount after the dragon as it pitched groundwards, seeking to escape, its movements laboured, the stench of charred flesh drifting in its wake.

The pegasus jinked and swerved to match the dragon's panicked descent, the more agile beast closing quickly as the dragon turned slowly to the left and right. Seeing that it could not escape, the dragon banked as sharply as possible, slashing its tail towards Morathi. She ducked, the armoured spine of the tail passing less than a hand's breadth from her head. Slashing up with her blade, Morathi carved a ragged wound across the base of the dragon's tail, pouring dark magic into the grievous laceration so that the exposed flesh and muscle boiled and bubbled, blood steaming into the sky. With a strangely piercing wail, the dragon rolled over, lashing out with its back legs. A claw caught the pegasus across the flank, leaving a wound as wide as Morathi's fist.

The queen of Nagarythe summoned up all of her scorn, ignoring the shrill cries of the pegasus, and plunged the tip of her blade into the dragon's exposed underside. With a feral howl, she channelled the dark magic from her spirit into the blade, pouring every vile curse and hex she knew into the belly of the dragon. As her pegasus turned limply away, blood streaming from the cut in its side, she watched the dragon's scaled hide erupting from within. Decay burst out from the wound in its gut, spreading rapidly, scales withering and flaking away, flesh turning to dust, bones crumbling.

The creature that had lived for millennia was engulfed by the rotting of eternity, body parts falling away, flesh dropping in mould-encrusted clumps, turning to scattering motes on the breeze.

Exhausted by the magic coursing through her, Morathi allowed the dark pegasus to fly back to the ground. Slipping from its back, she almost collapsed, gasping for air as daemonic voices whispered in her ear and the flame of Chaos fluttered in her mind. For a moment, the cloud that followed her closed tight, forming a ring of tiny whirling figures, each miniscule fanged face laughing and jeering at her.

Straightening, Morathi sheathed her blade and cut her other hand through the whirling mist, breaking the ring. She took a breath and snarled.

'No. The time for your payment has not yet come. Leave me in peace, you filth of the other worlds.'

Exerting her will, she gathered in the tendrils of dark magic that had been leaking away, locking them up within her mind, whispering an incantation of control and calm. The cloud settled, seeming to drift into her body, sucked in through every pore, leaving Morathi's pale flesh glowing with unearthly light.

When she had the Aein Yshain, she would have no need of such dangerous pacts. All of Ulthuan's power, and all of the magic of the vortex, would be at her command.

A TREMOR OF fear washed through the army defending the Gaen Vale as a second dragon tumbled from the sky. Yvraine felt the dread wash over her like a cold wind. Now was not the time for faint hearts. The Everqueen knelt in the grass, her green robe seeming to merge with the earth. Sinking her fingers into the dirt, she closed her eyes and let herself become one with Avelorn.

She gasped with pain, feeling the felled trees like cuts, the scorched glades like burns on her skin. The stain that was Morathi's presence seared into her, her tread corrupting the ground beneath her feet. Fighting through the agony, Yvraine touched upon the lode that was the Aein Yshain. Gift of Isha, goddess-mother, the sacred tree pulsed with the energy of life and the light of love and harmony. The Everqueen tapped into that golden stream, healing the wounds upon her spirit caused by the destruction of her forest. She allowed the rays of warmth to flow from her fingertips, spreading through the fertile earth.

Around the Everqueen bushes and flowers blossomed into life. Rippling out in a circle, the life energy spread through the elven army, bringing with it the scent of spring and the warmth of summer. She felt Isha's power touching upon the hearts and minds of her defenders, leaving an imprint on each, filling her army with renewed faith and resolve.

Trumpets rang out defiance, drowning out the drums and horns of the druchii. Clear voices rose up in song, the anthems of the assembled kingdoms ringing out in a developing harmony, silencing the curses and war cries of the Naggarothi.

Yvraine reached further, out to the shores of the isthmus, tasting the salt of the Inner Sea and the tang of the weeds beneath the water. She sailed upon the waves, bodiless and free, beyond the taint of the smoke to where the sun shone bright upon the water. Drawn up by the sunlight, Yvraine danced amongst the clouds, ethereal hands beckoning the winds to her, swirling and circling at her whim.

The breeze was light at first, just a quiet susurration in the treetops. Yvraine concentrated, pulling in the elements, coaxing the currents of the air to follow her. The wind strengthened, setting banners flapping and crests flying. Stronger and stronger it blew, bending the branches of the forest, tugging at cloaks and robes, flattening grass. Still Yvraine called on the wind for more. Keening through the canopy of the forest, it became a gale, trunks creaking with the strain, fallen branches and leaves were whipped up by the wind, turning around and around, faster and faster.

The songs of the elves fell silent, the last syllables carried away by the howling wind. Deeper and deeper Yvraine reached, kept to her body by the most slender of silver threads, almost lost within the spell she had cast.

The wind struck the Naggarothi as a solid wall, hurling elves from their feet, slamming horses into one another, tearing standards from their poles and the poles from the grasps of those holding them. Bolt throwers were picked up, scattering their missiles, sent tumbling over the sward of the isthmus. Monstrous creatures bellowed, eyes slitted against the hurricane, while the druchii tumbled into each other, spears breaking, shields flying.

Then came an explosion of dark magic from Morathi. Like a black fire, her counterspell raged through the winds, burning up their energy. Wind and fire contested and in their meeting, Yvraine's mind touched upon that of her foe.

The Everqueen and sorceress recoiled from one another, minds flung apart by the contact. Yvraine was snapped from her immobility and collapsed to the ground; Morathi sank to her knees.

The moment had been so transient as almost to have never happened, yet Yvraine felt herself tainted by it throughout her being. The darkness of Morathi had seeped into her; Morathi felt sickened by the touch of the Everqueen, the light of her nature like a fire in her mind.

Mutually spent, the two queens sought the help of their followers; Morathi staggered to her cabal, Yvraine to the Maiden Guard. While they recovered, the two armies marched upon each other.

TEN YEARS OF bitter war left no room for mercy. The elves of the Everqueen and the Naggarothi threw themselves into the battle with pitiless fury. Repeater crossbows savaged the opposing spearmen. The air was thick with the missiles of the bolt throwers on both sides. The surviving dragon rampaged through the knights of Nagarythe, while hydras, basilisks and other Chaotic creatures brought from the pens beneath Anlec ravaged their prey with claw and bite and petrifying gaze.

When the elves of the Everqueen gained the upper hand, the druchii had only to think of the price of failure to redouble their efforts. When the Naggarothi pressed for advantage, Avelorn's defenders looked to Yvraine for strength, knowing that perhaps they fought for the future of their whole race.

The bloody fighting continued for most of the day, with neither side gaining any significant advantage. Morathi's sorceresses hurled dark bolts of magic while mages of Saphery cast shimmering shields over their troops to ward away the missiles of the enemy. The spirits of the forests fought alongside the elves, treemen and dryads wreaking havoc amongst the Naggarothi infantry surrounded by wisps of arboreal magic. Naggarothi princes mounted on half-tamed manticores laid about the Silver Helms of Cothique with flaming swords, their bestial mounts roaring and biting, stinged tails puncturing breastplates and barding.

Crushed together by the thin strip of the isthmus, the battlefield was clogged with the dead and the dying. The groans and shouts of the wounded were louder than the fierce battle cries of those still able to fight.

Morathi laughed at the carnage and hissed threats to her commanders, urging them to finish off Avelorn's protectors. Yvraine wept at the slaughter, the blood of elves poisoning her lands, tainting the aura of Isha that guarded the Gaen Vale.

Dusk was approaching when the breakthrough came.

Chasing down a squadron of fleeing knights, Prince Melthiarin and his dragon strayed too close to the massed bolt throwers of the druchii. Black shafts filled the sky, engulfing dragon and rider, piercing the monster's hide in many places. Seeing their foe grounded, the fleeing knights rallied and charged, finishing off the Caledorian and his monstrous steed with lance and sword; though a great number fell to the prince and dragon before they were slain.

The fighting lulled and the two armies briefly parted, the leaders of both sides recognising that their fates were about to be revealed.

Their strength almost spent, the druchii knew that their last chance for victory was at hand. Taking a steed from one of her commanders, Morathi joined her troops, waving them forwards with her sword, the air crystallising with mystical ice around the enchanted blade. Around her the druchii mustered for a final push, even the wounded dragging themselves to their feet lest they be deemed cowardly for not fighting to the last.

The line of elves pitted against them was thin, a sliver of silver and gold and blue against the treeline of the Gaen Vale. Clarions sounded the rally and they gathered about their standards, clearing away the piles of the dead so that they could form up behind their shield walls and thickets of spears.

As the druchii advanced, a lone figure emerged from the ranks of the defenders. Her green and yellow gown trailing on the breeze, Yvraine came before them, long locks of hair streaming, arms outstretched.

'The Gaen Vale will never be yours!' the Everqueen cried out, tears pouring down her cheeks.

'You cannot stop me!' Morathi shrieked back. 'All I have to do is reach out and take it.'

'That cannot be allowed,' replied Yvraine.

The ground began to tremble and the light within Yvraine grew brighter, gleaming from her eyes, particles of energy flowing from her splayed fingertips into the ground.

Althinelle dashed forwards towards the Everqueen.

'We can win!' shouted the Maiden Guard's captain. 'Do not do this!'

Yvraine turned her head, light glimmering from her mouth as she spoke.

'It is too late,' said the Everqueen. 'Ulthuan is wounded, but the Gaen Vale must survive.'

'But your power...' Althinelle cast down her spear and reached out an imploring hand towards her queen.

'Better that it is gone than is stolen for evil purpose,' replied Yvraine. 'We can no longer be trusted with it.'

'What are you doing?' screamed Morathi, spurring her horse into a gallop, whipping her sword from its scabbard.

The ground heaved, throwing both armies to the ground, sending Morathi toppling from her steed. Only Yvraine remained standing, as immobile as the Aein Yshain itself, an eternal part of Avelorn. From behind her, at the heart of the Gaen Vale, a golden glow filled the sky, burning away the late afternoon clouds, stilling the wind.

'Run,' said Yvraine. 'Run while you can.'

Pushing herself to her feet, Morathi heard these words and glared at Yvraine. She was about to spit a retort when the ground moved again, ravines cracking apart the isthmus from shore to shore. A wall of foaming water crashed along the welts rent in the earth of Avelorn, descending upon both armies.

The elves needed no encouragement. The remnants of the Naggarothi fled back into wasted Avelorn while the defenders headed for their boats on the very edge of the Gaen Vale. Morathi, caught in the middle of the destruction, looked left and right and behind her, and saw that the water would be upon her before she could reach the higher ground.

'Spirits of Anaekhian, hearken to your dark mistress!' she cried, throwing aside her sword to lift up her arms. 'It is time to play your part in our bloody contract!'

Thousands of black moths erupted from the flesh of Morathi, their wings marked with red runes of Chaos. They engulfed the sorceress, becoming part of her, turning her body to shadow as they bore her upwards even as the two walls of the inrushing sea crashed together beneath her.

The waters swirled around Yvraine, bearing her up also, a spiralling waterspout carrying the Everqueen gently back to the Gaen Vale as the isthmus sank beneath the waves. Many from both sides had been too slow and were swept away, Althinelle amongst them; the bodies of the dead covered the swirling, frothing sea, tossed this way and that by the tumult of the waves.

Alighting on the shore of the Gaen Vale as the ships of the other elves were pushed out by the foaming currents of the new strait, Yvraine looked at the druchii army retreating from the far shore. She sighed, feeling empty and exhausted. No more were the Gaen Vale and Ulthuan linked together, the breaking of the isthmus symbolic of the magical rent the Everqueen had wrought between her sanctuary and Ulthuan.

She turned her back on the settling waters and walked into the woods, heading for her chambers beneath the Aein Yshain. She had protected the sacred glade, but at the cost of the eternal diminishing of her powers. The trees parted for her, opening up a wide avenue to the Glade of Eternity. Ahead, the shining tree of Isha dimmed, its leaves losing their shimmering gleam, its bark no longer bright with golden energy.

The Everqueen still ruled Avelorn, but the true power of Ulthuan would now reside with the Phoenix King.

PART THREE

The Bloody-Handed God; The Witch King Rides Forth;
Assault on the Eastern Kingdoms;
The Battle of Maledor;
The Sundering

─◄ FOURTEEN ►─

Rivers of Blood

THE CARNAGE IN Avelorn and the Everqueen's dramatic actions brought a cessation to the open fighting. The absence of marauding Naggarothi armies lessened the pressure on Caledor, though the mustering of the force to Avelorn had depleted garrisons across the eastern kingdoms and the cultists increased their sacrifices and murders.

A relative peace descended upon Ulthuan, as both sides regrouped and considered their next strategies. In the last days of the autumn, the princes were again called to the Isle of the Flame for council, and as before they were divided over the best course of action. Caledor spoke little, and allowed the princes to argue amongst themselves.

'The Naggarothi cannot recover from their latest defeat,' insisted Dorien, addressing the council in full armour. 'Now is the time to press an attack into Nagarythe.'

'We suffered badly too,' said Tithrain. 'What troops I managed to raise were all but slain in Avelorn. The cytharai worshippers run amok through Cothique. To send what remains of my army now would be to abandon my people.'

'Tithrain is right,' said Carvalon, the ruler of Yvresse. 'With the Naggarothi beaten back, we should make efforts to secure our homes against attack from within.'

'The Naggarothi are not beaten,' said Finudel, slapping a gauntleted hand on the table at which he sat. 'There are still many of them in northern Ellyrion. We should muster our strength there and drive them back across the mountains.'

'Do not forget Tiranoc,' said Thyriol. The mage tapped his fingers in agitation, eyes moving constantly between the other princes. 'It would be a mistake to think the druchii have fled back to Nagarythe. They still hold several passes across the mountains and threaten Caledor, Ellyrion, Chrace, even Eataine. We cannot defend all of these places at once.'

'Has there been any news from the Anars?' asked Athielle. 'Do they still wage war within Nagarythe?'

'Alith Anar is dead,' replied Caledor.

Athielle gasped in horror and there were murmurs of unease from the other princes.

'The druchii have been crowing about it for some time,' explained the priest, Mianderin. 'Apparently Morathi's assassins caught him. We can expect no aid from inside Nagarythe.'

'The last time we waited for the Naggarothi to act, Avelorn was all but destroyed,' Dorien snapped. 'Which kingdom will be sacrificed next?'

'The druchii will not move again until spring,' Caledor declared. 'Use the winter to root out the cultists that persist in your kingdoms. The dragons will patrol the mountains, and we will set garrisons to guard the passes. We will gather what forces we can in Ellyrion, Caledor and Chrace when the season turns again.'

As the Phoenix King commanded, so it was. The warriors of Chrace and Caledor, whose kingdoms had been freed of the cultist threat, followed the Phoenix King on a purge through Eataine and Yvresse. Progress was slow, for the cultists were skilled at hiding in plain sight and when discovered fought to the death, knowing that they could no longer expect mercy. By the time the winter had passed, Lothern and Tor Yvresse had been secured, and all passage in and out of the cities was carefully watched to prevent the cultists returning.

In the spring, the securing of Yvresse occupied the Phoenix King. This task proved even more difficult than he feared; the many isles that lined the kingdom's coast provided hundreds of hidden sanctuaries for those that sought to undermine the Phoenix King's rule and strike out at those who followed him.

The ships and Sea Guard of Eataine were placed at Caledor's disposal, in return for two dragons sent to guard Lothern against possible druchii naval attack. Even the most experienced ship pilots found the straits and channels of Yvresse a troublesome prospect, as small flotillas prowled the coastline seeking to intercept the cultist groups as they sailed to the mainland on their raids.

Caledor was frustrated by every delay, but was not a leader to abandon a pledge simply because it proved difficult. Day after day he consulted with the captains and cartographers, plotting the patrol routes and launching expeditions against the larger isles to eradicate any cult encampments. The Phoenix King occasionally joined these maritime forays on Maedrethnir, flying above the fog-shrouded isles seeking telltale signs of cult inhabitants. Several innocent fishing vessels and villages were terrified by the arrival of the Phoenix King and his monstrous mount, crashing out of the skies ready for battle.

Eventually, as spring became summer, Caledor prepared to move on to Cothique with a smaller army, having despatched a number of warriors and his dragon princes across the Inner Sea to help guard Ellyrion and Chrace. The druchii had launched nothing more than a few raids since the autumn and the Phoenix King suspected that Morathi planned a new offensive.

Ever wary of the occupation of Tiranoc neighbouring his home kingdom, Caledor appointed Dorien as warden, effectively giving his brother rule while he immersed himself in his duties as Phoenix King. Dorien was displeased by this development, thinking that being sent back to Tor Caled was some kind of punishment for his outspoken views on taking the fight to Nagarythe. Despite the Phoenix King's assurances to the contrary, and emphasising the trust he was placing in him, Dorien sent frequent messages from Caledor demanding that he be allowed to lead an army to free Tiranoc.

Worried that his brother would do something rash, Caledor paused in his advance to Cothique, thinking to return to his kingdom to settle Dorien's spirit. On the morning he was due to fly south, a messenger hawk bearing a crystal from Thyriol arrived. The bird flew directly into Caledor's tent, startling the Phoenix King and his Chracian guards.

'Leave it be,' said the king as one of the White Lions stepped towards the bird of prey.

Caledor abandoned the maps he had been studying and took the pouch tied to the bird's leg. Several times had Thyriol sent word in this way, but as Caledor took the crystal from the bag and set it upon a low table he felt the bird's hasty arrival foreshadowed important news.

He was right.

Thyriol's shimmering image appeared in the centre of the pavilion, pacing back and forth across the rugs. The mage was fidgeting even more than usual, wriggling his fingers and shaking his head as he spoke.

'King Caledor, I fear my eye has been drawn away from Saphery too long,' the mage said. 'While I helped you spy out the cultists in other kingdoms, darkness has festered in my own realm. Though I have striven to suppress them, agents of Morathi have long attempted to sway some of my followers to the dark path. I thought I had taught them the folly of seeking the power of sorcery, but my warnings have fallen on ears deaf to them. Only this day I have discovered the practise of sorcery within my palace. My grandson Anamedion is dead and my daughter Illeanith has fled with the dark mages.'

Thyriol paused in his striding, lifting a hand to his brow for a moment, head bowed. He straightened and resumed his pacing.

'That is of no consequence directly. The palace is secured and I have moved it to a safe place in the mountains. If you wish to return a message to me, the hawk will find me. The sorcerers are free to wreak whatever ruin they can. They have corrupted some of my students and I cannot overstate the harm they may yet do.'

The mage stopped and reached a hand towards the crystal, half imploring, half in apology.

'I regret that until this threat has been dealt with, my mages must return to their kingdom and seek out these dark practitioners. I know that this leaves you with little defence against Morathi's sorceries but it must be done. The towers of Saphery hold many precious secrets that cannot fall into the hands of the druchii. I also know that you can spare few troops to aid us at this time, but any that you can send to Saphery will be invaluable. Even more than Cothique or Yvresse, we are not a kingdom ready for outright war. Yet it has come to us and I know in my heart the battles to come will be terrible.'

Thyriol gave a perfunctory bow.

'I must go and prepare for the coming battles, my king. I will send word again when I know more.'

The image shimmered and disappeared. Caledor frowned at the crystal, annoyed that he could not respond immediately. Instead, he called for a scribe to take a letter and composed a brief message to Thyriol, promising his immediate support. Another herald was summoned to travel to Dorien, telling the king's brother that Caledor would not be returning. With this done, the Phoenix King summoned his princes and commanders to discuss their next move.

The news of Saphery's turmoil spread through the camp. Several captains from Eataine and Yvresse, bordering Saphery, sought leave to return to their princes so that their kingdoms could be protected against any threat that spilled from the imminent war between the mages and sorcerers.

Caledor flatly refused all such requests and announced that the army would march to Saphery to assist Prince Thyriol. It was also in the Phoenix King's mind that this would bring his forces closer to the Inner Sea, should the Naggarothi make any fresh move in the west.

The following day as the army was forming up in column to march across the mountains to Saphery, a group of riders hastily entered the camp bearing the colours of Prince Tithrain. The exhausted heralds refused all refreshment and insisted they be admitted immediately into Caledor's presence. The Phoenix King met them on the open field as servants broke down his pavilion ready for the march.

'What is it?' said the Phoenix King, fearing that the inexperienced ruler of Cothique distracted him with some petty concern or imagined fear. It would not be the first time.

'The Naggarothi have returned,' said the chief herald, sweeping his helm from his head and bowing low. 'Cothique is under attack!'

'How?' demanded Caledor. 'How have they come through Chrace so swiftly?'

'They have not, my king,' said the herald. 'They arrived in a huge fleet and landed on the coast not more than six days ago. An army at least thirty thousand strong marches inland across the Anul Annurii. Prince Tithrain cannot hold them back with the few thousand troops he has.'

For a moment Caledor was stunned. How had the druchii held back such an army until now? And where had they got so many ships to carry them? The answer came to him quickly enough.

'Elthin Arvan,' he said.

'I'm sorry, my king, I don't understand,' said the herald.

'The druchii have abandoned Athel Toralien,' said the king. 'They have brought back all of their warriors from the colony to launch a fresh attack.'

'As you say,' said the herald. 'With what message shall we ride back to our prince?'

Caledor did not reply for some time. He could march north immediately, but his army and the dragons were spread across Ulthuan. To confront the enemy with the host at his disposal would be pointless. He needed to pull as many troops as possible back from the west, though he was wary of leaving Ellyrion and Chrace unguarded.

'Tell Tithrain to hide,' he said eventually. The declaration was met with stunned expressions from the messengers. Irritated, Caledor expanded on his instructions. 'He must avoid battle at all costs and preserve as many warriors as he can for my arrival.'

'What of the people of Cothique?' asked the horrified herald. 'What will they do while our prince hides? How can you abandon them?'

'They must hide as well,' said Caledor, hardening his heart to the decision. 'Or they will die.'

THE MOANS OF the prisoners and the shrieks of those dying on the altars were a symphony in the ears of Hellebron; an orchestration of pain and suffering and death that seemed like the anthem of Khaine Himself. She raised her voice in praise to the Bloody-Handed God as she watched another Cothan dragged to Khaine's altar, futile in her attempts to wrest free of the cultists' grip as they threw her over the bloodied stone table.

The pyre raged some distance away, so hot Hellebron could feel its flames on her skin though it was more than a bowshot from her. The column of smoke and fire reached high into the heavens, taking the spirits of the sacrificed to the Lord of Murder. Hellebron felt a thrill of exultation as she looked at the massive pyre and thought of the hundreds that had already been slain. Thousands more would come, until all of Cothique had fallen beneath the Khainites' blades.

The kingdom was ample reward for her slaying of the so-called Shadow King. It was recompense for the death of her sister at the hands of the Anar prince. More than that, it was recognition for her deeds in the cult of Khaine, and had come with praise from the lips of Morathi. Hellebron had savoured every plaudit, basking in the adulation of the assembled commanders and princes as Morathi had listed Hellebron's achievements as an example to them all.

She had returned to the waiting fleet as swiftly as a ship could take her, accompanying her father Prince Alandrian. In name, the army was his, the dispossessed host of Athel Toralien, but Hellebron knew they belonged to her in spirit. Through the long years of siege endured by her home city in the colonies, she had inculcated the populace into the ways of Khaine. As the forces arrayed against them had grown, the people of Athel Toralien had embraced the Bloody-Handed One.

The other elves of the colonies had shown their weakness of spirit, and had fallen at the walls of the city time after time, their bodies recovered so that they might be offered up to the Lord of Murder in thanks for His protection of Athel Toralien. Those attackers who reached the ramparts had been taken prisoner, and their long screams had kept the besiegers awake at nights while the elves in the city celebrated in the name of their bloodthirsty deity.

At first Hellebron had been distraught when Alandrian had informed her and Lileath that they were to surrender Athel Toralien to their enemies. Only when she learnt that the city was to be razed and the entire populace return to Ulthuan was Hellebron pleased. The Athel Toraliens had proven themselves even stronger than Nagarythe, and now returned to their ancestral home to aid the princes and captains that had once looked down upon them.

Smiling from the memory, Hellebron joined her personal guard. Their captain was Liannin, once maidservant to Hellebron, now the fiercest of her followers. The three hundred warrior-women Hellebron called the Brides of Khaine had been the first off the ships, falling upon Cothique like a bloody storm.

Skilled in Khaine's deadliest arts, Hellebron's guard were naked save for a few scraps of cloth and metal, eschewing armour in favour of speed, trusting to kill before they were killed, demonstrating their faith in Khaine's protection. Their hair was styled with elaborate spikes and braids, held in place with matted gore. Their pale flesh was tattooed and branded with runes of devotion to Khaine, and their lips reddened from drinking blood. Many had glazed eyes, chewing narcotic leaves that left them impervious to pain, and all proudly showed their scars of battle, their old wounds painted with elaborate designs to attract attention. In battle they took other drugs to drive themselves into a frenzy, and using the secrets taught to them by Hellebron and her late sister they coated their blades in the deadliest poisons. In Athel Toralien they had been the scourge of the attackers, fighting where the battle was fiercest. In Cothique they had yet to test themselves, a fact that rankled them.

'When will we face an enemy of worth?' asked Liannin. She rested her hands on the twin swords scabbarded at her waist and licked her lips, savouring the blood spattered on them. 'Khaine is forced to feed on peasants.'

'When the fires of Khaine can be seen from Caledor's throne room, the Phoenix King will be forced to come,' replied Hellebron. 'When the screams of Khaine's sacrifices can be heard at the Shrine of Asuryan, Caledor will have to face us.'

'Until then?' said Liannin.

'Until then, Khaine will lap up such scraps as we can throw Him,' said Hellebron. 'Refugees have been seen hiding in caves, in the hills to the west. Several hundred of them. Take them alive if you can. If not, slay them with the name of Khaine upon your lips.'

⤙ FIFTEEN ⤚

The Hammer of Vaul

FROM OUTSIDE THE tent came the muted sound of weeping; inside the pavilion the grief and anger of those who had escaped Cothique was much louder. A handful of princes and nobles had escaped the kingdom with their households, before the routes out of the kingdom had been cut off by the druchii. Tears streaked Tithrain's face as he listened to the impassioned pleas of the dispossessed, while Caledor looked on impassively, keeping his own thoughts to himself. Tithrain had done the right thing and obeyed the Phoenix King's command, bringing three thousand knights and infantry south into Yvresse to join Caledor's army. More troops came from further afield, swelling the camp that occupied a stretch of land between the forested hills of the Annulii and the Great Ocean.

'We cannot return,' Tithrain answered those who pleaded for the prince to save those trapped in Cothique. 'We should die also in the attempt, and our cause would be no better for it.'

'We sent warriors to the other kingdoms,' argued one of the nobles, his gaze on Tithrain but his words directed at Caledor. 'Where now is the pact we made to fight together?'

'Cothique will be liberated,' said Tithrain. He glanced at Caledor and received a nod of agreement. 'You have my oath on that. The Sea Guard of Lothern will join us shortly, with a large part of the fleet of Eataine. Another army gathers on the Ellyrian shore, ready for the march to Lothern.'

'That will take too long,' said another elf, his fine robes tattered by hasty

895

retreat. 'It has been almost half a year since the druchii arrived. Why can these reinforcements not sail across the Inner Sea?'

'Saphery is no longer safe,' said Tithrain. 'The druchii have spies everywhere, and it would be best that they do not realise we weaken our guard in the west.'

'Our people bleed and die, while you do nothing!' This shrill accusation came from an ageing elf lady, who pointed a finger at Caledor. 'You just sit there and do nothing.'

The Phoenix King had heard enough complaints to last a lifetime.

'Who was it that did nothing when first I called for aid?' Caledor snapped, rising from his chair. 'I told you to give me an army and was told that there was none that could fight. Do not blame me for the consequences of your own inaction.'

The lady was silenced by the outburst, but the noble who had first spoken took up her cause.

'With what would we fight?' he said. 'Goblets and forks? We were promised weapons, armour. Where are they?'

Caledor frowned, surprised by the question.

'The forges of Vaul burn day and night to equip our armies,' said the Phoenix King. 'Shipments leave for every kingdom with each new moon.'

This was answered by a barrage of questions and denials.

'No shipments have arrived in more than three years,' said Tithrain, waving for his people to quieten. 'We thought perhaps that they went to other kingdoms.'

'That is not right,' said Caledor, shaking his head. 'Hotek assured me that all who wished it would receive helm and shield, spear and scale.'

'Perhaps they were waylaid by the enemy?' suggested Tithrain. 'The arms did not reach Cothique.'

'For three years?' said one of the nobles with a derisive snort. 'It was an empty promise, admit it!'

'Leave me,' said the king, sitting down, chin in hand.

There were a few quiet protests, quickly stilled by Tithrain. The prince led his people out of the tent, casting a worried glance back at the Phoenix King at the door.

'What does this mean?' asked the young prince.

'Nothing good,' replied Caledor.

When he was alone, the Phoenix King summoned Carathril and dictated a letter to Hotek, instructing the high priest of Vaul to meet him in Tor Caled to explain the discrepancy. Another letter he sent to Dorien, informing his brother that he would return shortly and to expect Hotek's arrival. He chose not to pass on the news of the missing shipments, fearing his brother would react for the worse.

Before he could depart, Caledor had to make sure that Yvresse was free from threat. The border with Cothique was narrow, flanked by the mountains and the sea. The terrain had allowed the druchii to seize the kingdom with relative ease, but also made the route into the neighbouring kingdom predictable and simple to guard. As long as Thyriol held sway over Saphery and the Lothern fleet protected the Shifting Isles that stretched from the Yvressian coast, the druchii could not launch a surprise attack.

Not that Caledor expected any further offence soon. From the reports of the lucky few who had crossed the border since the new invasion, the druchii were more concerned with subjugating those already within Cothique.

The Phoenix King spent a considerable time with his commanders, making detailed dispositions for the army. The dragons were his greatest weapon, though far from all-powerful as had been demonstrated, and it was the princes of Caledor that would form a hard-hitting reserve, based in Yvresse. Should the druchii attempt to cross into Yvresse, the dragon riders would respond in strength while the rest of the loyal forces gathered to meet the threat.

Confident that he could return to his kingdom to address the issue of the armaments, Caledor took flight on Maedrethnir. On his way to Caledor, the Phoenix King met with Thyriol in Saphery and Prince Aerethenis in Lothern. All was as well as could be expected. The dark mages had ravaged much of Saphery with their sorceries but had been driven into the mountains by those loyal to Thyriol. Aerethenis assured him that his fleet held the Inner Sea against any encroachment from northern Ellyrion or devastated Avelorn.

There was little news from the west, which troubled the Phoenix King, but for the moment he was convinced the focus of the druchii was on Cothique. Diverting to Tor Elyr for several days, Caledor spoke with Finudel and Athielle, who kept watch on the druchii-held fortresses in the north and the keeps guarding the mountain passes. There was little activity to report and it seemed that for the moment the war had shifted to the east in its entirety.

Worryingly, all of the princes spoke of receiving fewer weapons than had been promised, and none for some time. Caledor hoped that Hotek would offer reasonable explanation for the deficits – a shortage of ore perhaps – but he feared forces more sinister were at work, though he could not see in what way. If there were traitors in the Caledorian fleet he would have thought their treachery would have been revealed by now; the druchii sorely needed ships to contend with the vessels of Lothern.

Finally coming to Tor Caled, the Phoenix King was greeted with little ceremony. Such warriors as might present a guard of honour were more gainfully employed patrolling the border with Tiranoc. Dorien met him with a handful of household servants and the two of them made their way to the throne room.

'I feel like a caged animal,' said Dorien as Caledor settled into his throne. Retainers appeared with food and wine, but Caledor waved away the fare, concerned by his brother's attitude.

'I cannot be king unless I know Caledor is safe,' he replied. 'I have entrusted its guardianship to you, because I know you will protect our lands before all other things.'

'There is no war here,' complained Dorien. 'There is not a whisper of battle from Tiranoc, and I sit idle. Finudel does not need my aid, and there are no cults to drive out. I am wasted here, Imrik, when I could be fighting in Cothique.'

'When I am ready to drive the druchii from Cothique, I will call on you,' said the king, ignoring his brother's use of his old name. 'You are the first I would have fighting beside me.'

'So why are you here and not leading your army into Cothique?' said Dorien, helping himself to some wine.

'Has Hotek not yet arrived?' said the Phoenix King.

'No, I have not seen him for more than a year,' replied Dorien. He noticed his brother's grim expression and shared his frown. 'Is something amiss?'

'I do not know,' said Caledor. 'The supply of weapons has dwindled. I summoned Hotek to meet me. He should have arrived by now.'

'Perhaps his labours occupy him,' said Dorien. 'He spoke to me of his desire to create the greatest artifices since the war against the daemons. He has forged several magical blades for the princes of Caledor.'

'Whatever it is, it can wait for the moment,' said Caledor. 'We will go to the shrine tomorrow. Tonight, I will spend with my family.'

And so it was. Anatheria and Tythanir met the Phoenix King in his apartments. His wife's welcome was genuinely affectionate, much to his surprise, though his son carried himself with polite aloofness.

After a meal, the three of them sat on a balcony overlooking Tor Caled. For the first time in more than three years, Caledor wore robes instead of armour. He savoured the wine from his crystal goblet – a vintage from before the war – and enjoyed a brief moment of simple contentment before wider affairs crowded his thoughts again.

'When do I learn the words of dragon-taming?' asked Tythanir.

'When you are old enough,' replied Caledor.

'I will reach my maturity in two years' time,' said his son. 'Dorien refuses to teach them to me. How will I be ready to join the war when I come of age if I do not know how to be a dragon prince?'

'Dorien is right,' said Anatheria. 'You are too young to think about such things.'

'When I am an adult, you will have to teach me,' said Tythanir.

'I am Phoenix King,' said Caledor, smiling grimly. 'I do not *have* to do anything.'

'And I am your heir,' replied Tythanir. 'One day I will be Phoenix King. I learn the sword and spear and bow, and as a prince of Caledor I have the right to know the secrets of the dragons! Would you rather your successor knew nothing of war?'

'The other princes will choose the next Phoenix King,' said Caledor. His smiled faded. 'I could die in the next battle and you would certainly not be chosen. If you become king, welcome it. Do not expect or desire it. Look to the folly of Malekith if you feel otherwise.'

'Nevertheless, I will one day rule Caledor, and it would be shameful if I was not a full dragon rider.'

'You have still to master your weapons,' said Caledor. 'Do not think yourself ready to fight.'

'I shall be one of the greatest warriors in Ulthuan,' declared the young prince. 'A leader does so by example.'

'And so does a father,' said Caledor. 'When you are old enough, I shall teach you the secrets of the dragons, but not before.'

Annoyed, Tythanir excused himself and left the king and his wife looking over the city.

'He is proud to be the son of the Phoenix King,' said Anatheria.

'He should be proud to be a prince of Caledor above all other things,' the king replied. 'No good comes of seeking high station.'

'Do not hold him back with your own reluctance to rule,' replied his wife. 'Ambition is not always the same as greed.'

'It matters little,' said Caledor. 'I strive for victory, but it is not close. A year from now, who can say how the world will be? I cannot see tomorrow, and Tythanir's future is a long way away.'

'Do not be disheartened,' said Anatheria. She moved from her chair to sit on the couch beside Caledor, laying a hand on his knee. 'I spoke with Carathril and he told me of what happens in Cothique. It is not your fault that the people suffer. You did the right thing.'

'I know that,' said Caledor. 'I do not regret my decision.'

'And if Athel Toralien has fallen, you can expect reinforcements from the colonies.'

'They have not yet arrived,' said Caledor. 'The only cause for delay can be reluctance. I fear that with the Naggarothi driven from Elthin Arvan, the leaders of the other cities are not so concerned with the fate of Ulthuan.'

'As king you must make it their concern,' said Anatheria.

Caledor nodded in half-hearted fashion.

'We shall see,' said the king. 'Let us see what tomorrow brings.'

TOMORROW BROUGHT AN overcast sky and a chill wind as Dorien and Caledor flew south to Vaul's Anvil, greatest shrine to the crippled Smith God of the elves. The evening was settling fast when Caledor saw a bright fire in the distance. Situated at the very end of the Dragon Spine range, separated by a wide valley from the rest of the mountains, a solitary peak cast its shadow over the water's edge, shrouded with cloud and fume. To the northern slope the dragons turned, where steps were carved into the black rock, winding back and forth up the steep incline leading to a carved opening flanked by two gigantic pillars. Atop the columns were statues of bent-legged Vaul; on the left the god of craftsmen laboured over an anvil, a hammer of thunderbolts in his hand; on the right he was bound in chains, weeping over the Sword of Khaine he had forged.

Before these pillars landed the dragons. Their arrival did not go unnoticed, and acolytes garbed in heavy aprons and thick gloves came out of the shrine's opening to assist the dragon princes in dismounting.

'Your arrival is unexpected,' said one of the young elves, his undamaged eyes wide with surprise. 'Is it Hotek you seek?'

'It is,' said Caledor. 'Take us to him.'

'He is busy at the moment,' replied the acolyte. 'He and the principal smiths have been working hard in the inner sanctum. I shall send word that you are here.'

Caledor permitted himself and Dorien to be led into the caves of the shrine. They were taken to a side chamber whose smooth rock walls were covered with thick tapestries showing the various labours of Vaul and his priests forging weapons for Aenarion. The sound of hammers rang through the bare corridors and the smell of sulphur tainted every breath.

The two princes waited for some time, each keeping his thoughts unsaid, until they were stirred by the echo of raised voices. The words could not be discerned through the distortion of the shrine's maze of chambers and tunnels, but there was anger in the tone.

'Hotek seems displeased to have guests,' said Dorien with a smile.

'This is something more,' said Caledor, standing up.

As the king got to his feet, a scream of pain rang down through the shrine followed by panicked cries. Caledor dashed from the chamber, sword drawn from his belt, Dorien close behind.

After a short distance, they came upon another room, lined with barrels. A surprised acolyte greeted them with wide eyes.

'Where is Hotek?' demanded Caledor.

The acolyte dumbly pointed to one of the two doors leading from the other side of the room and the Phoenix King ran on as more screams sounded from the shrine's depths.

They came out into a wide cavern, split by a river of fire over which a narrow bridge arched. More statues of Vaul flanked the crossing, each bearing the lightning-bolt hammer in upraised fist. On the far side of the chasm, through the fire and haze of the lava river, elves clad in the robes and accoutrements of priests struggled with each other.

Caledor dashed across the bridge with Dorien at his heels. Reaching the height of the span, he saw two huge bronze doors were open in the wall at the far side of the chamber. Beyond flickered the light of furnaces, and he could feel the trickle of magic seeping from the open portal.

Running down the other side of the bridge, Caledor was unsure what was happening. There were almost a dozen priests fighting, some with forge hammers, others with knives or swords snatched from the armouries. A few wrestled with bare hands, trying to drag their opponents towards the fire chasm. Four bodies lay between the two sides, blood pooling on the bare rock.

Caledor did not know with which group to side. There were five priests holding the path to the open doors and the others were trying to get past. He did not know if the traitors were attempting to seize the inner shrine, or if they were the ones stopping any interference.

'Make way for the Phoenix King,' bellowed Dorien, running past Caledor with sword in hand, answering the question for him. The priests trying to get into the sanctum forge parted; the others closed ranks against the Caledorian prince.

Dorien ducked under a swung hammer and drove the point of his sword into the wielder's gut. Caledor reached him, charging shoulder-first into another traitor priest, sending him tumbling to the ground. His sword found the priest's chest, opening up ribs and breastbone with a trail of fire.

Behind him the other priests rallied, charging into the elves holding the door with fierce shouts. The air crackled with magical energy as rune-etched blades and hammers clashed. Caledor hacked the leg from another foe and leapt over him as he fell. Without a glance at the others, he sprinted into the inner sanctum.

The shrine room was a large cavern overlooking the main crater of Vaul's Anvil. A sea of fire boiled, kept at bay by magical wards, redirected into the furnaces lining one side of the temple-forge. There were several anvils and workbenches, but at the centre of the room was the main altar-anvil. Gilded and carved with runes, it glowed with mystical power, the force of it stopping Caledor in his stride. Several acolytes were hurrying out of a side entrance, carrying what appeared to be pieces of black armour.

Caledor spared them only a glance. Behind the altar-anvil stood Hotek.

He was clad in his ceremonial robes, bare arms covered with enchanted torcs and bracelets, an iron collar about his throat. In his left hand he held a sword, its blade like a sliver of midnight, a black streak in the air. In his right he hefted the Hammer of Vaul, used for the forging of the elves' greatest artefacts, its golden head inscribed with lightning bolts.

'Surrender!' shouted Caledor, taking a step.

'Stay where you are,' warned Hotek, raising the Hammer of Vaul above his head.

'What have you done?' said the Phoenix King, circling slowly to his right, seeking to get between Hotek and the tunnel down which the acolytes had fled.

'Who was it that crippled our god?' said the priest, a manic edge to his voice. 'Who was it that bound him to his anvil to labour on the deadliest of weapons?'

'Khaine,' replied Caledor, knowing the myth well.

'And who are you to do the same to me?' said Hotek. 'Why labour for the servant when one can labour for the master?'

'You are in league with the druchii,' said Caledor, taking a few steps closer to the priest.

'The "Dark Ones"?' laughed Hotek. 'How simplistic! You are blinded by your name-calling. They serve a greater purpose and will see our people restored to greatness.'

'What purpose?' asked Caledor, edging closer still.

'To rule the world, of course,' said Hotek.

'What did Morathi offer you?' Caledor was almost within reach of the priest, a leap and a slash of his sword away from ending this. He hesitated, wanting to hear the reply. He heard a shout from Dorien at the doorway and turned briefly to wave him back. 'What could a servant of Vaul desire?'

'The secrets of the dwarfs,' replied Hotek. 'I have tried for an age to understand the workings of their runes, but they defy me. But with the power of true magic, the strength of sorcery, I have prised those secrets from the dwarfen trinkets. The power will be mine and with it I shall surpass even the Dragontamer in my accomplishments for Vaul.'

'You are corrupt,' said Caledor. 'Everything you have made is tainted.'

The Phoenix King tensed, ready for the lunge.

'I am blind but still see your intent,' shrieked Hotek. 'I warned you!'

The priest brought the hammer down onto the anvil with all his strength. The cavern filled with an explosion of light and heat. The shrine reverberated with an almighty crack, as if at the centre of a storm cloud, the floor and walls shaking with the detonation. Forks of energy flared from the anvil, blinding Caledor. A bolt struck him in the shoulder, sending him spinning to the ground, sword falling from his numbed grasp.

Through streaming eyes, Caledor saw Hotek unharmed, running into the side tunnel. Dizzy from the wave of power that had smashed into him, the Phoenix King stumbled and fell as he tried to get to his feet. He raised a gauntlet to his top lip and saw blood on his finger from his nose. His ears rang with the after-echoes of the hammer's striking and blotches of white swam across his vision.

Rolling over to see how Dorien fared, he saw his brother lying against one of the open doors, head to one side. For a moment the Phoenix King feared his brother dead, neck snapped, but Dorien moaned weakly and lifted a hand to the side of his helm.

The surviving priests and acolytes came running into the room. Their calls came as distant, tinny shrieks and Caledor could not understand a word that was said to him. He allowed himself to be hauled to his feet, head spinning. He waved the priests towards the tunnel where Hotek had fled, but they shook their heads vehemently, their arguments lost amidst the rushing in Caledor's ears and the pounding of his heart.

* * *

A THOROUGH SEARCH of Hotek's chambers uncovered a series of journals and a number of strange artefacts the priests identified as crude experiments in rune-forging. The most recent manuscripts were missing, presumably removed by Hotek's followers, but Caledor sat down with the others and spent the night reading them while Dorien went with the priests in a search of the tunnel labyrinth that criss-crossed the volcanic rock into which the shrine had been carved.

They returned shortly after dawn, reporting failure.

'None knows the tunnels better than Hotek,' said one of the priests. 'He has spent centuries exploring them. I fear he had his escape long-planned and even an army would not find him, and we have only two dozen at best to search.'

'Where do you think he will go?' said Dorien.

'To his masters, and mistress, in Nagarythe,' said Caledor, lifting up a journal. 'Morathi ensnared him with pride and curiosity long before the war began. She gave him dwarfen treasures to investigate, a riddle she knew he could not solve. When he reported failure, she sent one of her sorceresses to aid him. With dark magic they unlocked some of the rune-forging secrets and Hotek was trapped upon a traitor's path.'

'He has spent many years on a secret labour,' said the priest, looking through one of the leather-bound volumes. 'He has kept meticulous notes, but I cannot decipher many of them; they refer to practices of dark magic and sacrifice that I do not understand.'

'He is making a suit of armour,' said Caledor. 'I saw his followers flee-ing with it, and his journal speaks of such an endeavour beginning just as the war with the Naggarothi started. For what purpose he did not record. The other priests under his control have been using the forge to supply the druchii with enchanted weapons, and diverted the arms shipments to Nagarythe.'

'It is a long treachery,' said Dorien, 'and an injurious one at that.'

'He has taken the Hammer of Vaul,' added the priest. 'Without it, our forging is much diminished. Hotek was the most accomplished of us, and now the greatest enchantments are lost, no doubt to be turned against us by the druchii.'

'It is a sour year indeed,' said Dorien. 'It seems the forces arrayed against us continue to grow, while we are sapped of our strength.'

'Yes,' said Caledor, nodding mournfully.

'We must find a way to strike back, even the balance,' said Dorien.

For the first time since becoming Phoenix King, Caledor felt the task ahead impossible. For every victory he had won, the enemy came again. Every advantage he thought he possessed – the dragons, the mages of Saphery, the power of the Everqueen, the artifices of Vaul – had been taken from him. Not in thirteen years of war had he considered defeat, but now he could not see how victory might be gained.

He looked at Dorien, saw faith and determination written in his brother's expression. The priests of Vaul waited expectantly, perhaps with some desperation, for the Phoenix's King's reply. He had no answer for them. There was no grand strategy that would turn the current situation. He felt helpless and hopeless, and the burden of duty weighed more heavily upon him than ever before.

'We fight on,' he said, the words sounding hollow in his head but bringing encouragement to the others.

THE BURNING WOULD not stop. It raged in Malekith's mind long after his body was dead to the pain of the flames. Had his father felt like this? Is this what drove him to the Sword of Khaine, to escape the touch of Asuryan's blessing?

The thought calmed the prince of Nagarythe. As his father had endured, so would he. What was his torment but another chance to prove his superiority? When he next stood before the princes to declare his right to be Phoenix King none of them would argue. It would be plain for them to see the strength of his character. Who of them could deny that he had passed Asuryan's test? He smiled at the thought, cracked flesh creasing across the remains of his face.

Their resistance was fuelled by jealousy. The usurper, Bel Shanaar, had groomed Imrik like a prize stallion, though in truth he was nothing more than a plodding mule. The other princes had been blinded to the truth by the whispers of Bel Shanaar. When the evidence of Malekith's acceptance by Asuryan was presented, they would see through the falsehoods woven by the Caledorian and his supporters. Perhaps even Imrik would bend his knee, as Malekith had so graciously done at the foot of Bel Shanaar.

The curtain surrounding the bed stirred and Morathi bent over him. Malekith tried to rise to kiss her cheek but his body failed him. A spasm of pain along his spine trapped him beneath the covers, as though a great weight was laid upon him. His mouth twisted into a snarl of anguish.

'Be still, my beautiful son,' said Morathi, laying a hand on his brow. 'I have someone you should greet.'

An emaciated elf moved up beside Malekith's mother, face almost white, eyes pale and unseeing though they fixed upon the prince.

'Greetings, your majesty,' he said. 'I am Hotek.'

The memory of the name surfaced through the fires of Malekith's mind. The priest of Vaul. The one who would restore him. If he was here, that meant...

'It is ready?' said Malekith, voice cracking with joy. 'It is time?'

'Not yet,' said Morathi. 'Caledor chased Hotek from his shrine and he has come to Anlec to finish his work.'

'The interruption, the loss of the shrine, have added perhaps only a year to my labours,' said the priest. 'Yes, I am confident. Four more years and the work will be done.'

Four years? The prospect made the flames rage through Malekith's thoughts. Four more years imprisoned within this husk of a body. Four more years could see his armies destroyed, his kingdom overthrown. Why did the torment have to continue?

In the chambers below, the elves going about the palace paused as a piercing cry of agony and woe rang through the rooms and corridors. Shrugging, thinking that Morathi tormented some fresh victim for purpose or pleasure, they continued in their work without a second thought.

LOOKING AT THE tips of her fingers, Illeanith wondered if the black stain had spread since the day before. Her fingernails were utterly black and the flesh of her fingertips a darkening grey, touchless as she tapped them gently along the flat of her dagger's thin blade. It was not just her fingers that disturbed her – something sat in the pit of her stomach, a malign presence that seemed to be feeding from her, draining her strength and spirit. Only the dark magic kept it suppressed, and only the dark magic kept back the necrotism crawling up her fingers.

The gagged sacrifice looked at her with wide tear-filled eyes, the blue of them ever so bright in the candlelight. He had stopped struggling against the iron chains that bound him to the stone altar and now watched Illeanith carefully, eyes returning again and again to the rune-carved knife in her hands.

'Your death will have a greater purpose than your life,' she told her captive. He was a tailor, she remembered. He had once fashioned a silk cloak for her father, Thyriol. She looked at his hands, so slender and nimble as they had wielded thread and needle. 'Those lovely fingers, when they twitch their last, will bring life back to mine.'

He was naked, his skin already prepared with the unguents and runes she had learnt from the grimoire. She had studied its pages at length, in secret, and knew many of the incantations by rote. This one was trickier, incorporating not just elvish words, but phrases and noises from the Dark Tongue, the language of daemons and the beasts of Chaos.

Illeanith read aloud, moving the point of her knife to the prisoner's throat. She stopped, distracted, trying to remember the unfortunate's name. It did not matter. She pushed aside the thought and started again, this time more forcefully, concentrating on every syllable.

As she spoke, the brands and scars upon the prisoner's flesh began to weep a thin stream of blood. He grunted in pain, teeth gritted, chest heaving. Illeanith ignored him, focussing on the enunciation of every verse, ensuring that she spoke every word precisely and correctly. She could feel the dark magic gathering in the chamber, seeping up from the lower levels of the tower like a tree drawing nourishment from its roots.

The coils of dark energy mingled with the blood, turning it to a deeper red. The prisoner was panting heavily, eyes roaming the room as tenebrous shapes gathered around the white-painted rafters and shadows coiled across the bare pale stones of the walls.

Finishing her incantation, Illeanith gently slid the dagger into the captive's throat. He gurgled and died, slumping to the slab without any undue fuss. Blood bubbled from the wound as the sorceress placed the dagger to one side. Illeanith dipped her fingers into the crimson stream and quickly drew a rune upon each of her cheeks with the thick fluid. The bloody runes upon the body were glowing now, their gleam edged with a disturbing darkness, flowing together to form a shifting aura of power.

'Mistress!'

Illeanith turned, scowling as one of her acolytes burst into the chamber. She snapped at him to get out and returned her attention to the ceremony.

'Something approaches from the north, mistress,' said the acolyte. 'A strange cloud that does not move with the wind.'

Illeanith stopped just as she was dipping her fingers into the sheen of magical energy encasing the body. She took a breath, ignoring the concerns that suddenly crowded her thoughts, and wove a sigil with her fingertips. Where they passed, her hands left trails of glimmering darkness.

She stopped, uttered a few final words and drew the magical energy into herself.

'It is Saphethion, mistress.'

Illeanith knew this already. Now was not the time to be distracted. She shuddered, a low mewl escaping her lips as the life force of the dead elf flowed into her body. The thing lurking in her gut subsided and she held up her hands, watching the greyness recede. Still there was a faint darkness about her skin and nails, the corruption not wholly expunged by the spell.

She turned to her acolyte, picking up her knife. She saw others crowding at the doorway.

'I said I was not to be interrupted,' Illeanith told him.

'But mistress, Saphethion...'

Illeanith rammed the dagger under the acolyte's ribs, puncturing his lungs. He collapsed to the stone floor with a gasp. The sorceress looked at the others in her cabal.

'No interruptions,' she snapped. 'Do you want be torn apart by daemons, or dragged to the Realm of Chaos?'

'We have to leave here,' said Andurial. 'The floating city will be here before dusk.'

'No,' said Illeanith. 'We have prepared. We do not run any more.'

'We cannot face the might of Saphethion,' said the sorcerer. 'It is folly. We have not heard from the others. We may be the last of our kin to remain in Saphery.'

'And if we leave, we shall never return,' said Illeanith. She strode out of the chamber, Andurial and the adepts falling behind her as she made her way to the staircase that spiralled up to the tower's roof. 'We shall show them that we are not defeated yet. Morathi has promised support and we will not fail her.'

From the flat roof of the tower, Illeanith could see the length of the valley stretching northward. The slopes were covered with snow, a uniform blanket of whiteness that lay across the frozen streams and dark boulders, swathed fir forests and hid the caverns and lodges that dotted the mountainsides.

Against the grey sky there was a lighter patch of cloud, tinged with a golden gleam that had nothing to do with the sun dipping below the peaks to the west. Illeanith watched it for a while, her followers silently standing behind her.

'Bring up all of the prisoners we have left,' she said, looking at her acolytes. 'You know what to do.'

'We can still get away,' said Andurial. 'The tunnels beneath the tower lead to the south. Why stay to be trapped like rats?'

'They killed my son!' snarled Illeanith. 'He killed my son, his own grandson. I will make him pay for such a crime with blood. Cease your cowardly doubts and begin the preparations.'

FROM HIS OWN pinnacle at the heart of Saphethion, Thyriol looked south towards the citadel jutting from the forested slope of Anul Tinrainnith. He could feel the dark magic that haunted this place and knew that he had correctly divined Illeanith's hiding place. She was the last of the sorcerers and sorceresses that had turned against him. And she had come here, to the tower where she had been born. It was so predictable, Thyriol was a little disappointed.

In the valley below, covered by the shadow of the floating city, four thousand archers and spearmen marched towards the tower. Thyriol suspected that Illeanith had followers of her own who would fight – cultists and agents of the undergods, friends who had remained loyal after her treachery, locals bewitched or threatened into service. For all that, the ruler of Saphery knew that this battle was unlikely to be decided by an arrow or spearpoint. Magic was the weapon both sides had employed, and it was magic that had laid waste to so much of his kingdom.

Even though it was his daughter he faced, Thyriol had no thought of mercy for the sorceress he was to face. She was blighted by her hunger for power, and countless were the lives that had been taken on her quest to master the darker arts. Thyriol could detect the taint of blood sacrifice in the winds of magic.

As the sun was almost set, the sky coloured deep red and purple to the west, Saphethion reached the tower. Thousands of magical lanterns gleamed from the windows of the city, creating an artificial field of multicoloured stars over the valley.

The tower also shone, with light of unnatural yellow hue and forbidding red. The ruddy glow dappled the snow-tipped trees and reflected from the icy slopes above.

In the chambers beneath the palace, the mages of Thyriol gathered to begin their work. He could picture them now, gathered in a circle around the giant crystal at the centre of Saphethion, clad in white robes, laden with charms and bracelets, crowns and rings; the chanting would be calm and quiet, slowly drawing the magic of the world into the shining diamond-like heart of the city.

In contrast the mountainside and the tower's courtyard echoed with pained screams and shrill incantations. Thyriol felt the churning of dark magic below as his followers brought Saphethion closer to the citadel. Beasts of the mountains bayed and howled as they were let free to run amok in the valley. Hoarse shouts announced the emergence of a column of black-armoured warriors from the tower's gate, their jagged spearpoints gleaming in the flickering light of torches.

He let his mind touch upon that of Menreir, who was leading the ceremony within the city's depths. All was ready and he commanded his followers to unleash the power of Saphethion's heart.

Magic crackled across the city, leaping in sparks and bolts from the tips of the towers, crackling along a latticework of crystal woven into the structure of every building upon Saphethion's craggy foundation. The city shone like a star for a moment as the magic blazed along streets and across rooftops.

The crystal lodes within the city's bedrock glittered into life, bathing the tower below with white light. Thyriol gave the order and the mages unleashed the fury of Saphery.

Blue lightning rained down upon the tower, forks of magical energy streaming from the underside of Saphethion. Bricks exploded and roof tiles shattered, stones crumbled and flagstones erupted into splinters under the onslaught. The magical storm raged across the walls and towers, flaring in intensity before dimming and then flaring again. Gatehouses collapsed, their thick doors turned to ash, their ramparts hurled into the air.

Yet the central spire remained untouched, surrounded by a miasma of curling black energy that leached away the power of the magical onslaught. Illeanith knew well the power of Saphethion, had learnt the enchantments that powered the city, and had devised counterspells to protect her cabal.

More than this, she knew the city's weaknesses too.

Thyriol felt the surge of dark magic and almost retched at the sensation as dozens of sacrifices were made, their bloody, horrific deaths sending a pulse of noxious energy through the winds of magic.

Balls of fire erupted from Illeanith's towers, hurled upwards on columns of dark energy powered by the blood of the slain. They crashed into the rock of Saphethion, smashing the crystal conduits, shattering the geodes and channels that linked the city's magical web together.

For a long time the two sides battled, exchanging lightning and fire that melted the snow and set fires in the forest on the slope above the tower. The sounds of fighting drifted up from the valley where Thyriol's soldiers met the followers of Illeanith.

Saphethion slid over the tower like an eclipse in reverse, obscuring the citadel from Thyriol's view. The city shuddered with the impact of every magical bolt and hummed with the power of high magic. Around him the mages fought for control of the winds of magic, wrestling with the followers of Illeanith below, each trying to draw in more power than the other. Thyriol had his mages and the crystal heart of Saphethion; Illeanith had her cabal with their bloody knives and a seemingly endless stream of victims to sacrifice.

Slowly Thyriol won the duel, the vortex raging and swirling around the floating city as he struggled for control. The fires from the tower diminished and then died out altogether, yet still the dark shield around the central keep held firm against the renewed storm of Saphethion.

Thyriol called for the attack to cease and left his tower for the courtyard. Here servants waited with his pegasus. Mounting the winged steed, the Sapherian prince flew high above Saphethion, joined by dozens of lesser mages on the backs of giant eagles and more pegasi.

With blazing staff in hand, he signalled for them to descend on the tower.

ILLEANITH WATCHED THE mages cascading over the edge of the city towards her, each holding a gleaming staff and burning sword.

She had miscalculated.

'Turn them back,' she snapped at her followers. She waved a dagger at the remaining sacrifices, no more than a dozen left amidst the slaughter atop the tower. 'Use them all.'

She hurried down the stairs to her chambers as the snap of magical lightning and the shriek of the sacrifices erupted from the tower roof. Wrapping a thick cloak about her shoulders, she hastily filled a bag with books and sorcerous accoutrements. The sounds of her adepts dying rang down from above and she quickened her pace, dashing down the steps towards the catacombs. The tower shuddered again, sending plaster dust showering from the ceiling. Debris filled the stairways and passages, and twice she had to use her powers to clear a route, blasting through the obstacles with raw bolts of magic.

As Illeanith descended the ebb and flow of magic increased. The stones of the tower vibrated with energy and the air was thick with dark power seeping up from the rocks below. Flames crackled and unnatural wails sounded from above.

She heard her father shouting her name, his voice echoing along galleries and down stairwells. Illeanith did not hesitate in her flight, slamming shut a portcullis behind her with a wave of her hand as she ran into a rough-hewn chamber under the citadel. With a few prepared words, she muttered an incantation as she ran. The rock walls throbbed with power and the ground rumbled for several heartbeats. With a deafening crack the ceiling behind her collapsed, sealing the vault.

Ahead the dark tunnels stretched under the mountains. She pulled a wand from her belt and its tip gleamed with power, the light bouncing from moist walls and the uneven, puddle-littered floor. The drip and trickle of water was everywhere.

It was not the end she had anticipated, but she was not yet dead. Illeanith was not so proud that she could not admit defeat. One day she would avenge herself upon her father.

As she reached a fork in the tunnels she felt the surge of magic and heard a pounding against the rockfall she had created. Her pursuers were not far behind and it was a long way to Nagarythe.

─◄ SIXTEEN ►─

A New Power

As BEFORE, THE war had ground to a stalemate. Still reeling from the shock of Hotek's betrayal, Caledor was heartened by news from Saphery. Thyriol and his mages had triumphed over the druchii and driven them from the kingdom, though much of Saphery had been devastated by the magical battles that had raged and most of the dark practitioners, including his daughter, had survived to blight the world with their evil magic. The sorcerers and sorceresses had fled, presumably to Nagarythe, and the prince was quick to invite Caledor to a fresh council in his palaces to discuss their next move.

The princes gathered at Caledor's summons, and they marvelled at the floating citadel of Thyriol. Though its white towers bore the scars of bitter fighting, the huge gliding edifice was awe-inspiring as it lifted from the ground, the assembled princes on the palace balconies with their retinues watching the world drop away below them.

As the castle drifted over the hills of Saphery, Thyriol called the council together. Representatives from all of the kingdoms save for Nagarythe and Tiranoc were present; even Yvraine had deigned to send a delegation to speak on her behalf, though for the most part they spoke only to say that the Everqueen could do little else to help in the war and all of her attention was focussed on the rebirth of Avelorn. She had done it before, after the war of the daemons, and seemed content to let the war rage across Ulthuan without further interference.

Pledges were renewed, by Caledor and the princes. The sacrifice of Cothique had been a hard blow to the princes, who had feared that their own kingdoms would suffer a similar fate. True to his word, Caledor had not allowed the druchii to spread beyond Cothique, and with the securing of Saphery there was general consensus that the war in the eastern kingdoms had reached a plateau. This was not to the liking of Tithrain.

'You speak as if we were at peace,' said the prince of Cothique. 'My people still suffer misery and torment at the hands of the Khainite horde unleashed upon them. Do not make the same mistakes we did and believe the threat has passed. One day, maybe not for many years but as sure as the sun rises, the druchii will bore of the sport they make of my people. They will come for yours, and where then should I lend my support?'

'You make a good point,' said Finudel. 'I would gladly lead the army of Ellyrion across the Inner Sea and attack from Saphery. If others strike from Yvresse, we would trap the druchii between us and see to their destruction for good.'

'A worthy plan,' said Carvalon. 'As neighbour to Cothique, Yvresse does not sleep soundly knowing that the druchii could be at our doors at any time. Give me a year and I will assemble as many companies as I can. I will draw such troops from the colonies as can be spared'

'A year?' cried Tithrain. 'A year more of torture and sacrifice for those I swore to protect!'

'A year,' repeated Carvalon. He looked at the other princes and received nods of agreement, and finally turned to Caledor. 'If the Phoenix King wishes it, of course.'

Caledor regarded the faces of those sat in Thyriol's throne room. He saw determination, expressions grown hard from the time he had first set eyes on many of them more than a decade before. Then, at the outset of the war, the threat had seemed distant, perhaps even imagined. Now they had all seen the menace posed by the druchii. The marshalling of armies was quickening, as the common folk of every realm suffered daily the tales of woe brought about by the Naggarothi. Those who had long professed a love of peace were now resigned to bloodshed.

'I agree,' said Caledor. 'A year from now, the kingdoms will join together as we should have done long ago. We will drive the enemy from Cothique. When that is done, we shall turn our eyes westwards and free Tiranoc from its overlords. Nagarythe shall be isolated.'

The year passed without great incident. Rumour abounded of fighting in Nagarythe, and Caledor heard stories that the followers of Alith Anar had renewed their war against Morathi's troops. As the princes lent their full backing to Caledor and used all of their political might and skill, ships of elves came back across the Great Ocean, from Elthin Arvan and further afield, ready to serve the Phoenix King. Most were of second and third generation colonists, who were setting foot on Ulthuan for the first time. They brought a strange atmosphere of optimism, their visions of their homeland coloured with nostalgia, free from the taint of war's reality.

The druchii were not entirely idle. They continued to make forays into Chrace, seeking to take the kingdom and link Cothique with Nagarythe by land; the Eataine fleet still ruled the seas and frequently intercepted ships taking supplies back to the Naggarothi kingdom from the occupied eastern lands.

From those freed in these boarding actions, the Phoenix King's followers learned of the terrors unleashed upon Cothique. The druchii were ruled over by a savage Khainite priestess called Hellebron, herself a child of the colonies. The populace had been enslaved, set to work in the fields and mines with whips upon their backs, to provide food and ore for Nagarythe. All resistance had been broken. Any elf that so much as looked wrongly at the druchii overseers was dragged to the temples of Khaine that had sprung up across the kingdom.

Fear ruled Cothique and the slaves believed they had been abandoned. Without hope of succour, many had turned to the druchii way, embracing their dark worship of the cytharai, and so turned upon family and friends.

It was this news that most disturbed Caledor. The slightest hint that co-operation with the druchii was possible could not be allowed. The alliance between the kingdoms was fragile. A fresh setback would splinter everything that had been built, common cause divided by selfish interest.

Caledor did not sleep well for that year. He expected to hear of a new druchii attack at any moment, and since the episode at Vaul's Anvil, he suffered occasional seizures of the mind and body brought about by after-effects from the blast of the Hammer of Vaul. He missed Thyrinor's friendly counsel, and longed for the solitude he had once enjoyed. He returned once to Tor Caled, but could not find respite from his worries; Dorien and the rest of his family were a constant source of distraction and interruption, and after only a few short days Caledor left for the sanctuary of the Isle of the Flame.

The ministrations of Mianderin and his priests did little to improve the Phoenix King's disposition, but at least the Shrine of Asuryan was quiet. The silent Phoenix Guard continued their vigil, but their presence, and their reluctance to speak of his fate, added to Caledor's frustrations. He spent a long time standing on the shore, looking out across the calm waters of the Inner Sea, seeking some source of stability, some spark of hope.

Mianderin found him there one day, gazing at the sunset.

'Not even Aenarion knew such troubles as you,' said the high priest.

'You knew him?' replied Caledor, surprised.

'No,' said Mianderin, with a lopsided smile. 'I was speaking figuratively.'

The Phoenix King snorted with disappointment and returned to looking at the orange-dappled waves.

'The enemy was clear for Aenarion,' the priest continued, ignoring Caledor's rebuff. 'When we fight ourselves, when do we know we have been victorious?'

Caledor said nothing, but stopped short of telling the priest to leave him alone.

'What you fight is a taint, a malaise of the spirit,' said Mianderin, stepping up beside the Phoenix King. 'It is not something you can pierce with a spear or cut with a sword. Aenarion was victorious not because of the weapons he wielded, but because of the symbol he became. He could not defeat the daemons alone, but he fought and that inspired others. They invested him with their hopes, and that made them real.'

'You have a point?' snapped Caledor.

'A question,' replied the priest. 'Why does the Phoenix King hide here, away from his subjects?'

Caledor turned and began to walk up the white beach, his back to Mianderin. He had little time for pointless philosophy.

'Think about it,' the high priest called after him. 'When you know the answer to that question, you will know what to do!'

CALEDOR RETURNED TO Yvresse to find a host of warriors awaiting him. True to their oaths, the princes had striven to provide him with an army worthy of the Phoenix King. Nearly thirty thousand elves awaited his command; ten thousand more were with Thyriol and Finudel in Saphery, ready to march across the mountains and attack from the west.

Battle-plans were laid and messenger hawks flew back and forth between the armies as Caledor finalised his strategy. His army would strike fast along the coast, supplied by the Lothern fleet. Cut off from their ships, the druchii would be caught between Caledor's force and the army arriving from Saphery. As a last measure, Koradrel was despatched back to Chrace to shore up the defences of his kingdom, lest the druchii launch an offensive from Nagarythe to link up with their army beset in Cothique.

The appointed day came, early in the summer. Caledor felt something of his old pride as he mounted Maedrethnir and watched the column moving along the coastal road. Years of reaction and inaction had sapped his will, but on this morning he felt in control of his destiny again. Should the campaign go well, his army would be well poised to march through Chrace and take the fight to Nagarythe.

Two dragons had been sent to Chrace and two more to Saphery. The rest of the dragon riders took to the skies alongside their king, Dorien amongst them, and for the first time in many years Caledor was greeted by cheers from the elves below.

The Phoenix King looked down at the winding river of silver and white moving between the deep blue of the sea and the lush green of Yvresse's forested hills. From on high he remembered the beauty of an army on the march; for a moment he was happy. The feeling passed as he remembered he marched not against savage beastmen or crude orcs, but against his fellow elves. The thought did not sadden him, but roused in him a deep resentment. The ambition of the Naggarothi had turned him into a kin-slayer, and for that he could never forgive them.

The army crossed into Cothique unopposed. What they found was more disheartening than any army set to fight them. Villages lay ruined, the doors of houses and farms broken in, occupants dragged from their homes. Fresh bodies littered the roads and fields. Huge flocks of crows and other carrion eaters wheeled in the skies, while the settlements the elves came across were almost overrun with swarms of rats gorged on the feast left by the druchii.

There seemed no sense to the slaughter. Fields had not been razed and the storehouses had not been looted. Some of the dead showed signs of ritual sacrifice, chest splayed open and organs removed and piles of burned bones, but most were simply slain and left to rot, throats slit and guts carved open.

As they moved further into the kingdom, the presence of Khaine's worship became more pronounced. Caledor's followers came across shrines bedecked with bones and entrails, the altar stones notched with many strikes of the sacrificial knives. Here the pyres had burned high, and mounds of blackened bones dotted the countryside. All cheer at the prospect of reclaiming Cothique drained away and the elves marched in stolid silence; there were some that were overcome by what they witnessed and broke down in tears, unable to continue the march.

In the larger towns, the carnage was even worse. Squares and plazas were choked with the dead, from newborn to elder. The cobbles were stained red with blood, the walls daubed with gore in the shape of Khaine's runes. Caledor despatched Carathril and several other messengers back to Yvresse, to seek out priests and priestesses of Ereth Khial to come and make proper preparation of the dead. Caledor did not envy them the task, and knew that many years hence the survivors of Cothique would still be burying their dead.

For several days they marched, and met no resistance. Here and there they came across stunned survivors who had hidden in caves and woods. Some had buried themselves beneath the mounds of the dead to avoid the murderous attention of the druchii. They described the orgies of bloodletting that had swept across the kingdom since the turn of spring. Whole villages had been cut down as the druchii had rampaged through the woods and fields.

It was senseless, even for the atrocities of Khainites; slaying for its own sake.

As more days passed, it became clear that the druchii had not long abandoned Cothique. Further north there were more refugees, first in their dozens, then the hundreds, coming down from the high mountains. Caledor's host joined with Finudel and Thyriol's army, who brought with them more than three thousand more elves who had fled the massacre.

'They have been recalled to Nagarythe,' said Thyriol. 'To what purpose, I do not know.'

'Why such slaughter?' asked Athielle, who remained stern-faced despite the horrors encountered.

'Rage,' replied Thyriol. 'The Khainites struck out in blind rage, perhaps angered by the call back to Nagarythe. Knowing they were going to leave, they resolved to kill as many as possible before they went.'

The grim news did not cease. They came to Anirain, the capital, and found it a burned husk, the walls cast down, every building razed nearly to the foundations. The tangled mass of bodies in every home and shop, every tower and palace gave testament to what had happened; locked inside by the Khainites, more than ten thousand elves had been burned alive as their city was put to the torch. Such was the charnel stench that the army was forced to move away; desertions amongst the companies increased significantly as distraught elves fled back to their homes in their hundreds.

Caledor's mood matched the devastation that surrounded him. Eight days earlier he had found a glimmer of optimism, a seed of hope that might be nurtured into victory. Such thoughts were far from his mind as he watched soldiers with scarves wrapped across their faces carrying the dead from the ruins; a labour that seemed like it would take an age.

His anger was spent. There was no ire left for those who had committed such slaughter, its scale too vast to comprehend, its evil too dark to contemplate. Caledor took himself away from the army and with Maedrethnir flew up into the mountains. Asking leave of the dragon, he found a quiet mountain lake and sat at its rim, staring at his reflection.

He wept for the whole night. From sunset to sunrise, Caledor gave vent to the grief that had built within him for thirteen years. He shed tears for the dead, for his cousin Thyrinor and the thousands of others whose lives had been claimed. He cried for his son, for a world he would grow into that allowed such things to pass. And at the last, the Phoenix King of the elves wept for himself, out of pity and weakness and raw despair.

When the sun rose, he gathered his thoughts and flew back to his army. The world had not ended and the druchii had not yet won. The withdrawal of the army from Cothique clearly signalled some new shift in the war; one for which Caledor was determined to be prepared.

THE LAMENTING OF the prisoners rebounded from the rough stone walls, moans and wails of misery amplified by the great dungeon in which they were chained. Several black-robed elves stood over the captives with curved daggers in hand, the blades shining with grim runes.

In one wall a cell housed a furnace, its coals kept hot by a bellows worked by two scar-backed slaves. Beside the forge stood Hotek in his full panoply, the Hammer of Vaul in hand, a sheaf of parchments in the other. He studied his notes as Morathi swept into the room followed by three sorceresses. Behind them came more slaves, their eyes put out so they could not see the burden they carried.

On a bier strapped to the bent backs of the elves rode Malekith. His wasted form was propped up by silk cushions, a blood-flecked sheet across him to hide his ravaged body. His eyes stared from a mask of blackened flesh, and the prisoners' wailing increased in volume at the hideous sight. At Morathi's command, the slaves lowered the prince's seat in the centre of the chamber before being driven out of the dungeon by the lashes of their overseer.

'He will need to stand,' said Hotek, glancing with dead eyes at the reclining prince.

'I cannot,' whispered Malekith. 'The flames took my strength from me.'

'Not for much longer,' said the priest of Vaul with a sly smile. 'Soon you will be stronger than ever.'

'I will give you the strength,' said Morathi.

She strode up to one of the prisoners and grabbed her long hair, dragging the bedraggled elf to her feet. With her other hand, Morathi gestured to the acolyte beside her and received the adept's dagger.

The sorceress-queen began an incantation, the words harsh, spat from reddened lips like curses. The prisoner writhed weakly in her grasp, eyes roaming the dungeon for escape. With a quick gesture, Morathi drew the dagger across her captive's throat and handed it back to the acolyte. Holding up the drooping corpse by the hair, she cupped her free hand and filled it with blood gushing from the wound. This she swallowed, smearing her face with crimson.

A tenebrous presence coalesced around the dead girl, snakes of shadow coiling about her, probing the open wound in her throat. Morathi dragged the body across to Malekith, leaving a trail of blood on the bare stone floor. The shadow-creature followed, tendrils drifting as it did so, seeking the life fluid it craved.

'Drink,' said Morathi, using her hand again to catch some of the blood, holding it to Malekith's lipless mouth. He lapped at the red liquid like an animal, painfully gulping it down.

The shadow slithered along Morathi's arm, tinged with droplets of blood, sliding across her shoulders to rear up beside Malekith. The formless thing wavered for a moment, dabbing its incorporeal limbs at the blood on the prince's fleshless chin. When these drops were gone, it contracted, sliding into his open mouth.

Malekith gasped and shuddered, rocking left and right on the bier. His lidless eyes stared at his mother as clenched fists beat at his side. With another rattling hiss, the prince slumped back, fingers twitching. He lay motionless for a moment.

Malekith's quiet laugh silenced the plaintive noises of the prisoners, chilling their hearts. With deliberate care, the prince sat up, pushing aside the bloodstained sheet.

'Life from life,' he said, some of the timbre returned to his voice.

'It is fleeting,' warned Morathi, taking her son's offered hand.

He swung one leg from the bier and then the other. With his mother's support, Malekith stood, swaying uncertainly. Morathi released her grip and stepped back. The prince took a faltering step, and another, all the while his haunting chuckle echoing from the walls. As his strength returned, he straightened and turned to face Hotek.

'I am ready.'

The priest nodded and signalled to his attendants. Each of them carried a piece of blackened metal, curved and rune-encrusted. Some were recognisable: breastplate, vambraces, gorget, gauntlets. Others seemed utterly alien, strangely shaped, trailing sheets of black mail or fixed with awkwardly angled hinges.

The first piece was put into the furnace. The slaves were whipped to increase their labours at the bellows. Muttering prayers to Vaul, Hotek fanned the flames with magic, until they burned white-hot. Reaching his bare hand into the fires, he retrieved the piece of armour. Impervious to the heat, he carried it to Malekith, who watched the proceedings with the remains of his brow knotted in concentration.

'This will burn,' said Hotek.

Malekith's reply was a shrill laugh, tinged with madness.

'I can burn no more,' whispered the prince. 'Do it!'

An acolyte brought forwards a smoking rivet in a pair of tongs. Hotek and his assistant crouched, the priest placing the hot piece of metal against Malekith's flesh with a hiss of vapour. Malekith giggled.

'Now,' said Hotek.

The acolyte pushed the rivet into place. With a few whispered words of enchantment, Hotek struck lightly with the Hammer of Vaul, tapping the hot rivet through its prepared hole and into the bone of Malekith.

The prince snarled with pain, and swayed for a moment. He wished he could close his eyes. Instead he set his mind aside, going to the place he had created for himself in the cold depths of his thoughts.

He pictured himself on a golden throne, wearing his father's armour. Prince after prince came forwards, kneeling to kiss his booted feet while a chorus of maidens sang Malekith's praises. The sun shone down upon the ceremony, casting stark shadows. In a nearby cage something insubstantial writhed; the shade of Bel Shanaar brought back from Mirai to witness the coronation of the true Phoenix King.

With a start, Malekith was dragged back to reality. Two bodies lay at his feet. His body burned with fresh fire, but it was no more than he had grown used to. Acolytes moved around him, painting blood from the sacrifices into the runes carved upon the pieces of armour put in place, following each curl and line with brushes made of elven hair.

His lower legs and feet were clad in the smoking black iron. He did not remember lifting his feet, but realised he must have done so. He could feel the rivets hammered into heel and toe and laughed at the thought of being shod like a warhorse.

There was chanting. His mother looked on silently, but her adepts' words swished around the chamber, verses overlapping, creating an arrhythmic harmony of magic. More rivets were driven into the scrawny flesh of his thighs, and links were riveted into place through the sides of his knees.

The pain was becoming too intense again as more of the hot metal was placed against his flesh. It was a physical pain, nothing like the soul-searing agony of Asuryan's blessing, but it was pain nonetheless and he retreated from it.

A thousand white doves flew into the blue skies to mark his ascension to rulership, while a thousand clarions rang out his tribute.

When next he perceived clearly what was happening, he was clad from foot to neck in the armour. Every part of him trembled. He could feel the energy of the spirit he had consumed slipping away.

'Too soon,' he muttered. 'I am falling.'

Morathi hurriedly beckoned to an adept, who sacrificed another captive and brought the blood to Malekith in a cup of ancient silver. Malekith took the cup and then stopped. He realised he had not held a thing for more than a decade. He examined the fingers of his new hand, each perfectly articulated. He recognised the dwarf-work that inspired the design and smiled to himself. Even now, his great adventures of the past were still bearing fruit.

Drinking the blood, enjoying the flex of the armoured arm as if it were his own flesh, he dropped into pleasant memory; sharing a goblet of wine with his good friend, the High King Snorri Whitebeard.

He remembered the old dwarf's confused expression. The taste of elven wine was nothing like the brewing of the dwarfs. Snorri had gulped down the glass in one draught. Malekith poured him another and told him to savour it, to let it roll across his tongue and moisten the inside of his cheeks. Always ready to try something new, the High King did as was suggested, making great exhibition of swishing the liquid in and out of his cheeks. He tossed back his head and gargled, making Malekith laugh with surprise.

Smacking his lips, Snorri...

Snorri was dead.

The memory changed and Malekith's heart sank. He knew that part of him had died with that noble dwarf. Not since had Malekith allowed himself to trust anyone as he had trusted Snorri; not since had he ever allowed himself to know the weakness of friendship. It was too painful, the heartache of loss, and Malekith had lost himself in his grief.

The fires flared anew and Malekith was brought back to the present. A film of red covered his vision. His own blood, he realised.

He blinked.

The simple motion caused him immeasurable joy. The thinnest slivers of black metal had been fashioned into eyelids. Malekith blinked again, and then closed his eyes. He enjoyed the darkness and more time passed.

'IT IS DONE,' announced Hotek.

Malekith flexed his arms and bent his legs, trying out his new body. It felt like his own flesh, though the burning had not lessened. Half a dozen dead elves lay sprawled at his feet, throats slit, their blood anointed upon his forged form. He could feel their spirits sliding around him, trapped within the runes of the armour.

'Not finished,' he said. 'My crown.'

Hotek looked confused and turned to Morathi for explanation. She summoned an acolyte who brought forth a velvet cushion on which was placed a circlet of dull grey metal, spikes jutting at strange angles like a crown conceived by a lunatic.

Morathi reached a hand towards it, but Malekith grabbed her wrist. She howled in pain and tore free from his grip, backing away. There were burns on her flesh.

'You cannot touch it,' said Malekith. 'It is not yours, it is mine.'

He took up the Circlet of Iron. It felt icy cold to his touch. While Morathi fussed over her burnt wrist, Malekith raised the strange crown to his head and placed it on his brow.

'Weld it,' said the prince. 'Make it a piece of the helm.'

Hotek did as he was bid, striking more rivets into Malekith's skull before securing the circlet in place with molten metal. Malekith reached up and tugged at the circlet, assuring himself that it could not be removed.

Satisfied, his closed his eyes again. He let his thoughts free from his body, tasting the dark magic seething around the dungeon chamber. He felt the inrushing of power and rode the wave of energy, spearing up through the roof of the chamber, passing through the many floors of his father's palace like a meteor called back to the stars. Anlec dwindled below him and he shifted from the plane of mortals into a realm of pure magic.

As at the first time he had worn the circlet, he looked at the Realm of Chaos, the domain of the Chaos Gods. On this occasion he had no fear. He materialised in his armoured form, burning white hot, his presence blazing across the dominions of the Chaos Gods as a challenge.

Sentiences not of any mortal recognition stirred. Malekith felt their attention slowly drawn towards him.

'I am Malekith!' he declared. A flaming sword appeared in his hand. 'Son of Aenarion, the daemons' bane. Hear my name and know me, the rightful king of the elves!'

As a comet of power, he plunged back to his body. The runes of his armour exploded with dark flames as he re-entered his artificial form. He opened his metal eyelids, revealing orbs of black fire.

He looked down at the elves around him. They seemed small and insignificant. His voice echoed strangely from the mask of his helm, filling the room.

'I have returned,' he declared. 'Pay homage to me.'

All present fell to their knees, instantly obedient to his words; save one, who fixed him with an expression of utter happiness.

'Hail Malekith!' cried Morathi, golden tears streaming down her face. 'Hail the Witch King of Ulthuan!'

SEVENTEEN

More Blood on the Plains

IT WAS TOO much to believe that the ambition of Morathi and the druchii had been finally thwarted, though there were some amongst the princes that believed the abandonment of Cothique signalled as much. Carvalon and Tithrain were the chief proponents of this view, arguing that the druchii army had surely been withdrawn to shore up the defence of their home kingdom. They went as far as to suggest that embassies be sent to Nagarythe to initiate discussions for an accord.

Caledor was far from convinced by this argument and warned that not until Morathi had been slain and the druchii brought to their knees would they ever consider any kind of peace. It was a difficult debate, made all the harder for the Phoenix King by his own desire to end the war.

'It would be the easy answer to believe we are on the brink of victory,' he confided in Thyriol one evening.

The two of them shared a jug of wine on a balcony of the mage's floating palace, looking down across the moonlit Inner Sea. So tranquil was the scene, it was almost possible to forget the woes of the past thirteen years. Almost, but not quite. Caledor could not rid himself of the things he had seen, especially the carnage he had witnessed in Cothique.

Thyriol seemed much changed by his personal battles too. His daughter and grandson had turned against him, and he had slain the latter. Several mages Thyriol had once counted close allies, friends even, had been corrupted by the lure of dark magic, and sorrow lay heavily on the Sapherian ruler as he stood beside Caledor at the rail, his shoulders sagging, back bent as if weary with burden.

'I must concur with your assessment,' said Thyriol. He let out a drawn sigh and swirled the wine in his goblet, eyes gazing into the distance. 'We face a foe every bit as irrational and determined as the daemons. They will not capitulate and they will not accept an easy peace. Part of me thinks you should allow an embassy, if only so that its failure will curb these false hopes that erode the resolve of our allies.'

'That would be unwise,' said Caledor. 'Any hint of weakness will be seized upon by the druchii. And such entreaty will simply offer them an opportunity for manipulation. I would rather some of the princes harbour doubts than give our enemies a means to divide us even more.'

'You are right, I am thinking poorly,' said Thyriol.

The ancient mage fell silent and for a change it was Caledor that felt the need to speak, to fill the quiet to avoid the company of his own bleak thoughts.

'We have achieved nothing,' said the Phoenix King. 'So many deaths, so much devastation, and for no gain by either side. Again I must wait, fearful of what the druchii will attempt next. How is it that a single kingdom can be a match for the rest of Ulthuan?'

'Greed and dread,' replied Thyriol. 'The druchii fall into two groups. There are those who serve their personal greed, their desire for power and dominion. There is another part, who fear their rulers, Morathi most of all, and know that to despoil and to fight is a better fate than the one that awaits them if they disobey. Such are the benefits of tyranny.'

Caledor gulped down his wine. He was a little drunk and in a more melancholy mood than even was usual for him. He leaned over the rail and looked down, past the edge of the hovering citadel, seeing the moon-dappled waves lapping gently at the Sapherian coast.

'I do not regret our decision,' said Thyriol.

'What decision?' said Caledor, eyes fixed on the shore.

'To make you Phoenix King,' said the mage. 'You are the best of us, Caledor.'

'I was the best choice,' agreed the Phoenix King. 'I wonder if this could have been prevented if I had acted sooner.'

'None of us could foresee Malekith's madness,' said Thyriol. 'Of all the princes, you were the most reluctant to let the Naggarothi scheme and plot.'

'But I did not act,' said Caledor. 'Had I agreed to be Bel Shanaar's general, perhaps this war might have been avoided.'

'I do not disagree,' said Thyriol. 'It was a selfish act, but no more selfish than many others that were undertaken at the time.'

The mage-prince took Caledor's cup and moved to a low table, refilling both goblets with the last of the wine. He turned and offered the drink to the Phoenix King.

'You are not prone to regrets,' said Thyriol. 'It does not suit you to start wearing them now. When the future seems so dark, it is tempting to regress to the past and relive our mistakes rather than face the present. It is not in your nature to do that, I feel.'

'No,' said Caledor. 'I have had little to regret in my life, and less time for it than most. If there are lessons to be learned, I have learned them.'

Taking a deep breath, Caledor raised his glass and directed a lopsided smile towards his companion.

'A toast,' said the Phoenix King. 'To deaf ears and unreasonable stubbornness.'

The mage frowned, confused by the proposal.

'Why would you laud such things?' said Thyriol.

'They might prove to be my best qualities,' laughed Caledor.

THE FOLLOWING SEASON brought no fresh attack, adding fuel to the fires of speculation amongst the princes loyal to Caledor. Those who sided with the Phoenix King were divided on the question of where the next assault would come: Chrace, Ellyrion or perhaps even Caledor. Those who believed the Naggarothi had spent their strength argued harder than ever for some form of engagement with the enemy. These calls were hard for Caledor to deny without seeming a warmonger, but deny them he did.

The council was summoned to the Shrine of Asuryan as summer become autumn. Tithrain was noticeable by his absence, though it was understandable given the dire circumstances in his kingdom. The rebuilding of Cothique was the first topic to be raised in the council.

'Yvresse will provide such supplies as are needed,' promised Carvalon. 'A weak Cothique is a threat to my kingdom. We have been fortunate enough to avoid the worst depredations of war.'

'Such aid as we can spare we will send to Cothique,' said Aerethenis of Eataine. 'I fear my kingdom has not fully recovered from the Naggarothi invasion, but the fleet is at the disposal of this council as ever.'

'Saphery can offer little help,' admitted Thyriol. 'Our fields have been devastated by the sorceries of the druchii and what little we have must go to our people first.'

Caledor allowed the princes to continue, content to allow them to organise a relief fleet to be sent to Cothique. There was little he could do as Phoenix King, and no spare food to offer as prince of mountainous Caledor. When the arrangements had been agreed, the conversation turned to the matter of the cults.

'Barely a murder or sacrifice has been perpetrated in Saphery since the routing of the sorcerers,' said Thyriol.

'Since the purge, there has been no trouble in Eataine,' reported Aerethenis.

'The same is true of Yvresse,' said Carvalon. 'Not a cultist has been uncovered this past year.'

'That is not good,' said Caledor.

'How so?' said Finudel. 'Surely this is cause for celebration. Perhaps we have not yet defeated the druchii, but their agents and sympathisers have been expunged from our kingdoms.'

'I fear otherwise,' said the Phoenix King. 'They have gone to ground, but that does not mean they have disappeared entirely.'

'They bide their time?' said Thyriol.

'Maybe not,' said Carvalon. 'I am inclined to agree with Finudel. Even if we have not rooted out every last cultist, they see that the tide has turned against them. Their Naggarothi masters have abandoned them.'

'Let us not be complacent,' said Aerethenis. 'At the siege of Lothern, the traitors were content to remain concealed as assault after assault failed. These creatures are cunning, knowing the time to strike when it will cause most strife and destruction.'

'True,' said Caledor. 'They will not show themselves again until our attention is drawn elsewhere. They wait for a new Naggarothi offensive to move our gaze from them.'

'There is little enough we can do to combat that,' said Thyriol. 'If they choose to hide, it will be all but impossible to draw them out into the open.'

'There are more subtle weapons we have than dragons and spears,' said Mianderin, who had seemed to be sleeping in his chair, but evidently had been listening carefully to the exchange. 'Far be it for a priest of the light of Asuryan to suggest falsehood, but it would seem to me a wise move to give the cultists false hope. If we wish the cults to show themselves, we should appear weaker than we are.'

'A classic manoeuvre,' said Finudel. 'A feint, of sorts. Perhaps these spies will even take word to Nagarythe and prompt an ill-considered move.'

'What shall be the lure?' said Thyriol.

'An attack into Tiranoc,' said Caledor, an idea quickly forming. 'We will muster an army in Ellyrion, but in truth we will also strengthen the garrisons keeping watch for the cultists.'

'The army will need to be dispersed for the winter, regardless,' said Athielle. 'There is not a single kingdom that can now keep so many troops fed during the season of ice. Spread rumour that the army has moved to Ellyrion, the fleet of Lothern can make it seem so by some crossings of the Inner Sea, whilst we send the companies back to their barracks.'

'What if we succeed in the deception and the druchii decide to launch an attack?' said Koradrel. 'Chrace cannot stand alone, nor can Ellyrion.'

'There is too little time left for the enemy to take enough ground before the snows come,' said Caledor. 'Nagarythe is a harsh land and the enemy will have even harder supply problems than we. If they seek to act in any way, it will be through the cults. If they are foolish enough to venture forth they will find little to sustain them.'

'And in the spring?' said Thyriol. 'Whether the cults are drawn out or not, their destruction will not force the enemy's surrender.'

'A double bluff,' Caledor said with a smile. 'We let it be known that the plan to attack is a ruse. In reality, we will bring the army to Ellyrion as quickly as we can and strike at Tiranoc. I am sure there are many still in the kingdom who would be happy to swell our ranks.'

'Attack?' said Carvalon. 'Are we so sure of our strength that we would risk it?'

'I am sure that delay will make us no stronger,' said Caledor.

The plan was set in motion. Messengers were despatched openly to the garrisons, informing them of the proposed deception in the hope that the orders would be intercepted and passed on to the druchii. Meanwhile the princes returned to their kingdoms with the real plans, under strict instruction not to entrust them to any other. In the spring, Caledor would send word for the army to be gathered to Thyriol, who would in turn inform the princes by means of his message crystals. By the time the druchii heard of the army gathering in Ellyrion it would be too late for them to react.

For the first time in many years, Caledor left the council with a little confidence. Wary of the optimism that had been dashed by the retaking of Cothique, the Phoenix King did not indulge too much hope, but was nevertheless pleased to be taking positive action again. He spent the winter in Tor Caled with his family, whose company he was better able to tolerate than on his last visit.

The Caledorian winter was especially harsh. Strong winds and driving rains lashed the mountains for the whole season, and no elf ventured out except when no other option presented itself. The dragons sought refuge in their caverns, and Caledor spent much time at the palace windows gazing to the north, wondering if the fierce weather was some conjuration of his enemies.

In the last days of winter a hailstorm engulfed Tor Caled, balls of ice the size of fists hammering into the tiled roofs and crashing upon the cobbled streets. Ice rimed the eaves of the houses and palaces, and the sentries on the walls sought the shelter of their guard rooms, warming themselves beside the fires of magical braziers.

Amongst the downpour appeared a lone figure, heavily swathed against the onslaught from the skies. He rode up to the gates of the city and demanded entry, revealing himself to be Carathril, the Phoenix King's chief herald. Knowing that nothing but the most urgent news would bring the messenger forth in such horrific weather, the guards conveyed Carathril to the palace as swiftly as they could while messages were sent ahead to warn Caledor of his arrival.

The herald was a bedraggled sight as he came to Caledor in his throne room. He had divested himself of his heaviest furs and cloak, but his long hair hung lank across his soaked robes, a blanket thrown about his shoulders by the Phoenix King's servants. The king ordered hot wine to be brought for his herald, waved him to one of the seats that circled the throne, and sat down next to Carathril.

'The druchii march,' said the herald between chattering teeth. His face was pale and drawn, exhaustion dimming his eyes, lips bloodless. 'Word came to the Isle of the Flame from Finudel. The fortresses of northern Ellyrion have been emptied, their garrisons gone. An eagle came, warning that a dark army marched south along the Annulii, heading for Eagle Pass. Finudel and Athielle will muster what army they can but request that you summon your host to meet the attack.'

Attendants appeared with food and drink. Caledor commanded Carathril to rest and restore himself while he considered the news he had brought. The Phoenix King met Dorien in his chambers and told his brother of what was happening.

'I will ride to the dragon caves,' said Dorien. 'While I rouse the drakes from their hibernation, you must take what troops you can to the aid of the Ellyrians.'

'Send your swiftest riders to Lothern and have the Sea Guard make haste for the coast of Ellyrion,' said Caledor. 'I will send Carathril back to the Isle of the Flame to take the news that we march. Bring the dragons to Tor Elyr, and the princes shall ride with me.'

'The druchii are mad to march in winter,' said Dorien. 'In Nagarythe the snows must have taken their toll.'

'Something has driven them to it,' said Caledor. 'Unless they control the elements. Perhaps our ploy to lure them out has succeeded better than I had hoped.'

'It will have succeeded only if we can defeat this army,' said Dorien. 'This pre-emptive assault has caught us off-guard.'

'It is troubling,' agreed the Phoenix King. 'I fear our secrets have not been kept and the druchii know something of what I intended. What other explanation is there for such a rash campaign?'

'Do not ponder it too long, brother,' said Dorien, opening a chest in which his armour was stored. 'The druchii do not think rationally, and to attempt to understand them is to share their madness.'

Caledor bid his brother a safe journey and returned to the throne room. Carathril looked a little restored from his wintry ordeal, and wore a resigned expression as Caledor explained that he would have to leave the next day to bear messages to the other kingdoms.

'I wish you could enjoy the hospitality of my realm a while longer,' said Caledor, laying a hand on the other elf's shoulder. 'None have given more energy to our cause than you.'

'It seems that Morai-heg has chosen a life in the saddle for me,' said the herald. 'My ship awaits my immediate return. There is no point delaying, I will ride again tonight.'

Caledor nodded his thanks and gripped Carathril's shoulder even tighter.

'Bel Shanaar made many mistakes, but his choice of herald was not one,' said the Phoenix King.

Carathril managed a smile, hands clasped to a steaming mug of mulled wine. Caledor left the herald and went to his wife and son to explain that he would be departing soon.

THE MARCH NORTH was unpleasant, the winter storms not abating in their violence as the army of Caledor pushed on through the wind and rain. The mountain roads were more like shallow streams, and mudslides and tumbled boulders frequently blocked their path, making progress even slower.

As they descended into the foothills between Caledor and Ellyrion, the weather eased, though was by no means conducive to a speedy march. The army travelled light of supplies and equipment, the baggage wagons left at Tor Caled due to the harsh conditions. The Ellyrian army would be similarly bereft of war machines – such engines did not suit their fast-moving columns of reaver knights – and so Caledor devised a strategy to suit the forces he would have at his disposal. To attempt to contain the druchii in Eagle Pass would be reckless, and he would have to persuade Finudel and Athielle to allow them onto the plains where the Phoenix King's dragons and cavalry would have their greatest effect.

The weather improved steadily as they crossed into Ellyrion. The storms became showers and eventually abated when the spires of Tor Elyr appeared on the horizon. Caledor was relieved to see a great many pavilions and herds around the Ellyrian capital; the kingdom's army had not yet set out. His confidence improved further when he saw six dragons in the skies above, keeping watch for any approach of the enemy.

His meeting with Finudel and Athielle was brief. They agreed to his plan and despatched squadrons of their lightly armoured cavalry to Eagle Pass to watch for the arrival of the druchii, two dragons sent as escort to ensure they would not be waylaid. The combined army was moved west for two days, the better to keep Tor Elyr safe from attack.

It was a tense wait. None knew the full extent of the Naggarothi host and it was always in Caledor's mind that the attack was a diversion, created to draw his attention from some other objective. He despatched one of his dragon princes to the north, to warn Koradrel in Chrace that the druchii might attempt a fresh attack on his kingdom, assuring his cousin that he would march to his aid as soon as possible if this proved to be true.

The reavers sent to watch for the enemy returned three days later, confirming that a large body of druchii had moved out of Eagle Pass and was heading for Tor Elyr. A black dragon came with the army, along with several riders on griffons and manticores. These did not overly concern the Phoenix King; his dragons would be the match of the druchii beasts.

With the agreement of Finudel and Athielle, Caledor ordered the army to march. The sooner the druchii were confronted and destroyed, the happier the Phoenix King would be. With this latest assault driven back, he would be free to respond to another offensive or, as he hoped, be able to muster his army for an attack into Tiranoc in the early spring.

The sky was overcast as the armies of Caledor and Ellyrion headed towards Eagle Pass. Winter had not relinquished its grip entirely and flurries of cold rain swept the plains, brought down from the mountains.

The scouts reported that the enemy had made camp in the foothills of the Annulii. It appeared their intent was to guard the entrance to Eagle Pass, confirming Caledor's suspicion that they had been despatched to head off any attempt he might make to breach Tiranoc. In light of this, the druchii's hasty march south made more sense, and hinted at a change of strategy from earlier years.

'Perhaps Carvalon and Tithrain were right,' suggested Finudel as he played host to Caledor in the pavilion he shared with his sister. The army was two days from the druchii encampment, and Caledor had called the princes and captains together for a final council before the battle. 'The druchii have spent their energy and can no longer spare the troops for their assaults on the other kingdoms.'

'No,' said Caledor. 'Why not defend the western end of the pass? The only reason to come east is Tor Elyr.'

'What difference does it make?' said Dorien. 'The enemy have made a mistake and we should capitalise.'

'I agree,' said the Phoenix King. 'We attack as planned. The Ellyrian cavalry will form the southern wing of the army and swing around the enemy camp to the west, cutting off the route to Eagle Pass. The rest of the army will press the attack.'

More detailed plans followed, using the enemy dispositions brought back by the scouting squadrons. The druchii had occupied a line of hills that ran south-east to north-west, protected to the east by a lake. The body of water was no obstacle to dragons and Caledor would make use of the oversight, leading the dragons across the lake to attack the exposed flank of the enemy while the infantry assaulted from the south.

When the plan was settled, the princes and captains returned to their companies. Caledor remained with Finudel and Athielle.

'If I have erred in my plans, say so now,' the Phoenix King told them, detecting a hint of reluctance from the prince and princess.

'The plan is good,' said Finudel, but exchanged a glance with his sister.

'Yet if it fails, the route to Tor Elyr will be wide open,' said Athielle. 'If we are not victorious, we will be pushed south and west, away from the city.'

'Better that we do not fail,' said Caledor. 'No battle is certain, but we cannot allow the druchii to establish themselves in strength east of the mountains. To abandon northern Ellyrion to move to the south suggests that the druchii might intend to use your kingdom as a step towards an invasion of Caledor.'

'Not to be harsh, but would that be so bad?' said Finudel. 'Caledor has suffered little and its defences are strong.'

'They would have to destroy Tor Elyr,' said Athielle. 'It cannot be left to threaten their staging camp.'

Finudel was dismayed by the thought.

'So we return to our earlier concern,' said the prince. 'Perhaps the druchii have another army in the pass, waiting for us to expose our flank with an attack on the encampment.'

'If you see some other way to proceed, tell me now,' said Caledor. 'If not, we attack in two days.'

No better plan was forthcoming from the rulers of Ellyrion and so Caledor returned to his tent. He dismissed his servants and sat deep in thought, trying to discern the purpose of the druchii encroachment. Whichever way he looked at the situation, either a diversion or a first probe towards Caledor seemed the most likely reason.

Whatever the ploy of the druchii, Caledor was resolved to destroy their army and deal with any consequences. To lose himself in second-guessing the intent of the fanatical Naggarothi was a pointless exercise, as Dorien had warned.

THE FRESHENING WIND brought a chill from the mountains, and the low clouds were a uniform grey sheet across the sky. The vanguard of Finudel's reavers fought a brief skirmish with druchii outriders in the mid-morning, driving the pickets back to their camp. Caledor's army arranged itself in the line of battle as warning horns sounded in the enemy encampment and rows of spearmen and crossbowmen formed up alongside the tents.

A barricade of sharpened stakes defended the approach from the south. A brief foray by a squadron of knights revealed ditches had been dug too, making a cavalry charge impossible. This was not a revelation for Caledor, who had not planned to commit his knights in a frontal attack. As several thousand druchii assembled for the battle, he was convinced his plan would work. The enemy gave little thought to an aerial attack across the lake.

Amongst the black and purple of the Naggarothi were several red banners decorated with Khainite symbols. The sight of these caused a ripple of anger through Caledor's army as the atrocities of Cothique were remembered. The Phoenix King sent stern words to his captains that they not allow thoughts of revenge to affect their judgement. They would follow the plan as it had been outlined and not seek to enact retribution against the Khainites if it meant any deviation.

Receiving assurances that all would proceed as the Phoenix King demanded, Caledor took to the skies atop Maedrethnir. The dragon was in a surly mood.

'A wet day for a battle,' rumbled the beast. 'You bring me from the comfort of my lair for this rabble?'

'Look there, to the west of the camp,' replied Caledor.

Atop a rocky outcrop, a black dragon flexed its wings. From this distance

Caledor could make out no detail of the rider, who seemed oddly positioned to support his troops. Two manticore riders and a pair of griffons flapped into the air above the camp, but the dragon rider did not move. The creature he rode was immense, towering over the pavilions of the druchii. There was no doubt in his mind that such a mount would belong to a high-ranking druchii prince.

There were other creatures in the army, goaded into position by the druchii beastmasters. Clouds of steam and smoke wreathed the monsters as they lumbered through gaps left by the infantry.

Flying low, Caledor signalled to his captains to sound the advance. Trumpets blared along the line of silver and white and as one the Phoenix King's army moved forwards. Finudel and his reaver knights broke to the left, heading westwards, while Athielle and her cavalry cut a more northerly route, putting herself between her brother and the enemy to ward away any counter-attack.

Not wishing to reveal his intent too soon, Caledor circled over his troops with the other dragons. When the enemy were within bow range, they would head east and come at the enemy from across the lake.

From his vantage point, he examined the layout of the druchii camp. It was like several he had seen before, arranged in orderly lines, although he noticed several clusters of tents dotted along the periphery to the south and east. It seemed quite large in comparison to the number of troops that had formed up, giving the Phoenix King a momentary pause for thought. He reasoned that this confirmed his suspicion that the encampment was intended as a staging ground, and had been prepared to receive more troops in the future as fortifications were built.

Some of the cultists could not hold their positions and sallied from the druchii line. Their wails and screams could be heard as Maedrethnir swept along the line of Caledor's army. The spear companies did not pause in their advance, leaving the Khainites to be dealt with by the archers, who stopped in long lines, bows at the ready.

As the first arrows were loosed, the Khainites broke into a charge, heading for the centre of Caledor's army. They were engulfed by a cloud of arrows, cut down in their dozens by the disciplined volleys, leaving a trail of semi-naked bodies in their wake. Heedless of their casualties, the cultists pressed on, heading for the archers.

Not a single cultist reached the line, but their suicidal assault had broken the coherency of Caledor's army. The spear companies were coming into range of the enemy repeater crossbows, unsupported by their archers. If they waited for the bowmen to rejoin them, they would suffer from the enemy missile fire; if they pressed on, they risked being outflanked by a counter-attack.

'Go with the spears!' Caledor called out to Dorien, waving his lance towards the enemy. 'Take Anatherion with you!'

His brother signalled his understanding and the two dragons dived down, swiftly catching up with the spear companies. The enemy had concentrated their line to meet this attack, further weakening their flank, still trusting to the protection offered by the lake. Caledor signalled to the remaining dragon princes to follow him as he headed east towards the water.

Dorien and Anatherion swept along the druchii line, their dragons breathing fire into the repeater crossbowmen as Caledor's spearmen struggled across the defensive ditches. The manticores and griffons dashed across the camp, and soon an elaborate aerial melee was rising and falling above the two lines of infantry, the smaller beasts attempting to separate the two dragons and concentrate their numbers on one of them. Dorien and his companion were aware of the risk and climbed higher, almost wingtip to wingtip, leaving the manticores and griffons behind. After a brief discussion, they descended again, both dragons spearing towards the manticores with flame and claws.

Caledor kept an eye on the main battle as Maedrethnir arced across the lake, his wing beats sending ripples across the placid waters. The spearmen had almost reached the druchii and the archers were moving up swiftly in support; Athielle's cavalry had reached the hills to the west of the camp and were turning north to come at the enemy from behind; in a few moments Caledor and his dragons would reach the eastern end of the camp and the druchii would be surrounded.

A flurry of movement in the encampment caught the Phoenix King's eye. Dozens of tents were quickly cast down, revealing massed batteries of repeater bolt throwers. As soon as they were revealed, the war machines began launching their deadly shots. Spearmen were scythed down by the score by the first devastating volley as they navigated their way through the walls of stakes.

Caledor found himself flying into a cloud of iron-tipped spears, each shaft glowing with a deadly rune. Maedrethnir did his best to avoid the barrage, but bolts clattered and ripped along his flank as he turned north. A shaft tore clean through his wing, leaving a burning hole, the dragon letting loose a snarl of pain.

Behind Caledor, Imrithir and his mount were not so lucky. Caught full by a flurry of bolts, the prince slumped in his saddle, a shaft piercing his chest; his dragon flailed at two bolts transfixing its throat and plummeted into the lake with a tremendous eruption of water.

Faced with such a weight of fire, the spear companies struggled to make any headway. Those that successfully negotiated the stakes and bolts were easy targets for the repeater crossbowmen and they died in their hundreds. Caledor sped north, out of range of the bolt throwers, seeking some other route into the encampment, but saw that a ring of engines surrounded the entire hill.

The battle had turned in a moment. Athielle was forced to hold back her charge, leaving the infantry to struggle on into the teeth of the enemy without support. Hydras and chimeras charged into the fight, crushing and biting, gouts of fire and petrifying gas taking a heavy toll.

Above the camp, Dorien and Anatherion did their best to menace the druchii war engines, but were repeatedly driven back by the diving attacks of the manticores and griffons. At risk of being shot down, the two princes were driven further and further north, away from the embattled infantry.

Now that the bolt throwers had been revealed, Caledor could see the genius with which they had been placed. Any dragon landing to destroy a battery would be an easy target for at least two others. He flew high across the camp, looking for some chink in the defence to exploit, but found nothing. Faced with the massed war engines, the infantry captains had sounded the recall, retreating the line back to the ditches where at least there was some cover from the incessant war machine volleys. It was only a temporary respite though; at some point they would have to advance or retreat from their position and would be cut down as they did so.

Caledor needed to think quickly. The druchii infantry were reforming after the melee, readying to press forward their advantage. The situation was bad, but a decisive move now could swing the favour of battle back towards the Phoenix King's forces.

He noticed that the Naggarothi dragon rider had not moved. Perhaps the prince was wary of committing himself to the fight, or was merely leaving his options open. Either way, Caledor would not be confident of victory unless he could draw out the black dragon, preferably luring it away from the protection of the bolt throwers.

As Maedrethnir circled again, too high for the druchii bolts, Caledor saw more movement in the enemy camp. From on high it was impossible to see anything clearly, but it looked to the king as if patches of shadow worked their way from tent to tent.

'What do you see?' he asked Maedrethnir, whose eyes were even keener than the Phoenix King's.

The dragon turned his gaze groundwards and stopped in the air, beating his wings slowly to hold station. An odd reverberation sounded from Maedrethnir's chest, a draconian noise of surprise.

'It looks like shadows that walk,' said Maedrethnir. 'I cannot see the figures that cast them.'

As he watched, Caledor saw the puddles of darkness converging on one of the bolt thrower batteries. There seemed to be a struggle of some kind, the crew drawing their swords against some foe that Caledor could not discern. Whatever attacked, it did not take long to overwhelm the crews of the war engines. The battery fell silent and the darkness dispersed, moving through the camp before coalescing next to another line of bolt throwers.

'Attack!' cried Caledor, seizing the chance. 'To the east!'

Maedrethnir did not hesitate. The dragon folded his wings and dived. He felt a tremor run through the dragon's body as they came within range of the bolt throwers. No volley was launched and the pair plunged down further. Closing fast, Caledor saw black-cloaked elves fighting with the war engine crews. He did not know what was happening, but knew that there was no time to waste.

A glance above showed that the other dragon riders had noticed their king's safe descent and with roars and bellows of flames, they plunged down, eager to wreak revenge on the druchii that had tormented them. Seeing the dragons attack, the infantry surged forth with trumpets blaring the assault, while Athielle and Finudel were finally able to signal the charge of the cavalry.

Caledor glanced at the black dragon and saw that its rider had made no move in response to the turn in the tide of battle. There was a more immediate threat as a manticore and its rider launched from the druchii line, heading straight for the Phoenix King.

'Beware of the sting,' said Caledor.

'This is not the first manticore I have slain,' Maedrethnir replied with a laugh. 'Deal with the rider and I will show you how it is done.'

The druchii sat astride the roaring beast wielded a spear wreathed in crackling energy. Caledor took the hit on his shield, the magic flaring brightly from the protective enchantment bound within the ithilmar. The Phoenix King's lance found the manticore rider's thigh, piercing armour and bone to slide into the flank of the monster. It gave a pained howl and lashed its sting at Maedrethnir's underside. The dragon caught the flailing appendage in one of his rear claws, and with the other seized the manticore by the throat.

With powerful sweeps of his wings, Maedrethnir headed upwards, dragging the manticore beneath him. The rider was not yet dead and swung his spear at the dragon's throat, but its point was knocked aside by Caledor's dipped lance. Turning, the dragon changed its grip slightly, moving the manticore's tail from back claw to front. With a single bite, Maedrethnir severed the tail, the sting dropping away as the manticore raged, twisting and snarling in the dragon's immovable grasp.

'And now the finish,' declared Maedrethnir.

His jaw snapped again, clamping around the rider and shearing through the manticore's backbone. Vertebrae shattered as the dragon ground his jaws, blood spilling in showers to the camp far below. With a last effort, Maedrethnir flexed his body and legs, ripping the manticore in half. He let the blood-spewing remnants fall from his grip, the rider's mangled corpse falling free as the manticore's remains spun groundwards.

As soon as he looked back at the druchii infantry, Caledor knew the battle was won. The enemy were streaming back through the camp in their hundreds, abandoning their positions in a massed rout. There would be no escape from Finudel and Athielle sweeping in from the other side of the encampment. Many of the druchii threw down their weapons, begging for mercy. Their pleas fell on deaf ears as knights and spearmen converged, slaying every foe in their path.

Both griffons and their riders had been slain by the other dragon princes, and the surviving manticore headed west, its rider deciding that a timely withdrawal was in order. Caledor looked again to the black dragon. There was something unsettling about the way its rider was content to watch the massacre. He wondered if it was perhaps some illusion conjured by the druchii and told Maedrethnir to head towards it. As soon as the king and his dragon were heading in its direction the drake took to the air, massive wings casting a huge shadow over the camp.

Out of spite, the rider swept over a squadron of Athielle's reaver knights, shredding dozens of riders and horses, billowing clouds of noxious vapour from his dragon poisoning even more. With a languid turn, the black-scaled monster arced westwards. Caledor saw a brief glimmer of shining blue, a flaming sword raised in mocking salute, and then the dragon rose towards the clouds. It had too much of a head start to catch and soon disappeared into the clouds over the mountains.

Unnerved by this display, unsure what it signified, Caledor directed Maedrethnir to land. Most of the camp was already overrun. The only resistance seemed to come from a group of black-swathed elves who had taken refuge in a small copse of trees on the northern slope of the hill.

'I shall burn them out,' said Dorien, sweeping past on his dragon.

He was out of earshot before Caledor could reply, rising higher and higher in preparation for his swooping attack. Caledor followed his brother with his eyes, raising his head as prince and dragon climbed into the clouds.

A shout from the left attracted his attention.

'Call off the attack!' cried Finudel, galloping hard through the trampled tents, his knights struggling to keep up.

'They are allies!' shouted Athielle, riding just as hard from the west.

Prince and princess reined in their steeds next to Caledor, horror written in their expressions.

'The Naggarothi in the woods are not the enemy,' said Finudel. 'I recognise them.'

'They are the Shadows of the Anars!' gasped Athielle. 'Do not harm them.'

Cursing, Caledor barked at Maedrethnir to launch himself. They headed for the stand of trees as Dorien began his steep descent, smoke and fire trailing from his dragon's maw. Caledor knew there was no point in shouting; his brother would hear nothing over the roar of the wind.

'Get in front of them,' he told Maedrethnir. 'Quickly!'

The dragon raced towards the trees, wing beats scattering the elves below with huge draughts of wind. Caledor ducked low and raised his shield to direct the rushing air over his head, to avoid being broken upon his saddle by its force.

Dorien did not slow, probably thinking that Caledor joined the attack. Against the buffeting wind, all the king could do was grip tight to lance and shield, peering ahead through slitted eyes.

Maedrethnir roared, his whole body shaking with the effort. The deafening bellow struck a chord in the mind of Caledor; for a moment he was overwhelmed by a primal fear and almost let go of his lance. It was a challenge, a hunting cry, a claim of territory that no other creature could match.

Dorien's dragon responded out of instinct, veering away from the woods to charge headlong at Maedrethnir, roaring his response. Almost thrown from his saddle-throne by the change of direction, Dorien lost his shield, which tumbled into the trees as Maedrethnir and the other dragon hurtled towards each other.

Caledor realised that in uttering the challenge, Maedrethnir had reverted to his most feral state. He barked the incantations of the Dragontamer, trying to break the dragon from his instinctual behaviour; he guessed Dorien would be doing likewise.

Maedrethnir gave a strange yelp of pain, snapping from his fury. He folded his wings, dropping like a huge stone so that the other dragon passed overhead. He could only half open them again before he hit the ground, legs splayed to lessen the impact. Trunks exploded into splinters and branches scattered as the dragon ploughed into the woods. In a deluge of green and brown, dragon and rider slid down a shallow slope, Maedrethnir's claws gouging deep furrows in the earth as he slowed himself.

They came to a stop and the dragon sagged to his belly, panting hard. Caledor's neck flared with pain and he realised his teeth were gritted together so hard the muscles in his jaw had locked. With an effort, he opened his mouth, pain surging down the sides of his neck.

Maedrethnir shook his head, puffing smoke as he recovered his senses.

'Are you all right?' the dragon asked, arching back his head to look at Caledor.

The Phoenix King grunted and nodded as best he could, unable to speak. He dropped his shield and lance to the ground and wrenched off his ornate helm and gauntlets. Rubbing his neck in his hands, he stretched his back, fearful that his spine had been broken. There was no stab of pain and he relaxed, slumping forwards to pat the dragon on his shoulder.

'We are not alone,' said Maedrethnir.

Caledor looked around and found himself surrounded by several dozen black-swathed elves, bows bent with arrows pointing directly at him. One of them stepped closer, the bow in his hand a beautiful object of silver and white, its string no thicker than an elf maiden's hair. Dark eyes regarded Caledor coolly from under the elf's hood. He slowly lowered his bow and the other shadowy elves did the same.

'You must be the Phoenix King,' said their leader, pulling back his hood to reveal a slender silver crown. 'The one who calls himself Caledor.'

'You must be Alith Anar,' Caledor replied. 'The one who calls himself the Shadow King.'

THE ELLYRIANS WERE searching the woods for Caledor. The Phoenix King heard Finudel calling his name. Another, lighter voice called for Alith: Athielle. At the sound of the princess's voice, a change came over Alith's demeanour. He beckoned for Caledor to dismount and dispersed his warriors with a snapped command.

Maedrethnir settled, allowing Caledor to unbuckle his harness and drop to the branch-strewn ground. Standing next to the Shadow King, Caledor found Alith to be a lot shorter than he had imagined, and a lot younger too. He was probably not even a century old, yet from his exploits Caledor had thought him a veteran of war.

'Malekith is alive,' said Alith.

At first the Phoenix King thought he had misheard.

'What did you say?' said Caledor.

'Malekith, prince of Nagarythe, still lives,' said Alith.

'You are wrong,' said Caledor, shaking his head. 'He was burned by the flame of Asuryan. I have spoken to those that saw it.'

'And I have spoken with him, not so long ago,' replied Alith with a hint of a smirk. 'Which of us is wrong?'

'How can that be?' The idea was beyond Caledor's comprehension. The testimony of Thyrinor, of Carathril and Finudel, spoke of the ruin that had been carried from the Shrine of Asuryan.

'Sorcery,' said Alith. 'He wears an enchanted suit of armour, the colour of midnight, though it burns still with the heat of its forging. He asked me to join him.'

'He did what?' Each revelation was more unbelievable than the last. Caledor looked at Alith carefully, trying to detect any hint of subterfuge. He saw nothing and could think of no reason why the last of the Anars would fabricate such a ridiculous tale.

'Malekith lives on, sustained by his magic, and now calls himself the Witch King,' Alith explained. 'You saw him today.'

'The dragon rider?' said Caledor.

'Yes, that was the Witch King,' said Alith. 'When he came to me in the ruins of Elanardris he offered me a place at his side. I said no.'

'I have only your word that is true,' said Caledor. 'How is it that you survived?'

'By running,' Alith replied with a lopsided smile. 'Running very fast. They pursued us into the mountains, but we know the peaks and passes better than any other and escaped. I followed Malekith south, and learned of his plans here.'

'You have my thanks for your part, though it was not necessary,' said Caledor.

'Not necessary?' Alith's laugh was edged with scorn. 'Your army was being destroyed.'

'I was about to order my dragons to attack the bolt throwers at the same time,' said Caledor, crossing his arms. 'We would have wiped out half the war machines in a single moment. The battle was far from lost.'

'I did not fight for your thanks,' said Alith, taking a step back. 'As I told your brother and your cousin, I fight for Nagarythe and that is all.'

'Prove to me you do not owe loyalty to Malekith,' said Caledor. 'Swear your allegiance to the Phoenix Throne.'

'Never,' spat Alith, his hand moving to the pommel of the sword at his waist. 'I will swear no oath to any king again. Nagarythe is not yours to command, it is mine.'

'My father was there when Malekith bent his knee to Bel Shanaar and swore his loyalty,' snarled Caledor. 'Who are you to do any less for me?'

'I am the Shadow King,' said Alith, touching a hand to the circlet on his brow. 'This is the crown of Nagarythe, worn by Aenarion himself. My grandfather was the last of the great princes, equal to your ancestor. Do not think that because I wear shadows for my cloak I have abandoned my lineage.'

'I will not offer my protection to any that will not swear their obedience,' said Caledor.

'I do not need your protection, Nagarythe does not need your rule,' said Alith.

The scion of the Anars glanced over Caledor's shoulder and again his expression changed; his anger faded, to be replaced by a grim look. The Shadow King spoke quickly.

'Do not think you have seen the worst of this war, Caledor. Morathi has known all along that Malekith lived and has been nurturing an army for him. They are the deadliest of Naggarothi, the knights of Anlec at their heart. They have been hidden away, even from me, upon the Blighted Isle, studying the deadliest skills of Khaine at His bloody altar. Nothing you have faced is like them. You have not seen yet half of Nagarythe's strength. Prepare yourselves for the onslaught.'

'There cannot be such a force left in Nagarythe,' said Caledor. 'The druchii have suffered many defeats these past years. What of the army destroyed today?'

Alith laughed bitterly, a sinister sound that cut at Caledor's spirit.

'Today you slaughtered frightened Tiranocii,' said the Shadow King. 'They are terrified of the Witch King, and fight as conscripts in his army. They would rather die on the swords of your warriors than face the Khainites that Malekith has at his command. News of Cothique's fate has spread far indeed.'

The sounds of the search were approaching close; the devastation left by Maedrethnir's fall would not be hard to find. Alith's discomfort increased and he darted a look at Caledor. He suddenly again looked to be the young prince Caledor had first seen close at hand, worried and alone.

'Many thought I was slain, and with good reason,' said the Shadow King. 'Tell Finudel that I am still alive; I leave it to his discretion whether Athielle should know. I would rather she did not see me.'

'You would rather not see her,' said Caledor, reading Alith's expression.

'I cannot, I forfeited that life when I became the Shadow King.'

'You are a strange person, Alith Anar,' said Caledor. 'I do not like that you call yourself king, but if you need my aid, send word.'

'The elf who takes his grandfather's name and has a dragon for his best friend calls me strange?' Alith said with a laugh. He grew serious. 'I am no hunting dog, to be called when you choose. I am the wolf, and I hunt in my own way. I will fight the druchii, but not at your command. I tell you again, Nagarythe is not yours, it is mine. Stay away.'

Alith turned and dashed into the darkness of the woods, swiftly vanishing into the shadows. A moment later, Finudel called out from behind Caledor and the Phoenix King turned.

'Who was that?' asked the Ellyrian prince.

'We will discuss it later,' said Caledor, his thoughts full of Alith's dire warnings.

EIGHTEEN

The Phoenix Resurgent

THE PLAINS OUTSIDE the walls of Anlec were still hard with frost, the air steaming with the breath of thousands of warriors. Armour dark against the white ground, they waited in rank after rank for the command of their king. Malekith looked down at his army from the eastern gate tower, overshadowed by Sulekh, the Witch King's dragon. The black-scaled monster loomed over the gatehouse with wings half-spread, her hide pitted and scarred from many fights with her brood. None had been able to tame her until Malekith, and now that she was broken to his will the black dragon was his bodyguard as well as steed.

The ring of heels on the stone steps of the gate tower announced the arrival of Morathi. The sorceress-queen strode onto the rampart and stood beside her son to survey the host of Anlec.

'They are a fine coronation gift,' said Malekith, fiery eyes regarding the massed companies below. 'You were wise to save them for me.'

'I knew you would return to us, one day,' replied Morathi. 'All that remains is to use your gift to seize the throne of Ulthuan.'

'We shall inspect the troops,' announced the Witch King.

He held out his right arm and the flames that played about his armour died, leaving wisps of smoke in the air. Morathi laid her hand on the proffered arm and the two of them made their way down the tower and headed out of the city.

'You have met Hellebron already,' said Morathi, waving a hand towards the Khainite high priestess. Her hair had been bleached white and stood in spikes and a mask of dried blood covered her face.

'Hail the Witch King, son of Khaine!' she shrieked, lifting twin blades above her head. The Khainites let out ululations of praise, howling and screaming as they flourished their weapons.

Witch King and sorceress moved on past the wailing cultists to where a dozen princes and commanders stood waiting, their companies of spears and repeater crossbows standing in stolid lines as the cold wind keened across the open plain. The crews of a hundred bolt throwers stood ready beside their machines, flanked by five thousand heavily armoured knights on black steeds.

'The host of Anlec,' said Morathi.

Malekith nodded and at a shouted command, the thousands of Nagga-rothi crashed spears and swords against shields and stamped their feet.

'Hail the Witch King!' they roared, lifting their weapons in salute.

Further north were the beast pens, where the black dragons lazed, sur-rounded by a fog of noxious gas. Manticores paced their iron cages and roared their frustration. Griffons and hydras strained at their chains, their rasping growls and hisses dying to silence as the Witch King approached. Even the manticores seemed cowed by Malekith's presence, settling to their haunches in deference, submissive whimpers echoing from their cages.

Other warriors there were too; lightly armoured scouts and foot knights who wore long coats of mail and high-crested helms. Morathi's sorcerers and sorceresses, a dozen in number, lowered themselves to their knees as Malekith came near. Assassins branded and tattooed with the marks of Khaine abased themselves, presenting poison-edged daggers of black crystal as a sign of obedience.

'What is your plan?' asked Morathi as mother and son turned back towards the city gate.

'Chrace must fall,' announced the Witch King. 'Tor Achare must be taken if we are to stage any campaign against the eastern kingdoms.'

'That will take us into the territory of the Anars,' said Morathi. 'Many an army has not returned from those mountains.'

'It is my territory!' Malekith snarled, snatching his arm away from his mother. Flames rippled along his armour, burning dark blue, the inside of his helm glowing with the same hue. 'I will crush the Anars, as you should have done a decade ago.'

'It is fool's errand to attempt a conquest of the mountains,' Morathi snapped back. 'Many of my incompetent minions lost their lives attempting the feat.'

'I did not say I will conquer Elanardris,' said Malekith, 'I said I would crush the Anars. The march to Chrace will be too tempting a target, and when they attack I will trap them and kill the last of Eoloran's spawn. With-out Alith, their resistance will crumble.'

'We thought him dead for many years,' said Morathi. 'He is sly.'

'I know him,' said Malekith. 'I have seen him. He is nothing more than a boy. He will not outwit me.'

They passed under the gate as the commanders dismissed the army back to their camps. The huge iron portcullis descended and the gates closed as the pair emerged into the late winter sun that shone down on the plaza within the walls.

'You said you will take Tor Achare,' Morathi prompted.

'With Tiranoc and Chrace in my possession, Ellyrion will soon fall. Avelorn is a spent force, to be finished off at my leisure. Cothique lies ruined, and so Saphery will be the next objective. Thyriol is not the match for either of us, and together we can destroy his gaggle of mages and rob Caledor of their enchantments.'

'You seem to have everything considered,' said Morathi, as the two of them crossed the square towards the road leading to Aenarion's palace.

'I have had a long time to consider my plans,' replied the Witch King. 'When the pain was not too great, I thought hard on what I would do. I will isolate Imrik, take from him every advantage and ally, and when he is left alone, I will offer him the chance to hand over the throne of Ulthuan.'

'He would never accept,' said Morathi. 'He is far too stubborn to admit defeat.'

'I do not wish him to accept,' said Malekith. He held out a flame-wreathed hand. 'When he refuses, I will seize him by the throat and he will burn. He will not know one-hundredth of the pain I knew, but it will still be an agonising death. I will slaughter his people and cast down Tor Caled. The dragons will be broken and turned to our cause and when all of this is accomplished, when Imrik knows that I am the master of the elves, I shall burn him to death.'

Malekith shuddered with delight as he pictured that glorious moment. It had overtaken the visions of coronation in his dreams. He could feel the charring of the usurper's flesh on his fingertips and hear his strangled cries of mercy. Malekith knew well the stench of burned flesh, but the smell of Imrik's immolation would be sweeter than the finest incense of Cothique. Skin would bubble and his eyes would melt. Flesh would rupture and bone turn to ash.

'I have the measure of him,' said the Witch King, freeing himself from the daydream with some effort. 'My foray into Ellyrion has proven I am the superior general. He is guilty of extremes, veering between cautious defence and over enthusiastic attack. He was never my equal.'

'Yet he beat you in Ellyrion,' said Morathi, darting a glance up at her son's masked face.

'It was not my intent to defeat him,' replied Malekith, holding his temper in check despite the accusation in his mother's voice. 'The Tiranocii conscripts would never be an army worthy of my command. And I have taught Imrik a lesson, one that will make him nervous of attacking my army again.

I will use that uncertainty to my advantage when I strike for Tor Achare.'

'What of Tiranoc?' said Morathi.

They had reached the plaza in front of the palaces. Sulekh swept over the city, her massive shadow blotting the sun from the square as she flew to a perch atop one of the palace's ancient towers, stones and tiles crumbling to dust as she found purchase with her claws. Malekith glanced up at the dragon, amused by her behaviour, as loyal and dependent as a hunting dog.

'Tiranoc?' he said, recalling the question. 'It is safe. Imrik dares not launch an offensive while his allies are under attack. He will have to defend Chrace, or lose the loyalty of his supporters. That is his weakness. He cares what his subjects think.'

'That is not a problem for you,' said Morathi as they mounted the steps up to the palace doors. 'Our people adore you.'

'They can hate me, for all that I care of their opinion,' replied Malekith. 'As long as they fear me.'

As LOATH AS he was to leave his army, Caledor was forced to convene a fresh council at the Isle of the Flame so that the matter of Malekith's return could be discussed. To the Phoenix King the only thing that had changed was the quality of his opponent. As ruler of Nagarythe, Morathi had been prone to acts of spite and was not a natural military leader. Malekith was a far more worrying proposition. It had not been by luck that he had conquered much of Elthin Arvan.

Leaving Maedrethnir to recover from his wounds in Tor Elyr, Caledor travelled with Finudel and Athielle, while Dorien remained as the general of the combined armies of Caledor and Ellyrion. They took ship to the Shrine of Asuryan, and were met by the delegations of the other kingdoms, hastily gathered for the conference.

The first day tested the Phoenix King's patience, as every prince offered forth his own theories on how Malekith's survival had come to pass. Some questioned the veracity of the report, but were convinced of Alith Anar's trustworthiness in this matter by Athielle, who had been in sombre mood since learning of the Shadow King's own apparent resurrection. Caledor ended the day's session early, realising that no real business would be done while the princes were still taken aback by the revelation of Malekith's return.

He fared little better on the second day; the council seemed determined to discuss their own ongoing woes and how these affected the promises they had made in the previous council. Caledor detected no small amount of back-tracking from the plan that had been agreed upon, and a call was made to debate a new course of action.

The Phoenix King left abruptly as Finudel was making a speech, striding from the shrine in a foul temper. Mianderin caught up with him on the marble road that led to the quays where the king's ship was berthed.

'Your departure is hasty,' the priest called out, holding up a hand to wave the king to a halt.

'Empty oaths,' snapped the Phoenix King, turning to face the high priest of Asuryan as he hurried up the white causeway, robes flapping. 'Promises were made and now they argue the most eloquent way to renege on them.'

'They are scared,' said Mianderin.

'Of what?' replied Caledor.

'Of Malekith,' said the priest.

The Phoenix King did not know what to say to this. Mianderin took his frown of confusion as a sign of anger.

'Do not be so harsh on them,' said the priest, taking the Phoenix King's arm to lead him to a curving bench on an immaculate lawn beside the road. 'Some of them saw Malekith emerge from the flames, and even if not for that remarkable survival, his reputation cannot be ignored.'

'He scares me as well,' admitted Caledor, pulling aside his cloak of feathers to sit down. 'That is why we must be united and strike first.'

'Your fear drives you to action,' said Mianderin, seating himself beside the Phoenix King, hands held neatly in his lap. 'Their fear makes them cautious. Something they once believed true has proved false and every other doubt they have is magnified.'

Caledor rubbed his chin and considered this. It had not occurred to him that the other princes would react in this way.

'You must allay their fears and dispel their doubts,' said Mianderin. 'They will follow you, they have shown that, but you cannot drag them with you.'

'As we speak, the druchii could be on the march,' said Caledor. 'We do not have time for endless debate.'

'And in this, you show your fear to them.' Mianderin turned his head to look at the shrine. 'You cannot bully them, as Malekith found out. No matter how weak you think them to be, they are princes of Ulthuan, rulers of their kingdoms, and they have their pride.'

'Vanity.'

'Perhaps, but no more than yours,' said the high priest. 'What else but vanity would make you believe that they will follow you without question?'

'Necessity,' replied Caledor.

'They see the world differently. They look only at what they have to lose, while you see what can be gained. That is why they chose you, to provide them with the vision they lack.'

'I am not that sort of leader,' said Caledor. 'I do not make speeches or waste words.'

'And you do not have to,' said Mianderin. 'But your actions can be misinterpreted. What does the council think at the moment? Have you abandoned them? They do not know your thoughts.'

Caledor looked at the gleaming pyramid of the shrine like it was a fortress to besiege, his heart heavy. He took a deep breath and stood up with a glance at Mianderin.

'Let them know my thoughts?' said the Phoenix King.

The priest nodded with a smile of encouragement.

'I can do that,' said Caledor.

He strode back to the shrine, the Phoenix Guard at the door parting their halberds to allow him entry. The Phoenix King stopped and looked at the two silent warriors.

'Summon your captain, I will speak with him shortly,' said the king. The guards nodded their assent and Caledor passed into the shrine.

He strode back to his chair but did not sit down. The conversation of the princes died away and all watched him closely. The Phoenix King took off his winged helm and set it on the seat of the throne. He then opened the clasp of his ceremonial cloak and cast the mass of feathers over the throne's back. Caledor turned to face the others, arms crossed.

'I am Imrik again,' he said. 'Forget the cloak and the crown. Forget the Phoenix King. Listen to Imrik, dragon prince of Caledor, who you all turned to in your time of desperation.'

He strode purposefully across the shrine, armoured boots ringing loudly on the tiles, filling the silence. He stood before the table where Thyriol sat and leaned forwards, fists on its wooden surface.

'Did you choose me to be your king?' said Caledor.

'I did,' Thyriol replied with a nod.

'Why?'

The mage looked at the others before he answered.

'You were the best suited to it,' said Thyriol. 'Your skills as a warrior and a general, your determination and your principles made you the best of all the princes.'

'Is there another that now surpasses me in that regard?' Caledor's eyes bored into the mage's as he waited for the answer.

'No,' said Thyriol.

Caledor straightened and looked at the other princes.

'If any of you disagree with Thyriol, who alone amongst us has chosen two kings, speak your mind now.'

None of the princes spoke. A few exchanged glances. Finudel smiled and nodded, while Koradrel raised a fist in salute. The Phoenix King walked back to his throne and put on the cloak and war helm before sitting down.

'I am Caledor, the Phoenix King, your ruler,' he said leaning forwards, fists on the arms of the throne. 'While I live, we will not be defeated. That is my oath.'

Heartened by this bold declaration, the council agreed to halt the discussions until the next day, when they would hear the Phoenix King's proposal. As the princes left the main chamber of the shrine, a tall warrior entered, his silver armour gleaming, halberd in hand, flowing white cloak trimmed with embroidered flames of red and gold: the captain of the Phoenix Guard, Elentyrion.

Caledor sat down and waved for the shrine's chief protector to approach.

'You are sworn to the protection of Asuryan's flame,' said the Phoenix King. 'Malekith will extinguish that flame if given the chance. He will suffer no other to pass through it. Do you understand?'

The captain nodded once, his eyes not leaving Caledor's.

'Your defence of Asuryan's shrine cannot start and end at the Isle of the Flame,' the king continued. 'Should I fail, should we all fail, Ulthuan will be overrun, including this shrine. The Phoenix Guard must fight alongside the Phoenix King if they are to do their duty.'

The commander of the Phoenix Guard considered this for some time, his face expressionless. Caledor thought the warrior's passive response was a refusal but he eventually bowed to one knee and nodded, placing his halberd at the feet of the Phoenix King. Caledor picked up the weapon – it weighed almost nothing, forged of ithilmar – and told Elentyrion to rise. Handing the captain the halberd, Caledor allowed himself a brief smile. Malekith might have kept an army hidden, but how would they fare against the sacred warriors of Asuryan?

THE COUNCIL WAS called together early the next day. Caledor was keen to say what he wanted before the princes had time to start their own discussions. As a concession to the time of day, Mianderin had food brought into the shrine and the atmosphere was one of a convivial breakfast as Caledor spoke.

'We must not underestimate Malekith,' said the Phoenix King. 'Yet we must not also overestimate him and his army. There have been times when all has seemed lost. Remember those first years, when the dragons slept and Lothern was besieged. Remember the peril we all felt as Avelorn burned. Remember the dread of Cothique left to its fate. We can remember these things because we have survived them.'

'Malekith's return is like nothing we have faced before,' said Carvalon. He wiped crumbs from his lip with a silk napkin.

'Malekith cannot be everywhere,' replied Caledor.

There were looks of confusion from the princes.

'Neither can you be everywhere,' said Tithrain. 'Nor the dragons. It seems to me that we have returned to where we began, waiting for the sword to fall so that we might turn it aside if we can.'

'No,' said Caledor. 'That will not work. I do not know if I can beat Malekith.'

This announcement was met with dismay from the princes. Caledor raised his hand to quiet them but their protests continued.

'Only yesterday you promised us victory,' said Athielle. 'Today you tell us we cannot win.'

'I did not say that.' The Phoenix King rose from his throne and began to walk around the shrine, looking at each of the princes in turn as he spoke. 'We do not have to defeat Malekith. We have to defeat the druchii. Take away his army and he is just a lone warrior. A powerful one, yes, and gifted with sorcery too, but just one elf.'

'Not from what I saw on the Ellyrian plains,' said Finudel. 'He rides the largest dragon I have ever seen, and after what he has endured I am not so sure he is mortal any longer.'

'We will test his immortality,' said Caledor. 'He cannot defeat an enemy that will not face him.'

'You said the same before, and Avelorn was almost destroyed,' said Athielle. 'And what of Cothique?'

'This war will be hard, but it cannot go on forever,' Caledor assured them, his confidence growing as he spoke. 'Avelorn was not destroyed. Cothique is wounded but survives. Ulthuan is stronger than Nagarythe. We are stronger than Morathi and Malekith. Their greed and their hate drives them. Our duty and our loyalty must be as strong.'

'What do you propose?' asked Thyriol, who had been busily eating his breakfast while the others spoke, and had not spoken before. He pushed away the remains of his meal and rested his hands on the table. 'How do we isolate Malekith?'

'We must offer resistance where he advances, but not commit to open battle,' said Caledor, continuing to pace. 'While the druchii attack in one place, we attack them in another. The Anars had it right. We cannot risk this war being decided on a single battle. Malekith will give us no second chances.'

'Chrace will bear the brunt of the fighting,' said Koradrel. His shoulders heaped with his white lion cloak, the prince of Chrace seemed to dwarf the others in the room as he stood. He looked at Finudel and Athielle. 'As will Ellyrion. In Chrace, we know very well how to hunt. The enemy will not breach the passes without casualty.'

'We Ellyrians are not so well versed in mountain fighting,' said Finudel. 'However, we can wage war on the move as well as any Chracian hunts. Malekith will not find us easy to catch.'

'And I will give the enemy another problem,' said Caledor. 'It is still my intent to retake Tiranoc. I will muster the army in Caledor and strike north for Tor Anroc.'

'Do not expect this to be swift,' warned Thyriol. 'This plan of yours will take years to come to fruition.'

'Aenarion did not destroy the daemons in a day,' Carvalon said with a laugh.

'Aenarion did not destroy the daemons,' Caledor corrected the prince, sitting in his throne. 'My grandfather did.'

'And your name will sit easily alongside his in our histories,' said Tithrain. He stood and raised a goblet of fruit juice. 'It is too early for wine, but I salute you with all that I have. Cothique has suffered, but we will fight with you.'

The other princes stood also, offering their agreement. Out of the corner of his eye, Caledor glimpsed Mianderin standing at the door of side chamber. The high priest was nodding, a contented smile on his face.

THE RAIN RATTLED from Sulekh's scales and hissed into steam where it hit the Witch King's armour. Rivers cascaded down the mountain slopes, swelled to bursting from the spring deluge. The low clouds clung to the peaks like a shroud, swathing the pass in a thick haze. Malekith's army picked their way down a slope strewn with boulders and fallen trees, a winding column of black that disappeared into the grey mist.

Closing his eyes, the Witch King felt the bubbling winds of magic washing over the Annulii. With the circlet, he could see every slender strand, the smallest ebb and eddy of mystical energy. He searched for disturbances hidden to normal eyes, seeking the telltale swell and whirl of living things. Giant eagles nested in the heights of the peaks; mountain goats bounded up the slopes in large herds, gorging themselves on grass revealed by the recent thaw; a bear ambled from its cave seeking food; the trees were delicate slivers of life burrowing deep into the soil.

There was something else.

Further down the pass, Malekith detected the glow of fire, drawing the magic of flames to it. A camp. Several camps. Around them he spied the silvery flicker of elven spirits. He turned to the cluster of messengers who sat astride their black horses a short distance from Sulekh, their blinkered mounts trembling with fear.

'Warn the vanguard,' said Malekith. 'There are Chracians on the northern slope, where a bridge crosses a river. It may be an ambush.'

One of the riders nodded and headed off down the mountainside, his steed galloping hard, grateful to be heading away from the presence of the Witch King and his dragon.

It was almost an insult, thought Malekith. Did Caledor rate him so lowly that he thought the Witch King would be caught by such a simple trap? His armour creaking as he turned, Malekith cast his unnatural gaze back towards the west, where his army was still crossing the last shoulder of the mountain. It would be noon before they were all in the valley. It did not matter, he was in no hurry. He wanted his enemies to know where he was.

Malekith looked up, rain hammering into the mask of his helm. Droplets danced and spat on the hot armour. He tried to remember when he had last drunk water. He could not. The fires that burned inside him left him with a ravening thirst but he could not quench it. It was the same with food. Not a morsel had passed his lips since he had been sealed inside the armoured suit. Sorcery alone kept him alive; the magic sustained by the sacrifices bound within the plates of his artificial skin. It was sad in some ways, liberating in others. He could taste nothing but the ash of his own near-destruction, but he could dimly recollect the sweetness of honey, the richness of wine.

Simple pleasures, taken from him by cowards and traitors. The jealous priests of Asuryan had cursed the flames so that they would not accept him. Yet their trickery had not succeeded. He had emerged from the flames with the blessing of the lord of gods. He would throw them into the fires they had tainted with their subterfuge and let them know what their god's judgement felt like.

The ground trembled. Malekith sensed it through a shift in the magical winds, a turbulence that flowed south along the vortex. His ravaged ears could hear little over the constant crackling of the flames, but the Witch King's magical sense was far more accurate. Boulders and logs tumbled down the slope from the camps by the bridge. He heard the screams of the warriors who had crossed over to attack the Chracians and felt their bodies crushed by the avalanche unleashed by the mountain-dwellers. The spirit of every dying elf flickered briefly, a pinprick of darkness that was swallowed up by the ever-shifting tides of magic.

There were more shouts and sounds of fighting. A column of march was no formation for battle and the vanguard had allowed itself to be surrounded, despite Malekith's warning. With a growl, he jerked Sulekh's iron reins and the monstrous beast launched herself from the rock, plunging down the valley in a swirl of cloud.

Nearing the bottom of the pass, Malekith saw several hundred Chracians fighting against his warriors. He saw the slew of debris blocking the bridge over which the vanguard had crossed, cutting off any reinforcement. Naggarothi warriors called for axes and bars to be brought forward so that the blockage could be cleared.

'Stand back!' Malekith roared as Sulekh landed on the near side of the river, clawed feet sinking into the soft mud of the bank.

He waited while the startled soldiers hurried back from the bridge. When they were clear of the crossing, the Witch King extended a hand, drawing in the threads of magic that invisibly wound down the valley, crushing them into pure energy with his force of will. He felt the icy touch of the circlet in his mind as he shaped the magic, a bolt of forking lightning leaping from his fist to smash into the boulders and hewn tree trunks. Stone and wood splinters exploded upwards, cutting arcs through the mist before drifting down onto the foaming water of the river.

'Is it safe?' one of the captains called out. The bridge had taken some of the blast, its stone wall collapsed for half its length on one side.

'That is not my concern,' said Malekith. 'Follow me!'

Sulekh leapt across the river and with a single flap of her vast wings carried Malekith up the far slope to where his embattled soldiers were encircled by axe- and spear-wielding Chracians. Some wore the prized white lion pelts for which their kingdom was famed, the furs heavy with moisture from the rain.

As soon as they saw Malekith approaching, the Chracians scattered, breaking off their attack to sprint back into the woods. Not all reached the safety of the eaves; Malekith unsheathed his sword, Avanuir, and launched a flurry of fiery blue bolts at the retreating warriors, slaying a handful with each detonation. The Witch King drew in more magic and with a shout unleashed it in a broad wave. Where it struck, the trees exploded into black flame, the fire quickly raging up the slope, engulfing even more of the Chracian hunters. Sap exploded and leaves turned to ash as the wave of fire continued along the mountainside, engulfing the tents and wagons of the Chracian camps.

Sustaining the magical fire took all of Malekith's concentration; as he weaved his metal-clad hand back and forth the fires spread further and further, the heat of the flames dissipating the mist as they engulfed the mountainside. The surge of dark energy flowing through him resonated with the runes of his armour, igniting dead nerve-endings, sending a shiver across the metal's plates as if it were his skin.

With an effort, the Witch King cut the flow of dark magic, pulling himself back from the brink of intoxication. The mystical flames guttered and died, revealing blackened stumps and bones littered across the mountain. The clatter of armour attracted his attention and he turned to see a squadron of knights galloping across the bridge.

'Captain, come to me,' Malekith said, beckoning to the elf who had been in charge of the vanguard.

The captain came forwards, a bloodied sword in his hand, breastplate rent open from a Chracian axe. He dropped to one knee, eyes averted.

'My apologies, king,' said the soldier.

He knelt trembling, head bowed, as Malekith steered Sulekh to loom over him. The crest of the captain's helmet fluttered with each of the dragon's breaths, wisps of poisonous vapour coiling from her nostrils. The Witch King could feel the elf's fear dripping from his shuddering body.

'Do not fail me again,' said the Witch King. The captain looked up, surprised and delighted. 'Continue the march!'

The officer bowed and hurried away, anxious that his master might have a sudden change of heart. In truth, the captain was ordered into the trap by Malekith and could not be blamed. His mother might dispense summary executions in such a situation, but her acts of spite were wasteful. The Witch King suffered no illusions about his opponents and knew he would need every soldier if he was to claim Ulthuan for his own.

Uncertainty keeps soldiers alert, Malekith told himself. He would not want to become predictable.

WHILE MALEKITH'S ARMY navigated the difficult passes into Chrace, Caledor's host was poised to descend from the Dragon Spine mountains into southern

Tiranoc. The border was heavily fortified, the Phoenix King's scouts reporting a dozen citadels had been erected since the druchii occupation had begun. Caledor would have to lay siege to each if he was to advance on Tor Anroc.

The westerly winds brought the freshness of the sea and the spring sun was bright as Caledor led his army out of the mountains. At the foot of the valley were twin castles, situated at the narrowest point, a massive iron gate between them. Flying above his army, the Phoenix King could see more ramparts had been built into the mountainsides. Batteries of bolt throwers were stationed to create a killing field in front of the gate.

He signalled to Dorien to follow and instructed Maedrethnir to land on a spur of rock just out of range of the war engines. There was frenetic activity on the walls of the keep, a mass of soldiers boiling up to the ramparts from their barracks within.

'A tough proposition,' said Dorien as his mount settled a little below Maedrethnir's perch. 'This could be bloody.'

'Yes, it could,' replied the Phoenix King as he analysed the defences guarding the pass.

The fortifications protecting the bolt throwers were little more than slits in the rock, allowing no room for a dragon to land. It would be possible to fill them with fire, but any dragon doing so would have to fly slowly into the teeth of the war machines' fire. Even if the outer defences were neutralised, the keeps themselves were solidly built, and would provide plenty of cover against dragonfire and lance. It would take some time to build siege engines that could breach the gate.

'How do we attack?' asked Dorien, showing little of his usual enthusiasm as he looked at the forbidding fortress.

'From Lothern,' replied Caledor.

THOUGH THE WASTED march pained the Phoenix King, he had realised that it would be far better to attack Tiranoc from the sea. As the army headed back eastwards, Dorien confronted him in his tent one night.

'Why did we not sail to Tiranoc from the outset?' his brother asked. 'Spring will nearly be summer by the time we return.'

'I had to have a look,' answered Caledor. 'If we attack by ship, we must retake Tor Anroc. A retreat to the fleet will be very dangerous. Should we be cut off, the passes of the Annulii stand between us and sanctuary in Ellyrion. A hard withdrawal also.'

'And when we take Tor Anroc, what then?' said Dorien. 'There are druchii outposts all over Tiranoc. We will be an island in a sea of enemies.'

'We will not be staying,' said Caledor. 'We need to hold the city long enough for Malekith to respond. When he does, we will leave and sail to Chrace to threaten from there.'

'Why not dispense with all of this play-acting and simply land on the coast of Nagarythe?' said Dorien, who had not been at the council and had confessed some doubts over his brother's intentions when he had been informed.

'Enough!' snapped Caledor. 'You do not tame a dragon by putting your head between its fangs. Malekith has always known victory. When I deny him, he will become frustrated and make mistakes. That is when we strike, and not before.'

Dorien did not seem satisfied by Caledor's explanation, but did not raise the matter again on the march across Caledor and Eataine. By the time the host arrived in Lothern, the fleet of the city was waiting for them. It took several days to embark the army upon the eighty ships, but the winds held fair for the journey around Ulthuan's western coast.

Since the destruction of the captured Tiranocii ships at the siege of Lothern, the greatest disadvantage of the druchii had been a lack of vessels. Though they had enjoyed a brief naval ascendancy when the colony fleet had returned, several battles along the Cothique and Yvresse coasts had restored the advantage to Caledor's forces.

So it was with justified confidence that the Eataine captains sailed their vessels to the coast of Tiranoc, expecting little resistance. Aided by pilots who knew the waters off this stretch of shore, Caledor had selected four landing spots; isolated bays and small harbours that were unlikely to be defended. Even if the Naggarothi left their port at Galthyr the moment the fleet was spotted, it would still take them four days of hard sailing against the prevailing winds to reach the closest landing. By then, Caledor was determined to be at the walls of Tor Anroc.

As the Phoenix King had expected, the landings went unopposed. Five thousand knights and four times that number of infantry marched east along the neglected roads of Tiranoc, converging on the capital from the west and south. They encountered a few small garrisons, most of whom tried to flee upon seeing the approaching army but were chased down by the dragon riders.

The people of Tiranoc were in jubilant mood, crowding the roads and villages to welcome their liberators. Unlike Cothique, the Khainites had not been let loose and the kingdom was for the most part prosperous. That was not to say the druchii occupiers had been gentle or subtle in their domination; Caledor heard many woeful tales of their oppression as he passed through towns and hamlets thronged with cheering and singing crowds.

Eager to press on, he found little time for the celebrations that were thrown in his honour, and even less time for the local dignitaries that threw them. Every delay niggled at the Phoenix King's patience. Grateful Tiranocii filled the roads and slowed the march and it was five days before the army sighted Tor Anroc.

Unsure of the enemy's strength, Caledor spent a day scouting the city and surrounding countryside from the back of Maedrethnir. The other dragons he sent north and east to look for druchii armies on the march, along with Thyriol and Finreir on their pegasi and a prince of Yvresse, Namillon, who rode a white-feathered griffon. The flying patrols spied no druchii force larger than a company, while Caledor's inspection of the city's defences was curtailed by a hail of bolts from the towers as Maedrethnir swept over the city.

Though not one of the great fortresses of Ulthuan like Anlec, Tor Achare or Tor Caled, Tor Anroc was still an imposing city. The capital of Tiranoc, once the seat of the Phoenix King, was built atop a white-stoned hill that was bordered by steep cliffs facing west towards the approaching army. About the foothills of the mount were white buildings roofed with red tiles, some of them abandoned and half-ruined. They nestled amongst poorly kept fields that were dotted with wooden sheds that had not been built when Caledor had last visited. The stench and swarms of flies revealed the purpose of these outhouses: abattoirs where meat was still hanging on the hooks, recently deserted.

There was only one approach to the city, from the east. Caledor split his army and they circled north and south around Tor Anroc. Knowing that there were likely secret tunnels through the rock of the mound, the Phoenix King left several companies camped beside the cliffs, far enough away to be out of bolt thrower range but close enough to keep watch on the cliff sides.

From the east the city looked even more spectacular, though its white walls were marred with cracks and swathes of unpainted plaster and fresh stone. Caledor regretted his abortive attempt to enter from the mountains, judging that the defences had been shored up with the forewarning that the expedition had given the druchii. He dismissed his worries; there was nothing he could do to change the past.

Spearing straight across the landscape from the mountains to the east, a road of pitted hexagonal tiles ran up to the closed gate. Wide enough for five chariots abreast, the wood and iron of the massive portal were exposed, the plates of gold that had once gleamed in the sun stolen by the city's invaders. A great gatehouse barred the approach to the city, a bastion upon a wall twice the height of an elf that arched backwards into the mount itself, all carved from the naked rock. Two pale towers flanked the roadway, devoid of openings except for high arrow slits that looked upon every approach. On each of the flat tower tops stood a bolt thrower, mounted upon an assembly of bars and thin ropes so that they could be swung with ease in any direction.

Beyond the gate, the road split and spiralled east and west towards the city proper. From high walls, the black and purple flags of Nagarythe flew on banner poles, the spring wind teasing out the long pennants. There were other more grisly decorations; the heads of elves hanging from chains and impaled atop spears, and skeletons and half-rotted carcasses sealed in gibbets that stirred in the breeze. Towers and citadels carved from the white rock broke above the curving crenellations of the curtain wall, but these in turn were dwarfed by a central spire that pierced the morning sky like a shining needle.

Once that tower had burned with a blue flame, signalling the occupation of the Phoenix King. Now the palace of Bel Shanaar was in disrepair. Even from outside the city Caledor could see broken windows, sagging tiled roofs and crumbling balconies. While he had held no deep affection for Bel Shanaar, to see the legacy of the city he had built so shamed brought the Phoenix King's ire to the surface and he snapped orders at his commanders to make camp either side of the road.

The elves erected their pavilions in the ruins of walled orchards, where rows of apple and cherry trees were breaking into blossom, a strangely bright and cheerful apparition amongst the aura of gloom that seemed to emanate from the occupied city. Caledor's household erected his tent in the grounds of a farm protected by high walls of white stone overgrown with creeping plants, the gateways empty, the silver and gold gates that had once lined the road taken like those of Tor Anroc.

Little was left of the summer manses of Tiranoc's nobles. Many of the white towers that stood atop the surrounding hills were tumbled or blackened with soot. Caledor despatched companies to investigate each of these, in case they harboured enemies that could launch raids from behind the siege lines.

Caledor also sent a large company to the wooded hills north of the city; Chracian woodsmen and artisans from Lothern. They were to fell timber and construct the siege engines that would be needed to assault the city.

As rows of red and white and blue tents rose up in a second city around Tor Anroc, Caledor summoned his princes and captains to discuss his plans for the initial attack.

FAR TO THE north, the druchii pressed on towards Tor Achare. Villages and towns had fallen to their advance, and another was about to. Spearheads clattered harmlessly from Malekith's iron skin, as dozens of Chracians tried to surround the Witch King. He swept his flaming sword from left to right, parting spears, shearing through shields and slashing through armour and flesh. Stepping over the burning bodies of the dead warriors, the Witch King drove his sword through the shield and chest of another foe. Overhead, Sulekh flew back and forth, clouds of green vapour billowing from her maw as she hunted through the narrow streets of the town. The black dragon landed atop a row of houses, the roofs buckling under her weight.

Another group of Chracians dashed from a side street, axes swinging. Malekith blocked their blows with his massive shield, the rune of Khaine on its surface blazing with baleful energy. With a growl, he smashed his sword through a handful of attackers, separating limbs and heads with one blow.

As the Witch King's warriors advanced up the street, the Chracians fell back, disappearing into a warren of gardens and alleys.

Striding after them, the Witch King noticed an elf crawling into the shadow of a collapsed wall. He sheathed Avanuir and dulled the flames of his armour before reaching down and seizing the Chracian by his ankle. Dragging the unfortunate elf across the rubble, Malekith released his grip on the elf's leg and seized hold of his breastplate, lifting him from the ground.

'Where are they hiding?' growled the Witch King.

The Chracian said nothing, his face a mask of defiance. The elf did not even attempt to struggle, but hung limply in Malekith's grasp, blood spilling from a wound in his shoulder. The metal of the Chracian's breastplate buckled and tore as the Witch King tightened his grip.

'Where is Imrik?'

'King Caledor will fight you when he chooses,' replied the Chracian. 'He has more important things to attend to.'

With a snarl, Malekith hurled the elf against the collapsed wall. The Chracian's broken body crumpled to the ground, neck snapped.

'Kill everyone, destroy everything,' the Witch King bellowed.

He turned away from the fighting, seeking to calm himself and master the frustration that boiled within him. For the whole of the spring he had fought his way across the mountains. Every valley and peak had been a struggle for his army. Never gathering in one place, the Chracians had gnawed at his army like rats, emerging from their holes to nibble away at his troops before scuttling back to their lairs. It mattered not how many towns he burned, how many villages he put to the sword, his enemies refused to meet him in true battle.

Only the day before he had received word that the Anars were raiding the supply caravans to the west. Companies sent to forage in the woods came back bloodied from ambushes. They had broken the bridges across the raging rivers and blocked the roads with felled trees. None of their actions could halt his advance, and even the casualties they inflicted were tolerable, but the disruption and delays were a source of constant irritation.

As he watched Sulekh ripping down the tower of a noble's manse, Malekith pushed back his anger and reviewed the situation. Despite the Chracians' tactics, he was less than five days' march from Tor Achare. The plains of northern Chrace were open before him. Caledor would have no choice but to meet him there. The alternative was to allow Tor Achare to fall, giving Malekith a stronghold from which to launch further attacks into the Inner Kingdoms and the east; even Caledor could see the folly of allowing an enemy such a fortress.

A strange whispering distracted the Witch King. He sensed an odd flow in the winds of magic: a daemonic presence. Turning to his right, he saw the flames of a burning cottage glowing red and purple. As he watched, the fires coalesced into a diminutive figure. It jumped down from the pile of burning timbers, awkward and lopsided, stubby wings trailing sparks from its back. Its face was beaked, though the daemon's features constantly shifted, the number of eyes and mouths changing from moment to moment in the dancing flames.

It padded forwards, gangling arms swaying like branches in a wind, pink smoke bubbling from its fiery body, a line of little ash footprints left across the slabs of the street. Stopping just in front of Malekith, it squatted down and looked up at the Witch King with a scowl.

'I have been bid to deliver you a message,' the creature said, its annoyance obvious.

'Then deliver it,' said Malekith.

'The glorious Morathi, queen of the elves, mistress of the black spheres, sends warning,' said the daemon, the words delivered in a bored monotone. 'The treacherous Imrik and his followers have laid siege to Tor Anroc. She of the Thousand and One Dark Blessings entreats you to make haste to lift the siege lest the southern border of Nagarythe be threatened.'

The daemon stood up and turned away.

'Wait!' snapped Malekith. 'I have a reply for you to take to Anlec.'

'I never agreed to a reply,' said the daemon, not looking back. 'Take it yourself.'

With a growl, Malekith extended his hand, fingers splayed. Magic twisted, forming a net of barbed darkness that surrounded the daemon. It squealed and tried to run back to the flames that had birthed it, but Malekith tugged back his hand, dragging the infernal creature across the road.

'Even one of insubstantial form such as you can suffer a multitude of torments,' Malekith told the creature. The daemon howled and squirmed as the dark net tightened and lifted into the air, guided by a gesture from the Witch King. Malekith closed his fingers a fraction and the daemon screamed as black thorns dug into its flaming body. 'All I have to do is close my fist.'

'All right!' wailed the daemon. 'What is the message? I shall take it to Anlec.'

'To the sorceress Morathi, delivered to her alone, my words exactly,' said Malekith.

'Of course,' replied the fire-daemon. 'Your exact words. I swear.'

'Tell Morathi that I have received her message,' said the Witch King. 'She is to send ten companies from the Anlec garrison to fortresses on the Naganar. She is to do nothing else without my command.'

'Don't trust her not to go charging off?' laughed the daemon.

Malekith tightened his fingers and the daemon let out a piercing screech.

'I did not ask for your opinion,' said the Witch King. 'Deliver my message and return to the realm that spawned you.'

'I will, I promise!'

Malekith released the spell and the daemon fluttered down to the road like a burning leaf. Grumbling and muttering, it shuffled back to the burning building and climbed within the flames. It turned to Malekith and made an offensive gesture of contempt, before melting into the fires with a cackle.

The Witch King stared into the flames long after the daemon disappeared, weighing up his options. Imrik was making a gamble, believing Malekith would not be willing to give up Tor Anroc for Tor Achare. For that to work, the usurper would have to convince Malekith that he was willing to use Tiranoc to attack Nagarythe directly. The Witch King doubted Imrik had the mettle for such an assault. The sensible thing to do would be to proceed with the capture of Tor Achare to call Imrik's bluff.

However, a shadow of doubt crossed Malekith's mind. To capture Tor Achare was a simple matter, to keep it was another. It was vulnerable to attack from Avelorn, Ellyrion, Cothique and Saphery, not to mention a possible landing on the coast. Perhaps Imrik really was willing to sacrifice Chrace in the knowledge that occupying the kingdom would weaken the defences of Nagarythe. He had allowed Cothique to fall beneath the blades of the Khainites, and that demonstrated a ruthless nature Malekith could admire.

He wracked his brain for a third alternative, a means by which he would force Imrik into battle. The Isle of the Flame sprang to the Witch King's mind, but was quickly dismissed; he had not nearly enough ships for an expedition across the Inner Sea. Lothern was a similarly valued prize, but was too far away from Nagarythe for an extended campaign without possession of Tiranoc.

Tor Achare or Tor Anroc? The question nagged at Malekith as he sent word for his commanders to attend him. Push on to the capital of Chrace and subjugate the east, risking an invasion of Nagarythe? Another factor entered his thoughts: Morathi. He could not wholly trust her to be obedient to his wishes. It would take some time to capture Tor Achare, leaving his mother to make her own schemes. She would take it as a personal affront that Imrik threatened Nagarythe and would respond. Such a reaction would be reckless, committing Malekith to a war both in Chrace and Tiranoc.

The runes of the Witch King's armour glowed white hot as his anger returned, stoked by Imrik's cowardly plans and his own uncertainty. Malekith's subordinates converged on the central square of the town as buildings burned and the fighting continued. They kept some distance away, eyes narrowed against the fiery glare of their master.

With a deep growl of annoyance, Malekith made his decision. He could not allow Imrik to recapture Tor Anroc, but there was no reason to take the circuitous route back through Nagarythe.

'Rally the army,' he told his commanders. 'We head south, to Ellyrion.'

THE STREETS OF Tor Anroc rang with the clash of battle. The smoke-choked tunnel-roads of the city were packed with spearmen of both sides, while about the palace the dragons of Caledor laid waste to the citadel's defenders with claw, fang and flame. The great doors of the palace were barred, but Tor Anroc's central spire had not been designed as a bastion of war. Druchii warriors on tiered balconies fired volleys from their repeater crossbows, while the Phoenix King's mages hurled lightning bolts and balls of fire through the high windows into the halls within. Stained glass was shattered, tapestries and curtains burned.

Black-clad soldiers dashed from one of the tunnels leading into the palace square, pursued by the silent Phoenix Guard, their halberd blades slick with blood. After them came Caledor's favoured White Lions, who broke towards the noble houses surrounding the plaza, which had been quickly fortified by druchii defenders. A swathe of spearmen and archers followed, pushing towards the palace doors.

Maedrethnir settled on the roof of a tower overlooking the west gardens, where bolt throwers unleashed hails of spears from behind ornamental hedges and beneath blossoming fruit trees. Claws scraping gouges across the stained stones, the dragon launched himself at a battery of the engines situated behind a white-painted wall. Sweeping overhead, he bathed the lawn with flame, setting fire to mountain roses and sunpetals, scorching grass that had once been carefully tended by a small army of gardeners.

Stowing his lance and unhooking his harness, Caledor dropped from the back of his mount, landing sure-footed beside a shallow pool that gently steamed, dead fish floating on the surface. A shadow swept over him as Dorien's dragon flew past, bathing the roof of the great hall with fire.

The Phoenix King drew his sword and ran up to the glass-panelled doors that stretched along one wall of a feasting hall. He dimly remembered eating in the long chamber as his armoured boot crashed against a lock and sent the door crashing from its hinges. Plunging inside, he found broken furniture barricading the doors into the rest of the palace. Lathrain cut through the upturned tables and chairs with ease, and within moments Caledor was through the door into the corridors of the palace proper.

He headed north towards the great staircase that led to the upper levels. The gallery was deserted, the sounds of battle outside muted as his boots rang on the marble floor. Busts of Tiranocii princes sat in alcoves on either side, each broken and defaced by the druchii.

As he reached the entrance chamber, he came across a group of druchii guarding the main doors. They turned at his approach, swords and shields raised. Lathrain blazed as Caledor cut them down, even as a deafening boom sounded from the doors. Twice the massive portal shook. On the third, the oak doors exploded inwards, filling the entrance hall with splinters that rattled from the Phoenix King's armour. In the smoke and dust, Caledor saw a slender figure approach.

It was Thyriol, his raised staff glowing with power. The mage's eyes were alight with golden energy, his skin writhed with magic. His pale hair surrounded his head like a nimbus, streaming with its own life.

'I thought it polite to knock,' said the Sapherian prince, smiling.

As the mage stepped over the threshold, more of Caledor's followers poured up the steps, their war cries echoing around the large hall. Caledor led them up the eastern staircase, heading towards the royal apartments where Bel Shanaar and his family had once lived.

Footfalls muffled by the thick carpets, the Phoenix King and his warriors moved from chamber to chamber, searching for foes. They found much evidence of the druchii's depravity: trophies taken from victims, tomes of evil prayers, fetishes of the cytharai adorned each apartment.

Coming to the chambers of the former Phoenix King, Caledor kicked open the door, sword in hand. The apartment was empty of the living, but two bodies lay sprawled near the window. The elves, one male and one female, were dressed in the finest robes and jewellery. Flopped over a low couch, their faces were painted pale, eyes surrounded by dark kohl, lips black. A broken crystal phial lay on the floor close by and Caledor could smell the distinctive scent of black lotus.

'Cowards,' the Phoenix King said with a sneer.

There was a fire in the grate, books and parchments used as fuel. Crossing the chamber, Caledor saw a pool of blood leaking from the door leading to the bedchambers. Steeling himself, he opened the door.

On a blood-soaked bed lay three children, the oldest no more than fifteen years. They too were dressed in rich robes and gems. On the floor around the bed were the bodies of five more elves, garbed as servants, their throats slit. Disgusted, Caledor turned away, slamming the door closed.

Feeling sickened, he tossed Lathrain onto a table and slumped into a padded chair. The city was his, the capture of the palace a certainty. He could let others do the fighting for a while. Exhaustion tugged at his mind and body. Closing his eyes, he drifted into a light sleep.

He awoke to find Dorien standing over him, a grim smile on his brother's lips.

'We are victorious,' said Dorien. 'The druchii are all slain.'

'Good,' said Caledor.

He hauled himself to his feet, retrieved his sword and strode to one of the windows opening onto the royal balcony. Dorien followed him out onto the white parapet, which offered a magnificent view of the city. From here, high in the palace, the breaches in the wall looked small. The bodies littering the square below merged together, druchii and loyalist heaped alongside each other in death. Fires burned across the city and a column of elves were streaming down the roads and out of the shattered gate.

'A sorry sight,' said Dorien. 'Bel Shanaar's legacy has been humbled.'

'Better Tor Anroc than Tor Caled,' said Caledor, leaning on the balustrade.

'True,' replied his brother. 'I am sure Bel Shanaar would understand. Let us hope that Tor Achare has not suffered a similar fate.'

The Phoenix King did not reply, his attention drawn to a shape against the clouds to the east. As it neared the city, it resolved itself into a pegasus and rider. It was Anamatheir, one of Thyriol's adepts. The mage flew straight for the palace.

'Such haste cannot bring good news,' said Dorien, following his brother's gaze.

DRIVEN ON BY their relentless master, the druchii surged south through Avelorn and into Ellyrion. Day and night the army marched; a winding serpent of black and gold in the sun; a ghostly line of torch and lamp by moonlight.

The army did not burn, did not slaughter. Ellyrion was not the Witch King's target, though he faced a difficult decision as he approached Eagle Pass. Two days east lay Tor Elyr. It was an easy target, with no wall or keep, no bastions or towers. For that reason, it was also a worthless target. The destruction of the city would take several days for no reward save the misery of Finudel and Athielle. Tor Elyr was not a capital like Anlec or Lothern; the Ellyrians spent most of the year with the herds, and even the nobility spent all but winter in camps spread across the plains. Though it would add only six days to the march, the city's destruction would be a distraction, one that might allow Imrik to escape.

Malekith's decision did not sit well with his commanders, who had spent a fruitless spring chasing Chracians and being ambushed. Their protests were not voiced, but the Witch King could tell by their sullen demeanours and pointed silence that they did not approve. He did not care one bit. Any that spoke against him, openly or in secret, would betray their lack of loyalty and would be dealt with accordingly.

The army turned west and marched for Eagle Pass and Tor Anroc.

THAT SPRING SIGNALLED the course of the next stage of the civil war. Malekith force-marched his army across Tiranoc, only to find the capital abandoned by Caledor and his troops, the ancient city deserted save for vermin. The Phoenix King's army travelled north on the Lothern fleet, raiding Galthyr in the midsummer before they moved eastwards and landed in Chrace to reinforce Tor Achare.

Rather than chase his elusive enemy, the Witch King set about rebuilding the fortifications of Tor Anroc. From here he could easily move north to counter any invasion of Nagarythe, whilst threatening Caledor and Ellyrion. Morathi joined her son as summer became autumn, riding south with a caravan of cultists and other strange elves. Malekith was not of a mood to welcome her in extravagant style and refused her thousands-strong entourage entrance to the city.

Furious, Morathi made her way to the palace of Bel Shanaar where Malekith had formed his new headquarters. The citadel was half in ruin; the disrepair of the druchii occupation and the damage caused by Caledor's forces had left whole wings as piles of rubble or burnt-out shells. Through broken windows the setting sun streamed jagged shadows across the floor of the throne room as Morathi entered.

'Why must my people live like cattle in the fields?' she demanded, striding across the cracked slabs.

'There is little enough room in the city for my army,' replied Malekith. He sat on the broken remnants of Bel Shanaar's throne, the wood blackened by his armour. 'If they do not find conditions to their liking, they can return to Nagarythe.'

'It is an irritation that I must come here at all,' said the sorceress. 'Why do you dally here, when you could be marching south to Caledor?'

'Do not think to advise me on strategy, mother,' said the Witch King, the visor of his helm glowing with pale flame.

'And yet I find I must do just that,' said Morathi. She sought amongst the broken and burned furniture for an intact seat and eventually found a bench. Righting it, she sat down, legs crossed, her eyes fixed on her son. 'Why do you waste your time in this hovel?'

'I cannot invade Caledor,' Malekith said, resting gauntleted hands on his knees. 'We have been fortunate that more dragons have not woken. Should Sulekh and her spawn enter the mountains, I am sure the other dragons would be roused by it. There is another reason. The moment I cross into Caledor, Imrik will surely set out from Tor Achare to take Anlec. Do you desire that I swap my father's palace for that of the Dragontamer?'

Morathi's scowl was deep but she had no quick answer to Malekith's taunting question. She tapped black-painted nails on the pale surface of the bench, small sparks of dark magic flickering between her fingertips to earth themselves in the wood.

'What is it that you intend?' she said eventually. 'Surely you do have a plan?'

'I have a strategy, but it will not be swift,' said the Witch King. 'While Imrik has his fleet, he can move much faster, along the coast or across the Inner Sea. If I march on Chrace through Ellyrion he will move back to Tiranoc. If I advance through Tiranoc and Nagarythe, he will come south via Avelorn into Ellyrion or Saphery.'

Malekith raised a finger and drew a circle of smoke and fire in the air.

'I could spend eternity chasing Imrik around Ulthuan and never catch him.'

'Then we are at an impasse,' said Morathi, speaking as if the words pained her to say. 'Imrik is willing to leave any kingdom to our mercy, and we can hold no place hostage to force him to battle. Yet he will not fight us directly, and so neither side can achieve a lasting victory.'

'It is a duel,' said Malekith. He laughed, a harsh metallic noise that rang coldly around the empty hall. 'Feint and thrust, parry and counter-attack. The first to flinch, to blink, to make a mistake will lose.'

'I hear you say a lot, but I am no wiser regarding your plans,' said Morathi. 'How will you break the deadlock?'

The Witch King stood and approached his mother, dimming the flames of his armour so that he could stand over her. He reached down a hand and graciously helped Morathi to her feet.

'What is this weakness?' she asked. 'What have you seen? One of the princes, perhaps? One who can be turned to our cause?'

'No, they are all loyal to Imrik,' said Malekith. 'Imrik is the weak link in the chain.'

'You are mistaken,' said Morathi. 'He is considered by some to almost be your equal. Nonsense, of course, but he is not without intelligence and skill.'

'I have no doubt that eventually I would prove myself superior, but the world might turn an age before that happens,' said Malekith. He walked towards the doors, Morathi hurrying to keep up with the long strides of her son. 'He is the finest of the princes, in battle and as a leader. That is why our enemies look to him, why they follow him. That shall be their undoing'

'Our foes have one weakness, one chink in their armour to exploit,' said Morathi, gaining understanding of Malekith's intent. 'They rely on Imrik. It is his stubbornness and his bravery that keeps them fighting.'

'Precisely,' said the Witch King. He stopped and picked up a lump of masonry that had fallen from the vaulted ceiling. It turned to powder as he closed his fist. 'Without him, resistance will crumble. Imrik knows that he cannot defeat me and seeks to destroy my army piece by piece. I know that I cannot destroy his army if I cannot catch it. So, I will march to and fro, keeping his eyes on me, testing the resolve of his allies. His determination to avoid open battle will be his weakness. I am not so proud that he must die by my hand. There are many ways to slay a foe.'

Morathi smiled as Malekith thrust open the doors to the hall and stepped into the antechamber. The Witch King's voice filled the room.

'Kill Imrik and we will win the war!'

—◆ NINETEEN ◆—

A Deadly Dance

As Caledor had predicted, the druchii lacked the strength for an all-out assault across Ulthuan. Refusing the pitched battle that Malekith needed for victory, the Phoenix King and the princes allied to him were able to temper the druchii offensives whilst minimising their losses. Sometimes Caledor took the initiative, probing at the passes between Nagarythe and Ellyrion, sending expeditions to make joint raids with the Anars across the border with Chrace. Always Caledor tried to goad his foe into a rash move, but the Witch King was too canny a general to split his forces or over extend his advances.

This duel of armies continued for several years as the druchii tested the resolve of the Phoenix King and his followers. Towns were burned and populaces driven out, but as soon as the army of Nagarythe was drawn elsewhere, Caledor would visit the devastated regions, showing unity with the people he ruled.

The Phoenix King remembered the question asked of him by Mianderin and knew that he had been afraid of fully becoming the ruler of Ulthuan. He had shunned his responsibilities, choosing to focus on the weaknesses of his allies rather than his own deficiencies as king.

Though still short of temper and curt of tongue, Caledor endeavoured not only to lead by example but to encourage those around him. In battle he was implacable, striking hard from the back of Maedrethnir, always at the forefront of the fighting. In the times when retreat was necessary he was there also, his presence bolstering the resolve of those whose homes would be burned, displaying his defiance for all to see.

As Caledor was the inspiration for Ulthuan's defenders, Malekith was

965

the driving force of the Naggarothi. None could match him in battle, for strength or sorcery. On occasion he would ride forth with Morathi and they would sweep all before them; Malekith with his disciplined veterans, Morathi with her wild cultists. The Witch King alone was worth ten companies of spears, and when he rode Sulekh to battle there was not an army to match him.

Four years after Malekith's return, the summer was long and dry. The army of Nagarythe was encamped on the banks of the River Ilientath that bordered Chrace and Avelorn, and looked poised to strike into Cothique once again. Tiranoc was under druchii control, its defences much improved under the regime of the Witch King. Caledor mustered his army in Saphery, hoping to lure the Witch King into the kingdom of the mages, while ready to sail across the Inner Sea to Avelorn to come at Malekith's advance from the rear. For the whole of the summer the two armies camped, separated by no more than ten days' marching; for the whole of the summer neither the Witch King nor the Phoenix King was willing to show his true intent.

As had been agreed in the pact between Caledor and his princes, Koradrel had left Chrace when the druchii had launched their latest attack. No prince was allowed to remain in an assaulted kingdom, lest they fall in battle or, worse, be taken prisoner and turned against their allies. Though many had never expected to become rulers, under Caledor the princes of Ulthuan had formed a close bond with each other, and the petty rivalries of the past had been forgotten, overshadowed by the common threat of the Naggarothi.

Caledor spent the hot afternoon relaxing alone in his pavilion, having invited his Chracian cousin to dine with him that evening. Riders and dragons patrolled the northern reaches of Saphery, ready to bring word of any movement from the enemy, and the Phoenix King was content that all was in order. Wary of complacency, he had spent the morning reviewing the dispositions of his forces, but could find no weakness that might be exploited by the Witch King.

The heat of the summer and a long, tense battle of wills had taken their toll on Caledor's stamina. Having removed his armour, he dozed in his throne clad only in a loose robe of white, embroidered with the phoenix flames of Asuryan. He half-heard the shouts of the captains as they drilled their companies on the parade ground at the centre of the camp. There were clatters of plates and goblets as his servants prepared the adjoining chamber for the evening's meal.

Still feeling drowsy, the Phoenix King roused himself at the arrival of Koradrel and a few of his Chracian princes. Servants came in with trays of wine jugs and goblets, though Caledor ordered water be brought for him, fearing his thirst would make him drink too much.

The group moved to the banquet, which consisted of the finest fare Saphery had to offer. Caledor took little part in the idle conversation, content to allow the Chracians to swap well-worn hunting stories and gossip from Tor Achare. More wine flowed and a heated debate erupted as the princes argued over who had slain the most foes.

The evening had begun to cool the air and Caledor suggested that the party move outside. He had eaten little, as usual, but his guests appeared uninterested in the suggestion. Their earlier animation had dwindled and the Phoenix King noticed that Koradrel and the others were sluggish, their speech slurred. Acharion, one of Koradrel's nephews, attempted a toast but stumbled as he stood, eventually collapsing to the ground, face red and swollen.

'Poison!' hissed Caledor, slapping the goblet from Koradrel's hand as he raised it to his lips.

The Chracian ruler reacted slowly, turning his head with a confused expression.

'You spilled my drink, cousin,' he said, brow knotted, hand still halfway to his lips.

'The wine, it has been tainted,' said Caledor.

The Phoenix King turned to the three servants who stood at the far end of the table.

'Fetch the healers,' he demanded. 'Who brought the wine?'

None of the servants answered. At first Caledor thought they had sneaked a sample of their master's cask, but the notion was dispelled as all three reached into their robes and drew forth curved daggers. The Phoenix King saw the red glint of Khainite runes and the sheen of poison on the blades as the three advanced, two to his left and one to his right.

'Assassins!' roared Caledor, snatching up a carving knife from the carcass of a fowl.

The one to the right came first, blade flashing for Caledor's throat. The Phoenix King ducked and lunged, his weapon passing harmlessly across the assassin's chest as the elf stepped back. Caledor dropped and rolled to his right to avoid an attack from his left, sending a side table laden with fruit flying as he surged to his feet, the carving knife ringing against a dagger aimed at his gut.

Heart hammering, Caledor leapt onto the table, scattering dishes and plates, shards of broken crockery punching into his feet through his thin boots. The assassins broke apart, quickly surrounding him. Turning left and then right quickly, trying to keep all three in view, Caledor side-stepped to the foot of the table, towards the doorway.

Koradrel rose groggily to his feet, swinging a fist at the nearest assassin. The punch connected with the elf's shoulder, sending him reeling into the side of the pavilion. Distracted, the attacker trying to circle behind Caledor was too slow as the Phoenix King whirled on his heel and drove a booted foot into the assassin's face. The assassin snarled, blood dripping to his lip, and leapt up to the table.

The carving knife met the assassin's chest, punching through ribs into lungs. The assassin's momentum carried him into Caledor, knife blade nicking the Phoenix King's chin as the dying elf's weight bore him down into the serving dishes with a crash.

Pain flared along Caledor's jaw. The wound had been minute, but the poison on the blade spread quickly, seizing the king's tongue and throat. He gasped for breath as he pushed the assassin's body from him and rolled off the table a moment before another dagger plunged into the wood.

There were shouts from the doorway as Caledor staggered towards it. The carving knife was still in the chest of the dead assassin and he was unarmed. He watched helplessly as the attacker floored by Koradrel jumped back to his feet and plunged his knife into the Chracian prince's eye. Koradrel made no sound as he toppled backwards, head bouncing off the edge of a chair.

The Phoenix King felt like he was drowning. With a flailing arm he managed to seize a lamp from its chain and hurl it at the closest assassin, sending burning oil splashing across his attacker's arm. His chest was growing tighter and tighter and his throat was raw. Dizziness made the pavilion spin and he was only dimly aware of shapes rushing past. They looked like beasts of the Annulii, white-furred with massive silver claws. Every breath rasping, Caledor managed to stagger out into the main part of the pavilion where more of the pale creatures were dashing in. He fell to his knees, choking, tasting blood.

Hands grabbed him and lifted him bodily into his throne. Another shape appeared and Caledor heard a calming whisper, though he did not comprehend the words being said. He felt hands on his face and warmth replace the chill in his limbs. There was a golden light. He reached a hand towards it and felt soft skin.

'Rest,' said the quiet voice.

Caledor dimly recognised it as belonging to Thyriol. He slipped into a sleep, dreaming of bright meadows, though the skies above were tainted by storm clouds.

THE ATTEMPT ON Caledor's life sent the army into turmoil. While the Phoenix King was caught up in a deep fever, Thyriol took charge, organising a thorough search of the camp. The bodies of three servants were found hidden in a copse of trees close to the river where the army took its water. Worse still, when the assassins were examined, they seemed identical to those elves that had been killed. Thyriol dispelled an enchantment that had been cast upon them and their faces reverted to their own, revealing the pale, harsh features of Naggarothi, cut with runes of disguise.

Distrust and paranoia ruled, verging on panic. All in the camp were potential suspects and new watch rotas were drawn up. Soldiers were swapped between companies and all were commanded to go about their duties in groups of at least ten. Thyriol enacted a curfew between dusk and dawn, save for the guard patrols which were reinforced to thirty-strong parties drawn from the White Lions and the Phoenix Guard, who were reckoned the most loyal warriors of all.

Scouts returned the next day, reporting that the druchii had broken camp. No doubt expecting the assassination to have succeeded, Malekith was making his move. With Caledor incapacitated and the army in dread, the princes quickly agreed that a retreat was the only option. Determined that no advantage would be gained by a hasty rout, the princes organised an orderly break of camp and a withdrawal southwards to the shore of the Inner Sea. Thyriol despatched messenger hawks to the Lothern fleet, asking for immediate help.

Attended to by healers and Thyriol, Caledor's fever broke on the sixth day, but he was still weak from the poison. He was coherent only in brief snatches, but was able to add his endorsement to the princes' plan of retreat. The Naggarothi came east through the ruin of Avelorn, marching hard for Saphery.

The princes had no choice but to split the army; to wait for enough ships to evacuate all of the king's warriors risked being caught by the swiftly advancing army of Malekith. Thyriol took Caledor and a quarter of the troops east, summoning the city of Saphethion to provide sanctuary. Half of the army continued south, before crossing the mountains into Yvresse. The remaining force, acting as a rearguard, awaited the arrival of a fleet from Lothern.

Too few ships arrived to take all of the troops that had been left behind. Tithrain, who had volunteered to remain as commander of the rearguard, ordered that lots be drawn to find out who could embark. To their credit, every elf in the small army refused, their commanders passing on the message that they would all live together or die together. Mindful of Caledor's decree that no prince be slain or captured, Tithrain was in two minds whether to remain with his troops or leave with the ships.

Tithrain elected to stay, determined that he would not abandon his people again. The army spent what time it had fortifying the shoreline. Repeater bolt throwers were brought from the ships to create defensive batteries, and every spare plank, mast and spar was used to construct ramparts along the grassy dunes that lined the beaches. Trenches were dug and filled with oil from the ships' lanterns and stores, ready to be set alight.

When the scouts reported that the druchii were only a day away, Tithrain ordered a feast dedicated to Asuryan. All of the food left with the army was cooked and prepared and the tables sagged with the weight of it, brought out under the sun for the banquet. The prince of Cothique laughed and joked, saying that he would rather such fine food was not left to the Naggarothi, whose palates could not appreciate its quality.

Beneath the jollity was a current of fear. Smiles were strained and the conversation purposefully light-hearted. Yet as the day wore into evening, there were many in the army who set down to compose their death poems, or sang mournful dirges, accompanied by sombre pipes and lyres.

As the soldiers settled down to sleep their final sleep, Tithrain walked about the camp. There was an air of calm, the army resigned to its fate. He walked to the shore and stared at the dark expanse of water, the stars in the clear skies reflected in the rippling waters.

He was about to leave and return to his pavilion when he saw a light far out from the shore. At first he took it to be a shooting star, as the light seemed to move across the sky. Then another appeared, and another, shining white and red and blue, and growing brighter as he watched.

Soon there was a swathe of bobbing stars, of every colour of the rainbow. Tithrain wondered if he was asleep and dreaming. A shout from the warships at anchor not far from the beach attracted his attention.

'Sail to the west!' The cry was taken up from every masthead.

In the moonlight and glow of their lamps, a flotilla of small vessels approached the shore. Fishing boats and traders, coastal barges and oar-propelled scows appeared out of the darkness. There were dozens of them, and even more lights were coming nearer.

Something blotted out the stars above and Tithrain caught the distinctive crack of a dragon's wing beats. The monster dropped down to the beach, the draught of its landing kicking up a storm of sand. Tithrain stared in surprise at the golden-armoured figure upon its back.

'Stop staring and rouse your troops,' the Phoenix King shouted down to the stunned prince. 'There is no time to waste.'

As the word spread through the camp and the small ships beached to take on as many warriors as they could, their crews explained that Caledor had been racing up and down the Sapherian coast, entreating every village and town to put any ship it could claim onto the water. The larger vessels towed small boats, some of them holding only half a dozen elves, and it was a slow process to bring them up to the beach, which was not large enough for the boats all to land at the same time.

Dawn was tinging the horizon and the blaring of the druchii horns could be heard. There were still nearly two thousand warriors to embark. Naedrein, a captain of Cothique who had survived the Khainite purges, approached Tithrain and Caledor.

'My company will man the bolt throwers,' he said. 'We will hold back the druchii and give the others time to get away.'

'You will not survive,' replied Caledor. 'Are you sure you wish to do this?'

'We are sworn to it,' said Naedrein. 'All of us lost loved ones to the druchii scum. We consider a score requires settling.'

'It is an honour to have such warriors fighting with me,' said Tithrain. 'Hold them for as long as you can, and watch for Malekith. He will make short work of the defences if you allow him to approach.'

'If we are lucky, we might even kill that accursed dragon of his,' said the captain.

He raised his sword in salute, the gesture returned by the prince and king, and marched away.

'Kill as many as you can!' Caledor called after him.

Naedrein and his warriors were as good as their word. While the sun was still rising, the sound of the bolt throwers was carried along the shore.

'Perhaps we should help them,' Maedrethnir said to Caledor. 'Those elves will not hold back Malekith for long.'

'If we fight the Witch King, we will die,' Caledor replied. 'That cannot happen.'

'You consider yourself too important to risk battle?' said the dragon, a note of disapproval in his deep voice.

'That is one reason,' said Caledor.

'And the other?' asked Maedrethnir.

'I have no desire to die,' the Phoenix King admitted. 'Not without good purpose.'

The dragon rumbled with laughter and took to the air, carrying Caledor up to where he could see the advancing druchii and his own followers. The last of the small vessels were sailing away and the remaining troops were being shuttled to the warships by boat. It was clear that the last of them would be aboard before the druchii reached the shore, but the Inner Sea was no barrier to the Witch King and his mount. There was still considerable harm that could be suffered.

Looking at the enemy army, the Phoenix King realised his concerns were misplaced. Malekith held back, the dark shape of his dragon looming behind the massed ranks of infantry that advanced on the beach, wary of the bolt throwers.

'I am not the only one that wishes to live,' Caledor remarked.

THE ASSASSINATION ATTEMPT and subsequent retreat shook the confidence of the princes and Caledor had to work hard to keep them sworn to his strategy. The loss of Koradrel was also a bitter, personal blow. So far the druchii had claimed Caledor's brother and two of his cousins, as well as a number of more distant family from Caledor and other kingdoms. A memorial was held for the dead Chracian prince, and his body interred in the mausoleum at Lothern until Chrace could again be secured.

There was no obvious successor to wield Achillar, and Caledor feared that infighting over the rulership of Chrace would bring more turmoil. It was with some surprise that he received a visit from the most powerful claimants, all three distant cousins of the Phoenix King. They presented Caledor with an agreement that they had all signed, along with many other nobles of Chrace, nominating Caledor to be bestowed the title of regent in the absence of any clear claimant. The Phoenix King duly accepted, and just as swiftly chose Thuriantis, the oldest cousin, to be his representative in Tor Achare.

'If only we could all be so pragmatic,' remarked Thyriol when Caledor related this meeting to the mage at the next gathering of the council.

THE ATTACK IN Saphery was only the first of several such incidents over the following years. Ambushes were laid to waylay Caledor as he travelled between the kingdoms, and there were more attempts to poison him. Despite every precaution the guile of the Khainite killers, and Malekith's determination to see the Phoenix King slain, meant that he was in constant danger. The cults, though much diminished in size and power, still had their agents and networks, and the only place Caledor felt truly safe was on the back of Maedrethnir or during his infrequent returns to Tor Caled.

Another leader might have been cowed by the incessant threat, growing paranoid. Caledor refused to let the enemy dictate his movements and actions, and though ever watchful for the next attempt on his life, the Phoenix King would not be driven into hiding nor give over his direct command of the army to another.

Not only physical attacks threatened Caledor. For a whole winter he was plagued with nightmares and headaches. Fearing sorcery, he summoned Thyriol, who confirmed that a curse had been laid upon the Phoenix King. The mage wove counter-enchantments and brought forth talismans from the vaults of Saphethion to protect Caledor against these hexes.

There were less subtle magical assaults as well. During a crossing from Ellyrion to Saphery, Caledor's ship was engulfed by a devastating storm. The sky boiled black and lightning rent the darkness. The Inner Sea was whipped to a frenzy, waves as tall as houses crashing over the prow of the hawkship as it was flung about by the howling winds. Dozens of crew were washed away, but the steersmen bound themselves to the wheel and the captain lashed himself beside them, guiding their hands.

For what seemed like several days the storm continued, cracking the mast and ripping up the decking. The sailors worked tirelessly, cutting away debris and patching the holes in the hull, barely keeping the ship seaworthy. Eventually the storm abated, its fury spent, and the ship limped to Lothern. The crew bailed day and night to keep the vessel from sinking, and even Caledor took his turns, using the fabled war-helm of the Phoenix King as a pail.

Each brush with death served only to increase Caledor's determination. It was noticed by others that when vexed he would rub the scar left on his chin by the assassin's blade, and they knew to offer no further argument against their king at that time. The hottest days of summer sometimes brought the king to the brink of fever, the effects of the poison never being wholly eliminated.

Despite these frequent distractions, Caledor was always attentive to every detail of the war. Every trick and ploy, every advance, feint and countermove by Malekith met with failure. Ten years and more since the Witch King's first attack, victory was no closer for either side.

Those years had seen the fortunes of both Malekith and Caledor wax and wane, but as the Phoenix King had foreseen, the longer the war dragged on, the more it turned against the druchii. The enemy lacked the numbers to hold any ground they took, and in Nagarythe the continuing shadow war of Alith Anar took a slow but steady toll. Tiranoc became the favoured battleground of both sides, a contested region that acted as a barrier between Nagarythe and Caledor. Slowly, with each cautious campaign, the Phoenix King's armies cut away at the druchii forces. Eagle Pass was retaken and the keeps built by the druchii were garrisoned by troops loyal to Caledor. Griffon Pass fell to the Phoenix King in the following year, and Unicorn Pass in the next.

Caledor almost went too far in his attempts to seize Dragon Pass; a swift and deadly counter-attack by Malekith almost caught the Phoenix King's army, which was pursued halfway across Avelorn before the Witch King relented, fearing he was being lured from Nagarythe as part of some grander scheme.

In the twenty-fifth year of his reign, after two and half decades of war, Caledor once more called his council to the Isle of the Flame. The princes were filled with apprehension as the Phoenix King entered; it had been several years since he had brought them all to this place.

'We are winning the war,' the Phoenix King declared as he sat on his throne, though his expression was grim rather than jubilant. The council members exchanged confused glances, unsure what this meant. 'Our armies are blooded and our tactics well tested. The druchii are weary, labouring out of fear of their rulers. Now we strike.'

'For Anlec?' asked Dorien, making no attempt to hide his joy.

'For Anlec,' Caledor replied.

CALEDOR'S PLAN WAS a simple one, which he considered the best kind. Late in the spring, he launched another attack into Tiranoc, reclaiming Tor Anroc from the druchii. On this occasion he did not stay in the city, but drove northwards, driving the druchii before him. By midsummer he came to the Naganar, the fast-flowing river that separated Tiranoc from Nagarythe. Here he made a great show of camping his army, marching east and west as if looking for a suitable crossing. On the opposite bank, the Naggarothi shadowed his movements, ready to contest any crossing he might make.

The manoeuvres were a subterfuge. While the druchii had retreated, Caledor despatched parts of his army eastwards, replacing them in camp with fresh recruits, and even elves too young or old to fight dressed in fake armour and given hastily-made spears. Dorien took command of this force – from any distance two gold-clad riders on red dragons were indistinguishable – and Caledor flew across the mountains in secret. It was a tremendous gamble, the only one Caledor had ever taken. If Malekith had any hint of the deception, he would be able to sweep across the Naganar and destroy the false army, and continue south into Caledor.

The true army mustered in northern Ellyrion, every soldier and knight from each of the allied kingdoms marching and sailing to the border with Avelorn. Beneath their banners they gathered. Spearmen and archers, Silver Helm knights alongside reavers from Ellyrion, mages and princes; the Phoenix Guard of Asuryan came from the Isle of the Flame and the White Lions led the Chracian host. The sight of the gathered army filled Caledor with trepidation. All of his strength was brought here, enough in his reckoning to take the Witch King unawares and smash his army, but if not the last of Ulthuan's strength would be spent.

If he was victorious, the road to Anlec would be open. If he had judged wrongly, there would be no force in Ulthuan that could stop the Witch King. For the first time since walking into the sacred flames, the Phoenix King said a prayer to Asuryan. When he was finished, he gave the signal for the army to march, heading north to Phoenix Pass. He hoped the name was a good omen.

For good or bad, this would be the last battle of the war.

'YOU WOULD LEAVE Anlec defenceless.' Morathi's shrill protest jarred Malekith's nerves. 'An army camps on our border and you would have our troops simply leave them.'

'It is a ruse,' said Malekith.

He waved a hand and a glimmering image of northern Ulthuan appeared in the air in front of his huge throne. It was more than a map, it was a picture of the region, every river glittering as a thin line, every road and field, farmhouse and ditch recreated in minute detail.

'If Imrik intended to attack, he would not have paused at the Naganar, but would have pressed straight across while the defences were weakest,' the Witch King explained.

'Why are you so sure that he attacks from the east?' said Morathi, poking a finger through the hovering apparition of Nagarythe. 'Why Phoenix Pass?'

'Your memory is short, mother,' Malekith replied calmly. 'Do you not recall, when I retook Anlec?'

Morathi's only reply was a spat curse.

'You were wrong then, and I was victorious,' said Malekith, enjoying his mother's indignant expression. His humour faded as he considered the impudence of Imrik. 'The upstart thinks he can trick me with the strategy I devised? No, that will not happen. I will remind him of his folly as he begs for my forgiveness.'

'So what do you plan to do?' Morathi glared at the gently drifting image. 'Call the army back to Anlec. It is the best course of action.'

'Again, that served you so well,' laughed Malekith.

'The treacherous Anars were the only reason you took Anlec from me,' Morathi snapped.

'Who can say that they will not do the same again?' said the Witch King. His voice turned harsh. 'Is not my crown upon the head of Alith Anar, stolen from this palace while you looked on? Your cultists are worthless as warriors, and worth even less as guards.'

Morathi stalked away, hair and gown billowing like a storm cloud.

'Here,' Malekith whispered to himself, pointing a burning finger at a stretch of barren land between Anlec and Phoenix Pass. It was perfect. Marshes bounded it to the north, while any army trying to escape south would come against the cold waters of the Lianarrin River. 'Here is where I will wait for you, Imrik. At Maledor.'

—◄ TWENTY ►—

A Fateful Clash

IT WAS DORIEN that voiced the concern in the minds of all the princes. They were gathered outside Caledor's pavilion, dressed in full armour, cloaks swirling in the strengthening breeze.

'Can we win?' asked the Caledorian prince. It was Dorien who had first seen the dark blot on the horizon from the back of his dragon and reported the druchii army waiting to the west. 'For years we have avoided this clash, by your desire and command.'

'We must win,' replied Caledor. 'If not now, then never. To retreat would be to admit defeat and destroy the morale of the army.'

That army was gathering on the rugged heathland of Maledor. Every kingdom loyal to Caledor was represented. Spearmen and archers from every realm gathered beneath standards displaying the colours and runes of their princes. Amongst them were the serried companies of the Lothern Sea Guard, decked in armour that shimmered like fish scales, armed with both spear and bow, their robes and banners of sea green and turquoise picking them out amongst the expanse of white-clad soldiers.

Knights of Caledor and Eataine formed up in long squadrons, their lances decorated with bright pennants, their silver helms adorned with fabulous crests of feathers. Batteries of bolt throwers were erected, protecting the flanks of the mustering host.

Overhead flew the pegasi of Saphery, Thyriol's mages weaving their protective enchantments over the army with flashing staves and gleaming wands. There were more of their order amongst the regiments of the kingdom, wielding swords of flame, shielding the troops with golden arcs of power.

The centre of the line was held by the Chracians. Flanked by companies of spear and bow, the White Lions, Caledor's chosen warriors, waited with long-hafted axes. To their left stood the silent ranks of the Phoenix Guard, their cloaks shimmering in the sunlight, halberd heads gleaming.

To the south, the left end of the line where the ground heaped up over bush-covered hummocks, the massed reaver knights of Ellyrion waited for the return of Finudel and Athielle. Their horsehair plumes tossed in the wind, which carried their laughter and conversation to the rest of the army.

Last were the dragons. Eight had survived the long war. Surrounded by a smog of fumes, they rumbled and growled to each other in their own language, Maedrethnir standing proud at their centre with wings outstretched.

'We can win,' Caledor said again. 'Be bold and stay strong.'

The battle-plan was agreed and the princes returned to their troops. The Caledorians mounted their dragons and took to the air while Athielle and Finudel joined their reavers. Tithrain rode to the head of Cothique's small company of knights and Carvalon mounted a griffon that had been nurtured by the prince since it first hatched. Thyriol's pegasus climbed towards the clouds as the mage-prince flew to his acolytes.

Trumpets were raised and their clear notes rang out over the plain. The shouts of the captains echoed the command and as one the host of Caledor advanced. To the west, a spreading darkness approached.

As the dragons of Caledor soared into the sky, Sulekh let out a deafening screech, neck arched. Her three children roared in reply, the terrifying sound rolling over the advancing army of Nagarythe.

At the forefront of the army were Hellebron and her Khainites, supported by her father Prince Alandrian with a force of knights from Athel Toralien. The two were in stark contrast; the near-naked Brides of Khaine howling and wailing, eyes wide and wild from frenzy-inducing drugs, hair spiked with the gore of sacrifices, bared flesh pale in the sunlight beneath an icon of Khaine made from bone and draped with entrails; the knights armoured from head to toe in plate and mail, their black steeds protected by heavy caparisons of golden scale, the banner of Athel Toralien proudly flying above.

To either side stretched the legions of Nagarythe, rank after rank of spears and repeater crossbows. Standards of red, black and purple fluttered in the wind, and the sun shone from twenty thousand barbed spearpoints. Runes of Ereth Khial and Atharti, Khaine and Anath Raema adorned their shields. Drums of elfskin sounded the beat of the march and gilded bone horns blared the call to war.

The air above the army writhed with dark energy. Like a black pall, daemonic forces churned, held in check by the incantations of Morathi's acolytes. Malekith could see them more clearly with the aid of his circlet;

horned and fanged monstrosities that bayed and growled as they clawed at the sky seeking entry into the mortal world.

The beastmasters had brought forth every creature of the mountains: hydras and manticores, hippogryphs and chimeras. Packs of savage hounds with spiked collars and iron-tipped fangs and claws howled and strained at their iron leashes. Whips cracked and goads were thrust into scaled hides to propel the beasts towards the enemy, flames and smoke wreathing their advance. The winged monsters took to the air in a mass of feathers and fur and leathery wings.

Just in front of the Witch King advanced the pride of Malekith, his knights of Anlec. Across Elthin Arvan they had crushed armies of orcs and goblins, slaughtered hosts of forest beasts; across Ulthuan their charges had scattered the elves of the Phoenix King and cut them down as they fled. Their lances gleamed with magical power, fashioned by Hotek and his smith-priests. The runes on their shields and armour flared with power as the winds of magic surged, the mystical energy that swept across Ulthuan whipped into the storm by the coming battle.

Malekith could feel the magic around him. Fire and blood drew it, gold and silver harnessed it, fear and hope swelled it, life and death shaped it. Through the circlet he experienced the constant flow, through the air and the ground, in every arrowhead and heart.

When the upstarts were crushed, there would be no power in the world greater than the Witch King. The conquests of the past would pale in comparison to the empire he would build. He had brought the elven people to the brink of destruction, but it was from the ashes of that war that they would arise stronger than ever. When he was Phoenix King, he would lead his people to even greater heights of glory and power.

From his throne on Sulekh's back, Malekith turned to his mother, who was sat to his right astride a newly tamed raven-hued pegasus.

'At last I shall have my battle,' the Witch King said. 'Imrik has misjudged a step and it is time to end this interminable war.'

'You shall see him humbled,' replied Morathi. 'The usurper will bend his knee as you were forced to bow before Bel Shanaar. He will weep at your hands, begging forgiveness for taking your throne. The blades and acids of the Khainites will eke out every drop of agony from his wretched body. My sorcery will visit upon him every nightmare ever conceived.'

Malekith regarded his mother with burning eyes, bemused by her vehemence and melodrama. He no longer dreamed of a broken Imrik pleading for his life; his visions were filled with the pure joy of standing over the usurper's corpse. For twelve years it had been only a dream. For twelve years he had suffered humiliation and torment, the thought of which hurt as much as the pain of his still-burning flesh.

'I would rather he just died,' said the Witch King. He let out a moan of pleasure at the thought. 'The sooner, the better.'

He wrenched on Sulekh's chains with unnatural strength, signalling her to launch into the air. The other black dragons followed as Malekith steered his mount over his army. Holding Sulekh's reins in his shield hand, the Witch King drew Avanuir. The magical blade burst into blue flame and Malekith's voice roared out his simple command.

'Attack! Kill Imrik!'

GRIPPING SHIELD AND spear tightly, Carathril advanced at the head of a company of spearmen from Eataine. His skin felt oily and slick from dark magic and he nervously eyed the convulsing cloud of darkness gathering over the moor. There were whispers on the edge of hearing, cruel and seductive, beguiling and threatening. He drove them from his thoughts, focussing on the enemy ahead.

Arrows and bolts flew in clouds from both armies. The cries of the dying and the wounded were already loud. A hail of spear-like shafts slammed into the company of elves to Carathril's right, ripping a hole through their ranks. Bolts clattered from shield and scale coats as the missiles of the druchii fell into the advancing elves of the Phoenix King.

There was little Carathril could do but trust in fate and believe that Morai-heg was not so cruel of humour that she had carried him through this war so far only to have him spitted on a bolt or punctured by quarrels.

A hideous beast, an unholy hybrid of lizard and dog and lion, the size of a horse, padded across the spongy ground towards the Eataine company. A thick miasma surrounded the creature, pale yellow in colour, its sulphurous stench carrying to Carathril. Behind, beastmasters goaded it forwards with long-tined tridents and lashes barbed with cruel hooks, the faces of the druchii swathed with scarves.

'Basilisk!' Carathril shouted in warning.

As the beast approached, Carathril hoped that one of the bolt thrower crews would sight the beast and slay it, but as the basilisk broke into a run, baring fangs like black knives, he knew the hope was empty.

The company halted to receive the monster's charge, shields raised and spears lowered. Carathril swallowed down his fear, his mouth dry.

The basilisk barrelled full-pelt into the spear company, roaring and slashing. Shields were rent by its claws and scales of armour shredded by its teeth. Spears snapped upon its thick hide as the elves struck back, though not all were turned aside and bloody wounds were opened in the basilisk's scaled flanks.

Where its blood spilled forth, the filthy fog spilled also. Its touch was corrosive, flaking metal and melting skin. The elves that were unfortunate enough to breathe in the toxic mist fell back with hoarse screams, dropping their spears to claw at burning throats. The merest touch of the deadly fume petrified flesh, turning eyes and hands into a rough, grey, stone-like substance.

Recovering from the initial shock of the basilisk's attack, the spearmen closed ranks, using their shields to waft away the poisonous fog. Eyes closed, they thrust blindly at the monster, trusting to instinct and elven senses to guide their blows.

More fell to its teeth and claws, but eventually the holes and cuts upon the basilisk's hide were too much. Ichor and blood oozed from dozens of wounds as it collapsed, sending up more of the foul vapour. The creature's handlers fled as the spearmen parted around the rapidly rotting body of the basilisk.

Carathril gasped, drawing in a ragged breath. Through stinging eyes he saw the druchii spearmen advancing to meet the line. The bitter tang of the basilisk clung to Carathril's robes and his face itched from the passing of its fume.

These distractions fell away as he looked upon the sneering, shouting faces of the enemy. He thought of Prince Aeltherin burning himself alive. He remembered the hard days of riding back and forth for Bel Shanaar. He recalled the bloody mess of Ealith and the seductive wiles of Drutheira. The carnage of the Shrine of Asuryan haunted him still. Twenty-six years of war crowded into his mind; the siege of Lothern and Aerenis's death by his hand foremost amongst the many dreadful things he had witnessed and done.

It was not in his nature to hate, but for that moment he was filled with loathing for the elves that came towards him. It did not matter if they were as scared as he was. It was of no consequence that many would have families. Some he might even have fought alongside before Malekith's treachery. All such considerations were irrelevant. They were the druchii, the dark elves, and they would kill or enslave all of elfkind if they were victorious.

'For Caledor!' Carathril shouted, raising his spear, the call echoed by those around him. Though no command was given, the company broke into a run, heading straight for the oncoming druchii. Carathril relaxed, knowing that if he died he would know peace. The enemy surged forwards in response and Carathril shouted again.

'For Ulthuan!'

THE FIRST CLASH of the armies crashed across the moor. Flying high above the battle, Thyriol watched the lines of black and white undulating as first one side and then the other pressed forwards and fell back. The Witch King's attack was focussed on destroying Caledor, his army driving forwards on a narrow front. The Phoenix King had predicted this and laid his plans accordingly. Using himself as bait, Caledor had placed himself in the centre of the army, a lodestone for the fury of the druchii.

The White Lions and Phoenix Guard bore the brunt of the first assault, while archers poured arrows into the advancing druchii knights. The phalanx of Caledor's spears pushed forwards as far as possible, creating a funnel effect that further encouraged the enemy to attack towards the Phoenix

King's best warriors. Dragons and griffons and manticores whirled about the skies, forced high by the massed bolt throwers on both sides, the riders of each army duelling for dominion of the air.

While spear and sword, axe and lance contested the battle on the ground, a far more esoteric but no less deadly fight was being waged in the air. The winds of magic churned, ripped this way and that as Morathi's sorcerers and Thyriol's mages struggled with each other. The daemonic cloud that roiled over the battlefield filled the Sapherian prince's mind, sitting heavy in his thoughts like a coagulated mass of darkness.

Lightning split the air from staff tips and balls of fire screamed across the clouds. Hails of glittering crystal spears sliced through the druchii while whole companies of Caledor's soldiers were swallowed by great maws that opened in the ground beneath them.

The air was thick with spell and counterspell, forming a glittering land-scape no less real than the moorland below. Inhuman things screeched as they erupted from the Realm of Chaos, plucking knights from their saddles and devouring horses. Fire-bodied eagles soared over the heads of the Phoe-nix King's soldiers, their flaming wings incinerating the clouds of bolts and arrows launched at them by the enemy. Cascades of white energy fell from Thyriol's sword as his pegasus swept low, the magical sparks setting fire to a battery of bolt throwers as the mage-prince passed over them.

A sudden pressure, a build-up of dark magic, drew his attention to the north. He felt a wave of daemonic energy tearing at the fabric of reality. The ground erupted and an immense serpent with a fanged maw and dozens of writhing tongues burst up beneath a regiment of archers. Lashing tentacles ensnared the helpless warriors, tossing their bodies into the air and dragging them into the creature's slavering mouth.

With a word to his mount, Thyriol turned towards the daemonic appari-tion, words of banishment in his mind. As the creature devoured more elves, the mage dived down towards it, chanting the incantation of unbinding. A golden glow enveloped the summoned monster, turning pustule-pocked flesh to shimmering dust. The daemon thrashed, letting out an unearthly wail, appendages rippling, its clustered black eyes glaring at Thyriol. Channelling the winds of magic through his staff, the mage hurled a bolt of white into the creature's maw, setting a white flame burning within it. Its scream still linger-ing on the wind, the daemon was consumed, burning away to nothing.

Occupied by his banishment of the daemon, Thyriol had not noticed a black-winged shape approaching closer, a trail of black flames left in its wake. Too late he felt the sorceress's presence and looked up. He saw a hate-filled face wreathed with a halo of black hair, and felt the rush of dark magic from the skull-tipped staff in her hands.

He threw up a silver shield to counter the spell, but the wave of dark magic blasted it aside, turning it to falling magical splinters. Thyriol braced himself, his amulets glowing protectively, but the next spell was not directed at him.

His pegasus gave a choked cough and spasmed, blood pouring from thousands of small cuts that appeared in its flesh. Feathers fluttered from its wings as it fell. The mage could feel bones breaking in the body of the pegasus, as if a giant hand was crushing it. With a last whinny of terror, the pegasus died and Thyriol plummeted towards the ground.

MORATHI LAUGHED AT the spectacle of the falling mage. His robe fluttered and his staff fell from his grasp as he frantically waved his arms, perhaps trying to imitate a bird. Her laughter died away as a pair of insubstantial silver wings shimmered from the mage's shoulders, bearing him lightly to the ground. As the sorceress circled around for another attack, the mage brushed down his robes and held out a hand, his staff flying into his grasp from where it had fallen.

Sword in one hand, skull-headed staff in the other, Morathi plunged towards the impudent mage. As she came closer she recognised Saphery's ruler and she remembered bitterly the mage's role in the insults and woes that had been heaped upon her. He had spoken at the First Council, and it had been his wards that had imprisoned her within Bel Shanaar's palace.

Thyriol turned, sensing her approach. A shaft of blue energy sprang from his eyes. Morathi countered the spell with a snarled incantation, a shadow uncoiling from the tip of her staff to meet the column of light. The two spells clashed with an explosion of energy that sent Morathi reeling against her mount and hurled the mage to his back.

Pulling herself upright as her pegasus landed, Morathi pointed her sword at the supine spellcaster. Energy flickered around her blade, coalescing into an icy spike that flew towards the mage's chest, splitting into thousands of shards. The mage lifted his staff at the last moment, a disc of gold appearing in front of him. The ice storm deflected from the magical barrier, turning to a cloud of mist.

Pushing himself to his feet, the Sapherian lifted an open hand towards Morathi. Whispering a dispel, she watched as a dove appeared in the mage's palm. It took off and circled around the mage's head, cooing gently. Morathi laughed again. It was a cheap cantrip used for the entertainment of children, nothing more. She summoned more dark magic, her mind reaching up to the daemonic cloud to tap into the raw power of Chaos.

As she prepared to unleash her next assault, the dove began to circle faster, the arc of its flight growing wider and wider. Its eyes glittered like crystal, mesmerising as it dipped and rose, weaving a complex series of curves and angles around the mage.

Morathi snapped away her gaze, just in time to rein in the dark power that was building inside her. Her skin crawled for a moment with excess magic, her teeth buzzing and her nerves dancing. The dove grew in size, its feathers changing to every colour of the rainbow, wings becoming iridescent trails of flame.

The phoenix hurtled towards Morathi, its keening cry ringing in her ears, driving into the core of her mind. She clenched her jaw and tightened the grip on her staff as the dark magic thrashed inside her, trying to escape. The phoenix-spell struck her full force, setting fire to her hair and throwing her from the back of her mount.

Crashing to the ground, Morathi gasped for air, tendrils of black energy escaping her throat. She gritted her teeth and surged to her feet, sword thrusting towards the mage. Crescent blades of black iron appeared in the air, spinning towards the Sapherian. The mage again summoned his golden shield, but Morathi had expected as much. The scything blades became needle-fine darts, each a tiny sliver of pure magic. They punched into the mage's shield. Most were stopped, but some smashed through, reducing the shield to golden shards before engulfing the mage. The Sapherian's robes were reduced to tatters in a moment and his flesh was a mass of grazes and scratches.

Extending more power, Morathi followed the path of the spell with a spat curse, the dark magic winding along the course followed by the bolt, seeping into the open wounds in the mage's flesh. Every tiny cut began to suppurate, blistering outwards with small explosions of pus and blood. The mage cried out in pain, falling to his knees. Morathi stalked closer, pouring more and more magic into the hex, driving the infection deeper and deeper into the Sapherian.

With a defiant shout, the mage flung out his arms. White fire erupted from within his skin, burning away the magical plague. He staggered to his feet as the flames continued to rage, his eyes blinding orbs, hair dancing wildly in the mystical fire. With visible effort, the Sapherian brought his hands together, still clutching his staff. The flames burst along his arms and out of the staff, engulfing Morathi.

Out of desperation, the sorceress hurled herself to the ground, clutching her arms to her chest, turning her skin to stone. The flames washed over her, touching but not burning. They raged for a long time, while she was cocooned within her own flesh. Morathi fought back the dark magic that flowed through her blood vessels and caused her heart to pound.

Eventually the fires dissipated. Morathi reversed her spell, but the transformation was slow. Like a waking statue, her limbs turned back to flesh and she straightened. Dust flaked away from her face as she opened her eyes.

The mage had fled, borne aloft on the magical wings that had saved him from his fall. For a moment she considered chasing after him, but a screeching cry from above drew her eye.

Out of the clouds dropped a griffon, claws extended, red and black wings held back as it stooped. On its back rode a prince clad in golden mail and blue robes, a sword of sapphire in his fist. His long shield bore the symbol of Yvresse, against a background of midnight stars.

* * *

MALEKITH TOO NOTICED Carvalon's attack. He had been watching the progress of the battle with some satisfaction. His knights had broken through to Caledor's war engines and were wreaking havoc amongst the bolt thrower crews. The line of the Phoenix King's spears had been halted and was slowly being pushed back. Everywhere he looked, Malekith saw a constricting ring of black and silver closing in on Caledor.

Sulekh launched towards the prince of Yvresse as Carvalon dived towards Morathi. The sorceress flung an arm towards the griffon, black lightning springing from her fingertips. Fur and feathers burned and the monster pulled out of its dive, swerving to avoid the crackling energy.

The black dragon struck like a thunderbolt, claws ripping through the griffon's smouldering wings. Malekith saw the prince's eyes widen with shock within his visor as the Witch King crashed Avanuir down on Carvalon's shield, splitting it in two.

The griffon was cawing and screeching in agony as Sulekh tore bloody chunks of flesh free with her massive jaws, parting muscle and sinew, snapping bone. Carvalon leapt from the dying beast's back, landing on Sulekh's shoulder. Surprised, Malekith reacted slowly as the Yvressian prince slashed his sapphire-bladed sword across the Witch King's chest.

Sparks flew from the wound and molten metal trickled like blood from the gash in Malekith's breastplate. He looked down, astounded, and then felt the pain.

Snatching hold of one of Sulekh's spines, Carvalon raised his sword for another blow.

Enraged, the Witch King struck, thrusting Avanuir into the prince's chest. Enchanted armour buckled and then split as the blade erupted from the prince's back, flickering blue flame igniting Carvalon's robes and hair. Malekith reached out and grabbed hold of the prince as he was about to topple. Burning fingers seared through gilded pauldrons and sank into flesh.

With a snarl, Malekith brought up Avanuir, shearing through spine and ribs, parting Carvalon like a roast hog. Blood splashed onto the Witch King and hissed into nothingness on his hot armour. Feeling nothing but contempt, Malekith let go of the prince's split body and brought down Avanuir, striking off the head as the corpse fell from Sulekh.

Sheathing his sword, Malekith dabbed a hand to the wound in his chest. The metal that had bubbled free was already cooling, forming a weld across the breach in his armour. The pain subsided, but it was a salutary lesson: he was not immortal.

Looking down at the unfolding battle, the Witch King saw a swathe of pale skin and red driving through the line of Imrik's army, like a spear aimed directly for the usurper.

Malekith smiled. Perhaps the Khainites would slay Imrik for him.

* * *

DUCKING BENEATH AN axe blade, Hellebron slashed the sword in her right hand through the white pelt cloak of the Chracian in front of her, slicing off his arm, while plunging the blade in her left into his eye. Kicking aside the falling body, she leapt over a swinging axe, burying both blades through the helmet of the elf wielding it.

Around her, the Brides of Khaine shrieked praises to the Bloody-Handed God as they battled the Chracian bodyguards. They ducked and dodged the slashing axe heads of their foes, poisoned blades licking out like serpent's tongues, finding exposed flesh. To Hellebron's right, a Bride was cleaved from shoulder to gut, spattering the Khainite priestess with blood. Hellebron licked her lips, savouring the taste.

The Chracian stepped over the mangled corpse and swung his axe at Hellebron's neck. She dropped to all fours, legs split, the blade whistling over her head. In an instant she sprang up again, slashing both blades across the Chracian's throat. He fell back, arterial blood coating Hellebron like the blessing of Khaine Himself. Heart pumping, she vaulted over the crumpling corpse, plunging a sword into the back of another warrior.

Over the melee, Hellebron could see the towering form of the usurper king's dragon, the accursed Caledorian on its back. She swayed aside from another axe, eyes fixed on Imrik, and cut off the hands that wielded it. Without a pause, she swept a blade across the warrior's face. The carnage thrilled her, fuelling her body, sharpening her mind. Blood racing, the sacred brew of Khaine flowing through her, Hellebron stalked on. Through the rushing of blood and the pounding of her heart, the ring of metal engulfed Hellebron, a symphony of destruction that gave voice to Khaine's gift.

Senses heightened to a preternatural degree by the narcotic leaves she had ingested, Khaine's Chosen One eluded every blow aimed towards her while her blades were a constant flicker of silver leaving dead and dismembered foes. She fought without thought, reacting to the slightest movement, her swords moving as if they had a life of their own.

A new sound pierced the haze of death: the clear note of a trumpet. The ground was trembling underfoot. Despatching another Chracian with a backhanded slash, Hellebron turned towards the sound. Over the heads of her Brides, she saw a wall of white horses and silver-clad riders bearing down.

IN A WAVE of streaming horsehair plumes and green pennants, the Ellyrians crashed into the Khainites with lowered spears. In Finudel's hand blazed the ancient spear Mirialith. Dozens fell to the charge, caught on spearpoints and crushed beneath galloping hooves. Finudel struck left and right as his horse surged through the press of foes, every thrust slaying a Khainite.

Burning with anger at memories of the atrocities he had seen in Cothique, the Ellyrian prince fell upon the Khainites with merciless ferocity. Beside him, Athielle carved a path through the enemy with her silver sword, her long hair flowing like a cloak behind her.

The prince and princess drove into the heart of the Khainites, pushing towards the grisly standard, their reavers following behind. Finudel's eyes met those of a feral witch, her face caked in blood, hair outlandishly spiked and braided. The prince lowered Mirialith towards her in challenge and urged his horse on.

As the impetus of the Ellyrians' charge diminished, the Khainites swarmed around them. Finudel lost sight of the Khainite leader for a moment as he was surrounded by a press of shrieking faces and poisoned blades. He slashed with his magical spear, hurling back the wild attackers.

The Khainite witch reappeared to his left, somersaulting onto the back of a horse, her blades leaving a red gash across the rider's chest. With unbelievable dexterity and balance she sprang from the horse to another, slashing the head from another knight before jumping again, leaping from one steed to the next, leaving a trail of falling bodies behind.

In the melee, Finudel and Athielle became separated. He glanced over his shoulder, relieved to see his sister still fighting, her sword rising and falling in shining crescents as she cut her way through the Khainites. Kicking a booted foot into the face of a Khainite that leapt towards him, he directed his steed at the priestess who was slaying so many of his warriors.

She seemed possessed, paying no heed to the many marks and cuts upon her body. Standing in a circle of bodies, the Khainite leader twirled and leapt, slashing the legs from horses and cutting down their riders. She fought with a strangely wild grace, ever moving, each motion bringing a perfect moment of death.

The Khainite was oblivious to Finudel as he broke free from the press and lowered his spear. He whispered a command to his horse, which broke into a gallop, and aimed the point of Mirialith at her naked back.

A sudden chill struck the prince as a shadow swallowed him. He smelled a dreadful stench and his horse baulked, rearing up in terror. He turned just as a monstrous black claw closed around his body.

THE SOUNDS OF shrieking metal and the screams of the dying Ellyrian prince were drowned out by Sulekh's roar. Malekith swept down his sword, a blaze of fire disgorged from the blade to engulf the reaver knights. Sulekh's tail toppled a score of riders, crushing bodies, spearing them on its bony spines. A cloud of noxious gas bubbled from her mouth, choking and corroding, blinding and suffocating.

The knights around the Witch King fled in terror, their panicked shouts sounding muffled to his ravaged ears. He threw more magical fire after them, incinerating steeds and boiling the riders in their armour.

As Sulekh lunged after the fleeing Ellyrians, Malekith noticed a group of riders several hundred strong had not turned to run. At their head was a golden-haired princess, her face a mask of hatred. She lifted her sword and signalled the charge.

Yanking on the reins, the Witch King guided Sulekh towards the approaching reavers. Spears shattered on scale as the knights charged home. Sulekh swiped with her front claws, beheading and disembowelling dozens of Ellyrians. Their princess avoided a slashing claw, her blade carving a bloody furrow along Sulekh's foreleg as she rode under the dragon's body.

Malekith twisted, looking for Athielle to emerge from beneath the dragon's bulk. Sulekh hissed with pain and staggered to the right, revealing the princess with bloodied sword, gore spilling from a wound in the black dragon's underside.

Sulekh's tail lashed, smashing into Athielle's horse, turning it to a pulp of blood and broken bones. The princess was flung through the air and landed heavily, left leg twisting beneath her. Malekith channelled dark magic, ready to unleash another blaze of fire to finish off the Ellyrian. A movement caught his attention, a swiftly approaching blot against the clouds. He looked up to see a massive red dragon plunging towards him, a golden-armoured figure on its back.

'Finally,' the Witch King said, all thoughts of Athielle forgotten. He raised his voice in challenge, his words a metallic roar that carried over the din of battle. 'Come to me, Imrik! Come to me!'

THE COMPANIES OF the White Lions and Phoenix Guard surged forwards into the Naggarothi below while Malekith's black dragon leapt up to meet the Phoenix King head-on. Maedrethnir plunged down from the clouds uttering a roaring challenge. The shock of the dragons' impact almost threw Caledor from the saddle-throne, the two titanic beasts slamming into each other in a ferocious welter of claws and fangs. The Phoenix King thought he heard mocking laughter from the Witch King as Maedrethnir bathed the other dragon with fire.

The two beasts parted and circled, gashes pouring blood from both dragons. Caledor levelled his lance for the next pass, aiming for Malekith's chest. The rune upon the Witch King's shield burned into his mind, writhing and shifting. The blood-red symbol, the True Name of Khaine, bombarded Caledor with the cacophony of war and the taste of blood filled his mouth.

Shaking his head to clear away the effects of the dread rune, Caledor saw that Malekith was almost upon him. He swung his lance as Maedrethnir rolled to the right, the weapon's shining tip scoring a wound across the flank of the black dragon as she passed by overhead.

The black dragon turned swiftly, almost catching Maedrethnir's tail in her jaw. The dragon dipped in the air to avoid the attack, exposing Caledor to the beast's raking claws. He turned and brought up his shield just in time, claws as hard as diamond ripping across its surface as protective energies blazed.

Gliding towards the ground, the two dragons closed again, snarling and roaring. Fire sprang from Malekith's sword, surrounding Caledor with crackling intensity. The enchantments of his armour protected the Phoenix King from harm, the blue flames passing around him harmlessly. Maedrethnir grappled with the black dragon, their longs necks swaying as each sought to sink fangs into the other. Claws raked back and forth, sending scales and blood spilling to the ground.

Bucking and twisting, the dragons descended, locked together by jaw and claw. Caledor let his lance fall from his grasp and pulled free Lathrain, just as the Witch King lashed out with Avanuir. The two swords met with an explosion of lightning and blue fire. The shock numbed Caledor's arm and it was with a surge of will that he parried the next attack, turning aside Malekith's blade as it screamed towards the Phoenix King's head.

The dragons gave no thought to their riders as they savaged each other. Caledor was tossed left and right as Maedrethnir struggled with his foe, wings flapping and tail whipping. Malekith clung to his iron reins with his shield hand, steam and smoke rising from his armour.

The gaze of the Phoenix King met the eyes of the Witch King. They were like bottomless pits filled with black fire, dragging his life from him. The Sapherian charms hanging on Caledor's armour glowed as they warded away the Witch King's sorcery. Again he turned aside a stroke from Avanuir as the two dragons came close enough for Malekith to strike.

The battle continued to rage around them. In their frenzy, the dragons trampled over friend and foe without distinction, Khainites and Ellyrians, White Lions and Naggarothi clawed and trampled by the two behemoths.

Caledor kept his focus on the Witch King, seeking an opening to strike. When the black dragon reeled back from an attack from Maedrethnir, the Phoenix King saw his opportunity. His sword cut down into the Witch King's shoulder, biting deep with a scream of tearing metal. A wave of energy pulsed up Caledor's arm, sending agony shooting through every part of his body.

Maedrethnir gave a pained howl as the black dragon's claws found purchase around his neck. Jaw snapping, Caledor's mount seized hold of his enemy's wing, biting through bone and sinew until the black dragon released its grip in a spasm of pain. Blood was gushing from Maedrethnir's neck. The red dragon stumbled back leaving a stream of crimson on the rucked earth.

As the Witch King wrenched on the chain of the black dragon's reins, the beast lunged at Caledor. Her jaw closed around his arm, teeth cracking against the ensorcelled ithilmar. The Phoenix King's arm was already numb with pain and Lathrain tumbled from his grasp. The straps of the Phoenix King's harness parted as the black dragon shook her head, dragging Caledor from the saddle-throne, casting him to the ground.

Heaving in a gasping breath, Caledor pushed to his feet, seeking Lathrain. He saw the glitter of metal in a tussock not far away and set out towards it, hand outstretched.

A massive blow caught him in the back, lifting him through the air. The Phoenix King crashed down amid the bodies of the slain Ellyrians, coming face-to-face with Finudel's dead visage.

Lying on his chest, Caledor felt the ground trembling. He rolled to his back, expecting to see the black dragon looming over him. It was not. Malekith wrestled with the beast's reins, trying to direct her towards Caledor. The black dragon struggled, eager to pursue Maedrethnir, who had withdrawn, limping heavily, flanks scored with dozens of ragged gashes. The black dragon had fared little better, her wings tattered, face and neck marked by claws and fangs.

The will of the Witch King prevailed and the dragon's head was steered towards the fallen Phoenix King. Flapping ragged wings, the black dragon pounded forwards, jaws wide, dripping bloodied saliva.

Caledor looked up into the dragon's glassy eyes, seeing himself reflected in the black orbs. There was nothing to read there, just reptilian coldness. He heard Malekith's triumphant laughter.

A RUSH OF hooves engulfed Caledor. A squadron of knights galloped past, some of the steeds leaping over the prone Phoenix King as they charged. Lances crashed against the scales of the dragon, while fire roared from Malekith's sword.

When the last of the knights had passed, Caledor saw that they flew the colours of Tithrain. Discarding their broken lances, they drew gleaming swords and rode around the black dragon, hacking at its flesh. The dragon struck back, stomping a clawed foot onto one of the knights, crushing rider and horse, while its jaws engulfed another.

Caledor tried to stand but pain shot up his back from his right leg. He fell to the side, hands sinking into the blood-slicked mud. Looking down, his saw his leg was twisted, the armour buckled and ruptured. Pushing back the pain, he sat up again in an attempt to see what else was happening.

The battle was still in full flow. Dragons and manticores ripped at each other above. Spells of destruction and protection flared and the whine of bolts and arrows tore the air. Still the dark roiling cloud of the daemons stretched across the sky, bubbling and burning with infernal energies. The spear companies clashed, the roars of their battle cries joining with the ring of metal, the ground trembling beneath the hooves of charging horses and the booted feet of thousands of warriors.

Caledor dragged himself across the bloody grass and propped himself up against the body of Finudel's horse. He looked at Malekith and the black dragon and saw that more than half of Tithrain's knights had been slain and still the beast and its master lived.

As he watched, Tithrain was lifted from his saddle in the dragon's jaws. The prince rained blows upon her face with his sword, opening up welts in the scales. Then the jaws closed fully and Tithrain was slain, his limp body hanging from the black dragon's fangs as it opened its mouth to let out another cloud of noxious vapour.

With the death of their prince, the nerve of the knights broke. As they fled, Malekith again struggled to direct his mount towards Caledor while it wanted to pursue the retreating riders. Under the Witch King's urging, the dragon took three steps closer to Caledor, blood streaming from dozens of wounds. This time Caledor looked up at the Witch King, whose flaming eyes blazed red. The Witch King had his arm upraised, Avanuir pointed to the sky.

The Phoenix King felt strange warmth fill him. His vision danced, half-blinded by the sun setting behind Malekith. He thought he saw a figure in the rays of the sun, a lithe elf with hair of ivy and eyes of blossoms. The figure drifted towards him surrounded by an aura of gold and green, and the smell of grass and trees came to his nostrils.

'Victory will be yours, Caledor,' said the apparition. 'You just have to reach out and take it.'

The Phoenix King glanced at Malekith, expecting the mortal blow any moment. The Witch King seemed frozen, as was the rest of the battle. There was no sound save for the sighing of wind through leaves and the creak of swaying branches.

The maiden looked down to Caledor's right and smiled, the expression sending a wave of strength through the Phoenix King's body, driving away the exhaustion and pain.

With a thunderous crash of returning noise, the vision passed. The foetid breath of the dragon passed over Caledor, making his skin prickle. Not knowing what he did, he reached out his right hand to where the apparition had looked, eyes still set on the Witch King.

His gauntleted fingers closed around the haft of a spear, its touch warm with magic in his grasp.

The black dragon pulled back its head, ready to lunge, drawing in a massive breath. Caledor looked at the cracked and bloodied fangs, and saw the monstrous forked tongue tasting the air.

He brought his arm forwards with all his strength, hurling Finudel's spear.

MIRIALITH GLEAMED AS it flashed towards the open maw of the dragon. The spear punched through the roof of the dragon's mouth and into the creature's skull.

Sulekh roared and reared, her whole body thrashing in her death throes. Iron links parted and the chains of her harness snapped. Malekith was cast backwards and to the left, falling from the black dragon's back. He slammed into the ground with a crash of metal, flames and steam billowing from his armour.

Still jarred from the impact, Malekith raised himself to one knee, throwing aside his shield to free his hand. Beside him Sulekh continued to writhe and thrash, keening loudly. The Witch King fixed his baleful stare on Imrik, who lay slumped over the body of a horse. The usurper met his glare with a defiant stare.

A moment later, Sulekh's body slammed into Malekith, crushing him into the ground. Pinned by her massive weight, he heaved at her mass, trying to free himself, letting out a bellow of frustration. He dropped Avanuir to the ground so that he could use both hands to push at the massive corpse that lay on top of his legs and waist.

A prickle of sensation shuddered through Malekith; the touch of magic. He turned his head to the left seeking the source.

A wave of white fire poured towards him. It was beautiful, glittering like moonlight on the sea, flecked with gold and silver. He recognised the flames. He had stood within them to receive Asuryan's blessing. Now the lord of gods had come again to aid Malekith, as he had Aenarion.

With a surge of power, Malekith heaved free the body of Sulekh. He stood up and faced the oncoming fire, arms spread wide to receive Asuryan's blessing. The white flames crackled closer and closer, a chill wind against his red-hot armour. He closed his eyes as the fire engulfed him, waiting for the release from the agony that had been his companion for more than two decades.

Fresh pain seared through his chest and arms. Malekith gave a cry and opened his eyes.

It was not the flame of Asuryan that surrounded him, but the halberds of the Phoenix Guard. Each blade burned with the white fires of Asuryan, every blow they landed upon the Witch King igniting the flame that had been set within his flesh by the lord of gods.

The physical pain was as nothing compared to the pain of betrayal. As his iron flesh was rent and ripped by the swinging halberds of the Phoenix Guard Malekith realised he had not received Asuryan's blessing. His father had not endured the agony he had endured.

The Witch King's delusion fell away and he saw his punishment for what it was. Asuryan had shunned him, cursed him with everlasting torment. The shock of it brought Malekith to his knees as more blows rained down upon him, carving furrows in his black armour.

The moment of woe passed, quickly replaced by anger; a deep-rooted rage fed by the burning that seethed inside the Witch King. His armour exploded with fire, hurling back the Phoenix Guard, their flesh withered, armour melting, hair and cloaks in flames.

Lacking any weapon, Malekith set about the servants of his tormentor with flaming fists, his iron hands punching through breastplates and ripping off limbs. Towering above the Phoenix Guard, he summoned dark magic, feeding off the escaping life force of his foes, twisting it to his own ends.

He tried to draw the magic into himself, to heal the rents in his armour. The dark magic swerved and writhed, failing to take purchase in his body.

Where the blades of the Phoenix Guard had marked him, tiny golden flames burned, keeping the dark magic at bay.

Dread filled Malekith's heart. Unable to heal his wounds, which streamed with rivulets of molten metal like blood, he realised he was about to die.

'Never!' he roared.

He drew himself up to his full height. The dark magic he had summoned to cure his wounds swirled around him, forming blades of blackened iron that slashed through the Phoenix Guard. With a final pulse of dark magic, he blasted the forest of magical swords into his foes, driving them back.

Leaking metal and fire and blood, Malekith turned and ran, leaving burnt prints in the bloodied grass. He would not die yet; not here on this dismal moor, with the usurper looking on, laughing. The Witch King drew on the power of his circlet, reaching out into the winds of magic, grabbing all of the power he could. An oily black cloud formed around him, flickering with lightning, obscuring him from his pursuers. It spread further and further, a churning, living mass that snatched up the Phoenix Guard who came after him, twisting their bodies and snapping their bones.

So it was that Malekith the Witch King fled the field of Maledor and returned to Anlec, broken and bitter-hearted, his ambition destroyed upon that bloodied heath.

MORATHI SAW THE flight of her son and knew that the battle had been lost. Yet she was not yet convinced that the war could not be won. Long she and her son had spoken of their most ingenious plan, that would guarantee victory. Leaving the army to fend for itself, she sent the command to her sorceresses to withdraw and turned her pegasus westwards.

THE LOSS OF the Witch King was a blow from which the druchii army could not recover. Seeing their lord and general flee broke the spirit of his followers. Such princes and knights as could escape followed their master, fleeing westwards to Anlec. Here and there Naggarothi companies managed to break loose and retreat to the south towards the keeps guarding the Naganar, Hellebron and the remaining Khainites amongst them.

Caledor was in no state to command the army and it fell to Dorien to lead the pursuit. The army of the Phoenix King swept to the west, driving the remaining druchii into the marshes north of the battlefield. Many druchii drowned in that mire, dragged down by their armour, but the treacherous ground halted all pursuit save for the three dragons that had survived and a lone Sapherian on his pegasus.

As night fell, Dorien was forced to return to the army, his remaining foes disappearing into the darkness, fearful for the welfare of his brother. He flew back to the Phoenix King and found him being tended by the healers. The White Lions stood protectively around Caledor, the silent ranks of the Phoenix Guard close by.

There was no sense of victory, no jubilation amongst the warriors of the army. The princes of three kingdoms had fallen to the Witch King and their armies were wracked with grief. The elves wept at their losses; many thousands would never return to their homes. The strength of Nagarythe had been broken, but at tremendous cost.

As the night deepened, Caledor was numb in body and mind. He refused to leave the battlefield until all of the other wounded had been attended, sitting against Finudel's steed where he had slain the black dragon of Malekith.

Campfires were lit, far from where the fighting had taken place for none wished to look upon the heaps of the dead; a grisly task that would wait until the next day. Finally Caledor allowed himself to be lifted onto a bier. He was about to be taken back to his pavilion when a shout of challenge cut the darkness.

By the flickering glow of the fires, indistinct figures could be seen. Hooded and cloaked, they hovered on the edge of vision. Caledor heard a whisper from one of the elves carrying him.

'The spirits of the druchii!' the captain hissed. 'Even in death they hate us.'

'Not so,' said a voice from the darkness.

The White Lions brought up their axes as a black-clad figure emerged from the shadows. He pulled back his hood, revealing himself to be Alith Anar.

'There are still some Naggarothi alive on Maledor this night,' said the Shadow King.

'You are late,' said Caledor.

'For your battle?' said Alith, his voice tinged with scorn. 'I told you that I do not fight for the Phoenix King.'

'What do you want?' said Caledor, too tired and sore for an argument.

'I want you to leave Nagarythe,' said Alith. 'You are not welcome in my lands.'

'Your lands?' barked Dorien, his hand moving to the hilt of his sword.

Alith moved quickly, so fast it appeared that one moment he was standing with arms crossed, the next he had his silver bow in his hand, an arrow pointed at Dorien's throat.

'*My* lands,' said the Shadow King. He spoke to Caledor, but his eyes did not move from Dorien. 'Three thousand of my warriors surround your camp. If any of your soldiers raise a weapon against me, they will cut you down.'

Caledor looked into Alith's eyes and judged that this was no empty threat. He waved Dorien to stand down.

'Malekith has survived, so too Morathi,' said the Phoenix King. 'I must go to Anlec to finish this.'

'You have done your part,' said Alith. 'What remains is the business of Nagarythe and no other kingdom.'

'You need my help,' said Caledor.

'I have never needed your help,' replied Alith. 'I wish you no harm, but if you try to march on Anlec I will be forced to stop you. Do not interfere any more in the affairs of the Naggarothi. When Malekith and Morathi have been dealt with, you will hear from me.'

Looking at the young Shadow King, Caledor saw nothing but determination and sincerity. The Phoenix King knew that the shadow army could not stop him, and Alith had to know that as well. That did not make the prospect of fighting a fresh battle any more encouraging. The druchii had tried for more than twenty years to defeat the Anars, what chance did he have?

'You have my agreement,' said Caledor. 'For the moment. You cannot allow Malekith to regroup. I will return to Nagarythe in the spring with my army to finish this, if you have not done so already.'

'You would be given commands by this Naggarothi whelp?' snarled Dorien, taking a step.

'Shut up, Dorien!' snapped Caledor.

'Listen to your brother, Dorien,' said Alith. 'Your tongue will be your death, and the deaths of many others.'

Growling wordlessly, Dorien stalked away, flicking a dismissive hand at Alith as he departed. The Shadow King lowered his bow, though the arrow remained nocked to its string.

'Thank you,' said Alith. 'I will leave now, but be assured we will be watching. When you have taken care of your dead, march east.'

Caledor said nothing. The Shadow King withdrew into the darkness, merging with the night. Caledor waited for a while, until reports came back from across the camp that the shadow army had also gone.

In his heart he knew he could not trust Alith Anar to deliver on his promise. Even with the army of Nagarythe all but destroyed, Anlec would be no easy victory. Malekith and Morathi would not submit until the last of their strength was spent.

Now was not the time to pick another fight. The Phoenix King would give Alith a chance to try and fail, and would return in the spring with his army to finish the war for good. If anything, the shadow army would wear down the last resistance, making the final task easier for Caledor.

As he drifted off to sleep, Caledor was filled with relief. The fighting was not yet done, but the war was almost over. Nagarythe's armies would not swiftly recover from their defeat, if at all.

There was nothing the Witch King could do now, his last gambit had failed.

❯ TWENTY-ONE ❯

The Sundering

THE THRONE ROOM at the heart of Aenarion's palace was shrouded in darkness. The only light came from the glow of the Witch King's armour, casting flickering shadows from the twelve figures that stood before him.

The humiliation hurt more than his wounds, though they were grievous; the blows of the Phoenix Guard had reignited the fire of Asuryan that had been set in his flesh. Malekith did not retreat from the pain as he had done before. He embraced it. He nurtured it. The agony in his body fuelled the rage in his spirit.

'I will not be denied,' Malekith growled.

'We are defeated, master,' said Urathion, the sorcerer-lord who ruled over the citadel of Ullar. 'There are barely enough troops to defend the walls and the army of the accursed Anars will surely come soon.'

'Silence!' Malekith's shout reverberated around the hall, echoing from the distant walls. 'There will be no surrender.'

'How can we resist with our armies scattered?' asked Illeanith. The sorceress, daughter of Thyriol, asked the question in a whisper, voice full of fear. 'It will take too long to withdraw our garrisons to the city.'

'We will have a new army, one that Imrik and his fawning minions will never defeat,' said Malekith.

The Witch King stood up, armoured feet ringing on the stone floor as he took several steps closer to the ring of wizards. He held out a smoking hand and cut the air with a finger. A line appeared, bulging with energy; a torrent of formless colour and noise screamed from the tear in reality. The line widened to a gap, pulled apart by clawed hands to reveal leering daemonic faces. A scaled arm reached through.

The rift into the Realm of Chaos wavered. The arm withdrew as the rent sealed itself, disappearing with the sound of tearing metal. It had lasted a few moments, but left no trace of its existence.

'Daemons?' said Urathion.

'An endless army to command,' said Morathi, stepping into the circle, her skull staff in hand. 'Immortal and impervious. What better host to serve the lord of Nagarythe?'

'It would take all of our power to summon a handful of daemons,' said Drutheira, once an acolyte of Morathi, now a fully accomplished sorceress. Her dark hair was twisted with silver and her pale skin painted with runes. 'There are yet the artifices of Vaul that can destroy a daemon's form; enough weapons to defeat any host that we might conjure.'

'We do not have to summon them,' said Malekith. 'We need only to break the bars that keep them imprisoned in the Realm of Chaos.'

There was silence as the cabal considered what this meant. It was Urathion that broke the quiet.

'You mean Caledor's vortex?' said the sorcerer.

'It cannot be done,' said Drutheira. 'The vortex is powered by the lodestones of Ulthuan. We would have to destroy them, and most are in the lands of our enemies.'

'It can be done,' said Morathi. 'Not by destroying the lodestones, but by overloading them.'

'A sacrifice,' said Malekith. 'Together we will create a surge of dark magic, enough to disrupt the harmony of the vortex. Its own power will do the rest, dragging that blast of energy into its heart.'

'Is this wise?' asked Urathion. 'Without the vortex, the Realm of Chaos will be set free upon the winds of magic. Not even together can we control that power.'

'It does not need to be controlled, simply directed,' said Malekith. He raised a smouldering finger to the circlet set into his helm. 'With that power turned to our ends, I have the means to focus its energies. Our enemies will be swept aside by a tide of daemons. Only those favoured by me shall survive. I will have both victory and vengeance in one stroke.'

The cabal looked at each other. Some seemed eager, others more concerned.

'What other choice do we have?' asked Auderion, dragging black-nailed fingers through his white hair. His gaze flickered nervously from one member of the cabal to another, never stopping. 'We cannot hold out forever, and our lives will be forfeit.'

'Our spirits are already forfeit,' whispered Illeanith. 'Bargains we have made and promises of blood have not been kept. I will not go easily to that fate.'

'Imagine their terror,' said Drutheira. 'Imagine the horror unleashed upon those that scorned us, abandoned us. We will rid the world of the Dragon-tamer's legacy, reverse the mistake he made and erase the insult upon Aenarion's legend.'

Some of the cabal remained silent, not daring to speak though their unease was as palpable as the heat from Malekith's armour. Worried eyes glittered in the gloom.

Urathion bowed his head to Malekith.

'Forgive my objections, master,' he said, dropping to one knee. 'What must we do?'

'Return to your castles and gather such acolytes and slaves as you still possess. Morathi will furnish you with the details of the ritual you must undertake. At the appointed hour, midnight ten days from now, we will begin. The blood of our sacrifices will draw the dark magic and our incantations shall send it as a storm into the vortex.'

'What of the Sapherians?' said Illeanith. 'My father and his mages will try to stop us.'

'How can they?' said Morathi. 'By the time they know what is happening, it will be too late for them to intervene.'

'Even if they do, they do not have the power to stop us,' said Malekith. 'The vortex was wrought by Caledor Dragontamer at the height of his strength. Not even your father can contest with such a spell.'

There were no further questions or objections. The sorcerers and sorceresses bowed and departed, leaving Malekith alone with Morathi.

'If you are wrong?' said Morathi. 'If we cannot harness the vortex?'

'The daemons will rampage across the world and all will be destroyed,' said Malekith.

'And you are sure you wish to risk such an end?' said Morathi.

'Risk it?' Malekith replied with a harsh laugh. 'I embrace it! If Ulthuan will not be mine, then none will rule. I would rather our people perished than see them laid low by the hand of another. Better it is to see the world torn asunder than suffer this eternal torment.'

As HE HAD sworn to Alith Anar, Caledor withdrew his army across the Annulii, back to Avelorn. Many of his warriors he sent back to their kingdoms; some to solemnly bear the bodies of the princes who had been slain. Dorien was despatched to Caledor to take the news of the Phoenix King's victory, while Carathril was sent into the ruins of Avelorn seeking to convey the same to the Everqueen.

Thyriol remained with the army, concerned by the Phoenix King's wounds. Though he professed publicly to be regaining his strength, Caledor confessed in private that he was weak. He did not feel ready to return to the Isle of the Flame, and so stayed in Avelorn with the army, ready to respond should things go badly for the shadow army in their attempt to overthrow the rule of Anlec.

The days were shortening and Caledor spent most of his time in his pavilion, resting and pondering what he would do next. One evening, twelve days after the battle at Maledor, he asked Thyriol to join him.

'You must find another Phoenix King,' said Caledor.

'What is wrong?' asked the shocked mage, hurrying to the Phoenix King's side. 'Your wounds, do they not heal?'

'It is not my body that is weak, it is my heart,' Caledor answered. 'The war will be over soon. My time as king should end with it.'

Though still concerned, the panic left the mage and he sat down beside the king's throne, tucking his hands into the voluminous sleeves of his robe.

'You think that you will not be a good leader in peace?' Thyriol asked.

'I know it,' said Caledor. 'You know it too. I am not made for audiences and councils. You will need a better leader than I to rebuild Ulthuan and start afresh in the colonies.'

'Princes are thin on the ground of late,' Thyriol said with a sad smile. 'There is no other, I think, who could wear the crown.'

'You could,' said Caledor. 'You have the wisdom and the experience needed. You see the hearts of our people better than I.'

'Please do not say anything to the others about this. At least let us ensure that the druchii are truly defeated before we turn their minds to what happens after. Morathi is like a manticore, with a spiteful sting when cornered. Talk of peace is premature.'

'Perhaps you are right,' said Caledor. He leaned back in his throne, his bones aching. 'It will seem a strange world.'

'I think you will be pleasantly surprised,' said Thyriol. 'Life demands a certain harmony and will tend towards that state. In a few years, in your lifetime, you will see the world returned to the way it was. Cities can be rebuilt, and children will still grow up. Like your father, you will be glad that generations from now will prosper free from the blight of war. That will be your legacy.'

The thought brought some little comfort to the Phoenix King. He rested his weary body, eyes closed, and tried to picture Ulthuan as it had been. He could not. Wherever he looked with his mind's eye, be it at Cothique or Lothern, Avelorn or Chrace, he saw the death and destruction brought about by the war.

He lifted a hand to his chin, to the small scar where the assassin's knife had nicked his flesh, and he wondered if the druchii had forever poisoned Ulthuan. Would the evil they had unleashed, and the violence he had committed to stop them, ever be expunged from the hearts of the elves?

He heard Thyriol stir, a murmur of unease coming from the mage's lips. A few moments later Caledor felt that which had disturbed the mage. There was an undercurrent in the winds of magic, a dark eddy of power.

He opened his eyes and thought for a heartbeat that he was under attack. The lanterns in the pavilion seemed to dim, the shadows deepening. He realised that he did not imagine the thickening gloom; the lamps were extinguishing themselves.

Thyriol stood, the tip of his staff glowing.

'Sorcery,' the mage whispered. 'Stay still.'

The pavilion was now utterly dark, save for the small circle of light that surrounded the Phoenix King and the mage. Noise came, the sound of running water and wind howling over rocks. The darkness shifted, paling in places, shapes merging to form an image.

'The magic is not here, though,' muttered Thyriol. 'The spell is cast somewhere else.'

The spectre of an elf appeared in the gloom, hooded and swathed in black. He pulled back his hood to reveal a haggard face, hair hanging lankly about his shoulders. Sunken eyes looked first at Caledor and then Thyriol. It was to the mage that the apparition turned.

'I am Urathion of Ullar,' said the elf. 'I do not have long and will not reach you in person. Malekith has sent the raven heralds after me. Heed my warning, Thyriol, and prepare.'

'Prepare for what?' said Caledor.

'The vortex,' said Urathion, his shade still looking at Thyriol. 'Malekith and the other sorcerers attempt to unbind its powers, letting free the Realm of Chaos.'

'Madness!' exclaimed Thyriol. 'Ulthuan will be destroyed.'

'Yes, it is madness,' said Urathion. 'I have done evil things and I do not regret them. The power I have wielded and the things I have seen have been reward enough. Yet even I see that this cannot be allowed. Malekith would rather see the world destroyed than live in defeat.'

'How will he do this?' demanded Thyriol. 'Tell me of the spell and I will thwart it.'

'A huge sacrifice is planned,' said Urathion. 'Malekith and Morathi will infuse the vortex with dark magic and let loose the hosts of Chaos upon you. It is too late to prevent the ceremony, you must prot–'

The apparition of Urathion gave a strangled gasp and stiffened. As the shadows lightened, Caledor saw the sorcerer fall to his face, a bolt jutting from between his shoulders. Beyond was the silhouette of a cloaked rider with crossbow in hand. The light of the lamps returned to obscure the image, bringing with it a sense of unreality.

Caledor looked to Thyriol. The mage's brow was furrowed in thought and his fingers tapped nervously along his staff.

'Do you think this is a trick?' said the Phoenix King. 'Perhaps Malekith seeks to lure you into a sorcerous trap.'

'That is a risk I must take,' replied Thyriol. 'If it is true, Malekith must be stopped. Urathion did not exaggerate. If the vortex is destroyed, we are doomed. Even if Ulthuan survives the loss of the vortex, the daemonic hordes will return. You and I are not Aenarion and your grandfather, we cannot stop such an invasion. Our people will be slain and enslaved by the powers of Chaos. I must go now.'

'Where to?' said Caledor. 'Can this spell be stopped?'

'The Isle of the Dead,' said Thyriol, answering the first question and avoiding the second. 'The centre of the vortex.'

Chanting a spell, the mage drew an arc in the air with the tip of his staff. The air parted where the staff passed, creating an arch of golden energy. Within its arc, Caledor could see ghostly apparitions; robed elves as immobile as statues, frozen within a glimmering aura.

'Your battle is won, now I must win mine,' said Thyriol.

The mage stepped through the magical door, which vanished with a shower of falling sparks. Caledor stayed in his throne, gripping its arms with white-knuckled hands. Shaking himself from the shock, he pushed himself up and walked outside on weak legs.

The sky was clear, the stars a bright swathe across the heavens. Caledor looked west, to the Annulii, where the vortex made the air shimmer around the peaks.

'Asuryan, lord of the heavens,' he whispered. 'You did not answer the prayers of Aenarion and I do not expect you to listen to me. Yet for all that, I am your king and rule in your name, and upon me your blessing was laid. If you love my people, do not let them be destroyed.'

His short prayer finished, Caledor knew there was nothing else he could do. He remained where he was, eyes fixed on the Annulii, and drew Lathrain. If the daemons came again, he would not die without a fight.

THE HALL WAS awash with blood. It moved with its own sluggish life, hissing and sizzling at Malekith's feet, lapping over the twisted bodies of his victims. Morathi chanted, staff held above her head, an incantation calling upon all of the daemons and powers with which she had made pacts during her long life. The air seethed with dark energy, flowing from walls to ceiling, making the symbols and runes painted in blood on the stone glow with ruddy power.

Through the circlet, the Witch King could feel the rising tide of dark magic across Nagarythe. In castles and towers across the barren kingdom his followers despatched their sacrifices and used their deaths to draw on the winds of magic, the mystical forces congealing together under the sorcerous influence of the Naggarothi.

Morathi's incantation was reaching its crescendo. Her voice was a wail, her body shuddering, the coils of dark magic thickening and strengthening as they whirled around the throne room.

Reaching out his hands, Malekith felt the slick touch of the magic on his iron skin. The circlet gleamed on his brow and filled his mind with ice as the Witch King grasped and manipulated the formless energy with his will, shaping it, turning its convoluted waves into a rhythmically pulsing cloud.

'Now!' screamed Morathi, her staff blazing.

Malekith flung the dark magic up, spearing its energies through the palace of Aenarion. He could feel the other columns of power erupting across his kingdom, pillars of pure magical energy roaring up into the heavens.

THE MAGIC HISSED liked a serpent, throwing coils of power around the dungeon chamber, thrashing wildly. Illeanith gritted her teeth and spat words of control, almost imploring the dark energy to obey her. She staggered back as another surge of magic rose up through her, bursting from her open mouth.

Eyes wide, the sorceress gasped every word of the incantation, speaking them over and over and over, cajoling and threatening the creatures that existed on the other side of reality's veil. The blackness that tainted her skin was spreading. Already her hands were completely ebon, and the corruption was leeching up through her darkening veins, making them pop out of the skin of her bared arms.

Illeanith's lips and gums were fizzing with magic and her eyes ached with the power. Her long hair writhed like rearing serpents, sparks flying from the flaring tips. The whole of the tower shook and the clean-hewn stones groaned and ground together.

The other world, the Realm of Chaos, started to intrude through the swirl of magic. Illeanith half-glimpsed maddening vistas of trees of finger bones and clouds that rained molten silver. The squeals and screeches, roars and howls of the daemons filled the chamber, echoing from the walls while simultaneously fading into distance.

Something hunched and ruddy, its bulbous head elongated, globular eyes white, burst into the room. It whirled around orientating itself with the surroundings, its wiry limbs tensed, a bronze sword in its hands dripping thick blood.

Illeanith shrieked and backed away from the creature, which fixed upon her its lifeless stare. In her fright, the sorceress stumbled and fell, one hand passing through the symbol of salt she had laid upon the floor.

With the mystical sigil broken, the dark magic was let loose. It rampaged around Illeanith, smashing the walls, ripping up the tiles of the floor, prodding and slashing at her, pulling her hair and tugging at her teeth. More of the daemons formed in the mayhem, snarling, predatory things that immediately set upon the first with fanged maws and slashing tails. Illeanith struggled to her feet, weeping blood. A thick tar-like substance leaked from her mouth, choking her as she clutched at her throat. The sorceress gurgled a cry of agony as her veins burst, magic boiling like sludge from her ruptured blood vessels.

Bones cracked and splintered, ripping forth more wet screams from Illeanith. She crumpled, falling face-first, her arm snapping beneath her as she tried to stop her head hitting the slabs. The daemons swarmed around her, their fang-ringed mouths gnawing and tearing at her spirit as well as her flesh.

Her last cry died away, but the damage had been done. The dark magic flowed from the breach in the rune, burrowing through the stones, prising apart the blocks with tenebrous tendrils of power. The daemons' forms lost cohesion and they evaporated into the miasma, which continued to spin and roil, seeking escape.

With a thunderous detonation that hurled stone and earth high into the air, the dark magic exploded from the dungeon, toppling the tower. It spiralled and spun, bubbling across Nagarythe towards the Annulii, joining the other streamers of dark power cutting across the cold night.

CALEDOR FELT THE ground shudder. It was faint but strong enough that soon the elves of the camp were leaving their tents, fearful questions being asked. The Phoenix King ignored them and continued to stare at the glimmer over the mountains.

One by one the stars seemed to wink out of existence. The aura of the vortex strengthened, becoming something more than a hint on the edge of vision. Caledor could see the whirling energy, pick out the strands of magic cascading down the peaks, swirling in pools in the valleys.

He looked overhead and saw the darkness spreading, leaching the light from the stars. The air grew colder as the dark magic funnelled down the vortex, drawn towards the Isle of the Dead at the centre of the Inner Sea. Forks of energy played along the glowing ribbons of magic. Turning east he saw the magic plunging down like a tornado, growing thicker and brighter with each passing heartbeat.

MALEKITH STRODE TO an iron balcony adjoining the chamber, Morathi hurrying after him. He turned his flaming gaze to the east and saw the ravening energies gathering across the mountaintops.

'It is done,' said Morathi.

She pointed high into the heavens, to the north. Lights burned in the sky, silhouetting the horizon with a rainbow of colours that were constantly shifting. The magical aurora flickered, spitting bolts of energy to the ground and up towards the disappearing stars.

Malekith could see through the anarchy of shape and colour. Towering spires of crystal and rivers of blood; cliffs with screaming skull-like faces and forests of waving tentacles; castles of bronze and a huge dilapidated mansion; plains covered with splintered bones and white beaches rippled by purple waters; clouds of flies and miniature suns that glared with cyclopean eyes.

And he heard the roaring and the howls, the screaming and the growls. Marching and slithering, swooping and leaping, a host of daemons poured forth.

'The Realm of Chaos opens,' he rasped, feeling triumphant. 'My legions awake!'

* * *

STAGGERING AGAINST THE buffeting of the magical gale, Thyriol pushed himself on towards the distant figures of Caledor Dragontamer and the other mages. His whole body was afire with magic, exhilarating and painful in equal measure.

He could feel the counterspells of his fellows, given hasty warning by their prince. Counter-currents and whirling siphons raced around the vortex as the mages of Saphery tried to claw back the power being unleashed.

Thyriol could see that their attempts would be in vain; it was like trying to empty the Inner Sea with a thimble. Overhead the vortex grew stronger and stronger, the weight of it on his shoulders making every step a near-impossible effort, every breath a ragged gasp for life.

He heard the wailing and roaring of the daemons before he saw them. At first they were nothing more than motes of energy cast around by the vortex; brief glimpses of fanged faces and sharp talons that were soon swallowed by the mass of power. As he pushed on, the daemons fed on the magic, forming bodies of pure energy, dancing and twisting along the circling currents of mystical power.

Their whispers came to his ears, threatening all manner of cruel torment.

Thyriol drove all other things from his mind, focussing on his goal, giving no thought to any other desire or need that might be perverted by the daemons. His staff cracked and then exploded into a shower of splinters, unable to hold the magic coursing through it. The charms upon his bracelets, the amulets around his neck, spat and hissed with power, whirling about as if caught in a gale.

He pressed on.

'TO ARMS!' CALEDOR bellowed. 'Protect yourselves!'

Faster than any mortal host, the daemons poured down from the mountains, riding upon the waves of magic. A beast with a slug-like body and fanged maw fringed with writhing tentacles materialised in front of the Phoenix King.

All thought of pain and weakness were gone. Caledor slashed Lathrain through the creature, parting it in a blaze of fire and magical sparks. Gibbering, wretched things plunged from the sky on wings of darkness, to be met with the shining blade forged for Caledor Dragontamer.

Around the Phoenix King, the elves of his army did their best to fight. Their arrows and spears did little harm to the immaterial creatures that attacked them. A few wielded heirlooms from the last daemonic invasion, spears and swords and axes forged in Vaul's Anvil now turned again to their original purpose.

The ground was thick with magic and the sky filled with a roiling storm cloud of pure energy. Caledor glanced up as he thought he heard a deep rumbling laugh, glimpsing for a moment a monstrous thing of no particular form but unimaginably terrifying. He fought without thought, hacking and thrusting at any daemonic thing that came within range.

For an age the elves had survived, building an empire and thinking that peace was eternal. As the daemons cackled and shrieked around him, Caledor realised how fickle that existence had been. He wept as he battled, thinking how cruel a world it was that his grandfather's greatest legacy was undone.

BLINDED AND DEAFENED, his whole body a searing torrent of ecstasy and pain, Thyriol clawed his way across the ravaged ground. He was guided only by his inner magical sense, feeling his way through the anarchy of the vortex's heart. With every laboured heartbeat he felt the vortex weakening, the lodestones unable to cope with the magic of the druchii and the power of the daemons. Very soon it would collapse entirely and all would be lost.

The mage felt like a speck of dust in a hurricane, physically and in his spirit, but clung on with every shred of willpower to maintain his sense of self and purpose.

As if passing into a gap between realities, Thyriol felt everything disappear. The noise, the confusion, the pain all vanished, leaving him with a sense of pure peace. He had reached the eye of the vortex, the very centre of the magical storm.

He did not know if his plan would work, but he had spent his life studying the work of Caledor Dragontamer and the principles of the vortex. If he was wrong, it would only hasten the vortex's collapse.

He had nothing to lose.

Pushing himself up to a kneeling position, Thyriol bowed his head and folded his hands in his lap. There was no ground beneath him nor sky above him. He was utterly isolated, floating in nothingness. He was not even sure if his body had survived. In this place, in the tiniest sliver between realities, the grey edge between light and dark, the cusp of life and death, such things as immortal and mortal, body and spirit, were irrelevant.

Within his clasped hands, he released the tiny mote of magic he had brought with him. It was barely anything, perhaps enough to give life to the smallest insect. He opened his hands and the tiny particle of magic floated up, a minute glimmer in nothingness.

Releasing his grip upon the magic, he allowed it to interact with the void.

The magic exploded, turning into an infinite sun, filling the gap between worlds. The barriers between the real and the immaterial fell away, breaking the last bonds that held the Realm of Chaos in check.

The vortex was complete, a solid whirl of magic whose reach stretched across the whole world. Far to the east, dwarfen runesmiths paused in their labours, wondering why the runes they worked on guttered and died. In their ancient, jungle-devoured cities to the west, the immortal servants of the Old Ones paused in their calculations and contemplations. Alien intelligences turned their attention to the sudden change in the world, coldly assessing its importance.

Opening his eyes, Thyriol found himself still on the Isle of the Dead.

'I see,' said a voice behind him.

Thyriol turned, coming face-to-face with an aged elf with a thin face and silver hair. The mage recognised him instantly, from a hundred statues and a thousand paintings: Caledor Dragontamer.

The influx of magic had broken the stasis as Thyriol had hoped.

The greatest mage of the elves appeared calm even as the vortex raged and bucked around him. Other mages appeared out of the anarchic storm, robes flapping in the unnatural breeze, staffs in hand.

They formed a circle around Thyriol, eyes cast upwards. The prince of Saphery joined them and saw a pinprick of night amidst the magic, the briefest glimmer of a star.

'This will not end well,' said the Dragontamer, 'but it cannot be helped.'

The assembled mages lifted up their staffs and began their chants. At first nothing happened and Thyriol could not divine their purpose. Slowly, imperceptibly at first, the vortex slowed. Centred around the circle of mages another vortex began, running in the opposite direction.

Gathering power this second vortex created ripples through the magical storm. It grew larger and larger, feeding off the magic, gathering pace even as the main vortex slowed. Thyriol watched amazed as Caledor Dragontamer turned the vortex against itself. Where magic had once been drained from the mortal realm, now it was being channelled from the Realm of Chaos. Faster and faster the counter-vortex whirled, erupting with flashes of dark amidst the light, bubbling clouds of pure energy flowing against the roiling winds of magic.

The two conflicting vortices reached parity and the world froze.

His sword slashing the throat of yet another blood-skinned daemon, Caledor felt the ground lurch, almost throwing him from his feet. As one, the daemon horde fell still and silent, even more unnerving than their shouts and screams. They turned unnatural eyes towards the vortex as the ground bucked again.

Light detonated to the east, surging up through the funnel of the vortex. A moment before he was blinded by it, Caledor saw the daemonic host bursting into flames, the cinders of their bodies turning to crystalline dust.

Another convulsion of the earth toppled the Phoenix King, who fell heavily to his side. He heard and felt a deep rumble, coming from the bowels of the world. Looking up through slitted eyes he saw the mountain peaks swaying, the vortex rippling and pulsing. Avalanches crashed down from the peaks and cliffs tumbled, toppling down the slopes.

Thyriol has failed, he thought. This is how the world ends.

'No!' screamed Morathi.

Malekith felt it too, a presence he had not known for more than a thousand years. The Dragontamer had returned. The Witch King did not know how, but he would not be defeated so easily. He poured out all of his scorn and hatred, looking to wrench control of the vortex from the elf who had betrayed his father. Morathi sensed what he was doing and added her own sorcery, seeking to overcome the Dragontamer's spell.

The two waves of magic clashed within the vortex, detonating with a blaze of multicoloured light that swept away the storm, converting both high and dark magic into a huge detonation. Malekith felt it as a shockwave that pulsed across Ulthuan, flattening trees and toppling towers. He sensed the mountains lurching as the vortex spun again.

He felt something else too, like the world was tipping on its axis. The magic unleashed rocked Ulthuan, ripping earth and sky with its power. A crack appeared in the city wall of Anlec as a huge fissure opened up in the ground to the north. Roofs collapsed and walls toppled as Anlec convulsed. Everywhere across Nagarythe the dark magic earthed itself, mighty spires of rock erupting from the ground while huge pits and crevasses dropped down.

'What is that noise?' said Morathi, looking to the north.

IN ONE OF Nagarythe's northernmost towers, Drutheira laughed gaily at the magical battle being fought. She delighted in the clash and merging of energies, marvelling at the patterns of light and dark wrought across the stars.

Her laughter died away as she felt the first tremors of the earthquake. Around her tall candle holders fell to the flagstones and lamps of elf fat spilled from their sconces. She staggered to her left as the world lurched, the beams holding up the ceiling creaking alarmingly. A cloud of mortar showered down on to Drutheira as she struggled to remain upright.

The whole tower swayed and cracked, like a tree in a gale. Its movement sent her reeling into the wall, next to one of the narrow windows. Grasping the sill, she looked outside and saw the stars spinning overhead. In the light of the crazily dancing moons she could see the rocks of the coast.

The shore stretched away into the night, far further than any natural tide. She could see fish flopping on the dry land and splashing in small pools left between the rocks. It was if a god had come down and taken a titanic draught from the seas, leaving mud and wet sand covering a massive expanse to the north and west.

It was then that she heard the rumbling and saw the first glimmer of surf in the distance. She knew immediately what it meant and hastily returned to the pentacle drawn in blood at the centre of the chamber.

The magic was a wild, bucking stallion that refused to be broken to her will, slipping and rearing from her grasp as she chanted madly, trying to reach into the maelstrom of energy for the power needed to cast her spell.

She finally latched on to a straying aura of dark magic. Slitting her breast with her sacrificial dagger, she offered up her own blood to seal the conjuration. Dark magic rushed into her, as the sea rushed to fill the gap that had been made along the shore.

Drutheira plunged her spirit down into the foundations of the tower, carrying with her the formless cloud of dark energy. She allowed herself to seep down into the rocks and tunnels on which the tower stood, breaking them free from the strata of the earth beneath. Further and further she stretched her spell, opening up massive cracks around the outer wall of the citadel, lifting the entire structure from the bedrock.

Returning to her body, she stared out of the window and saw that she had cast the spell just in time.

MALEKITH TURNED, GRIPPING the rail of the balcony tight as the palace swayed on its foundations, turrets and towers crashing down onto the buildings below in a flurry of broken stone and tiles.

To the north was a wall of white. It looked like fog at first, a bank of cloud swiftly approaching from the north-west. It brought an odd hissing, which deepened as the cloud came closer.

Malekith felt a moment of dread as he realised it was not a cloud that approached, but a wall of water. As though the ocean had heaved itself up in protest, a tidal wave stretched across the horizon, shining in the moonlight, as high as the tallest tower of Anlec.

THE WAVE BURIED Nagarythe under its titanic assault and crashed across the Naganar into Tiranoc. Sweeping everything before it, the onrushing ocean crushed towns, flattened forests and cast down city walls.

IN ELANARDRIS ALITH Anar looked on in horror as the kingdom he had claimed as his was drowned. The water surged up the mountain valleys, washing away the remains of the manse of the Anars. The foaming surge drove up the river valleys, obliterating everything in its path.

Shouting warnings to his followers, the Shadow King led them higher up the slopes, abandoning their rude huts and cave dwellings to the encroaching sea. Many on the lower slopes had no time to escape. Tents and campfires were engulfed by the frothing mass, which swallowed up hundreds of elves, young and old, dragging them to their deaths and crushing their bodies with uprooted trees and grinding boulders.

THE RUINS OF Tor Anroc were drowned. Water coursed along the ancient tunnel-streets of the city and poured through the shattered remnants of the palace. The great white cliffs crumbled and the orchards of cherry and apple were obliterated. Bel Shanaar's throne room filled with water, the benches and throne rising with the water, swirled and smashed together by the torrent raging through the broken windows.

The alleys and passageways became swirling rivers, the rising sea smashing through doors to fill the subterranean workshops and stores, the walls and buildings of the noble manses pulverised by the deluge. The great towers at the gate were cast down, crumbling stone by stone into the all-encompassing flood.

Finally the great pinnacle of Tor Anroc toppled. Magic flaring as the needle-like structure fell, for a brief moment the blue fire of the Phoenix King burned again, before it too was drowned by the incoming waters.

FAR TO THE south, Dorien was awoken from a deep sleep during which he had dreamed of an army of daemons besieging Tor Caled. Roused from his slumber, he sat up in bed, haunted by the strange voices that lingered after the dream had passed.

He felt the first tremors shaking the bed and was filled with foreboding. Pushing himself to his feet, he was hurled off the ground as the whole of the palace rose and fell in a moment, followed by an ear-splitting crack.

Alarm bells and gongs were ringing all across the city. The prince fumbled his way to the great windows that led onto the balcony overlooking Tor Caled. Throwing open the doors, he moved out to the rail and turned to look back at the mountains, which shouldered up over the city.

Fire burst from the peak of Anul Caled. Flame and smoke wreathed the mountaintop and burning rocks sailed high into the skies. Cracks were opening up on the mountainside, venting flame and vapour, rivulets of lava beginning to pour from the breaches.

There were shouts and screams from the city below. Dorien looked down across the levels of Tor Caled and saw torches and lamps moving in the darkness as elves fled from their homes. The fortifications were tumbling down and buildings collapsing as Tor Caled continued to buck and heave alongside the volcanoes' eruptions.

The moat of lava surged and raged against the magical wards holding it in check. The bridges across the fiery river swayed and fell, their stones disappearing into the red depths. Dorien looked on in horror as those trying to flee the city were plunged to their flaming deaths.

They were trapped inside the city.

A cloud of hot ash swept down from Anul Caled, a billowing miasma of darkness and death that engulfed the city in moments. Dorien fought for breath in the superheated air, choking on the fumes and heat of the cloud. Along with thousands of those over whom he had been guardian, the prince was quickly engulfed by the ash, his clothes and hair burning, his skin peeling away even as his flesh petrified.

TO THE EAST, across the great expanse of the Inner Sea, the mages of Saphery had been lending their weight to the duel for control of the vortex. In the palace of Saphethion, Menreir and a cohort of fellow mages chanted and channelled, seeking to avert the disaster befalling their isle.

They too felt the reappearance of Caledor Dragontamer and paused in their incantations, wondering at the import of the event. As they watched the counter-vortex begin to take shape, the crystalline nervous system of

Saphethion started to resonate with the new wave of magic pouring into the world. The diamond-like heart of the city quivered and shook in its golden nest, vibrating in tune with the whirling storm of magic and anti-magic raging through the vortex.

With a detonation that resounded in the minds of the mages, the crystal heart shattered, rocking the city from within. Magic exploded along the crystal lodeways, splitting rock with showers of fire and lightning.

Saphethion seemed to sag in the air.

Horrified, the mages could do nothing as the floating city descended towards the foothills of the Annulii. The streets outside the palace were quickly thronged with elves, screaming and shouting, while eagles and pegasi launched from the stablehouses, taking their riders to safety.

Menreir and the others did what they could to slow the city's descent, but it was too little. Towers and buildings were flattened as Saphethion crashed into a hillside, roofs collapsing, filling the streets with debris, crushing hundreds of elves with falling masonry and beams.

Secondary magical detonations rocked the city, causing blazes to spread through some quarters as tanneries and workshops caught fire. The palace itself was wreathed in magical energy, lightning forking from tower tops to walls, while within the building the many magical artefacts and devices of the Sapherians burned and glowed, hissed and spat with more magic than the world had seen for an age.

IN NAGARYTHE, MALEKITH'S sorcerous followers watched in horror as the tidal wave engulfed their lands. They used the last of their dark powers to protect their citadels, casting enchantments that sundered the foundations of their towers, allowing them to be lifted up by the wave like immense ships.

In Anlec, Morathi wreathed the palace of Aenarion with her magic, though she could not protect the rest of the city. Water crashed against the towering pinnacle, smashing away stone and brick. Calling upon her daemonic allies, the sorceress ripped the immense palace free from the city, the water boiling and frothing below it as the massive edifice rose up above the waves and Anlec was tumbled into ruin.

—◄ EPILOGUE ►—

THOUSANDS HAD BEEN slain by the catastrophe. Whether slain during the brief but deadly daemonic incursion, drowned by the tidal wave or crushed by the earthquakes, all of Ulthuan had suffered the wrath of the vortex's detonation. Caledor made his way immediately to the Isle of the Flame, knowing that it was to the Shrine of Asuryan that the princes would come.

Over time they did, each bringing tales of woe and loss from their kingdoms. Thyriol did not arrive though, and Caledor sent an expedition to seek him. They returned from the Isle of the Dead with the grim news that they had found the Sapherian prince, locked in stasis surrounded by Caledor Dragontamer and the other mages of old.

Of the druchii there was no sign.

Word was sent to Alith Anar, who despatched Carathril back with a bitter message full of grief and hatred. Western Nagarythe was destroyed and the east ravaged by the vengeful wave. It was a dead land now, laid to waste by the hubris of Malekith. Tor Anroc and the surrounding countryside was now a chain of islands, surrounded by treacherous waters that still spumed and boiled. The druchii sorcerers who had managed to escape had steered their towers north, towards the ocean.

'And of Malekith and Morathi, the Shadow King believes that they still live,' concluded Carathril. 'Anlec is a ruin, but there is no sign of Aenarion's palace. What do you think that means?'

1011

Caledor's reply was simple.

'The war is not over. We shall never know peace.'

THE STORM-WRACKED SEAS crashed against a harsh shore of rock pinnacles, foaming madly. The skies were in turmoil, blackened by dark magic. Through the spume and rain dark, massive shapes surged across the seas; towering edifices of battlement and wall.

The castles of Nagarythe followed in the wake of the largest floating citadel, upon the highest tower of which stood Malekith. The lashing rain steamed from his armour as he turned at the sound of Morathi's voice from the archway behind him.

'This is where we flee to?' she said, anger flashing in her eyes. 'This cold, bleak land?'

'They will not follow us here,' replied the Witch King. 'We are the Naggarothi, we were born in the north and in the north we will be born again. This land, bleak as it is, shall be ours. Naggaroth.'

'To build a new kingdom?' sneered Morathi. 'To accept your defeat and start afresh as if Nagarythe had never existed?'

'No,' replied Malekith, flames leaping from his iron body. 'We will never forget that which has been taken from us. Ulthuan belongs to me. If it takes a thousand years, ten thousand years, I will claim my rightful place as king. I am the son of Aenarion. It is my destiny.'

Dramatis Personae

AERENIS – friend of Carathril, lieutenant in the Lothern Guard, cultist dedicated to Ereth Khial. Aerenis has turned to the cult of the dead in an effort to contact the maiden he loved (Glaronielle, killed during the raid by Carathril and Aerenis in *Malekith*). When Lothern is besieged by the druchii, the cultists attempt to rise up within the city and Aerenis's allegiances are revealed.

ALITH ANAR – the Shadow King of Nagarythe. Alith is an avowed enemy of the druchii, but also a strong advocate of Naggarothi independence. He is distrustful of Caledor (both the realm and the king) and refuses to swear allegiance to the Phoenix Throne. However, he concedes that while the druchii exist, he has more enmity for them than the Phoenix King, and fights alongside other elven armies on several occasions.

ATHIELLE – princess of Ellyrion, horse mistress. An even more able rider and warrior than her brother, Finudel, Athielle is the true heart of the Ellyrians. While her brother is utterly devoted to her, she places the pride and safety of their people above Finudel. Often hot-headed, she nevertheless understands best of all the princes and princesses what sacrifices need to be made in order that Nagarythe and its allies are stopped.

BEL SHANAAR – Phoenix King of Ulthuan, ruler of Tiranoc. Bel Shanaar was chosen for his calmness and wisdom to succeed Aenarion, and becomes the object of Malekith's hatred. Knowing that the Naggarothi will never truly bend their knee to him, Bel Shanaar allows Nagarythe to go into self-isolation, but is taken aback when the cults of pleasure surface with so much vehemence. He ultimately pays the price for his complacency when Malekith poisons him before the massacre at the shrine, though not soon enough to prevent Bel Shanaar sending a letter to Imrik naming the prince of Caledor general of Ulthuan's armies.

CARATHRIL – originally a captain of the Lothern Guard, now herald to the Phoenix King. Before his assassination, Carathril is entrusted by Bel Shanaar to carry a message to Imrik, nominating the Caledorian prince as general of Ulthuan's armies. After the massacre, Carathril must seek Imrik in the wilds of Chrace, and arrives shortly after the attempted slaying by Morathi's assassins. After this, Carathril breaks off his service to the Phoenix King and returns to Lothern, but when the city is besieged by the druchii, he is swept up in the fighting. Trapped in the city, Carathril ends up facing his friend in the fighting, after which Carathril is all but broken.

CARVALON – prince of Yvresse, grandson of ruling prince Haradrin. Slain by Malekith during the Battle of Maledor.

CHARILL – ruling prince of Chrace. Charill is amongst those princes slain at the Shrine of Asuryan, leaving Koradrel as ruling prince. Carries the weapon Achillar, whose double-headed blade crackled with lightning in his hands. His son Lorichar bears the banner of Tor Achare; the head of a lion in silver thread upon a scarlet background. Present at the assault on Anlec, both were killed in the massacre.

DORIEN – younger brother of Imrik. Arrogant and tactless, Dorien is all for defending Caledor and leaving the rest of Ulthuan to its fate. Fights at the first battle of Ellyrian Plains, where he breaks his leg and briefly meets Alith Anar.

FINUDEL – prince of Ellyrion, horse master. Typically carefree and adventurous like his people, Finudel is an optimist with a great faith in his fellow princes. He is the most shocked by the turning of Malekith, whom he adored, but comes out of his shock as one of the fiercest opponents of the Naggarothi, if somewhat lacking in wisdom and forethought. Utterly devoted to his sister, Athielle. Slain by Malekith during the Battle of Maledor.

ILLEANITH – daughter of Thyriol, mage of Saphery. Illeanith is corrupted by the teachings of dark magic and flees Saphery to join the druchii. She is killed when Malekith's attempt to overload the vortex is thwarted.

IMRIK/CALEDOR – prince of Caledor, dragonlord, grandson to Caledor Dragontamer, future Phoenix King. Imrik has none of the magical aptitude of his grandfather, but is possessed of the same stubborn will. He is not talkative, sometimes downright taciturn, and is immensely practical in his outlook. It is to Imrik that the other princes turn when Malekith betrays them, and he takes his grandfather's name upon being crowned as Phoenix King. After the sacrifices his family have made protecting Ulthuan from the daemons, he will go to any lengths to protect the isle and its people against the renegades. He leads by example, sacrificing his own pleasures and future to become a defiant warleader. His father is Menieth, who attended the First Council and died fighting in the colonies to the east. Wields the sword Lathrain (Wrathbringer).

HELLEBRON – a young, ambitious priestess of Khaine with a secret desire to overthrow Morathi. Utterly ruthless and dedicated to the Lord of Murder; after 'slaying' the Shadow King Alith Anar, she is a scourge of the elves in Cothique but is forced to flee with the other druchii during the Sundering.

HOTEK – high priest of Vaul. Hotek and some of his followers are corrupted by the druchii and begin to fashion magical weapons for the dark elves in secret. When they are discovered, Hotek abandons his minions and flees to Nagarythe with the Hammer of Vaul. There he forges the Armour of Midnight that turns Malekith into the Witch King.

KORADREL – prince of Chrace, cousin of Imrik. Pragmatic and fiercely loyal, it is Koradrel and his hunters that save Imrik from Morathi's assassins. After this, Koradrel convinces Imrik to accept his fate to become the Phoenix King of Ulthuan. Present at the assault on Anlec. When Charill and Lorichar are slain, Koradrel takes up the mantle (literally – he wears Charill's lion cloak) of ruling prince of Chrace, fighting in the north of Ulthuan while Caledor concentrates his efforts to the south.

MALEKITH – son of Aenarion, prince of Nagarythe, dwarf-friend and elven general beyond compare. Malekith was passed over to succeed his father as Phoenix King, and Bel Shanaar was chosen in his place. At first it seems that Malekith stays true to his loyalties to the Phoenix Throne, but in his heart he is wracked with bitterness and disappointment. He believes that only a son of Aenarion can replace his father, and fears that Phoenix Kings not of his line will diminish the power of Ulthuan. He feels he remains true to the elves and their future, but in his quest to regain his throne he is eventually corrupted by Chaos, and becomes utterly bitter and vengeful against those who rejected him. Attempting a coup, Malekith traps the other princes in the Shrine of Asuryan while he walks through the sacred flames – and is hideously burned. He is believed dead for the following twelve years, while being nursed back to health by Morathi, before returning as the immortal Witch King armoured by Hotek. In his twisted mind, Malekith is still the true Phoenix King – after all he *has* walked through the sacred flames and survived like his father, albeit almost killed by the experience.

MAEDRETHNIR – dragon of Caledor. Following the death of Aenarion and the demise of Caledor Dragontamer, the dragons of Caledor returned to their slumber, save for a few, chief amongst them the dragon Maedrethnir. Maedrethnir is reluctant at first to become embroiled in the woes of the elves, but Imrik convinces the dragon to bear him into battle. Seeing the danger posed by the druchii and the affront of the Naggarothi black dragons, Maedrethnir rouses others of his kind to aid the dragon princes against Malekith. Maedrethnir is wounded by Malekith's dragon, Sulekh, at the Battle of Maledor but survives the encounter when Imrik slays Sulekh.

MIANDERIN – high priest of Asuryan, who bestows the Phoenix Crown and Cloak upon Imrik and wards him with spells when Imrik steps into the flame of Asuryan.

MORATHI – wife of Aenarion, mother of Malekith, chief architect of the pleasure cults. Morathi is the power behind Malekith and has been fuelling his ambition to further her own. Once her part in the pleasure cults is revealed, she revels in her notoriety, enjoying the freedom from the elves' complex religious and social traditions. As the partner of Aenarion she once enjoyed great power and she will do anything to regain it. She is far more cynical than her son, and is already well on her way to becoming a corrupt yet extremely powerful sorceress. After the massacre at the shrine, Morathi resumes rule of Nagarythe and unleashes her cults and armies against the other kingdoms.

THYRINOR – prince of Caledor, cousin to Imrik and Dorien. Slain by Morathi.

THYRIOL – mage-prince of Saphery, one of the survivors of the massacre at the shrine. Thyriol takes on much of the diplomatic and civil governance of Ulthuan after the massacre, leaving Caledor free to concentrate on the war. When Malekith unleashes the Sundering upon Ulthuan, Thyriol gives his life to help the returned Caledor Dragontamer and other mages restore the vortex, joining them in limbo upon the Isle of the Dead.

TITHRAIN – young prince of Cothique, forced to take the rulership following the massacre. Has to deal with druchii reinforcements returning from the colonies, led by the Khainite cultist Hellebron. Slain by Malekith during the Battle of Maledor.

URATHION OF ULLAR – prince of Nagarythe, sorcerer. One of Morathi and Malekith's protégés, Urathion learns the dark arts, but when Malekith finally reveals his plan to unbind the magical vortex he flees for sanctuary and warns the Phoenix King of Malekith's insane plan before he is assassinated.

YVRAINE – Everqueen of the elves, daughter of Aenarion and Astarielle. Although the spiritual protector of the elves, Yvraine cannot combat the sorceries of the druchii as Morathi's followers crush resistance in Chrace and march into the forests of Avelorn. Aided for a time by Alith Anar and the spirits of Avelorn, the Everqueen holds out until King Caledor can free the forests of the druchii. Desperate, Morathi personally leads a final attack against the Everqueen's realm. Her strength almost spent, Yvraine and her followers retreat to the Gaen Vale, and the Everqueen collapses the land bridge connecting the Gaen Vale to the mainland, destroying Morathi's army but also isolating the Gaen Vale forever.

ABOUT THE AUTHOR

Gav Thorpe has been rampaging across the worlds of
Warhammer and Warhammer 40,000 for many years as both an
author and games developer. He hails from the den of scurvy
outlaws called Nottingham and makes regular sorties to unleash
bloodshed and mayhem. He shares his hideout with Dennis,
a mechanical hamster sworn to enslave mankind. Dennis is
currently trying to develop an iPhone app that will hypnotise
his victims. Gav's previous novels include fan-favourite *Angels
of Darkness*, the Time of Legends trilogy, *The Sundering*, and the
Eldar Path series amongst many others.

You can find his website at:
mechanicalhamster.wordpress.com

TIME OF LEGENDS

THE WAR OF VENGEANCE

THE GREAT BETRAYAL

NICK KYME

An extract from The Great Betrayal
by Nick Kyme

On sale November 2012

THUNDER ROLLED ACROSS the slopes of Karag Vlak, shaking the earth for miles. Fire wreathed the darkling sky. It warred with the furnace at the mountain peak, glowing hot and angry through swathes of pyroclastic cloud. Shadows lurked within it, drifting against the wind on thin, membranous wings...

Thurgin Ironhand eyed the enemy racing at his throng across the hellish plain and scowled.

'They are swift,' he said, feeling the tremor of their hoof beats through his iron-wrought armour. Runes of warding fashioned into its breastplate began to ignite in a chain of forge-bright flares that painted the metal like parchment.

Never before had the dwarfs waged war against such a foe. All of the urk and grobi festering beneath the Worlds Edge could not come close in number to the glistening horde riding down upon them now.

Two hundred feet away from bloodying his axe and Thurgin gave an order, growled through the mouthpiece of his war helm and carried to every warrior of his throng through its runecraft.

'Lock shields!'

Across the slopes of Karak Vlak, ten thousand dwarfs obeyed.

That was but the first rank.

Deep into the valley, standing upon the Fist of Agrin, Thurgin knew the High King fought alone. It was said of him that he could break the stars.

To witness that rune blade he bore, gripped two handed and splitting heads as effortlessly as barrels, Thurgin could believe it.

The enemy closed, coming fast and hard on hooves of silver flame.

Thurgin, thane-king, felt the solidity of his clan brothers at either shoulder and smiled.

This would be a good day for the dwarfs.

Vengeance would be won.

He bellowed, his voice louder than a hundred war horns, 'Khazuk!'

The throng answered, its many ranks adding to the fury of their reply, 'Khazuk!'

Axes and hammers began to beat shields, rising in tempo as the riders closed.

'Khazuk!'

Thurgin slid the ornate faceplate over his eyes and nose until it clanked and the world became a slit of honed anger.

His brothers' chorus resonated through his helm, chiming with the clash of arms.

'KHAZUK!'

It meant war.

War had come to the enemies of the dwarfs.

GLARONDRIL THE SILVEN spurred his riders to greater effort. The enemy was close, a thick wedge of mailed warriors clutching blades and shields.

Twenty thousand noble lords at his command, armour glittering with the falling sun, lowered their lances.

They had ridden hard and far to reach this hellish plain. Glarondril would not be found wanting on the slopes of the mountain. He would see it through to the end, even if that meant his death. Whispering words of command to his mount, he drew the riders into a spear tip of glittering silver.

'In the name of the Phoenix King,' he roared, unable to keep his battle lust sheathed any longer. A sword of blue flame slid soundlessly from his scabbard. 'For the glory of Ulthuan!'

So close... Glarondril saw their hooded eyes, shimmering like moist gemstones, and smelled the reek of their foul breath, all metal and earth.

'None shall live!'

The blue-fire sword was held aloft as a thicket of lance heads drew down upon the enemy.

THURGIN FELT HIS body tense just before the moment of impact.

'Hold them, break them!' he raged. 'No mercy. Kill them all!'

Here before them was a foe worthy of dwarfish enmity.

The shield wall dug in, backs and shoulders braced.

Over fifty thousand in this single throng; his muster from Karak Izril was large but far from the largest of the hold.

Behind them he heard the slow tread of the *gronti-duraz*, felt the resonance of their advance as the low, sober chanting of their masters compelled them. Thurgin was glad to have the stone-clad giants at his back.

Lightning cracked the sky as magical anvils were made ready.

On the far mountain flank, obscured by rolling fog, the bolt tips of ballista twinkled in the dying light like an endless celestial array.

Dwarfs did not need the stars, or the sun. They were dwellers of the earth, solid and determined. They would need those traits today as they would need all the craft of the runesmiths and the engines of the guilds.

Never before had the dwarfs faced a foe such as this. They meant to drive them from the Old World forever.

The enemy reached them.

Thurgin knew there would be no quarter given.

GLARONDRIL AND HIS knights swept into the armoured horde piercing flesh and shattering bone. Incandescent fire reaved from the jaws of their mounts in a tide that burned the foe to ash. No defence was proof against the Dragon Princes of Caledor. No foe, however determined, could resist their charge.

Hundreds died in the first seconds, their corpses left to ruin in the fell sun. What began as a contest swiftly became a slaughter.

'For the king!' shouted Glarondril above the eager roar of his mount, as he took the enemy leader's head.

'FOR THE KING!' urged Thurgin, chopping into the riders blunted on the dwarfs' wall of shields. They buckled as they hit it, mounts and riders sent sprawling only to be crushed by those that followed or butchered by dwarfish axes.

'Forward!'

The throng of Karak Izril moved slow but inexorably, like a landslide and with the same momentum. Already broken against the dwarfs' resilience, the riders were scattered. Hounded without mercy, the enemy cavalry had lost two thirds of its warriors before the charge was ended.

Seeing no gain in pursuit, Thurgin called the throng to a halt.

He looked to the sky at a vast shadow approaching him out of the sun.

'We have the east flank in our fist,' he called to it.

Glarondril landed with a grace the dwarf had not thought possible for the winged monsters he rode, and bowed in the saddle to the thane-king. So too did his beast.

'Well met, Thurgin son of Gron.' He wiped the ichor-blood from his sword before sheathing it.

'High prince,' the dwarf answered with a nod of deference, standing amidst a host of sundered daemon corpses.

'We had best make the most of our good fortune then,' remarked the elf.

'Indeed…' Thurgin turned his eye northwards.

Four behemoths, avatars of Ruin all, towered in the distance. Before them the innumerable hordes of Chaos made flesh.

And on a stool of rock, miles across, still farther away stood High King Snorri Whitebeard and the elf lord Malekith, alone and besieged by hell.